SUPER SALES

SUPER HEROES

By William D. Arand

Dedicated:
To my wife, Kristin, who encouraged me in all things.
To my son, Harrison, who now lets me sleep, but wants to help me "type type" on my keyboard.
To my family, who always told me I could write a book if I sat down and tried. I've now written five.

Special Thanks to:
Niusha Gutierrez
Caleb Shortcliffe
Austin Youngblood

Thanks to my Beta Readers:
Alston Sleet
Cory Grimes
Dominic Harney
Ezben Gerardo
Florian Cadwe
Kegan Hall
Robert Magdaleno
Tim Burago

I appreciate you reading through an unedited nightmare

Chapter 1 - Not So Black Market -

Felix couldn't keep himself still. He practically gyrated with nervous energy. He jumped at every noise in the alley. From a mouse scratching at cardboard to a streetlamp that started to buzz.

This is a bad idea. Stupid idea. Trying to buy something from the black market.

Well. The not-so-black market anymore. What exactly do you call a black market when a supervillain runs your city?

He very nearly shouted in alarm when the garage door behind him opened abruptly, the chain rattling as it moved.

A black man in a dark brown trench coat was waiting for him on the inside.

He looked about Felix's age.

Well, maybe not. He's a bit younger? Maybe like five years younger? Call it twenty-five?

He looked like any number of people you'd pass on the street and never give a second glance to. He might just barely hit six foot, or so Felix thought, measuring him against the frame of the garage door.

The man's posture was relaxed, his hands in his pockets, watching Felix with a partial frown.

"You're a little early there, Felix," the man said in a smooth baritone. "It is Felix, right?"

"Yeah! Felix, Felix Campbell. Pleasure to meet you," he said, holding out his hand.

The man stared back at him, his eyes flicking from Felix's hand and back to his face.

"I, uh, I came early with the van," he said, gesturing to the unmarked vehicle next to him.

"So I noticed."

"I didn't want to be late. I can't stand being late. Though I think coming early didn't do me any favors for my nerves, sorry," Felix apologized lamely.

The man smirked at that and then chuckled softly. "Yeah, I hear that. I wouldn't want to stand around in this alley much longer either. Snidely's come prowlin' often enough. Come on."

"Snidely?" Felix asked, stepping quickly to catch up to the man.

Felix was by no means a short man, but nor was he tall. Sitting at an unimpressive five foot eight, he was as average as you could be.

The clack of the man's polished shoes echoed dully. Realizing how immaculately dressed the man was, Felix felt like a slob in his work uniform, minus nametag.

"Snidely? Snidely Whiplash? You know, villain? Great 'stache? Dorights and Snidelys? Never mind." The man shook his head.

"Sorry. I don't watch TV. What channel is it on?" Felix asked. Then he shook his head. He had to get this done and get it done right. He needed this. "Actually. Forget that. What do I call you?"

"You don't," said the man, stepping up to a rectangular wooden crate. On top of that crate was a black box and a sheet of white paper. "I call you."

Felix took a breath and then pulled out a wad of money from his pocket. This deal had cost him two thousand. What little he had left after that was in his hand in a roll, amounting up to three hundred dollars.

All that he had till his next paycheck.

"Then maybe you can call me when you get similar merchandise in the future." *Damn, that sounded good! At least I think it did.*

The man tilted his head to one side and then smiled widely at Felix, showing a set of bright white teeth. Taking the money from Felix's hand, he nodded his head, thumbing back the twenties.

"Well alright. I can do that. Call me Marcus, it'll do for today," said the man now known as Marcus, putting the wad of money in his pocket. "As for the market, no buyers for this stuff. You're already paying basement price of what it cost to get it here and out of where it was with only a slim margin for us. So I'll keep you in mind, but no promises."

Marcus turned and picked up the black box and the paper, then handed both to Felix.

"Ownership papers and one owner's box. We call 'em Pits. Go ahead and stick your finger in that hole," Marcus explained, holding out the box.

"Uh, shouldn't the seller put their finger in first for these?" Felix had heard about them. Apparently, Pits were well regarded for transactions among supers, since they had a magical element to them.

"Not for this purchase. For future purchases, we can just use this Pit again. Now go ahead and get that paw up here..."

Felix lifted his index finger and slipped it into the hole.

He felt the sting before he even thought about what was going to happen.

"All done. You'll feel that tomorrow," Marcus said, shaking his head with a grin. Turning his head, Marcus whistled at a forklift that was sitting dormant in the side of the warehouse.

Felix flinched as the vehicle came to life. He hadn't even noticed it. In fact, he hadn't even looked around at what he'd walked into.

Way to go, idiot.

Marcus pointed to the van. "You go hop in and wait. We'll get this loaded up in a second." The man hesitated for a second, then continued, "You know, I'm glad someone's buying this. We were considering tossing it into the river, but... that never works out."

"I should think not. It wouldn't be as bad as, say, lead, but it'd eventually create some problems with the water," Felix said, nodding his head.

A big shipment of bismuth really could cause problems. I mean, how do you explain buying a shipment of heavy metal that then ends up in a river?

Marcus looked at him in a strange way at that and then laughed with a wave of his hand. "See you later, Felix. You're a strange cat."

Felix wasn't quite sure what to make of that exchange, but he waved back. "Later, Marcus."

Felix hurried off back to the panel van and got in. The forklift operator went about his business and had Felix loaded up in under a minute.

There was a smack on the rear door, and then the garage started sliding shut a second later.

Felix adjusted his mirror, catching a look at himself in the process. He looked pale. Pale as ever. His gray eyes stared back at him. Listless.

Even his hair looked defeated. Limp. It hung on him in its way, the brown strands overly worked with hair gel.

He looked incredibly tired for a thirty-year-old.

We're changing that. Starting with this. We can do this. We saved, we scrimped, and now we'll succeed.

Popping the radio back on, Felix pulled out into the alleyway.

"Tonight, we have a guest speaker from our new leader's cabinet. Please wel —"

Felix cursed as he jammed the brakes. A superhero in a costume stumbled out in front of him from a side alley.

The van clipped the caped crusader and sent him spinning.

At the same instant, another costumed weirdo appeared. That person pounced on the hero as they stumbled back from the van and began plunging a knife into their chest over and over.

Felix kept his eyes straight on the road and hit the gas again.

"Didn't see anything. Didn't see a super being murdered. Nope, not a thing," Felix said, staring straight ahead.

The closest Felix had been to crime was watching the loan shark across the street from his work operate.

Even that felt too close for comfort sometimes.

Ever since the supers in charge of the city's defense had lost, it'd become open season. Anyone not in line with the new power structure was free game.

Which was pretty much every and any superhero out there. There'd been a mass exodus and only a few had remained. And of those who remained, the vast majority were poor slobs who thought that they could tough it out till relief came.

In fact, a lot of people said the relief had come at the same time as the original attack.

Which made sense; no one else ever came.

Felix doubted anyone else would come at this point.

For people like Felix, the everyday man, life hadn't changed much from the turnover.

Vice laws, like slavery, prostitution, and drugs, were legalized. They were now given government protection, and were expected to meet the same or similar regulations that other markets had.

And let's not forget taxes.

Taxes were of course levied on all those vices. Being legal, the price had rapidly inflated, crashed, then flatlined. The city raked in the cash and started immediately spending it back on city programs.

Like drug rehabilitation centers.

Then Skipper, the villain now in charge, had promptly lowered income taxes. Since there were no federal taxes anymore, that meant people overall were paying significantly less, unless they were partaking of the new legal frivolities.

Which set off another round of vice spending and purchasing in general.

Suddenly, not only were the heroes not receiving support, but if anything, they were being asked to leave.

Or hunted and killed.

" — to be here, Mike! I'd like to start off by reminding everyone we have a ten-grand reward for anyone with information leading to the capture of a hero. Five grand for a kill with the body as proof."

Or hunted, apparently.

The audience cheered at that reminder. Felix had heard something about that but had brushed it off as rumors. Apparently, it wasn't.

"As our government is only here in this city, we need to secure ourselves. The longer we have threats inside, the longer it takes us to begin to branch outward," said the guest.

"I heard that one of the first cities we'll be taking is — "

"Now, now, Mike. You know I can't talk about that. Though speaking of targets, I'd like to warn our listeners out there: Violence towards the other humanoid races, such as Dwarves, Beastkin, or anything other than a Human, won't be tolerated. It'll be punished. Severely."

"No arguments here! Glad to hear justice will be applied evenly."

"I heard the old federal government isn't even bothering us anymore. That they've left the recapture of our city to the Guild of Heroes. Is that true?"

"It is, it is. Skipper is regularly on patrol and watching for anything. So far, they haven't retaken an inch."

Tired of the political whitewash he was sure was going on, Felix flipped the radio to an eighties station and drove onward.

Shutting the door with a thump, Felix looked around the spacious garage. Much like every other area in this house, it had the feel of his family. It was their house, after all. He was merely living here as the clock ticked down on them being proclaimed dead. Death in absentia.

They were at year seven of ten.

His aunt and uncle had simply up and left one night when Felix was twenty-three. Give or take a few months.

Leaving him alone in a home that had been paid off completely. Their bank accounts, stock, and everything else was being managed by a group of lawyers through a trust.

He had rights in the trust to insure they weren't spending money frivolously, but he had no rights to the money itself.

Sighing, Felix moved around to the rear of the van.

"This'll change everything. Once I get this squared away," Felix said to himself, opening the rear doors. "Then I can quit. Quit that hellhole of a job and just... just do whatever. Yeah. Whatever.

"Sit around, pick my nose, and watch game shows all day."

Felix grabbed the edge of the rectangular box and heaved once. It slid out by a foot.

It was at this moment that he realized he had no way to get it from the bed of the van to the garage floor.

A quick hunt of the garage got him the motorcycle ramp his uncle owned.

Wedging it against the van, and getting it in a stable place, he heaved on the crate again.

Groaning, it slid free of the van, hit the motorcycle ramp, and slid down it.

Wood cracked and popped when it hit the floor. It managed to come to a stop the same moment it came off the ramp.

Felix sighed and closed the van doors and put the ramp back.

Getting a hold of the latch at the top and bottom of the box, he took a slow breath, then unbolted them at the same time and tipped the lid backwards.

Looking inside eagerly, Felix felt dumbstruck.

Instead of a load of bismuth, which he'd hoped to turn into gold with his own superpower, there was a corpse.

The face looked like it'd gone through a factory furnace. Like something out of those old slasher films his uncle loved.

There were no eyes. Dry, empty sockets gaped at him. There were no ears, but instead two nubs of flesh no bigger than the tip of his pinky. Two gaping holes sat in the middle of the ruined face, right where a nose would be. Should have been. No lips remained to cover the broken and shattered teeth.

It was a real horror show.

"No more," mumbled the not-corpse almost like a mantra. "No more, no more, no more, no more, no more."

Felix looked down at the ruined husk of what had once been a human being and pressed his hands to his face. This wasn't something his brain could comprehend right now.

"No more," the body whispered.

His brain slowly lurched into gear and a thought sent him for the passenger door. Popping open the door, he grabbed the paperwork and started to read over it.

Paperwork was on the rise as of late since the taxmen had to collect taxes. And taxes needed accurate paperwork.

National ID cards, too.

Finally, he found the listed items sold. No mention of bismuth came up at all.

Only the purchase of a slave and one slave control box. One superheroine, to be specific. One previously owned by the government.

That's a woman? Holy crap.

Felix felt his thoughts starting to spiral rapidly out of control. Hunching over, he put his head between his knees and took some deep breaths. Right when the world stopped spinning crazily, he stood back up and breathed more regularly.

Setting the paperwork down back next to the Pit, he considered his options.

His money was already spent and gone; even though he'd clearly received the wrong package, it wouldn't be good for him to whine about it. They'd just laugh at him and ask him what the problem was. He'd accepted the bill of goods as it was. Who was to say this wasn't exactly what he wanted?

Maybe this won't be so bad after all. I wanted to transmute bismuth to gold. What if she can do more than that? What if she can make gold? Or find gold?

This might actually be even better than he'd expected. Provided that he could fix her.

That is, if he could keep her alive long enough to fix her.

A super with a decent power set would be worth a lot more than gold. Especially in the current environment where slaves were legal.

He started to think of any number of things supers could do and how he could profit from it.

Closing the passenger door, he walked back to the crate.

"Can you, er, can you hear me?" he asked her.

There was no response. Her chest rose and fell in labored breaths. Now that he looked at her body, he found the rest of it as horribly disfigured as her face. It looked like her fingers had been removed. Her breasts. Most of her skin. She was a real mess.

Could he even fix her?

His face twisted into a frown as he tilted his head to consider her.

He hadn't used up his power today. It wasn't as if he had any plans to use it before he went to sleep, either. In fact, if he was up past midnight when his power set reset, he could try again.

Solidifying his decision, he concentrated on her. She was his, he owned her, she was his property.

Felix was actually a superhero or villain candidate. He could modify any item he owned. Make it new, change it into another substance, make it better or worse quality.

Anything, really. The scope was incredible.

The problem was that the more he modified an object, the more it would take from his power pool.

And his power pool barely had enough juice in it to fix a crack in a toilet.

Felix had always thought of it like batteries.

Most heroes and villains had a pretty decent-sized battery. There were those who had smaller ones, and those who had larger ones.

If he had to compare himself in relative terms to others, Felix was a triple A battery that had been left outside in a puddle. The lowest measured superhero or villain before Felix would be akin to a golf cart battery.

Up to this point, the best use of his superpower had been repair jobs. Mostly maintenance, to tell the truth. He couldn't modify or change big objects, but he could limit wear and tear for sure.

He'd tried minor transmutations with success. Leading to this moment here and now with the hope to change bismuth into gold.

In using his power, the change would simply occur over a few seconds.

The precursor to that, though, when he used his power, was a virtual window that appeared in front of him. It had the look of a checklist sheet with sliders on one other side.

It was all very strange, really.

Focusing on his unexpected guest, Felix struggled to activate his power.

To ultimately no result.

Scratching at his cheek, Felix thought on the problem. She was his possession. Legally.

Up to this point, that'd been all he had to do.

Taking a different approach, he tried using a character sheet. Generic, and yet taking root from hundreds upon hundreds of role-playing games he'd played.

Why not?

He saw it in his mind's eye first. A piece of white paper. At the top, there was basic information and vital stats. Things that anyone would have regardless of being a super or not.

Below that, all of the powers, abilities, and functions that made them unique.

These sheets would contain everything from blindness, being sick, or even having a genetic disposition to heart attacks.

Then he opened his eyes and saw the exact same form he'd been visualizing floating in front of him.

Only he could see it. When he'd tried to explain it to his family, they'd thought he'd gone crazy at first. Only after showing them an example of what he could do, where he took a faded and dirty penny and made it new, did they believe him.

At first, he'd thought perhaps he was indeed crazy. What kind of superpower presented itself like this? This wasn't a normal power. In fact, it'd been classified as unique. Nothing even similar.

Felix had become contemplative after that information had been given to him by the guild.

To him, that meant that he either was the one doing the visualizing of his power, or another entity had set it up for him.

Both answers disturbed him.

The reason why Felix had never gone any further with his talent was his lack of power.

At the bottom right of the sheet floating in front of him was where the cost would be to make the modifications he wanted. They were always more than what he had available for anything useful.

After much experimentation, he knew he had roughly one hundred and fifty points he could spend on things before he ran out. He could always tell if he ran out because the confirm button would simply go away.

That was a pretty small number when compared to the things he could change. Like turning a table into solid gold.

With a sudden thought, he tried to flip to the "second page" that his power normally offered up.

The real meat and potatoes of his power.

The upgrade page.

The viewing window changed.

It now looked like something out of a role-playing game character creation page.

He could modify anything about her, providing he paid the power cost. Strength, intelligence, reflexes, weapon skills, languages, skills, height, weight, senses, anything and everything that you could think of.

The list was extensive and a touch overwhelming. The possibilities for a living person were infinitely more complex than a simple item.

Felix shook his head to clear it. He'd have to worry about that later after he'd fixed all the problems.

Maybe try to limit what came up to what he wanted to change.

Focusing back on the here and now, Felix started to read through the list of debuffs this person was suffering from. It looked endless at first.

He began to feel sick at the problems listed. Some of them were rather horrible. She'd apparently been cut open and had a number of her organs removed. He couldn't even begin to think of a reason for that.

"Waaaaaah…" he groaned. "That's just sick perversion, isn't it? Who the hell did this?"

This wasn't going to be a quick fix; it'd take months to spend enough power to make her human again, let alone whole. That wasn't even mentioning how long it'd take to get her back into a condition to be useful.

It'd take months to make enough money to buy a shipment of bismuth again anyways.

Besides, not like I'm doing anything else with this power. I could clean up some coins. Scrub the shower. Ooooooh, impressive.

Fine, let's Frankenstein's monster this shit.

Felix grunted and looked to the sheet again.

The cheapest thing to change, and which would refund some points he could work with, was putting her in a coma.

A single thought later and "Coma" appeared in the debuff list. One hundred points with a negative sign popped up in the bottom right corner.

Flicking through multiple options, he found that replacing her teeth would be relatively simple and cheap. Her lips came at a discounted price since it was all in the same area and some of the reconstruction could bleed into the other.

Then he was spent. That was all he had.

For a start, it was great. He'd take another crack at it when midnight rolled around and his points reset.

Before he clicked the confirm changes button at the bottom, he stopped. Below the confirmation button was a slider. One he hadn't imagined or put there.

No time like the present to figure it out.

The slider simply read "Draw" and read from zero percent to one hundred percent. It was set at zero right now.

Moving it to one hundred percent, he checked to see if anything had changed. Nothing.

Back to zero, no change.

Back to one hundred, still no change.

Leaving it at one hundred, Felix shrugged his shoulders. Maybe he could figure it out tomorrow. For now, he'd leave it a hundred to see if anything changed.

Mentally popping the confirm button, he looked up to the body in the crate.

Instantly, teeth began to straighten themselves, growing anew. Where teeth were missing, new teeth broke through the gum line. In ten seconds, she had a healthy set of lovely teeth.

Then her lips started to warp and fan out as they regrew themselves next, until finally she had a pair of full lips hiding those resplendent teeth.

Felix sighed and looked around the garage. He had an hour or so to wait till midnight.

Going inside the house didn't appeal to him. It was empty. Dark.

Devoid of life.

Here in the garage, with what was essentially a corpse, at least he wasn't alone.

When midnight finally rolled around, Felix felt like his skin caught fire for an instant.

It wasn't painful, but it certainly wasn't comfortable. Normally when his power reset, it only felt like he'd caught a mild sunburn. This time felt like he'd been in a furnace.

Felix popped open the window and then hesitated. He might as well get it out of the way now. He'd been thinking while waiting for midnight. If he couldn't fix some of the truly awful things, what was the point?

He selected the box for blindness: left eye, and looked to the corner. Six hundred points.

Despair welled up in him.

Eyeballs aren't simple things like teeth or lips. They're intricate organs and —

The confirm button was lit up.

Chapter 2 - Spend Money to Make Money -

Felix adjusted his necktie as he shifted in the seat of his rundown coupe. Glancing up in the rearview mirror, he found it almost looked right.

Almost. There was still a hint of a pleat in the middle.

The horn coming to life behind him made him jump in his seat. Felix gunned the gas and then jumped forward. Only to slam on the brake when he realized the light was still red.

Ha ha, ass hat.

Doing his best to not make eye contact with anyone, Felix slunk into his seat. He remained in "stealth" mode all the way until he pulled into the parking lot of work.

Felix looked up to the rotating hamburger above the squat red brick building. The windows were decorated with saccharine-sweet mascots and kids who looked like they'd been fed a steady stream of cola.

Pressing his lips together in mute disappointment, Felix clipped his name badge into place.

"Felix - Manager" read the top line. Underneath that was his "time served," as employees called it.

"Eight years serving you," he muttered aloud.

Eight years of serving up burgers, fries, and every other assortment of fast food under the sun. Eight years of watching young people roll in and roll back out when they realized fast food wasn't easy and didn't pay well.

It certainly wasn't rocket science, but it had its own challenges. Namely the customers, really.

Whoever had coined the phrase, 'the customer is always right,' had clearly never worked in retail or customer service.

And if they had, well, then they'd need to be hauled out into the street and beaten to death with plastic spoons.

His phone began to chime gently, signaling his need to go clock in for his shift.

Felix huffed and then exited his car. Silencing the alarm, it took him all but a minute to drop his card past the electronic reader.

The day went by in a blur. Not to mention he had a hard time concentrating. His mind kept wandering back to the woman in her makeshift coffin in his garage.

He'd shut the lid and latched it back closed. Then he'd left her there, as he wasn't quite sure what he wanted to do. Most of the night he'd spent tossing and turning, thinking about the fact that he now had a total of nine hundred points to spend.

It'd taken a bit of tinkering with options to figure that out, but he'd done it.

And he still had all those points to spend at the end. After cycling through all the options available, he'd ended up not being sure what to do.

In the end, he'd reverted the changes he'd made to her, since he didn't plan on breaking the coma from her yet, and then gone to bed.

"Felix. Cover the window for me, I'm going to take a break," demanded the imperious voice of Janessa.

Before he could even object to the lovely young woman's demand, she pulled out her phone and wandered off.

The last one she'd thrown at a customer and he'd had to play go-between to appease the customer and get Janessa in the back room.

She was the most recent pet project that had been pushed his way by the regional manager. One that really wasn't working out in any way, shape, or form.

So much so that had it been anyone else, Felix would have let her go already.

Felix didn't doubt for a minute that Joe had ulterior motives, and wasn't quite prepared to go up against him right now. Not over a woman who would end up quitting in the end. It wasn't the right time or place to call the regional manager out on it.

Can't trust anyone named Joe.

As the store manager, he had to deal with whatever the regional made him do as long as it was within company policy. Though he was slowly preparing all the right paperwork to walk the woman out despite that.

Beautiful, built for the eyes, and whatever else she may be, but an annoying, lazy, monster that could only be a shrew to whoever she was dating.

In his shame, he couldn't deny he'd been infatuated with her for a short period. Days, maybe. That was how long it had taken before she'd revealed her dumpster fire of a personality.

"Hello? I'm ready to place my order," said a voice in the headset at the window. She'd simply set it down and walked off without another word.

Vibrating his pocket, his phone demanded his attention at the same time.

Pulling out his phone, he glanced at the caller ID.

Restricted, unknown caller.

The regional manager liked to call him at all hours on different phones to test him.

Another worker slipped into his line of sight at that moment, and Felix thanked whatever luck he'd been granted at that moment.

"Steve, get the window, please? I'd really appreciate it," Felix said to the young man with a smile. He flipped open his phone at the same time, which he hoped would end any argument before it could happen.

"Sure thing, boss," said the young man.

Felix assumed part of that was the fact that Janessa would have to talk to him when she came back.

Holding the phone up to his ear, Felix said, "This is Felix."

"Afternoon, Felix," came the cool response.

He recognized that voice. He couldn't quite place it.

"I happen to have two more items that fit your request for merchandise."

Marcus!

"Ah! Marcus. Yes, yes. That's great news," Felix said, and he meant it. Where one super might give him a significant point boost, what would several more do?

He was pretty sure it all hinged on that slider at the bottom. The "Draw" slider. Nothing else had changed otherwise.

Looking around, he realized this wasn't the best spot to have this conversation. Walking into the back office where he normally did performance reviews or paperwork Felix shut the door.

"Marcus? Ah. Nah. Today I'm Caldwell," said the previous Marcus, now Caldwell.

"Alright. Caldwell. What's the fee?"

"Five. This'll be a delivery to boot. We were going to dispose of these two Dudleys, but I figured… why not make green on the side?" Caldwell chuckled at that.

"Definitely. Definitely. Do you need that fee today?" Felix opened his work computer and flipped to the Excel spreadsheet he kept his finances on.

Negative three hundred and sixty-two dollars and fourteen cents.

"Yep. I'll have a courier pick it up out of your mailbox tonight after everyone's out in that sleepy little neighborhood of yours. That is, if we have a deal?"

Felix chewed on that mentally. He didn't have the money, and wouldn't have the money. But… how often did you get a chance to power up your abilities?

I can go get a loan. My car isn't in that bad of shape. I can sell it if I really need to clear the loan later. I don't have any debt, either.

Get six thousand. Buy the two, set up a room that they can convalesce in. Use all my vacation and sick time. Get those three up and running to a point that they can care for themselves.

Then use that to upgrade things and make money.

Felix blinked.

It was a lot like those games he used to play when he was a kid. Spend money to buy upgrades. Use those upgrades to make more money, to buy new things that would help you make more money. Which in turn would let you buy upgrades for those items.

His power was literally that game, he realized. He might as well call himself Upgrade Man.

"Done."

"Great, I'll have it delivered to your place in an hour. They'll pop the garage and leave it there. No need to meet us or even disarm your security. Don't forget to use the box. You'll need to do that for their loyalty and your safety to finalize.

"See ya later, Felix."

The line disconnected suddenly.

Felix pulled his phone from his ear and looked at the screen.

From being essentially a nobody, to owning slaves.

He knew that the owner's box he'd been given could hold up to ten thousand slaves without a problem. It used magic to bind them to their master's will. That they couldn't harm or work against their master.

Couldn't use it on someone against their will, though.

It did leave open the ugly loophole of giving someone no choice but to allow it, but that wasn't his problem today.

Looking to his phone, he dialed in the regional manager's number and mashed the voicemail button the moment it started to ring.

"Hey, Joe. This is Felix over at number forty-two. I'm going to be heading home sick for the rest of the day. I'll be out tomorrow as well. Sorry about the short notice. Just not feeling well. Everything here should be covered."

Felix ended the phone call and then opened the browser on his smartphone.

He was generations behind the newest wrist phones, but he liked his old phone. It had a big screen and... well, it was one of the few things he'd been able to successfully modify.

It had taken him peeling it apart and upgrading individual components, but it had worked.

Tapping in a request for directions to the closest branch of his bank, Felix laid out plans to get the loan, buy supplies, and head back home. He'd have to build an impromptu ward and start treating his cash cows.

Having them die on him would be gut-wrenching now that he'd figured out how to increase his power.

Now that he could be somebody.

Before all that, though, he'd need to head over to the law offices. Today was his monthly visit with them.

Felix wasn't looking forward to it. He never was, really. It only made him realize that those he cared for were gone.

Bank, supplies, home, meeting, home.

With a nod of his head, Felix started what he believed would be the changing point in his life.

Pulling in front of the office building, Felix shook himself and then ran his fingers through his hair. He hated doing this, but it was something he had to do to make sure his family dues were taken care of. Both in this life, and wherever they ended up.

Getting out of the car, Felix looked up at the sign hanging above the entrance to the building.

"Reznik, Blacketer, and Troy," the sign read. Supposedly they were the ones who owned the business, though Felix had nothing to do with them.

Walking up to the front door, he pulled the handled and stepped inside.

Waiting for him was the same steel-haired matron he always saw behind the reception desk.

She never smiled, she didn't say anything out of line, and Felix wasn't even sure if she blinked.

Maybe she's a robot.

"Felix Campbell. Monthly meeting for my trust," Felix said, picking up the clipboard and signing himself in.

"Take a seat, they'll be with you shortly," said the woman without a hint of anything resembling a personality.

Rolling his eyes, Felix sat down in a leather recliner. The lobby was empty, and he couldn't help but feel like they were making him wait to prove a point.

That they could make him wait.

Felix picked up a magazine and started to leaf through it.

He was halfway through an article about the fact that the economy was on the rise since the takeover before they called him in.

Tossing the magazine negligently onto a table, Felix followed behind one of the young associates as they led him to the same conference room they always went to.

She gestured to the lone chair that he always sat at.

Felix took the proffered seat. Looking up, he found himself facing the eight lawyers his aunt and uncle had contracted should something happen to them.

One of the clauses of those worst-case scenarios was if they happened to be missing. And that they were to be declared dead in absentia, providing that it was the appropriate amount of time they were missing.

Along with that provision came an impressive and full set of rules they'd had to put together to protect themselves, their estate, and Felix.

"Good afternoon, Mr. Campbell. Good to see you, as always," said the lead legal expert. The group that had been put together was evenly split by men and women, though they seemingly came from every background imaginable.

The head honcho of this little group was an older man in his fifties by the name of Mr. Joseph, who had a head of salt-and-pepper hair and a clean-shaven face. He looked like your next-door neighbor — minus the fact that he was a bloodsucking bastard without a soul.

"First order of business, we've reviewed your request to have a regular gardener take care of the front and back yard," said Joseph.

He'd gotten sick of mowing the massive yards and decided he might as well make use of the maintenance money that was set aside.

"It's been approved and we'll be hiring an appropriate candidate to take care of the grounds. Salary will be paid out of the maintenance account, of course."

Felix nodded at that. That was fine. He didn't like them picking the candidate, but he wasn't going to argue with them. They'd just start quoting clauses and subsections at him.

"Second, and I apologize for this, as I don't believe this is fun for anyone, we need to discuss your living arrangements."

Felix lifted his eyebrows at this. "What about them? I've been living in that home for as long as I can remember. Grew up there."

"Yes. Well. As you're living there, we believe you should be paying rent. Should have been paying rent as well."

Felix shook his head, his mouth opening and closing twice.

What the actual fuck? What stupid horse shit is this?

"To that end, we need to collect roughly one hundred and fifty thousand dollars from you in overdue rent."

"Are you fucking kidding!?" Felix stood up, pressing his hands to the table.

Four of the people on the other side of the table looked uncomfortable, while the other four seemed sure of themselves.

"It's all perfectly accurate, I assure you."

"You want me to pay rent for living in a home that I've been in since as far back as I can remember?" Felix shouted at them.

"That's correct. The amount is in your favor, I assure you, since it's mostly free of interest. I'm sure this is a shock to you, so we'll conclude our business with this item," Joseph said with an oily smile.

"To that end, I believe if we were to set up a simple payment method, from you to your parents, and put it at a set rate, as well as your monthly rent, we can get this taken care of without a problem."

"And what exactly are you thinking is the rent?" Felix asked, his anger starting to make his vision blur as his heart thudded in his chest.

"Well, according to the survey we conducted of the area…" Joseph said, looking for a paper in front of him.

A survey? They've been planning this. This isn't random or ill-thought-out.

"The rent for the house would be roughly twenty-three hundred a month. Though since you're a relative of the owner, we believe fifteen hundred would be more comparable."

Felix shook his head slowly. This couldn't actually be happening. This was insanity at a level he'd never thought possible.

This was something you saw on a terrible movie.

"I see that this has upset you greatly. We'll discuss restitution and repayment at our next meeting," Joseph said, stacking the papers in front of himself.

"No, we'll discuss it now. Give me a damn copy of the agreement, now, as I know I'm entitled that, and show me where this is possible," Felix said, grinding his teeth.

"That or I call the police and we have them sort this out."

That got their attention. Suddenly everyone was a lot less confident.

Joseph blinked, and then withdrew a packet of papers from his briefcase. Coming over beside Felix, he set the papers down and flipped through a couple pages. Laying on the table face up was an entire section about "living in the house" and appropriate rental rates.

Damn it. Seriously? What the hell is this?

Felix started to read through the mind-numbing legal jargon before giving up. He was in no mood to try and ferret out where this clusterfuck of a shitshow went.

"Fine, we'll talk again," Felix pushed the words out between his teeth. Snatching up the documents, he stomped out of the offices, making sure to slam every door in his way.

It wasn't until he pulled onto the road that his head cleared at all.

"They're trying to drive me out. I'm sure there's something they want. Something they're after. Okay, during this week-long vacation, we're gonna sit down and really go over the contract and will. We'll get this figured out. Yeah."

Felix sighed, and gripped the wheel tighter.

He couldn't afford the rent, to be frank. A fast food manager didn't exactly make stacks of cash. Not in the least.

No, this would end up with him falling into a never-ending pit of debt to his own family.

Growling, Felix slammed his hand into the steering wheel as his anger spiked again.

Chapter 3 - It Begins -

The garage was utterly silent as he stared at the three open wooden coffins.

Without realizing the impact of what he was doing, he'd opened all three boxes, made sure each one was in a coma, and confirmed the draw at one hundred percent. Then he'd wandered off with his supplies and set up the "ward," as he was calling it.

Dropping the money off as instructed, he'd gone back into the garage.

Only on his return did he now realize he wasn't sure who was the one he'd bought first, and who were the two he'd just purchased.

He'd reverted all his modifications back to the baseline to get his points back.

They all looked the same. He really hadn't paid much attention to anything that would have made the first one stand out from the others.

They all looked as if they were corpses that'd gone through a meat grinder.

Ah well. Doesn't matter. It's not like this is a stupid story where the first heroine on the scene gets all the fans.

Felix grumbled to himself and then set to work. That meeting with the lawyers had really thrown him off.

Pretty badly, in fact.

Felix changed his thoughts as fast as he could before he settled back into a violent anger.

He carefully lifted each woman, one at a time, and carried them to the ward. Once he settled them in the bed, he reused the slave box on each individual. Luckily, they each had at least one toe or finger he could fit in the box.

Now that he was really paying attention as he shifted them into their new homes, he realized they all had different heights.

He couldn't really tell what their body types were, though. Especially given the fact that they'd had their entire body mutilated. They were scarred and horribly disfigured.

Whoever had done this to them truly hated them. Selling them in this condition had been the final insult, he imagined.

Sighing, with his hands on his hips, he regarded his three sleeping corpses. He'd dressed them in simple pajamas he'd purchased and had put them in diapers.

He'd have to work fast to get them to a point where he could at least get nutrients in them.

Not being a doctor, or having any clue about medicine, he gave himself two days. He could keep them going through his power and forcing their bodies to repair, but that was a short-term solution that would inevitably end their lives.

No, he had to work to get them to a point where they could drink and eat. To live and keep themselves alive.

Beyond that, everything else was superficial.

Looking around his ward, he did a mental check of it.

It was one of the big master bedrooms that had been turned into a guest room. The attached bathroom with tub and shower would be perfect for a temporary ward.

He wasn't quite sure how long they'd be laid up, and giving them a bath close to their sick bed would probably be ideal.

He'd also attached a smart TV to the wall in case he got bored. Hours spent waiting around for living corpses didn't sound great to him.

Three occupied twin single adjustable beds with matching sheets were the big-ticket item in the room. Not to mention they took up most of the space.

It had been a little more expensive to get the adjustable ones, but he figured being able to sit them upright would help for meal time.

Then there was a single stool for him to use, so he could sit next to those beds. Standing next to them as he worked didn't really sound all that fun.

He'd also purchased a sleeping bag for himself in case he had to sleep in here.

There were also three rolling trays like the ones found in hospitals that could slide over beds. Eventually they'd be eating and drinking again.

And a veritable slew of supplies that he would probably need during their convalescence. Bedpans, more pajamas, diapers, cups, bowls, utensils, anything he could think of that they'd need.

Dropping down into the stool with a clank, he looked around nervously.

"Hah, they can't hear me. What am I thinking?" Felix said to no one.

Pushing off the ground, he wheeled the stool around to the first bed.

A fraction of a thought from him and the window popped open. He cycled through everything that was wrong with her.

"First things first. The ability to eat and drink," Felix muttered.

Two changes and she had teeth and lips. She still had a tongue, and as far as he could tell, everything was working as far as her plumbing and digestive system went.

Frowning, he contemplated some of the mental issues listed. He didn't bother to read them off. It was apparent she'd been tortured to near insanity.

Even if he managed to get her to a point where she could eat, would she be a raving lunatic?

Tilting his head to the side, Felix focused on the idea of wanting her to lose her memories of the last month.

He'd chosen a month since that was about the time that the heroes of the city had started to take real losses.

And the sought-after negative trait appeared. "Short-term amnesia" popped up as if by magic.

In the same instant that he selected it, the negative mental problems turned gray. Gray as in no longer active. That they wouldn't be a problem any further.

The traits weren't really gone, but they would no longer be able to make an impact anymore.

It even had the added bonus of giving him points back, since amnesia certainly wasn't a good thing.

"Neat," Felix said. He confirmed the changes and slid to the next bed, repeating the process for the other two women.

Upon finishing on the third, he realized he still had about three hundred points or so left. The amnesia had really offset the costs and pushed him into a better point bracket than he'd thought he would be.

Shrugging, he looked at the clock. It was about ten minutes till midnight.

The whole midnight reset thing still bothered him, but not enough to question it anymore.

Standing up, he stretched his back and then prepped three cups of water, three bowls of chocolate pudding, and three bowls of lime Jell-O. There was no telling if they'd be hungry. Or thirsty, even. But he'd rather be safe than sorry. Not to mention, it might help him earn some brownie points with them.

Cooperative slaves were preferable.

Then he walked in front of each bed at eleven fifty-eight p.m. and disabled their comas one by one.

Deciding that he'd rather be perfectly safe without a concern for what they might do, he then took the restraints he'd purchased and looped one around each woman's waist. They'd be unable to get up unless he undid the buckle that ran around the back of the bed.

It took only a few minutes, but they all began to stir at roughly the same time, their arms twitching and their lips fluttering as they came back to life.

"What's going on?" one asked.

"Why can't I see? Get this blindfold off me," someone else said.

"My fingers, my fingers are gone!" shouted a third.

Felix bit his lip and took a deep breath. "Good evening, everyone," he said.

All three stopped, their eyeless heads swiveling in his direction, trying to track him.

"First, don't panic. You're in a safe place while you recover. While you're put back together.

"Second, there's been some serious changes in the city. You three were captured by a villain who took over the city. They run it completely, from top to bottom."

Felix took a breath before he continued. "You've been... you've been tortured to the point that you should be dead."

Felix felt his stomach flip over. This wasn't the best way to start.

"I've removed your memories for the last month and I've begun working to... to fix you. To put you back to rights. I swear I can do it. You'll find that at this moment, you're a normal human with... severe injuries.

"The city has fallen. Heroes are being hunted and killed in the streets for bounties, or being turned over to the government to handle. Also for a bounty. Heroes are pretty much outlawed right now, and there doesn't seem like there is anything that can be done to change the situation.

"In fact, the population supports everything, as the economy is now booming. Unemployment is way down, economy is up, and they pushed through universal healthcare."

Three hairless heads made tiny bobs as if they agreed or understood that.

Odd.

Now the hard part.

"The only way that I was able to retrieve you was to purchase you as slaves. Slavery now being legal, that is. Slave contracts are enforced magically and permanently binding. I can shift your ownership to someone else if I chose.

"As your slave contracts appear to be a punishment, rather than for a set limit or cost, there is no going back for you. You're slaves for the interminable future."

At this point, all three women sat up straighter, their spines stiffening. One lifted her battered arm to gesture wildly at where she probably thought he was.

They started asking questions at the same time, all demanding an answer of him. Loudly. Annoyingly.

"Be quiet," Felix finally got out, raising his voice. Then he closed his eyes and counted to ten in his head.

He had to tell them exactly what was happening now. There was no room for there to be misunderstandings or changes down the road.

This was where he set it all up.

All three had fallen silent from his command.

"Sorry, but you don't seem to understand your position. I own you. I've bound you in a slave contract. I'm no hero. I'm not doing this for charity.

"I don't want you to suffer, nor do I want you to be disfigured for life. I do want you for what you can give me, though. My power seems to increase in power by the number of people I have in a contract. I imagine it works for villains or heroes. Probably even civilians, to a lesser degree.

"Oh, and you'll not discuss any of this with anyone. This is confidential, for us alone."

Felix sighed and put his hands on his knees. The woman in the center bed was struggling with the strap around her waist. The closest one had the stumps of her hands pressed to her mouth. The one in the furthest bed looked... disoriented but unafraid.

"You can speak now. Please don't yell. And since none of you can see, there's three of you here. Nor do I know your names. Let's start there. My name is Felix."

"I—"

"My nam—"

"Stop," Felix cut in. "Let's do this. I'll touch you on the shoulder, you say your name." He got up and walked over to the woman on the far left. He gently touched her shoulder with a finger. "What's your name?"

"My name is Miu. Miu Miki," said the woman.

"You may ask one question before we move to the next person," Felix said. He was trying to be fair, but he also wanted to get moving with this whole thing.

"What do you plan to do with us?" Miu asked.

"Plan to do with you? Nothing. You'll end up living with me while you recover. After that, I don't know. Maybe get jobs and have a normal life? Next."

Felix tapped the woman in the middle on the shoulder. "Name?"

"I am Ioana Iliescu, the War Maiden, and you'll release me—"

"No, I won't. Sorry. Like I said, this is a villain's city now. As long as they're in charge, you're my property, and I'll be using your powers to my benefit.

"Now, Ioana, do you have an actual question?"

"I have a statement. If you even try to rape me, I'll rip it off."

"Good to know. I have no plans to abuse you three against your will. I stand by my earlier comment, this isn't charity. In the same breath, I'm not a villain, though. You'll live, work, and stay with me, but you do still have certain rights. I think 'not being raped' is definitely one of those rights."

Felix walked around Ioana's bed and approached the third woman. He tapped her shoulder gently.

Her head turned up in the direction she probably thought he was, and then smiled.

"My name is Kit Carrington. I can't hear your mind. I can't hear anyone's minds. Everything is silent. Is everyone dead? Are we all dead?" she said wonderingly.

"No. The takeover went rather smoothly. Only heroes ended up dead or missing. Pretty sure all the civilians were allowed to walk out with a clean slate. I'm pretty sure I've depowered you, and boosted my own power. Do you have a question for me?"

Her earlier question felt more like a panic response than an actual question.

She processed that and then nodded her head.

"Can you fix me completely without repowering me?" she asked.

"I can and plan to do that. You'll be as fit as any other human out there. More so if we have the time to bump up your stats. Though even if I did repower you, and I might, depending on what my needs are, I could just as easily turn it back off."

Kit nodded her head at that and then lay back down comfortably in her bed. "If you can keep it as quiet as it is right now, I'll serve. Willingly. Call me Kit."

The woman named Ioana made a sound of disgust at that.

"Kit Carrington? You're Augur?" Miu asked.

"I was Augur. I'm Kit now. Only Kit." The woman sighed and snuggled into her bed, adjusting her sheets. "Can I have some water, or tea, and maybe something to eat? I'm not hungry, but I think I'd like a snack and a drink."

Augur. As in the strongest telepath? Arguably the world's strongest? Who rumor said she spent hours at a time in a catatonic state when her gift would overwhelm her? Wow.

"Oh, yes. Here." Felix loaded up a tray with a bowl of pudding, Jell-O, and one of the jugs of water. Wheeling over the cart to her, he set a spoon in her palm and then gently wrapped medical tape around it so she could use her mangled hand to some degree.

Then he adjusted the bed so she was sitting up, taking a moment to reset her blankets.

"The bowl on the left is pudding, the middle bowl is Jell-O, and on the far right is water.

"I wasn't sure what condition you would all be in once I woke you, so we're sticking to simple things for now. Things that you can digest regardless of whatever condition your insides are in."

"Good plan. Makes sense," Kit said, dipping the spoon into the pudding and then trying to guide it to her mouth.

"Could you get me some as well?" Miu asked, her voice soft.

"Of course, give me one second while I get that all prepped," Felix said, moving over to her.

"So, you can fix amputations. Quite a power set. What do you plan on replacing next?" Kit asked, closing her mouth around her spoon. "Oh, chocolate."

"Either your hands or your eyes. I can only do so much in any given day. It resets at midnight every night. Then I can do it all over again."

"Hands, please," Miu said. Felix adjusted her bed and then wheeled her full tray over. "Eyes can wait if I can take care of everything else myself."

Kit nodded her head as she tried to reposition her spoon. "Maybe hands. I think maybe eyes, personally. I'm not keen on being blind so far."

This was all rather unexpected. They were actually reacting better than he'd thought they would. That or they were playing with him, waiting for an opportunity to do something.

Wouldn't matter, though, since they were magically bound in their contracted states to him.

Behind him, Ioana grunted and then said with a stern yet soft voice, "A tray for me as well, if you please. I admit the same as Kit. I do not hunger, but... I think I would enjoy having something to drink and eat."

Felix grinned at that. "Sure thing, Ioana. I'll take care of that."

Chapter 4 - Point of View -

All three of the heroines had passed out as soon as they'd cleared their bowls.

Rather than working on them as they slept, he decided to wait till morning.

Staring up at the ceiling of the ward room, it took him a minute to orient his thoughts.

Sitting up, he rubbed at his eyes with his hands, the sleeping bag bunched up around his middle.

"Good morning," Kit said pleasantly, her eyeless face swiveling towards him.

"Uh, yeah. Good morning," Felix said, coughing into his hand. Stretching his arms over his head, he inspected his supers.

Ioana slept, Miu looked... lost, and Kit seemed chipper.

"Miu," Felix said. Her head slowly turned towards him, but she said nothing. "What's wrong?"

"I... can't see anything," Miu said slowly.

"Yes. Your eyes, well, they were removed." Perhaps they hadn't accepted everything as easily last night as he had thought.

"I'm blind. I'll never see again," Miu murmured, her head sinking.

"Ah, no, I can restore them." Felix stood up from his bag and walked over to her bed.

"Lie," Miu hissed. "No one can do that. You only wish to use us."

Felix couldn't argue with that. He did want to use them. Instead, he opened up Miu's window and selected the Blinded condition.

"Left or right eye, Miu?" he asked.

"What? What do you mean?" she asked bitterly.

"Left or right eye?" he asked again, not giving her any more information.

"Right," she said in a mocking tone.

Felix picked the right eye of the blinded condition, then hit confirm.

Miu sucked in a breath as the dark socket of her eye started to boil and shift. A few seconds in and already he could tell her right eye was regrowing itself straight out from her brain, behind the sunken eyelid.

Ten seconds from the confirmation button and all was still on Miu's face.

"Try opening your right eye. Don't be shocked by what you see. As I said, and have now demonstrated, I can fix it." Felix left her there and wandered over to Kit's bed.

"I... I can see! I can see... oh my God," Miu said, her voice catching. "What did they do?"

"They did what only the truly evil can," Kit explained. "And yet, here we are. Alive, under care, and being given the chance at a normal life. I'm grateful. I choose the left eye; it's the least problematic of the two. I might even be able to see the TV. I'll need to get a new pair of glasses."

Felix smiled to himself as he focused on her sheet. She did indeed need glasses originally. Since the eye was being rebuilt, though, it'd only take a few extra points to modify it. To make it so she wouldn't need a prescription.

"That's a pity. I'm afraid you won't be able to leave the house for a while," Felix said, mentally thumbing the confirm button.

Kit smiled sadly at that but didn't respond. In ten seconds, her left eye had been reformed.

"Then again, I fixed your eyesight. You won't need eyeglasses anyways," Felix said with a prideful snicker.

Ioana had been stirring as they spoke. She'd probably wake soon.

Felix turned around to face her. Picking her right eye, he hit the confirmation button. After it activated, he walked over and sat down on his stool.

Amazingly, he still had points left. He wasn't sure how many, but he still had some. He was at least twelve times as strong as he used to be just by going by the point values already.

"That's quite impressive, Felix," Kit said, looking around with her one eye.

"Anything I own, I can modify," Felix said with a shrug. Ioana's single eye fluttered open.

"What?" she muttered.

"We started with a single eye for each of you, Ioana. It seemed like a good demonstration that, yes, I can repair you completely, and that, yes, it's exactly as I described to you. Seeing is believing, after all."

Felix looked over his shoulder at the unpowered TV. Pointing at it, he continued, "The remote to this is in the bedside between Ioana and Miu. Full cable access and every station under the sun.

"I'll be undoing your restraint today as well. I'm telling you to stay in this house, though, and please do not attempt to contact anyone else."

Felix sighed and looked back to the three one-eyed women. "All you'll accomplish is bringing the authorities down on us. You'll get sent to... wherever they send supers, and I'll probably be fined for not handling you correctly."

"Fined? For not handling us?" Ioana asked darkly.

"Yeah, fined. I told you, the city is run by a supervillain now. Heroes are little better than lampposts right now. All the borders are under checkpoint and patrolled by supers and the military alike."

Felix shrugged and stood up. Working quickly, he undid the restraints for each woman. They still looked like the walking dead, but they seemed energetic enough. They weren't in pain, either.

"How long will it take... take to fix us?" Miu asked.

"I really have no idea. I've never done anything at this level. I do plan on taking the next week off for vacation, though, to get you three put back together as much as I can."

Felix looked at each of them in turn. "Any other questions?"

Kit got her feet onto the ground and then flipped her sheets off. "Can I wander the house freely? You wouldn't mind whatever room I went into? I'd like to explore a bit if I'm going to be cooped up here for a while."

"Uhm, sure. You're all allowed to wander the extent of the house without restraint. Just please don't go outside, contact anyone, or even *try* to contact anyone." Felix scratched at the back of his head. He had hoped to keep them locked up in the ward, but that had gone out the window.

"Thanks, thanks," Kit said. "Oh! Slippers."

Kit stuck her feet in the blue slippers and shuffled her way out the door into the living room.

Miu took a second but immediately did the same, following Kit out without a word.

Ioana stared at Felix with her one eye, watching him as if he would attack her at any moment now that they were alone.

Holding up his hands, Felix walked out of the ward to the kitchen. "I'll make breakfast."

His week of rebuilding heroines was coming to a close. For the last five days, it'd been nothing but updating them on events of the city, remaking their bodies, and generally hanging out around the house.

All in all, it was actually rather enjoyable after the first couple awkward hours. Miu and Ioana had started doing some limited training in his basement with his uncle's weight set, and Kit had simply enjoyed herself.

Though the three of them really did infinitely more eating than him. Truth be told, they ate through his entire pantry. He'd already gone to the grocery store once to restock.

He'd heard supers could put away calories, but this was impressive for people who were in their condition.

They were taking a giant bite out of the small amount of money he had. With this trip, he'd be going into the negative on his credit cards.

A loan, debt on my cards… this is going to get worse.

Felix gave himself a small shake, breaking himself free of his thoughts. Turning the keys, he killed the engine and looked to his passenger.

Kit looked uncomfortable. She watched people going in and out of the grocery store like they'd attack her.

She was dressed in a sweater and a pair of jeans.

The ladies were able to face the public on a general basis. Mostly. He hadn't fixed any of the flesh, muscle, and bone that was covered by clothes. They were still quite lacking of breasts and were all scar tissue.

The points involved for that were simply much higher, and progress was slowing down. For the most part, though, they were restored to normality.

Kit ran her fingers through her hair, pulling it to one side, and then looked to him.

Now that she didn't look like a corpse, he'd call her cute. She had wavy dark brown hair, brown eyes, and a finely featured face. She wasn't pretty, but she wasn't unattractive either.

Then again, she didn't look quite healthy yet. Or even put completely back together. He got the impression that might change his opinion of her not being "pretty."

"I don't think I can do this," Kit said quietly.

"Sure you can. I guarantee you won't hear them unless you want to." Felix unclipped his seatbelt and pushed his keys into his pocket.

"Promise?" Kit asked, her hands balling into fists in front of her.

"I do. Come on, let's go. I've noticed Ioana gets feisty if she isn't fed regularly." Felix wasn't really kidding, either.

Pushing open his car door, he stepped out into the fall morning.

Adjusting his windbreaker, he looked across the top of his car. Kit finally opened her own door and stepped out. With a quick tap of the door control, he locked the car and shut it.

Felix stuck his hands in his pockets, looking around him as he walked to the front of the store.

"I was thinking. The way you described your power," Kit said from beside him. "It's... strange. One would think someone else planned it for you."

Felix sighed and looked over to Kit, who met his eyes and then looked away.

"Yeah. I know. Same thought I've had about it. That or I'm crazy. It makes no sense, though, when you consider that I didn't even have enough points to use my power."

The doors slid open and Felix grabbed a shopping cart. Angling it towards to the left, they started off into the produce aisle.

"That makes me wonder. Have you tried visualizing other things? Like, a bank account listing how many points you had, and from what source?" Kit asked, picking up a sack of potatoes.

"Huh. No. Never thought about it. And I don't talk to people about my power, so it's not like I have a sounding board for it." Felix adjusted where the potatoes sat in the cart and picked up a sack of oranges.

"Give it a try? I'm going to go get carrots and celery. Making soups and stews will stretch the pantry further."

Felix shrugged and concentrated on what she'd suggested. A bank account-looking screen that showed all of his points — where they came from and how much he had for the day and where he'd spent them.

Much to his chagrin, the screen instantly appeared.

	Received	Spent	Remaining
Daily Allotment	150	0	150
Miu Miki	400	0	400

Ioana Iliescu	800	0	800
Kit Carrington	1,500	0	1,500
DAILY TOTAL	**2,850**	**0**	**2,850**

"Shit," Felix said, closing the window.

"Worked?" Kit asked, dropping both carrots and celery into their cart as she returned.

"Yeah. You're worth twice as many points as Ioana. Miu isn't even in the same league you're in." Felix reached into the cart and readjusted everything till it fit the way he wanted it to.

"Not surprising. Telepathy is kinda rare in comparison to battle senses or inhuman strength. Miu is more or less on the lowest end of the power spectrum and is more like an enhanced human." Kit stopped talking and picked up a bottle of salad dressing and dumped it into the cart.

Felix frowned and moved the bottle. Not saying anything, they cleared the produce aisle and started working their way up and down each lane.

"How about this?" Kit said suddenly. She held up a skillet in front of her. Felix opened his mouth to tell her he had to own it first, but she kept going. "Let's try to take it one step further. Focus on this and try to use your power on it. Except I want you to… envision it as a hypothetical. As in, what would be available to you if you owned it?"

Frowning, Felix did as she instructed, and the skillet's window popped up immediately.

Tilting his head to the side a fraction, he closed the window and looked up to her.

"Worked, didn't it?" Kit gave him a bright smile, going from cute to "attractive" in a heartbeat.

"Uh, yeah. It did." Felix set the skillet back into its place on the rack. "This only makes me more nervous, though. Were these prepared in advance, are they reacting to my desires, or am I just… crazy?"

"Who cares?" Kit asked laughingly. She picked up a carton of toilet paper and slid it under the cart. "Your power works, and it's truly unique."

Felix couldn't argue with her right now. Everything she'd made him do so far had worked. Results always spoke for themselves.

"Alright. Next test. Can you give me back my powers?" she asked, turning her fingers inwards to point at herself.

"I can. I… yeah. What percentage of it do you want back?" He scratched at his jaw and turned his head; it made him nervous when she stared at him.

"Oh! That's perfect. I thought it'd just be an on/off switch. Let's try… ten percent?" She grabbed the front of the cart and got them rolling again as she spoke.

"Ten, okay," Felix agreed. Flipping open the window as Kit took control of the cart, he lowered the draw to ninety percent and accepted.

Kit slowed for a second, but then continued on as if nothing had changed.

Felix said nothing, and instead held up the list he'd made. Scratching off toilet paper, he looked around himself to figure out what was next.

"They're so quiet. It's like constant muttering," Kit said, reaching up to pull down a pack of paper plates. "Put it to one percent."

Felix obliged, and then checked his account balance.

Kit was listed as one thousand four hundred and eighty-five points now. Exactly ninety-nine percent of her value.

"I really have to focus to hear anything. To the point that it hurts. Urgh. How about five percent?"

Felix flicked the slider over four percentage points.

"I can hear them if I think about it. That's... rather nice, really. Do you mind leaving it there?"

Felix wasn't going to worry over something like seventy points right now. Not when he could always take it back just as quickly. "Sure."

"Thanks. You're an okay guy for a slaveowner."

Felix chuckled at that and shook his head. "You're a smart, telepathic lady. Read my thoughts. You'll find I'm not that nice."

Kit stopped dead in her tracks and slowly looked at him. She tilted her head to one side, then the other. "I can't. I actually can't... read your mind. I've never had that happen. Put it to one hundred percent real quick."

Doing as she requested, he popped it up to zero percent draw and looked to her.

She staggered as if struck and then looked at him. Her eyebrows drew down, and he got the feeling she was exerting immense pressure to open his mind.

Felix looked around to see if anyone was watching. It looked more like she was angry at him than anything. It was honestly rather embarrassing.

An old woman passed by them, eyeing Kit, then him. Felix made an apologetic gesture at the woman and gave her a weak smile.

"I can't," Kit said finally, shaking her head. "I actually can't read your mind."

Felix flipped her back up to ninety-five percent draw and then shrugged. "Okay? Goodie goodie for me. I'm betting it has to do with the slave master thing."

Stepping in front of Kit, he took the cart and got them rolling again.

"No, you don't understand. I can't tell if you're lying or telling the truth."

"Okay? Yeah, that's normal. Welcome to being human." Felix shook his head and turned the cart across the back aisle towards the dairy section.

"You're right. So, tell me, then," Kit said, grabbing a two-gallon jug of whole milk.

"Tell you what? The slaveowner thing?" Felix scratched off milk from his list and then pointed at the cheese section.

Kit nodded her head and grabbed a bag of shredded cheese.

"You're a source of power. A battery. Income," Felix explained slowly. He wasn't sure why he was telling her this. He was giving up some power over them in favor of... trust, maybe?

"Ah. I see. Keep us happy, healthy, and cooperative and it's easier for everyone." Kit nodded her head, dropping the cheese into the cart.

Felix grunted his agreement, immediately moving the cheese into the right spot.

"Smart. I get it. I think I'd probably do the same. Well, if we—" Kit stopped, a smile frozen on her face. "Someone is watching us. They recognized me as Augur. The things he's pushing at me mentally are... can you turn it off? Please?"

Felix nodded his head and pushed her back up to a full draw.

Kit blinked and then laughed suddenly, pressing her hands to her stomach. "Oh, that's rather nice. No helmet required, just... boop, gone. Haaaaa. Other than the whole slave thing, this is rather nice. What's next on the list?"

Looking to the list, Felix scratched at his head. "Meat. Ioana wants a lot of meat."

"Meat!" Kit said loudly. She jumped up on the back of the cart, sending it skittering forward as she pointed towards the indicated section.

Sighing, Felix followed along behind her. He didn't blame her for her actions. He imagined her life up to this point had probably been full of the thoughts and emotions of others.

She lived for herself now.

Well, through me, for herself. All fifteen hundred points of herself.

Felix stopped dead, staring at nothing.

He had two thousand eight hundred and fifty points.

A grin popped up over his face, and suddenly, the world seemed a much brighter place.

Felix smiled at Miu and Ioana as they opened the garage door. Felix turned the keys and shut the car off. Opening his door, he tossed the keys to Miu.

Giving them a quick wave, he slipped by them and entered the house.

"What?" Miu asked, catching the keys and looking to him.

"If you could please unload the car, I'll take care of lunch in a bit. I'm sorry, and thank you," Felix said over his shoulder, heading straight to his uncle's study.

"Why? What's wrong?" Ioana called after him. "Felix!"

"Gotta check something. Might just solve a whole buncha problems."

Felix opened a dresser drawer and pulled out a solid ingot of lead. It weighed five pounds and had been one of his early experiments.

He knew that he didn't have the points to turn it into gold.

Focusing on the heavy metal, he called up the window for it.

Picking the "material" section, he changed it to silver, then looked at the point value needed.

Two thousand points. Exactly as he remembered it from when he'd tried different materials.

Grinning, he hit the confirm button. The five-pound lead bar was replaced with a five-pound silver bar.

Laughing, he picked up the bar and flipped it over in his hands. It was real. It existed. It worked.

"We're in business."

"And what business is that?" Ioana asked from the door, her arms folded across her chest.

Felix looked to her and gave her a big smile. "Whatever we want it to be. First, we need to buy a lot of cheap metal. Whole lot of it."

Then Felix realized something even better. He could quit whenever he wanted if this went as he hoped it would.

Chapter 5 - Slow Joe -

"Alright," Felix said finally, looking over to the three women standing in the doorway. "I'm going to head out to a pawn shop and sell this."

Wagging the silver bar at the women, he gave them a smile.

"Why a pawn shop?" Ioana asked.

"Because they're less likely to ask questions. After that, I'll need to pick up some more lead bars. This one I got from an auction sale for a scuba school. I figure I can hit another one for more weights. That or fishing supplies. They use weights, right?"

"What if they're not pure lead?" Miu asked quietly.

"Then it might cost a few extra points, or fewer. So long as most of it is there, it should be relatively the same. Besides, I can check it now before I buy it. Thanks to Kit."

Felix wormed his way between the three of them and grabbed his uncle's keys.

He wasn't going to be using his car anytime soon since it still had groceries in it.

Sliding the door open, he hopped in and jammed the keys into the ignition. As the garage door started to open, Miu opened the passenger door and got in next to him.

"I will accompany you," she said. Reaching for his hand, she snagged the silver bar from him and then buckled her seatbelt.

"Alright," Felix said uneasily. A single glance over his shoulder to confirm it was clear, and he backed them out of the garage quickly.

He really only knew of one pawn shop. It would have probably been a good idea to do some research and figure out the best one to go to.

Felix couldn't help himself, though. He was excited.

An income that couldn't be taxed, written off through cash, and done on a daily level.

No, he was beyond excited.

Miu said nothing the entire ride over. She quietly flipped the bar over and over in her hands as she sat there.

She'd apparently gotten a hold of one of his hoodies and looked very similar to Kit in her style of dress.

As her name would imply, she was clearly of an Asian heritage. He'd have guessed Japanese, but he was truly awful at figuring out people's ethnicity. That and it didn't matter that much to him.

In a world filled with Elves, Dwarves, Beastkin, and every other fairytale creature under the sun, race didn't matter that much.

She was a touch prettier than Kit, though her face held no emotion. She seemed more akin to a doll at times.

Felix shook himself from his thoughts as he pulled into a parking spot in front of the pawn shop.

"May I handle the sale?" Miu asked, patting the silver against her palm.

Felix looked at her and then nodded once. "Sure. You might be able to get more than me anyways. Being pretty helps.

"Sell it, don't pawn it. I was hoping to get at least eighty percent of the melt value for silver."

Miu nodded her head and then got out of the car, walking straight for the front door. Felix locked the car and fell in behind her.

Right up until she headed for the sales counter.

Felix turned off to one side to look around.

All around him were things that the pawn shop had purchased and was reselling. Jewelry, instruments, weapons, anything and everything.

And if I were the owner of this shop, I could upgrade and resell at an even higher price.

Screw transmutation. Pawn shop! We'll do this alchemist thing for a bit, buy a pawn shop, then really get the money rolling in.

Felix grinned, leaning into a display case and doing hypothetical point checks on watches, rings, necklaces, earrings.

It was all well within his power to turn these low-grade metal pieces into much more expensive ones. Even if he only did everything in silver. Or converted a low-value gold into a higher-value gold.

Or diamonds.

Technically, diamonds would be easier than gold, since diamonds are more common. Hah. This is it.

Or if he got really lucky, a damaged antique.

Fixing something that had a low material value but a high intrinsic value.

That's the real money.

"I got you ninety percent." Miu sidled up next to him. "Going to buy us jewelry?"

"No. Besides, this is all rather cheap. But this trip did give me an idea. A big one, in fact." He turned and exited the pawn shop quickly, getting back into the car. It wasn't until they were both seated and the car had been fired up that he continued.

"We're going to buy a pawn shop. Or make one. We'll pay a bit more than others to purchase items to draw customers in. Then I modify, fix, or whatever, then we sell it at a higher return. It's perfect."

Miu digested that, turning her head to one side. Black hair as dark as night covered her deep brown eyes. "Yes. I think that would be a good direction. Though I do not think you have the money for this, no?"

"No. Not yet. But you have to spend it to make it. And that," Felix said, pointing to the money in Miu's hand, "is the start. Off to buy some lead. Then I have to get ready for work tomorrow. If I can get myself fired, they have to give me a paycheck immediately. I think I have something like four weeks of vacation accrued and several weeks of sick time. By law, they have to pay it out to me as it was earned time, not given."

Miu raised her eyebrows at that, then gave him a small smile. "Bold. And stupid. Craven, too."

"Sounds like me, I guess." Felix shrugged, backing up out of the parking space.

Felix walked through the front door of the fast food restaurant where he spent his days with a big shit-eating grin. Dropping his time card into the punch clock two hours early, he immediately called his regional manager.

Much to his surprise, he heard a phone going off from his office. Spinning towards the door to his office, he lifted the handle and turned it.

It opened easily enough and he found Joe hunched over his computer. Pecking at the keys, he glanced up as Felix entered.

"There you are. Kind of you to actually show up. Now, I need—"

"Fuck off, Joe," Felix said with a grin. "Actually, first. Janessa!"

The woman whom Felix had learned to loathe jerked in response to his sudden shout. She was in the back, putting on makeup, of course.

"You're fired. Here's your final paycheck. I took care of it this morning through accounting. Go finish your makeup in your car." Felix held out the final check to her.

He'd spent the better part of his morning going over Joe's head to HR, payroll, and legal.

Joe was going to be in a world of hurt once HR started up its investigation. For now, this was more of a means to an end.

Janessa snatched the paper from his hands with a squawk. She looked between him and Joe, then fled the building quickly.

Felix entered the rest of the way into his office and then closed the door. He sat down in a chair in front of Joe with a huff.

"What the fu—"

"Shut up, Joe." Felix shook his head and rolled his eyes. "We all know you only kept her on to try and bang her. Don't worry, I'm sure you can hire her on somewhere else."

He grinned at the sweating regional manager. It'd only make it worse for him when he had to explain that.

"One more word and I'll have you fired—"

"Then do it. Fire me. Now."

"Felix, what the he—"

"Fire me, you disgusting bastard. Do you have any idea how many times I've covered for your incompetence? No? Whatever. Fire me."

"You're asking me to fire you."

"No, I'm calling you a disgusting piece of shit."

Joe glared at him and then leaned forward with a sick smile. "You're fired. Effective immediately."

"Great. Here's what you owe me. I've already made sure of everything with payroll and accounting in advance. Let me just get them on the phone," Felix said, laying down a slip of paper with his balance sheet on it. In the other hand, he dialed up HR.

It was going to be a hell of a final paycheck that would probably screw up Joe's entire bottom line for the month. With any luck, the store would underperform at the same time.

Going to be a bad month for you, Joe.

"Hello, this is Susan."

"Hey, Susan? This is Felix. We spoke earlier. Joe has officially fired me."

"I see. Could you please put me on speaker so I can confirm this?" came back the voice on the other end.

Felix set his phone down in front of himself and thumbed the speaker phone button.

"You're on," Felix said.

"Hi, Joe, this is Susan over at Human Resources. I understand you've terminated Felix from his position?"

Joe looked confused, glaring first at Felix then his phone. Clearing his throat, he leaned over the phone. "That is, we were—"

"You told me I was fired. Effective immediately. Did you not?" Felix said, grinning at Joe.

Hesitating for a moment more, Joe finally nodded his head. "Yes. Felix is terminated immediately."

"Thank you," came back Susan's voice.

Felix flipped it off speaker and put it back to his ear.

"Alright, Susan, you're back with me now. Was that all you needed?"

"Yes. Was this immediately after you terminated Janessa?" Susan asked.

"Sure was. About two minutes."

"I'm sorry about this. We'll be in touch with you soon. I've cleared your final paycheck to your account."

"Whatever. Doesn't matter," Felix said, disconnecting the line.

"Alright. With that, I'm done. You're a scumbag, Joe. I hope you get what's coming to you in the future," Felix said brightly.

Getting out of the chair, Felix opened the door, tossed his name badge on a counter, and walked right back out the front door.

Stepping outside, Felix stretched his arms over his head and then sighed with a smile.

That had been refreshing.

Felix jumped when his phone started ringing in his hand.

Looking down at the caller ID, he frowned. He didn't recognize the number.

Lifting it to his ear, he thumbed the call accept button.

"This is Felix," he said, walking to his car.

"Hey, Felix," came the smooth voice of Marcus. Caldwell.

He didn't give a flying pig's ass what the man called himself.

"Hey, Caldwell. More merchandise already?"

"Hey, hey. It's Leon today. And yeah, merchandise. Kind of. There's an auction going down in three hours. I only found out about it a few minutes ago. Got you an invitation.

"Different this time, though. No damaged goods. Price will be higher accordingly, of course."

Felix looked down at his feet, his keys forgotten in his hand. "How much higher would that be?"

"Last numbers I looked at, it seemed like the average price was about ten to eleven thousand per."

He grunted at the number. He didn't have that and wouldn't have that. It was beyond his means. A pity, since—

"Alright. Give me the address," Felix said, making a snap decision.

Sell my car and pull out the paycheck in the bank, that's about twelve.

"Alright, alright. I'll text you the address. See you there, Felix."

Looking up from the hood of his car, he saw the loan shark across the street. The man operated out of a restaurant that he coincidentally owned.

This is a terrible idea. This is truly an awful idea.

He couldn't manage a thought other than how much of a bad idea this was. Right up to the point that Felix found himself standing in front of said loan shark.

"I need twenty grand," Felix said without preamble, introduction, or thought.

The loan shark blinked and looked at him in confusion. Then he started laughing and pointed at Felix.

"A man who knows exactly what he wants and doesn't waste my time. I'm Dimitry."

"Felix." Holding out his hand to Dimitry, he shook it briefly. Then he was pulled in close to the man, who pulled open Felix's shirt to look inside.

"No wire, either," Dimitry said, lifting Felix's arm to run his fingers down his side. "Or a piece."

"No. I'm just—"

"Yeah, yeah. Sorry. One of those things. Twenty grand?" Dimitry asked, looking at Felix first, then over his shoulder towards where he'd worked up until about ten minutes ago.

He'd undoubtedly seen Felix a number of times while he was working. Felix could even remember intervening once between a worker and Dimitry when they'd messed up an order.

Dimitry knew exactly who Felix was.

"I don't normally lend so much to someone I don't know. I don't know you, but I know of you. I want forty back from you in three months. If you try to pay up early, it'll still be forty grand. These are my terms."

"I accept." Felix said it with as much authority as he could.

Dimitry sniffed and took a drag of the cigarette in his left hand.

"Fine. Go inside. Here's some markers. Head inside, talk to the hostess, get your money." Dimitry pulled out four tokens from his pocket and handed them to Felix.

Taking the plastic circles, Felix realized there was no going back from this point. Closing his fist around them tightly, he went into the restaurant.

"See you in three months, Felix Campbell," Dimitry murmured with a shark-like grin.

The skin on the back of Felix's neck prickled at the use of his last name.

Getting out of the cab, Felix walked up the driveway towards his aunt's oversized SUV.

He tried not to use their vehicles since they weren't technically his.

Opening the rear door, he tossed in the thirty-three thousand dollars in a briefcase and then shut it.

"Where's your car?" Ioana asked from the corner of the garage, startling him. He hadn't even seen her or realized she was there.

"Sold it. There's an auction that's going to start. They're selling... slaves. I needed money so I could participate. If I can get more supers, I can make money faster."

Ioana wrinkled her nose at that, yet said nothing. She eased herself back into the chair and ignored him.

Felix darted into the house for a quick change of clothes, something a bit more professional and anonymous. Put together in a simple black business suit, he slipped into the large black SUV with its tinted windows.

His aunt had disliked being seen.

Looking over, Felix found he wasn't alone.

Kit waved from the passenger seat, dressed in her street clothes.

"I'm going! You'll need me anyways. You'll need to set my power to about twenty percent, I bet. We should probably stop and get me some clothes to match your own. You can spend a few points to fix up what the clothes can't cover.

"Miu and Ioana have offered up one eye each, their left arms, and their toes to get me presentable."

Felix cringed at the morbid nature of the discussion, but then sighed and nodded his head.

They'd been quick to convene and discuss it since he'd only been home a short while.

"Fine, let's get this over with."

At least it won't be painful for anyone.

Felix gave his name at the front door. A paper was checked and he was allowed in after a cursory pat-down.

The building they'd been directed to was a large thirty-floor building that served multiple governmental needs.

One of which was apparently auctions on slaves.

"It's almost like an industry," Kit murmured, walking along beside him.

She'd chosen a simple black dress with long sleeves. They'd only had to do some minor work to restore her exposed skin.

She was also functioning at thirty percent of her original power, as she'd suggested.

"It isn't like an industry, it *is* one. This is where debtors, prisoners, and other malcontents who meet certain qualifications end up. I imagine the bulk of the money generated here ends up in the hands of the government itself." Felix moved at a regulated pace. This wasn't a normal auction, per se.

All of the "goods" were on display on different floors and rooms. From what he understood, after a few hours, everyone would be asked into various meeting rooms. Everyone would be given a simple button remote that tied into the Wi-Fi and would register their bids.

Everyone would be anonymous. He imagined it would help to increase bids and prices. If no one knew who won an auction, he figured it was better for everyone involved.

"No," Kit said, as they walked by a glass-walled conference room. Inside was a number of men and women seated in chairs with placards in front of them. "None of them will be worth our time. They'd only work against us."

Us?

Felix was taken aback momentarily at that statement. Kit had always been supportive, oddly so. He didn't like it. It didn't make sense to him.

Nonetheless, he had to agree. From the look of them, they all valued themselves highly and would be accordingly attributed so. They weren't for him.

Kit turned her head slightly, as if she were looking into the roof.

"Two floors up, that's where we want to be. Everything above that isn't worth our time, and everything below that will be out of our league."

"And how do you know this?" Felix asked casually.

"Powerful enough to be useful, smart enough to fall in line, not prideful enough to raise problems. Trust me."

He didn't like that. Didn't want to. Trust wasn't easy, wasn't really in his vocabulary or his dictionary.

"Alright, alright. Makes sense. Anything we don't spend here we can use to buy lead," Felix said, agreeing to her desire.

They walked over to the elevator and Kit hit the button to call it.

"I think you should limit yourself to three at the most. Six will strain your ability to keep everyone in check. Once everyone is more settled and up to speed, you can increase the size again," Kit said as they stepped into the elevator and the doors closed.

"Thank you for the advice. Are you my consigliere now?" Felix asked.

"Better. I'm someone who wants you to succeed because it gives me what I want, while providing me with the least number of problems. So I'm an involved, and willing, party to all of this."

"Uh-huh. We'll see," Felix muttered as the doors swung open.

This floor was definitely different than the others. There was a tension in the air that was palpable.

Felix couldn't pinpoint the problem or why it was so different. Instead, he looked to the conference rooms on each side of him and saw a very similar display to the ones on the floors below. There were less interested parties, but it was roughly the same type of situation.

"They have villains and heroes both on this floor. Everything below this was heroes with a certain mindset or civilians with talents."

Felix couldn't help but feel confused about that. Villains selling villains.

"I wouldn't worry about purchasing villains. They'll serve just as well. You do realize Ioana isn't a hero, right? She falls more on the villain side of things," Kit explained, pulling him into a conference room.

"I thought you didn't know her." Felix was rapidly losing control over the whole thing.

"I didn't, I looked her up on the internet. She fights anyone who she feels is stronger or a better warrior than her. Often, she kills them if they didn't live up to her expectations. She's called War Maiden."

"Oh," Felix said intelligently.

Chapter 6 - For Sale -

"Do you think we should talk to them?" Felix asked, looking at the information displayed on terminals in front of the conference room.

Kit was standing next to him, flipping through a similar terminal.

"Doesn't matter. I can read their minds. I think we're better served by you using your hypothetical screen to get an idea of what we're working with."

"That almost seems like cheating. Reading their mind for every answer you'd like." Felix looked at the men and women in the first conference room.

Kit sighed and looked into the room as well. "It made dating impossible. No room for white lies. Let's start with this group, then. Give me a bit. You read through the terminal while I sort through them."

Felix shrugged and started to read through the information available to him. In minutes, he wasn't really reading it anymore. It didn't matter.

Kit would tell him if these people fit the bill or not.

"Hey, Felix." The voice jolted him from his wandering thoughts.

Looking up, he grinned as he realized who it was.

"Leon. How's it going?" Felix asked, holding out his hand.

"Good, good. Holy shit, is that... it is," Leon said, shaking Felix's hand.

"Yeah," Felix said, looking back at Kit as she did her thing. "So what's up?"

"Huh? Oh. Nothing. Working the crowd. Building contacts. Apparently the brass were real pleased. Getting rid of their castoffs and making money at the same time really turned a head or two.

"You'll have to tell me some time how you managed to—"

"You're welcome," Felix said, interrupting him. Then he turned to look back into the conference room. "Thanks for the invite, by the way. I'll not forget it."

"I'll hold you to that, man, I'll hold you to that. Alright, I'm going to go keep making rounds. Most people think she's dead, by the way, so make sure you stick to that story."

Felix nodded, glancing back at Kit and then to the terminal as Leon left.

Fuck that. Marcus, Caldwell, Leon, whatever. From now on he's Mr. No-Name.

"See ya later, Mr. No-Name." Felix tapped at the screen, pulling up the rap sheet on the woman he was looking at again.

Felix shifted in his seat and adjusted his tie again.

"Stop, it looks fine. Besides, no one can see you," Kit said, lounging in the recliner next to him.

Being invited here by No-Name had provided them with a few benefits he hadn't expected. Like being sequestered in a small office and watching the auction on a TV screen.

"Though this is going to be a lot easier to talk. I was a little concerned about how we were going to do this." Kit sipped from the soda can she'd gotten from somewhere.

"Yeah, true. Hey, should I be concerned about people recognizing you?" Felix asked, putting his thoughts out there. He'd been mildly concerned about it for some time but kept putting it into the back of his mind. He hadn't wanted to consider it.

"Not really, no. Most people who knew me as Augur knew that without my helmet, I was fairly susceptible to forced thoughts."

"Forced thoughts?" Felix asked as the announcer on the screen rambled on and on. Until they got to the actual auction portion, he wasn't that interested.

"My helmet protected me from what basically came down to people thinking nasty thoughts at me. I don't have a way to block them out. Er, well, didn't have a way to block them out. Now I just have you turn down the volume."

"So… you don't think we should worry because most can't recognize you without the helmet, and the ones who do would try to break your brain?"

"Yup. Besides, you can always change my hair color with your fancy powers, can't you?" Kit asked, swiveling her head around to peer at him.

"Actually, I think I can do that."

"So, yeah, not worried about it. Wouldn't matter if they did. Oh, here we go," Kit said, turning back to the TV. "Lucky us, it's even one we were thinking of."

Felix nodded his head. They'd spent most of the time in the conference rooms figuring out who they were interested in and how many points they'd give back to him.

The man on the screen was a big, brutish thing. He looked more in line with a classic representation of a caveman than a modern-day human.

Before Felix could press the button to bid, the price listed over the man's head jumped into the twenty-thousand-dollar range.

"Damn," Kit muttered. "Not surprising, though. To be perfectly frank about this whole thing I think I already know the three we'll end up with. Mostly because others will see them in a certain way, even if we know better."

Felix sighed as he watched the price go ever higher. He'd wanted this one. If nothing than for the simple fact that he was worth in excess of eight thousand points.

"I never dealt with him personally. I'd heard of him. I hadn't realized he'd come into the city," Kit said conversationally about the man on the screen.

Felix wasn't really interested in him anymore. He was far and away out of his price range.

"What was Miu, exactly? She clearly knows you. Well, it seems like she knows you, but you don't know her," Felix said. The auction closed out on the man and someone he wasn't interested in took their place.

"Miu. She was internal security forces. For civilians. I knew of her, but didn't really interact with her. She'd applied for higher-end teams but never put in the training or time to do it. She's actually got a good power. Anything she is, or can do, is multiplied.

"If she could normally lift eighty pounds, she'd be able to lift one-sixty.

"So if she became a real bodybuilder, she'd probably be on par with the one we just saw get purchased," Kit said, with a small frown curling her lips.

"That's… odd. I wonder why she didn't do just that, then," Felix said.

On the screen, the auction continued, sale after sale concluding, none of which held any interest to him.

"I probed her once. A little. She's… different. Her brain works in a way that I wasn't really familiar with. Got out of there quick after that. Unique minds are touchy things. Think of the geniuses of an age and those are all unique minds.

"Her motivation isn't there, though. It's like she's lacking one key thing."

Felix shrugged his shoulders at that. "Maybe I could order her to train more vigorously?"

"Oh, oh. Here we go. We liked this one. She was the magic user."

"Magic us—oh. Her." Felix didn't really care for this one. She was a powerful magic user alright. One that had fed on the souls of other supers to increase her own abilities.

She was a powerhouse. A powerhouse who was a walking demon.

Long black hair flowed down her back and shoulders, and an aura of energy crackled around her. She had black eyes that seemed too big for her face and skin that was as pale as porcelain.

Her features were sharp and elegant, something you'd expect more out of a fashion model than a villain who tore the souls out of the living.

She'd been called many things, but the name that stuck with the masses was Mab. The fairy queen of legend and story.

No one seemed to know her actual name.

Felix didn't really get the connection or care what name she used. What he did care about was the fact that her point value was significant.

Two thousand five hundred. A cool thousand above Kit even.

That and he was pretty sure people weren't going to bid on her. Something about stealing people's souls made everything touch and go.

The opening bid was set at five thousand.

Nothing happened.

After a minute, the bid dropped to four thousand.

Again, nothing happened.

As if sensing the problem, the moderator in control of the bid dropped it down to a thousand dollars.

Felix thumbed the button, his own number of forty-two popping up in the top right of the screen.

The bid locked in a green color. Below that, an increment bid of five hundred appeared with a question mark.

There were no counter bids. They'd underestimated how much people had been unnerved by the soul-taking thing.

The number turned black and "sold" was written across the screen.

Mab was taken away and the next person was brought up.

Curious, Felix mentally opened his "point account" as he had taken to thinking of it. He also deliberately tried to skew his thoughts about tomorrow's projected point values, rather than what they were today.

Today's points were a mess of body parts and other things that he'd have to put to rights before the day ended.

PROJECTED	Received	Spent	Remaining
Daily Allotment	150	0	150
Miu Miki	400	0	400
Ioana Iliescu	800	0	800
Kit Carrington	1,500	0	1,500
Lilian Lux	2,500	0	2,500
DAILY TOTAL	5,350	0	5,350

"Her name is Lilian Lux. Lily." Felix shook his head and closed the window.

"I doubt her parents knew what she'd become when they named her."

"Yeah, but Lily Lux? That's just…" Felix snickered, shaking his head.

Next, a man was brought up. He had the look of a man in his thirties who'd spent his life working outdoors.

This was another person they'd decided on trying to pick up, Aeric.

His power had been rather straightforward—he could move with unheard-of speed and grace. It put quite a strain on his body, so he'd trained himself to cope with it.

The bid started at ten grand, which Felix happily pressed his button for.

"Oh good, we might have a sho—" Kit started when there wasn't an immediate incremental bid.

Then it jumped to fifteen thousand.

Felix gritted his teeth and thumbed the button again. They'd gotten Lily cheap. He could spend a bit more on Aeric.

He saw his bid flash on the screen, then vanish as it was replaced several times, ending at twenty-two thousand.

Felix hit the button again. It was probably his last possible bid he could throw up.

Before his number had even finished materializing, it was gone, the bid rocketing up to thirty thousand.

"Fine, whatever. For fuck's sake," Felix grumbled.

"It's alright. I wasn't expecting to get him anyways."

"And who are you expecting we'll get, then?" Felix asked, still grumpy.

"Andrea Elex and Felicia Fay."

"Those were… the multiple one and the inventor?" Felix asked after a moment.

"The very same. Felicia was at my own point value, I think, and Andrea just under it, right?" Kit asked, tossing her empty soda can across the room to clatter into the trash bin.

"Yeah. I think they were about that. Why so sure on those?"

"Mind reading. There's some seriously bad vibes going through here. But those are two names I haven't really heard from anyone else. And those that are interested are going for the lowball bid."

"Huh. You're way more useful than I gave you credit for. Sorry, Kit."

Kit shook her head and then started to laugh softly. "Yes. World's strongest telepath. Useful for getting good buys on slaves."

"Sorry. You're not... er, I don't care that you were Augur. Never paid much attention to supers anyways. You're just Kit," Felix said, slinking into his chair.

"No, I get that. It's fine. Just... unexpected. Ah, here's Andrea."

Felix looked up to the screen as a young woman stepped into frame. She looked like a college student to him. Or so he thought, based on her face and demeanor. It made her seem out of place.

That impression was ruined when he took in her clothes.

She was wearing what looked to him like a harness and webbing for military hardware.

You could easily call her cute, maybe bordering on the side of "girl next door" pretty.

Two large ears peaked through her mess of dirty blonde-colored hair. One eye was a crystalline blue and the other a dark brown. Behind her was a limp, bushy tail that swept outward. She looked to be about five foot six and held herself awkwardly.

"Huh, she's a Beastkin." Felix thumbed the bid button the moment her price of five-thousand popped up.

"Yes, and she'll be very useful for us. She's a multiplier. Creates clones of herself.

"I think you'll get her for six or seven, but our last one will cost us." Kit sighed and pressed a palm to her forehead. "Can you dial me out to ten percent?"

Felix nodded and flipped her draw up to ninety.

"That... is so special," Kit murmured, melting into her chair.

Looking back to the screen, he realized Andrea was now at seven thousand. Felix thumbed the button, pitching it up to eight grand.

The bids stopped and nothing further came through. Then Andrea was his, and she shuffled off the stage.

The camera shifted its view to center a young woman who couldn't have been taller than five feet.

She had dark brown curls that hung short around her face. She had a petite look to her and a small hourglass frame. Her face was on the cute side of the equation, but held a fiery look to those light brown eyes.

"Oh, there's Felicia. Lucky us. She's an inventor. After this, we can relax.

"I almost forgot, there's supposed to be a new season of that dating show starting tonight. The one we were watching last week. I forget the name," Kit said, snapping her fingers as if trying to remember.

"You said she'll be pricey?" Felix asked as the woman lifted a hand and yelled at someone off stage.

"Think so. Probably about twenty. She's worth it. The Fiancé? What was it again?"

Felix acted quickly when the screen flashed to Felicia's starting price of five thousand. He jammed the button ten times.

And up her price jumped. From five to fifteen in a second, with Felix's number in the corner.

Someone else pushed it to sixteen, to which Felix flicked the trigger twice. Pushing it straight to eighteen.

The bids ended as quickly as they came in. He was pretty sure he'd made his point to whoever else was bidding.

With a buzz, Felix now owned an inventor.

Then the channel switched as Kit held up the remote, changing the channel to normal cable.

"Wish we had snacks. Snacks would be kickass. Dial me to zero?" Kit asked.

No-Name popped in eventually with his three new slaves in tow.

"Sorry, Felix. Didn't realize they'd put you in here."

"I know, awesome, right? No need to be quiet or even worry about eavesdropping. Remind me to get you to invite me again next time," Felix said, standing up.

"Yeah, really helped. Hey, are there any snacks around here?" Kit asked, leaning her head back on the headrest of the recliner

"Huh? Oh, yeah. Across the hall, actually. As long as you're happy, then, Felix."

No-Name stepped to the side and let the three newcomers file in.

"I'll need the purchase amount in full. Once I've got that, these are yours. I'd recommend using your Pit immediately."

Nodding his head, Felix picked up his briefcase and counted out twenty-seven stacks of one thousand dollars. They were still wrapped in the numbered bands from the bank.

No-Name pulled up a briefcase Felix hadn't noticed and transferred the money into it.

"Great, pleasure doing business with you, Felix. I'll hit you up again if I hear of another auction. Similar merchandise? Willing to settle for less? Or more?" No-Name asked.

"Sure, hit me up for any of that. Not a problem. Let me guess, you get a cut with me as your guest?" Felix said with a grin, holding his hand out to him.

"Damn skippy," No-Name said, shaking Felix's hand. "See ya, Felix."

"Later, No-Name."

"Leon."

"No-Name." Felix shrugged his shoulders and rolled his eyes as No-Name left.

Turning to the three newcomers, Felix fished out his owner's box. "Index finger please, Felicia."

Felix held it out in front of the diminutive woman. She said nothing, but glared at him as she stuck her finger into the box.

"You're up next, Andrea."

The Beastkin's ears lay flat to her head as she glared at him from under her bangs. Then promptly put her finger into the box.

Moving to the beautiful magician, he smiled and held out the box to her. "You're up, Lilian."

Lilian's eyebrows drew together and she stared at him for a long second. "And how do you know that name?" she asked finally, pushing her finger into the hole of the box.

"What, that your name is Lilian Lux? Does it matter?" Felix put the small box back into his coat and then adjusted it. "Time to go home. You three need to earn your keep tonight.

"First, though, we need to go buy some things."

All three women eyed him.

Opening the rear van doors as he passed by, Felix picked up the weights and went inside house.

He'd already taken the time to revert Kit to how she was pre-auction. He wanted to put Miu and Ioana back together to a more normal state before the newbies saw them.

Both Miu and Ioana were in the living room, watching TV. He targeted Miu and put her back together, then Ioana.

If he didn't get them put back to rights before the points reset at midnight, they'd be lost points.

Waste not, want not.

Glancing over his shoulder, he watched as Kit herded his new recruits into the house.

Setting the weights down onto the coffee table, he activated his current point balance.

	Received	Spent	Remaining
Daily Allotment	150	0	150
Miu Miki	400	0	400
Ioana Iliescu	800	0	800
Kit	1,500	0	1,500

Carrington			
Lilian Lux	2,500	0	2,500
Andrea Elex	1,300	0	1,300
Felicia Fay	1,550	0	1,550
DAILY TOTAL	**8,200**	**0**	**8,200**

He'd bought a bunch of fishing weights that weighed out at about half a pound each. They looked more like cannonballs than fishing weights.

Then again, he'd never been fishing.

Seemed boring.

Focusing on the first half-pound fishing weight, he pulled up the upgrade screen and selected the material.

To convert a half-pound fishing weight to gold was five thousand points.

It'd leave him with over three thousand points left over.

Hitting the confirm button, Felix chuckled as the weight became pure gold.

"Damn," Kit said from over his shoulder.

"Yeah. So that works. Can't keep doing this, though. Someone will eventually wise up. Hence the pawn shop idea."

"Pawn shop?" Kit asked.

"Miu and I were talking about it the other day. A pawn shop would be a great way to launder my powers into money, without raising the ire of our overlords."

Felicia's hand shot forward and she picked up the golden ball. She smacked it into one of the other lead weights. She immediately pulled it up to her eye, intent to inspect it.

The dent it had caused was easy for everyone to see.

"This is gold," she said, her voice a surprisingly low tone.

"Yep. It sure is. It's also how we pay back the bank, the loan shark, and get our pawn shop." Felix leaned back in his chair, resting his hands behind his head.

Chapter 7 - Investment -

"You will wake up now." The melodic voice brought Felix out of a deep dream. Blinking a few times, he managed to slowly focus on Lily standing above him.

"Morning, Lily," Felix said, and then yawned. Looking over at the clock, he saw it was a touch past seven. "Little early to wake up. I don't have a job anymore. Self-employed."

"You will release me," said the lovely soul-stealing monster.

"Uhm, no? Seriously. What'd you wake me up for?" Felix rubbed at his eyes with the palms of his hands.

"I... you will rele—"

"No. I won't. And just a hint, none of your powers will work on me. The Pit pretty much ended that problem. On top of that, I took your powers away to fuel mine.

"Completely. You're just a beautiful young woman right now. That's it."

Felix swung his legs over the edge of the bed, sending Lily scurrying backwards a few steps.

Sighing, he bent over his knees and slapped his hands into his temples twice. "Breakfast. Need food."

"No... my magic can't be gone. It can't. I can't... I can't do anything. This is... no," Lily said, making strange hand gestures.

"Well, temporarily gone. I can turn it back on whenever we need it. Is something burning?" Felix asked, sniffing the air.

"Temporarily? Give them back to me!" Lily stepped in close and loomed over him.

"Yeah, no. Seriously, though, it smells like burnt toast." Felix stood up and pushed Lily back with one hand as he left his room and headed for the kitchen.

"Now, you'll give them back now!" Lily shouted at his back, trailing him.

Entering the kitchen, he found Felicia sitting on the floor with what looked like a toaster spread across the tiles. She looked very confused, her hands holding the shell of the toaster.

The grunting snores coming from the living room on the other side of the island drew his attention. Sprawled out on a couch and sounding much akin to a chainsaw going through a zombie was Andrea.

"I can't fix it. It wasn't working right. I can't make it work." Felicia mumbled. She looked up to him and held up the toaster shell. "I'm broken."

Letting out a slow breath through his teeth, he pressed a hand to his head.

"Powers! Now!" Lily shouted in his ear.

Andrea snorted and fell off the coach, jumping up to her feet. She threw her arms to the left and then the right while yelling incomprehensibly.

Her face twisted up in a confused frown and she hopped in place twice.

"I can't split. I can't split? I can't split!" Andrea yelled while looking at Felix.

"Be quiet for two minutes, all of you. For fuck's sake." Felix sat down on a stool and shook his head.

Kit, Miu, and Ioana stepped out of their shared room. All three looked confused, or annoyed. Ioana somehow managed both.

"Sorry. They're just now figuring out I took their powers. I probably should have explained more last night," Felix apologized to the three. "I'm going to set everyone to a small percent of their power back. This isn't permanent."

Felix called up each woman's screen and set the draw to ninety-five percent. That left him with seven thousand eight hundred some odd points.

"There, you all have a fraction of your power back. Except for you, Kit, I have yours still off."

"Thanks, leave it off. Are you making breakfast today?" she asked, sliding into a stool across from him.

"Was going to, but Felicia decided the toaster had to die. So that removes anything from the toaster menu.

"Whatever. Maybe we should go get some breakfast or something. Need to sell that gold and do another conversion today. Then use the rest of the points on you three."

"You will give me my powers back. Now. All of them. Then I'm leaving," Lily demanded, her hand resting on his shoulder.

"Lily, what part of this haven't you gotten yet?"

"My name is Mab!"

"No, it's Lilian Lux. You're twenty-six years old, and you don't have magical powers. You actually have ethereal projection. You honed it to the point where you could draw magical symbols and runes with it.

"Now, here's something you should know."

Felix looked over his shoulder at the enchanting face. "You're my property. You can't harm me, or tell me what to do. So far, I've been tolerant, and I will continue to do so. That tolerance will eventually run thin."

Felix blew out a breath and then scratched at his head.

"I don't plan on using you against your will, but you will remain my property. You can live a fairly normal life, but you won't be running rampant with your powers again. Any questions?"

Lily's mouth hung open, her jaw worked as she seemingly tried to find the words.

"No? Alright. Felicia," Felix said, turning to the woman with his toaster. "Did you murder it, or can you fix that with the small amount of power I put back in you."

"I can fix it," Felicia said, already hard at working putting the whole thing back together.

"Goodie."

"I can make pancakes!" Andrea said loudly, bouncing back and forth in one spot. Then she separated into two people.

Felix looked from one, to the other, then back again.

"We can do it! Leave it to us," they said in unison.

Picking up a marker from the table, he looked to the Andreas. "Which one of you is the prime?" he asked.

The Andrea on the left held up her hand high above her. "Hooooooi. That's me."

Felix walked over to the prime Andrea, pulled the sleeve of her shirt up, and wrote a big "P" on her shoulder.

"We'll need something more permanent. I'm betting metal won't be duplicated when you clone yourself. Maybe a ring or a necklace. Anyways.

"Right. Start in on those pancakes. Thanks, Andrea Prime and Andrea One."

The Beastkin and her clone looked at each other. "We never thought of that," they said at the same time.

Then they cheered in unison and they both leapt over the couch to get into the kitchen.

"I suppose today can be interview and job assignment day. Each of you, please come see me one at a time in the study. We'll get this sorted out now before we get any later in this whole..." Felix made a jerky vague movement with his hands as he spoke. "Whatever this is."

Sliding off the stool, he pushed it under the counter and went to the study. He popped the power button on his computer as he went, sitting down behind the desk.

The door slammed shut and Felix looked up.

Lily sat down in the seat across from him, her hands pressed to the desk.

"You will start with me," she said ominously.

"Hooray," Felix deadpanned.

"Do not mock me," Lily said, leveling a finger at him.

"Why not? So far all you've done is bitch and moan. All I've done to you so far is drain your powers. Give me a reason to not treat you like a spoiled, conceited little princess."

Felix typed in his password and flipped through a few virtual pages that came up on the desk terminal.

Firing open a spreadsheet with an attached word processor, he began writing in her basic information.

"I don't—no. Stop. You will not do whatever you like."

"Yes, I will, Lily. Keep it up and I might lose my temper and tell you to sit in a corner for the day. You'd be forced to obey. That or I tell you to never speak again."

Felix angrily hit the holographic enter key and glared at her across the desk space.

Lily frowned and then looked at the desk. She clasped her hands together and then glanced back at the shut door behind her.

"You don't fear me," she said, looking up at him through long lashes.

"Not in the least. Now, let's start with where you are now and what you're worth." Felix called up her character sheet with his power.

Name:	Power:
Lilian Lux	Ethereal projections
Alias:	**Secondary**
Mab, Soul Stealer, Demon	**Power:** Mana Manipulation
Physical Status:	**Mental Status:**
Healthy	Confused
Positive Statuses:	**Negative Statuses:**
None	Fear

A quick glance and he confirmed everything was as he'd expected.

"Did you know you technically have a second power? Mana manipulation. Not sure if that's intrinsic or learned."

He flipped it over to the second sheet.

Looking over the information there quickly, he gave it a once over to make sure everything was there.

Strength:	37	Upgrade? (370)
Dexterity:	55	Upgrade? (550)
Agility:	53	Upgrade? (530)
Stamina:	42	Upgrade? (420)
Wisdom:	67	Upgrade? (670)
Intelligence:	88	Upgrade? (880)
Luck:	21	Upgrade? (210)
Primary Power:	64	Upgrade? (6,400)
Secondary Power:	59	Upgrade? (5,900)

On a cursory inspection, it seemed as if all attributes were in multiples of ten. Likewise, all power increases were in multiples of one-hundred.

All nice and neat. It was almost too neat, really.

"Hm. Alright. I have a pretty good idea about you, Lily, from a power and abilities perspective. That's all without the context of who you are, though," Felix said, rapidly filling in the information into the spreadsheet. "I'd appreciate it if you could tell me about you."

Lily squirmed in her seat, wringing her hands slowly. The strong, violent mage was gone. All that was left was a woman who seemed more scared than anything.

"You can really see all that?" she asked, looking at the spreadsheet from the other side.

"Sure can. It's my power. Up until recently, it wasn't very useful," Felix said a touch self-consciously. "It is what it is, though."

Lily, pursed her lips, then spread her hands out in front of him.

"I was never anything special. Went to school, graduated, went on to get a legal degree," Lily said, tracing the wood grain in the desk with a fingernail. "Then I had a case. Involved black magic. The kind they warn you not to get involved in."

Lily shrugged her shoulders. "I represented him. I believed in him. Believed he was innocent. I was wrong.

"I don't want to go into the details, but he tried to kill me, and I knocked him out instead. He wasn't dead, but I didn't think he'd live longer, either.

"He'd locked us in his library when he tried to kill me."

Lily sighed, turning her head to the side.

"There wasn't much to do. I couldn't break the door down; it was reinforced by magic, I think. So, I started reading from the book he had laying out.

"It was full of diagrams, instructions, warnings. Spells.

"Suddenly, I pulled his soul out. I felt incredible. I... felt powerful. After a while, the magic on the door faded and I was able to escape. I called the police and they came over. It was ruled self-defense."

Felix nodded, fascinated.

"Then later I had another case. I knew she was guilty. She'd told me so. So... I killed her and took her soul. Then another. And another. Eventually, it caught up with me, of course.

"You can't make your clients disappear every time they appear guilty without someone noticing."

Lily let out a slow breath and leaned back into her seat. "That's when the goody goodies got involved. Killed a few of those, and suddenly I'm on a titanic level of power. Super souls are worth a lot more. A whole lot more.

"End up doing my own thing for years. I haven't aged a year in a decade. And since your own power said I'm twenty-six, it sounds like I really have stopped aging. And here I am."

Felix held up a finger. "You were a lawyer?"

"Yep. Was a trial lawyer. Defense. Did pretty well with minor crimes," she said, a small smile sneaking across her face, only to disappear as quickly as it came.

"Great. Here," Felix said, reaching down into a drawer. He'd stuck his contract there after coming home. Fishing it out, he laid it out on the desk in front of him. "I'd like you to read over this and tell me your thoughts.

"The problem is the board is trying to get me to pay rent that they claim I should be paying for living here. Once you're all caught up on that, we can discuss it and see what we can do. I'm sure I'm missing something. I leave it to you."

Lily looked at the packet of paper, then back to him. "You would have me... be your lawyer?" she asked in a small voice.

"Well, legal counsel, at the very least. I'm not sure if you were disbarred or not? It would be nice if you weren't, though. Maybe we could get you back on track for that? Look into it and see what it'd take."

Lily seemed awestruck at that. She picked up the packet and then looked to him. She gave him a tiny nod of her head. "I'll do that."

"Alright, that's it for now. Could you send in the next person?" Felix said with a smile for her.

"Yeah. I can do that. Do... you want me to have Andrea bring in pancakes when they're ready?"

"I'll eat last. This is a bit more important for the moment. Thanks, Lily," Felix said, closing the drawer and then folding his hands on the desk.

Lily walked to the door, opened it, and stepped out of the study quickly.

"Pancakes!" came back a shouted duo of voices as Lily exited. "Catch!"

There was a splat-like noise, followed by a growl and a screech.

Felicia stomped into his study, the short woman slamming the door shut with the back of her fist.

"So, you've stolen my wits, have you?" growled the short woman. "Made me as inept as an Elf with a weight set?"

She stomped up to his desk and slapped her hands onto the surface, glaring at him over the top of it.

"I'm not as daft as that magical tart that just left. What do I have to do to get my wits back?" she spat at him. "Do I need to start taking my clothes off here and now? Despite all your pretty words? You wouldn't take advantage because we'd be offering?"

"Wait, stop talking," Felix interrupted her, holding up a hand. Then he gestured to the chair. "Please, take a seat if you would. I propose a simple solution to what clearly is going to be a problematic conversation for us both. You ask a question, I'll answer, then we go back and forth till you're satisfied."

Felicia glared at him, her jaw working soundlessly.

After a minute of what truly looked like she was shouting at him wordlessly, she held up her arms and looked as if she would split down the middle.

"Please, calm down, and let's talk. Once you've seated yourself, I'll remove the compulsion."

The sound of her panting dominated the room. Slowly, she eased herself in the chair, staring murderously at him with a red face.

"You can speak. Now please, back to the beginning. What do you have to do to get your wits back was your first question.

"Now see, that's the problem. If I give you your 'wits' back, I lose out on all the points that your power offers.

"And you give me one thousand five hundred and fifty. That's a lot."

Felica's face scrunched into a scowl. She opened her mouth, then closed it, pressing her hands to her stomach.

"I see. Or at least, I think I do. I offer a trade. Barter, if you will."

Felix tilted his head to one side. He was curious. What could she offer him that he couldn't take by force?

"You say you can't give me my 'wits' back because it takes your points. What if I use my wits to get you more points?"

Felix put his elbow on the desk, and then his chin into his hand. "I'm listening."

She gave him a bright smile and leaned forward. "I'm a genius at inventing things. I can build things that would hone, empower, and build up these girls' powers. Perhaps even a machine that could enhance them permanently. But I'd need my wits to do it."

"It'd need to be permanent for it to affect my point pool," Felix said. Sighing, he sat upright again. "Give me a bit with your points. I need them for a time. Then we can see about giving you your wits back. There's a lot of work to be done right now in the short term."

"Unless you want to give me a specific order for every little thing, you'll be giving me part of my wits back," she said.

"I can't. But I'll make you a deal. What can I do for you now that you'd accept as an act of good will? Something you want for yourself that would show you that giving me some time is truly in all of our interests."

She eyed him, her argument frozen on her tongue. "How much can you change? One of them ninnies said you can change us."

"Quite a bit. What'd you have in mind?"

"Can you make me taller?"

Felix stopped himself from instantly replying. Kit had opened his mind to new possibilities.

Instead, he focused on Felicia and what he believed would be more in line with her "character sheet" for things relating to her physical appearance.

Much as it had happened before, a new window surfaced. One that had all of Felicia's measurements in it.

Her height was listed at a paltry four foot eleven. And it would only cost him a hundred points to bump her up an inch.

"I sure can, what kind of height did you have in mind?"

"Ah. Oh. Ergh," Felicia mumbled, scratching her shoulder. "Maybe, five foot four? That's still short, but… not child short? I guess?"

Felix looked back to the screen and tapped it five times. It'd cost him six hundred points in total. The height was still below average, so it didn't seem to cost that much.

"Done. Anything else?" he asked, looking up at Felicia.

She whispered something that he didn't quite catch.

"Sorry, I missed that. One more time?"

"I want to be a D-cup," Felicia said angrily, meeting his eyes.

Felix blinked, unsure of how to respond.

Then he shrugged. It didn't matter to him what breast size she was. A glance at the window told him she was an AA cup.

Below average again. How much will it cost?

Felix flicked the button four times and the cost went up to fourteen hundred points even. It was less than what she was worth for one day. It'd only take him a day to replenish his point values. If he had to do this for everyone, it'd be annoying, but not the end of the world.

He'd call everything a bargain and spend today lounging around. Maybe convert something small to silver.

"Done. Anything else?" Felix asked again.

Felicia looked to her chest, then back to him. "I don't—"

"Once I confirm the changes, they'll happen. You may want to unhook your bra. Going from AA to D... yeah, it's going to be significant."

Felicia turned a deep scarlet red and then reached behind her back and into her shirt. There was a soft click and her clothes shifted.

"I'm ready."

He hit the button and leaned back to watch.

Felicia stood up rapidly in surprise. Her body began expanding rapidly in multiple ways.

Ten seconds later and it was all over. Her clothes had split at the hip and shoulders, and her increased bosom pulled the fabric tight in the front of her shirt.

"Glad we had this talk, Felicia. Now, could you send in the next person?" Felix said with a smile at the half-breed Dwarven woman, who now looked much more like a human than her heritage would have normally allowed.

Chapter 8 - Boldly -

The two Andreas were looking at him, unspeaking.

He'd already gone through everyone else, each person having minor requests here or there. By the end, he'd spent five thousand of his points.

"Want me to go make more pancakes?" Andrea One said.

"Let us make you more," Andrea Prime said.

"No, no. I've had my share. Remember?" Felix asked. He was concerned. She'd already said that twice.

"Yes," they said in unison.

"But pancakes make people happy," Prime said.

"And you seem sad," One said.

Felix shook his head and pointed at Andrea Prime. "How long can your clone remain with you? How many can you have at one time?"

"She can remain forever. There's no time limit or anything. It can get annoying to sleep in the same bed. We often combine back together at night.

"As to how many... I'm not sure? We can't count how many are inside of us. I think we had two hundred out at one time? That was a hard day," Prime said. One nodded her head at that, crossing her arms in front of her.

"I... see. So, rather than clones, it's more like multiple versions of you existing at the same time?" Felix asked slowly.

Andrea Prime blinked, and then looked at him with a smile. "Want more pancakes?"

"Ah, no." Felix pressed the fingers of his right hand to his temple. "Andrea, do you want anything?"

He began to call up her window for her stats and powers.

Name: Andrea Elex	Power: Multiple Self Projections	
Alias: Andrea, Andie, Lex, Myriad.	Secondary Power: Partitioned Mind	
Physical Status: Healthy	Mental Status: Happy	
Positive Statuses: None	Negative Statuses: None	
Strength:	44	Upgrade? (

		440)
Dexterity:	62	Upgrade? (620)
Agility:	71	Upgrade? (710)
Stamina:	51	Upgrade? (510)
Wisdom:	81	Upgrade? (810)
Intelligence:	17	Upgrade? (170)
Luck:	53	Upgrade? (530)
Primary Power:	31	Upgrade? (3,100)
Secondary Power:	79	Upgrade? (7,900)

"I'd like to get married one day," Prime said with a smile.

"Have children," One added.

"Oh yes, children. Dating is hard, though. We keep getting tricked by bad men," said Prime.

One looked at Prime and patted her on the head gently.

Felix was quickly losing himself in the meandering nature of Andrea. That and it was depressing.

He'd briefly considered changing some stats as he went through the meetings, but he ended up leaving everyone with their starting numbers.

He'd almost increased Lily's luck, since it was so awful, but had decided against it.

Here, though, talking to Andrea, he wasn't considering it—he was already running out the numbers in his head.

For two thousand one hundred and fifty points, he could push her intelligence up to twenty-six. It didn't seem like much, but maybe it'd put her on par with a teenager.

Quickly making the adjustments, and tuning out the conversation she was having with herself about dating, he hoped there would be immediate improvements.

Prime and One both immediately stopped talking, their heads whipping around to view him.

"You changed us," they said in concert.

"I did. Is that a problem?" Felix asked carefully.

They looked at each other, as if they were speaking without speaking, then looked back to him.

"No. Why spend points on us? We're not like the others. We're not really good for anything. You covet your points."

Felix couldn't answer that. Yes, talking to her was annoying, but he could just as easily have sent her out of the room.

"I don't know. They say ignorance is bliss, but... I don't know. Never mind that. Is there anything else you want now?" he asked, diverting the question.

Mostly because he couldn't answer it. He didn't like the thoughts he was having. Andrea was too close to his own social ineptitude from his teenager years.

"No. But... thank you. I'm happy being me. But maybe later you can let me bring out more of me? They get crowded in there after a while and it's easier the more I can bring out."

"Uhm, yeah. Sure. We could work something out. Though I think it'll be a bit," Felix said cautiously.

"Okay! Do you modify yourself at all? I don't think I could resist the temptation if I could," Prime said.

"I can't. I've tried many times, but... I can't. I don't know why."

"Oh. What about the house? You should modify it."

"I don't own it."

"Buy one, then! Then upgrade it! We need more bedrooms," Prime explained. One nodded along next to her.

Felix started to argue with her, then realized she was right. Beyond right, even. It was so obvious it hurt. He wasn't thinking big enough.

A pawn shop is good, but a house... A house I could build into a massive mega house with custom defenses and...

"You're brilliant, Andrea," Felix claimed, smiling at her.

"First time I've heard that," Prime said.

"Me, too," One agreed.

Time moved faster than Felix thought it could have. In no time at all, a month had passed since his last estate meeting.

He was dressed in a business suit again, staring up at that horrid sign that had come to represent so much hate for him.

So much anger.

Up until a few days ago when Lily had come to see him.

What had felt originally to be an unfair match now felt to him as if he had the high ground. The high ground and more troops.

And a nuke.

Grinning, he looked across to the passenger seat. Lily was dressed smartly in a black jacket, a slim black dress, and a red blouse. She'd pinned her hair up and had the look of someone going into battle.

"We ready?" he asked.

The soul-eating mistress of death glanced at him and then gave him a cocky smile. "We'll tear out their souls."

"I'll leave that to you. The whole beautiful soul-eater thing isn't me," Felix muttered. He pulled the keys from the ignition and stepped out of his aunt's SUV.

"Remember what I said," Lily reminded him, opening the front door and walking in ahead of him.

"Yes, dear," Felix said in a whiny voice. Lily turned her head and gave him a piercing glare, blocking the doorway. "Sorry, yes, I remember."

She arched a brow at him. It reminded him that she'd supposedly killed a couple hundred people in her career as a villain.

Only after having ripped out their souls to use as power.

After another second of Felix being forced to bear that heavy stare, she finally relented and moved forward.

"Felix Campbell and associate," Lily said in a firm voice to the receptionist.

The receptionist blinked at Lily, then looked to Felix. "I… alright. Please follow me."

They usually make me wait.

Lily gestured to the ground with a subtle move of her hand. Felix took the indicated spot, one step ahead of her and to the left.

As they moved to the conference room that he always ended up in, Lily grabbed a chair from an office that was empty as they passed.

The receptionist gave her a look, but then wisely decided she didn't want to argue with Lily.

The looks on the faces of the normally placid board changed dramatically when they saw Lily.

Felix couldn't place it, but he was sure they were annoyed and hoped they were afraid.

"Mr. Campbell, good morning. May I ask who you've brought with you today?" one of the board asked.

"This is Lilian Lux. She's an associate of mine I've recently employed," Felix explained. He'd been warned repeatedly by Lily that she was not legal counsel, but only there to provide her opinion and advice to him. Especially since she wasn't a lawyer.

"I'm afraid that we can't allow you to retain your own counsel, Mr. Campbell," Joseph started.

"She's not a lawyer. She's here simply to provide me with her advice and opinions," Felix clarified. "Please proceed."

Joseph looked rattled. Clearing his throat, he looked to his paperwork in front of him and back to Felix.

"The first order of business is the discussion of the rent you owe," Joseph said slowly.

"Good. I agree. First, do you hold to the statement that I owe payment for rent to the amount of one hundred and fifty thousand dollars. Yes?" Felix asked.

Joseph looked to the others on the board and they began to nod their heads. "That is correct, we—"

"Next. Who has deemed that I am the renter? In other words, who is the named landlord?"

Joseph turned his head a fraction of an inch to the side and then gestured to another person. "Mr. Jen is the landlord."

"Good. That means you've collected wages for the seven years up to this point as landlord?" Felix asked, turning to Mr. Jen.

"I, uh… yes," said the man.

The room was getting more tense by the minute. Lily had coached him very well, and it was clear she knew what would happen. Each question was provoking responses.

"Would you agree that the amount of that pay would be… roughly four hundred thousand dollars? Plus five percent of the rent as a bonus."

Mr. Jen nodded his head.

"Could someone please provide me the document in which I agreed that Mr. Jen would be the landlord?" Felix asked, looking around the room.

Everyone froze. No one responded.

"If no one can provide that document, I'm afraid we have a problem."

"No, no problem here, Felix. There's no requirement that you—"

"Yes, there is. Per…" Felix had to look at the sheet of paper in front of Lily. "Section six, subsection c, listed as 'approving of contractors and personnel,' I'm listed as an approver. I did not approve. Therefore, the selection is invalid."

Joseph opened his mouth and then closed it. "I… that is—"

"You are in breach of contract unless you can provide that document this very minute. Are you in breach of contract?"

Again, there was no response.

"If you do not provide the document in the next minute, or state that you can provide it in the next ten, I'm moving to have you in breach."

Joseph swallowed and held up a hand. "Perhaps we should move to set this entire situation aside and—"

"I rule you in breach. Now that you're in breach, under section ten, subsection a, all accounting will now be done through me. I am officially moving to hire an accountant this evening who will now be part of this board."

"Now see here—"

"In addition, I move to elect myself the landlord of my own property," Felix said, cutting Joseph off.

"Those in favor?" Felix asked.

No one but he raised their hand.

"Those against?" Joseph raised his hand immediately, as did Mr. Jen and a few others.

"Per my rights as the primary beneficiary to dismiss two people from the board every quarter, I move to strike two people from this board. Mr. Joseph and Mr. Jen. You're no longer needed, thank you. Per my rights of breach, I move to strike one additional…" Felix looked at one of the men with his hand up. "You. You can leave as well."

The three he'd selected were dumbfounded.

Felix picked up a packet that Lily pulled out of the case she was carrying.

"I have here a formal grievance for Reznik, Blacketer, and Troy. Once I send this, I'm sure I can have every one of you replaced. And have myself as the approver of every single person who comes into the board next.

"Now. With the departure of Mr. Joseph, Mr. Jen, and whatever his name is, I cannot remove anyone until the new quarter. Which happens to be tomorrow. I'll be convening an emergency meeting tomorrow.

"Just to make sure everyone understood my previous question, I'd like to ask again to be made the landlord of my own estate and ask for a vote," Felix said with a grin for the remaining five people on the board.

Felix raised his hand, and all five of the remaining people on the board raised their hands.

"Good. I'm glad you've realized the severity of this situation. Let's hope you all remember this day.

"Now for you two," Felix said, looking at who he believed to be the instigators of this situation. "I expect to be paid the entirety of the four hundred thousand dollars by this evening, Mr. Jen, Mr. Joseph.

"Otherwise, I will be forced to move to the next section of the breach clause, which is when I hire an attorney for myself, and you lose all access to the trust, as set up by my aunt and uncle. Then Reznik, Blacketer, and Troy get a black eye when I report it to the media. I imagine they'll hold you liable and you probably will never work in your chosen career again."

Lily slid a card in front of him. "Thank you, Lily," Felix said, smiling to her. "This here is my bank account. I'll be checking it promptly at eight o'clock tonight."

Felix stood up and stretched his arms above his head. "Whew, that was fun. Do you have any questions for me before I leave?" he asked, addressing the five remaining members.

"No? Good. I'll see you five tomorrow, and you three, never again."

Felix collected his papers, leaving the card on the table, and left the room. Lily followed at his heel.

He didn't say anything until they got back into the SUV, where he let out an explosive breath and doubled over. He rested his forehead against the steering wheel.

His stomach hurt. The anxiety and stress of the situation rubbed him raw.

He really needed to use a bathroom.

"That was well done. A little dramatic, but... well done," Lily said from the passenger seat.

"Thank you, Lily. Without you, that would have gone much worse."

"Not over yet. We need to get our money first. But I think they'll pay it all up. I imagine you might even get a phone call once they're done, asking you to please not discuss the situation with their bosses, or why you asked them to step down. They'll probably spin it as if they themselves asked to step down.

"For what it's worth, it's probably worth letting it go at that point. It'd earn you a win with those who remain on the board."

Lily clicked her seatbelt into place and crossed one leg over the other. "Take us to lunch. Then we need to hire an accountant. I'll handle that."

Felix nodded a bit. He felt drained. He wasn't cut out for talking to people. Slowly, he sat up and got the SUV moving.

They'd ended up not needing to hold that second meeting after all. Lily took care of the accountant that evening, and the books were cleaned up that night.

The rent would still need to paid, as it had been initiated.

He still owed the hundred fifty grand in rent, the forty grand to Dimitry, and the five grand to the bank.

The annual salary from the landlord's job, about fifty-five thousand, would definitely help.

The bank debt could wait, as could the rent, since he was his own renter. He'd also get that percentage back.

The only problem was his debt to Dimitry. He had about two months to get that paid off or he'd be liable to get stabbed. That or be turned into a permanent debtor.

All of this was good to know, and hadn't stopped Felix at all in purchasing a storefront that doubled as a home.

It was more of a warehouse with an attached front office, and a set of rooms at the top level that somehow had been zoned and approved as a live/work residence.

The front office would do the job of the storefront, and the warehouse as the "shop floor" for work. Which could be anything. Or even just housing purchases.

The neighborhood was decent and seemed on the lower side of middle income. There'd be no problems with clients being afraid to visit. Nor would there be access issues, since it was right off the freeway exit.

No, the biggest problem would be spreading the word. Advertising. They wouldn't be able to purchase ads or anything like that.

It'd cost him almost every penny he'd made from the landlord back payments, and the gold he'd been turning into cash.

Now, though, now he could really start to make money. Everything he did here, he could also disguise and legitimately pay taxes on.

First, he'd need to transmute a few lead weights into gold over a few days. That'd be the seed money to build up his pawn shop purchasing.

Then he could start converting that quickly and easily into items. Items into sales.

Word would spread quickly about a pawn shop that bought almost anything.

Hell, in this day and age, in a month he could have an online store open to sell everything he bought locally.

That'd have to wait for another day, though. Today was moving day. They'd spent some time making sure only items that he owned went with them.

The rest of the furniture they'd had to buy from wherever they could get the right piece for the right price.

Miu had been ideal to take with him on those trips. She had a knack for getting people to accept less than they wanted.

Andrea had offered herself up as the moving team. There was now something like two hundred Andreas running around the rear delivery entrance and throughout the building. Felicia was acting as floor supervisor for them and directing them as they needed.

They'd backed up a moving truck into one of the loading bays and let her have at it. In return, she'd been allowed full control of her power for the day.

Most of them were exactly like Andrea Prime, though there were a few who were clearly very different.

They carried themselves differently, spoke in a different tone of voice, or even responded in a different fashion to the rest. They'd look right at a sudden noise, and one would cower and take cover.

Ioana had simply followed him around, dressed up in leather biker clothes. He wasn't sure when and where she'd gotten it, but the hilt of a long sword angled out from her hip.

Now that he thought about it, everyone was running around today in clothes and things he knew he hadn't purchased

"Ioana?" Felix asked, turning to look at his escort.

"Mm?" grunted the warrior. Her eyes swept the street up one side and down the other.

"Where'd you get the sword? In fact, where did everyone get all these clothes? I don't recognize any of it. I'm not mad, only curious."

Felix looked back to the storefront where Miu, Kit, and Lily were setting up the interior of the store.

Ioana met his eyes and then gave him a feral grin. "We raided our own safe houses. Whatever they did to us, we didn't give them the safe house locations. Bank accounts are cleaned out, though."

Didn't trust me enough to tell me, and I didn't think to ask about it.

"Probably got that through your bank cards. I imagine they probably raided your homes," Felix said with a sigh.

"You think this'll work?" Ioana asked him, throwing a thumb at the building.

"Can't be any worse than what we were doing. Not to mention, I didn't want to sit around and wait for things to change.

"No, playing it slow up to this point was excruciating. It's time to make it work on my own terms."

Ioana turned her head back to the street, watching it. "Good. The bold live more freely, even if with less time."

Chapter 9 - Changes -

Felix flipped the vase over in his hand. Then he viewed it with his hypothetical ownership window.

Name: Imitation 19th century glass vase	Created In: 2013
Appraised Value: $10.00	Created By: Frank Putz
Actual Value: $10.00	Condition: Lightly worn
Asking Price: $3,200.00	Durability: 90/100
Mint Price: $12.00	Cost to Repair: 50 points

Shaking his head, Felix pushed the vase across the countertop. "I'll give you ten for it, and that's because I can probably resell it for twenty. It's fake. Sorry."

"What? You can't possibly know that, if you—" started to complain the man who owned the vase.

"Sorry, not interested in it for anything more than ten. Is there anything else I can help you with?" Felix leaned onto the glass counter and looked around the shopfront.

The man grumbled, and walked out without another word.

Ioana opened the door for him, watching him with a hawk-like stare as he passed.

Kit, Lily, and Miu were working the shop counters. Andrea was working with Felicia in the back.

Felix was on appraisal duty. Kit had once again provided him with insight into his own power he didn't realize he had. Rather than focusing on the upgrade and material aspect of his power, she had him focus on the ownership and item side of it.

Now he was an antique appraiser with an instant turnaround and perfect accuracy.

Word had spread about the eccentric pawn shop that had an employee who could appraise anything in minutes.

They now charged a small fee for his time, but provided no documentation. At least not yet.

Lily was working on that.

Sure is nice having a lawyer on the team.

Felix let his eyes wander over to Lily while thinking about her. He'd lucked out so far. Everyone he'd picked up had their own area of influence and ability.

The villain known as Mab was happily chatting with an official-looking older woman.

Beyond that, Miu and Kit were engaged in individual sales.

Miu was responsible for haggling and Kit was on mental sweep duty. Her power was dialed up to ten percent, and she casually monitored the store as she worked.

This was temporary. They'd need to hire more people soon. They were far more busy than he had expected.

It'd only been two weeks and they were drowning in merchandise and money.

"You the antiques and memorabilia guy?" came a man's voice in front of him.

Felix nodded and didn't bother looking at the person. "Yep. Put it right here," Felix said, indicating the counter in front of him.

He didn't lift his eyes, ask for a name, nothing. He didn't care to meet another person, hear another sob story, get told another lie.

Everything and anything someone could do to get him to pay more.

I can only imagine Kit's life now. Always knowing the other person's thoughts.

Looking up across the room at the mind reader in question, he caught her staring at him.

Probably pissed this guy off and that got her looking this way.

He gave her a lopsided grin and turned back to his counter. The man had put a torn-up baseball covered in signatures on it. It looked like it'd been roughed up pretty bad.

Felix picked it up and activated his power.

Name: Historical Signed Baseball	Created In: 2001
Appraised Value: $40.00	Created By: *Truncated for size limits
Actual Value: $50.00	Condition: Extremely Damaged
Asking Price: $100.00	Durability: 13/100
Mint Price: $42,000.00	Cost to Repair: 1,150

"It's the game-winning ball from the first all-Beastkin team. It was the last time an all-Beastkin team was allowed as well. Everyone signed it, including the coach. This is the ball that drove in the last run," said the would-be customer.

"Do you have a letter of authentication and ownership?" Felix set the ball down and looked up at the customer finally.

He was interested in this item. It would be easy to repair and resell at a much higher price. These are the kind of items he was looking for. Waiting for.

They didn't pop up often, maybe once every few days, but he'd found a few. Most didn't have as much of a resale value as this one did, but they added up.

"I have ownership papers, but no authentication," admitted the man, now unable to meet Felix's eyes.

He looked ordinary, everyday. See them one minute, gone the next.

"I'll give you one hundred for it," Felix said. Reaching under his counter, he pulled up an electronic pad that he used for sales forms.

"Done."

Felix nodded his head with a grim smile.

Miu was due to make a trip to the other side of the city and sell all of their antiques, memorabilia, and other items to collectors and museums. It was how they'd really started pulling in the money. Everything else they simply repaired and resold here.

The buyers had been hesitant at first, having everything appraised and certified.

Now they paid out the requested amount and had the appraisal and authentication done afterwards.

Felix wanted to preserve that mentality, so he made sure nothing ever went over to them at an incorrect price or listing.

He'd take care of this fixer-upper beauty tonight and add it to the shipment with his notes on the expected price.

Felix's phone started buzzing on his work desk. He sighed audibly, working through the purchase entries for the day on his virtual work screen.

Andrea slammed bodily into his desk in her haste to get to his phone. She groaned in pain and held up the phone to her eyes.

Felix looked up at her with a small smile over his virtual workspace.

"Well, Miss Beastkin secretary? Who is it?" Felix asked. She was cute in an adorably dense way. Always happy, and sometimes said the most profound things.

"I'm your secretary? That's great! What's my salary?" Andrea said, bouncing from foot to foot, her ears twitching back and forth. "I promise I'm worth it, whatever it is."

Felix chuckled and reached out to take his phone from her hands and flipped it over.

"No-Name."

He tapped the accept button and held it up to his ear. "Good evening, No-Name. How are ya?"

Wedging the phone between his ear and shoulder, he went back to work.

Or tried to.

"What are my duties as your secretary? The only thing I know about them is they usually sleep with their boss. Wait, do I have to sleep with you?" Andrea asked, scratching her head.

Felix frowned and looked back to Andrea.

"I catch you at a bad time, Hoss?" No-Name said, amusement clearly in his voice. "I can call back later after you've worked out your job duties with your secretary."

"Unnecessary," Felix said.

"But why not? I mean, I don't think I want to, but maybe I do? I've never been propositioned before. Oh goodness, it's warm in here. I should go talk to Lily about my promotion. She'll know what to do," Andrea said with a squeal, then skittered off.

Dashing out of the office, she bounced off a crate, apologized to it, and kept on running.

"She's excitable," No-Name said.

"Yes. She is. It's cute. Like watching a baby bird trying to figure out how to fly."

Felix looked back to his work, then saved and closed the program.

"So what's up?" Felix asked

"Big auction coming up. Lots and lots of supers. No previewing this time, though. It'll be as is, as seen. Most powers will be a guess," No-Name said.

"That's... odd. What's the deal?" Felix asked, leaning back into his chair. Felix hesitated on calling on anyone else. Then he reached over to the intercom and thumbed it twice in rapid succession. "Hold on a second. I need to get a pen and paper."

Felix muted his phone and set it down on the desktop. Pulling out some paper and several pens, he then waited.

Kit and Lily came into his office at the same time. With a gesture at the chairs in front of the desk, they seated themselves.

He'd long gotten used to the idea of them being his "Intelligence Center."

Between the two of them, they had enough intelligence and experience they could give him advice. Advice that would be better than his natural decisions.

He was smart enough to know they were smarter than him.

"No-Name has another auction coming up. He was just starting to give me the details. Was stalling for time," Felix explained. He pulled off a single sheet of paper from the pad and set it in front of himself and took one of the three pens.

Kit and Lily looked at each other, then back to him.

Apparently I'm the only one with a bad memory.

Felix popped the mute button again. "Sorry about that. Alright, so you said that you won't even know what powers they have, but it's a big auction. Why the lack of info?"

No-Name chuckled and the sound of a chair creaking could be heard over the line. "Funny story for another time. The short and sweet version will do for now. A bunch of Dudleys and Snidelys teamed up and launched a coordinated attack on our glorious leader. They were defeated without fatalities on either side. Now we have something like... four hundred of them up for grabs."

"Got it. That's quite a few. You were pretty accurate on the sale price last time around. What are you thinking this time?" Felix asked.

"Not really sure. Since the powers are all going to be a guess, based on what our people saw during the battle, it could be high or low. Might be dirt cheap, might be astronomical. Sorry, Hoss, not a lot of knowledge here."

"Right. Give me a second. Need to look at my books."

"Sure, sure," No-Name said.

Felix flicked the mute button.

"Thoughts?" he asked, looking to Kit and Lily.

"I don't know. We have a lot of debt right now. We're doing very well, but there's no guarantee it'll continue to go this well," Kit said, then looked to Lily.

"Kit's right," Lily said, holding out a hand towards the telepath. "We're well in the black right now. We could easily pay Dimitry, the bank, and about one hundred thousand of the rental debt we owe to your family's estate."

Lily reached out and tapped the desk as if to emphasize her next point. "But, buying more supers would increase your power load. I'm all for increasing power. Worst case, we kill Dimitry, I take his soul, we buy some time while they figure out what happened."

Kit grimaced at that and laid a hand to her temple. "You're so bloodthirsty, Lily. We could pay off Dimitry now and take the money for the rent to the auction anyways."

Lily rolled her eyes and sat back into her chair. She folded her arms across her chest and then nodded her head. "You're right. We could. Though, if we did increase my power, it would increase his power, too," Lily said, looking to Kit.

Kit frowned and then shook her head. "Yes, that's probably true, but—"

From the back of the warehouse there was a crash, followed by several shouts.

"Intruders!" came Ioana's shout from somewhere in the warehouse.

Felix hit the mute button. "I'll call you back, No-Name. We're on board, though, so send us the information and the invite." Hanging up, Felix pulled up his character screens for each of his people and put the draw to zero.

"You have your powers," Felix said quickly.

Kit's head snapped around at the same time that Lily's body burst into an electrical aura.

"Lily, no deaths if possible. Immobilize or stun if you can. We need Kit to run rampant through their heads to figure out what they're doing here. You can pop their souls after," Felix cautioned.

Lily didn't respond, but instead made a sigil with her hand and vanished.

There was a chorus of shouts, followed by the crash of metal.

Felix didn't kid himself, he was no use in a fight. He'd wait for this one to run its course before he did anything.

An explosion of light and the crackle of electricity running free filled the building.

Seconds ticked by before he finally heard one of his girls call out.

"Safe! Come over," Ioana yelled.

Felix and Kit left the office, walking towards the back corner of the warehouse. It was the back of the building that adjoined the alleyway.

Lily stood there, one hand held above her head and lightning crackling along her fingers.

Ioana stood by her side, a club resting on her shoulder, her sword still in its sheathe.

On the other side of Lily was Miu, her hands loose at her sides, though her knuckles looked bloody.

"Six unconscious scumbags. A couple have dents in their skulls, but I think they'll live.

"Snuck in earlier, I'd wager. Were waiting for us to go to bed. Just happened to stumble across them during my patrol," Ioana said, using the club to prod at one of the unconscious men.

"Good work, Ioana. I'm not sure what I can offer in thanks, but let's chat later about rewards," Felix murmured, squatting down next to one of the men.

Lily closed her hand with a pop, the glow fading immediately. "The others live, though I may have fried nerve endings."

"That's fine. Andrea?" Felix asked, looking around.

The Beastkin girl popped out from behind a box and nervously looked around. "I'm here."

"Can you split a few times and help Miu get these... people... into separate areas? I imagine interrogating them individually will yield the best results."

Kit nodded her head at that, her fists clenched.

"You alright at one hundred percent of your power for now, Kit? I can dial it to—"

"I'm fine. I'll tear the secrets from their minds. I'll leave nothing left. I've been resting for a long time. I could handle anything right now," she said. Her voice sounded nothing like what she normally sounded like.

Can't forget she was a hero first. They're not exactly bloodless. Deaths happen.

"Thanks, Kit. Felicia, you around?"

"Here, you nitwit. Look right over me, did ya? Do I need to ask to be taller? Make 'em bigger?" grumped the half-breed Dwarf from the side.

"No, I'm sorry. I'm a bit frazzled. You all might be used to this kind of thing, but I'm new to this. Felicia, Lily, come with me while they tend to our guests."

Felix shook his head and stood up.

It's never ending. Always something else going wrong.

A brief walk back to his office helped him clear his thoughts. This was a time to act. To move forward and take steps toward preventing this sort of thing.

He wasn't sure who was behind it, but he doubted they were simply here for a smash-and-grab.

No, a smash-and-grab would have hit the front office. Not the rear.

Which meant they were directed. By someone.

Annoyed, and angry, Felix sat down on the edge of his desk. Lily and Felicia took the seats in front of the desk and looked to him.

The Dwarf looked angry, as always. Though she certainly filled out her clothes better now. He doubted her personality would ever change.

"What?" Felicia said, meeting his gaze.

"I need you to build a machine. Preferably sooner rather than later. I need it to be able to dispose of bodies efficiently. I need it to leave nothing, and create no waste. I'll expand the warehouse to have a basement tomorrow for you to work in," Felix said, laying out his need.

"I can do that… I'll need my wits," cautioned the Dwarf.

"I know. You actually already have them back. I'll give you a week. After that, we'll have to figure out something else," Felix said. Looking to Lily, he gave her a feral grin. "When we're done pulling out their thoughts, you'll be killing them and taking their souls. Any concerns?"

Lily grinned at him and shook her head. "Do I get to keep my powers for a bit?"

"Sure. Till about a minute before midnight. So you've got a few hours. Maybe you could see about putting some magical wards on our home?" Felix said, gesturing at the walls. "Anyways. Do you need anything, Felicia? Is it too much to ask?"

The Dwarf scoffed and stood up, adjusting her blouse. She'd definitely been wearing clothes that emphasized her figure as of late. "No. I'll get you what you want. Though it'll be sad to give up my wits after that."

"Do a good job. Show me your worth. I guarantee I'll have more jobs for you that'll require your wits. The more you show me, the more I want, the longer you keep your wits. It needs to be worth more to me in your head than as points."

Felicia grimaced at first, then frowned. After a moment, she laughed and clapped her hands together. "You've challenged my abilities, then? I'll win, you wait and see. You'll be begging me to use my wits. You wait and see."

With a snort, she left him there with Lily, stomping her way out of the office.

Lily ignored both of them and began to make sweeping gestures with her hands. Blue energy coalesced and flowed into shapes and patterns, creating sigils and runes in the air between them.

Felix watched, enjoying the impromptu lightshow for a minute. Then he returned to his logs.

There was always work to be done.

Roughly an hour later, Kit came back into the room.

A single glance told him that it'd be in his interest to push her to one hundred percent draw. Taking a second, he did just that.

The tension in Kit fell off instantly, her shoulders sagging and her taut face smoothing out.

"That is so refreshing," Kit said, a smile slowly creeping over her face.

"Glad to help. So, what do we have?" Felix asked, closing his desktop window.

Lily shook herself out of her own private thoughts and listened in.

In fact, everyone was here. Andrea was resting against the desk, Miu was sitting on the couch, Felicia had been tinkering with some device in a corner, and Ioana stood by the door. Ever the watchful guardian.

"Honestly, I'm not completely sure," Kit admitted, taking a seat in one of the chairs facing the desk. "Their minds were fairly well wiped clean. What I got was fragmented. Using all six together gave me a direction, though.

"A restaurant across from what I think was where you worked. There were pictures of you in your uniform.

"There was also a black-haired man, with narrow eyes and a small face. Couldn't have been taller than five foot one."

Felix frowned and leaned forward over his desk. He propped his chin up in his hands and tilted his head.

"Well, that rules out Dimitry. I wonder, maybe one of his peers? Or his boss, even? I suppose it isn't out of the question," Felix mused aloud.

"Isn't Dimitry our friend? As your secretary, I'll call him and set up a meeting! Then we can make this all right," Andrea said triumphantly. Her hands went to Felix to probably dig around for his phone. "I'll make pancakes and it'll be fine."

Andrea clawed at his clothes, her fingers trying to get into his pockets.

"Andrea, stop. It's okay. I don't think Dimitry is the problem. Promise," Felix assured her, fending off her quick hands and quicker fingers.

"Secretary?" Miu asked softly.

"Misunderstanding," Kit said, turning her head to the ex-security officer. "She thinks Felix gave her a job. She thinks one of the job duties is sleeping with him, and she can't decide if she wants the job or not."

"Oh. I see," Miu frowned prettily, her dark eyes fastening on Felix.

Felix slipped his phone from his pocket and under his ass. He held up his hands and let Andrea do as she would and then looked back to Kit.

"Anything else?" he asked as Andrea opened his breast pocket and stared into it. Her nose twitched, then her ears as she seemingly considered the problem.

"Not really. I get the impression they were here to kill us, though. Not rob us. They were waiting for us to fall asleep." Kit tilted her head to one side, watching him.

He imagined she was evaluating his response.

"Then they die. Let's keep them alive for a few days while Felicia builds me my corpse dispose-o-matic machine.

"Lily gets the souls."

Felix stood up and thumbed the computer off with his right hand, his left hand covertly grabbing his phone.

"We'll have a long day tomorrow. Let's get those six secured. I'll build a basement tomorrow for Felicia to work her magic in. I'll be reverting everyone to zero for the night. Except for Andrea, who will remain at a fraction so she can have a few extras watching our guests, and Felicia, as I'm sure she'll keep working."

Felix sighed and ran his hand through his hair. "Any questions?"

"I'm not sure if I want the job or not. I've only been intimate a few times, and that was years ago. I'm not that easy.

"I mean, well, I might be willing. Your scent is amazing, after all. And you are kinda my type," Andrea said slowly. "Can I use one of my Others for the first time?

"There's a couple who already said yes."

Felix pressed his palms to his eyes.

Chapter 10 - Sausage -

Creating a basement from scratch with just his powers hadn't worked. The price had been too high with only his normal point allowance.

Instead, he'd bartered with Andrea.

He'd offered her the job of assistant, which didn't need her to sleep with him. But her job duties would be random and assigned as needed.

When she was doing tasks he assigned, she'd also be given her power back to let out her "Others," as she called them.

So, he'd opened up a shaft big enough for a person to go down, into what would eventually be the basement.

The foundation was a problem. They weren't quite sure how deep it went, or what it would support, or if they'd be cutting into it.

Felicia assured him there'd be no problems with it, and that she'd make sure everything worked out in their favor.

On her Dwarven heritage itself, she swore it.

Then again, she had an army of Andreas to direct as well, so it might happen exactly as she said.

He didn't decline and left her to it. Which had Andrea now digging out a basement with an unending workforce of herself. Felicia, of course, was directing them. They listened to the angry Dwarven woman.

They'd make excellent progress. To the point that they could dump their would-be murderers in the basement and leave them there with no way to get out.

Felix couldn't sleep, though. He felt like he was missing something. He'd spent his remaining points on converting gold and settled in for paperwork.

Hunched over his workstation, he stared at the six folders in front of him.

There wasn't much overlap; except for Miu, who had a generalized skillset, and everyone had their own area of expertise. As he'd been conditioned to do in a corporate scenario, he created an employee file for each.

Flipping open the one on top, he found a picture of Felicia.

Her appearance was quite different than when he'd purchased her. Someone had been going over the finer points of fashion with her.

Her details remained the same, though.

Felix set her file aside. She was simple and easy to maintain. A workaholic if presented with a challenge. The type of employee that would go to ruin if left without a task, project, or job to manage.

Opening the next, he found Andrea. Smiling, throwing a thumbs-up, and standing in a ridiculous pose.

Felix chuckled at the memory of it. She'd insisted he write "Personal Assistant" in her file after he explained what he was doing.

She was infinitely useful for her power, and incredibly cheerful. What she lacked in intelligence, she made up for in good-hearted concern for everyone. Though she could see to the root of a problem fairly quickly, which led to some interesting decisions. Wise, but lacking foresight.

Opening the third and closing Andrea's, he found Lily. Her picture was odd. He'd taken it while she'd had her powers active. She'd immediately doused her sigils and rearranged herself more for a business photo.

She was a curious one. Ruthless, cynical, and willing to eat the souls of those she beat.

Yet she bent herself to the tasks he gave her. Especially the non-mystical ones.

"She would rather work on something that doesn't require her purchased through blood power," Felix murmured.

He'd have to work on her. For now, it was simple enough to engage her in intellectual pursuits and let her work on them.

Right now, her primary duty was their financials and inventory counts. It kept her quite busy. Thankfully so.

Glancing into Miu's folder, he nearly shut it as fast as he'd cracked it open, but stopped. He put some true thought into her rather than dismissing her.

She was a mystery still. A question mark.

She tended to avoid him whenever possible. She never skirted any duty he gave her, however.

She did everything he asked to the fullest of her ability, and then some.

He looked to her picture and had to wonder about her all over again.

She was attractive. Almost beautiful, even. Clearly of Asian lineage with the features to match. Clean, petite, elegant. Black hair and dark, dark brown eyes.

After he'd finished repairing her body, he'd found she had an athletic figure that most women tried to achieve and never did so.

Her multiplicative power seemed to function on every level. There was nothing that didn't get amped up from its base setting.

Which meant her workouts were simple and easy.

"Infinitely pissing off," Felix said, closing Miu's and picking up the next folder. "Ioana. The War Maiden."

Felix thumbed the cover back and stared at the imposing figure of the woman. She was big. Muscular. Toned and fit.

She was what you would call handsome, but her ever-present lethality culled any thoughts of her being something you could spend time with.

She'd gotten her thick dark hair into a ponytail and wore it as that. Nothing else. She didn't go in for makeup at any level, either.

Put together and looking for all the world like a warrior, she reeked of death. Setting her down, he picked up the last one and hesitated.

"Kit Carrington, also known as Augur. Pretty, a body built for sin, smart, and insane," said a voice at the door. "A true loose cannon that's a danger to her team, as much as the enemy. Unlikely to ever lead. Or so my old team leader would tell me."

Felix looked up from the unopened folder to find the very same "loose cannon" speaking to him.

As she'd said, she was definitely easy on the eyes. And after he'd restored her to normal condition, he couldn't disagree.

Definitely right inside that strike zone, bud.

"I dunno. She's pretty handy so far. As to the pretty and sin thing... sure? I mean, yeah, you're hot, but... so are a lot of women?"

Kit shook her head slightly with a confused look on her face. Her mouth twisted up in a frown. "What?"

"You're hot. Totally an eight or a nine out of ten. So are other women. As to being smart? Completely agree. More than most people would be comfortable to admit, because I'm pretty sure you're smarter than I am.

"Keeps me on my toes. Insane, though? Not at all. Loose cannon? Not so far," Felix reiterated, leaning back in his chair.

Kit snorted and then moved from the door frame and flopped into the couch. "Uh-huh. Because you keep me dialed down nice and low. I'm not complaining, mind you, but it's not exactly like I'm in control of it."

She laid out on the couch, draping one arm over her face, the other hanging down at her side.

"You sure you can't upgrade it for me? I'd be thankful. Maybe not as thankful as Andrea, but..." she said in a teasing voice, making a vague gesture with her hand. "Grateful."

"Yeah. Sorry, the most the screen ever says is—" Felix stopped. Looking down to his desktop he frowned. He hadn't really considered it or thought about it.

He'd always just assumed upgrading a power was more about the power level.

Focusing on the normal character screens, he tried to pull up Kit's. It flashed up easily. There was no way he could increase her Power's ability.

Name: Kit Carrington	Power: Area Telepathy	
Alias: Augur	Secondary Power: None	
Physical Status: Healthy	Mental Status: None	
Positive Statuses: None	Negative Statuses: None	
Strength:	51	Upgrade? (510)
Dexterity:	54	Upgrade? (540)
Agility:	48	Upgrade? (480)

Stamina:	46	Upgrade? (460)
Wisdom:	72	Upgrade? (720)
Intelligence:	78	Upgrade? (780)
Luck:	41	Upgrade? (410)
Primary Power:	91	Upgrade? (9,100)
Secondary Power:	--	Upgrade? (--)

Pushing his mental focus towards the idea of modifying her power to a controlled power upgrade, he stared at that power function.

He willed it to change.

And then a window popped up.

Power Upgrade: Directed Telepathy	Required Primary Power: 80 (Met) Required Intelligence: 70 (Met)	Upgrade? (5,000)

With Felicia and Andrea running around with their powers, it was practically his entire pool.

"How grateful?" Felix asked, looking up from the window.

"What?" Kit asked, her head turning to the side to look at him.

"How grateful would you be?" Felix sighed and rested his cheek on his right hand, watching Kit.

"Uhm. Pretty fucking grateful. I mean, well…" she said, clearly at a loss. "Can you?"

"I can. It's pretty much an entire day's worth of points."

"Well. I—that is…" Kit looked at the ground. "I'm already your slave. I'm not sure what else I can do that you can't order me to."

Felix thought about that. Having someone do your bidding was one thing. Having someone work for you, because they chose to, was entirely different.

She was already that for him. But how much further would she go if he did this for her?

"Be you. Be who you were up to this point. Fight by my side, rather than for me. I need you, Kit."

Felix hit the accept button on the power and then stood up, his stomach falling out from under him.

A whole day wasted.

Opening her screen, he flicked her power draw down to zero. "You're at one hundred percent, and I upgraded your power. Practice with it.

"I'm going to bed. Did Andrea wander up that way?"

He tapped open Andrea's character screen and increased her intelligence by a single point with the points he had left.

Might as well.

Moving to the other screens, he pushed everyone's draw to zero. Tonight would be a free night since he had no points left anyways.

"I uh, no. She's in her bed. I double checked," Kit said, staring at him.

"Good. See you in the morning."

Walking into his room, he collapsed into the bed and immediately fell asleep. Only to feel as if he'd only just fallen asleep when his phone started going off.

Moaning, he slapped at the phone with little accuracy.

A sudden beep sounded above his head.

"Good morning," came Andrea's chipper voice. "Felix's phone."

Groaning, he rolled over and sat up.

"He was sleeping, but he's waking up now," Andrea said, smiling at Felix. "Me? I'm his personal assistant. I was his secretary, but I wasn't sure if I should sleep with him. Do personal assistants sleep with their boss?"

I can't tell anymore if she genuinely doesn't understand or is actually fucking with me.

"Oh. I see. That makes sense. I started thinking I might have been wrong. Kit told me I was, but... what? Oh, sure," Andrea replied, holding the phone out to him.

"It's for you."

Felix gave her a pained smile and nodded his head. Taking the phone from her, he checked the screen.

It was early morning, and No-Name was calling.

"I bet your bed smells great," Andrea said, crawling past him and dropping to all fours in the center of his bed.

"Hey," Felix said into the phone. He watched Andrea as she spun around a few times and dropped down into the spot he'd been sleeping in.

"Smells like Felix," Andrea said into the mattress.

"You made her your personal assistant?" No-Name asked, chuckling.

"Not really. Kind of self-promoted. Sorry about not calling you back last night. I'm all in for the auction. When's the date? You made it sound like it was soon."

"Few weeks from now. They're healing everyone up first and then getting them prepped for the sale. You want a private room again?" No-Name inquired.

"Definitely. Not sure how many I'll bring with me, though. Three seats should be enough."

Lily, Kit, me. That should be more than enough brainpower between those two.

"Done. I'll get it set up for you. Going to have lots to purchase. Bring deep pockets and a party wagon."

The line went dead before Felix could say anything else. Shaking his head, he set the phone down on the nightstand.

A sharp snore from behind him alerted him to the fact that Andrea had fallen asleep.

"She's tired. She woke up early and sat outside your door waiting for you," Miu told him from the doorway.

"I see. Morning, Miu. Everyone has their power back today. I made some late-night changes and spent everything up. Today is going to be a lab day for me. Figure out where to build our house up. Anything going on?"

Miu shook her head. "Ioana and Lily are running the store. Kit is assisting them and setting up appraisal appointments for you. There's also a mountain of pancakes in the kitchen."

"Andrea?" Felix asked, getting to his feet.

"Andrea," Miu confirmed.

Felix padded past Miu and glided through the kitchen. He picked up a dry pancake and wolfed it down while grabbing a sheet of paper. Then he went to sit on the couch in his "office," as they'd taken to calling it.

He didn't feel like staring at a computer screen right now, so he settled for taking notes in pen.

Flipping the pad open to the first page, he started jotting down the names of the rooms, areas, or sections of the home.

My bedroom, all of their bedrooms, office, study, kitchen, dining room, living room.

He paused as he considered the next area. It hadn't been done intentionally, but the basement entrance was smack dab in the middle of the warehouse. When he checked on what he could upgrade for the house, "Basement Entry" had been listed separately from everything else.

Really, everything up here will become secondary as we move underground. We'll need to disguise and guard the entrance to the basement. I'll have to consult Felicia on how she wants to do this.

"What are you doing?" Miu asked, standing near the doorway.

Felix glanced up at her and noted her posture and position.

She's always near an exit with me.

"Trying to get an idea of where to start with our home defenses and point costs. They're fairly straightforward for the most part right now. Reinforcement, removal of certain windows, making sure everything can withstand a blast. That sort of thing."

Felix sighed and kept writing in details for each room. "It won't really get detailed or intensive until we get the basement outfitted. Once we start building underground… then I can start upgrading individual doors, furniture, defenses. Mostly after Felicia starts building.

"Rooms, designs, machines, whatever it may be. Then we'll really get moving. That's after she finishes up the dispose-o-matic."

"Is that the thing she built last night?" Miu asked.

"Huh? Last night? She finished?" Felix asked, ignoring the pad of paper in his hands entirely now.

"Yeah. It's this strange-looking contraption that looks like a wood chipper." Miu nodded her head as she spoke, taking a step back from him and into the other room.

"Fantastic. That was quick. Is she awake?" Felix asked, setting aside the pen and paper.

"Yes. She's in the basement still."

"Would you mind relieving Lily? I need to borrow her for this next bit, I think. I'd really appreciate it, Miu," Felix said, trying to catch the woman's eyes.

She avoided looking into his face; instead, she looked to the side and nodded her head. "Of course. I'll take up her job duties and have her sent to you."

And with that, she was off. As mysterious as ever.

Moving to the basement, he brushed off the thoughts of Miu. As long as she cooperated, he'd not complain.

Reaching the entrance, he leaned over the hole and peered in.

"Felicia, are you down there?" Felix called down.

"Aye, where else would I be, you daft shit? Trying to get a bit more efficiency out of this before the first test," she called back.

Felix started to climb down the ladder rather than shouting back down to her.

Reaching the floor, he found the whole area was fairly rough. It'd been hacked, chiseled, shoveled, and mined. They'd have to spend some time or points to get it looking like a proper basement. But that was for later.

Walking to the center of the area, lit by lamps plugged into extension cords running up out of the hole, he found "the wood chipper."

"Looks like a giant wood chipper attached to a dumpster," Felix said, peering into the machine.

"It is," Felicia said, coming over to stand near him. She brushed her forearm across her forehead. "My machines aren't pretty, just like me. They'll get the job done."

"I disagree. With the changes Felix made, you're very easy on the eyes," Lily said, coming up behind them. "I prefer men, but even I can appreciate your looks."

"What she said," Felix concurred, pointing at Lily.

Lily made a curious face at that.

"The first part. Not the into men thing," he clarified, realizing where the confusion came from.

Felicia grunted and then pulled a switch on the strange control box in front of them.

"Pick one out, do your thing. We'll put him through after that." Felicia stumped off.

"She doesn't take compliments well," Lily said, arching a brow.

"Whatever. Go pick out your first meatsack and drain him like a juice box. Try to kill me and mine... Fuckers," Felix muttered, shaking his head.

"Touchy," Lily countered, looking to him.

"I don't like it when people mess with my things and people," Felix said, wrinkling his nose.

Lily watched him, then sauntered off to pick one of the squirming, screaming, mumbling, bound-and-gagged men who they'd wrapped up in tarps.

"I'll need my powers back," Lily said, dragging one of the struggling men over to the front of the machine.

"Been back since last night."

"Really? I didn't even notice. That's what I get for not trying," she said with a grin.

Lily then slammed her palm onto the top of the struggling tarp. A purple haze surrounded her, the man, and a few feet around them.

A gut-wrenching scream was heard on a level Felix couldn't explain. Then it cut off with a pop.

The man stopped moving and lay there like a corpse.

"It's done. His soul was foul," Lily muttered, shaking from head to toe.

"Sorry, didn't realize they, uh, had a flavor. Felicia, do we just stuff him in?" Felix asked.

"Oh, aye, just pop him in." He couldn't see her, but her response was clear enough.

Shrugging, Felix eased Lily back from the body and then lugged the whole thing up and into the chute.

For whatever reason, Felicia, thankfully, had attached a rubber flap that swung back into place after the body passed it.

There was a grinding noise to start. Then the wet squishing that sounded like hamburger meat when you were turning them into patties. Followed by the sick crunch and pop of bones being splintered.

Felix raised both his eyebrows. "It really is a wood chipper."

Lily pressed a hand to her mouth. "That's awful."

"You're one to talk, you damn prissy princess. You rip out a man's soul and then get all doe-eyed when we dispose of the corpse? Pah." Felicia came back into view and pulled another switch.

"For what it's worth, Felicia, I appreciate it. If it does what I asked, I'll never say a cross word about the dispose-o-matic," Felix said.

The Dwarven women grunted and then pulled a third lever.

"Does more than you asked. It'll turn their body into a paste. Thinking it'll look like blood sausage. Should improve the body or power of whoever you feed it to."

Felicia pointed an accusing finger at Lily. "I doubt the princess has ever had a sausage in her mouth, so she's probably out."

"Right," Felix frowned. He wasn't quite sure he wanted to force someone to eat the ground-up paste of a dead person. "I'll... make everyone aware of what it is and that they can have it if they choose. Good work, Felicia.

"Wait. He had clothes on, and a tarp? Where does that go?"

"It gets ripped off and flamed. We only lost a little bit of mass with it, so it's fine."

He managed to not shudder at the idea of what had just happened as a whole.

Right up until the point that the dumpster made a noise like a toaster. Then a metal plate slid upwards, and a rack of what looked like sausage swung out on a shelf.

Then he shivered, his throat clenching up.

She's an evil genius. A brilliant one.

In the end, Miu volunteered to eat it, and Felicia convinced Ioana to try it.

Chapter 11 - Places to Be -

Felix checked himself over to make sure he had everything he needed.

Money, papers, Pit, portable work terminal... I think that's everything.

That wasn't quite true, though. He didn't have any money on him at all. He'd pre-arranged everything with the bank so that he could make large electronic payments tonight.

Having met with the bank manager directly, it'd only been a matter of explaining the situation, and that it was a government-funded event.

No-Name had taken care of the other side of the equation and gotten the information they needed to make everything ready to go.

Setting aside three months of mortgage payments, since that was the one thing he wasn't willing to default on, they'd put together roughly two hundred thousand dollars.

They were leaving from the rear loading bay that Felicia had converted into a garage.

Felix looked to the dark-windowed, black-colored, powerful sedan next to him.

The car was a recent acquisition. One of the nice things about owning a pawn shop was people brought in all sorts of things to sell you.

Like broken-down or accident-destroyed cars. This one was especially bad.

A luxury sedan, last year's model, that had been twisted into a heap of nothing.

Felicia had spent some time ironing it out when she was bored. She'd done the majority of the work and had left the irreparable bits to him to tidy up.

It had cost him two days of points, but they'd brought it all the way up to mint condition, and then improved upon it.

Felicia had treated it more as hobby, since she spent most of her time doing the basement work with Andrea.

"Your tie is sloppy," Lily said angrily, walking over to him. She was dressed in a black jacket, blue blouse, and black skirt with matching heels.

Her hair was loose and bounced around her neck and shoulders freely.

She looked beautiful and immaculate.

"I hate ties," Felix said disdainfully. Turning around, he looked into the reflective surface of the rear passenger window and began to fix it.

"That's a shame, since you actually look presentable in a suit and tie," Lily said dryly.

The window slid down to reveal Andrea staring at him with a smile from inside the car.

"Hi! As your personal assistant," she said, slapping his hands away and immediately trying to fix his tie, "I can do this."

"Andie, you're making it worse," Lily said, watching the Beastkin trying to fix the tie. "Stop, no, pull it through there."

Felix grunted as Andrea pulled him to one side.

"No, no. Other way," Lily said, indicating to something Felix couldn't see.

"Like this?" Andrea asked, tightening the tie to the point that Felix was uncomfortable.

"Here, wait." Lily roughly pushed Felix to one side and then yanked on his tie. After three swift jerks, jostling him around while doing so, she stepped back to view her handiwork.

"Better. Don't touch it. Get in the car. I'm driving," Lily said, dismissing him with a wave of her hand.

"I thought I —" Felix was interrupted when Andrea opened her door suddenly. She managed to even hit him with it.

"Get in! We can talk in the back while they get us there."

Andrea's hands snapped out at him as he stumbled backwards and dragged him into the car by his jacket.

She pulled him bodily across the seat before letting him go. Then she leaned over him, sticking her knee into his shoulder as she shut the door.

"This'll be fun!" Andrea said, getting back to her own seat and grabbing her seatbelt. "Put on your seatbelt, Felix. Don't just lay there."

Felix grumbled, getting his feet placed and then sitting up. Adjusting his jacket, he pulled the seatbelt down and clicked it into place.

Lily was adjusting the mirrors from the driver's seat. The passenger door popped open and Kit slid in.

"Ready when you are," Kit said, looking to Lily

"All the runes are up, just need a trickle of power. Are we all set, Felix?" Lily asked, looking at him in the rearview mirror.

"Ah, yeah. You, Kit, and Andrea are all at one hundred percent. Ioana, Miu, and Felicia are at twenty percent each."

He hadn't been happy to give over so many points, but Kit had convinced him it'd be for the best.

"Good," Kit said.

Lily made a gesture with her hand and the interior of the car flashed white for a second.

Between himself and Felicia, the luxury sedan had been turned into a racecar-level monster with the durability of a tank.

Unfortunately for him, Lily had found out about its driving performance and refused to drive it at anything less than full speed.

To her, the brake pedal didn't exist.

Felix looked to the back of the seat in front of him as Lily turned the engine over and revved the monstrous engine twice, making the whole car shudder.

Felix distracted himself and focused on his point allocation screen.

	Received	Spent	Remaining
Daily	150	0	150

Allotment			
Miu Miki	1,000	200	800
Ioana Iliescu	1,100	220	880
Kit Carrington	2,250	2,250	
Lilian Lux	2,600	2,600	
Andrea Elex	1,400	1,400	
Felicia Fay	1,550	310	1,240
+ Loyalty Bonus	460	0	460
DAILY TOTAL	**10,510**	**6,980**	**3,530**

Kit, Miu, Ioana, and Felicia had all gone up in point values. Kit because he'd upgraded her power, Lily through her soul snatching, and Miu and Ioana through their continued eating of the "power sausage," as it had been termed.

They'd only had to eat it once, then been told of the increase, for them to request it going forward.

Everyone else, while intrigued about the increase, declined.

Even Felix had his limits.

"Are you looking at our points?" Andrea asked, pushing up next to him. She stuck her hand through the space that held his view and then moved it back and forth.

"I am. Even with all of those points missing, I'm sitting at roughly three thousand five hundred points."

"That's great! Maybe I should start eating the power sausage." Andrea clapped her hands together through his points screen. "I can't feel it."

"I imagine not," Felix said, looking up at the odd girl.

"Such a strange thing. It almost speaks of something more. One wonders about your power. It seemingly changes at your whim, functions at a level on which no one has ever heard of, and seemingly has a mind of its own."

Felix didn't respond to that. It wasn't something he hadn't already considered.

The sudden acceleration of the vehicle as Lily gunned it pressed him into his seat.

Closing his eyes, he did his best to tune out the world.

Kit and Lily could get them there safely.

Felix wasn't sure if his breakfast would make it there with them, though.

Lily got them there with time to spare. This auction was certainly more secretive than the previous one. Cars were being routed into a parking complex. Each car was privately directed into sectioned-off parking spaces.

They were asked to wait in their private parking space for their pickup.

In their case, it was No-Name. No words were exchanged, though a handshake was.

They were escorted quickly and quietly to a private room that thankfully wasn't an office this time. It was a large conference room. On one side of the wall was a series of buffet tables that were laden with appetizers, small meals, snacks, and drinks.

A table with a number of chairs around it sat in the middle of the room. Several monitors were set up around the room, all presenting the same feed. Everyone would see the same thing without having to strain.

"This is great, No-Name," Felix said, looking around.

No-Name shrugged his shoulders with a casual, smooth smile. "My pleasure. Auction should start in—" He paused to glance at his watch. "—twenty minutes or so. They managed to get some info from a few people, but not much.

"The ones with information will be later in the auction, so I'd save your money till then if you're feeling unsure."

Felix only nodded his head, Kit, Lily, and Andrea going straight to the buffet table.

No-Name glanced to them and then back to Felix.

"If you hand me your Pit, I'll make sure they all get registered with you as we go. Oh, and here," No-Name said, holding out a tablet to him and taking the cube Felix offered. "This will act as your bidding tool, and confirmation of payment. Take a few minutes and get all your information in so it'll go quick."

No-Name stopped talking, and looked like he was mulling over his next thought.

"You sure you're alright with those three? Augur, Mab, and Myriad, of all people. More blood spilled than most from any one of those, let alone combined."

"Huh? Myriad?" Felix asked, looking back to No-Name.

"Myriad? The Beastkin solitary PMC? Takes more or less any contract that suits them and drowns the opponent in bodies all of her?" No-Name asked.

"Uh… nope. Did she live somewhere else?" Felix asked. His eyes slowly went back to Andrea. "Never really paid attention to whole thing."

He'd known about Kit and Lily. They were rather well documented, and he'd seen or heard of their exploits.

Never heard of Myriad.

"Huh. Guess that could be why you don't know. Yeah, she was. She killed a number of people for whatever reason she came up with. Almost as coldblooded as they come."

No-Name followed Felix's gaze.

"Whatever, your problem. Catch ya later, Felix." No-Name turned on his heel and left right after that.

Felix frowned and scratched at his chest. "Hey, Myriad," he said finally.

Andrea's head whipped around. Her eyes unfocused for a second, then she realized he'd been the one who called her.

A smile bloomed across her face. "What is it?" she asked.

"Nothing. Anything good over there?" Felix asked, walking over. He didn't particularly care who she'd been before she had become his.

Her smile grew even wider. Without responding, she picked up a second plate she'd been filling that he hadn't noticed.

"Here! As your personal assistant, I was filling you one."

Kit laughed and shook her head, dropping into a chair. "He didn't realize you were Myriad, Andie."

Andrea's smile fell, the plate in her hand outstretched and forgotten. "Oh."

"And I don't care. To me, you're Andrea. Now, as my personal assistant, can you guarantee I'll like this plate?" Felix asked, taking the plate from her. He leaned over it and poked at a few things with a finger.

Andrea's face nearly split into two with the grin that came over her. "Yes! I can't find any candy, though. Always need candy. Do you think there's a vending machine nearby? That'd have candy."

Lily sat down next to Kit and said something under her breath to the telepath.

Kit snorted and turned to her to reply.

Felix smiled and looked to Andrea. "I dunno. But I don't think we're supposed to leave. We'll get some on the way home.

"Now, how about you tell me how you and Felicia did yesterday? I haven't had a chance to look."

Andrea nodded excitedly, moving over to the table and seating herself by dropping into the chair.

"We finished up the second basement floor. We need you to smooth it all out and make it pretty, but they're mostly there," Andrea said.

Then she frowned and stuck her hands on her hips. "'That daft fool we call a master can make this a place we can all live.' I don't think you're daft. You're really nice."

"Felicia is welcome to her opinion of me. She's done all she promised and more, so far. She's done her job," Felix said. The monitor on the wall came to life, catching his attention.

A timer flashed up on it and started to tick down.

"Speaking of job, when do I get my first paycheck?" Andrea asked, stuffing a French toast triangle into her mouth.

"Huh? Paycheck?" Felix said confusedly, his eyes flicking back to Andrea.

"Well, I'm your personal assistant. I was wondering when I'll get my first paycheck. Actually, I don't even know how much I'm being paid." Andrea lifted up a chicken leg and began devouring it, her elongated canines making an appearance.

"Huh. Honestly, I hadn't even considered it. What would you need money for?" Felix asked.

"Clothes. Things. You're not really providing us with much so far."

Felix couldn't argue that. Giving them a salary would probably cost less than trying to provide them with everything.

"Lily, let's set up a payroll function and get salaries for everyone," Felix said, looking toward the woman who he was quickly thinking of as his chief operations officer.

Lily blinked and raised her delicate eyebrows. "Of course. I'll make sure it's taken care of."

Everyone fell silent after that. They ate, drank, and more or less waited, watching the clock wind down.

At some point, Andrea got bored and laid down in a corner, falling immediately asleep.

As the timer hit zero, Kit took the chair on his right, and Lily the one on his left.

"Felicia had her up late. It'll be easier to be quiet if we're closer together," Lily explained, taking the electronic pad from Felix. "Ah, good. You set it up."

Lily set it back down in front of Felix.

There were no introductions, explanations, nothing on the monitor.

It was a black screen with a clock, and then it was a live stream of what looked like a lobby.

"What's our goal here?" Lily asked.

"Kit reads their mind, while I pull up a hypothetical on them, and we figure out their power. Then we determine if we want them and could be useful." Felix drummed his fingers on the table.

"Okay, but what are we looking for?" Lily pressed. "Powers are as unique as people."

"Errr, well…" Felix drew out his answer. He hadn't consulted them, but his thoughts had been running down corporate lines. Felicia, Ioana, Kit, and Lily all becoming supervisors for relevant or similar powers that they could work with. "I was thinking that we'd discuss them as they came up. As far as what kind… Any? I'm not that picky."

Saved from further questions, a group of four men were pushed out in front of the camera.

Looking to the pad, he saw the opening bid was set for four thousand dollars. No information on them whatsoever.

"They're brothers," Kit said, before Felix could even think of opening his own power. "They're all strength-type powers. They're good at fighting and have practiced a fair amount of martial arts. They'd make good security forces or front liners."

Lily grunted and crossed her arms in front of her midsection. "I'd say worth at least eight thousand, then. Worst case, I can take their souls, and we turn them into sausage."

Felix tapped the bid button with a shrug of his shoulders. She was right. "Good point, Lily."

"This is… incredibly easier," Kit said, scratching at the table with her index finger. "I'm not sure I've said it yet, but… thank you, Felix. The… upgrade… really changed things. It's like working with a scalpel instead of a machete. I can still use it as if there was no change, but it's at my choice now. So… thank you."

"Wait, you can upgrade powers?" Lily asked, surprised.

The pad in front of them chimed. The word "Purchased" flashed across the screen, followed by a box that took up the whole window as it asked, "Authorize payment?"

Felix thumbed the confirmation box and looked to Lily. "I can indeed. Why, something you don't like about your power?"

"I hate using my hands to write the sigils. I'd rather use my mind because it'd be so much faster. Instantly projecting them instead of drawing them out," Lily said, turning her entire body around to face him. "Can you do that?"

Kit froze in her seat, her eyes stuck to Lily.

"Maybe, one second." Felix focused on the idea of changing Lily's power. From a physical ethereal projection to a mental one. That the projections would be instant and from her mind's eye.

After a few seconds, the upgrade window came into existence.

Power Upgrade:	Required	Upgrade? (
Mental Etheral Projections	Primary Power: 50 (Met) Required Intelligence: 80 (Met)	10,000)

"Yeah. I can. The price is hefty, though. Ten thousand points. So it'd take an entire day's worth of points," Felix said, looking back to the pad.

A woman in her forties was brought in front of the camera.

"Do it," Lily demanded.

"Do what, upgrade you?" Felix asked. Then he motioned to the pad. "Kit?"

"Builder. She's mechanical, though. Nothing magical about her. If she's cheap, pick her up. Worst case, she can keep everything working."

The price that flashed up on the screen was only a thousand.

Felix hit the bid button.

"Do it. Tonight. After we've bought everyone, you'll have more than enough points." Lily had inched closer to him; she was practically in his face now.

Looking at her with a small frown, he sighed. "Why? What benefit do I get, Lily? I know what Kit's bringing to the table for me. What the change in her powers did.

"Besides. Your powers are useful, but... up to now, you've been far more important to me for your mind and your thoughts. More of Lilian Lux than Mab.

"If anything, I'd rather spend the ten thousand points pushing your intelligence and wisdom up."

Or that awful luck of yours.

The pad chimed again. Looking only to confirm the auction win, and authorize the payment, he tried to keep his attention on Lily.

"You don't understand. I could cast spells that would currently take me minutes, hours, days, in seconds. My potential would become near limitless. I... no, you asked what's in it for you.

"I would be limitless potential for you. I'd do anything for you. Anything. I'll never fight with you, or make fun, or snark—"

"Stop," Felix said, holding up a finger in front of her. "I'll purchase the upgrade tonight. If I can do it before midnight, all the better. As for what you'll do, be you. Be who you were up to this point. Fight by my side, rather than for me. I need that elegant brain of yours, Lily.

"Not your powers. Deal?"

Lily turned her head to the side, watching him from the corner of her eye. Her lips were turned down in a pouty frown.

"That's it?" she asked suspiciously.

"For about five more seconds, yep. Next purchase is coming."

Lily held out her hand. "Your word on it, then. A deal."

Felix shook her hand and turned back to the screen.

A teenage boy took the stage. Felix put him at probably eighteen years old.

He looked roughed up but healthy enough. Clearly, he'd continuously tried to either provoke his captors or escape.

While he didn't seem to bear any wounds, his clothes bore tears, smears, and rough wear.

Whoever was running the auction realized what people were looking at and put the starting bid at a low five hundred dollars.

"The boy is a mage. A natural one, though, not runic, mystic, or elemental. He focuses natural energies," Kit said.

Tapping the bid screen, Felix waited. The sale went through quickly and he confirmed the payment.

The handler who escorted the young man off the stage shoved him roughly off screen.

Almost immediately, he was replaced with another teenager. Felix put this one at fifteen. It was a little hard to tell, though.

Her face was swollen, her eyes puffy, and she looked like she would collapse any moment.

Whatever had been done to the teenager before this one now seemed light in comparison.

Her clothes were in far worse wear, and it looked as if she'd been pushed through a garbage chute.

Felix focused on the girl and popped open a screen for her as if she were already purchased, getting the hypothetical view.

Name:	Power:
Eva Adelpha	Intangibility

Alias:	Secondary Power: Mind Control	
Physical Status: Gravely Wounded	Mental Status: Shock	
Positive Statuses: None	Negative Statuses: Crippling Fear, Paranoia, Hunger, Thirst, Internal hemorrhaging	
Strength:	35	Upgrade? (350)
Dexterity:	43	Upgrade? (430)
Agility:	46	Upgrade? (460)
Stamina:	56	Upgrade? (560)
Wisdom:	41	Upgrade? (410)
Intelligence:	61	Upgrade? (610)
Luck:	84	Upgrade? (840)
Primary Power:	91	Upgrade? (9,100)
Secondary Power:	02	Upgrade? (200)

"What would you say, 'intangibility' means? Because that's her primary power. That and mind control, but that one's very, very weak," Felix wondered, pressing the bid button. She was only going for five hundred dollars too.

That and he doubted anyone would bother to look into that internal hemorrhage. He imagined that whoever bought her would have less-than-honorable intentions to begin with. She was as good as dead with anyone but him, he wagered.

"Hum," Lily mused, chewing on her lower lip. "I think I heard that mentioned once... I'm not completely sure, but maybe she can pass through walls?"

Kit made a soft humming sound and then tilted her head to one side. "Ah, there it is. Yes. Her mind control gives her a limited ability to shield thoughts. A touch of telepathy in that control. She's shielded her ability even from her own mind."

On the screen, the girl pressed her hands to her head and bent over for a second, looking around at everyone near her off screen.

Kit pushed a little hard, maybe?

Someone else bid it up to three thousand, to which Felix hit the button immediately on, moving it to four thousand.

Then it flashed "Sold" after a ten-second delay.

Tapping his thumb against the table, he waited. He'd need to get her looked at immediately. She could be incredibly useful with a power like that.

Felix raised his eyebrows with a sudden thought.

He called up his point totals.

	Received	Spent	Remaining
Daily Allotment	150	0	150
Miu Miki	1,000	200	800
Ioana Iliescu	1,100	220	880
Kit Carrington	2,250	2,250	0
Lilian Lux	2,600	2,600	0
Andrea Elex	1,400	1,400	0
Felicia Fay	1,550	310	1,240
Benito Hernandez	750	0	750
Carlos Hernandez	900	0	900
Enrique Hernandez	850	0	850
Ignacio Hernandez	1,100	0	1,100
Ruby Todd	1,300	0	1,300
Antony Adelpha	1,700	0	1,700
Eva Adelpha	1,600	0	1,600
+ Loyalty Bonus	685	0	685
DAILY TOTAL	18,935	6,980	11,955

He had far more than he'd expected, points wise, but that was whole reason he was buying people, wasn't it?

Next, he focused on Eva's Negative Status of Internal Hemorrhaging, and that he wanted to correct it.

Status Correction: Internal Hemorrhage - > Healed	Correct Status? (2,000 points)

"Kit, can you put a thought in the girl's head?"

"I can. Why...?"

"She's bleeding out internally. I'm going to fix it," Felix explained. "Let me know when you're done."

"I... yes. It's done. She's very confused and scared and trying to talk with me now," Kit said after a second.

"That's fine. Nudge No-Name and see if he's willing to bring her directly to us if you think it'd be worthwhile.

"Car might be a bit cramped, though. And..."

Felix tapped the button, confirming the status correction.

Sighing, he leaned back in his chair and looked to the tablet again. "There. I'm tired. Feel like getting some pizza on the way home?"

Lily looked like she was going to explode. She clenched her fists in front of him and took a deep breath.

"That'd be fine, Felix. Though I think we should probably discuss how much you really can do with your powers," Kit interjected.

"Probably a good idea. I had no idea I could fix an active wound until this moment, though. Cost two thousand points to fix her internal bleeding. Seems expensive. I mean, we knew I could do limbs and whatnot, but an actual bleeding wound? New."

Lily growled, shaking visibly. Slowly, she turned from him, facing the monitor. "Oh yeah, healing power the likes of which has never been seen before. Done in seconds. Doesn't even have to be nearby. Or actually see them. Expensive," she grumbled.

Chapter 12 - Building Upward -

Felix stared at his points screen and then poked at it with an angry grunt. Bending his will to it, he tried to force it to reorganize itself for him.

He didn't want to see every damn name. It felt like an endless list. He wanted it organized by power type under who it would be rolled up to. He wanted it organized like a corporation.

He knew those. Corporations made sense. Org charts kept everyone in line. It was a civilian military system.

Trying his damnedest to get his way, he used the example of the Hernandez brothers rolling up to Ioana because their power sets were similar. They'd end reporting to her as if she were their supervisor.

With over a hundred additional people, it was going to take some time to get it all sorted out.

Right now, they had some time. Felix had spent his time buying up the undocumented masses cheaply. The rest of those participating in the auction were now fighting over the high-value known individuals.

Felix couldn't deny his interest, but not at those prices. Instead, he got to work.

He had to check his terminal a few times to confirm his thoughts against his notes, but eventually he got it to a view he was happy with.

He left Eva out because he wasn't sure where her powers would fit best.

	Received	Spent	Remaining
Daily Allotment	150	0	150
Miu Miki	1,000	200	800
—Direct reports	12,875	0	12,875
Ioana Iliescu	1,100	220	880
—Direct reports	24,720	0	24,720
Kit Carrington	2,250	2,250	0
—Direct reports	20,600	0	20,600
Lilian Lux	2,600	2,600	0
—Direct reports	12,360	0	12,360
Andrea Elex	1,400	1,400	0
Felicia Fay	1,550	310	1,240

–Direct reports	13,905	0	13,905
Eva Adelpha	1,600	2,000	-400
+ Loyalty Bonus	1,610	0	1,610
DAILY TOTAL	**97,720**	**8,980**	**88,740**

"Weeeell. Ending total right now is just shy of one hundred thousand points. I'd say our money troubles are well and truly over. We'll need to be careful, though, and not overdo it and make ourselves too rich. That'd just draw attention we don't need.

"I say we go with the original plan. Use the pawn shop as a front to launder the points through into money," Felix said, closing the window.

"But I do your laundry," Andrea said sleepily from her corner.

"That you do. Hey, I wanted to ask you about that. I appreciate you doing that for me, I wasn't expecting it, but it feels like everything is off by a week."

"I don't understand?" Andrea asked, rolling over, putting her back to him and curling back into a napping position.

"The clothes you dropped off yesterday were from two weeks ago. It's... weird. It's like there's a delay."

Andrea started to snore softly, leaving Felix's question unanswered.

Felix harrumphed and looked to the screen. The amounts were getting ridiculous.

Pointless. I can turn Eva into a wrecking ball. Or the boy into a second Lily. Bidding on an end result is pointless for me. I can take the untrained and bring them up.

Trainer of newbs.

Felix smirked at his own thoughts and waited for the whole thing to end.

Looking at the young girl next to him, Felix kept himself from sighing. Technically, he'd told Kit she could do this. He had only himself to be upset at.

The rest of them were being shipped in busses tomorrow morning, since it was already late in the day by the time they'd gotten out of the auction.

No-Name had set it up for him and seemed rather pleased with himself. Felix didn't care. He imagined the man would get a cut of Felix's purchases, and that was fine with him.

It was a relationship they both benefited from.

"You bought my brother? You swear?" she asked again for the tenth time.

"If she asks me the same question again, I want you to put her to sleep, Kit," Felix said, ignoring her.

"Eva, he bought your brother," Kit said, turning her head to face the young girl. "Please don't make me put you to sleep. I won't have a choice in the matter. Remember what I said about his power and your power? It doesn't exist right now."

Eva shuddered, looking at Felix out of the corner of her eye. "And you're Augur?"

Kit nodded from the front seat.

"And you're Mab," Eva said, turning her head to face the rearview mirror.

Lily glanced up at the girl and then flashed her sparkling white teeth at her. "I am."

"And you're Myriad." Eva's finger pointed to Andrea, sitting next to her.

"Yep!" Andrea happily said, smiling at her from ear to ear. "I haven't killed anyone in a long time, and I don't have to anymore. Felix buys me all the pancake batter I want, and gives me fun things to do, and he lets me sleep in, and I get to build a basement and—" She paused to suck in a deep breath. "He smells awesome. When we get home, you'll see."

Andrea leaned in close to Eva and whispered conspiratorially, except her voice carried easily to everyone in the car.

"If you want something from him, all you have to do is phrase it in a way that will benefit him, and how he can't live without it. Works every time. Watch."

Andrea sat up and gave Felix a broad smile. "Felix?"

He shook his head looking at Andrea, laughing. "Yes?"

"He heard you," Eva whispered at Andrea, trying to stop her.

"Can one of my Others sleep in your room tonight? I think it would be good for you to have someone watching over you. Just in case.

"Your life is important and you should have a bodyguard."

Felix blinked at that and his smile faltered.

His inner paranoia kicked up a notch, and he found himself wondering what could happen at night.

It's not a bad idea. At all. I could probably use a bodyguard. Not to mention if it is one of Andrea's Others, it wouldn't really matter.

"Huh. Sure. That's not a bad idea, actually." Felix felt better in agreeing to that. It'd be odd at first, he was sure, but it'd help.

"See?" Andrea whispered to Eva, as loud as she was before. "Now I get to smell him all night long. I just have to make my Other me, and I get it all for nothing."

"Fuck, it worked," Lily muttered from the driver's seat.

"Sure as shit did," Kit agreed quietly.

"Now wait a—"

Felix was slammed into the door. All around him, the world became as bright as the sun. A fiery red sun.

Time passed in an angry roar and pulse of light.

Eventually, it faded and he found he could think again.

He felt his chest pulling heavily at the seatbelt as his body tried to slide to the car's roof.

"What... what happened?" Felix asked groggily.

"Someone tried to blow up the car. I think we got hit by a grenade, maybe," Kit said gruffly.

"Well fuck them. I'll tear their souls out," Lily hissed.

Looking around, he realized they were upside down.

He was, at least. So was Eva.

Kit, Lily, and Andrea had already undone their seatbelts and were leaning down, peering out the windows.

Andrea reached up and unclipped his seatbelt, and then Eva's without turning her head away.

"I count thirty," Andrea said. All trace of the bubbly, bouncy Beastkin was gone.

"Forty. Ten in the building above us," Kit corrected.

"One second." Felix grunted as he righted himself, slithering down to sit on the interior of the car's roof.

Grunting, he made himself as comfortable as he could.

Pulling up Lily's power window, he confirmed the upgrade without a thought.

Then, in an afterthought, he called up Lily's power draw and tried to force it to negative one hundred percent.

To pump more power into her instead of drawing it out.

A second later, and he saw the hash line jump to where he wanted it.

Snorting, he shook his head, then repeated the process for Andrea, Eva, and Kit.

"Right. I reversed the... flow... I guess. You're now all at twice your original strength. Lily, I also upgraded your power as you requested.

"Andrea, you're a PMC leader, what's the play?" Felix asked.

The Beastkin known as Myriad turned her head and stared at him.

It was strange. Clearly, she was Andrea, but not Andrea at the same time.

"You would defer to me?" she asked him.

"I'm not an idiot. I have no military experience. Besides, at this point, I think you could probably make about four hundred of your Others and drown them out by yourself if you wanted."

Andrea's mouth turned up at one side. "If I do that, I'll be defenseless and spent. I normally take hours to summon my Others and get them ready. This'll hurt. Would you carry me? Even though I'll slow you down?"

"I suppose I could? But wouldn't it be easier to have one of your Others carry you?" Felix asked.

Andrea flashed him a sharp-toothed grin. "Can't blame a girl for trying."

Andrea looked to Lily and Kit.

"Mab, run defense on Felix. We're fucked if he goes down. Augur, I need you to tell me info on positions, locations, and plans of the enemy. Then update my Others with new info as it comes in."

Both supers nodded their heads.

Lily lifted a hand and then lowered it again. In front of her body, a rapid series of runes spread out in ever-increasing speed.

Her pretty face became an evil smile as the runes doubled, then quadrupled faster than he could keep up with.

They spread throughout the vehicle and wrapped up around it in a bubble. Then it made a deep thrumming noise and turned from blue to yellow.

"Done," Lily said, looking to Andrea.

"All forty were sent by one person. They know only the barest details. I think it's our friend from the restaurant, but I can't tell," Kit said. "Most have automatic weapons, a few have sniper rifles. They're determined to wait and see what happens. Expect no mercy."

Andrea wrinkled her nose and lifted a hand to play with one of her ears.

"Right. When this is over, I'll need a buffet of food. Meat, preferably. And lots of spoiling. Looking at you, Felix," Andrea said. Then she sighed and opened the door. "Stay with Felix, Eva."

Andrea's Others began sprinting out of Andrea Prime in droves. She clutched the door as gunfire started to open up all around them. It struck the car, asphalt, everything.

Thankfully, the car was beyond armored, so it had no effect.

Screams and moans were heard as the Others clearly began dying.

Andrea crumpled, the Others still pouring out of her.

"Damnit, Eva, pull her over here. Kit, let's get the hell out of here. Which way?" Felix asked. Reaching across Eva, he pulled Andrea into his lap.

The Others had to take a few stumbling steps to get free of the car now, but they kept moving.

"West. There's an alley we can get into and move from there."

"Lily, you're on rear watch. Kit, you're on point. I trust both of you to do what you feel is best. Don't ask for permission, executive decisions only."

Felix's door was already westward facing. Popping open the door, he took a peek outside. Andreas were littering the street and the surrounding area. So was the enemy now, though. Quite a few were engaged in hand-to-hand combat. One Andrea had somehow gotten a hold of a rifle and was keeping the snipers pinned down.

"Eva, help me get Andrea on my back. Lily, how strong is your Glenda impersonation?" Felix grabbed Andrea by a shoulder and started levering her onto his back.

Eva started to help him, pushing the Beastkin up onto him.

Up in the front seat, Kit and Lily opened Kit's door and made ready.

"With that power amp you gave me... probably a tank shell, at most. Though sustained fire will be an issue, too."

"Kit, lead on," Felix said, taking a hold of Andrea's legs. "Hold on, Andrea."

The Beastkin woman nodded her head against his shoulder.

"Go," Kit commanded.

The group of five stormed out from the safety of the car, sprinting for the alley Kit had mentioned.

Bullets sprayed over the bubble they were in, spitting up chunks of the pavement.

What took seconds felt as if it were a year, finally getting into the cover the alley provided.

Kit kept out in front at a light jog, Felix and Eva a few steps behind her.

Above them, the maze of fire escapes twisted and turned. Kit had them turning at random locations down towards directions he hadn't considered.

There's either people following us, or people ahead of us.

It was the only logical conclusion.

"No restrictions if we run across an enemy. Kill 'em and move on," Felix huffed, balancing Andrea on his back.

"Understood," Lily said darkly from behind him.

"I can't shake 'em," Kit admitted in front of them. "They're ahead of us and keep moving to intercept. The ones behind us are long gone, but... I can't shake these."

"Fine. Give us a good place to fight from, then. Let's stop, peek into their heads, and figure out the place they don't want us to go," Felix said, pulling up short.

Kit's head swung to the right, looking at a wall. There was a high-pitched scream in the distance.

"They're supers. One down. Not dead, but... probably never to, well, never anything now.

"They don't want us getting into an open space. I think their team is primarily an 'up close and personal' one. Though their telepath is strong enough to keep me from turning anyone else into a carrot."

"Okay, that works. Which way, then? Get us an open space and we'll deal as best as we can. Preferably somewhere the three of us can hole up while you two deal with them."

"Felix, I can't really fight that well. I'm a telepath. Telekinesis isn't in my power set." Kit turned back the way they had come and led them off down the twisting alley.

"Huh. Well, it's a sister power to yours. So why not—"

Felix tried to focus on Kit's power set, adding telekinesis directly to it.

Second Power (Unlock): Directed Telekinesis	Required Primary Power: 90 (Met) Required Intelligence: 80 (Unmet)	Upgrade? (30,000)

"Goddammit." Felix fumbled with his screen and smashed two points of intelligence into Kit, getting her up to eighty.

The second window flashed green as her Intelligence now met the requirement.

Kit slid to a halt in a dead-end corner of the alley. It was an expanded circle that looked like it had once been a park.

"Hold onto your tits, Kit, you're getting a second power." Felix stabbed the upgrade button.

As it activated, he called up his character screen for her to check the result.

Name: Kit Carrington	Power: Directed Telepathy	
Alias: Augur	Secondary Power: Directed Telekinesis	
Physical Status: Healthy	Mental Status: None	
Positive Statuses: None	Negative Statuses: None	
Strength:	51	Upgrade? (510)
Dexterity:	54	Upgrade? (540)
Agility:	48	Upgrade? (480)
Stamina:	46	Upgrade? (460)
Wisdom:	72	Upgrade? (720)
Intelligence:	80	Upgrade? (780)
Luck:	41	Upgrade? (410)
Primary Power:	91	Upgrade? (9,100)
Secondary Power:	45	Upgrade? (4,500)

"Congratulations, it worked. I'm betting it works the same way as your telepathy," Felix said. Turning his head around to inspect the area, he found a dumpster.

Kit had staggered to one side, her hands going to her knees.

Trotting over to the dumpster, he pushed it open. Glancing inside, he found trash bags and nothing that looked like it'd hurt. Then he dumped Andrea in. "Sorry, Andrea. I'll make it up to you later. You'll be safe in there."

Andrea moaned as she hit the bags and lay there, limp and unmoving. "Eva, get your ass inside." Felix gestured at the teenager.

"What? I'm not getting in there." There was enough room for the two of them, but not if he tried to get in too.

"Get in. Now."

Eva's lower lip jutted out but she clambered in, unwilling to defy her master.

Once she was in, he lowered the lid into place and then got behind it.

"If I can help, I will; I'm no fighter, though." Felix wedged himself against the wall and tried to keep himself hidden.

Lily clapped her hands together and then shook them out. The bubble around the area disappeared in a flash.

Standing up, Kit hesitantly motioned to a trashcan and it zipped through the air to crash into a wall.

All around the two women, runes formed in thin air. They looped and wrapped around them faster than he could believe possible.

Then they tightened together and flashed.

Holding her right hand to her side, Lily conjured lightning into existence.

Kit hastily began arranging objects around the area. Moving them into specific positions that she could call on from any direction to attack with.

"I want a third power after this," Lily said.

"I just upgraded you. Why should I give you a third? Giving Kit a second one was expensive."

"Because if you do, I'll make sure you never regret it. You'll have a devoted soul magician till you die.

"I'll even bring your soul back from the grave if I can, just so I can serve you longer.

"I know what I want already, too."

Kit shook her head, perhaps still feeling a touch unsteady. "It hurts. It was like someone punched a hole through my brain."

"We'll discuss it after. Kill them, eat their souls, whatever."

"They're here."

Several seconds after Kit said that, a group of four men and women stepped into the circle.

They were all dressed alike in black spandex and black hoods. Their bodies were hard to gauge other than male or female.

Cosplay for the gimp.

One of the four dropped an unmoving fifth member to the ground to one side.

"Where's your master?" the one in the lead said. "We want—"

A rock carved into a block the size of a wheel flew in from the side. It bulldozed into one of the women's midsection and smashed her to a wall.

There was a sickening pop as she screamed and fell over to the ground.

"My back! I can't feel my damn legs!" she screamed.

At the same time the group started to react, a lightning bolt slammed down from the sky into the middle of them, sending them flying in every direction.

One of the remaining three pressed their hands to their head and squealed, dropping to their knees and then lying still.

The final two charged in. The first was a blur of speed, dashing straight at Lily.

He zipped around her in a circle, trying to catch her unaware. Lily watched him warily for a few seconds and her runic shield flashed as the man attacked her repeatedly.

"Too fast for you to use those runes, princess?"

Lily gave him a smile.

A band of runes sprang into existence in front of the speedster and wrapped around him.

He came to an abrupt halt, and the sound of his ribs breaking and his breath whooshing out was audible.

"My dear master upgraded me," Lily said, wrapping her hand around the man's skull. "I wonder what you taste like. I bet it's awful."

A purple haze burned the area around her, hiding everything from view.

The man started to scream.

Kit stood staring the last woman down. Unmoving, they looked as if they were two predators determined to have the other blink first.

"Where's your helmet, Augur?" said the woman.

"Don't need it."

"You sure?"

Kit chuckled and then tilted her head to one side.

"Very. This has been a rewarding experience. I haven't tested myself like this in ever. Shall I stop toying with you?"

"Funny. You were never that stro—" The woman choked on whatever she was going to say, falling to her knees.

Blood oozed from her nose and ears, her eyes rolling up into her head. Both of her hands were pressed to her temples, her teeth clenched together.

"Don't explode her head," Felix said loudly. "Her body will foul up if you do that. If you're willing to keep her alive, we can see about enslaving her. If not, at least preserve the body so we can put her in the wood chipper."

Kit snarled something between her teeth, then sighed. The woman collapsed to the ground at that moment.

"Fine. See if she'll take the slave status. Make her mine. I know her. She was always an uppity bitch who took every opportunity to put me down a peg. Or hurt me."

"She was a hero?" Felix asked, easing out from behind the dumpster.

"Yeah. They all were," Kit said. Sighing, she put her hands on her hips.

Lily's mist faded away and she dropped the speedster's living, souless husk to the ground.

Lifting a delicate foot, she kicked the man's jaw. "They made me ditch my heels. They were expensive."

"I'll buy you new ones." Felix lifted the dumpster cover and helped Eva out.

"Three of these we can interrogate for answers. Maybe get them to accept a slave oath willingly. That or go into the sausage machine.

"The fourth one over there is the carrot I made. And I think this speedster here is an empty juice box," Kit explained to no one's asked question.

"You alright, Kit?" Felix asked. He reached into the dumpster and started pulling Andrea out.

"My head hurts. It's like it opened into something else. I'm not... quite aware of it entirely yet."

Felix could only imagine.

Andrea limply clung to him as he wrapped his arms around her. Slowly and carefully, he turned around and got her up onto his back again. "There we go."

Eva looked at them and then at the bodies. Her eye twitched as the woman with the broken back started screaming again.

"Kit, put that one to sleep, please? Nothing permanent. After that, give Miu a call to get her down here with a truck."

The screaming cut off abruptly.

"Lily, can you start gathering up our... err... loot, I guess? Kit can probably float them wherever we need them after that."

"Uhm, if they attacked you here, wouldn't they attack your base, too?" Eva asked.

Felix blinked, shocked. Then he pulled up his character screen and slid Miu and Ioana upwards on their power draw. All the way up to a three hundred percent boosted level. Pushing them to a level that they'd probably never reach in their lifetimes.

If Eva was right, they'd need it. If they were alive.

If Eva was wrong, then he'd be out nothing.

Chapter 13 - House Call -

"She's not picking up," Lily said, holding a hand up to Felix while the other held the phone to her ear.

"Shit, alright. Uhm," Felix said, looking at his feet. "Shit, shit, shit. Andrea, any of your Others make it?"

Felix looked over his shoulder at Andrea's face on his shoulder.

"A few. I feel them. Don't know what they're doing. Probably absorbing the fallen," she murmured softly. "I have no way of contacting them, sorry. They're separate from me the moment they split, but I can feel them."

"Kit, can you—"

"I'm sorry, they're beyond my reach."

"Shit on a stick. Alright... fuck." He didn't want to give up on his trophies, but it was looking a lot like they'd hit his pawn shop at the same time.

"Ioana, Felicia, and the shop phone aren't being answered either," Lily said, lowering the cell phone.

Damn. I can try to get them back home, but that'll take time.

"Lily, take their souls, then call a tow truck for our car. Kit, call No-Name and tell him there's some heroes here for pickup. We can split the bounty with him."

Lily and Kit started doing as he'd requested as he fished out his own phone.

"And what are you doing?" Eva asked him.

"Seeing what our fastest route home is. If there's a used car lot nearby, that'd be the quickest. Cash talks, bullshit walks. A taxi is good, but that'd leave a trail. Mass transit is slow.

"No, no. We're going to crush this problem with our wallet."

Lily slid them into the garage in their new used car. He'd paid a prick price for it, but it'd gotten them home quick.

And too late at that.

Even as Felix stepped out of the car, he knew they'd been attacked. There was no question of that.

All around the warehouse floor were signs of violence. Corpses, body parts, smashed items, and even a fire.

Felix surveyed the scene and then lifted his hands to his mouth. "Hey! Anyone here?" he called.

There was a distant response from the front office. He couldn't make out what it was, but it was something.

"It's Miu," Kit said, stepping out of the passenger side. "No one here is a threat."

Felix took off at a trot towards the front office.

As soon as he crossed the threshold, he found all three of his people.

Felicia looked like her jaw had been shattered. It hung at a strange angle, and didn't look right. She also had a hand pressed to a bloody shoulder.

Miu looked more like raw meat. Wounds covered her arms and torso. Her forearm hung grotesquely from her elbow, attached by only a few bits of flesh. A tourniquet was tied around her bicep where it met the elbow.

Ioana was lying down on the ground, a sword wedged in her guts. Blood welled up around the weapon with every breath. Frothy bubbles gathered on her lips.

Her left leg was mangled and broken in several places. Bone jutted out from her lower shin.

Her glassy eyes found him and seemed to focus for a second.

"Stop lying down on the job," Felix said to Ioana, calling up her window.

Name: Ioana Iliescu	Power: Enhanced Reactions	
Alias: War Maiden	Secondary Power: Combat Mastery	
Physical Status: Fatally Wounded	Mental Status: Shock	
Positive Statuses: None	Negative Statuses: Bleeding Out	
Strength:	84	Upgrade?(840)
Dexterity:	73	Upgrade?(730)
Agility:	62	Upgrade?(620)
Stamina:	77	Upgrade?(770)
Wisdom:	36	Upgrade?(360)
Intelligence:	41	Upgrade?(410)
Luck:	51	Upgrade?(510)
Primary Power:	31	Upgrade?(3,100)
Secondary Power:	82	Upgrade?(8,200)

Status Correction:	Correct Status?

Expand for List (Over 200 items) -> Healed	(10,000 points)

Felix hit the accept button and then drew up Miu's screen.

Name: Miu Miki	Power: Multiplicative Base		
Alias: Miu	Secondary Power: None		
Physical Status: Gravely Wounded	Mental Status: Flustered		
Positive Statuses: None	Negative Statuses: Concerned		
Strength:	43	Upgrade?(840)	
Dexterity:	53	Upgrade?(730)	
Agility:	51	Upgrade?(620)	
Stamina:	52	Upgrade?(770)	
Wisdom:	46	Upgrade?(360)	
Intelligence:	40	Upgrade?(410)	
Luck:	49	Upgrade?(510)	
Primary Power:	75	Upgrade?(3,100)	
Secondary Power:	--	Upgrade?(--)	

Status Correction: Expand for List (Over 50 items) -> Healed	Correct Status? (5,000 points)

Felix hit that accept button on her, too.

Next, he turned his thoughts to Felicia.

Name: Felicia Fay	Power: Mechanical Understanding	
Alias: None	Secondary Power: Magical Enhancement	
Physical Status: Wounded	Mental Status: None	
Positive Statuses: None	Negative Statuses: None	
Strength:	62	Upgrade? (620)
Dexterity:	57	Upgrade? (570)
Agility:	29	Upgrade? (290)
Stamina:	44	Upgrade? (440)
Wisdom:	41	Upgrade? (410)
Intelligence:	78	Upgrade? (780)
Luck:	31	Upgrade? (310)
Primary Power:	62	Upgrade? (6,200)
Secondary Power:	64	Upgrade? (6,400)

Status Correction: Broken Jaw -> Healed	Correct Status? (2,000 points)

Tapping the accept button, he looked back to Ioana. The sword that had been embedded in her stomach simply reappeared next to her, swathed in blood.

The warrior queen stared at him uncomprehendingly, her eyes clear and no longer holding over the glaze of pain and imminent death that they had before.

"You done sleeping? I'm tired of the game we're playing with these fools. Soon as midnight hits and our points restock, we're going to go storm the damn place and take their heads."

"Sweet mercy and grace of the gods above and below," Eva said from behind him. "She looked like a corpse. They both did."

Felix looked to Miu, who had turned her head in a different direction, avoiding his eyes. It was clear she was in perfect health again.

Felix grunted and then walked off back to the car.

He had a promise to keep to a certain Beastkin.

"He healed them instantly. Instantly!" Eva nearly shouted at Kit.

"Yes, I know. Get a mop and a broom. We'll need to clean this place up. Andrea's not going anywhere for a while, so she won't be able to get working on this," Kit said to the young girl. "Truth be told, neither am I. My head is killing me."

Opening the rear passenger door, Felix reached in and gathered up the spent Beastkin. He did his best to not pinch, crimp, or bend her tail as he did so.

"Thank you," Andrea murmured as she oozed into his arms, laying her head on his shoulder.

Felix only grunted and carried her off to her bedroom.

"No, please don't," Andrea murmured softly.

Ignoring her, he managed to get her door open with one hand while still holding her.

Taking a step into her room, he now understood a few things that he hadn't previously.

His clothes were heaped up in a pile where her covers should have been.

"I'm sorry," Andrea said.

Felix didn't respond, but instead carried her over to the center of that pile.

There, in the middle of his dirty clothes, there was a circle that looked like it was big enough to sleep in.

She'd turned it into a den.

Laying her in the middle of that circle, he adjusted her clothes a bit, trying to make her as comfortable as he could.

Andrea snuggled into her bed, and his clothes, and lay still.

Felix crept from the room, closing the door with a click behind him.

Popping open Felicia's character screen, he slid her draw to three hundred percent.

Moving to the front office, he found Kit was lying down behind the counter, fast asleep. He wasn't sure if she had fallen there or laid down.

Didn't matter.

"Felicia. I've put your wits at a level unsurpassed by anyone on this planet. Make our home a fortress. I expect plans by tomorrow morning," Felix said.

Leaving, he went to go find a place to nap for a bit. When midnight came, he wanted to be ready.

They'd parked around the corner from the restaurant and sat with the lights off. Ioana, Kit, Lily, and Miu were with him. Felicia, Eva, and Andrea were at home.

"It's them. These are the people who attacked us. I can feel their worry. They're wondering why no one has checked in. Everyone they sent out is hours overdue. They have people watching the street and everyone is twitchy," Kit said from beside him.

"We should tell them they're being turned into sausage. Ease they're minds on where their minions are," Ioana growled. "So help me, they'll be next."

Felix said nothing for a few seconds. "Any innocents in there?"

"Everyone in there is a criminal. It seems like they're a criminal organization almost like... well, a mafia. Or a gang. In fact, quite a few of these people know about other organizations in the city. I had no idea."

"Heroes really only looked at villains. Gangs and the like were left to the police," Felix explained.

"I suppose. Well, most everyone in there was in on the attack on us or knew about it. But..."

"But?"

"But not all of them. Some had no idea. Pretty sure Dimitry's people are in there, too. I don't feel Dimitry, though."

"Damn. I don't want to get Dimitry involved if we don't have to. He could be useful as information after this. Or even just an ally.

"Ioana, I want you through the front door. Get in as quick as you can. I don't want anyone escaping, and the longer we're in the street, the more likely police will be coming.

"Lily, stay on her heels and play long-range support. I doubt you'll get halfway down the street before they open fire.

"Kit, I want you to put a thought into everyone's head who wasn't in on the attack that tonight is a bad night to be brave. That if they were to lay down and not move, they might find themselves left alone. After that, stay safe here and do what you can.

"Miu, you're with me."

Felix opened the door and stepped out.

A second later and Ioana, Lily, and Miu did as well.

Lily and Ioana took off at a pace akin to a leisurely walk. Ioana unlimbered her sword and Lily began calling runes into existence. She was getting better every time with them. Faster. Denser.

In a handful of seconds, Ioana had a small silhouette of power outlining her body, followed quickly by one that enveloped Lily.

Whoever was on watch wasn't slacking. Twenty or so people rushed out of the restaurant the second Lily and Ioana crossed into the street. The muffled bark of pistols with silencers could be heard following that. They weren't waiting or taking chances.

Either they own the cops, or the neighborhood. You don't fire guns in the street that brazenly otherwise.

Guns with silencers are still loud.

Felix and Miu eased back around the corner and peered around.

Bullets crashed into the silhouette of power and fell to the ground.

Realizing that bullets were pointless, they switched from pistols to knives and whatever they could find close at hand.

Two men in trench coats stood to the rear of the battle. They started to glow faintly. One waved his arms through the air while the other held perfectly still.

A bolt of electricity crackled from Lily's palm and speared through the chest of the one holding still.

As Ioana walked forward, she swung her blade in wide, swift arcs when people got close enough. She took hands, arms, or lives with each flick of the sword.

"Once they're inside, grab whatever corpses or body parts you can and let's get it inside," Felix said distastefully. "While I doubt the police will be coming, I'd rather not tempt fate."

"I'll take care of that," Kit said from behind him.

Looking over his shoulder to her, he managed to keep himself from asking why she had gotten out of the car.

When he looked back, Ioana was just entering the building. Miu led them into the street at a slow walk, her eyes scanning the area as they went.

Bodies, both dying and dead, and body parts, were lifted from the ground and moved back to the restaurant in a parody of a parade.

Miu entered the building and then Felix followed behind her after a few seconds. The sound of battle could be heard from deeper inside.

A man in a white collared shirt rushed at them with a bat from a side room.

Miu stepped in front of him and swept her arm across her body, intercepting the man's arm. The man was disarmed before he could even swing his weapon.

Taking a grip on the bat, Miu brought it up from below and cracked into the man's chin.

There was a sick pop and he dropped to the ground.

Searching the room with her dark eyes, Miu confirmed there was no one else.

Felix patted Miu on the shoulder. "Good show."

Then he followed the trail of bodies and destroyed furniture Ioana and Lily had wrought.

The confidence the enemy had was surprising. Corpses were everywhere.

If Felix had been cornered like this, he would have had everyone scramble and get out.

Pride is a commodity that can be purchased again later.

One's life is not.

As Felix entered yet another back office, he caught only the tail end of Lily disappearing down a trapdoor.

"The hell is this? It's so damn cliché," Felix muttered.

"Clichés exist because they're based in reality." Miu shoved him gently to one side and entered the trapdoor ahead of him.

"She's not wrong," Kit said, pushing him to the side again when he tried to move to the trapdoor.

Felix couldn't argue with their demeanor. He was nothing more than a civilian.

Maybe I should have Miu and Ioana train me. This is getting pathetic. I might as well remain at the shop and send them out on missions like a starship captain.

Go get 'em, Number One. I'll sit here and mind the coffee.

Felix sighed and then dropped down the trapdoor.

At the bottom of the ladder was a simple entry room with a single doorway.

Ioana, Lily, Miu, and Kit were standing around what looked like a desk in the other room.

Felix walked in, looking around in each corner as he did so.

It was a rather well-decorated study.

My office looks horrible in comparison.

Sitting behind the desk was a man with an iron circlet around his brow.

He looked smug. A man without a care in the world.

"I can't get into his head. That pretty princess crown of his is keeping me out, I'd bet. Enchanted, probably," Kit said, turning her head to Felix.

Ioana grunted and then moved around to the other side of the desk.

Then he saw Felix. His eyes glazed over, his pupils rapidly expanding as if he were in complete darkness.

Then the man lifted a pistol from his lap that no one had noticed. He leveled it at Felix and pulled the trigger. The bullet slammed into the shield around Ioana, who stood between him and the gun.

Before the boom of the first shot even registered, the man swiftly placed the gun to his temple and pulled the trigger again without hesitation.

The two shots from the handgun in the small room made Felix jump. Blood began pumping out of the man's skull in rhythm with his still beating heart. It quickly covered the desk and started to pool on the ground.

That looked strange. As if he was commanded to.

"Lily, take his soul before it escapes. Kit, was this the man giving orders? On top of that question, I take it you can't read anything if his brain has a bullet in it?" Felix asked.

"It was him, and no, I can't read his mind now," she said softly.

Lily gave herself a visible shake and then laid her hand on the dead man's shoulder.

The purple haze surrounded Lily and the man for a few seconds and then vanished. It seemed quicker than usual, but Felix didn't care to ask about it.

Instead, he went to the coatrack in the corner and pulled a jacket off it. Walking back over to the man, he threw it over his head.

"Search the room for anything that might tell us information. Leave the valuables. Let's get out of here quick like. Once the bleeding dies down, let's take that thing he had on his head. I'd like to be gone in five minutes, so chop, chop, people."

It took a moment, but everyone started moving even as the man continued to bleed out.

Felix was angry. He'd hoped they'd find out who was behind this whole mess. It seemed now, though, that it was only going to get worse. To keep going. To keep draining his patience and resources.

Lily pulled the car into the garage. There'd been no one on the streets during their trip home, mercifully empty of onlookers or would-be heroes.

Lily sighed as the garage door closed behind them.

"I'm going to bed," Lily grumbled, opening the driver-side door.

"Good work today, Lily, Kit, Ioana, Miu. All of you did great. Thank you," Felix said sincerely.

Positive reinforcement for a job well done was always a good thing.

Kit, Miu, and Lily abandoned the car, stepping out and shutting the doors after themselves.

Felix and Ioana were left in the vehicle alone. For himself, Felix only wanted to sleep. He was exhausted and felt like he'd been running around far too long.

"Thank you," Ioana said, a grumpy frown showing up on her face.

"For what?"

"Fixing me. Again. Didn't have to."

Felix shrugged his shoulders. "No worries."

Ioana nodded at that, then slid over and left the car.

Sighing, Felix opened his door and dragged his feet to his bedroom. It took more concentration than he had available, but he managed it.

Crumpling into the bed, Felix was asleep instantly.

Only to be woken up too soon.

"Tomorrow would still be too soon," Felix mumbled, his eyes opening slowly.

Something squirmed against his side and then fell still.

Lowering his eyes, he found Andrea pressed up into his side. Her mismatched eyes were wide open and staring at him.

"Good morning," she whispered.

Felix let out a slow breath. "Morning. Something wrong?"

Andrea shook her head, her ears twitching atop her head.

"Weren't you sleeping in your own room?"

Andrea nodded her head.

"Why aren't you still there?"

The Beastkin wrinkled her nose and gnawed at her lower lip.

"You've seen me," Andrea finally said. Her tail lay limp against her legs.

"Often. Frequently making pancakes. And?"

"No, you've seen me. It won't be the same anymore. It's different when the... when the walls aren't up. When the Others and I are me."

"Okay? And?"

"You don't care? That I'm practically two different people?"

"I can't deny it's kinda schitzo, but whatever. It doesn't actually change who you are.

"Anything else? Long day ahead, I'm betting. Going to need to call Dimitry and see where we stand. I can't imagine he'll be happy that we gutted their organization last night."

"My Others returned last night. They absorbed everything from the Others who died," Andrea said, turning her head to the side. Her tail had lifted up a few inches and swished slowly back and forth. "None live who stood against you."

"Grand. Can I get up now? Could probably use a shower. And breakfast."

"So… you don't care? At all?" Andrea pushed herself up and stared down at him, her hands pressed to his shoulders.

"No. I don't care that you have multiple personalities. That was obvious, though, after talking to some of your Others. They're not all exact copies of you.

"So Andrea Prime has a military side to her. What about it? Seems useful. You all seem to have relatively the same intelligence and disposition. Only varying shades of it."

Andrea didn't let him go. She stared at him, her head tilting one way and then the other.

"I don't understand you. We will talk more about this tomorrow morning."

Andrea got up out of the bed, moving to the door.

"What do you mean, tomorrow morning?" Felix asked, sitting up in the bed.

"I'm your night guard, remember?"

Andrea opened the door and went out of his bedroom, pausing on the other side.

"Pancakes!" came the shout from an Other, probably in the kitchen.

The Andrea outside of his door smiled back at him. "Pancakes are ready, dear."

Chapter 14 – Speeches and Uniforms -

"There's only one entrance," Felicia said, pointing to the blueprint. "That entrance has several settings for it, from simply being open to requiring biometrics. Can change the sucker depending on the situation."

Felix nodded his head, chewing on the mouthful of pancake.

"More?" Andrea asked happily crowding over his shoulder.

"Yes, more?" asked the other Andrea, leaning over the blueprint with a pan in one hand and a spatula in the other.

"Sure, cake me," Felix said, holding out his plate. "Now, this is good, Felicia. But we have an entire boatload of people that'll be arriving today. Need somewhere to put them."

A blueberry pancake flopped onto his plate and he smiled up at the Andrea who had given it to him. "Thanks."

"Nn!" Andrea chirped happily and spun back to the stove top.

"Well, I looked at the ownership papers. We don't have permission to dig down too deep. Maybe a single basement's worth. So everything is going to end up needing to be shielded in lead and we'll have to be careful with who we tell. Will help keep discovery down. This'll be illegal." Felicia flipped a few sheets down on the rather large stack of blueprints.

How many levels is she planning? I admit I asked for a fortress, but...

"Okay, but what will be done? Is it a dorm? Individual rooms? A giant single room?" Felix forked up a chunk of pancake and shoved it into his mouth.

Felicia waved off his question with an annoyed hand gesture.

"Pah, it's more like a hotel. Everyone will have their own space. Once I decided we would dig downward, it made it easier. The annoying part will be building fast, strong, reliable elevators. But that's my problem, not yours."

"For now, I have a team of Andreas working on the whole thing. You'll need to go through and use some points to make it habitable, but... should be done by this evening."

Habitable. I wonder what she's thinking.

"Yeah. Picking up that many people is definitely going to raise the cost of food. We'll also need to put in places that we can have them all eat in, relax in, and train in." Felix shook his head. Suddenly he wasn't so keen on the idea of purchasing the sheer number he had.

"Already there. I assumed you'd need those. That'll be complete this week. The Andreas have really got a knack for things once you show 'em how to do it. Fastest build team I've ever seen."

"We just absorb each other and resplit over and over," Andrea said, working on more pancakes. "It shares our experiences and our energy. Every half hour, we have to make a few new Others from Andrea Prime to get the energy levels up," she said, pointing to the Andrea behind Felix.

Felix nodded his head and finished up the delicious pancake.

"Thanks, Felicia. That's great. Suppose I'll need to get working on making money tomorrow. Our current finances won't hold up under this massive number of people."

"Especially when you start paying salaries," Andrea said happily from behind him, clapping her hands together. "I want to buy some dresses. And some guns. I really need some rifles. Did we put in a gun range?"

"Yeah, a few. Also training rooms for hand-to-hand," Felicia admitted. "We'll need our security forces training in both. Can't have what happened yesterday ever happen again."

Felix couldn't argue that point. He didn't want a repeat of the situation either. And the best way to do that was to be prepared and trained.

"How are you two doing, by the way? I dialed everyone back to one hundred percent of their power, except you, Felicia. You're still at three hundred." Felix smiled at another Andrea who picked up his plate and whisked it away.

"Fine!" the three—or was it four?—Andreas in the room replied.

"I've got a wicked headache, but I've never had so many ideas before. I borrowed your portable terminal and started typing them all in."

"Mm. Purchase one in the pawn shop side of things and I'll upgrade it, then hand it over to you. Probably need one of your own anyways."

"You should buy the storefronts across the way and turn that into the pawn shop. This would then become our head office," Andrea enthused into his ear, suddenly hanging off of him. "Then we can turn this into a skyscraper in time and base everything out of here. Open pawn shops everywhere. Have them send everything here for distribution, and we ship it back out to other locations."

Felix froze. Those were great ideas. Great ideas that he probably should have thought of. It'd help disguise what they were buying and from where. It'd also increase their ability to take in other items.

All I'd have to do is give people an appraisal type of superpower for each location and they could judge if it was worth buying and shipping back in.

Brilliant.

"Or so Lily said. She's smart. I like Lily. She woke me up this morning and reminded me to watch over you," Andrea said.

Lily? Why didn't she come to me with that?

Felicia grunted and stood up, downing the rest of her coffee. She gathered up her blueprints and set off. "Going down to check in with my people. Send a new team down soon."

Felix raised his eyebrows at that.

Kit and Eva passed Felicia in the hallway with a brief nod of heads. Kit glanced over her shoulder to confirm Felicia was gone.

"She likes being in charge of a project like this. Sees it as something monumental. A fortress by her design with an unlimited workforce and budget. She's not a full-blooded Dwarf, but she certainly thinks like one."

Felix looked up to the mind reader and gave her a small smile.

"You poking around in everyone's head?"

"Not at all. In fact, everything is blessedly quiet unless I try. It's... serene. Now, we have a problem."

Kit turned and gestured to Eva continuing before Felix could say a thing.

"Eva is fourteen. By law, we're required to provide basic essentials for all minors, even if she is property."

Felix made an inarticulate noise. "I see. Any other minors we picked up last night?"

"Just Eva."

The girl in question ducked her head, looking at her feet. "I'm sorry."

"Not your fault. Whatever. Uh... so what do we need to do?"

"School. She needs to go to school, you idiot," Kit said exasperatedly, swatting Felix on the head with her palm.

"Oh. Alright. So go enroll her and —"

Kit interrupted him before he could finish.

"You have to do it. You're her legal guardian now. I've already arranged the meeting for you. It's tomorrow at one in the afternoon. You'll meet with the principal at the school and get all the paperwork filled out. Lily's going with you."

Felix sighed and shook his head. "Fine. Eva, what... grade are you in?"

"I'm a freshman," the girl said, shuffling her feet around. "I would have started school last week."

"High school? Ugh. Alright. Fine. Need to figure out how you're getting to school, too."

"I'm going to drive her!" the Andreas shouted as one.

Kit looked pleadingly at Andrea.

"We're going to use one of the cars and drive her to school. Kit said I even get to wear a uniform if I want," the cooking Andrea said, flinging her pan to the side. A pancake whipped out of it and splatted into a plate a different Andrea held up.

"Uniforms! I want a uniform for our personal assistant position, Felix. Wait, would I have had a uniform as a secretary? I might be willing to take that position now, especially if it had a sexy or powerful uniform," Andrea Prime shrieked, shaking him roughly.

Kit pressed one hand to the side of her own face and gave Felix a weak smile.

Apparently they'd already taken care of everything. He just had to sign the paperwork and be done with it.

"Okay, fine, whatever. Stop shaking me, Andrea," Felix grumbled, reaching back to grab at Andrea.

His hands passed over her ears, landing in her thick hair. Her entire body shuddered at the touch.

Instead of stopping, she lifted him bodily up from the chair and started giggling, swinging him around. "Uniform! I want a uniform!"

Felix managed to wiggle free and glared at Andrea, clenching his fists.

"Fine, we'll get you a uniform. Just... don't do that again," Felix grumped, folding his arms in front of himself.

"Ah, also, the new recruits will be arriving in about an hour and ten minutes. I went ahead and reserved an audience hall in the hotel across the way. It should hold everyone comfortably. Ah, I had it catered as well," Kit said, glancing to a notepad she held in one hand.

The Andreas were chirping happily at each other in high-pitched squeals and words he couldn't quite make out.

It was hard to stay angry with her when she was so happy over a simple uniform.

"Alright. That's a good move, Kit. Thanks for that. It should help get everyone on the same page quickly. How long did you reserve the conference hall for?" Felix slowly relaxed, his discomfort at being manhandled going away.

"All day. I also booked enough rooms to have two people to a room for tonight. That's in case Felicia isn't done by tonight.

"We can cancel at any time before seven tonight for a credit refund, but not a cash refund," Kit said apologetically.

"Wow, that's... actually pretty good. Well done, Kit." Felix smiled at her, genuinely pleased with the work she'd put in. "Remind me to reward you somehow. You seriously took an entire worry and a half off my plate with that one."

The Andreas stomped their collective feet and pouted. "I helped! I want a reward too," they said in unison.

"Uhm, what would you want?" Felix asked slowly.

"A unif—"

"Other than a uniform," Felix hurriedly interrupted her.

"Oh," Andrea prime said.

"I didn't think about it," a different Andrea said.

"Think on it, then. Alright, I'm going to go shower real quick and get dressed, then head over to the hotel," Felix excused himself from the room before it could get any weirder.

Heavy feet clomped up behind him.

Felix didn't have to turn around to know who it was.

"Hey, Ioana."

"Morning," said the warrior woman. She stopped somewhere behind him. He imagined she had her sword belted on and was staring out over the empty hall filled with chairs. It'd be filled with people soon enough. They only had about ten minutes left before everyone was due to be delivered.

At that point, an Andrea would escort them over here.

"So," Ioana elaborated intelligently.

"Mm?" Felix tilted his head back and looked up at the big woman behind him. "Spit it out. Whatever it is, it's easier if you say it directly. I'm not any good at subtlety."

Ioana's nostrils flared and she shifted her weight from one foot to the other.

"You're not a warrior," she said finally.

"Nope. I'm not. Probably the furthest thing from it," Felix agreed.

"You should let me train you."

"I should. I agree."

"With only a litt—wait, what?"

"I agree. You should train me. I'm about as useful as a kitten in a fight right now. You and Miu both should train me."

Felix looked back to the hall.

That was easy.

"Oh, okay. Yes. That'd… yes. Good."

Felix chuckled. He imagined she had had some grand speech prepared. He scratched at his cheek, trying to keep himself calm. "Gonna be a lot of people here."

"Any of them you plan on taking to your bed? Slip 'em the sausage?"

Felix guffawed at that, shaking his head with a grin. "No. I'm a slaveowner, a bad man, and I let an evil sorceress rip people's souls out of them and then feed you their ground-up corpses. I'm not taking any women to my bed who I own.

"It'd be rape."

Ioana let out a slow, deep breath. "I guess you're right. What if they wanted to?"

Felix shrugged at that. "Hasn't happened yet, so I dunno. Why?"

He glanced over his shoulder at the woman again.

"Oh, not me. Sorry, you're not my type. I guess… I guess I was wondering if Felicia was…" Ioana turned a faint red color and frowned.

"Ah. She's all yours if you want her. Not my type. Her personality is a bit much for me," Felix admitted, turning back to the hall. "You have my blessing or whatever, if you need it. Go get her, tiger."

"Thanks. I think I will," Ioana said, sitting down heavily in the seat next to him. "So… Lily, hot or not?"

Felix smirked at the sudden change in the woman and the conversation.

"Very hot, and very soul-sucking evil."

"She could suck me, I wouldn't complain," Ioana said casually, turning her head to face Felix.

Laughing, Felix shook his head. "Yeah, me too. Except the part where, you know, my soul goes away."

"What about Kit? She's got those legs that—"

"Yeah, I'll refrain from responding to that one. Forgive me, but she'll pop your head open like a piñata and look for the candy inside to get my opinions. She can't read my mind.

"Let's just say, Kit is pretty. Yes."

"Good point. I forget that. They're both pretty, but I don't think I'd want anything lasting. A quick romp and stomp, sure," Ioana said, shifting in her chair.

"Been there, got the t-shirt. Don't think I'm looking for anything fling-like anymore." Felix let his thoughts drift backwards in time for a second.

"Yeah, getting old. Not sure what I want, but it's not a fling."

"What about those dating sites? I hear there's a supervillains one."

"I'm not much of a villain. Or a hero. A civilian with a power that he can only use to influence others.

"But yeah, I get your meaning. I suppose I could try that."

Ioana leaned towards him and held an open hand.

"Andrea wouldn't say no."

"She's also a Beastkin. A wolf, if I don't miss my guess. That'd turn into something permanent for her quicker than I could get her to make me a pancake."

"That's pretty quick. They're pretty great pancakes, though."

"Yeah, it is. And yeah, they are. We'll see. I'm not averse to the idea, I just don't see it happening any time soon and being more than a one-night stand."

"Could you imagine if you talked her into using her Others, though? I mean, I bet they could—"

Felix started to laugh again as Ioana was getting into her own thoughts. "Stop. We have to talk to an audience in a bit. Getting me all bothered about Andrea isn't going to help me at all."

"What about me?" asked an Andrea, easing up from behind his chair.

"Nothing. Nothing at all. I take it the new recruits are here?" Felix said, standing up.

"Coming now. They'll be filing in momentarily. The food is on the way as well."

"Great," Felix said, shaking his hands.

He hated public speaking.

"What are you going to say?" Andrea asked.

"Same as ever. Don't talk about the organization. Don't disobey your superiors. Don't hurt each other directly or indirectly. Don't try to escape. Normal stuff. Then I'll let them know the same thing I told you all."

Felix leaned his head to one side and felt the pop he'd wanted so desperately. "Ah, that was a good one. But yeah, same thing I told you all. Live, prosper, be happy. Don't do anything stupid."

"Good. You're not going to hire a secretary, are you? I still might want the position."

Felix shook his head and stepped up to the podium that had been set up at the front of the hall.

Flicking the mic twice, he leaned in to it. "Test, one, two."

Leaning back, he looked to Ioana, who gave him a thumbs-up.

Trolleys laden with food, both hot and cold, were wheeled in from the sides. Almost as soon as they were set up, the front door to the hall opened and two Andreas strode in confidently.

They turned to each side and held open the conference hall doors as his new purchases began entering.

They looked more like a disorganized mob than anything. Which nearly turned into chaos when they realized there was food.

Felix leaned into the mic again. "Be calm. Make an orderly line, and get your fill of food, a drink, then take a seat. Once everyone is seated, we'll begin."

Instantly, there was order.

Can't give them directions like that without expecting it to happen exactly as I state it.

Felix blew out a sigh after he flipped the switch on the mic that muted it.

"Good, I'm glad to see you have them in hand," came the cool voice of Lily.

"I told you he would," responded Kit.

Both ladies seated themselves on either side of the podium.

"They looked like they were about to mob the buffet tables. Can't have that. That'd just devolve into a Mad Max breakfast.

"We don't really need them killing each other."

Lily shrugged her delicate shoulders and crossed her legs. "You're right, of course."

"A group of Andreas and Miu are running the store," Kit said before he could ask.

"Thanks. And what about Eva?"

"She's with Miu as well."

Felix grunted and looked back out to the throng of people.

Most were seated, and only ten or so remained at the tables, filling their plates.

All eyes were on him. He could read almost every emotion in the entire range of human capacity on their faces and in their eyes.

From hope all the way to suicidal despair.

Have to make sure I order them not to hurt themselves. Directly or indirectly.

Once the last person seated themselves, and the Andreas closed the doors, Felix flipped the mic into the live position.

"Good morning, everyone. My name is Felix Campbell. I'm your new owner.

"First, all of the following orders apply to you directly, and indirectly.

"Rule one, you will not discuss anything about our organization with anyone outside of it, for any reason. This is for everyone's safety.

"Rule two, you will not harm each other, or yourselves, for any reason if you can avoid it.

"That's it for the rules," Felix said.

He swept his eyes over everyone. Now was the part where he gave them hope and a chance.

The carrot.

"I expect you're all wondering what is to become of you. Honestly, that's a fairly simple answer. You'll live together and share a purpose to build an organization that puts us in a place to live comfortably. You were purchased for your powers and how they help my own.

"My promises to you as your owner are thus. I will feed you. I will clothe you. I will not spend your lives wastefully. I will not sexually assault any of you. You will be given healthcare on a level that you are not accustomed to. Dental included."

Felix paused for a moment. "I'm still considering if I should pay you a salary, but I'm leaning in that direction.

"Of course you're all wondering what's coming next, right?

"Either tonight, or tomorrow, you'll be given a room that you'll live in. This is your room and yours alone. You will not enter someone else's room without their permission, nor will you steal from anyone in the organization. It all belongs to me anyways."

Felix cleared his throat. He hated talking in front of people.

"After that, you'll begin training in whatever department you are best suited for. Lilian Lux and Kit Carrington," Felix said, gesturing to the women on either side of him, "will be placing you accordingly. Please cooperate with them to the best of your abilities. If I'm your CEO, they would be my board members.

"Serving as my chief of security is Ioana Iliescu." Felix pointed to the big warrior. "If any of these women tell you what to do, you'll treat it as if it were an order from me."

That should do it. Good speech.

Andrea slammed into his side and snatched the mic. "I'm his personal assistant and secretary! I may or may not be sleeping with him. I'm not sure yet. Actually, I am sleeping with him, but we're not having sex."

Andrea pushed his hand away as he tried to get her off the mic.

"He's my type, after all, and he smells awesome. Especially when he's sweaty or angry."

Andrea turned and smiled at him warmly, her mismatched eyes twinkling. Then she looked back to the crowd.

"I think I want some pancakes, then a nap. I can't wait to sleep in the clothes I collected this morning. They smell great. All that adrenaline from the gunfight really got his blood going, so they reek fantastically."

Felix couldn't help himself, and he face-palmed.

Chapter 15 - Building Bridges -

"It looks like a shithole," Felix grumbled, looking at the public school they'd stopped in front of.

Andrea turned around in the driver's seat and smiled at him. "It really does."

Lily sighed and shrugged her shoulders. "This is the school she'll be sent to, according to the system."

Eva ran a hand through her hair, peering out the window. "I've been to worse. Really. It's okay."

Felix snorted and then opened the door and got out of the car.

"No, no! That's my job. Stop, get back in the car," Andrea whined.

She hurried around to the rear of the car and pushed him back inside, slamming the door on him.

"You spoil her," Lily said, smiling at him in the rearview mirror.

"Shut up," Felix grumbled. Looking up out the window at the enthusiastic Beastkin, he waited.

Andrea opened the door and doffed her cap, holding it to her breast. "Sir."

Felix sighed and got out of the car, giving Andrea a small smile. "Thank you."

Eva exited behind him while Lily opened her own door and stepped out.

Andrea shut the door behind him and then folded her hands atop each other in front of her. "I'll wait with the car, sir."

Then she split into two people, another Andrea forming from the thin air beside her in the same outfit.

"And I'll go with you!" she chirped, bouncing on her heels.

The new Andrea saluted the other, who returned the salute.

Lily was already walking ahead, snapping open her messenger bag and pulling out several papers. Felix took a few long steps to catch up to her.

"We should be able to take care of this quickly," Lily said. Then she pushed open the front door and locked eyes with a woman behind a desk.

"Felix, guardian for Eva, here for Principal Meier," Lily said in a clipped voice. She handed one of her papers over to the woman.

"Ah? Oh! Yes, he'll see you immediately, he's right through that door —"

Lily thanked the woman curtly and took the paper back. Then, without another word, she walked towards the door the woman had indicated.

Opening the very same door, listed simply with "Principal" on the outside, Lily entered.

"Principal Meier, Felix Campbell to see you in regards to Eva Adelpha."

"Oh! Yes. I'm glad to see you, Mr. Campbell," said a mundane-looking man in his forties.

"Yeah. So, can you tell me about your school?" Felix asked, shaking the man's hand.

"Yes, yes. We're actually a growing district right now. We've recently put in plans to expand the school with a new grant provided."

Is that a clever way to say they're overcrowded?

"How many students per class?" Felix asked, getting to the point."

"I, uh, we're happily at thirty-five per classroom. We've had great success with it—"

"Uh-huh. Can I see your PTA calendar?" Felix asked, holding out his hand.

"Oh, of course."

The principal opened a drawer and then set a small flyer in Felix's hand.

Felix read over it quickly. All the events were simple social things aimed at fundraising and little else. "What's your current attendance count for the PTA?"

"Twenty-four."

"And how many students?"

"One thousand two hundred, give or take."

Felix grunted and then set the flyer down on the man's desk.

"I'm going to go walk your hall real quick and take a peek in a classroom."

"Now see here, this is unheard of. Our school is perfectly fine to accept your ward and—"

Felix growled and pressed a hand to his forehead, ignoring the man.

Damn Kit. Damn Lily. Damn Eva. I'm no parent.

He'd once had to help a young mother find a public school for her son. He'd done it because she'd been a good worker. So he knew a few things, but not everything.

"Sir, there's a fight in the east hall again. They think they need the police," said the woman from the front desk.

Oh, fuck this.

Felix left then, exiting the school and walking straight back to the car without a word for anyone.

Andrea saw him coming and popped open the door for him.

Felix waited for a moment, ushering Eva into the seat behind him.

The second Andrea slipped in close to the first one and she vanished into her.

Never going to get over that. Still freaky.

Getting into the car, he waited for Lily to get seated.

"Lily, solve this for me. Find a private school that'll actually get her an education that she can attend without fear.

"I don't care about cost. And if you get this taken care of quickly, and I don't have to do much, I'll get you that third power you wanted."

Lily's eyes lit up at that.

"You really can give people extra powers?" Eva asked, eyeing him again.

Felix ignored her. She asked the same questions over and over.

"Swear it?" Lily asked him.

"I do. I want it done soon. Like, two days soon."

"I already did it," Lily said, flipping open her bag and pulling out a paper. "I figured this might happen, so I took care of it. I just need your signature."

Felix smiled and took the paper. Reading it over, he realized it was a school charter. Taking the pen, he signed it and handed it back.

"You're beautiful, Lily. A beautiful genius. Hit me up tonight and we'll get that power squared away."

Andrea clambered into the car and turned the key in the ignition. Then she turned back to look at him, smiling and adjusting the cap on her wolf ears. "Where to?"

"I'm hungry. Weren't we going to get pizza last night? I still want pizza."

"I want pancakes."

"You always want pancakes."

Lily cleared her throat and held up a finger.

"I would suggest we call Dimitry. We just dismantled a large portion of his organization. It might be wise to provide him with information, as well as perhaps a peace offering."

Felix nodded his head slowly. Some type of blood money wouldn't be uncalled for. Might even be the best response in this situation.

"Worst case, we go back and finish the job," Lily concluded.

Good point. It would be good to have him as a friend, if only to have a friend.

Can always use more sausage if not.

An hour later and Felix was still hesitating. He knew that this call wouldn't go well.

Tapping a thumb on his desk, he shifted in his seat.

Lily stepped past two Andreas who were keeping him company, and dropped a brick of lead on his desk.

"Make this gold. I'm going to go buy those shops across the street," she demanded. She put her left hand on her hip and shifted her weight to one side. Her eyes watched him, a small smile quirking her lips. "You can give me that power tomorrow. You have nothing else on your point calendar today or tomorrow."

Another Lily invention. The point calendar.

A day planner that listed out all of his points and what he was scheduled to spend them on. It helped them plan out what the needs of the company were.

Things were changing, and Lily was at the forefront of most of it.

"I also have all the departments arranged for an appropriate corporation. I've submitted all the appropriate documentation for the company as well. Your first department head meeting will be next week, after the HR department gets everyone in the right spot."

Felix gave her a lopsided smile and spread his hands out in front of him. "Thank you, Lily. You've definitely been pushing us in the right direction. I appreciate it. Without you, this would have taken considerably longer."

Tapping the brick of lead, he converted it to gold and then looked back to her. "How are we doing finance-wise? All this gold and purchases have to come from somewhere and go back out."

"Loophole. You're now paying all your employees, who happen to be all your slaves. Effectively paying yourself for their work. They keep a percentage of it, but most of it comes back to you. This won't work forever, as I imagine they'll eventually close the loop. For now, it's perfect."

"And our people get some play money. What would I do without you, Lily?" Felix said, shaking his head.

Lily's face shifted at that; she looked uncomfortable. Just as quickly, she smiled even wider at him.

The left Andrea crossed her arms and glared at him over the piece of paper they were using for tic-tac-toe.

Right Andrea got up and moved over to his side, pressing her head into his shoulder.

"No need to be jealous, Andie. No one can ever take your place as his personal assistant and possible secretary. I'm only acting as his operations officer and legal officer," Lily assured the wolf girl.

Andrea harrumphed and rubbed her face back and forth on Felix's shoulder before returning to her game.

"I'll update your point calendar accordingly and forward it to your inbox. You did install the software I laid out for you, right?" Lily tilted her head to the side, her dark hair fanning out.

"Uh, yeah. I did. I also sent over all the information you needed," Felix said, glancing away. "Alright, thanks, Lily. I'm going to stop stalling and call Dimitry. Unless there was something else?"

"No. I took care of the police for today. We paid a hefty amount for our line and Dimitry's lines to be free of eavesdropping or recording. You'll be fine being blunt with him, and letting him know would help him make some moves today if he felt so inclined.

"I'll update your calendar as well. We'll speak tomorrow morning. Purchases, finance, and where we are on the company paperwork." Lily tossed her head, giving her hair a flip, and then exited his office.

Left Andrea continued to pout at him. "I don't like this."

"I don't either," Right Andrea said.

"Why? She's doing her job. And speaking of jobs, did you get a chance to get a hold of No-Name and buy the weapons you wanted?"

Both of them nodded in unison. "They arrive tomorrow. He got us a good deal. We should have enough equipment to arm one hundred Others."

Felix nodded his head. Then he picked up the phone suddenly and dialed Dimitry's number without a further thought.

Now or never.

The line rang twice and then flipped over. "Good afternoon. I'm afraid we're under reno—"

"Please put me in touch with Dimitry. Let him know it's Felix."

The man didn't respond to Felix's interruption. Instead, the phone went silent.

Seconds ticked by.

"A moment," came the response eventually.

Felix let out a slow breath.

One of the Andreas closed the door to the office and then sat down in front of it. The second Andrea came over behind him and laid her hands on his shoulders.

"This is Dimitry." The suddenness of his voice startled Felix.

"Ah, hey, Dimitry. Felix here. I wanted to talk to you."

"Your debt is not due for some time. Do you need more money?"

"I appreciate the offer, but this is actually about what happened to your... compatriots? Peers?"

He could hear Dimitry's breath catch.

"I don't understand what you're—"

"I'm responsible for what happened. I had people visit my home who wanted me and my people dead. I took offense to that, and killed everyone involved," Felix said slowly.

Andrea began to rub her fingers into his shoulders and neck muscles.

"We paid for a communications blackout on your lines today. No one is listening. I'd like to discuss how I can make amends with you and your organization. I'd like very much for us to be friends."

Felix heard Dimitry's chair creak as he probably leaned back. It was a lot to take in suddenly without warning.

"I see. You have me at a disadvantage. I did not know there was a problem. Nor did I realize you were... so formidable."

"There was, and I am. So, how do we make this work, Dimitry? The money you gave me is what allowed me to become as powerful as I am. I consider you an ally and want you to feel the same for me."

Dimitry grunted. "I appreciate you being direct with me. With reaching out to me before I found out. For not wasting my time. I shall do the same for you.

"I'm now in charge here. We're in the middle of a recruitment drive, and I am obviously weakened."

Felix nodded his head; this all made sense so far.

"Money isn't an issue. Though I will still collect on your debt, as that was previously agreed to."

"Agreed."

"I need guards. Guards and favors. You say you made it so this line is free of listeners?"

"For today. Would one of those favors include making it go beyond today?"

"Yes, if possible. That'd be helpful."

"As for guards," Felix said, looking to the Andrea in front of the door.

She smiled at him and tilted her head to one side.

"I can send over twenty-five armed soldiers tomorrow morning. They'll rotate out daily. I would be able to provide this for a month."

Andrea nodded her head. The one behind him leaned in to the ear he didn't have pressed to a phone.

"That'll be good for us. We can gain more experience and keep some of our Others busy."

"A good start. Very good start. I feel that three additional favors would be required for us to be even."

Felix didn't like it being open-ended, but at least it had a number.

"Three favors, though I have right of refusal if I believe it unreasonable."

Dimitry hesitated a moment. "Done. I look forward to our new partnership, Mr. Campbell."

The phone clicked and went dead.

Setting down his phone, Felix leaned his head back onto the headrest.

"That's done." Felix closed his eyes and enjoyed what Andrea was doing with her hands.

It was fantastic. Her hands seemed to know exactly what to do.

"One of our Others spent some time working as a masseuse. We have absorbed many jobs," one of the Andreas said

A knock came from the door.

"It's Eva," came a muffled response.

Felix opened his eyes and nodded at the door Andrea. The Andrea behind him stepped to the side quickly, flanking his desk.

The door swung inward and Eva stepped in, her hands pressed together nervously.

"What can I do for you?" Felix asked, leaning forward in his desk.

"You're going to be paying everyone for their work, right?" she asked hesitantly.

"I am."

"I've been working in the shop and… I was wondering if I could get a hold of that money? I want to buy some clothes for school, and supplies."

Felix waved a hand at that.

"Don't bother. You'll receive a wage like anyone else. Use it on other things you want.

"Your school supplies and basic essentials, though? That's something I'll provide for you regardless. Put together a list of everything you need and email it over to me. We'll get a purchase order put in immediately for it."

Eva nodded her head, smiling. "Uhm, okay. Thank you. Can we go out today, then? I want to go try on clothes and find some things."

Felix kept himself from rolling his eyes. Barely. He didn't want to go clothes shopping.

"Please? Me, you, Lily, and maybe an Andrea? I know you're busy, but… I'd appreciate it," Eva pleaded.

The Andrea near the door nodded her head enthusiastically.

Relenting, he shook his head with a smile.

"Alright. Fine. Though you'll have to check with Lily. She seemed like she had plans for the day. If she's willing to go, we'll all go."

Eva clapped her hands together, smiling. Then her face fell, her eyes going to the ground again.

"What?" Felix asked, trying to prompt whatever was coming next to happen, rather than waiting on it.

"Can I see my brother?"

"Oh, sure. He's across the street right now at the hotel, recovering. Everyone will be coming over here tomorrow and living in their new rooms downstairs. Speaking of which, I believe you have a room there too now.

"Talk to Felicia and maybe she can put you guys next to each other."

Eva gave him a bright grin and rushed him. She gave him a tight hug even as he sat in his chair.

"Thank you. I really thought our lives were over. We didn't even have enough money to eat when we were caught. Now we have a home, and I can go to school. A good one. Evan even has a mentor. A great mentor. Lily is known all over the world."

Felix felt awkward. He gently patted the young woman on the shoulder.

He was great in the corporate world. That all made sense to him.

Emotions, people, and this kind of stuff, though? Might as well have been Swahili.

"Yeah, no worries," he said lamely.

"Can I take an Andrea with me to talk to Evan and Lily?" Eva asked, pulling back.

Felix looked to the Andrea beside him.

She instantly split into two, the left one holding up her hand. "I wanna go!"

"Have fun, then. I'll be here. I'm sure Lily has sent me more paperwork and meetings that I'll have to sign and agree to."

Felix smiled as the new Andrea and Eva exited the room.

As the door closed, he opened up the terminal set in his desk.

He had forty-two unread emails.

"Maybe I should buy a new phone that I can link to this. Maybe if I try to keep on the emails, they wouldn't go so bad."

"I could read them for you," Andrea offered. "I mean, if I'm going to be your... I hate saying both. From now on, I'm your personal secretary, okay?"

"Okay," Felix said, grinning.

"If I'm going to be your personal secretary, maybe I should read your mail and sort out what's worth your time and what isn't. I can even keep your calendar in order and start getting you where you need to be on time."

"That sounds great, Andrea. Be sure to put in an order for a phone or tablet or whatever you like so you can do that."

"Nn! I'll take care of it. As Andrea Prime, I'll remain at your side."

"Thanks."

Andrea smiled and then hugged him tightly, wrapping her arms around him.

"Eva was right. This really is the best. You don't care about whatever we were before, you only care about what we are now for you."

Felix smiled tightly, patting Andrea gently on the back.

I don't really see how becoming a slave is a positive, but as long as they're happy.

Chapter 16 - The Color Red -

Once again, Felix sat at the breakfast table looking at the blueprints Felicia had laid down in front of him.

"Everything is done, as promised. Once you go spend your points for the living quarters, they'll be done. Which is on the point calendar, as Lily requested," Felicia said through gritted teeth.

The beautiful ex-lawyer and busty Dwarf didn't really get along. Keeping them in each other's company was very similar to putting two unfamiliar cats in a box.

"And while you're down there, you can finish off the dining halls. We made better progress than expected. Training rooms and common areas should be later this week. Since we don't have a facilities department yet, I put in the initial orders for everything the kitchens will need. Or at least I think I did. Might not be everything." Felicia shrugged her shoulders. "Not my problem. Off to work. See you later."

Ioana moved in and pulled out Felicia's chair as she stood up. The Dwarven woman eyed Ioana curiously.

A thought popped into his head. "Felicia, could you spend some time with Ioana for the training rooms? She'd know best what we need in terms of space and equipment."

"Eh? I could do that... fine. Come along, then," Felicia said softly, turning and leaving them there.

Ioana looked to him and gave him a grin.

Felix threw her thumbs-up. "Go get 'er," he said quietly.

Ioana took off at a light trot, chasing down Felicia.

"I didn't know," Eva said quietly around a forkful of pancake.

Kit smirked and tapped Eva's plate with her own utensil. "It was very subtle. We'll work on learning the difference between surface thoughts and things people hide. Maybe after you get home from shopping today."

"You sure you can't come too?" Eva asked, looking to Kit, then Felix.

"I can't. Felix needs people here at the same time. Besides, I'm putting together my department today, remember? It all starts with HR, which means me," Kit said apologetically.

Lily turned her head to Felix, smiling as ever.

He often felt like she knew something he didn't.

Too often.

"There's a public domain auction on slaves in two days. I plan on attending and will need Kit with me. They're all non-supers, just civilians. It'll be a chance to pick up some people for specific roles. Any objections?" asked Lily.

"None. Be sure you keep it cheap and run the numbers by Felicia so she can build out accordingly. If our FTE keeps going up, we'll have to build accordingly. It's not like we'll have attrition."

"FTE?" Andrea asked, dropping a pancake onto his plate as he finished up the third.

"Full-time equivalent, or full-time employee, depending. Attrition is when you fire people. Can't really fire a slave, though."

Lily pointed her fork at Felix. "Actually, we might end up having attrition. Not everyone will fit a role perfectly. Eventually we'll run out of places to put them if they keep fouling up. You'll need to consider what we do with those people. They're a poison and would eventually corrupt the rest of the workforce."

Kit sighed, placing a hand to her ear. Then she slowly shook her head and looked to Felix. "She's right. I don't like it, but she's right."

Felix shrugged his shoulders. He'd already thought of that to a degree. It wasn't something that would be pleasant, but a simple answer.

Sausage machine.

Felix pushed his plate away. "Sorry, Andrea, delicious as always, but I'm full."

Andrea smiled and took the pancake away. Then she suddenly leaned over the table, knocking over an empty cup while doing so.

Licking her thumb, she rubbed it against the corner of his mouth. "Syrup. Messy, messy."

Felix sat there, frozen in place, staring into Andrea's face.

"Thanks." He didn't know what to do in this situation.

"Nnnn! As your personal secretary, it's my job. Now, I'm going to go change so we can get going." Andrea pushed back off the table to her feet and then left quickly.

Lily started to laugh. Then Kit did, followed by Eva.

"Maybe she'll give us lessons," Lily said, turning to Kit.

Felix let his eyes wander around the department store. Lily, Andrea, and Eva were all in the changing rooms going through the clothes they'd picked out.

Kit, Felicia, Miu, Ioana, and a team of Andreas were back home working on moving their shop across the street. Lily had completed the purchase, pushed the paperwork along, and even rebalanced their books.

She was really showing a natural aptitude to corporate work. Then again, she'd trained as a lawyer, so it couldn't have been all that different.

A store clerk flashed by him, asking him if he was okay, and leaving even before he could fully respond.

Shaking his head at the lazy work ethic, Felix turned his mind to the rest of his day.

He still owed Lily her power buildout. Depending on what she asked for, he should have enough points left for the day. Felicia's finishing touches had cost him a good amount, but the effort hadn't bankrupted him.

"Flirting with the help?" Lily asked.

Felix turned to find Lily approaching him by herself. She was wearing a black dress that she filled out well. It pulled the eyes into dangerous territory.

"Not really. I don't really have time for that sort of thing right now." Felix stuck his eyes to her face and kept them there.

Lily tilted her head to one side, watching him. "I'd like my third power now."

"Alright. You still haven't told me what it is."

"I want to be able to store power. I'd prefer it to be in something physical so I could pass it off to others if needed.

"I want to be able to make Lily batteries."

"Oh. That's... not what I was expecting. I don't think that'd be too hard to add, since it's more of a utility thing."

"It differs?" Lily ran her fingers through her hair. "And what were you expecting?"

"Well, yeah. Bigger powers cost more. A utility power probably won't cost that much. As for what I was expecting... something destructive?"

Lily gave him another one of her feral grins, pearly white teeth slipping free of her pale pink lips. "I'm happy to surprise you. Realistically, though, you've given me a number of students to watch over. Being able to practice freely will increase their experience. To practice, they need power. I have it in abundance as of late since I'm not constantly under attack. So, Lily batteries."

Felix smiled back at her and held up his hands in defeat. "Makes sense. I'm glad to hear you taking your responsibilities seriously. Alright, let's see..."

He called up Lily's window and focused on adding a third power to her.

Third Power (Unlock): Energy Transfer	Required Secondary Power: 70 (Unmet) Required Stamina: 50 (Unmet)	Upgrade? (20,000)

"Huh. Your power isn't strong enough and neither is your stamina," Felix said, pulling up her character screen.

Name: Lilian Lux	Power: Ethereal Mental projections
Alias: Mab, Demon, Soul Stealer	Secondary Power: Mana Manipulation
Physical Status: Healthy	Mental Status: Happy

Positive Statuses: None	Negative Statuses: None	
Strength:	37	Upgrade? (370)
Dexterity:	55	Upgrade? (550)
Agility:	53	Upgrade? (530)
Stamina:	42	Upgrade? (420)
Wisdom:	67	Upgrade? (670)
Intelligence:	88	Upgrade? (880)
Luck:	21	Upgrade? (210)
Primary Power:	64	Upgrade? (6,400)
Secondary Power:	59	Upgrade? (5,900)

"That's... disappointing," Lily lamented, pressing a hand to her cheek.

"Gimme a moment. I'll just push your stats up, then get the power for you. The cost of the power is pretty low, so giving you the points needed isn't that big a deal."

Felix tapped in the individual point upgrades, pushing her secondary power to seventy and her stamina to fifty.

"I forgot that you could do that. Any chance you can kick my luck up a bit? You said it was pretty bad," Lily asked. She tilted one shoulder towards him, turning partially sideways while her hand slid from her cheek to her neck. "I am kinda unlucky."

The pose was ridiculous and he knew she was messing with him.

Felix pursed his lips and then moved her luck up to thirty-five. It was pretty low, and he could see that going poorly for them at the wrong moment.

"Fine." He hit the accept button and then gave her the third power.

Calling up the screen again, he confirmed the changes.

Name: Lilian Lux	Power: Ethereal Mental projections
Alias: Mab, Demon, Soul Stealer	Secondary Power: Mana Manipulation

Physical Status: Healthy	Third Power: Energy Transfer	
Positive Statuses: Protective	Mental Status: Happy	
	Negative Statuses: None	
Strength:	37	Upgrade? (370)
Dexterity:	55	Upgrade? (550)
Agility:	53	Upgrade? (530)
Stamina:	50	Upgrade? (500)
Wisdom:	67	Upgrade? (670)
Intelligence:	88	Upgrade? (880)
Luck:	35	Upgrade? (350)
Primary Power:	64	Upgrade? (6,400)
Secondary Power:	70	Upgrade? (7,000)
Third Power:	50	Upgrade? (5,000)

"Done. Consider this a promotion. Or a merit increase? Maybe a bonus? Something like that.

"I hope you work as hard as you did up to this point, if not more so." Felix dismissed the window and looked to Lily.

The soul-stealing mass murderer's eyes were clouded. She looked like she was in pain, even.

"Kit said it felt like someone had punched her brain. Do you want to sit down? Here, I'll get a ch—"

"No, I'm alright. I just need a second." Lily lifted the hand on her neck to her temple. "It felt like my mind expanded. I even know how to use it, I just... push my energy into it. There's no limit to how much I can put in an item, other than what I can personally channel in one sitting."

Felix checked his pockets to see if he had anything she could practice on. *Nothing. House keys, phone, and some lint.*

Looking around, he saw the cash register. Pushing off the pillar he'd been propped against, he moved over to the checkout stand. He started looking around for the impulse buys that any good checkout had.

Something innocuous. Something that people would overlook that you could charge. Something that would be —

Ah!

Sitting to one side of the register was a glass display case. Inside were a number of silver bracelets with charms.

The bracelet, and each charm, could function as a battery, he was willing to bet.

"Can I help you?" asked the cashier. He was a younger man, probably in his early twenties.

"Give me that," Felix said, pointing to the bracelet he'd been eyeing.

"Huh? The necklace or the bracelet?" said the clerk, leaning over.

"Uhm, give me one of each."

"Okay. That'll be four hundred and ten."

Felix flipped a credit card onto the space between them. "Hang on to that, they'll be out with a bundle of clothes, I'm sure."

Picking up the bracelet and necklace, he went back to Lily.

She'd watched him but hadn't moved at all. To him, she appeared as if she were still recovering.

"Here. Bracelet and necklace. Both have a bunch of charms on them. Maybe you can turn them into individual batteries?" Felix held out the two silver pieces of jewelry.

Lily held out her wrist to him. "Put it on."

Grunting, Felix laid the necklace on his shoulder. Holding on to the bracelet, he unhitched the clasp and then wrapped it around Lily's wrist. Slipping the clasp into one of the links, he let go. It dangled but seemed well fit.

Turning around, Lily lifted her dark hair up from her shoulders.

"You can put this on yourself," Felix grumped.

"Put it on," Lily demanded.

"Seriously, you—"

"Put it on."

Taking the necklace in hand, Felix reached around Lily and draped it across her neckline. With a quick flick of his fingers, he latched it shut.

"There. Practice away," Felix said. Taking a few steps back, Felix leaned up against the pillar from earlier.

Lily let her hair fall and glanced at him from over her shoulder. "Hmph."

Breaking eye contact with him, she walked back to the changing room.

Felix let out a slow, even breath as she went. Lily made him uncomfortable.

Maybe it's because she's too damn pretty. Kit and Andrea have their own thing going for them, but Lily is just… forbidden fruit, maybe? Soul-eating seductress. Maybe I should rename her to Succubus instead of Mab.

He chuckled, giving his head a shake.

An explosion of sound went off behind his head, and his entire head felt like it'd been struck by a hammer.

He felt his legs go out from under him, unwilling to respond to him in any way, shape, or form. There was another explosion from feet away, and this time his side exploded in red-hot agony.

The world flashed white as screams echoed throughout the department store.

Felix couldn't do much of anything. The cold of the tiled floor felt great on his face. The rest of him was a bubbling quagmire of pain and heat. Everything hurt.

In fact, he was pretty sure he was dying. There was too much pain for it to be anything else. Or so he believed.

He tried to roll over onto his side and accomplished... nothing. Fingers flexed against the tile, his shoes squeaked, and that was it.

A hand grabbed him by the shoulder and flipped him over.

Everything was blurry. Blurry and red.

Someone leaned down into his face. They said something. He couldn't figure out what they were saying. Now that he thought about it, those weren't screams he was hearing, but ringing. His ears were ringing.

Yanked to his feet, Felix tried to stand up but his knees wouldn't obey. He began to collapse as fast as he'd been stood up. His eyes felt heavy and he blinked.

Felix must have blacked out for a moment, because the next time he opened his eyes, he was being carried. His arms were held across two people's shoulders and they were practically sprinting with him between them.

"Hang on, Felix," said the one on the left.

"Stay with us," said the one on the right.

Oh, they're both Andrea.

Felix tried to ask what had happened, but only made a gurgling noise instead.

"He's awake!" the one on the left said.

"Good, keep him that way. Being awake is better," came back a call from up ahead. There was a burst of light, followed by an intense explosion.

"I need two Andreas up the left side. Clear out that hallway!"

Felix felt himself pressed up against a wall.

An Andrea appeared in front of him, smiling at him from an inch away. "Going to just take a peeky peek now. See if you're a leaky bottle of ketchup again."

Her fingers slipped along his side, which was apparently now bandaged and very red.

Red like blood.

There was a black marker line where the bloodstain ended, all the way around.

"Nothing new, but that's no guarantee," Andrea said. Then she stood up and gently turned his head to the side.

Felix's brain slipped out of his skull and hit the ground. Or that was what it felt like, at least.

Felix focused on the tile beneath him and the fact that he wasn't dead.

"No change here either. Damn. I wish we'd spent more time in that hospital. We need to send an Other there after this," whispered the Andrea in front of him.

"Nn, nn," said the second Andrea.

"Is he okay?" Eva asked. Her voice wasn't far, maybe behind Andrea. Maybe. Things didn't sound right.

"He's... alive. Lily! We need to move!"

Another explosion came from further ahead. "Clear, move up. Garage is right ahead of us. You think Chauffeur Andrea is still there?"

"We would never leave. We would die first," the two Andreas said in unison.

Before he could really start to follow the conversation, it was over. They picked his arms up and pulled him back over their shoulders again.

His head lolled forward, his eyes watching the tiles pass underneath his dragging feet.

Body parts and blood were liberally painting the floor.

As he watched, the tiles became dark pavement. A burst of gunfire tore through the air.

Return gunfire came from the Andrea on his right and from up ahead.

"In, in, in," shouted Andrea from ahead of them.

He heard car doors opening, then he was being shoved bodily into the rear seat. Eva was already inside and pressed up against the glass on one side.

As the Andrea who was guiding him in got him situated, her clothes blew out around her.

She dropped bodily into the car, her head falling into his lap.

In a last burst of strength, she somehow got the door closed and lay still, staring up at him from his lap.

Chauffeur Andrea got in and stomped on the pedal.

"Where's the other—" Eva started.

"I absorbed her. No room," Chauffeur Andrea said.

Felix laid his hands on the Andrea in his lap. Her mismatched eyes stared up at him. Her mouth was wide open as she gasped for breath.

"It's... my lung. Shot in... the lung," she got out between gasps.

Felix understood that at least. She was probably dying faster than he was.

Carefully, he brushed her hair back from her face. He gave her a smile and ran his thumb along her eyebrow.

"Sorry," Felix said lamely.

"It's... okay. I'll... come back. Myriad... never really dies," Andrea said, giving him a bloody smile.

Her face twisted for a second and she pressed her hands to her mouth, coughing into them.

Blood seeped up between her fingers, splashing down the sides of her face and neck.

"I'm sorry, Andrea."

Felix gently stroked her forehead, smoothing her hair back. She coughed into her hands again, blood spilling unendingly from her hands. Her eyes gazed up at him, full of pain and fear.

"Andrea, can you absorb her before she dies? I-I think she'll suffocate at this rate," Felix said lamely, looking up to the driver's seat.

Sunlight poured in through the windows as they escaped the garage.

"Kit, this is Lily. Felix has been shot. We're on our way back. Tell Felicia she needs to come up with something quick. Do we have any supers with healing powers?"

Chauffeur Andrea looked back at him when they hit a stoplight. There was no way she could run it since there was a constant stream of cars driving in either direction.

After what looked like a moment of indecision, Chauffeur Andrea reached back and pressed her hand to the Andrea in his lap, and she vanished.

She was there one moment, and then gone the next.

All that remained of her was the blood that stained his pants.

Letting his head sink back into the seat, Felix felt the world slip out of his grasp.

"Lily? Felix is..."

Chapter 17 - Catching Up -

The world was a groggy haze. Filled with snatches of conversation and alternating bright lights and deep darkness.

Occasional words would slip through, but none of them stuck.

In time, Felix began to feel as if he could keep a thought for longer than a few moments. Longer than a single breath.

His eyelids felt heavy. So heavy he couldn't open them.

That's good. Heavy eyelids means I'm alive. Right?

Swallowing, he concluded he must have eaten a desert, considering how dry his mouth was.

"Oh! Felix? Are you awake?" asked a soft voice.

"Mmnnuugh... wwaaaa..." Felix explained patiently.

"Water?"

"Yuuuuuuu," he energetically agreed.

A straw slipped between his lips. Felix set to the task and drank quickly. The cool, very wet, very delicious water brought life and happiness back to the wasteland that was his mouth.

Releasing the straw, he sighed, licking his lips.

"Thank you. I feel groggy," Felix said. His head felt heavy. Trying to open his eyes again, he only managed to get them open a crack.

Which immediately blinded him.

"It's been two days since you were shot," came a patient voice.

He couldn't quite place it. He knew it, but his brain refused to tell him a name.

"What happened?" he asked. Somehow, he managed to move his hand an inch, and suddenly found someone else's hand. Latching on to it, he laced his fingers into theirs.

At this moment, any human contact was preferable, even if he didn't know who it was.

"You were shot. The first bullet grazed your skull. The second nicked a lung, perforated your bowels, and exited your hip," said the definitely feminine voice that he knew. That he swore he knew. "We've kept you drugged up until a little bit ago. There were concerns about waking you early before everything could be finished."

"Finished with what? It sounds like I should be dead."

Felix struggled with his eyes again, finally managing to get them open. Everything was blurry and bright, but he wasn't blind.

"Felicia built a machine that would help anything mend. To heal. In such a way that it would defy science and modern medicine. It's more like a bed than a machine. You were in it up until this morning. I carried you to your bed so you could rest more comfortably."

The world began to come into focus, though aggravatingly slowly. As the kaleidoscope of colors and blurs became something recognizable, he realized it was Miu at his side.

The aloof beauty Miu, who seemed to always flee rather than speak with him. Smiling at her, he squeezed her hand. "Thank you, Miu."

"Of course. I've been watching over you since they brought you home. I shall not be leaving your side going forward. I'm going to be your personal bodyguard should you leave for anywhere until we can find someone more permanent for the job."

"I see. I assume this is something Ioana, Kit, and Lily agreed with?"

"They did not get the chance to disagree. I will be training at an increased speed to make sure I can handle any problems that come up as well."

Miu didn't elaborate on the fact that the others didn't agree.

"I won't even argue. Being shot sucks. Was anyone else hurt?"

"No, only you were. It was an impromptu attack. I believe they followed you, waited, and then planned the assassination from there."

"Assassination?"

"Someone tried to shoot you pointblank in the head. It's a miracle they missed. It's an assassination attempt. There can be no question of that. All that remains is to determine who."

Felix took a slow, deep breath and then nodded his head.

It made sense. There really wasn't any other possibility when you looked at it from that point of view. There had been no other targets, only him.

"Lily is the only reason you're alive. She was able to react quickly enough that the rest of the gunshots impacted a shield, rather than you," Miu admitted with a glum look on her face.

Apparently Felicia isn't the only one who doesn't like Lily.

"I'll be sure to thank her when I get a chance. So, what's the prognosis, Doctor Miu, will I live?" he asked, giving her hand a squeeze.

"Oh, ah, yes. Everything is as good as new, but you are very weak. Felicia's machine pulls the energy from you to make the repairs, as if you were to heal naturally. You will feel tired for many days."

"Delightful. Paperwork, antiques, and office work for me, then."

"Yes. Though, I fear we are about to have a visitor. She has—"

The door burst open, slamming into the wall. The clang of the doorstop heralded the fact that she hadn't put a hole in the wall.

"Felix!" Andrea shouted. Closing the distance in a single hop, she was suddenly up in his bed, rubbing her face all over his chest. Her arms were locked around his neck and she squeezed him tightly.

"You're awake. Kit said you'd be awake quickly. That you were stronger than people gave you credit for. I'm so glad," Andrea gushed. "It was so hard to not climb into the machine with you and hold you. Felicia said she'd cut off my tail if I did it. Then Ioana promised to turn it into a broom. Mean. Mean, mean."

Felix chuckled and released Miu's hand. He gently set his arms around Andrea and patted her on the back. "They were right to keep you away so I could recover, Andrea. Sorry, but they were being mean for the right reasons."

"I know. I still don't like it, though. You don't smell good. You smell like medicine. You need a shower. Come on, I'll wash your back."

"What? No, I don't—"

"Yes, yes now. Yes now, or else," Andrea threatened.

"I would agree with her. You smell of medicine and sweat," Miu said, a small smile turning up the corners of her lips.

"I don't—"

"No more talking. More showering and scrubbing." Andrea hopped off the bed and split into ten different Andreas rapidly.

In unison, they all clapped their hands together, then held up one arm. "To the shower! Strip him!"

"Hey now, let's taaaaoouuu—"

Felix had only a moment's notice before the Andreas descended on him and carried him off to the shower, Miu trailing along behind.

They were merciful. They stripped him, dumped him in the shower alone, and left him there sitting under the hot, steamy water.

He'd have to remember how invigorating a hot shower could be. He went from feeling sorry to himself, to being hungry, thirsty, and clean.

Hot water was glorious.

By the time he stumbled out of the shower, he found a set of clothes waiting for him to change into. Only Miu and a single Andrea remained when he finally left the bathroom.

"A pancake brigade has been assembled," Andrea said with a bright smile.

"I… that sounds great, actually. Thank you," Felix said sincerely.

"Lily and Kit are assembling a department head meeting for you."

Felix nodded his head and gestured at the two women. "Lead on."

Andrea happily bounced off, opening the door and stepping out.

Miu merely ducked her head to him and waited.

Keeping his tongue behind his teeth, and his wit, he realized he couldn't fight what they wanted to do to him. They depended on him being alive and healthy. After this incident, he didn't think he'd be wandering around alone anymore.

Giving her a tight smile, he followed the sound of Andrea skipping towards the dining room.

A handful of pancakes, a glass of orange juice, and a soda perked him right up.

Everyone gave him a chance to finish before starting in. The moment he admitted he was indeed done, they cleared the table, and all looked to him expectantly.

"Ah, thanks, everyone. I understand that I owe my life to Felicia?" Felix asked, looking to the builder.

The Dwarven woman crossed her arms in front of her chest and looked to the side, though eventually nodded her head.

"Thank you. Your work is fantastic, as always."

Felix then turned his gaze on Lily.

"And Lily, I understand you saved me from dying right then and there. Then managed a running offense to get us back to the car. I'm not sure how to thank you for that."

The woman in question arched an eyebrow at him. She looked as if she were hesitating, then gave him a shrug. "We can figure out something later. So far, you've done nothing but build up my power. Even as a slave, this isn't something I can easily write off."

"Fair enough. Andrea—"

"I want to sleep in your bed. I don't like only watching over you, I want to sleep, too."

"I, uh... what?"

"For my reward, I want an Other to sleep in your bed. She'll sleep at the foot. Your feet are warm. Thanks!"

Felix opened and closed his mouth twice and then nodded his head. It sounded annoying, but he didn't want to push her away.

She'd carried him bodily the entire way, and one of her Others had been mortally wounded for him.

"How's Eva, and where is she?" he asked, realizing that sitting around him were only those who had been part of the original group.

"In school, and she's fine. She got your credit card on the way out for you, by the way. We've taken her shopping several times since then, and she has more clothes than any teenager could want." Kit pulled out a single sheet of paper from her binder and slid it across the table to him.

Glancing at it, he realized it was a balance sheet.

He didn't care. He pressed a finger to it and passed it back without looking at it a moment more.

"Thank you. I'm glad she's in school. She like it?"

"So far. Everyone wants to know who her sponsor is. Apparently, getting into that school isn't easy." Kit didn't say anything more.

It left the entire thing open to a question. One he'd have to ask Lily.

Felix had to wonder how Lily had managed to get her in, but didn't feel like wasting his breath. If she wanted to be coy about it, she could. He didn't need to press them on every secret.

"So... I suppose that brings us to the department head meeting we should have had. Felicia, how about you start us up?" Felix asked. He spread his hands to the dwarf and waited.

"Hah. Ass. Why do I always have to start?"

"Because you're building our home. To me, that sounds like one of the single biggest, and most important, tasks to get updates on. First you go."

"Hmph. It's fine. Common spaces will need you to smooth them out, and the training areas are only about half done. I put them on hold since you were injured and haven't gotten back to them. Been working on the medical ward and its machines. You'll need to smooth that one out too.

"I've got everyone working with whatever best suits them. We got quite a few talented people out of that last purchase. We're fabricating all sorts of great toys and things."

Felix couldn't help but admire her progress, all things considered. "Great work, Felicia. You're a credit to your race.

"Ioana, let's go with you since you're next to her. We'll go clockwise from there."

"Security forces are being trained up. Miu is assisting me with the hand-to-hand combat. Andrea has taken up firearms. Everything else is under me.

"We'll have our first security team ready for deployment in about a month. Class rollouts should be every couple of weeks after that as we stagger the classes. We'll be drilling them one against the other for experience."

"That's far better than I'd been expecting. Good job, Ioana. I'd like to get some time in your classes once I get my energy back."

"You're already enrolled," Lily said with a smirk.

"Good. Kit?"

"HR, which includes counterintelligence, since we're all telepaths, is up and running. We've sorted everyone out by their abilities, tendencies, and desires. It'll take time for everything to actually get off the ground, but with everyone ideally placed, it should be easier.

"We did mark a few people who seem like they'll be problems. Only three seem intent to cause a problem."

"Alright. Give them to Lily first and then put them in the sausa—"

"No. Not yet," Kit interrupted hurriedly. "We'll give them time to adjust, counsel them, and only failing all of that will I... give them to Lily and the machine. There are many opportunities to get them on board."

"Whatever, attrition is your concern. And speaking of attrition, always looking for new hires. Did that auction happen?" he asked, looking between Kit and Lily.

Kit nodded her head and held up a hand towards him.

"It did. We picked up around two hundred unpowered normals. They didn't even cost a fraction of what you paid for the supers. We now have: marketing, finance, legal, IT, facilities, kitchen, janitorial, motor pool, medical, and I'm sure I'm forgetting some. We'll need to headhunt some key positions but by and large we did well."

Two hundred more people? I won't get as many points for them as I do a super, but points are points.

"We already expanded the housing project to accommodate them, and then doubled that for growth.

"Princess over there managed to get us a permit to dig as far down as we like," Felicia said, gesturing at Lily.

"I see. So... we're well beyond what a pawn shop could support. Did we pick up a few buildings in other areas to put in more shops?"

"That's been taken care of. It'll take a week or two to get them outfitted and staffed, but they'll be up and running soon," Kit said. "Our bottom line is alright, but it would be good if you could convert some bricks in the next couple days. We've had our newly created finance department running the numbers to figure out our taxes."

Felix shook his head with a smile. "Good show. I assume that means you handled all the paperwork, Lily?"

"Sure did. Everything is settled. I felt fun when I drew up the company name," she held up a hand. "Ahem, we are Legion. All of us in one. The new legal team is actually rather good, so we moved quickly."

We are Legion.

"Right. Anything else from the HR department, then?"

"People are asking about bringing their families on board. I admit I expected it to eventually happen. We can either allow visitation, and risk all that entails, or simply deny it."

"Can we buy their families?" Felix asked.

"What?" asked the telepath incredulously.

"Their families. Can we buy them? So far we've been picking up people based on if they went to auction. What if we made it an employee perk program?" Felix leaned back in his chair, feeling more at ease.

Solving problems of this nature always felt right to him. Corporate life never felt terribly difficult.

"If they put in good work and service, we can offer to purchase their family at a fair price. As they're selling themselves willingly, we would amend the contract to indentured rather than slave. They'd get a few more rights, like the promise of never having to face combat duty, the sausage machine, or anything like that."

Felix looked up to the ceiling as he thought.

"Heck, at that point we may want to consider buying the buildings around us and expanding our subsurface expansion to include family homes, schools, and stores."

Felicia sat upright in her chair, her fingers pressed to the table. Apparently, the idea of expanding the fortress to an underground kingdom tickled her fancy.

Kit sighed and trailed her fingernails down the inside of her forearm.

"I mean, I'm all for being self-sufficient, and it would help encourage people to work hard. Though I wonder at what eventuality that leads to.

"Can people begin purchasing themselves out of slavery and into indentured servitude? Do children born of such a relationship get born into indentured service?

"Or do we purchase a semi-limited contract on them that expires at eighteen, and all services remaining that weren't paid for become debt and they have to leave?

"In the end, it sounds a lot like building an empire," Kit said slowly.

He could practically hear Felicia demanding he start this action now.

"Mmm. We'd be a target. Well, let's start testing out this 'family package' plan with those who asked for now. See what happens. Maybe we'll get some serious work out of them. No one wants to work endlessly without a carrot, right?

"Anything else?"

"No. That's everything for me. I'll take the family plan idea back to the team and see what we can do."

"Great. Lily?"

"Legal, marketing, and planning are all fine. We're drawing up plans for commercials and some branding for the new stores. Get people in the door."

Lily paused to thumb a piece of paper out of her folio and spin it across the desk to him.

"I took the liberty of purchasing a parking garage. It used to have an attached office. We've already started to convert it to a mechanic shop and housing location. It's only a street away from here, so it's nice and close.

"Most of our fabricators who can't help out here are already holed up there. Everything is now closed to the public, and cars purchased at the shops are taken there.

"If you plan on expanding our purchases, do it in that direction so we can link everything up."

Felix nodded his head. The return on cars would be rather large since he didn't have to technically pay his people the normal amounts you would for a mechanic. "Nice. That sounds fun. We should use it as a way to start purchasing company cars as well."

"On it. On the second page there in front of you, I've assembled a list of cars to be purchased at market value if they're presented so we can convert them. Apparently, word spread quickly and people have been bringing cars in here. All purchased vehicles that fit the criteria are being stored in the parking garage."

"Huh. Lily, you're amazing." Felix gave her a grin, leaning forward.

The immaculately put-together woman blushed and looked to the side, her hands folding into her lap. "Thank you. I admit I'm enjoying corporate life. It's… straightforward."

Letting her off the hook with that, he looked to Andrea.

"Armory and arsenal are being stocked. Most of the weapons we're purchasing from No-Name and Dimitry.

"We're focusing on SMGs and pistols to get everyone trained quickly and have a common talent pool. Though we have set aside a budget for rifles once we have everyone equipped. Rifles cost more and require a bit more training.

"Uhm, for gear, we're looking into defense contractors. Vests, helmets, everything, all needs to be above military grade. Investing in the gear will keep your living investments safe."

Makes sense.

"Good show, Andrea. Your skills as Myriad are definitely showing through."

Andrea gave him a bright grin and leaned forward in her chair towards him, her tail sliding up from behind her to wag slowly.

"Miu?"

"Facilities and internal security are up and running. We have requisition orders for everything we need, but all should be well in a matter of weeks. Ioana has created an extensive training program, and we'll be fielding our agents from her security teams."

Ioana nodded her head approvingly at that.

"I'd like to put that indentured service program in place for security. We can purchase mercenary contracts with limiting factors dictated by our HR department. They can sign deals with our resident magician that would bind their soul to ensure cooperation and secrecy."

"Huh. That's a great idea. I approve of that. Let's get that one rolling. That'd be a good way to shore up our manpower and maybe get you a few more trainers, Ioana."

The big woman slowly nodded her head. "It would help."

"Great. That seems like everything. What's next on the agenda?"

Kit picked up a box of something from beside her and dropped it into the center of the table.

In the box were two crowns, and several bracelets. They all looked very similar to the one Dimitry's boss had been wearing.

"We were able to collect these from your attackers."

Ah. They haven't given up.

Chapter 18 - Power and Debt -

"So," Felix started, drumming his fingers along the table. "From home invasions to mid-day assassinations. I'd say someone really doesn't like me."

Ioana snorted at that and gestured to the box. "That's putting it mildly."

Kit pulled out one of the bracelets and laid it on the table.

"It's quality workmanship. Imbued with a high level of psychic defense.

"I couldn't break through to them when they were wearing the crown. I can't confirm it, but I'm betting the bracelet does the same thing, perhaps at a lower power, though."

Kit fingered the enchanted item and nudged it to the side an inch.

"That and the ability to control whoever is wearing it. I would suggest we let no one wear these, even to test them. I wouldn't want to find out simply because we're not sure how that mind control part of it activates. It would be rather awful to have someone suddenly being controlled by our enemy."

Felix sighed set his elbow down on the table, resting his chin in his palm. "Alright. Do we know anything? The one time we had a chance at information, he killed himself."

"Not a thing," Lily said, spreading her hands out in front of her in apology. "All we can do is wait for them to make a mistake. Or capture one alive before they can end their own life. For that to work, we'd have to incapacitate them before they could do anything, though."

Felicia slapped an open hand on the table. "What about nonlethal? Lots of that on the marketplace. I'll see what the lab can whip up and maybe we can catch a break."

"So long as we don't risk ourselves doing it," Felix said after a second. "It isn't worth someone dying over it to find out that whoever is doing this was smart enough to keep themselves hidden just in case.

"I mean, really now, do we honestly think that whoever is smart enough to do all this, keeping themselves in the shadows, would go to such lengths only to let someone see them because they're wearing a suicide device?"

Everyone sobered at that, frowns and creased brows spreading around the room.

"That's a good point," Lily murmured. "It's easier to believe our opponent is foolish or stupid."

Felix shrugged his shoulders with a wince. "Works out in my favor when I believe my enemies are smarter than I am. Overpreparation isn't a terrible thing."

Looking around the room, he met each person's eyes before looking back to the box.

"I suppose all we can do for now is prepare and be ready. If there's nothing else to be taken care of, I think I should probably go over the upgrades for the building and get back to laying golden eggs.

"All that sleep put me behind considerably."

Andrea stood up quickly, sending her chair tumbling as she scampered out of the room on whatever wild thought had taken hold of her.

Miu retreated to a quiet corner of the room while Ioana and Felicia left together. Kit and Lily looked at one another, then to Felix.

"Either you both need to talk to me privately, or you're working on the same problem from different angles," Felix said, looking from one to the other.

"You go first, Lilian," Kit offered, adjusting herself in her seat.

The sorceress looked to Kit and then shrugged. "We've gotten an emergency meeting request from Reznik, Blacketer, and Troy."

Felix quirked his brows at that.

"I'm not sure what they want, but they barred it to anyone who isn't legal counsel for yourself. Thankfully, I've been reinstated and my team is actually rather... accomplished." Lily gave him a bright smile, leaning forward on the table and tapping her folio.

"Glad to hear that. Did we have to drop a hefty bribe to get your license back?" Felix asked, curious.

"Not really. It only took the simple promise that I never head back to my home city. Which isn't a problem, since I cleared out my lair and don't plan on going back."

"Hm. Alright, set up the meeting. Sooner the better. I know it's out of nowhere and we have no way of knowing what they want, but prepare the best you can for it."

"Done. Thanks, Felix. You're a doll." Lily stood up, gathered her folio, and slipped out of the room.

Looking to Kit, Felix scrunched his face up in confusion. "Doll?"

"She likes you. Feels like you value her for who she is, rather than what she is," Kit explained.

"I do. Not a hard thing to do when she's as talented as she is," Felix said a touch skeptically.

"She's still listening at the door," Miu whispered from behind him.

Felix snickered at that. "Go, Lily!" Turning to Kit, he then gestured to her. "What's up?"

Kit's eyes flicked up to Miu and then started to move to Felix but stopped. She stared at Miu, her eyes focusing in on the self-proclaimed bodyguard.

As quickly as it happened, Kit broke eye contact with Miu and looked to Felix. "Right, uhm. I... I'm not sure how to say this."

"With words. Direct words that leave no room for misinformation," Felix prompted.

"Ah, yeah. It's hard since I can't read your mind. I can't get a fix on —"

"Welcome to what the rest of us do on a daily basis. Kit?"

"Yeah. Yeah, right, okay. I'm not a superhero anymore."

"Nope. You're not."

"I'm practically a villain. I've taken the lives of other heroes."

"Not a villain, per se, but definitely the life thing. Probably more down the road as well. Sorry, the price of living in this city now."

"I can handle being neutral, I guess, but I don't... I feel dirty. Ruined."

"Why? Turn the situation sideways. We have something like half a thousand people in our employ. They would have all been bound for more than likely worse conditions."

"Except for the ones you're going to send to the sausage machine," grumped Kit.

"Fine, no sausage machine. But you really need to figure out what to do with those who simply can't work with the team. Does that appease your sense of guilt?"

"A little. Can we use the medical facilities as part of a health plan to get everyone to perfect health?"

"So long as I don't have to arrange it, sure. Get the medical team on board and start conducting routine examinations on a semi-annual basis.

"You tell me what works. You're HR, after all, and benefits fall squarely in your purview."

Felix didn't think that was a problem, and if anything, it'd help. People loved benefits.

"Really?" Kit asked suspiciously. "Not just saying that to placate me?"

"Really. Not saying it to placate you. Put together a benefits package for me and we'll go over it later.

"And back to the villain/hero thing. Does it matter? The Guild of Heroes was more of a faction than anything. The city is well patrolled and has a fairly strict sense of justice right now.

"Last I saw, crime was on the decline."

"It is, it is, I just... I don't know. I was always a hero. Even when I was dangerous to teammates, I was a hero. And now I'm... now I'm the single strongest telepath in the world with probably the greatest sense of control.

"And, oh yeah, I'm suddenly telekinetic as well."

The pen in front of her lifted up off the table and spun wildly through the room. Dancing, twirling, the pen defied gravity as it flew.

Only for Miu to snatch it out of the air, click the pen top to withdraw the tip, and set it down in front of Felix.

"I could do so much. I could help—"

"Nope. Sorry. Not a hero anymore. If you really want to help, get to HR and put that benefits package together.

"Then link up with our marketing group, finance group, and see what we can do on a charitable level. Donations go a long way to help build a company's face value and lower taxes.

"We deal in antiques and equipment. Schools and museums seem like the obvious place to start to me." Felix never did like dealing with the passionate ones.

The ones who had to feel like they were making a difference.

It's a job. Work the job, do what you want in your personal time.

Or nothing.

"Ah! Really? I can do that?" Kit asked eagerly.

"Sure. Put it all together and get back to me. Was that it?"

"Yes, thank you. Yes. Thank you," Kit said, standing up.

Just then, her phone went off.

Turning her wrist over, she looked at the display on her wrist.

"Huh. It's Eva." Kit tapped the display. "Eva? What's wrong?"

"Kit! I'm at school and I need you to come get me," said his ward into her phone. Then the line went dead.

"Huh?" Felix looked to Kit, waiting for an explanation.

Kit blinked and then tapped her wrist display again. "Ah, well. Eva is having troubles adjusting to her new school."

"I see. Go pick her up, then, I'll just—"

Kit's wrist display lit up again as another call came through. The telepath couldn't hide her unease as she viewed the caller window.

Felix gave her a grim smile and waited.

Kit sighed and tapped the display. "Good afternoon, Principal."

"Good afternoon, Miss Carrington. Is Eva's guardian recovered enough to come deal with his hooligan of a ward?" came back the starched tones of what sounded like an elderly gentleman.

Hooligan?

"He has indeed. He'll be—"

"Good, he can come pick up his ward and a piece of my mind."

The line went dead once again.

Felix let out a slow breath and closed his eyes.

"That sounds like a lot more than adjusting."

"Yes... well. Yes," Kit said lamely.

Several Andreas came marching in before Felix could ask anything further.

They moved in a small group, armed with SMGs yet no body armor or gear to speak of.

When your life is expendable to the point that gear costs more, I guess I can understand.

The one in front took a spot directly to his side and then drew to attention.

"Reporting in, as per procedure. We've successfully repelled a group of supers who were attempting to gain entry. We killed one, wounded two, and only lost fifteen of my Others. All reabsorbed without incident," Andrea said, looking at the space above his head.

"What...? We're under attack?" Felix tried to confirm.

"Were under attack. We've repelled them. The body has been sent to the sausage machine after having Lily check for a soul.

"Request permission to return to post and split the Others back off."

"Yeah. Do that, Andrea. And could you send Andrea Prime over to see me later? Sounds like I need a few more Others," Felix said, pausing to look at Kit. "That and more information about the situation at hand. What say you take a seat, Miss Carrington? I think we have more to talk about."

The three-car-long dark sedan convoy moved sedately through traffic. Andrea wasn't taking anything for granted.

She drove each vehicle, as she could coordinate with herself without speaking, since it was herself. They'd think the same thing and come up with the same answers.

She also refused to run yellows or reds, and would simply stop early.

Kit and Miu were with him, along with two Andreas. Riding in the other vehicles were all Andreas. Every one of them dressed in a black pantsuit and armed.

Even Kit and Miu were dressed in a similar fashion. Not identical, but similar.

Miu wore something a bit more sporty that she could probably move better in.

Kit, on the other hand, had clearly picked her outfit from a fashion standpoint. She certainly caught the eye with it.

Felix didn't get what they were aiming for, and honestly, he didn't want to. He was sure it was some odd type of intimidation that Ioana, Miu, or Lily had cooked up.

Probably will work, too.

Didn't hurt that they'd stuffed him into one of the nicest suits he'd ever had the pleasure of owning.

The suit had been a custom job. Felicia had tailored and made it for him specifically from her R&D department.

Turning his wrist over, he checked the time.

"We'll be there in three minutes, dear," Andrea Prime said from beside him. She was the only one of the Andreas dressed differently. Where the others wore pantsuits, she wore a gray pencil skirt and dark jacket.

"Ah. Thanks. You look good in that, by the way," Felix said, pointing a finger at her.

"Thanks, babe! I knew you'd like it. I wasn't sure if it went with my tail. Does it? Look, look," Andrea said, turning to her side and shoving her bottom at him.

Her fluffy tail wagged a fraction, her bottom moving with it.

Quickly pulling his eyes up with a strained smile, he met Kit's eyes. "Yep, looks fine."

Kit gave him a smirk and pressed a finger to her lips, motioning him to remain silent about the humor of the situation.

"You're such a nice person. Thanks, dear. Wait till I show you my underwear. It really suits my skin. Here, take a—" Andrea said, shifting around to face him again.

"Ah, Andie?" Kit asked, looking to the Beastkin.

"Aww, fine. I'll show him tonight. Do you think he likes black and red?"

"I'm still here. It's not like I went somewhere," Felix said.

"Good point. Do you like black and red?" Andrea said, turning to him with a bright smile.

"We're here," Chauffeur Andrea said.

"Thank the saints," Miu murmured and opened her door, getting out immediately.

Felix moved to get out and had Andrea wrap a hand around his wrist. "Wait."

Looking back to her, he sighed and then nodded his head. The assassination attempt on his life had changed how he would be able to interact with the world at large.

The door had been closed, and now two rear ends in pantsuits were directly outside his window. He knew they had SMGs in holsters under those buttoned, fashionable jackets.

He also knew that Andrea was an incredibly fast draw.

Finally, one of them popped open the door and Felix was allowed to step out.

Taking in a breath, he stood up and surveyed the area quickly.

It looked like the definition of a private school.

Good-looking front entrance, decorated smartly yet tastefully; pathways leading up to the front gate; manicured lawns and trees providing a natural look; expensive-looking housing across the street; a decent-sized redbrick wall that circled the campus.

"I think I'd have been kicked out if I had gone here as a kid," Felix muttered.

"Me too," Miu said, standing on his right. "Then again, my schooling was very different. Fewer books, more swords."

"One of these days, I'm going to order you to tell me all about yourself, Miu."

"That'll be the day you learn secrets you wish you hadn't," said the severe woman. Then, surprisingly, she gave him an earnest smile. "But I appreciate the sentiment. Another time."

On his left, Kit flipped open her messenger bag and pulled out a manila folder. Taking a quick peek inside, she checked its contents and then held it out to Felix.

"This is probably everything you'll need. I put everything in there relevant to Eva. Just in case. Lily said she'll be available by phone if you need her."

Felix took the folder and started walking to the front door. Looking into the folder, he gave it a onceover, realized it wouldn't do him much good for the situation at hand, and closed it again.

Not her fault. Her school experiences were probably very clinical.

The Others fanned out in front of him, taking positions along the walkway and eyeing everyone nearby.

Students watched, enthralled with what was happening.

Felix shoved those concerns off to the side. It didn't matter to him because, realistically, the protection Andrea was providing for him was beyond what anyone could reasonably ask for.

His complaints about the situation would never cross his lips.

An Andrea held open the door for him inside. Several Andreas escorted him in, while a handful that had remained near the car moved up to take the ground between the cars and the door.

Entering the front office, he needed only to follow the Others. They had gone over the floorplan meticulously and would be herding him straight to the principal's office.

A receptionist started to stand up, before an Other shoved her back down into her chair. "Sit."

Shaking his head, Felix turned down the hallway, following the Others.

"It's necessary for your safety. We won't come that close again," Miu said.

"Never," Andrea agreed.

"This is the safest option for you, and for them," Kit concurred.

Felix didn't argue.

Ahead of him, an Other opened a door for him, and Felix walked right into the principal's office.

Trailing him was Miu, Andrea Prime, and Kit.

Inside of the office was a stodgy-looking man in his fifties, and Eva.

"Felix? Felix!" Eva squealed, jumping up. She wrapped him up in a tight hug.

"Hey there, yes, yes. Hug, hug. All good now? Maybe let go?" Felix said with a pained smile at her.

She only hugged him tighter. With a small smile curling his lips, Felix gave her a genuine hug.

"If you're done, we can begin talking about your hooligan's beh-"

"You can stop right there," Felix said, glaring over the top of Eva's head. "And if you don't stop, I'll have Miu here help you."

"I... You have no right to talk to me like that."

"You call her anything other than Eva, student, or ward, and this'll be the fastest meeting you've ever had."

Felix gently peeled Eva off of him and literally handed her over to Andrea, who happily hugged the girl and lifted her off her feet.

"Now, what's the problem?" Felix asked.

"She won't listen to her teachers. She makes no attempt to treat them with the respect they deserve. She hasn't done a single iota of homework. She's, quite frankly, one of the dumbest students we've had," grumped the principal, crossing his arms across his chest.

"Uh-huh. Eva?" Felix asked, turning his head to Eva. "What's the problem? No teenage drama. No bullshitting—"

"Language!" shouted the principal.

"And tell me. Don't even think of saying, 'you'd never understand,' because I guarantee I will."

Eva lifted her head up from Andrea's embrace and truly looked at him.

"The teachers single me out because I don't know the answers," she said finally.

Ah. I see. And from that starting point, I imagine everything else went to shit.

"How far behind are you? Guess if you don't know."

"I dunno... a year, maybe. Two... I'm sorry, I know I'm stupid, I just—"

"No, stop right there. You're not stupid. This is actually easy to solve," Felix said, smiling at her. Turning his head to the principal, he continued, "If people pulled their heads out of their ass long enough to take a breath.

"Did your teachers even attempt to redress this issue? To ask her where she was in her studies? There was no placement of any sort to determine what would be best for her? If she needed tutoring?"

"Well, I, that's not what we do here. We shape minds —"

"So, no. You didn't, and no, they didn't." Felix let out a short breath and then pulled his phone out of his pocket.

Kit frowned, looking annoyed and out of her depth.

She couldn't find it with mind reading.

Felix held up the phone to his ear as it rang.

Not everything can be solved by picking through thoughts, my lovely superheroine.

"Felix? Miss me already?" Lily purred into the phone.

"I did. I missed that mind of yours. So, Eva is behind in her studies. We'll need a tutor to get her up to speed of the school."

"Now look, this won't solve what she's done. I'm already in the process of having her expelled," said the principal loudly.

"Oh? Alright. Sorry, I should have thought of that myself. She did say she and her brother had been out of school for a while," Lily said. In the background, he could her rapidly typing at a keyboard. "Don't worry about the principal, by the way."

"Why's that, exactly? You do something crafty with that big brain of yours?" Felix asked, smirking.

"I did indeed. We needed something to sink money in that we could turn back around to our employees. The school has a bit of an ugly secret that it's trying to hide."

"Do tell. I await your honeyed words with bated breath," Felix teased. For whatever reason, Lily could draw him into banter.

"Honeyed? With what I've been doing for you, it damn well better smell like ambrosia.

"Suffice it to say, the school was a bastion for kids of superheroes. Those kids, who paid a whole hell of a lot in fees to be anonymous while going to school, are gone.

"The school overspent its budget by a drastic amount. Everything went on credit.

"They were so far in the red the school was going to be shut down. I bought up all that debt on the cheap; I only had to flash a smile a few times, and posted the loss against our taxes.

"I made sure the schoolboard knew we'd bought it all up, that we were willing to negotiate. I have a bi-weekly meeting with their board.

"Then I set the whole thing up so all future children of parents from Legion, or become part of Legion, get sent there for their K-through-H education. Put that one in as a massive tax write-off.

"Probably won't be completely approved by the government, but it'll do more than enough to get our taxes down."

"Huh, that's pretty crafty. I love it. It sounds like it'd break the bank, though."

"Might have. Our accountant is a wonderful lady, though. All the losses are going to be posted late in the year as it winds its way through every process from here to New Year's.

"In the end, we'll definitely get our money back, but it'll take time. Unless a cranky CEO decides to call in the debts a certain school owes. Then it'd be shut down that day."

"Lily?" Felix asked after digesting that.

"Mmm?" came back a smiling voice.

"You're fantastic. I owe you something nice."

"Spoil me. Corporate life is great. I get to be as evil as I can, you reward me for it, and I don't even have to get my hands dirty."

"I'll do that indeed. See ya later."

"Ta-ta."

Felix thumbed the display and pocketed his phone.

Turning to the principal, he smiled slowly.

"You know, this is certainly my year. I find myself in unbelievable positions of power.

"Anyways. Principal... whatever the fuck your name is. Let me spin you a tale. A tale of a school with no money. A school that had a white knight come riding in and buy up all their debt, and then tell them not to worry about it. That they'd negotiate and work something out."

Felix grinned and leaned over the chair, the wooden back creaking ominously under his weight.

"I'm not feeling particularly charitable right now. You called her a hooligan."

"Twice!" Andrea said happily.

"Twice..." Felix agreed.

"And he called her the dumbest they've ever had," Andrea amended.

Chapter 19 - Sentiment -

Felix looked to Lily at his side.

In the end, Reznik, Blacketer, and Troy had limited him to one attorney and no bodyguards.

That hadn't prevented a horde of Andreas spreading throughout the office and watching everyone.

Or the fact that Kit was in the lobby, more than likely pillaging the minds of everyone that she could find.

Miu had somehow been talked into remaining at home and drilling the teams with Ioana.

In fact, it was probably the overwhelming entourage that Felix had arrived with that sent the Reznik, Blacketer, and Troy lawyers scurrying. It was beyond all their expectations.

"So… thanks for taking care of the tutor thing," Felix said, tapping his fingers on the desk.

"Not a problem. It was easy to arrange and didn't cost us much. The check-in I had yesterday after the initial meeting confirmed that she's well on her way to being caught up. Maybe only a week or two of dedicated work is all it'll take. She wasn't as far back as she thought she was. Just missing a few fundamental things."

Lily brushed the concern off with a flick her of wrist, the cuff on her jacket snapping lightly as she did it.

"Fair enough. Still, thanks. I know Eva appreciates it as well.

"You put any thought into what you want? I did say I'd spoil you."

"Hm, not yet. Honestly, I have everything I want right now. I'm sure I'll think up something."

Lily sighed and crossed her arms in front of her. "They're stalling because they weren't expecting me here, Andrea in the lobby, or Kit staring through people's heads."

"Unsurprising, I suppose. She really does stare through people's heads, though. I don't think she's used to directing her talent yet.

"Maybe we should —"

The door across the way clicked open and a group of well-dressed men and women began filing into the room.

Felix vaguely recognized some of them from previous meetings, but there were of course several new faces.

"Sorry for keeping you waiting, Mr. Campbell," said a smartly dressed young woman, taking the center seat.

She was in her late twenties, brown hair, blue eyes, attractive, put together on the slimmer side, with a perfectly straight smile.

"That's alright, we're billing you accordingly," Lily said with a bright grin in return. "As this was an emergency meeting and fell outside of expected contracted calendar dates, you'll be taking the bill for everything.

"I don't think you'll like my rates. Especially when we factor in the costs of bodyguards and personnel."

"I… see." The woman's face had clouded at that. "My name is Lauren Aston. We'll try to keep this brief.

"We'll be halting all payments made to you as a landlord, until you are able to pay off the outstanding debt."

Felix raised his eyebrows at that and opened his mouth to ask a question.

Lily lifted a well-manicured hand and held up a finger, her face tilting to the side a fraction to catch his eyes with her own.

Nodding his head, Felix closed his mouth.

"Is that all?" Lily asked.

"Ah, we'll also be unable to process any other agenda items until it's taken care of, as you're still in breach of contract," finished Miss Aston.

"According to my notes," Lily started, opening her satchel and flipping through a series of papers. "The debt owed is… one hundred and fifty thousand dollars?"

"That's right. I'm afraid with that substantial amount of money owed, we really would need it taken care of first."

Weird. Wouldn't they assume I could just use the landlord back pay to crush the debt? Do they know I already spent it all? Do they think me broke because I opened a business?

"And who has deemed that this is the correct course of action?" Lily asked, picking up her pen and moving it over to her ledger.

"Ah, that is, we had a majority vote."

"That's fine. I'll need the names of who voted in favor of this action, though. I'm afraid your voting process isn't sealed," Lily said, smiling with her teeth.

As if to emphasize her point, she tapped the pen twice to her paper.

"Ah…" Miss Aston paused and looked to her left and right.

"Here, I'll make it simple. Who voted in favor of this action? Please raise your hand? If you don't have a majority, we can give you the bill for this meeting and leave."

Lily curled an errant lock of hair behind one ear and waited, moving her eyes from one person to the next.

Slowly, five hands raised into the air.

Lily made a point of reading the nameplate of each individual, which they had so graciously provided in their self-important routine, and writing it down.

"You can't dismiss anyone, as you're in breach," Miss Aston said, leaning forward over her section of the table.

Lily sighed and pulled out a checkbook. Filling out a check quickly and neatly, she set it down in front of Felix.

"Sign here." She indicated the signature line.

Felix accepted the pen, signed his name and slid it back to Lily.

"Here is your payment. When will you have the five percent for the landlord available?" Lily asked. With a quick motion, she popped the check clear of the book and set it down on the desk.

"I… tomorrow. As per our regulations." Miss Aston no longer seemed so sure of herself.

"Great. As this is a new quarter, we move to dismiss two people. We'll also be filing a complaint that we find the recent hiring practices to be unsatisfactory.

"As to who's dismissed…" Lily tapped her chin with a finger and then leaned back in her chair, looking to Felix. "Any thoughts? If nothing else, Miss Aston is pretty enough to keep around for fun. I mean, she's not me, but… you can't always stare at me. Even I'll get self-conscious after a while."

Miss Aston made a shocked noise, while the four who had raised their hands with her looked everywhere in the room except to them.

Felix smirked and shook his head, letting out a slow breath.

"I ever mention you're fantastic, Lily?"

"Several times. Don't stop."

"I'll leave it to you, Lily. I trust you." Felix didn't want any part in her power game right now. Instead, he pulled out his phone and updated Kit in a text message.

"Music to my ears. Great, you two are gone. Thanks.

"Now, Miss Aston, I do hope you'll be working for our interests here in the future. I'd hate to see you lose your job over it.

"We'll leave our bill with the receptionist, as well as our formal complaint. I made sure to have it notarized. Can't have it go missing, now can we?" Lily stood up from her chair, closing her satchel.

Felix got up as well, pocketing his phone.

Nothing more was said as they left. Lily was as good as her word and left both the complaint and bill at the front desk.

Felix adjusted his pants as they left the building. For whatever reason, he could never get his dress pants to sit quite right.

Stopping just outside, he reached down and pulled at the sides of his pants. "I swear to God, maybe we should hire a tailor. Felicia's great, but I think I'm abnormal and need a master tailor or something," Felix muttered.

All around him, a sudden and blinding bright white light encircled him.

A group of Others plowed into him and hustled him forward before he had a chance to even contemplate it.

What the fuck?

He was forced head first into the car. He ended up being smashed up against Lily with Andrea just about clambering on top of him.

He caught a glimpse of Kit in the passenger seat before the convoy took off.

"That was a sniper. Had to be miles and miles out. Didn't even hear the sound," Andrea said, still pressing into him. In turn pressing him into Lily.

The sorceress looked at him, his head wedged into her shoulder and chest. She gave him a weak smile and averted her eyes.

"The force on the shield was significant. Whatever they shot, it was a very heavy round," Lily said, adjusting her position without looking at Felix.

Andrea eased up off him as they blew through a red light and across into a section of street with taller buildings.

"Sorry, Lily," Felix said as he sat up. He tried to do it without pawing the woman unnecessarily.

"Better to be manhandled by you, than you dying. Property, like slaves, goes into a limbo state if the owner dies. Your health is important," Lily explained, her voice soft. She picked something off her skirt and then crossed her legs.

"Oh! Did that tire you out? Here, you can lean on me, dear," Andrea said delightedly. Grabbing him around the shoulders, she pulled him into her side and chest, holding to him tightly.

Felix growled, putting his hands to her to push away. Only to have her pull his head to her chest, and then lightly comb her fingers through his hair. "There, there, dear. We're all here for you. All you had to do was ask."

Felix closed his eyes before he could see Kit or Lily gloating at him. They seemed to delight in the fact that Andrea did as Andrea pleased. Much to his eternal dismay.

"Whatever. Now they're using snipers to take me out."

"Yes. They were outside of my range," Kit said from up front.

"I didn't see the shot," Andrea said, her fingernails grazing along his scalp.

"Nor I. It only confirms what we knew. They're out there, and very determined. Nothing has changed, except that we now know some of those poor excuses for lawyers are involved," Lily said with a click of her tongue.

"What?" Felix asked, cracking an eye open to look to Lily.

The soul-eating lawyer met his eyes and held up her hands in a gesture of futility.

"A sniper was prepared for your exit, with a perfect shot, and at an extreme distance. The whole thing was a setup."

Oh. Shit.

Things had calmed down since the shooting.

Everything was finally back to normal.

Or at least as normal as it could be when you were the head of a corporation boasting some of the strongest supers the world had ever seen.

Felix was on antique duty today. There'd been a large number of scheduled private evaluations while he'd been incapacitated.

Since coming back into the store, he'd given the superpower of "Item Identification (by touch)" to several people.

Having it triggered by touch had kept the point cost much further down than by sight.

It also meant that the other stores, and the auto shop, would be outfitted to have someone always on hand to get things cataloged. Which left Felix at HQ doing his own part.

Sitting in what used to be the storefront in the warehouse, he awaited the next client.

They'd be searched, brought in, and dropped off here with their item.

Today had been a very good day. Several high-end acquisitions had been made that'd turn their fortunes around quickly.

After all the cash outlays recently, their bank account was looking rather skinny.

Broken antiques, purchased at a higher price, repaired, and then sold, made everyone happy.

Most especially the people who sold those broken antiques for more than the value of it.

A man entered the room. He spent some time looking around at the various items dispersed throughout the office as decoration.

"Good morning," Felix said, standing up from behind his desk.

The man jumped and his head whipped around to lock on to Felix. "G-good morning."

"What can I do for you today, Mr....?" Felix held out his hand across the table good-naturedly.

The man took Felix's hand in a firm shake and then took a seat.

"Mr. White. I'm, uh, here to sell this." Mr. White pulled out a legal-sized sketchbook with drawstring ties.

"Oh?" Felix. "And what do you believe it is?"

He'd learned that asking this question was the best way to determine the intent.

"It's a sketchbook. My father bought it from a collector. The man claimed it was worth a couple hundred dollars at the time. It's filled with sketches from artists from the twenties and thirties, with a couple of knockoffs as well."

Mr. White said it humbly and without any emotion behind it. It was a sale to be made to him, nothing more.

He needs money and doesn't really care that much about the item at all.

Flipping open the sketchbook, Felix began to sort through them one by one.

They matched exactly what the man said. Sketch after sketch he flipped through and checked.

Fifty dollars here, a hundred there, ten for the next one.

Right up until Felix flipped it open onto a sketch that was very out of place. It had the look of something religious, yet drawn in an older style.

One that looked similar to the Renaissance era.

Name:	Created In:
Michelangelo di Lodovico Buonarroti Simoni Sketch	1502
Appraised Value: $32.00	Created By: Michelangelo di Lodovico Buonarroti

	Simoni	
Actual Value: $4,500,000.00	**Condition:** Moderately Worn	
Asking Price: $200.00	**Durability:** 69/100	
Mint Price: $22,000,000.00	**Cost to Repair:** 200 points	

"That's one of the imitations. Supposedly it's meant to look like Michelangelo. The attribution is missing since the corner it'd be in was torn off.

"It's well drawn, but without that attribution, there's no telling if it was a master or someone who liked his work."

Felix cleared his throat and delicately withdrew the sketch and set it aside.

Just buy it, just buy it, just buy it, just—aarrrrggh.

"Why do you need the money?" Felix asked quietly, folding one hand into the other and meeting Mr. White's eyes.

"I don't see why that matters. Can't you just buy it and...ugh. My son was apprenticed to some superhero. He doesn't even have powers, he just... wanted to help. Damn cops got him the other day when the hero he was working for... left him behind."

The man shrugged his shoulders and slumped low in his seat.

"I need to get the money together to buy my son. He's my only son. I've been out of work for a while now, living off my savings. Now this happens and I... they said it'd cost a significant amount of money to buy him. Because of his apprenticeship. Doesn't matter if he doesn't know anything, everyone will assume he does.

"And right now, the bounty on heroes has skyrocketed."

Felix could only nod his head. It had indeed.

Apparently there were some heroes still working in the city, and in the last day or two, the bounty had jumped into the millions.

Yeah, his son is going to be expensive. Not my problem, though.

Nodding his head, Felix pulled over the bill of sale and started to write it in for a thousand dollars.

It was more than generous on his part.

Felix stopped in mid pen stroke and looked at the pen he was using.

It was something Eva had given him. It was a rough cast steel pen that had been engraved by Eva's hand.

His name was front and center on the barrel of the pen. Taking up a sizable space. All around his name were engraved simple words.

Defender. Valiant. Fearless. Preserver. Vigilant. Guardian.

On and on it went, the pen completely filled with those silly words formed from a childlike innocence.

She'd spent hours trying to get the engraving just right.

She had given it to him in a little box and everything.

"Your weapon is a pen. Here's one from me, then," she'd said at the time.

Smothering the stupid sentiment welling up in himself, he set the pen down and pressed his hands to his face.

She'd hate me.

Felix shuddered at the thought of Eva staring at him after finding out about the sketch.

Especially if she got the full story.

"This actually is a Michelangelo sketch. It isn't an imitation. It's legit.

"In its current condition, it'd probably be worth four million if you could get professional attribution," Felix said between his fingers.

His energy leaked out of him as he spoke, slowly hunching over the desk.

"I can certify it with my own name, but I wouldn't be able to buy it from you, nor would it honestly get the full worth from it.

"I can put you in touch with the name of a contact I have who deals in some of the slave auctions. He could probably arrange something for you, though I doubt you'd get the full amount from the sketch."

"Really?!" Mr. White leapt to his feet, the chair clattering to the floor and scraping along the ground. "That'd be... that'd be great. I can't tell you how grateful I am."

"Uh-huh," Felix said without emotion. Setting his hands back to the table, he picked up Eva's pen. Staring at it for a second, he looked back to the sheet of paper and wrote it out as an evaluation rather than a sale.

"That'll be one hundred dollars for the valuation," Felix said, sliding the sheet of paper across to the excited man.

Mr. White gathered up the sketchbook and then looked at the valuation.

"I... I don't have it. I'm sorry. What little money I had, I spent on getting an invite to the auction that my son is being sold at.

"I don't have a job."

Felix groaned and scratched at his head. "Alright. What exactly do you do for a career?"

"I, uh," Mr. White paused. His words were cautious, uncertain. "I was the lead engineer on several projects for the super hero association. When the government changed over, I escaped and never looked back."

Felix's attention changed from the sketch to Mr. White. "What kind of projects?"

"Nanotechnology, energy weapons, and renewable energy. They're all kinda interconnected," Mr. White said with a small smile.

Ha... hahahaha. Seriously?

"Mr. White. How about you sit back down? I'll cancel my upcoming appointments, have lunch brought in, and let's have a talk."

Felix turned his head to the dark corner he knew Miu would be in. "Miu, could you coordinate with some of the Others to get things arranged? I'll also need Kit in here. I want to see where she ended up with the Indentured package.

"I'm going to make Mr. White a job offer here and I want to make sure we have an appropriate contract that we can put together."

"What do you mean, you're going to make a job offer? How can you offer me a job? This is a pawn shop, isn't it? Why would you need an engineer?" Mr. White's voice sped up as he asked each successive question.

Miu materialized out of the shadowed corner and lifted a hand to her ear. "Shadow to… Shadow to Pancake," Miu said between gritted teeth.

"Pancake here!" came Andrea's shouted response, which Felix could hear through Miu's earpiece even from where he was sitting.

Miu flinched at the sudden response and shook her head angrily.

Probably shouldn't have let everyone make their own call signs. Your own fault there, Miu.

Chapter 20 - Free Lunch -

Felix sat down with his tray in the first dormitory floor's dining hall.

Managing to surprise him, Felicia had built it to accommodate everyone on the floor and two below.

Everyone in Legion fit into this single dining hall. Felicia already had teams of Andreas excavating down, building out several more of these dining halls and attached dormitories. And every other type of room that they'd need.

Lunch today was actually rather good. Lasagna, garlic bread, and some type of vegetable medley.

After eating in the dining hall a few times, he realized he didn't care at all what his food costs were. Whoever their cook was, they were a master, and Felix would ply them with whatever ingredients they asked for.

Andrea dropped down beside him and immediately smashed her right side up into his left.

"Andrea, I can't really eat like this," Felix said, his left arm forced out behind her back.

"Ah! I'll feed you, then! Say ahhhhhhh," she said, holding up a forkful of lasagna.

"Andrea, I don't—mmphff!" His words were lost in the mouthful of food that she stubbornly forced on him.

Growling, he looked ahead as Lily sat down in front of him. She was dressed as she always was. Beautiful and professional.

Kit took the seat on his right, making a happy cooing noise over the food. She loved eating.

Lily had apparently seen what had happened and daintily scooped up a chunk of lasagna on her fork and then held it out towards him.

A perfectly pretty and evil smile turned her lips and she raised her eyebrows at him. "Don't leave a lady waiting, Felix; if she's allowed to feed you, I believe I am too."

Felix found himself getting annoyed and pointed his fork at her.

"Oh? You want to feed me? Certainly, certainly." Lily laid her fork down and then opened her mouth wide at him. Her tongue slowly moved up and touched her incisors and glided across.

Felix looked to his right, his cheeks heating up. Kit was watching him from that side as well. Her own smile was less predatory, though full of mirth.

"You do realize she gets a rise out of this. She, and I know this, gets off on the fact that you refuse her. That whenever you even get close to flirting or hitting on her, you run," Kit explained as if talking to a child. She ate a bite of her own lunch and then pointed back to Lily with the empty fork.

Felix slowly turned his eyes back to the soul-eating lawyer. She'd returned to her meal, her cheeks a faint red.

She's not wrong, is she? Lily was always the one being chased by suitors, police, and supers alike.

Didn't mean he wanted to mess with Lily right now. She'd give him twice as bad later any he gave her now.

Kit, though, Kit he could harass.

Looking to Kit, he swallowed and then gave her a grin. "As if you're any better. You prod at me to figure out my reactions so you can try and predict what I'm thinking. Since you can't read me.

"Should I share those thoughts with you? Should I tell you about what went through my head when I was putting you back together? Piece by piece? When I saw you for everything you were?"

Ha, two can play that game.

Kit immediately turned a bright, fuming red and turned her face forward. Her left hand came up to shield herself from his sight.

"Was that when she was all broken and meat and stuff? Ioana told me about that. That you were like corpses and you brought them back from death."

As soon as Felix turned his head to answer Andrea's question, she shoved her fork into his mouth again.

Grunting, he started chewing the mouthful and glared at Andrea.

Who only smiled at him, tilting her head slowly forward to peek up at him from below. Her mismatched eyes peered at him through her blonde bangs.

"You could take me apart and put me back together in whatever way you see fit. Or a few of me, if you like," she whispered in a promising voice.

Felix stopped chewing entirely and stared at the young woman.

She still made it a point to sleep in his bed every night. Sometimes at his feet, sometimes on him, beside him, or even on the floor. That arrangement took on a whole new meaning with that one statement.

Andrea was definitely attractive. Especially when she got coy or energetic. That girl-next-door charm of hers changed in a heartbeat when she tried.

"How was that? It was embarrassing, but I did it. Did it work?" Andrea asked, turning her head to Lily. "Did I melt his boxers? Will he want to sleep closer tonight?"

Lily choked on her food and pressed a napkin to her mouth.

Felix turned a wide-eyed glare on Lily, who was hiding behind her napkin.

"Felix, the indentured servant program is going well," Kit interrupted. "We've had a number of people ask for their families to be put into the program."

Kit fingered a paper out of her messenger bag at her side and laid it down in front of him.

Felix slowly turned his glare from Lily to the paper.

It was a balance sheet on costs and return on investment based on pay and job title.

They were well in the black.

Beyond in the black. The pawn shops were making money, but the estimated costs of the work everyone else was doing was all in savings. And it was a lot.

"All the children are being enrolled immediately, after an evaluation and tutors if they need it.

"The school seems to be enjoying the influx of children; the empty desks are filling up, and their tuition is filling their account."

"It doesn't hurt that we converted all that debt into ownership and controlling shares."

That little bit of business had soothed Felix's ire. The debt was wiped out, and instead they now owned a majority of the school. An eighty percent controlling share, no less.

Felix nodded his head, following along.

"We never did find out what auction Mr. White's son went to, but I'm happy to report they both turned up this morning.

"Mr. White is already in his lab at work. His son is training with Ioana."

"Pity. We could use more people. I think the auctions will become more and more scarce as time goes on," Felix said. He moved the sheet of paper back to Kit.

Andrea shoved another forkful of food into his mouth. He felt the Beastkin's tail swish back and forth against his back.

Sighing through his nose, he gave up. Picking up his plate of lasagna, he set it into Andrea's tray and then pointed at her own mouth.

"For me? Goodie! I'll feed you mine and eat yours. Being your personal secretary is great.

"It's kinda like when people date in movies.

"That reminds me!"

Before he could figure out what the wolf girl was doing, she handed her personal tablet to Lily and then grabbed Felix's face.

With quick, agile fingers, she rearranged his hair, brushed something off his cheek, and then forced him to look forward.

"Smile!" Andrea said, pressing into his side.

Felix did as instructed and smiled at Lily, not quite following along.

"Great! Get ready, Lily!" Andrea commanded. Andrea's fingers snatched his chin and turned his face towards her own.

Then she kissed him wetly on the corner of his mouth, pressing herself right up into his shoulder.

Pulling back from him and giggling insanely, she made grabby hands at Lily.

With a smirk, Lily handed the tablet over to her. "I expect you to return the favor."

"Of course, of course. Just let me know when and I'll get the Others involved," Andrea promised as she began flipping through what looked like photos of him and her that were just taken.

"What in the actual fuck did —" Felix started.

"Oh, Felix? Dimitry left a message for you about thirty minutes ago. He'd like to arrange a call to discuss his first favor with you," Kit interrupted him. Again.

His thoughts derailed at that, his anger instantly cooling. Turning his head to Kit, he lifted his right hand in a questioning gesture.

"He did? Alright. Let's set up a call or a meet for an hour or two from now. After this, I'm supposed to let Ioana and Miu kick my ass for a while."

Then another forkful of lasagna was jammed into his mouth.

"Mmmm!" Felix turned his head towards Andrea. Halfway there, he found Lily smiling at him with an empty fork, still in front of him.

"Eat up, dar-ling," said the demoness in her best impression of Andrea's voice from earlier. Her eyes were teasing and warm, her smile hungry.

"Oh, you have a little something there, dear," Andrea said, getting in front of him. She grabbed his face, licked her fingers, and began wiping at his face with them.

All around him, his people watched.

They were watching.

Felix began shuddering in absolute rage as Andrea patted his cheek.

Flopping into the chair, Felix watched Miu cross the room and take up residence in a corner.

Two Others took the door, while Andrea Prime was practically in his pocket. She was working on something on her tablet but stayed glued to him.

Tapping the screen on his desk, he pulled up Dimitry's number and hit the send button.

The phone connected on the first ring.

"Felix. Glad you could get back to me so fast. I need to call in one of those favors."

"Good to hear from you, Dimitry.

"And yeah, that'd be part of the agreement. What can I do for you?"

"I think I have an infestation and I could use an exterminator. Make sure you bring your mind reader to find the rats.

"Say, tomorrow morning, eight o'clock, my place."

"I'll be there," Felix said.

There was no response to that, since the line had already gone dead.

How did he know about Kit?

"Rats? I hate rats. I had to deal with them a lot when dealing with targets who were in not nice places," Andrea grumped unhappily.

Felix closed out his program and slept the desktop display.

"I think he means informants. People who work for the cops. Not actual rats," he explained to the Beastgirl.

"Oh, that makes sense." She poked at something on her screen and then bounced up and down twice. "There!"

She flipped her tablet around and showed it to him.

It was the background for her tablet. A picture of them smiling into the camera. One of those that had been taken earlier that day.

She tapped the desktop and it switched to the picture of her kissing him. She tapped the screen again and it was another photo of them together, but this time in the car.

Then it was a picture of a number of Andreas sleeping next to him in his bed. Though on him might have been more accurate. One was spread across his lower legs, another next to him had a leg thrown over his stomach and hips, and a third had wrapped herself up around an arm.

A fourth one was above him sleeping lengthwise across the pillows with an arm over his face.

Sleep hadn't been as refreshing as it used to be. That change certainly lined up with after she'd weaseled that concession out of him.

Now he knew why.

"Andrea... how many pictures like this do you have?" Felix asked, looking over the top of the tablet.

She gave him a grin and leaned forward towards him. "A lot."

"I... see. And you didn't give these to anyone, did you?"

"No, no. Of course not."

"Good."

"Just Lily, Kit, and Miu."

Felix felt his face screw up in a grimace at that.

"They're all well taken," Miu promised from behind him.

His intercom beeped once, then came to life.

"Mr. Campbell, I have a..." There was a pause as an Other questioned whoever it was for their name. "John Smith here to see you. He says he's here from the Department of Slave Affairs."

Thinking, Felix tilted his head down, staring at the ground. Reaching up, he thumbed the intercom button. "I'll meet him in the Gold conference room. Please have Kit and Lily notified."

Andrea Prime stood upright beside him and began tapping things into her tablet.

"I should be there in—" Felix paused as Andrea caught his eyes.

She held up one hand with all five fingers splayed. Closed her hand and did it again.

"Ten minutes," Felix finished.

Andrea Prime nodded her head and turned back to her tablet.

"Consider it done, Mr. Campbell." It had taken some serious work to get Andrea to be able, or at least willing, to call him Mr. Campbell when she used an Other to man the front desk.

In the end, it was Lily who had managed to get her to do it.

Now that he thought about it, those two were thick as thieves as of late.

"I have a couple Others preparing a suit for you. A squad of guard Others are setting up in Gold.

"Miu, I've taken the liberty of alerting your people of the situation." Andrea looked up from her tablet, waiting for a response from either of them.

"Good work," Felix and Miu said in unison.

Ten minutes later to the second, Felix sat himself down in the conference room named Gold.

Lily sat to his right, Kit on his left, Miu a half step behind him.

There was also an Other in each corner, armed with SMGs.

The poorly named John Smith walked into the room, took a look around, and then held up his hands.

He looked to be in his early thirties, brown hair, blue eyes, nondescript. Neither tall nor short, overweight or skinny.

One of the Others immediately moved in and frisked him roughly and thoroughly. She pulled out a handgun from a shoulder holster underneath Smith's jacket. Opening the door, she handed the weapon to someone else and continued with her search.

"Wearing a wire, nothing else," the Other reported, moving back to her corner.

"A little paranoid, Mr. Campbell?" Mr. Smith asked, dropping his hands to the side.

"I am indeed.

"You may want to turn off your electronics. Maybe put them on the table, even. I'd hate for all the electronics on your person to go dead. This building tends to eat electronics at times. My people constantly complain about it," Felix said in a flat tone.

Mr. Smith looked up to the corners of the room, finding himself on two different cameras. "Uh-huh."

Taking out what appeared to be a phone, with an attached cord that came up through his sleeve, Smith set it on the table. Then he pulled out a second device as well.

He deliberately showed both being powered off, then pushed them to the middle of the table.

"What can I do for you today, Mr. Smith?" Felix asked.

"As I said to your receptionist, I'm an agent for the newly formed Department of Slave Affairs."

Pulling out an identification card, he flipped it open and held it out to Felix.

It read literally as he'd described.

Slave Affairs. John Smith. Investigator - Field Agent.

"I'm here as you're a registered slave owner. Specifically, a major holder. We're reaching out to those with a large interest in slaves to discuss changes we'll be implementing."

"I'm listening."

"Glad to hear that, Mr. Campbell. Specifically, there is going to be a tax on all income generated by a slave equal to four percent of the value. This went live last month and this'll be the first month that it'll come due for payment."

Lily was taking notes into a holographic projection from her tablet. Kit was staring through the man's head.

The Others behind Mr. Smith had their weapons trained on the man's back.

"Message received. Anything else?" Felix asked. He didn't care, nor did he really want to deal with this right now.

Mr. Smith blinked at the casual acceptance and dismissal.

"Next year, the loophole caused by paying your own slaves will be eliminated," said Smith.

"I understand. Anything else?" Felix repeated once more.

Mr. Smith smirked and then gestured at everyone around Felix. "Could we perhaps speak alone for two minutes? That's all the time I need."

Felix sighed and then nodded his head.

Lily had already spelled a shield around him. It would remain regardless of where she was. He was as safe as he could be already.

"Fine. Two minutes. Everyone, please clear the room. Make sure the recordings are paused."

As one, they closed up their workstations, tablets, and messenger bags, packed up, and left.

The last one out the door was Miu, who he imagined was probably now standing on the other side of the door waiting.

"You've built quite a harem," Mr. Smith said, smiling at Felix.

"What was it you wanted to discuss?"

Felix had other things he had to take care of today and his calendar was booked. After this, he was due to sit down and go over possible upgrades for the building.

"We both know there's a multitude of loopholes right now with the slave system. Our beloved leader made it legal, but didn't invest any time in its infrastructure. The system. Taxes. Anything, really.

"What'd be illegal elsewhere isn't so at all here."

Leaning forward, Felix spread his hands out in front of him. "And?"

"And I'd love to spend some time with your ladies. You let me stop by twice a month for an hour or so, and I'll make sure those taxes you owe disappear. As if you'd paid them already.

"I'd prefer either of the two who were sitting next to you, but I could go feral on that dog girl," Mr. Smith said.

Huh?

Felix had to concentrate for a second to realize Mr. Smith was suggesting he use Lily and Kit as payment in lieu of taxes.

"She's a wolf. And no thanks, I'll pass. Unless there's something else, I believe that we can conclude this meeting."

Standing up from his side of the table, Felix gestured to the two devices.

Mr. Smith smirked at Felix and then got up. He pocketed the devices and then paused.

"See you real soon, Mr. Campbell. My offer remains open. You know, in case something changes and you need help."

Turning his back to him, Mr. Smith left the conference room.

Immediately, Kit, Lily, Andrea, Miu, and the Others came back inside.

"Well! Now that we know about it, we can set aside taxes for it. Sounds like we need to have yet another finance meeting."

Lily watched him curiously.

No doubt she wants to know what happened after they left.

"Yes. We probably should. We're in some trouble, but nothing we can't work ourselves out of with proper budgeting of both our finances and your points."

"Great. Let's just… do it here. We should probably get lunch sent up." Felix sat back down with a sigh.

Almost as if they had been waiting for that statement, a crew of Others came in and began serving pancakes and fruit juice.

Andrea immediately sat herself down on his left side and pulled his plate in front of herself.

Several of the cook Others crowded around him, watching.

Felix knew where this was going. He closed his eyes with a groan, pressing his face to his hands.

"Say ahhhhhhh," Andrea Prime said from his left.

Chapter 21 - Point of View -

Felicia slapped a hand against the dark black metal. A solid thud came back, which was surprising.

"It looks like... medieval armor," Felix said, tapping a finger against the chestplate.

"Oh, aye. It is, really. It's what we could whip up on the fly. It'll stop everything up to a fifty-caliber sniper rifle." The dwarf seemed proud as she hooked her thumbs into the clasps of her overalls.

"This'll keep you safe from most things. We're working on other things, of course. Better things. This'll do for today, though."

To be fair, metal armor that looked this thin stopping a high-powered rifle round was impressive.

"Better than even full body armor. No loss of movement, and the weight is minimal. Certainly ain't fashionable, but that's not the point." Felicia reached up and pinged the helmet.

Fashionable, no. Not at all.

"Alright. And you've tested this?" Felix asked. Picking up the helmet, he set it to one side and then drew out the chestpiece.

"Andrea shot the material up quite a bit. No penetration," Felicia explained.

"Great. Good work, Felicia. You and your team are phenomenal."

"Thanks. It's nice to work without limits."

She picked up the gauntlets and handed them to Kit.

"He's your boy, you dress him. I'm leaving before I have to see anything I don't want to." Felicia trundled out of the room, Ioana following her with her eyes.

"Go, Ioana. I already have enough people watching me."

Ioana nodded at Felix's statement and followed the Dwarf out.

"They're interested in each other, they just haven't taken that first step yet," Kit said, running a finger over one of the armguards. "It's cute."

Felix grunted and inspected the armor.

Smooth, sleek, and made with elegant lines, it had the appearance of modern tech. It clearly couldn't be anything else but a suit of armor, though.

Made of interlocking plates, it was bound and secured against the black padding that it was mounted on.

"Guess I should put it on. We're supposed to meet Dimitry in an hour."

Andrea clapped her hands together and Others started to leap out of her.

When six Others were standing behind Andrea Prime, she lifted one hand above her head.

"Get 'im!"

Felix was brought down under a flurry of hands trying to undress him so they could stuff him into his new armor.

Kit stood on his right. Spread out in a semi-circle behind him were many, many, Others.

Ioana, Miu, and Lily had to remain to keep the whole business running, but also defend it.

To that end, those three, plus Kit and Andrea, were all boosted at three hundred percent of their power.

"Remind me to go through the upgrades when we're done here. I keep putting it off."

"Sure thing, dear!" Andrea Prime said happily from beside him. She was dressed in a jacket, blouse, and pencil skirt that she'd taken as her uniform.

Tapping something into her tablet, she shifted her weight back and forth.

In sharp contrast to that, every Andrea around in the area was on sharp-eyed vigilance. They were all decked out in pantsuits, ballistic vests, and SMGs under their jackets.

He'd managed to convince her to buy a mass of the vests and hand them out to her Others.

At long last, the door to the restaurant opened. Dimitry stood there, staring at Felix in his suit of armor.

"Felix?" Dimitry asked slowly.

"Yup. Sorry. Going out in public has been a problem as of late. Can we come in?"

Dimitry nodded his head and then stepped aside, holding the door open for them.

He'd kept them waiting for twenty-some odd minutes.

"I apologize for the delay. There was some… dispute about people being excused from this test."

Felix waved a gauntleted hand at him. "No worries, no worries. Andrea, spread out and cordon off the building. Only bring a few in with you. We should be safe here," Felix said, turning his head to Andrea Prime as he passed Dimitry.

"Yes, dear."

Andrea stopped and looked towards her Others, who all looked to her. In an instant, they split up without any form of communication.

Once again, Felix had to wonder how they managed that. Was it a psychic link, or something else?

Two Others, Andrea, Kit, and himself were led into the basement. The last time they'd stepped foot here, they'd been on a mission of death and destruction.

This time it was a favor.

Hopefully there isn't a body count this time.

Dimitry opened a door that hadn't been there the last time they had come through. Inside was a large number of men and women sitting in chairs, standing around, and generally just waiting.

There was even a number of people hogtied and laid out along one wall.

"It's like that horror movie we watched the other day.

"You're not going to wear one of their faces like a mask, are you?" Andrea asked, looking at Dimitry.

"Ah, no.

"You can start with whoever." Dimitry flipped a hand at the people in the room.

Felix had expected it, to a degree. This wouldn't do at all. It'd reveal far too much about Kit's abilities.

"Do you have a room we can work out of? One-on-one interviews will get us the best results," Felix asked, turning his head to the crime boss.

"Hmph. Yeah, we can do that. Over there, it's an office that isn't being used."

Andrea pointed at one of the Others, who took off at a jog to inspect the room. After half a minute, she waved them on.

Felix took a chair in the corner and pulled off his helmet. Then he gestured to the chair behind the desk. "All yours, madam interrogator."

"Thank you. Thank you for both getting us out of that room, and the seat. I didn't really want to interview them in that room, with everyone watching." Kit sat down, adjusting her dress and blouse with a few gentle tugs.

"Stop, you look great."

"Really?" Kit asked, looking up at Felix.

"Course. Now get ready, Dimitry will probably start sending people in."

"The room is clean, no one listening or watching," one of the Others said.

Only a second or two later, two men brought in a bound and struggling third man and dropped him in the chair in front of the desk. "Him first."

Without another word, the two men left, closing the door behind them.

Kit smiled and flipped open a pad of paper and met the man's eyes.

"Let's begin."

To Felix, it was interesting. He imagined she probably had all the answers she needed within seconds of meeting the man.

Yet she spent time asking him questions, prodding at his answers, and generally conducting what felt like a police interview.

After a while, though, he noticed that her questions weren't linear. They tended to flow from the last question alright, but in a strange direction. Almost as if she was reading a thought and asked a question to clarify his answer, and read his mind at the same time.

After five minutes, and most of his responses being one-word answers, Kit had the two Others drag him out.

"Not a cop. Steals a lot, though. Has gone informant on a few people in the organization he didn't like, but not on the organization itself," Kit said, jotting something down.

"Oh. Did you know that right up front, or...?" Felix asked as the door closed behind the Others.

"I knew most of it up front. The questions help focus their mind on the thoughts I want.

"I couldn't read Smith very well the other day. He kept his thoughts close. I'd almost suspect him of having a minor-level telepath skill.

"This interview was easy in comparison. Certainly a lot easier since you… upgraded me.

"Still weird to say that."

Felix made a soft "hm" noise and settled into his chair.

After a few minutes, the Others dragged in the next person.

Twenty-some odd interviews later, Kit changed her approach.

It was subtle; he almost missed it.

She didn't write anything as the Others escorted a young man to the chair. Every other time, she'd already been writing as they brought the subject in.

The man looked scrappy, his face sporting a few scars, and angry eyes.

He seemed much like everyone else they'd interviewed. Built in a physical manner and clearly well suited to being part of a crime syndicate.

When the door shut, Kit laid her pen down on the paper.

"Pretty impressive. Pulling off a deep cover that long without being caught." Kit said in a complimentary fashion.

The two Others in the corners pulled out their weapons and drew a bead on the man in the chair.

Looking from one gun to the other, the man deflated in his chair, his hands resting on his knees.

"That easy, huh?" he said softly.

"That easy. Six years is a long time to be a deep cover cop."

"Huh. Yeah. Doesn't matter, though, when mind readers are playing merc, does it."

"Not really. Don't blame her, though, she's here because of me. So watch your tongue or I'll have one of the Others pull it out.

"That or we take you back home and put you in the sausage machine. Right after Mab gets a shot at you," Felix said, leaning forward, suddenly eager.

"Sausage machine?"

"Yeah. First we give you to Mab, she eats your soul, then we put your living body in this machine. It turns you into sausage that empowers people who eat it.

"Haven't tried it myself, but quite a few of my people swear it's tasty."

"It's gamey," Andrea said from beside him. "Didn't like it."

The cop looked from Felix to Kit.

"Tell you what. I figured this might happen, expected it, really, so I brought something," Felix said. Holding out his hand to Andrea, she set a sheaf of papers into his open hand.

"You can work for me, become an indentured servant, and continue on as a policeman. You get to keep your job, and get paid for both, while being in Dimitry's organization. Or I tell Dimitry you're a cop, and I get your soul anyways, and turn you into sausage. Your call."

"Why not make him a slave?" Andrea asked.

"That'd require a lot more effort and taking him down to a government-sanctioned slave officer. Can't just force anyone to be a slave, after all."

Silence took over. For ten seconds, no one said anything.

"What would you have me do?" asked the cop in a soft voice.

"Dunno. Probably have you feed bad information to your cop pals. Make you swear to say nothing about me, or my organization, to anyone. Honestly, I'd probably just have you feed me info."

Felix shrugged his shoulders and then dropped the contract in front of the policeman.

"Read it over if you like, but time's ticking. If we run out, or you say no, then we go on to the sausage option."

"No need to wait. I already have an answer. I'll be your damned servant. You leave me little choice. They'd go after my family if they found out."

"Two children and a wife," Kit said. "They live about an hour from here. We'll be able to protect them once you sign on."

The man blinked, staring at Kit.

Felix tapped the papers in front of the cop. "Read, sign, and then take this." Felix set down a pushpin next to the paper. "Poke a finger, smear some blood in that circle in the corner. Voila, you'll be done after that. Contract signed and magically binding. As easy as that. Then we move right along as if nothing happened."

The cop picked up the top few papers and started to scan through them. "Could you give me the abbreviated version?"

"Sure. Too long, didn't read, coming up.

"You work for me. You discuss nothing of me, or the organization, with anyone outside of it.

"You'll be paid for your work according to market value.

"You'll receive health and dental benefits.

"You'll be enrolled in a 401k.

"Your family will receive a life insurance payout if you die in the line of duty.

"Your life cannot be spent recklessly.

"Contract is valid for one year.

"That's the gist of it, really."

The cop frowned and squinted at Felix. "That sounds very... corporate."

"I guess? We're a company. We are Legion. Money is our goal."

The cop frowned, picked up the pen, and signed. Taking up the pushpin, he pricked his thumb. A bead of blood welled up. The cop pressed the blood droplet into the corner.

With a hiss, the blood boiled away, only to leave a nasty red stain.

"I feel like Faust."

"Hardly. If you were Faust, you'd be stuck for all eternity. This is only a year," Felix said. Picking up the contract, he signed it, then handed it over to Kit.

Taking the pen from him, she signed her own name at the bottom where it listed, "HR representative."

"I'll arrange your onboarding and orientation. It'll probably be sometime next week, when we have a new class starting," Kit said, tucking the paper away.

"Seriously?"

"Yup. Whatever, time for you to go... what's your name again? Never mind, doesn't matter. I'll probably not see you again. Your supervisor will work with you." Felix gestured to the man while making eye contact with the Others.

Picking the man up under the arms, they escorted him out.

Dimitry sat down in the interviewee chair and looked to Kit. "Well?"

"One thief who moonlights as an informant on occasion when he finds someone he doesn't like.

"That's it, though." Kit tore out the page she had taken her notes on. Giving it a final glance, she set it down in front of Dimitry. "There's all the notes you'll need."

"Huh," Dimitry said, reading over paper. "Handy."

"She's irreplaceable. Now, if that's taken care of, I think we'll be leaving," Felix said, standing up.

"Yeah, yeah. Thanks," Dimitry murmured, waving a lazy hand at them.

The Others left the room, leading the way.

Kit, Andrea, and Felix fell in behind them, moving to the exit without another word for anyone.

Hitting the street in under a minute, they started off for their convoy of cars parked nearby.

Halfway to the car, something crashed into the pavement nearby.

All around him, gunfire opened up as a man-shaped monster stood up. Dressed all in red, it roared and lifted its arms.

In its hand was a mangled Other, the head of the poor Andrea twisted all the way around and her chest flattened as if she'd been hit by a steamroller and dragged under.

Bullets sank into the hulking mound of muscle with no apparent effect.

Pulling the head off the dead woman, the man hurled it at a different Other. The gory projectile smashed into her leg and bent it backwards with a crack.

Kit, Andrea, and Felix took several steps back as the Others went to work. They moved in a wolf pack formation, the one behind firing to keep the monster busy, as the ones in front kept its attention moving.

"Kit, can you drop him?" Felix asked.

"No. I never could get into his head when he was on my team, and I can't now."

"What?" Felix's question was cut off as a bloody arm zipped by his head. It'd only missed because Andrea shoved him to one side, keeping him safe.

"His name's Tanker, he worked with—"

A lightning bolt tore free from the top of a building and hit Felix in the chest. The armor seemingly was built to take such a hit, and the lightning vanished.

The boom of the thunder practically rattled Felix's teeth out of his head.

Felix was pitched forward as something slammed into his back. Rolling head over heels, he fetched up behind an Other and dashed off towards the convoy.

Where he'd been a moment ago, there now stood a humanoid shadow with a blade, trying to fend off Andrea Prime. He could only barely make out the edges of the form, as it seemed to blend with the very shadows it resembled.

Apparently, Felicia's armor really could stand up to most anything.

Kit picked up the blurry wraith from the ground and levitated it into the air. Setting off at a run, Kit and Andrea joined him near the cars.

The struggling shadow was slammed into the ground several times, each bone-cracking pavement slap eliciting a groan.

Kit lifted the fellow and held them still. The moment the shadow twitched, she slammed them back into the ground again.

There was no further movement after that.

Andrea popped open the trunk while eyeing the ongoing fight with the savage monster man. Pulling out a set of jumper cables, she bound the shadow up, then tossed it into the trunk.

"We should get out of here," Kit said. "They won't be able to hold Tanker forever, and Bolt is still out there. That still leaves — "

"Well, I never. If it isn't Augur."

A man in a yellow-and-black spandex suit stood a few feet off. Even his head was covered in the material.

"You're looking great lately. If I di—"

Andrea buried the shadow's blade in the man's gut and ripped it upwards. Intestines spilled out of the man's stomach like spaghetti pouring out of a pot.

Whipping the blade back the other way, she decapitated the man. The shiny body suit material snapping down towards his bloody midsection as the head came free.

Picking up the head, which actually rolled its eyes, she tossed it at Tanker.

"Reabsorb and retreat!" Andrea called out. Getting into the driver's seat, she twisted the ignition immediately.

Kit and Felix wasted no time and got in.

Andrea slammed the gas before the doors had even closed and had them off like a shot.

Another lightning bolt crackled to life and shattered the road in front of them.

Andrea cranked the steering wheel one way, then the other, avoiding the massive ditch with a few scant centimeters to spare.

"He won't be giving up that easy. We'll need to keep an eye out. He lands one and the battery is toast," Kit just about yelled.

"Hmph." Andrea spun the wheel and took them off down an alley, the rear quarter panel rebounding off a wall.

"I texted Ioana and Miu. They'll lock down the facility and keep watch," Kit said, tucking her phone away.

"Kit, they knew you, you know them." Felix looked out the rear window as Others scrambled in every direction, absorbing the dead and escaping in multiple directions.

"They're former heroes, Felix. Of course I know them. I worked with them often enough. They were supposed to be there when we tried to take out Skipper." Kit was grasping the "Oh God" handle above her, her other hand pressed to the dashboard.

"You fought Skipper?" Andrea asked, skidding them out of the alley and into a street.

Horns went off all around them as she nearly hit several cars as she drifted through.

"I think so. Felix took my memories of the period before we... before we ended up as slaves. One of the last memories I have is of starting to draw up plans on how to fight Skipper. It was just after they'd entered the city and started to take over."

"Okay, so I've never heard who or what Skipper really is. Who is he? She?" Felix tightened his seatbelt after Andrea recovered from the multilane skid and blew through a red light.

"We don't know. We think it's a man, but we're not sure. Or at least, we weren't at the time. Maybe I should get those memories back from you soon."

"Yeah, sure, whatever. Let's just get the fuck home first, yeah?"

Andrea drifted through another turn and wiped out a speed limit sign, the metal post snapping and going flying off behind them.

"This is fun! Maybe we could do this some other time."

"Without the bad guys chasing us."

"We are the bad guys," Kit lamented.

"No we're not! We didn't attack them, they attacked us! Didn't ask us a question or anything. Bad guys do that," Andrea cheerfully crowed as she brought them out of the curve.

"They did, didn't they..." Kit said softly.

Chapter 22 - Old Friends -

As they sped along the streets, Felix had the distinct impression things weren't getting better.

Maybe it was the shadow they'd thrown in the trunk. Or the Others being slaughtered. Or the fact that Kit seemed nervous.

Or the massive flying, angry, screaming man that landed on the roof of the car.

Crumpling as if it were a soda can, the car folded in on itself.

Shouting with rage, the man known as Tanker started ripping handfuls of the roof off.

Andrea pulled a pistol out of somewhere and rammed the nose of it up into the man's junk, then pulled the trigger.

The yelling turned into shrieking as Andrea emptied the entire clip.

A massive hand came down swatting at her, before leaping free of the ruined car.

Andrea's arm was bent at an unnatural angle at the forearm. After a second, blood began pumping as the wrist and hand detached and fell free from her forearm.

The massive monster had managed to tear off Andrea's lower arm in a single hit.

Andrea screamed in pain, clutching to the wheel with the other hand as she kept them moving.

Felix leaned over the console and reached down towards Kit's midsection.

Grabbing a hold of her skirt, he yanked at it.

"Felix, this isn't the time!" shrieked Kit, her eyes wild as she looked at him.

"I need your belt," Felix replied. Pulling at her skirt again, he got eyes on the prize.

Unbuckling it, he snatched it free of her skirt and then grabbed the stump of Andrea's arm.

Looping the belt quickly around the elbow joint, he cinched it incredibly tight and looped it back around. Giving it a final jerk, he tucked the belt loop into itself.

"That'll hold you while I fix it. Keep going while I see if I can get your arm to grow back."

Felix called up Andrea's character sheet, then dismissed it when a thought came to him.

Half of Andrea's problem was she had no resiliency.

"Fuck it," Felix said, focusing on the idea of giving her extreme and controlled regeneration.

Third Power (Unlock): Directed Complete Regeneration	Required Stamina: 70 (Unmet) Required Intelligence: 40 (Unmet)	Upgrade? (35,000)

Felix immediately upgraded Andrea's stamina to seventy, and her intelligence to forty, and then upgraded her with a third power.

Name: Andrea Elex	Power: Multiple Self Projections	
Alias: Andrea, Andie, Lex.	Secondary Power: Partitioned Mind	
Physical Status: Wounded	Third Power: Directed Complete Regeneration	
Positive Statuses: None	Mental Status: Concerned	
	Negative Statuses: Bleeding	
Strength:	44	Upgrade? (440)
Dexterity:	62	Upgrade? (620)
Agility:	71	Upgrade? (710)
Stamina:	70	Upgrade? (700)
Wisdom:	81	Upgrade? (810)
Intelligence:	40	Upgrade? (400)
Luck:	53	Upgrade? (530)
Primary Power:	31	Upgrade? (3,100)
Secondary Power:	79	Upgrade? (7,900)
Third Power:	50	Upgrade? (5,000)

Andrea shuddered, her head dipping forward as the power opened inside her mind.

She groaned, dodging a head-on collision by inches as they barreled along.

Felix glanced at her right arm as he grabbed the wheel, keeping them in the right lane even if he couldn't control their speed.

From the ruins of her right forearm, the bones shifted, muscle growing outward, and skin immediately covering it. In a handful of seconds, her arm was regrown and whole.

"What'd you do?" Andrea asked groggily, her head lolling towards him.

"Gave you a third power. Andrea. Andrea! I need you to focus. Please. You're driving."

What was left of the roof tore off suddenly and went hurtling away.

A lightning bolt crackled across the street and caught Felix in the chest.

The armor took the hit, but the force of it sent him careening into the back seat this time. His helmeted head clanged off the glass and shattered it.

Groaning, Felix tried to move but felt like his arms and legs were made of pudding. Nothing was responding to his commands.

"Felix!"

Another lightning bolt zipped by as Andrea spun the wheel end over end, sending them down a cross street.

They bounced off another car and wiped out a mailbox as they went, car parts and letters filling the air.

Sitting up, Felix found himself staring at Tanker at the end of the street.

They herded us here.

It looked like they could swerve around him.

Felix's head was pounding. He couldn't tell if it was the lightning or using so many points so fast.

"I can't move him, he's too heavy," Kit called out.

"Brace yourself, Kit, and act as soon as you can," Felix said, calling open Kit's window.

He pushed her second power all the way to ninety, then focused on the idea of giving her another power.

Illusions. Illusions to the point of physical manifestations.

Third Power (Unlock) : Illusions (Physical Projections)	Required Intelligence: 70 (Met) Required Wisdom: 70 (Met)	Upgrade? (60,000)

Felix mentally slapped at the upgrade button.

Kit wavered in her seat, a hand coming up to her brow.

Tanker was seconds away.

Then he was sent tumbling to one side by a gigantic fist.

He blew through a wall and disappeared into the interior.

Blowing past at near seventy miles an hour, Felix only had the brief flash of the man Andrea had gutted and decapitated.

He was covered in blood and looked fine, hiding behind a wall.

Looking back, Felix saw the man lift a rifle to his shoulder.

"Down!" Felix shouted, standing up and lifting his arms behind the heads of Kit and Andrea.

Heavy rounds slammed into his back and arms, drilling him into the back of the headrests.

Andrea took another turn at incredible speeds. The tires skipped and skidded across the road as their rear end swung out behind them.

The car smashed into a streetlight with the fury of a wrecking ball. Unfortunately, streetlights didn't give way as much as street signs.

The rear right tire exploded from the impact, the car lurching towards the left.

Andrea floored it and took them into a parking garage. The wooden arm of the toll gate exploded into a shower of splinters as the car zoomed by.

Felix slumped into the rear seat, feeling as if he'd been beaten with a rubber hose all over his body.

Squealing around another turn, Andrea rushed up a ramp towards the second floor.

Grinding and scraping filled the entire parking complex as whatever was left of the tire went flying away.

Taking another ramp, Andrea bounced the car off a cement wall, and then off another car.

Feeling a lot like the ball in a pinball machine, Felix pressed his hands to both sides of his helmet.

"Sorry, handles like a bathtub on wheels right now. One more ramp?"

"One more ramp," Kit said, nodding her head.

Andrea charged the dying vehicle up another ramp, spinning them around the turn and bouncing the rear end from wall to wall.

Each crunch and impact left paint and bits of the car everywhere.

She pulled them into a secluded corner next to the slotted openings that looked out over the street below.

Felix hung his head, then crumpled completely into the floorboards of the back seat.

Eventually he felt hands on him. Hands struggling to get him moving. Or at the very least out of the car.

"Come on, Felix, time to go. We don't want to be here when they arrive."

"Yeah, yeah," Felix muttered. Trying to get to his feet, he got two steps before he collapsed to the cement.

"Oh, can't forget. I'll get the shadow," Andrea said.

There was the pop of the car trunk, and the thump of a body hitting the ground.

"Over here, Andie." There was the shriek of metal being torn and then the clang as it was dropped to the ground.

"Drop him on, then get Felix on it. Hold on tight to both of them. Not sure if this'll work, but... at this point, it's our best shot."

Felix was dragged a short distance and dropped. Then Andrea was there, holding tightly to him and pressing him to the ground.

Closing his eyes, Felix tried to get his brain working. Between the lightning bolt, the adrenaline wearing off, and probably spending so many points, he felt drained.

The world around him jolted.

Opening his eyes, Felix turned his head and saw the dead man, Tanker, and what looked like a living bolt of lightning sprinting up from the ramp.

The ground shuddered again, and then of all things, the ground vanished.

Rather than the simple sensation of floating away, Felix realized he really was. Floating away, that is.

As quickly as it had started, they were outside of the parking complex and speeding off into the sky.

Looking down, he realized they were on hood of the car.

Twisting his head around the other way, he found Kit standing nearby, her arms spread out in front of her.

A lightning bolt came out from the parking complex but died halfway to them as Kit continued to pour on the speed.

In a couple of heartbeats, they were soaring through the sky towards home.

"This is amazing," Andrea said.

"Felix boosted my power set again. Considerably so. Gave me the ability to make living illusions. Actual physical projections."

"He made me regenerate to the point that I think it'd be very hard to kill me. He also moved my intelligence up again," Andrea replied.

"Not sure how I feel about that. I think... I think I might now understand some things I wish I didn't."

Slowly, hesitantly, both women started to laugh as the wind whipped by them.

Felix closed his eyes and let himself drift off for a moment. They had it under control. They didn't need him right now.

Jolting upright as the car hood slammed into the ground, Felix looked around.

They'd touched down in the garage bay.

Home sweet home.

Felix sighed and slumped where he sat. It'd probably only been a few minutes that he'd drifted off, but he felt better for it.

"You okay?" Andrea asked. She was in front of him, bending down to meet his eyes.

"Yeah. Tired, but okay." Felix got to his feet, his armor creaking.

Kit clapped her hands together and then stretched her back out. "That was certainly unexpected. Though it definitely gives us some ideas as to who's been attacking us."

Felix reached up to pull the helmet off his head. Pulling at the locking latch under his jaw, he grunted when it came free.

The fresh, cool air bathing his head reminded him of why he generally despised hats and helmets. It always felt like he was being smothered in his own sweat.

"And what ideas are those?" Felix pulled his helmet up under his arm and looked around.

Everything seemed fine. There wasn't anything going on or out of the ordinary. Which meant the attack had been aimed primarily at him and no one else.

"Heroes association. Those were all heroes. Wraith here"—Kit indicated the living shadow bound at their feet—"is a hero. As was Tanker, Lizard, and Bolt."

"Okay?" Felix stood up. Ioana and Miu were going to lock everything down, or so he remembered. The fact that they weren't here was a little disturbing.

Maybe they're at a different location making sure everything is secure? This would be the most likely location to get through an attack without them.

The automated defenses that Felicia had been putting up were formidable. Turrets, locking bulwark doors, electrified rooms. She'd really gone for the full "supervillains hideout" cliché.

"That means that the people we've been fighting this whole time would seem to be the hero association. I honestly… didn't even consider it."

"Oh, but I did," said a cool voice.

Looking over, he found Lily walking towards him.

"Did you miss me?" she asked, walking up to Felix.

"Maybe. Though I think you missed teasing me more." Felix pointed at the paper she had in her hand. "Got something for me?"

"I sure do." Lily walked up and tapped his breastplate with a single fingertip. "I also have information."

"Stop flirting and tell him. I'm going to take Wraith here to 'the room' in the meantime. Meet me there," Kit said. She grabbed hold of one of Wraith's ankles and dragged them off.

Lily sniffed delicately, then held out the paper to him. "The hearing with those lawyers was indeed a setup. The entire firm was purchased by a holding company.

"Tracing that company took some time, it went through a couple others of course, but we found it went back to, surprise, the hero association."

Felix read over the paper, which listed out the owner of each company as it moved back up towards the real owner.

"Huh. Seems almost too easy," Felix muttered. He looked up from the paper to find Lily watching him with a smile.

"It was. So either they're incredibly stupid, and underestimated us, or they're a puppet.

"Oh, did I also mention someone is opening up pawn shops next door to ours at every location?"

"Huh? That's… strange." Felix handed the paper back to Lily.

Felix had noticed Andrea had been coming in closer, slowly, out of the corner of his eye.

Now she wedged herself between Lily and himself.

Both he and Lily looked at her with a bit of a surprise.

"I don't like it when you're so close to him," Andrea said. Her voice was soft, almost the point they couldn't hear her.

Then she looked from Lily to Felix and turned a bright red. Pressing her hands to her face, she fled, her tail hanging low behind her.

"What... did you do?" Lily asked. She'd watched Andrea leave, but now turned her eyes back on him.

"I raised her intelligence. It was the only way I could give her a new power." Felix shrugged.

Lily made a humming noise and tilted her head to one side. "I'll talk with her. No more upgrading people without consulting me." Lily smacked his forehead with the rolled-up sheet of paper. "I'm your account manager, both monetary and points; don't do things without consulting me."

"Yes, dear," Felix said in a mocking voice.

"Good, so long as you understand. How am I expected to balance the household income otherwise?

"And about our budget. We'll need to rely on you making our money for a while. These pawn shops are literally doing everything they can to drive us out of business."

"Huh. What exactly are they doing?" Felix set the helmet down at his feet, then reached up and started to take off his armor.

"Oh, the usual. Undercut our prices, buy things for more, sell them for less. Honestly, they're probably hemorrhaging money doing it.

"They're definitely making more money than we are, though, since we're not making any at all.

"Without you backstopping our finances, we'd be out of business in a few months."

Felix frowned at that, dropping the breastplate and its undergarment to the ground. "Which means they knew our finances when they concocted this plan, but not the extent of my powers. Interesting."

Scratching at his bare chest, Felix thought on that.

Reaching down, he pulled his boots off.

"I would almost think we had a rat, except for the fact that no one can discuss anything about us, with anyone. Maybe I should look into upgrading the building with anti-listening measures."

Lily nodded after a moment and then leveled her paper at his chest. "You've lost weight."

"Huh? Oh. Yeah. Miu and Ioana kick my ass daily, then make me work out." Felix looked down at himself as he spoke. He'd had a tummy when he'd been working. Free fast food saved money, even if it did nothing for his physique.

"Not eating fast food every day probably helped as well."

"Hm. Get a haircut and start shaving more regularly. You're not unattractive as you are, but with a little work, you might actually get a girlfriend."

"Heh. Who wants to date a slaveowner and be bound by an oath to not speak of anything they saw?

"No. My social life will be even worse than it used to be, I'm afraid."

"Why not date an employee, then? I'm sure there would be those who were willing."

"That seems almost worse. No way to tell if they were dating me for the perks, or for me."

Felix reached down and got the lower portion of his armor free.

After a second, he got it unlatched and stepped out of it, letting it clatter to the ground.

"Gah, free. Free at last." Felix twisted himself one way, then the other, getting his spine to pop.

Lily met his gaze with a smirk. She deliberately ran her eyes down along him slowly and then back up.

For whatever reason, getting out of his armor had taken precedence over caring that he was only wearing boxers underneath.

Now, however, standing such in front of Lily, he was forced to realize that this had not been a good idea.

Lily had no interest other than provoking and prodding him. And all he'd done was give her an easy target.

The fuck is wrong with me? Like something out of a terrible movie.

"Uh. I think I want a shower."

"Is that so? We can continue this discussion in your bathroom, then."

"Ah, no. That's fine. We can pick this up later."

Felix turned and marched off with as much dignity as he could muster.

Chapter 23 - Reactionary -

Felix had set himself up in the appraisal room for customers and clients.

There weren't any, since everyone was going to the competing pawn shop, but he still wanted to keep to his schedule.

To keep himself busy, he was going over the available upgrades and point purchases he could make.

"Dense materials. All exterior surfaces and materials are upgraded. Prevents listening equipment and superpowers from hearing anything inside the building. One-hundred twenty-five thousand."

"That sounds nice," Andrea said. She was seated at the end of his appraisal table, working on her tablet.

"Mm. Definitely seems like something worth taking. Add it to the list."

Andrea made a musical noise in the affirmative.

Felix kept reading through the listed improvements. There were a number of them that didn't seem to be worth the cost.

Stain-resistant floors. Upgraded insulation. Energy-efficient lights.

Felix shook his head and closed the window. They'd already gone through and picked out the ones that would be useful.

"Can you read the list back to me?"

"Mm-hmm." Andrea tapped at her tablet and then cleared her throat. She opened her mouth, and then stopped.

After a second, she dropped the tablet and turned her chair around to face him. "Actually, I want to ask you a favor."

Felix waited patiently. Andrea being serious was something out of the ordinary. "I'm listening."

"You... made me smarter."

"I did."

"Twice."

Felix had to think about that for a moment, but he nodded his head. He had indeed moved her intelligence up previously as well.

"I... understand things I didn't before. Things that seem obvious to me now."

"Okay. I'm not sure if you're complaining, or..."

Andrea gave him a small smile. "Maybe I am. Well, I'd like to ask if you can upgrade my powers."

Felix nodded his head. The request wasn't surprising. Not really. Not when he thought about it.

"Okay. And what do you want me to upgrade exactly?"

"When I... when I take in my Others. I take in all of their memories. And if they're dead, I take in their memories of their death.

"After a while, it... it can be overwhelming. All those memories of death. The pain. The suffering that comes right before. The emptiness and loneliness."

I can only imagine.

"After a while, I have to create a Death Other. I give them all my memories of death, the pain, the horrible things that happen. Then I send them out. They normally head to places that could use a vigilante.

"Where they can put our skills to use while trying to live with the burden we've given them."

"I see."

"I want you to upgrade me so that I can choose the memories I take back. That I can leave out the ones I don't want."

Andrea looked at him with wide eyes, her hands clasped in her lap, gripping each other.

It explained her partitioned mind power, as well as why she seemed disturbed and happy at the same time.

"I'll see what I can pull up. Why don't you call Lily in while I do that?" Felix turned back to the table. Focusing on her power, he tried to encapsulate everything she'd told him as part of an upgrade to her existing powers.

That and so that it didn't take as much out of her with each clone.

Power Upgrade: Multiple Self Projections	Required Primary Power: 40 (Unmet)	Upgrade? (5,000)
Power Upgrade: Partitioned Mind	Required Secondary Power: 50 (Met)	Upgrade? (5,000)

Expensive when you count in the cost of getting her up to Primary Power forty. Something like forty-five thousand points.

"You rang, dar-ling?"

Felix glanced up from his power screen. Lily was perched on her elbows on his table, her face resting in her palms.

"Yeah. Andrea wants an upgrade to her power set. Total cost is around forty-five thousand points. I think it's worth the cost. As far as I can tell, there's nothing on the point calendar today, either."

"There isn't. And no, I don't disagree with you on the upgrade for her." Lily's eyes flicked to the wolf girl, then back to him. "Though you'll need to upgrade Ioana, Miu, and Felicia after this as well. It wouldn't be fair otherwise."

Felix sighed, pressing a hand to his temple.

She was right, of course. Doing so much for Kit, Lily, and Andrea put him in a strange spot for the other three.

"Yeah. You're right."

"I know I am. Your point calendar is empty tomorrow as well, we were just going to have you make gold. Our finances are doing well enough in our other investments that we can spare the points."

Lily stood up, rearranged herself, then moved to sit next to him on his left.

Felix accepted the upgrade for Andrea as he turned to Miu in the corner. "Come on over, Miu. We'll do yours next."

Lily's head snapped around to where Felix had spoken to.

"I want nothing," Miu said from the shadows.

"You sure? Could give you the ability to blend in with shadows. Actually become one."

Miu was silent. The spot that he thought was her shifted. Barely.

"I will consider it. For now, nothing."

"As you will."

Felix sighed and looked to Andrea. "So? Was that what you wanted?"

Andrea gave herself a visible shake, her eyes turning to him. "Yes. Yes, it is. I'm... I'm going to go. I need to call my Death Others and bring them home. Those who are alive, at least."

Getting to her feet, Andrea moved to leave, her tail swishing back and forth behind her energetically.

Stopping at the door, she turned to him. She gave him a bright, warm smile. "Thank you, Felix. I'll repay you."

Then she opened the door and stepped out.

"My, my. I think she even gave me butterflies with that," Lily whispered in Felix's ear.

Flinching away from her, Felix tried to ignore her completely. "With that many points spent, I'd rather keep the rest just in case. Besides, we really could use the money."

"Not a bad thought. Just make sure you get back to Felicia and Ioana soon. And Miu, too, if she figures out what she wants."

Felix could only agree. Now the rest of the day sat ahead of him. There were no appointments scheduled, which meant it'd be time to catch up on paperwork.

"So. What ever shall we talk about?" Lily asked, smiling. "How about the fact that those boxers you had on the other day looked like they were ten years old?"

Felix was making the rounds today. Visiting each department, asking about the few people he knew by name, trying to learn the names of a few more.

Everywhere he went, he found people working hard in their various jobs and tasks.

He also got a chance to really explore the layout on foot, as blueprints and maps only did so much for him.

In his head, he now divided each "section" by three floors. For each section, there was one communal dining hall, a number of training rooms, classes, supply depots, section stores, armories, restrooms, kitchen, morgue, conference rooms, meeting hall, a number of break rooms, and a good number of recreation areas.

Felicia had truly aimed at producing in each section everything someone could ask for in their lives.

People worked shifts, were given an allowance, and could socialize freely. Nothing was restricted to them, except speaking of the organization.

Outside internet connections weren't available on personal PCs. It was accessible at public computers, through a VPN and firewall that scrubbed everything going out and in.

Somewhere along the line, they'd picked up a rather proficient IT team.

Then there was the other side of the "underground world," as some had taken to calling it.

The departments. With the main elevator bays acting as a central hub, half of the section was divided into the departments. The work areas.

Residential and commercial zones did not overlap.

Thumbing the biometric lock to get into the R&D lab, Felix waited for the door.

Mr. White had hired a team of people to work for him. All with the approval of HR and magically enforced Indentured contracts.

Every time he visited, which wasn't as often as he'd have liked, but probably more than he needed to, there was something new.

Felicia's team shared the workspace with him. Mundane engineers and supers working side by side to create the best tech for Legion.

The big security door moved aside, the three-inch-thick steel ominously silent.

Walking in, he found Mr. White and one of his team members fiddling with what looked for all the world like a soda can.

If soda cans glowed and had circuity that seemed to guide that glow.

Felix said nothing, as he didn't want to interrupt their conversation, but instead took a seat and merely watched.

The team member took the can and inserted it into a slot at the bottom of a box-like contraption.

With a flick of a switch, the box started to glow and gently hum.

"Good, take it to Felicia." Mr. White shooed the assistant off and turned to face Felix.

"Good afternoon."

"Good afternoon, Mr. White."

"You just witnessed the first time we had a successful energy cell power up something other than itself."

"The soda can?"

"Exactly. That soda can could power everything in this building for a few hours.

"And with that successful test, we've now solved the problem we had with our energy weapons. There was no way to supply a sufficient amount of energy, to create reliable weapons.

"Sure, it'd fire once or twice by conventional means, but that was it."

Felix had to admit that sounded like a pretty terrible problem. Why take a weapon that can fire twice, when you could take a firearm that could put hundreds of rounds downrange easily and still fire more.

"We should have a working prototype in a week. Felicia built a machine that creates those soda cans.

"Works off a similar principle to how Lily charges things, I guess."

"Makes sense. And yeah, that sounds like Felicia. Anything she can think up, she can probably build. Provided she can think it up."

Felix held out one hand towards Mr. White.

"How goes the progress with th—"

A deep rumbling brought Felix up short. He could even feel it on his body.

This particular lab was rather far below surface level, which meant whatever had just happened was huge.

Then the emergency lights started flashing, and a low buzzing could be heard.

"We're under attack," Mr. White said, looking up at one of the flashing lights.

"Take your position, then." Felix moved over to the security door and thumbed it open.

He'd be needed in central control. Being able to repair anyone, or anything, from anywhere in the building, made him invaluable.

But he had to see what was going on.

Another deep rumble overtook him. It was louder this time.

Did they fucking nuke us?

Setting off at a run, Felix felt like he couldn't get there quick enough.

Eight soldiers, as they couldn't have been anything else in the gear they were wearing, in front of the vault door for central command and security saw him coming. They were armed in what looked as if a modern-day soldier had gone through a science fiction novel.

Each was armed with a machine gun that was mounted to an exo-frame that was issued to the elite forces in Legion.

The weapons were belt fed from a backpack that hung off the back of the exo-frame.

Their tactical gear had the feel of blast gear that didn't seem to encumber them at all.

Their helmets were the stuff out of comic books. Much like the rest of their armor, it was dark, sleek, metallic. An eyepiece over one side of the dark black visor added to the strange look of it.

He'd seen these soldiers training with Andrea and Ioana. He knew they were superior in many ways. Quick, strong, determined, intelligent.

Those exo-frames weren't a joke either, and could power them along as fast as an Olympic sprinter for as long as they had power. They could lift things far beyond their capacity as a normal human.

Those frames put them on a level with low-powered supers.

Each of the fifty exo-frames they possessed had been created by Felicia's team by hand. They weren't able to be mass produced yet, as the energy source required hadn't been available.

That and it was inefficient as hell.

They ate up power. They were only good for three hours before needing to get recharged.

Until a few minutes ago, that is. Mr. White solved that problem.

The gigantic vault door began to unlock itself and hiss as Felix got closer.

By the time he was close enough to enter, it was already closing itself again.

Felix slipped inside as it clanged shut behind him, the massive locks engaging and closing them in.

Andrea Prime, Kit, and Miu were present in the room, as well as the command center crew.

"What the hell is going on?" Felix asked, moving to his "captain's chair" in the room. It was center stage in the middle of the massive wall display of cameras, feeds, and information.

"They bombed the building," Andrea said, coming up beside him. "Twice. No deaths, but a lot of wounded. Felicia's machines are patching them up so they'll live, but… you'll need to spend points to get them back to full capacity."

Felix grunted at that. "Of course. It's part of my duty to them. Did we engage our Telemedics?"

Kit came up to stand on his left. "We did. They worked splendidly. We had a full triage and medical evacuation within twenty seconds of the blast. They're the reason we have no casualties."

"Perfect."

The Telemedics had been a late-night thought of his own.

He had kept giving superpowers to those who already had them. He'd never stopped to think about giving powers to those who had none.

Putting out a call to those who, one, wanted to be on the medical staff, and two, wanted to receive a superpower to do that job, they'd gotten a large number of volunteers.

Each volunteer had been granted the power of teleportation for themselves and whoever they were touching. Then he'd given them a miscellaneous power, as he'd called it. They were all given the gift of a full education in medicine in the span of an hour.

As much of an education as you could get going through medical school, that is.

It was a strange superpower to give out, the knowledge of medicine and health.

Pretty much like a damn skill book out of a video game. A superpower granted by virtue of what was contained between the covers.

No one complained about suddenly being the equivalent of a medical doctor from it.

Finally, each was given a power cell from Lily and told to activate it when they were in danger. It would activate a shield for about thirty seconds that would keep them from harm.

They weren't issued weapons, though, as their primary function was to get in and get out.

And thus the Telemedic team was born. A group of twenty men and women given superpowers specifically to operate in a single function.

They'd practiced extensively but had had no actual experience until today.

"What else do I need to know?" Felix asked. Several of the cameras at the entrance and the front lobby were down.

"They've taken up position and are sieging us. There's been nothing on any police, fireman, or government frequencies. Lily is pretty sure a blackout has been purchased, as she can't even reach her contacts." Kit closed up her tablet and tucked it under her arm.

"I see. Who's leading the defense?"

"Ioana and Lily. They're working on shoring up defenses as well as probing at the attackers.

"Some of the Telemedics are taking it on themselves to snag wounded enemy combatants. They're being dropped off with... with Andrea's guests."

"Guests?" Felix asked, turning his head to Andrea.

"My Death Others. They all came in today. We're going to reabsorb them back into ourselves. Welcome them home. They've been gone a long while. Some died, but most lived."

"Death Others," Kit said, not really understanding.

"I had to fill an Other up with all of our deaths. And then send them out into the world. So many deaths piled up hurt us. We had to do it more frequently when we worked."

"Right. I take it your Death Others greet these wounded enemies with smiles and cookies?" Felix asked.

"They're... questioning them. Ask them to sign an Indentured contract. Then feed them into the sausage machine if they decline. Alive."

"Oh. They sound like they'd be great to have a game of Risk with. Let's go have a chat with them when this is over."

"When this is over?" Kit inquired.

"It's not like we didn't plan for this." Felix tapped the communication button on his display next to his chair. Then he hit the dropdown list and selected the R&D lab. "Mr. White, Felicia. I need the Wardens."

"Sending them up as soon as we're able. We put them through a series of trials earlier and they're still charging," came back the response. He wasn't sure who it was, but it didn't matter.

Felix held in a sigh. He didn't need the Wardens right now, but he wanted to use them.

"Wardens?" Miu asked from directly behind him.

"Wardens. I'd… tell you what they are, but why spoil the surprise?

"You were welcome to come with me when I was doing the department goal setting and those damned individual development plans the other week. This all came up then."

"I had enough of those tasks when we went through my own department." Miu had been nonplussed with the corporate mandates he kept laying out.

"Andrea?"

"Mmm?" asked the Beastkin, turning her head to him.

"I could really go for some pancakes. Did you get that tiny kitchen set up in here?"

"Pancakes!" shouted the Beastkin, who scampered off to a corner.

"You spoil her," Kit muttered.

"That I do."

Chapter 24 - Escalation -

The smell of pancakes cooking filled the room as everyone watched the screens.

His people held the security hall as it was intended to be used. A narrow choke point with overlapping fields of fire.

The enemy had taken the lobby and were attempting to do the same thing further in. Except that there was no cover, and there were murder holes from reinforced security boxes that lined the lobby.

It left their would-be attackers just barely inside the lobby, and his own people at the end of the security hall, and in the kill rooms.

Occasionally, one side or the other would put some lead down the security hallway or through the lobby.

"They've already lost twenty or so people. Most of those were in the initial push," said one of the techs at a terminal. "We've got about forty wounded."

"All satellite locations have reported in and are in their bunkers. Everyone is accounted for."

"Outstanding," Felix said around a grin. Leaning forward over his display, he pulled up the overhead map and centered it over the security hall.

"They've disabled all the cameras they can reach, so we've got nothing on the outside. Initial reports are that there is only minor damage outside of the lobby, though." The tech who was speaking fed an overlay to the map Felix was looking at, marking off broken cameras, problems, and assumed positions.

"That was where the bombs went off? The lobby?" Felix looked up to the monitors on the wall. The lobby was charred, smoking, and full of fragments of people and objects.

"Both of them. Yes, sir." The tech dropped the conversation and turned to the tech closest to him and started up a different conversation.

Something blurred across the video feed in the lobby. That same blur burst down the security hall.

Then stopped dead in its tracks in the center of the staging area at the end of the security hall.

It was a man in a dark spandex suit. He'd been picked up off the ground and was suspended in midair.

He rotated slowly in one direction as his legs pumped furiously at the air.

One of Felicia's tricks, he guessed. He wasn't sure what it was set up for, but it seemed as if its goal was to take whoever stepped on it and hold them in the air for a time.

One of the ceiling tiles shifted and a two-inch-long rod stuck out from the crack. It segmented itself and then extended rapidly, plunging a circular tip into the man's back.

Electricity crackled from the end of it, discharging straight into the man.

His mouth sprang open soundlessly as the room flickered and flashed.

"Do you want the audio feed, sir?" asked one of the techs.

"To what, hear him scream? No thanks, I'm not that twisted."

The electrical current cut off as abruptly as it started. The man hung limply, the only sign of life his eyes rolling around wildly in his head.

Retracting into itself, the segmented electric rod disappeared.

The floor rippled now, a number of floor plates sliding around. Then the man fell. He vanished into the open ground and was no more.

"I kinda feel like a Bond villain. I just need a cat sitting in my lap. I could scratch their ears while I chuckle at the fact that a superhero just fell into a damn pit trap."

"This is so cliché, it hurts," Felix said, shaking his head.

"Clichés tend to be founded in reality." Kit sighed and opened up a different screen on one of the unused monitors. "I believe Miu told you this previously, did she not?"

On that monitor was the appropriately named sausage room. It was only accessible by the main elevator, and it was rather deep down. If he had to guess, Felicia had put it roughly a hundred floors below.

Surprised he didn't go splat when he reached the bottom.

The man who had fallen through the floor was being strung up by his arms and legs by darkly dressed Andreas.

The Death Others.

They worked efficiently, coldly. A man in a chair was being questioned, while a different woman was sitting in front of a desk with what could only be an Indentured contract in front of her.

A cart was brought in by a normal Other, dressed in the standard Legion uniform the Others had adopted.

Moving quickly to the sausage machine, she started pulling down the long ropes of what used to be a human.

Once the cart was loaded up, she happily waved at the Death Others, and left.

The woman at the table signed the form and then laid her head down on the desk and started crying.

"Lovely. Yep, Bond villain."

Andrea happily dropped a plate of pancakes into his lap and handed him a fork. "Pancakes!"

Tanker appeared in the lobby, running dreadfully slow.

"Looks like the speedster was the one who was supposed to soften things up." Kit tapped at her tablet and focused one of the cameras on Tanker.

He trundled along as bullets slammed into him continuously. Even Tanker couldn't take that kind of punishment without injury. His arms came up to protect his face as he stomped along.

Bouncing off a wall, he stumbled into the security hall and kept moving. When he came out into the open area that the speedster had been trapped in, Tanker veered off to the left blindly.

"Oh, he missed the pit trap." Felix took a mouthful of pancakes and watched as Tanker closed in on a barricade full of his people.

A squad of supers stepped out of the barricade and surrounded Tanker.

Off to one side of the camera, Felix could see Lily and Ioana supervising.

Must be trying to give the newbies a taste of actual combat. Considering the Telemedics, it's not a terrible idea.

A woman with a thin sword stepped forward and blasted a lightning-fast thrust into Tanker's side.

The sword skittered across his skin, drawing a line of blood but nothing else. The swordswoman danced away as Tanker's arms came out, trying to grab her.

One of her partners stepped in and unleashed a flurry of kicks into Tanker's knees and thighs.

As soon as the big, nigh invulnerable hero turned, Eva's brother Evan stepped up and laid his hands on Tanker's back.

Lightning coursed through the hero at a level that could probably power an entire city.

Tanker arched his back, his body stiffening under the onslaught.

Evan kept using the man as a grounding wire before he finally took two steps back, falling to one knee.

Lily waved a hand at the young man and he was dragged backward out of the combat area by a burst of rune script.

Tanker started to fall over, his body still locked in an upright position from the shock. Then he somehow managed to take a few stumbling steps backwards.

The swordswoman stepped in again, her blade dancing out into Tanker's face. Once, twice, thrice.

Then she was gone again before Tanker could react.

Turning, Tanker started to flee towards the security hall.

Apparently, that was a signal, as Ioana and Lily stepped in at that point.

Lily smashed Tanker to the ground with an explosive concussion. Ioana casually walked up to the man and started kicking him in the head repeatedly.

Ten kicks in and Tanker's arms fell to his sides, unmoving.

Ioana visibly sighed and then looked off camera and gestured at someone. As she walked away from the unconscious man, Felix waited to see what would happen next.

"It's like watching a movie." Felix happily finished off one of his pancakes and dug into the next.

The floor around Tanker flowed, and carried him to the center of the room. Much like the previous attacker, Tanker fell down the hole and vanished.

Looking to the other screen, Felix waited. He really wanted to see what happened when they arrived.

After several seconds, Tanker was there, suspended in midair. Felix couldn't see how he'd arrived, but he assumed there was a hole in the ceiling.

Huh. So, the same way in which the first was caught is the way they don't go splat.

Two Death Others walked up and began discussing the man. Even now, he was waking up. On top of being as strong as he was, he apparently had a rapid healing factor.

Kit sucked in a sudden breath.

Felix's eyes jumped back to the main screen.

The swordswoman was down on the ground writhing. Lightning arced from one limb to the other. Blood poured from her eyes, ears, and nose. Her teeth were locked together as she convulsed.

Smoke even wafted up from her body as if she were being cooked.

Lily and Ioana were both nearby but could do nothing, and looked on as she shook.

Focusing on the woman, Felix called up her ownership window and the idea of fixing her.

Name: Victoria Volante	Power: Sword Mastery	
Alias: Vicky, Swift Blade	Secondary Power: Expanded Senses	
Physical Status: Fatal Heart Attack, Electrocution, third degree burns	Mental Status: Shock	
Positive Statuses: None	Negative Statuses: Dying	
Strength:	56	Upgrade? (560)
Dexterity:	88	Upgrade? (880)
Agility:	79	Upgrade? (790)
Stamina:	47	Upgrade? (470)
Wisdom:	58	Upgrade? (580)
Intelligence:	51	Upgrade? (510)
Luck:	45	Upgrade? (450)

Primary Power:	61	Upgrade? (6,100)
Secondary Power:	33	Upgrade? (3,300)

Status Correction: Fatal Heart Attack -> Healed	Correct Status? (15,000 points)

Seems cheap. Is it because a heart attack could be treated by a defibrillator?

Felix shrugged and waited for the lightning to dissipate. The moment it did, he hit the accept button to correct her status, then thumbed the communications button for the security hall.

"Get her up and moving. I don't want to fix her again if I don't have to." Felix let go of the button.

Everyone in the security hall jumped at the sudden use of the communication system.

The martial artist snagged Victoria and dragged her off into cover. The swordswoman, for her part, was still in shock, or so Felix guessed.

Not every day your heart explodes and gets instantly repaired.

As soon as she was behind cover, everyone refocused their efforts on the hallway.

Victoria lay there behind the shielding, staring up at the ceiling.

Not being able to spare her any more of his time, Felix turned back to the other displays.

His people waited calmly. Patiently. There was no reason to go charging out of the lobby and into whatever they'd prepared on the street. Everything they needed had been placed underground. Only the security hall and lobby were above.

The rest of the building was shipping, receiving, and an elaborate fake of a headquarters building.

Leaning back in his chair, Felix set the fork down on his plate. "Fantastic as always, Andrea."

The mercenary clapped her hands together happily. "Thank you, dear!"

Snatching the plate from his lap, she skipped away gleefully.

"I guess now we wait for their next move. They've lost two elite agents, a group of lesser agents, and gained nothing. I can't imagine the police can ignore this forever. We don't have to go out there, but they do have to get in here if they want whatever they came for.

"Probably my head." Felix folded his hands in his lap.

Curiously, Victoria remained lying where she'd been dragged, staring up at the ceiling.

An hour passed, with the occasional burst of gunfire from the lobby, but nothing changed. At some point, there would be a push or a retreat. It all came down to the opponent's belief in themselves.

"This is boring," Andrea said plaintively. "Can we play a game?"

"What game did you have in mind?" Felix asked. He was only barely paying attention to the screens. His people were unlikely to be hurt in any way, shape, or form.

The Wardens were hanging off to the side in a neutral, non-powered state, waiting for the call to be used.

"I dunno. What about a card game? That'd be fun.

"Lily wanted me to ask you to play a game the other day, but I think she was trying to trick me," Andrea grumped, her fingers playing with a button on her jacket.

Said sorceress was still down in the security hall defending.

"I wouldn't be surprised. She likes making you do things that she knows put me on edge." Felix looked around himself. Kit had left to go work on their guests in the sausage room.

Miu had shown up shortly after that, making herself part of a corner.

Everyone else had a job to do.

"On edge?" Andrea whispered, leaning in towards him. Felix felt his skin prickle and his stomach flop over at the nearness of her.

"Your scent changed." Andrea moved in even closer and took a deep whiff from his shoulder. "It smells like y—oh. Oh! On edge."

Andrea turned a bright shade of red and sat back into her chair. "On edge. I get it now. Yes, she was trying to make me put you on edge, then."

"Honestly, originally, I thought she was playing power games for the sake of playing power games. Now I'm not so sure."

"That'd make sense. Her scent changed recently, too. She kinda—"

Andrea broke off as every pair of eyes was drawn to the lobby on the main screen, where a flurry of activity was taking place.

Out of nowhere, people dressed in dark fatigues came in with sledgehammers. Walking alongside them and protecting them were others with portable ballistic shields.

Those shields were pressed to the kill slits. The men and women inside those reinforced security bunkers had been a primary point defense for keeping people out of the lobby.

With the shields so close, it made it a problem to fire, as bullets were unpredictable and could easily come back at them.

"Need energy weapons," Felix said, watching the feed.

"That'd help. Though they would send in energy reflective shields instead. Should get an over/under weapon. Energy weapon with a rifle under-barrel." Andrea's voice had taken on the professionalism of Myriad.

A few minutes passed in relative peace as the people with sledgehammers did... something. They were off screen and couldn't be seen.

- 202 -

He was lucky the camera left up in the lobby had been disguised as a water sprinkler. No one had paid it any attention, and it was their only means of seeing in right now.

Unbelievably, an armored car rolled into frame. Then a second. Before Felix could hit the PA and warn his people properly, both vehicles were off at full speed down the security hall, one after the other.

Slapping his hand down on the button, he shouted into the microphone, "Incoming! Take cover!"

Everyone on the exit point of the security hall took their positions.

On each side, the Wardens came to life.

They were, by all accounts, what people would call a mech. Something out of fantasy stories and fictional worlds. They were big enough for a person to be inside and pilot, similar to an exo-suit or exo-frame. Except that they were completely covered from head to toe.

They weren't the huge versions in movies.

Yet.

Felicia had come up with the idea when Felix had asked for the ability to have an entire section locked down by a single team of heavily armed and armored people.

Coming in at eight feet tall and humanoid, they were intimidating. Built out of an alloy the Dwarven inventor refused to explain, they were incredibly tough. The power source she'd created for them, once again stolen from Lily's power, was built for the Wardens specifically.

Each pair of Wardens worked as a team and had been built to assist its partner.

The far scarier-looking one was outfitted with a sword with a plasma edge, of all things, and a tower shield. That sword could eat through most metals and polymers with a frightening degree of ease. Thicker metals took longer but eventually could be gotten through.

The second Warden's armament was a giant railgun. The power needed to discharge the weapon was one of the reasons the power source was built into the Warden.

Its secondary purpose was that of medic. It had a small pod attached on its side that contained electrical repair tools, self-heating lower-grade alloy of the same type that the Warden was made of, and a diagnostic tool. The idea was that it could make spot repairs and keep them in the fight longer if they had a moment to take a step back.

The armor on the ranged Warden was slimmer and less thickly made. The idea was for it to be agile, and keep itself on target with its weapon.

All four Wardens went "heads up" at the call. Both Shield Wardens trundled forward, their swords held out at their sides as their counterparts brought their railguns to bear.

The armored cars screeched into the area and the back hatch dropped down.

"Shit."

Supers flooded out of the dropped gate, the cannons on the armored cars opened up, and the security hall was filled with enemy troops.

"Andrea, send the Others."

"On it." Andrea pressed a hand to her ear and turned her head to one side.

His people lit those armored cars up like they were range targets. The camera started to fritz as the armored cars continued to boom out round after heavy-caliber round.

The supers took cover behind the armored cars and began organizing themselves quickly.

His Shield Wardens got into place and neatly snipped the tips off the barrels from each of the armored cars. The barrels melted from where they were struck, the red-hot glow deforming them.

The next round from one of them exploded in the damaged barrel, while the other one failed to fire at all.

A gauss round tore through a super who tried to get a peek around the armored car, his head disappearing in a splatter of gore.

Then everything went to shit as the Others flooded in from the sides.

Felix simply couldn't keep up with what was going on as the whole thing devolved into chaos.

Hitting the comm button, he dialed into the Shield Wardens. "More coming down the security hall. Hold them there and keep them out. We need time to deal with the supers."

He got two acknowledgments in return as the Shield Wardens turned off to face the tunnel.

Lightning crackled one way, then fire in the opposite direction. Explosions detonated throughout the room as the battle raged.

Telemedics popped up here and there as they were able to, vanishing with a wounded comrade.

Feeling the weight of his lack of combat experience again, Felix had to turn to Andrea for help. "How's it looking? I'm no strategist, Andrea. I'm just a pencil pusher."

Andrea's glanced over at him, her mismatched eyes piercing through him. She gave him a warm smile, then looked back to the monitors. "We're winning. But not without losses. It shouldn't be much longer. It just looks like this because everyone is unleashing all their trump cards.

"Lily is scary as shit. I genuinely underestimated her."

Felix couldn't tell what she was talking about, but if he had to guess, it was the mass of lightning that was dominating one side of the room.

"Yeah, she hides the monster well."

"As to being a pencil pusher, that's okay, dear. You be you, you do you. You're not here to fight, you're here to help us fight. I enjoy the idea that you depend on us for your safety.

"It's not every day we get to rescue the damsel in distress. You'd look terrible in a dress, though."

"Yes, yes I would. I'll leave that to you and Lily. You two have certainly set a new standard for attractive and professional."

"You flatter me. Do it some more."

Felix frowned for a moment as he watched the mess that was the screen.

Andrea changed whenever she flipped her Myriad switch. Almost to another person. The intelligence boost only made it more obvious.

Might as well ask, I guess.

"You're like a different person."

Andrea blinked twice, her eyes unfocusing. She gave herself a tiny shake of her head, her eyes flicking back to the monitors.

"That's because I am. I'm me, of course, but, the one you call Andrea Prime isn't Andrea Prime. I died and we absorbed ourself through our oldest Other. We are Andrea, yet we are—I am—not."

Andrea's eyes scrunched up and she looked pained.

"This isn't easy to explain, and I'm making a mess of it."

"No, no I get it. I get it. It also makes a bit more sense. We'll talk more after this. I'd like to ask some questions about your Others and Death Others, too."

"Good, because this thing is over and we need to get down there to start picking up the dead and wounded."

Felix looked up to the screens and found she was right. The Wardens were holding the hallway, while the center of the screen was a bloody mess.

"Not quite. We still have to clear the lobby, and whatever they've laid in wait for us outside.

"This isn't over, I'm afraid," Felix said morosely.

Chapter 25 - Clearing the Field -

"I object to this. There's no reason to put yourself in harm's way," Miu said sternly, trailing at Felix's heel.

"Noted, but I really think I should be down there. So I'm going."

"I don't like it. I don't like it at all. What if you get hurt?" Miu's voice had changed pitch entirely, her voice bordering on breaking.

"Really, it'll be fine. Everyone is there. I'll stay back, but there's nothing I can see from the control room that'd help me."

Miu's breathing became irregular, rapidly speeding up over the course of ten seconds. Then suddenly it returned to normal, the sound of it being replaced by the sound of their shoes striking the floor.

Andrea skipped ahead and thumbed the elevator button. "It's okay, Miu. Everyone up there wants him to live as much as we do." Pressing her back to the frame of the elevator, Andrea pulled out her tablet and started to tap her screen.

"You alright, Miu?" Felix asked, turning his head to Miu.

"Yes. I'm fine. I don't like you risking yourself. It's troubling. You risk everyone."

He couldn't exactly disagree with her. She wasn't wrong. But nor did he really want to sit back the entire time and do nothing.

Her reaction was also pretty strange.

"I get that. I promise I won't take unnecessary risks."

"I'll kill anyone who gets close to you."

"I don't think you need to go to that extreme, but please do watch over me. I'm in your care." Felix gave her a smirk.

The elevator chimed and all three entered. Nothing was said as they rode the elevator up.

With a chime, the elevator stopped and opened up into a landing behind the security hall's opening lobby. This was meant as a fallback position and sheltered enclave to take wounded.

And wounded there were.

Laid out all around were his wounded. Those who suffered so that Felix could remain in power. Telemedics, medics, and doctors were working through everyone there. It was clear the truly worse off had been triaged to the medical facility, the rest being held here.

More of Felicia's beds would be needed in the immediate future.

When resources were available.

Heads turned his way as he exited the elevator. Bloodstained and weary, they looked to him.

"I appreciate your service. All of you. You will receive the best care to put you back to rights in every way possible.

"I will personally make sure you all are healthy, mentally and physically. There isn't anything I cannot fix given a day or two."

Heads nodded slightly, fingers unclenched from sheets, eyes softened.

"Let our very talented medical staff take care of everything they can. And everything that's beyond the purview of modern medicine will fall to me. Trust in your peers, trust in Legion." Felix bowed his head to everyone, then moved on.

Turning the corner, it was like walking into a slaughterhouse. Bodies, body parts, and blood were liberally smeared over and on everything and everyone.

It looked as if a massacre had taken place.

Meeting the eyes of anyone who looked his way, Felix refused to turn away from them. This was all for him and everyone in Legion. He'd feel shame to not meet their gaze.

Lily and Ioana were organizing what he could only guess was a counteroffensive near a back wall.

Before he even made it halfway across the room, a bubble of protective magic snapped into place around him.

"Felix!" Lily shouted, jogging towards him. Her corporate attire was gone, and in its place was tactical gear the likes of which he saw many of his people wearing. It gave her a different look, especially with her hair pulled back into a tight bun behind her head.

"What in the seven hells are you doing here? Miu, I thought we agreed to keep him out of this?" Lily turned her glare on the woman who had escorted him here.

"He overruled me. I pleaded with him."

"She did, and I did. I'm here. Deal with it. Might I also say you look rather fetching?" Felix tried for distracting her. It worked elsewhere, why not here?

"What? Don't be stupid. Fine, you're here. Come. You're staying with me and Ioana for now." Lily turned around and headed back towards Ioana.

She started talking into what he guessed was her mic to someone else.

Miu, Andrea, and Lily escorted him to Ioana, who gave him a death stare down the bridge of her nose.

"You are not to be here, Felix. Your strength lies elsewhere," said War Maiden, speaking from her old persona to the inch of it.

"I know, Ioana. I know. But I couldn't sit back and not show up at this point. Not after everyone already fought and bled for me. I can't. I won't."

Ioana narrowed her eyes, then suddenly nodded her head. "Good. I dislike you being here, but your reasons are good. Stand beside me."

Ioana turned her head and snapped her fingers, and pointed at someone in the crowd.

Felix wasn't tall enough to see over the sea of heads and bodies.

Then Victoria appeared, garbed in her lightweight tactical vest and sword baldric.

She was very similar to Kit in build and body type. Athletic supermodel sprang to his mind as a good definition. Tall and lanky, she had a body that looked lithe and swift.

She was also rather pretty. Not as striking as Lily or "girl next door" as Andrea, but definitely pretty. Certainly above the average.

Her hair was pulled back from her face in a similar style as Lily's, though a few dark brown curls had slipped free.

Probably when she got turned into a Christmas tree.

Large dark green eyes peered at him, her face turning a light pink in tone, her lightly tanned skin darkening.

Victoria stood in front of Ioana and went to attention.

"You're on guard duty under Miu. Keep Felix here out of trouble." Ioana jerked a thumb at Felix as she spoke. After having given the order, she turned back to the people she'd been working with when he'd arrived.

"Felix?" Victoria said softly, her eyes locking on to him.

"Heya. Sorry for ending up as my babysitter. I couldn't sit behind and wait."

"You're on point, I'll take the rear. Remain at his side," Miu said from behind him.

"Of course, Miu." Victoria bobbed her head, not taking her eyes off Felix.

Felix gave her a smile and then turned his attention to what was going on around him.

Teams of supers were working to haul the damaged armored cars out of the open area and to one side.

He imagined Felicia would get them to a garage somehow and rebuild them. She enjoyed those kinds of projects.

"Idiot. What are you doing up here? Don't you know your place? I know mine, and it sure as hell ain't here," grumped the woman he'd just been thinking about.

Meeting Felicia's stare Felix couldn't help but smile. "Ho there, friend Dwarf. If this isn't your place, what are you doing up here?"

"Doing your little princess a favor. She called me all worried about you getting your dainty ass hurt. Your mark two armor is this way." Felicia did an about face and marched over to where a team of her people were unpacking.

Felix was surprised.

Mark two?

From those boxes and crates, a suit of armor emerged. One that looked nothing like the set he'd worn previously. This one looked more between the first suit, an exo-frame, and the Warden.

"Uh… pretty sure I'm not going to be going to Mars to slay aliens or anything. So what's up with the Space Ma—"

"Shut up." Felicia slapped a hand onto his wrist and jerked him closer. "Stand there, and be silent. We'll get you outfitted. We've already put the pod in your room. That'll strip you of the armor and put it back on when you're ready.

"The mark two isn't completely done, but all that's left is getting the heads-up display debugged. It has a couple graphical glitches, but that's it."

Felix grunted and did as instructed. There was no point arguing with them. He'd either end up ordering them to stop, and pissing them off on a whole new level, or letting them do as they wished.

The latter option was easier.

He did as they asked, letting them guide him along the process. They had him step into the heavy boots and greaves first. Judging by those alone, it looked like this suit would completely cover him from head to toe.

Around him, Ioana and her team were getting ready, arming themselves and making plans with Lily's team.

The two groups were starting to work very well together. Training had definitely set the foundation for them, but nothing worked better than live firsthand experience.

"Chin up." A male tech prodded Felix in the jaw. Lifting his chin, the tech pulled a helmet down over Felix's head.

The helmet was depowered and dark, giving with him a view of absolute blackness.

Then the screen in front of his eyes popped on and flickered before stabilizing.

Amazingly enough, it was as if he were looking through holes in the helmet.

"Damn, that's impressive."

"Volume's a little low. You'll need to key that up. The helmet is tied into the electric impulses your brain puts out. So think about moving the volume up.

"As to the suit, my team thanks you. I'll relay to them your appreciation of their efforts. I'll be sure to remind you about this when budget time rolls around," said Felicia.

Felix chuckled at that and mentally thought about turning up the volume as she'd suggested.

"Mr. White is a smart man, but he's more built for outfitting a mass of people. My team and I are better at one-offs. Or stuff like your damned Wardens.

"We downloaded the footage from them, by the way, and will be going over it later for improvements.

"Anyways. Don't get killed. We're done here. Tell your princess to stop worrying." Felicia waved a hand at him over her head and left.

As she went, she stopped next to Ioana.

The big warrior looked down at the Dwarf, then gave her a truly kind smile. Ioana and Felicia shared a quick kiss, then separated, both going their separate ways.

"Ha, good for them. They make a great couple," Felix said. He'd been trying to keep his voice down, but apparently he'd pushed the volume up way too high.

Every head in the room turned to him, including Ioana and Felicia, at what to them had been a shout.

Ioana gave him a frozen wide-eyed gaze, while Felicia grinned at him.

"What?" Felix said, the helmet turning it into a shout.

Something slammed into his helmet, the servos in the neck whining under the impact.

"Lower the volume stupid," Miu told him.

Felix mentally tried adjusting the volume again.

"How about now?" he said.

"Better. It'll do."

Felix shook his head in annoyance and looked around. It was strange. He knew he wasn't looking at things, but at a display. Yet everything looked normal. As if he were simply looking through eyeholes.

Reaching up, he waved his fingers in front of the faceplate. Whipping them back and forth quickly, he saw no delay from action to visual relay.

"Huh. She outdid herself. A lot. Remind me to see what she wants as a reward."

"You give rewards?"

Felix turned his head to find it was Victoria asking him the question.

"Why wouldn't I? Best way to encourage people is with rewards. Only a fool thinks that the stick is the only way to motivate people. Luckily, I'm the owner of our experiment, so I don't have to run anything through anyone."

Turning back to the security hall, he saw the Wardens moving out.

They were lined up two by two, moving at a pace equivalent to an easy jog for a human.

"They're impressive," Victoria said softly.

"Yeah, they are. I told Felicia I want one for my own use, but with replaceable power units. She's working on it.

"I imagine this suit was a prototype that came before the Warden. She probably just built it halfway and then left it."

"You want a Warden?" asked the swordswoman.

"Of course. I mean, shit, what kid didn't grow up saying they wanted a mech? Didn't you?"

"Yeah. I guess you're right."

"I mean, what if we made a super lightweight one that was built around using an elongated sword?"

Victoria fell silent at that.

Felix started walking forward, taking up position behind the last team entering the security hall.

"Felix, n-no. Stop. You can't. You said you'd stay back," Miu said, her hands clamping around one of his arms. Her voice wasn't as firm as it normally was.

"And I will stay back, just not back here. Come on, Miu. Between you, Victoria, and this suit, I'll be fine." Felix kept walking, the servos and powered limbs not even slowing down despite Miu's immense strength.

"Damn it, Felix!" Miu cursed. Moving in front of him, the diminutive and deceptively deadly woman kept herself alert. "Fine, you'll remain in the entryway and not a step beyond.

"Or I will finally join Lily in turning Andrea on you."

Andrea made a chirping sound behind him. "Turning me on him how?"

That drew Felix up short. "I understand. I will obey," he said automatically.

The Wardens split off into the lobby up ahead. The individual teams that Lily and Ioana had put together broke off to assist in clearing the room.

After a minute, Ioana held up her hand in the center of the room. "Clear. Move to the exterior and sweep."

Intricate glowing runes filled the doorway leading to the outside. Flowing script swooped and circled endlessly as Lily called it forth into being.

As his people marched through the door, and the runes, blue glowing shields wrapped around them. The Wardens were too big to exit through the lobby door, so instead they took up defensive positions in the lobby.

Team after team filtered out the door till only Ioana and Lily remained of the assault group.

After a minute, Felix started to worry.

Then Ioana turned her head to one side, her hand pressing to her ear. Nodding her head, she looked to Lily, who held up her hands in an "I don't know" gesture.

Ioana swiveled her head to Felix. "Nothing out there. There's signs that the entire street was full of combatants, and the pawn shop across the street is a ruin, but that's about it."

Felix let out a breath and relaxed. "Good. This is over, then. Let's see about purchasing all the buildings on this street and get it all locked down.

"Lily, please let me know how much money we'll need and I'll get that together. I'd like to do this quietly and without people realizing we own everything, if possible. Money isn't an issue there either, so... yeah, just let me know how much we need."

Felix nodded to Ioana.

"You're on duty to make sure this area is a fortress. I don't want this happening again. Our defenses held, but I don't like it. Work with Felicia and her team to get it set up. Multiple fallback points, security bulkheads, traps, turrets, mines, whatever.

"And if we need something that we can't provide, I'll use points to get it done."

Shaking his head, Felix turned back to the security hall and went back into his complex.

He needed to get out of his armor and get to the medical wing. There were injured and wounded people who would need to see him.

First, those Death Others and our guests.

"Andrea, I want to meet your Death Others. Let's get me out of this suit and head there.

"Miu, go take care of your teams. I'll be fine from here on out."

"I understand. Victoria, you're now on detached duty to Felix for the day. Felix will not give you orders to the contrary, or my earlier threat will be carried out."

Fine, she can come. So grumpy.

"Understood," Victoria said loudly.

It took him thirty minutes to figure out how to get out of his new powered armor.

He didn't deny it was exactly what he needed to stay safe, but he still didn't like being closed up in it.

It was pretty fricking cool, though, by his own estimation. The armor made him actually feel like a superhero instead of a manager.

The elevator doors pinged open into the sausage room.

Hard-faced Andreas looked up from around the room.

They all wore different clothing in different styles and tastes. Every single one of them bore Andrea's face, but not all of them were Andrea. They weren't even an Other.

They were all battle scarred. A number of them looked like they'd been burned, shot, broken, or worse.

Before Felix could do or say anything, Andrea stepped out in front of him and immediately crossed the space between the two groups.

"Hello! Thank you all for coming. Thank you for helping out. It wasn't my goal originally, but things happened." Andrea wrung her hands in front of herself, her tail hanging low between her legs.

"I... I want to start by saying sorry. You all volunteered for your burden, and I allowed you to take it. That doesn't make it right, or any better."

The Death Others had taken a few steps back from Andrea when she'd entered. He finally came up with a reasonable assumption that made sense as to why.

They weren't afraid of her, they were afraid *for* her. Absorbing them would bring back everything they had taken on themselves to begin with. Their sacrifice would be nullified.

"I..." Andrea trailed off, her head dipping down.

Felix cleared his throat and stepped up beside Andrea. Setting his hand on her shoulder, he gave it a light squeeze.

"I'm Felix, Felix Campbell. Andrea is my slave. She has been my trusted lieutenant as both Myriad and herself. She's also my friend.

"I have the power to modify the abilities of any person I own at a cost. Andrea asked me for only one thing. To be able to selectively choose what memories come back to her when she absorbs an Other.

"I granted that wish."

Felix gave the Death Others his best smile, trying to meet the eyes of each one.

"To that end, one of the first thing Andrea did after getting that power was to call all of you. I believe she wants to ask if you'd be willing to return to her and rejoin the Andrea collective. She'd probably weed out any and all memories neither of you want, and you'd simply return to being an Other.

"Please keep in mind that Andrea is still a slave. And if you were to rejoin her, you would become a slave as well."

Felix released Andrea and stepped back into the elevator.

Putting his foot in front of the doors so it wouldn't close, he continued.

"I'll have a conference room set up in ten minutes for you to discuss this situation at length. I'll also have food and drink sent up.

"As well as Andrea's mini traveling kitchen, if you suddenly decide you want pancakes."

A number of Death Others smiled at that. At least a little.

Pulling his foot out of the door, the elevator dinged and closed.

Felix sighed and hit the button for his office. He'd need to go book a room and move some things around for them to get what he had promised.

"You can modify powers? I mean, we've heard about it, but... hearing it from you directly..." Victoria said slowly, as if she wasn't sure she wanted to say anything at all.

"You're alive, aren't you? You got turned into a goddamn lightbulb. You should be dead."

"I... I was dying, wasn't I? I was. My heart... it hurt so bad."

Felix moved his head a fraction to catch Victoria out of the side of his eyes. She looked pale.

"Yeah, you were dying. Fixed you all up, though. Good as new, no damage at all."

Victoria shook her head, and then smiled. "You saved me."

"Of course. Why wouldn't I?"

Chapter 26 - Smith -

Looking up from his office terminal, he saw Andrea standing in the doorframe.

"How'd it go?" Felix turned his eyes back to the spreadsheet. Lily had sent him over the finances involved with purchasing out the entire street.

Only the two stores on each side of his own refused to even discuss the matter. Nor did they owe anything, giving them no leverage at all over them.

They really did open them up just to get us. Next we'll need to find out if they had any involvement with this attack. If they did, I'll send a herd of Andreas over there.

"They're all with me again. I am... we are... thankful."

"Hah. Good. I kinda figured they would rejoin you. I can't imagine a reason why they'd stay.

"You all cleaned up, then? No death memories?"

"None. We kept all of our memories outside of the deaths. They... are not all pretty, but they are us."

"I've heard that before. Or something to that effect. Uh... 'the sum of what we are, our experience, is what we draw upon to make choices. It's what we use to defend ourselves from doubt. We compare them to things we've done previously and judge it based on what the outcome had been then.' Or so I remember it as."

Felix closed the spreadsheet, pulled open Lily's email, and gave her a quick reply. Sending it off, he locked his terminal and turned his attention on Andrea.

"They had many questions. Mostly about you."

"Oh? That's surprising. I thought they'd want to know more about what memories you'd strip from them."

"No, we share memories, for we are but one person. It's... complicated."

"I suppose it is at that."

Andrea came in from the doorway, walking his way slowly. She'd changed out of her normal corporate attire and was in a tight pair of jeans and a tank top.

It was very much not in her normal style.

Andrea had that girl next door thing down to a science. This was more like —

Lily.

"Well, is there anything else you need? Actually, before you answer that, I had a question. If an Other is wearing clothes, where do they go? And gear? Say, if they had a knife?"

Andrea came up to stand directly in front of his desk. Placing her hands on the wood, she leaned forward over it.

Felix kept his eyes fastened on her face, her different-colored eyes.

"Any fabric goes... somewhere. Everything else ends up on the ground. We can recall the fabric from wherever it goes so our Others are dressed."

"Oh, how odd," Felix said, leaning back in his chair, away from Andrea.

He was well aware of the women around him. Aware of their appeal. He wasn't stupid to think that they wanted anything from him like an actual relationship, though.

They all had their own moments where they teased or flirted, but that was where it would end and he knew it.

"We should build an Andrea armory. Where you can store all your Others' gear. That way they can arm up and move quickly."

Andrea tilted her head to one side, her hair cascading down to one side. Her ears twitched on the top of her head, swiveling backwards and then forwards towards him. Then her nose twitched as she made an audible sniffing noise.

"How many Others do you have, exactly?" Felix reached over and thumbed his terminal to life. He opened up an email to Felicia and started writing a quick letter about creating an armory for Andrea and her Others.

"Three hundred or so now."

Felix entered that it'd need to hold three hundred sets of full tactical gear and sent the email.

Andrea sat down in his lap, her tail moving up to press to the side of his shoulder and neck.

"You're not paying attention to me," she growled under her breath.

Felix's head snapped to her, his eyes catching yellow flickering irises.

Never seen that one before.

"With the return of our Death Others, we've realized a few things when we went over our memories. You keep me at a distance. You smell of desire and longing, yet do not touch. You watch me, roll your eyes over me.

"You even watch me at night sometimes."

Felix's eyebrows went up slowly, till it felt like they were in his damn hairline.

She wasn't wrong, of course. He was only human, and he hadn't gotten laid since before this whole thing had started.

Saying he had blue balls would have been an understatement.

Honesty would do the best for him here.

"What can I say? You're right. It would be wrong, as you're a slave and I'm your master."

Andrea chortled and her eyes flashed again. Reaching up, she poked him in the forehead. "I'm not as smart as the others, but I know this. I will mate as I will mate, when I mate. No one will tell me otherwise.

"You are the alpha. I can accept sharing you with others, but I cannot accept you saying no."

Andrea patted him on the chest and then got up off his lap. "I'm going to call all my Others in tonight. I'll let Miu and Ioana know about the gap."

Leaving his office by going into his attached bedroom, she disappeared without another word.

"Okay then... I'll just... finish up here and go to bed. I guess." Felix scratched at his cheek. There was a certain amount of excitement in his head. And his other head.

He was only human, after all.

At that moment, his phone went off.

Clicking his teeth shut, he looked at the display.

The fact that the name came up at all on the display was simple pride on their part.

"Agent Smith," Felix muttered.

Hitting the accept button, Felix pulled the phone up to his ear.

"Agent Smith," Felix said again, now for the benefit of his caller.

"Mr. Campbell, I'm so glad to have gotten a hold of you."

"I don't remember giving you this number."

"You didn't, but that's okay. I heard you had some guests earlier today."

Felix felt the hairs on his neck stand up on end. Was Smith involved in this?

"We did. They were escorted off the premises."

"Glad to hear it, glad to hear it. Unrelated, there was a real problem with the emergency circuits today. Apparently, a huge number of emergency calls and emails didn't get through today."

"Uh-huh, I imagine. A real shame. I hope no one had a problem with the lack of emergency services."

"No, no. The problem was a very small area, apparently. About a street long."

"I see. So, other than local news, to what do I owe the pleasure?"

"Oh, nothing really. Just wondering if you'd thought on my offer."

"Not really. I'll be honest with you, I haven't thought of you since you left."

"For shame. Well, I'll be by next week to see how things are going. Check on your slaves. Collect. You know, government job and all."

"Goodie."

"With that settled, I'll see you then. Good evening."

The click of the agent hanging up was all Felix heard.

Setting his phone down, Felix contemplated the situation.

Then his door opened, and Others began marching by.

They were all dressed in street clothes, most of them wearing jeans and a t-shirt, with very little diversity.

Each and every one of them made eye contact with him as they went by, though. Their cheeks turning a pale red and their eyes flashing yellow at the center as he met their eyes.

They all filed into his bedroom, a never-ending train of them.

The last Andrea entered the office, turned, closed the door, locked it, and then entered the bedroom. Watching her go, he waited for her to vanish from sight, and then he opened an email to Lily.

He filled her in on everything that had just happened with Agent Smith, and his questions and concerns, then sent it.

If anyone could figure out what was going on, it'd be Lily.

Getting up, he wandered over to his bedroom as casually as he could make himself be.

The door was already open and inside was a trio of Andreas, waiting for him.

This'll be fun.

I think.

A week passed in the blink of an eye.

Felix spent most of that time either making gold, or putting his people back to rights.

They'd only lost a few people in that final push.

Missing limbs, blinded, mental problems, everything was swept away under an onslaught of spent points.

He was also well aware of what that did for his reputation. Everyone began treating him as something much greater than a mere employer.

They all treated him like he was their personal superhero. That nothing was too great for Felix. That if for whatever reason something failed, Felix would be there to fix it.

Personally, Felix ignored it. He had other things to worry about.

Like the fact that their assets had been frozen and they couldn't access anything electronically that was directly tied into Legion.

That was a pretty big worry right now. They'd only been tied up for two days, but it was already enough to be a problem.

Lily had her entire team jumping through hoops to get it all figured out and sorted, but for the most part it seemed as if it was a government hold.

Which really only left Agent Smith.

No one else knew them or had even tried to put any pressure on them from a government position.

"Now I don't feel so bad about sending Wraith after them," Felix said, leaning back in the chair in front of his personal computer.

Wraith, the incorporeal shadow hero they'd captured, had signed on as an indentured servant. It was that or get his, her, whatever, soul ripped out and stuffed into the sausage machine.

Since Wraith had never revealed their form, Felix wasn't even sure how to address them. Not that he cared how to address them. They were Wraith. That was all that mattered at the moment.

And at that moment, they were infiltrating Agent Smith's organization and doing a bit of intel gathering.

The speedy guy and Tanker had both declined his generous offer. For some reason, they had seemed to think he wasn't going to go through with killing them.

Felix wasn't your average cliché villain, though. He did what he said he would do.

Tanker had been turned into many, many sausages. Most of the enemy captured prisoners had been in fact dumped into the machine after having their soul stripped, just like Tanker.

After they'd all been thoroughly interrogated, of course. Any who were willing to sign a contract were given a chance and were being put through their paces.

"Why would you?" asked Victoria. She rarely left his side now. After Miu had attached Victoria to him, Miu had taken a back seat and was working with her team more frequently.

"Dunno. Seems rude to do that to someone who up to this point has genuinely only been annoying rather than a problem." Felix interlaced his fingers behind his head. "Whatever. Wraith will figure out what they can and report back. I think Lily said she was expecting something today or tomorrow."

"She did!" Andrea chirped happily at his side. She tapped at her tablet and then nodded her head. "She has another meeting tomorrow with you."

Victoria took a number of steps to one side, and then paced back the other way. Her sword clicked as she turned and started back the other way.

"Stop pacing."

"Sorry. I'm not used to this yet. I was just on a security team a bit ago, and now I'm protecting you."

"It's been a week already."

"And? Still not used to it."

"Whatever. Take a seat or Lily is going to be annoyed. Miu would tell you to post up near the door. Probably."

"She would," Andrea confirmed. Her eyes peered at him for a second over the top of her tablet.

She'd changed since they started actually started sleeping with each other.

She was her normal and chipper self; she touched him casually a little more often, but nothing obvious.

Then there were times where she touched him when they were alone somewhere, times when her touch was far more intimate.

The door opened and Lily entered. She was dressed in a dark black jacket, white blouse, and dark black pencil skirt. Her hair was tied back in her professional style, though most surprising was that she was wearing glasses.

"Agent Smith should be arriving in fifteen minutes." Lily crossed the distance to where he sat at the conference table and dropped into the chair next to him at his left side. "Andie, Vicky."

Both women nodded their head to Lily.

Felix quirked a brow, smiling at Lily.

Reaching up, she adjusted her hair with a touch and then looked down at herself. Looking back up to him, she frowned. "What? You're looking at me in a strange way.

"And not in the normal, stripping me of my clothes and devouring me way."

Felix snorted and reached out. He pushed her glasses up higher on the bridge of her nose. "Didn't realize you had a prescription.

"And how would you know what I do to you in my mind while looking at you?"

Lily pressed her lips together into a line. "Yes, I'm a bit nearsighted. I ran out of contacts and forgot to order more."

"Wear the glasses more often. Your eyes are lovely, it brings the focus on them."

Lily smiled at him, then looked to Andrea over his shoulder. "He's been much more of a smooth talker since you tamed him."

Andrea chuckled, not arguing the point.

Felix wasn't quite sure how he felt about the fact that everyone knew Andrea and he were sleeping together.

"Anyways. My eyes aren't the topic, though thank you for the compliment. Agent Smith is definitely the reason we're all tied up financially. I also found out what's going on with that slave tax bologna."

"Bologna?"

"Complete bologna. Yes, there will be a tax, but it isn't being put into place for a while yet. They're still going through the assessment faze. He's trying to shake us down.

"The freeze on our assets is probably part of a toolset to help them determine what we should be paying when the tax goes live.

"Best I can tell, it'll be repealed tonight."

"Huh. Good work. How'd you find all this out?"

"Wraith and our police informant. Doesn't hurt that we kept all that petty cash on hand. I've been using it to grease wheels. We'll need more."

"You know what, Lily? You're fantastic. I cannot imagine Legion without you."

"You still owe me, remember? Now you owe me two nice things. Spoil me, already."

"Fine, whatever. Two favors of your choosing. Get it put down in a meeting and we'll take care of it. No limit, except anything along the lines of 'free me,' cause that ain't going to happen. Sorry, too valuable."

Lily lifted up a hand with one finger held up. Her shoulders were set and her body had gone rigid. "Anything?"

"Well, anything within reason. But yeah, I can promise to be receptive to whatever you ask."

"I'll hold you to that. We can talk after this meeting. I do have a favor already in mind. I've been working on getting it set up, one of the reasons I didn't bother you about it yet. I finally got most of it taken care of."

Felix was curious now. He really didn't know much about Lily. She kept to herself when it came to her past and about herself in general.

"You damn tease. That's all you're going to say, isn't it?"

Lily's tension melted away in a heartbeat, replaced with the vibrant soul-stealing monster.

"Of course. I have to keep you coming back for more. Ever since you started playing bedroom games with your wolf over there, you don't pay me as much attention."

Andrea started giggling at that. "Bedroom games?"

"There's lots of games. We're having lunch tomorrow, aren't we?"

"Uh-huh. You promised me a different type of pancake. Creepies or something."

"Crepes, but yes. Not quite pancakes, but similar enough.

"We'll talk about games then. We haven't talked recently. I think our little leader here has been trying to keep you away from me."

"No. Just busy. We were setting up the Other armory."

Felix sighed and looked to Victoria as the two kept chatting.

"As you can see, I'm a passenger most of the time. Just along for the ride."

The swordswoman shrugged her shoulders. "Most of us kinda assumed you were already sleeping with Lily and Andrea. There's even a pool going as to how big you're going to make your harem and who's next."

"A pool? Seriously?"

"It's not that surprising. People bet on anything. And you do kinda own everyone."

"Huh. So, who's in the lead in the pool right now? Maybe I can swing it in my favor with a rumor and split the payout with the person."

"Ah... that is..." she started.

"What, Kit? Ioana? I mean, seriously. Ioana isn't my type, and she's with Felicia. Kit... don't get me wrong, she's pretty, but she's a touch on the girl scout side for what I do for that to work."

"Right now, it's me. I spend the most time with you among anyone in your senior leadership circle. I'm... I'm at the top of the pool."

"That's... unexpected. I mean, you're definitely in my strike zone, but we just met a week ago."

Felix shook his head. He never quite understood how people perceived relationships in that fashion.

He tried to deal with everything from a black-and-white perspective. Relationships were very much not black or white.

" —then I gagged and almost threw up," Andrea said sadly.

"You need to practice first." Lily shifted in her chair and leaned towards Andrea.

Felix sat up straight and jumped into their conversation.

"Yeah, no. That conversation is over. Let's get ready for Smith," Felix said quickly, slapping his palms to the table.

It was one thing for everyone to know he was sleeping with Andrea. It was altogether too much for him when they discussed their sex life aloud as if it were polite dinner conversation.

He turned a full glare on Andrea, who only smiled at him. She lifted her tablet up in front of her face, only covering her nose and mouth, her eyes watching him.

"Seriously, is there anything I need to know?"

Lily shook her head and then lifted her hands up in surrender. "Realistically, there's not much more we can do but wait to talk to him. We can't do anything more till then."

Andrea tapped her tablet and Lily's chimed in response.

Lily picked her tablet up, tapped at it, then laughed.

Oh my God, they're sending messages about it since I told them to stop talking.

Chapter 27 - Favors -

The conference phone in the center of the table started to ring.

Felix quirked a brow, forgetting Lily and Andrea altogether.

Tapping the accept button, he leaned over the speaker.

"This is Felix."

"Mr. Campbell, I have Agent Smith on the line. I believe we were expecting him in person, but… he's trying to call in," came back the Andrea secretary's voice.

"Alright. Patch him through, then."

Felix didn't care for this; it felt weird and didn't make that much sense to him. Smith had set this meeting up and had asked for it to be in person.

Tapping the mute button, he looked around the room.

"This isn't right. Lily, any chance you can get a report from Wraith as soon as possible?"

Lily nodded her head to that, already working in her tablet. "On it."

"Mr. Campbell, so generous of you to pick up. I wasn't sure if you would," Mr. Smith's words came floating in through the speaker of the phone.

Felix sighed and flicked the mute button. "Yep, I'm here. Though I thought we were supposed to meet in person. You requested it. Even went so far as to request the attendees, who are here."

"Ah, that's a shame I can't see it. I'll be sure to make an appointment to swing by later. Sorry."

Felix didn't respond. Silence would be his weapon in this battle. The less he offered Smith, the better.

"Felix?" came the eventual question.

"Yes?"

"Ah, sorry. Anyways. We were going to talk about your taxes and what that number is for you."

He's being rather vague, isn't he?

"Yup."

Felix swore he could hear a chair creak and papers being shuffled.

"Ah… well, uh." Felix smirked at the verbal pause to fill the gap. People really didn't handle silence very well in general. "That number is going to end up being rather hefty. We're not done assessing it, but I can safely tell you it's already going to be higher than a hundred thousand."

Looking to Lily, Felix's hand was halfway to the mute button.

She already had a hand up in a placating gesture, nodding her head at him.

Okay, so that falls within her own projections. Or at least close enough.

"Got it," Felix said. He idly began tapping his thumb on the table, his index finger hovering over the mute button.

"As we discussed previously, I'd be happy to work with you to get this handled."

"I see. And when is the money due in whole?" Felix decided to cut to the chase and see if he could catch the man lying. He'd feel better about it if he could.

"Not yet. Again, we're still assessing things. I'm sure you noticed your assets are frozen. I'm afraid that was our doing, as we needed to get an idea of your finances."

Rolling his eyes, Felix waited. The man wasn't very good at the "government agent" thing he was trying. Then again, it probably helped that Felix had a group of people who were watching out for him.

Once again, he treated Smith with silence. A big, happy heaping helping of it.

"Felix?"

"Yes?"

"Err, never mind. So, yes, your account is frozen for a bit."

"I noticed. When will you be releasing it?"

"I'm not sure. I could swing by tomorrow and talk to you in person about it."

In other words, come by and sleep with one of my people.

"Afraid I'm all booked up, Agent. With our account being frozen, everyone is certainly a lot more busy right now."

Felix didn't want to leave anything to chance, or give Smith a chance to not state something. "Any idea on when you think that'll unfreeze?"

"Not at this time," Smith said in a clipped voice.

"Alright. I'd appreciate it if you could send over the agency directive name and passed regulation that allows you to freeze my account. Along with all the pertinent details about what's allowed. For documentation purposes, of course.

"Oh, and please also send me all the tax law information as well. Trying to get everything put together."

Smith was silent. Maybe Felix had pushed it a bit too far, but he wasn't in the mood for games. Smith was actually hurting his business and his people at this point.

"Sure. I'll get that over to you today. Have a good day, Felix."

Shaking his head, Felix hit the disconnect button.

"Fuck him and the horse he rode in on." Felix leaned back in his chair.

"Kit said he wanted you to prostitute one of us for favors," Andrea said.

"That he did. Which is why after he rides back out on his horse, the horse can fuck him."

Felix pressed his hands to his face, closing his eyes.

"Whatever. Lily, let me know when we get in touch with Wraith."

"Of course, though there's another problem. I just got another emergency meeting request with Reznik, Blacketer, and Troy."

"Great, now what?"

"They wouldn't say. They're sending their people over now to see us. This was after I told them we were unable to leave the office today.

"They'll be here in—"

The conference phone in front of them buzzed.

Felix dropped his hand on the phone, hitting the connect button blindly.

"Yep?"

"Mr. Campbell, I have a group of people here representing Reznik, Blacketer, and Troy to see you."

"Tell Miss Aston we'll see her shortly, we're finishing up a meeting."

"Of course."

There was a pause. "Mr. Campbell, Miss Aston is no longer with the company, but they're waiting."

"Huh. That's interesting." Felix opened his eyes and rested his chin in his palm. "Now why would they get rid of her? She didn't seem unintelligent."

"She's actually pretty good, as far as lawyers go. Graduated near top of her class, multiple offers for employment, spotless contract record," Lily agreed, a frown crossing her pretty face. "I didn't specify that Miss Aston was a problem in our complaint, nor did we ask to have anyone removed in it. If they got rid of her, it's for their own reasons."

Which means she refused to play ball, probably.

"Victoria," Felix said, looking to his bodyguard.

The swordswoman came to attention, her head snapping around to him.

"Get me a Telemedic, the petty cash briefcase, and a brick of lead."

Victoria hesitated, looking to Andrea.

The Beastkin apparently understood something he didn't, as she suddenly split three times. The three Others left the room immediately, Victoria remaining in position at the door.

"Uh..." Felix started.

"She can't leave her post. Don't worry, my Others can handle it."

"What are you planning?" Lily asked, leaning towards him. Her moist lips were parted in a predatory grin. "You've got something in mind."

Felix shrugged, eyeing her. "How would you feel about hiring Miss Aston to work in your department? I'm betting she's unemployed right now and looking."

"Knowing you, you've researched her top to bottom and even know her address. Your praise is never given freely, either. For you to compliment her, that means you actually think she's worthwhile in some way.

"Telemedic taxis you to her, brings you and her back, we have a lovely meeting with her old team as she debriefs you on the way.

"Cash for whatever you need up front, gold bar to replenish the money you spend."

Lily's eyes scrunched up in delight and she leaned forward towards him. She reached out with her right hand to pat him on the chest. "I love it. And yes, I'd hire her in a heartbeat. I'll draw up a standard Indentured contract for her."

Thirty minutes later and Felix welcomed the team from Reznik, Blacketer, and Troy to have a seat at the conference table.

Victoria, Lily, Andrea, and now Lauren Aston were present, the latter three sitting with him on his side of the table.

Every person from the opposing team noticed Lauren sitting on Lily's right hand side.

Apparently, Lauren had been blackballed by the community. So, when Lily had shown up with a cash in hand offer, a contract, and a new home to work out of, she had only had a few questions.

Her belongings would be arriving later.

As an Indentured, she would be offered a place to live on site, with the understanding that she could move out whenever she liked.

So far, no one had turned down the offer to live on site.

And when we buy up this street, we'll see about expanding our subterranean kingdom. We'll just use the buildings for defenses and other things.

From what Lily had told him after hiring her, Lauren had been dismissed for what they'd surmised. She'd sent a complaint to the ethics board about what her bosses had forced her to do.

What she'd attempted to do to Felix, that is. It wasn't personal, it was business, and her job.

She hadn't agreed with it, had sent a formal complaint, but had been nonetheless forced to go along with it if she wanted to keep her position.

Since she'd gotten fired shortly after the whole thing had gone down, it sounded like someone in ethics had sold her out.

All in all, she was a great acquisition even if she couldn't offer any insight into what this meeting was about.

"Good afternoon, everyone," Lily said. "What can we do for you today? Please keep in mind, you've once again filed for an emergency meeting outside of protocol. Our bill will be in the mail."

"This'll be quick," said a man Felix had seen several times but never bothered to learn the name of. Dropping a paper in front of Lily, they turned and left without another word.

Felix was confused. All that fuss, and for what?

Lily had already picked up the paper and was reading through it.

"If we ever wanted proof they're in league with our enemies, this would be it. They didn't bother to cash our check. When they finally did try, it was when our assets we're frozen, which means the check bounced. We're now in breach.

"I'm sorry, Felix. I didn't even think to check to see if they'd cashed the check."

Felix waved it off. "Doesn't matter. We don't need the money from the landlord job anyways.

"I mean, don't get me wrong, this sucks. And it puts a lot more weight on the points bank, but it isn't anything we can't get through."

Lily sighed and set the paper down in front of Lauren. "Please get to work on this immediately; we'll reconvene tomorrow for a department meeting. I'll introduce you formally to the rest of the team. Until then, get settled, get a tour, get some food."

Lauren picked up the paper, her messenger bag, and nodded. A few seconds later and she was out the door and on her way to start her first day.

"She's eager. I think she'll be a great long-term employee. I didn't tell her much, as she wasn't under contract, but the little I did tell her seemed to make her happy."

Felix shrugged and then sighed, slumping into his chair. "I think we were supposed to talk about something next, weren't we?"

"Yes, my first favor," Lily said, folding her hands in front of her on the desk. Apprehensive would have been a good description of her.

"Okay, sure. That'll at least be fun. Probably even solvable. Whatcha got for me?" Felix scratched at his head.

"I want you to fix my little brother. He's... not well. I've got him in a full care facility right now. Technically, I'm his guardian. I've been working on getting everything together to have him transferred here."

Rather surprised at the request, Felix didn't know what to say.

"As of course, being your property, my property is yours. As his guardian, I've written him up an Indentured contract."

Lily slowly set a paper down in front of him. It was indeed a contract and had been completely filled out.

"My favor is... please, sign the contract and then help him?" Lily finally turned her head towards him, her hands gripped together in front of her.

Her eyes were wet, and it looked like she was fighting to keep herself from crying.

"He's one of the reasons I got into magic. I wanted to find a way to help him."

"What exactly is wrong with him?" Felix picked up the paper and looked over it.

There was a momentary flicker of annoyance, a whisper of indifference to the situation.

Both vanished and were replaced by the simple fact that he wanted to take care of Lily. That he didn't want her to suffer if he didn't have to.

Pulling the pen from Eva out of his front pocket, he ran his thumb along the words.

Guardian indeed.

"We're not sure. He just... fell asleep one day and never woke up. His brain is active, he's not... he's not braindead. He just won't wake up." Lily sniffed, her voice breaking. Her fingers were locked into one another, intertwined.

Felix nodded his head and signed the contract. "Let's go get him, then. If we can get him put to rights today, we'll do it."

Lily let out a sudden sobbing breath, a smile breaking free. Then she launched forward and wrapped him up in a tight hug, her arms firm around his shoulders. "Thank you, thank you, Felix. Thank you."

Awkwardly, he patted her on the back. Lily shuddered and Felix realized she was crying.

Catching Victoria's and Andrea's eyes, he motioned them towards the door, hoping they'd get the hint. Both women left without a word.

Felix held on to Lily, not saying a word.

The sobbing sorceress of death, the incredibly strong lawyer, the ravishing temptress, broke down.

All that was left was a woman who was carrying the burdens of an older sister who only wanted her brother to be well.

"It's okay, Lily. We'll get this taken care of. How old is he right now?"

"Sixteen. If he wakes up—" Lily took in a shuddering breath. "He'll be so far behind. What kind of—" Another shoulder-shaking sob. " —life will he even be able to have?"

"Well, I'm sure I can cheat and use points to get him up to speed. I wouldn't worry about it too much. I mean, come on. I can practically bring people back from the dead. There's not too mu—"

Felix blinked at a thought that tore through his head.

I own their corpses, don't I? Why can't I just… bring them back?

Lily didn't realize he'd stopped mid-sentence, but had buried her face in his neck instead, holding tightly to him as she cried.

Felix followed his thoughts as he comforted Lily.

Standing at the foot of the bed, Felix was surprised. The young man looked wasted away. Years of immobility, of not moving his muscles on his own, had caused them to atrophy.

He looked as well cared for as one could be in a coma, though. The facility was very high end, and Lily had paid for its treatment of her brother for another hundred years in advance.

She'd been concerned what would happen to him if she was killed or captured.

Smart sister.

The boy had a faint resemblance to Lily, but Felix had a hard time seeing more than only a hint of it. The sunken cheeks, waxen and pale skin, took too much of the life out of the kid.

"No time like the present," Felix said. Calling up screen for the teenager, Felix looked to the character sheet.

Name: Lucian Lux	Power: Astral Projection
Alias: Luke	Secondary Power: Eidetic Memory
Physical Status: None	Mental Status: Lost, terrified
Positive Statuses: None	Negative Statuses: Lost,

	atrophy, intellectual disability	
Strength:	17	Upgrade? (170)
Dexterity:	23	Upgrade? (230)
Agility:	15	Upgrade? (150)
Stamina:	11	Upgrade? (110)
Wisdom:	31	Upgrade? (310)
Intelligence:	91	Upgrade? (910)
Luck:	47	Upgrade? (470)
Primary Power:	91	Upgrade? (9,100)
Secondary Power:	95	Upgrade? (9,500)

"Huh. He fell asleep because his power woke up. He's an astral projector."

"He's just lost," Felix said. Turning his head to Lily, he gave her a smile. Only she, Victoria, and Andrea had accompanied him here. They'd arrived by Telemedic and would be leaving the same way.

"Really?" Lily asked hopefully, her voice threatening to break again.

"Yup. Here, go stand next to him. Don't touch him immediately, he might be groggy and a little out of it. Let him wake up.

"I'll do a little bit of power tweaking and we'll see about him waking up."

Felix didn't mention the intellectual disability. It wouldn't help, and he could just remove it. The atrophy he'd leave alone, though, because it'd help get Lucian to have a goal.

First, the disability.

Focusing on removing that, he waited.

Status Correction: Mental disability - > Healed	Correct Status? (5,000 points)

A tap of the accept button and Felix moved on.

Next, the upgrade.

He wanted Lucian to have the ability to return to his body no matter what, at any time, regardless of how far he traveled. That it would cost him nothing to do so, and be as simple as opening his eyes.

Power Upgrade: Astral Projection- (Instant Recall)	Required Primary Power: 80 (Met)	Upgrade?(20,000 points)

Felix grunted and hit the accept button again.

Closing the windows, he looked up to the sleeping boy.

"Wake up, Lucian. Your sister is waiting for you, and we have a lot to do today. First of which is hiring you some tutors, getting you some clothes, and getting you into a physical therapy program," Felix said, intoning it all as a command. The Indentured contracts were more or less a timed enslavement. He owned Lucian, and Lucian would have to obey. "Open your eyes and recall already."

Just like that, Lucian's eyes flipped open. Lily let out a soft crying noise, her hands clenching into her clothes.

He blinked several times. His eyes slowly focused on the ceiling.

It really is like watching someone wake up.

Languidly, those eyes began to move, looking at each person in the room, as if cataloging them.

After each person was examined, the boy's head turned towards Lily, his eyes fastening on her.

"Lily?" he asked in a croaking whisper.

"Hey, bud," Lily said, tears rolling down her cheeks. Picking up a pitcher of water at the bedside table, she poured a small amount into a glass and then leaned over him. "Here, take a sip for big sis."

Lucian nodded his head, and took a drink from the glass. Then several more.

"Thanks," he said. His voice didn't sound as raspy now. "I was lost. I couldn't find home, or you, or... me.

"I was wandering around in a forest just now. I was following some hunters and... and then it felt like someone knocked a hole through my brain. Like... shutters and curtains that had blocked out the light were ripped free and thrown aside.

"It felt like I'd been carrying weights around in my head. Then they vanished.

"And then I suddenly knew where my body was. I was told to open my eyes and... I'm here."

Lily let out a chuckle that sounded like a sob. "Yeah. That'd be Felix here. His power is... unique. He made it so you could come back, and it seems like he fixed you, too."

Whoops. Apparently the mental problem was something that existed before he went to sleep.

"And I'll be talking to him about that later. For now, though, he's right. We need to get you home. I already have a room set up for you."

"Home?" Lucian asked, his head having slowly turned towards Felix.

"Felix's home. I live with him now. He said you could live with us, so... we're going home."

"That sounds nice. When we get home, then can we eat? I'm hungry."

"Sure we can," Felix said with a grin. "I know someone who is always itching to feed people pancakes."

Andrea nodded her head happily from beside him, her hands immediately coming together in front of her.

"Thank you, brother," Lucian said, a smile on his face.

"Brother?" Lily asked. She had moved over to the intercom to call the nurse to prepare discharge papers.

"You're married to him, aren't you? The way you said everything, it sounds like you're married. Mom and Dad must be so happy.

"You were always so intimidating. Dad always said that you scared off all the boys. Mom and Dad worried you'd never get married. I'd heard them sometimes talk about it. So I'm glad you married Felix."

Lily made a squawking noise, her cheeks turning a deep red as she hurried back to Lucian's side and began whispering to him.

Felix chuckled at that, turning his head to Andrea.

"Call the Telemedic back, we'll be leaving shortly. Then you can make everyone pancakes."

"Pancakes!" Andrea shouted.

"Pancakes!" Victoria agreed.

Chapter 28 - Mostly Dead -

A medical attendant pulled open the door. Felix waited as the man grabbed the slab and drew it towards them. On that slab were the remains of one Jordan Taylor.

He wasn't a super, or someone remarkable. He was average, really. Talented enough to make the cut for the internal security team, but that was it.

He was also agnostic, and had no living family. Thus, he became a perfect test subject.

"You're welcome to remain, but I order you not to speak of anything that occurs in this room with anyone else in any way, shape, or form. Not until I tell people myself.

"Do you understand?"

The masked medical attendant hesitated, then left the morgue quickly.

Turning back to the dead man, he felt his skin prickle. Half of his face was gone, including a sizable portion of his skull.

You wanted a test, Felix. This is it.

First, he focused on putting Jordan's body back together. Exactly as it had been before his death. A week in the morgue had probably slowed down the decay of everything.

Hadn't stopped it, though.

Status Correction: Expand for List (Over 5,000 items) -> Healed	Correct Status? (35,000 points)

Felix accepted the change. It was costly, but if it was a successful test, then that'd be worth it.

Jordan's body rapidly regenerated all the missing bits and pieces. His body reformed itself as if he'd never been touched.

Though he drew no breath, and his chest remained still.

Pushing his awareness into the man's character sheet, Felix looked to see if there was anything that could give him a clue on how to proceed.

Name: Jordan Taylor	Power: --
Alias:	Secondary Power: --
Physical Status: Decaying	Mental Status: Dead
Positive	Negative

Statuses: None	Statuses: Dead	
Strength:	53	Upgrade?(530)
Dexterity:	57	Upgrade?(570)
Agility:	48	Upgrade?(480)
Stamina:	67	Upgrade?(670)
Wisdom:	41	Upgrade?(410)
Intelligence:	52	Upgrade?(520)
Luck:	36	Upgrade?(360)
Primary Power:	--	Upgrade?(--)
Secondary Power:	--	Upgrade?(--)

It's not that simple. Is it?

Redirecting his focus, Felix hammered at his mind on the simple idea of Jordan coming back to life.

He'd put his mind and body back together to the point right before he died. If he could get him to breathe and get his heart beating, then he'd be alive, right?

That or we make a zombie.

Status Correction: Dead -> Living	Correct Status? (50,000 points)

Reaching up with one hand, Felix rubbed at the back of his neck.

Maybe I should ask someone to come stand with me... just in case.

Moving to the entry door, he popped it open.

Looking around, he found Lily working with some of her team. She'd accompanied him down here at his request, but had remained outside, also by his request.

"Lily, I need a hand."

She nodded absently, still talking to one of her people. A full minute later and Lily was done, coming in to join him in the morgue.

"Okay. What's with all the cloak-and-dagger mischief?" asked the woman as the door closed behind her.

"And why are you playing with corpses?"

Felix didn't answer at first, moving over to stand next to Jordan. "Raising the dead."

"I... see."

Lily came over to stand next to him. "And what am I doing here?"

"Checking to see if he has a soul. Or blow him up if he becomes a zombie. Maybe both?"

Not giving her a chance to answer or argue, Felix spent the points.

Jordan Taylor, dead for a week, with a good part of his brain being blown out, took a deep, gasping breath. His eyes flew wide open and his body spasmed.

Coughing, the man's hands shot up to his head, his eyes wide.

Looking around himself, Jordan continued to cough.

"Easy there, Jordan. Easy. You're okay," Felix said soothingly. Stealing a look to Lily, he asked under his breath, "He is okay, isn't he?"

Lily was shocked, her eyes wide, skin pale, her mouth hanging open. After a second, she lifted a hand towards the man and then nodded her head.

"He's... fine. His soul is his and it's there," Lily said in a whisper.

Jordan had sat up by this point, his hands covering his naked body as his head jerked back and forth between Lily and Felix.

"What... what happened? We were fighting in the lobby... the man in front of me had a shotgun," Jordan said in a quivering voice.

"You died. That man shot you in the head with the shotgun."

"I died?"

"Yeah. You died. You've been in the morgue for a while. About a week."

Felix fell quiet. Jordan seemed to be taking it pretty well. No need to overburden the man if he didn't have to.

"I don't understand. I died, but I'm not dead?"

"Yeah, you're not dead. I brought you back."

"Back."

"Yeah, from the dead."

"Oh. I'm a zombie, then... or something?"

"No, not at all. Lily is here, and she already confirmed for me that you are exactly as you were before you died. It's as if you never died at all."

"But... why?" Jordan seemed calm still, so Felix saw no reason to end the experiment.

"Why bring you back? Why not? It said in your file you were agnostic, so there was no religious reason not to put your s—put yourself back together. No family, either."

"Yeah... no. Neither. So... I just go back to work?"

"Take a few days off. We didn't report your death, so no worries on that end. You can just... pick up where you left off."

"Yeah. A few days off. Okay, I can... I can do that. Nothing's different?"

"No, nothing's different. You might have to get a new room assigned, and get some new clothes and things, but nothing HR can't fix up, I'm sure.

"I'll have an Other come in and get you squared away, alright?" Felix asked Jordan, patting him on the back.

"Yeah, okay. Did... did we win?"

"Decisively so. Look forward to seeing you around, Jordan."

Felix turned on his heel and left the morgue, stopping only to give Andrea instructions.

"Felix, how many points did that cost?" Lily asked, her gait slowing down as she caught up with him.

Victoria and Andrea trailed behind.

"Fifty to bring him back to life. Thirty-five to get his body put back together."

"You do know what this means, right?"

"That I should probably go buy the corpses of some of the strongest supers in the past and bring them back?" Felix responded, hitting the elevator button.

"Er. You could do that, yes. But I think first and foremost you should have HR get everyone to sign a 'life after death' policy. Not everyone may want to come back," Lily said. She entered the elevator when the doors slid open. Andrea and Victoria entered as well, though they were still silent.

Maybe this was a bad idea.

"Yeah, I kinda figured. It's why I picked Jordan. Agnostic, no family." Felix hit the button for the floor to his office. "Next thing on the to-do list: buying the street."

"Ah, we've had some success with that. It'll take some time to buy everything, but considering our assets are still frozen, that's fine.

"We need to meet with an inspector tomorrow to go over all the buildings and make sure they're up to code for a purchase. I already sent you the invite, and you accepted, but I don't think you actually read the invite.

"Not that we care about the inspection anyways, since we can just send in our teams and fix anything, but those are the regulations." Lily leaned up against the back wall of the elevator as the doors slid shut.

"Great. Why is my entire life meetings? And meetings to prepare for meetings. Maybe this is why owners hire a CEO and then wander off." Felix shook his head, his mouth twisting up in a grimace.

"No CEO would ever care as much as the owner does. That's just the reality of the situation. You're doing fine," Lily said in response.

Felix huffed as the doors opened in front of him. Setting out for his office, he couldn't find fault in her words. No one would care as much as he did.

"Yeah. I'll get with Kit and have HR run up a new policy and get everyone to indicate their preference. I'll also have them discuss the fact that Jordan is indeed alive, and no longer dead.

"I imagine I'll get a number of people trying to get me to raise dead family members."

Felix thought on that for a moment as he opened the door to his office.

"I suppose that's doable… but we'd have to have them as a different contract. I don't think a single year under the Indentured contract would cover the points."

"Ah, good news, then. We've been experimenting with HR on the contracts. We can build a contract that lasts five years now. It took some doing with verbiage and how much magical power to put into the seal, but it works.

"Binding that contract with a return from the dead is more than enough oomph to seal the deal sufficiently."

"Huh. So the nature of the deal helps enforce the contract?" Felix spun his chair around and sat down heavily in it, calling up his personal terminal.

Victoria took up her position at the door, and Andrea lay down on the couch. Neither spoke.

Their silence was becoming eerie. He imagined they'd have to consider the choice and its implications.

He was blessedly unable to resurrect himself, so his choice would never come.

"Magic can be finicky when it comes to people signing things with their souls. This would work.

"The hard part is getting a family member who owns the dead. I mean, who really owns a corpse? I imagine it might come down to if they left a will, and if they left an estate to someone. That'd probably qualify."

Felix nodded his head, the conversation falling off as he started to get lost in the day-to-day minutiae of running a company.

Andrea was on high alert.

Her Others swarmed the streets, roaming up and down them. They covered the corners, stared people down when they got close to Felix, and generally made asses of themselves. To the point that people would cross the street to avoid the mess.

He'd even caught sight of a few Others clearing and utilizing the rooftops.

Victoria was at his side, of course. He'd finally heard from Ioana that she was happy Victoria was at his side. Apparently she was a master swordswoman and could even fight Ioana to a standstill.

Felicia and the inspector had disappeared inside a building ten minutes ago and were going through the entire thing with a team, as well as the owners.

Andrea turned her head to one side as someone probably relayed something to her.

After a second, she turned her eyes back to the building they were standing in front of.

"It looks like vomit. It's vomit yellow. I want to paint it. Can we paint it?" she asked.

"I don't care? Pretty sure Felicia and her team are only interested in the guts of the building. You'll have to link up with design," Felix said offhandedly.

Andrea hadn't said anything about why she'd gone silent yesterday after he had pulled Jordan back from the grave.

By and large, Legion as a whole was rather impressed with the news that death was not the end for them.

At least, if they opted for that in their HR policy.

Much as he'd predicted, the yes and no responses were divided by religion. *Makes sense. Maybe she's religious? I mean… why not ask?*

"Andrea," Felix started, his voice unsure. "Why were you so upset yesterday after you found out I could raise the dead?"

"Huh?" she asked, her eyes not meeting his own. "I don't understand. By the way, after this I want to—"

"Andrea, if you don't want to talk about it, just tell me that. I'll leave it alone. And I ask because I care."

The Beastkin winced, her tail drooping.

"It was just surprising… really. I think I've got you figured out, and you do something I never even though about.

"I mean, I'm not smart, right? I'm scared that maybe you're sleeping with me for a reason I'm too stupid to figure out."

Oddly reasonable… though a bit late to worry about that sort of thing, isn't it?

"Well. I can tell you I'm sleeping with you because you're beautiful, and I care about you. I'm not sure where we'll end up, but I can tell you that it's not just sex.

"Is that fair?" Felix tried to get it all out as straightforwardly as possible. Andrea was a simple and straightforward girl, after all.

The Beastkin's mismatched eyes were glowing faintly, staring into him. Her tail was lifted and swishing back and forth slowly, her entire body angled toward him. All around him, the Others had shifted as well. Many were watching him, their eyes glowing and intent.

"Really?"

"Yep. Look alive, your Others are watching," Felix said with a grin and a vague gesture around them.

As one, Andrea and the Others returned to their normal pose. It was strange and unnerving.

"Lily was right," Andrea whispered, the ears on her head swiveling around.

Before Felix could question her, Victoria pulled her sword from its sheath. Her eyes were fixed on a man heading their way.

The rather large individual, who had shouldered his way through several Others to get past them, stopped dead.

Victoria had taken several steps out in front of Felix and was in the process of leveling her blade out in front of her, pointing the tip towards the man.

Looking at it closely, Felix realized it wasn't the same sword she'd had previously. It shone in the light. A cold, deadly shimmer.

Upgrade from Felicia?

That large man looked at Victoria for another second before he doubled back the way he came and took the crosswalk to the other side of the street.

Victoria gave her blade a flourish and sheathed it. Sniffing disdainfully, she wandered back to Felix's side.

Felicia and the inspector chose that moment to pop out.

"Nothing terrible with that one. Elevator needs an update to the electrical, but that's it," Felicia said grumpily. She marched up to Felix and glared up at him.

She was viewing the entire exercise as a waste of time. He couldn't disagree with her, but it still needed to be done.

"Okay. Get it written down. Where to next?" Felix did his best not to sigh.

"Nowhere. Mr. Inspector Man needs a break. He and his team are going to break for thirty. Union and all. I say we hit the cafe," she said, pointing across the way.

The cafe in question had already agreed to the purchase. The staff, after being informed of the purchase, seemed happy that nothing was changing.

Doubly so when the volume of customers skyrocketed after it was made known Legion was buying into the place, and would be subsidizing the costs for employees starting immediately.

"Come on, money bags, you can expense it." Felicia walked out into the street and started crossing without a thought towards the cars.

In a creepy scene out of a thriller movie, Others flooded the street and began blocking traffic in both directions.

Felix couldn't help it now and sighed, stepping out into the street and following along.

"What are you doing about Agent Shithead?" Felicia nearly yelled over her shoulder at him.

"Who, Smith? I have an appointment with his boss after this. Going to see if we can get our assets unfrozen. Lily prepped me with a lovely document showing how we can file a lawsuit and claim damages if they don't."

"Ah, the princess. You porkin' her yet? You're already porkin' the wolf."

Andrea left his side and skipped ahead to be next to Felicia. "He sure is! Me, that is, not Lily. Not yet. We're trying to get him to settle for both of us, and only us. Lily says she can share with me because I have as much guile as a knife. I don't mind sharing with her because she's honest with me."

"Oh? Good on you two, then. May your porkin' be rough and messy." Felicia slapped Andrea on the ass, getting a squeal out of the Beastkin. Then Felicia stepped past her and into the cafe, shoving the door aside.

Victoria gave him a strange look as she passed by him entering the cafe.

Felix could only wonder at what the hell Lily and Andrea were up to.

A soft chirping came from his phone. Felix waited till he sat down next to Andrea before he checked to see what the notification was.

It was an email from Lily. Opening it, he felt his temperature rise and his teeth clicked together.

His meeting with Smith's boss had been canceled without a reason. Their assets were still frozen and now he had no recourse.

He wouldn't bow to Smith and whore out one of his people. He knew he didn't have a moral compass that pointed north, but even he wouldn't sink that low.

No, no, he had other alternatives that he could employ that would be worse, but not as bad for his own people.

He tapped in a response for Lily. He wanted her to get a hold of Wraith for a meeting.

No sooner was his message away than did another message come in for him. This time from Kit.

"Ugh." Felix turned off the display and picked up the menu. All three women had turned their heads to him at his noise of displeasure.

Before they could ask, he opened his mouth again. "None of the shops are buying gold anymore. Someone figured out what we were doing, I'm betting.

"Which means we need to figure out where to make our money next."

"Cars," Felicia said, slapping her menu closed. "They can't stop us from selling cars to the public. Get all our cash together and buy as many junkers as we can. My team will repair everything we can, and list out the parts we're missing.

"Then your stupid ass comes through and magics up whatever we're missing with your points. The end."

Felicia held up her hand towards the waitress and gestured at her angrily. The Dwarf didn't wait for anyone or anything.

Cars, huh? That's not a bad idea. We can hit the scrapyards and buy as many junkers as we can and push them all through private auctions or the used car lots.

Chapter 29 - Moral Compass -

The sun hadn't even risen yet. The pre-dawn gloom was a grungy haze outside.

Felix stared into his terminal as he contemplated the call he was about to take with Wraith.

Smith hadn't really left him any room at this point. They really did need access to their accounts.

Sure, they could function without for a long time, but at a cost.

"Thinking about it?" Lily asked from the couch.

Everyone else had been cleared from the room, and Andrea was still in bed.

"Yeah. Everyone up to this point had always felt... vindicated in some way. This one... less so," Felix said, rubbing at his jaw with one hand.

"Then why do it? You have alternatives."

"Because those alternatives don't do me any favors for my own people. And I refuse to put my people over a table—literally, in this case—if I don't have to.

"Smith can take his horny self to a bar." Felix shook his head as he said it. He knew his reasons for doing it, but it didn't make it any easier.

"For what it's worth, I appreciate it. You're not exactly a shining beacon of moral righteousness. Then again, you're not the same person I first met anymore," Lily said.

Felix scoffed at that, his mind going to Eva and her blasted pen. "Yeah, tell me about it. From resources to employees. Definitely a change in my own plans as well."

"That and you keep putting those precious money-making points of yours back into your people."

"They need it."

"The person who can split into multiple people and is practically immortal needed regeneration?" Lily asked, her tone becoming mildly antagonistic.

"Well, no—"

"Or Felicia needed that makeover you gave her?"

"That was part of a deal—"

"Or even Kit, our beloved psychic, who is now a telepath, telekinetic, and a master of illusions. She clearly needed all of that?"

"We were escaping from Tanker. We needed—"

"No, you didn't. I've talked to Kit and Andrea. They were both under the impression they could swerve around him. He's strong, not fast."

Felix thought on that. On all three, really.

In each case, he had had a clear reason for doing it, or so he'd believed at the time. They still felt justified.

Sort of.

"What do you want me to say, Lily?" Felix pressed his forehead to the desk. His call with Wraith was due any second now.

"Nothing. Only that you should realize that you aren't doing things entirely for a 'necessary' purpose. Now, Wraith is going to call you in ten seconds. Get your game face on."

"Ten seconds? How would you know that?" Felix asked curious. As he lifted his eyes from the desk, they went to the phone, then to Lily.

She was dressed in dark colors that hugged her frame but were modest and professional.

Much as she always was.

Instead of responding, she pointed to the phone.

As if by magic, the phone rang.

Controlling his response, and trying to do the same for his heart, Felix accepted the call.

"Wraith," came the sibilant voice on the other end.

"Thank you for calling." Felix took a breath and went with his chosen course of action. "Can you kill Smith and make it look accidental?"

"Yes."

"Can you do it after forcing him to unfreeze us?"

"No."

"Kill him. Return for debrief after you complete your duty."

"Done."

The line disconnected and went dead.

Felix pursed his lips and set the phone down.

"That was easier than it should have been..."

"Not really. You knew what you wanted to do a while ago. This was only the culmination of that. For what it's worth, I'm glad you made the decision. Smith was a problem."

"That he was. I'm not looking forward to telling Kit about this." Felix turned back to the window, watching the first fingers of light reaching out above the buildings.

"She won't be happy. She's still a hero at heart. She'll need some placating and maybe something to soothe her conscious. I'll ask her privately later if she wants me to take over counterintelligence. The dirty side of the business."

"Thanks. Not sure if she'll take you up on it, but I appreciate you offering it to her all the same."

"Anything for you," Lily murmured from directly behind him. She'd snuck up on him.

Felix didn't have it in him to react right now to her provocations. In fact, this was probably a good time to go on the attack.

"Andrea mentioned you were trying to get me, yourself, and herself into a three-way relationship."

"I'm not surprised; it was only a matter of time before she mentioned it. She's a good girl, but has about as much guile—"

"As a knife," they said at the same time.

"Yeah, she really doesn't have a cunning bone in her body. But what about you, Lily? You're a beautiful woman who could have any man she wanted. I can't imagine you willingly signing up to be a plaything."

He could feel Lily standing behind him. Felix didn't even need to look at her to know she was there. It was something he'd noticed about her a while ago.

She put out an energy, what he assumed was magical energy, and anyone nearby could feel the pressure of it.

Or so he assumed. He'd never actually asked anyone about it.

"You're right. I'd never sign up to be a plaything. And you'd never treat me like one. You're the type of idiot that, once he starts sleeping with a woman, happily shuts down that entire area of his life. To literally have eyes for no one else."

Felix blustered for a moment at that. Then deflated. She wasn't wrong.

His experience with women was almost entirely dependent on them taking the lead. He was a follower when it came to that.

Monogamy felt right and he didn't look elsewhere.

It was also why the idea bothered him about having two women.

"Much as you told Andrea, we'll see where this goes. No promises, but it's a start. Besides, I can't deny I'm interested in you. You're fascinating in a strange way.

"I'm not brave enough to jump into your bed as easily as Andie did, but we'll see where it all goes. Like I said."

Snorting, Felix shook his head. "Only you would ask a man to date her while saying that."

"I know, and that's why you're taking me to dinner tonight." Lily's lips pressed to his cheek. "Doesn't have to be fancy, but I do expect it to be just us.

"Well, other than Vicky. See you at the department meeting later. I've gotta run. Need to pick out a nice dress."

Andrea's fist landed cleanly on his jaw and sent him crashing to the ground. Felix felt like his head was spinning.

That and he heard this high-pitched whining noise. It was really freaking distracting.

"Get up! I'm coming for you," Andrea called out to him as she closed in on him and struck him twice more. Once to the shoulder, the second to his midsection.

Stumbling to his feet, Felix managed to get his hands up in time to fend off a punch.

"Good! Faster next time, dear. Faster. Your opponent won't wait for you to get up to your feet." Andrea got in closer and sent a fist towards his stomach.

He sidestepped correctly, but wasn't fast enough. She caught the side of his stomach and sent him to the mat again.

"Pah, he's done," Ioana said. The sound of her heavy footfalls departing were like the sound of accusations to him.

Too slow. Too weak. Too much thought. That was what they kept saying.

He'd asked for this, and he was getting better, but he was starting to regret this course of action.

Panting, Felix managed to at least keep himself up on one knee, rather than flopping into the mat.

"Better. Quicker, though. If you can't be quicker, block it. Expecting to dodge attacks is honestly a good way to get hit.

"Silly dear. Don't worry, I'll make it all better tonight." Andrea was leaning over the top of him, her hands patting his shoulders.

"Yeah. Thanks. Did Lily tell you about tonight?"

"She did! I look forward to hearing how it goes from her later." Andrea's tail was swishing back and forth happily as she said it.

She was genuinely happy for Lily.

"By the way, I know I say this every time, but I appreciate the training. I know it isn't easy to teach someone with little to no aptitude." Felix groaned and got to his feet.

"Aptitude is merely a way to measure how quickly one learns something. In this case, you just need more time." Andrea gave him a bright smile and then wandered off.

Victoria replaced her, holding out a wooden sword to him.

Felix sighed and took the sword from her hand.

"Training while tired —"

"I know, I know. Training while tired is more difficult, but doesn't hinder learning." Felix grumped and then fell back into the neutral pose she'd beaten into him days previous.

Her training blade came up into the same pose, then darted forward.

She'd done that to him almost every time, forcing him to expect an attack immediately every time they started.

Managing to get his blade up in the appropriate deflection, he stepped in and struggled to bring his weapon across as quickly as he could.

Victoria was gone before he even finished the block, having stepped backward out of his range.

"Good. Now, let's start," Victoria said with a sickening amount of enthusiasm.

Victoria did much the same as Andrea had, beating him forwards and backwards across the mat. Giving him a number of bruises and welts with each pass.

Eventually, Victoria released him from his hell and sent him off to the medical room.

Bruises and welts were fine, but there was no sense in having them beyond the original lesson if you didn't have to.

Felicia's machines did a great job of getting a person back to normal for most anything.

Especially since he couldn't do a damn thing to himself. It always ended up coming back to that.

The inability to modify his own parameters. To upgrade himself so easily as he did others.

After the medical fixup, and a quick snack, Felix was the first person to the department head meeting.

He normally was. It gave him some time to refine his agenda and get everything laid out how he wanted it.

Before he even had a chance to start, Kit came in.

"Good. I was hoping to catch you alone," she said, dropping down into a chair directly in front of him.

Felix could only nod his head, not even bothering to open his terminal. Instead, he folded his hands in front of him and looked to the telepath. "What can I do for you?"

"Lily told me about Wraith and Smith. I'm not... really sure this was the right path."

"Alright, what options were you considering instead?"

Kit blinked and then looked to the table. "Other options? I mean, we could have just waited, couldn't we?"

"Could we have?"

"Well, er... yes. Yes, we could have."

"Okay, what are our finances?"

"Our finances?"

"If you're confident in our ability to wait, then clearly our finances are good. What are our finances?"

"They're... no, they're not good. Unless something changed, we'd barely have enough capital to pay our bills on time. Not including Dimitry's loan is coming due."

"Okay, if our finances aren't good, and we'd be in trouble soon, what other options did we have available?"

"I... don't know. But we didn't have to kill Smith!"

"No, we didn't. Yet as I've been directing your own mind to the problem, I could not myself find another answer."

"Killing someone isn't an answer!"

"It is when they're not a good person, and are demanding that I prostitute you out to service them. That was another option, you remember. It seems unlikely, but would you have preferred that to killing him? He'd be back next month for the same thing, mind you."

Kit chewed at her lip, her eyes scrunching up. "No," she said finally.

"The choice isn't on you, Kit. You had nothing to do with it. This is all on me, and it's my burden to bear. Not yours.

"Now, is there anything else you wanted to talk about before the others came?"

Kit shook her head, her eyes still glued to the table.

After a handful of heartbeats, her gaze moved up and met his own. "I'm not very good at this. In the beginning, I was bitter, jaded. It felt right. Now, though... now I feel as if I'm abusing my powers."

"The powers I gave you," Felix clarified.

Kit nodded her head once. "The powers you gave me."

"Have I asked you to take a life that you felt wasn't justified?"

"No."

"Have I asked you to harm anyone who wasn't attempting to hurt us?"

"No."

"Have I asked you to do anything against your will?"

"Yes... well, no. You listened when I told you I didn't want to use the sausage machine on our people."

"Then what's the problem, Kit? I don't understand. Help me understand."

Kit licked her lips and then made a vague gesture at him, then back at herself. She shook her head a fraction and then took a partial breath and held it. Then just as suddenly let it out.

"I don't know."

"Is it because you can't read my mind? Never had the problem of not being able to verify a thought, concern, or problem without a proof positive?" Felix said it as gently as he could.

It was the only thing he could think of. Kit and he hadn't ever really disagreed on many things, but small little things could have added up in her head. And without her ability to rifle through his thoughts, he imagined she had no way to verify her own judgments about situations.

"I... could that be it? It just sounds so selfish. So childlike."

"How do you confirm what someone believes?"

"I do exactly what you said. I look into the mind of others to see how it was received or thought of and adjust."

"Have you considered not doing that? Taking people at their face value?"

"Why would I?"

"For fun. See if you can hone in on what psychiatrists and psychologists have been doing for years. Up to you, though, merely a question.

"As to the problem at hand, I wouldn't worry much about it. Nothing has changed since our last talk. You're our conscience and our moral compass. I expect you to continue pointing due north and provide me with a counterbalance."

The door to the conference room burst open and Felicia entered, followed closely by Ioana.

Before the door could close, Lily, Andrea, Victoria, and Miu trooped in, taking their seats.

Victoria took up a spot behind Felix's right shoulder.

"Welcome, one and all. This department head meeting is more than likely a critical one, as I have one update that must be shared. I'm sure you have topics you want to cover as well, so I'll be quick about it.

"If no one has any objections?"

Felix looked around the room to each member to confirm there were none.

"I've tasked Wraith to kill Agent Smith. He should be dead by tomorrow. At that point, I'll be heading over to their office to demand to speak with our case worker. With any luck, we'll get a new one that will take one look at the length of time our assets have been frozen and undo it."

Everyone had different reactions. Ioana, Miu, and Felicia nodded their heads. Lily had no reaction, as she had already known. Andrea looked thoughtful, and Kit still seemed frustrated.

"Beyond that, everything is as you heard it last. Assets frozen, gold is no longer being purchased in the city, the two stores on each side of ours steal perhaps ninety percent of our customers, and the estate lawyers deliberately held on to a check so it'd bounce.

"We're under attack. It's just no longer a physical attack."

Grim faces were turned to him around the conference table. Everyone knew what the score was, and no one could doubt what was happening.

"We'll start with Felicia, as she had a brilliant idea on how to generate some cash flow. Felicia?"

All heads swung towards the diminutive woman.

"Exactly as planned. We're overhauling all the cars we could get our hands on from the junkyards. By the end of next week, we'll have them all ready for sale, providing you can carve out some time to get your ass in gear and magic us up some parts."

"I can make that happen. Any initial estimations?"

Felicia wrinkled her nose and then shrugged. "Not really? Price of all the cars we bought in mint condition, with working parts, would probably be several million. Our investment wasn't large, so that'd be good. Won't know till we run an auction. We're already distributing flyers about a car show and auction."

"Great. Anything else?"

"No. Weapon work is going good. Tiny robots, too. Power source is coming along. Your personal Warden was started earlier. That'll be up and running soon. Getting my people experienced with the cars first. Similar in some ways."

"Great. Next, Lily?"

"Legally, we're rock solid. Everything we're doing is actually above board, so it makes our job relatively easy. Nothing really going on there. Though everyone and their mother is trying to get the paperwork together for dead relatives."

Felix could only nod. That'd been a concern, and he wasn't that worried about it. It'd only help bring up his numbers and his people. This financial crisis was a temporary problem.

"Finance would be next, I suppose. And that's where the problem lies." Lily sighed and pressed her fingertips to her brow, just above her glasses.

"We've got enough capital to go maybe two weeks. Three on the outside. It's not going to go very well if they don't unlock our accounts."

"I see. Is there anything we can do to help shore up those numbers?"

"No. There isn't. We'll be declaring bankruptcy soon if that car auction doesn't work out.

"That's the reality, and there's no changing it."

He hadn't thought it possible to feel worse than he had minutes ago. He was wrong.

"I'm going to make pancakes. Pancakes make everything better."

Andrea stood up and held up an arm; several Others leapt out of her and held up an arm each.

"Pancakes!" they shouted in unison.

Unable to help himself, Felix lifted his arm with a smile. "Pancakes."

Chapter 30 - The Bait -

This was a risk. A risk to come to a location he'd ordered someone killed at. A risk to step outside in public where he was attacked every time he'd done so. A risk to go to something that he'd called and made arrangements for the previous day, giving his enemies time to prepare. A risk to go make demands of a department that didn't care a whisker about him or his people.

Yet here he was, sitting in the lobby of the government agency that seemed hellbent on screwing him over.

Victoria was with him, of course, along with Andrea and a number of Others, but that was it.

Everyone else was busy trying to scrounge up material, capital, or favors to get them through this hardship. They'd only allowed him two companions to accompany him anyways, so any more would have to wait in the lobby.

Felix was dressed up in one of his nicer suits. Andrea looked as if Lily had dressed her, as she was striking and modest at the same time. A blood red blouse, a black jacket, and black pencil skirt.

Victoria had chosen something more mundane. A suit jacket, slacks, button-up shirt, and ballistic vest.

That and her very real, very high-end sword hanging from her hip.

No one had attempted to take it from her, though Andrea's handgun had been confiscated.

After getting a pat-down and being asked what their business was and who they were here to see, they were promptly told to wait. They sat them down in the lobby right there without another word or direction.

That was an hour ago.

"Can we go home? You smell great, and every time your eyes fall on me, I can smell your need," Andrea said, laying her head on his shoulder.

Victoria snorted at that, shifting from one foot to the other. She hadn't relaxed her guard, and seemed as tightly wound as she'd ever been.

"No, we need to stay and make sure this gets taken care of. You heard what was said at the meeting. No more questions about that; I'd rather not discuss our business out in the open. Who knows what's being recorded."

"Fine. I'll be good. Lily told me that when I'm good you're supposed to reward me.

"Oh! That reminds me, how'd the date go? Lily seemed really happy this morning."

Felix felt his lips curl into a smile. "We decided to postpone it till this evening because I couldn't get a reservation."

"Huh? Then why was she happy?" Andrea asked, her tail sliding up behind him to curl around his hip.

"Because he's taking it seriously," Victoria answered. "He didn't want to just take her out, he wanted to take her to a nice restaurant."

"Oh. Hm. You can make pancakes with me and then we'll mate in our bed. That'd make me happy," Andrea said, pressing up closer to his side.

"I'm all for that, but I think maybe right now isn't the best place to talk about it. Or cling so closely to me. It's pleasant but distracting."

"What if we started making out? Do you think they'd want to get rid of us if we started making a scene?"

Felix felt the sweat pop out on his brow, his skin heating up several degrees.

"I don't think that'd be wise," Victoria said critically. "How could you protect him at the same time? They disallowed your Others in here, remember? I need you helping me here."

"That's no fun. Besides, when I said it, Felix got really excited. I could practically hear his heartrate speed up, and the scent was strong."

"Really? That strong?" Victoria asked.

"Maybe he wants you to watch. Oh! Or maybe he wants you to join? Not sure. We should ask Lily. She'll know what to think of this."

"Uhhhh, I think that—"

At that moment, a man in a suit opened the interior lobby door and held it open. "Mr. Campbell?"

Standing up happily, Felix left the two women behind with the speed of his escape.

Andrea and Victoria scrambled to catch up with him as he dodged past the crony and into the hallway beyond.

"This way, please."

Felix didn't bother to respond as he followed the man down the hallway. They wouldn't have anything to say to him that would be worthwhile anyways. And if they did, they certainly wouldn't tell him prior to his meeting with what he assumed would be their boss. Or at least someone higher up in the corporate ladder.

People who fetch guests in the lobby don't typically have a lot to add at this point.

They were led to a glass door, which the man opened for them. "Mr. Chirk will be with you shortly. Have a seat."

Felix dropped into a chair and rested his left ankle on his right knee. "More waiting. Goodie. It's a shame we can't bill them for our time. This'd be a hell of a lucrative trip."

Andrea shrugged her shoulders, wandering over to a window. Her head turned one way, then the other, peering out of the glass. Then she held a hand up to her ear.

"This is Pancake, request street actual check in. Pancake actual is in south side of building, floor two, window. Confirm overwatch," she said.

Felix watched her back as she easily slipped into her role of Myriad. He could vaguely hear responses from the Others, but nothing concrete.

Victoria was busy searching the room, looking for anything out of place that could be a problem. Even going so far as to open the desk drawers looking for weapons.

"Pancake receives, maintain overwatch on this position."

Andrea turned around and looked to Victoria while folding her hands behind her back. "All is well and accounted for. Can you confirm the room is clear?"

Victoria popped open an electrical device she pulled out of her tactical vest. Thumbing the side of it, she looked down to what he assumed was a display.

"Listening devices, nothing outside expectations. Room is clear," Victoria said, closing the device up. She walked to the door and took up a position there.

"Good work." Andrea turned to Felix and gave him a grin. "Room clear, street is covered."

Felix gave her a small smile and felt weird about the entire thing. He knew their precautions were necessary considering the number of attempts on his life, but they still made him feel strange.

He still felt like Felix, the fast food manager. Felix, the lonely man who barely made enough at his dead-end job.

Now I'm Felix, the one with twenty-four hours a day, seven days a week bodyguards who sweep and clear buildings that I'll be entering.

"Thanks, Andrea. Hopefully we can get this taken care of and get moving. I'm looking forward to not fearing payroll every day.

"Costs keep rising, even if we can't get a hold of our accounts. This whole thing is fucking ridiculous."

Felix shifted, slouching into his chair.

"Agreed, but we do what we must."

Felix opened his mouth to retort when the door opened behind them. An older man in a dark suit walked in. His eyes snapped to Victoria, whose hand was resting on the sword at her side, then to Andrea, whose hand had dipped into her jacket.

Felix wouldn't have been surprised if Andrea had managed to slip a holdout pistol through security.

"I see. Mr. Campbell?" asked the older man, looking to Felix.

"That'd be me. I'll cut to the chase," Felix said, getting to his feet. "My accounts have been frozen for longer than the statute al—"

At that moment, his phone went off. Pausing long enough to rotate his wrist, he glanced at the linked screen.

Eva Adelpha.

"I'm sorry, this might be important," Felix apologized. Tapping the screen, he fished his phone out of his suit pocket and held it up to his ear.

"Eva wha—"

"The school is under attack! We'r—"

As abruptly as she'd started talking, the phone went dead.

Feeling his heartbeat speed up, he dropped the phone to his waist. He quickly thumbed through the security screen and pulled up his contacts. Tapping Ioana's line, he held the phone back up to his ear.

"Mr. Campbell, if you ca—"

"Hush," Victoria commanded at the man, stepping between Mr. Chirk and Felix.

"Ioana," came the strong voice of his War Maiden.

"Eva called me, said there was an attack on the school."

"What? Give me a second."

"Now see here. Mr. Campbell, if you can't give me your attention this moment, you can leave."

Felix's eyes tracked back to Mr. Chirk. They'd kept him waiting for a long time.

Long enough that Felix had gotten angry. Long enough that the anger had turned into a cold, quiet rage. Long enough that he'd been tempted to send Wraith in and clear out the entire agency.

"I mean it. You can leave and we can schedule an appointment at another time. I believe my calendar is open in two weeks. Until then, nothing will change with you or your accounts."

Felix blinked. That was quite a threat. It'd put them well outside the point that they'd more than likely become insolvent.

"We've got confirmation," Ioana said in his ear. "There's an attack going on alright. I'm sending multiple squads and all four Wardens. I'd appreciate it if you could suit up and join us. Having you there should cut through red tape since you own the school."

"Well?" Mr. Chirk asked.

Felix blinked, his thoughts grinding to an immediate halt.

Because there was no need to debate the choice.

Guardian indeed.

"Apparently my weapon of choice is a pen. You'll be hearing from my lawyers, Mr. Chirk. Mr. Smith tried to blackmail me and my people, then held our accounts hostage. I do have proof of it.

"I plan on taking this up with Skipper. I hope you're ready to get your entire organization cracked open."

Dismissing the man with a flick of his free hand, he turned his head to the side to focus on the call.

Victoria, taking his intention as something else, shoved the older man out of his own office, and shut the door.

"I'll be there. Send me a Telemedic to pick us up. We'll have the Others bring the cars back."

Only minutes after having received the call, everyone was on site. The Telemedics had earned their keep several times over today.

Felix would need to increase their capacity and give them some combat training. That and increase the number of them.

All over the school, his people were swarming the grounds.

Squads were actively working to clear the entire school. Each squad was made up of twelve people. Each one of those squads were hand assembled to form their teams. They were filled with both mundanes carrying amped-up gear and supers to provide force multipliers.

On top of that very deadly force, the four Wardens were released. They were being utilized separately of each other. The long-range models were used to clear open areas that could be a killing field. The Shield versions were being sent into the close-quarters area to clear any combatants that could be hiding and waiting in ambush.

After their arrival, it was obvious the school was in lockdown. Students and teachers were huddling in their classrooms. The classrooms that would have had students from Legion, however, were conspicuously empty.

Ioana and her team moved as only trained professionals could.

Having been given a huge budget and open recruiting was clearly paying off.

Training rooms, equipment, extensive mental conditioning through HR, the best in medical care.

Ioana's people had been showered in everything that could and would make them lethal, deadly, and balanced mentally.

Those soldiers, as if they could be called anything else, were clad in dark black tactical gear from head to toe. Armed with high-end weaponry, both prototypes from Felicia and White's lab, and standard armory issue. Equipped with spell-powered gear built by Lily and her corps of magicians.

They were a force that could probably stand toe to toe with actual special forces, and win.

Even if they fell, providing they'd signed the appropriate form, they would rise again for the next battle. Wiser, having gained experience most paid for with their life and were unable to act on.

At least that mountain of money was worth it.

Felix tried to marshal his thoughts and mind back to the situation. He was standing there in his powered armor like a daydreaming fool.

Around him, his people worked.

And they really were his people. Someone had been building him a team to function around him in the field.

A command team.

Those people had assembled as soon as word had spread that he'd be taking the field. Bodyguards, techs, Telemedics, and supers who would be useful for communications.

They'd put together an instant communications hub and headquarters for him in two minutes of arrival.

He'd have to check in to see who had set this up for him. It was incredibly effective, and he felt like he was tied into the whole operation even without being there.

Kit, who wasn't far away, was acting as if it was completely normal and expected. Making her the prime suspect.

He was watching as a Warden began its approach on the library building. It was a massive stone-faced thing that looked as if it had been a truly large endowment from a wealthy contributor.

Probably to buy the silence of the school as well as entry for the child of a well-known super.

Or a delinquent.

As the Warden made its way across the field towards the building, the tension mounted. This would be a defensible area, for both students to find shelter, and for a hostile force to make home.

When the Warden reached the halfway point, a missile flared to life from an upper window.

In a second, that missile closed the distance and exploded into the Warden. A ball of flame went up around the figure, the camera feed giving way to static and red glare.

Two seconds later and the Warden was visible again. Around it, a blue glowing shell flickered.

The Warden angled itself backwards and engaged the jump jets on its legs and fired, sending it rocketing back the way it had come.

As it flew, the Warden spun around, bringing its railgun up to its shoulder. It lined up a shot, and fired. Having fired, it finished its spin, putting its back to the building.

The massive round lit the air on fire as it boomed out. The slug went through the window the heavy explosive had come from.

Switching from the Warden's camera to an aerial drone, Felix flipped over to its heat camera.

All around the interior of the window and ground was the bright red of heat. Splattered liberally in every direction, the Warden had landed their shot, and blown apart the combatant.

"Enemy down," reported a tech over the comms. The Warden who had been engaged on came to a graceful landing behind a building.

"Damn good shot," Felix muttered.

"Thank you, sir," came back the immediate response.

He hadn't meant to congratulate the soldier, but whatever.

It really was a great shot.

The other long-range Warden was moving to the other side of the building now to set up a crossfire. The two Shield Wardens continued to clear and search.

Half of the deployed squads broke off and began to cordon off the library.

Curiously, one squad broke away and was making their way back towards the landing area.

Routing his helmet's feed to a drone in that area, he found the reason.

Crates had been dropped in by Telemedics after the area was secured. Telemedics could carry quite a bit with them, but the original power had been built around the measurements of humans.

The crates themselves looked as if they'd been designed to maximize what a Telemedic could bring with them.

There was a squad watching over ground zero and those crates, but there was no indication of what was in those crates.

Turning his focus back to the library, the Wardens were watching for heat signals in the windows. They weren't cleared to fire yet, as they couldn't ID those targets, but that wouldn't be the case for much longer.

Part of each squad was assigned an electronics warfare and reconnaissance member.

A number of small drones were being launched, both into the air and on the ground.

Making sure his voice wouldn't carry, and that his comms were on silent, Felix cleared his throat.

"I'm glad to see that constant training preparation is paying off. Remind me to approve whatever Ioana wants after this."

He meant it, too. This was smooth. He couldn't deny they were reacting to the enemy movements, but this was a planned reaction. Planned reactive movements.

"You already did approve everything she asked for. I'm still surprised you approved the armored cars," Victoria said, watching one of the monitors.

Felix cast his mind back. Now that he was thinking about it, he couldn't remember not approving anything Ioana asked for.

Everything had been drawn up with plans, expectations, and costs that had seemed acceptable at the time.

"Armored cars," Felix said slowly.

One of the techs directed a camera to the roadway entry. There sat six armored cars, blocking traffic on both sides of the street. Their turrets were pointed down those open streets.

They were painted a dark black, with white lettering and a logo on the side.

He didn't need to read what it said. There would be only one thing that would be written there.

A serial number, a garage loading bay, maybe even what unit it belonged to. Above all that, though, it'd say one word.

Legion.

"This'll be on the news for sure," Andrea said, clapping her hands together. "Can we go do an interview? I always see the after stuff on the news when I visit somewhere, never during."

"I promise not to mention that I'm your personal secretary and that we're sleeping together."

After a moment, Andrea tilted her head to the side, looking at him.

"Do you think they like pancakes?"

Chapter 31 - Outplayed -

"Let's not and say we did." Felix started flipping through the monitors and feeds in his helmet.

A blueprint had been shared on the war-net, their version of a privatized shared working space for information. That and more info was being quickly drawn in and hostiles counted and placed.

The drones were earning their keep and then some.

A light on the inside corner of his helmet turned on. It was a deep red color. The kind that screamed "warning" without the word.

Felix focused on it and a screen came up.

One of the squads had gotten their drone into the center of the library. There, hunkered down in a sphere of magical energy, were his kids. There were wounded amongst them, but it looked like everyone was there.

A man was pounding on that shield, his fists glowing red with each strike. On the opposite side, someone was firing a never-ending stream of rifle rounds into it.

Pausing only to reload and shove a new magazine home.

Before he could say anything, the screen he was looking at was forcibly changed as Ioana began documenting orders there.

Flipping back to the overview of the library, Felix watched as a super with speedster powers moved around the library.

The tactically loaded super stopped at each squad, handed over what looked like a black piece of sheet metal with handles, and left for the next group.

As if it was by designation, a member from each squad ended up with that black piece of metal and moved to the front of the group.

A timer began ticking down in the corner of the war-net from two minutes.

Felix looked away from that, focusing his view towards what was actually happening around him.

He caught the eye of the Telemedic team lead and then crooked a finger. "We have eyes on the kids," Felix said as the woman came in close. "I'm betting you can't get through as long as that shield is up?"

"That's correct, sir. We can't through barriers if they're sealed up."

"Okay, I want your people familiar with the location, and be ready to bounce in, grab one, then bounce out if that shield goes down. Be ready as soon as possible, because we have no idea how long that thing will hold. Lily builds 'em tough, but it can only take so much.

"Use the monitor feed to familiarize yourself. Got it?"

The team lead nodded her head. "Yes, sir. We won't fail you."

Turning his head back to the screens, Felix accessed his helmet feed and routed it back to the war-net.

At one minute, the timer turned yellow. The two long-range Wardens opened up, their railguns coughing out their high-powered rounds.

Drones recorded several kills before everyone took cover inside. The long-range cover kept the windows clear.

At fifteen seconds, the Shield Wardens sprinted forward. Several of the hostiles tried to return to the window, only to be driven back. Both melee Wardens reached the walls before the timer hit zero.

Not stopping there, both Wardens began scaling the building. Nimble as a spider, they leaped from window to window to the top.

Reaching the end of the countdown, the squads moved up.

That black sheet metal was gone now, and in its place was a tall and wide shield. Angled at the sides, it would protect and block an entire squad on approach.

Held by the point position, it was supported by another person on each side. The glow of magic infused it.

The shields weren't needed, though. The squads reached the entry points without resistance.

A ten-second timer popped up in the corner as the last squad made it to their assigned position.

The Shield Wardens on top, now positioned in opposite corners, brought their swords down into the roof.

Withdrawing their weapons, each reached into a pod on their side and pulled out what could only be a grenade.

At five seconds, they pulled the pins and dropped them into the holes they'd made.

The Wardens on the outskirts began firing into the windows, if only to force people to keep their heads down.

Once more at zero, the squads moved in. Doors were battered aside and the teams began to enter.

They cleared the entry lobby, checked corners, and began a systematic sweep of the building.

On top of the building, the Shield Wardens burst through the roof. They would be clearing their way down.

To Felix, it was mind-numbing and hard to follow.

Instead, he focused in on the children.

The shield was still up, but flickering with each strike from the super strength goon who was pounding on it.

Then the shield went down.

Before Felix could even think about yelling out, the Telemedics were there. Teleporting in, and out, in the blink of an eye.

In the Telemedic loading area, the kids popped into existence. Being ferried here as quickly as his people could manage. As fast as they could.

Before the brute could think to attack the kids, they were all gone. Whisked away at the moment the shield failed.

Expanding the Telemedics is now a definite. Yep. Lots more.

Felix couldn't stop the smirk that spread across his face. Disconnecting himself from the feed, as there wasn't much he could add and he doubted there'd be much left to do, he moved over to the kids.

Sifting through them, he quickly found Eva and Lucian in one corner. Both appeared whole and healthy. Which meant Lily wouldn't murder him.

"Felix!" Eva said, seeing his approach. "You came."

"Of course I did. Hard to be your legal guardian if I don't take care of you. Everything alright?"

"Yeah," she said, looking to the others. Those who were wounded were already receiving treatment on site. Those who needed immediate attention were ported off back to home base, he imagined. "They stormed the school, demanded to know where we were. They shot the principal when he wouldn't tell them what class we were in. That's what we heard, at least."

Felix suddenly felt poorly about how he'd treated the principal.

"They were looking for you, specifically?" he asked.

"Yeah. They were."

"Alright. Sounds like we need to open a school of our own, then," Felix said with a sigh.

He couldn't leave the kids out in the open like this if they were going to be targeted.

I'm so tired of only reacting. Reacting to their attacks. This needs to end. Now.

"I think this is over. I'll head back with the first group and start talking to the kids. Make the entire department available to talk to people," Kit said.

Honestly, Felix had almost forgotten she was there with how quiet she was.

"Sounds like a plan. Thanks, Kit. I appreciate it." Felix turned his head towards her. He tried out a smile, only to remember that she couldn't see into his helmet.

She gave him a smile and a casual wave of her hand. Then, pressing a hand to Eva's shoulder, she guided her away from the group.

She led her over to the Telemedic party where she began talking to them.

"Kit's nice. She says she likes talking to me because I speak my mind," Andrea said, taking several steps forward. She leaned down and started to fiddle with the ground, her fingers pushing into the soft dirt.

"I can imagine." Felix turned back to the monitors, watching his people sweep and clear the library.

"Smells funny," Andrea said. Looking over, he found that Andrea was digging like a dog now, sending handfuls of dirt behind her.

"What does?" he asked.

"The ground. It smells like…" Andrea paused, considering her words.

Felix noticed out of the corner of his eye the moment the Telemedics took Kit and the children back to headquarters.

"Like explosives," Andrea said, recapturing his attention.

As his eyes flicked back to Andrea, she held something up in one hand.

Then it blew up.

Everything blew up.

All Felix knew was fire, the sound of detonations, and tremendous forces buffeting him.

He could see... nothing. He could hear nothing. He felt nothing.

That wasn't quite accurate. He could feel pain. A lot of pain.

He just couldn't feel anything besides that.

Which means I'm at least alive.

Felix managed to lift an arm, then the other.

Am I blind or...

Reaching up with both hands, Felix tried to unclasp his helmet.

Fumbling blindly with unfeeling fingers, it wasn't an easy task. It was damn near impossible, really.

Eventually, he managed to get the locking clasp open, then rotate the lock and pull the helmet free.

Blinking, he tried in vain to clear his vision. Acrid smoke and dust hung in the air all around him. The smell of blood was overwhelming.

And the low sound of moans gave everything a surreal, hellish feeling.

Rolling to one side, Felix came face to face with the mangled remains of Andrea.

Most of her head was missing, as was a good portion of her chest and one arm. There was no life there in the remaining eye.

Even her powers of regeneration wouldn't help there. It was directed regeneration to help keep points down.

Shuddering away from that, Felix sat up quickly. Then threw up all over his leg plates.

Spitting a chunk of digested food into the grass, Felix started to slowly rise to his feet.

Taking a moment to steady himself, Felix allowed himself to look around him.

Ioana was there, the lower half of her body simply gone. Her hands were pressed into her guts as if she had tried to hold herself together in her last moments.

His stomach rose up as if to try and empty itself again.

Turning his back on his dead War Maiden, he distanced himself a little.

Lying in the grass, fetched up behind a monitor, was Victoria.

Every inch of exposed skin was blistered and cracked with burns. Her hair was just gone.

She looked alive, though. Her chest rose and fell slowly.

Nearby, he saw the remains of several Others, all dead and decimated.

Reaching down, he gently shook Victoria's shoulder.

Her eyes cracked open, then closed. Grudgingly, they opened again, as a groan escaped Victoria's lips.

"It hurts," she hissed.

"At least you're alive. Can you get up?" Felix asked. He left her alone, looking around for other survivors. Here and there, people were going through the wreckage and bodies.

Victoria somehow got to her feet, looking more akin to something that'd been flash fried.

"I think you took the blast, but the fire went around you," she ground out between burnt lips. "I can't feel most of my fingers. I think the nerves are burnt."

"They probably are. Don't worry, I can fix you after this."

"Can you fix them?" Victoria asked, one hand indicating Ioana and Andrea.

"So long as they said yes in their HR documentation... and that I have enough points to do it. I'm not sure, and I really don't want to look right now, but I'm betting I lost a good number of points."

"Oh," Victoria said, one hand drawing her sword and flexing around the hilt experimentally.

It also means I really can't afford to spend any points until I know what's going on.

"Sorry, Victoria, I'd fix you right now, but I have no idea what we'll be up against here. I mean, for all I know we're still under attack."

People were forming squads and teams to begin rounding up the wounded and then triaging them.

Ioana's people were trained well. Very well.

Even if she isn't here to lead them.

"That's fine. I'd do the same. What do we do now, though?" Victoria asked, sheathing her sword.

"Contact the Telemedics, get them out here, sta—"

Felix's wrist started buzzing softly, interrupting him. Lifting up his hand, he looked at the scratched and fizzing display.

"Kit's calling," Felix said apologetically. He had to tap the icon several times before it recognized he was trying to accept the call.

"Felix? What's going on? The Telemedics are saying they can't get back to you. There's a magical barrier between them and your location."

"We were attacked. An explosion. Everything blew up. Everything. Ioana's dead. So is Andrea. I... don't even know where to start."

"I'll send people over immediately. We'll get this sorted out and then—"

Kit stopped mid-sentence. Felix could hear someone telling her something in the background.

There was a pause.

"Felix, we're under attack here. I'll do what I can to hold them off, but we're seriously understaffed. We'll do all we can."

"Kit, they've already gotten through the security hallway. They'll be here in a second, we need to go!" shouted a voice.

"I'll call you when I can. Be safe," Kit said, then disconnected.

Felix let his arm fall down to his side.

"They played us. They brought us here deliberately. Deliberately so they could cause the most damage without us being able to resist.

"And now that that phase is done, they're attacking HQ. We walked right into this," Felix muttered.

Victoria grimaced, her burnt, hairless face scrunching up.

"What's the call?" she asked him.

Felix sighed and shook his head.

He wasn't a warrior. No combatant. He was a glorified CEO at best.

"Felix, you need to give everyone orders," Victoria said softly, for his ears alone.

Looking around, he realized a few people had started to turn towards him. Waiting. Watching.

Steeling his resolve, he held up a hand above his head for a few seconds, gathering his wits and what he wanted to say.

"Protect and gather the wounded. Provide medical treatment as best as you're able. Get them into a building for shelter and let no one on the school grounds. Though I'm doubting anyone will show up. I'm betting everyone was paid off."

Several heads nodded at that.

"Beyond that, gather our dead. Try to get as much of their body as you can. Don't start doing that till all our wounded are taken care of, though. Prioritize those who are alive, but let's not neglect our dead."

Felix looked around himself to make sure everyone had heard him and had no questions. "Spread the word," he said, dropping his arm.

Dropping down to Andrea's side, he stared at her dead face.

This wasn't the first Andrea Prime. She'd suffered quite badly in her knowledge of not being the original Andrea. He imagined a third Andrea Prime would only make that worse.

A piece of light-colored fabric lay nearby. It was about the size of what had probably been a t-shirt.

Snatching at it, he laid it flat on the grass. Taking a breath, Felix then haltingly dipped his finger into the ruins of Andrea's rib cage. Taking his bloodstained finger, he began writing on the fabric.

Do not Absorb. This is Prime.

Eyeing the work, he felt like it'd have to do. Then he carefully took the stained canvas and wrapped it around the upper half of Andrea's remains.

Any Other would be sure to see it and read it first.

He hoped it would convey the message clearly enough.

Looking to Victoria, he shook his head, not quite sure what to do next.

Then his mind kicked into gear and went back to his previous thought.

I'm so tired of only reacting. Reacting to their attacks. This needs to end. Now.

"Get your gear. We're taking an armored car back to HQ." Felix turned and started off towards the front of the school. Tossing his broken helmet to one side, he realized it was time to act.

Time to do something—anything—rather than sit around and wait for others to act.

"We should have washed your armor," Victoria said as they cranked the armored car into gear and down the main street leading in.

"Probably. But at this point, I didn't want to waste time on smelling fresh. Need to get home and help if we can. They're under attack."

"An armored car showing up in your flank is a good way to get your shit kicked in, I'm betting." Felix pulled the shifter into gear and looked around through the portholes.

Behind him, the other armored cars were heading into the grounds to take up defensive positions and protect everyone.

Up ahead, Felix saw ever more proof that they'd been outplayed and set up.

Armed enemies behind a barricade of cars, preventing anyone from driving in or out.

Angling the front of the vehicle at a spot between two vehicles, he floored the engine.

Bullets began pinging off the armored front. After a second, it went from a light rain sound to a hailstorm to rival that of an angry god.

His foes had underprepared on this one point, though. All the arms they had didn't seem as if they had enough power to penetrate the armor of the vehicle.

They hadn't counted on actual armored vehicles.

With a deafening crash and a jolt, Felix smashed into the makeshift barrier.

Twisted metal and sparks showered everyone nearby in wreckage as the cars were torn asunder and pushed to the side.

Holding tight to the wheel, Felix wrestled with the behemoth to keep it straight. The wheels bounced and shuddered one way and then the other, the vehicle careening off as it broke through.

Fishtailing wildly, the rear end cracked against another car before it evened out.

With the pedal still pressed to the floor, they began to accelerate away.

"Get back there and take a peek through that rear hatch. In fact, maybe get into that gunner's seat and get that turret spun 'round," Felix called to Victoria.

"What? You want me to use the turret?"

"Sure as hell isn't there for decoration. What're they going to do, shoot back? They already did."

"What about the police?"

"If they're not responding to an explosion, I'm betting they're not responding to anything today."

Victoria sat there for a second. Then she got up and went to the back.

One of the lights on the complicated dash turned red and started flashing.

Giving it his attention for a moment, he realized it was a safety switch.

Thumbing it quickly, it turned a solid red.

The moment it did, the turret came to life, the chattering of rounds being fired out of the beefy cannon echoing throughout the hull.

The clatter of brass tinkled over the top and sides of the vehicle.

It didn't take long for Victoria's sustained fire rate to become the trained burst fire that Andrea had drilled into everyone.

Dreading the results, and with a great trepidation, Felix activated his points screen.

	Received	Spent	Remaining
Daily Allotment	150	0	150
Miu Miki	1,000	0	1,000
—Direct reports	4,150	0	4,150
Ioana Iliescu	0	0	0
—Direct reports	3,050	0	3,050
Kit Carrington	3,000	0	3,000
—Direct reports	8,600	0	8,600
Lilian Lux	3,100	0	3,100
—Direct reports	7,100	0	7,100
Andrea Elex	0	0	0
Felicia Fay	1,550	0	1,550
—Direct reports	11,808	0	11,808
Eva Adelpha	1,600	0	1,600
+ Loyalty Bonus	1,010	0	1,010
DAILY TOTAL	**46,118**	**0**	**46,118**

He didn't have enough points. A single resurrection took fifty thousand. No one would be coming back from the dead until they could get more points. And there wouldn't be more purchases without their assets being unlocked.

Suddenly, everything was falling apart, and Felix didn't know if he could fix it.

Chapter 32 - Gear Check -

"They pulled back after I got the lead car," Victoria shouted from behind him.

"Great. Keep it that way. Feel free to fire on whoever or whatever."

Felix wedged himself between the cars in front of him and nudged a car out of the way with his armored bumper.

Forcing himself through the traffic, Felix slowed down to look both ways and then ran the red light at full speed.

No cops stopped them, traffic was light, and there were no firetrucks or ambulances, either. That wasn't normal.

Too quiet.

The city knew something was going on, and to him it seemed as if the emergency responders had all been bribed into silence.

Bribed and scared into noninterference.

There would be no help from anyone outside of Legion.

You know what, fine. Fine. Suits me just fine. Means I don't have to worry about getting arrested when I run people over.

Fuck this. Fuck them. Fuck everyone.

Felix growled and bounced up over a curb and started driving on the sidewalk.

Everyone out to get us? Fine, I'll be out to get everyone. Everyone who isn't on our side is my enemy.

Mailboxes, benches, and trashcans were crushed or knocked aside.

"Are we on the sidewalk?" Victoria screeched.

Instead of answering, Felix dropped the pedal, the engine roaring as it rushed forward.

Sidewalks didn't have traffic. At least, nothing that could stop or slow him.

The drive was uneventful, if you discounted running red lights, crushing things, and generally causing enough chaos to make a certain video game named for stealing a car raise an eyebrow.

It wasn't until they turned onto the street where the front of their HQ stood that things changed.

Certainly not for the better, either.

There were bodies all over the entryway. Packed bloody and deep. Blood, body parts, corpses, and weapons.

Felix was looking out through the viewing ports and found no one moving.

"A grave," he muttered.

"Stay here," Victoria commanded. She drew her sword and exited the rear hatch, closing it behind herself.

Not bothering to argue with her, Felix watched the burnt and injured Victoria move amongst the bodies. She watched both the corpses and her surroundings, picking through and making sure of her foot placement. She eventually disappeared through the front door into the lobby.

Fidgeting, Felix did his best to keep calm and aware of his surroundings. Sitting out here didn't help his anger and annoyance.

The problem was the moment his mind found a quiet place, it went straight back to the fact that so many people were dead.

His rage would flame up like a stoked bed of coals and he had to force himself to remain seated.

It felt like he was missing something, on top of everything else.

At least Andrea's not gone. If I can't revive the prime, I can at least have an Other abso-

Felix's train of thought stopped dead. Feeling his breath catch, he called up his point screen again.

	Received	Spent	Remaining
Daily Allotment	150	0	150
Miu Miki	1,000	0	1,000
—Direct reports	4,150	0	4,150
Ioana Iliescu	0	0	0
—Direct reports	2,725	0	2,725
Kit Carrington	3,000	0	3,000
—Direct reports	8,600	0	8,600
Lilian Lux	3,100	0	3,100
—Direct reports	7,100	0	7,100
Andrea Elex	0	0	0
Felicia Fay	1,550	0	1,550
—Direct reports	11,808	0	11,808
Eva Adelpha	1,600	0	1,600
+ Loyalty Bonus	1,010	0	1,010
DAILY TOTAL	**45,793**	**0**	**45,793**

"She's at zero. That... means her Others are gone, too. Right?" Felix asked softly to no one.

Even Andrea, then. The legendary Myriad. That must have been a lot of explosives to manage to bag every single Other.

Thinking back on it, it really had been a huge amount of explosives. Most of the school had been leveled.

In fact, he could've sworn he'd had forty-six thousand points earlier.

My wounded are dying. People are still dying.

Victoria reappeared at the entry to the lobby and waved him in.

Exiting via the hatch, Felix did all he could to not look at the bodies. He knew he'd find some of his own people in there.

Or at least he thought he would. That'd be more than enough to keep his eyes up and forward for now.

"Hurry up, she doesn't have much time."

"What?" Felix squawked in confusion. Picking up his pace, he entered the lobby and followed along behind Victoria.

Turning the corner into the security hall, he got his answer.

Miu was propped up against a wall; blood stained her lips and jaw. It also covered her chest and stomach as if she'd thrown up on herself.

Her eyes turned up to see him approach, a weak, bloody smile crossing her lips. It was one of the few smiles from Miu he'd have called real. Not the fake mask she put on for others.

"Felix. Felix, you're alive."

"Hey, Miu. Just... hang on and we'll get you fixed up."

Miu shook her head and then coughed violently, blood gushing out from her mouth. It was a fountain of bright red vomit.

"Unnnggh, no. They're after you. Want you dead. Won't stop. Took Kit.

"Activate Wraith's receiver. Ordered him to follow. Follow Wraith," Miu said. She took a slow, deep breath. Then her head slowly lolled to the side as she exhaled.

Her eyes locked to a point somewhere above his head as her body went still.

"Miu?" Felix asked, getting down in front of her. There was no response.

Mentally focusing on her, he tried to call up the correction window. To correct her condition. Make her healthy again.

Status Correction: Dead -> Living and Healthy	Correct Status? (65,000 points)

The accept button was grayed out, of course. He didn't have that kind of points available to him.

"I can't... I can't fix her. I don't have enough points to resurrect her, let alone resurrect her and fix her.

"I don't..." Felix trailed off, staring at Miu's lifeless face.

"Felix, we'll get through this, but I really need you to get a hold of yourself," Victoria said, getting in close to his side. "You're the only one who can bring everyone back, but only if we make it through this."

Felix gritted his teeth and turned his head away from Victoria and Miu both.

She was right. Absolutely right.

"Didn't you hear her? They want me dead. That's the goal. They won't stop till it happens. Which means we have to kill them first. So that's what we do.

"Kill them all."

Swallowing, he got to his feet. Reactions weren't going to win the day. Actions were.

Bold, direct actions.

If they're not with me, they're against me.

Standing up, Felix went to the elevator. He knew what he needed to do. What he wanted to do.

And it'd go his way, or he'd die trying.

Victoria stood at his side, her sword back in its sheath. She'd become his shadow and support.

He'd not forget it.

"Remind me to make you incredibly deadly after this."

"I will. I also signed my form. If Ioana doesn't kick your ass, I will."

"Noted."

The elevator dinged and the doors slid open.

Inside was a mess of blood and gore, staining the walls, ceiling, floor, everything. It was like someone had dropped a body into a giant blender.

Standing at the center of that blender with energy crackling all around her was Lily.

Power undulated across her body back and forth.

She was coated liberally and painted red. Her clothes were ripped, torn, burnt, and hanging on her by sheer will and a few threads.

Seeing him and Victoria, she let the blue storm of death wink out.

"Felix… you're alive," Lily said, her lips twitching as if she wanted to smile, but didn't have the energy for it.

"Alive and angry. I'm going to go get my toys," Felix said, stepping into the elevator. He stepped in close to Lily and waited for Victoria.

"Toys?" asked the sorceress.

"My toys," Felix said. Reaching over, he thumbed the button for the research and development floor.

The very floor where Mr. White worked on weapons, and Felicia was building his personal Warden.

"Nice look, by the way. Real post-apocalypse flavor."

"Oh? Does that suit your tastes? Dream of a fantasy world where you keep a harem of sex slaves?" Lily asked, her tone changing. Gaining a touch of her usual teasing self.

"Ptff, sounds like a teenage fantasy. Give myself a good strong name like Vince and run around a continent sleeping with slave women."

"Of course. Can't forget that you'd be a hero, though. Protecting all those women."

Felix snorted.

Then again, that'd be pretty awesome. If I had to pick an alternate life...

Lily slapped him behind the head. "Stop thinking about it. You have enough on your plate."

Grinning, he let it drop.

Going through the normal security quickly, Felix was happy to see everything looked normal.

Which meant Felicia and Mr. White would be safe and sound. Safe and sound and ready to help him get prepped.

When he finally opened the lab door, he was almost beyond relieved to find several squads of Miu's internal security forces waiting for him.

Guns drawn and pointing in his direction, but still waiting.

"Felix?" Felicia called out from behind a console. Beside her was Mr. White, his hands clutching a pistol leveled at Felix's chest.

To the rear of the room were both their teams, waiting for directions and pressed together, looking much akin to a flock of nervous sheep in white coats.

"Yep. Here to pick up some goodies, then go take the fight back to these bastards. Get Kit back as well and end this whole thing."

Rather than waiting for her to ask, he'd get it out ahead. Maybe it'd help strengthen her resolve.

"They killed Ioana, Andrea, and Miu. I mean to return it back to them."

Felicia started to blink rapidly, her throat flexing, her face twisting. "Did you bring her back? Ioana?" she asked curtly.

"Can't yet. Can't bring anyone back. Not enough points. After we kick the shit out of them, I'm going to rob everything they own, take slaves, make sausages, and get more points. Then get everyone back who signed the form."

Felix shuddered, his entire body shivering for a second with the amount of anger he held.

"Everyone," he said, emphasizing the point.

Felicia nodded her head quickly, then brushed her hand across her eyes. "Good. Ioana signed the form to come back. She'd kick your ass the moment you died, ya daft fucker, if you didn't bring her back."

Felix chuckled at that. "Yeah, she would. Down to hell and back up. Now, let's see how far you got with my Warden. I want to get it moving, even if I have to spend today's points to do it. Then we're going to do the same with your weapons, Mr. White."

Felix gave them both a tight smile. "Then I'm going to go pay a house call."

Everyone on their teams turned to face a corner of the room. One of the walls there was clearly a sliding wall.

Mr. White gave Felix a considering look, then moved back to that wall. He grabbed a hold of it and heaved it to one side.

Felix, Victoria, and Lily stood staring at what lay inside.

There stood a black-and-red Warden unit. It had a similar look and feel to the others, but it was clearly different. It had the look of both versions in regards to utility and defensive capabilities, but more.

All around it and mounted to the walls were various weapons that looked as if they'd been designed specifically for this unit.

"It's got all the same gear of the earlier models. Half the weight, though, so double the battery capacity on a normal battery.

"Mr. White and his team helped fix a few other battery design problems, so you've got quadruple the power output of the traditional units on top of needing less," Felicia said generously, even waving a hand at the man as she came up to stand beside Felix.

"Yes, yes. We've taken all the different projects and combined them. The energy output is considerable, and can recharge itself to a degree. So we built an energy weapon to hook into the unit. It can put out enough power to punch through six-inch-thick steel.

"In addition, we put together a standard armament set for you since your weapon uses energy. No need to carry ammo, so we used the space for other things."

"Standard armament?" Felix asked.

"Energy pistol, high-explosive grenades, flashbangs, a hand axe Felicia made that she assures me will go through steel, and other things. Those are the big ones, though."

Felix blew out a breath and looked to Felicia. "So what's wrong?"

"The wiring. It's not done, and it won't be anytime soon. It's a complicated mess of electronics with some intense shielding," said the dwarf.

"It'll take a few days of dedicated resources," Mr. White added.

Felix instead focused on the unit and the fact that he wanted it ready to go per Mr. White's and Felicia's standards.

Equipment(Legion's Fist): Build out complete	Warden Unit will be completed per specifications.	Upgrade?(25,000)

Felix hit the accept button and sat down on the ground to start pulling off his boots. "Help me get dressed for this. People to slaughter.

"As to all of you, I'm willing to take whoever wants to go, but realize, if you fall, there's no guarantee I can bring you back.

"I mean, that's my goal, but at this time, I'm not able to."

"I'm going," Victoria said. "I'll be in the armory."

"As will I," Lily agreed. She patted Felix on the top of the head and left with Victoria.

All three squads volunteered as well, and promptly went to join the ladies in the armory.

Getting up in nothing but his undershirt and skivvies, Felix clapped his hands together. "Alright, let's get my stupid ass into Legion's Fist here so I can go kill people."

"You're no soldier, Felix," said one of the techs as another keyed the Warden to open the cockpit.

"No, I'm not. But even I can aim a rifle." Felix turned around and backed up into the Warden. Stepping into the cockpit, he slid his legs into place, then his arms.

"Is your aim any good?" asked the same technician.

"Guess we'll find out how much first-person shooters carry over to real life." Felix placed the back of his head into the helmet. "Close it up."

There was no response to his command, but the Warden whirred to life. The cockpit began to close up around him, the helmet coming down into place around his head.

In front of his face, four displays came to life. Three provided him with his front and peripheral cameras, with the fourth giving him a rear view.

"Testing, one, two, three. Please confirm external microphones picking up audio," someone said.

"Reading you," Felix confirmed. He shifted himself as the harness began to tighten up around him. After a few seconds, he felt like he was held firmly in place.

"Testing communication system. We're also releasing the servos. Do you know how to pilot it?" That'd be a tech manning a console nearby.

Felix turned his head to focus the camera on the individual. As if he were moving his own body, the Warden moved. "I hear you, and I'm sure I'll figure it out. No time like the present."

"Most of the controls will be reading the signals in your brain to help coordinate the movements of your body. You'll notice the longer you're in there, the better it'll get. Learning mode should be complete within two hours, or depending on how much you use it."

"Anything else?"

"It utilizes all the same cues your mark two did. Use the war-net just as you did previously."

"Right."

Stepping out of the loading bay, Felix had the impression that he could move freely. There was no delay from his body's commands to the movement of the small mech.

"Looks like everything is running smoothly. Any questions?"

Felix turned towards the arsenal and pulled down the energy rifle. There was a connection port and locking mechanism that the Warden's hand fit into perfectly.

With a pop, his HUD changed, turning red. A crosshair in the top left of the screen came to life. In the top right, the silhouette of his energy rifle and an energy bar showed up.

Pulling the rifle up to his shoulder, the crosshair changed its location, matching up with the direction of the rifle.

"Two questions.

"Where is Wraith's tracker, and how do I get out of the lab? Time is money." Felix pulled the rifle's muzzle up and held it against his shoulder.

He was ready.

Now, if only his opponents weren't, this'd be a lot easier.

Chapter 33 - High Voltage -

He'd taken the four Wardens after finding out they had survived the blast. They'd only needed a minimal amount of re-equip and repair, and would meet them at the location once ready.

In addition to that, he'd taken all three of the internal security squads from HQ. With Victoria and Lily, that completed his small army, and they'd set off for Wraith's location marker.

Felix was looking at the war-net virtual map. He was slowly going over all the notations and markers that his people had been adding as they scouted the area.

Looking up to his screens, he tried to imagine the map overlay with the actual layout.

They'd ended up at a large, sprawling... farm.

An actual farm on the outskirts of the city-state.

It had the look of a militia holdout farm. Self-sustaining, armed mundanes wandering around on patrol, and paranoid signs disavowing the local government.

An organization of supers, mundanes, and others who had targeted him personally, masquerading as an anti-government mundane militia.

His long-range Wardens had set up in the distance, both providing cover and vision. The melee Wardens had been assigned each to a squad, leaving the third one with Felix. Victoria was with team one, and Lily with team two.

"Tee-one, guard change," crackled the radio in his ear.

This was it.

They'd only been here for a short time, but they already had a solid idea of what they were walking into. The entire complex was regularly patrolled, but the number of people didn't match how many heat signatures they got from inside.

Which meant this was much like his own base.

Underground.

"El-ef actual, engage and take both. Confirm," Felix said into his mic.

"Tee-one actual, copy. Tee-two actual, copy. El-ef, copy."

"Engage." Felix watched his displays.

His people quickly overran the enemy positions. There was no noise, no gunshots.

"Tee-one, confirmed."

"Tee-two, confirmed."

The squad leader for his own group moved ahead now. Felix took up the rear guard and leveled his weapon.

The squad fanned out and moved at a quick jog, sweeping and clearing the field as they went.

Their goal was the farmhouse wall ahead. There were no windows or overlook to it, which meant the approach was ideal. The two closest patrols were built in such a way as to watch the area.

When they hit the halfway point, Felix heard his comms pop to life again.

"El-ef, phase one complete. Go phase two."

There was no response to the command, but Felix knew they were moving towards the third and fourth guard positions.

He couldn't spare a thought to look, as he was making sure he was doing his job.

Felix swept his head to the left, then right, confirming that their flanks were still clear.

The squad reached the wall and sidled up to it. Four members of the squad broke off and rushed to each end of the wall.

"El-ef two, west clear. Sight on tee-one, on engage."

"El-ef four, east clear. Sight on tee-two, post engage."

Felix moved to the wall and squatted down, turning himself into an impromptu ladder. Kneeling with nothing to do, he pulled up the war-net.

The plan was going accordingly. There were only two more patrols that they knew of. Catching them during the guard change would eliminate the most hostiles, but was also the most risky.

Then he heard something he didn't want to. Something he'd dreaded.

A gunshot.

"Tee-one, shots fired, post engage."

Felix licked his lips. It wasn't the worst outcome; they'd managed to clear a good number of the patrols before this point.

Maybe they didn't hear it.

"Ess-one, hive active. Clear shot, engage?"

They heard it.

Two members of his squad had vaulted over him and onto the roof of the building. That was the end of him being a ladder.

Turning his face to the wall, Felix took a deep breath.

"El-ef actual, weapons free. Move to final."

As he finished giving the command, Felix burst forward, activating the jump jets.

Plowing through the wall, Felix brought his energy rifle up in a low firing position. Wood, cement, and rebar exploded out from his dynamic entry.

Stopping dead a foot inside the building, Felix immediately cleared the corner to his left, then swept right.

There were two doorways.

Triggering the communications button for his own squad, he moved to the right. At the same time, he dropped his left hand into the armored ammo pod on his thigh and fished out a grenade.

"El-ef five six, left doorway, seven eight, hold room."

Activating the high-explosive grenade, he tossed it through the left-hand doorway and then focused on the right.

Two men with assault rifles were stepping free of the doorway as Felix centered his crosshair.

Pulling the trigger on his rifle, it discharged a brilliant white beam of light.

The powerful discharge turned the first man into a flaming pillar, before cutting through him. The man behind the first went up in flames next.

Before either human torch hit the ground, the grenade Felix had lobbed into the other room went off.

Stomping forward, Felix moved towards the right-hand room.

With his left hand, he slapped both flaming dead men aside. Entering the next room, Felix acquired a target at the end of the hallway and pulled the trigger briefly.

He'd held the trigger down last time. He wanted to see what a quick trigger depress would do.

As the bright light of the discharge struck the man, he immediately burst into flame. The energy cut off almost as soon as it touched him, though.

The man screamed, dropped his weapon, and ran off down the hallway.

Felix started to look into each room as he cleared the hall, making sure there'd be nothing behind him as he went. The chatter of weapons fire behind him alerted him to the fact that his people had encountered resistance.

Drawing his energy pistol in his left hand, Felix lifted the weapon and fired it several times into the torso of an unarmed woman trying to get into her clothes.

Smoking holes appeared in the woman's chest where the rounds hit her. She dropped to her knees, her eyes widening, then slumped over.

Felix dismissed her from his mind and went to the next room, re-holstering his pistol.

The next two rooms were empty. Felix pulled up short at the exit to the building. Activating his mic, he looked out into the interior of the complex in front of him.

"El-ef actual, right doorway and adjoining rooms clear."

"El-ef six, left doorway clear. El-ef five was KIA."

Felix felt his lips peel back in a grimace. Every life counted right now since he couldn't bring them back.

"Tee-one, tee-two, sitrep," Felix called into the void.

"Tee-one actual, final complete. One KIA."

"Tee-two, final complete. Actual plus two KIA."

"Ess-one, clear."

"Ess-two, clear."

"El-ef actual, sweep and clear. Find entry."

Felix killed his mic and then set off to look for the entry.

"I don't understand," Felix said slowly, looking at the corpse of Victoria.

A bullet hole marred her forehead, damn near directly in the middle of it.

"There was a super in the group. Before he could attack us, she engaged him, killed him. Before we could cover her, someone got a shot off. We dropped him after that first shot, but it was already too late," said the new leader of squad two. "I'm sorry, sir."

Felix took a slow breath, then shook his head. "Don't be. It wasn't your fault. She died doing exactly what she wished. We'll bring her back with us.

"Take the bodies somewhere safe and mark the location. We'll pick them up afterwards."

Wraith materialized out of a shadow nearby. "Found the entry. I couldn't get past the first checkpoint without setting things off," said the shadow. "There's no doubt they know there's something going on up here, but I wasn't sure how you wanted to proceed."

Felix blew a raspberry and then shrugged his shoulders.

"Doesn't matter. They do know were here and are probably expecting an attack. I'll take point, follow in behind me."

Checking his display, he saw his batteries had recharged thirty percent of the fifty percent he'd used.

They really had done wonders with this Warden. And this was only the first iteration.

Tapping the open command for the armored pod on his left hip, he reached in. Using his HUD to verify what was in it, he pulled out the black metal shield his squads had deployed at the school.

The metal snapped to his hand at the connection point and then expanded rapidly to its full size, then shrank back down to the starter size. It wouldn't get in his way, and he could activate it quickly.

Felix looked to Wraith and nodded his head. "Lead on."

The black shadow that was Wraith flowed back in the other direction.

Following along behind, Felix felt his thoughts slide off into a new direction.

He had to wonder if this was what it had felt like for his attackers when they'd tried to invade his base the first time around.

Both of their attacks had been brute strength with little in the way of coordination or strategy.

Could he believe that'd be their response while even on the defensive?

He needed actionable intelligence.

Wraith oozed up next to a wooden door like one would normally find leading into a basement or root cellar.

"Once I get their attention, I need you to phase in and do what you can to cause havoc and figure out where to hit them.

"I'll be playing distraction. If I can manage to soften them up at the same time, great. Otherwise, I plan on pulling back after an initial probe."

"Understood."

"Great," Felix said, and then jumped forward. His feet slammed through the wood and he dropped into a cement-lined tunnel.

At the end of the tunnel was a machine gun slit and a big steel door.

Bringing his rifle up, he centered the crosshair and held down the trigger.

In such an enclosed space, the light put out from the muzzle was blinding.

Felix kept the beam flowing for another three seconds, moving as fast as he could. It was a fairly narrow tunnel and his arms were brushing against the walls.

His displays filtered out the light quicker than his eyes could have. The machine gun was gone, and the room it was in was a roaring inferno.

Reaching for a grenade, he came up against the machine gun position. Pulling the pin, he stuffed the explosive into the slit and then moved back several feet to aim his rifle at the heavy door.

He focused his reticle on the point where he assumed the door was bolted or barred on the other side and then fired.

For five seconds, the beam weapon unloaded into the door. Then the muffled boom of the grenade going off could be heard.

The door gave out, weakened from the extreme heat the energy rifle put out and then capitulating under the confined explosion of the grenade.

Blowing outward, it hung on the frame brokenly.

Charging ahead, Felix drew out his pistol, trying to give his rifle a second to cool off. The heat gauge next to the outline had gone from yellow to orange.

Slamming the door to the side with his shoulder, Felix scanned the room.

There were men and women all over. Wounded, dead, dying, all of it.

His HUD rapidly marked each target and Felix lifted his pistol.

Methodically, with precision, he shot each one in the head. They were against him. They were the enemy.

A woman sat up slowly, her eyes slowly focusing on him. She was beautiful.

Felix pressed the tip of his pistol to her forehead and pulled the trigger.

The back of her head blew out and splattered her brains all over the wall.

Sweeping the room one more time, Felix found no hostiles. Holstering his pistol, he moved towards the hallway that led into the machine gun nest.

Dark and without light or noise, it was clearly a trap.

Activating the night vision camera, he found it was nothing but an empty concrete hallway.

Unfortunately, he couldn't see to the end of the hallway.

Taking a breath, Felix leaned up against the wall and trained his rifle on the hallway.

"El-ef actual. Front position secured. Tee-one, move up and hold this position.

"Detach Mel-War one and two and prepare for assault."

Closing his eyes, he tried to calm himself.

The enormity of the situation wanted to overrun him. He was no soldier. No warrior.

But I'm a murderer. Killing wounded and unarmed people. They were my enemy, though. They were against me.

But they didn't even have a chance.

His mind flashed back to the confused look the woman had had on her face a moment before her brain had been turned into a microwave dinner.

Felix felt his lips tremble, his mouth going dry as his stomach pushed upwards, threatening to make him throw up.

Miu, Victoria, Ioana, Andrea. Miu, Victoria, Ioana, Andrea. Doing this to bring them back. Miu, Victoria, Ioana, Andrea. Save Kit, bring them back. Doing this for them.

Felix muttered in the quiet dark of his Warden, no one hearing him, no one seeing him.

Alone with his thoughts.

"You in there?" Lily asked, her finger poking at the camera, getting his attention.

"Huh? Yeah," said Felix. She'd caught him off guard; he hadn't noticed her arrival.

"Open up, let me see you." Lily folded her arms across the tactical gear she'd put on from the armory.

"Lily, I'm fine. If I do th—"

"Open up." Her voice was calm, clear, and commanding. There would be no arguments.

Felix triggered the opening sequence. The smell of the room hit him in the face. Coppery and rich. The stink of blood was all-encompassing.

"Yes. That smell. Remember it. You can never go back from here," Lily said, pinning him in place in the open cockpit with her glare. "There is no hemming or hawing in this situation. You did this. You killed them. And that's something you have to live with for the rest of your life."

Reaching into the Warden, she pressed a cool hand to his face.

"But you won't hold that guilt alone. This is to save our people. Your people. You did this with good intentions and a belief that it's what you had to do.

"It's only death. Death isn't the end. They're all already moving on.

"I'm afraid I realized that fact after the first time I took someone's soul." Lily sighed while giving him a bitter smile.

"You, on the other hand, Mr. Campbell, have to help me carry my burden as well. I expect to be spoiled."

Felix nodded his head slowly, digesting her words.

She was right, of course. In many ways, she probably carried more guilt around than he ever could.

"Thanks… Lily. You're right. And yeah, I'll do my best to spoil you. Haven't had our first date yet, though. Kinda hard when we keep having to reschedule."

Lily's tragic smile turned bright at that. She leaned in and kissed him on the cheek. "I'll make sure to make it memorable, then, so it overshadows all the problems we had getting there. Now. Button yourself back up and get ready. There's a number of people waiting for us, and we can't keep them waiting, can we?"

She leaned back away from him, her eyes glowing in the soft light, her smile truly bringing out her beauty.

Then a lightning bolt sprang out of the dark hallway and went into one side of her head and exited the other. Her hair caught fire, her skin crisped, and her ears smoked.

Her body locked up into a rigid pose, and then collapsed.

In that moment, Lily fell to the ground.

All around him, his people opened up with their rifles, firing down the dark hallway.

Desperately, agonizingly, Felix pulled at his character screen for Lily. He wanted to make her healthy, put her back to rights. Victoria had been struck by a similar attack and had gone into cardiac arrest.

Maybe this would be easier or fewer points or—

Status Correction: Dead -> Living and Healthy	Correct Status? (60,000 points)

She's dead.

Felix stared at the smoldering corpse of Lily. The fire in her hair went out on its own, and all that was left behind was the sickening smell of burnt flesh and hair.

Lilian Lux was no more.

Chapter 34 - Hitting Rock Bottom -

Felix stared at Lily as she lay there unmoving.

He didn't understand. It was the same type of attack that had nearly killed Victoria.

Why did it kill Lily outright? It's not fair.

It's not fair. It's not fair. It's not fair.

It's NOT FAIR. IT'S NOT FAIR!

The Warden's cockpit closed up on Felix and he turned down the hallway.

He lifted up the black metal shield and activated it. Setting his feet, he did his best to get into a stable stance. Then he flipped on his jump jets.

Leaning forward behind the expanding magical shield, he rocketed down the tunnel.

"IT'S NOT FAIR!" Felix screamed.

His shield bucked and smashed into his arm as if struck by something. Felix didn't care. His shout carried him onward as the jump jets continued to build up speed down the tunnel.

As rapidly as he gained speed, he lost it. All of it.

He slammed to a standstill against what he could only assume was the end of the hall.

Deactivating his jump jets, he pulled his shield to one side to take a look around it.

Smashed between his shield and the wall was the hero who had killed Lily. The damned electrical spawn of the devil.

Felix smiled when he realized the man was alive. Moaning, breathing heavily, and looking like he'd been hit by a car, but alive.

The metal shield flickered and went out, the magical enchantment having been completely spent.

Disconnecting the shield and tossing it to one side, Felix hung his rifle on one of his ammo pods. Then he reached out for the hero with both hands.

Grabbing him by the arms, Felix got a good hold. Then he yanked his arms apart, one to each side with as much strength as he could.

With a sickening crunch and pop, one arm tore off from the man's torso and the other crackled sickeningly and went limp.

Flinging the torn arm over his shoulder, Felix pressed his free hand against the man's torso.

The man had been screaming since the moment Felix had started. Rather than deal with it, Felix lowered the receiver, then pulled again on the man's remaining arm.

With a wet squish, the arm came free. Dropping it to the ground, Felix pushed the dying hero to one side.

Pulling his rifle free, Felix stomped over to the door and kicked it in with a single boot strike.

His low-light vision flickered on and he could immediately pick out where the enemies were.

Pulling the rifle into position, he began firing quick one-second-long shots at each hostile.

As they were turned into bonfires, they began to return fire at him.

The rounds pinged off him, doing little to no damage to the Legion's Fist.

Felix moved forward, slinging his rifle and pulling a grenade out of his pod. As the men and women around him screamed, burned, and died, he casually stepped amongst them and threw a grenade down the next hall.

Lining up his rifle, Felix waited.

The explosion was a dull echo, but he moved the moment he heard it.

This time, he happened upon a group of stunned and disoriented enemies.

Using his rifle as precisely as he could given the blood-curdling rage he felt, Felix kept moving forward.

A wounded man was squirming around on the ground at the center of a hastily put-together barricade.

Felix aimed his foot and stepped down hard on the man's skull as he went by. The wet pop and crunch of his own skull was probably the last thing the man heard.

Felix couldn't get his breathing under control; he was panting, gasping, and shivering inside his cockpit.

Reaching the end of the hall, he found a heavy-duty service elevator bay.

There was no elevator, though.

Looking down the shaft, Felix let out a choked huff. There was nothing but darkness below him.

Stepping into that abyss, Felix braced himself.

Seconds passed by as he plummeted down.

"Down, down to goblin town," Felix said, snickering into his microphone between heaving breaths.

His Warden slammed to the ground, warning lights going off all over the cockpit. The resounding boom of his landing echoed upwards.

Taking two steps towards the bay doors, he inspected them for a second. Rearing back, Felix threw as heavy a punch as he could.

One of the doors peeled away and bent outward while the other broke in half.

Crawling out of the wreckage of the elevator shaft, Felix tried to get back to his feet.

The Warden refused to cooperate with him. The flashing red lights became solid red lights.

Son of a bitch! That's what you get for not thinking, idiot. Did you even try to slow your fall? No. You just jumped down a giant dark hole in the earth.

Think, think, think.

How bad is it?

Glancing at the warnings, Felix decided he'd have to go on without the Warden. Both legs were damaged and the servos were locked.

There was no way it was going anywhere.

Unbuckling himself he hopped out of the cockpit before it even fully opened. Snatching up the energy rifle he turned the big weapon over to inspect it.

Running a hand through his sopping wet sweaty hair he looked at the connection point in the handle.

Now to check a battery.

Reaching into the cockpit, he fingered the control for the Warden to open up its battery compartment.

The lower back half of the torso slid open.

Felix yanked on one of the straps that had held his hips in place. Pulling the knife out of the sheath on the Warden's belt, he quickly cut the belt away.

Moving back to the rear of the Warden, he looked at the batteries. They were connected by a single cord each to something else.

Yanking the cord out of that point, he flipped over the connector to look at it.

"Looks right," Felix muttered, his breath slowly coming back under control. Pulling the cord closer, he tried to fit it into the handle of the rifle.

Two seconds of wildly trying to insert it, he got it to seat itself.

With a pop, the energy rifle hummed to life as the cord fed power to it from the battery.

Setting the rifle down against the Warden, Felix took out the strap and tied it into a sling through the carrying handle of two of the batteries.

Tying it closed like a bandolier across his chest, Felix tied the second connector cord to the first.

"Gotta make sure the reload is quick," he muttered to no one.

Hefting the rifle, he went to the front of the Warden. Reaching into the pod, he fumbled around blindly to find any grenades he could. It was hard when the system didn't tell him what he was accessing.

Getting a hold of three of them, he attached them to his harness. Turning towards the hallway in front of him, he took a deep breath.

Then set out again.

"Shit to do, people to kill."

Getting to the door, he found his first obstacle.

The damn locked door itself. The Warden could get through it, but not Felix.

Looking up at the edges of the door, he found that it was only held up by two hinges.

Heading back to the Warden, he spent a minute hunting in the pod. He was hoping that for some reason someone had thought to include some C4 or a breaching charge or anything.

Unfortunately, there was no such luck.

Grumbling, Felix went around to the battery hatch and dragged out two more batteries. Lugging them over to the door, he detached the rifle from the battery on his back.

Snatching the cord up from one of the two at his feet, he clicked it into the rifle.

Aiming it at the top hinge, he pulled the trigger. It only took him a second to get the beam into place, and then he waited.

Holding the trigger down.

Twenty seconds in and he finally let go.

The hinge was slag. It'd turned molten and oozed its way down.

"One down."

Aiming at the lower hinge, Felix pulled the trigger.

The beam was decidedly less bright this time.

Rather than mess around, he let go and pulled the cord out. Kicking the spent battery away, he attached the second one and went back to work.

Twenty seconds in, and the lower hinge was gone.

Turning the rifle and its sizzling, smoking barrel away, he disconnected the second dead battery.

As he moved up to the door, he reattached one of the batteries on his back to the rifle.

Staring at the door, it was clear he'd really messed it up. The entire thing was warped and bowing outward.

Pulling a grenade free, he wedged it into the hot, bent metal, then pulled the pin.

Jogging off as quickly as he could, Felix didn't stop until the grenade exploded.

Turning around, he headed back the way he'd come. As the smoke cleared, he could see the door was done.

The entire upper half was torn out, and it was hanging on the other door.

Rather than risking it and giving people a clear shot on him as he went through, Felix did the only sensible thing.

He wedged a grenade in the bottom of the door and repeated the process.

As the smoke cleared from the second explosion, he watched as both doors swung slowly open. The busted one fell out and slammed to the ground while the other kept opening.

"Are you done?" a voice called from inside.

Felix blinked, his shoulder pressed up to the space next to the now open door.

He hadn't expected someone to talk to him.

"No. You're not dead yet, and I don't have Kit. How about you send her out and I'll let you live today?" Felix lied.

None of them would leave this place alive.

"Forgive me if I don't believe you."

"Then you get to die. Last words?" Felix called out.

He started taking deep breaths, rocking himself up against the wall.

Throw in the last grenade, then shoot him.

Find Kit, get out.

"Felix?" Kit called out.

Shit, Kit.

"Uh-huh," Felix responded.

"Leave me here. They put a control crown on me."

That definitely explained why she wasn't fighting back in any way.

"They want me to fight Skipper for them. To free the city."

"Can't do that, Kit. The only way they get to keep you for themselves is my death."

"What?" Kit asked someone else.

There was quiet discussion back and forth.

"Did they tell you they blew up the school to kill me? Ioana, Andrea, Lily, and Victoria are all dead.

"Eva's probably dead, of course. Since, you know, they blew up a school. I'm sure Lucian is too. And you know, every other kid there.

"Real snazzy bunch of heroes. Totally in it to save the city. One dead child at a time."

"That's—" shouted the male voice, trying to argue with Felix and assure Kit at the same time.

Felix decided this was it. Sprinting around the corner, Felix went down to one knee and slid across the cement as he crossed the doorway.

Two men were standing next to Kit. One he knew, the incredible regenerating man, and the other he didn't.

Felix pulled the trigger, the bright beam of his rifle stabbing outward.

Mr. Regeneration was cut in half outright.

The second man got the beam across his head, and dropped instantly. His head simply disintegrating.

Then a third person stepped out of the shadow in the corner. They leveled their weapon, and fired.

Bullets tore into Felix's leg, stomach, and side.

Tracking the target, Felix pulled the trigger again, the beam lancing out once again.

It connected with the weapon and the hand holding it.

Screaming, the attacker hunched over, then vanished, leaving their gun behind.

Felix felt his breath catch and lay down on the cold cement.

"Damn," he hissed.

Pressing a hand to one of the bullet holes, he lay there, staring up at the ceiling.

"Shit, that hurts," said someone else, presumably the guy he'd shot. "Didn't your mother tell you that cutting people in half isn't nice?"

Felix felt his body failing even as he lay there.

He didn't care anymore. Everyone was dead.

"Be your own hero, Kit. Don't let them use you as a weapon," Felix managed to say. He blinked, staring up at the ceiling, not seeing it. "You deserve more than that."

He'd put in a word with No-Name a long time ago. If he died, release and free everyone from their contracts. Both slave and indentured.

"You just wait. When I get myself back together, I'm going to b-urrrrrrhhhhhnnn," groaned the ever-regenerating hero.

Kit leaned over Felix, her hands gently pushing his hand away and pulling at his clothes.

"Damn," she said.

"Sorry," Felix gasped, his breathing getting short. "Couldn't leave you here. Needed to at least try."

Kit gave him a bitter smile and looked back to his wounds. "Stay with me, alright?"

"Sleepy," Felix said softly. He really was sleepy. Everything was warm and nice. Closing his eyes, Felix sighed.

"Damn you, wake up," Kit growled at him. Then it felt as if someone were bathing him in fire. Someone had clearly pulled out every nerve in his body and then set it on fire.

Arching his back, Felix's eyes shot open. Kit hovered above him, exactly where he'd seen her last.

Where'd that regenerating guy go?

"Regenerating hero," Felix mumbled. "Everything hurts."

"Dead. I killed him. After your stupid attack the crown deactivated. Threw it off," Kit said, her fingers pressing into his side. "Sorry it hurts. Doing it to help you. You need to stay awake."

Then she paused and looked off to one side. "Let's hope this works," she whispered.

"Huh?" Felix asked stupidly.

His arms and legs dangled at his sides as he was lifted up into the air. Felix rolled his head to one side, catching sight of the regenerating hero. He wasn't split in half anymore, but he didn't move. His face was slack, drool sliding free of his mouth, his eyes unseeing.

"Oh," Felix said, then closed his eyes.

His nerves caught fire again. Groaning, Felix opened his eyes, trying to curl up into a fetal position.

His limbs wouldn't respond to him. They wouldn't move. Looking to his body, he found his arms and legs were strapped down. Tied down to a gurney.

How did I get on a gurney? Was it an illusion? It had to be.

Looking to the side as he was being rolled along, he passed his Warden.

"Did you jump down the shaft?" Kit asked from the head of the gurney.

"Yeah… no elevator," Felix tried to say.

"Shhh. Rest, try not to move."

Felix leaned his head back and attempted to listen to her orders.

"Up we go," Kit said, moving the gurney into the decimated elevator shaft.

Except that when they entered, it was a fully working elevator. One that hadn't been there a moment ago.

Kit reached over his head and flicked one of the buttons.

Felix closed his eyes as the hum of the box carried them upwards.

Only a second or two later, he opened his eyes as quickly as he could. He didn't want Kit to hurt him again.

Taking a slow breath, Felix looked down to himself.

He was covered in blood. Almost to the point that it looked like he was made out of blood.

"Am I dead?" Felix asked, watching blood pour out of one of the bullet holes.

"You should be. You're full of... you're full of illusionary blood. I'm creating illusionary blood in you as fast as you're losing it."

"That sounds impossible. Impossible and hard."

Felix felt strange. Lethargic and on the edge of passing out, but not.

"It's hard. Very hard. But not impossible, it seems. Shh, concentrating."

Felix fell into silence, his mind stubbornly fighting through what he'd been told.

"Make sure they collect all our corpses. Need them," Felix said. As soon as he said it, he felt unbelievably tired.

Despite his best efforts, his eyes slid shut.

Every now and then, he managed to get his eyes open.

All around him, things were changing. Hallways, rooms, his own people flashing by.

The interior of a car.

Open sky.

Clouds.

A bird.

Then impenetrable darkness.

And the quiet hum of a machine.

In that darkness, Felix thought.

He planned.

He questioned.

He had a lot of questions. Lingering questions. Questions that he was sure he needed answers to.

The crowns and how they worked. How Kit could toss one aside.

The vanishing hero who escaped after Felix attacked.

Why the heroes never bothered to approach him if all they wanted was Kit.

For all they knew, he would have agree.

Too many questions.

Epilogue

Lily's eyes popped open. Her pupils dilating wildly as they adjusted to the overhead light.

Taking in a deep, choking breath, her hands came up to her face.

"I died," she said.

"That you did. Have no fear, though, I put you back together, and now you're back in the land of the living," Felix said happily, leaning over her. "Or so I hope. Got any extra parts I should know about? Probably didn't make it back with you."

Lily's eyes snapped to him and held fast to him. "I don't remember being dead... there wasn't... anything."

"I should hope not. Your memories are a result of your brain, not your soul. Want to sit up? That tray is pretty cold."

Felix took a step back and picked up her hands, giving her a tentative tug.

Lily didn't argue, and she got herself into a sitting position. "How long...?"

She hesitated, as if not wanting to ask the obvious question.

"About three weeks. Forgive me for the delay, but we had to get everything put back together before we could start resurrecting people. Didn't have the points for it."

Felix moved off towards the corner of a room and came back with a pair of jeans, blouse, socks, running shoes, panties, a bra, and a windbreaker.

"Sorry, I kinda raided your room for clothes," Felix apologized, laying her clothes down next to her.

Lily looked down at herself, finally realizing she was in nothing more than a medical apron.

Turning his back to her, Felix walked over to the door. "So there you have it. I do have to apologize for something else, though. You had no file on record on whether you wanted to be resurrected or not. I chose for you.

"I was selfish and couldn't think of a... a Legion without you."

The rustle of clothes was all he heard behind him. Lily didn't seem very talkative, and he could understand.

Not every day you're brought back from the dead.

"The form. I... hadn't decided on if I wanted to be brought back. Part of me was afraid that... well... I can't imagine ripping a soul out of someone does me favors to get into heaven. I doubt asking to be resurrected like a zombie would make it any better, either.

"I forgive you, though. For both actions. Fill me in here, what happened? I remember we were attacking the base, but that's it."

"You were hit by a lightning bolt. Went through your head. Dead before you hit the ground.

"After that, we killed everyone, saved Kit, and got out."

"Just like that?"

"Well, not quite just like that. I got shot. A lot. Getting shot hurts.

"Kit patched me up with illusionary blood and got me back to headquarters where Felicia stuffed me into a machine that put me back together. Took two days.

"Anyways, after we got out of that base, we gave No-Name a call to see if we could get bounty payouts for that entire base. Since the vast majority of them were all heroes."

Felix shifted his foot from one to the other.

"Got a pretty large payout from that. Hit up auction after auction and bought anyone I could with a decent point value.

"Took some time, but we hit fifty thousand points last night. You've been in mint condition waiting. On ice, so to speak. Proverbial Sleeping Beauty."

"Beauty, huh?" Lily asked, a small hint of amusement in her voice.

"Obviously. I'm making the rounds and going to start bringing people back. It'll take some time, but we'll get everyone back up on their feet."

"Good. What ever happened to our money?" The sound of shoes squeaking on the ground was a good sign she was getting close to being done.

"Oh. That. It got unfrozen pretty quick after word spread that Legion eliminated the Guild of Heroes and everyone a part of it. The car auction went very well to boot. We're flush with money and buying up as many new heads as possible to get our points up, so I can bring back our people."

"Where's Andrea? Or Victoria?" Lily asked from directly behind him.

"Andrea is in number forty-two, Victoria in thirty-two," Felix said, pointing at the shelves in the wall. "I haven't brought them back yet."

"Wait. Am I first?"

Felix turned his head to the side, looking at her out of the corner of his eye. "Ioana was first. Felicia wouldn't have left me alone until she was back with us.

"And to be fair, it was her tactics and doctrine that saw our people trained so very well.

"You're first after Ioana. Andrea will be tomorrow. I miss her. Far more than I feared I would. She kept everything fun. Happy. Energetic.

"Today though, I needed my Lily. Hard to run this place without you."

"Oh," she said, eyeing him.

"That and you owe me a date. You've kept me waiting long enough."

"Oh," Lily said again, grinning now. "Everything is okay, then?"

"I wouldn't say okay, but we're definitely back on track. Only a matter of time now."

"Which means we can go on our date tonight?"

"We can definitely go on our date tonight.

"Right after you hel—"

"Nope. Date first. Tonight. Work tomorrow."

Felix shook his head with a smile and relented.

"Date first. Work tomorrow."

"Now, where are you taking me? I expect to be spoiled. Spoiled rotten. I haven't eaten in weeks. I'm sure I'm famished."

Thank you, dear reader!

I'm hopeful you enjoyed reading Super Sale on Supers. Please consider leaving a review, commentary, or messages. Feedback is imperative to an author's growth. That and positive reviews never hurt.

Feel free to drop me a line at: WilliamDArand@gmail.com

Keep up to date—
Facebook: https://www.facebook.com/WilliamDArand

Blog: http://williamdarand.blogspot.com/

LitRPG Group: https://www.facebook.com/groups/LitRPGsociety/

SUPER SALES ON SUPER HEROES

Book 2

By William D. Arand

Dedicated:
To my wife, Kristin, who encouraged me in all things.
To my son, Harrison, who now lets me sleep, but wants to help me "type type" on my keyboard.
To my family, who always told me I could write a book if I sat down and tried.

Special Thanks to:
Niusha Gutierrez
Caleb Shortcliffe
Austin Youngblood
Michael Haglund
Steven Lobue

Thanks to my Beta Readers:
Michael Cramer
Eric Leaf
Daniel Schinhofen
Chris Chan
Alexander Hodge
Timothy Schwemmer
Chris Prochaska
Nogard53

I appreciate you reading through an unedited nightmare

And finally:

"Ha!! Please tell me I'm very interesting."~Steve Middleton being told that he was in book two of Super Sales on Super Heroes. 11/19/17 2:15 PM MST

Rest in peace Steve. Thanks for making me feel special as an author.

Chapter 1 - What They Understand -

Felix was roughly pushed into the chair, practically falling out of it with the force of the shove.

"Sit," growled out the heavyset officer.

Looking up at the man with an unamused face Felix laid his hands flat on the table. Sitting there quietly he inspected the room they'd put him in.

White bare walls, table with four chairs, a single entry, and a very obvious one-way mirror.

Before the pudgy uniformed police officer could do or say anything more, a woman in slacks and a blazer strolled in. She held a binder under her arm and seemed to be in her mid thirties.

Quirking a brow Felix turned his attention to the woman.

"Mr. Campbell," said the woman. "I'm Detective Torres."

"Morning, Detective Torres," Felix said evenly.

"I'd like to ask you a few questions, and then have you look at a few things," she said as she took the seat across from him.

"And you're gonna be real helpful," muttered the cop, looming over Felix.

Eying the man Felix contemplated the situation.

He didn't have to be here. They weren't actually holding him on anything, and the moment he got resistant they'd probably be forced to cut him loose. Or admit they had nothing.

If they really wanted, they could hold him for twenty-four hours on nothing.

But that was okay. They'd left early from Skippercity for this very reason. He didn't want to spend any time here, but it fit within his expectations.

"Uh huh," Felix replied, looking back to Detective Torres.

She was an attractive police officer. Darker skinned, brown eyes, short black hair. She had a hard set to her mouth and eyes though. Felix could only imagine she worked and fought her way through the ranks.

Battling her coworkers as often as crooks, he imagined.

"First, what's your reason for coming to Tilen?" asked the officer.

"Business. Our ventures in Skippercity have reached a bit of a plateau. Only so many antiques and heirlooms in one city. You know how it is. Expand, grow, or die," Felix said honestly.

"And what business is that exactly? Slaves?" said the detective, leaning forward in her seat.

"Hardly. Slavery isn't legal here. We're looking to expand our pawn shop business, and we're also considering a few other opportunities. In fact, we've already got all the prerequisite licenses and approvals on behalf of the city. It's one of the reasons we came here openly," Felix said, leaning back into his chair.

He kept his posture open and loose. He wasn't hiding anything and he didn't want her to think he was.

"I'm very much aware. I pulled all your paperwork to give it a once over and everything does appear to be on the up and up.

"Moving on. Do you know these individuals?" she asked, flipping out several photos in front of him.

Victoria Volante stood in all her glory with a sword upraised in front of her. Dark brown curly hair and dark green eyes.

The picture next to that was Kit in her Augur costume, her dark brown curls slipping out from the bottom of her helmet, the beautiful face hidden.

Last was Miu, dressed in a security uniform and with a no nonsense look on her serene Asian features.

"Yep. Head of internal security, head of HR, and head of my personal bodyguards," Felix said, identifying each one.

"And these two?" asked Torres, pulling out two more photos.

The first was Andrea with a sub-machine gun pulled in tight to her shoulder in a firing stance. Her hair was pulled back in a ponytail, the bright locks pulled back from her "girl next door" features.

You couldn't see her mismatched eyes, but he was sure they were flat and dead. She was clearly in her Myriad persona.

The second was a photo of Ioana. Clad in leather armor, a sword held out in front of her, one boot smashed into the pulpy remains of someone's head.

Plain featured, huge, with a shaved head. She was every bit the intimidating warrior he knew her to be.

"Yep. The big one is the chief of external security for Legion. The other is my personal secretary," Felix said, holding the photo up. "Never seen Ioana with no hair though. Can I get a copy of this? Felicia would probably like it."

Detective Torres' mouth became a thin line and she took the photo back from him.

"She's responsible for the deaths of multiple Heroes and Villains. She's a murderer," said the detective.

"Supposedly. She's never actually been convicted of anything. In fact, I do believe there's been a recent change in all of the pending charges against her. The vast majority were ruled... well... inconclusive really, due to a lack of evidence," Felix said, giving the detective a smile.

"And that brings me to the next one," said Torres, ignoring him.

She picked a photo out of her folder and dropped it onto the table.

It was Lily.

She stood in the middle of a photo that had been taken at considerable distance. She was wreathed in red and blue sigils and was clearly fighting with someone else.

"Yes?" Felix prompted, not giving up anything they didn't have.

"Mab."

"Uh-huh"

"Killed her own clients."

"Supposedly," Felix said neutrally, fighting a smile.

In truth, Lily, Lauren, and Kit had spent the last three weeks going through HR records. Every charge they could find, they argued and filed against in whatever fashion they could cook up.

Lauren Aston, Lily's new legal apprentice, apparently had a real knack for that work. Lily had praised her several times to him.

Combine those three great minds with the resources of Legion and those charges were rapidly vanishing under oceans of paperwork. It'd take time to get everything muddied, dropped, or blackmailed off, but it'd happen eventually.

It was one of the reasons Felix allowed himself to be taken into custody.

The large cop slammed his hands into the table, glaring at Felix.

"She's killed cops! Heroes! There is no supposed about it!" shouted the officer.

Felix felt the corner of his mouth twitch as he fought a smirk.

Is he the bad cop then?

"Supposedly," Felix said calmly, staring into the cop's face.

Then, surprisingly, the cop smashed his fist into Felix's jaw.

Rocketing out of the chair and crashing to the floor, Felix couldn't help but be shocked. Having Victoria, Miu, Andrea, and Ioana train him daily had put him through much worse though.

Playing the situation for what it was, Felix lay limp on the ground.

The bastard had taken a cheap shot at him. He figured he might as well earn some points from it.

If this was a stand up fight I would have cleaned his clock, too.

There was the sound of shouts and a door slamming open as Felix recovered.

Before he could get back to his feet, the officer had been hustled out of the interview room.

"Yeah, no. We're done," Felix said, getting to his feet. Feeling around in his mouth with his tongue he could taste copper. Taking aim, he spat a mouthful of blood onto the table. "I'll also be filing charges against that officer for assault and suing the city for every penny it's worth. My lawyers are quite good.

"I'm formally refusing all medical assistance until this is documented and my wounds photographed. You can testify or I can have a mind reader verify the truth of the situation," Felix said, giving her both barrels. He didn't want this going anywhere he didn't want it to.

Detective Torres stood there, her face now an angry snarl and her hands clenched at her sides.

"You have my sincere apologies, Mr. Campbell, perhaps you could let this matter drop?" she asked him.

"Are you fucking kidding me?" Felix asked while laughing. "What kind of request is that? Why would I do that? I'm going to happily see that hulking gorilla tossed out on his ass, and then collect a big fat paycheck."

Felix brushed his clothes off carefully, but made sure not to touch his bleeding lip. In fact, he let the blood flow freely down his chin and neck.

"We can hold you for a while," Torres said.

"You were already going to hold me. Your offer changes nothing. You have about ten seconds to say something that makes sense before I ask for a lawyer, and this whole thing ends."
Felix turned his head to stare into the one-way mirror.

Torres followed his gaze and then went over to the mirror and tapped on it twice.

A few seconds passed before a tap came back in return.

Turning her head to him, Torres gave him a grim look.

"I'd consider it a personal favor. I'd also turn you and your entire crew loose today," Torres offered.

Oh? A personal favor might be worth it but…

Felix reached up with his left hand scratched at his ear with a finger.

"I dunno. Are your personal favors worth a few hundred thousand dollars? You're just a detective, aren't you?" Felix asked seriously.

Detective Torres was clearly gritting her teeth. He couldn't imagine she was enjoying this situation very much.

"You know what, don't answer that. I'll take you up on it, provided you can get me and my people out of this precinct in the next," Felix said, pausing to look at his watch, "ten minutes."

Never hurts to have a policeman in your pocket. This is turning out to be an interesting trip already.

Detective Torres must have had some pull.

Since Felix, Miu, Kit, Lauren, Victoria, and Eva were all on the street in front of the security convoy with all their possessions returned in under five minutes, it seemed like a logical conclusion.

Miu was staring at Felix while Lauren got into the lead car of the security detail, just wanting to put the situation behind them.

Those dark eyes of Miu's bored into him, demanding an answer to her question.

"Ok, yeah. Something happened. Some cop punched me. Because of that, we got turned loose, and the detective in charge of my questioning owes me a favor," Felix admitted. "May not count for anything, but it seemed like an easy favor to take."

Miu's face turned pale. Her face became murderous and she looked as if she were going to march into the police station and start killing

"Miu, stop, please. Just… let it go for now. This'll work out to our benefit, I'm sure. Now… how about we get in the car, and head off for the new Tilen Legion pawnshop, our headquarters. We need to get set up and start hiring with the new contracts we prepared," Felix said. "I'll let you dictate security and I won't even argue. Ok?"

Miu's eyebrows drew together as she glared at him. "You won't complain?"

"Nope, not a word. You and Victoria can do everything you like," Felix promised in the most charming voice he could manage.

He opened the passenger door and motioned inside. Looking to Kit he gave her a wave as well. "Come on, hop in, and let's get going. I'll sit in the back with Victoria and Eva like a good boy."

Kit shrugged her shoulders and gave him a small smile.

Things had been strained between them since the "incident" two months ago with the Heroes guild.

To be fair, it wasn't every day that your companion is kidnapped, doesn't seem to fight, and a school full of children gets blown up.

Not one of those every day kind of affairs.

And since then, there'd been an uncrossable distance between them.

A gap that was too wide right now to cross. They'd made some progress, but it was slow. Difficult.

Kit couldn't read his mind and he could only tell her everything was fine so many times.

Having been a mind reader for so long, she didn't have the trust and faith in people that normal humans did.

He imagined it'd eventually right itself.

Moving to the driver's seat, Kit got in.

Miu finally got into the passenger seat, glaring at him the entire time.

Closing the door, Felix let out a breath.

"She worries about you, that's all," Eva said with a smile, patting Felix's arm.

"Yeah, I know. And are you sure this'll be alright? You're good with your studies right now?" Felix asked, opening the rear passenger door for Eva.

"Yes. I'm fine. I'm ahead actually. The new Legion school is great. I know everyone there is happy that you built it into Headquarters, but it's nice to get out. The fun part for me though is it doesn't matter how many students we have, we just make the school bigger and hire more teachers. So you won't lose track of any of your friends, they'll just be in a different part of the campus," Eva said, getting into the car.

Huh. Well, at least Felicia is on that. I'm sure she already planned for number increases. Ahoy future planning.

Victoria grabbed the door and then became immobile.

"I know, I know. Middle seat," Felix said.

Victoria smiled in return to his comment and nodded her head, waiting.

Clambering into the car, he made himself comfortable.

It was a good thing they purchased luxury sedans and upgraded them. Middle seat in those was at least moderately comfortable.

And Andrea isn't here. Which makes this even better. I won't have a Beastkin crawling all over me.

Victoria slid in next to him and pressed into his side. Her lithe athletic figure reminded him that he hadn't seen Andrea in a few days.

Clearing his throat uncomfortably, Felix felt excited.

"Let's go see the new building first, Headquarters," he said.

Kit nodded her head and got the car going. They sped off quickly down the road.

"So… are you going to do what you said?" Eva asked. She reached up and tucked a dark brown lock of hair around an ear.

"What, about the new pawnshop? Yep. I also want to explore what we did with the Telemedics. I think that could be something we can use to train people up a whole heck of a lot faster. I've already got some things to test out.

"The hard part is getting in the door, then getting them to buy the pitch," Felix admitted with a frown. "It's like any job, right? You get interviewed as you interview them. They find out if they want to work for you, work for the company, and if it'll do right by them."

"That seems hard," Eva said.

"It can be. Especially if the number of jobs outpaces the workforce. Then you end up in salary wars, one hiring away the employees of the other and constantly raising their rates. We'll see though. I think we'll be able to make enticing offers. Well, provided that new indentured servant contract Lily drew up is valid and legal," Felix said seriously. "I mean, this whole trip will be pointless if the contract doesn't bind them to me in the same way."

"Speaking of," Kit said from the front seat. "Are we technically no longer slaves?"

Frowning at the question, Felix called up his point screen.

	Received	Spent	Remaining
Daily Allotment	150	0	150
Miu Miki	1,250	1,250	0
—Direct reports	14,315	0	14,315
Ioana Iliescu	1,100	0	1,100
—Direct reports	25,170	0	25,170
Kit Carrington	2,250	2,250	0
—Direct reports	22,170	0	22,170
Lilian Lux	2,600	2,600	0
—Direct reports	14,750	0	14,750
Andrea Elex	1,500	3,000	-1,500
Felicia Fay	1,600	4,800	-3,200
—Direct reports	14,125	0	1,600
Eva Adelpha	4,900	4,900	0
Mr. White.	300	900	-600
—Direct reports	21,090	0	21,090
+ Loyalty Bonus	5,030	0	5,030
DAILY TOTAL	**132,300**	**19,700**	**100,075**

"Everything is still there. So your contract works. That or you're still a slave. Won't know until we test the new contract on someone else," Felix said.

After a while the vehicle came to a slow stop as Felix tinkered with his screen. He'd spent any number of hours fiddling with his views. Trying to get the most out of them.

It was beginning to seem more like an anxiety response.

At least the huge increase in points from all the unpowered they bought certainly had paid off. Though their costs in finances was still annoying. Their profit margin shrunk by a few percentage points.

He had to constantly spend points to keep a thousand and one things on track and moving in the right direction. The point calendar looked like an ever-increasing bank balance that always had more withdrawals than he liked.

How else were we going to bring everyone back to life, though? We needed those people.

Not like you can magic up points. Gold? Sure. Points? Not really. And converting one to the other is damned expensive.

Victoria opened the door and stepped out, Miu doing the same.

"No hostile thoughts," Kit said, holding a hand to her ear.

There was a muted response from the earpiece.

Felix waited quietly as he promised he would.

"Holy cow, that's the new building?" Eva asked, peering out the passenger window from her side of the car.

Looking up, Felix found himself staring at a rather large skyscraper.

Tall, dark, and ominous, it was a rectangle. There were no accents or artful designs.

A giant rectangle stabbing into the sky.

Felix kinda liked the simplicity of it.

It went up what he'd guess was fifty floors.

Looking back down he found the entry was a vast and open area that funneled down into one single entry. The rest of the building on the ground floor was made of concrete.

He could definitely see why Miu, Andrea, Victoria, and Ioana were all happy with the building. The entry was a death trap. A real choke point without even being reinforced or upgraded.

Makes sense.

"Where's... where are we living?" Eva asked softly.

"I'll be modifying it to be an exact replica of our current HQ in Skippercity. At least, everything from the ground floor down. You'll be living in the exact same room you do at home, I suppose," Felix said.

Going to be most of your points for the day there, Felix old pal. You won't be doing much after this at all.

In fact, it would be all of his points. One hundred thousand and five hundred points. And that'd only take care of the first floor and down.

It'd take another several days to get the upper floors into what they wanted.

Kit and Lily had run the numbers on how much it would cost. In the end, using Felix's points and several days of his time was simply the cheapest method. Even if all he did was make gold all day instead.

"Oh. Where's your office going to be? Top floor?" Eva asked.

"Pfft. Only a villain, a hero, or a fool would live that high up. Nope, I'll be in my office below ground. If I can't be there, then I'll be on the second floor when I have to be. With a window I can bust open and a comfy bush below it I can jump into," Felix said dismissively. "Top floor will be a dummy office that I 'work out of' but it'll really just be an elevator going really slow for one floor. Mr. White put together this weird display for the windows to mimic the top floor. It's too technical for me, but it works."

"That seems overly elaborate," Eva said.

"It is. But it made them happy to solve a problem I didn't care about. So we let them solve it. He'll be here in a few days anyways so he can explain it then if you want."

Victoria came up and rapped on the glass twice, waited five seconds, then opened the door.

Sighing, Felix slid out of the car and stood up with a stretch.

All around him, spreading out across the entire entry area, were people in tactical gear. They carried loaded and locked weapons, all checked out, licensed, and legal.

It was as if a private military company had been contracted for security detail.

Well, after the training Andrea gave them, maybe they are a PMC.

Thinking about what he wanted done to the building, he watched as the window floated up from nothing in front of him.

Then he thumbed the accept button.

"Let's go settle in then. Today is moving day, and I imagine there'll be a number of trucks showing up soon. Probably need to have you and your HR team ready to scan the locals as they help out," Felix said, turning his head to Kit.

Sighing, she nodded her head and gave him a small smile.

"You're right of course. I'll get my people moving," she said.

"Good. I'll be in my office going over our quarter to date results," Felix said eagerly.

Spreadsheets were still what made sense to him.

Despite all the changes.

Being trained in combat and guns.

Even changing his mindset to be proactive.

He still enjoyed spreadsheets and data.
They made sense.

Chapter 2 - Now Hiring -

Several days later and everything was up and running.

Now it felt almost as if he were in the Skippercity HQ.

Minus Andrea and Lily.

Felix shook his head to clear the thought. It didn't help any, and it would only make the situation worse for him to dwell on it.

The best cure for morose thoughts was work.

And work we have aplenty.

Looking to his display he called up his itinerary and began to read through it.

Andrea had marked out everything he needed to take care of for the week.

Lily had updated his points calendar to reflect his upcoming meetings and Legion needs.

Kit had sent him all the appropriate documents and talking points.

Everything was prepared in advance for him. Now he just had to start hiring for the pawnshop, recruiters, and their other ventures.

The overarching goal was to make the lives of Legionnaires comfy.

This of course was actually all secondary.

Yes, these were all valid things that they wanted to accomplish. But the real reason they were here in Tilen was that it had an active Heroes guild location.

During her time as a prisoner, Kit managed to siphon a good bit of information off of her captors. Unfortunately it was all done through conversation and being observant.

Nothing was ever directly confirmed.

That device they made her wear really did a fair job of keeping her locked in her own mind, unfortunately.

From everything that they'd been able to piece together, their enemies wanted Kit herself.

Felix was a means to an end for them. They'd even gone and deemed him as necessary collateral damage.

Their goal was simple. They were going to kill him to break the contract. Once that was done, Kit would be put into a limbo state with the government.

Beyond that, nothing was said. The assumption everyone in Legion was working off of was that they wanted to secret her away before anyone was the wiser. Before the government of Skippercity could reclaim her.

And yet, there really was no reason stated for this whole thing. At least that they discussed. No clue, no hint. Nothing. Not a word.

Or even how Kit had ended up with Skipper, and then been sold.

It didn't make sense.

The guild only wanted Augur. No one, and nothing, else. She was apparently so important, no one had even bothered to simply ask Felix if they could purchase her.

That's the world though. Full of fools. Supers, Villains, and unpowereds alike.

Wouldn't have sold her anyways. Too damn important to me.

Have I told her that?

Standing up, and chasing his thoughts away before he could settle on any one, Felix buttoned his coat and gave his lapels a quick tug.

"Need to tell her how important she is to me," Felix muttered. Lifting his hands up he smacked his cheeks with his hands. "Time to go put on a show."

Walking out of the small office they'd let him prepare in, Felix set off for the school gymnasium.

The halls were quiet as he passed, but up ahead was a roar and crash of noise. He knew it was hundreds of excited teenage voices talking at the same time.

This assembly had been scheduled by Lily in advance. All she'd had to do was promise a few things. The first was that all applicants of Tilen High would be given preferential status over other applicants for Legion entry level positions for the next six months.

Second was of course a small donation that the school didn't ask for, but didn't decline.

All to test a contract, and how to teach people quickly.

Pushing the double doors open, Felix stepped out into the gym.

Plastering on his best customer service smile, remembering to crinkle his eyes slightly at the corners in the parody of a genuine smile, he headed for the center.

Standing there were Victoria, Lauren, Miu, and Kit.

No wonder there's so much discussion. Every guy here is probably wondering how to get a chance to talk to them.

"Everyone, settle down," said a man in a suit with a microphone. He was fairly average in all things, with brown wavy hair and blue eyes.

He apparently did have some credit with the student body though, as they all quieted down in decent order.

"We have a guest speaker today. He'll be talking to you about his company branching into our fair city of Tilen, and an offer he's making to Tilen High specifically. Please help me welcome Felix Campbell. Owner and CEO of Legion."

There was a moment of silence, followed by a respectful amount of applause.

Smiling, Felix bowed his head incrementally to the principal and shook his hand when he got close.

"Thank you. And thank you, Tilen High," Felix said, taking the microphone and holding it up. "I'm here today because Legion is expanding. We're setting up a branch right here in Tilen."

Several hands shot up into the air and Felix couldn't help but grin.

"We'll save questions for the end, but I'm sure I can guess a few.

"Yes, I'm from Skippercity.

"Yes, I own slaves.

"Yes, the beautiful woman standing next to me is Augur.

"Yes, Mab is in my employ, as well as War Maiden, and Myriad.

"No, they aren't here today.

"How many questions did I answer with that?"

Looking around, he saw almost all of the hands drop down.

"Great, save those questions for the end though, as I might answer a few as we go. Have no fear, this'll be a quick assembly. Even though some of you might wish it was longer," Felix said with a chuckle.

There was a collective snicker at that.

Everyone loved assemblies. It meant they didn't have to do anything.

"Legion is hiring. We're looking to hire many of you. This'll not just be pawnshop jobs either. We're hiring into all departments and aspects of Legion," Felix said. Moving to the other end of the gym, he made sure to look to both sides of his audience. Trying to bring them all in.

"Because of course some of you are wondering how you could ever work at Legion with no experience. We're going to be showcasing a new training methodology we're perfecting. Should you be hired on, this is something you'd be given access to. Miu?"

Turning to look to his internal security chief he gave her a smile.

With a glance to the other set of double doors that led out to a patio, Miu said something into her headset.

The doors swung open, and four men and five women came into the gym, wheeling in a large platform. It looked like a bathroom stall with a roof and only a single door.

"Inside of this is that very same methodology we just spoke of. I'll first need several volunteers. I won't be selecting anyone though. In fact, you can elect your own volunteers and send them up. Those lucky volunteers will get to see it firsthand, and experience it."

Felix turned away from the crowd. With a few swift steps he reached the spot his people were setting up.

"We all set, Kit?" Felix asked, thumbing the mute button on the microphone.

"Yes. I've also been scanning the area. There are several Heroes spying on us. It would seem choosing this location really was ideal. Picking the high school directly across from the Heroes guild hall was a solid idea," Kit said with a smirk.

"Hey... before we go any further in this. I just wanted to say, you're important to me. Very. Don't ever think you're not," Felix said, catching Kit's eyes with his own.

"O-oh. I see. Yes. Thank you," she said, breaking her gaze away after a second.

Lifting the microphone back to his mouth, Felix turned around to his audience. Two young teenage boys and a girl were walking his way.

"Ah, good show, good show. Congratulations and welcome! You'll be our first job applicants. Though I'm afraid, it'll be for today only, and the skillset you learn won't be of much use. Well, maybe," Felix said, grinning.

Several of his assistants had left and now came back carrying boxes of varying sizes. Some so large it took two people to move them.

"Alright, you, Mr. Letterman jacket. Pick a box," Felix said waving a hand at the parcels being set down.

"Uh... sure," said the kid.

Walking over to a medium sized one, he picked it up and looked to Felix.

"Go ahead, open it," Felix encouraged. Moving over to stand beside the young man, he tilted the mic towards him.

"Kay. Uh..." Pausing, he opened the box and peered inside. "It's a... Rubik's cube?"

"Great. Ever solve one of those before?"

"No. They uh... they don't make sense to me."

"Perfect. First, I have to ask you to sign this waiver. It's very simple. This is your agreement that you're allowing us to train you in... how to solve a Rubik's cube. To do that, we have to go into your head, put the training and experience there, and then get back out.

"It also says that this training will only last for a year. And everyone here just heard me say this, and that's the legally binding contract. I've had your faculty read over this beforehand of course, and they felt it was acceptable.

"Of course, it does say that you won't be sharing any of what you see in that teaching booth with anyone else."

Almost on cue, the principal nodded his head and gave a thumbs up.

Thanks, Chief. Remind me to actually use this school as a recruiting grounds instead of just on paper.

"Uh. Ok. I just... sign?"

"Yep, right there," Felix said, pointing to the specific line. He took the Rubik's cube from the boy and began mixing it up.

Lauren held out a pen to Mr. Letterman, who took it and signed his name. Which was apparently Jeff.

"Go ahead and open that door there, Jeff, step behind the curtain, and follow the instructions."

"Kay."

Real conversationalist there. Destined for a job in a back room.

Jeff opened the door and stepped in. One of Miu's people shut the door.

"Now, folks, this'll really only take a minute. So while he's doing that, how about you two go pick a box?"

The girl immediately went to the largest box and set about opening it.

The other boy picked up a small sized one.

He managed to get his open first and held out his prize.

"How to speak Japanese," he said curiously.

"Oh, that'll be fun," Felix said.

The girl yanked the side off the box and stared at what looked like a desk with tools on it.

"Woodworking. I wonder what you'll build for us. Maybe you'll be an undiscovered artist," Felix said with a laugh.

The door to the training cell opened, and Jeff stepped out. He looked a touch dazed, but fine.

Hm. Need to check on the skill books and see if converting them into a video format changed a few things. The books worked for the Telemedics after all.

"Ah, good. Here ya go, Jeff. Solve this as fast as you can," Felix said, tossing him the mixed up Rubik's cube.

Jeff looked down at it, confused.

In the next moment, his eyes focused on the cube and his hands started moving. Rotating and shifting the cube faster and faster.

In under a minute, he solved the cube and held it up.

"I did that? I did that... I can solve a Rubik's cube," Jeff said with a laugh.

"Here, try again. Each one you solve in under a minute I'll give you a fifty for," Felix said. Pivoting on his heel, he took an open box from one of the assistants. Inside were ten Rubik's cubes.

Setting it down in front of Jeff, he turned back to Kit as the second boy was being escorted into the cell. Thumbing the mute button he gave her a critical look.

"It's working. I can read everything in their heads. Without them even knowing. Check your point values?" Kit asked.

Nodding his head, Felix turned back to the Rubik's cube master.

Focusing in on Jeff, Felix wanted to know what it would cost to change Jeff's hair color.

But only if he owned Jeff. Not a hypothetical option.

Physical change: Blue Hair	Required Ownership: (Met) Required Permission: (Met)	Change?(400)

Below that was the accept button.

The contract worked, and the training worked when changed to a video format instead of a book. Which meant they could probably train an entire class at the same time.

"We're golden," Felix said, dismissing the window.

Kit gave him a relieved smile and then nodded her head.

Holding up an arm, Felix pointed to the two doors his people had come in from.

"Those who want to see the other two lessons may of course remain," Felix said into the mic. "Those who want to find out what departments are hiring in Legion, all of them, and speak to someone about that, step right on outside."

Two of the movers had anticipated his statement and were waiting at the doors. As soon as he invited everyone outside, they opened the doors. Light from outside flooded into the gym.

"Thank you, everyone, for your attention, we're going to move to the Q and A session now. All questions regarding certain departments should be taken to their respective booths. Generalized questions to HR." Felix stopped next to one of his people. "Or you can speak directly to me if you like. Enjoy the career fair. I hear the corndogs are awesome."

Handing over the mic to the black suited man, Felix walked outside.

All around him were booths and tables. Decorated and labeled by their respective departments. From janitorial to HR. Motorpool to security. Everything was here.

Victoria was beside him, matching him pace for pace. His destination was obvious. There was a booth at the center of everything that had one empty chair behind it.

The placard on the top of the booth read "applications." Beyond that was an area with arranged tables, chairs, pens, and men and women waiting on hand for questions.

Felix could smell the sweet siren call of the food stands off to both sides. Everything was free to anyone who could provide their school ID.

We really did go all out on this.

"I think we're going to be drowning in applicants," Victoria said from his side.

"That's a good thing. If we can catch them out of high school, and do it right, they'll never want to leave," Felix said, nodding his head.

Moving around to the back of the booth, Felix sat down in the chair. He didn't bother to offer the other one to Victoria, she wouldn't take it.

She'd be too busy staring everyone down who came close.

Instead, he picked up a stack of applications and a pen. Giving the top of it a click he checked to make sure the ink could write.

Sighing, he retracted the pen tip and set it down next to his right hand, arranged the stack of applications, then folded his hands one over the other.

High schoolers were spilling out of the doors in droves. They were looking around as they went, and then heading immediately to whatever booth they were interested in.

"Hm. How are things?" Felix asked to Victoria.

"Same as ever. I did catch a few Powereds trying to get in close. I made sure that they understood there was a limit to my patience," Victoria said. "The change in my secondary power helped," Victoria amended softly.

"Wasn't that big a deal. We just moved your observations to heightened reflexes. Didn't even cost much. Though… do you find yourself fighting it at times? Is it an always on kind of thing? I know you said it's almost as if time slows down when you're pushing it."

"It's controllable for the most part. I find myself knowing things I don't want to. Smells, changes in body posture, pupils constricting, increase in heart rate. All signs of people lying or… or other things. Overall though, very beneficial. Definitely makes it much easier to babysit you," Victoria said with a smile in her voice.

"I'll give you something to babysit," Felix said. "Maybe I'll decide we need to go on a late night trip to a fast food joint at two am and I'll be eating on the curb."

Victoria snorted at that and didn't respond.

Yeah, pretty unlikely.

From inside the press of teenagers, a small open area formed at the back.

Grinning, he already knew it was Miu and Kit. They were the only people he knew who could make a path like that without hurting people.

Proving his thoughts true, Miu and Kit stepped out of the throng of young people.

Catching Kit's eyes, Felix smiled genuinely.

"Your heartrate sped up and you're leaning forward. I'm not sure which one has you so interested, or both, but your tongue might as well be hanging out," Victoria said softly. "The problem with me noticing these things, though, is I'm sure Kit has read my thoughts and knows these things as well."

Felix froze as he processed all that.

Then he shrugged.

"Don't care, they're both extremely attractive in their way. Besides, Miu can read lips. She just doesn't like to let people know. Don't you, Miu, you beautiful tiny princess who I'd like to see in a pair of yoga pants and a sports bra," Felix said.

Miu tripped over nothing, catching herself immediately as her face turned a deep scarlet.

"See?" Felix asked with a snicker.

"You're a horrible man," Victoria replied.

"Only with Miu. She's a delight to prod at because her reactions are so… sincere. It's not my normal disposition to flirt," Felix said honestly. "All of my previous girlfriends asked me out first."

It really wasn't his inclination to be the aggressor. Almost all of his relationships were something someone else initiated.

Kit had turned her attention to Miu and was making sure she was alright. Only letting it drop when they stood in front of Felix.

"Well," Kit began. "Everything is pretty much what we suspected. There's a few memories here of people seeing me across the street. Or hearing of me being there. We're on the right track."

"Great. That's what we were hoping to confirm. One step closer to finding out what they wanted you for. One step closer to getting them off our asses," Felix said grimly.

"Sorry. We can—"

"Stop talking," Felix said, interrupting her, pointing a finger at her. His eyes turned cold and dangerous. "Not a word. You're important to me, and I'll not hand you over to people who blow up schools to justify their goals. They're petty, stupid, and intolerant. That'd be like someone dropping a nuke on Skippercity," Felix said hotly.

"What?" Victoria asked, shocked. "That's just stupid."

"You and I would agree. But there are some crazy, very stupid, very basic, low IQ individuals who would do something like that. They'd damn hundreds of thousands of people, to take out one villain. Poison the earth for hundreds of years. Kill thousands upon thousands with the radioactive fallout afterward. All for one villain who was in control of a city, and running it, rather well all things considered.

"It sounds insane, and bizarre, but there are those people out there. Some upper echelon nutjob with a name like… Corinne, David, Victor, or Noah. Yeah," Felix said with a sigh, naming off previous employees he remembered.

Everyone collectively shook their heads at the thought of it.

"Anyways, that's beside the point. Don't even think to offer up a suggestion like turning yourself over, as that's pure idiocy.

"Besides, you're not even a slave anymore. You're only indentured. You were able to break your contract the moment you came to Tilen with me," Felix said, looking back to Kit again.

It'd be a heck of a break price, but you could do it.

The telepath said nothing and merely stared back at him.

Then with a small smile she nodded her head a fraction. "And here I'll remain. You're not a Hero, Felix, but you're not a Villain either."

"Pretty much. Just a guy looking out for his own. Oh, here we go," Felix said with a bit of excitement in his voice.

A group of six teenagers were walking up to his booth, questions in their faces, arms braced against themselves with nervous energy.

Felix gave them a smile and waited. Whatever questions they had, he'd answer them honestly. *And with any luck, I'll be giving them an application.*

Forty minutes later and Felix had managed to clear his queue. He had doubted that it was going to last as long as it had, but he was glad to have finished up that group fully.

No sooner than they cleared out, Jeff came trundling up with a wheeled trashcan. Behind him was two younger girls who vaguely resembled Jeff. Each one of them had a trashcan they were pulling as well.

"Jeff, to what do I owe the pleasure?" Felix asked. He leaned over his desk and set his chin on his folded hands, watching.

"I wanted to collect on that deal. You didn't give me a time limit or anything so…" Jeff said hesitantly.

"Go on," Felix said. He already figured out what Jeff had done and was doing his best not to laugh.

"So I went across the street. There's a toy store. I bought as many as I could afford and… solved them," Jeff said. He pulled his trash can over to Felix and lifted the lid.

Inside was nothing but solved Rubik's cubes.

Unable to help himself, Felix started to laugh. Looking up at Jeff, he clapped his hands together a few times.

"Well done. You're absolutely right, and I'll pay out. On the condition that you put in an application, Jeff. I like that kind of thinking. Quite a bit," Felix said.

He needed more people to throw into Lily's department. Smart creative thinkers were dangerous in legal departments.

Chapter 3 - Omission -

The evening of the career fair found Felix hunched over his desk.

He was peering at the display of all the applicants on his virtual desktop. He wasn't sure, but it seemed like over ninety percent of the senior class had applied. He'd be able to get a final count later on when it was all pushed into an excel sheet.

Every department got at least one applicant.

"Quite a few interested in security," Felix said, flipping through the applications. "Even a few with existing powers. I didn't realize they had Powereds in the school."

His bodyguard said nothing. Instead, he stood at the corner of Felix's desk, doing his best impression of a men's suit mannequin for a war zone.

Dressed sharply in a tailored black suit, clearly wearing kevlar underneath, and toting a SMG, he had the look of a trained operative.

Not surprising. We did start with our own people on the training program with the singular books. They might very well be the equivalent to some special forces.

The woman at the corner of the room gave him a glance, then resumed her duties. She was dressed similarly to the man, armed the same way, and had the same lethal air around her.

Sighing, Felix missed Andrea.

There was something about the bubbly Beastkin that made even the quiet moments... different.

Closing his terminal with a flick of his fingers he leaned back in his chair. Staring up at the ceiling, he tried to order his thoughts as best as he could. There was quite a bit to do, still.

Before he even got through a mental list of every task, let alone sorting them, his phone started buzzing on his wrist.

Falling into a normal sitting position he glanced at the display on the front.

Lily?

Tapping the connect button he pulled his earpiece out of his front pocket and slipped it into his ear.

"Hey, beautiful," Felix said, grinning. "I miss you. You and that big brain of yours."

"You say the most wonderful things. You compliment me on both sides, and reassure me that you want me for my mind," came the purring voice of Lily on the other end of the line.

"I want compliments, too!" said Andrea, clearly in the same room.

"Stop, Andie, you know he compliments you endlessly," Lily said with a laugh.

"I miss you both," Felix said simply.

There was no response to the sincerity in his tone. Both Lily and Andrea seemed flustered.

"Well," Lily began again. "That'll be over soon. Wraith is on their way over to you. Should be there in an hour or two."

That means the job is done.

Every witness who was lined up for every charge against anyone in Legion had been taken care of. Silence purchased, intimidated, or simply eliminated.

Hopefully as little of that last one as possible.

"Only two," Lily said, as if she'd heard his thoughts.

"That's great," Felix said, feeling better.

Two out of six hundred was pretty low on how bad it could have been.

Me and mine first. Anyone else is an enemy. Legion first.

"We'll be waiting about a week, and then joining you," Lily said a touch breathily.

She missed me, too?

"Lauren's been sending me status reports. Seems like everything is going splendidly," she immediately continued on.

"Ah, yeah. Everything is. We had a really good turn out for Tilen High. We'll probably be visiting all the other high schools after this. They'll all get second tier preferential treatment, but still preferential," Felix said, leaning back in his chair again.

"Good, good. Stop it, just—ok. Ok. You don't need to give me that look, stop multiplying. Ok, here," Lily said. "One second, Felix, Andie wants to talk."

Felix laughed and nodded his head, even though they couldn't see him. "Alright."

"Felix!" came a thundering of voices practically shouting into the phone. Then it devolved into a tumult of voices. It sounded as if there were at least twenty of them all crowding around the phone.

"Any possibility of you getting down to Andrea prime? It's a touch hard to understand with so many of you talking at the same time."

The Andreas got quiet, and one of them was directing the others.

"I'll go first," said an Andrea into the phone. "I love you, Felix. I miss you."

The directness of the words struck him at his core, and he felt his skin prickle insanely. There was a heavy feeling just behind his forehead and eyes.

"I... I love you, too, Andrea," Felix said thickly. For the first time. And he meant it. Which was surprising.

"Nn! Feelings received. We'll be there soon so just... just wait for us," Andrea said huskily into the phone.

"Ok, next!" she shouted to someone else.

The phone made a rustling noise as it was clearly passed off.

"Felix! This is Andrea," said Andrea.

Unable to help himself he chuckled. "Hi Andrea," he said, wondering which one it was.

"This is number three. I was with you the night before you left," she said in a conspiratorial whisper. "I love you, Felix. I miss you."

"I love you, too, Andrea," Felix said for the second time.

They're not going to pass the phone off to every—

"Nn!" said the Andrea, and then the sound of the phone being passed could be heard.

"Felix? This is Andrea!"

Oh god they are.

"Hi... Andrea. How many... others... are there right now?" he asked neutrally.

"All of us! We made a line. Myriad got us in order like when we're prepping for a mission. She said she'll go last so it's fair. This is number four. I was a Death Other and you brought me back."

"Ah. I should have guessed," Felix said resigned.

"I love you. So much," the ex-Death Other cooed into the phone.

Sighing, Felix settled in for what he suspected would be a long phone call.

Pulling the earpiece out, Felix blew a raspberry with his mouth and closed his eyes.

A deliberate shuffling of feet caught his attention. "Wraith is here?" Felix asked.

"Yes, sir," said one of the bodyguards.

"Everyone please leave after Wraith enters. Please also track down Eva and send her over. Only people allowed in are Victoria, Miu, and Kit," Felix ordered.

He heard everyone leave quickly, the door opening and closing only once.

"Wraith?" Felix asked quietly.

"Here," came the echoing whisper.

To this day, Felix wasn't entirely sure what Wraith was. His ability page seemed to say one thing, though his appearance countered it.

Since he was a conscripted employee, Felix didn't really trust him.

"We'll wait for Eva," Felix said, relaxing into his chair. He was still processing everything that had just gone down with Andrea.

Five minutes ticked by before the door opened again.

Opening his eyes, Felix found Eva standing there in the doorway.

"Felix? What's up?" Eva asked.

"Come on in, take a seat. Wraith is going to go on a mission tonight and I'd like you to accompany him. Time to test out those skills we put in your head, and some of those new powers," Felix explained.

Eva nodded her head with a smile. Coming into Felix's office, she closed the door.

After what happened at the school, and spending a long time getting everyone back from the dead, he'd begun experimenting.

Modified powers with massive detriments that made them cost few points.

Eva was a very good example.

He'd given her super strength. On par with some of the mightiest in the world. Except it only worked for a short period of time given certain circumstances.

As strange as it was, the power cost a touch under one thousand points. It was an economical power that was undeniably useful.

Then he gave her Lilly's powers, with the same limitation.

Then Kit's.

And Andrea's.

Eva had an altered version of many powers. She was his personal nuclear warhead. Eva... was probably the single strongest super in his employ. Provided it only had to last a day or two.

And she didn't even know it.

Because each and every power he gave her had a limitation. She had to have Felix's approval to use them, speak the name of the power, and after the usage, that power would fade away.

Nor did she know about it. She had no idea about all these powers he'd put into her.

In fact no one did. They were originally just experiments.

After his success with these one-off powers, he'd begun making the books with similar powers within, instead of just medical training.

And soon, the library will be done.

Breaking free of his thoughts, he slid a small skill book across the desk to her. It'd been an expensive skill book to make. It had cost him a number of points.

"This is Wraith's power set. I want you to go with him tonight on his mission. Learn from him. Let's see you put to use all those other skill books we've been feeding you," Felix said with a grin.

Every skill book created for every other department was given to Eva as well. She was a walking encyclopedia of the working knowledge of Legion.

Eva gave him a small smile and picked up the book. A few seconds later and it vanished into nothing.

Part of keeping the cost of books down was making them all single usage.

Now if only I could use those damn books myself.

Much to his chagrin, not a single book was usable by him.

At any level.

It lined up with the inability to modify himself.

Or to modify others to have his own power.

"When you're ready, head out with Wraith. Oh... Lily and Andrea will be joining us in a week," he said.

Eva had bonded with both of them. Lily for being Evan's mentor, Andrea for helping her adapt to Legion life.

The young woman smiled brightly and couldn't help but clap her hands together.

"Really?" she nearly squealed.

"Yes. Really. Now," Felix said, turning to Wraith. "Your mission. I need you to infiltrate the local Hero HQ. We're trying to find out why they want Kit. We know they want her. To the point that they're willing to blow up schools. But not why.

"I want to know. Take a head set so I can follow along. Shouldn't get in your way at all."

Wraith, the black silhouette that he was, made no move to obey the order.

About the time it took for a single breath passed before he answered.

"Why not look into their memories?" Wraith asked.

Felix had contemplated that one already.

It wasn't outside of his power, but it would involve hunting around in their heads. There was no guarantee that if he popped open those memories he'd locked out they would be containable.

Or that he could re-blank them after.

He'd done it while they were insane with agony and suffering. Truth be told, he wasn't even positive he hadn't damaged them in the process. Right now it was a risk he wasn't willing to run.

Not when he could find the information through other means.

"It's something I've considered," Felix admitted. "Not something I'm willing to pursue at this time. Anything else?"

"No."

"Go. Make sure you protect, take care of, and guide Eva. Assume she could eventually take your place since she can fade through objects," Felix commanded.

"Of course," Wraith said. Without turning around, Wraith inverted into himself and began walking to the door.

Eva gave him a nervous, yet excited, smile, and dashed off after the black shadow.

She was a bit too excited, but it was a mission where she was mostly on her own.

After the door closed, Felix let out a nervous breath. Pressing a hand to his temple he steadied himself.

"Gotta succeed on their own eventually. All you can do is prepare them. And she's as prepared as someone who's lived lifetimes," Felix said, trying to assure himself.

Eva might be his wrecking ball, but she was also as close to a younger sibling, a daughter, a niece, as he had.

Part of giving her so many one-off powers was an insurance card. That she could get out of any situation should the need arise.

Provided he finally told her about it.

The problem was that the moment he told her about it, she'd probably try to volunteer for more dangerous duty.

Sighing again, Felix wondered if this was what parents went through.

Wraith slid along the external wall, dipping and diving through the shadows. Passing around and past guards as if they were standing still and looking the wrong way

From Felix's point of view, Wraith was walking along obviously and should have been noticed.

He knew better though.

If Wraith didn't want to be seen, and you weren't aware of him to begin with, you simply wouldn't see him. That was more or less his power.

The ability to kill someone in a single breath was actually all trained.

Wraith's head turned fractionally and Eva was just in the corner of the screen. She was pressed in low to the solid thick wall and was more than halfway melted into it.

That's one way to hide yourself.

Gliding forward, Wraith was off. They scampered along the perimeter and slipped inside without anyone the wiser, Wraith slipping between two guards, and Eva simply passing through the wall completely.

Felix couldn't help but frown when they made it onto the main grounds. It was a wide open space. There was no cover, no greenery, nothing.

It was a blank enclosure that would highlight anyone trying to get across.

Felix suddenly felt as if he'd made a mistake.

This didn't make sense and didn't feel right.

Wraith would do his best to get through, but even he had his limits. Especially with Eva tagging along.

So why didn't he say anything?

"Wraith, this is Felix. Double back, we're done here. That's a death trap," Felix said into the mic.

Waiting, he watched as Wraith's head swiveled back and forth, surveying the field.

"Wraith?" Felix called. "Retreat. Head back to home base."

"Felix, I don't think he's wearing his earpiece," Eva whispered softly.

Wraith's head whipped around as Eva spoke.

Why wouldn't he—shit!

"Eva, tell him Felix said stand down. Quickly!" Felix demanded.

From Wraith's view, he saw Eva's head dip down then back up as she got her orders.

Before she could even open her mouth, Wraith was darting across the no man's land. Dodging between suspicious clumps in the ground Wraith kept on. His feet carried him onward at a breakneck speed.

He was doing his best to avoid everything and carry out the orders Felix gave him. The orders that he was forced to follow.

Damnit. I didn't even think of him disobeying through the minutia of the orders.

Wraith was following all of his directives. Felix suspected that there was no way for Wraith to actually beat this section though.

"Stay put, Eva. Actually, belay that, get back here immediately," Felix said.

All it would take is a thermal camera pointed in Wraith's direction and that'd do it. Right? He might know about them, but without knowing where they are, he can do his best by moving quick.

Felix sighed and hoped the suicidal run wouldn't be just that. He wasn't optimistic though.

The Hero had played Felix rather well.

"I suppose that's what I get for relying on a press-ganged recruit. Everyone else is mostly here of their own volition at this point," Felix muttered to himself.

Wraith twisted around a corner as alarms started going off all around him. His view spun as he surveyed the scene and immediately adapted to the best of his ability.

"And now… he's going to commit suicide while following orders. He'll even do so in such a way that it'll alert the entire Hero's Guild," Felix said. Shaking his head he felt the helplessness in his stomach. "He signed on so he didn't die needlessly, then throws his life away to warn them? Why? What changed?"

A line of security officers with rifles sprang out in front of Wraith and leveled their weapons while firing.

Twisting as best as he could Wraith charged headlong into the riflemen.

Bullet after bullet struck the living shadow, the first several sending him crashing to the ground.

There was no letting up though. Felix couldn't see much anymore as the headset had twisted around. All he could see were boots.

Boots and muzzle flashes.

Only when empty magazines hit the ground did the flashes stop.

There was no movement from Wraith. He'd been cut down and killed instantly from what Felix could guess.

Frowning, Felix berated himself again.

He should have seen it. Using Wraith was opening himself up to problems.

Felix knew better, too. His paranoia should have warned him.

Though that left him with only two people who could fill Wraith's role now.

One was Miu, the other was Eva.

And Eva sure as hell isn't being sent out on something like this.

Which means we need to upgrade Miu.

The view on the monitor changed, grabbing Felix's attention.

A dark black pair of boots stood in front of the camera. For a second, as the newcomer tilted Wraith to one side, Felix got the view of a handsome man in a black and white costume.

Then inky darkness took over the camera, and the feed died.

And that was that.

Felix grunted, and rewound the footage. He took a screen-capture of the black and white costumed man and sent it over to Lily.

Closing up his terminal, he laid his hands on his desk and thought.

The best option was to power up both Miu and Eva.

Doing so to Eva would reveal everything else though.

Making a decision, Felix looked up at the closest bodyguard.

- 307 -

"Please get Miu, and send her over to me. We've hit a snag and I seek her counsel," Felix said.

Nodding his head, the bodyguard turned to one side and said something into his mic.

So be it. We'll need to go about this another way I suppose. The Hero guild might not be the only one who knows.

What about the Villains? Nothing wrong with seeing what they know, right?

Maybe they'll even trade me for the information.

The enemy of my enemy is my friend.

Right up until I have to kill them, at least.

Chapter 4 - Hopscotch -

Miu came quickly. Stopping in front of his desk and then standing at a loose sort of attention, her eyes boring into him.

"Everyone out," Felix said. "If your department head can't protect me, no one can."

The night crew of bodyguards only left after Miu gave them a quick nod of her head.

Felix laid his head back against the head rest of his chair when the door clicked shut.

"Wraith committed suicide while obeying orders," Felix said simply.

Miu stood stock still for a moment, then nodded her head once.

"I'm considering upgrading you, and powering you up, in such a way as to replace him. The problem being that you're also the department head for my bodyguards. I'd like your thoughts," Felix concluded.

Miu shifted her weight uneasily from one foot to the other then clicked her tongue.

"I dislike it. But I agree that I am probably the best candidate. My natural power makes me formidable with even the least bit of training," Miu said, her mouth turning down into a frown. "Victoria could take my place as department head, and probably should. She's who they look to if I'm not around. To be honest the position was never permanent for me. I was only filling in."

"And what position do you want then? You're the mystery, Miu. I've tried to get into that head of yours. Heaven knows I've tried. But I can't seem to get anything out of you. I want to know more. Know your desires. Your wants," Felix said, leaning forward now.

He didn't get too many opportunities to get into Miu's comfort zone. Not ones that she brought up herself.

Miu's nose twitched and she looked away to one side. After what felt like forever, she turned her eyes back to him.

"You would use that information to beguile me into working harder for you. Your carrot, as it were," Miu said.

"I can't deny that. But is that so bad? To be rewarded for your efforts? It's not as if you're not doing the work anyways," Felix said, doing his best to sound reasonable.

Miu's lips pressed together tightly, then shook her head.

"My wants and desires wouldn't be attained easily," Miu said.

"Try me, I'm open to suggestions."

"No, you are not. This isn't something that could be given," she reaffirmed. Her voice had an odd pitch to it, and her eyes flashed in a peculiar way.

Kit had once said your mind was unique. Different even.

What are you hiding in there?

"And how would you know unless you asked?"

Miu shook her head again, then folded her hands together behind her back, and went into a rigid stance.

Recognizing it for what it was, Felix let the subject drop.

"List out everything you'll need training- and power-wise to do Wraith's job, if not better. I'm willing to dump a ton of points into you if that's what it'll take," Felix said. Leaning back into his chair, he felt tired and drained.

"Understood," Miu said. "I'll have it for you by tomorrow at noon."

"Thank you, Miu. You can go," Felix said. There would be no further conversation without dragging it out of her.

And that wouldn't really get him what he wanted.

Not really.

Grunting, Felix decided to wait up for Eva.

Then he'd crawl into bed and wait for tomorrow.

And whatever joys the day might bring.

Felix scoffed once and pulled up his terminal again. He might as well get some work done.

Before he even started to type, even before his bodyguards retook their positions, his phone went off.

Glancing down at the display he frowned.

Dimitry?

Tapping the accept button he pushed his earpiece a bit deeper.

"Felix here," Felix said into the phone.

"Felix, it's Dimitry," said the Russian loan shark.

"What can I do for you?" Felix caught the eye of one of his bodyguards, pointed to his phone, then held a thumb up, then turned it down, then back up while shrugging his shoulders.

"Line's clean, boss," said the bodyguard.

"And by the way, line is clean on both ends," Felix said, making sure to be direct and to the point.

Dimitry chuckled darkly.

"My thanks. I'd like to call in that second marker I have," Dimitry said slowly. "It's a simple meet and greet. I'm somewhat cut off from the rest of my organization here. It would go a long way to have a proxy relay information face to face about the situation. Having you do it in person would... I'd feel much better about it."

That doesn't seem like everything. What else does he want? I mean, he could just call someone or send an email in a cryptic way. Couldn't he?

"I'd also appreciate it if you could give them two hundred thousand in cash," Dimitry finished.

Felix mulled that one over. He owed Dimitry two more favors. Transmuting items to gold, changing it to cash, and then handing it over wouldn't be terrible.

Not exactly pleasant, but not horrible.

"And that'd be your second favor? That's all? Deliver the money, this is from Dimitry, thanks bye?" Felix asked. He wanted to clarify the situation. To make sure everything required was stated simply.

"That'd be it," Dimitry confirmed.

"Alright. Send me the contact information. I'll see if I can take care of it tomorrow or the next day. It'll be done before the week is out though, I can promise that," Felix said.

"Ah, thanks, Felix. I appreciate you keeping your word."

"I wouldn't be a good ally if I didn't, now would I? Oh, I was wondering about that order of rifles?"

"Ah, yes. I turned those over to your personal bed assistant. She was quite eager to get another order of them."

"Eh? Alright. I'm sure she has something in mind."

"Wait, so she is?"

"Is what?"

"Your bed assistant?"

"For a bit now. Why?"

"She's Myriad, right?"

"Yeah," Felix said slowly.

"Does she... uh..."

"Does she?"

"Multiply... as well?"

Felix let the line hang open for a few seconds, a small smirk on his face.

"She does."

It was two days later before Felix finally managed to make the time for Dimitry's chore. That and to get the gold transferred to cash without creating a serious issue.

The IRS was probably watching Felix like a hawk. He had no doubt a few government agencies had suspicions about his newfound wealth.

In the end, he'd resorted to having a few trusted people take ownership of the gold and transfer it.

How many villains would trust their employees with that much cash, after all? None.

So no one watched as his people walked around with all that money.

Which led up to him sitting in the car.

Nervously sitting in the car.

Drumming his fingers along the case full of cash, Felix stared out the window at the passing homes.

"You're fidgeting," Miu said from his left side.

"And?" Felix asked.

"Stop."

Making eye contact with the newly trained assassin, Felix drummed harder.

"Felix?" Victoria asked from his right.

"Mm?"

"Please stop?" the swordswoman tried.

"I'm nervous. I'm allowed to fidget," Felix complained.

"You are, but it'd be nice to get there without Miu contemplating how to make your life miserable when Andrea arrives," Victoria offered. "She hasn't seen you for a bit. I can't imagine she'll be entirely stable."

Miu's eyes brightened at that, her frown turning into a devil's smile.

"Ah, yeah," Felix said, his fingers stopping instantly. "That's uh... a very good point."

Then again. It really isn't Andrea who'll need the attention.

It's Lily. Far be it for anyone to ever suspect she's actually a cuddle bear. A cuddle bear that needs attention and affirmation.

Over and over.

"Are we sure about this?" Victoria asked, hijacking the conversation.

He'd have to thank her later for giving him an easy out.

"I'm sure that it's Dimitry who asked. So it's probably a criminal boss of some sort we're supposed to see. That's about it. That's why you're both here," Felix said.

"And why you're in body armor. And wearing Lily's locket," Miu added.

"Yes, and that." Felix reached up and fingered the small cylinder that hung around his neck. She'd told him to wear it whenever he felt his life could be in danger. That it'd provide a shield that'd give him enough time to get out of harm's way.

Or enough time for her or someone else to show up and save my dumb ass.

The driver gave the wheel a turn and brought them into a parking garage. The exchange was going to be simple.

Get out, put the case down in a numbered parking space, and wait.

When a black car showed up and parked in the space next to it, Felix had to make himself visible so the occupants knew everything was on the up and up. After that, he could get back into his car and leave.

The End.

Felix wasn't really sure if he liked the plan or not. It had the potential to be so simple it couldn't be messed up. Yet it also was so simple it couldn't be anything but messed up.

He certainly didn't like the part where Dimitry had made him the face of this exchange. If Dimitry hadn't, he would have just sent Miu and Victoria in his place. There wasn't really a need for him to be here.

Unless it was a setup.

Thy name art paranoia.

Holding back a sigh, Felix handed the case over to Miu when they stopped.

Twenty seconds later, and Miu was back in the car, minus one case full of money.

"Done," Miu said, putting her seatbelt back on.

"Hmph," Felix said, eying her then the case critically.

"Your paranoia is getting worse," Victoria said. "Is it because you don't have Lily or Andrea around?"

Feeling his eyebrows come together and his mood turn sideways, Felix glared at Victoria.

"What? It's an honest observation," Victoria said, defending herself.

"Leave him alone. His paranoia in this situation is warranted," Miu said defensively of him. "Even if he does miss his bedroom buddies."

"Hey—"

"Hush," Miu said, interrupting him. "Headlights."

Following the pointed finger of his assassin, Felix saw light trailing along the wall on the far side. They were turning through the ramp.

Gradually, a black sedan came around the pillar. It swung into the lane and drove slowly towards them.

It shifted into the exact parking spot it should, and went into park.

Getting out of the car, clambering over Miu in the process, Felix stood up and made sure he was visible for at least five seconds.

Then he got back in, shutting the door behind himself.

"Time to go," Felix said quietly.

The driver, one of his bodyguards he didn't know the name of, put them into drive. They were off and away.

Right up until twenty men with rifles stormed out of a fire escape and started unloading on both vehicles.

High powered rounds were no match for the tanks that Felicia, Mr. White, and Felix put together.

But that didn't mean he wanted to stick around and test that stunning durability either.

The bodyguard spun the wheel, bounced them over a parking bump, and floored it down the lane.

"Damn," Victoria cursed. Reaching to her hip, she pulled out the pistol Andrea had been training her in. After her death at the farm with a bullet-hole between her pretty eyes, Victoria had trained determinedly with pistols. "Considering they're firing on the other car, this wasn't a setup. Right?"

"Dunno. Did they get away as well?" Felix asked. He'd ducked down low in the seat. He trusted the vehicle but didn't at the same time.

"Yes," Miu said. "One of them even got the briefcase."

"Well that's stupidly heroic," Felix muttered. The driver slammed them around a corner, the tail end of the car fishtailing out wide behind them, and drifted the whole car through the turn. Bringing the vehicle back under control, the bodyguard kept their speed high. Felix was suddenly very glad specialized driving lessons had been part of the special training program for his bodyguards.

There was a deafening crash as they barreled out of the parking garage.

Smoke, steam, and sunlight were all around them in the street. The car had come to a dead stop.

Whoever had kicked this off had put something at the entrance to try and block everyone in. Powering through it as if it were nothing, the car had rolled right over it.

Leaning over Miu, Felix looked down to the ground. Their wheels were spinning wildly in the air, and the bottom of the car was wedged up on something.

"Time to beat feet," Felix said. "Hit the street running. Any path you want to take, Vicky? Miu?"

Miu bit her lip in a rare display of nerves, looking to Victoria.

The swordswoman growled, her head turning left then right as she looked down the street in both directions.

Then she looked up.

"The building across the way. Apartment complex. Roof should give us access to the other building. The buildings from here are all lower or even. We can hop the gap between certain ones and make our way out of this," Victoria said.

"Interesting... plan," Felix said. Getting behind Victoria, he laid his hands on her shoulders. They'd have to bolt fast.

"Came up with it after we got the address. Did a quick search and checked it out by satellite. Just in case. As you've said before, no plan survives enemy contact," Victoria said, grabbing the door handle.

Behind him, Miu slid up against his back, her hands on his hips.

In the driver's seat Felix watched his bodyguard. The man gave himself a once over, then pulled out his pistol. Shifting over the center console he moved to the passenger side and got ready.

"Go," Victoria said, opening the car door. She hit the pavement at a sprint. Felix scrambled out behind her. Getting his feet under him, he got moving.

Behind him, he heard the bodyguard and Miu bringing up their rear.

Victoria popped open the door to the building that was their target and ducked inside.

There was a muffled shout and curse.

Felix was only a second behind her, shoving the door open as he charged through.

Victoria had a blade buried in the throat of a wide-eyed man with a shotgun next to him. His heels were drumming the ground as his hands futilely worked to pull the knife out.

"They're everywhere. This isn't a simple attack," Victoria said, pulling her knife free.

Giving the dying man a glance, Felix realized Victoria had severed everything in the man's throat. Her weapon had only stopped because it hit the spine.

He'll be dead in a minute, tops.

"I've never seen the uniform either. Is this a super villain group?" Victoria asked, standing up.

Miu sauntered over and blasted her elbow into the man's forehead. His head dropped to the ground unmoving.

Unconscious.

"I'm not familiar with it if it is one," Miu said. "Lily or Andrea would know. They've had more dealings with them."

The bodyguard had made it inside as well. He was at the door. He had it cracked open by a scant inch, and was looking out of it.

"Can hear them out there," said the bodyguard. "They're arguing about who has the money. Us or Dimitry's guy. They're here for a cash grab."

"Damn. That settles the concern over Dimitry though. Alright, up we go," Victoria said, moving towards the stairwell off to one side.

Felix grabbed hold of the unconscious dying man and dragged him along the ground. Finding the underside of the stairs empty, Felix moved the body that way.

Shoving him underneath, Felix left him there to bleed out and darted after Victoria. He didn't think it'd help, but taking ten seconds to possibly save them minutes or hours seemed like a good gamble.

Flight after flight they climbed. Passing by a number of fire escape doors that probably led into apartment corridors.

Up ahead, Victoria went out through the door leading onto the roof.

Felix shielded his eyes as he came out into the open air.

In front of him were two men, staring back at Victoria as she charged them.

One had a scoped rifle and the other binoculars.

Before Victoria could get a hold of them, one man got a hand to his earpiece.

"They're on the roof! On top of—" His voice cut off as Victoria's sword cleared its sheath, the blade coming around in an arc and separating his head from his shoulders.

The second man had slower reactions, and Victoria took two more steps to reach him. Her blade flashed out, the tip of it sliding through the man's chest.

With a soft gasp, the man collapsed to his knees, his hands closing around Victoria's blade.

Placing a booted foot on the man's chest, she yanked it out of his body and spun.

There was no one else on the roof.

"We need to go. Now!" Miu said. Putting action to her own words, Miu started running for the opposite side of the building.

Pushing himself onward, Felix followed. Even when Miu sped up and leapt off the side of the building, Felix poured on the speed and doggedly pursued her. Getting his feet right before he reached the edge, Felix stamped down and jumped. Sailing across the gap between the buildings, Felix caught sight of an empty alley beneath them and his stomach flipped.

Then he was rolling across the top of the building. Managing to not fall too poorly, Felix got to his feet and stumbled after Miu.

Victoria and the bodyguard landed better than Felix did and caught up to him quickly.

"How many more like this?" Felix asked as Miu dove off the side of the building in front of him.

"Four more. But... but then we have to make a choice," Victoria said.

The conversation paused for a moment as they all took a running leap off the building.

Gritting his teeth, and feeling the bruises his knees and elbows were already developing from landing hard, Felix cursed whatever god did this to him.

Getting up, he managed to get next to Miu before she bolted off again. He laid a hand on her shoulder, and held on to it tightly, keeping her stationary.

"I'm not made for this. I'm built for spreadsheets," Felix muttered. Then more loudly he asked, "What choice do we have to make?"

"We can head into the streets to the west. Where the buildings reach a ground level that we can get to easily. That runs the risk of being seen and being on the run again. It's very possible they're not even there though, but it's a risk. There were a lot of people back there, and they were trained, equipped, and prepped. I'd imagine they have a large swathe of the area encircled," Victoria said. "Or we keep going over the rooftops to the south. It'll end up dropping us off near an industrial complex where it runs out of room."

Felix could smell there was more to that statement. Smell it a mile away.

"And?" he prompted.

"And it's the safer of the two routes to choose if we think they'll keep after us," Victoria said.

"And?" he prompted again.

"And... and it's supposedly where a villain known as Neutralizer is supposedly building a base. The Heroes don't know about it, and we only found out about it because Lily keeps in touch with her old contacts."

"I don't know him. Give me the tourist two sentence version," Felix said, looking around nervously.

"He uh... anything within a mile, he can exert his power over," Victoria said. "And before you ask, his power is to remove the power of others. He can only hold down about five people, which is why the Heroes guild doesn't ever have too much of a problem with him. His counter is simple. They just send two squads for him."

"Except for us right now, who don't even number more than four, he's a problem," Felix finished for her.

"Yes. But that's if he is even there, and assuming that he wants to make a problem for us," Victoria said hurriedly. "It really is the safer option. If we get down, and find them waiting for us, either we'll end up in a fight on the streets, or being chased."

"Where the hell are the police? The Heroes? Shouldn't they be working on this?" Felix asked in an annoyed tone. Opening his phone he stared at the screen. "Are you kidding me? No signal? On top of a building? That's not normal. Something is very not right. This is beyond well coordinated."

"I'd bet that communications have been cut in a few key places," Miu said. "That or a few people were paid off. It can happen. I was the target of many bribe attempts in security."

"So, it becomes more of a question of, do we believe that those chasing us were more well equipped than we thought, or that a villain may have an interest in us," Felix said.

Everyone stopped talking. Far to the northwest, the sound of a helicopter could be heard. In fact, it was just barely within eyesight.

"That isn't a news-chopper," said the bodyguard.

"South it is," Felix replied.

Chapter 5 - Insane Devotion -

"Right," Miu said. They were all watching the helicopter. Everyone was assuming it wasn't there to help them. There was little chance of it and there was no point in taking the risk.

Miu instead sprinted southward. She took a running jump from the building they were on to the commercial building next to it. Felix followed right behind her.

The roof cracked with Felix's impact, shattering and sending cracks out in every direction. Rolling forward Felix managed to get out of the space even as the entire thing began to fracture and come apart.

Scrabbling for traction, a grip, anything, Felix crawled and scuttled forward.

More and more of the roof fell inward, giving way. The bones of the building were starting to tremble as the weight of the whole thing began to shift.

Did they just fucking ignore all their maintenance? Holy shit!

Miu grabbed him by an arm and hustled him towards the edge of the building. Taking a monstrously strong grip on his shoulder, she jumped, dragging him along through the air.

In the middle of the jump, Felix got a good look backward.

Victoria and the bodyguard were still on the previous building They watched as the entire roof gave way.

Landing with a crunch, Miu fell to her knees. Felix was sent rolling to one side. Lifting his head he caught sight of Victoria looking like she was going to jump anyways. Waving his arm at her, he caught her attention.

"Go! We'll meet back up at home base. Keep yourselves alive," Felix shouted at them.

Not waiting for a response, Felix got up, pulling on Miu's forearm.

"Come on, Miu. We need to get rolling. Did you break something, do I need to repair you?" Felix asked, pulling at her arm.

"I… no. I'm fine just… stop, let go of me!" Miu screeched out, her voice breaking. She was trembling from head to toe.

She afraid of heights or something?

"No time to really argue. Get moving, Miu," Felix said, releasing her. Putting himself into motion, Felix took off, jumping to the next rooftop as soon as he got near the edge.

Several minutes were spent simply leaping from roof to roof. Checking occasionally to see where they were, and if they needed to keep going.

Victoria had been the one with the plan after all. Not them.

Miu wasn't doing very well either. She had been shivering this entire time and couldn't seem to stop herself.

"I mean, she said it would run out, right? This has to be it," Felix said, staring down at the street below them. They were only two floors up now, and there were no buildings around them to leap to.

"I think so," Miu said.

"Alright, good enough. Down we go then," Felix said.

Turning he made his way to the roof access door.

"Step aside, please," Miu said, slipping past him and through the door when he opened it. She managed to do it without even touching him.

"Fine, whatever, just go," Felix said.

Ahead of him there were shouts, exclamations of surprise, and a few harsh words.

Quickly enough though, they were leaving the building and exiting out onto the street itself.

It wasn't much of a street. Clearly this area was an industrial park. There were a number of warehouses, 'closed to the public' signs, and general warnings of "you don't belong here" throughout.

Felix frowned, wracking his mind for a plan. Glancing at his phone, he found the signal was still nonexistent.

"We need to get out of here. Find somewhere to… Miu?" Felix paused, watching as Miu started walking off towards what looked to be a warehouse.

"I need… I need time. I need to get control. I'm not in control. I need control," she said to herself. Her voice was so low, Felix almost didn't hear it.

Jogging a few paces to catch up to her, Felix laid a hand on her shoulder. "Miu—"

Only to have it thrown violently to one side. Miu stared at him with eyes that flickered and quivered.

Miu was gone.

Whoever, whatever, this was, wasn't his cool, collected assassin.

"No, no, Felix. Please, no," Miu said. Turning her face forward, she started walking again towards the warehouse. "No control. I need it. Need time. Need to… need to put myself together."

Felix stared at her, unsure of what was going on. He'd never seen her like this.

She wouldn't hurt him, he knew that. But he was starting to doubt if she was sane.

Going to need to have Kit do a deep dive into that head of hers. She said she was unique, apparently that stands for batshit crazy.

Miu slammed a palm into the door in front of her, blasting it to the side and walking in.

Felix bit his lip and eventually followed her in. It was better than standing around alone by himself out here.

"Miu, we really shouldn't—"

Something pounced on him from the side, blindsiding him.

A woman pressed down on top of him, her hands closing in on his throat.

"Hold, hold still, baby. I need… I need a fix. This'll be quick, I promise. Just your cash. I'm sorry, I'm sorry, it'll be painless," hissed a crazy-eyed drugged up woman. She smelled like the back end of a garbage truck and had the face of a life lived hard and short.

There was a shrieking yell and a fist crashed into the crazy woman's temple before Felix could throw her off.

She went down in a heap next to him.

Before he could even think, Miu was on top of her. Miu screamed even as she grabbed the now unconscious woman's arms and gripped them tightly.

"He's mine! Mine! MINE!" Miu shouted into her face.

"Miu, stop! We don't need to kill her. A corpse is the last thing we need," Felix said, pressing his hands to her side.

"No! Don't touch me!" Miu shrieked, shrinking away from Felix as he touched her. Cowering low, she slunk to one side and moved into the shadows of a corner. "Don't… don't touch me. I need control."

"Miu, what the fuck is going one? Control over what? I don't understand," Felix said, following but giving her some distance.

"No. You can't know. You won't know," she said. Foamed spit was visible on her lips, her eyes darting off into every direction.

"Tell me. I think I'll understand," Felix said soothingly, holding out a hand to her, but not touching her.

Miu tightened up until she was unmoving. Rigid. Stone-like.

Then she deflated in on herself.

"Your touch burns me. Your eyes scorch me. Your words penetrate me. My soul resonates," Miu said tonelessly. "I have to hide it. Bury it. Fight it. You know my power, yes?"

"Yeah. Your natural abilities are multiplied. Twice as strong as any other person kind of thing," Felix said.

Miu flinched, her head teetering as if on a rubber band.

"Yes, and yet no. Everything… is doubled. Everything. If I hate someone, I loathe them. I would harm myself to see them hurt," she said.

"You loathe me?" Felix asked.

"No. I love you. I love you so much it hurts. I want to kill Andrea… I want to turn her skull inside out. I want to kill Lily in her sleep. I've stalked them both. I watch them. I know their patterns. I could kill them both so easily. They shouldn't touch you. I should touch you. Not them. Not them.

- 316 -

"No! No, no, Miu. No. Control, you need control," she said, trailing off into a repeating loop of muttered curses.

"I love you. I love you in a way that you should be loved. They don't deserve you. I deserve you. I'll kill any woman who looks at you. Victoria minds her distance, but I want to kill her for touching you earlier. No one should touch you. Only me," Miu said, looking up at him.

In those eyes was madness. Madness and devotion.

Oh shit she's crazy.

"Ok. I... understand. So... everything is doubled. Which means you're..." Felix paused, unsure how to describe it.

"I'm a Yandere, if you need a word for it," Miu said, a fractured smile slipping across her face as her head jittered back and forth. "It fits. I looked it up once."

Whatever that is, it doesn't sound like a good thing in her own mind.

"Don't know what that means, but alright. The long and the short of it is... you love me to the point that you want to kill any woman around me," Felix said.

"And eat them. I want to eat them so that I can absorb whatever they took from you," Miu added to his statement. Her eyes dilated for a minute as if whatever went through her head with that thought struck a bit too deeply.

"But you haven't done anything like that," Felix said. Hoping to god that this was all in her head, and hadn't been an action.

"I haven't. I want to. I've tried. Your commands forbid me. I have to... I have to stay away from HR. They'll read my mind. They'll know. I fill my head with thoughts of slaughter whenever they peek. I can always tell when they peek. Their eyes start to unfocus when they look into me. Blood, death, massacres. That... gets most of them. Some of them it doesn't. I start screaming at them instead. They leave. They always leave," Miu said woodenly.

"How can I help?" Felix asked. He let his hand fall to his side. He imagined touching her might not help at this moment. "I could modify your powers to —"

"No! I am me, and always have been. Don't change my power. I... just need control. I'll be fine after that," Miu said, interrupting him. "I am me."

"Ok, and how can I help with the control?" Felix asked. He genuinely wanted to help.

Miu suddenly made a lot more sense to him. All the way around, even.

She wasn't avoiding him, she was controlling herself.

She didn't despise him, she loved him, and hated herself.

"Don't... look at me. Let me rebuild my defenses. I just need time. If I can get a f—" Miu stopped, her eyes unfocusing. "Someone is suppressing my power."

"Isn't me, but Victoria did mention that villain around here. Come on, we need to go," Felix said. Looking around, he found the exit and started making his way over.

Miu grabbed him and pulled him through a doorway and into an office. She immediately went about reorganizing the room, moving things in front of the door to block it.

"They already know we're here, I could hear them, right before my power was squashed. We're surrounded. We'll have to hold out till help arrives," Miu said grimly.

"Miu, no one knows we're here," Felix said, watching her from the corner.

"I know. But the good news is in squashing my power, they also gave me my control back," Miu said, shoving a filing cabinet over.

Felix shook his head. That was a strange thing to be happy over when people were slowly encircling you for god only knows what.

"Come on out. We'll be taking everything off you, then deciding what to do from there," called a voice.

Yeah, fuck that. That usually ends up with a gang bang and a bullet.

"Don't answer that, we'll pretend we're deaf for the time being. Ammo count?" Felix asked.

Fumbling through his pockets, holster, and belt, he found he had his pistol and all three clips.

"Didn't plan to. Offers like that never stand up. Forty-eight rounds," Miu said. She'd moved everything heavy to the door, and now was crouched low in a corner nearby.

"Hey now, come on out. We can make this quick and easy. Painless even," called the voice again.

Felix pulled two of his clips from his belt and underhanded them to Miu. "You're a better shot," he said by way of explanation. He kept the clip that was in his pistol, and a second for himself.

Settling back into his original position he held his pistol in both hands, waiting.

"So… you're not… sickened with me?" Miu asked.

"Huh? Oh, no, not really. You sound a bit on the cracked side but… so do most of you. I mean, you should have heard Kit before I started poking around in her power set," Felix said seriously. "I'm flattered in a way. Not sure what I did to deserve your attention."

"I'm unsure myself, but I cannot help but admit I was attracted since the start. Not in love, but attracted. It built slowly," Miu said, leaning her head against the wall. "And here we are. I finally lose it, you find out, and don't even seem to care. And we're going to die here."

Pursing his lips, Felix couldn't exactly disagree with that sentiment.

Looking around the messed up office, he tried to take stock of everything, and what he had available to him.

There really wasn't a whole lot. Everything you'd expect in an office.

Even an old landline phone.

Felix snatched up the old cordless phone and pulled the receiver off the hook.

He got an immediate dial tone.

"Ha, no signal to block or deny. It's a hard-line," Felix said. Flipping his wrist over, he checked his personal phone. With a flick of a finger, he looked at his address book.

Who to call? Who would be the most likely to get here as quickly as possible. They could rush us down at any second.

Wait.

No.

Lily and Andrea worked in these circles. Let's… let's try them first.

Looking from the phone to his wrist display and back, he began to dial Lily's phone number.

"What are you doing?" Miu asked.

"Calling Lily," Felix said, pushing in the last number.

"Lily? What?"

Smiling at Miu, Felix pressed the phone to his ear.

The line began to ring.

Felix held his breath. He didn't stop to consider what to do next if she didn't pick up. Or if her signal was bad as well. Or if —

"Legion, this is Miss Lux," came the silky voice of Lily.

"Oh thank god," Felix thunk into the phone. "Lily, it's Felix. I've got a bit of a problem here."

"Felix? What are you — wait, no. What problem? How can I help?" she asked.

"Do you know anyone by the name of… what was it, Miu? Neutralizer?" Felix asked.

"Yeah, Neutralizer," Miu said.

"Neutralizer?" Lily repeated curiously. "I'm not sure. It sounds familiar. Andie, do you know Neutralizer?"

"Huh? Vaguely. You sure you don't want another pancake? Who are you talking to? Can we leave yet? I want to see Felix," came the faint voice of Andrea.

"I ask because he's got us cornered in an office. Miu and I, that is. His special power is literally neutralizing others' powers," Felix said.

"What!? How'd that happen! Where's Vicky?" Lily asked in a dangerous tone.

"Long story. Short version, lots of shit," Felix said. "So, anything on this Neutralizer I can use? Kinda stuck h—"

"Andie… Andie. Andie! I need Myriad, Felix is in trouble," Lily snapped at Andrea.

The chattering on the other side of the line went deathly silent.

"What?" Andrea asked finally after a few seconds.

"Someone named Neutralizer has Felix cornered. Do you know anything about him he can use?" Lily asked, the phone slightly muffled.

"Yeah, put me on the phone with Felix," Andrea said.

"Ok, here. One second Felix, here's Andie. Oh, before I go, does Neutralizer know it's you? That it's Legion? Start there," Lily said.

Then the phone was audibly passed to someone else.

"Lily is right, first check and see if he knows who you are. This might be easily avoided," Andrea said into the phone. Her natural personality was gone.

Myriad was here.

"One second," Felix said, covering the phone receiver. "Hey! My name is Felix! Felix Campbell. Owner and CEO of Legion. I think we should talk before this gets any worse."

"Oh! A CEO? Great. Let's talk about your bank numbers," called back the same voice.

"No go. They don't know me. If they do, they don't care," Felix said back into the phone. "Any possibility they'd know you? Can I use you and Lily as leverage and a fear factor?"

"Yes. Throw the phone at that idiot. I've met him a few times. I can end this immediately. I'll tell him exactly what's going to happen if he doesn't fuck off and leave you alone," Andrea said into the phone.

"Hey! Does it help if I tell you Mab and Myriad work for me? In fact, Myriad says she's even met you. I have a phone in here with me and she'd like to talk to you," Felix called out.

There was silence in return.

Seconds ticked by and Felix was starting to wonder if this was about to go sideways on him.

"Myriad and Mab?" came the voice again. Less confident this time.

"Yeah, they work for me in Legion. Along with Augur and War Maiden," Felix added, sensing this might be his chance to make this swing in his favor.

Again the silence for a response.

Miu smirked and shook her head. "I now wish I had worked harder to make a name for myself. To inspire fear in the hearts of your enemies."

"Well, considering I pushed your powers into a whole new dimension the other day by giving you all of Wraith's and a few others', I'd say earn your name now. In Legion," Felix said.

He really had given her Wraith's entire powerset along with an on/off switch. The only problem was that it was just as vulnerable as her normal powers to this Neutralizer fellow.

"I... think I will do so. To be known for my work in supporting you would be acceptable. I'll need a good name though. Miu is not very impressive," said the crazy woman who wanted to kill and eat the women around him.

"Actually, Miu is a decent name for that. Just have to make it work for you. I mean, if w—"

"Throw me the phone. I'll talk to her," came the voice from outside.

"Turn our powers back on first and I'll get the phone over. Otherwise it'll take a while to be able to get the phone out," Felix called in response.

A second later and Miu shivered from head to toe. Her eyes glazed over and her hands trembled.

"Miu, I need you to get in control. Now. For me," Felix said, imploring her.

Ordering her.

If I have a crazy person in my employ, maybe I can use that crazy as a control rod?

The trembling, shivering, broken Miu froze, and then became much more like her former self.

"Yes. For you, by your command," Miu said, her body becoming loose and fluid again.

"Punch a hole in that wall, Miu, so I can shove this thing out to them. You there, Andrea?" Felix asked into the phone.

"It's Myriad," said Myriad.

"No, it's Andrea. Who is also Myriad. We've talked about this before. Knock it off," Felix said.

"I... yes, dear. It's... it's Andrea... who is Myriad... Myriad and Andrea who love you," said an unsure Andrea with Myriad's voice.

"Good. Love you, too," Felix said.

Miu promptly punched a hole in the wall with far too much force and held out her hand to Felix. Her face was hard, stony even.

Gotta remember to play down the other women in front of her crazy ass.

"See you later. Giving you to Neutralizer," Felix said, then promptly gave the phone to Miu.

Miu shoved her hand back through the hole with the phone held out. She stared at the wall impassively.

"So… since we're way past the point of no return. Any chance I could talk you into training me in hand to hand combat? I get the impression you're far more lethal then you've ever let on." Felix asked.

Miu's eyes went wide and she turned her face to him. Her cheeks flushed a deep, dark crimson. Then she licked her lips, her eyes dilating slowly.

"Yes. So long as I don't have to be in control," she said finally.

"Alright… I can agree to that, but maybe we should talk about what that control means," Felix said.

I wonder just how insane she'll get at that point.

"And privately," she amended.

"Alright, and privately."

"I'll be sure to wear yoga pants and a sports bra," she said with a strange edge to her voice.

…Shit… don't tease the crazy person.

Chapter 6 - Catching Up -

"Hello?" asked a muffled voice on the other side of the wall.

Miu retracted her hand from the hole, and took a few steps away.

"I... yeah. Neutralizer, yeah. Yeah. Wait, no. I didn't—no, of course not. But I—you what?!" asked the man in a strangled voice.

"No, no, no, no. Not a thing. I swear. Yes! What? A frying pan...? I get it. I get it. Yes! I get it! Wait, who? Mab?" asked the voice.

"Uh, hello? Yeah. No, I already—" The man stopped talking. "I promise. I swear. Yes. I understand. I'll make sure it happens. Yes. Tomorrow? O-ok. Yes. Goodbye."

The silence after that strained one-way conversation was odd for Felix. He could only imagine how both Andrea and Lily had torn into the man. Felix felt a certain sick sense of pride. He wasn't responsible for it, but he did take a certain glee in it.

"Mr—Mr. Campbell, I go by the name Neutralizer. I'm so sorry for this misunderstanding. I do hope you can forgive me for it," said a voice from directly outside the door.

"Not a problem. I assume my people have arranged an exit strategy for me?" Felix called out.

"Yes. Yes they have. I'm going to escort you personally back to your Headquarters. Mab—ah, Mab told me to come back tomorrow when she arrives. She'd like to discuss my current... current job status with her," said Neutralizer.

"Oh? She doesn't take recruitment lightly. She must know something about you that she's willing to take a chance on," Felix said. "Alright then. Well, time to go I suppose."

Felix didn't like trusting this man, but the alternative really wasn't much better.

So... trust it is.

A heavy and sudden weight crashed down on Felix's chest.

"Felix!" shouted that weight.

Staring wide eyed and half asleep at Andrea as she nuzzled his chest, Felix tried to catch up mentally.

It was the day after their return, the previous evening being spent mostly trying to figure out what exactly happened.

Dimitry had been calling Legion HQ non-stop trying to get a hold of anyone.

Apparently his contacts had been run down in the end, the money taken, and their lives ended. Dimitry swore up and down he had no idea what was going to happen.

For Felix's part, he believed that. Because Dimitry had to know Kit was going to send someone over from HR to sweep his mind at some point. And there'd be no hiding the truth from them.

"H-hey Andrea. When did you get in?" Felix asked, wrapping his arms around Andrea's shoulders.

"Two minutes ago," she said into his shoulder. "It's about six am. Lily wanted to leave early. I didn't get to make pancakes."

"Lily did?" Felix asked.

"Yes. I did," said a voice from beside his bed.

Looking up, he saw the pale beauty staring down at him with a small smile.

"I... missed you. And I didn't like being away from everyone. I mean, really, the only two you left behind with us were Ioana and Felicia. They're so into each other right now, it was like they were on a different planet," Lily explained. "Better to leave them there by themselves."

Andrea's face was smashed into his chest, and she was taking deep huffing breaths.

"I couldn't smell you. Your clothes lost their scent," she said between massive gasping inhales.

"Andrea, you're going to faint," Felix said, pressing at her shoulder.

With a final deep breath, Andrea nodded her head. Then she started rubbing her face back and forth on his chest.

Then several Others popped out of Andrea. Three of them immediately leapt onto Felix, while another two set off for the door that led out of his room.

"Pancakes!" the ones that were leaving shouted

"Pancakes!" replied the ones that were clinging to Felix.

Lily laughed and shook her head.

"I'm going to unpack. While Andrea unloads all that pent up Wolf Tribe stuff on you. We should talk a bit after this. Make sure everyone is on the same page," Lily said, waving her hand at him as she left.

Great.

Felix wasn't sure being left alone with several Andreas was a good thing right now.

Then he realized that it could be a good thing.

If he wanted it to be.

Felix sat down in the middle of the large conference table. Tapping at the display in front of him, he pressed his thumb into the scanner. Two seconds later his desktop popped to life from his office. Before he could even settle in and do some busy work, everyone began filing in.

Andrea, Lily, Kit, Miu, and Victoria all took seats around him.

Glancing at the clock, he saw it was 8:59 am.

Dismissing the desktop with a finger motion he folded his hands into one another.

"I'm sure you've all read the report Miu and I made after we got back. I'd like to start with questions on that. Does anyone have any?" Felix asked, looking around from person to person.

"Do you think it was targeted?" Kit asked.

"The initial attack, no. Nor was Neutralizer," Felix said.

"And the cell signal?" Kit asked, redirecting him.

"That one... that felt weird. It blocked all of us, but from what I can tell, no one else. That seems directed," Felix admitted.

"I would agree," Lily said, folding her arms across her chest. "As far as I can tell, and I've dug quite deeply, that was directed only at you five. That's odd, to say the least."

Felix frowned and placed his chin on the tops of his hands, resting his elbows on the desk.

"Alright. So, two out of those three things weren't aimed at us. The third was, but in a passive way. There was no direct threat in it, other than that we couldn't get in touch with anyone," Felix murmured. "But no one would have known of the attack until it happened. That wasn't exactly planned. It doesn't make sense."

Kit sighed and pressed a fingertip to her temple.

"I say let it lie for now. We'll keep looking into it, but there isn't much we can do with it. It's more or less an unknown," she said.

Felix nodded his head glumly. "Lily, please consider that your takeaway. Press your contacts, see who bought that service if you can."

Lily nodded and scratched something into her notepad with her pen.

"Any other questions about the whole thing?" Felix asked. He wanted to make sure no one left anything on the table.

Felix noticed Kit was now staring at Miu, who was staring back at her.

Trying to let whatever was going on continue without calling attention to it, Felix turned to Victoria.

"I read your report. You more or less broke contact immediately and vanished. They weren't interested in you," Felix said.

"That's right. Strange as it is, it simply ended. Though I do hope no one comes calling for us to pay for that rooftop," Victoria said with a smirk.

"Hmph. Alright. If there's nothing else we'll continue on. The next item I have is that I wanted to talk about our progress. Figuring out why they were so interested in you, Kit, is definitely one of those topics," Felix said. Hopefully she was done finding out whatever Miu wanted her to know.

Kit's eyes broke from Miu and locked onto his.

"I... no. There is no progress at this time. I've been sitting there every day in the counselor's office, talking to high schoolers day after day. None of them know anything more than we thought. In addition, the few times I've seen a hero across the street, they were clearly being shielded," Kit said.

"In other words, Wraith really did a number on us with that suicide swan dive," Felix said.

"Yes. Yes, he did. But... we still have options of course. Lily has been in contact with a number of hackers. Data thieves. The vast majority of them are willing to take a paid job with Legion. Apparently the benefits and protection are worth more than their own personal freedoms for most. Lily, it's your project, would you like to take it from here?" Kit asked.

Sighing, Lily ran a hand through her dark hair, pulling it to one side.

"I don't mind at all," Lily said without a hint of unpleasantness.

The two of them had actually been playing nice for the last month or so. To the point that Felix wondered if they'd had a conversation on the side.

"I just wasn't sure if I wanted to bring it up quite yet I suppose. Mostly because I'm not done. But... I do have a dozen or so... individuals... who are willing to sign on to Legion. They're primarily interested because we can get them whatever equipment they want." Lily paused as if considering. Then she smiled and shrugged her shoulders. "That and the fact that I told them that we can teach them whatever they want. Predictably, a number of them said kung fu."

Felix closed his eyes at the predictable answer and felt a sigh trying to break free.

"Alright. I suppose that's all good news. I assume you have a plan for them?" he asked.

"Fairly simple one. Smash through the server on the Hero side of things, and see what they have in their systems. It's not exactly rocket science or a mastermind type of scheme, but I think it'll do," Lily said with a small vicious smile. "And I may tell them to leave a few things behind. Maybe download their files. You know. Corporate espionage?"

Felix opened his eyes and quirked a brow at her.

"Maybe I'm being a little vengeful," Lily said placatingly.

Felix didn't say anything but just stared at her.

"Ok. Yes, I am. Do you not want me to do it then?" she asked, looking annoyed.

"Nope, just keeping you honest. Be sure to redirect all their web-traffic from their web page to something different. Like 4chan," Felix said with an ugly smile.

"What is—you know what, I don't want to know," Lily said, sighing. She looked down to her paper and scratched something in quickly. "I'm sure they'll know what it is."

"Great. So... back to the point at hand though... we have nothing. Right?" Felix asked.

All around he got slow head nods.

"I suppose that takes care of that for now. Let me know if you make any headway later on." Felix glanced down at his blank terminal.

Really wish I had brought an agenda or notes or... well, anything.

"The last thing I have is more about our actual business. Legion, that is. I know part of the whole reason we moved here was to try our hand at diversifying ourselves. I mean, all it would take is for Skipper to change employment regulations or something along those lines and we'd be well and truly fucked," Felix said. It was a bit blunt for him, but that was the situation.

Kit and Lily exchanged a look. Lily pointed at herself with the pen, to which Kit nodded.

Lily pursed her lips and tapped her pen against the pad of paper.

"Finance is fine. Our growth is stagnant, but we were expecting that. There's only so much business any pawnshop can do after all," Lily said. "As far as our new venture is going... it's going well? I'm not sure how to put it into a perspective we could measure."

Felix grinned and held his hands apart in front of himself. "Try. I promise I won't fault you for not having a power-point ready for me. Though, hey, in the future, power-points are great. Especially ones with graphs I can paper walls with. Bright colors and attached numbers. Love power-point decks."

Lily looked nonplussed. With a slow blink she continued on as if he hadn't spoken.

"We've got a number of high school children who are interested. Enough to easily fill several classrooms if we follow the original college plan. The negotiations we started before coming here are progressing well enough. Though now that we're here, they seem rather… tight fisted… to say the least. They're looking for any and every loophole to deny us the school campus," Lily said.

Felix couldn't help but nod.

It made sense. It was the exact same thing he'd do in their place.

Except he might have sent Wraith to kill them all.

Maybe I should send Miu instead? I mean… she wouldn't mind, would she?

Casting his eyes to Miu, he found her staring at him unblinkingly.

Or… maybe not using the insane assassin is a better idea.

Quickly looking back to Lily he made a dismissive neutral hand motion at her.

"Alright, that's close to what we were expecting. Anything else?" he asked.

Lily scratched a fingernail back and forth against the paper in front of her.

It raised Felix's nerves. Something was on her mind.

"Not really. The accreditation is all done. We'll be on par with everyone else."

Uh-huh… so what is it that's wrong?

"Lily," Felix said, waiting for her to lift her eyes to meet his own. "What?"

Pressing her lips together into an angry line, she held up a hand and pointed at him.

"Don't do that," she said.

"Don't do what?"

"That."

"That what?" Felix asked, confused.

Lily growled and leaned back in her chair.

"Oh! Oh! I know!" Andrea said loudly, clapping her hands together.

"Andie, no—"

"She wants you to enroll her brother into the training school! That's all!" Andrea said.

Huh?

"Is that it, Lily? You just want Luke to go to the training school?" Felix asked.

Lily was glaring at Andrea, who for all the world didn't seem to notice.

Instead, she was spinning in her chair, still smiling at having solved the problem.

Realizing there was absolutely no point to her anger, Lily looked back to Felix.

"Yes. If… if we have him go through the school, and load him up with some work skills, he could probably live a normal life in Legion. He missed most of his education. It'll be hard enough for him to catch up in a regular school. He's technically in Legion, just… not really," Lily said.

Alright, leave it at that, idiot. Her personal affairs don't need to be the subject of a board meeting.

"Consider it done. I know we probably gave him some tutors, but can we get better ones? Worst case, I'll see if I can put elementary education into a skill book for him."

"Put in the paperwork for all of it, I'll sign it. Anything else though? It seems like everything is on the right path. Or at least, heading in the right direction," Felix said.

Once again, he looked to each person around the table. Inviting them to add anything.

"Everyone is free to go then. You get," Felix paused, looking at his watch, "forty-five minutes back in your day."

Victoria, Kit, and Miu got up and immediately left together. He imagined they were going to go over the situation reports from yesterday some more.

Andrea and Lily took flanking positions on his left and right sides.

"Hang back for a second, Felix," Lily said softly as Felix started to stand up.

Felix felt like this was going to be a problem, but he didn't feel like arguing right now. Sitting back down heavily in his chair he immediately pulled up his workstation from the desk.

"Ok? What's up?" he asked, quickly flipping through the windows on his screen. Pulling up the blueprints for the school they were purchasing he stopped.

They were both silent. Which was never a good sign.

Putting his attention on Andrea, she looked away rather than meet his eyes. Moving his focus to Lily, she nearly did the same thing.

"Uh… what's the problem?" Felix asked, his paranoia ramping up several levels.

In front of him, there was a static hiss. The type you hear when you turn on a television set that's not plugged into anything.

A small blue dot appeared in mid air, drawing everyone's attention.

"What in the world..." Felix said, staring at it.

As if it had always been so, the blue dot blew apart into an oval of crackling energy and distortion.

Through that oval, that window, that dimensional gate, as what else could it be, Felix could see three people.

A man, a woman, and a Beastkin.

Each looked road stained but dressed more akin to what he saw in movies about apocalyptic scenarios.

They were standing at what looked like an old-fashioned control station from an old TV show. There was little else in the room save for other control stations and bones.

"What the..." Felix said, squinting to get a better view.

Andrea reacted first, pulling an SMG out from under her jacket and positioning it up against her shoulder. She neatly clicked the safety off and slipped her finger into the trigger guard.

"Andrea, wait!" Felix said, hoping he could stop this before it turned into a bloodbath.

A dirt stained and beautiful pale skinned Beastkin, she looked like a cat-tribe type to Felix, leapt on top of the control panel.

Andrea could only be considered domesticated in the face of this feral version.

The Beastkin had hot glowing red eyes. She arched her back and hissed at them, her eyes dilated to slits and clearly on the defensive.

Lily stood up and held out a hand, blazing red runes spreading out in every direction around Felix, Andrea, and Lily.

A woman who looked more the part of a beauty queen held out a staff as she stepped up next to the man in the portal. Bright green energy started to blow out from her, quickly filling the room the three people were standing in and creeping through the portal.

The man moved something in front of him, and the portal winked out of existence.

Felix stared at where the portal had been, the hair on the back of his neck standing up straight. His skin was tingling.

His thoughts were dull and slowed.

Lily and Andrea seemed equally surprised and at a loss.

After the span of several breaths, Felix woke up from his stupor.

"Get me White and Felicia on the line, Andrea. At the same time, Lily, have someone find me Kit," Felix said.

Opening up his desktop terminal again, he started plowing through all the files he had on super powers.

Portals, portals, portals. Who can make portals? Who were they? How did they do that? Can I do it? Can I make a machine? Can I give it to Eva?

What if I can. Can I use it as a weapon? What... what if that was another world? Can I branch not just out of the city of Skippercity, but the very planet?

Felix was lost in his thoughts. The possibilities were spinning endlessly out in front of him.

He had work to do.

Chapter 7 - Thinking with Portals -

Felix drummed his fingers along the edge of the terminal. He'd been sitting there unmoving since the strange portal popped open in front of them earlier.

"Felix?" Kit asked, coming into the conference room. Five Andreas twitched in unison at her entry, one in each corner, and one at Felix's side.

"What's wrong? Everyone is running around in a hurry," Kit said, her brows knitting together.

"Hm? Oh... ah... someone opened a portal out of thin air. Right over there in fact," he said, motioning to the exact spot. "Opened up like it was always there. Poof. Then vanished just as quickly. I want to see if I can't get that for ourselves."

Kit frowned at that, her eyes set on the area he'd indicated.

"Anyways. Have a seat. I think we should talk," Felix said with a practiced smile. He indicated the seat directly across from himself at the table.

"No conversation has ever gone well that started that way," Kit muttered. "And I should know. I'm in HR."

"Ha... very funny," Felix responded, still pointing to the chair. "Sit your booty down."

Rolling her eyes, Kit did as instructed. She gave him her best "HR knows best" look as she did so.

"Should I make pancakes? Pancakes makes every situation better," Andrea asked.

"No, Andrea, it's fine. This actually isn't a bad conversation, though... I doubt it'll be comfortable."

"And diving right into that. Kit, I'd like to talk about the fact that you don't trust me," Felix said without regard to how it came across.

"I... what?" she asked, her eyes narrowing.

"Of course she trusts you!" Andrea argued, slapping a palm against his shoulder.

"No, she doesn't. Not in the way you're thinking. You never did, not fully, Kit. I think that's partially due to the fact that you can't read my mind," Felix said, folding his hands together in front of himself.

He kept the eye contact steady, his tone neutral, but direct.

Don't scare them, but don't let up. Come from curious.

"It's very possible that I've misread the situation. I wouldn't doubt it for one minute. Maybe you could explain it to me from your own perspective?" Felix asked.

Kit's mouth twitched as she fought whatever emotion had attempted to gain traction.

Andrea pouted at him. She was fond of Kit, he imagined she didn't quite care for his accusations. The four in the corner were in their Myriad impersonations, all holding an SMG ready.

"I mean, if it was exactly as I said, I'd understand. You've spent your entire life being able to simply source the truth from someone's mind without having to trust in them. I imagine that now, after you're very invested in this whole thing, not knowing my thoughts is more of an annoyance than the gift you thought it was," Felix said. "Or so I'd believe if I were in your position. Could be wrong."

He watched her as he spoke, attempting to catch the subtle tells that people gave off. A partial head nod or shoulder shrug, leaning in close to him or pulling away, folding her arms or putting her hands under the table.

What he got from her was... nothing.

She didn't even twitch.

Kit just sat there as if she'd been hit in the back of the head.

Letting the silence take hold, he waited.

Silence and steady eye contact could crack even the most obstinate of people.

Well, most people.

Felix waited. Letting the time pass.

Instead, Felix turned his thoughts to his task-list. He even began sorting out what he wanted to do with the portals if and when he could get them functioning.

"I hate it when you do that," Kit said, leaning back in her chair away from him.

Defensive.

"Hate what, when I wait for you to talk?" Felix asked.

"Yes. That and your stare. That cold stare that burns through me and leaves me no room," Kit grumped. Slowly, she folded her arms across her midsection.

Defensive again.

"So, let's cut to the chase. I want to change your power, and give you the implicit ability to read my mind. I think that'd be the easiest way to solve this dilemma. Your dilemma," Felix said as nonchalantly as he could. "Once we go down that road though, we can't really go backwards. You'd have popped open the seal to my thoughts and rummaged around in there.

"Also, you don't need to worry about Miu. I know… what she is. What she thinks. We had a good long talk about it."

"I know. She didn't fight me earlier when I started poking around. One thing led to another and I watched the whole thing unwind from her own point of view. Are you sure you're actually comfortable with that from her? It's… not normal. It is legitimately insanity. The thoughts that she has in the darkest places were… extreme. Even for me and what I've seen," Kit said carefully.

"Yep. I know. I looked up the definition the other day for the term she gave me. There was a number of examples in media of characters that fit it," Felix admitted with a shrug of his shoulders. "She's insane. And would do anything I asked, even if I told her I wanted her to capture every blue-eyed woman named Jane Smith in Skippercity that had more than two fillings."

"Exactly. I mean, you heard her, she wants to kill me and ea—"

"Yeah, I know. But she can't," Felix said hurriedly. It'd be best if Andrea didn't know the depth of Miu's devotion.

At least, not yet.

"Besides, she's devoted to me. Do you know how much I can get done with that kind of loyalty? Lots. Also, we've trained her up to the point she can take Wraith's spot. She's our blade in the dark now. For better or for worse, we can't exactly change that at this point," Felix said. "Anyways, no changing the subject allowed. Mind reading me. Yes or no?"

"I want to read your mind," Andrea said, grabbing his forearm with both of her hands.

Felix snickered at that and gave her a look.

"What… It'd be fun to read your thoughts," Andrea said defensively.

Looking back at Kit, Felix focused on her again. Kit grimaced at the attention, her fingers flexing on her forearms. Before he could even start to give her the staring treatment, she sighed and hung her head.

"This seems wrong. To make you do this just so I can stop having a crisis of faith," Kit mumbled.

"Why? This isn't a silly book, or a story, or a TV show. People don't just trust for no reason. Everyone wants to know that they're making the best decision they can. And in that way, we all seek confirmation of our choices," Felix said.

"To quote a favorite saying of mine," Felix said. "'The sum of what we are, our experience, is what we draw upon to make choices. It's what we use to defend ourselves from doubt. We compare them to things we've done previously and judge it based on what the outcome had been then.' In your case, you have no experience dealing with people at face value, and not plumbing their minds for the truth."

"I trust you," Andrea said, trying to get his attention once again.

Kit groaned and held her hands up to her face.

Taking the moment that she distracted herself, Felix leaned in close to Andrea.

"Please, help me? This is her problem, and I need your help. Please," Felix said, inaudible to anyone other than a Beastkin.

Andrea's eyes held confusion at first, then determination. She gave him a fierce nod of her head, her ears twitching atop of it.

"Thanks," Felix said, and then kissed her once. Pulling back, he saw Andrea had a silly grin on her face, her tail swishing slowly back and forth behind her.

As if he'd never diverted his attention, he set his eyes back on Kit.

"Is it so terrible to admit a simple truth? Shall I assume that's a yes? You can just nod your head, you don't have to say it," Felix offered.

Kit's shoulders tightened up, and then she slumped into her chair.

Defeat.

"Nod your head. I promise it'll be fine, and once you see inside, you'll feel better. Then we can get back to the business at hand," Felix said.

Kit nodded her head once.

Done.

Forcefully, he put his attention on modifying her power. Modifying it so that she could actually get into his mind as if he were anyone else.

Except he put in the caveat that it was something that he could deactivate whenever he wanted. It'd limit the scope of the power, give him a back door, and maybe lower the point cost.

Or so he hoped.

Power Upgrade: Directed Telepathy (Owner included)	Required Primary Power: 80 (Met) Required Intelligence: 70 (Met)	Upgrade? (2,500)

"That's not so bad at all," Felix said to himself. Activating the upgrade button, he deliberately made sure to keep his mind tranquil and open. As if it were nothing more than a closed file folder and wouldn't require any effort to look into at all.

Kit lifted her head up, her hands hanging down in front of her knees. She met his eyes, and he suddenly felt her. Like a finger poking around in his memories.

She was gentle about it, but he could feel her power. The strength of it.

The speed that she went through all of his thoughts.

An absolutely astonishing level of power.

He was suddenly very glad she was on his side. Before he changed his train of thought, he deeply implanted in his own mind the need for her to send him an email.

An email with all the answers to the questions he needed answered, that he was sure she could see in his mind.

Kit smiled and then quirked a brow. "Yes. I can answer those for you. And Lily would be annoyed."

"Huh? About wh—oh. Hey, hey. Thoughts are private things and aren't meant to be shared aloud. You said you wanted to look in, that goes with all the baggage that comes with it," Felix said defensively.

"I don't think every man wonders about people in his employ quite like—"

"Nope! Not going there. Stop. You're done. Now, unless you have anything useful to add, like helping me remember something I've forgotten, we should change the subject. Like to if you're feeling better about everything and your doubts are dispelled," Felix said, desperate to get the topic changed.

"Not going where?" Andrea asked. "Why would Lily be annoyed?"

Kit let out a shuddering breath and gave him a bright smile her eyes flickering to Andrea.

"Nothing, Andie. I was just teasing him. To your own point, Felix. Yeah. We're good. Also, I'm glad to know you think that way, but I think you've got your hands full already."

"I have no idea what you're talking about," Felix said deliberately, his eyes widening at the edges.

Please god, read this thought and stop right there. Please. Andrea will drag me off for hours if she even thinks I have thoughts about other women.

"Fine. I'll say no more," Kit said with a self-satisfied smile.

Andrea looked from him to her, and back again. She didn't seem to notice anything out of the ordinary.

Safe?

"For now, at least. And yes, I'll take on another power. I saw it in your head. It'd work and I like the idea of it. Though we'll have to prepare some teams to go with me and make sure everything is clear," Kit said.

"Yeah, that's fine. Arrange it with Ioana and Andrea. Oh, and by the way, I set it up so I can turn your ability to read my mind on and off at will. As you no doubt saw in my memories. Let me know if and when you want it on or off. Now, if there is nothing else more pressing, we should probably get moving on the new power," Felix said with a waggle of his fingers.

"Mm, no. Though, we did get the most recent suggestions back from Skippercity just after that meeting. One was interesting and I thought it might be worthwhile to discuss," Kit said.

"Oh? I'm always open to suggestions."

"It was from one of the security people. Alex was the name, I believe. He wanted to know why we don't have pancakes available that are at the level of Andrea's skill. And on top of that, why don't they operate in the same fashion as power sausage," Kit said.

Uh... what?

"Pancakes!" Andrea shouted. "Make a robot of me that only makes pancakes. But make the boobs bigger."

Andrea looked down at her kevlar vest and cupped herself experimentally through it. "Maybe... Lily's size. Or Victoria's, she squishes them down. But not Felicia. Those look like they'd hurt under a vest."

Felix ignored Andrea and frowned in thought as he contemplated what Kit had said.

I... actually that's not a bad thought. Why aren't we doing that? Can Felicia use something other than corpses to make power sausage? Even at a lesser degree? And pancakes wouldn't be that hard either. All she'd have to do is make a machine that would do both, right?

Or do one, and I upgrade it to do the other.

Shaking his head to clear his thoughts, Felix held up his hands in front of him.

"Good idea. Put it on Felicia's project calendar and send Alex a bonus for the month. I'd like to encourage good ideas in the future. Now... about that power," Felix said.

Kit scratched at her ear with a smile. "I'm ready. And... do you really believe I look better with the short hair? I know I've let it grow out long, but all of your..." She paused at that. Thankfully she continued on, skipping whatever word she had originally planned on using. Her eyes flickered to Andrea for only a moment. "They were of me when my hair was really short."

This was a terrible mistake. All a terrible mistake. Oh my god what have I done.

"Felix likes short hair?" Andrea asked Kit.

"He does. He especially likes your hair length right now or a bit shorter," Kit said.

"Oh! Good. I keep telling Lily she should get her hair cut short like mine," Andrea said.

Forcing his thoughts to the task at hand, Felix imagined giving Kit another power.

Her fourth major power.

A power to control portals. That lead to anywhere. Any place.

Even different worlds.

Only Eva had as many powers, but hers were all conditional things.

Fourth Power (Unlock): Portal Control	Required Intelligence: 70 (Met) Required Wisdom: 70	Upgrade? (125,000)

Felix winced. It'd take an entire day's worth of points. Everyone would practically be at zero.

We'll keep Felicia amped up, I still want a technological version of this portal power. Kit can handle this for now. With any luck, we can use this to our advantage. Portal directly into the Hero HQ.

Then we can just leave her memories alone. No need to go digging into that quagmire.

It'd just hurt everyone to have those memories brought back, and it'd have to start with Kit.

Not doing that.

He tried to not think about the three mummified women. How he had met Kit, Miu, and Ioana. Whatever was done to them had broken their minds. There was no reason to go back there, even to find out what he wanted.

"Alright, I'm going—" Felix paused. Kit was staring at him. Her shoulders were tight and her spine ramrod straight. "What… what is it? Are you alright?"

I didn't turn on the power, did I? She said it hurt last time. I can't imagine opening a fourth power would help at all.

"No. I'm fine, I just… hearing your thoughts… they come non-stop. I've met those with faster, but very few. And… and I'm thankful. You worry over me, even though you have such a cold and icy exterior. I… I think I'd like it if you turned off my ability to hear your thoughts. For now. I'm reassured but… I don't think I like it. You were right. About everything, and I appreciate your consideration. For now, let's turn it off," Kit said, repeating herself.

Felix didn't have any reason to deny her request. So he mentally deactivated the extension of her power, and then purchased her fourth power upgrade.

Kit's head dipped down and she pressed her hands to her temples.

"God, I hate that," she said. "It's not painful but… it's unnerving."

With that done, the next task on the chore list was getting a hold of Felicia. He needed to get her running on creating a portal machine that could accomplish the same thing that Kit could now do.

Beyond that, he'd have to start dealing with the local and federal government. He needed to put a stop to both branches of the government interfering with his plans. They kept trying to halt his plans for the college campus.

Lily and Lauren are ideal for that. Take Victoria and Andrea for protection.

Kit can stay here and start practicing with the new power.

So much change so fast.

How far do I push everyone as well? At what point can I justify popping open their memories and subjecting them to whatever hell they went through.

Again.

Finding himself with no answers to that, Felix opened up his terminal.

Flicking open the address book inside, he typed in a quick email to Felicia.

If she hasn't responded to phone calls, that means she's buried elbow deep in some machine's guts. So… email to her and White.

Adding White in to the CC function, he snapped off the email with a finger flick.

"With any luck, she'll get back to me before I get bored and tell you to just open a… actually, let's just do that," Felix said. "Kit, you feel up to trying out that new power?"

"I… yeah, I think I could. Doesn't seem to be that difficult honestly," she said, raising her head up to meet his eyes. "Similar to the telekinetic side of things, but not quite?"

"Is that a question or a statement? Nevermind. Just… try to open a portal to Skippercity HQ. Preferably the Labs. I want to talk to Felicia," Felix said, getting up from his chair.

"Alright. I can do that," Kit said. Spinning in her chair, she focused on a point at the end of the table.

Slowly, much more slowly than the previous portal had opened, a sphere appeared. Starting no bigger than a baseball it began to inexorably open up into an ever-growing oval.

It wasn't large enough to get through yet, but he could clearly see the lab on the other side.

Walking over to it, Felix leaned down and stuck his head through the opening. On the other side of the portal were a number of lab techs. They were all staring at Felix.

"Oh, hey everyone. Could someone find me Felicia and Mr. White? I need to run something by them," Felix said.

The closest tech slowly nodded their head in the affirmative, and walked away stiffly.

Leaning back out of the portal, Felix watched as it kept growing. Andrea squealed and ran over to it.

Then promptly stuck herself halfway through the portal. She was waving at everyone on the other side and trying to start conversations with them.

"Good work. With a bit of practice, I'm betting you can get this opened up rather quickly," Felix said, looking to Kit.

She gave him a bitter smile and glared at him at the same time. "Happy to see you try. We could always swap if you like. You might find my own 'shower thoughts' interesting, too."

Felix blinked, did his best to forget her comment, and looked back to the portal.

Would that I could, my dear. If I could make changes to myself, this would all be… so much easier.

That or I'd already be an extreme super villain.

Probably.

"Felix! You dumb asshat. What the fuck are you doing to my lab?" came a shouted call from the portal. "Move, ya dumb wolf."

"Ah, the ever pleasant shriek of my employees who are so joyous to see me," Felix muttered.

Andrea squeaked and was shoved bodily out of the portal. She landed in a heap on the ground. Felicia's angry and annoyed face was on the other side of the portal, staring up at him.

"What did you do!? You ignorant goat's ball-sack. Do I need to ban you from the lab?" she shouted at him. "And you know Andrea isn't allowed down here. Not after last time."

"You weren't responding to people trying to get a hold of you. If you want to blame anyone, look to yourself. Maybe I should put in an intercom down there to yell at you from whatever office I'm in. Did Ioana drag you to a closet or something?" Felix asked.

Felicia's face turned a deep scarlet at the accusation, and immediately crossed her arms in front of herself.

"Well, I'm here. What is this… thing then?" she asked.

Ha. I was right about the closet? That's actually funny.

"It's a portal that Kit can open up. We got the idea from a different piece of technology doing the same. I want to see if you can do the same, or better. Did I mention the tech looked as if it were at least fifty years old?" Felix asked.

That should rile her up.

Felicia's eyes opened wider and she snorted.

"Oh, I'll build you a damn machine that'll do this. I'll build it and it'll open a portal straight to your godforsaken asshole so we can shovel all the shit you spew out back in!" Felicia declared.

"Ah. Good. Think you can have it done by the end of the week? Or do I need to give up on your R&D department and have Lily recruit me a bunch of people who can make portals after I upgrade them with a super power," Felix said. He put as much disdain into his voice as he could manage.

She was always the type to rise to a challenge. And Lily was her most hated rival it seemed.

"You keep the damned Princess to your own bed and away from me and mine. I'll punch her right in her nethers if she comes down here, you hear me? Bah, I have things to do now," Felicia said, turning her head to one side. If Felix didn't miss his guess, she was already pushing her power towards the goal. "Going to need to get White on this with me as soon as possible. Betting this'll end up being a tech special. Like the beds."

"Anything I can he—"

"Fuck off and die," Felicia said, waving her hand at him.

At least I know she's that way with everyone. Actually, other than Ioana, I might be the person she treats the nicest.

"You can drop the portal, Kit, we've made the point. It may not be any of my business, but you might want to practice open and closing it repeatedly. Distance might be a thing, might not."

Felix yawned abruptly and held a hand over his mouth.

Andrea clapped her hands together from below, staring up at him.

"I want one. So I can get into your room whenever I want. You and Lily always lock the door. I listen sometimes but all you ever do is talk," Andrea said.

"Actually, can you open a portal to the break room? I think I'm going to need a candy bar or something. My tolerance level for things is rapidly diminishing," Felix said.

"Don't bet on it. It takes far more effort on my part than any of my other powers," Kit said, not even trying to open another portal.

"I can make pancakes! They're like candy!" Andrea shouted.

Chapter 8 - No Brakes -

Felix watched as the projector screen slid down from the ceiling.

One of Lily's analysts turned off the lights as another one turned on the projector. A power-point presentation popped on an introductory slide.

"You know," Felix said. "I'm not sure I actually meant to make a deck, but I'm impressed at the same time."

Lily snorted and didn't bother to look his way.

"Start when you're ready, Jim," she said. "Felix is just being ornery today."

"Of course, right away," said the man at the end of the table.

Murdering his stray thoughts, Felix took a quick look around the room. Miu, Andrea, Victoria, Kit, Lily, and two of her analysts were the audience. Though Andrea was working on her pad with a stylus, and clearly not paying attention.

Probably sorting my mail again.

Leaning over, he took a peek at what she was doing.

She was using a virtual coloring book.

I... didn't I increase her intelligence? Repeatedly? Does she just enjoy coloring?

"—is a mock-up of the finished campus," said the analyst.

Felix immediately pinned his attention on the screen. It wouldn't do to miss this, especially since he was the one who'd asked for the information dump.

"Yeah, I appreciate that, but to be honest, I'd like to move on to the parts that we're getting pushback on," Felix said.

It wasn't that the representation was bad, or even poorly thought out, he just didn't care.

"That is, I... of course, sir, I'm sorry, sir," Jim said. Holding up the control in both hands the analyst began flipping forward through the slides.

Slide after slide went by with depictions of the grounds. The areas around it. Expanding the campus into more of the surrounding territory.

Projections for land value and expected changes flashed by on graphs.

"Hm. My compliments to the reporting team. That's quite a lot of data for only a day's time to prepare," Felix said, shifting in his chair.

Jim bobbed his head, though he didn't change his attention from the slides.

Some twenty slides later he stopped.

On the screen was listed a set of bullet points with the title of "challenges."

Ugh. Calling it challenges, opportunities, or whatever else it might be, is still calling it a problem. Just changing the damn word. Stupid fluffy corporate self-help crap.

"Ok, so these are our problems," Felix said, emphasizing the word. "Walk me through them, and as you do, tell me what we're currently doing to solve them."

"Of course, sir. Ah... first is residency. The city put in a requirement that any business or corporation that wants to own land to the degree that we do, with the expressed purposes of education, must have a residency in the state," Jim said.

"That's odd. I mean, the simple fact that we'd be buying a building should grant residence. Did they put this in recently?" Felix asked, leaning forward.

"Yes sir, almost as soon as they realized that we were buying in. As for solving it, we simply bought existing businesses that have had a long history of ownership and residence. It's enough of a loophole that they can't reasonably close it without us being able to get litigious," Jim said.

"In other words, we could hit them with a lawsuit saying they're discriminating against us directly. Good. Next?"

"They're having teams of surveyors and engineers going through the entire grounds and fining us for everything they can think of. We're just paying the fine and having the work completed as quickly as possible," Jim said.

"Well, that's a good short-term solution, but I feel like it invites problems down the road," Felix said. "How do we get them to stop it in the future?"

"I'm working that one, Felix," Lily said. "I've demanded that they show me the protocol for this amount of scrutiny. I've also requested all the documentation around it to show me where it's been utilized on other companies. It's likely that it'll take a week or two, but we should see it lessen."

"Great. Next?" Felix asked.

"Uhm. Yes, next. Next we have the guild itself. They're trying to push a law through that will grant them the ability to inspect the facilities at any time so long as they have probable cause. Unfortunately, we're fairly certain that they'll use it more as a way to disrupt operations," Jim said. "We're pushing the details of the law out to the press. Through a leak of course."

Felix nodded his head at that.

That'll get the entire country up and moving about in a butt-hurt sort of way.

"Alright. So far everything you're describing doesn't seem like issues to me. What's preventing us from launching the campus tomorrow?" Felix asked directly.

"Ah... yes... that is..." Jim said. After his pause went on for a second longer his eyes latched onto Lily, as if seeking rescue.

The soul-drinking lawyer looked at Felix.

"There really isn't a problem. The real issue is that the company we used to leverage the purchase and the mortgage is dragging their feet. They're waiting for the very last minute of each deadline to process it. All within legal limits but... it costs us. The delays are starting to mount and we're probably behind schedule by a week already."

Felix shook his head and then pointed at the two analysts. "Turn on the lights, and please exit the room. Thank you for your time. It was a good presentation, I'm afraid I'm just not the right audience for it today."

That shook up everyone in the room.

Even Andrea put her pad away and stopped fooling around.

When the door closed, Felix folded his hands on his desk.

"Do we know who the processor is for the purchase?" Felix asked. "The actual person, not the company."

"Yes, of course," Lily said.

"And the mortgage, too?"

"Yes."

"Great. Miu?"

"Yes?" asked the security guard turned assassin.

"Slip in, and have a discussion with them both. Take one of the Fixers with you. See what the hold up is. If it's them, kill them. If it's their bosses, kill their bosses. Accidents only. Have the Fixer pop a blood vessel in their head, get creative, don't be repetitive. I hear accidents are going around these days," Felix said in a deadpan voice.

Fixers were a recent creation of his and part of the HR team.

Where Telemedics were there to help people and get them away, the HR Fixer was there to fix memories. Or simply end people with a minor expulsion of telekinetic energy. Fixing a situation either way.

"Ah..." Miu said softly.

"If you do it perfectly, I'll let you drop the control for a few hours in a public setting and I'll even take responsibility for it," Felix promised.

Carrot goes so much further. Even with the crazies.

Kit squirmed in her chair, and Miu sat up straighter, her eyes fixating on him.

"I'll make sure it goes off perfectly," she promised, a hint of zealotry in her tone.

Eva wouldn't much care for this... and to think she won't get it out of someone's head is infantile.

"Kit... if Miu ends up taking care of this problem, let's see if we can't make sure their families are taken care of. Actually, Miu, amend that order a bit. See if they're willing to be bought. Offer them jobs, bribes, whatever," Felix said uncomfortably.

"I'll make sure that a death is the last possible action," Miu promised.

"Thanks," Felix said, shaking his head. "Anyone else being a problem?"

"The education board doesn't much care for our presentations. Any school we've visited has gotten us a twenty to fifty percent attendance to application," Kit said. "Give it two years in our system and you'll have triple the workforce today."

"Goodie. A bunch of kids who grew up without knowing what the world was like before the Internet all working for me," Felix grumped, feeling like an old man. "Whatever. Can't fault them for being born, but can we at least do some head-scans to make sure we're only getting people we actually want?"

Kit laughed and gave her head a shake. "I assumed you'd be that way. We're already doing it. Of the applicants we've received, only about seventy percent are being admitted."

"Though I did force them to admit a few spies. I'd like to keep track of them," Lily said.

"Oh? Good. Get a Fixer assigned to each one as a counselor. Any shape shifters in the lot? Or more specifically, any non-minors?" Felix asked.

"One or two," Lily admitted.

"Have the Fixers take their memories after they sign on, ship 'em to Skippercity. They can join the main workforce and vanish. That agreement was designed for minors," Felix said dismissively. "Anything else?" he asked.

Andrea leaned over next to him, practically pressing her mouth into his ear. "You promised to upgrade Felicia and Ioana a few times already," she whispered loudly in the way only she could.

"Felicia and Ioana... yeah, that's a good point. I'll set up some time with them later and take care of it. Ioana will just want something combat related I'm sure. Felicia... I have no idea. What do you give to a woman who can make whatever she wants?"

"The ability to make more things!" Andrea said, lifting her arms above her head. "And I'll book your meetings for you. It's my job."

Not... a bad idea.

"If there isn't anything else then, I'll cut this one to a close and we can go about our business. That business being, how do we get inside of that damn guild and find out why they want Kit so bad," Felix said.

"Can you make Miu stop killing my Others?" Andrea asked. "It's not that big a deal since I don't have to absorb their memories anymore, but the constant change of clothes and cleaning up the mess is getting tiring."

Uh... what?

Felix looked to Miu who started to tremble slightly, her lips twitching in what looked like it might be a smile.

"It doesn't harm her. I asked her many questions to make sure. So long as it isn't Prime, it does her no harm at all. I asked," Miu said, staring back at him. She nodded her head as she spoke, her control clearly starting to slip little by little.

Andrea nodded her head, then frowned, looking at Miu. "Why do you keep killing me by the way? I never asked."

Miu's grin tightened up and it was clear she was fighting herself.

"Nevermind, Andrea, I doubt you'd understand it," Felix said shaking his head. "Even I barely do."

Felix felt a headache growing. He felt like calling it Miu, but he wasn't sure it was entirely her fault.

Closing his eyes, he rubbed at the bridge of his nose with a thumb and forefinger.

"Someone schedule me a meeting with the governor while we're at it. I should probably have a chat with him," Felix said.

"I assumed you might want something like that," Kit said. "You already have an appointment for him later today. I've made Lauren and one of my people available to go with you as well."

"Goodie," Felix said blandly. "I do so love meetings with politicians. I wonder what I'll have to promise or bribe him with."

The next several hours were more of the same. Details, reports, work-ups on people or departments, and generally feeling out where everything was in Legion.

By and large, it was on track. The pawnshops were going in without a problem. Most of the competition was packing up and leaving, or selling their premises over to Legion directly.

It made the whole thing rather pleasant, since they didn't even have to get into undercutting or aggressively buying things.

Thinking on that did remind him of those pawnshops back in Skippercity though.

Did we ever figure out who was running them? I mean, I know it led to the Hero guild but… we never found any links other than the paper trail.

Which seems just odd.

Very odd.

"—e from there. I don't think it should be too bad," Lauren said from the front passenger seat.

"Oh?" Felix said. He hadn't heard a word she'd said really. He didn't care much either.

Right now he was wedged in the backseat between Andrea, who was alternating between touching him, and playing online tic-tac-toe with some of her others, and Victoria.

Who had wedged her elbow into his side and seemed ready to hurl him out a window at any given moment.

He wasn't really sure if she was protecting him, threatening him, or annoying him.

Maybe all three.

"—ot listening," Victoria said.

"What? Why?" Lauren asked from the front seat.

"Don't know. Sometimes he gets like that. See, he's listening now," Victoria said, grinding her elbow into his side.

"Yeah, so, I didn't think being between two women would be so unpleasant. Mind pulling that sword you call an elbow out of my kidney? Last time I peed blood I was still in Felicia's machine," Felix grumbled, pushing at Victoria's arm ineffectively.

"But, we tried it with some Others and—" Andrea started.

Felix laughed with a hint of insanity to it and pressed a hand to Andrea's mouth.

"We talked about this, remember?" Felix asked, staring into her eyes.

Andrea nodded her head slowly, then held up her tablet for him to see.

On it, an Other was excitedly chattering on about something he couldn't hear.

"I don't understand?" Felix said, releasing her mouth.

"It's my turn. You were making me waste time," she said, wrinkling her nose at him.

"Yes… I see," Felix said, settling back into his seat.

My life is insane.

"We're there," Lauren said as the car stopped.

"I'll wait here!" shouted chauffeur Andrea from the front. "Maybe I'll have time to get out the portable grill in the back and make pancakes. Pancakes for dinner would be great."

"Pancakes!" shouted Andrea next to him.

"Pancakes!" silently replied the Other on the tablet, holding her arms above her head.

"We… have a grill in the tr—no, nevermind. Vicky, get the door open. I don't want to be in here anymore," Felix said, turning and putting his hands on her back.

"Vicky?" she asked, opening the door and stepping out.

"It's what everyone else calls you, why do I have to stick with Victoria," Felix said. Rather than letting her close the door on him, he put his hands on her rear end and shoved, moving her forward.

"Wait, I haven't—"

"Don't care, done now," Felix said, stepping out of the car.

Spurred on by his actions, eight Andreas appeared out of the other sedans in the convoy and fanned out around him.

With his patience splintering rapidly, and the headache from earlier getting worse, Felix nearly jogged to the front door of the city government building.

"Felix, stop," Victoria demanded, shoving him out of the way. Grabbing the door handle she opened the door and entered. Two Andreas flanked him and kept him outside even as he tried to follow her in.

"Calm, calm, love," the Andrea on his left whispered.

"Let us do what you asked us to," the Andrea on his right said.

Felix forcibly made himself relax.

They were right.

They were all right.

He was behaving like a child because his frustration was getting the better of him.

"Yeah… yeah. Sorry. You're right," Felix said pressing a hand to his temple.

"Don't worry, Lily has a plan for your date tonight with her. I'm sure she'll make it all better," left-Andrea said, patting his back.

"Yes!" right-Andrea said cheerfully. "She even asked us questions about how you spend your nights with us."

Headache… getting worse.

"It's clear, and the receptionist said he's already ready to see you," Victoria said, holding the door halfway open.

"Great! Good! Let's go before I put my head through a wall just to see if it hurts less," Felix said.

"It doesn't," left-Andrea said.

"We've had our head smashed many times," right-Andrea said.

Is… is that it? Are her concussions cumulative? Something to check later.

Thankfully Victoria was right, and they were whisked right on through the lobby and into an office.

A short fat man with a red face sat behind a desk.

His hair, what little he had, was overly-worked with hairspray, and his eyes were a pale watery blue. He had to be in his late forties, but he didn't look too roughly worn. At the front of the desk was a name placard that read Nicholas Callas.

Yeah, I'd call him ass. Felix immediately thought to himself. There was a definitely and clear ass like quality to the man.

"Ah, Mr. Campbell," said Nicholas as he stood up and came around the desk. "I'm Mr. Callas, you can call me Nicholas."

"Felix will do," said Felix, shaking the man's hand.

It was a weak wristed thing that felt more like a half dead fish.

Hiding his displeasure, Felix smiled instead and let the man's weak handshake go.

"Your people set up this appointment but didn't seem to want to discuss what it was about, other than your company's move here," Nicholas said, moving back around his desk to sit in his chair.

"Yeah… that's kind of what it's about. Vicky?" Felix asked, turning to address the swordswoman.

"Clear," she replied.

"Andrea?" Felix asked, moving his focus.

One of the Andreas fished something out of an inner coat pocket and laid it down on the desk. A second one moved over to the computer sitting on Nicholas's desk and pushed a thumb drive into the rear of it.

"What are you doing?" asked Nicholas.

"Just securing the room," Felix said calmingly, taking a seat in one of the chairs facing the desk. "Can't have people listening in now, can we?"

A third Andrea walked over to the only window, and placed a small object against it that was no bigger than the thumb drive they'd used earlier.

The first Andrea turned her head and spoke into a microphone, too softly for even Felix to hear it. After she apparently got a response, she turned her face back to Felix.

"All secured. Neutralizer has the surrounding area locked down," she said.

Definitely a worthwhile recruit. Memo to me, thank Lily.

Lauren and the HR rep he didn't know the name of took the other two chairs around Felix.

"That's better," Felix said, looking to Nicholas. "So... you're making problems for me. I'm tired of it. I'll make this simple."

Nicholas looked scared now.

Whatever he was expecting, this wasn't it.

"Get on the train, or get the fuck out of the way. This thing has no brakes, and I'm going to run it right up your fat ass and across your back," Felix said. He rested his ankle on his knee and leaned to one side in his chair. He propped his chin on his fist.

"So it's your choice. You can get on board, and I'll give you whatever it is you want from me for that cooperation, or I have your memory of this wiped clean. And have my Fixer here give you an aneurysm in a day or three. Then I ask the next governor the same question.

"You're not the end all, be all, you know. You're an elected official," Felix said with a grim smile. "Eventually I'll find one of you I can buy."

Chapter 9 - Buying Pork -

Nicholas stared at Felix, much as a fish would when it's been landed.

Felix waited quietly. Silence was always one of his best used tools. People couldn't deal with being stared at silently very well.

Most would immediately babble or start to lose their cool.

Nicholas shifted his entire body around in his chair, first leaning forward, then backward.

Uncomfortable much?

And… is this worth all the trouble? What if I ran for governor myself. It isn't a terrible idea and I could probably make a decent run of it.

What would it take?

"I… see. Ok. Yes. Ok," Nicholas said.

Felix smiled, interrupting his own train of thought, and waited some more. He wasn't about to offer anything up until the fat man croaked for it.

"That is, I mean, I understand your position. I can certainly promise you—"

"He's lying," said the Fixer. He watched the governor unblinkingly.

"Oh, did I mention, lying won't work or save you? I brought with me one of my Fixers," Felix said with a grin.

Nicholas stared at him. He looked a bit like a frog right now.

"He's been under orders from the national government to stonewall you," the Fixer said. "Some pressure from the Heroes Guild, but not that much."

"Oh? That's a little unexpected. I thought it would be the other way around," Felix said.

"No. It's mostly from the national government. I get the impression they want you to go to them, and then they try to turn you into an informant. His memories are a little jumbled but not bad. I think they've had similar people such as myself work on him. It's a rare powerset, sure, but it's not as if there aren't millions of people to sort through. Just not as good as what your training puts out," said the Fixer.

"Happy to know we're the best in the business," Felix said. "Any chance of him agreeing, or should we just wipe him now?"

"Hey, I'm right here! Don't talk over me," Nicholas said hotly.

"Maybe. He's getting some flack from his voters for employment rate. That and the relocation is starting to go up for the area. People are leaving for education elsewhere. He was at first delighted when we started to move in and make our plans. He only got hesitant afterward when he found out who we were," said the Fixer.

"Ah. Alright. Nicholas. What will it take to get you on board? A specific number of jobs created? Taking on more students? We're fully accredited. What will it take for you to get off my ass?" Felix asked.

"Twenty minutes," one of the Andreas said aloud.

"And the clock is ticking," Felix said, acknowledging Andrea's statement.

"I… wait. You're… bribing me?" Nicholas said.

"Are you listening at all? Catch up already. I'm telling you that you need to get on board or I'm going to have you killed. What will it take for you to agree to the deal?" Felix said, his patience long since gone.

Nicholas spluttered at that, his face going from red to pale, and then red again.

Holy crap. I hate dealing with people. Elected officials should require an IQ test. Or maybe a comprehension test?

The Fixer audibly sighed and shook his head.

"I'm not sure he's worth it. He still thinks this is all some political ploy. Maybe we should consider his replacement?" said the Fixer.

Felix groaned and closed his eyes.

He really just wanted to go home, slam several types of headache medication, and pass out.

Wait, no. Can't do that either. Lily stole my calendar for the evening.

"Fine. Whatever. Wipe his memory. We'll need to set up an appointment with his replacement," Felix said.

Lauren cleared her throat and gave him a lopsided smile.

"Lily already arranged one for you. It's right after this. She wasn't sure if Nicholas here would be cooperative," she said.

"Great, let's clean this up then and get moving. Maybe he or she can see us early," Felix said, standing up. "Uh. Just dump his memories all the way up to this point. We'll go with the 'hey are you alright, you don't look good' thing."

Everyone stood up, including Nicholas.

"Now wait! I can make this work. We caaaaoouuuuuu…" He moaned, slumping into his chair.

"Damn, I can't seem to get my control as good as Kit's," said the Fixer. "We're good to go."

Nicholas lifted his head up and looked at them, his eyes glazed. "I don't feel good."

"You don't look so good, either," Felix said. "We can continue our conversation later if you like. We were talking about supporting you in the upcoming election."

"We were?" Nicholas asked. "Oh. Yes… that'd be… good."

"Andrea, can one of you go get his assistant? I don't want to leave him here like this."

"Nn!" came an Andrea's response.

The door opened and closed quickly. Only to open again and a middle-aged woman rushed up to the governor's side.

"What happened?" she asked, looking around the room.

"We're not sure. We were talking about supporting him in his upcoming election, and what he needed from us as a company. He said he felt weak, was dizzy, and then this," Felix said. "We'll get out of your way so he can recover."

Without another word, or giving her the chance to stop them, Felix and crew exited the office.

"God, I hope this goes easier," Felix grumbled. "I'm over today. Over everything. I hate being on top sometimes."

"You weren't on top last night, I was," Andrea said happily from his side.

Felix adjusted his blazer, shifting it to one side, and then the other. He was dressed well, but not overly so. Andrea and Kit had made sure to help him pick out the right clothes.

"You'd think we could get this to fit right with how many people we have on staff," he muttered.

"It isn't a problem of staff, it's that you're putting on muscle, and losing weight," Kit said from behind. "Besides, Lily doesn't care. Now, is there anything else I need to know? Or is what's in the report everything. You have a tendency to leave things out I'd rather know."

"Uhm, nope? Besides, a Fixer was there. Go through his thoughts, or better yet, mine. Here, and while you're in there, make this headache go away," Felix said in annoyance.

He mentally flipped the switch on her being able to read his mind and went over to his desk.

"I… oh… ok. Yes. Ok," Kit said, as if speaking to his memories.

"Uh huh, so while you're talking to yourself, about that headache? Anything you can do?" Felix asked. Opening a desk drawer, he pulled out a bottle and popped open the top. Pulling out two of the pills he swallowed them dry. "Blegh. Remind me to bring a water cooler in here or something."

"Huh? Oh, sure. You know… you often start thinking about your inner circle when your mind wanders. You called them shower thoughts, but I begin to think that's all that's on your mind," Kit said.

"You know what? One of these days, I'm going to hit you with a fantasy as dirty as I can make it. Just to watch you swim through it. Alright? Cause right now, I'm at about a thirteen on the one to fuck you in the eye-socket scale of in pain," Felix said, leaning forward over his desk. "So if you want to get right down into it, I'll be happy to drown you in a sea of damned seme—"

As bad as the headache was, it was the sudden relief that took his breath away.

"Better?" Kit asked, coming up beside him.

"Yeah… yeah, it is," Felix said, closing his eyes and hanging his head. "Sorry, I felt like there was a piston pounding at the back of my skull."

"You definitely were having some tension problems in your neck and base of your skull. I've been going through that library you put together. Read about it in your thoughts," Kit said happily.

"Un?" he mumbled.

"I took one of the medical books for things relating to the head and brain. Helpful, yes?" she asked, a hand pressed to the middle of his back.

"Yeah. Helpful. Very helpful. Super helpful. You need a bonus," Felix said, simply enjoying the lack of the headache.

"I'd like you to make some more books like the one I took. I need one for everyone on my staff," Kit said, her hand patting his back.

"Sure thing. Whatever you want," Felix said, nodding.

"Good. Now, you have a nice date with Lily, and please turn off the mind reading. I'd really rather not hear your thoughts later tonight. I also have a report I need to put together for you. I know those questions are burning holes in your head, but it's all rather silly. It's embarrassing, really," Kit said.

Should have let her into my head earlier. Ever since she got free rein in there she's about as passive as could be.

Popping the ability into an off-state, Felix stood up.

"You're right, gotta get going. I'll see you later," Felix said. Waving at her he stepped around his desk and left his office quickly.

Lily caught him right on the other side. She was in a knee length grey dress with a black jacket that ended at her elbows, and a white blouse underneath.

"There you are. I see Kit's turned you loose. I also approve of her choice," said Lily as she walked up to him.

"You would. You enjoy seeing me being uncomfortable. Maybe not in pain, but uncomfortable," Felix said, trying not to let his eyes make the elevator trip down and back up.

Which he imagined he failed at since her smile spread.

"I'm no mind reader, but I take it you approve?" Lily asked, glancing down at herself.

Felix wrinkled his nose but didn't rise to the bait.

"So, where are we off to then. You've kept me in the dark long enough," Felix said.

"Ah, ah, not spoiling it quite yet. But we'll get there. First we need to take a trip back into your office. Kit should be ready by now," Lily said, making a shooing gesture with her hands.

Now without the miserable headache that had been plaguing him all day, his patience for her nature was at an all-time high.

"Alright, sure," Felix said, turning around.

Only to have two hands press into his back. "Faster already."

"Har har, maybe I should drag my feet and see if you can push me?" Felix said, moving a bit quicker despite his words.

Opening the door to his office after having only left for a minute, he was surprised to find an active and open portal in the middle of it.

"Ah, fantastic. Thanks, Kit. I owe you one," Lily said from behind Felix.

"I take it we're going through then?" Felix asked, walking up to it and peering through.

"As soon as I finish our disguises, yes."

"Disguises? The heck do we need disguises for?" Felix asked, leaning in through the portal.

"Get out of there, silly. You'll ruin it," Lily said.

Sighing dramatically, Felix leaned back and gave Lily a bright smile.

"Only cause you do look good. Otherwise I'd be half tempted to walk through just to see if I could incur the wrath of Mab. You haven't gone all high-and-mighty on me in a while," Felix said, looking to Lily and Kit.

"Sorry. He's being insufferable and it's partially my fault," Kit said.

"No, he's always insufferable. Alright, make sure I do this right? I can't see it since I'm on the other side," Lily said to Kit.

"Of course. Go ahead and put them on."

Missing something here. Put on what?

Lily turned and stared him down. Hard.

Like he was a bug, kind of stare.

And as quickly as she did, she looked to Kit and held up a hand.

"So?" she asked with a touch of hesitation in her voice.

"They look good. Pretty much right in the middle of average. Good show," Kit said with a smile for her.

"Grand. Open it up tomorrow morning? I'm sure we'll be ready by about eight or so," Lily said. Turning, she grabbed Felix by the elbow and led him through the portal.

"Have a good time!" Kit called behind them, and then closed the portal shut.

Lily looked around as soon as they stepped out of the portal and smiled to herself.

"Perfect. This is literally right outside," she said as if to herself.

"Uh, where are we exactly? I'm guessing it's further away than an hour long car ride?" Felix asked.

It looked familiar to him, but he had no memory of the place.

"You really haven't explored your own kingdom, have you," Lily said dejectedly.

"Ok, by that comment I can assume we're back in Skippercity then?"

"Yes. And in the lower habitation levels. The ones shielded by about ten feet of reinforced concrete with steel plates. You paid a lot for them? You don't remember?"

"I sign many things. I think I want to buy a stamp with my signature on it. It could just sit on my desk. 'Oh, sign this', stamp," Felix said, feeling playful. For the first time in a long while, he wasn't being drowned in paperwork, working a headache out, or dealing with something.

"You do realize how quickly that'd end up in Andie's hands, yes? Then everything would have your signature on it. Including her, I imagine," Lily said, pulling him along through an archway.

"Ah... yeah. That's... yeah. Good point. Ix-nay on the stamp," Felix said.

As they passed the arch and got deeper into the room, Felix realized they were surrounded. It started with a few people, and almost immediately climbed into a throng of men, women, and children running about on whatever chores they were doing.

"These are..." Felix started, watching as people streamed in and out of what looked to be stores. Grocery stores, knick knack shops, even an electronics boutique.

"These are your people, living in their underground world that you carved out. You subsidize almost all of their costs, so the fact that almost everyone's salary is the same, doesn't matter at all. And since you actually pay them their full salary now, that goes pretty far with the subsidizing. Shame about that loophole. I really thought that would last a while. Or at least, longer than it did. It got wiped out pretty quick in the grand scheme of things. Skipper realized how much they were missing out on in taxes," Lily said.

"Yeah. Skipper is definitely paying attention. I imagine that probably shored up some gaps in the budget for Skippercity, too."

Lily only nodded her head and led him along as they walked down the street. There were no cars or bikes, just pedestrians.

Everyone moved about as if they were simply out and about. Enjoying an evening after work in a shopping district.

There were even dark gray security guards on patrol making their rounds.

It was obvious they were treated vastly different by the crowd in comparison to how most people acted with the police.

The security patrol smiled and nodded to friends and acquaintances as if they were still at the office. Quite a few stopped and chatted with others.

"It's a little strange," Felix said softly, watching.

"I suppose it is. At first. Mostly everything turned out this way, because it's us against them. Legion versus everyone else. Sense of a shared purpose. And with everyone getting the same treatment, even down to the same living spaces dependent on family size, there's little room for envy," Lily said.

Felix nodded his head at that, not responding.

He hadn't meant to do it, but it was a very normal tactic in business.

- 342 -

And warfare.

Or taking over countries.

"Don't feel bad about it. If you are, that is. They have purpose, drive, and unity. In fact, part of where we're going tonight is to show you that," Lily said, giving him a clue finally.

"Ok. Also… and this is starting to make me a touch crazy, since it doesn't seem like anyone has noticed, do they not see us?" Felix asked.

"Oh they see us, but they don't see us. We look like normal employees. Not Felix and Lily. I doubt we'd get a true experience of your city within a city otherwise," Lily admitted.

"That—ah. That's why you wanted Kit to take a look at you. I mean that—"

"PANCAKE!" shouted a crowd of people off to one side.

Felix blinked and stared in that direction.

"Let's… not go over that way," Lily said.

"No, we're going over that way. I want to know," Felix said, moving off towards the sound.

Felix managed to get up to the crowd before he was practically knocked flat with another shout.

"Holy crap," he said, lifting up a free hand to rub at his ears.

"They tend to get loud. Especially when there's a crowd," Lily said. "I'll be over here by the fountain."

Looking over at her, he found she was smiling in a bemused fashion, indicating the statuary nearby.

"I'll be right back then. I'm very curious. Can't help it," Felix said.

Forcing his way up to the front, Felix found himself face to face with an eerily accurate yet clearly mechanical Andrea.

From the hairstyle, down to the eyes, and even the smile, it was Andrea.

Just not Andrea.

The machine held up a plate to him that had a pancake on it.

The machine had just pulled it out of some type of oven that was behind her to one side.

"Want a pancake?" it asked in Andrea's voice, moving the plate closer to him.

"Uh… sure," Felix said, taking the plate.

"Pancake!" yelled the Andrea, holding her arms above her head.

"PANCAKE!" came the reverberating shout from the crowd.

Felix winced and ducked his way back through the mob of people.

As he went he finally realized that this wasn't the same crowd, but was a constantly filtering group of people. Coming and going all at the same time.

He found Lily exactly where she said she'd be. Sitting down next to her with a pancake on a plate, he felt a touch strange.

"That was… different," he said neutrally.

"Oh yes. Remember when you said you wanted a machine that could turn out pancakes that increased power? Like the Power Sausage? That'd be that," Lily said, indicating the pancake. "Besides, it's hard not to like Andie. She's practically the mascot of Legion. Everyone knows her and loves her. Most remember your first speech and her stealing the show."

"Err. Is it made out of people?" Felix asked, changing the topic. He wasn't quite sure what to do with it.

He'd never been that keen on the Power Sausage. Even though he'd made that promise to actually eat them, he'd never been able to

"No. Thankfully not. Though I do hear that the security team seems to prize the Sausage when it's made. A 'successful encounter' is how they describe it when it's available. Hand that off to someone, you'll spoil our dinner. We should be off anyways," Lily said.

She got up and set off at a leisurely pace, clearly knowing where she was going.

Felix stood up and made eye contact with a teenager and held out the pancake to him.

"Hey, eat this," Felix said with a grin. Handing off the plate to the kid, he jogged a few steps to catch up with Lily.

The kid mechanically picked up the pancake and began eating it, the order of the CEO of Legion being something no one could resist.

Chapter 10 - Break Out -

Lily seated herself comfortably at the table and then smiled up at Felix as he took the chair across from her.

They'd been brought to their table rather quickly. In fact, he'd swear it had only been maybe ten minutes since he'd witnessed the pancake worship.

"Alright. So this is all rather interesting. You've got me there," Felix said, looking around at the rather upscale restaurant in Legion city. "But I'm curious why you picked this of all places."

"To get you away from everyone, mostly. That and to show you all the good you do. I know sometimes you get bogged down in... well... ordering people's deaths and conquering companies, banks, and local governments. It's good to see the good you do, no?" Lily said, leaning forward over the table.

Felix bobbed his head back and forth as he thought on that.

He couldn't deny that earlier today had been bothering him. He'd more or less went full villain mode and ordered the death of the governor, and forced a deal on his successor.

Part of him wondered if it wouldn't be easier to just run for governor after all, but that was besides the point.

On top of that, he'd realized that this wasn't over by a long shot. If the government was trying to get to him to use him as leverage in Skippercity, that'd bode well for no one.

"No... you're right. It was... yeah. It was getting to me, I admit it. Well. Since you're playing the part of my therapist and girlfriend, what do you recommend?" Felix said.

"I have no idea. Never been here. Girlfriend?" Lily asked, flipping open the menu.

"That's the part that gets you strung up? Not the therapist?" Felix asked, staring at the top of the table.

"Not really. They're the same thing anyway," she said. She paused to read something on the menu that caught her attention. "That looks nice. I'll do the tilapia. I've always liked tilapia. You'll do a hamburger. Because you're easy. Don't bother opening it you'll just confuse yourself."

Felix snickered at that and slid the menu to one side. "Yes, dear. Thank you, dear. Am I paying?"

"You're welcome, and yes, you are. Don't worry, I'm worth every penny," Lily said, giving him a dazzling smile.

"Are you now. Definitely gotten my money's worth out of how little I paid for you," Felix said, watching a waiter heading their way.

"That the best you got? You'll need to do better than that," Lily said. She gave her head a shake, her hair swishing back and forth as she refused to rise to the bait.

"Good evening. Welcome to Legion's, what can I get for you to drink?" the waiter asked, looking from Felix to Lily.

Legion's? Really?

"Wine for me, he'll have a soda. And we're actually ready to order already as well. I'll have the tilapia. He'll have the Legion's Fist," Lily said, holding out her menu.

"Ah, good choices. I'll have that all brought out immediately." The waiter picked up the menus and scurried off.

Felix smiled and let out a slow breath.

It was refreshing to not make choices.

To lead a company of people through a cesspit of humanity was hard. Being that he had both Villains and Heroes present was doubly so.

"Felix... why are we in Tilen?" Lily asked him softly.

"Hmm? To figure out who's after us. To offset our risk with the whole slavery thing as well. Why else?" Felix said. Perhaps a bit too quickly.

"That's a very good reason. Why else?" Lily asked. "I know there's another reason, Felix. It isn't like you to spend as much as you have on this enterprise simply to find out who attacked us. Knowing you, you'd make like a turtle and sit inside Legion until you had a chance to fight back. This is out of the ordinary for you."

He wasn't surprised.

Lily knew him fairly well. Knew what his habits were and what he liked and didn't like. This move into Tilen was pretty far outside his normal tendencies.

"That obvious?" Felix asked, finally meeting her eyes.

"Only to me. Kit, too. Everyone else either doesn't care, or doesn't know," Lily said, holding her hand out to him across the table.

Felix gave her half a grin and set his hand in hers.

"Ya got me there. Yeah, there is another reason. After everything that happened in Skippercity, I had to take a step back. Reevaluate everything. Figure out what was my weak point. Ask myself, if I started over today, what would I change," Felix said.

"And what I found was that the one thing I'd change is my reliance on slaves. Sure, it's a great way to hold everyone in check. Keep everyone in the same path. But all it would take for Skipper to end me, us, would be to make slavery illegal. And that'd be the end," Felix said honestly.

"You mentioned something about that before, but I didn't take it to the obvious conclusion. Outlawing slavery would… definitely hurts us," Lily said.

"I know. It's dumb, right? But that's all it'd take. Hence our adventure to Tilen. If we can make this work, and it is so far, then all I have to do is change the contract everyone is on." Felix shrugged and gave Lily's hand a squeeze. "And there it is. I need to get this all hammered out. My only saving grace right now is how many people would be insanely pissed off if Skipper outlawed it today."

Lily closed her mouth and opened it again, only to close it once more.

"I didn't even think about it. It's… such a simple thing to do, too," she said finally.

"Yep. It really is. Like I said, the one thing I'd change would be that. But hey, most of the way there already. Kit is pretty sure we'll have this all buttoned up in time. She's been going over everything we need from a HR perspective. We'll have the contracts over to you and your legal team by next week I imagine to finalize any of the wording and clauses. But enough of this, you didn't ask me out here to talk about work, did you?"

"No. No, I didn't. Not at all. I'm glad to hear that you're being proactive though. Very glad," Lily said, giving his hand a squeeze and smiling. "Now, how about we talk about something else entirely. Like that we're going to go see some art from the Legion after this."

"Art?" Felix asked, raising a brow with a grin. "We have art?"

"You said you wanted everyone to have a place. A position that fit them. If everyone earns the same, and costs are incredibly low, anyone can work doing anything without fear. There are a number of people in your employ who create art, write books, or make music," Lily said, her teeth flashing as she smiled at him. "Kit took your meaning directly, and now we have many, many jobs that wouldn't normally exist in a corporation."

"That's… actually rather interesting. I'd love to see it. You said we're going after dinner?" Felix said, actually feeling rather interested in the whole prospect.

"That we are. Then after that we'll see where the wind takes us. Legion is a city that doesn't sleep since we have graveyard shifts in almost every department," Lily said with an adventurous grin.

Felix wasn't one to normally feel like he wanted to go explore the unknown, but right now, he was happy to be in Lily's company, and let her dictate the pace.

Lily took a few steps out in front and held up her arms. "Well?"

"I had fun," Felix said, nodding his head with a smile. They'd spent quite a while walking around the exhibit.

"That's it? Just… fun? That's all you can give me?" Lily said, exasperated.

Looking around Felix realized they were alone out here in the plaza. The art exhibit exit behind them wasn't the same one they'd gone into.

An impromptu walk in the park, and a long conversation later, and they'd ended up on what seemed like the other side of the city.

Must be on the backside.

"Fine. You want to hear it?" Felix said with a chuckle. Taking several steps forward he caught up with her and slid an arm around her waist, drawing up close to her.

"I had a fantastic evening, Lily. One of the best dates I've ever been on," Felix said seriously.

Lily dropped her arms around his shoulders and smiled at him. "Is that so? Does that come from a wealth of experience? Because I'm betting it doesn't."

"Har har. No, it doesn't come from a wealth of experience. It does come from a genuine place. A realistic one. One that I have trouble expressing and putting into words. But I'm doing it, and will try to be more open with it," Felix said, making sure he kept eye contact with her.

Lily froze up at that, her smile faltering till the point that she had a neutral expression.

"Really?" she asked finally.

"Yeah. Really. I mean it. I'm not the best at it, but I can definitely put in the effort. I want to put in the effort. You're worth it. Especially when you've clearly put so much work into me and my needs," Felix said honestly. "This isn't something that you came up with on the fly."

"No... it isn't," Lily said, not pulling away from him. "Then what would you say all this is? It's not exactly a normal relationship. You have a Beastkin—a Wolf, no less—that you sleep with," Lily said. Then looking down and to the side, she continued in a softer tone. "I'm not quite sure what to make of all this myself, actually."

"I... don't know. I don't even claim to know enough to give an honest opinion. When it comes to you and Andrea, I... don't have a plan or even a direction. I've mostly just been going along with whatever pace you two set. Or so it feels like at times," Felix said.

Lily nodded her head once and then turned her face back to his. She gave him a lopsided smile and then a soft peck on the lips.

"Good. I think for now that's the right direction. Now, unless you plan on causing a scene here and now, you should be letting me go so we can head back. I imagine that Andrea is probably waiting either to pounce on you, or chat me to death to find out what happened," Lily said.

Felix didn't really care for her response, but he could understand.

She was an independent woman who gained her powers through the death of others. Many others.

Her very nature had been changed as of late, and he couldn't imagine she was in the most stable of mindsets.

"Of course. In this, you lead, I'll follow," Felix said.

"Just the way it should be," she said, grinning at him.

Neither of them moved however, and Felix wasn't about to be the first one to let go.

After ten seconds passed, Lily laughed softly and pressed her forehead to his.

"You can let go. I promise I won't run, and this isn't the end. I... just feel cautious all of a sudden. That's all. I'm interested, obviously, and Andrea and I have talked about this quite a bit. I think I want a bit more time though," said the soul-stealing sorceress villain.

"Yeah, not a problem," Felix said and released her. "What did you—"

Felix stopped as his phone started to chime in his pocket.

"I thought I told no one to call you," Lily said with a touch of heat in her voice.

Pulling out the wristband from his pocket he flipped it over. He'd pulled it off as soon as their date started just case he felt tempted to look at it.

"It's... Kit? That's odd. You'd think she'd be the one person to listen to you," Felix muttered. Sliding his thumb across the screen he accepted the call, buckling it to his wrist.

"Kit? What's—"

"Felix, there's a problem," interrupted Kit.

"I kinda figured since you called me, but—"

"Shut up and listen. There's been a super-villain breakout. Literally. That isn't the entirety of the problem though. The Heroes guild is handling that. The other part of the problem is that in their breakout, they smashed a supermax prison apart and there's a flood of prisoners and convicts running around the city," Kit said.

Felix sighed and closed his eyes. He pressed his free hand to the middle of his forehead.

"Pull everyone in, get the generators up, and set the defenses on active," Felix said.

"What's happening?" Lily asked.

"Prison breakout," Felix said, pulling the phone from his mouth.

" —id all that. We're safe and everything's buttoned up. But I was thinking. This might be a good opportunity to mobilize some of our resources. I mean, we have emergency responders for this situation. We should use them, the Telemedics, the Security teams, even the Fixers. Put Skippercity on a lockdown and transfer the resources here," Kit said.

Huh. I guess we could. Might help a bit with our local PR problem. Thankfully we're not getting into a dirt flinging contest with the guild.

The guild!

"Is the Heroes guild responding as well?" Felix asked, his entire attention now on the matter at hand.

"Yes. They're dividing their forces up. Half to go for the villains, the other half to work in the city," Kit said, her voice sounding weary.

"Alright. See if Felicia got the portal up and running for everyone else. I'll need you to put a portal down to my current location. Do I need to tell you where I am or can you call it up with a camera? Oh, and don't worry about checking on Felicia. Just tell her you wanted to see what her progress is. Chances are she already got it up and running just to spite me. I'm betting it's already working. Get all the resources over after locking down Skippercity HQ. I need Miu, Eva, and a Fixer who's been trained to multi-skill out to Miu's department," Felix said.

"I'll take care of it. What else do you need?" Kit asked.

"A huge number of GPS transponders. I want one for about… three hundred Others," Felix said. "We're going to arm up the Andreas and send them out in a massive patrol but I want to recover any corpses they leave behind."

"On it. Anything else?" Kit asked again.

"Nope. Date went fine, you didn't interrupt anything. See you later," Felix said, closing the phone and turning it off.

"I take it that was work?" Lily asked, the irony not lost on him.

"Indeed. And this time, I think we can use it to our advantage. The Heroes guild is going to be distracted with this. We're sending Miu, Eva, and a Fixer in to get the information we need. At the same time, we'll be assisting the local government and working on our public image. Get your pretty face ready to go smile into the camera, Lily. You're about to go do some meet and greet with the press I imagine," Felix said.

With one hand he started to work through a series of menus for the Skippercity HQ. Calling up pre-existing modifications he'd built in that he was now activating.

"Why me?" Lily asked.

Felix snorted at that and closed up the screen. He was ready.

Then a blue dot appeared to the side and started to slowly open up.

And there we have Kit's portal.

"Why you, you ask? Because you're the most attractive woman we have in Legion, and have a smile that matches. Doesn't hurt that you've got a killer intellect on top of that. Now, I hate to date and run, but I think this is our ride out of here, and Kit doesn't have the best control over it yet," Felix said.

"I can hear you, Felix. Don't make me close this up on you while you're halfway through," Kit said from the other side.

Felix froze in place and then shook his head. "Actually, can you keep it open for a bit? I need to zip up to my office and grab my armor. I'm thinking it might be best if I was on the scene and helping to organize the efforts from an operation base. I think everyone would agree with me doing that in the suit."

"I… yes. That'd probably be wise. I'll start opening a portal inside your office, and move this one to the staging area in SC:HQ. Be a dear and activate the right protocol? I'm sure you already turned on all the right upgrades, but don't forget the people," Kit called through the portal, and then closed it.

"Protocol?" Lily asked curiously.

"HR loves having a process and procedure for everything. Leadership is expected to read through them all, it's those online trainings that everyone gets pushed to their work stations or tablets," Felix said. "I would hope since you're in Legal you'd be—"

"Yes, yes. I've read all the ones pertinent to me. I just didn't realize there was one specifically for a prison break," Lily said.

"There isn't one. But there is one for mobilization. Now. Let's go get my armor," Felix said, setting off at a jog, moving with the crowd.

"Do you even know where you're going?" Lily called after him.

"The same place everyone else is, the elevators," Felix said back.

All around them, people were starting to get messages from co-workers. They were all looking at their wrists or phones.

Felix imagined it was them being told about all the modifications going live. They would all be assuming something was about to happen.

Word tended to spread with something like that.

Those who had been notified first were already on their way to the elevators was Felix's guess.

Sure enough, when he lifted his eyes to the horizon, he could see the outline of a massive column reaching up into the recessed lighting above.

That'd be the place.

An alert chirped on his wrist and he flipped it over to check the screen.

It read "R&D lab" and was from Felicia.

Well, she's quick on the draw. New suit, maybe? Also should probably find out how she knew.

"We're heading for R&D," Felix called over his shoulder to Lily.

As they got closer to the elevator, he could see that it was part of a large plaza.

Sitting in the center of that plaza was the wrecked mech Felix had piloted.

Legion's Fist.

It looked no different than what he remembered, half salvaged by his own hand.

Except that when he finally got up close to it, he realized the entire thing had been bronzed or recreated in bronze.

I thought she was repairing it. I'll have to ask.

Felix noticed the placard as he passed and quirked a brow.

Legion's Fist-Year One: Piloted by Felix to eliminate the Heroes Guild of Skippercity.

He wasn't quite sure how he felt about being immortalized like that, but he wasn't about to naysay them right now.

The time was right to strike.

Chapter 11 - Mobilized -

Felix stepped out of the elevator and found himself in the middle of a fantastic mess.

Felicia and White's people were scurrying around in every direction. Loading crates, packing boxes, and generally making ready as if they were going into the field.

Everything was being shifted to a gigantic freight elevator in the back. It required both White and Felicia to unlock it to actually be used.

"Over here!" called the voice of Felicia from a corner.

Felix ducked his head at the shout and followed it.

He'd lost Lily somewhere along the way. He imagined she probably went to talk to her department for one reason or another.

Probably to get ready for the camera and prep anything legal-wise.

"Felicia, I'm not sure how many more times you can upgrade the suit before it hits a plateau," he called out over the hubbub.

"Obviously there was at least one more, idiot. Get your scrawny ass over—oh, there you are. Stand in the bay," Felicia said, stomping over to a large pod.

It was reminiscent to the medical pods she'd been building for the hospital ward.

"Uh, alright? And what is this going to do exactly?" Felix asked, stepping into the indicated position.

"Put your armor on, what else? You ask the stupidest questions sometimes. It's a wonder we're doing as well as we are," Felicia grumped.

"You know what? I'm going to cut funding to your department one of these days. Just to see what you can do with a shoe-string and some gum," Felix said, looking up into the darkness of the machine above him.

"No. You won't. You like the toys I build you too much. Stop whining and put your arms down or you'll lose them," Felicia said, slapping a button he only noticed as she hit it.

"I'll what!?" he shouted and pressed his arms down to his sides. "Swear to god, Felicia."

The Dwarven woman snorted and moved to the other side, holding up a tablet.

"It's more or less the same as your last one. Just better firmware and some onboard hardware. Nothing out of the ordinary. You're so damn hard on everything though, I decided to shield it a bit more. That's a bit more power draw than I thought it would be," she said absentmindedly, staring at the tablet.

"What is? Wait, if this is the same suit, why this alcove thing?" Felix asked, still holding still.

Before she could answer, or choose to, the whole thing roared to life around him.

Metal doors slammed closed in front of him and shut him in the darkness. Felix felt his body being pressed in tight by padding, and then become rather chilly as his clothes simply ripped away. Unable to prevent a shriek from escaping, Felix wanted the ride to be over.

He also suddenly wondered if this was anything like the corpse-o-matic sausage machine.

Before he could finish that thought, the padding was pressing down on him again.

A series of rapid clicks and a hiss was the only warning he had before the entire thing opened up again and he was staring through his helmet at Felicia.

"Going to hurt you," Felix said, his voice coming out at a natural volume through the helmet.

"No. You're not," Felicia said, looking up from her tablet. "Everything is fine. Your gear was already packed up. Sorry. I'll have it shipped to the operational base. Get the fuck out of my lab."

Waving her hand at him, Felicia wandered off, going about whatever it was she had been doing.

Mr. White stepped up and gave him a grin. "She must like you. Always takes the time to actually talk to you. Other than me, that's rare."

"Hm. Anything I need to know?" Felix asked, looking at White.

"No. It really is the same as the previous, just some upgrades in it. Anything you need?" White asked, holding up a tablet.

"No?" Felix replied without any confidence.

"Great. Use the elevator in the back, it'll take you to the staging area." White left as quickly as Felicia had.

I think I need to hire someone with a bit more of a social personality down here. Like an assistant or something.

Heh… or an Andrea.

Plotting his own version of revenge, Felix trod over to the elevator and waited with the crates. He synced his system up with his phone and then dialed into Lily's.

"Felix? What is it. I'm trying to get ready with my department," came Lily's voice

"I need to get a hold of the governor. Make sure he's on board with us actually moving in to assist."

"No one can find him. His lieutenant-governor has taken over for now but he's not being proactive in the least. He's honoring the deal we made with him, but he's useless."

"Damn. Get him to agree, just a yes in a written format, preferably with a signature. I'll get everyone moving as if he had already done so. I'm going to go set up a forward operating base in the city. Probably a library or something mildly government based. Better sense of authority."

"Alright, I'll get on that. Are you heading back to your room or—"

"No, heading down to the staging area. You use the portal in my room. Signing off," Felix said and promptly disconnected the call.

Pulling up the war-net, he activated the mobilization process formally.

All the lights immediately dimmed. Blue running lights came to life along the sides of the walls. On every display a single word showed up: "Mobilization".

Five seconds later and the monitors returned to normal.

The freight elevator turned on, and took its load down to the staging area.

During that ride down, Felix began to contemplate a run for governor. It'd solve a number of problems, put him charge, and give him more than enough leeway to leverage Legion desires.

Felix for governor. Governor Campbell?

Governor.

Felix stared out at the streets below from the top of the library steps.

The early morning sun was providing them with some light to see by. A lot of their arrival and setup had all been done in the darkness with limited visibility.

This location wasn't where the reporters were, though. That was elsewhere.

Far, far from here, the reporters were trying to interview refugees from the safety of the police barricades.

Where Lily was. Doing her job.

Being the face of Legion and putting on a show for the entire country to watch.

Watch a company take control of a city, quell a riot, return order to the city, and establish peace.

No, where Felix was was where the operation was actually being run from.

All along the perimeter of the library were his security forces. They were dressed in full gear for an assault or defense.

Kevlar enforced armor and helmets with automatic rifles in hand. The entire area was on lock-down. It was also where refugees were being directed, and funneled through manned barricades.

His people were screening the refugees for weapons, then sending them into the library to be processed.

Fixers were actively screening the refugees as they went by and were processed. Working alongside their armed counterparts in similar gear. They were discreetly tagging anyone of interest for one reason or another to be picked up. Those special people were grabbed by Telemedics and dropped at SC:HQ to the tender mercies of the rehabilitated Death Others.

Those survival-driven Andreas had taken it up as their personal duty after returning to Prime. They seemed ideal to be guards and interrogators. Loners who preferred to work in the dark and quiet with situations that seemed unpleasant. Felix could only imagine their personalities were skewed from being Death Others.

Not that they acted any different around him, but he didn't doubt they were probably different.

When Legion arrived, Felix and his crew had quickly broken into the library. The basement was promptly cleared and pulled apart. It was now a fully functioning medical ward, and the entire building was a refugee center.

There was also a steady stream of Legion vehicles making runs from the library's enclosed parking lot to the front line of the police barricades.

For the wounded who couldn't wait, the Telemedic squads were making the leap from site to site.

Legion as a whole had gotten their formal approval from the lieutenant-governor in the form of a signed letter to act within the confines of the law to bring order to Tilen. Which meant Legion was free to act with impunity.

And illegally, provided there were no witnesses.

The sound of gunfire, distant shouting, and muffled thuds that were probably explosions could be heard. It was all coming from deeper in the city.

Once the power went out, and there wasn't any possibility of getting it back on any time soon, sections of the city had broken down to rioting and looting.

"What a mess," Felix muttered to himself, staring down the street.

"It really is," Victoria said at his side. "Security teams are actively expanding the perimeter. Ioana is leading the way down the center towards the prison. They're working with standard Rules of Engagement."

"Remind me to put in weapon, armor, and supply caches throughout the city in our buildings. In fact, let's buy buildings just to do that. If we had people stranded out here, this would have been the time it could have helped them," Felix said.

"I'll coordinate it with Kit and Lily," Victoria said immediately.

Mentally Felix called up the war-net map and then reviewed it. The map was filled with dots. Blue, Red, and Green.

Blue was obviously their own people. Red were known locations of combatants. Green were noted refugees or holdouts operating in areas.

The Legion security dots were gradually, slowly, expanding through the city. They were taking the city back block by block.

Armored cars and Wardens were acting as the mechanized backbone, providing the hardened center that could soak up attention.

Suddenly Felix was quite happy he'd had the number of Wardens and Armored cars increased dramatically.

"Mm. Everything seems like it's going in the right direction. I want to step off to the side for a second and check up on the other operation. Think you can play goalie here for a bit and keep people busy? Or at least out of my way?" Felix asked, turning to look at Victoria.

She nodded her head and rapped her knuckles against his breastplate. "I can do that, Felix. Just keep an ear out if I start calling for you."

"Right, right," Felix said. Waving his hand at her he took several steps towards a planter that put him out of line of sight from the street.

Felix then focused in on his war-net map, filtering out everything else from his mind. Multiple windows popped up in front of him as he opened up a number of items with a thought. Flipping through several maps, he found the one he wanted.

It was on a secure channel on the war-net, and buried under a clearance wall that only allowed him, Kit, and Lily to see it.

Eva, Miu, and a Fixer Kit sent along were in the process of infiltrating the guild of Heroes in Tilen. They'd been dropped into location from a portal. It opened up directly onto the roof of the guild.

Kit had dropped them there behind a screen of illusionary empty space. Kit literally was shielding them from being spotted while holding open a portal at the same time in case they needed to get out immediately.

Need to reward her. She's putting in the work lately. Pavlov would be proud of me.

Clicking into the cameras that each of the three were wearing he checked each one. He wanted to get a better view of the situation.

Settling on Eva's viewing frame, he found he could see most of what was going on.

Miu was holding what looked like a penlight and was drawing circles on the roof over and over. The same circle repeatedly and endlessly.

Felix watched for a moment before pinging Lily with a screen-capped image of the action. The attached was only "What?"

He figured it'd get his point across enough. If she saw it in time.

Chances were she'd probably see it much later since she was working the PR angle right now.

Switching back to the live view from Eva he couldn't really tell if there was any change. Deciding not to sit there and wait, he flipped to the camera for Ioana.

He got a view of a street, with manned barricades at the end of it. Ioana was storming down towards them at a dead sprint. Behind the barricade were men and women in colored jumpsuits on the other side. They'd armed themselves and were clearly resistant to surrendering and being taken into custody.

In fact, one of them threw a Molotov cocktail that burst into liquid fire out in front of Ioana. She simply ran through it and burst out the other side.

Felix waited for a few seconds more as Ioana leapt over the barricade.

It was long enough to watch a sword swing into view from the side and cleave someone's head from their shoulders, before he switched again.

Don't need to watch a snuff movie right now. Enough of that on Reddit.

Grunting, Felix disconnected from the war-net. He closed almost everything down to a base desktop level and then opened up a web connection.

He tapped into the live broadcasts on the internet and flipped to the news. He wanted to know how the coverage of the event was being handled, and if he needed to do anything more. He trusted Lily implicitly, but he would never be anything if not paranoid.

The player paused for a moment and buffered the feed.

" —ing to help everyone in the city," said Lily as the screen popped open in front of him. "I know our CEO is on the scene himself and working to bring order to the situation. Our entire goal is to bring peace and order to the city."

She looked amazing. She normally didn't go all in on the makeup and dressing to accentuate her looks, she was a bit of a natural beauty, but she'd clearly put in the time for this one.

"Ah. That's a relief to hear, though I wonder, is it really Legion's place to do this? This almost seems like something more suited to the national guard. In fact, most would say you're acting the part of a private military company," said the newscaster, then pointed the microphone back at Lily.

"It isn't our place to be here. We don't deny that and regret our involvement. The moment the government, national guard, or a federal agency shows up, we'll be happy to turn over everything to them. We're a company with a security team, not a military force.

"Right now we're acting as an emergency stop-gap measure. A relief group to provide aid and safety. The governor could not be found when we started to ask around to find out what was going on. The rest of his people were sitting on their hands waiting for help to come to them rather than seeking it when we finally got a hold of someone," Lily said. Her tone was pleasant, even if her words were acidic.

There was no mistaking that as Legion's spokesperson, she was laying the blame squarely at the feet of the local government.

"We stepped in because no one was doing anything, though we did get permission first from the lieutenant-governor. We're acting well within the limits that were given to us, and are holding to the very letter of the law," Lily concluded.

"Of course. That makes sense," the newscaster said, looking into the camera. "We've also received word that the Heroes guild won't be able to assist as they're currently combating the Villains who caused this situation."

Lily laughed with a silken voice at that, drawing the attention of the newscaster and the camera back to her.

"The Villains didn't cause the situation. The situation was caused when the guild decided to put a prison in the middle of Tilen. Right next to a power plant no less. One need look no further than who made that zoning happen to find responsibility," Lily said, and left it at that.

The question that everyone would ask who saw this broadcast would be the same.

Who was responsible for this situation then? Who approved that jail?

Most would find fault with either the local government, or the heroes guild, or both. No one else could have allowed the prison.

Perfect. There's no reason she would bring that up unless she could implicate the governor and lieutenant-governor.

Felix grinned and then turned off the monitor. That was more than enough already.

Half of taking power was eliminating whatever power base would support the official. The other half was the speed with which you could do it and hold the purse strings.

There was no second place in politics after all.

In this case, support was the constituents. A governor was of course an elected position, whose power base was built off of voting blocks.

Next will be attacking the group of essential backers that are holding the governor and lieutenant-governor in place. That'd be whoever is funding them, and whatever business is gaining. Leaders of voting blocks, businesses, or religious leaders.

I'll pin that one back to Lily for later. For now... I'll just send an email to the marketing team to get them working on a 'Felix for governor' build up.

Start framing this whole thing as a failure to protect the citizens and how Legion could do better, and already has.

I imagine Lily already knows exactly how this came to be and whatever measure was passed for it to happen. They'll need to sync up to get the right ads out.

Elections are only a few months away and this'll be a firebrand to burn them with, and set myself up as governor.

Finishing up that email, Felix flipped back to the war-net map of Tilen to review what had changed in the last few minutes.

His forces had expanded out to the police cordon on each side. The rear had already been secured.

The rest of the push would be straight into where the prison break occurred. Re-establish peace and allow work crews to get in and start restoring power to the people.

Everything really was on track and going according to the plan.

Which means this is where it goes wrong, isn't it?

Cycling to Eva on the war-net, he opened up her camera.

Miu was still using the pen-light on the roof, but there was now a clear difference. A thin line of blue energy was spiraling round and round in the same spot Miu was working. The energy was cycling downward at the same time, slowly sinking into the roof itself.

Then all of a sudden, the section of the roof that she'd been working on fell inward. Light flooded up from the hole and bathed Miu's face.

She had an evil grin spread from cheek to cheek.

Miu dove into the hole headfirst. The Fixer followed behind, then Eva.

Turning off the camera, he found he couldn't watch. His stomach had flipped over and twisted in on itself.

Felix wasn't a brave man, he wouldn't watch what could be his people diving into a trap or worse.

Changing the screen back to the news, he did his best to not think on it. For now, there wasn't much to do but wait.

Chapter 12 - Always Watching -

There wasn't much else he could do right now. He could hunt down whatever station Lily was talking to now. He didn't think it'd be anything different than what she said the first time around.

It'd be the same message, maybe with a few different words, but the same statement.

Bracing himself, and realizing that there wasn't much else he could do right now, he linked into Eva's camera.

And pulled up a view of Miu holding someone down to the ground. She twisted the person's head up, revealing it as a pretty young woman. Her forearm flexed around her windpipe and the woman spasmed, then went limp.

Miu released the woman almost as soon as she passed out.

Reaching down, Miu took a hold of the back of the woman's head. Glancing around at the hallway they were in she seemed to assess her options.

Eva tracked the same place Miu was looking, and they found a cord snaking out of a runner. The runner wasn't secured very well and the cord had started to slip upwards.

Miu stood up, holding the woman like a doll and held her over the runner as if she were measuring something.

As cool as could be, Miu slammed the woman's head into the steel doorframe halfway down. There was a sickening pop and crunch as her skull was stove in on the hard edge.

Miu released the woman and let her fall naturally. Leaning down, Miu inspected the work.

"She's gone. The swelling in her head will take care of her," came a male voice from the side.

Eva's head swung around to the speaker. Felix found the Fixer staring at the body.

"Good enough. It'll look suspicious for sure but... not that we were ever here, but more like someone murdered her. Let's go," Miu said.

That'll be an ugly tombstone. Died by possibly tripping.

Felix flinched when the call incoming screen popped up in front of his view. The sound was ear splitting and dominated his entire helmet.

Damn it! I need to change that setting. Somehow. This is when it would have been a good idea to get a F.A.Q.

Felix mentally smashed at the accept button on Lily's phone icon.

"Hey there," Felix said, minimizing the window.

"It's a magical battery. I had Felicia put a discharge tip onto them," Lily said.

Huh? What... oh. I sent her a screenshot of the thing.

"Ah. Alright. Was interesting to watch. Cut right through the roof," Felix said, watching through Eva's camera again.

"It's definitely a useful item to put in a tactical kit. I can't make them that quickly, so don't go expecting everyone to have one," Lily said.

He could hear people talking in the background. It sounded as if she were in the middle of someone giving an interview in fact.

"Sorry about the noise. Some administrator showed up and is trying to do damage control. Too bad for them the documents relating to the zoning approval by the governor are already making the rounds on the net. Shame that the lieutenant-governor is also on the same approval," Lily said. Felix could hear the smile in her voice.

"Have I mentioned you're quite good at this whole corporate thing? You really missed your calling," Felix said.

Miu stepped to one side and pointed to a door. The Fixer walked up and pressed his forehead to it.

"I won't deny I'm enjoying myself. Did you watch the broadcast?" Lily asked.

He wondered if she was fishing for a compliment. Admittedly he had no reason not to compliment her.

"I did. You looked amazing. I'll be asking for a high resolution digital copy of it for me to watch later," Felix said.

The Fixer shook his head and said something to Miu.

In response, Miu turned and kept moving down the hallway.

The sooner they found what they were looking for, the better. Every minute they spent wandering around was more time to be discovered.

Miu at least had experience as an internal security guard for the guild, and knew the normal patterns and protocol.

Every major city had a guild, but they all shared the same procedures. It was a hell of a gap, but honestly, how often did they have to worry about someone who was foolish enough to break in?

"And here I thought you were already captivated by me," Lily purred into the phone.

"I was, I just realized that you're a natural ten, that goes up to eleven when she wants," Felix said.

Miu gestured to another door and the Fixer pressed his forehead to it.

Several seconds later he nodded and stepped back.

"Well, everything is exactly as you asked. What's next?" Lily asked.

Miu stepped up to the door and then opened it, charging inside.

The Fixer and Eva followed behind, shutting the door after all three were in. It was a rather simple office space that any manager or director would probably have.

"For you? I need you to keep playing the beautiful PR lady for now. Though when you get back to a computer, I could use you putting in some time at a terminal. Need to find out who the funding for the politicians are. We need to neutralize their spending power as quickly as possible. I'm going to be a third party candidate, so we'll have to plan for both Democrats and Republicans. The sooner we shut down their money, the better. After that, we'll need to look into what public works they were sponsoring and which ones were favors and to who," Felix said.

Felix watched as Miu picked up a man slumped over a desk and laid him out on a couch. She adjusted him into as close to a natural position as she could.

The Fixer moved over and stood over the couch, watching the sleeping man. Eva went and stood next to the desk, lifting her right hand to her earpiece.

"This is Worm. Dirt is ready, need a hole. Mole actual, please confirm," Eva said.

Whatever response Eva got, Felix didn't catch it.

"That makes sense, didn't realize you wanted to run for governor though. We can talk about your reasons later, but I think I already understand," Lily said, competing for his attention at the same time as everything else was happening. "I'll get on that immediately. Do you want to bury any of the candidates? I'm sure I could dig up quite a bit of mud."

"No. If anything, we need to expand the playing field. See if we can funnel money into any of them to run a separate campaign apart from their party. We'll need to use a..." Felix paused as a portal opened up next to the desk.

"... use a shell company. Make sure it's not traceable back to us," Felix finished.

"You want to increase the number of people running against you?" Lily asked skeptically.

"Yep. Their votes will be divided between the candidates. It's why almost every political race ends up as one runner from each party. It's how they solidify voting blocks," Felix said.

A pair of hands reached out to the computer on the desktop and turned it sideways. They pulled the Ethernet cord out of the computer and pulled it into the portal.

"Understood," Eva said, apparently to whoever she was speaking with. Looking at the rest of her team, Eva made eye contact with Miu. "Metal Detector will be done in ten minutes. Order is to stay with the dirt. Hole is to remain open until then."

Miu nodded her head and stalked to the door, readying herself if anyone should enter.

"I... you're right. I never really paid attention to politics," Lily said.

"It's a lot like corporate life, really. In this case, we want a lot of them running. Muddy the field and spread it around. When we find out who the financial backers are, and eliminate them, it'll be chaos," Felix said.

"As for what we offer, that's easy. Jobs, protection, and separation from the guild of heroes. Our own brand of security, with regards to protection. Contracted out specialists who work with whatever needs and desires the companies or corporations have. It sounds terrible, but that's how we win over the corporate backers," Felix said.

Nothing was going on in Eva's room, so he opened up the war-net map instead.

"Jobs, economy, and education will swing the masses over to our side. Jobs we're already doing, so that's just a matter of making it a known fact. Economy… well, the jobs take care of that. And the pawnshops tend to boost areas that we're buying in. And education was the whole setup for us being here, which brings us back to the first point. Making sure everyone knows."

Felix sighed and studied the map a second time.

Ioana and her team were deep into enemy territory. The rest of the security forces were fanning out and clearing everything behind her.

He imagined she wanted to get into the heart of this and tear it out. Remove the leader, end the resistance.

"That's… all very clinical, Felix. Have you thought about this before?" asked Lily.

"Before Legion? No. It's just what they'd want, isn't it? It's what anyone wants. Security, money, and the ability for their children to do better. It's all rather simple. Everything else is detail work and an opinion that matches what the majority of the voting blocs want to hear," Felix closed the war-net.

Looking back to Eva's camera he found that nothing was changed. He didn't think anything would change either, now that he thought about it. The attack was successful, and his IT people were on the guild's network.

Access was always the hardest problem with any attack on a network.

"Sorry, Felix. I have to go. Another reporter is coming my way and I'm betting they want an interview, too," Lily said.

"Knock 'em dead, dear. Give them that dazzling smile," Felix said and cleared his windows.

"Will do, bye hun," Lily said, closing the connection.

Felix looked out into the streets, watching as the stream of displaced citizens continued.

"This is Tip to Throne, actual," said a voice on the war-net communications network.

That message could only be on the leadership channel if it was to Throne.

Tip would be Ioana as the spear tip. Throne being his own code that she generously bestowed on him.

Activating his own com link, Felix walked back to Victoria.

"This is Throne, actual. Go Tip," Felix said.

"We're under heavy attack and request assistance. Minimum force suggested is three wardens to neutralize threat," said the Tip communications officer.

"Understood. Reinforcements en route," Felix said.

Turning his head to Victoria, Felix lifted a hand.

"Send four wardens out to assist Tip," Felix said.

"We only have two. I'll get them moving," Victoria responded, picking up a tablet she'd set down on a planter.

Felix frowned, staring down the street.

"I'll go as well. I'm not at a warden's level of power, but I'm sure I'll be able to make up the difference," Felix said, starting to go down the library steps.

"No! I'll go instead, you remain here," Victoria called out from behind.

Before Felix could argue, turn around, or change his mind, a number of refugees pulled weapons out of their clothes and began attacking his people directly in front of him in the line.

Guns fired, people screamed, weapons clashed on armor.

There were even clearly Super Villains in the sudden battle with the Legion forces.

Then Felix's Supers sped out of the library to engage, and the battle escalated.

Three men charged straight for him, two with clubs and a third with a blade.

Victoria was out in front of him in a heartbeat, her sword speeding outward to pierce the closest man through the eye and into his brain.

He dropped like a stone.

Felix had been in action as well. He drew the pistol from his holster and racked the slide. As he pulled the muzzle up he was already slipping his finger onto the trigger.

He trained the iron sight on one of the hostile targets rushing him and then fired twice. Both shots struck the man center mass.

Moving to the next target, Felix pulled the trigger twice more. Again, both shots hit the chest.

Both enemies went down, groaning, screaming, bleeding out on the ground. Begging for help as they gasped for air.

Felix didn't care.

They weren't his people.

Marching forward, Felix maintained proper gun control. Looking for targets that he could fire on cleanly, he had no choice but to wait.

Clearing the dying men, Felix found two more targets and put two shots into each of them.

Eight spent, seven left in the clip.

Victoria danced ahead of him, her enhanced super powers making her a whirlwind of death. Her blade snaked out, skewering enemies on its length.

Legion security forces were highly trained. Drilling almost all day, every day. The simple reality was that their job was to prepare for situations worse than this.

They worked in tandem with their super partners, wardens, and coordinated the fight. Officers made snap calls on the communication line and the defensive line firmed up.

By the time Felix made it to the line of combat, his people had ejected the remaining attackers from the field. Who were then forced to cut and run, leaving behind their dead and wounded.

Confirming there were no active threats in sight, or on the war-net, Felix thumbed the clip release on his M9.

Catching the clip with his free hand he reached down to his left side and pulled out a fresh magazine. He turned the half spent magazine so that it didn't fit right in the slot and slid it into the now empty space.

His goal was to make sure he could identify it later if he needed to.

Popping in the fresh magazine he thumbed the safety and returned it to its holster.

"This is Throne, actual. Team leaders, cart your wounded and dead back to HQ. Telemedics are to prioritize Legion." Felix paused to consider the fallen enemies. Smirking to himself, he made the choice. "Power sausage the enemy wounded. Pile the dead."

Apparently Felix's dour mood was shared with his people, as he could actually hear the collective dark chuckle.

"Mole actual, this is Worm. We have contact," said Eva's voice over the high level security channel.

Felix turned his head down and to one side, pulling up the Eva's camera with a thought.

Everything was more or less how he left it. Eva was pressed up to the door with her forehead touching the wood.

"Need a time on the hole. Farmer is about to notice," Eva said again.

"Mole actual reads. One minute on the hole," Kit said into the void.

"This is Worm, actual," Miu said into her headset. "Moving to Hole. Prepping."

The Fixer and Miu got up and went to the portal, stepping through it and to the other side. Back into SC:HQ, he imagined.

Eva twisted the lock into place on the door and moved to the portal and then stepped through. She was staring back at the side of the computer and its missing Ethernet cable.

Felix knew that it'd be ideal if they could do this without being caught. Information was always best when it was retrieved with no one the wiser.

Turning her head around, Eva gave Felix a good view of where the portal opened up to.

Sitting in a rolling office chair was Kit. A tablet held in one hand, she was watching the tablet and the portal in equal measure.

She was surrounded by a crew of what could only be IT computer engineers who were all working on laptops that were wired into a router. That router had the Ethernet cord from the guild splitting the network feed between them.

An IT dungeon. They're all working to crack the network.

Near the rear of the room was a handful of men and women in black suits with SMGs pointed towards the portal. Their fingers were inside the trigger guards and it was clear to him they were ready to fire.

Good protocol. This portal is a way into the base as much as it is a way into the guild. We should build a portal control room where we can launch sorties out of, and defend too.

Should probably talk to Felicia about it. Her machine would need to be moved wherever we put the launch room.

"Done. Everyone log out, I'll leave the connection open as if I forgot to shut down," said one of the engineers.

Everyone else started typing furiously into their laptops. Each of them closed their laptop lid after they finished whatever it was they were doing.

The engineer who'd spoken reached out and unplugged the guild cord from the router and held it out to Eva.

"Good to go," he said.

Eva snatched the cord and ducked into the room. She was halfway in, and halfway out when someone started banging on the office door.

There were muffled shouts that were clearly punctuated by a curse.

Flinching, Eva dropped the cord. Immediately she bent down to grab it.

Smashing her forehead into the desk in the process.

Pressing one hand to her head, she grabbed the cord and then slipped it into the network port in the back of the computer.

Stepping back quickly she came back into the IT dungeon.

Kit shut the portal without any visible gesture as the sound of a door being opened could be heard.

"We'll have data in a day or two. It's all there though. Once we were in the network it was over. That was a lot easier than spending weeks trying to break in first," said one of the engineers.

Felix couldn't help but nod at that.

He could only imagine it was significantly easier being on a network line inside of the building.

"Alright. Good work. Let's get this all spun up. I'll need to let Felix know about it and send him a status report," Kit said. "You alright, Eva?"

"Yeah, I'm fine. Smacked my head pretty good," Eva said.

He couldn't see it, but Felix imagined it was probably more than a smack. The noise that came through the microphone was pretty loud.

"Alright. Good work everyone, you're all dismissed to return to your posts," Kit said. Everyone got up and immediately left, catching the intention behind her words.

Kit then got up and came over to Eva.

Felix felt his heart speed up a notch with how close Kit was to the camera.

She tilted Eva's head to one side and began to inspect the injury.

"It's going to be a heck of a bruise. We'll need to make sure Felix doesn't see it. He worries incessantly over you," Kit murmured. "It might even be worth asking Felicia to put you in one of the tanks for a few minutes."

"Huh? He doesn't worry about me. He doesn't worry about anything," Eva said.

Kit released Eva's head and chuckled softly.

"You forget I've seen inside his head. He's done quite a bit of worrying over you. He's also done a lot of things to protect you," Kit said. "You're probably the closest thing he values to what he'd consider family."

Felix felt panic rising up in his heart. If she told her what he'd done, she'd want to go on many more missions. He'd have to tell her about the changes he'd made in her and how little they cost point-wise to do.

"What? Really? What exactly—"

"This is Throne, actual," Felix said, activating his microphone and interrupting Eva. "Status report on operation Farmer."

Kit's eyes immediately flicked to the camera on Eva's head. The corner of her mouth quirked upward as she stared into it.

"This is Mole, actual. Operation Farmer was a success," Kit said knowingly. She didn't openly call him out on it, but he was certain she'd considered it. "Expect a report within two hours."

"Thank you. Throne actual, out," Felix said and closed his mic.

"He was watching the OP, wasn't he," Eva said. Felix had no idea where she made that jump in logic, but he was proud for a moment, before being horrified that the conversation hadn't stopped.

"He was. Pretty sure he still is. And he's not watching from just any camera either. Want to guess which camera? Or rather, whose camera?" Kit asked, still looking into the recording device.

"Mine? I don't... he really worries that much? About me?" Eva asked uncertainly.

Kit didn't say anything to that.

"Felix? Can you hear me right now?" Eva asked.

He contemplated not saying anything. Then realized it would only damage their relationship.

"Yeah," Felix said into her comm alone. "I'm here. We'll talk later."

"Ok. Thank you, Felix," Eva said.

Felix disconnected from the camera and went back to work.

He had a campaign to plan.

Chapter 13 - Quid Pro Quo -

Felix was staring down at the after action report on his desk. They'd finished up their operations in Tilen this morning. The national guard had shown up and taken control over the situation.

Luckily for them, the situation was already under control. All that was left to do was maintain the peace.

Legion had lost thirty-some odd security officers, two Fixers, and a single Warden.

Of those lost, everyone had signed the resurrection request to be brought back.

Felix sighed and tapped the report with a thumb.

Which means I'll be converting gold bricks for points later.

Part of the contract for resurrection was putting aside enough pay to purchase five pounds of gold. The gold was purchased in advance for the person signing the contract, and the pay was deducted on the back-end over time.

In the case of death, Felix would convert the gold to something worthless, like dirt, and use the points to resurrect people.

He planned to never be put in the same position that he was in previously, where he simply didn't have enough points to bring people back.

Setting the report to one side, Felix pulled over a tablet. He put in a meeting for himself to go into the vault, then the morgue.

"And that's that. Everyone should be up and running by tomorrow," Felix said. "Might take a bit longer for that Warden though."

Victoria looked up from the corner she was lurking in at the sound of his voice. Realizing he was talking to himself she went back to whatever it was she was doing on her phone.

Andrea made a humming noise at his side but said nothing either. She wasn't quite pleased with her role the other day. She'd been asked to split into hundreds of herself and to secure and hold both T:HQ and SC:HQ.

"I promise that next time you can have a few Others around me. I mean it. I just couldn't trust the HQs to anyone else, Andrea," Felix said, looking at her.

"Yeah?" she asked, not meeting his eyes.

"Yeah. Promise."

"Nn. Kay. I just wanted to be there for you."

"You were right where I needed you, protecting our home-front," Felix said. He meant it too.

Andrea smiled and ducked her head, nodding. "Okay."

Felix didn't want to read anything more in the action report. He'd already read it through twice.

Something like a hundred people had been turned over to the Sausage Machine. There was no looting, pillaging, or crime on Legion's part, other than taking no prisoners of those who attacked their security forces. All in all, it was a successful OP. Many of his people gained real world experience, they gained a massive amount of positive PR, gave the Heroes Guild a black eye in the media, and even managed to steal everything on their private network completely.

His office door opened, Andrea, two Others, and Victoria all coming to attention.

Only to relax when they saw it was Kit and Lily coming through the doors. No one but his inner-circle would be coming in the door in the manner they did, but it still set his guards on edge.

"Felix. I think it's time to talk about your plans to run for governor," Lily said without preamble or even so much as a greeting. She slumped down into a couch and seemed to ooze into the cushions. Kit took the seat next to her and crossed one leg over the other, looking the part of the ever present cool collected head of HR that she was.

"Alright. You ok by the way?" Felix asked.

"Tired. Very tired. I've done nothing but interviews and press conferences with interested parties," Lily said, laying a hand over her eyes.

"Oh? How'd that all end up by the way? Seems like everything went well according to the reports," Felix said, setting that very report back down on his desk.

"It did. It did go well. Even the National Guard was quite happy with us. They didn't have to do much and weren't the bad guys. I made sure that whenever we talked about them, it was always neutral or positive. They don't control their own deployment, of course, so it's not their fault."

Felix nodded at that. She really had been careful about the wording for them. He imagined it might make some people happier about it. Especially military veterans.

"The new governor is furious of course. He won't do anything directly since he took our bribe, it'd implicate us both, but he's definitely no longer a friend," Lily said. She didn't sound concerned about that. "The Heroes are in a tizzy. This isn't just a black eye for them, but an embarrassment. As for the people themselves… they're beyond grateful. In the end, our rapid response, recovery, and peacekeeping kept damage and looting quite low. Far lower than the expectation."

"Great. Good work, Lily. You'll have to tell me how to reward you for this one," Felix said. He earnestly meant it to.

"Tell me that again after I get you elected. Half of my team is already running up everything we need to get you legally ready for office," Lily said. "The other half is starting to go through the paperwork on donations and who's sending what to where. The election itself and how to run it is all Kit's."

Kit smiled and rearranged her hair with one hand. She'd cut it short late last night, and had a hairstyle very similar to what she looked like when he first met her.

"We're also digging through who the players are on the governor's spot. Pay, donations, business deals, all the like. As for running the campaign, I think that'll be rather easy. We just flood the radio, TV, and Internet with ads," Kit said. "We just do it exactly as you told Lily. Focus on the essential items that the voters want."

"Good. At the same time, I want you to talk to all local elected officials below the governor, as well as the police chief, fire chief, and local federal agent liaison. See if we can get them on board. I'm open to promises of support to them, either for public funds, private donations, or equipment," Felix said.

"Do you need their help though?" Andrea asked. "It's a voting thing. You just need to get everyone to vote for you."

"Somewhat. Votes are only half of it. I need to expand the number of people who are supporting us, and decrease the number supporting the governor. The fewer he has in his coalition, the harder it is for him to maintain power. And if we can take away the replacement backer pool he'd draw from, it makes it ever harder for him. Those people are who others turn to for direction and support. The more of them we get in line, the better. Actually, in addition to all of those people, contact their opponents, and subordinates who would be considered if their boss lost their job."

Kit frowned at that and rubbed a finger against the back of her hand.

"The people I use to take power, may not be the same people I use to keep power," Felix said. "I have to consolidate my power base almost as soon as I take office and the people who put me there will more than likely cost more to keep in my pocket than who can replace them.

"We'll also have to get an idea on the city treasury within a day or two of taking office. So let's get some new accountants ready and set to dig through a lot of shady bookkeeping. I imagine we'll end up using Legion funds at some point, but I'd rather do that as a last resort. Making the books balance for both the city and Legion after that would be annoying. And costly."

Andrea lifted her head and stared at him with a glum look. "I don't like this. Do you have to be a governor?"

"I don't have to be, but it's the easiest way to get approvals all the way around for Legion. This is a golden opportunity, and I'll leverage it for all it's worth," Felix said.

Andrea sighed and then leaned forward, resting her forehead on his shoulder. "Ok. I understand."

Felix grinned and patted her lightly on the head, taking a moment to rub her ears.

"It'll be ok. Besides, this'll be good for us. You'll probably get to be on TV at some point. You're my personal secretary after all, right?"

"Yeah?" she asked, her voice muffled in his clothes.

"Yeah."

"Felix," Kit said, getting his attention. "That all makes sense. None of it should be an issue. The real problem is going to be conflicts of interest. They're going to have a field day with us. We're opening a college after all."

"That's why we have our lovely and talented Lily over there," Felix said, indicating the lawyer. She pulled her hand from her eyes and met his gaze. "Use Miu, hire more people, do whatever you need to do. Just make sure we don't have a problem."

Lily paused for a second to reflect on that, then nodded. "Alright. I'll take care of it."

Turning her head to the side she addressed Kit. "I might need a Fixer. I'd be willing to pay the head-count to your department to have one on loan for a few months."

"Alright. I think we can manage that. Send me a meeting invite when you're ready, and we'll go through the candidate pool," Kit said agreeably.

"Oh, and Felix?" Kit asked. Felix had let his eyes fall back to the report. "You have a meeting scheduled in an hour. It wasn't originally on the books, but they wanted an interview with you. You just so happened to be listed as touring the campus since construction and refit is complete. So now you have an inspection, and an interview to give at the same time."

"Ah. Well, that's to be expected I suppose. Might be a good opportunity to announce my candidacy for the gubernatorial race," Felix said, thinking on it. "Probably. It'd set the precedent that interviewing reporters have a chance to get information that isn't released yet. Is it a female reporter they're sending?"

"They are indeed sending a girl. I think she's barely old enough to drink. Quite pretty, too," Kit said. She couldn't quite hide the annoyance in her voice.

Felix wasn't sure why she'd be annoyed, except maybe that she took issue that the news team thought Legion could be so easily manipulated.

Then again, if I actually release the information about my run for governor, that'd only feed into that belief.

"Well, I hate to encourage their assumptions, but this'll work out in our benefit. If they think sending reporters our way is to their benefit, all the better. We can scour their minds for information and find out what stories they're working on and which way they'll go with it," Felix said.

Kit snorted and then sighed. "Alright. I'll make sure one of my people is with you whenever I can."

"I could always take Eva with me," Felix said.

"She's technically not old enough to work and doesn't fall under any department. She's still in Legion school," Lily said.

Oh yeah. Still need to have that talk with her.

"Got it. Schedule a meeting with her for me later tonight as well. Probably should start talking to her about what she wants to do in the future. School won't last forever. How's her brother doing?" Felix asked suddenly. He hadn't checked on Evan in a while.

He and Eva had bonded through their shared experiences. Evan and he really didn't have much contact at all.

"Fine. He'll never be a master magician, but he's certainly above average. He doesn't have the killing nature that one needs. To gain power, one must make sacrifices," Lily said dryly. "He'll be good for Legion and you. He's lucky you can increase his power whenever you want, rather than being tempted down the road I went."

Felix shrugged at that and then opened up his terminal.

"The road you walked led you straight to me. Forgive me if I don't share your regret," Felix said. He opened up the most recent sales report from the used car dealerships that Legion owned.

Between the pawnshop and the car lots, they were making money hand over fist. The number of super powers Felix had given out to simply fix or repair things was higher than both Telemedics and Fixers combined.

The business of fixing and selling was great.

We should start buying junkyards and clearing them out. I bet we could make a killing on it.

Looking across the school grounds, Felix had a sense of déjà vu. He'd actually visited the Legion school previously, the day after the Andreas had finished construction.

The Tilen campus was a near mirror of the Legion campus. There was more visible security here on the Tilen campus, especially since it wasn't behind the same defenses the Legion campus was.

It was a sprawling complex. There were a number of multiple-story buildings littered throughout. The huge stadium in the far corner was gigantic.

"We can compare with any state college, at any level," came a voice.

Felix glanced over to find an older man in his late forties walking up to him. He'd walked past Felix's bodyguards as if he belonged, which meant this person wasn't a threat. Even the Fixer who'd been assigned to Felix's security unit only gave him a single cursory look

"My name is Sean. Dr. Sean Rithe. I'm the president of the Tilen university. I was hired by Kit," said the man, holding out his hand to Felix.

"Ah. Good to meet you. I'm F—"

"I think everyone employed by Legion knows who you are, sir," said Sean with a smile.

Felix snickered at that, shaking the man's hand. "So I continue to find out."

"I'm glad you were able to accept my invitation for a tour," said Sean, releasing Felix's hand.

"Of course. Though I must confess, we're expecting a news reporter any minute. I'm afraid that, as limited as my time is, I have to combine meetings whenever I can," Felix apologized.

"Not a problem, not a problem. I understand completely. Honestly though, I'm looking forward to it. It'll be a chance to advertise the school. I have a fully staffed faculty, empty classrooms, and a budget one could only wish for. I'll take any opportunity to bring in more students," said Sean.

Felix could definitely understand that sentiment. The rule of thumb in Legion was to put everything at maximum capacity, and then fill it. If you needed more after that, you doubled the whole thing, and repeated the process.

"Ah, and here she comes. I can't help but notice she looks young enough to be a student," Sean said, looking over Felix's shoulder.

Taking a steadying breath, Felix turned his head with a smile.

It was a young woman, a young man, and a cameraman.

Surprisingly to Felix, she was a Beastkin. A Fox breed. Or so he judged based on the brown coloring, the bushy tail, and the triangular ears. She was on the taller side of the scale for a small breed Beastkin, hitting right around five foot eight if he had to judge.

"Ah," Felix said.

They're trying to match Andrea? I didn't realize it was public knowledge.

The reporter's ears twitched at Felix's voice, her sharp hazel colored eyes locking onto him.

And apparently her hearing is phenomenal.

She was pretty, with certainly more than a handful for a chest and a waistline that gave her an hourglass frame.

He'd peg her at somewhere in her twenties.

Kit hadn't been kidding. They really had picked something they thought would hit him in the strike zone.

She was dressed in the same type of women's jacket and dress that you saw on most news reporters, which gave her a mature look as well.

Good thing Felix already had two women he was handling. That was already more than he wanted. Only a fool tried to take on more than one woman.

Even if she was amazing looking.

Truth be told, he still wasn't sure what Andrea and Lily saw in him. He couldn't even identify if it was infatuation simply due to the fact that he saved them.

"—ame's Jessica! Jessica Perreira," said the Beastkin. "It's such a pleasure to meet you."

Felix kept the smile on his face as he shook her hand. He'd missed whatever she'd said at the start but he didn't think it mattered.

"Felix, Felix Campbell. The dignified presence next to me is Dr. Sean Rithe, president of the Tilen Legion college," Felix said, releasing the reporter's hand and then gesturing to Mr. Rithe.

"Dr. Rithe," said Jessica, shaking his hand. "I'll be honest, the station wasn't expecting you to agree to the interview. Let alone to give us a tour of the Legion campus at the same time. How did you gentlemen wish to proceed?"

"Yes, yes. I thought perhaps I could give you the tour as if you were a prospective student. It would give you a good amount of footage, I imagine," Dr. Rithe said. "Unless you have a different idea, sir?"

"No. No, I'm only here to provide an interview while getting my own tour. You're the man with the plan, Doc," Felix said, clasping his hands behind his back.

Sean smiled at that and then turned and held a hand out to gesture to the campus. "Then let me show you our campus," he said.

The cameraman, who Felix had failed to catch the introduction for, fell in next to Sean and immediately began asking questions.

Jessica slid up next to Felix and looked at him. "That leaves you with me. I don't even see any of your minders nearby," she said, looking around at the bodyguards. "Only your security."

They'd discussed previously that it'd probably be better if none of his inner circle were here. It'd create a better opportunity for the reporter to think she got information out of Felix directly.

"Ah, yes. They had other duties they couldn't get out of. That's the problem with an ever-expanding corporation. Always more work, never enough hands," Felix said with a grin for the Beastkin.

She smiled back, revealing her canines. They were a bit longer than average, he thought, but then again, Beastkin weren't humans.

Thankfully he didn't have to deal with the problems behind the issue of race in Legion. Legion was a complete meritocracy. Species didn't matter.

"I'll take that as me getting lucky with you. So, Felix—can I call you Felix?" she asked.

Sean, the cameraman, and the other reporter were moving forward now on the tour.

"You can at that. Honestly, I'd prefer it, Jessica," Felix said, deciding to help perpetuate whatever false assumptions she and her station would make from all of this.

"With the campus complete, and the approvals now in your favor, what's your next step?" Jessica asked. She moved her hand to hover beneath his chin, a hand-held recorder in her grasp and recording.

"Our next step? With the college? We'll be working to increase our student body size. We've already hired an entire faculty. From president to groundskeepers," Felix said. Sean was leading them across an open area. It had a number of tables, benches, and seating areas.

"Yes, we've heard about that. There's been a lot of complaining lately from other colleges," Jessica said.

Felix chuckled at that. "I imagine. We went around and offered some of their best professors a job. So long as their demands were within reason, they were met. This institution will strive to have the best of the best in all departments," Felix admitted.

"That isn't limited to just education though, is it?"

"No. No it isn't. We made sure to hire leading collegiate coaches."

"My understanding is that you hired a number of them."

"Football, soccer, baseball, basketball. We did hire the appropriate coaches and support staff for each."

"And you made the same offer to them that you did the professors?"

"We did. Though the coaches asked for more facility and resource type of things."

"That's all rather interesting, but I can't imagine it being very profitable. In fact, from everything we gather, tuition will be almost nothing. That it'll actually be affordable, provided a student is granted a seat."

"You're right about tuition. And no, this whole thing is not profitable, and likely won't be. At all," Felix said while laughing. "At least, not for a long while. Thankfully Legion is a private company, and I own all of it. Every loss is my loss. This year is going to be brutal for the bottom line. But worth it."

Jessica didn't say anything to that, but instead shifted her hand, re-angling the microphone.

He got what she wanted, and decided to give her it.

- 365 -

"I believe in the youth of our country. Tilen will be the first to go through this campus, but not the last. There is no expense so great that it would make the education of the next generation not worth it. Have you seen how much debt these kids are being saddled with as they head into the real world? It's unimaginable. They won't be paying that off any time soon. If ever."

"Why put so much effort into educating them, if their first three years in the real world must be spent in Legion? Isn't that part of their tuition agreement?"

"It is. And those three years will be paid at market parity. They'll earn a healthy living, gain real world experience, and be given a job immediately after they graduate. Name any other college that can do that."

"That's a fair point. I can't. Between you and me though, Felix," Jessica said, her arm brushing up against his as she lifted her hand to his chin again. "What's next for you?"

There it is, and here we go.

Felix wrapped a hand around Jessica's hand and stared into her eyes.

"Let's talk off the record for a minute. A little quid pro quo conversation, and a contract between you and me."

Chapter 14 - Discrimination -

" —Campbell is indeed running for governor," said Jessica. On the screen, footage of the campus was rolling as Jessica gave her report.

"In fact, when I questioned him about that decision, he admitted that it was all due to the prison breakout. He told me the story of how his Legion security forces spent the better part of an entire day and night bringing order to the situation.

"I did some fact checking after my interview with him. Everything he said was exactly as was reported by the National Guard. I took some time to speak with residents in the area as well, and they had nothing but praise for Felix and his Legion.

"By all reports, both official and unofficial, Legion held the line and protected the citizens. Brought order to the situation. And ended what looked like it could destroy a good portion of the city."

The television switched to Jessica sitting behind a desk, smiling into the camera.

"As a Beastkin, and knowing how Legion works, I can't deny I'm curious to see how Felix will do in his bid for governor. Back to y—"

Felix turned off the screen on his phone and looked back to the crowd of students all flooding into the campus.

"And she got a promotion out of it," Kit said into his earpiece.

"Good for her. And good for us. That story was everything we wanted and more. That's some extreme level exposure for our college, and my run for governor," Felix said.

"Speaking of your bid for governor. The racists are already lining up to crucify you. Your relationship with Andrea, and endorsement from Jessica, has put them on the other side of us. Of course, they don't call it racism. Amounts to the same thing in the end," Kit said. "And then there's the fact that you own slaves."

Felix could only nod at that. With so many races running around of every different flavor under the sun, there was no question about intermingling.

The larger issue was that people couldn't escape mentalities of inferiority or superiority.

It all went back to the simple fact that some races were better at things than others. Like an all-Beastkin baseball team.

As a rule, humans were fairly average at all things. Elves, Beastkin, Trolls, Ogres, Dwarves, everything else, all had a niche they could own for themselves.

Many humans took that with a heavy helping of fear.

Felix just thought of it as being the baseline. Everyone needed baseline employees. Never a five, never a one, always a three or a four. If you were lucky, they made up the majority of your workforce.

"Nothing we can do about either situation," Felix said nodding his head at a young woman who passed nearby him.

She must have recognized him as she quickly looked away and ducked into the entry hall for the administration building.

Everyone who recognized him shied away immediately. Those who didn't sometimes stopped and talked to him, or asked for directions.

He was happy to help. It was enjoyable.

His security detail wasn't far off either, and they didn't seem to mind the people at all. Andrea was on his left, watching everything with an ear to ear grin.

"Besides, they were already after me before when they realized Legion University accepts all races. If anything, this'll just draw all those in favor of equality into my camp," Felix said. "It's doing me a favor. Less backers I have to worry about soothing. They can be part of the pool of essentials and need little in the way of effort."

"Ok, I'm tired of you talking about this. I don't understand what you mean by essentials, and the pools, and backers and—"

"Sorry. It's how I think of everything when it comes to having power. An essential is someone I need and/or must secure to get into power. In this case, I need certain people in the community to back me and press for votes," Felix said. He paused to smile and nod to a young Beastkin man who looked up from a pamphlet.

"In this case, I was never going to secure the votes for Humanity First. There was no point in ever trying to get their votes. Now, for the non-human communities, the opposite is now true. I can use them to drum votes in my direction with little or no effort on my part."

"So... why aren't they essential?"

"Because with or without my attention, they'll push for my governorship. This isn't true for those who respect the police chief. Or those who follow the business leaders of the community. Those are essential for my election, as are their backers. I'll need their support. So I have to figure out what they need or want from me, and either make that promise, or figure out who I can use otherwise."

"And that's why you wanted to know who their replacements and competitors were," Kit said.

"Yep. Unlike most politicians, I have options available to me. A competitor is a valid piece for me, when it wouldn't be for anyone else. Hence my need to determine my essentials and backers. It'll also come down to offering public policies that the general populace want to secure unaffiliated voters."

"And that's why you combined the interview with the tour. I think I understand. So... what's next?"

"We've already made promises of education, and are carrying out on that. Above board, cheap, easily readable contract, and a job. Security for businesses would be next. I have some ideas on that already," Felix said. "We do have some seniors transferring in, don't we?"

"We do. Their contract for work is only set at a year. Why?"

"Send me a list of everyone interested in security, military, or defense. Both physical and intellectual."

"I can get that," Andrea said from his side, rapidly typing into her tablet. "It'll only be a few minutes. I've been thinking about what you were saying the other day. Me, holding down the homefront."

"Oh? Thank you by the way for getting me that data, Andrea."

"Yeah. I don't want to be security anymore. I want to lead a department. Or directing security if I have to stay in that. I've been speaking about this to Victoria and Ioana. They're both on board with it. I've been making plans to pull all the Others out and put them into other positions. To learn more about Legion, and be in the know for anything you need. To truly be your personal secretary."

Felix was a bit shocked at that. Andrea hadn't really displayed any desire for that course of action previous to this.

What changed?

Calling up her character screen, Felix started to read it over.

Name: Andrea Elex	Power: Multiple Self Projections	
Alias: Andrea, Andie, Lex.	Secondary Power: Partitioned Mind	
Physical Status: Healthy	Third Power: Directed Complete Regeneration	
Positive Statuses: None	Mental Status: Happy; Determined	
	Negative Statuses: None	
Strength:	44	Upgrade? (440)
Dexterity:	62	Upgrade? (620

		)
Agility:	71	Upgrade?(710)
Stamina:	70	Upgrade?(700)
Wisdom:	81	Upgrade?(810)
Intelligence:	40	Upgrade?(270)
Luck:	53	Upgrade?(530)
Primary Power:	31	Upgrade?(3,1 00)
Secondary Power:	79	Upgrade?(7,9 00)
Third Power:	50	Upgrade?(5,0 00)

Nothing appeared out of the ordinary.

Everything was exactly as he remembered it.

"I'm curious. What drove you to this? It couldn't have just been me asking you to defend to the HQ," Felix asked. He could practically hear Kit asking the same question over the earpiece.

"I... I spent last night with all of my Others with me. No one liked what happened. That we were given a task that took us away from you. That not one of us could be left somewhere else. None of us liked it. We're going to change our role to fit what we want. We want to be your personal secretary.

"Now we will be. We have Others in almost every department, and spread throughout the ranks. We also enlisted some of the tech department to provide us with a way to communicate with one another privately. I'm... I'm going to be your Andrea-net," said the Beastkin, looking up from her tablet and meeting his eyes. "And the Andrea-net won't fail you."

There was a soft chime on his wristwatch signaling an incoming email.

"I sent you the list, as well as everyone's scores, home lives, and potential for hazard-duty assignments. I also put in a list of all business owners who were impacted by the prison breakout, and all those who were close enough that they could have been impacted," Andrea said.

Felix raised his eyebrows at that.

"Remind me to reward the Andrea-net," Felix said.

"I figured you'd eventually offer something like that," Andrea said, looking to her tablet. "I need you to sign this requisition form. It'll build out a floor specific to my Others and me only. It'll be the Andrea-net, and where we will gather to consolidate information."

"I... I see. Alright, sure, I can sign that. It makes sense," Felix said.

Turning his wrist over he opened his mailbox. Almost immediately a requisition form popped to the top of the list. He opened it and pressed the "approve" button that Andrea had attached to the bottom.

It filled out all the appropriate information automatically and sent it off to only Andrea knew where.

"Thank you, Felix. As a mate, you're good to me, and as a boss, you're better. It isn't simple infatuation. You're a good man, and you do good things, while protecting our pack. You're a good Alpha," Andrea said, peering up at him shyly.

Felix only nodded his head, he wasn't quite sure how to respond to that. Though he had to admit, it gave him a bit more insight into why Andrea wanted to be with him.

Now to build out a security plan for businesses.

"On second thought. Could you use the Andrea-net to gather up everyone you think would qualify on that list for hazard-duty, after all? I want to have a meeting with those seniors and present them with the opportunity to get into a new Legion business expansion. Security. Probably should get a Fixer in there, too."

Andrea grinned at him, flashing her bright white teeth. "Nn! Consider it done, boss."

"Kit, we'll need time to prep the seniors who volunteer and skill them. In the meantime, could you get me in front of whatever board is in control of the prisons?"

"Of course. I'll have it set up as soon as possible," Kit said.

From here on out, there is no backtracking.

And on top of everything else, there's been no news on the data we stole from the heroes. No news at all tends to mean that there is nothing to report that's favorable, or they can't even get in.

Everything is just getting more complicated.

Felix adjusted the cuff on his left arm.

Out of habit he touched the ring on his right hand. He'd taken to wearing it since the prison break a few weeks ago. It was a construct Lily, Felicia, and White had built for him.

A very simplified version of the crown, which only blocked the powers of other mind readers. The only exception to that was anyone wearing a Fixer's version of the ring.

It was a simple silver band. The crown of it was flat with a red background. Stamped in the middle of that was a black L.

Everyone in Legion was being issued one with the instructions to never take it off.

Mind reading was the easiest form of espionage. Just because Kit was the strongest, didn't mean there weren't others who could read your mind as easily.

Unthinkingly, Felix then checked Lily's charm that rested on the inside of his dress shirt. He could feel it just under his tie.

"We'll be right here," Victoria said. "Should anything go wrong, we'll be in there in a heartbeat."

Miu fixed him with her flat stare.

He knew her mind now. Knew her fractured thoughts.

She didn't want him to be alone in there and was contemplating disobeying him. Felix feared her twisted mind could rearrange his orders into whatever she wanted it to be. He'd been getting large doses of her crazy as she began to teach him hand to hand combat in a more unhinged fashion. There was no doubt in his mind she was insane.

Andrea nodded her head emphatically at his words, and the other two calmed at her unspoken cue.

Kit and Lily were already talking about something privately and had taken seats.

"It'll be fine. I'm just meeting with the prison board. This should be a productive meeting," Felix said with a smile for them.

Reaching out he turned the doorknob and opened the door. Stepping into the conference room, he found seven men and women staring at him.

The door shut with a quiet click behind him.

"Good afternoon, Mr. Campbell," said the woman in the center position.

She was older with touches of gray at her temples. She also looked exactly as he expected. Stern, pale faced, and bureaucratic.

"Good afternoon, chairwoman," Felix said with a smile.

Running down the line of men and women, he found there was an eighth chair off to the side of the table, and one chair facing those eight.

Felix moved towards that chair and took a seat, unbuttoning his jacket and letting it open at the front. He set his manila folder down on the table and then folded his hands into one another.

"We're waiting for—"

A side door opened and a man in a super hero outfit walked in, causing the chairwoman to pause.

The Hero looked at Felix, then sat down in the eighth chair.

"Ah, we're all accounted for. A representative of the Heroes Guild asked to be here to represent their interests," said the chairwoman.

"As you will. First, I'd like to have permission to record this meeting," Felix said. After a pause he produced a recorder from his pocket. Laying it down on the table he continued. "With my governor bid, I want to make sure that all of my dealings are above board, and without any type of conflict of interest."

"That is... I see no reason why not," said the chairwoman.

There was no grounds to stop him from recording the proceedings. He'd already had Lily look into it. If they had tried to shut him down, he would have recorded the meeting anyways and released it to the public at some point.

"Great," Felix said. Tapping the record button he glanced at the display. "This recording is a meeting between Felix Campbell, CEO of Legion, and the committee of prison affairs. The date and attendees are as follows—"

Felix said the date aloud and then read through the names for each of those attending. He paused, staring at the hero.

"We've been joined by one representative of the super heroes guild by the name of..." Felix paused, waiting for the man to introduce himself.

"Not needed," said the man.

Felix nodded his head.

"The representative has refused to identify himself. He's dressed in a dark black outfit with red pinstripe accents running up and down both the arms and legs. Estimated height at five foot ten," Felix continued.

Without missing a beat as he talked, Felix pulled his phone out of his pocket and took a photo of the super hero.

"I've taken a photo of the hero for my own notes on my personal cell phone—"

"You can't do that!" shouted the hero, standing up.

"I can do that. It's perfectly within my rights to take a photo whenever and however I see fit. This is not a closed door meeting, and recording was allowed by the chairwoman. Nor is this under any type of government oversight. This is a contract meeting," Felix said.

The hero continued to close in on Felix, coming around the table.

"I don't recommend that," Felix said. Miu and Victoria were both on the other side of the door. Both had enhanced senses. "You have no right to touch me, my person, or my belongings. I'll ask you to stop right there."

Apparently the hero wasn't used to someone telling him what to do. His response was anger, and what could be seen of his face was telling.

Miu appeared between Felix and the Hero. She stood stock still, her arms hanging at her sides.

Victoria opened the door and stepped through, her blade moving backwards as she prepared to lunge forward towards the hero. Andrea was a step behind her, an SMG snuggled up into her shoulder.

"Stop," Felix commanded.

Victoria came to a rest, her blade held at the ready and a single muscle movement away from impaling the Hero.

Miu stood as she had previously. Waiting for the Hero to get too close.

"Now, I'll say it again. I'm a citizen, in a meeting that is being conducted publicly," Felix said. He caught Lily and Kit entering the room and closing the door behind themselves. "You are acting in a hostile way that will force my bodyguards to defend my person. You can take your seat, and we can begin this meeting, or you can leave. It's that simple."

"You're telling me what to do!?" shouted the hero. He'd stopped two feet from Miu and was glaring down at Felix. Ignoring the petite woman.

"I am. Because you have no right to do anything to me. I'm giving you the best advice you'll ever get. And probably the only warning you'll get," Felix said.

He didn't think this situation was going to deescalate. The guild of heroes was full of people who believed they knew what was right and wrong.

He doubted this particular Dudley would hear the reason in Felix's voice.

Reaching over Miu, the Hero made for Felix's phone.

Miu snatched the man's wrist, bent it to one side, then turned his arm around with a crackling sound. She held his arm back behind his head as her left hand snaked down around his throat.

"Miu, don't kill him. Release him," Felix said.

The Hero fell to the ground, shrieking and holding his broken arm.

Sighing, Felix turned back to the committee. "My apologies. Often I find myself the target of discrimination on the part of the Heroes guild. Kit, could you get him out of here and seated in the lobby? Lily, could you notify the guild of the situation and that I'm contemplating charges?"

"Of course."

"I'll see it done."

"Great. Now, madam chairwoman, could we please move on to business? I'd like to make an offer towards taking responsibility over a number of prisons," Felix said. "We have no interest in any prisons containing super villains, as that's the domain of the guild."

The chairwoman was staring at him.

He imagined she was shocked at what had just happened. Heroes weren't supposed to lose. Be overpowered. Cowed. Beaten with logic.

"I would like to operate them as non-profit entities. Any and every penny the prisons in my care would make would be reinvested back into the prison itself. Higher walls, more guards, more rehabilitation programs, more opportunities to curb their behavior. We can't save them all, but if I can save even a fraction of them, I'd consider it money well spent," Felix said.

"Non-profit?" she asked. She seemed as if she were coming back to the world.

"That's right. I don't need to make money off the prisons. I'd rather spare the tax payers, and give them some security," Felix confirmed.

Miu was standing on his right, in almost the same position she'd appeared in. Victoria on his left. Kit and Lily had both already left to take care of the matters he'd asked them to.

Andrea was lurking behind him. He couldn't see her, but he could feel her there.

"I... we have a lot of contracts with the guild. They—"

"Failed," Felix said, interrupting her. "And the citizens suffered for it. Paid for it. Are still paying for it. Legion and I can handle all the normal prisons. The guild and their super villains can go outside of the city. It'd be best for everyone," Felix said.

He now had every intention of releasing this recording to the public later on. If the committee turned him down, it was likely that there'd be a harsh backlash from the public. Felix idly wondered if the chairwoman realized that she was effectively trapped. Taking a moment he looked into her eyes and saw anger there. Amongst her wariness and dislike of him was pure anger.

She knows.

Felix grinned at her from across the table.

Good.

Chapter 15 - Litter -

"No. You can't force it. You have to draw the runes. Each finger must take part for it to construct itself accordingly," Lily said.

Felix froze at the sound of her voice. He hadn't seen her since the prison meeting the previous day.

"I can't. It's too hard," came a young man's voice.

"Of course you can. I did it for many years before Felix adjusted my powerset," Lily said encouragingly.

Realizing that Lily didn't know he was there, Felix crept around the corner. Peering into the training room, he found Lily and Evan standing with their backs to the entry. They were both facing the far wall. It was a steel-reinforced, magically-backed monstrosity. Built for the sheer purpose of absorbing attacks.

Evan looked the same as Felix remembered.

Cleaner though, and certainly looking far more healthy.

Felix didn't spend much time with him though. Much in the same way he didn't spend much time with Lily's brother.

They had their own things going on.

So why do I spend so much time with Eva?

Felix frowned at the thought. It wasn't something he wanted to explore right now. Especially since he owed a conversation to her about what he'd been doing to her.

On her behalf.

Without her knowledge.

"Can't you just ask him to change my powers for me?" Evan complained. "Make mine just like yours? Everyone says he's more likely to do things for you or Andrea since you're his girlfriends."

"I could ask him. And he'd probably do it for me if only because I asked. That doesn't solve your problem though. You need the control and the practice. Changing your powers now wouldn't help you in the long run," Lily said. "Learning with your hands and fingers first is ideal. Master that, and I promise I'll ask Felix."

"This would be so much easier if —"

"No. Try again," Lily said firmly.

Evan sighed dramatically and lifted his hands up.

Slowly, painfully, he began to draw in the air with his hands. Runes and symbols began to glow in the air. Faint and shimmering, they were translucent.

Even Felix could tell they were not at the level of power or clarity that Lily could put out. Nowhere near close.

"Good, good. That's actually fairly accurate. Your will isn't forming it completely though. See how it wavers? How it looks misty? You have to focus as you do it," Lily said.

"Ok," Evan said. "I'll... I'll just try again, then."

"Good. Concentrate. Move through the spell sigils slowly, and build them correctly," Lily said. She demonstrated with her hands, the spellwork flowing up immediately and trailing her fingers.

It was as solid as if it were real, strikingly so. It radiated power and certainty.

As ever, it was beautiful.

Elegant.

Just like her.

Felix smiled, and slipped out of the entryway.

Andrea gave him a curious look but said nothing. In her new role as the Andrea-net, the day to day hadn't changed. At least around him, that is. He knew the floor she'd requested had already been built out, and that her Others were occupying it.

Turning down the hall, he left Lily and Evan in the training room alone and moved on down the hallway.

He didn't want to intrude on her lesson, as he couldn't imagine it helping at all. Though he thought about asking her about it later. In fact, he probably needed to get involved a bit more with the up and coming Legion members with powers. They'd need training and assistance.

Something to talk with Kit about.

Right now though, he was here to help Miu adjust her powerset, and to give her orders.

As was her fashion, she had chosen the last training room. She had also more than likely brought a lock so that she could secure the door.

And more than likely cut the feed to the cameras and audio sensors.

Taking a moment outside of the closed door into the training area, Felix gave himself a quick once over.

He had dressed in clothing he could move in. Clothes that he could add padding to if she brought it. Clothes he could rough-house in and go tumbling to the mat.

Miu was anything but gentle with him in their one on one sparring sessions. She figured he could hop in a healing tank as easily as a bath tub, and so she was essentially causing him no harm.

Even if she broke his arm.

"I'll get the tank ready," Andrea said happily. "Do you want to have lunch after this? You could come down to the Andrea-net!"

"And there'll be pancakes?" Felix asked with a knowing smile.

"Of course! But other things, too. Doctor Andrea said we need to try and balance your diet," Andrea said.

Doctor Andrea? They did requisition a medical skill book. I wonder what she's up to.

"Thanks, dear. Yeah, let's do lunch after this. I'll see you after she's done with me," Felix said.

Andrea gave him a wide grin then nodded her head once.

Opening the door, Felix stepped inside.

"Lock it," Miu called from the center of the room. She was dressed in yoga pants, a sports bra, and was barefoot. She seemed to delight in wearing outfits like this in their training now. As if it was some type of victory in doing exactly what he'd teased her about.

And that was a lesson learned. Don't make fun of the crazy person.

Felix locked the door, clicking the padlock into place as she'd instructed him. Then he stepped out into the center of the training area.

It was a simple square room, sized for lots of movement and empty.

She gave him a wide frantic smile, her eyes glued to him.

Clearly she'd already dropped her control over herself and seemed ready and eager.

"I want to adjust some of my powers after this, but first, I think we should do some hand to hand sparing," Miu said, putting her hands on her hips.

"Alright. Let me warm up and we'll—"

"No. You'll go into this cold. As if it were a fight you weren't expecting. Here I come," Miu said, then promptly charged at him.

Her fist practically blurred with the speed of the punch she threw at him.

Stepping into the attack, Felix blocked her inner forearm and drove forward with an elbow. Miu caught it easily with her free hand and shoved it to one side. Her doubled strength was enough to knock him off balance. Felix did his best to move with it, working to keep his footwork and balance in check.

Turning around he caught sight of a fist just before it caught him in the mouth. Stumbling backward under the force of the blow, Felix got his hands up.

Miu wasn't the type to let up, and dropping your guard after a hit would only invite another.

Seeing him defensive, ready for her, she stopped.

"Good. Your reflexes are getting better," Miu said.

He knew for a fact that she was incredibly talented in martial arts. Her powers made her gifted in everything and anything.

Lately she'd been training much more diligently as well. Her strength, speed, and agility were skyrocketing.

Felix sniffed, and rubbed the back of his wrist against his mouth. Looking at it he saw bright red blood.

"You hit like a freight train," Felix said. Or tried to. His mouth was actually filling with blood rather quickly.

Poking around with his tongue, he found he'd split the inside of his lip open. Sucking on it for a second he spat out a mouthful of blood onto the mat.

Cleaning crews were assigned to clean up bloody messes just like that, Felix reasoned. He didn't worry about it.

Miu's fractured smile spread across her face. She looked from him to the blood, and then back.

"I hit much harder. I've been training. I'll be your bloody blade, gladly," she said.

Felix didn't let his guard down. Instead, he started to slowly back up, trying to give himself a bit more space. Miu had a tendency to attack when he wasn't expecting it.

He figured she was practicing her own techniques at the same time, but that didn't mean he was going to make it easy.

"Speaking of being my bloody blade, I wanted to give you your orders," Felix said.

Miu began to move as well, stalking him. Though she was moving much slower.

"I want you to go through the personal lives of some people. In particular, all of my opponents who have a similar disposition as I do, who might be going after the same voters. I need to clear the field of anyone with the same base as I do," Felix said. "The goal is to do it with pressure if possible. Giving them an opportunity to drop out if we know the skeletons in their closet. After that, probably a subtle bribe from Lily. If that fails... you or a Fixer finishes it."

"So... non-human supporters. Anyone who thinks the Heroes guild is too big for themselves. And anyone promoting better security and defenses," Miu summarized.

"Kinda, yeah. I mean, everyone ascribes to some of that. But I want to make sure I'm the one pushing it the hardest. So anyone who's running it as part of their main platform would be on the target list," Felix said.

"I shall take care of this for you. Now..." Miu said, pausing.

She reached down and dragged her fingers through the blood on the mat.

The blood he'd spit up.

With shivering fingers she wiped it across the bridge of her nose and down her cheek. Then she licked her fingertips and quivered from head to toe.

Gasping, Miu closed her eyes and began sucking on her fingers. She pressed her left hand to her chest as if she couldn't contain herself.

Slowly, only after she'd cleaned her fingers completely of blood, she opened her eyes. Opened them and locked them on him.

Or to be precise, locked on what felt like his bloody mouth.

The look that she gave him was a mixture of desire, revulsion, and need.

Exactly what he expected from her.

"Let's see how you do, and what you've learned. Then we can go over what powers I need," Miu said, and then sprinted at him.

Crazy and dangerous. Thank god she's on our side.

Felix braced himself and was ready for her.

Stumbling out of the training room, he practically ran over Eva.

She was sitting next to the door, working on a tablet.

"Holy crap," Eva said, looking at him.

Felix knew he looked as if he'd gone twelve rounds in a heavy-weight bout.

Partially because he had. Miu looked diminutive but had the strength of a champion boxer.

"Training," Felix said.

"Eva said she needed to talk to you," Andrea said, smiling. "I saw you had a note that you needed to have a meeting with her so I scheduled it for right now. We can go have lunch and put you in the tank after."

Felix sighed but couldn't disagree. It was a conversation he needed to have.

"Oh, and Kit sent over an email to you. She listed the contents as secure and your eyes only, so I didn't read it."

That'd be the answers she promised me.

"Right. Thank you," Felix said. He was only mildly annoyed, but that was more about the situation than what Andrea did.

She was only doing exactly what she felt was right, he couldn't blame her.

And it was right, he just didn't like it.

"Come on, Eva. We'll talk over lunch in the Andrea-net."

"Andrea-net?" Eva asked. She got up, giving her bottom a brush off.

"Yeah. It's where all the Andreas gather and do Andrea things," Felix said. "I don't think she lets anyone else in, so consider this the only chance you're likely going to get to see it."

Andrea smiled at them when they both looked at her. "We know Eva is important to you. We'd let her in if she asked."

Felix wasn't sure how to respond to that, and fell silent.

Eva and Andrea chatted back and forth and left him out of the conversation, for which he was thankful. He was using the time he had to try and figure out how he wanted to have this conversation with her. He hadn't planned on it being so soon, but he knew this was as good a time as any.

Lost in his inner turmoil and thoughts, Felix didn't break free until they stepped out of the elevator.

Two Andreas with SMGs gave him, Eva, and Prime a once over before they even cleared the doors.

"Thank you," Felix said earnestly for their dedication to the job.

He smiled at the two Others as he followed Andrea out.

"Felix," they said in unison.

Everywhere he looked were Andreas. Working at various desks, monitors, and tables.

At the sound of his voice, ears began swiveling around towards him. Slowly, every Andrea he could see, was looking his way.

Giving them a grin, he held up his hand and waved. "Afternoon, Andrea. Here for lunch. Anyone care to join me?"

"Nn!" came the chorused response. They began closing or putting away whatever they were all working on. Chattering with each other excitedly as they put their tasks on hold.

Being caught up in the flood of Andreas, Felix and Eva were escorted to what could only be a lunch room.

Chairs and tables were spread throughout the room haphazardly. Seats were being filled quickly as certain Andreas broke off into smaller groups to eat with others.

Prime caught him at the elbow and guided him to a seat at the center of the room. Seating him, she took the chair to his right and indicated the chair to Felix's left.

"Sit right there, Eva. Food will be along shortly," Prime said, smiling widely at them both. "It's so exciting to have you here, Felix. You should eat with us more often."

Felix couldn't help but laugh and spread his hands out in front of himself. Andrea always managed to put him into a good mood somehow. "I just might do that. Especially if you can cook other foods as good as pancakes."

"Yes! We're good at all breakfast foods. Lunch… isn't that bad, but not great. Dinner is better off as breakfast," Prime said.

In other words, it's sandwiches or breakfast food. I'm not surprised in the least.

"I suppose it's a good thing breakfast is the best meal of the day then," Felix said. Looking to Eva, he found she was trying hard not to stare at him.

He figured she was probably trying to figure out what he wanted to talk about, and what had happened previously.

"Eva…" Felix said. Her eyes snapped up to him, her body going rigid. "Calm down. Nothing's wrong, first and foremost. Yes, I wanted to talk, but it's all positive. I promise."

Eva gave him a flat smile and bobbed her head. "Ok."

"So… yes. Kit's right. I treat you differently and I worry over you. Perhaps a bit too much, but I do. I'm not really able to express it in words any better than that. But there it is," Felix said.

"I kinda get it. I've been thinking on it. Is it how you'd worry over a family member? Like a niece or… or a daughter?" Eva asked.

Feeling the awkwardness settle over him like a blanket, Felix wasn't sure how to answer that.

"I don't know. I don't have any family. All my life my family members have vanished or died around me. I think so, though? I mean, it seems like it? I don't quite understand it myself," Felix admitted.

"Ok. Uhm. It feels like you worry over me the same way Evan did when we were younger. So… I think I'll go with that," Eva said.

Felix wasn't any good at this sort of thing. He could help develop people into whatever version of themselves they wanted to be. But explaining his own feelings and emotions?

Not a damn clue.

"Alright. With that in mind, and that I do worry, I've been… modifying… your powers," Felix said. His volume was low, and his speech slow.

This was much harder than he thought it would be.

"You've been modifying me?"

Felix nodded as an Andrea laid a plate down in front of him. It had a toasted sandwich of some sort on it with a small salad to one side. She laid a napkin down next to the plate and put down a tall glass of water as well.

"It's a grilled cheese sandwich with ham, tomatoes, and thousand island dressing. You'll like it. Promise," said the Andrea practically in his ear.

Then she was off and away, serving up a meal to another Andrea before he could even say thanks.

Prime was eating already, watching the conversation without saying a word.

"Yes. Well, no. They're all one use activation powers. They'll last for a period of time, then fade away. I'd have to put them back for you to use them again. Because they're single use, they cost very little in the way of points."

"What kind of powers…" Eva said. She picked up a french fry from her plate and started chewing at it. He hadn't even noticed an Andrea had dropped her off a hamburger with fries.

Eva, though, never broke eye contact. Her eyes were drilling holes through his skull.

"More or less every power that my inner circle has. I have a list somewhere in my office if you want to read it over," Felix said. He picked up the sandwich and then took a bite of it. Eva looked like she was figuring out what she wanted to say next, so he'd give that time.

Damn. Andrea was right. It's pretty good.

Felix eyed the sandwich and took another bite, enjoying this lunch quite a bit.

Whenever he tried to take lunch in the cafeteria, or a restaurant, he got beaten down with stares and whispers. Eating amongst the Andreas was weird, but not unpleasant.

"What's the activation?" Eva asked, her eyebrows drawing down.

"One is permission from me to utilize them. Which I now give you. The second is knowing the power you want to use and thinking the name of it in your head. Followed by the desire to use it. That'll activate it."

"How long does it last?"

"Not really sure. When I made the powers I was shooting for twenty-four hours, but this was all experimental at the time. Yours are the strongest, tailor-made versions of the powers I've been handing out. For all I know, you might be able to focus all of a power into a few minutes for a massive use. Or maybe slow it down and use it for months. Dunno."

Eva grunted and set down the hamburger. "Why make me a guinea pig? What if it went wrong?"

"Then you'd have a power I never authorized you to use, and you'd never have known about it. As for why you… because… I worried. I worried what would happen to you or what could happen or if someone tried to kidnap you and use you against me or—"

"Ok, ok, I got it. Just... just in the future, ask me?" Eva said, looking down at her plate.

"I promise. I will," Felix said. He felt better coming clean about it.

"So, could I take Ioana or Miu in a fight?" Eva asked

"Power to power? Definitely. Skill and experience? Dream on, kid," Felix said, grinning at her.

Andrea clapped her hands together in a happy way and then leaned forward over the table.

"You're like his daughter!" she whispered loudly. "When I have my first litter, will you be their big sister?"

Eva started at that, her hands freezing in mid air. Then she started to laugh.

Reaching out she grabbed Andrea's hands with her own. "Sure. I can do that, but it'll be a while before I call you mom."

Andrea grinned and bounced in place at the table.

All around, the Andreas were bouncing in place, clapping, or reaching over to pat Eva.

Litter?

First litter?

Chapter 16 - Rapport -

Felix watched the screen mounted above him.

He was sitting in a green room, waiting for them to call him up to take his place.

The moderator was going through introductions and explaining the format, and what everyone could expect. As far as he could tell, Felix thought everything was fairly generic.

"You're not nervous at all, are you," Lily said from his side.

"Not really. It's no different than spending a few days at a management summit. Those are pretty brutal," Felix said, still watching the monitor. "Everyone argues about the best way to do things. About why they're right and you're wrong. More often than not they'll spend more time arguing one point than talking about what their actual policy is."

"I take it your goal is to stick to your policy points then. Try and keep the back and forth to a minimum?" Lily asked.

"Somewhat. I'll look for any opportunity to debate a point when I have a superior idea that fits the voters. Otherwise, yeah. I might spend some time addressing their issues with a sentence, but nothing more than that. I'm sure a portion of the audience, both here and at home, will be watching for the drama of it. They want to see the back and forth. Watch the candidates draw blood and argue. Our goal, Legion's goal, is to get our message out."

Felix paused as the female moderator of the pair finished introductions and then started to address the audience directly.

"Commercials and ads get skipped in today's world. Record, watch later, fast forward. We'll buy just as many ads as everyone else of course, but it doesn't have the same impact it did, say, fifty years ago. This debate though... people will tune in to watch specifically. Then there will be reviews, summations, opinion papers, forum posts. No, we're here to make sure our message is loud and clear."

"And put yourself in harm's way. We didn't have to do this debate. They invited us more as part of the spectacle than anything," Lily said with a touch of annoyance in her voice.

"We'll take the opportunity for what it is. As far as danger... not really. I have my charm, my ring, and all of you," Felix said. "Besides, we both know everyone is here and on guard."

"Yes. Miu and Victoria are both in the audience, working the crowd. Legion security forces are spread out around the building in plain clothes, and Kit will be on the side of the stage," Lily said.

"Good. That means all I have to worry about is all the bloodsuckers up on the platform with me who are out for blood," Felix said.

A small light set to the side of the TV went from red to yellow.

"Ah, time to go and take my place I suppose," Felix said. Standing up he turned to face Lily directly. "Let's catch up after this. Maybe go hit a restaurant with those handy disguises of yours?"

Lily made a humming noise and smiled up at him. "Asking me out? Well. I'll take you up on that. You'll have to tell me where the courage came from as well."

"I'll tell you right now, since it's actually rather simple," Felix said, walking to the door that would lead him behind the stage. "I already know you're interested, and that you're just as nervous as I am. That makes it a lot easier to deal with."

Lily was watching him with an amused look.

"Lost my mystery, have I?" she asked.

"Not at all. Far from it, in fact. It's just different knowing it's mutual," Felix said, then left, getting the last word for once.

Ten seconds after leaving Lily in the green room, and Felix was waiting again.

He was standing atop a position marker that had his named painted on it. This was his assigned spot.

Trying to get an idea of his surroundings, Felix looked around. As a whole, the backstage wasn't very well lit and everything was dipped in shadow. He didn't know why but assumed it had something to do with lighting for the stage.

Kit slid out of the darkness from one side, coming to a stop at his side. "Did you have any further questions about my answers?"

Shit! I didn't read them. Really need to take care of that.

"You didn't read them," Kit said with a flat tone.

Is she reading my mind? Think dirty thoughts of her to test it out. Kit with short hair taking a shower and—

"No, I'm not reading your mind. You're just… much easier to understand now. After having read your mind, that is. You can stop thinking dirty things about me, unless you want to," Kit said. She held out a small deck of index cards to him.

"I know you said you didn't need them, but I made some quick note cards for you. Only a few sentences on each card. Bullet points if you will. Short enough that you can read them in a glance. I sorted it out by person with tabs on the side," she said, indicating the said tabs with a finger.

"Thanks, Kit. I appreciate it," Felix said, taking the cards from her. "Anything I need to know last minute before heading out there?"

"Not really, no. Though you're supposed to give an interview later today. It's not one of the networks that'll probably give us favorable coverage, but it's not one of the ones that'll set out to try and end us either. It might be a good time to drop the news about the prison contract if it doesn't come up here. Maybe earn you a favor," Kit said. "And if not the prison contract, then the contracts for corporations. Lily approved what I put together and we're ready to start up the program."

"Fantastic. Between you, Andrea, and Lily, Legion damn nearly runs itself. I'm not sure I could do it without you three," Felix said and meant it.

"Good thing we're not going anywhere," Kit said.

The light set in the ground next to his marker turned a solid green.

"Go get 'em, boss. You're looking rather smartly dressed and ready," Kit said, running her fingers over his lapel quickly. "It's a shame most of that doesn't count for much for those who think you're simply too young. I'll be on the side playing spy as we go. This'll be a good opportunity to go diving for secrets," Kit added, unable to keep a chuckle out of her voice. "It's a good thing telepathy powers aren't that common, otherwise the world would be run by us."

Felix couldn't help but agree with that sentiment.

Stepping forward he exited the backstage. He pressed through a slit in the curtain in front of him and stepped out onto the main stage.

Lights beamed down from above, and Felix had a hard time seeing what was in front of him.

"Felix Campbell, founder and CEO of Legion," said a female voice over the loudspeaker.

Whoever was manning those spotlight beams from hell took pity on Felix. They thankfully shifted away from sitting right on his face.

Felix could finally see the audience. It was full.

Full of people, cameras, reporters, and security.

The entire place was packed from wall to wall. There wasn't an empty chair in the building or even standing room.

Waving with a smile, Felix walked up to the podium that had been set out for him. Setting the cards Kit gave him down atop it, he looked to his sides.

He found at least half of the other candidates standing at their podiums as well. They were men and women who had been in politics for quite a while. There were also quite a few people Felix had given money to so that they'd run, even if they weren't the primary candidate.

He gave them each a polite nod of his head and a smile. It never hurt to be polite when other people could see.

Letting his eyes wander to the crowd, he focused on himself. Keeping himself calm and collected. The introductions continued on, giving Felix a chance to settle his mind.

"Ladies and gentlemen, we'll now begin the debate. First will be a simple question and answer session. Each question will be directed at one candidate at a time. Each candidate will have two minutes to answer the question," said one of the moderators. "These questions were all submitted by the audience prior to this evening. We'll go left to right to keep things simple."

The moderator picked up a piece of paper from their desk. "The first question is, in light of recent events regarding the prison break, what do you feel is the best course of action with regards to the heroes guild?"

Damn. They're not playing around. That's a pretty loaded question to answer. This'll separate those who support the Heroes from those who don't right at the start.

Felix watched, and waited. He listened and tried his best to memorize what each man or woman was saying and their position.

They all had rather bland answers. Of course they supported the Heroes guild. They wanted more oversight over zoning but didn't feel the guild was responsible at all.

On and on they went, praising the guild and extolling their virtues. While also heaping criticism on the missing Governor.

Felix thought the man was dead somewhere, the aneurysm the Fixer had prepared having come to fruition in some dark corner of nowhere.

"Mr. Campbell, your time starts now," said a moderator. Felix turned his head to the moderator and smiled.

Damnit, Felix, not the time to be losing track of yourself.

"To repeat your question, what is the best course of action with regards to the guild of heroes," Felix said, giving himself a moment to catch up. "Do I support the guild? Yes, of course. I'd be foolish not to."

"Sure have a weird way of showing that," said someone to his right.

Looking over, Felix found the speaker. It was Dave Nectar. A copper skinned short manchild with a huge ego and eyes as dark as tar.

He had to be at least forty and his vanity was clear to everyone considering how much time he clearly spent on his looks. Felix wouldn't have been surprised if he drove a giant truck and lived at the gym.

Didn't help matters with a name like Dave Nectar. It sounded like a moniker someone in the adult video industry would use.

That and seeing a woman young enough to be his daughter.

Felix wasn't unfamiliar with this pitiful man. He was a leading member of humanity first, and happily espoused the view that anyone who wasn't human shouldn't be in Tilen.

The problem was that many conservatives fell into that mindset out of fear.

In that moment, Felix realized the moderators weren't on his side, since they said nothing to the breach of etiquette.

Staring at the man for several seconds, Felix turned back to the crowd and grinned.

"Someone will have to remind Mr. Nectar about the rules later on, and teach the moderators how to moderate. I'm sure I can arrange some training at Legion University if any of you are interested. Tuition is very affordable," Felix said with a snicker.

The audience chuckled at that, joining Felix in his laughter.

"Now. I do support the guild. What I don't support is the attitude, or current procedures. Had the jail been constructed outside the city, none of this would have happened with a jail break. I'd like to ask them why it was built in the city to begin with. Was it for the convenience of the heroes? I'm fairly certain they're paid quite well by the guild to be heroes. I can't imagine they're not able to afford bus fare or a car?" Felix asked, looking around.

There were nods at that, people frowning in thought.

"For the rest of us, our taxes will be spent repairing a city that was damaged through the neglect of the current local government, and the guild. Thankfully, Legion security forces brought relief to the situation and were able to hand the reins off to the National Guard on their arrival. I applaud the Guard's efforts in keeping the peace and giving my people the chance to get back home. So yes, I support the guild. I don't support their recent choices, or procedures."

"You support them so much, you steal their prison contracts," said Dave.

"Goodness me, Dave. I think we'll have to teach you some manners if you visit the college since your parents didn't."

"To answer your point though. Yes, Legion is taking on the prison contracts that the guild was handling. We're doing it as a non-profit, and re-investing every dollar we make back into the prison system. In fact, the contract will be made publicly available after this debate," Felix paused to make sure everyone got that.

A number of people were hurriedly writing down notes.

"Legion will, of course, be hiring more guards, and possibly rebuilding some of the prisons. If you're looking for work and have the qualifications, be sure to drop a resume off with Legion. Our goals with these contracts is to offer better accommodations and opportunities to inmates, while also offering more protection to the citizens. I would like to point out that we're not taking on the super villains though. That is still the domain of the Heroes guild."

Felix took a good look around. He saw numerous heads bobbing along as they considered his words.

Good. Reconfirm our promises to the voters, and pull them in with the sweet song of logic.

"Moderators, could you actually moderate please?" Felix asked, looking to the man and woman sitting at the desk. "I'd like to donate the rest of my time so you can review the rules with Mr. Nectar. I'd hate for him to break them another time and make you look like you're not doing your job. Again. Though the offer to attend the university is open, of course."

That actually got the room to laugh darkly. Felix didn't think it was particularly funny, but he was pulling the audience into his domain.

Both of the moderators looked annoyed and caught at the same time. He could only imagine they were on Nectar's payroll.

"I... that is," said the male moderator.

"Our apologies, Mr. Campbell. I'm sure Mr. Nectar will respect the rules going forward," said the female moderator pointedly.

"I look forward to the rules being upheld," Felix said, leaning forward over his podium and resting his chin on his palm. "And you doing your job. Finally."

The audience laughed again at that.

Swagger will do just dandy right now.

"Yes... moving on. Mr—"

Felix shook his head with a smile and stood back up, tuning the moderator out. There wasn't much of a point to listening to the rest of the answers. They'd all be variations on a theme about supporting the guild, or so he expected.

Looking to his cards, he flipped through them. Each one really did have some good information for each person up here on stage with him. Most of it was repeating what he already knew. It did help to refresh his memory and reinforce what he thought he knew, which was helpful.

He was appreciative for the simple fact that Kit had done it for him without asking, despite his resistance.

Damn, her email. I need to read that after this. Read the email after the debate. Read the email. Read it.

Stacking the cards, he set them back down in front of himself, and did his best to pay attention to the answers being given.

As he'd predicted, everyone stood with the guild completely. Felix ended up being the only one speaking against them. It was odd to a degree, at least to Felix.

Maybe there's something behind that.

When they finally pop open the data on their server, it'd be good to find out if they're using some type of leverage in the political world.

The next several questions were all much softer. Taxes, environment preservation, public works proposals, and propositions on how to spend money.

None of these were controversial or even concerning. As a governor, the power of the position only stretched so far.

Then the debate portion opened up and everyone began talking back and forth about their points and positions they'd stated earlier.

Everyone, including Dave, avoided talking about the guild. They also avoided talking about the prison break. Even when Felix brought it up and reiterated his points, his plans, and what he wanted to do, no one questioned him.

If anything, Felix was thankful for that. It made him unique in his platform, and in giving tired, scared, and frightened citizens an answer.

"And now we're going to ask some questions directed at individual candidates from the audience," said the female moderator.

Felix blinked and looked up from the podium. He'd been wondering how they'd come at him next. This seemed tailor-made for that purpose.

"Mr. Campbell, I'm afraid that the vast majority of the questions were directed towards you," said the male moderator. "We—"

"I'll answer them all," Felix said with a wide smile. "Please, let's begin."

Give me all your air time. I'll take it all.

The moderators stared at Felix, stupefied. Either at his answer, or for interrupting them.

"I'm more than happy to answer all of them. Begin whenever you're ready," Felix said, making sure it was clear to everyone watching he would do it.

The moderators looked at each other and then back to Felix.

"I don't think we could do that," said the female moderator.

Felix shrugged and held up his hands.

"But we'll definitely start with you," she continued. "The first question we have is, what are your feelings regarding non-humans? Do you feel you can separate the issues humanity faces, given that you're in a relationship with a Beastkin?"

Felix nodded his head. It was definitely a question he was expecting.

Though he'd half expected them to start with slavery, really.

"First, I'll address the unasked question. Yes, I'm in a relationship with a Beastkin," Felix said. He had no reason to hide it, and didn't have a desire to either. If anything, the public admission would only cement his relationship with the backers he wanted.

"Now to the actual question. Our state itself is made up of many different racial profiles. In fact, we have one of the most diverse racial makeups of any city, here in Tilen. This is especially true for the more rural areas, where certain humanoids can excel at whatever profession they choose. That doesn't mean we should be sending them all to live somewhere," Felix said, emphasizing his point by hitting the podium with his palm.

"All citizens, regardless of race, are given the right to vote. They do, however, have different needs. What proposals would work for, say, a Troll, wouldn't work for an Elf. Or a human," Felix said, leaning over his podium again. "My feelings are pretty straightforward. Are you a citizen, or not? If you're a citizen, you're due all the rights anyone else gets. But can we make everything to accommodate everyone? That's another problem entirely. I can't exactly get an Ogre a motorcycle that'd fit him without it being custom made."

Felix took a breath and looked around at the audience. "The answer to that one is more to do with making sure that businesses aren't segregated, or treated differently. A shop that specifically caters to Ogres or Trolls could and should be opened anywhere they wish."

"And is that how it is in your communist state known as Legion? Everyone is the same in the eyes of Felix?" Dave asked, the disdain practically dripping from his lips.

"Everyone is indeed equal in Legion. There are no benefits given for being any race. No preferential treatment of any sort. It's a meritocracy, and everything is earned," Felix said immediately. "Legion pays salaries to all of its people, we subsidize all of their living expenses, and offer them the ability to shop at Legion owned stores. We don't require it... but it's certainly hard to beat our prices. I shop there myself. The price on white bread is outstanding."

That got a chuckle from the audience.

Felix grinned and looked to the moderators. "Next question please. I'm delighted to address our state tonight. Though, I really do worry about those rules. Invitation remains open, of course."

Chapter 17 - Understanding -

By and large, Felix was pretty happy with the outcome of the debate. He'd successfully turned it into the Felix Campbell and Legion show. Their points and platform were obvious, and defined.

He'd even managed to set himself up as a rival for the lead contender for what he'd consider his opposition party. When it came down to it, being the rival of the lead contender to a party almost always gave you more credibility.

Other than feeling worn out, Felix felt successful.

Staring out the window, he could only wonder what would be coming next.

Other than that interview tonight.

Or the Email!

Felix sat back in his seat in the back of the sedan. Reaching to the side he opened up his messenger bag and pulled out the tablet that Andrea had purchased and set up for him.

He didn't want to try and read the email on his phone, he imagined this might be a rather lengthy email.

Tapping the device on, entering his password, and navigating to the email interface, he found her email. It was marked as important, filed to the "read me" section Andrea had set up, and unread.

Opening it, Felix began to read.

Hi Felix,

Among your many questions, the predominant one was why didn't I try to escape from the guild. The answer to that is... well I want to say it's complicated, but it's not.

I was being selfish. Selfish and not very understanding of you.

Or Legion.

I felt like as Augur, with my powers, I could have done so much good for the world. But only because of all the changes you made to me. Only because you made my life so much easier. That you fixed what was wrong with me.

For all of the good I've done in Legion, and the community, I felt like I could do more as a hero. And I selfishly wished to go back to that life, despite everything that had happened.

Then you were there. Fighting your way through a base filled with super heroes to get me. To take me back from what you believed was forced captivity.

I didn't know what to do with myself, except that I knew I didn't want you to die. So I involved myself at that point.

As for how I was able to act... the crown didn't work on me. If I had to guess, either your ownership of me, or the slave magic, were too much for the crown to overcome. It was just a really heavy hat.

I'd imagine that it doesn't work for anyone in your employ, under contract, or slavery. Your power might simply be too strong.

For everything that happened after that... it was too hard to talk about. To discuss. To try and work things out with you, because I couldn't see a way through it.

Then you opened your mind to me. Let me see everything from your point of view.

You were right. I couldn't function without being able to see behind the curtain. Not everything is so easy for the non-telepathic. But you cut right to the heart of it and solved it.

For me.

And the only thing I saw in your mind, was everything that you'd been telling me.

Minus the shower thoughts.

I'm unsure of how to express this, so I'll say it directly.

I'll never be Augur again. But that's by choice. Augur ceased to exist when she was turned into a corpse and sold. And I'm comfortable with that. She wasn't very fun to be.

Who am I now is different.

I'm Kit.

I'm Legion.

I'm one of many.

I'm yours.

Felix closed the email and frowned. She didn't answer all of his questions.

But she did answer the one he actually needed an answer to.

He needed to get the crowns out to Tilen and do some tests. Have a test study and do some variable elimination to determine what it worked on, and didn't work on. Knowledge like this would be ideal to plan how to handle whoever it was that was making these things. If there was no fear of the crowns, then it was a trump card to hold on to.

There was no hiding the warm and fuzzy feeling he felt bubbling up in his chest. Kit had definitely put to rest any concerns he had with that email.

Everything she said made sense for her personality as well. He found no fault with it, or her logic. He imagined that many might have made a similar choice in her position.

Chauffeur Andrea opened the driver's door and stepped in.

"Hi dear!" she said, looking at him in the rear-view mirror with a wide smile.

"Hello," Felix said, grinning. "Are we all set?"

"Nn! Victoria and Miu were going over some preparations for your interview later with Lily," she said. She adjusted her mirror and then went through a systems check for the car.

Chauffeur Andrea took her responsibility seriously. He hadn't been driven by anyone else since the Andrea-net went active.

Andrea Prime opened the rear driver's side door and slid in next to him. At the same time, Miu did the same on the right.

At first she seemed hesitant, having to be so close to him. She met his eyes and he gave her a small nod to her unasked question. Her lips twitched, and she pressed her shoulder, leg, and knee up to his, getting in close to him.

Victoria opened the front passenger door and got in and gave him a glance, then a hooded look for Miu.

"Vicky lost!" Chauffeur Andrea said from the front. "So Miu gets to sit next to you."

For his part, Felix only shrugged.

"Ready to go?" Andrea Prime asked.

"Let's hit the road. If possible I'd love to use the restroom and get a bite to eat before the interview," Felix said, nodding his head. "One never knows what's going to be thrown at you. Best done with a meal and a restroom break."

Chauffeur Andrea said something into the microphone on her lapel and then eased the car out into the road.

Felix smiled politely and waited for the next question.

"—brings us to your life. Your family specifically. How about you tell us about them?" asked Charles. He was an older man with brown hair fading to white. His brown eyes were soft, and the way he dressed matched a statesman's air.

He had a history of sometimes going off on wild tangents, but those were few and far between. Mostly in his youth. Charles was extremely well respected in the television interview circuit.

"It's a rather simple story. No brothers, no sisters, one paternal uncle. A very small family full of only children, really," Felix laughingly said.

"My parents were out of the picture at a young age, and I ended up in the care of my uncle and aunt. They took me in rather than make me a ward of the state thankfully. It was a whole mess of paperwork at the time," Felix said. He could remember his uncle signing for what seemed like hours at a time.

Looking back from an adult's perspective, it was more than likely only minutes.

"Much later, they went on a trip and I haven't seen them since. The estate is moving forward with a death in absentia. At the time I felt it was a betrayal. How dare they say they were missing and probably dead. As if they'd given up hope on them."

Felix frowned and looked at the ground.

"In retrospect it was a good call. I'd have waited far too long. Believing that if I somehow moved forward with the case, I'd be admitting they were gone."

"I can definitely see how that'd impact a young man. You were in your twenties at that point?" asked Charles.

"That I was. Twenty something and feeling like the world was collapsing down around me. That the world was conspiring against me. I took a job at a fast food chain that'll remain anonymous thank you," Felix said, smiling for Charles and then the audience. "Let's just say I had time served."

A number of audience members smiled, laughed, or nodded their heads. Quite a few people had similar starts in life at the very same chain, he imagined.

"Then Skipper came," said Charles.

"Then Skipper came," Felix repeated. "The strange part is… nothing changed in our daily lives. The only glaring thing was that Heroes were on the run instead of Villains, and most vices were legal."

"That seems fairly hard to believe," said Charles.

"And yet there it is. And here I am. I travel freely back and forth between Skippercity and Tilen without a concern."

"But this was when you founded Legion, isn't it?"

"It is. I took out some money, scraped everything I had together, and made a purchase from what was now called the grey market. I leveraged that purchase into the great river of trade and began to build Legion, brick by brick," Felix admitted.

"Done through also purchasing slaves, and using their powers and bodies to set your foundation," Charles said.

Felix didn't quite like the way he'd phrased that, but it wasn't wrong either.

"I bought anyone the government was trying to get rid of, that I felt I could save, help, or use. A large number of those people are now free, working here in Tilen for Legion. Slavery of course isn't legal here, so that all expired the moment they crossed the borders with me."

"And they stay with you."

"They stay with me. I've had people leave Legion. But that's to be expected with any large corporation," Felix said.

"We've actually talked to a few people who left about Legion. No one is willing to say anything about it at all. Even when pressed or coerced. They won't say anything. Or they can't," Charles said.

A warning sign began to flash inside of Felix's mind. He definitely didn't think this was going into territory he liked very much.

That was a good amount of digging for what was supposed to be not much more than an interview.

"Legion is a family. I'll be happy to confirm there is a non-disclosure agreement between everyone who joins Legion and the company," Felix said. He kept his answer much shorter than his previous answers up to this point.

The interview should be winding down, and Felix was feeling a bit paranoid.

"Speaking of family. When we were looking into yourself and Legion, we found a number of connections between you and a known loan shark by the name of Dimitry," Charles said.

With his heart lurching in his chest, Felix smiled and nodded his head, doing his best to look unconcerned.

That's a loose end if I ever had one. I need to get that taken care of. Immediately.

"I won't deny I know the man, because I do. I borrowed money from him. A personal loan. It was part and parcel of how I founded Legion."

"More than that though, isn't it? My understanding is you actually do business with them directly. Buying guns, selling information, helping each other?" Charles pressed.

"Goodness, no. Our dealings have been very limited since I borrowed the money. Mostly it's repayment of that loan, and borrowing more money," Felix said with a laugh. "Do I look like the type to be having dealings in those kind of sectors? I think I'd lose my mind if I was in a situation like the one you're describing."

Charles didn't immediately respond. Instead he turned to the monitor between them on the wall.

"This footage was recorded during the prison break out. The camera was confiscated almost immediately and so this is all there is," said Charles.

The monitor popped on, and on came a cell phone video. It started after a second and the sound picked up.

It was kept low to the chest, filming upwards as they walked. Clearly it was being recorded without the Legion security forces knowing.

The dark uniforms that looked somewhere between soldiers' uniforms and SWAT team outfits were everywhere. They were funneling, checking, assisting, and guiding the citizens.

"This way everyone. This way," called a voice off camera. "If you have elderly or children that need special accommodations, please approach anyone in a uniform for assistance."

"Thank god," said a woman to the camera holder's right. "Thank god. We're safe."

There was no aggression on the part of the security forces. Everywhere the camera was directed, Legion was actively working to help and assist citizens.

Felix knew the reason for that. The Fixers were scanning minds and tagging people. Security really only had to protect civilians and work the lines.

Behind the cameraman was a shout.

Every single member of Legion froze for a second, then as one lifted their weapons and converged on an unseen target.

"Everyone get down!" shouted multiple voices from Legion security forces.

The crackle of gunfire was immediate after that and everyone dropped to the ground.

The camera was cradled tightly, and the view half obscured.

Looking like something out of a sci-fi movie, a suit of futuristic looking armor stepped into frame.

Shit.

It had a raised pistol, fired twice, and continued off frame.

Twenty seconds later and Legion security was rushing back into positions.

"Don't panic," came a raised but calm voice. "The situation is under control. Everyone please look around you for anyone wounded. If there is, please flag down a security officer immediately."

The cameraman stood up just in time to see the suit of armor heading back up the library steps.

All around the courtyard, soldiers with pistols, bags with a red cross on them, kevlar vests, and helmets simply appeared. They began to fan out, taking hold of anyone who had even a minor injury, and vanishing as soon as they got a hand on them.

"Oh thank god. Thank god," said the same woman's voice.

A hand came into view and snatched the camera away, and the recording cut off immediately.

Felix tried to look pleased and nodded his head. Looking to Charles he waited.

"I'd like your thoughts on that video," Charles said finally.

"It was the prison break, as I'm sure everyone could tell. That was the Legion processing center. Where Legion security forces were acting out of," Felix said calmly, confidently. "As you saw in the video, we did our jobs quite well that day. Loss of life, possessions or property was minimized. That was an incident where a large group of prisoners were trying to infiltrate into the citizenry and escape. They were identified, neutralized, and removed. Not a single civilian was lost in that brief encounter, though a few were injured by stray rounds fired from the prisoners."

"And that armored soldier?" Charles asked.

"A member of Legion. The suit is something we're testing. It's part of a few initiatives we're working on," Felix said.

"Were the people who appeared and disappeared the same thing?"

"That they were. Very similar in scope, but different function."

"What happened to all the wounded prisoners?"

"There were no wounded. Legion security forces are all marksmen certified with their weapons before they're allowed to carry them on duty. Unfortunately, all of their shots resulted in fatalities," Felix said.

And the ones that weren't immediate were turned into sausage after having their souls pulled out.

"The bodies never turned up. There are a number of missing prisoners," Charles said. It wasn't really a question.

"I can't speak to what happened after Legion quit the field. We left the corpses behind to be policed and recorded appropriately," Felix said. It was the truth, too. Anyone killed then and there was left on the field. Only the wounded were carted out to be used.

"The National Guard did confirm that. There were even some super villains you left for them."

"Indeed. Legion security is extremely well trained, outfitted, and ready. We're not just a pawnshop, anymore. Not at all. We're in the automotive industry. Primarily used cars. Antique identification and restoration works too. And we're always looking to explore other options," Felix said with some pride.

"As has become readily apparent as of late. I even saw a news report that you've been purchasing every junkyard willing to sell for a reasonable price," Charles said.

"I can't deny that, and won't. It's nothing secretive. We're in the business of restoration. Why does it have to be limited to cars and antiques? Why not anything and everything that we can? It's a simple enough shift of scope. And with today's online market, it isn't as if we can't reach a market. We'll have our own shop, and make it available to other online retailers," Felix explained.

He hadn't intended on revealing that. At this point though, he honestly thought this interview would get heavy ratings for the clip of the prison break alone.

Felix had every intention of making that work for Legion's benefit.

"That makes a lot of sense. I can definitely see the appeal," Charles conceded.

"I mean, take it a step further," Felix said, leaning forward. "Instead of dumping your old product at the junkyard, as you would normally do, what if you could simply have it repaired there? Cheaply, too. Much more so than buying a new item, or having it refurbished."

"I'm pretty sure that'd invalidate any warranty the product had," Charles said with a small upturn of his lips.

"Oh, and then some. But if you were going to throw it away anyways..." Felix stopped, leaving his open-ended statement hanging.

It was easier to let people finish the thought on their own. It never hurt to do it, and it always helped with the adoption of new ideas.

"I... yes. I see what you mean. Well, I think that's all the time we had. I wanted to say thank you for coming out and talking with us. I know you're a rather busy man. Especially with your bid for governor," Charles said, leaning over his desk and holding out his hand to Felix.

Uh huh. You were hoping to watch me fall on my face.

Felix smiled and took Charles' hand in his own and gave it a good shake.

I'm going to buy this broadcasting station eventually and put your show on at two in the morning, and have it recorded at three in the morning.

Chapter 18 - Blood Price -

Felix got into the car and waited long enough for Victoria to slide in next to him.

Andrea Prime was on his other side, Miu in the front with Chauffeur Andrea.

"Andrea," Felix said. "Get me a meeting with Dimitry. Use our secure channels. Tell him we'll meet him in his office at the time. I'll need a Fixer or Kit, Victoria, and one of your Others."

Miu turned around and stared at him.

Asking me if you can go, huh? Not this time, my little psycho.

"Miu, I need you to get ready to infiltrate the police station that undercover cop of ours debriefs at. I want to know what he's been reporting. You might need to take a Fixer with you, so be sure to take one who can keep up with you," Felix said, meeting her stare dead on. "Let me know when you're ready to run your operation."

She blinked then nodded. Turning towards the front of the car, she seemed content to know she had her own mission for him.

"I'll take care of it, Felix," Prime said from his side, rapidly typing something into her portable terminal. He couldn't remember when she'd switched from her tablet, but it seemed like it was working out better for her.

In fact, now that he looked at it, he was a touch envious. Apparently Felicia had built her a wrist communicator that doubled as her phone, and light terminal entry with an actual display.

Andrea must have felt his eyes on her as she paused, her ears flicking to one side and swiveling towards him. Then she tilted her head and looked up at him shyly.

"What is it?" she asked.

"Nothing. Sorry, thanks, Andrea. Be sure to include one of your more combat oriented Others with me. You'll have to stay put and man the ANet for me. Keep me looped in. I can't deny the ANet has been extremely beneficial and helpful."

"I will…" she said, her cheeks reddening slightly.

"Good. Alright. Let's get back to Tilen HQ," Felix said. Pulling out his own light terminal from his bag at his feet, he flipped it over and opened up the email section.

He needed to get Lily working on a contract that'd work to cover a third party vendor as if they were Legion, with all the same protections a normal member would have.

Legion had a leak, and he had to plug it.

One way, or another.

Kit ripped open the portal directly into Dimitry's office. Victoria, a combat geared Andrea, and a Fixer in a Legion Security outfit darted through.

Ten seconds later someone called back.

"Toss through the bag. Got ears," Andrea called.

A second combat Andrea picked up a bag off the ground. Taking a few steps forward she heaved it through the portal.

Got ears meant that Dimitry's room was bugged. Either the policeman they'd turned had wriggled out of his contract, or Dimitry had picked up another spy.

One way or another, it'd be fixed tonight.

Felix had erred here. He had let something into Legion that wasn't part of Legion.

All because he wanted to have an ally.

Shaking his head, Felix couldn't help but berate himself again. This was all his doing, and it was up to him to get it resolved immediately. If this had gone any further south it could have cost him his governor run.

A minute passed in near silence.

Kit watched him from across the room as she held open the portal. She was concentrating on it, making sure to hold it steady.

I should up her control over that or something. That or have Felicia put a second gate creator here in Tilen. Having it in Skippercity is nice… but not so useful when we're working out of somewhere else.

As if she could hear his thoughts, which she couldn't he reminded himself, she cracked an eye open and gave him a smile.

Closing her eye she went back to holding the portal open.

"We're clear," Andrea said.

Ducking into the portal, Felix stepped into Dimitry's office. Victoria was standing near the door, Andrea in the corner of the room, and the Fixer right in the middle.

Dimitry was sitting behind his desk, glaring at the remains of what looked like listening devices on his desk.

"Clear, Kit. I'll flip you a text when it's time to come back," Felix said, looking back through the portal.

She opened her eyes, nodded her head, and the portal winked out as if it had never existed.

"Evening Dimitry," Felix said.

The loan shark looked the same as ever. A little older maybe. Touch of gray in his temples.

He was aging and fast.

"Felix," Dimitry said, looking up. "While I'm thankful for this," he said, indicating the devices. "I can't say it's good to see you. You never come without mixed news."

Felix had to nod ruefully at that. "True."

Taking the seat in front of Dimitry's desk, Felix sat down and got comfortable.

"Found 'em," the Fixer said.

Felix glanced back at the woman and lifted a hand. "And?"

"Skippercity government spy. Slipped in a month ago. Been feeding information to the police, Skippercity, and… the guild of Heroes," said the Fixer.

"Pop a vessel and let them die easy," Felix said with a sigh. He put his attention back to the loan shark. "Suppose that answers that. I wasn't sure what was going on, but that does explain a few things."

"Done. Everyone else is clean, though not entirely loyal," the Fixer said.

"That's not unexpected," Dimitry said, shaking his head.

"No. It isn't, but we're here to fix it," Felix said.

"Here to kill me then?" asked the loan shark. He seemed resigned. "I've been wondering if you would since the incident with the money drop."

"Huh? Why would I? That had nothing to do with you, and everything to do with a robbery," Felix said dismissively. "No, I've come to make you a job offer. You'll not be part of Legion directly. You'd be more of a… satellite organization. Same benefits as Legion, actual pay structure, non-disclosure agreement, and restrictions. Just not Legion in name."

Dimitry lifted his eyes and met Felix's. "And why should I turn over my organization to you? Hm?"

"Because I don't want your organization. I want it to remain as it is, but to support it, and know that it isn't a loose end for me," Felix said. "Right now, it's a liability for our relationship. The moment we turn your organization into a branch of Legion, you can expand."

"I can't even begin to believe that this would all come without strings. So let's skip to the part where you tell me what I can and can't do if I took your offer," Dimitry said, leaning back in his chair.

"Well. Since everyone would receive a salary, I imagine you might not need to go so deeply into criminal enterprises. At least, not the petty things. I'd say your only limitation is… don't bring down too much heat. Operate as you see fit, and be sure to benefit Legion whenever you can," Felix said.

There was a thump from the other room, followed by some muffled voices.

"Ah, that sounds like you're going to have a visitor in a moment," Felix said, looking backwards to the door.

"Yes," Dimitry said flatly. Getting up he walked to the door and opened it. "What is it?"

Someone said something back that Felix couldn't quite make out.

"Okay. Dump the body. We'll send his stuff to his widow," Dimitry said, and then shut the door. He laid his forehead against the wooden frame.

"That was the traitor?" he asked.

"Yes," said the Fixer. "They were hired and directed expertly on how to infiltrate your organization. I couldn't get much in the way of who ordered them, as it seems their mind was cleaned. That was the only one so far though. There may be others, if not everyone is here."

"I... yes. Not everyone is here," Dimitry said. "I have your word on all that, Felix? Exactly as you said it?"

"That you do. I even brought a non-standard Legion contract. Specifically for you and your people. It's not written in lawyer speak. It's fairly straightforward. Though I do have to have you sign a non-disclosure agreement before you see the contract," Felix said.

"And I'll be the head of this... satellite... organization," Dimity said, unmoving from his place at the door.

"You would be. You'd answer only to me," Felix said.

Dimitry fell silent.

Felix let it grow. Silence was his weapon. His friend.

Ever his ally.

"I'll sign," said the newest member to be of Legion, and the first employee of the Legion's satellite group.

"Probably should come up with a name for your department." Felix paused to open his messenger bag and pulled out the non-disclosure and set it down on Dimitry's desk. "There's the first one."

Dimitry came back over to his desk. With a heavy thud, he sat down in his chair and picked up a pen. Without reading the document, he signed, and slid it back across the desk.

"Good, good. And here's the contract," Felix said, picking up the NDA and replacing it with the contract they'd drawn up for Dimitry.

Again, Dimitry signed the paper without bothering to read it. Sliding it back towards Felix, Dimitry slumped into his chair.

"What's next then, boss," Dimitry said.

Felix smirked at that, and then attempted to make the changes to Dimitry he'd called "The Buildup" package.

Power Upgrade: The Buildup Expand for List (Over 100 items)	Upgrade?(180,250)

He already knew what the cost was to make the changes he wanted. It was a cost he didn't want to pay since he'd had to convert a number of gold bars to dirt to get the points to make the change.

"As part of the contract you just signed, I'll be modifying you to a degree," Felix said, looking up at Dimitry. He could have just made the change without worrying about it. In this case, Dimitry had signed without even knowing what he was signing.

"I... what now?" Dimitry asked.

"Modifications. I'm going to give you some super powers. Strength, extra speed, low grade regeneration, resistance to injury, slow the aging process, and boost your ability in general. You'll also go back to about thirty-two years in age," Felix said, giving the man the summary version of the extensive list of changes.

"You can do all that?" Dimitry whispered. For the first time that Felix could remember, Dimitry sounded unsure.

"Indeed, and you're about to go through it. Brace yourself, I understand it's a bit of a... thing... I guess. Anyways, here we go."

Felix hit the button.

Dimitry went limp and slid out of his chair, curling up into the fetal position on the ground.

Raising a brow, Felix turned his head to Andrea. "That's done then. Let's start pulling everyone in one by one and having them sign. Once they sign, we'll give them their non-Legion Legion rings. If anyone disagrees or doesn't sign... well..."

Felix shrugged his shoulders instead of concluding his sentence. He didn't have the luxury of time. Which meant he couldn't be gentle about this.

So many things to do, and never enough time.

"Of course," Andrea said, hesitation in her voice. "Though... when we're done... can we go get some food? I'm hungry."

"Yeah. We can do that, Andrea."

Two hours, a mass of signatures, and a single death later, and Dimitry's entire organization was incorporated. Felix left instructions for him on how to recruit new people.

He also gave Dimitry a desktop terminal that was encrypted and locked for Legion personnel, and was part of the Legion network. This was to be how he kept in touch without making it obvious. Felicia and Mr. White had taken extreme precautions to protect the terminal from outsiders, theft, or hacking.

As far as Felix knew, it was one of a kind and wasn't likely to be replicated without serious effort. Dimitry was the only one off network, after all.

Both Skippercity and Tilen were connected through a "portal network" that Felicia had installed. They were linked to the same network, closed off from the outside world, and completely hardened. The only way to access the Internet was using specific terminals put in place with that purpose. To Felix, it was a ton of infrastructure he was glad to have, but had no idea how it had all come to be.

That's proper management though. Isn't it? Build, train, and enable your people to make executive decisions without you. To work towards the betterment of the company, without input.

Leaders are what I need, not grunts.

Sighing Felix stared out across the buildings below him. The Skippercity HQ had been brought up to the same height as the Tilen HQ building. Everything was mirrored both ways. The buildings were twins of one another.

A calling card, is the way Felicia put it. A Legion HQ would always be noticed.

And a wonderful distraction since we all live underground.

A breeze blew up over his shoulders and Felix hunched into his jacket. Miu had told him to be up here. She had accomplished her meeting and was bringing what he'd asked for.

"It's cold," Andrea said from beside him. She pressed her side up to his and then pressed her icy hands to his sides.

"Damn, your hands are like a freezer," Felix complained. He didn't push her away though. It was only her and him up here right now.

Kit was only a text and a portal away.

Felix had realized that she out of everyone was best utilized as a hub, and asked her to remain at Tilen HQ. At least until Felicia could put in a secure portal network that could be accessed from outside either HQ. One that would protect itself from someone getting hold of a portal device and using it against them.

For now, Kit was their impromptu taxi service. Being used to send and receive Legion agents from all over the country.

"I don't like Fall. Or Winter. I like Spring and Summer," Andrea whined.

"You can go inside. It's just Miu," Felix said. "She's not going to hurt me in any way."

"Nn... I know... I just want to be with you," Andrea said, her head dipping down and pressing into his shoulder.

Felix couldn't help but smile and lifted a hand to lightly scratch at the base of her ears. "Ok. Promise me you'll head inside when you truly get cold though. No sense in both of us freezing."

Before she could respond, Andrea's head lifted up, her ears twitching around almost randomly.

Her hands slipped to her waist and came back up with a pistol. She aligned the barrel with the sky above them and began tracking something.

"What's wrong? You're all—"

Felix was interrupted by something flashing down from above. He saw a flash of Miu, and realized she was coming down fast. As if she'd jumped from something above them or teleported there.

She crashed down onto the roof, the thump of her feet making him wonder if she'd just broken her legs or ankles. She fell to one knee casually, as if landing as she did had been nothing more than a hop.

A second later a Fixer landed behind her. Apparently the power this one had chosen for travel had been flight.

The Fixer was dressed in standard Legion security combat attire with the Fixer rank insignia affixed to their collar.

"Sir," the Fixer said.

Miu stood up only after catching Felix's eyes with her own. Her hands moved to a sack attached to her belt. Unfastening the drawstrings, she reached in and scooped out its contents. With a wet splat, she dropped a severed head to the ground between them.

Eying the bloody spectacle, Felix realized it was the cop they'd turned. Brought into fold as it were.

"He was using every possible avenue to press the bounds of the contract. He was slowly letting information out about the Legion. Not enough to be harmful, but that's the reason why the Skippercity agent was there," the Fixer said. "Or that's my guess. They'd gleaned some information from the police and used it as a line to trace back to us."

Nodding his head, Felix stared at the bloody head. "That contract wasn't as enforceable without constant watch, or so Lily feared. Thank goodness she's improved them since then. Did he suffer?"

"It was quick," Miu said softly. "He felt no pain. The body is disposed of. He didn't fight. I spared his family."

"Good," Felix murmured. "Tonight has been a real cluster-fuck. At least we caught it now, rather than later in the campaign."

The Fixer rechecked his SMG and unloaded the magazine, and expelled the chambered round. "Permission to retire, sir."

"Go. Thank you for your work tonight. You and your department are a credit to the Legion," Felix said.

It wasn't idle words either. The Telemedics and Fixers were indispensable to Legion.

And the next group, even more so, Felix thought, looking back up to the skyline as the Fixer left.

He needed spies. Spies that could slip in, read thoughts, spy, and get back out safely.

Wraith had been a starting point. Miu the logical progression for a single individual. Now he wanted a team of covert operation specialists.

They were planned to have invisibility, limited mind reading, teleportation, enhanced agility and dexterity, and some skills one would associate with thieves and pickpockets. More than likely he'd add more training to that, but that was his starting point for now.

"Felix," Andrea said, lifting a hand and pointing to a distant speck on the horizon.

That spec was rapidly becoming a dot, then a smear, and suddenly two bodies.

There was no mistaking that they were moving at maximum speed, and heading straight for Felix's current position.

Turning his wrist over, Felix laid his thumb on the screen. Activating, it cycled for a second before bringing up Kit's contact information.

Miu and Andrea both got in front of him, drawing their weapons. Miu pulled out a short sword from a sheath he hadn't noticed previously, Andrea snuggling her SMG up to her shoulder.

A woman and a man came into view. The man was dressed in bright yellow and grey. He looked the part of a Super, though that'd be strange since they were outlawed here in Skippercity.

The woman was dressed in very expensive looking clothes, and was wearing a thick fur coat.

Coming to a halt at the edge of the building, the man stepped onto the edge. Stepping down from the man's side, the woman looked at Andrea and Miu, then dismissed them. She had eyes for Felix and Felix alone.

He gave her a quick once over, finding her neither attractive nor unattractive. She simply… was, with brown hair and blue eyes, average height, and average build.

The picture of mediocrity.

She stared at him for long seconds. Felix stared back at her, unperturbed, waiting.

"In every instance I check, you say nothing until I do. And if I do anything other than talk, you summon Augur," said the woman. "You're annoying."

"A—"

"Skipper," said the woman, crossing her arms across her chest. "My name's Skipper. You should know it."

Chapter 19 - Photo OP -

Thinking quickly on that, Felix considered all the possibilities. From what the woman said, it meant her power was about possibilities.

Eventualities, perhaps? Able to see what may or may not happen. What might or might not. That means that she just spent all that time staring me down to measure out all the possibilities, right? In all of those possibilities, I would have acted accordingly with my behavior.

Normally I wouldn't try to anger the leader of the city. Her annoyance seems to stem from the fact that I would summon Kit. That means Kit is... something she doesn't want me to do.

Therefore if I make the choice to push the button right now, and she can see what I'm going to do, then I'll get a response.

Let's push the button.

Skipper sighed and her mouth screwed itself into an angry scowl.

Looks like I guessed right.

Felix mashed the button, sending the text to Kit, not wanting to wait.

A second later, and Felix could hear Kit's portal open up behind him.

"Felix?" called Kit through the portal.

"Come on through, Kit. We have a visitor and I could use your help," Felix called back without breaking his stare-down with Skipper.

"What? Fine, fine. I'm coming," Kit said.

"Sometimes I wonder what he's thinking when I can't read his mind," Kit was muttering to herself. "Out of nowhere and—"

Kit paused as she stepped out of the portal and came to a stop beside Felix.

"Kit, Skipper," Felix said. He wasn't sure how she'd respond. In theory, this was the person who had turned her into a living corpse.

And no one can do that to another person without extreme hate, or they're just plain evil.

But then again, I turn people into sausages. Am I any better?

Skipper had frozen in place, still staring at Felix. But he got the impression Skipper wanted to look at Kit.

There was certainly a lot more here, but for the life of him he couldn't figure it out.

"I like your ring," Kit said. "The design, specifically. It's simple, yet tasteful."

Felix glanced down to Skipper's hand. The ring looked eerily similar to the same rings he'd seen on his enemies. The ring version of the crown.

Does that make her my enemy then?

Or their leader?

Skipper jammed her hand into her pocket, hiding the ring. Looking at Skipper's face, Felix was confused.

If Skipper can see eventualities. Possibilities.

The future, really.

Why didn't she see that Kit would notice the ring?

"To what do I owe the pleasure, Skipper?" Felix asked in a neutral tone. "I believe I'm up to date on all my forms, taxes, and requirements."

"Oh, you are," said the city leader.

Felix didn't kid himself one bit. This was the single villain who routed the entire guild of Heroes. It was one thing to put her off balance if possible, it was another to actually insult her.

He didn't need more enemies right now.

Especially if she was already one privately.

"I honestly hadn't planned on paying you a visit, but I saw you were up here on my way back from a meeting," Skipper said. She casually let her eyes fall to the severed head still sitting on the ground. "Apparently one of my agents has vanished. I was looking into it to see if I could discover anything."

"Oh. I can definitely understand. We were working on something extremely similar ourselves," Felix said, with a gesture at the head. "Unfortunately, we found one of our informants. Dead. Perhaps they're linked occurrences? Could you tell me about the one you're investigating?"

Skipper's brows came together as she scowled at him. "I don't have proof it was you, but we both know that's not something I actually need."

"I'd say that... if someone were infiltrating an organization, one that dealt in very dangerous things and people, one would have to expect they run a certain risk," Felix said evenly.

Sliding his hands into his pockets, Felix checked their contents.

Nothing.

"Andrea," Felix said. "Go ahead and empty your weapon. I think we're more than safe in our glorious leader's company."

Andrea flashed him a glare, then thumbed the clip release. She caught it with her left hand and tucked it away. After securing that, she reached around and ejected the round in the chamber. Catching it deftly, she went to put it into a pocket.

"I'll take that," Felix said, holding out his hand for the ejected unspent cartridge.

Andrea looked confused, but handed it over to him.

Truthfully, Skipper actually did look mildly relieved when Felix returned his attention to her.

"Anything I can do, I'll be happy to. Just let me know how I can assist," Felix said.

"Hmph. I'll keep that in mind. I think for now, I'll just tell you that you should keep to your business, and mind yourself," she said.

"That's the plan. I have no desire to do anything other than living my life, and running Legion."

"Good," Skipper grumped.

Felix nodded his head slowly, rolling the round between his fingers. Pinching it between thumb and forefinger, he aimed as discreetly as he could.

"Here, a memento," Felix said, even as he flicked the round at her.

It spun through the air, and bounced off Skipper's shoulder. She flinched at the sudden contact, and took two steps backwards.

She doesn't have her power. She didn't expect that. It surprised her, even.

Skipper had a shocked expression. Her eyes unfocused slightly as she stared down at the cartridge rolling around on the ground.

As casually as could be, Skipper pulled a pistol out of her pocket, turned, and fired it into the head of her companion. Before the man could fall, she pulled the trigger twice more.

His body jerked as his brain was forcefully ventilated, halfway to falling to the ground already. He hit the edge of the building as his brain stopped sending valid signals, and he fell off the edge of the building.

Sighing, Skipper turned back to Felix. "I suppose that answers that. You wanted to get me something? Get me a coffee while I wait. It's going to take someone at least twenty minutes to come pick me up."

Miu drew herself up, putting herself between Felix and Skipper.

"Sorry about the mess behind your building. Just put it in a trashcan," Skipper said, putting the pistol back into her pocket.

And I thought I was cold.

Kit, Lily, Andrea, Victoria, and Miu were all sitting around a table. In the middle sat a phone with Felicia and Ioana on the other end. A second Andrea was in the corner, minding the ANet.

"And she just shot him?" Ioana said.

"Yeah," Andrea said. "Three rounds into his brain."

"But why?" Victoria asked. "I mean, if he was wearing one of those rings, he was her puppet, right? They're not as strong as the crowns, but close. Yeah?"

"Yeah, they are. And that's what the cleanup crew said, he had one of the rings on him," Lily said, leaning back in her chair. "As to why... I think it's because Felix showed him something he wasn't supposed to know."

"Huh?" Ioana asked.

"When he threw the bullet at her, he showed everyone that her power wasn't working," Kit said.

"And what's her power?" Andrea asked. She looked down at the table.

"Rumor was that it was time control. Seems more like it's the ability to see into the future," Lily said. "At least, to a limited degree."

Felix nodded his head, his hands clasped in front of himself on the desk.

"That was my guess based on her statement when she landed. Or something akin to that. At first I thought she could only see possibilities or... something along those lines," Felix said. "The only thing that changed from when she arrived and had control of her powers, and when it stopped, was Kit."

Everyone in the room looked to Kit.

"I couldn't read her mind. The ring blocked me. When I couldn't read her directly, I used my general area telepathy. Sometimes I can get hints and feelings through it, even with a ring or crown involved," Kit said.

"That leaves that ability as the culprit for why she couldn't use her own power," Lily added. "So... why?"

Everyone fell silent. No one had any thoughts on it.

"Doesn't fucking matter," Felicia said on the other line. "And this doesn't matter to me at all. Felix, I'm going back to work. I put in a request for some more people. I want to get our hardware upgraded for our security forces. I know we can bring their dumb asses back when they die, but a bit of preventative work could make that happen less."

"Alright. I'll see what I can do. I might be sending you some high school graduates who applied with mechanical aptitude," Felix replied.

"Bah. Whatever. Hands are hands," Felicia said. There was a pause.

"Bye, love," Felicia said, much more softly and distantly. It was as if she hadn't expected anyone to hear it.

"See you," Ioana responded.

Clearing his throat, Felix leaned forward across the table. "Felicia's right. It's almost irrelevant. We have information now. Information that makes us targets and dangerous."

Pausing, Felix couldn't help but shake his head. "Though I can't help but wonder if Skipper thought we had it to begin with. They've known for a while that Kit is in Legion. It also explains why the guild wanted Kit so bad as well. That they wanted you back so they could fight Skipper. Without her power... she's probably much more easily handled."

Lily blew out a breath, looking up at the ceiling. "We never did find anything on the guild's network, drives, or files with anything. They lost all contact with the Skippercity guild when the city fell," she said.

"Well, it's kinda pointless, isn't it?" Victoria asked. "The guild had crowns and rings in their upper echelon."

Felix blinked, his heart lurching.

He'd forgotten about that.

Forgotten it entirely.

It changed the perception of the situation in a scary way.

"The reports we got from both the guild and the Skippercity faction indicate that while there was a shift in the leadership mentality, they all went along with it. In fact, the guild wrote up several endorsements for the steps they took," Lily said, flipping through her papers, looking for something.

"That means Skipper wanted me in her custody, and Felix dead. It also means that while the guild wasn't in charge of the Skippercity faction, they endorsed it. On top of that, doesn't that mean that the government doesn't care? The minders installed at the guild headquarters would have had to have signed off on the orders and endorsements for Felix to be killed," Kit said.

There was no surprise from anyone. Everyone had been moving to the same thought that Kit voiced aloud.

I'm in a shadow war with Skipper, the guild of Heroes, and the government. Certainly explains why all of the attacks, and lack of investigation, seemed so odd.

They're not working together, but they all want the same thing.

Felix harrumphed and looked up from the desk.

"Nothing actually changes, other than our viewpoint. We weren't exactly on speaking terms with any of them anyways. We continue on, knowing what we do now. Is there anything that we need to change? Any type of change in our scope or position that we need?" Felix asked.

"I'm going to put in a req to have a change to your bodyguard detachment," Victoria said. "I want several of them to have the ability to project an energy shield around you, like Lily's, at all times. What this sounds like to me is the perfect opportunity for a vigilante."

"Actually," Ioana said, the phone coming to life, "I think that sniper attack was a vigilante. We never did track that one down. Not completely, at least. Vicky's right. Best to put measures in place now before they're needed. It'd only take a single sniper rifle to end you. I'd go further and get a few people who have Neutralizer's power set as well. We already had it on the books to have several of them at each HQ, why not in your bodyguard section?"

Felix checked a sigh and nodded.

They were right of course. Even if it did end up restricting his movement further.

"I understand. Put the forms through and book the point calendar accordingly. What else?"

"I think we should begin considering an exit plan," Miu said. "Perhaps we should reach across federal lines to our neighbors in the south. See if we can't secure a government deal to begin expanding that way."

With a turn of his head Felix looked to Andrea. "Send an email to their embassy. See if the glorious nation of Wal would like to enter into negotiations. It'd be good to have a third location out of reach for our enemies. Besides, last I heard, Wal was doing rather well for itself. They might be happy to have a company such as ours building a facility there."

Around the room heads nodded in agreement.

"Anything else?" Felix asked. "No? Good. Let's move to the next subject then. The governor run. How are things looking?"

Lily pressed her hands to her forehead and then closed the folder in front of her.

"That bad?" Felix asked.

"What? No. Sorry. I couldn't find what I was looking for. Ah, the governor bid? It's fine," Lily said.

"Define fine. Looking for some details here so I can plan," Felix said.

"I... sorry. You're right," Lily said.

"You alright?" Felix pressed, leaning forward over the table.

"Yeah. Tired. I think I need to promote Lauren higher and delegate some work off to her. I feel like I'm being run down," said the ex-super villain.

"Defeated by paperwork. The fall of Mab. Definitely promote Lauren, and then go wade through the new high school recruits. I'm sure there are some that would fit," Felix said. "Jeff comes to mind."

"Jeff?" Lily asked, looking up at him.

"Rubik's cube kid. Caught me in a verbal loophole. I liked him," Felix said. "Anyways, the governor run?"

"Oh, yes. You're not in the lead, but you're in the lead when it comes to everyone on a similar platform. The problem is your voter base is being split a few too many times. Candidates who run on wishes and the belief that simply because they try, they could win and change the system," Lily said. She pulled out a different folder and flipped it open. "The closest candidate to your platform is taking about fifteen percent of what could be your own vote. Or so we're estimating according to polls and what we can estimate."

"Right. That makes sense. It's the same thing that's happening to the other candidates that we're sponsoring. They're cluttering up the field and eating up votes that could be used elsewhere. The classic problem with a single vote system—it always comes down to two parties," Felix said. Looking to his hands on the table he tapped the wood a few times.

"Do you want me to take care of those taking your votes?" Miu asked, her voice tinged with a desire to be set loose.

"No. Not yet, at least. And if I do send you out, that'd only be after we tried to blackmail them out, buy them out, or to get them to buy into our platform. I'd rather exhaust every other avenue first. Then I'll send you out," Felix said, making his choice. "When there's about three weeks left, we'll see about getting them all out of the race. That'll give voters enough time to reconcile themselves to voting for me, and to their candidate no longer being in the running."

Kit didn't say anything, but Felix could feel the dislike of the situation coming from her.

"I'd like to stress again, that we'll pursue every possible action that will cause the least amount of hardship first. Only when all those options fail will we turn to the more damaging possibilities," Felix reasserted. He didn't make eye contact with Kit, or look her way, but he hoped it would soothe her mind.

She might not be Augur anymore, but she'd always be a good and kind-hearted woman. Someone who wanted to do good.

"In fact, start reaching out to those individuals and feeling them out. It might make it easier down the road to get them on board if we begin now."

"I've got that," Andrea said, typing something into her terminal. "I'll also take on the meetings with Wal. We should be able to relay everything effectively between the departments."

"Great. Thanks, Andrea," Felix said.

"Nn! Also, I'm arranging the company picnic. It'll be ongoing for an entire week in the Tilen HQ. Felicia said we can use the portals," she said, closing her terminal and turning towards him.

"Oh? I didn't realize we were having one," Felix said. He really didn't know, but it sounded like something someone would put together.

"Yes! It's going to be fantastic. I've booked lots of fun things to do. Lots!"

"Uh... hopefully it's not all facepainting or—"

"I did book some facepainting, but that's for the kids. They'll like that. I also talked Felicia into getting involved. There should be lots and lots of fun giveaways and the like. She said it'd be a good opportunity for her to test her new people," Andrea said.

There was a chuckle from the phone.

"Stick to that story, Andie. It's better than admitting you hounded her for two weeks till she finally gave in," Ioana said.

Andrea blushed for a second, the nodded her head sharply. "Nn!"

"So much fun stuff! There's even going to be a dunk-tank for all department heads. I've already planned it all out," said the excited Beastkin.

"I see. Well as—"

"What's generated a lot of interest so far was lunch with Felix, and the photo booth. I originally only planned to have it open for about three hours a day, but it looks like it'll be more like five."

Felix felt his eye twitch at that. He didn't much care for the idea of standing around taking photos for hours at a time.

"I want an hour to myself in the photo booth," Miu said from the other side of the room. Her eyes were wide, her hands pressed flat to the table, and her body quivered a little.

"Sure!" Andrea said happily. "I'll book it right after my own hour."

The eye twitch evolved, and Felix could feel his teeth grinding together as well.

"I'd like an hour as well. That'll give me time to get some department photos with Felix, and some for myself as well," Lily said.

"Oh! That's—"

"Yes! I'd like—"

Me, too. Depart—"

Everyone started to talk over one another with the idea of having their entire departments take photos with Felix.

To which Felix could only respond by staring at Andrea with burning dread.

She responded with a smile at him, and a wiggle of her ears. "Going to be so much fun!" she said as the others all began to talk about photos.

Chapter 20 - Faust -

"Come on, Mikey. Let's see if you can get a strike," Felix said loudly.

He stared down the lane in front of him, at the man with the baseball held tightly in his hands. The distance was twenty feet, give or take a few inches.

Felix's job was to rile up the crowd, and get them to spend game tokens for the honor of trying to dunk him into a pool of ice cold water with ice-cubes floating around in it. The ice-cubes were a present from Felicia.

Seeing how annoyed it had made him had only enamored her with the idea of punishing him. She'd gone ahead and dragged out an ice maker and set it up nearby for an eternal supply of ice.

"Maybe when you're done getting yourself into the zone you could let someone else try!" Felix cat-called.

All around people laughed. They all seemed to be enjoying themselves with the picnic, and watching their CEO and founder being dropped into an ice bath seemed hilarious to them. Even though it had already happened twelve times, everyone acted as if it were the first time, each time.

Michael, who was a janitor by trade, was all seriousness. Winding back, he hurled the ball downrange towards the target. A circle no bigger than a catcher's mitt.

Felix didn't see it hit, but he heard the clang. The seat he was perched on dropped out from under him, and Felix was dumped into the vat of near freezing water.

He could hear the cheer of everyone around even under the shockingly cold water.

Rising as quickly as he could, Felix came sputtering to the surface, gasping for breath.

"Cold!" Felix squeaked and scrambled out of the tank. Flopping to the ground he shook himself out, trying to soak up the sunshine instead.

"Good throw, Mike!" Felix called out from the grass.

If they managed to hit the target and send him to his watery fate, they were awarded twenty raffle tickets to spend as they saw fit on the prizes.

Getting to his feet, Felix shook himself out.

"You've got a thirty minute break," Andrea said, sliding up next to him. "Here's a towel. Go get something to eat and maybe wander around. Say hi to some people. Have fun!"

Felix could only shake his head with a smile. Taking the towel, he draped it over his shoulders. He was glad he wore a simple t-shirt and shorts for this. Otherwise it'd be unbearable to be this cold, and this wet.

Sunshine or not.

"Thanks. I'll go for a walk then. I heard Ioana is queen of the pugil sticks right now and taking all challengers. That might be fun to watch for a spell," Felix said.

"Nn! That'd be fun! I think there's a corndog stand near there, too. I'll come check on you when it's time to get you back up there. Right now it's Kit. People seem just as eager to put her into the tank as they were you," Andrea said.

Felix had a momentary flash of a thought to stick around and watch, but then realized she'd probably dig through his memories later at some point. He didn't want her reliving him enjoying her in a bathing suit.

"Good luck with that," Felix said, pulling the towel up over his head. Felix gave Andrea a smile and started walking towards the pugil arena.

"Hi Mr. Campbell," said a female voice on his left.

Looking to his side from inside the towel, he found a female Beastkin keeping pace with him. She had long rabbit ears sticking up from a mass of dark black hair. Light brown eyes and a pretty face looked up at him. She had soft features that invited someone to confide in her.

"Hello there, Miss?" Felix prompted.

"Call me Erica! I'm with channel thirteen," said the woman excitedly. She pulled a recorder out from an inside pocket and checked that it was running.

Of course she's a reporter. All the smart networks send me young Beastkin types to see if I might give them more info.

Surprising it's only one of them, though. I thought I'd get swarmed.

"Erica, then. What can I do for you?" Felix asked, looking forward towards his destination.

"I'd love to ask you some questions. If you don't mind?" asked the young woman.

"Sure, if you answer me one first. How'd you manage to catch me alone?"

"I planned which way you'd probably exit from the tank, put myself on the far side, and bet on the fact that someone would run blocker for you," said Erica. "Sure enough, Myriad had a number of security personnel screen your departure. Everyone else was too close."

"Smart. Ok, ask away."

Felix wormed his way past the crowd and into a corner area. The arena was rather crowded and it didn't look like there was much room to see from.

He made his way to one side where an area looked rather clear, only to find a security guard and a closed gate. The security guard noticed him and opened the gate immediately, smiling.

"Sir, I guarantee no one will bother you here," said the female security guard, her eyes flicking to Erica.

"Eh, let her come with me. We invited the media after all, and she earned a few questions," Felix said. "Thanks a bunch, by the way. Appreciate it."

The guard nodded as Felix and Erica slipped through the gate, then shut it behind him.

They were in an alcove set aside for some purpose Felix couldn't discern.

"Why did you invite the media, by the way?" Erica asked.

"Everyone always asks what Legion is like. This…" Felix said, gesturing to the arena, and everyone around it. "This entire thing is Legion. We're more a family at this point than an organization."

Ioana stood atop a column in the middle of the arena. In her hands was a pugil stick. She remained there, waiting for someone to challenge her.

"It definitely feels that way! Everyone is so kind and charitable to each other. Is this more of a publicity stunt then?"

"Not at all. This is a company picnic, that the media was invited to. That's really about it."

A smaller man took a pugil stick from one side and stepped up onto the column.

Ioana had a feral grin plastered to her face as she swung her weapon lazily in an arc.

"What do you think about the accusations that your opponents have made about you?"

"Which ones? Some are true, some aren't. The fact that I'm in a relationship with a Beastkin is quite true."

"How about the one that you're secretly in league with Skipper? And spying for them? That Legion is actually a front?"

"Lies, all of it. I don't work with Skipper in any capacity. Legion supports Legion and the people who are its customers. That's it," Felix said sternly. "I dare anyone to show me proof at any level. Any shred of evidence at all."

"Ah—" Erica said, her voice cutting off in a squeak at his tone.

"Sorry. I'm not mad at you for asking, I'm mad at them for making the accusation. It's so patently stupid, it's infuriating. Skipper doesn't need my help or anyone else's. She took Skippercity all on her own. Now she has even more power than she did," Felix said, his tone softening.

"That's ok. I understand completely. I take it from your tone you don't care for Skipper?"

Felix didn't respond at first. He watched Ioana toy with her opponent for a minute. Even going so far as to offer advice to him, before promptly knocking him off the column with a jab of her stick.

"I neither like or dislike Skipper. Skipper is a government entity that I work within the scope of in her city. That's the extent of our relationship," Felix said.

"Anything to add about the fact that Skipper has been massing their forces? It almost looks as if they're planning to make a move to the east. Do you think they're looking to expand?"

That was a bit of a surprise. He hadn't heard anything about that.

Need to link up with Dimitry and get some of his people in position to watch this.

"I have no comment. I'm more focused on my work and my governor bid."

"Speaking of work. Any chance I could get you to talk to me about this business security venture we've heard about? There's been a few things here and there, but nothing really about what it is. What it does," Erica asked, pushing for her story.

Reaching over without looking, Felix hit the stop button on her recorder.

"What do I get, Erica?" Felix said, not taking his eyes off of Ioana.

"I-I-I beg your pardon?" Erica asked.

"Say I give you your story. What do I get? What I did with Jessica wasn't on accident."

"I don't — I'm not, I'm not willing to sleep with you for a story. That is, it's not that I'm not attract — "

"Stop. Not what I meant. What I want is your support. Will I get a positive story out of it? Spin it in my favor? You do that, and we can talk about the story, and future stories," Felix said. "I need long-term relationships in the media. Pretty young girls don't normally get story breaks, or opportunities to get them. I know what my direction is, and I know I'll be in the news. I need a few more reporters in my corner."

Turning his head, Felix finally met her eyes and gazed into them.

Erica stared up at him with wide eyes. Her ears were rigid, her face pale.

"If you don't want this offer, just say the word, and it never happened. You want your story? I want you," Felix said.

Blinking rapidly, the Beastkin slowly nodded her head.

"I'm yours. Your reporter," Erica said. There was a touch of shock in her voice that Felix detected. *Well, she is incredibly young, isn't she? Need to get her the same contract I had Jessica sign.*

"Good. We'll draw up a Legion contract later. You and Jessica will be welcome to discuss it amongst yourselves of course, and any others I include. Though I'll be looking to only pick up one or two more," Felix said.

He thumbed the recorder back into the on position. "Why not? The business security idea is something we're putting together for companies. After watching what happened with that prison break, I realized that I could offer a service. Security. Wholesale security tailored to the needs of each business and reasonable pricing. If they're afraid of a super attack, they could easily hire super security from Legion. Expecting normal everyday bank robbers? PMC trained security officers ready to take the job. This would be at every level of businesses."

Erica took in a quick breath and then gave him a smile. "Got it. Any chance of that expanding to a residential side? I imagine there might be some interested parties after what happened in the city."

Felix shrugged his shoulders, looking back to the arena for a second. Ioana had just cleared another opponent from the column. Turning his eyes back to the rabbit, he smiled at her.

"Maybe. Residential is harder since the scope would be much more limited. At that point, I'd rather buy an existing security company, run it into Legion, and have it as a branch company. Starting up completely new departments is the pits."

"I could definitely see how that'd work out. It's certainly an interesting project," Erica said. Then her face locked up. She turned off her own recorder and stared at him with a sense of panic that was obvious.

"Why me? I know they only hired me a few weeks ago because I'm a pretty Beastkin. They hired me and sent me over here to you because of it. I'm barely out of college! They were hoping you'd make a move or give me a story. All because you clearly show a preference to female Beastkin. Is it just because I'm a Beastkin? Is it because I'm pretty? I don't understand. I don't want... I don't want to look a gift horse in the mouth, but..." Erica paused, her mouth hanging open.

Felix snorted at that.

"Don't get me wrong, you're definitely... yeah, definitely beautiful, but I'm already in a relationship. As to why, partially your determination, partially your intelligence. Now turn your recorder back on and stop worrying about it. I'll also be paying whatever your salary is today, and then tripling it, by the way. So I'm effectively your employer," Felix said, tapping the recorder. "So how about we keep this moving?"

"I, yes. Yes of course. I'm sorry. This is just all so unexpected," Erica said. She turned the recorder back on. Staring at it, she was visibly collecting herself.

Felix exploded backwards flipping through the air. A blue glow came up around him as he crashed into a back wall.

He could faintly hear Erica shrieking, and the sound of sustained gunfire.

With a shake of his head, Felix got to his feet and stumbled to one side. Trying to get out of the line of fire. Or so he assumed. There was only one direction a clear shot could have been taken on him.

He didn't know if it was a rifle, magic, or a power, but regardless of the source, he didn't want to stick around.

The charm resting on his collarbone popped loudly and shattered.

Damn, that was strong, whatever it was.

Taking a leap and a guess, Felix rolled in a tumble behind a crate. Laying flat to the ground, he squirmed around until he limited what could be seen of him. Then he did the only thing he could in a set of bathing shorts and a towel.

Wait.

Felix had been well trained, but he wasn't an idiot.

"Erica, get out of sight and behind cover!" Felix yelled

He could hear the sound of gunfire, shouts, and the pounding of feet as every member of Legion acted.

Deafening booms and the crackle of power punctuated the annoyance and fear in Felix's mind.

The explosions and sound of gunfire fell off sharply.

It only took a few seconds after that before Felix could hear verbal commands being issued. Then the PA system that'd been setup came to life with a crackle.

"Security check, gather the sheep and begin shearing," Kit said over the loudspeakers. The sheep would be the reporters, and the shearing would be their memories of the attack.

No one would be the wiser as to Legion suffering an ambush. That'd been the plan when they invited the media in case something happened.

"Code Black, Eagle is missing. Repeat, Eagle is missing," said Kit over the PA.

"Damnit. I need to get up and flag down a security officer so they don't start ripping everything apart," Felix said to himself.

Getting up to his feet, Felix went back over to the gate he'd come in from. When he'd taken only a few steps in that direction, the female security officer broke into the alcove and immediately locked eyes with him.

"My charm broke, but I'm fine. The attack was directly on me," Felix said quickly, trying to reassure the officer.

Apparently it worked, because she stopped dead in her tracks. Her left hand shot up to the microphone on her shoulder and she began speaking into it.

Looking around, Felix needed to find Erica. He'd have to take her over to the Fixers to have—

She was laid out on the ground, blood pooling around her rapidly.

"Code Black canceled, Eagle has been sighted. Need a TM and a SB to section forty-two, south gate. Fro—"

Felix tuned Kit's voice out and ran over to Erica's prone form.

She was breathing hard, her hands pressed to her stomach. Her large eyes darted to him.

They were large, dilated. Full of fear.

"I've been shot," she said, as he came to her side. "I'm shot."

"Yes. You have. You're also in shock," Felix said. Looking over his shoulder he saw the security guard. "Hey! Tell the Telemedic to bring a number three contract with them. And to hurry, that's an order."

The guard immediately began talking into her mic, moving to exit the alcove quickly.

Grumbling, Felix knelt over Erica and pressed his hands to hers.

"Hey there. A little bit more truth for you than most people get before they sign a contract with me. I have a super power. I can modify or change anything I own," Felix said, trying to hold her eyes with his own.

The sheer amount of blood seeping into the ground beneath her was unnerving. He couldn't imagine she had much blood left in her at this point.

"You're a powered," she said. "That explains so much."

"Yeah. So, with that said, I have a modified contract system that gives me temporary ownership of you, as my employee. Which lets me modify or edit you as a person," Felix said slowly. He was trying to keep her with him. An explanation of why she needed to sign her contract immediately seemed like a great place to start.

"I? I need to sign?" Erica asked, her voice getting softer. "What do I sign?"

"A contract. I need you to sign a contract," Felix repeated. She wasn't anything to him, but he didn't want to see her die. She'd only been trying to get a story on him.

A victim by being in his vicinity, only.

"Oh. I already signed a contract. I got a job! I didn't think I'd... I'd get one so quickly. Beastkin have to try harder," Erica said.

"Yes, but you have to sign another. As soon as it gets here." Felix looked around as soon as he finished talking.

If they don't get here soon it won't matter a damn bit. I thought we pla—

A young male Telemedic popped into being a few feet away from Felix. In a heartbeat, the man had crouched down beside Erica and handed the contract to Felix.

"Erica, I need you to sign this, ok?" Felix said, pulling the contract open.

It was the right one.

Thank goodness for small miracles.

"I don't have my pen," Erica muttered. "It's with my... my notes. In the car. It's cold here. Can I have a blanket?"

Felix looked to the Telemedic, who stared back at Felix.

There's no pen.

"That's ok," Felix said, taking Erica's right hand away from her stomach. "Pretend your finger is a pen, and sign right here, ok? Sign your agreement. I can't do it for you."

Erica's hand lifted up and pressed into the page. She grabbed it with her thumb and forefinger and lifted her left hand instead.

"Left han...ded," Erica whispered, then her hands dropped down to the ground at her sides.

Her eyes fluttered, and she let out a slow rattling breath.

And died.

Felix blinked, staring at the bloody contract in his hand.

Her bloody fingers had left a smeared trail along the signature line.

Blood counts, right? People used to sign with blood. That's right.

People signed in blood back in the day. Before the populace could sign, right

"That's fine, Erica. Signing in blood is fine. That's fine," Felix said to the corpse. "This'll work. I'm sure."

Felix looked at the contract and then tried to call up her character window.

"Get back to HQ and get the appropriate resources for however many people we need to raise, plus one," Felix said to the Telemedic.

He didn't want to see him right now. The lack of a pen was an oversight on both their parts. Felix didn't ask for one, and the Telemedic didn't think to bring one.

Resurrect Erica. Bring her back to life because she signed her contract. She's an employee. Bring her back.

The Telemedic got up and immediately vanished, flitting away through the space between places that they zipped through.

No screen popped up.

Felix wasn't looking for a hypothetical, he was looking for an actual screen. Which meant it'd only come up if it was a binding contract.

"Come on, Erica. You signed in blood. You even used a fingerprint. That's a valid signature, right?" Felix said, trying to pull up the screen again.

Nothing.

"Oh, come on!" Felix shouted at Erica's cooling body. "Look, I know... I know my power isn't normal and it changes by my wishes at times. The only way that's possible is if someone is watching up there."

Felix waited for a few seconds and tried to pull up the window again.

Nothing.

"Come on... she was willing to sign. She wanted to sign. She put her bloody thumb on it. That's a signature," Felix muttered, sinking down into a sitting position.

"Consider it a favor owed," Felix said.

Erica wasn't anyone to him other than a resource. But she died because of him, and had done him no wrong.

For the first time in a long time, Felix felt some guilt.

Regret.

"I'd owe you two favors?" Felix asked, a bitter smile crossing his face as he realized no one was listening.

Name: Erica Newberg		Power: --	
Alias:		Secondary Power: --	
Physical Status: Decaying		Mental Status: Dead	
Positive Statuses: None		Negative Statuses: Dead	
Strength:	35		Upgrade?(350)
Dexterity:	41		Upgrade?(410)
Agility:	42		Upgrade?(420)
Stamina:	45		Upgrade?(450)
Wisdom:	58		Upgrade?(580)
Intelligence:	55		Upgrade?(550)
Luck:	31		Upgrade?(310)
Primary Power:	--		Upgrade?(--)
Secondary Power:	--		Upgrade?(--)

Status Correction: Dead -> Living	Correct Status? (15,000 points. Two Favors Owed.)

Felix stared at the last message for several seconds. His breathing was strained and it felt like his chest was being crushed.

Two Favors Owed.

Someone or something was listening.

And I struck a deal with it.

Chapter 21 - Separation -

Felix stared at the machine dully. He'd had a hard time functioning since the picnic ended. Somehow he'd managed to keep it all together during the event, but only just barely.

Legion's morale was riding high. Especially when Felix had resurrected everyone who died at no cost.

With every attack on them, every assault, every insult, Legion proved to be the stronger.

They came out on top.

Stomped their foe to the ground and tore its head off.

Confidence could be a dangerous thing, but as long as there was a reset button that could be hit, his people would always learn from mistakes.

Especially fatal ones.

But that's the problem.

Felix shook his head, his thoughts going back to the debt he now owed whoever controlled his powers. Or influenced his powers.

Or made me.

Shuddering from head to toe, he could actually feel the anxiety and panic washing over him.

There was nothing comforting in knowing there existed a higher power for Felix.

Lily had once told him that she didn't sign the form because she'd feared what would happen to her in an afterlife. At the time Felix had dismissed it.

There'd been no reason for him to believe. Sure, Lily was eating souls, or what people believed were souls, but there had been no proof of that.

Now Felix believed it.

Believed in souls.

That something was watching him. That modified his powers so that he could bring a young Beastkin back to life.

To put her soul back into the husk of her body, and allow Felix to put her body back to rights. That wasn't something casual.

Someone else held a power that controlled how his own interacted with the world.

"Felix!" Felicia shouted in his ear, causing him to start.

"What?!" he shouted back, staring down at her. His annoyance was plain and his ear was ringing.

"You're not listening to me! You arse-faced idiot. I've been talking to you for at least a minute. Did you hear anything?" Felicia asked in a raised voice.

Freezing up, Felix couldn't answer that. He actually hadn't heard a word she'd said. The existential panic he'd been floundering around in had consumed him.

"No," Felix said, his shoulders dropping. "I didn't."

Felicia's eyebrows came down and she put her fists on her hips. She opened her mouth and closed it again. Her face went through a series of emotions he couldn't identify, but it settled on something surprising to him.

Concern.

"I'm no good at figuring out people," she said finally. "Give me a toolbox and a machine and I'm good. But... I'll help how I can. Ioana would say the same. Just tell us what we can do."

Felix felt his lips flicker to a smile and he huffed.

"Thanks. It's not something anyone can fix, though. I just had someone upend my plans is all. I have to do some revisions, just kinda stuck in a negative loop. I'll be fine," Felix said. "Now, I'm sorry for not listening. How about you tell me again what you were saying."

Felicia considered that, glaring at him for a moment more. "Fine. It's what you asked for. A security function and an override."

Nodding his head, Felix looked to the portal machine once more. It looked like a tunnel entrance that led nowhere. Directly behind it was a wall.

"The security function is that it'll only process people with Legion rings. Anything within a foot around them will go with them. Including air by the way, that was fun to find out. Makes a boom with each person. It's why we had to move it down here to its own level. Shook the goddamn teeth out of your head. We've minimized it as best as we can."

"Great. That's definitely a good way to handle a security lockout. What happens if someone goes through without a ring?"

"They get dropped into a holding cell deep under SC:HQ. I figured it might be a good idea to simply not tell anyone about the security function. Everyone in Legion has a personalized ring after all. It only works for them. There's no reason for them to ever take it off. This becomes a passive feature, and we never have to worry about it," Felicia explained, patting the control panel.

Felix couldn't deny he saw the appeal in that. It'd be an unspoken security feature that anyone of Legion would always pass without ever knowing.

"And the override?" he asked.

"Three different lockouts. First is a retinal scan. Go ahead and cozy up to this here," Felicia said, pointing to what Felix couldn't see as anything other than a submarine periscope viewer.

"Uh huh..." Felix muttered. Stepping forward he pressed his face to it and was instantly blinded by a red flash. "Holy fucking shit."

Felix jerked away, rubbing at his eyes.

"Oh, yeah. It's a bit bright. You'll be fine. Next is—"

"Voice confirmed. 'Holy fucking shit' registered as the passcode for Felix Campbell," said a robotic voice.

"Next is voice registration. Good. The last is a simple typed mechanical password. Use the boxed in keyboard there."

Felix opened his eyes and could barely see beyond the white spots in his vision. What she'd been talking about was a keyboard with raised walls so one couldn't see what was being typed from other angles.

"And what do I type?" Felix asked, putting his hands into the keyboard.

"Whatever your network password is," Felicia said from the other side of the panel.

Grumbling, Felix typed in the code.

Immediately the portal machine activated and a giant blue wall sprang to life in front of him. A second after that, it flashed brightly, and all Felix could see was an endless sea of green grass.

"This is the world we ended up going with. It matches everything you listed. I have it set and locked it for now as the destination. I have other things that are more important than babysitting you," Felicia said, stomping off towards the door to the elevator.

Staring through the portal, Felix wasn't sure of himself anymore.

This was something he'd arranged the day before the picnic started. In fact, Felix had forgotten about it, right up until Felicia booked the slot on his calendar for a six hour meeting.

Exactly as he'd requested.

"Well, shall we go?" Lily asked from behind him, causing him to look over his shoulder.

He hadn't heard her enter. With her was Victoria, a squad of Legion security, three squads of Legion employees in work clothes, a Fixer, a Telemedic, an Other and Andrea. They were all dressed for combat, wearing the equipment and gear they'd put together specifically for combat engagements.

Felix himself was in combat armor, and wearing all the various charms and things his people had prepped for him. They'd decided it wouldn't be good to make the trip in his usual armor.

From Andrea's scouting reports, the world was inhabited by tribal humans who were barely starting to enter large farming communities.

Though their system of government seemed barely to scratch the surface of feudalism.

It was likely that his usual armor would cause more of a problem than relying on other defenses.

"Yeah... let's head in. Everyone, follow your orders. Lily, hang back with me, I want to ask you a few questions," Felix said. Making a sharp turn, Felix walked into the portal, and onto another world.

It was more or less another Earth, as far as they could tell.

Everyone went through the portal and spread out, going about their tasks.

"Something's been on your mind for a bit," Lily said casually, standing beside him.

You don't fool me. You've all known something's up. Kit has been the most persistent, asking twice to get the ability to read my thoughts turned on.

"Don't make that face. I'm trying to be nice. Kit said I'm still coming across too strong at times," she said. Apparently he hadn't been as neutral as he'd thought reacting to her statement. "I'm still getting used to this whole, everyone isn't trying to scam me, kill me, or rape me thing. Corporate life is certainly more fun than being a villain."

"You and her have certainly been getting along," Felix said. "I almost wonder if that friction I imagined ever so long ago even existed."

Lily blew out a breath. "Don't change the subject."

"I think you were right," Felix said, watching his people working. They were putting out stake markers, measuring off distances, and general prepping what would be their base camp. "There is a higher power. Or at least, one that has control over my own powerset."

"I... don't understand. What do you mean?" She sounded concerned to Felix. He could only imagine her dilemma, as having taken the souls of a number of people certainly wouldn't endear you to the heavens.

"Erica didn't sign her contract. She tried to, but died before she could."

"But if that were true, you wouldn't have been able to bring her back. And I know you did. We watched her report yesterday evening. She's on Legion payroll."

"And that's all true, and correct. Except the part where she signed her contract. She managed to press a bloody thumb to it. That was it. She died. And I wasn't able to bring her back."

One of the Legion employees leaned to one side and spoke into a microphone.

They must be getting the materials ready.

"Then I started talking aloud. Arguing that she signed the contract. With her blood and thumbprint," Felix said.

Behind him he could hear carts being rolled out of the freight elevator as everyone began getting ready for the second phase.

Watching them go by, Felix took in a slow breath. "I said something about knowing someone was there. That my power was too... directed, for there not to be. I offered up a favor, if they'd agree that Erica had meant to sign."

A breeze came through the plain and ruffled Felix's hair.

It was strange to have the interior of a building behind him, and an open field in front of him.

"Then I offered two favors. I don't know why I did, but I did. Then a window popped up after that. It had a point cost, and said that I owed two favors, and Erica would come back to life," Felix said. "The point cost was rather low. Far too low. Which means that the favors had some type of value attached to them. That'd mean that it was a choice. Planned, calculated, and thought out."

Large wheeled carts skirted around him and Lily, moving to the designated area markers. Stacks of bricks, paving stones, steel, bags of cement, and all sorts of construction materials were being hauled over.

"That... that definitely sounds like you've come into contact with a higher being. A god? I don't know how to take that, really," Lily said after the last cart trundled by.

"Yeah, pretty much where I'm at myself. It throws a number of things out of perspective for me. I was never one for religion... not really. It all sounded so strange growing up. Now I find that not only was it not so strange, but real. Where does that leave me? And why did it, they, him, her, whatever, decide to answer me. That seems really... the whole thing feels weird."

"Ok... so... what did you want to ask me? I'm guessing you wanted to talk about souls, given the conversation."

"I did. But I'm not sure it matters anymore. I kinda answered it myself. There's not much I can do. Until such a time as they decide to collect a favor, at least."

"That's true," Lily said. "How about a subject change. I've read the reports that Andrea sent back. I read through the basic outline you put together for department heads. But you always hold back and keep your thoughts out of those. As if you're worried they might go further than you want."

Felix snorted at that and started walking off to one side of the area his people were working in. He wanted to keep moving.

Standing still didn't feel right anymore.

Victoria noticed him moving immediately. She made a gesture he didn't recognize to Andrea, and began to move parallel to him.

She kept her distance as he'd requested though.

"Honestly, my plan was to turn this world into a recruitment drive. As far as we can tell from what the scouts sent back, it's a world inhabited by humans and beasts. There aren't any other humanoid races. At all. Not one. Just humans," Felix said. He gestured to the west. "The closest settlement is several rather large tribes over that way. Large enough that you could probably consider them the local powers. With any luck, we'll be able to start working with them."

"You want to… work with the locals?" Lily's skepticism was palpable.

"Yes. I do. And not in the conquering explorer kind of way either. I want to offer them things in exchange for service, materials, and other things. I don't plan on giving them any technology, or letting them into our encampment without being in Legion. But I'm not against giving them food. Leather, hide. Basic cloth, even. I wanted to turn this world into Legion's world. Now though…" Felix trailed off, staring westward.

"Now you worry that you might piss off a god who doesn't take kindly to you mucking around on different planets," Lily finished the statement.

"Yeah. I mean… in the ancient history of our world, it's said many times that originally it was just humans. Medieval humans.

"Then the humanoid races came. From where they're not sure, but they were just there one day. In cities, villages, and homes as if they had always been there. Everywhere, not just in localized places.

"I have to wonder if that wasn't an intervention. And if I'd be provoking another one."

"I'd say let the god tell you that when they decide to talk to you again. If they didn't want you to, would they even have let you come here?" Lily asked. "Assume the answer is permission granted, until shown otherwise. In fact, I would argue just by having this conversation aloud, you force the god into an unstated acceptance until otherwise said."

Leave it to the lawyer.

Felix smiled and shook his head. "I suppose that's about right. At least, that's all I can do until otherwise stated. And the day after tomorrow, the Death Others will be returning with the three leaders of those tribes."

"Death Others? How do you know?" Lily asked.

"They all volunteered for security, guard, or interrogation work. Apparently being on your own for that long gave them a different outlook on life. I can't imagine their personalities would have merged very well with Andrea after that. It's the very reason she cut them out to begin with. The memories will be gone, but does that change the personality?"

"Hmph. That'd explain why the Security Others are separate from the Corporate Others now," Lily said.

Stopping in his tracks, Felix glanced over to Lily. "What?"

"Huh? Oh. Probably not my place. You should talk to Andie about that. I'm going to head back to the site. I have a few jobs of my own to do, you know. My boss gave me a list of things he wanted done, and I'm clearly not working on them," Lily said, giving him a grin.

"Uh huh. Maybe I should order you more often."

"It's a wonder you don't. Talk to Andie."

And with that, Lily left him there, heading back towards the setup area.

As if knowing that they'd been talking about her, Andrea Prime came over.

"Felix? Are you better now?" she asked, moving in close to him.

I must have really worried them all. I'll let Kit inside my head when we get back so she can pick through my thoughts. Once that's done, everyone else will end up being better off as well.

"Yep. Doing much better. But I wanted to ask you a question or two if you don't mind," Felix said, wrapping an arm around her shoulders.

"Nn?"

"Did you separate Myriad out from yourself?" he asked directly.

Andrea went rigid in his arms, her shoulders as stiff as a board.

"What?" she asked, as if she hadn't heard him.

"Did you separate Myriad out?"

"I... that is..."

"You did."

"Nn..."

"Why?"

"Because, Myriad isn't me. And I'm not Myriad. You were right. We're all the same person, but we're also not. We talked it over. A lot. We weren't going to tell you, because we want you to treat us all the same as you always do. But... but the Security and Combat Others are all going to be in a different... Prime... of sorts. And everyone else is coming to me."

"So... there's an Andrea Prime, and another Prime, now," Felix said, trying to clarify the situation.

Andrea hesitated for a moment before nodding her head. "Yes. We... we've successfully split and everything is working. In fact, I played her part the other day, and they were me, and no one noticed. We can still perform each other's functions, memories remain after all because we split them, but... the Others..."

"Were swapped around. Ok, I think I get it. And you want me to treat you two as if there was no difference?"

"Nn..." Andrea said, pressing her face to his shoulder.

"I can definitely try to do that. I think you might find that as time goes on you'll become further and further separated. Though regardless of that, I think the new Prime needs a regular name if only to designate who I'm trying to talk to. If you're Andrea, and she's your twin sister, how about... Adriana?"

"Adriana?" Andrea repeated. "Adriana."

"Adriana and Andrea Elex," Felix said.

"Twin sister. Can... can you try something for me?"

"Sure, what is it?"

"Could you try to pull up Adriana's window? As if she were her own self?"

"I can do that," Felix said, smiling down at the Beastkin.

Taking a step back from Andrea, since it was just easier if the window didn't go through people or things, Felix focused his mind.

He conceptualized the idea that Adriana Elex, formerly Andrea, was a separate entity. Equal in every way to Andrea, but not Andrea.

That he wanted to modify her, and not Andrea.

Nothing came up at first, and Felix was afraid that it wouldn't work. That Andrea and Adriana weren't able to be separated in the way that Andrea wanted, and would always and forever be Others.

A window popped up suddenly.

Status Correction: Joined Personality -> Separated, yet able to Join, Personality	Correct Status? (20,000 points. I would have chosen Alexa instead.)

Felix took a slow breath, reading the window again.

The panic that had threatened him previously fell away in a rush.

Lily had been right.

This... thing... whatever it was, would intervene or interfere if and when it decided it wanted to. For now, it seemed content to watch.

Felix hit the button to accept the change.

"Andrea, you're officially twins, though I suspect you could still reform into one person if you wanted," Felix said, looking up at the now smiling Beastkin.

Chapter 22 - Trump Card -

The ex-marine snorted and stared out across the field.

"Any particular reason you chose me?" he asked. "Don't get me wrong. Nice view and all, but you're asking me to be the ugly end of the stick for an entire… world."

"Because you're qualified, can function independently, and were given a Fixer rank. According to HR, Michael Haglund does very well when put into the worst situation and given little in the way of support," Felix said "I'd say manning a fort in the middle of a hostile planet counts for that. Your heavy weapons specialist title doesn't hurt either. I figure you'll have this place tighter than a shoelace budget at the end of a fiscal year."

"And you brought me here to show me the site and offer me the job," Michael said, scratching at a beard far too long for a man so young. Blue eyes that'd seen a bit too much during deployment held a dull glow to them as they stared into Felix.

He looked very much the part of ex-military trying to make it back in the real world.

Maybe being at a fort on the edge of a wild world will be just what you need.

"That, and you and your wife both listed relocation as an option," Felix said, nodding his head. "This would be relocation."

At the mention of his wife, Michael's eyes flicked over to the small, dark-haired Beastkin frolicking around in the tall grass.

Felix wasn't one to judge, given his relationship with Andrea, but they seemed an odd pair.

"Veronica does seem rather happy," Michael said gruffly.

Felix took a moment to watch the cat-eared Beastkin dive into a dense growth. "I've noticed they tend to do better in wilder environs, yes. Can I assume that's a yes?"

"Can I pick my own security assets?" Michael asked, looking back at Felix.

And there we go. That's all done, just a matter of him formally agreeing.

"You do, but you'll lose your HR status and be forced into a leadership role. A separate HR Fixer will be assigned and report up through Kit. A representative of Legal will, of course, be on hand as well. Everything else is a material or personnel requisition form," Felix said, holding out his hand.

Michael had a sour look on his face, but shook Felix's hand.

"Oh, planet's named Legion. I've claimed it by territory rights. I plan on listing the ownership of said planet locally here, and at the HQs back home. I figure ten years is long enough for a legal claim against it," Felix said with a grin.

"Figures," Michael said, grinning back. "Legion first."

"Legion first," Felix repeated.

Michael let go of Felix's hand and turned back to the field. Leaving him there to contemplate his new home, Felix went to join Kit.

"He's happier than he lets on," Kit said when he got within earshot. "He has a hard time showing it."

"Good. You done reading through my brain yet? Can I turn it off?" Felix asked.

"Yes. I'm done. I did take a minute to really go through your thoughts about the dunk tank though. It was surprisingly — "

"Going to drown you in horrible thoughts if you finish that sentence," Felix threatened. "If you really wanna know what I can dredge up then we can go right on down to hard-on hotel and I'll make you wish you could bleach your own thoughts."

"Ah… yes. I'm done. I'd agree with Lily and her assumption, based on what I saw from your mind. And yes, we are getting along, and for the reasons you suspect," Kit said.

"Hm. Good," Felix said. He didn't want to talk about it. His suspicions were rather simple. Kit was sharing his thoughts with Lily, and acting as a filter for her.

He disabled her ability to read his mind with a thought.

"You ready for our guests? They should be arriving soon enough," Felix asked.

"I believe that'd be them over yonder, actually," Kit said, indicating a group of people off to one side. "Victoria and a Fixer cornered them as soon as they got here. I'm afraid there's some problems that we'll have to discuss before you even go over there."

"Oh. There's always a problem. That much is certain. The question is… what is it this time?" Felix asked, looking to the group of people.

"Security brought in three people. Supposedly they're the representative leaders for each group. One is, the other two aren't," Kit said. She pointed to the two older gentlemen of the three. "They're maybe third in line, and come from a dictatorship form of government. They're here because their leader didn't want to risk themselves."

"Alright, not exactly a bad idea when meeting with someone you have no idea about. I can't deny that if I had someone show up wearing things that didn't belong, with tech that I didn't understand, I might be reserved as well. Is that the problem though? That doesn't seem —"

"One of them has knowledge that their tribe is attacking the other even as we speak. They were hoping they'd send their leader and were going to use this as an opportunity," Kit clarified.

"Huh. Not a bad plan. I mean, we did something very similar if you remember. Who exactly are they attacking?"

"The other dictatorship. They don't view the council-run one as much of a threat."

"I imagine not. Especially if they aren't a warrior based community. Taking a guess here, this third one has only survived this long because the other two would attack the other the moment they went to take over the third?"

"Something like that," Kit said, nodding her head.

"Right. Well, the only one who acted in good faith was our dear little community run tribe. That's fine. They're probably preferable to work with anyways. With a larger pool of essentials in their community, I imagine that they have far more to gain through a deal. The other two would have just wanted wealth so they could distribute to their backers. Politics is always so fun," Felix said in a flat voice.

"Put a thought in Victoria's head to send the other two away," he continued. "Bring the democratic one. I'll need Michael sooner than I thought. Give him a brief rundown of the situation and have him meet up with me.

"At the same time, I'm going to need you to mobilize say… an entire battalion of Legion Security. Armed for full combat. Engage their mech attachment as well," Felix said, running down the plan in his head.

"That's… quite a firm response. Did you want the Powered element activated as well?"

"No. Let's keep that under wraps for now, but do ask for the appropriate number of Fixers and Telemedics. After that, get yourself back to HQ. I need you making sure the ship stays on course. I'll be over that way," Felix said, pointing at a boundary marker.

"Oh, and get me Miu," Felix called over his shoulder. "Let her know in advance she'll be off her leash."

Flipping over his wrist he did a quick check for any new messages or email, and then tapped the alert indicator for Andrea.

A second later and her face popped up in the display. She was clearly in the ANet and working on something.

"Felix?" she asked. "What's going on? I just saw a number of things light up and go active at the same time. I thought you said you didn't need me because this was going to be simple."

"Yeah. Looking like we're going to have a bit of a fight out here on Legion world. Is uh… is Adriana available? I think I'm going to need her," Felix said. He wasn't quite sure how to refer to the two of them yet. It'd only been a day after all.

"Nn! She is. Want me to send her your way? Full combat rigging?" she asked.

"Yeah. And an Andrea of course. Not you though, not Prime. Or Adriana's Prime. If I don't have to spend points I'd rather not," Felix said.

"Got it!" chirped the Beastkin, and promptly shut down the channel.

Almost at the same time, Victoria brought over a middle-aged man, and Michael came up from the other side.

"Great, everyone's here. First up, did the Fixer finish up with English?" Felix asked, looking to Victoria.

"Yes. Your servant gave me your language," said the man.

Felix gave him a second look and found that he was fairly ordinary. Brown hair, dark brown eyes, and a face weathered by work and toil.

His age may not have been what he'd originally thought. In fact, now that Felix really looked at him, he might be in his thirties and simply suffering a hard life lived rough.

"Good. And your name?" Felix prompted.

"Hern."

"Any surname attached to that or just—"

"Hern."

"I'm going to assume you meant that your name is simply Hern, and not Hern Hern. Anyways. My name is Felix. These are indeed my people, and this is going to become my camp. I originally asked all three of your tribal leaders to come speak with me to discuss things. Though I've just found that apparently your two neighbors are already engaged in what sounds an all-out attack on each other. Best guess is they'll turn on you when they're done," Felix said, keeping it simple.

Hern blinked once and then started to turn to the side, as if he wanted to run straight home.

"I'd like to make you an offer," Felix said, trying to head the man off before he ran off with his emotions. "One that would be equitable for both of us. I want to—"

Felix paused as he realized he was probably talking past the man, if not far above him.

"I want to work out a deal that's good for both of us. I want your people to join me, if they're willing, and I want to trade you in… stuff," Felix said. He wasn't sure how else to call it other than stuff. They hadn't even figured out what they'd need yet.

Other than the basics, that is.

"I'm afraid that won't work," Hern said. "Because as soon as one of those two kills off the other, they'll turn on my people. We're not… we're not a warrior tribe." Hern shook his head, looking at the ground. "I should have listened. We should have moved long ago."

"About that. I think the starting point for an agreement might be as simple as say, an alliance?" Felix said.

The dark brown eyes of Hern jumped up to Felix's own and stayed there.

"You do not have the number of warriors needed to defeat them. You offer something that you don't have."

"Don't worry about that part. I'll need a yes or a no, and your signature. Wait, do you even have a written language?" Felix asked, halfway to pulling out a sheet of folded paper he'd prepped in advance.

Hern had the look of someone listening to a crazy person.

"Right, no written language. A thumbprint worked for Erica so, let's try that. How do you feel about a blood-oath?" Felix asked.

"Fine. And what is this blood-oath needed from me and mine? Would you have me become your property to simply avoid becoming their property?" Hern asked.

"Honestly, it's simply a straight alliance with nothing promised other than mutual defense and cooperation. By my honor, that is all," Felix said.

"And you'd put your own blood-oath mark on it?" Hern asked.

That's new.

"I would be willing—"

Hern pulled a small knife from his belt and cut it across the ball of his thumb. He then promptly pressed his thumb to the paper, while holding the knife out hilt-first to Felix.

Taking the knife, Felix eyed it for a second, then repeated the same action Hern had.

"Michael, I took the liberty of getting you a battalion worth of Security. The attached mechanized unit was activated as well. I need you to take the field and protect our new allies," Felix said, looking to the local force commander.

"Understood. ROE?" Michael asked.

"One warning, then engage until they break. Don't chase. No limit on amount of force inside of conventional means," Felix said. "Dismissed."

Michael saluted, out of habit or reflex Felix wasn't sure, and went off towards the portal gate.

Hern looked between Felix and Michael, and then decided to follow the soldier.

Felix couldn't blame him, he was no warrior.

The sound of booted feet announced an arrival from the portalway. Expecting the Security forces, Felix was surprised to find thirty Andreas dressed in full combat gear marching swiftly in his direction.

An additional one dressed in corporate clothing walked along to one side of them, holding a messenger bag under an arm.

They even had their own rankings and insignia on the collars.

Coming to a stop in front of him, the lead Andrea looked up at him.

"Adriana, reporting. Adriana Prime is with Andrea Prime in the ANet," said the Beastkin.

Right. Adriana. I need to change her hair color or something. Wait, would she even want to?

"You're in a defensive role. We'll be rolling into a hot area. Victoria and Miu have both been activated as well. Coordinate with them for anything you need or want. Any questions?" Felix asked.

The Adriana looked backwards towards the Beastkin arranged behind her, and back to Felix.

"None."

"Great. As you will, then."

Every Adriana pulled up a shortened rifle to their shoulder, one Felix couldn't identify, and racked it in unison.

There wasn't much to do until the mechanized units got here and loaded them all up.

Somehow he'd convinced the Adrianas, Miu, and Victoria that he should be allowed to view the scene from the turret of the personnel carrier.

Surveying the field, Felix found it was more or less what he expected. Hern's people were living in buildings of wood, hide, and a few of stone.

"They don't even have a wall," Felix said.

"I don't think a wall would have helped. If anything it would have drained resources," Miu said. She was standing atop the personnel carrier just behind Felix.

"Fair. Still… I can't help but worry. What if this lack of foresight continues," Felix said.

"Then you'd correct that," Victoria said, sitting on the edge of the personnel carrier on the other side. "Simple enough, really."

Michael had been working this whole time, setting up a number of heavy machine gun positions. They were traditional hard points with overlapping fields of fire.

Each had been stagger stepped to provide coverage for the other, creating a funneling effect as well.

It'd be a field of death.

"You realize how silly this is," Adriana said from inside. "I've been watching the feed from a UAV and this is nothing more than a berserker's brawl. You're putting up weaponry better used against a traditional army."

"I plan on making an impression. Michael has experience with heavy weapons, this is what he knows. Though I figure if he was in cavalry, he'd be asking for helicopters. Or tanks if he had been in an armored division. For here, this works perfectly. Massed enemies. Charging," Felix said.

"A bloodbath," Miu said.

"Speaking of. I need you to go ahead and work through their officers, leaders, or whoever they look to for direction. Wipe 'em out. Do a great job and I'll let you off your leash in public with a mask from Lily," Felix offered.

He felt a little bad about making such a strange offer, but he'd use whatever carrot he could.

"Done. Can I start now?" Miu asked, her voice cracking on the last word.

"No. But you can go get ready if you w —"

Miu vanished before he even finished talking.

"She's going to kill anyone who opens their mouth to give an order," Victoria said softly.

"Probably. But that's what she's good for."

"I'd say the lead elements will be here in under ten minutes," Adriana called up. "Still only seeing melee combatants with simple weapons. They've finished up with the other tribe, and are sending everyone over this way. They're not even stopping to pillage, loot, or anything. Surprising given their mentality."

Felix laid his hands flat against the metal, and rested his chin on them.

Hurry up and wait.

Truth didn't match expectation though. As soon as the warriors saw Hern's peaceful community, they started towards it at a sprint.

"This should be short and ugly," Felix said to no one in particular.

Clearing the grasslands at a fast run, they ran onward towards Michael's defenses.

Later than Felix thought it'd happen, Michael apparently gave the word. The deep rapid chattering grunts of the machine gun positions opened up.

Warriors in leather skins and naught but a hand-held weapon dropped as the scythe of bullets swept across the field.

"Technically, this is a defensive action," Felix shouted over the din of fire. "I'd say we're well within our rights to protect our allies."

"I'll make sure all the reports indicate that. Wouldn't want this to be ruled a war crime in the history books," Adriana called back.

Well that's rather dark, isn't it.

Then again, she's not Andrea.

A minute in, and the grass was only a foot high from the point that the machine gun line started.

Nothing stood in that barren field.

Man, tree, or bush.

It'd all been cleared.

"Is that it, Adriana?" Felix asked, looking down below him into the carrier.

He saw an Andrea staring back up at him with her tablet in hand. She looked to the side, probably at the Adriana in front.

"There's a mass of them out of range on the other side. They're all grouping up and... I don't know. It looks as if they're facing outward and talking to one another. Hard to tell from this angle."

"Probably Miu hunting them. I imagine she's cornering anyone trying to issue orders," Felix said.

Straining to see into the distance, Felix didn't manage to catch sight of anything.

Almost too softly to hear, he picked up the faintest sound of chanting.

Unbelievably though, it began to rise in volume. As if it were being shouted by far many more voices than were actually possible.

"I think they're chanting," Adriana said. "It... sounds like praying, but I don't know their language. But it has that same kind of quality to it."

"Why would they be praying?" Victoria asked.

"Not sure. Maybe it's part of their culture?" Felix asked. "Pretty loud though. It doesn't... feel right."

A crack of lightning came down out of the air from a clear sky. It exploded when it hit the ground, and the ground rumbled.

As the dirt cleared and Felix could see again, he was surprised to find a group of ten or eleven people standing side by side across the field from him.

The radio in the personnel carrier crackled to life.

"I can't read them," said the Fixer assigned to the mission. "And the brief snatches I get are strange. It's all strange—"

One of the people lifted an arm and a blue streak of light flashed out across the distance and hit the lead machine-gun nest.

It exploded in a burst of white fire and rounds began cooking off.

"Damnit. What is that?" Victoria asked, standing up.

" —feels like something I've never felt before!"

Felix thought about the possibility of changing the status of the person who'd just attacked. If he hypothetically owned them, what would their status be?

Name: Abera		Power: Mastery of Ice	
Alias: She of Frost; Ice Queen; War		Secondary Power: Goddess	
Physical Status: Immortal		Mental Status: Enraged	
Positive Statuses: None		Negative Statuses: None	
Strength:	4,200	Upgrade?(40,200)	
Dexterity:	3,900	Upgrade?(30,900)	
Agility:	5,100	Upgrade?(50,100)	
Stamina:	9,000	Upgrade?(90,000)	
Wisdom:	8,420	Upgrade?(80,420)	
Intelligence:	7,800	Upgrade?(70,800)	
Luck:	3,010	Upgrade?(30,010)	
Primary Power:	N/A	Upgrade?(N/A)	
Secondary Power:	N/A	Upgrade?(N/A)	

"Holy shit it's a god," Felix said. "They're all gods."

Abera, the Ice Queen, drew her arm back and threw another bolt of whatever it was. Another emplacement went up just like the first.

How do you even fight a pantheon? And why is there a pantheon? What the actual f—wait. Wait wait. Don't I have my own card? Maybe?

If they're listening?

"Hey, I'm not sure if you're listening," Felix said aloud. "But if you want to collect on those two favors later, it probably won't be possible if that Ice Queen over there tears my head off. And no. I don't plan on withdrawing. I'll be honoring my commitment to Hern."

"You'd force my hand then?" came a voice from nowhere and everywhere. It was masculine, and human sounding. There was an immense pressure in Felix's head suddenly.

Where Kit had been strong, she'd also been gentle.

This presence was anything but. His mind was laid bare, stripped, and beaten.

"You would. Annoying. And amusing. Right, then. You'll not call on me in this fashion again. Ever. Or I'll turn your head inside out," said the voice.

A shape appeared in front of the distant pantheon.
A lone silhouette to battle a dozen.
There was no sound.
No movement on either side.
Not even a discernible confrontation.
The gods and goddesses lined up on the other side simply fell to their knees.
Uh?
Felix tried to do the same thing to this new arrival that he'd done to Abera. To see their status. To get anything at all.

```
Don't test me, Felix. Good try though.
Do not interfere with the local
beliefs. If anything, you'll encourage
them and their beliefs in their gods.
Spare those who surrender.
This situation is handled and done. Do
not do anything like this again.
If you do, I'll destroy you myself,
and turn your soul into toilet paper.
```

As if they'd never even been there, the pantheon simply wasn't there anymore. They were gone. The shadow silhouette disappeared as well.

Chapter 23 - The Return -

"Adriana," Felix said, not wanting to lose the chance his nameless benefactor had given them. Ducking down into the carrier he met the lead Adriana's gaze.

"Get out in the far field and get over to the other camp. Let's curtail any pillaging and looting before they get a chance. I need it done at a run, so take whatever mechanized units you need. Questions?" Felix asked.

Adriana shook her head, getting up from her seat.

"Oh, and Adriana... what do you think about changing your hair color permanently? Something to distinguish you from Andrea. I promise to treat the two of you the same, and you can always recombine later on, but it might be good to have at least one unique feature," Felix said. His words had started to ramble a bit at the end. He wasn't sure if he was making a situation out of something that wasn't there.

Adriana stared at him for a moment, then gave him a smile.

"Nn. I think that... I think that'd be a good thing. Though I think we'll choose brunette. We are, and are not, Andrea. I'll discuss it with my Prime when I rejoin her," said the Beastkin.

"Good. As much as I love staring at you in that harness, you need to go get going," Felix said, gesturing at the door.

"Oh? I'll let my Prime know that, too. Maybe she'll wear it for you tonight."

Adriana slipped by him without another word, leaving him alone in the carrier.

Huh. Those are two very separate personalities... long-term troubles maybe. As long as I treat them the same, I suppose, it isn't my problem.

Standing up, Felix found Victoria waiting. She opened her mouth and before she could get started, Felix held up a hand.

"We're staying here in the carrier. Adriana is going to go hit the other camp and curtail the pillaging, raping, and killing. I can't imagine yonder warrior tribe taking their loss easily. They'll take it out on the other one," Felix said. Then he shook his head. "No. We'll end this one here and now. We take the other tribe into the alliance, force them to work together with Hern, and banish the third. That doesn't break any of the decrees that were set down."

"Decrees?" Victoria asked.

Felix felt his stomach lurch. He didn't really want to think about it if he didn't have to.

"Did you see a silhouette on the field? Right before that enemy conga line of gods vanished?" Felix asked, his voice soft.

"Yeah. I did. It just... appeared. They all... knelt before it, it looked like."

"Yeah. They did. That silhouette is someone... or something... I owe some favors to for a change in my own powers I wanted. I kinda forced it to intercede here. It left me with a few commands I am quite loath to break," Felix explained.

Victoria nodded her head, looking out to the field again. "It sounds like the world is a scarier place than I thought it was," Victoria said.

Felix heard a chime in his ear signaling an incoming call.

I had no idea we got reception on another planet. They must have put up some temporary signal relays or something.

Reaching up to his ear, Felix tapped the button.

"This is Felix," he said.

"What the heck just happened?" Kit asked him, sounding completely out of breath.

"Huh?" Felix muttered. "What do you mean? Weren't you watching the feed? That was the whole reason we outfitted so many people with cameras. You wanted them specifically for HR."

"I was watching! We even tried to record it. Every single camera has a blank spot. I could see when those people appeared, one started attacking, then the recording goes white," Kit said, her tone curt. "Every. Single. Camera."

"And... did it come back on?" Felix asked. He had a sneaking suspicion but he didn't want to believe it.

"The cameras? They did, yes. They all turned back on as if there wasn't even a problem. The people were gone and the field was empty," Kit said. He could hear the loud thump of her sitting down heavily in a chair.

"Well. Something did happen. It might be good if we waited for me to make it back to HQ to talk about it though. It might even be best to let you read it from my head and a few others. It's... it's honestly hard to explain."

Kit sighed from her end of the line. "I imagine so. Because that's not all that happened."

"Oh?"

"I'm sending you a few clips of video. These happened minutes ago but are all over already. Watch them but don't hang up. Your wrist terminal should be able to display them fine."

"Alright, alright. Send it my way then," Felix said. Turning over his wrist, he opened up the display, flipped it to his email, and waited.

Crap. Need to call Miu off before she murders her way all the way down to the peasants.

Typing off a quick command into an email, he sent it Miu's way. She was well outside of radio range he was betting. With any luck, the notification would catch her interest if the signal relay could get it out to her.

Several video clips fed into his inbox. Opening the first one he cleared his throat. "So what is it I'm looking at here? While it loads, that is. Any type of—"

"Just watch," Kit said.

"Fine, fine."

Biting down his impatience, Felix managed to wait quietly.

The video blipped once, then turned on.

It was a church service.

He couldn't recognize the religious iconography in the video on the walls. There was no point in guessing at the religion for Felix. He'd never had a mind for worship so there simply was no base knowledge for him to work off of.

A man stood on a raised dais and was standing in front of a podium. Felix assumed the man was giving a very good sermon since he was being drowned out by applause.

Finally noticing the look of horror on the man's face, Felix realized it wasn't applause.

It was a grinding, shuddering rumble that was increasing in volume every second. To the point that it was simply too loud for the microphone on the camera to pick up anything else.

Light began to shine from a symbol on the wall. One that was smaller than the others. It was dull at first, then it exploded into a blazing beam of scorching whiteness.

The video cut out after that.

"Was that a bomb?" Felix asked, moving to open the second video.

"No. It wasn't. In fact... the next two videos are the same, though one is from outside of a museum. A museum of religion," Kit said.

"Alright. I'm not sure what's happening here. When did this happen exactly?" Felix asked.

"A minute or two after the recordings blanked out."

That means that whatever my friend did here... affected Earth. But in what way?

"Ok. I'm up to speed. But... what does it mean? Did anything happen afterward? I mean, did they just go back to normal?"

"Yes... and yet no. A few religious leaders... exploded. A number of people simply died. Stranger still, some recovered from terminal illnesses and diseases. Some that they simply shouldn't have been able to," Kit said.

"I... I don't even know what to say to this. It doesn't make any sense," Felix murmured. He really didn't either. None of it registered with him as anything that connected with what he knew.

"Maybe it'd help if I told you that every single spiritualist, from the weakest clairvoyant, to the strongest necromancer... passed out. When they woke up, they were all changed. By and large, most of them are incredibly stronger than they were previously. Especially those devoted to religions or cults.

"You know how Witches and Warlocks were believed to simply be a lower form of Magic or Wizardry?"

"Yeah. Their magic was very similar, but it couldn't put out enough power to be useful."

He'd actually looked into it at one point. Most of them used fairly mundane relics and simple beliefs to fuel their spells. Once he'd realized that it would only do enough to get him in trouble, Felix had dropped the study fairly quickly.

"Every Witch and Warlock in our employ reported in. They experienced a massive upsurge in power."

"They did?"

"Orders of magnitude greater. They also reported something else."

Felix was in a bit of a hurry and didn't really have time to play this game, but he imagined Kit was enjoying herself.

"Oh? And what's that," Felix said amiably.

"Sorry, I know this bugs you. It's just so exciting. They all reported that... that something reached out to them. Reached out to them and they suddenly felt complete. Whole. The spiritualists said something similar."

Something reached out to them?

"This is a guess but... you said that they were gods that you saw? Gods and goddesses?"

"Yeah. Apparently the enemy prayed and—oh. You think...?"

"What I think is that in the tales passed down, priests were magicians of their own caliber. Before the non-human races appeared."

Frowning Felix looked up and out onto the bloody grasslands. His history was shaky at best.

"Quite a few people thought it was the end of the world back then. I mean, the non-human races just appeared one day, and by all accounts, magic was at an all time low.

"And now... we opened a portal to another world and all of the... the religions... woke up," Kit said.

"That seems pretty far fetched," Felix said.

"I would agree. Except that we actually have a priest or two in our ranks. They also reported similar events to the Witches and Warlocks," Kit said. "And apparently, they got a more direct message."

"And that was?"

"'We have returned.'"

"That sounds ominous," Felix said, feeling like he'd done something incredibly stupid.

"That it does. Way to go there, Pandora. Let's pray hope is still in the box. I can't imagine gods from thousands of years ago being up on today's morality and society. I've already notified Lily and she's working to get whatever info we can. She still has contacts in the magical community after all."

Felix pressed his hands to his face.

Everything kept getting more and more complicated.

"I've got Jessica on the line," Andrea said, looking up from her terminal.

Felix closed his eyes and rubbed at them with his palms. It'd been a few weeks since the battle on Legion world. Election day was literally around the corner now.

Tomorrow, even.

Felix was feeling tired and run down at this point. He was quite glad for the governor race to be over soon. Win or lose.

"Yeah?" he said.

"She said she linked up with Erica. They have some others from other stations they want to bring in. She'd like to schedule a meeting with you to go over it," Andrea said.

"Uh huh. And pump me for a story as well. Her career has really skyrocketed since we've been feeding her and Erica stories," Felix muttered. Opening his eyes he blinked a few times, trying to get everything to come into focus.

"They're pretty," Andrea said suddenly.

"That they are. And I'm already with a lovely wolf Beastkin and her sister. Go ahead and schedule the meeting for today. I wanted to drop those stories off with her to sink the other candidates tonight anyways. I'll pack things up and head over that way. I need to stop by Felicia's lab first and see how things are rolling. She promised me a peek at the new Fist," Felix said, standing up.

"Nn!" Andrea said, her cheeks turning a faint red. "Adriana is happy... by the way. We joined briefly the other day. They're happy being Adriana and our sister."

"Good. Off to see Felicia," he said, leaving the ANet and entering the elevator.

He'd taken to hiding here whenever he needed some time to himself. Few people would venture into the ANet floor willingly.

Two Adrianas smiled at him as he passed by, watching him intently. Practically staring at him. *They're quite a bit more intense than the Andreas.*

A few minutes later and Felix couldn't help but wonder if this had been a bad idea. Felicia had been excited to see him.

Which made every inch of skin on his body crawl. She was never happy to see him. *Unless she wanted something*

"Felix! Great timing. I wanted to talk to you," Felicia said as she stumped over to him as he was cleared through security.

"Oh? And what does my armorer need?" Felix asked, unable to help himself.

"Eh? More people, honestly. But I wanted to talk to you about Legion's Fist, and your points," Felicia said. She smacked the back of her hand against his stomach and went in the opposite direction she came from. "This way. I want you to look at this."

Felix followed along. Unable to help himself he looked into every lab room, desk, and terminal he saw as he passed.

Everyone was working on something. He could see prototypes, modeling, data points, even an entire meeting that looked like it was talking about testing protocol.

"—ee if we can't make upgrades simply based on your power! I mean, when we really dug into the original Fist we found a lot of things we'd never even considered. That's why we tore it apart, put it back together, and then retired it," Felicia said.

"Huh. Yeah, that makes sense. I suppose we could see what the point cost is. No idea how much it'll do or how far I can push it though. Some of that more subjective stuff gets weird," Felix said.

"Excuses already? You're the naysayer today, are ya?" Felicia said.

She slapped her hand into a panel next to a doorway. The door slid open and she made to enter immediately.

"Come on then, come take a look at the Fist and let's see what we can do," Felicia said as she walked through the doorway.

Felix followed along and stopped almost immediately just inside.

It was bigger than the last one. At least double the size in fact. The weapons were similar, but sized up. There was even what looked to be a gigantic cannon sticking up over the shoulder and pointing skyward.

How would you even use that?

This new Fist was clearly designed for a battlefield, and not for a building.

"I know what you're thinking, and you're right. This isn't for going into buildings. Your normal armor is for that, and excels at it. Why create another tool that does the same thing?" Felicia said.

Stopping in front of a console, she began typing something in.

"White and I have been working pretty heavily on this one. We took a lot of his other work and built it in. Nanotech, rail guns, better energy sources, better alloys," Felicia said.

She typed something rapidly in and the Fist began moving.

It was eerie how little noise it made as it lowered itself to the ground.

The torso opened up, the lower half forming a stairwell, and the upper half moving out of the way. The cockpit inside looked as if the original one had been mirrored.

He wasn't quite sure how that'd work if he was supposed to control it as if it were his own limbs.

"Similar helmet design to your armor. It feeds in, and responds, as if it were your body. We spent a lot of time getting it right," Felicia said.

"Am I that easy to read?" Felix grumped. Lately it felt like everyone knew what he was thinking as he thought it.

Felicia stopped what she was doing and turned to look at him.

"No. But we all talked to Kit about your thoughts once she got into your head. It's… good to know you're exactly what you say you are. Also easier to understand. Even if you are an ass."

Should have known. Not a problem, though. She's not sharing anything I wouldn't already tell them if they asked.

"Good, I suppose. So… you want me to try to upgrade it?" Felix asked, starting to draw up what he wanted his popup to do.

"Yep. I want you to more or less do what you did last time. We figured out a lot of things that would've taken us time to get to, and we would have, but time saved, ya know? So… more of the same," Felicia said, facing him. She leaned up against the console and folded her arms across her chest.

"Fine, fine. By the way, how are you and Ioana doing? I don't get to see much of her. She's always working," Felix said.

He focused on Legion's Fist, trying to think back to what he did last time. He'd simply wanted it completed at the time. To be what it would be if they'd had the time to finish it.

"We're… we're doing well. Too well. I keep expecting something to go wrong," Felicia said after a moment.

"That's a silly way to look at it. Why predict a negative when you have no reason to? Focus on the now or lose it," Felix said with a touch of anger in his voice.

A number of people he'd met in his life had always focused on the problems. The concerns. The negative what ifs that could happen.

They spent their lives worrying and complaining, instead of working to fix it.

Ah, let's do that then. Let's apply that thought to this.

Making that his driving thought, Felix wanted to see what the Legion's Fist would be if Felicia and Mr. White had another year to work on it.

To see the state of the mech at that point.

Equipment (Legion's Fist II): Build out extended by one year	Warden Unit will be completed per specifications.	Upgrade? (53,000)

"Well. I got the answer. About fifty-three thousand points," Felix said.

"And what'd you do exactly?"

"I wanted to see what'd it'd be like if you had another year to work on it."

"Huh. That's definitely one way to look at it. Change that though. What would it look like if we upgraded it to the next version," Felicia suggested.

Nodding his head, Felix altered his desire.

Equipment (Legion's Fist II): Build out changed by one iteration.	Warden Unit will modified by one development cycle.	Upgrade? (112,500)

"Damn. Jumped up to one-hundred and twelve. Give or take."

"Ok, go up another version."

Felix frowned and decided he'd humor her.

Don't exactly have that kind of point value, you know.

Equipment(Legion's Fist II): Build out changed by two iterations.	Warden Unit will modified by two development cycles.	Upgrade?(359,250)

"Three hundred and sixty. Roughly," Felix said, shaking his head. That was a massive point investment.

"See, that's a big point jump though. It isn't a straight multiplication. Which means the development on that one is much bigger. Ok, do that one," Felicia said, nodding her head.

"Hah. And where do you think I'll get those points? It's not like th—"

"Ah. That's right, I haven't told you. I've been converting some of my budget into gold. Right now I have enough for about a million points. This is what I want first," Felicia said, waving her hand in the air. "Your point budget right now is at about one hundred, I'll take up two-hundred and sixty of that on my own."

... Damn. I never even thought about doing that. That's not a bad idea. Have departments turn their budget to gold to convert to points instead of straight funding.

"I also told everyone else what I was doing the other day with my budget. I expect they'll probably be doing the same."

"I would be, too" Felix admitted.

"Alright. Do you have the gold handy or do we have to do some transfers?" Felix asked.

Felicia looked back to the console and poked a button.

"Oi, bring in two hundred and sixty thousand points worth of gold," Felicia said, and then looked back to Felix with a wide grin. "I can't wait to see what we would have made in the future. This'll jump us ahead by years I bet."

Felix began turning gold into dirt as soon as the lab assistants started to cart it in. As soon as it was altered, the dirt was carted right back out.

By the time three minutes had passed, Felix mutated enough gold to make economists twitch.

And when it was all done, he only took a moment to pull up a window and make the upgrade.

Legion's Fist began to rapidly change in front of them.

The design went from sleek lines to hard edges. Weapons melted and reformed themselves into vaguely similar designs, but clearly different.

Overall, it was a similar design, but was clearly a different machine.

"Yes, yes!" Felicia shouted, clapping her hands together. "I can't wait to start poking around in it. Shit in my beer, is that a portal device on this thing?"

Chapter 24 - Shakedown -

Shaking his head, he couldn't help but feel some mild amusement at Felicia's excitement over the Fist.

Felix's wrist terminal made a deep chiming noise.

One he hadn't heard since he selected it as an option. It was a sound he knew intimately and had hoped to never hear it.

Ignoring Felicia's antics, he brought his wrist terminal up and tapped the flashing red indicator. It was an email from Dimitry, and it had only one word in the subject line, the body of it was empty.

Hannibal.

Taking a shuddering breath, he did his best to control himself.

He needed to clear his head, to think, to be ready.

Hannibal meant that Skipper was on the move. On the move and moving towards Tilen.

Ok. First things first. Don't panic.

Emergency recall protocol. That's first.

Even if this is false, we can use it as just another drill.

Opening up a quick window with his power, Felix changed the status of Emergency Recall from deactivated to activated.

Felicia's wrist terminal chimed three times in succession.

"What just happened?" she asked suddenly, looking at the recall notification.

"Skipper's on the move, I don't know exactly in what way yet, but she's on the move. For Tilen. I need to get to the ANet," Felix said.

Spinning on his heel he took off at a trot for the elevators.

Next is confirmation and response.

Pressing a finger to his earpiece call button, he held it down for five seconds.

There was a notification chime that came over the PA system.

"Emergency Recall is active. This is not a drill," Felix said as he stepped into the elevators. "Code is Hannibal. I repeat, Hannibal. Response is Alpha-Alpha-One at this time."

The lights dimmed as power conservation went into effect. Red, blue, and green running lights went up along the walls in the labs as the building operators began activating the appropriate programs and systems.

The elevator clanged as it went into a safety mode.

Felix pressed his ring into the security panel made specifically for the Legion rings, and pressed the button for the ANet with his other hand.

Lurching into motion, the elevator flew towards the designated floor, moving well past normal safety considerations.

Feeling the pressure in his stomach, then his knees when it came to a rapid stop, Felix groaned.

When the doors opened, he was greeted with the barrels of guns, and two angry looking dark-haired Adrianas.

"Felix!" the one on the left said.

"Get in," said the one on the right, lowering her weapon and pulling him out of the elevator. "The Primes are waiting for you and they've received notification from Kit, Lily, and Victoria. They're on their way. Miu and Ioana are on mission."

"Great, thanks," Felix said, moving quickly towards the command center in the ANet.

Most of the emergency and command functions had been transferred over once the ANet had been formed. The previous site operated independently as a backup now.

Just in the case the worst happened in the ANet.

Contingencies. Always contingencies.

Stepping through a door guarded by several Adrianas, Felix was in the command room. It was a hardened room, both physically and network wise. Andreas and Adrianas were throughout the room, working.

Both of the Elex Primes had taken their ANet job seriously and devoured any and every skill book Felix allowed them to have.

At this point, they were as qualified as anyone else in Legion to do any job.

As one, the Elex sisters looked up at him, then went back to their tasks.

Both of the Primes, designated now by a bright silver clasp on their right ears, were situated behind his command chair.

"Felix, I've got several general confirmations so far," Andrea Prime said from her work station. "Our hack into the Tilen Heroes guild shows that they're seeing the same thing we are. Army and the government also see it, but not as many confirmations."

"Alright. Recall status?" Felix asked. He needed to get his people and their families into cover. Everyone should be able to make it back to an HQ within thirty minutes. Those who were further than that had Telemedics assigned to them.

Taking a seat at the center of the room, he started to pull up his display screens. He'd have to get them where he wanted them.

"Eighty percent accounted for, another fifteen in flight. The remainder haven't reported in, but their transponders show they're en route to TM pickup locations," a different Andrea responded.

"Let's assume this is th—" Felix stopped as Lily and Kit arrived at the same time. They immediately went to their own positions and started to settle in.

"Let's assume this is the real deal, and Skipper is on her way in to take Tilen. Based on the mockups we ran, this is already abnormal. Last time her people were already in place before she launched. What changed?" Felix asked.

"Unsure at this time. Dimitry was the first to spot it because a Skipper-super showed up and prevented them from leaving. The Fixer on site read everything from there and relayed it up. I'm sure we'll get more later," Kit said.

"Felix," came Felicia's shout from the War-net bridge. It had been piped in through the command center and was working as the central communication hub. "Portals are open and functioning. We're ready."

"Great. Who's on duty at SC:HQ?" he asked.

"Sir, uh, that is," said a voice on the War-net bridge.

"Neutralizer?" Felix asked, recognizing the voice.

"Yes, sir!"

"Good. Keep the building on lock-down, bring everyone in past the first defensive line. Sacrifice the lobby and all adjacent buildings if need be. Anyone show up on your power?" Felix asked.

"Ah, a few. I didn't rub them out though. I didn't want them to know we knew. Should I ha—"

"No. That's perfect. Stick with it, and keep an eye on them.

"Legion world?" Felix asked next, moving down his check-in list.

"Michael here," came the rough voice of his site-commander. "Entry point is locked down and ready to receive."

"Perfect. Last, anyone from Wal?"

"Ioana here. Operation is progressing smoothly. We haven't made contact with anyone yet, so we're safe. Miu checked in and is laying low on an objective."

That was good news at least. Ioana and Miu had been sent to the nation of Wal to begin setting up for their branch out. It was good luck and chance that they'd not made contact yet. Had they, there was no telling if Skipper would make a move on them.

Who am I kidding. We're not even sure if she'll give a crap about Legion when she takes Tilen. After all, Legion exists in Skippercity and she leaves us alone.

For the most part, at least.

"Felix, last time Skipper ambushed everyone. There wasn't a lot of resistance at the beginning because of that," Lily said, leaning out of her seat towards him. "This time, there's going to be warning. A lot. That means there's going to be a pretty big ugly fight up there, right?"

"That'd be my guess," Felix said, agreeing with the assessment.

"Do we want to open the emergency bunkers? We built them for a situation like this, didn't we?"

Frowning, Felix thought on that.

The emergency bunkers had been built for public safety. They hadn't planned on revealing that information until tonight or tomorrow morning, just before people went to the voting polls.

It'd be that final confirmation of a promise he'd made when campaigning.

Defense and safety.

But does it even matter now? If Skipper takes the city, you won't be governor, Felix. And they're not part of Legion.

Eva would ask me why I didn't, and to think she wouldn't find out is stupid.

"Open them up, send up some Wardens and security forces. The moment everything becomes obvious, start directing people in. Engage if engaged, otherwise safe and escort rules of engagement," Felix said. "We'll turn them loose once it calms down a bit and bid them well. Maybe we'll do some recruiting for those who want to apply as well."

"I'll get that set up with your site commander for SC, Ioana," Lily said, starting to type immediately.

"Thank you," came the warrior's voice over the com.

"How far out are their lead elements?" Felix asked.

"A minute or less. It's a large group of powereds, helicopters and… I think drones," said Adriana Prime. "We're honestly in the dark. They're in between the cities right now. We only know as much as we do because we started to tap into every camera in Skippercity. A few were able to be pointed skyward but… not enough."

"Call coming in for you," Andrea Prime said, a second before his screen flickered.

The Fox Beastkin Jessica came into focus on his screen.

He'd forgotten about their meeting entirely.

"Sorry, Jessica. I'm afraid I'm going to have to cancel our meeting. We're doing a recall. I know you're not technically—"

"Felix. We need your help. A group of people broke into the station and they're rounding everyone up and killing them! They're burning them alive. Down to ash and then take the ashes!" Jessica hissed into her terminal.

Killing them? That doesn't make a damn bit of sense. Unless Skipper knows there's some Legionnaires there… at which point she'd just clear out the whole building and fill it with news reporters loyal to her.

Not only that, but if they're going that far to destroy the body, I'm not sure I'd even be able to bring them back. That'd be on a whole different level.

How did she even know about that, too?

"Show me the room you're in, we'll get a Telemedic to you immediately," Felix said. "Just lift up the terminal and show it the room."

Jessica lifted her hand and showed them all the room they were in. Erica was just on the side of the frame, as was a few other Beasktin he didn't know.

A small message popped up in the corner of his screen.

"We won't be able to get to them. All of the Telemedics are on missions, and won't be checking in. They are literally zipping in and out as fast as possible without a break -Lily"

Felix fought the grimace that threatened to take over his countenance.

So on top of not being able to send someone their way, I overspent my points today in a severe way. And trying to add Teleport to anyone here would just take too many points.

Looking to the side, Felix thought furiously as Jessica continued to broadcast the layout of the room to them.

"I keep trying to open a portal," Kit said. "I can't get it any bigger than a foot across though. Something is blocking it."

Damn. Did Skipper already find a countermeasure? Why did I have Kit show off the portal ability right in front of her. That was stupid, Felix. Stupid!

He wasn't willing to lose Jessica and Erica. He'd made a significant investment in both of them, and they were his people after all.

"A foot?" Felicia asked.

- 428 -

"About. The size of a dinner plate, really," Kit confirmed

"Is that why I did that?" Felicia said almost to herself.

"Felicia, you got an idea?" Felix asked.

"I do at that. Or I think, my future self did. The Fist. It has a Portal function attached to a disk. 'Bout the size of a table coaster. Fucking thing didn't make any sense to me. Does now though if we lost those two in a situation like this. If you want to save those little Beastkins of yours, pilot the Fist," said the Dwarf. "And I already checked. It's fit only for you, and only responds to you. I'm not sure why I did that, but I did."

Felix thought for a second, then sighed.

He wasn't meant for combat. He didn't like fighting. Having to resort to things of this nature felt like a loss.

"Tell Victoria to meet me in the lab," Felix said, making his choice. "Let's go, Kit. Adriana, I'll need some security forces I imagine. Time to show off, so suit up for a fight with Powereds."

Kit opened a portal in front of them as big as she said earlier.

Felix flipped the small disc through and then turned, clambering up into the Fist.

"I don't like you going in," Victoria said. Her voice was a touch distorted. She was sporting a new suit of light powered armor that Felicia had built her. It was almost an extremely lightweight version of a Warden.

"We don't either," a group of ten Adrianas said in unison.

"And yet, we're all still going. Seal the lab. The Fist will lead the way. Legion first," Felix said, closing the hatch of the Fist.

"Legion first," everyone said back at the same time.

The displays that popped up as the Fist locked him into place were very similar to his armor. Everything tightened up around him, preventing him from moving. Pressing down onto him.

Then the mech shuddered and stood up.

A single red light in the middle of his view turned green, and he could move again.

It felt natural. Fluid. There was no delay between his actions and the mech responding.

Thinking about the disc, a screen popped up in the corner.

Activate Portal?

Felix mentally hit the confirm button, and a portal slammed open instantly. It was huge, swirling, and loud.

Jessica, Erica, and a host of others flooded into the lab.

"Everyone remain calm," Felix said through his microphone. "Everyone will be escorted to a holding area and processed. No exceptions."

Adrianas began tagging and guiding people as they ran into the lab. They needed to make sure they didn't bring anyone inside that would be a problem later. He'd not be inviting in a worm or a mole now. Not when everything was on the line.

As if they'd been waiting for this moment, a group of men and women in various suits of armor, costumes, and clothes charged the portal.

There was no mistaking them as anything other than enemies.

Because they weren't Legion.

He could probably close the portal here and now, but he'd lose the disc that had created the entry point. Realistically, Felicia might be able to replace it, but there was no guarantee of that.

Not to mention he didn't want to hand over technology to the enemy.

"Engage," Felix said, making his choice.

Victoria flashed out, her sword blazing with light as the plasma edge carved through the air. Four Wardens with their standard issue Railguns opened up.

Enemy fire began rattling in as they lowered weapons and fired into the mass of Legion troops. A few Adrianas went down in the fire, and a number of rounds pinged off of the Fist.

Felix's mind blanked for a second, and then he thought only of utilizing his weapons.

His screen flashed and Felix had the strangest sensation of the Fist actually giving him instructions. At first it suggested the missile pods that were apparently what was mounted to the left shoulder. Which Felix quickly dismissed. That'd cause more problems right now.

The Fist instead helped Felix with what it called a FX-PC01.

Moving down on one knee the Fist settled itself into position quickly as rounds continued to bounce off it. The cannon mounted on the right shoulder unfolded itself and positioned itself like a bazooka there.

Reaching up with one hand, Felix steadied the cannon and an aiming reticle popped up on his view.

Targeting a huge muscled man in kevlar armor, Felix discharged the weapon. A blast of pure light and heat leapt from the cannon and vaporized the man's chest. His arms and legs fell to the ground, the head rolling away in an opposite direction.

Bright yellow and flashing, an indicator light came to life on a panel.

Tracking another target, Felix fired off another load of whatever it was. The second target tried to dodge, and instead of losing their chest, lost the entire left side of their body. She went down in a screaming, bleeding heap.

The yellow light went to an orange color and began to flash more rapidly.

It only has about three shots before it's empty or has to... something... One shot left I'm betting. Let's save it.

Pushing the command to holster the cannon, Felix stood upright and hefted the rifle that the Fist had hooked into a hip pod.

Pulling the trigger as soon as it settled onto his shoulder, Felix felt and heard the heavy impact of the heavy railgun discharging. The rifle had an attached ammo belt that could feed into several ammo pods throughout the Fist. It was limited in ammunition, but it at least carried a significant amount with it.

Victoria and the Adrianas hadn't been idle this whole time either. They were systematically working to eliminate all enemy combatants as they came in.

Victoria, moving at full speed and taking hits that would have killed an unarmored human, was shaking off her inexperience with her armor rapidly.

It was her first time using it, and she was now getting the hang of it.

Soon it was clear that Legion would take the victory

As if there had been any doubt.

"Deploy a boundary, no escapees," Felix called out.

Several Adrianas darted forward and hurled what looked as if they were glowing baseballs. They soared over the fight and landed against the far wall. Each Andrea looked to their wrist terminal and entered in a few commands. Giant blue walls of light erupted from those balls, blocking the door off behind solid magical energy constructs.

Realizing there was no escape, a number of their attackers began to surrender. Another number began to beat and attack furiously at the walls preventing their retreat.

"Waste 'em," Felix called through the War-net.

Without hesitation, the Adrianas began systematically moving into the surrendering numbers and giving them each a few rounds to the temple.

What'd been a battle, was now a bloodbath.

The forces Skipper had sent here weren't up to the task of actually engaging with Legion. They were a cleanup crew that could deal with security forces and a number of Powereds.

Victoria took the head off a woman who had her hands up, pleading for mercy.

And the room was silent.

"Leave the corpses, take the weapons and gear. Felicia likes that stuff for scrap and testing. Once we're out, toss in a firebomb," Felix commanded.

The surviving Adrianas, after consuming their fallen Others, went about their business.

Operation complete. Now the question is... what happens next, and does Skipper plan on attacking Legion. If she leaves us be, then we leave her be.

But I'm not so sure Tilen will go as easily as Skippercity did. Either her confidence got the best of her this time, or she was forced to move early.

And if she moved early, why?

Chapter 25 - Self Eval -

At first, it seemed as if Skipper's forces would steamroll right over the local police, government, and armed forces.

Then the government sent in the army and the air force. The guild dispatched numerous heroes. Vigilantes began pouring into the city of Tilen from the surrounding areas.

Doubling down on their attack, a second government army was sent to retake Skippercity, even going so far as to employ hundreds and hundreds of mercenary Powereds.

The ANet was keeping tabs on the situation by deploying a number of drone assets that Felicia had developed. Many of them would have to return and refuel, but those were exceptions with specialized functions.

An overwhelming majority of them had power supplies that could resupply themselves through other means. Solar, wind, and even a few that could tap into the grid directly. Those could remain in the field indefinitely.

Legion forces had been tasked to sweep, clear, and evacuate the upper floors of the HQ buildings for both locations.

After that, Felix had activated the security protocol, and his powers, that would seal up both locations from the outside world.

It'd appear as if there was never anything below the ground floor.

Legion was effectively safe behind a thick cement barrier and deep underground. Anyone who came to call on them would find only an empty building, and not a trace of them.

The only thing that anyone could find, and this wasn't something they could change since it was the point to be found, were the emergency civilian bunkers.

They'd filled to capacity immediately, and immediately gone over it. Now they were locked down and closed shut. That didn't mean the bunkers were invisible though.

Several times Legion Security had been forced to scare off, or eliminate, threats that came to the front entrance. It was an unfortunate reality, but Legion was already taking care of more than their expected responsibility.

Felix was now sitting in his actual office below ground.

It'd only been about eight hours since the attack started. Already the infrastructure of both cities had broken down. It was being carved into two different sectors: the actual government, and Skipper's. The middle ground was a contested area where both sides clashed.

Whenever Skipper showed up at a location, the government pushed at the other. Skipper was only one person after all. The strength of her alone was immense, but she simply couldn't be in two places at the same time.

"She doesn't trust her people to do what they need to do. She can't conceive of giving them the power to uphold their own sectors, because it'd be the power they need to overthrow her. Even though she practically controls them like puppets through the rings and crowns," Felix said, reading through another report.

"Nn," Andrea said at his side, typing into her terminal at the same time.

"Not everyone owns their employees," Lily said. She was sprawled out on a couch nearby.

She'd been coordinating efforts between the various villainous organizations, the magical societies, and Legion.

Felix snorted at that. "Uh huh. Everyone in Tilen was never a slave, but an employee. Technically speaking, everyone who's come to Tilen became free instantly. You'll remember I had everyone sign a second contract when they entered. The contract breaks might be steep, but nothing someone couldn't live with. You should know, you wrote part of it, Miss Lawyer Lady."

Lily waved a hand at him dismissively.

"Yes, yes. I admit it. I could have walked away. Everyone could have." Lily paused and seemed to dwell on her thoughts. "Maybe if it had happened early on I might have even left. But now... Legion feels like home. Like the place I want to return to. I have friends here. Coworkers, colleagues, respect, and a support group. Even the lowest employees are given all the same things."

"Yeah, you've mentioned that before," Felix said, closing the report and opening one from Dimitry.

"And I stand by it. Even people who fight, disagree, and argue are still coworkers at the end of the day. Everyone wants to simply better Legion. Everyone is equal, no one is different, and everyone spends their money in the way that they want. You're somehow walking a fine line between capitalism and socialism, and it's working."

"A cult, maybe?" Felix said offhandedly. Skimming through the report Dimitry had sent up, he couldn't help but be mildly concerned.

As a whole, the world of crime in Skippercity was going through an apocalyptic level of change. Dimitry wasn't sitting on his hands either. He'd leveraged all of the assets Felix had given him, and expanded their territory, membership, and area of control by three times its original size.

Felix had the unfortunate regret of having not created a Dimitry here in Tilen. Even if Legion had to board up its windows, Dimitry would be able to function and provide almost all the same functions that could be done legally. It would have just been catering more to the unsavory types, rather than the general public.

"A cult fits," Kit said from her chair. She was slouching in it, her fingertips pressed to her temples. "The simple adoration that everyone thinks towards you is overwhelming at times. The constant praise. The unyielding determination to be noticed and move up. One of the big benefits to a meritocracy, I suppose."

Felix shrugged and started writing a response back to Dimitry. Wondering if he could get someone he trusted to start up operations here in Tilen.

Dimitry had a Telemedic on duty after all. It was a bit late to start, but it didn't hurt to try.

"Now that word has spread about Legion world, everyone is asking when they can put in for a transfer," Kit continued. "A world built from the ground up from a Legion point of view seems to fit with a lot of view points. Since we have too many mouths to feed here, I've approved a large number of temporary transfers from both Tilen and Skippercity. Michael is drowning under resources right now. I imagine the next time we visit that tiny outpost might be a fortress. Or so I—"

Kit went silent as Victoria trooped in, still dressed in her combat armor. Her blade was sheathed at her hip, the click of the baldric as it swung back and forth as she walked was audible.

It was the look of her that'd gotten everyone's attention, however.

Blood was splattered up one side, and ash and soot down the other. She looked very much the picture of someone who'd gone through hell and back.

"We fought off a government incursion that wouldn't take no for an answer," Victoria said. "Then bounced back an attack from Skipper. I think both sides will leave Legion territory alone. I sent your communication to both sides, per your orders."

Felix finally broke his attention completely from his computer and turned to face Victoria.

One must give respect where it's due. And the greatest respect must be given for a hard job done well.

"Thank you, Victoria. You and your department weren't meant for combat duty on the front line, but you're performing extremely well. Please give everyone my gratitude, and that I'll not forget this," Felix said, meeting Victoria's eyes evenly.

She blinked twice and then nodded her head slowly. "Of course, Felix."

"Great. If they listen to the message, and actually heed it, then we'll be in the clear without anyone worrying about us. I'd like to play the neutral party if possible, and let them blast away at each other until they tire of it," Felix admitted. Sighing he shook his head and smiled ruefully. "I should have been celebrating my successful bid for governor by now, rather than worrying about military matters."

"Isn't that why Skipper attacked?" Andrea asked. She was leaning over her terminal, poking at something with one finger. "I mean, the day before you were more or less guaranteed to become governor, and take ownership of the city. Perhaps not in a purely contractual sense, but certainly as a temporary caretaker. I can only imagine the resources you'd have at your disposal then."

Everyone in the room went still.

It makes sense. She wasn't ready. Her takeover of Skippercity was so much more planned out. So much more... ready.

Already set in place. It was merely a matter of springing the attack.

This time was nowhere near that level.

"I really wanted to ride on a helicopter, too," Andrea Prime whined. "That or go to a fancy five star restaurant with the governor. See if they can make better pancakes than me. I bet they can't. I'll turn Skipper into a Sausage and then feed it to a dog."

"Not to mention how many of me have died," Adriana Prime said from Felix's other side. "It's a fortunate thing we don't have to create Death Others anymore. We'd have three more already."

"Stupid Skipper!" the Elex sisters said in unison.

Stupid Skipper? Stupid me! I'm the instigator in this whole thing. If I had taken control of Tilen as a whole, could I have leveraged it to take Skippercity?

Maybe? It's possible.

The better question here, though, is would I even want to?

I just wanted to live comfortably. The idea of being anything more than Legion is... terrifying.

"What do you want to do with all those civilians?" Lily asked him. It was in the small hours of the morning. Everyone else had shifted off at this point to grab some sleep.

With how much was going on, Felix didn't feel like he could actually sleep right now.

"Dunno," he said honestly. "Everything is just... going to hell. And so quickly. It's only been a day and already it's becoming clear that this isn't going to be a victory for either side. I think this'll become a city under siege, with the citizens losing, no matter who wins."

Felix was sitting on the couch in his private room. He was tired of looking at screens, reports, and files. The only thing he wanted to see right now was the back of his eyelids.

"It does seem that way," Lily agreed. She flopped down onto the couch next to him, her skirt slipping upward with the movement. She went to adjust it, then sighed and let her hands drop. "I think I've recruited more magic based Powereds today than I have in my entire career in Legion. If anything, I can certainly say that this war is certainly driving our recruiting."

Felix nodded his head a bit at that. "Safety in numbers, and Legion has a track record for taking on the odds and winning so far. We've matched against Powereds and come out on top. It's only fitting, really."

"Oh, there were a few spies in those reporters you brought over with your new pet Beastkins, who are desperate to speak to you by the way. The Fixer on duty dropped the spies off as soon as there was time. Last I heard they were under the fine ministrations of the Death Others."

"Hm. Those really are rather separate from Andrea and Adriana. Maybe they need a third sister after all."

"Maybe. They seem to split the Death Others between them and let them circulate freely. I get the impression they're acting as information carriers and welcomed between both. Still surprising that they separated into two, though."

"Yes and no. Andrea Prime wasn't actually the original Andrea. Or Myriad, as it were. I get the impression that Myriad was the original personality, and Andrea... Andrea was what was left over when a horde of Myriads converged on a location and lost. Died."

Lily frowned, her eyebrows lowering over her eyes. Leaning to one side, she rested her head on Felix's shoulder.

"That makes sort of sense. And also why Andrea is... well... different. She's the remainder... so to speak."

"Somewhat. Definitely makes you think. I think them separating into two different personalities is probably a good thing in the long run. We'll see. Good, bad, neutral. It's done, and she was the one who wanted it."

Felix sighed and laid the back of his head on the couch, staring up at the ceiling above.

"I find myself wondering how Skipper managed to do all that she has. Is she seeing the future? Alternate universes? What ifs? And if that's the case, how does she not lose herself in it. I imagine I'd probably chain a what if scenario to a what if scenario to move ever further into the future and find my path."

"Does it matter? Whatever her power is, she uses it to her advantage in all things. She also keeps a tight lid on it from others. I imagine the guild has some thoughts on it, but not the reality. As does the government," Lily replied.

"Uses it to her advantage. Am I any different? I use everything I can to build myself and my people up. To the point that we find ourselves here, today."

"Yes, yes you are."

Lily jabbed a finger into his side and dug it in. Felix grunted and brought his elbow down to fend her off.

"You know how Skipper empowers her people? Hm? Those she can't corrupt to her side of things?" Lily asked, getting her finger into his side again despite his efforts. "She uses her power to view every instance of what it would take to power them up, make them stronger, more powerful, more anything, so long as it isn't something she can't handle, and then does it. Regardless of what it might do to them, the problems it'd cause, she does it."

"Quit it," Felix complained, turning sideways on the couch to face Lily. "And how do you even know that? There's no way you could."

"Kit and her people have been filtering in to active roles on missions when they can. Scanning minds when the possibility presents itself. Buried in those wiped minds, those empty thoughts cleaned of personalities, is a story of broken men and women forced to endure.

"She's filled me in on the situation. I was curious about it, since the rings and crowns clearly serve a purpose, but wouldn't empower these people as they have. I've seen a few people I recognize with powers I don't remember them having, or strength they didn't."

"Great. And? I'm not exactly any different. You'll remember I've been forcing powers on people for a while now."

"No. You haven't. In fact, you seem to go out of your way to make sure the powers you do hand out match personalities or existing powers. You're not turning people into living bombs either, which I get the impression Skipper would do."

Felix snorted at that, eying the sorceress warily.

"Ok, you want a more clear-cut example?"

"Sure, why not," Felix said, the sarcasm dripping from his voice.

"Miu."

"What about her?"

"Miu is insane. Clinically so. She murders the Andreas and Adrianas that sleep with you. She paints her walls in their blood and dyes her sheets in it. That isn't a normal thing. The only thing holding her in check is you, your commands, and her contract with you."

"I'm aware," Felix said dryly. He'd gotten the biggest helpings of Miu's personality that anyone had.

Other than the Andreas she killed.

"Why not fix her?" Lily asked.

"Huh?"

"Why not just... remove that part of her personality. Eliminate the insanity. You could. Easily."

"I..."

"Go ahead. Try. Pull it up. Tell me how many points it would cost."

"I don't think—"

"Do it, Felix. I want to know. Humor me."

Annoyed, tired, and frustrated, Felix felt like arguing. He had no intention of doing what she wanted. Gritting his teeth he lifted up his hand.

"Please?" Lily asked. Her voice was soft and there was an entire undercurrent he'd never heard from her before in it.

Deflating, Felix hung his head. His anger cooled instantly and his will to battle fled.

"Alright."

Felix focused on the simple concept of making Miu's power a positive thing. To remove the negative aspect that drove her towards insanity. Or at least, controlling that aspect so she could be free of it.

Status Correction: Insufficient Control -> Sufficient Control	Correct Status? (11,150 points.)

"Well?" Lily prompted when it was clear Felix wasn't going to immediately offer the information.

"Eleven thousand. That's all it'd cost to give her control over it."

"What about removing that aspect entirely?"

Chewing at his lip, Felix tried again. Simply wanting to eliminate the negative aspect to Miu's power.

Power Upgrade: Multiplicative Base-Positive aspect only	Required Primary Power: 70 (Met) Required Wisdom: 60 (Unmet)	Upgrade?(35, 000)

"Thirty-five thousand. With a few point changes in another category," Felix admitted.

"In short, you could make Miu into a better person."

"Sure could."

"And why haven't you? Or changed my luck? As far as I know, you haven't modified anyone without them asking you to."

"I changed Andrea's intelligence a few times."

"If I remember correct, she complained to you about it, and you modified it. That's the way she tells it, at least."

Felix thought back on that. He could vaguely remember Andrea complaining that she'd been taken advantage of.

The more he wracked his mind, the more he felt like Lily might be right. His modifications and changes were always in his interest. Always.

But they were never counter to the person's wishes either, or at the very worst, they were neutral.

"The single defining character trait that you have, that makes you so different from Skipper, is you genuinely care about your people. It shows," Lily said, leaning in closer to him. "Everyone sees it. From the lowest, dirtiest job, to the highest heights of your inner circle. No one would ever mistake you for not caring for your people. Sometimes you say or do dumb things, like wanting to put people who don't belong into the sausage machine."

Felix mentally winced at the memory of that. He'd thought on that one a number of times. His reaction had been dismissive and not at all thoughtful.

"Kit tells me you berate yourself for that one. And I'm glad to hear that."

Meeting her eyes, he didn't look away. "And why's that?"

"It makes it so much easier to care for you. Knowing that you're just as human as the rest of us," Lily said with a grin.

She laid a hand to his jaw, leaned in, and kissed him tenderly.

When she finally pulled away, Felix felt like the world was spinning around him.

"Now. How about you treat me to a meal, and we try not to think about all this for a bit," Lily whispered.

Chapter 26 - Taking Stock -

Stepping out into the sunshine of Legion world, Felix took in a deep breath. The clean smell of grass and the fresh air washed over him.

It'd been an entire day since he'd seen the outdoors, let alone sunlight. The battle for Tilen was ongoing and had fallen into a lull of sorts.

Felix didn't dare step outside for the simple memory of the last time a sniper took a shot at him. They had been quite far away, and had nearly ended him. The lack of security in the city meant that everywhere that wasn't under direct Legion control had the potential for an ambush.

Looking around, he found the camp that he remembered was long gone. The portal led out onto a platform that was similar to a landing pad for a helicopter.

All around him was the interior of a place that looked more like a gigantic military camp than anything else. It was massive in size, and all along the perimeter were stone walls.

Sitting at the center of the entire complex was a gigantic stone keep. Something that looked like it belonged in a medieval story with knights and catapults.

Decorating the keep, the walls, and randomly spaced throughout were large metal poles that stuck straight up into the sky for at least twenty feet.

Something very odd going on here.

"Felix," Andrea said at his side. "I'm... I want to—" Andrea paused, her hands opening and closing. She looked torn.

"Want to go run around?" Felix asked, smiling. He knew what she wanted, even if she couldn't bring herself to quite ask for it.

It was a normal Beastkin reaction to this world.

"Nn!" Andrea said. She leaned in close to him, her tail trembling behind her.

"Well, run along then. My understanding is the surrounding area isn't completely safe though, so be on your guard."

Andrea nodded rapidly, then split into seven different Others and took off at a run. One remained behind with a sad look on her face. Felix noted that even the Prime had taken off.

"Don't worry about it, Andrea, I promise to spoil you later for taking one for the team."

The Andrea Other gave him a big grin, her ears twitching atop her head.

Adriana Prime assumed that permission had been given to her as well, apparently, since she split six times and sent her Others chasing after Andrea, though Adriana Prime remained.

"I'll stay with you," Adriana Prime said, peering up at him. "I want to be spoiled."

Taking a moment to collect his thoughts as he laughed at that comment, Felix wasn't sure if he really wanted to ask the question that was at the forefront of his mind.

The more he thought about it, the more things didn't quite add up for him.

"Good. I meant to ask... and you don't have to tell me but... where did Myriad go? You and Adriana are... well you're fairly similar. And you clearly have all of Myriad's skills, but I haven't seen her personality in a while. It's almost as if she's been submerged too deeply."

Adriana looked down, her shoulders tensing up. "She left. Myriad didn't feel like an Andrea or an Adriana, she said. That she didn't belong. She promised to keep in touch but... she still left. She's out here on this planet somewhere."

Frowning, Felix couldn't help himself from shaking his head. "I'm sorry to hear that. Was it something I did or something I didn't do?"

Adriana's head whipped up, and the Andrea grabbed his arm. "No!" they said in unison.

"She just didn't feel at home. The Death Others feel the same way at times.," Andrea said.

"The Death Others feel like they are still one of us, though," Adriana said, picking up where Andrea stopped. "Myriad... didn't. I think it's partially that she was the original Prime."

Suppose that makes sense. I wonder how that worked out in the end. I mean... she didn't even say goodbye and Andrea and Adriana didn't want to bring it up.

A problem for another day.

There was a deep whumping noise that made the hairs on the back of Felix's neck stand up. An Adriana stepped in front of him and began tracking something to his left. Turning his head, Felix found a bright red flare in the daylight sky. Then it got brighter, and bigger. Belatedly, he realized it was a fireball, and it was heading straight for the base camp.

The sound of the crackling fire could be heard as the giant ball of flame got closer and closer.

A beam of white energy shot out from the base camp and met the fireball. It broke apart into fiery shreds and burnt out into nothing, as if it had never been there.

"That was different," Felix muttered. "And I'm starting to wonder if Michael owes me a bit deeper of a report. There was no mention of giant flaming balls of death."

"That'd be because those only started up after my last report," Michael said. Felix looked to the man as he approached.

He hadn't noticed him. The fireball had been a real attention-grabber. "They also have tried lightning. One of the main reasons we've got all that lovely iron-age decoration everywhere. It's all grounded deep in the earth."

Felix grunted at that, holding out his hand to his site commander.

Michael shook his hand with a smirk. "Welcome back to Legion. We've been calling this place Fort One. Not very creative, but it describes it accurately."

"Considering I named the planet Legion, I'm not one to complain," Felix said, releasing Michael's hand. "So what's with the lightshow?"

"Locals are all up in a rage that we don't worship their gods. No one from Hern's group, or the group we saved," Michael said.

"Hm. I take it my mercy is reaping its reward?" Felix asked.

"And then some. It's not terrible, but it's growing. Come on, let me show you what we've accomplished. The attacks are annoying, but ineffectual so far."

Michael gestured towards the nearest wall and started walking. Felix wasn't quite ready to let the subject drop, but he was more than willing to let Michael show him around.

There'd been a lot of change since the last time he'd been here. It had the look and feel of a functioning military encampment now.

Michael led him up a set of stairs and straight to the wall. Laid out in front of him was what looked like what he saw in old war movies. A training camp made of tents, wooden buildings, and areas with long benches.

Men and women moved around the entire length and breadth of it. They were clearly working as both groups and individuals.

"This is our first batch of recruits. First class everyone has to pass is of course learning the language. Only after they get a mastery in that do they move on. Our lone Fixer has been killing himself simply working on the new recruit entry, let alone anything else," Michael said. "For those who look like they'll fail the language, they get put with him to see if they're worth training directly."

Nodding his head, Felix could well understand the problem. "Identify some candidates. We'll do some training the trainer once they get a pass from Kit. It wouldn't be a terrible thing to start the new talent in an HR role. They'll be better able to understand the situation," Felix said.

"Understood. We can do that, sir," Michael said. "That'd help immensely."

Pausing, and clearly reordering some things in his head, Michael continued, "The vast majority of the new recruits are going to be brought up to speed in security, infrastructure, and the basic jobs. As much as I'd love to have a department for everything, gotta start with the foundation."

Can't disagree there. Especially in a hostile location. With everyone pulled in, we really have too many people right now. Kit said she was getting a lot of transfer requests. What if we just moved them before they even asked.

"My understanding is Kit has approved a number of transfers to here. With the recall, I can't imagine a universe where that number hasn't already skyrocketed. And since we're all in defensive bunker mode, a lot of normal functions won't be carried out." Felix turned to Andrea. "Let's put a meeting on the books to talk to Kit about doing a massive temporary move. It'd help morale and get people working, rather than sitting around doing nothing and worrying."

Andrea nodded her head as she recorded a note down.

Felix's wrist chimed a second later, and Andrea lifted her head with a grin. "Done, dear," Andrea said.

Michael blinked and looked from Andrea to Felix. "I get the impression I should have been asking for things sooner than this."

"You have your budget, Michael. Everything else is a request. They may or may not be granted," Felix said. "Now, how about you continue the tour. I'm curious to see how you've done, and I don't really want to head back to HQ yet. It's been nice to stand outside without worrying about sniper fire and being attacked."

"Do the fireballs count?" Adriana asked, a serious look on her face.

She's as bad as Andrea is, just not in the same ways.

Sitting at a table in the center of camp, Felix had been answering questions from the locals for an hour. Andrea and Adriana had just finished shooing everyone away when it was clear he was getting weary.

Taking that moment to return, Michael was allowed to pass through the ring of Adrianas.

"And where did you slip off to, hm?" Felix said with a trace of irritation.

"Anywhere else. Politics isn't for me, and honestly, I try not to attend any meetings here I don't have to. I typically leave it to the HR and Legal people. I'm just a Jarhead. Give me a target and a rifle, and I'm good to go," Michael said.

"Too bad. Sit down. Hern is supposed to be arriving relatively soon and we'll both be meeting with him. I'd like to talk to him about what he knows of those attacks, and then figure out what we can do to try and put an end to it if possible," Felix said.

Grimacing, Michael took a seat on Felix's right hand side.

Andrea looked from Felix to Michael and then back again.

"When are you going to spoil me?" Andrea asked in that loud whisper of hers.

"Tonight. I plan on heading into Legion city tonight and have a meal. In person, no less. Without a mask. And you and Adriana Prime will be coming with me," Felix said.

Andrea's ears perked up and she clapped her hands together excitedly.

Adriana Prime, who was standing five feet away, nearly had the same reaction. Though with an SMG in hands it was a bit muted.

"Yay!" they said in unison.

The other Adrianas began immediately talking in hand signals between themselves.

"They're arguing about who gets to go with her," Michael said, watching the exchange.

"Mm, maybe I need to get someone to teach me whatever that language is that they're using," Felix muttered.

"Don't look at me, I actually have no idea about the language, but an argument is an argument, and that one seems pretty obvious."

Felix couldn't help but start to laugh. Now that he was watching, it was obvious to anyone that the Adrianas were arguing.

Overthinking things, Felix... overthinking things.

Michael shrugged his shoulders. "Doesn't hurt that I'm a Fixer. Their thoughts are about as subtle as a knife."

"Felix, here comes Hern," Andrea said, standing up from the table.

Michael and Felix did the same, holding their hands out to Hern.

It wasn't until Hern shook his hand, and a bit strangely, that Felix realized that handshakes might not be the custom here.

Another thought for another time, but it might be part of the very problem we're facing here.

"Hern, welcome. I don't want to waste your time, as I know it's valuable. I'll keep everything short and to the point," Felix said, indicating the seat directly across from himself.

Hern grunted and sat himself down. He looked as crotchety and grumpy as ever. The man stared at Felix and waited for him to continue.

"How are you feeling about our arrangement?" Felix asked, getting straight into it.

Hern fought to keep something from showing on his face before he wrinkled his nose. "Everyone said you were direct... I'm happy with the arrangement so far. I worry about the fact that you'll not share your magic with us without us signing one of your papers... but I understand. Magic is a powerful weapon," Hern said, his voice slow as he puzzled out what he wanted to say.

"Indeed, it isn't a matter of faith or trust in you, it's more of a belief that our foes are stronger than we wish. Now, is there anything you'd want to add to the deal as it exists today?" Felix asked, redirecting the conversation.

Hern looked at the table, his thoughts clearly turning inward. "Not that I can think of."

"Ok, do you feel like you're being cheated in any way?" Felix asked

"No... but I do worry that eventually we're going to run out of recruits for you... at that point... what happens to our arrangement?" Hern asked, setting a hard stare on Felix.

"It remains. There's one thing you need to keep in mind, and I think this might be a great opportunity to discuss it. When word spreads about what's going on here, there will be many, many people who migrate and move here," Felix said, laying his hands flat on the table and leaning forward. "And when they come, they will see your community as the entry point. And while many will join Legion, not everyone will. In fact, I imagine quite a few will have family in your community, even though they work for me."

Hern had become motionless, listening intently to Felix.

"So while you're losing many of your people to Legion now, that's only your original investment. Your return will be coming as word spreads. Especially that the local pantheon was summoned, and then left. While they may power spells and beliefs still, their direct intervention is no longer possible."

"The thirteen will hear you," Hern whispered, making some type of warding sign on his chest.

"If anything, I'd prefer that they did hear me. The more their followers attack this camp, the more we'll be forced to retaliate. I don't want to have to fight, but I'll not hesitate if I feel like we're under attack. I'll not stop their beliefs, but I will take their lives without a thought," Felix promised.

Hern glanced upward, and waited.

Nothing happened. There was no response of any sort.

And that's part of the problem, isn't it. Gods are real. You've seen some, Felix. How do you even counter that? How does one protect against that?

Need to figure out something, because believing they won't attack us directly is naive.

I'll put in a request to Lily to add a "no worship of any deity that is not sworn to Legion" clause. It sounds awful, but not taking the preventative steps now would create more problems down the road.

He couldn't help but sigh over what he knew would be a contentious point. It was likely they were about to lose some people. That was better than opening themselves to attack later though.

"Speaking of that, what do you know of the attacks that have been ongoing? I saw a fireball heading this way earlier," Felix said.

Grumbling, the old man tore his eyes from the heavens and looked off to the side.

"The young and stupid, the overly zealous, and the cast offs. They lure people in with the promise of an amazing afterlife for service to the gods. Few of my tribe hear them out, less even consider their words," Hern said.

It didn't take a mind reader to realize he was embarrassed and ashamed at the same time.

"Hm. Radicals, then. I suppose that's fairly straightforward. Have there been any attacks on your people?"

Again, Hern's face flickered with something Felix couldn't quite discern. "Nothing serious. A beating, and some harassment."

Felix drummed his fingers on the table. This was a question of ideology, rather than combatants.

He could easily hunt down people, storm houses, and round them up in the way a modern army might do.

But we have so many more tools than they do.

"I understand. Great. I think that's more or less everything I need. It's been a pleasure to meet with you again," Felix said. He stood up and held his hand out to Hern.

- 441 -

The older man stood up as well, shaking Felix's hand.

"Thank you. I appreciate your direct nature. Goodbye," Hern said, turning and heading back the way he'd come.

Once he was out of earshot, Felix made his decision.

"First, let's get eighty percent of the long range Wardens here. They're not doing much sitting underground right now. We'll need to construct platforms for them to use, but they should make excellent long range defenders," Felix said.

"Additionally, while we're waiting on training up a contingent of local Fixers, let's pull about thirty of the Fixers from Earth's pool. For those thirty, I want them trained in guerrilla warfare, special operations tactics, and counterinsurgency. Then I want them to spend every day and night in those camps," Felix said, his eyes hard. "Tell all of them that this'll be a weapons free operation. If a target is discovered, they're to act with their own discretion."

That might actually help us figure out what we need to do at a cultural level here as well.

"I'll get that done," Andrea said, immediately diving into her terminal.

"I'd suggest monthly check-ins with a few of the counselors back at HQ. Make sure they're not overloaded," Michael said at Felix's side. "It's one thing to get desensitized to the whole thing, it's another to lose yourself."

Felix gave a brief nod of his head. "We'll need a new name," he said offhandedly, staring out at the encampment.

"A new name?" Andrea asked.

"Fixers are for HQ and security. What I just ordered put together is anything but that," Felix said.

Andrea puffed her cheeks out and furrowed her brows. Then she smacked one hand into another and turned to him with a grin.

"Minders!" she said happily.

Not exactly what I was looking for but... not bad. It'll do.

"Great. There we go then. A new department for HR is born. Though I get the distinct impression this might have some overlap with Ioana. Oh, speaking of, has Miu checked back in?" Felix asked.

"Nn! An hour or two ago. I think she finished debriefing a while ago and was prepping to head back to Wal," Andrea said, her eyes jumping back to her terminal.

"Call her in. I want her here for a few days. I think Ioana can survive without her for a time. If not, we can train up a second Miu for her," Felix said. "List of candidates for that please, by the way."

"Got it, dear," Andrea said, typing into her terminal. "I've notified Miu. She's probably on her way."

"From everything I hear about her... the fact that it's Felix asking for her means she'll be here as fast as a dead sprint can carry her," Michael said under his breath.

"Faster," an Adriana said. The ring of Adrianas shifted their positions to create a slight gap that faced towards the portal.

I wonder what that's about. She's not killing even more of them lately, is she?

... I bet she is.

Looking beyond the space the Adrianas had cleared, Felix could see the portal. It was left open at all times and guarded from both sides right now.

Someone came sprinting through the portal as if the blazes of hell were behind them. They came to a sudden halt almost as fast as they'd arrived.

Felix got the distinct impression that they were looking his way.

Then they were off again at a dead sprint.

Straight for him.

It only took a few seconds for him to realize it was Miu.

He really should have known, too. The more he accepted her personality, her behavior, the more she let her control slide in a different direction.

Especially once he deliberately took ownership of her actions and need for control. She seemed to delight in asking him for direction and then doing what she wanted free of restraint inside of those parameters. Without fear of him judging or holding her accountable for her actions.

He felt it was strange that she wanted to know his exact orders at times, but she seemed to enjoy it. Knowing her exact boundaries.

Taking responsibility for her control was her favorite reward now.

Taking no time at all, Miu came to a stop inches from him. Her hands fluttered between them, her fingers curling and uncurling.

Again with the grabby hands. The subtlety has long since gone.

She stared up at him with wide unblinking eyes. Amazingly, she wasn't even panting. All her work lately was to further increase her powers and abilities.

To be more useful to him.

"Felix," she said with a neutral tone. "I'm here. You want me?"

"Thank you for coming so quickly. I have a bit of a hard one for you," Felix began.

Andrea snickered from the side, followed immediately by the Adrianas.

Really, ladies? Felix mentally sighed and pressed onward.

"I need you to track down whoever is leading the attacks on our camp here. Once you find out who they are, and the general structure of it, report it all back here to Michael," Felix said, aiming a thumb at his site commander.

"I shall do this," Miu said severely.

"Do it quickly, and without accidental deaths, and I'll give you four hours where I'll take personal responsibility for your control."

Miu visibly spasmed at his words, then nodded her head.

"Go," Felix said.

His personal psycho was off in a flash, leaping off the wall and vanishing.

"At least she can't kill me tonight," Andrea muttered.

"Or us," the Adrianas said in unison.

Adriana Prime could only smile sadly at that, as she and Andrea Prime were the only ones Miu spared.

Chapter 27 - Negotiable -

Felix watched as the locals were being sworn in. This was the first group of individuals who had passed their language lessons and had been put into actual Legion training.

The first of Legion world from Fort One to join Legion directly.

Right after this would be given proper Legion training after being provided with their new recruit equipment.

One of the things they'd found out early about the skill books Felix made was that they tended to do a great job with information, but application of that information could be problematic at times.

There hadn't been many mistakes in the past because a lot of it had been context dependent.

Having to bind up a wound only had so many ways to be done.

The problems showed up when security forces were being deployed in early training exercises. Too many possibilities for how to approach something.

Solving that was having constant training.

All that drilling was for situations that could and would happen in the field. Which they had knowledge of, but needed to know how to apply it without thinking.

Just like the military, according to Michael and Adriana.

Gripping the edge of the wall, Felix shifted his weight around. Even though there wasn't much to do here, it was better than sitting around in the dark underground of HQ.

The sun, wind, and open skies were considerably better than small dark rooms.

With Fort One being stable, other than the occasional ball of fire or lightning bolt, they were actually having people come through here regularly. If only for a break and breath of fresh air.

Both SC:HQ and T:HQ were sending people on field trips regularly. It did wonders for morale to be able to escape what was viewed as a siege. When you could simply walk through a doorway and end up on another planet without a care, suddenly nothing seemed that bad.

It seemed like it wasn't a siege.

"Things aren't going well back on Earth I take it?" Michael asked, easing up next to him.

"Well enough for us. We're supplied for a few years as far as foodstuffs and water goes. Ioana has an operating portal up in Wal now as well, so we could always start putting in massive orders there, and shipping it here," Felix said with a smirk. "I never thought I'd become a smuggler, but with the portals, we've got the ability to do exactly that."

"Sounds like a good way to get people out of the cities, too," Michael said.

"Definitely been doing that. We've been having a large number of visitors who enter the Legion shells. They come asking for help, looking for it, trying to find us. Me."

Felix paused, watching as the recruits got up from the benches. They moved over to a series of lockers and equipment chests. Making an orderly line, they all began to move through the area, coming out the other side with gear.

This was their recruit assignment. The day they all got the equipment they'd be personally maintaining and using throughout training.

"For anyone brave enough to do that, and passing a Fixer scan, they get a few options. Join Legion, leave, or pay to get shipped off to Wal. We don't give them any documentation, so they're on their own once they arrive, but most seem happy enough to just escape."

"How much of a fee are you charging?" Michael asked curiously.

"Five a head."

"Five hundred a head?" Michael repeated.

"No. Five a head. It's about as much as it costs us to feed them while they wait for the next batch to be teleported. We put them up in the bunker until it's time to go."

Michael snorted, then started to laugh at that. "And how many actually teleport over after that? None?"

Frowning, Felix mulled that one over. He didn't quite understand what he meant.

"We teleport them all of course. I'd not let our people cheat them," Felix said a little defensively.

"No, I didn't mean it like that. I meant, how many actually want to teleport after you casually give them an option, charge them about as much as it would for fast food to provide them a meal, and give them safety at the same time while waiting for the next group."

"I don't know... I never looked into it."

"Not many," Andrea Prime said from his left side. She was still a bit sulky after he pulled in the Andrea Other and Adriana Prime on his night out, and she hadn't been allowed to go.

"Interesting. I suppose seeing is believing since the offer is made while they're still in the shell," Felix said.

"Is it?" came a cold voice from above him.

Craning his neck around, Felix found no one there.

"What are you doing?" Andrea asked.

"Does your neck hurt? I'm sorry, I shouldn't have asked you to do that to me," Adriana Prime said.

Andrea Prime had confusion written across her face when she looked at her sister.

"You didn't hear that?" Felix asked, looking from the two Beastkin to Michael, ignoring Adriana's comment entirely.

"Hear what?" Michael asked.

"They can't hear me," came the voice again. "I wish to bargain. Go to the top of the tower. Alone. We will speak."

Felix looked back to the training field, not really seeing anything. He wasn't sure who had just spoken to him. If he followed his gut, he'd bet on it being a god.

"You alright?" Michael asked.

"Yeah, I'm fine. I think I could use a minute alone and see the lay of the land at the same time though," Felix said, turning to face the tower coming up out of the keep.

It was a massive stone structure reinforced with steel and magic. Felicia had come out personally to build and set it up. It could theoretically withstand a direct hit from a tank shell or an artillery round. Which meant on this world it was practically untouchable. Since the enemy force couldn't really muster anything near that level of power, that was.

It served as an observation post that had great defense.

Thankfully it had an elevator, but it was a slow ponderous thing that moved more through magical application than actual machinery. Apparently most of the tower had to be forfeited to its integrity needs, which forced some things to be sacrificed.

Like elevator speed.

Michael waved his hand at him and started walking away. "Have fun with that. I personally only go up when I have to. Elevator takes for-fucking-ever."

This better be worth it.

"I'm here," Felix said, standing at the very top of the tower. There were numerous viewing slits that were all fitted with extremely thick laminated glass.

The elevator ride had been every bit as slow as everyone said it was.

Thankfully the top was enclosed and heated, otherwise this might have been an abysmally chilly adventure, as well as boring.

A woman and a man appeared as if they'd always been there. The woman was attractive, older, and built like she ate only when she wasn't working off the calories. Additionally she was tall, wide of frame, and clothed in animal furs. Hooked to her belt was what could only be described as a battle axe.

If she wasn't a warrior, Felix would give up his ownership of Legion.

Standing to her left was a shorter, chubby man that was practically drowning in furs. Each and every finger of his hands was adorned with gold rings. He had pale blond hair and grey eyes. He'd probably be attractive if he wasn't overweight.

"I am Abera," said the woman. "This tub of lard is my husband, Desh."

Smiling, Desh said nothing in response. He bowed his head fractionally to Felix.

"You are Felix. Leader of your country," Abera stated.

"I am," Felix said.

He knew Abera had been the one who had attacked his people in the field. Felix didn't know who or what Desh was, but he could assume he was from the same pantheon.

"I have watched your people for a while. Some of your people worship the old ones, but few. As a country, you have no god," Abera said.

"That's correct. Legion has no shared religion."

"You should turn to us," Abera said, taking a step forward towards Felix.

"I see no reason to. I'll not put on your yoke," Felix said, staring up at the goddess.

"Do you not fear me? You should kneel before me," Abera hissed.

"No. I made a deal with a third party who I believe you know. My agreement was to not influence your religion, and I believe your side made the pledge to not directly attack me or mine. I'm not sure if they'll come back to renegotiate for you, but I could ask them just to see, if you like?" Felix asked.

Maybe this'll be a chance to see and w —

"No! No. I will abide by the arrangement. There is no need to bring... them... here," Abera said quickly, taking three steps backward.

Desh had the appearance of a man who wanted to hide somewhere with the change in conversation.

There was no reason for them to be trying this unless they were desperate. He wasn't sure about Desh but he'd bet he was the god of trade from what he could see of the man.

Which Legion had effectively crushed when it entered into negotiations here. Almost all trade was done with, in, or on Legion territory.

And War, Abera's domain, wasn't much of a possibility anymore in this neck of the woods.

Legion stomped the local military into the dirt. There would be no war in this area that Legion didn't get involved in.

Then immediately crush.

No, they needed him for those reasons, but he got the impression there was something else going on as well.

He'd bet it was an internal issue in their pantheon. One large enough that "the band was breaking up" so to speak, and they needed a place to lay their heads.

Or that was Felix's guess at least.

Lucky for them, Legion needed a defense against gods. Gods fighting gods seemed like a valid defense.

And right here and now seemed like a prime opportunity to get the best deal for himself.

"I take it you're having troubles on the home-front?" Felix asked as casually as could be.

Abera froze up at the question.

Her head turned just a fraction towards Desh. Felix almost missed it. Almost.

Abera needed to work on her body language. Everything he wanted to know was answered in that one second.

"I'll take that as a yes, then?" Felix asked.

Desh let out a slow breath, literally deflating before Felix's very eyes.

"You have the right of it," said the man in a deep voice. "Our home has been torn asunder. When we formed together, many many years ago, we took in gods from other worlds. Those with no power, but experience. Our world was young then. Very young.

"Now that the portal has opened, many of those very same gods have returned home. Leaving us with missing aspects. Holes."

Makes sense. And also explains all the new religions cropping up back home. Or old religions, as it were.

"I think I can make an offer —"

"We were told how you maintain power in your country. We'll not subject ourselves to ownership. That's simply not possible," Desh said, interrupting Felix. Desh's voice was firm, giving Felix the hint that there'd be no budging on that.

Huh. I wonder who they got that from. That kinda narrows the possibilities, though.

"I'm afraid I wouldn't be willing to allow your worship as a god or goddess. For the same reason you wouldn't wish ownership, I wouldn't wish a future power problem. I think putting myself in a beholden position to someone else would do that," Felix said with a smile.

Abera and Desh both looked annoyed at that, but unsurprised. Felix had the unfortunate feeling that he was only catching up to where they thought the conversation might go.

"We didn't think you'd allow it, but we still wanted to try," Abera said forlornly. He wasn't sure who she was talking to.

"Let's not be hasty," Felix said quickly before they could vanish as quickly as they'd come. "Let's discuss something else. I'd like to learn a bit about you. From where I hail, there were no gods previous to the portal opening. I know little of your needs and wants."

Desh and Abera were more human than he expected, as they shared a moment to look at each other before turning back to him.

"Keep in mind, anything you tell me will be kept in confidence, and I'll not move against you, unless you move against me," Felix offered up. "I can also make that oath on the mediator of our previous pact."

There was a pregnant pause as the two deities seemingly waited for something to happen.

"Is there a problem with that? I've only spoken with him – it is a him, right? – twice but he seems reasonable. I'd be happy to abide by his mediation," Felix said.

He knew he was pushing it. Whatever this entity was, it was powerful enough to cow an entire pantheon.

"That... I suppose that's alright. We are empowered, and live, through the power of worship. It is directly proportional to the amount, and belief, of that worship. We know you've taken no action to hinder our religion in any way, per our arrangement, but nonetheless, we are no longer confident in our ability to survive the storm," Desh explained.

Ok, that all kinda lines up with what I was expecting.

"If you do not allow worship of us, and we won't allow ownership, we appear to be at an unsolvable impasse," Desh continued.

Abera nodded her head, her right hand resting on the axe-head at her side.

Desh noticed where Felix's gaze had landed and he smiled apologetically. "Forgive my wife. She's a warrior. Things of this nature are not in her disposition. As I'm no warrior, we complement each other quite well."

Chuckling at that, Felix couldn't help but relate on a few levels. He had a number of people who filled out the gaps he had.

"Don't go anywhere. I'm going to make a quick call. I've got a crafter in my employ who... honestly she's a genius. Her only limitation is her own creativity, which is somewhat lacking, unfortunately," Felix said, turning his wrist over. "This should be quick, but I think it'll be enlightening for both of us."

With the number of signal repeaters and towers the construction teams had been putting in, there were few places in Fort One that were off network.

There are few places within thirty miles that are off network, in fact. They went overboard.

Tapping in a command to dial Felicia, he lifted his other hand to his earpiece.

It only took two rings for Felicia to answer.

"What?" she said in a flat tone.

"Hey Felicia. I have a new challenge for you," Felix said, his tone of voice bright and chipper.

Felicia responded to challenges, and if you were happy about it, it only made her angry.

Angry Dwarves were determined Dwarves.

"I just finished up your last challenge, you pox ridden sex toy," Felicia grumbled.

"You're right, of course. If you need a break and can't handle this, I could see about spinning up a second team so you can —"

"What the fuck do you want!? Spit it out already," Felicia shouted through his earpiece.

"I want a machine that converts all the faith, energy, and worship that people seem to place in me, and send it elsewhere. Think of it as a magical power source, and we need an adapter to change the flow and direction," Felix said.

The line went absolutely dead. He imagined Felicia was standing there as that beautiful mind of hers melded with her power and began spinning off as many possibilities as it could.

"Huhn. Well... that's definitely a challenge," Felicia said after several seconds. "Did you have a specific destination in mind?"

"I did indeed. It would be to certain contract holders. You could easily use the agreement as a target point."

"Uuun. That'd work. I can do this but I want an off-cycle budget increase," Felicia said, her tone changing rapidly.

"Oh? What's the price tag?" Felix asked. He was curious where she'd go with it. Her pursuits were different than most.

"Points, and some of your time. I want to use your power to start combing through future builds and plans. You're a walking time machine if we do it right. So... that's what I want."

Now it was Felix's turn to freeze.

She was right. With the right application and a healthy dose of points, Felix was a time machine to a limited degree. Especially with things that would have a set value. Like the Fist.

"Done. Put in the request and kick it up the chain. Gotta go. I should probably have those contracts to you later today, or tomorrow. Need to have Lily take a look at 'em," Felix said.

"Be sure to have the princess take a look at your sausage while you're at it," Felicia responded, then promptly disconnected the call.

"She's a vulgar thing," Abera muttered. Her face showed nothing but disgust at the moment. "A disrespectful creature."

"And incredibly loyal for all her faults," Felix said, pulling up another contact in his wrist device. "There is something to be said for that trait outweighing every other. I'd take a loyal psychopath over a disloyal warrior."

"And what are you doing now?" Desh asked, watching Felix closely.

"Calling up my lawyer so we can begin the negotiations on a contract. I'd like to get this put away as quickly as possible. If possible, I'd really like to walk away from this with you two as allies and partners to Legion. You'd receive your power from Legion based on how much my people are invested in me. I think that'd be the best way to play the middle for us both. You'd be free to seek worshipers outside of Legion, but gain power from it simply for supporting it. And I'd keep control over my own company without a concern."

Abera snorted and Felix wasn't sure how she felt about it.

Desh, on the other hand, nodded his head, laying a hand on Abera's forearm. "I think that'd be something we could work out. This all seems... negotiable," said the god of trade. "And negotiable is a great way to start a deal."

Chapter 28 - The Way It Is -

It was late in the evening, everyone else had turned in for the night, gone to bed, or gone off watch.

Here, with only Eva, Felix had no need of guards or assistants. Originally he'd been alone until Eva asked if she could just work in his office with him.

The quiet scratch of Eva's pen was the only sound Felix could hear. The soft scritch of it as she swept it back and forth across the page.

Having been around constant noise, sound, and people moving around for so long, Felix couldn't do very well with absolute silence.

It was deafening.

So quiet that you could actually hear the silence. That it throbbed in your ears and made your ear drums ache.

That it grew so loud you could swear it was the roar of thunder.

"Felix?" Eva asked, the sound of her pen stopping.

"Mm?" Felix responded, staring at the window he'd called up.

"The assignment I'm working on is arguing for a point of view that I don't hold," Eva said. Nodding his head, Felix dismissed the window.

Time to try another angle of approach. "Ok? Sounds like a good way to expand your horizons."

"Yeah, I get that but... I don't know. I think I've run out of things to say."

"Well, what did you pick to talk about?"

Felix thought again on what he wanted to accomplish.

He wanted to see a documentary he was going to have people from his media team work on for the previous year, he'd have it put together in a year from now.

Effectively giving him a year in retrospect, and a way to see the future.

Equipment(Siege of Tilen and Skipper City): A retrospective over the last year	Documentary made available.	Upgrade?(112,493,128,312,489,500)

It's almost as high as when I tried to give someone else my own Powers. What the actual hell.

"I'm taking the position of allowing Skipper to take over, rather than fighting," Eva said.

"Huh. That's... definitely an interesting point of view. Let me think on it for a bit. Maybe let your subconscious chew at your assignment. And while that's happening, let me throw a question at you," Felix said.

"Sure! Is it what you've been working on?" Eva asked excitedly, bouncing up from her seat and walking over to his desk.

"Yep. So, you know what I did with the Fist, right?" Felix asked.

"Yeah! That was pretty cool. I never realized you could use your power as a way to view the future."

Eva stepped up to the other side of his desk and picked up the pen she'd made for him. He kept it with him most of the time, and pulled it out whenever he sat at his desk.

"I'm trying to do something similar, but different. I want to see a documentary I'm going to have made in a year, about the previous year."

"Uh... oh! I get it. That makes sense. Considering the way the Fist turned out, that should work, right?"

"And it can. It just costs enough points that I'd have to turn the entire gold reserve for the country into dust to do it. Which obviously isn't possible."

"Hm. That's… ok. How can I help?"

"I think I'm missing something. The Fist was much further than a year out if I don't miss my guess."

"Yeah, but the Fist isn't going to alter the actual future. If you had this completed, you'd be able to change, avoid, and alter everything that had already happened."

"Fair point. What if I did it for two years instead of one…"

Felix paused to try just that, working through his power quickly.

"So?" Eva asked, her excitement clear in her voice.

"It uh… it only went up by about a hundred thousand points."

"Ok, so if one year is that high in cost, but the year after isn't, that means that something happens this year that is incredibly monumental," Eva said, crossing her arms over her chest and nodding her head.

"Or apocalyptic," Felix countered.

"Sure, that's a possibility. But it could just as easily be that you somehow cured cancer or AIDS. I'd say that's monumental enough to skew quite a bit of history if you changed it or avoided it."

"Hmm. That's… fair… I just don't like it."

"Why, because I said it?"

"No, because it's optimistic. Optimism gets people killed."

Eva laughed at that and shook her head. "Felix, I swear. You're such a grump sometimes."

Unable to help himself, Felix crossed his eyes and stuck out his tongue sideways at her.

"You call it grump, I call it reality."

"Grump, grump, grump. Grump-o-saurus-rex."

"Har har. Fine. Go, get back to your assignment. You've made your point. I'll just have to try again from another angle."

The entire office churned into a sudden blazing red maelstrom of crackling power.

Felix shot to his feet at the same time as he slammed his hand down on the panic button.

Shimmering and growing denser, the red energy began to spiral rapidly in a circle.

Then everything exploded and Felix felt like his stomach was turned inside out and used as a stool at a dive bar.

When his vision cleared, Felix could see the stars above him, and the outlines of buildings ominously hanging over him.

Looking around, Felix realized he was in the middle of a street. An empty, barren street, full of wreckage and debris.

And he was naked.

Stark butt-naked.

"Felix, what happened?" Eva asked from behind him.

Taking a moment to glance over his shoulder, he saw Eva, naked, behind him in a similar position to his own.

"Don't know. Questions later, action now. We need to get off the street. Immediately," Felix ordered.

All around him were businesses that were burned out, looted, or simply destroyed.

"Mechanic's shop, there," Felix said, indicating the building.

Getting into a low crouch, Felix started making his way over.

"I'm naked!" Eva hissed.

Felix ignored her, focused entirely on getting out of the street. It didn't matter where they were in Tilen, being on the street at night was asking to get shot by anyone with an itchy trigger finger.

Without hesitating, Felix entered through the broken door and went straight into the building. Taking account of his surroundings as he went, Felix felt rather certain that the building was unoccupied. No one would choose this location to hold out in since it had no roof, too many entrances, and was unlikely to have anything of value.

For the moment, it served his purpose perfectly.

Ducking into an office, Felix started to sort through the wreckage to see if he could find anything usable.

"Felix! What are you doing? Where are we? What happened?" Eva asked, entering the office behind him.

"Surviving, don't know, don't know. We need to arm ourselves and get clothes. After that, information gathering. Did you notice any street signs by the way? I didn't see any," Felix said, opening a desk drawer and sorting through it quickly.

"What? Street signs?"

"Yeah. I figure we're somewhere in Tilen. If we know what the street is, that'll help. Well, if we know the street, it will. If we don't, not so much. But hey, information is information. Ah, a knife. That's a start."

Felix pulled out a six inch folding knife from the bottom of the drawer and flicked it open. Seeing the action was working, he thumbed the locking mechanism and closed it.

He set it on the desk and went back to digging.

"Felix, I... I don't—"

"Two options, Eva. Sit down, be silent, and get yourself together. Or start helping me dig through this office. We'll have to clear this building out completely and then figure out which way to go from there. Wait, do I own this knife now?" Felix asked curiously.

If he did, he could use his points to modify it into something better. Or clothes, even.

A quick check revealed that the knife did indeed belong to him now. Which meant the owner was dead and had no will or heirs, abandoned it willingly, or... something else entirely.

Smiling, Felix pulled up his point screen.

	Received	Spent	Remaining
Daily Allotment	150	0	150
Resources Inaccessible/Blocked	—	—	—
Eva Adelpha	4,900	4,900	0
+ Loyalty Bonus	1,010	0	1,010
DAILY TOTAL	**6,060**	**4,900**	**1,160**

Staring at the point screen, Felix had to fight to keep himself together.

Something seriously wrong happened. Very, very wrong. Ok, keep it together. We still have some points.

Sliding Eva's points away from herself, and into his pool, Felix continued in his search for resources.

He needed to keep his mind occupied and working.

Occupied and working was much better than shock and inactivity.

Behind him, he could hear Eva starting to shift things around as she started to search.

Good. Good. Let's see what we find.

The building was empty of people, unless you counted the corpse they found curled up in a fetal position out behind the building.

The shop did however have a few things that were usable as far as resources went.

Some of what they found still had owners, some of it didn't. Everything that Felix could get his hands on that didn't have an owner he turned into dirt if he couldn't use it immediately.

For a mechanic's shop, there happened to be some seriously expensive gear. Felix was more than happy to dust it all for points.

Three sets of mechanic's jumpsuits, oil smeared and everything, were welcome additions.

Other than the knife, though, they found no weapons.

"We have... a total of fifty thousand points, give or take," Felix said. They were hunkered down near the side entrance of the building that had been used by employees.

It was locked from the outside, but they could leave in an instant from the inside.

"Is that enough to give me a teleport power? Or portals?" Eva asked.

Felix grimaced at that. He'd actually already tried.

Adding any power at all to her would require upwards of a couple hundred thousand points. Even something simple like increased eyesight.

For the life of him he couldn't figure out why it would cost so much. It wasn't normal. It didn't seem correct on any level.

Which means there's an outside influence here. But I don't think it's my friend who I owe favors since... well since this is more likely to get me killed than anything.

"Honestly... I don't have access to any of the points for Legion. Only your points and mine. And when I try to add any powers to you, I get a cost that's... not realistic. At all. Something very wrong is going on with my power. I'm also starting to think the goal wasn't to drop me here. Something... someone... intervened. If I had to guess... Lily maybe. Or Neutralizer," Felix said, staring into the darkness of the vehicle bays.

"Oh... so... we're stuck out here then," Eva said a touch lifelessly.

"For the moment. How far did you get in your hand to hand training with Miu and Ioana?"

"Not far. They said I'd be better off sticking to my powers. I don't have a knack for it, I guess."

"How about guns? Did you work with anyone?"

"Yeah. Andrea, or Adriana I guess. I'm not a marksman or anything but I did alright," Eva said defensively.

Felix sat there thinking to himself.

It really left it up to him unless he wanted her to start spending her one shot powers. He'd sent her all the names and activations a while back.

"Let's do our best to not use your powers. There's no guarantee I'll be able to get them back any time soon," Felix said. "For now, leave it up to me. I think our first immediate need is information. I'm not keen on risking it but... that post office across the street might be ideal."

"What? The post office?" Eva asked.

"I figure it's less likely to have people there, and if we're lucky, it'll have a route map. A route map would tell us where we are in the city. Or so I hope. Worst case... empty building with nothing for us," Felix said.

Eva sighed, pressing her hands to her face. "This is insane."

"It's definitely not good. I think you need to realize that this will probably get worse though. Optimism and trust are probably the quickest ways to get killed out here. The teams we sent out to scout typically come back with some pretty bad stories about what was going on." Felix paused and took a shaky breath.

"I guess what I'm trying to say is... I wouldn't be surprised if this got worse, and we end up hurting people. Or worse. I normally try to limit the amount of harm I cause but... this isn't going to be fun. Or easy."

Eva choked off a broken chuckle that almost sounded like a sob. "So you're telling me you're going to murder people."

"Probably. And if I have to kill fifty people to protect you, I will. And that isn't something you can stop, prevent, or talk me out of. It isn't your fault, and isn't your doing, so you can't be responsible for it. But if — and I hope it's only an if — if it happens, I won't hesitate," Felix said.

Eva didn't respond to that. Instead, she looked away from him, unwilling to meet his eyes.

"Alright, let's go. I'll take the lead. Stay close to me and don't hesitate to pop a power if you think we need it," Felix said.

Wish I had given her some more utility powers instead of all the combat ones. Teleport or Portals would be rather nice right about now.

Opening the door, Felix slipped out and started back towards the road. Reaching the sidewalk, he hesitated, listening intently for whatever he could.

There'd been no working clocks or watches in the mechanic shop, but it felt like it was the small hours of the morning. They'd have to act quickly and maybe find a place to hunker down for the night. It might be easier to move about in the daylight when people were less likely to shoot at a shadow coming near.

Felix mapped out the path he wanted to take across the road. There was a truck he wanted to search but he didn't dare.

Not right now at least.

For all he knew, he was next door to Skipper's Headquarters. The last thing he wanted to do was get caught out in the open by her. He had the distinct impression she'd do awful things to him.

Taking in a slow breath, Felix got low to the ground and crept out into the street.

Sure steps and smooth movements carried him across the road quickly.

It wasn't until he stepped off the sidewalk and onto a side approach for the post office that he let out the breath he'd been holding.

Not waiting for people to come investigate if they did see him, Felix went up the steps quickly. Easing up to the side of a sliding glass door he peered in to see if he could catch a glimpse of anything.

There was the briefest flicker of an orange glow. Deep, deep within the post office. He couldn't be sure, but he'd swear it was a fire.

Which to Felix sounded like a pretty awful idea. Sure, it was cold out, but not that cold.

It was a risk he'd never take, that was for sure.

"Is that a fire?" Eva asked from beside him. "I'd love a fire."

Maybe it's a group of people with a similar mindset to Eva?

Pulling the knife from his pocket, Felix flicked it open as quietly as he could. Grimacing at how bright the damn thing was he looked down to the ground.

There in the corner he found some dark disgusting filth he couldn't identify. But it was sticky, and dark.

Which was exactly what he wanted.

Reaching down, he scooped some of it up onto two fingers and liberally coated the blade in it. It wouldn't do to have the knife reflecting in any way.

That bit of yuck done, Felix moved forward, entering the post office.

He kept to the far wall, half of his mind working in overdrive to keep himself from tripping over things, the other half trying to figure out where the firelight came from.

"—it!" came the faint sound of a heated whisper. Felix held perfectly still and cocked his head to one side, listening.

"No, I won't!" came back an equally angry whisper.

Back room. Sorting room? Behind the service desk.

Doing a quick check of the room, he found two different doors that could possibly lead into the back area. It had to be where he'd spotted the faint light.

Moving to the second door, Felix listened intently. If he could just figure out if they were on the other side or not, this'd go easier.

Then he heard a sound that could never be mistaken for anything else.

The clack of a gun being chambered.

Opening the door as carefully as he could, Felix pulled it open a centimeter at a time. Getting it past two inches he peeked in through the gap.

Two men and four women were pressed up to a wall in a defensive huddle. Not far from them were three men and a woman who were clearly the aggressors.

They also had the gun.

"Just give them to me. It'll be easy. And then we can both go our separate ways and act like nothing happened," said the man with the gun.

"No. I already told you. Just leave, you don't have to do this. It doesn't have to be like this," said one of the men in the defenders' camp.

"But it does," said the man with the gun, raising it up to eye level.

Chapter 29 - Never Again -

Goddamnit. If he pulls that trigger every idiot nearby will know something is going on here.
Taking a firm grasp on the blade, Felix thought furiously.

He wanted the gun. He wanted to stop this before it got out of hand and brought every fool down on them nearby that thought they could benefit.

He also wanted everything these people had on them, and anything in this building he could claim. Being after midnight, his points would hold until tomorrow night.

If he built up a big enough value, he could eek something out.

First, the gun.

Even if he never fired it, having it would help level the playing field. At the least, it'd be an intimidation factor.

Then we're resolved. We take the gun.

Miu would tell me to take out the one least likely to be missed, and move on quickly. If I do this right... I can drop two before they realize. Maybe three.

Doesn't have to be perfectly clean, just enough to drop them.

Incapacitate them.

A quick inspection of the area got him a chunk of brick, and a small rock.

Taking both up, Felix transferred the brick and knife to his left hand, taking the rock in the right. Gliding forward, he hefted the rock twice to get a feel for it.

"What now then? Huh? Hand 'em over. Or I'll just kill you, take 'em, and get out of here before anyone comes to check," said the man with the gun.

He was clearly enjoying his moment of power over these people. Hopefully he would be too caught up in that to notice Felix.

Amazingly, or perhaps not considering how hard Miu had trained him, Felix closed within two feet of the rearmost enemy. He was a man of short stature and seemed distracted. Felix flicked the rock to the far side of the building. He'd been aiming for a space that would take all the eyes off his targets.

Before anyone even reacted, Felix switched the knife to his right hand, and brought the chunk of brick up into the back of the man's head.

There was a solid clunking sound that Felix ignored immediately.

Flowing forward, Felix drew up alongside the woman and drove the brick into the back of her head as well.

The sound of the first man collapsing drew the second man to start turning towards Felix.

Leaping forward, Felix buried all six inches into that man's throat. Ripping the blade to the side, Felix did his best to continue on towards the gunman.

Only to find that man was already starting to lift the gun towards Felix.

Eva's fist crashed into the man's jaw, turning his head to one side with the force of the blow. The man fell to his knees, his head clearly ringing with the strike.

Moving in quickly Felix brought the brick down on the man's forehead. Chasing the man to the ground as he went, Felix brought the brick down twice more in rapid succession. Tossing the brick to one side, Felix scooped up the gun, rolled to one side, and came up with it aimed on the other group.

The men and women were staring at him unmoving.

"Keep an eye on them while I finish the others," Felix said, looking to Eva.

"Do we have to?" Eva asked plaintively.

Felix didn't respond to her, and instead went to the man he'd stabbed in the throat.

He was bleeding out fast and was already slipping into unconsciousness.

That one's done.

"Seriously, do we have to?" Eva asked again.

"What would you have me do?" Felix asked, moving over to the woman. "Do you want to tie them up? Let them go? Try to talk them onto our side? Hm?"

"Actually, wait," Eva said. "Hey, what territory is this? Where are we?"

The collective response from the huddled mass was jumbled and confused.

Felix got down on the woman's shoulders, pinning them down with his knees. Her face was covered in dirt and small cuts. She had the look of someone who was probably pretty, but had seen the ugly side of war and was coming out the other side changed already. She was breathing, and if he didn't miss his guess, she'd probably be mobile within an hour or two. Though still with the giant goose egg he'd given her on the back of the head.

"Where. Are. We. Who owns this block?" Eva repeated.

Felix put a hand behind the woman's head and grabbed a fistful of her black hair. He tilted her chin upward to get a good line at her throat.

"This is Skipper's turf," said one of the men.

"Wait, Felix! Don't kill her. If this is Skipper's territory, doesn't that mean you could take them as slaves? Yes?" Eva said.

"Nothing to bind it with," Felix said, pressing the bloody blade to the woman's throat.

"Wait. We can make this work. You gave me that one, didn't you? I could make that one work," Eva said, pleading. "I can use magic, throttle it out for two months, and use that as the binder. Lily told me all about it. Said it didn't take much if it was a blood oath to slavery. It's how the Pit works."

The woman beneath him cracked her eyelids open slowly. Her green eyes were rolling around in her head as she tried to focus on him.

"Mmmauuuhhhh," she gurgled beneath him. He must have really brained her.

Felix looked up at Eva. He wanted to do right by her, but this was foolishness.

Foolishness that'll scar her forever if I don't do it.

Sighing, Felix looked towards the other man he'd smashed with the brick. Unfortunately for that one, he wasn't breathing.

Must have hit him harder than I thought.

"The other one is already dead. Can't really fix that," Felix started.

"I don't care. Don't do this," Eva said. She apparently had realized she'd gotten some traction somewhere in this conversation and was pressing on it.

Felix couldn't help but smirk at the situation.

She adapts so well to the situation regardless of what it is.

"Fine. This'll be the first one I guess. That or I finish what I started. And you," Felix said, gesturing to the six people. "You'll be given the chance to join as well, but I'll be frank with you. I'll expect you to do what I tell you to, when I tell you to. This isn't a democracy."

Shaking his head, he looked back to the woman under him.

"And you, my dear thug, are very lucky," Felix murmured, wiping the bloody, blackened blade off on her shoulder. He watched her intently, wondering if she'd agree, or if he'd be finishing her off later.

"Lluuuuuuuu-fy," she groaned before her eyes closed again.

Eva was quickly explaining the situation to those six people.

Felix didn't really care anymore. He needed to start exploring the post office as quickly as he could.

If he could figure out what was of value here as quickly as possible, he could get moving.

Clear the building, dust everything for points we can, find a better location to hold out.

Once we have that… information, food, water.

And a plan to get the hell out of here and back home.

Not waiting for Eva to finish, he began to work over the entire post office from one side to the other. Quickly exploring to find anything he could claim, and convert to points.

Or at least chart everything out that he could so he could draw upon it later.

It felt like he'd only been gone for a few minutes when Eva stopped him while he was checking over a massive machine. Felix thought it might be a sorting device but he really had no idea.

All he knew was it was a mass of thick metal sheets and looked as if it were older than the building itself.

She'd hustled him into the main room everyone was staying in.

Sitting down on top of a desk, Felix folded his arms in front of himself. He let his eyes slowly roll over the seven people who had just sworn themselves to him on a blood oath. They'd all been given a chance to refuse, save the thug, and all had opted to join him.

Eva hadn't told them much, other than that Felix and she had a place where, if they could get to it, everyone would be safe.

She didn't specify where, who, or how, which was good, but they all seemed to eager to have a way out.

"So they were here for… your food?" Felix asked, staring at the man who'd been so defiant in the face of a gun.

"Food. Women. Both. Didn't matter," he said. "They weren't going to get anything from us."

"Admirable, if a bit suicidal. Your name is…?" Felix asked.

"Steve. Steve Middleton," Steve said.

"Derek. Derek Bissell," said the second man, without any prompting.

"Nancy Boltman," said the woman next to him.

"Amy Inocencio."

"Katy Hendricks."

"Lauren Romick."

Felix took that all in and nodded his head.

Looking to the thug he'd bound against her will, Felix waited.

"Julia Crawfird," she muttered, standing up straighter under his gaze. She still seemed a touch out of it, but was quickly recovering

She was a remarkably tall young lady.

"Welcome aboard, one and all. Sunrise comes in an hour or two, everyone get some sleep. I'll take the first watch, and we'll organize in the morning. And so you know, our goal tomorrow is barricading this building. As far as I can tell, and after searching through it, it's defensible. With a clear exit that's actually not obvious, or even visible from the street."

In fact, it opened up out into a private parking lot on the other side of the wall.

"It'll need some work, but once we get holed up, we'll have a better chance of keeping others out," Felix finished.

"What then?" asked Katy.

"Food, water, intelligence. I'd like to know who is controlling each block of the city. Who the local players are. How they're operating and what their activities are. Once we know that, we can better plan our moves, and how we get out of here," Felix said. "Go to bed everyone, I'll see you all in the morning."

Standing up, Felix checked the pistol and knife, and went towards the front of the post office. He could hear Eva trailing along behind him.

"Well?" she asked quietly when he stopped.

"Well what. I'm going to watch the front entrance. You'll be watching in a similar fashion when daybreak happens so I can get a nap in," Felix said. "So you might want to hit the sack while you can."

Eva snorted at that. She partially turned to leave and stopped. "Thank you… I know you did that for me."

Felix nodded his head at that, not even trying to deny it. "I did."

Smiling at that, Eva moved behind a desk, curled up, and promptly dropped off to sleep.

And when the morning comes… we'll find out what we're dealing with.

"Engineer," Steve said. "National Guard."

"Huh. And why are you out here in the city and not deployed? Last I heard they were all holed up with the army," Felix asked.

Looking out through the broken entryway, Felix could see the morning gloom. He figured daylight wouldn't be far off from now, and he could send his people out to begin gathering information.

"Wasn't on the clock when it went down. Didn't think I'd make it across the city so I didn't try. From what I can tell, it was the right choice too."

Felix made a curious noise but didn't look away from his task. He needed to be ready if someone decided to drop in for a visit.

"In those first few days, a lot of people got shot simply for being in the wrong place at the wrong time. Blue on blue situations," Steve elaborated.

"Ah. That makes sense," Felix conceded.

"But you wouldn't know that. Would you?"

Sparing Steve a dangerous glance Felix deliberately slipped his finger into the guard.

"As soon as everything went down, Legion sealed itself up tight and hunkered down. No one's seen much of you all since it all started."

"Interesting theory you have."

"Not a theory. I was there when we took over. I know you, Mr. Campbell."

"And you decided to put yourself into slavery to me anyways? Considering all the rumors out there, I'd be curious to know why you did that."

"Because you're not supposed to be out here. The fact that you are means that Legion is probably now on a warpath trying to find you. Either you'll find them, or they'll find you, and that means a free ticket out of here for my people and I," Steve explained.

Felix couldn't help but appreciate the cold logic of it. It made sense.

He liked it, because he'd do it himself.

"That's a fair point, Steve. For now, let's work on improving our lot. I'd be much obliged if you could start working on getting a bunker of sorts in place here. Turn this single entryway into a choke point. We'll barricade the back door to a degree, but nothing that can't be dismantled in a hurry if we have to bail," Felix said.

"Would if I could. I kinda need materials for that," Steve said, shaking his head. "Steel would be great. Even if I can't patch it together, getting it in place with a backstop would still do wonders."

Wish I could help ya there. But as far as I can tell, doing anything that requires modification at any level balloons the points I need to an astronomical level. I can't even make a — wait.

"Eva," Felix called out softly.

"Mm?" she replied from where she was dozing. She hadn't seemed to Felix as if she'd been sleeping very well.

At best she might have caught an hour or two of actual sleep.

"If you don't mind, I'd like you to take the watch. I need to try something before the day gets started," Felix said.

"Mm-hmm."

Eva slowly got her feet, rubbing the palms of her hands into her eyes.

"Remind me to better appreciate what we have when we get back," she grumbled.

"Noted. Need a minute to hit the bathroom or anything?"

"No. No, I'm alright. You only need a couple of hours?" she asked.

"Maybe less than that if I get this to work. We'll see."

Eva trudged over to him and leaned up into the desk. She held out her hand to him, still blinking rapidly to clear her vision.

"Shoot first, ask questions later," Felix said, laying the pistol in her palm. "Safety's off and should remain off."

"'Kay."

Smiling, he patted Eva on the shoulder, and went back towards the rear of the post office.

"Come on, Steve. Things to do, no time to do it," Felix called over his shoulder, making a beeline for the machine he'd seen previously.

"What are you doing?" Derek asked when Felix passed by the sleeping area.

"If you're awake, get ready to work. We'll be moving out in an hour or so. Otherwise, get back to sleep. Going to be a long day," Felix said.

Stopping in front of the massive machine, Felix gave it a once over.

"What are you looking for? And how is this going to help us?" Steve asked, walking up next to him.

"What I'm looking for is thick steel plates like this," Felix said, tapping one particularly worn and dented example. "If I pried this off the machine, would this do what you wanted it to?"

"Uh... well, I guess. I mean, I don't have any of my tools, it'd be whatever I could scrounge up and put together but... yeah. I think I could do something with it... but I'd need more. The backing I can fabricate easily enough."

Steve had started to inspect the plate now. "Don't know how you're going to pry this off though. It looks like it's been welded and riveted in place at the same time. That's just overkill."

"Get ready for a surprise," Felix said.

"A surprise?"

Felix concentrated. He didn't want to actually modify this machine too much. He merely wanted to turn everything to dust that wasn't suitable for the task at hand.

Which was creating a bunker and choke point.

And he'd need every plate large enough or thick enough that'd work towards that goal.

With any luck, it'll infer what I need and simply do it. And since we're not modifying anything, this'll be a zero point cost.

Or so we hope.

Equipment(Steel Plates): Scrounging metal	Unneeded material converted	Upgrade?(-4,050)

Wincing, Felix hesitated. It'd give him what he wanted, but it'd cost him a potential point loss of around ten thousand. The plates were worth that much in points.

Not like ten-k would actually do me any favors though.

Felix thumbed the upgrade button and took a step back.

Steve practically jumped backward when the entire machine went up in a flurry of dust. The steel plates clanged and banged into each other, or simply fell to the ground from up on high, as the machine became nothing.

"What the actual fuck," Steve said. "You're a powered?"

"Indeed. Keep in mind, if you reveal that to anyone, you'll meet Miu at some point. People don't enjoy that meeting," Felix said.

Reaching over, he rapped his knuckles against one of the thick plates. "This'll do then? You can make this work?" Felix asked, looking back at Steve.

"Yeah. I'll make it work. You were thinking just a kill zone?"

"Yep. With any luck we'll make a raid tonight and get supplies. Food, water, weapons. Daytime is for trading information and intelligence," Felix said.

Sighing he got up and brushed his hands together, futilely wiping dirt from one hand to the other.

Yeah. Need a portable portal device. Or a Telemedic call signal. Or anything.

Never let this happen again.

Ever.

Chapter 30 - War Crimes -

Frowning, Felix shifted his weight from one foot to the other.

They'd camped out in the old hull of a small knick-knack shack and were waiting for nightfall. This had been home-base for Julia and company.

The supplies at this location had already been carted back to the post office with Katy and Lauren. Eva was on duty there, guarding the entrance with Derek.

He was staring at the crude map Julia had brought in for him. It was drawn by hand by one of the men he'd killed, and though simple, at least had information.

Information was beyond priceless right now.

Apparently her group had been in the area for a while and had been working on establishing a "turf" of sorts.

The building he was interested in right now was a pawnshop that was only a street away. It'd been one of the purchases Kit had made on his behalf after the prison break. He'd wanted caches stored away for usage around the city. The idea of his people being trapped in a prison break without the means to survive had bothered him.

"You say there's a gang there?" Felix asked.

"Yeah. We crossed paths with them once or twice. They left off when Ca... when we got the gun. They've been trying to build out in the opposite direction that we were. Mostly protection money stuff. There's some small camps here and there." Julia shrugged her shoulders.

"Mm. Alright. How many do you think there are?" Felix had decided that the first move was to see if they could get a hold of the Legion cache. There was a strong possibility it'd have a line back to HQ. If it did, he could summon reinforcements and get out of here as quick as could be.

"Twenty? We didn't really get a good count. They left us alone after we... after we killed a few. Guns are power," Julia said.

"Any reason they chose the pawnshop, by the way?" Felix asked as casually as he could.

"Uhhh? I think someone said they found a door. Steel door. They got that open and didn't find anything though. Was empty. Someone beat 'em there. They stuck around because it only has the one door in the front, no windows," Julia said after a minute of thought. Her face was twisting into a grimace. "Didn't believe them though and kept digging for information."

Good. That's perfect.

Though I wonder if she was the one with the knife when they were asking for that info.

"Don't grow a conscience on my part. I've done far worse to people I liked better," Felix said, standing up. "That's the plan then. We go take the pawnshop and clear the building."

"And just how are you going to do that?" Steve asked.

"Two nasty things that when you mix 'em together cause a problem," Felix said, pointing to the bag in the corner.

When he'd found the products, he'd realized he could weaponize it. All he had to do was find a building he could use it on and not worry about innocent casualties.

Most everyone in the city seemed to be operating under the idea that this was all going to blow over sooner than people feared. Felix was of a differing opinion, and was treating this as if it were the end times. With that perspective in mind, Felix didn't really care much for any rules or laws that'd prevent him from protecting his people and himself.

He wasn't positive, but he was pretty sure that the pawnshop would have a vent he could dump it all into and then cover up the entry with a thick blanket.

These cache buildings only had their sub-basements modified. Everything else was left as is for both the building, and the occupants.

Case in point, the vent system would be a very normal everyday thing that probably had a exhaust vent that'd be turned off without any power.

"I don't understand," Katy said, looking from the bag to Felix.

"Don't worry about the details, but we're going to bug bomb them. Just be ready to welcome anyone who comes out. Preferably with your weapon. They won't exactly be sticking around once they see what's going on. After that it'll just be a matter of waiting for the gas to clear out," Felix said.

Moving to the corner he picked up his bag and exited the room. "Get the map, Julia," he called over his shoulder, not waiting or looking back.

He kept their pace fast on their way there. It wasn't far but it wasn't exactly close either. Depending on how much they pulled out, it could be a rather long trek back, too. Guessing on the outcome, it was likely they'd spend the day at the shop until nightfall.

He was glad he'd already warned Eva of that possibility as well.

When they finally got there, he'd been surprised to find the fire-escape had already been pulled down to street level. It'd made access to the roof easy and practically without a problem.

The harder part was keeping quiet as they got on the roof.

"You do realize this is a war crime," Steve whispered, peering down into the vent below them.

"You'll have to tell me what they think about it when I'm done," Felix replied, spinning open the top to the bleach.

"What do you mean? They won't be thinking at all. They'll be dead."

"That'd be my point. You know, you're a good person, Steve. I don't think this is the life for you. Remind me to transfer you to something that isn't on the front line. Like teaching or providing expertise. No sense in wasting a resource." Felix upended the bleach into the vent above the pawnshop.

"What? I just don't like the idea of gassing an entire building full of people. It's not wrong to believe that."

Felix shrugged and pulled out the second bottle. Not bothering to check the label, he knew what the contents were and what they'd do, he turned it upside down over the vent.

"Get that blanket ready. This is going to go bad pretty fast. We need to get out of here as soon as we're done, too," Felix said softly.

Steve shook his head, clutching the blanket a bit tighter to his chest.

Felix couldn't fault him for his attitude. Steve was a good person, trying to do the right thing, in a bad situation.

Those were the type of people who people wrote stories about.

Counter to him was Julia, who simply acted for whatever her interest was. She was much closer to Felix in sentiment.

"Toss it on, we're done here. Let's get back down and get ready."

"Can't we—"

"No. No prisoners. Nowhere to put 'em. Just… give the wounded to Julia. She has her orders. No need for you to bloody your hands. This isn't your call, and you can't save them. But I can at least spare you that," Felix said.

Turning on his heel, Felix moved as quickly as he could manage while keeping silent. Right about the time he slipped in close to Julia's left side, he could hear coughing coming from inside the building.

"What'd you do?" Julia asked.

"I made it so we could take them out as they come out. If they don't come out, they'll die in there anyways. No prisoners, Julia. I expect you to leave no one alive. Take anything worth a damn and set it to one side," Felix ordered.

"Huh? Why?" Julia griped.

"Because you're probably the only person, other than me, with blood on their hands. Did you notice all the weapons our compatriots chose?" Felix asked.

Julia's head turned towards Steve, Nancy, and Amy. "The weapons they chose?" she asked under her breath.

The coughing was growing louder.

"All blunt weapons that I'm betting they'll use on arms and legs. Or torso and shoulders. Hoping they'll fall down unconscious or in pain. No… this'll be you and me, I'm afraid, and some ugly blade work," Felix said. "Now get ready, here they come. Remember, fatal attacks if possible upfront. Less to deal with on the backside."

Julia nodded her head to that, gripping the machete in her hand tighter.

Felix had decided to stick with the blade he'd found the night previous. He'd already blooded it after all.

That, and the gas more than likely took his opponents' ability to see clearly.

Or so he hoped.

A man burst out of the door and stepped out into the night, hacking and coughing heavily. Light green vapor wafted out behind him before the door closed.

Worked like a charm.

The man was rubbing at his eyes with both hands, not even looking at his surroundings. Julia smashed a rock into the man's temple, dropping him to the ground. Grunting, she pushed the body of the man up against the door, then leaned up against it.

"Fuck you and your 'fatal attacks' and whatever else you wanted me to do," Julia said. Sliding down to her bottom atop the unconscious man. She wedged her shoulders and braced her feet. "They can all stay in there and be on your own conscience. Not mine."

Nancy and Amy were there before she even finished talking. Gripping the door handle, Amy held onto it while Nancy sat down right next to Julia.

"Overcomplicated bullshit. Are all your ideas like this?" Julia complained.

"Huh," Felix said, standing up slowly from his crouch. "That works, too. We're going to work out just fine together, Julia."

Felix could hear shouting and coughing from inside the building. The pounding of fists and feet on the door.

Probably a few shoulder checks.

Nancy and Julia bounced with each hit, but neither woman budged away from their job as a door wedge.

Well. We'll give it a few hours, then pull the cover off the vent to help it disperse.

Figure by morning we should be able to get in there and take a look around.

Maybe.

Hopefully.

Felix had spent last night and early this morning on trying to figure out what he could do with his points.

However... everything he tried was astronomically inflated.

There was nothing he could do.

With anything.

To anything.

Owning it or not, something was terribly wrong with his power. To the point that he was now certain that there was an outside source influencing him.

Focus, Felix. Focus.

Breathing in through the wet cloth, and redirecting his thoughts, Felix stepped over the bodies in the entry area of the pawnshop.

There were at least fifteen bodies right here, crowding each other at the door.

Guess that worked pretty well.

He didn't dare wait any longer since dawn was coming. They didn't want to be out in the street when daylight came.

No one wanted to be out unless they had to.

Hoping that the stupid wet cloth would work as an filter well enough that he didn't die, Felix pressed on. He didn't bother with the corpses and instead went straight into the sales room.

Most of the pawnshop's sales floor was littered with stolen loot, food, resources, and camping items. It was clear this group had been here for a while.

Ignoring it all, he kept on, making his way to the backroom.

There in the corner he found the no longer concealed trapdoor. That led to a steel door that'd been ripped off its hinges. He had no idea how they'd managed that.

That led straight into a concrete room with nothing in it. There were chips in all of the walls. It was clear that whoever had checked the room had tried to determine if the walls were truly concrete.

Standing in the center of the room, Felix cleared his throat and lifted the fabric up from his mouth.

"Felix Campbell," he said to no one.

Nothing happened.

Really, Felicia? I know you said you did, but I was hoping you were kidding.

Sighing, Felix cleared his throat again.

There was a slight burning sensation in his mouth and eyes.

He had to make this quick, it didn't seem as if the gas was quite gone.

"Felix Campbell, holy fucking shit."

A grinding noise came from the floor itself. Looking down, he realized the entire thing was divided into six portions, and the two on the furthest side from the door were moving.

They were literally sliding into the wall.

"Felicia, I hate you, and love you," Felix said in a muffled voice, pulling the wet fabric back down over his mouth.

Waiting only long enough for the floor to make a hole wide enough, Felix dropped down into the hole it'd made. It was a staircase that spiraled downward for at least thirty feet. He only went two steps down before he decided it'd be better to go back and get everyone else.

Returning two minutes later, Felix started to make his way down the steps.

"So, it's true then," Julia said from behind him.

"Which part?" Felix asked.

"That you're Felix Campbell, the CEO of Legion," Nancy said.

"Yes, he really is," Steve confirmed.

Felix ignored them all. He didn't feel like answering, and they seemed perfectly happy to answer for him.

When he reached the bottom, Felix found exactly what he was hoping for.

Sealed Legion crates.

They were all hermetically sealed and packed tight. Made and built at machine standard with no expense spared so that they could be shipped and held in reserve if ever needed.

The need had come first for planet Legion.

Michael had literal tons of these cases in store rooms to arm his recruits if he needed to. At least until they could build up a suitable force on site with an armory.

"Holy shit," Julia said.

"First and foremost…" Felix said, moving to a glowing panel off to one side. He pressed the activation button. Lights flickered on, and multiple displays to the right of the panel he was working in turned on.

Pressing a finger to the "close door" function, Felix heard the cement above grinding closed. Before the entry had even closed, Felix pulled the wet cloth free and flicked it towards the stairwell.

"Figure out what you want, but don't open anything. Every crate should have a contents list on the top," Felix said. Moving over to the next panel he pressed his thumb to the security reader. The screen flickered and opened up into the launch page and he started to read it over.

"This… this is incredible," Julia said, moving to the closest crate. "I've never seen anything like it."

"I get the impression this is a small cache," Steve said, leaning over a crate, scanning the list.

"Why do you say that?" Amy asked, staying close to his side.

"The crate itself has an entire designation, and at the end is a dash with the letter S. If I don't miss my guess about our intrepid leader," Steve drawled. "The S denotes this is a small crate, or a small cache, or a small load-out."

"Yes," Felix said, then promptly tuned them out.

He was gliding through the screen to figure out what he had access to.

Manifests, shipping logs, inventory and warehouse expectations, distribution, links to the other caches... where's the communication panel? This is all localized to the city, but nothing linking back to Legion HQ.

A sickening fear starting to build in his heart, Felix closed this panel down and moved to the next.

Mashing his thumb into the security scanner he impatiently waited. As soon as the screen opened up, he began to flip through the settings and windows. This one was more about the building itself. Everything and anything to do with the pawnshop.

Grunting, Felix closed that one up and moved to the last panel. Barely managing to keep his fear in check, he crammed his thumb into the security window.

The landing page opened with the single word "communications" as the title.

Ah, here we are. I was getting worried.

Managing to get through the windows he began to cycle through all the available options. Finally he found what he was looking for. A simple message system that tied all the caches to the local HQ.

Opening the program, Felix began to type in a quick rescue and recovery request to pick him up. It wouldn't take long for someone to get out here with enough forces to break through, retrieve him, and get out.

Snapping his finger down on the enter key, he reached up with his other hand and hit the send button.

Perfect. Now we just sit back and wait for rescue. This wasn't too bad.

Though definitely learned a few things.

The hourglass icon on the screen flipped over and then froze. It changed into a spinning circle, and a window popped up.

Error. There is no connection to HQ. The message could not be sent. The diagnostic tool reports that there is a signal interruption that appears to be a fiber cut.

Would you like to log your message and send it once the connection has been re-established?

Felix ground his teeth together and selected the no option.

He wasn't going to get the quick exit he'd been hoping for.

"Alright. Let's figure out everything we want to take with us, and get some shut-eye. We'll need to be ready to move tonight with whatever we can carry. We can always make a second trip if we need to, but I'd rather not," Felix said, turning around to his small group. "I'll pop open a camping supply crate and start pulling out what we need for a decent rest. Sleep in turns so everyone gets a chance to go through the lists and sleep. One person up, everyone else sleeping. Questions?"

Everyone shook their head.

"Let's hop to then. Quick quick like a bunny," Felix said, clapping his hands together.

Chapter 31 - Reinvigorated -

The ground itself shook and rumbled, knocking Felix out of a dead sleep.

Staring blearily around himself, it took a few seconds to remember he was still in the Legion cache bunker.

"What the fu—"

Everything trembled and shook. The rumble of what sounded like a freight train passing overhead was audible.

"Oh my god," Steve said from the stairwell, staring upward. "What the hell is going on?"

"No idea," Felix said, the way he was woken up clearing his mind pretty quickly. "But it sounds bad. Have there been any super fights in this area?"

"No. They all went to the front. The worst we get is patrols. Usually bored ones that are more concerned with getting back to base," Amy said.

Before Felix could respond, a massive shaking took over everything. Cases and supplies went tumbling about in different directions as the world seemed as if it would come apart.

The sound was deafening as well. Even as well sheltered as they were, the sound was as if he'd stuck his head into a machine.

Dust fell from the flickering lightbulbs above them as the cacophony of sound continued.

Felix got his feet under him and started to secure their cases and supplies. He was helpless to whatever was going on above him. He could at least be productive here and get things ready.

Motioning to the others, Felix set to work and got down to business. Hopefully it would distract him as well as he planned, and for everyone else as well.

Julia didn't hesitate and started to work as a pair with Felix, taking guidance from his actions and finger directions.

Steve managed to shake himself out of the daze. He rounded up the others and started to work on sorting out cases they'd tagged to open, and the ones they had no interest in.

Everyone got to work, and did their best to ignore what sounded like the world ending above them.

There were few breaks in the onslaught of sound and shaking.

Right at ten o'clock—and Felix only noted this because the panel chimed once at the top of every hour and he actually heard it—everything had gone calm.

Quiet.

Silence filled the room. Felix could actually hear his ears ringing now. What had sounded like constant explosions had ceased.

Felix and all of his people were all staring at the stairwell. As if they could somehow see to the pawnshop above.

"Amy, check it out. Don't go too far though. Just see what you can see from the stairs," Felix said. It felt strange to use his voice.

To talk.

There'd been no possibility of saying anything since the shelling had started.

Moving over to the security panel, Felix tagged the entrance to open.

Amy nodded her head and unhesitatingly scurried up the stairs. The grinding of the bay doors was loud, but not half as loud as what they'd just gone through.

When she got to the top she stopped.

"I can't get out," she called down. "The entire room is collapsed. I can see the sky above though. We might be able to climb out? Oh my god…"

"What is it?" Felix asked

"I can see Powereds fighting in the sky in the distance. It's… there's so many. I think… I think they shelled the city," Amy said.

There's no way they'd shell the city, would they? The goal isn't to kill their own citizens. To destroy their own cities.

They'd want to them back, wouldn't they?

Unless… unless they felt like they couldn't win. That they were losing. And destroying the city was preferable?

Does that mean… that they'd nuke the city?

Felix froze at the thought. It was an unrealistic scenario a few months ago, but now?

Now it might not be unthinkable. If they're willing to bomb the city, what's to stop them from dropping a nuke? We have to get out of the city. Have to get out, and now.

"Gear up. Now. Don't bother taking anything that you don't plan on carrying for long. Because we're only going to stop long enough at the post office to give everyone else their gear. We're done with Tilen," Felix commanded.

"Why not stay here?" someone asked. Felix wasn't quite sure who it was.

"Because an artillery strike is only the first move. And honestly there's no escape routes from here. This is a dead end," Felix answered. Moving to the closest case, he picked up the rifle he'd secured for himself. It was a shortened version of a military battle rifle. Andrea had drilled him repeatedly with it and several SMGs. This was one that he'd been relentlessly trained on. She'd told him repeatedly that standard use rifles weren't going to be useful in most city fights. Being that Legion operated in a city, it was all she would allow him to work with.

Need to thank her. Somehow. Both of them, since they both worked on this with me.

He'd already donned the dark fatigues, tac vest, and webbing. Felix was fully loaded with clips, grenades, a knife, and anything else he thought he'd need in city fighting.

Grabbing one of the extra clips from the case he slipped it in and felt it click into place. He pulled the charging handle and took a slow breath. The nerves were starting to creep up on him.

The plan was to take a group of people, with only one who had any rifle experience, another who was little more than a street thug, and two who were probably homemakers straight out into the street that was now an active war-zone, and try to get home.

All the while dodging Skipper and her people.

You got this.

"Mount up. Steve, you're on point. I'll take the rear. Everyone else, pick a case, and get ready to hump it all the way home," Felix said.

Being the only other person with any sort of experience with a weapon, he was the logical person to take the front.

They made their way up the stairs and met with their first obstacle of what felt like it was going to be a very long night.

Hanging around the entry in broken walls and shattered objects, the pawnshop was a ruin.

Whatever had gone on up above ground had landed squarely atop them. Only Felicia's knack for safety measures had spared them.

Clambering over and through the broken husk of a building, they eventually managed to get onto the street.

Only to find it was as bad, if not worse, as the pawnshop had been.

Gigantic craters littered the streets and holes were torn out of buildings all around.

The city of Tilen had been attacked with artillery. This was a scene of a city not under siege, but in a war with active combatants.

"Oh my god," Julia said, standing on his right side. She rolled her shoulders under the weight of her bulging backpack. "I… I can't even begin… I mean… This wasn't a staging area. This was all civilians… we weren't… we were just trying to survive."

"Unfortunately, someone decided that it was worth it, if it took care of a local Skipper resource. That's my guess at least, but I'm pretty confident in it," Felix said.

Shaking his head, he started down the sidewalk, weapon couched in his shoulder and finger in the trigger.

Having the situation elevated meant that everyone else would either be hunkering down, or panicking. Given that the city was already on edge before this point, and most of this entire territory seemed like it was living under apocalypse rules, Felix was betting on the latter.

"Only one warning," he said. "Then you fire. Keep the number of rounds low if possible to conserve ammo. It's unlikely they'll give you a second chance, so don't give them one."

"You're a nasty asshole, boss," Julia said. "A man after my own heart."

"I'm going to give you to Miu when we're done here. She could use a second. Then you can tell me if I'm a nasty asshole, or just a realist," Felix said. "Let's cut the chatter, keep an eye out."

Felix kept himself on high alert as they walked down the street. There were several times they heard noises from the alleys, and investigated none of them.

This wasn't the time to play investigative detective, and he wasn't about to split the party either.

At long last, the post office came into sight. Or what was left of it.

It'd clearly taken a direct hit and the entire front was a wreck of broken bricks.

"Move to the rear entrance. That's probably still intact simply because of the way it's positioned," Felix said.

Steve swung out to the right, his rifle held steady as he changed their direction.

Turning the corner through the alley, they arrived at the rear parking lock and secured entry. Standing around in large groups around the lot was what could only be citizens. It was hard to tell clearly what was going on since they were only going by the light of the moon, but he could see enough.

They were gathered around something on the ground in the corner, in the center where it looked to be an argument, and a bunch of people were battering on the rear door of the post office.

"Back up," Felix hissed.

Steve backed up slowly, everyone else doing the same.

"Drop gear and prepare for a firefight. I didn't see any guns, but that doesn't mean they don't have any. Make sure you're chambered, safety off, and have your clips ready. Try to keep your finger moving. Burst fire only. No full auto," Felix ordered.

Twenty seconds later, and everyone had dropped their cargo. Julia and Steve looked sure, the others looked sick.

"You two will be up front, kneeling. I want you to try to only shoot if people start heading our way. Got it?"

The two of them nodded at Felix.

"Great. Julia, post up on the right and keep it clear. Steve, the left. I'll hold the middle. Keep your fields of fire clean. If I move, move with me. To start this party off, I'll fire a single shot over their heads. If I fire after that, light 'em up," Felix said.

A single breath and they were staring back into the parking lot.

Nothing had changed.

Everyone got into position quickly, their weapons trained on the targets.

Aiming just above their heads, Felix fired a single round.

In an instant the world changed.

The single round cracked the air and echoed.

"Clear out!" Felix called. "Now! Only warning!"

Apparently the situation was far worse than he had thought it was. Because they all turned towards his group, and charged.

Sighting the individual who had started moving first, Felix pulled the trigger for a split second. Before he could even determine how bad he'd hit that one, he moved on to the next target.

Then everyone opened up and muzzle flashes lit the night.

Nancy and Amy spent their entire clip in seconds. Both freezing up on their trigger and holding it down.

Steve and Julia fared better, each tracking targets and firing selectively.

They got within thirty feet of Felix and his squad, before it was clear to everyone that this wasn't going to work. The rounds were penetrating multiple people and bodies were piling up rapidly.

What had started as a mob rush, now quickly became a full-on retreat. Everyone tried to head back the way they came, scattering as they did.

"Drop as many as you can. No survivors if possible," Felix called, shooting one of the fleeing people in the back with a burst of fire.

A dead round locked up his rifle as he sighted a woman who had almost made it to an alley.

Hitting the bottom of the clip with his left hand he checked the trigger and found it unresponsive. Reaching up he yanked the charging handle and sent a round flying.

Re-sighting his target, he pulled the trigger just as she cleared the corner. The two rounds he got off hit the building.

Scanning the area, he found no upright targets.

"Clear?" he asked.

"Clear," Steve responded.

"Fuckin' dead," Julia said.

Amy and Nancy said nothing.

"Walk the field. Julia, Steve, any survivors get a blade. If you think they're a threat, put a round in their head instead. Don't risk getting close. Amy, Nancy, get on that door and see if you can't get anyone inside to answer," Felix said. "I want to go see what they were so interested in over in that corner."

Pulling his magazine free he looked into it. He couldn't tell how many rounds were left in there, and he didn't really want to find out at a critical moment. Slipping it into one of his pouches, he put in a fresh clip and then headed off for the corner.

Keeping his distance from the unchecked bodies, Felix let his eyes scout the path out for him.

Reaching the corner, he found something surprising.

An Adriana.

She was alive, though she looked like she'd been thrown through a wood-chipper from the feet up. There wasn't much left of her from the hips down. Her left arm was gone from the forearm down as well.

"Fuck off," she muttered, her head turning away from him.

One of her eyes were clear, and the other looked like it'd been partially torn out.

Though he could see why everyone had been crowding around her.

It was slow, probably because of the extent of the injury, but it was obvious she was healing. Growing tissue anew.

"Hey there, dear," Felix said, squatting down near her head. "It's Felix. Going to get you some place to rest, hydrate, and put some food in your belly. I imagine if we can get you some energy and time, you'll be right as rain. Good thing your sister passed on that regeneration power, huh?"

Adriana turned her head back towards him and smiled brightly. She visibly relaxed from her position on the ground, tears trickling out from the corners of her eyes.

"I found you. I found you, Felix. I found you," she said.

"That you did. Now, how about you let me carry you inside and we get you comfy so you can put yourself together."

"They threw several grenades at me. No idea where they got them," Adriana muttered. "Bet they didn't expect me to survive. They had to rush me when I was reloading with one hand."

"Yes, dear. You're quite soldier. Maybe we should consider pumping your power up into a crazy level and drown the world in Adrianas," Felix said. Reaching underneath her, he gently scooped up her broken body and pulled her in against his chest.

Adriana immediately laid her head on his shoulder, her right hand clutching at his back.

Standing up, Felix went over to the rear entry door. Amy and Nancy were there, talking to someone through it.

They both stopped at his approach, eying what probably looked like a corpse to them.

"Open the door. Now. Or I swear by the dark-side of my asshole I'll—"

The door swung open rapidly. Derek stepped out and held it open for them. "Felix! I'm so glad you're back. Everyone got back ok, but with the shelling, we were worried about you. Then all those people showed up and—"

Walking past Derek without a word, Felix walked into the post office and headed straight for his sleeping bag.

"Oh thank goodness. I'm so glad to see you—oh my god. Adriana?"

Eva appeared at his side, her hands immediately going to the wounded Beastkin.

"She'll be alright. Her power just needs fuel to work. Start feeding her until she throws up. Fill her up with juice or food. Anything with sugar, and high in calories," Felix said. He kicked his sleeping bag open and then slid Adriana inside.

"Smells like you," said the Beastkin, her one good eye focusing on him.

"I would imagine so. Now. Anything I need to know immediately or can I debrief you later?" Felix asked.

"Later. It can wait," Adriana said, nodding her head.

"Great. Lauren, Katy, Derek, with me. We need to move some crates inside and re-secure the door. We'll also need to clear the front so we can get out. Having only one way in or out is making me itchy," Felix said.

He gently pulled the sleeping bag closed around Adriana and snuggled it up to her chin.

"Rest. We'll talk more after you've got more than a single limb."

"Nn…" Adriana said, closing her eyes. "I found you."

"Yes. You did."

Felix felt better. Having her here, in his time of need, was reality changing.

He was positive he could get through this now.

Taking a quick minute, Felix checked the front entrance of the post office and found that it was mostly intact, just collapsed. With a few quick checks of his power, he found he'd be able to clear it relatively quickly for an escape.

"With me, everyone—except you, Eva, take care of Adriana," Felix said as he passed by everyone.

Outside there was a single shout, followed by a groan. "Bastard. You're not getting off that easy," Julia growled. "Try to stab me?"

Felix stepped outside just in time to see her stomping on a man's skull.

"Julia, finish him up and move to the next. Better we're not out here if anyone decides to return. We'll need to figure out our next steps, too."

Grunting, Julia dropped her booted heel on the man's windpipe, and moved to the next body without a word.

Miu's apprentice, indeed.

"Get everything and get it in. I'd love to believe we won't have any more visitors but I'm not built for optimism," Felix said.

Drawing his rifle up partially, Felix remained posted at the entryway. He scanned the alleys and watched the corners. This was a bad situation and he didn't want his people out here any longer than they had to be.

Julia and Steve finished up their grisly task and helped to bring in the last of the crates.

Not waiting around, Felix got everyone inside and closed the door. He slid the locking mechanism in place. It wasn't until the solid steel door was closed, locked, and sealed that he felt his anxiety lessen.

Thank god to whoever decided to drop such a paranoid door in .

Turning on his heel, Felix made his way back to Adriana.

Eva was patiently spooning a constant stream of food into the Beastkin. There was almost no time to chew or even breathe.

Felix could see why Eva had taken such an extreme approach immediately.

Adriana looked better. Much better. Her eye and eyelid were now recognizable as an eye and were quickly reforming themselves.

"Nuh mooh. Feel shick," Adrian gurgled out between heaping spoonfuls.

"Give her five minutes, then stuff her full again," Felix said, squatting down by Adriana.

Adriana whimpered at that and pouted at him as she chewed. "Get shick and faht," she complained.

"Uh huh. Wanna give me a rundown of what's going on while you get an eating break?"

Adriana swallowed and then nodded her head once. "After you... what happened to you?"

"Don't know. Was in my office with Eva, then was on the street."

"Nn. Lily thought it was something like that. She could feel magical residue, she said. Anyways," she said, shifting around in his sleeping bag. "After you vanished Lily and Kit stepped in. They shored everything up and kept everyone moving. They were concerned, but not worried, ya know? They said that you were clearly still alive since all the magic of Legion was still in place. It just felt muted."

Felix couldn't help but agree with that sentiment. "My points are blocked, and everything I try to modify is about thirty times the expense that it should be. Someone, or something, is definitely interfering with Legion."

"Nn... that's what Lily thought. The two gods you contracted got to work yesterday after Felicia put that machine together. They were battering away at whatever was working against us. Especially the big lady. Ioana and her get along well," Adriana said.

Hm. If it wasn't for the artillery, and the possibility of someone dropping a nuke on us, I'd say we could probably hunker down and wait for Abera.

"We, the ANet, didn't feel like we should wait. We've been combing the streets looking for you. And before you ask, we each removed a pinky and left it with our Prime so we could be re-summoned by you after we found you in case we died while out on patrol.

"We knew we would find you. Us or Miu, but we trust her," said the Beastkin.

"Miu?" Felix asked.

"She's been looking for you as well. She's been carving her way through the ranks of Skipper's officers. Listening to their communications and ambushing them. She thought it was one of them who took you away. We weren't really sure."

From the rear of the post office there was a bang, as if someone had hit the door. It was followed by repeated strikes and booms.

"And our guests have returned," Felix said. "Alright. One up on the rear door. Everyone catch a nap if you can. We're out of here in three or four hours. I'll clear the front door when it's time."

Chapter 32 - Over a Candy Bar -

Felix felt like there was no time like the present. Rolling to his feet, he gave himself a quick brush off.

The strikes from the back of the post office had quit hours ago. Apparently they were figuring out a better way to get in, or had given up for the time being.

Either way, Felix wouldn't be using that door anytime soon.

Moving quietly around the rooms, he began to gently shake everyone awake, or get them up and moving if they already were.

There was no time like the present and moving at this hour would be beneficial.

Finally, he got to Adriana.

Eva had stuffed her to bursting, to the point that Adriana actually started to look like she might vomit.

Taking the corner of his sleeping bag in hand, he carefully raised it up to peek in to see if her legs were completely mended.

She was completely restored. Though he doubted she was recovered. Being fully intact wasn't the same as being healthy.

"Darling, are you going to join me? I'm not so sure with so many people around though," Adriana said, her eyes glowing softly with her Beastkin heritage as she stared up at him.

He hadn't even noticed she'd woken up.

Her teasing smile gave her true intention away.

"Cute. You're quite a bit darker and more playful than your sister," Felix said.

"Yes. We are. When we divvied everything up, we realized we would soon start to develop our own personalities. We thought this was ok," Adriana admitted.

"Mm. Eventually I'm going to corner you or Andrea about what really happened with Myriad."

"We know... we've been discussing it on the ANet... if possible... leave it be? For now?"

"Speaking of the ANet, I take it you have no way to contact home base?"

"It was destroyed when they fragged me. I had a radio and a transponder," Adriana said, frustration tinging her voice.

"Time to go out on a maneuver. Can you perform?"

"Yes... but I'm no good as anything other than a rifle right now. I'm feeling pretty weak," Adriana said, her eyes breaking contact with his.

"Great. You can walk the middle with Julia. That'd be a load off my shoulders. We have some no-combat experience helpers with us. In about ten minutes, be ready to roll out," Felix said.

Adriana's eyes flashed as they snapped up to his, freezing him. Her right hand slowly snaked out of the sleeping bag and drew him down, planting a firm kiss on his mouth.

"I'll be ready, darling," she said, releasing him.

Blinking twice, Felix got to his feet and went to the front of the post office.

Very different. Getting more so every day.

Staring at the entryway, Felix had pulled up multiple windows. The rubble was rubble, and had no owner.

It was trash.

Clearing unowned rubble was as easy as could be.

"Missed my calling in demolition work," Felix muttered with a grin.

"What, dear?" Adriana asked from his right side.

"Nothing. Nevermind," Felix said, shaking his head. Looking around, he saw everyone standing loosely behind him, all holding packs, crates, and weapons. "We all ready then?"

There was a collective nodding of heads.

"Suppose that's it then. The goal is to get out of Skipper territory. They're going to target anything owned by anyone else. We'll be heading in the same direction as Legion HQ as we do so," Felix explained. "Keep it quiet. Keep it simple. Keep it tight. Goal is to make it through without being seen or heard. Steve, you're on point again. Keep it to the back channels."

Felix activated the panels and the entire front of the post office fell away into nothing. In the span of ten seconds, it ceased to be and no longer existed.

Steve immediately moved out first, his rifle raised and on a swivel as he took point. Clearing the entry, he paused long enough to scan both sides of the street, and then started moving again.

Everyone fell in behind Steve. Felix and his small group set off in the gloomy pre-dawn hours.

They'd managed to make decent progress. Nowhere near as fast as Felix had hoped, though. Much of the city was in ruins, or now populated by angry citizens who were forming their own gangs.

Dropping shells on the city had only galvanized it into a support structure for Skipper.

Whatever idiot had decided this plan of action had altered not just the scale of this fight, but the complexity of it.

As they slunk through alleys, and broken buildings, and did everything possible to stay out of sight, they'd managed to get an eyeful of the change.

Murdering one's own civilians tended to radicalize a population. Tilen was no exception to that, and if anything, had gone to an extreme in that regard.

Partially so because of what Felix was now witnessing.

They'd been forced to take a breather when noon rolled around. Up ahead was a street crossing that they'd have to make and doing that in broad daylight didn't seem like the best idea.

Most especially when right in the middle of the intersection nearby was an entire congregation of people, that were clearly caught up in some true zealotry.

The screams were audible even from this far out.

"Sickening," Julia said, her mouth twisting in a sneer. "I'm not one to squirm away from killing, but this... is barbaric."

Felix didn't respond, but only made a soft humming noise instead. There was no point in saying anything. It'd all already been said by everyone else.

He could add nothing of value.

In the middle of that intersection, for their god or goddess, this group of people were setting people on fire and letting them burn to death.

Unable to watch them pull out another person to throw onto the pile of burning wood, Felix turned away from the sight.

He paused halfway as the sound of chanting voices could be heard.

It was faint.

Almost inaudible.

And coming this way from down the street.

"Felix, I can see a large group of people," Adriana said from a different window. "They're coming up the road. They're... glowing?"

Glowing?

Keeping himself patient and still, Felix waited at the window, his eyes glued to the direction the glowing chanting people were coming from.

At the same time, the murdering crazies who had been using people to make a bonfire were now organizing themselves. With several groups of people at the center, they formed up into a shapeless mass facing down the street.

When the newcomers finally came into view, Felix was surprised to find it was exactly as Andrea said, and yet not at all.

They really were glowing, but not in the way he had been expecting. Each person had auras shining out from their bodies. Right from the very center of their chests.

They all came to a sudden stop, in a much more organized fashion than the other group.

"I don't even—" Felix started to say, but fell silent quickly when he saw someone step out from the new group.

It was a woman with a bright glow coming out of her. She took several steps forward and held her fist up above her head.

A thick white miasma that made Felix's eyes water spun up around the woman's hand.

Flinging that same hand forward, the white ball spiraled off towards the other group.

It detonated on impact.

Fresh screams and the crackle of power filled the street.

Men and women with weapons in their hands charged out from the bonfire group. Their hands burst into orange flames.

Flames that twisted and licked up their arms and flared with light.

"I'm only getting snatches but... I think... I think they're all being powered by faith magic. I know we'd seen and heard that there'd been a change but... this is far beyond what anyone had even hinted at," Eva said.

"I imagine not. This would change the game for religions. Some of the biggest ones would now have an army inspired by their beliefs. No... this is..." Felix paused as he thought for a second. "This might just be all the world needed to finally go up in flames."

The weight of those words seemed to drive everyone into the floor. Everyone immediately thought about the ramifications of what was likely to happen as these kinds of scenarios escalated.

Grew larger.

Took on the guises of a country that's entire military would be its own belief.

"I think we're going to find many a deity at the head of a nation here real soon," Felix said softly. "Or so my worst fears tell me."

In the street below, the fiery armed worshipers had now clashed with those who glowed from within.

It seemed to be a low power fight between supers. Some threw their faith, others wielded weapons, but it was obvious they were all using a similar energy.

"Maybe," Steve said. "I think you're misjudging the situation a bit. There are quite a few deities who preach peace and benevolence."

"And you'd be right. As I said, my worst fears. Let's hope it's exactly as you said. And let's use this and get across the street while we can." Turning from the window, Felix moved to the rear stairwell and made his way quickly to ground level.

Taking their positions, his people got back into their original formation.

Looking at the crates of supplies, Felix realized this wasn't going to work. They were simply weighed down too much by it all. Luck and fortune had been on their side so far, but there was no guarantee it'd continue.

If they ended up with a sudden need to fight, four of his people would be scrambling to drop crates and ready weapons.

"Pack what you can into your kits. Leave the crates. Plan on being safe in two days, or finding a new source of food and water. Ammo is harder to come by than food and water right now, I'd wager. Pack accordingly. You got three minutes," Felix said.

Moving into the alley Steve had led them in from, Felix posted up near the wall and waited.

Adriana followed him out immediately, her eyes bright, scanning in every direction.

"Felix," Adriana said softly, coming up to him.

"Mm?"

"Your hands are shaking."

Looking down to his hands, he found they were shuddering and jerking every which way. He hadn't even noticed it.

"Put them in your pockets for now or hold your rifle. You're starting to lose it," Adriana murmured for his ears alone.

Laying his hands to his rifle, he gripped it tightly. Trying to stop the shaking by force of will alone. He could feel his mind threatening to unravel as he began to consider what his mind didn't want him to.

"It's normal. Very normal. You're under a lot of stress. Training doesn't prepare the mind for being surrounded by it," Adriana said, getting closer to him.

Her hands pressed to his neck and jaw. Cool fingers gently stroked his skin, her eyes digging through his own.

"You're doing fine. There's nothing wrong. It's a perfectly normal response," she said, her tone soothing and light. "No one ever walks away from things like this the same. Nothing compares to a life being lived in a heightened sense of fight or flight all day, every day. It's not something you can be ready for."

Staring into Adriana's face, hearing her words, her very reasonable and accepting words, Felix nodded.

"It's just anxiety. It'll pass and only you will remain."

Laughing at that, Felix felt his lips curve into a strange smile. "Anxiety? I've never had anxiety like this before."

"And you've never been dumped into a live or die situation where everyone wants to kill you for a candy bar, either."

That brought him up short. He was a planner. Someone who was almost always in the rear with the gear, so to speak. His excursions to the front of the action were limited and far between.

"Do you feel this way?" Felix asked.

"Sometimes. We've learned to control it. When we get home, I'll make you a nice batch of blueberry pancakes. I know you like those best," Adriana promised. "Then we can relax, talk about it, and have Kit maybe do a bit of spring cleaning in your head."

Soft and feathery, her fingers trailed up and down the sides of his neck and lower jaw. Briefly moving upward to trace the line of his ear and back down.

"Okay. I like that plan."

Adriana snickered at that, her eyes watching him. "We're well aware of what you like, darling. Just get us out of here, and we'll take care of the rest."

"Ready," Steve called from the front of their small column. Julia had sidled up next to him, preparing to walk point a step behind him.

Adriana gave him a charming smile and then patted his cheek.

"Nn, we're ready," Adriana said, turning around and lifting her rifle up to her shoulder. "Lead on."

By the time the team took three steps, Felix had caught up and was walking beside Adriana. He'd pulled his rifle up to his shoulder and was back to where he'd been before the brief stop.

The ongoing sounds of the battle a street over were ever present. A lot of it sounded like small arms fire and low yield explosives.

Focus on the now. Focus on here. You can fall apart after.

"Contact!" Steve shouted from up ahead.

Both Steve and Julia went to one knee and two bursts of gunfire crackled down the alley.

With so many people in between himself and the front line, Felix didn't feel confident that he could get a solid sight on the target without risking his own people.

A streak of bright red fire came from ahead of them and passed screaming over their heads, going wide.

Nancy, Lauren, and Amy started to fire off rounds as well, as they moved to the sides of the alley. Then almost as quick as it had kicked off, it was over.

"Forward," Adriana called out. "We need to get out of this alley double-quick. Let's get across. Fast."

No one argued that the order didn't come from Felix. They were all off at a trot and moving.

As they went by, Felix slowed only for a second to get a look at who'd they had just exchanged fire with.

They were clearly from the bonfire group of people, as flames were now covering their bodies. Burning them from the inside out it seemed.

Not sparing any more time for his curiosity, Felix kept his head on a swivel as they exited the alley.

"Intruders!" called a voice off to their left.

Felix pivoted as he went, sighting his rifle at who'd called out.

There were several people all clustered together. Pulling the trigger as he ran across the street, Felix managed a decent spray towards the group. Two dropped immediately and a third dove to one side.

Felix felt his toes catch on something and he almost went sliding to the asphalt. Getting his feet back up under him with only a minor bobble Felix ducked into the destination alley.

"Gonna need a rear action," Felix said to Adriana. "I dropped two, and one got away. Might be friends coming."

"On it. Keep them moving. Tell Steve we need to break contact," she said, pulling a grenade from her rigging and stopping in her tracks.

"Steve, we need to break contact. Throw us down a different alley if possible, and then another. We can keep on a parallel track!" Felix shouted up to Steve.

After that, the only thing Felix could hear was the sound of the faith battle fading away behind them. That and the stomp and crunch of booted feet echoing over and over.

From the rear there was a single explosion. One that Felix assumed had to be a grenade.

Turning down an alley to the left, Steve led on, moving according to the command he'd been given.

A moment of fear slammed into Felix's thoughts as he realized Adriana hadn't caught up yet. Slowing down, he started to turn around.

Right as Adriana caught up to him with a grin.

"Darling, were you slowing down?" she asked excitedly. "For me? For an Other?"

Picking up his speed again, Felix glanced over at her. "Other, Prime, either, you're still Adriana. You're worth no less than Prime, it's just easier to bring you back," Felix huffed out between heavy footfalls.

"Nn... when I tell Prime she's going to insist on rewarding you," Adriana said, her cheeks coloring faintly.

She can blush while she runs and isn't even out of breath? Beastkin are crazy.

He was so caught up in this brief exchange, he ran right into Julia and practically went up her back with the force of the impact.

Tumbling to the ground, he ended up on top of her, her face pressed into the ground.

"Damnit, Felix. I'm not your bed toy. Get off me," Julia grumped, pushing him off her.

"Sorry, Julia. I'm not cut out for this."

Getting up to his feet, Felix looked up to try and figure out why everyone had stopped.

There, in the middle of what had once been a very large park, was a military encampment.

Sprawling in every direction, it was a haphazard arrangement of thrown together buildings, lean-tos, and tents.

There were people everywhere inside. Moving about on tasks, lazing around, or engaged in other diversions. Even from here Felix had the impression of it being a dirty hellhole of a place.

Skipper's flag hung limply in the wind at the center atop a larger building. There in the middle of it all was a series of put together buildings that had more permanence to them.

"What the hell is it?" Katy asked.

"Processing center," Derek said. "It's... it's where Skipper sends people. To be recruited, killed, or... or simply become entertainment. I heard from a couple people about it. Those patrols we saw were out looking for people. If they found what they wanted, they headed back. They only knew about it because a few people managed to escape and talk about it. Apparently a lot of this place is underground. Dug out into maintenance tunnels below the park."

"Great. We'll wait till nightfall and just go around it. With them being there, that means all eyes will be on them, and not us. We might just make it to the other side without a problem," Felix said.

Perfect.

"Why can't we help them? I bet if I used some of my powers I could get in, get out, and be done quickly. We could save them all," Eva said.

"To what end? It's not like we can take them with us. We'd only be giving them a brief window to flee, and probably be recaptured," Felix said, shaking his head.

"So? That'd be better than the chance they have now, wouldn't it?"

"Eva. They're not Legion. Legion first. We can't—"

"Why? Why is it always and ever Legion first? Don't you care about them at all?"

"No! I don't. Not at all. They're strangers to me, and this isn't some made up fantasy story about how the heroes save the day! This is real life, and real life doesn't work that way!" Felix said, his voice getting heated with the exchange.

Her morality and ideals were a positive in his life, but right now, they were sorely pressing him. *This suicidal need to help others is inconvenient, to say the least!*

"Felix, we can hel—"

"No. And that's that. We rest here, stay till nightfall, and then move forward when it gets near one a.m. or so. The end. I'm sorry," Felix said. "We have a lot of people counting on us getting back safe and sound. We owe these people nothing in comparison."

"Damn right," Julia said, squatting down right there and pulling her pack off her shoulders.

"I don't know," Steve said, looking at the camp. "If she could—"

"Discussion is over. You bleeding hearts are going to get us all killed," Felix muttered.

Chapter 33 - The Price -

Felix woke up gradually. His head felt full and empty at the same time.

Not enough sleep. Need more sleep. Can barely think.

Forcing his eyes open, Felix tried to focus on his surroundings.

Right, the alley. Skipper's fort. Is it time to go?

Julia was on his left, Adriana on his right. Across the way the rest of the group lay curled up and sleeping. Derek should be around the corner on guard duty with instructions to get everyone up and moving when the only wristwatch between them all said one a.m.

He wasn't sure, but it felt like about the right time to get going.

"Derek," Felix whispered, getting up from the ground.

There was no response.

Moving as quietly as he could, since there was no reason to wake anyone yet, Felix crept towards where Derek should be.

Turning the corner, he found Derek sitting right where he should be.

Except he was sleeping. Chin down on his chest and snoring away.

Grumbling to himself, Felix made his way over and shook Derek gently.

"Hey, wake up. We should probably get going," Felix said.

Derek lifted his chin up. "Wuuuh?"

Frowning, Felix leaned in close to Derek's face.

His eyes were dilated. Huge, even.

"You alright?" Felix asked.

"Feel shick. Think Evash drink ish bad," Derek gurgled out. Then he promptly turned to one side and threw up.

Eva?

Spinning on his heel, Felix stalked back to where everyone was sleeping.

Checking over each person, he felt his blood run cold when he realized there were two people missing.

Steve and Eva were both gone.

Goddamnit!

Peering at the distant encampment, Felix had a pretty good idea of where those two had gone.

Gritting his teeth in frustration and anger, he went back to Julia and Adriana, waking them.

"Time to get up. We'll need to be ready to move," Felix whispered as he got them both to open their eyes.

Once it was clear they were up and moving, Felix slunk to the other side of the alley and proceeded to do the same.

When everyone was up and getting ready, Felix set about getting his kit together.

"Eva's missing," Adriana said. There was no real question in her voice. In fact, Felix didn't even detect the unspoken question of where they went.

Felix nodded his head before realizing not everyone would be able to see it.

"Yeah. Her and Steve. I imagine they're in Skipper's fort over there. Not much we can do about it either, except be ready to go," Felix said, cinching up a strap.

"Huh. Let's just go," Julia said from his left. "They made their choice, they can catch up later, can't they? She's a powered after all. Right?"

Not exactly wrong but... this is Eva.

"We're not leaving without her," Adriana said from his other side. "We'll wait for her here. I'm sure they'll be back in no time at all."

And at that moment, it was obvious she'd jinxed it. The sound of a single gunshot rang throughout the fort.

Followed by a whole lot of gunfire and a small detonation.

Everyone looked to the camp as the sound of gunfire continued.

Damnit. Damnit!

"You're all free to decide what you want to do. Stay here, fend for yourself, come with me, whatever. I'm going in for her," Felix said. Chambering his rifle, Felix set off at a trot to the fort.

Damn you, Eva. I'm going to flog you and give you to Victoria to train in a mountain range for a decade.

Closing in on the fort, the sound of screaming, yelling, and people shouting could be heard through the din of the gun battle.

A Skipper soldier stumbled out of a tent, and went down almost as suddenly as he appeared.

Julia had appeared on his left in that moment. And not only had she joined him, but she'd taken the first shot.

Reward that loyalty later. Heavily.

"I told the others to go around," Julia said. "Take Derek and clear the alley on the other side of the fort. Give us an exit route."

Drown her ass in rewards.

Adriana snickered from his right, her easy gait, athletic grace, and feral beauty shinning through.

"The one-time thug is earning her keep," Adriana said. Felix saw the front of her rifle come up an inch or two. A burst of rounds exploded free of the muzzle.

Off to one side, he saw two soldiers drop to the ground.

"Don't try to make a claim on my Felix though. I won't kill you, but Miu might," Adriana said.

"Why does everyone treat this Miu as if they were a walking death machine?" Julia asked.

"Because she is. Follow the sound of the battle and let's keep out of sight when and as we can," Felix said.

Then they were in and amongst the tents.

Shifting their speed to a swift walk, Felix kept tracking towards the sound of battle.

As they got closer and closer, they started to see fallen bodies. At first there were wounds and corpses that looked like they'd been shattered or simply crushed.

Super strength.

As they got further from whatever had kicked this off, and closer to the battle, the wounds changed.

Now the bodies had clear bullet wounds mixed in.

Brass casings were everywhere in the grass. Glinting in the soft camp lights.

"Up ahead," Julia said.

Focusing on what was directly ahead of them, Felix saw several soldiers taking cover behind crates.

Lining his rifle on them, Felix pulled the trigger. Julia and Adriana did the same, and the enemy soldiers dropped in a hail of fire.

Reaching the position the enemy had been holding, Julia made sure the enemies they'd shot were dead. A quick knife to the throat for each of them.

Didn't even bat an eye.

Adriana set up on the cover, scanned the view, and hesitated.

Looking out to the area in front of him, Felix paused.

There were a number of Skipper soldiers throughout. All with their backs to them, staring down a concrete ramp that led downward into the ground.

The gunfire was these soldiers simply firing blindly down into that ramp.

Julia rested her weapon on the crate and took aim. "Light 'em up?" she asked.

"Take left, work inward. Adriana, the right. I'll start moving out from the center. On my first shot," Felix said.

Setting up carefully, he got in position and readied himself.

Then he pulled the trigger on a woman straight out in front of him.

Her clothes puffed out around her as the rounds struck her, and she dropped to the ground.

Sighting up his next target, Felix pulled the trigger again.

And again.

And again.

When it finally came time for him to change his magazine, there were only two targets left in his field of view.

By the time he exchanged the empty with a fresh one, there was no one left to stand against them.

"Move," Adriana said. Standing up on top of the crates in front of them, she stepped over it and dropped to the other side.

Before Felix could process it, she was off at a run.

Julia slid over the crates leaving Felix alone behind cover.

Right.

Scrambling over the tops of the crates, Felix tried to catch up to the two women.

They had to be quick. The goal was simple. Get Eva, get Steve, get the fuck out. Before the rest of the base could respond and lock them into place.

"Friendly!" Adriana shouted down the ramp as she disappeared downward. "Friendly coming in!"

Adriana rounded the corner and vanished around the bend. Julia was only a few steps behind her.

When Felix managed to do the same he almost crashed into them.

Eva was down on the ground on one knee, blood flowing out of what looked to be gunshot wounds. None of them looked fatal, but they looked freakishly painful.

Steve was pressed up against a wall to one side, his rifle couched in his lap and wedged into his hip. He didn't look very good either.

"Grab 'em up, we're out of here," Felix said, turning in place and moving back up the ramp.

There was a storm of gunfire that came down towards him. It felt like his leg exploded, and then went out from under him.

Screaming, Felix went with the fall and did his best to roll down the ramp and back towards the turn.

Concrete shattered around him as rounds impacted the ground and walls.

Coming to a stop at the edge of the corner, Felix felt someone grab his leg and yank him back around the turn.

Adriana squatted down over him and grabbed his leg. She deftly ripped his pant leg open, revealing flesh and blood.

Sucking in a breath she pulled the fabric free and cleared the area two inches above the problem area.

To Felix it didn't look like one bullet wound, but several.

Reaching for his belt she started to unfasten it.

"I don't think this is the time or place," Felix said.

Adriana gave him a ghost of a smile and looped the belt around his leg just above the bloody mess, and then yanked on it till it was tight.

Shifting it around until the buckle was on the side of his leg rather than above the wound, she pulled on the tongue of it.

She expertly tied it into itself and gave it a tug to test it.

"Your leg is done. That'll keep you up for around two hours but... we're on a timer now," Adriana said, her face turning a pale white. "Lose the leg if we wait too long, maybe bleed out if we remove it."

Eva was staring at him from a few feet away. Her regeneration power must have been active, because the wounds she had were closing up.

"Felix, what are you doing here? Why?" she asked.

"Because you fucked up and got caught. And if I didn't come to get you," Felix said, sitting up, "then I'd never forgive myself. I hope your goddamn bleeding heart morality doesn't cost us all our lives though. Did you even manage to free them?"

"No... they... someone shouted for the guards when they realized we were freeing them. One of the prisoners did. I don't... why?" Eva asked, her voice tight.

"Because people are the best and worst things about our world. Someone probably didn't want to give up the power they had over other prisoners. This isn't a fairy tale. Remember? It's life. When we're done here, I think maybe it's time you got a real world education," Felix said. Levering himself up on one leg, he pressed his shoulder up to the wall.

Julia slipped in under his arm and pulled his around her side. "Come on, let's head back a bit. It'll only take a genius to get a grenade launcher around the corner."

Adriana grabbed Steve by the back of his vest and began dragging him along behind her as she followed Julia and Felix.

"Broken ribs," Steve panted out. "Something...wrong. Hard to breathe," he said in a strangled voice.

"Stab wound?" Adriana asked, not bothering to check him.

"Yes."

"Maybe a punctured lung. You'll be alright for now so long as you're not bleeding into it. If you are, you're probably already done," she said clinically.

"Great," Steve wheezed.

"I'm so sorry, Felix," Eva said, wringing her hands together, getting in front of him.

"Shut up and watch behind us. Use my rifle if you lost yours. Worry about your self-righteousness later," Felix grumped.

Looking crestfallen, Eva bobbed her head quickly. Taking his rifle she moved back behind them.

"That was a bit cold, darling," Adriana said after Eva got further away.

"And the world is cold. If you hadn't noticed, we're probably going to die down here."

"Nn. All the more reason to be kind to her."

"Don't be a dick-bag, boss," Julia said, agreeing with Adriana.

Sighing, Felix fell silent. He didn't want to talk about it right now.

Julia dropped him down into a chair next to an old laptop and a corpse. Taking her weapon in hand she started to move things around from the nearby areas to create some shelter and cover.

Adriana laid Steve out next to Felix and then checked on his leg again.

"That bad, huh?" Felix asked, watching Adriana's face. She had a pretty solid poker face, but when you spent almost every day with the same people, you tended to learn their mannerisms.

Her ears laid flat to her head and she froze, looking up at him.

"Yes... darling. It is. We need to get you out of here."

Unable to keep himself from grimacing, Felix thought hard on the situation.

There wasn't much they could do. He didn't think there'd be an exit out of the tunnels. They were pre-existing and he doubted Skipper's people really wanted to provide a way in or out of the fort.

There wasn't any way to contact Legion either. They'd never managed to find a cell phone with a signal, landline, or working computer.

Everything had been shut down by Skipper's techs and her control of the area.

What about radios? Or better yet, isn't Miu listening?

Turning his attention to the corpse, Felix started pulling at the uniform of the dead woman.

"Felix, what are you doing?" Adriana asked.

"Looking for a unit radio. There was a tower above us, which means this probably gets broadcasted, right?"

"Uuhhhm? Oh! Here," she said, picking up something that was under one of the woman's legs. Taking the radio from her hand, Felix checked it.

It was on, powered, and on whatever communication channel it was encoded to.

"You said Miu was listening, right?"

"She was last I saw her... Judging from the rank insignia, that's an officer. Leave it on whatever setting it's on."

Thumbing down the transmit button, leaving the settings as they were, Felix leaned over the device.

"Shadow. This is Throne. I need you," Felix said, trying to be as clear as he could be, while still protecting what little information he could.

It was enough to get her attention if she was listening.

A burst of responses crackled through the speakers. From people demanding that he identify himself, that he get off the channel, and just asking what the hell was going on.

Eventually, when no response was forthcoming, it all died away.

Nothing came back.

Silence.

Leaning back in his chair, Felix sighed.

She wasn't listening.

"She might be out hunting. We should try again in—"

"Where?" came the single word across the space and depth of hopelessness Felix held in his heart.

"What park is this?" Felix asked Adriana.

"Aaaa… I don't know," Adriana said.

"Tradewinds," Julia interjected. "I saw a sign for it when we were crossing in. Tradewinds Park."

Smiling, and feeling just the smallest bit of hope, Felix looked back to the radio.

It'd be a massive risk to give a location, but it was the only way he could give her the information at the same time.

He took a breath and pressed the transmit button.

"Tradewinds Park," he said.

Another flurry of messages came over the radio as people started talking about what was going on.

In the span of a heartbeat, between several people talking at the same time, Miu responded.

"I'm coming."

It was lost in the chatter almost immediately, but he'd heard it.

Closing his eyes, Felix couldn't help but smile.

His psychotic, devoted, maniacal, deeply disturbed assassin was coming for him.

"She's going to murder the shit out of me," Adriana said under her breath.

"Why?" Felix asked, opening his eyes and looking to Adriana.

"Nothing. Something Lily explained to us. We will endure. Now, we just need to hold them off until she arrives," Adriana smiled at him.

"None of this would have been possible without you. I needed you. Not for your skills, but just the emotional support," Felix said.

"Nn! Good. I expect to be rewarded. A lot. Also, my Prime has not yet selected a second. You should tell her to choose me."

Chuckling, Felix gave her a smile. "I'll do that. Reward you, and tell the Prime to make you second. Is there some type of reward for being the second?"

"Better access to you," Adriana said. Turning to Julia, she pointed to the woman. "Guard Felix, I'm going to go hold the line. When a scary woman shows up, let her do what she wants."

Not waiting for a response, Adriana walked off, heading for where Eva was positioned.

Watching her go, Julia eased up next to Felix. "I take it this Miu is on her way then?" she asked.

"That she is. I'm not sure how this is going to play out but… I have a strange question for you."

Julia grunted, not responding.

"If you died, would you want me to bring you back to life?"

"You can do that?" she asked, looking at him.

"Provided I have something of you I can… well, regrow, yes. I can. Is that a yes?"

"Hell yes. So, what do you need from me?"

"Well. A pinky would probably work. An ear. Something that you can function pretty well without. We can get it regrown once we get back to Legion HQ so don't worry about it being permanently gone or anything."

Julia grimaced at him, but released her rifle with one hand, and drew the blade at her side.

"And while you're at it… Steve, in or out?"

"I'm in," he rasped.

- 481 -

"Julia, be sure to collect something from Steve, and Eva as well. Thanks."

Julia shook her head, muttering to herself.

"Strangest and best job I've ever had," she said.

Then she chopped off her pinky finger.

Chapter 34 - Setup -

Felix had been drifting in a haze of pain and fear, his thoughts fluttering around wildly. Sitting, waiting, hoping that Miu showed up before they got rushed, was playing with his mind.

The sudden chatter of rifle fire shook Felix from his thoughts. It was deafening in the stark quiet that'd been squatting over them.

Lifting his head up, Felix focused on his people.

Julia, Eva, and Adriana were all lined up behind the crates. Julia's muzzle flashed as she fired another burst of rounds.

Following the line of fire, Felix saw the problem.

Skipper troopers were trying to get down into the tunnels with them. Either this was the only entrance, or they thought they could simply muscle their way through.

It'd cost them two people already. They were groaning and rolling around on the floor. Their arms flopping back and forth as they bled out.

Shifting in his chair, Felix's leg screamed at him.

The pain of the wound and tourniquet itself were kept his thoughts scattered. Bouncing around in his head like a couple of screws in a tin can.

"Save the ammo, let them bleed out," Adriana said.

"But, we could try and sa—"

"Do you really want to finish that sentence?" Julia said, interrupting her. "Haven't your goddamn goody-two-shoes wishes given us enough trouble?"

"I didn't mean for thi—"

"No, you didn't, and you didn't think a damn bit of what could happen. You just charged in because you wanted to help. If you didn't notice, your dad back there is dying because of your need to help," Julia hissed at her. "Shut your stupid mouth, and let the adults fix your mess."

"Julia… this isn't the time or place," Adriana said. "Stow it."

Scoffing, Julia gave her head a shake and muttered something under her breath that Felix couldn't make out.

Eva got quiet after that.

He didn't doubt for a second she was more than likely boiling with guilt and anxiety about the situation.

But he wasn't going to correct Julia either.

Unfortunately, even though he cared deeply for Eva, he didn't feel like Julia was wrong.

Soft headed morality was the shortest and quickest route to getting yourself killed, hurt, or taken advantage of.

You don't have to step on the heads of others to get ahead, but you'll never do it by letting others step on your own head. Then again, people in Legion are different. We're all united in our purpose and cause.

As his thoughts started to slip out of his control, several groups of armed Skipper troops came sprinting around the corner.

They all opened up as they came.

His Legionnaires returned fire and started to drop targets

Rounds shattered into walls, the ceiling, and passed all around in both directions.

Felix threw himself to the ground, trying to limit his profile. He wasn't good to anyone right now and was a liability.

Adriana spun to one side and went down in a heap.

Several heartbeats later, the bullets stopped flying, though there was a clinking sound he'd never heard before.

Rolling around between himself and his people was a small green sphere.

A grenade? A grenade.

Felix froze, unsure of what to do. He didn't think he could get away quick enough with his leg in such bad shape.

Julia dove on top of the grenade before Felix could come up with a valid plan.

She covered it up completely with her chest and stomach, lying flat over the top of it.

Her head shot up and she locked eyes with him.

"Bring me back, or I'll haunt you," she said, and then exploded.

The blast was particularly large, cutting her in half and emptying out her chest cavity as if the armor she'd been wearing had done nothing at all to protect her.

Her torso flopped to one side, her eyes wide open and alive.

A bullet passed through her temple as she took in a struggling breath and exited the back of her head, her eyes going glassy and flat in a moment.

"She'll thank me later," Adriana said, turning back to the ramp after having delivered the mercy shot.

"This is all my fault. All my fault," Eva said, her voice breaking.

"Keep your head in the game, Eva. I need you right now," Adriana shouted, her rifle opening up again as more enemy soldiers stormed down the ramp.

This time Adriana returned the favor, tossing a grenade as they turned the corner.

The detonation dropped half of them, and the other half was dazed.

Holding the trigger down, Adriana dropped them all and emptied the clip at the same time.

With a rapid magazine change that'd impress even the hardest of soldiers, Adriana leaned back into the cover.

Waiting.

"Damn. That was close," Felix muttered.

Levering himself up to a sitting position, Felix swiveled around to face Steve. "How you doing over the—"

Felix stopped when he realized Steve wasn't breathing. His head was leaned back against the wall he'd been propped up against.

Unmoving.

Dead.

Looking away, Felix wasn't sure what he could do anymore.

This is why you stay in the rear, with the gear. Remember? Sure, they trained you up just in case, but this isn't your forte.

The sound of movement came from the tunnel.

Felix briefly wondered how many more waves they could survive.

A large black mech stomped around the corner. It had a large sword in one hand and the other was empty.

Emblazoned on the shoulder was Legion's brand.

He didn't recognize it as one of the Warden models he'd seen.

Sliding around behind the Warden, because that was clearly what it was, came Victoria in her personalized suit.

Feeling a hiccupping laugh escape his chest, Felix lifted a hand and waved.

Not trusting himself to talk, that was the extent he could handle right now.

The Warden oriented itself on him and then moved quickly towards him, only stopping when it loomed over him.

"Felix. I'm here," came Miu's voice through the speakers.

"I'm glad to see you," Felix said. "I'm afraid I have another hard one for you. Get me, Eva, and Adriana out of here."

Victoria was talking to Adriana and Eva, a hushed conversation with violent gestures.

"I understand," Miu said. "You are wounded."

"Yeah. It's... not good. I think it's worse than Adriana is letting on. Think you can get us out?"

"No." Turning in place, the front of the Warden faced Adriana.

"If the Beastkin lets me kill her, we can escape quickly. She left a piece of herself at HQ and can be brought back easily," Miu said. "It would increase our speed."

- 484 -

Adriana stopped talking to Victoria and stared up at Miu. After three seconds she looked at Felix. "She's not wrong, darling. I'm healing but not fast, I'd slow you down. I'll take care of it in a moment. Please remember your promise, won't you? I'm currently designated as forty-two," Adriana said.

Not sparing them another word, she returned to her conversation with Victoria.

The Warden rotated around and lined up on Felix again.

"I will take Felix, and go back to HQ," Miu said. She reached behind her back and the sword clanged into place in its holder.

A pod attached to the left hip of the Warden cracked open. Kneeling down in front of him, Miu indicated the pod. "Medical kit. Use the painkillers," she said. "You need to stay awake, and I think the pain might become unbearable once we set out."

Reaching into the pod, Felix pulled it out and cracked it open.

There were several pre-set injectors hooked into the sides. The idea was that anyone could use the kit even without training.

Felix didn't know what was in them, or how to use it, and didn't even care.

Instead, he pulled one out, flicked the tip off it, and jammed it into his forearm.

Miu leaned in after that was done and scooped Felix up under his armpits and knees.

She's not actually going to princess carry me... ah crap she is.

"Throne acquired," Victoria said to what he assumed was the communication network. "Hook returning, requesting escort along R-2."

Felix saw Eva clamber onto Victoria's back at the same time that Adriana put her rifle down between her knees, put the rifle to her brow, and pulled the trigger.

The single boom and the explosion of her skull splattering the ceiling was shocking for some reason.

Crumpling to the ground, Adriana's corpse went rigid.

Miu didn't stop, and stepped over the blood-gushing corpse and started towards the ramp.

She turned the shoulder of the mech as she got up to ground level. Felix had a momentary thought that she'd done it to shield Felix in case there were more troops. At the same time, Felix got a view of the back of the camp.

The pain in his leg was rapidly fading away.

He wasn't sure if it was a good thing or a bad thing, but at the moment, it sure felt good.

There was a straight line of wreckage through the camp that led right here.

Nothing tried to stop them as Miu headed out of the camp.

"We sent a group of people towards the back alley," Felix said.

"We found them," Victoria said, loping along beside Miu as the Warden began to gather speed. Eva was wrapped around her back like a backpack, clutching tightly to her. "They're already being evacuated."

"I sense a but in there," Felix replied dryly.

"Skipper figured out where you were. She's mobilizing everything. A lot of the new religious forces are apparently moving as well. The only group not interested in eradicating you is apparently the federal forces," Victoria said.

"I... see. What you're saying is... we're going to have a lot of company real quick," Felix summarized.

"Legion is already taking the field. Everything is being turned loose. The new recruits from Fort One as well," Victoria said. "We did send all the students and their families on to Wal though. They weren't ready for this. At least, Lily and Kit didn't think so."

"Where are they," Victoria said, her head swiveling around.

"Where is—" Felix stopped when he saw an entire platoon of Wardens stomping their way towards him. They were fully loaded, and looked as if every Warden across the entire country was there.

As if it were by plan, the Wardens closed in around Miu and Victoria. A solid shield-wall of mechs and munitions.

"Hook is ten minutes out," Victoria said.

Either she's extremely nervous and forgot to turn off her external speakers, or she's taken damage.

From a side alley of the street they were running down, a group of Skipper soldiers stumbled out. Several Wardens on that side turned as they ran, leveled their weapons, and fired. Solid magnetic projectiles launched from the railguns and bodies literally exploded.

The entire group didn't even miss a beat in their running speed.

"Had contact. Position may be compromised," Victoria said, pausing as if listening to a response.

"Understood," she said, several seconds later. "Line change, R-2A."

The platoon began shifting towards the left side of the street. At the next intersection, the group turned left down a large street. After that they took the next right into another street.

They shifted over one to try and break contact. It must be much worse than I—

Up ahead there was a checkpoint of sorts. The center of the intersection was hastily barricaded with gutted cars and broken chunks of anything. Arrayed behind that haphazard cover were four squads of Legion security forces in full combat gear and two armored personnel vehicles.

The squads stood up when they saw the Wardens heading their way. Their officers made a couple of quick gestures and everyone began rapidly piling into their heavily armed transports.

Before Miu and the rest had even cleared the barricades, both vehicles had started forward.

"Good," Victoria said. "That helps."

The turrets were manned, and the vehicles slowed to match the Warden's pace. The designation on the rear of the APC marked it as belonging to SC:HQ though.

They now had a point guard from vehicles that shouldn't be here.

"You actually mobilized everything?" Felix asked.

"Everything," Victoria said. "No one was told a lie, everyone was aware you were gone. We were united in purpose, but we all knew you'd be found. Was only a matter of time."

"Felicia had to expand the portals from base to base. All Teleport and Portal functions outside of the city HQs don't work though. It's like someone took Neutralizer's power and threw it on the entire city. Otherwise we'd have already ported you out with a Telemedic," Miu's voice startled him when she started talking. She'd been quiet for a while.

This wasn't an accident in any way, shape or form. This was an elaborately orchestrated attack to kill me, specifically. But it doesn't quite make sense.

"Speaking of Neutralizer, he said the night you disappeared he felt a power trying to reach into HQ. He disrupted it as best as he could, but he'd never encountered it before and didn't know how to do it," Victoria said. "He's confident he can block it if he runs up against it again though. He also shared his knowledge with his department."

"I wonder if that's why I ended up where I did. They didn't get to use it the way they wanted, maybe," Felix said. "Remind me to thank him. Actually, I have an entire list of people I need to reward and thank."

A boom sounded out from somewhere to the left. It was a deep, resonating thing that shook the pit of his stomach.

Gunfire filled the silence afterward, only to be drowned out by a deep rumbling of a high powered machine gun.

The APCs entered what appeared to be a large single level parking lot and peeled off to the right.

When the Wardens made it into the lot, Felix realized it was anything but empty. It was bristling and full of Legion forces and equipment.

Machine gun emplacements, vehicles, even Powered soldiers were everywhere.

For all the world, it had the appearance of a fort perched on the edge of a battlefield that'd be held to the death.

Then people started to realize Miu and her Wardens had just passed the perimeter.

It started as a single cheer, and quickly progressed to a deep rumbling roar.

The Warden guard came to rest at the center of the fort.

Felix wasn't sure where it had come from, or if it had been there, but he was happy that there was a building there. One that looked like it had thick walls and maybe a nice seat.

Kit, Lily, and Ioana trooped out of that building, and rushed over to him.

He was surprised when he saw them because they were all wearing costumes.

Kit was in what looked like her original Augur outfit. He knew she'd kept it in a locker, and hadn't touched it since she retrieved it.

Lily was wearing a suit of the light combat armor that Miu typically favored.

Though this one was different. The black fabric had red stitching and graphics worked throughout it. The shimmer of magic bled back and forth across it as she moved. She'd clearly spent some time enchanting and modifying it.

Ioana was in a suit of armor similar to Victoria's, though much more bulky.

"Felix!" Lily said, quickly moving to his side as Miu set him down. "Oh, thank god. Oh my god, you're wounded."

Unable to help himself, he smiled as Lily began to methodically check him over, her fingers light and tender.

Andrea and Adriana Prime squirmed in at Lily's sides.

Adriana began to quickly go over his wound while Andrea fussed with his face and hair.

"Stop, back up, he's fine. But we should get him under cover," Kit said, muscling her way between everyone. "Here, I've got him."

Lily, Adriana, and Andrea all took a step back. They all wore worried smiles, but were clearly glad to see him.

Pulling her helmet off her head, Kit smiled at him, her short hair blowing out around her. Without a gesture or word, Felix floated up off the ground. Completely supported and weightless.

The door to the building opened on its own, and Felix was floated inside.

"I imagine Miu gave you the rundown," Kit said, following him in.

"She did. I'm not sure what good I am though. My powers have been messed with. I assume it's a unique powerset or… well… divine intervention," Felix said, trying not to panic at the fact that there was nothing between him and the ground.

The room was simple. A few chairs, a table, and a computer desk with a huge bank of monitors with live camera feeds.

"That's not a problem," Ioana said from the doorway. "Your job is to build us up and guide us. Fighting is the job of me, and my people. You've done everything possible, now it's our turn to show you what we can do."

Kit lowered Felix down into a padded chair.

Relaxing, Felix oozed into it, trying to get comfortable.

"Then you have my permission to engage as you see fit, and do what must be done. I place my full trust in you, Ioana. My Warmaiden," Felix said.

Ioana stood up straighter, her hands clenching. She seemed as if she couldn't respond to that.

"Go forth and conquer," he added.

Saluting smartly, she spun on her heel and charged back outside.

Lily leaned over him, hugging him tightly, pressing his face into her shoulder. "We were all so worried," she said into his hair.

Then Adriana and Andrea were there, hugging everyone at the same time.

"Sorry. I did everything I could to get back as quickly as I could. And before I forget… Adriana, one of your Others found me. Helped me. Provided assistance above and beyond. I'm not sure if you have a second, but I think it'd be a suitable reward for what she did for me," Felix said.

"Nn, I can do that. Where is she?"

"Dead. She took her own life so we could move faster in escaping. She said she left her finger with you. That her current designation was forty-two," Felix said.

Adriana nodded her head and then kissed him.

Followed by Andrea doing the same.

Lily only wrinkled her nose at them.

"I'll wait till later, when you're not covered in Wolfgirl slobber," she said with a broad smile.

Chapter 35 - Last Mile -

"Sounds like this was all part of some scheme by Skipper," Kit said, sitting next to him.

Everyone other than Lily and Kit had cleared the room. They all had things that they needed to do and see to.

"And we're not out of the woods yet," Lily said. "Best guess is we're about to be drowned in Skipper and other forces."

"They mentioned that," Felix said dryly. Grimacing he looked at his leg.

The tourniquet had been on for too long. He knew there was going to be muscle damage, but he figured Felicia could repair that. Bleeding out wasn't going to be as easy to solve, so it remained right there.

"Yes. It's not good," Kit said. "The leg is probably lost or severely damaged at this point. But so long as it's still intact and we get you to Felicia sooner rather than later, it'll be fine."

"Speaking of, how are we getting out of here?" Felix asked.

"Most of us are going to get out the same way we got in. Load up, move out. You, though, are being flown out by helicopter to an airfield. Felicia's there with a medical bed ready for you and a much larger plane. It's bound for Wal. We've already made a number of deals with them to acquire a sanctuary there," Lily explained.

"After everything that's happened... yeah. Tilen and Skipper City aren't going to be safe for us to operate out of. And with the religions getting militarized, I imagine global politics are shifting rapidly," Felix said.

"That they are," Kit agreed. "Wal is looking forward to our operational relationship as much as we are, I think. Their military was never large. We've taken on a contract to act as a standing army for them. PMC for an entire military, so to speak."

"Interesting. Michael will be happy about that."

"Which Michael?" Lily asked. "There's a lot of them."

"Fort One Michael."

"Ah, yes. He's already sped up his recruitment to help fill slots for that contract," Lily said.

There was a short klaxon-like sound, followed by a long high pitched whistle.

Kit sighed and put her helmet on, pulling it down tight. "I'm afraid your ride out hasn't arrived yet, but our enemies have."

Lily stood up and brushed herself off quickly. Leaning down, she gave him a quick kiss and then fled the building.

"She was rather worried. She might seem like everything is fine, but there were a few times where it was clear she was falling apart," Kit said. "I... must admit I felt very much the same. It was eye opening how much we rely on you when you're suddenly not there. Now... I'm going to go lead my Minders and Fixers into the field."

"Where'd Eva go?" Felix asked, wondering where she'd ended up.

"She's in an APC. I think there's a few Andreas with her. She's..." Kit's voice trailed off.

"Yeah. I get it. I'll talk to her later about it all."

Kit nodded, and then left the room, leaving Felix by himself.

Sighing, he levered himself up, and hopped and hobbled his way over to the computer desk. Sitting heavily in the seat, he managed to get himself mostly comfortable.

Fixing his view on the monitors, he watched as his people went about their tasks. Ioana, Kit, Lily, and Andrea were at the center. Around them were their lieutenants and assistants. Victoria, Miu, Adriana, and Neutralizer were much closer to the front, though clearly going through very similar circumstances.

On the next monitor, Felix found himself looking at one of the perimeter views. At the edge of the view-screen, he could see people making their way towards the Legion position. They were numerous. Something akin to a horror movie where a horde of zombies were rushing in, to be exact.

Legion forces opened fire, the heavy machine guns, rifles, and SMGs unloading. The turrets on vehicles, Wardens, and emplacements began firing as well.

Skipper's Powereds began filtering in amongst the enemy troops. Some literally came down from buildings to try and land amongst Legion's forces. Legion's equivalent met them head on, working in groups and in tandem to their advantage.

From another direction, on a different monitor, Felix watched as a group of what he assumed were militarized religious priests came running down a street. The only reason he even assumed that was that they were all glowing in a similar way to the group he'd seen the other day.

At that moment, the screen frizzed out. Almost immediately after that, every monitor died.

Not wanting to miss what was going on, and figuring he could probably do this safely, Felix decided to leave.

Picking up a helmet someone had left inside, he pulled it down over his head, becoming a faceless soldier, and not a standout target.

Exiting the building, he didn't go far. He leaned up against the wall, and looked towards where the religious order had started to come from.

There, floating in the air above, were several impressive looking men. They were garbed in nothing but energy, and seemed to hold weapons made of the same stuff.

Gods. Great.

Abera and Desh materialized over the Legion forces. Desh folded his arms across his chest and leaned his head back, laughing. Abera howled, gripped her axe, and leapt towards the three deities.

One lifted what looked like a sword to block her attack, only to have it shatter into bits, and her axe buried into his head.

Screaming triumphantly, Abera turned on the other two, yanking her weapon free of the god with the split skull.

More gods started to appear, until Desh and Abera were facing twenty or so of them.

"Come then," shouted the goddess of war. It was audible to everyone. As if it were enhanced and multiplied. "I'll bury you all! In the name of Felix and Legion, I will crush you. Crush you to goo."

The result was instantaneous. Whatever machine Felicia built was clearly working. Abera suddenly burned like the sun as Legion screamed their agreement to her words.

Desh turned a bright white then exploded, a golden halo sweeping out from him and covering everyone nearby.

As it passed over him, Felix suddenly felt lucky. Incredibly lucky. Like if he were to buy a lottery ticket right now, he'd win.

If he bought a ticket for every lottery, he'd win every one.

Turning into a golden meteor, Abera launched herself headlong into the enemy gods and goddesses, and began to wreak havoc amongst them.

Standing on a rooftop nearby, a dark robed man began to build rune-script out of the air.

Not far from where Felix stood, bright blue runes popped into being.

Evan stood there, his hands making sharp gestures as perfect, clean runes formed. Rapidly formed.

He was clearly proceeding with his spell in a much quicker fashion than the other man.

No sooner had the rune closed the pattern, than Evan clapped his hands together and shoved them forward. The rune formed a gigantic icicle and sped off towards the black robed man. And went through him.

Crumpling where he stood, the enemy magician tumbled off the roof and disappeared.

Evan wasted no time and started up another spell, the runes coming almost as fast as Lily's did before he upgraded her.

A rumbling crunch to the left got Felix's attention as an armored car with a turret mounted on it came into view. It started to fire into the ranks of his people.

Only one round got through before a wall of glowing red runes appeared. It was sloped to force rounds to glance upwards and away, Lily standing at the center of the formation.

Kit stood beside her, and wherever she looked, enemies fell in twitching heaps.

All around him, the forces of Legion battled and held their ground. There was no getting around the fact that Legion were outnumbered.

While everything Legion had had indeed been mobilized, that didn't mean everyone had already made it here.

And even if it was, Felix and his forces were fighting against multiple enemies. Holding out was a definite, and winning was almost guaranteed.

But it wasn't assured.

There was a chance it could all fail and fall apart. Most of this entire situation was because of Skipper.

She viewed him as a problem. A hurdle.

He was a rival for Tilen and Skipper City.

But what if he wasn't?

Hobbling back into the building, Felix wondered if this ploy would work, or doom them.

Yanking off the helmet he tossed it into a corner. With a hop and a graceless flop, he landed back in the computer desk's chair. Taking a deep breath, he picked up the speaker that was perched in front of the stand of monitors, and thumbed the button to turn it on.

"This is Felix Campbell, head and CEO of Legion. I'd like to parley with Skipper," Felix said. He could hear his voice amplified over the loudspeakers outside. More than likely it'd be passed back to Skipper.

"If she'd prefer to meet in a virtual space, I'll be on—" Felix paused to look at the radio nearby to read off what it was set to. "Two-seventy MHz. I'll be waiting for ten minutes, then assume you want to continue wasting your resources here. I'm sure the federal government is just watching and waiting to make their move. I know I would be."

Felix let go of the button and picked up the headset, pulling it over his head.

Before he'd even sat there waiting for a minute, Kit entered the room, her helmet clutched under one hand.

"What are you doing?" she asked immediately.

"Hopefully, I'm getting us out of here quickly. I mean, loss of life isn't a concern for us, but I'd rather not waste resources if we don't have to. Do you have any idea how much gold it'd cost us if this kept going?" Felix shook his head at thought of it. "No, if I can get us out quickly and easily, that'd be ideal."

"We're winning out there. Completely."

"Of that I have no doubt, but that doesn't mean there isn't the possibility of defeat. In this case, I'm going to be risk averse," Felix said, shrugging his shoulders. "Sit your pretty ass down and keep me company. Maybe you can block her from reading the future. Oh, and here, this'll catch you up. Also let you listen in technically if she decides to respond."

With his left hand, Felix opened up the command to allow Kit to read his thoughts.

"Felix," said a voice over his headset. "What the fuck do you want. Before my army crushes you and your peasants."

"Not much," Felix said, pressing down the microphone button. "Though I'm not so sure about you crushing anything. Have you taken a look at your losses yet? I have. Not looking so good. You lose too much more and you won't be able to fight when they roll over your forces in Tilen and swing to Skipper City."

"Hmph," Skipper said, and went silent.

Letting go of the button, Felix laughed. "She's so obvious. She relies on her power too much. Without it she can barely function. Right now she's probably trying to get reports on what's happening here. But your presence might be making it harder or impossible to do it with her power."

Shaking his head, he laughed again.

"I mean, we already know her infrastructure is garbage. If—"

"Well?" Skipper asked.

"Ah, to be continued, Kit my dear," Felix said.

He paused for a moment at that comment. His head felt funny, and the pain hadn't come back yet. Things weren't feeling quite normal.

Painkillers?

Except right now wasn't the time to worry about it.

"I was hoping to make you an offer to end this early. I don't want to sit here murdering your entire army just to pack up and leave when you finally figure it out. So I'll make you an offer. I have nothing I want in Tilen or Skipper City. I'll retreat, remove, and release all matters pertaining to Tilen and Skipper City for at least five years. This goes for everyone in my employ as well," Felix said, dragging a wrist across his brow.

"Un. And what do you want from me. Hm?" Skipper asked.

"I want the same from you that I'm offering. That you'll have no interest in Legion in any way for five years, and you'll withdraw from this fight. I want to leave, and the sooner you call your pets off, the sooner I can do so," Felix said.

Skipper didn't respond. The line went dead.

Outside, Felix could hear his people continuing their grim work. They'd been able to prep a position that they could hold from.

He wasn't in a rush. For now, his people held the upper hand.

Silence was his ally.

Always.

"Deal," Skipper said. It was clear she was frustrated and angry.

"Great. Go ahead and pull your forces back. We'll be on our way as soon as we can. Legion won't be your problem by the end of today. Though I recommend not sending people into our buildings. I'm going to demo them," Felix said. "Signing off."

Letting go of the button, Felix dropped the headset on the desk. Spinning in the chair, he turned to face Kit. "And there we have it," he said.

Kit was watching him intently. Her eyes were narrowed as she stared.

Lifting his eyebrows, he waited a beat. "Yes?"

"Nothing," she said, visibly relaxing. "Should I tell the troops to lay off as they retreat?"

"No. I don't want to give Skipper a chance to change her mind. We'll remain vigilant, aggressive, and ready. Though you can go ahead and tell everyone what's going on," Felix said.

"Done," Kit said, still watching him, though not as intensely. "I think when we have some time later, I'd like to sit down and discuss what all happened."

"We can do that. Definitely," Felix said, smiling. His head felt light and he wanted to lay down.

Sitting in a room with Kit and watching her as she dissected him didn't seem like a bad idea down the road. Maybe she'd even wear something fun. He just had to remember to make sure she couldn't read his thoughts. His minded tended to wander at the best of times.

Wait. Can she read them right now?

Did we turn it on? Or off?

Closing his eyes, Felix pressed his hands to his face and tried to collect himself. He felt like his control was unraveling.

Leaning forward in his chair, he took in a deep breath, and could only smell blood.

His blood.

His leg was soaked in it.

Sitting up straight, Felix forced the image of Julia exploding out of his mind. Of Adriana blowing her own head off.

He'd seen worse. He'd done worse. So why did those images haunt him right now?

No, no, no. Got to get—

"Felix," Kit said, pressing her warm hand to his cheek. "Calm down. Just… relax. The chopper is landing right now, and we'll be getting out of here in a moment."

"Alright," Felix said. "It's landing?"

"Yes. Right now."

Listening intently, Felix heard it then.

He was amazed he'd missed it up to this point. It was so loud.

Had he lost some time there?

"Come on. Everyone is getting out now. A squad of Adrianas is staying behind to organize the retreat, everyone else is getting on the chopper with us," Kit said.

Trying to stand up, Felix felt his leg go out from under him. Collapsing to the floor, Felix couldn't understand what'd just happened.

Oh yeah, that leg doesn't work now.

More than one pair of hands lifted him up, and he was situated between two people. Letting his head hang, Felix let himself go with the movements. Someone lifted him up into the interior of the helicopter, and belted him in. A number of other people joined him in the helicopter till someone eventually slammed the door shut.

Lifting his head a bit, Felix was staring out the window of the helicopter as it started to take off. Everyone was packing it in rapidly. Pulling out and putting tires to the road. Once Skipper's troops had backed out, the religious fanatics had found themselves under extreme attack by the concerted efforts of Legion.

Or so it seemed to Felix.

That's what it looked like to him right now as he watched them run away as magic, ammo, and other things rained down on them.

Abera and Desh stood side by side in the middle of the air as the enemy forces went tumbling back. Legion's forces taking the chance to dash away from the line and to their mechanized transports.

When it was clear that there would be nothing coming back their way, Abera and Desh vanished.

Lifting into the air, the helicopter swung to one side, and Felix's view of the field of battle was gone. Soon enough they were lifting up above the buildings and heading towards the south.

All along the route beneath them there were bombed out buildings, husks of cars, and wrecked pavement. The city wouldn't be useful for anything other than collecting debris.

Whoever won this battle would gain nothing.

In fact, he'd be surprised if someone didn't decide to start shelling it again.

Or bomb it.

Pressing his forehead to the cool glass, Felix closed his eyes.

That was all a problem for another day.

Right now, he just wanted to sleep.

- Epilogue -

Dear Felix,

I'm sure by now someone has told you that I've left.

Don't blame Andrea or Adriana, this was my choice. Looking back, I can honestly tell myself it was mostly due to the fact that I wasn't Prime anymore. That I wasn't the lead personality, even though I was the original.

I was Andrea Elex

I was Myriad.

It was hard to carry that in my own head, honestly. Hard to think that I was the original, but was no longer.

That I died.

With how much power, intelligence, and honestly everything you gave us, we became extremely stable. To the point that Adriana was able to split off into a person.

I decided to take that opportunity for myself, and split off as well.

Now I wander this interesting planet with a squad of Myriads. So long as I'm careful, and utilizing that lovely regeneration power you gave us, I don't think there will ever be an issue.

And yes, I know I can always come home whenever I want and you'll take me back with open arms. I appreciate it.

As for Legion world...it's fairly straightforward. Things are brutal and violent.

Simple.

I definitely appreciate the fact that you've launched satellites into orbit almost everywhere, by the way.

I can't help but wonder if you did this specifically for me, since there isn't anyone else on this entire planet but me who could use the Legion network via satellite.

The fact that my access is open, clear, and the same as it always was speaks for itself to a degree as well.

In closing, I'm well. Everything is fine, and I'll report back everything I find.

Be safe, darling.

Myriad

Felix looked up from the email and stared out the window.

They'd moved everything to Wal two months ago. During that time, they'd expanded rapidly into Legion world and built it out as if it were a normal city.

A normal HQ location, that was now the hub for everywhere else.

Every other HQ.

Satellites, roads, everything that they'd need to conduct Legion business.

Everything had settled down and Legion was back up and running to its previous stride. It'd only taken that long for them to branch out in every direction according to their previous successes: junkyards, used car lots, pawnshops, security for businesses, and the PMC contract.

He still regretted having to demolish the HQs in both cities, but he wasn't about to leave them standing for someone else. Though the underground portions for both buildings existed today, and were still thriving.

Legion would abide by the agreement it struck with Skipper, but it wouldn't give up its underground kingdom.

It'd only taken that single night to seal it all off as if it had never been there.

That same night his power returned to normal. As if there'd never been a problem in the first place.

Getting to his feet, Felix walked over to the window and stared out of it.

A vast and open plain was there.

He preferred to work in the main HQ on Legion world. There was no chance of being attacked by anything that could actually do him harm.

Which meant he was allowed to have a window.

With an actual view.

"Felix," Andrea said, getting his attention.

"Mm?" he asked, looking over his shoulder.

Andrea Prime was dressing in a similar fashion to Lily now, her hairstyle changing as well. She was sitting at the desk she'd brought into his office that was specifically for her, and her work as the ANet coordinator.

On the other side of the office, Adriana Prime had a similar desk. Though she still wore her combat gear everywhere.

"Have you decided what you wanted to do?" she asked.

"What, about Skipper and the rest?"

"Unn."

"Nothing. We're going to do nothing for another four years and ten months. I'll abide by the contract. Until then, we're going to build up and leverage everything. I have no desire for power, but I'll not be forced out again," Felix said, shaking his head.

"Nn. Oh, what about the portals? We have that project coming up to explore a few more worlds," Andrea said.

Felix had been mulling that one over for a while. He needed resources, and the other worlds offered up an opportunity for it.

There was a sudden knock on the door that broke Felix's thoughts. Turning, he frowned. No one knocked on his door because the Adrianas outside of it never let anyone in they didn't announce first.

Opening, the door swung inward and a man stepped in.

He was about five foot nine, Felix would guess. With average looks and build. Dressed in business attire, he looked like any office worker.

His eyes were unique though.

They were bright blue. Eyes that popped out with their vibrancy, and a shock of dark black hair that contrasted with them.

"Hey Felix," the man said, stepping into the office.

Andrea shot to her feet, her hands going down to the inside of her jacket.

Adriana was quicker and had brought her SMG up to her shoulder in a second from her position.

"Ah, that's enough of that," said the man, pointing a finger at Adriana and then Andrea.

Both Beastkin Primes froze stock still. Their eyes still moved, they breathed, but they were statues otherwise.

"They're unharmed of course. But we can't have them shooting at me right now. It'd just cause more problems than it's worth," said the man.

Felix blinked and then clasped his hands behind his back, trying to cover up his anxiety and nerves.

"To what do I owe the pleasure?" Felix asked, walking over to his desk and then taking a seat behind it.

"Ah, well, I'd like to talk to you about your portal experiments," the man said, taking a seat in one of the open chairs in front of Felix's desk.

"My portal experiments," Felix repeated. "Ok, and what about them exactly?"

"I'd like you to stop. Entirely. You're welcome to use them on your world and this one, but no more traveling to other worlds," said the man, nodding his head.

"Ah..." Felix said, unsure how to proceed.

"Right, then. I'll put it another way. You owe me two favors," the man said, leaning forward in his chair and holding up two fingers. "I'm calling one in."

Felix felt his blood run cold and his heart stumble in his chest.

It's him. This is him.

"I understand. I'll cease all portal experiments immediately for anything off-world related," Felix said, nodding his head.

"Great, that's grand. See, I knew you wouldn't be a problem. I think with that I'll get going. Lots to do today," the man said, standing up again.

Felix stood up quickly, holding out a hand to the man.

He had to try and work out a deal. A communication line.

Anything.

This entity was infinitely powerful.

"Ah, could I perhaps—"

"No. And realistically, it's better that way. The more you interact with me, the worse it'll be for you. There comes a point of no return where it'll no longer make any sense. Sooner rather than later as well. Especially for people like you," the man said, shaking his head.

"Can I at least ask you about the future and—"

"I have no idea how it'll all turn out. I'm omnipresent, not omniscient."

"Then you are a god after all," Felix said.

"No. I'm not," the man said. He paused, scratching at his jaw with one hand. "Eh... I'll be listening if you need something from me. But I still have one favor left, and there isn't much I need from you other than what I already have the favor planned for. Just don't expect me to respond. And if you try to play any games with me..."

The man stopped and walked over to Andrea and put a finger to her head. "I'll pull her soul out—" He paused to point at Adriana. "—and hers. Do you understand?"

"I... yes," Felix said, well and properly frightened.

"You're smart, Felix. Sometimes too smart. If I didn't tell you exactly what I don't want you to do, you'd think a way around it."

"Ah... can I at least ask you a question? Please?"

The man seemed to think on that, looking at Andrea.

"Right, then. I'll answer. If I can," he said finally.

"Are my aunt and uncle alive?" Felix asked.

Sighing, the man looked away from Andrea and focused on Felix. "Your aunt is long since passed. Your uncle is alive, but there's no way for you to ever see him again. Consider him lost to you, but yes, he lives," the man said.

Felix nodded at that, his eyes lowering till he was looking at the carpet.

"She died quickly. Painlessly. She's in a better place. Your uncle did everything he could to help her. They both left with regret about not being able to see you again," the man offered up. "I'll... I'll let them know you're thinking of them."

"Mm. At least I know, now," Felix said. "Thank you."

"Knowledge can be cruel. Ah, and before I go," the man said. Taking a moment, he snapped his fingers. "They'll not hear me for this next bit, and when I leave I'll wake them both up."

That got Felix's attention. Prying his eyes off the ground, he looked back to the man.

"You should probably remove the barren thing from both of them. Or have an honest conversation with them about not having kids yet. They're starting to worry they're never going to have children. I'm not sure how it'll turn out but I would guess it'd break them. I mean, I get it. I'd do it myself, but keep it up at your own peril," said the man, indicating both Beastkin women. "That's your freebie for not being a douche-canoe. My personal opinion is... knock 'em up. They want it, it'd make them happy, and honestly you could use some joy in your life yourself."

The man walked over to the door and opened it up.

"I'm outta here. I need to take a wicked shit in my crap-castle. See ya later, Felix," the man said and closed the door behind himself.

Andrea and Adriana immediately came to life again, both holding their weapons and scanning the room.

"He's gone," Felix said. "Don't bother raising the alarm or trying to find him. I get the impression he was a god. Or something like it. He used the door for his own convenience."

Andrea and Adriana didn't seem to care for that one bit.

"Darling, I don't understand..." Andrea said.

"Mm? Which part. He's the one I made a deal with. I owed him two favors for it. He called one in," Felix said.

"I… suppose. Unn," Andrea said, her ears twitching.

"I don't like it," Adriana muttered. Her own ears had gone flat to her head.

"And yet there it is," Felix said. Sitting back down at his desk, he folded his hands, one into the other. "We're canceling all portal experiments that aren't related to our world, or Legion world."

Felix looked off to one side. There were things to do, a war with Skipper to plan, and many things to consider.

Like how to tell Andrea he didn't want kids yet and had given her a barren status.

That or remove it and let her get pregnant to her heart's content.

He did suggest simply doing just that, didn't he?

Maybe that's a conversation better had with Lily first since she's sharing our bed too, now. See what she thinks about the twins getting pregnant.

Shaking his head, Felix looked up with a smile at the Beastkin.

That was the least of his problems. He still had a conversation he'd been planning to have with Eva later today. Hopefully… they could get through the problems and start to heal.

Together.

There was also the need to check in on Julia and Steve to make sure they were adapting well to life in Legion.

"Well. What's next?" Felix asked, grinning.

Thank you, dear reader!

I'm hopeful you enjoyed reading Super Sales on Super Heroes. Please consider leaving a review, commentary, or messages. Feedback is imperative to an author's growth. That and positive reviews never hurt.

Feel free to drop me a line at: WilliamDArand@gmail.com

Keep up to date—Facebook: https://www.facebook.com/WilliamDArand
Patreon: https://www.patreon.com/WilliamDArand
Blog: http://williamdarand.blogspot.com/
LitRPG Group: https://www.facebook.com/groups/LitRPGsociety/

If you enjoyed this book, try out the books of some of my close friends. I can heartily recommend them.

Blaise Corvin- A close and dear friend of mine. He's been there for me since I was
nothing but a rookie with a single book to my name. He told me from the start that it was clear I had talent and had to keep writing. His background in European martial arts creates an accurate and detail driven action segments as well as his world building.

https://www.amazon.com/Blaise-Corvin/e/B01LYK8VG5

John Van Stry- John was an author I read, and re-read, and re-read again, before I was
an author. In a world of books written for everything except harems, I found that not only did I truly enjoy his writing, but his concepts as well.
In discovering he was an indie author, I realized that there was nothing separating me from being just like him. I attribute him as an influence in my own work.
He now has two pen names, and both are great.

https://www.amazon.com/John-Van-Stry/e/B004U7JY8I
Jan Stryvant-
https://www.amazon.com/Jan-Stryvant/e/B06ZY7L62L

Daniel Schinhofen- Daniel was another one of those early adopters of my work who
encouraged and pushed me along. He's almost as introverted as I am, so we get along famously. He recently released a new book, and by all accounts including mine, is a well written author with interesting storylines.

https://www.amazon.com/Daniel-Schinhofen/e/B01LXQWPZA

SUPER SALES
ON
SUPER HEROES

Book 3

By William D. Arand

Dedicated:
To my wife, Kristin, who encouraged me in all things.
To my son, Harrison, who likes to just play on the ground with his toys in my office now.
To my family, who always told me I could write a book if I sat down and tried.

Special Thanks to:
Niusha Gutierrez
Caleb Shortcliffe
Michael Haglund
Steven Lobue
Eric Leaf

Books by William D. Arand-

The Selfless Hero Trilogy:
Otherlife Dreams
Otherlife Nightmares
Otherlife Awakenings
Ominibus Edition(All Three)

Super Sales on Super Heroes Trilogy:
Super Sales on Super Heroes 1
Super Sales on Super Heroes 2
Super Sales on Super Heroes 3

Dungeon Deposed Trilogy:
Dungeon Deposed
Dungeon Deposed 2 (To be released 2019)
Dungeon Deposed 3 (To be released 2019)

Books by Randi Darren-

Wild Wastes Trilogy:
Wild Wastes
Wild Wastes: Eastern Expansion
Wild Wastes: Southern Storm
Omnibus Edition(All Three)

Fostering Faust Trilogy:
Fostering Faust
Fostering Faust 2 (To be Released 2019)
Fostering Faust 3 (To be Released 2019)

Chapter 1 - Changes -

Felix smiled and leaned to one side in his chair. He looked from the microphone, which hung between himself and the rabbit-eared Beastkin, to the camera behind her.

He waited for the next question. This in-between time from question to question often got cut.

"Mr. Campbell, this next one is a bit of a loaded inquiry, so I apologize in advance," Erica said, giving him a broad smile, her brown eyes and soft features inviting him to confide in her.

Other than her dark black hair having grown quite long, she hadn't changed since he'd first met her at the company picnic.

Bright, energetic, and cute.

It was no wonder her news segment had become extremely popular in Wal. That went for the entire country, not its same-named capital city.

Everyone loved to watch her, and she always seemed to get the best stories, the most hard-hitting interviews.

Didn't hurt that she always looked stunning on the television.

Nor when Legion hand-feeds her every story of interest, now does it?

"Please, don't worry about it. I'd expect nothing less from you, Miss Newberg, and I knowingly accepted your invitation to the interview," Felix said, playing into his role. "Despite knowing your predisposition."

Erica had proved to be a perfect lightning rod for negative and neutral stories about Legion.

Her counterpart, Jessica Perreira, was where all the positive and political support stories went.

Everyone thought the two women hated each other, given that they seemed to represent opposing views.

Personally, Felix found the reality hilarious. He knew for a fact that they were very close. He'd even say they were each other's best friends on the surface of it.

Erica's smile tightened just a fraction, her eyes going a touch flat. It was obvious to him, as it had always been, that she hated her job and role.

Hated what she was doing to him.

"Recently, some reports have been circulating that Legion has been contracted to do more than just acting as a backup for the police.

"That your company has been tasked with providing policing and security for all government buildings of Wal, in addition to taking over every police precinct," Erica said. "Is that true?"

Felix wrinkled his nose and changed his posture slightly. It was all part of the act between him and Erica.

Questions that were meant to be hard, but that he had given to her to ask, and him acting uncomfortable.

As he shifted though, he had a momentary flashback to Tilen five years prior and a no-nonsense detective.

Interrogating him.

What was her name again... ah! Torres. Detective Torres.

"Well... it is true that Legion has been asked to step in and take over for the police. They're understaffed, underpaid, and unable to keep up with the workload," Felix admitted. "But it's also not true. Legion will be taking over the vast majority of the needs of Wal throughout the country, but the police will still remain employed and working in the same capacity they were previously."

"In other words, the police will become the backup for Legion," Erica said, boiling Felix's answer down. "You're reversing roles.

"But what about security for government buildings? You didn't answer that."

Felix nodded slowly.

"In the—I can't remember if it's four years or five years since we came to Wal—but in the five years since we came here, we've supported the government at every turn.

"They've asked us to up the security we can provide. That includes personnel, technology, and procedures," Felix said.

Erica lifted a finger up, her ears perking.

"Before you ask for clarification," Felix said with a smile for the Beastkin. "Yes, we'll be taking over security for government buildings directly."

Erica raised her eyebrows and jotted something down on her pad of paper.

"I do believe it's been four years and eight or so months, by the way," Erica said as her pen glided back and forth.

Felix didn't reply but merely smiled at the reporter.

"Speaking of security," Erica said, moving to her next question. "What are your thoughts on the violence going on with our southern neighbors? Or any of our neighbors, actually.

"By and large, it seems as if the entire continent is shattering apart as of late. Multiple armies are embattled on every front possible, warlords are acting as faith leaders for their religions, and it seems that there is no going back from this. More and more governments get caught up in ever-increasing disturbances."

Frowning, Felix reached up and drew a finger along his jawline.

Last he'd checked through a drone, Skippercity was little more than a giant radioactive crater. Tilen was a corpse of a city. A ruined, rotting thing that was beyond hope.

And all Skipper did was move on to the next target. Turning it into a battleground as well.

"I would say that… the government of Wal has done a fantastic job of limiting the influence of the old gods here.

"While I recognize the… problems… caused by outlawing certain religions, worship, and gods, I can't fault the results," Felix said. "By and large, Legion isn't called in that often anymore, and those found practicing illegal or warmongering religions are exiled from Wal."

Barbaric, but effective. And needed.

There really wasn't another option, given what happened in Skippercity. Saw that one first hand.

"Of course you'd support Wal in their efforts to eliminate dissenting religions. Those are the same people who run against the current governing body," Erica said, pointing her pen at Felix. "Or do you have a response to that as well?"

"I would say that I support Wal in its efforts to protect its citizens. While I don't morally agree with the actions taken, I can definitely understand why they were taken, and I support their implementation," Felix said.

"In other words, no. You don't disagree with Wal," Erica said, making a point of this.

It was critical for Erica to maintain her status as a counter to Wal and Legion. It helped them keep the focus of the populace on the stories they wanted them to focus on.

Which meant she had to deliberately seem to provoke Felix at times. After which Felix was required to smile, let it pass, and do nothing.

To any public figure other than Erica who spoke out against Legion, the response was always swift and deliberate.

Brutal, even.

Economic attacks, character assassination, and blackmail.

Tying everyone and anything up in legal problems miles long.

That didn't even cover those who worked in the shadows to cause problems for Wal, Legion, and Felix.

Dimitry had become an essential player to Legion in the last several years in that shadow war.

Working as Felix's blade in the dark, keeping the other factions down, or eliminating them outright.

"I see," Erica said. "Well, that was the last question I had for you, Mr. Campbell. I appreciate your time today."

"Of course, Miss Newberg, of course. I'll always make time for you," Felix said.

Turning to the camera, Erica crossed one leg over the other and folded her hands in her lap.

"Well, this is Erica Newberg signing out for the evening. I thank you all for joining me in tonight's interview," said the Beastkin. "I caution everyone out there to be safe, be vigilant, and be watchful.

"Goodnight."

Several seconds passed as Erica stared into the camera. Eventually the red dot at the top of the equipment began blinking.

"Aaaaaand… we're out," said the cameraman at the same time as the dot vanished.

Erica let out an explosive breath and spun around immediately toward Felix.

"I'm so sorry, Felix," she said, leaning toward him across the table.

"Don't worry about it. If anything, I should be apologizing to you," Felix said, standing up. "You've taken on a role you hate, for the betterment of Legion. I appreciate you and your sacrifice of your happiness."

Erica's ears bobbed as her head tracked him.

"Legion first," she said.

"Legion first," Felix replied, bowing his head to her. "Now, if you'll excuse me, Erica. I need to get a leg on.

"Felicia wants to go over a new iteration of the Warden. She thinks she's worked out a number of the problems the magical interference was causing."

"Of course! Tell everyone I said hi. I should have some free time this weekend. I plan on going to old Legion city.

"If you don't have any plans, maybe we could go to dinner together?" she asked, her voice softening.

It wasn't the first time she'd asked him out.

Simply put, though, Felix had his hands full with Lily, Andrea, and Adriana. Having three girlfriends, two of whom could multiply into as many as they liked, was too much.

Are they even what I can call girlfriends anymore? Andrea and Adriana are more like wives.

Hell, even Lily is at this point.

"As much as I appreciate the offer, I must decline," Felix said, walking past her.

"Of course you must, but I'm still going to ask," Erica said. "Maybe you'll surprise me one day and say yes."

Waving a hand at her as he exited the Legion-secured newsroom at Erica's employers building, Felix turned his thoughts to the rest of his day.

"You have lunch plans with Kit and I, then training," Miu said, coming up beside him.

Around him, several men and women in combat armor and armed with SMGs formed a column.

Glancing to the diminutive psychopath of Asian descent, Felix smirked at her.

"Thanks. I don't suppose you'll take it easy on me today?"

"No. I want to see how much of your blood I can take. It also gives me a chance to wrestle you to the ground. Touch you, run my hands over you," Miu said, her eyes boring into his. They widened slowly, her cheeks coloring at the same time. Her eyes started to take on that glassy gaze she tended to pick up as her true self started to slip free.

"Control, Miu. Control. You've been in control all month so far. Just a few more days and you get your reward, remember?" Felix asked.

Blinking twice, she suddenly swallowed and turned her face forward.

"My apologies. You're too close right now, and you were looking me in the eye," Miu said. "I'm fine. Now, we should go. I imagine the Elex sisters are bored."

Sighing, Felix could only agree.

"Never wise to let them get too bored," he said.

In silence, Miu walked Felix down to the entrance of the building.

Stepping to one side, he waited. He was well trained now.

Miu and a bodyguard walked outside, holding the doors open. At the same time, a woman slung her SMG around her middle and pressed a hand to Felix's back. Immediately, a small bubble of magical power enveloped him and her.

"Clear," Miu called from outside.

Letting himself be guided by the sorceress at his side, Felix was escorted outside.

Victoria, Adriana, and Andrea were all waiting for him inside the black sedan parked out front. The Legion banner was painted on the side of the doors, proclaiming to one and all that Legion was here.

There were two other cars in the same convoy with identical markings.

"Felix!" squeaked chauffeur Andrea. Her blue and green mismatched eyes lit up with life when she saw him. She reached up and curled some of her dirty-blond hair around an ear and under her cap. With her free hand, she pulled open the door to the back of the sedan and bounced in place as she stood there.

Adriana was a bit more subdued than her twin sister. She even managed to not call out to him as Andrea had.

Opening the front passenger door, the brunette got in the car and shut the door promptly.

Victoria moved around to the far side of the sedan and got in without a word.

She must still be annoyed with me.

"She's still mad at you," Andrea whispered loudly, confirming his thought. "She thinks you're overlooking too many security risks."

Felix got into the car and slid up next to Victoria's side.

"And you are," said the swordswoman. "Without you, Legion would crumble. You take too many risks."

"You should just listen to me."

Turning her head slightly, she glared at him, her dark-green eyes angry. The violent motion of her head made her short, dark-brown curls bounce.

"Sorry. I promise we can sit down over dinner or lunch and go over everything you want. I'll listen and do my best to implement whatever you suggest," Felix said in a conciliatory tone.

"Lily doesn't like it when you take other women out to eat," Miu said, her tone cold and flat as she pushed in next to him. "She's willing to share you with Andrea and Adriana, and myself to a degree, but I don't think she'll let you have more women."

Victoria frowned and peered at Miu. "My interest is in his safety, not him. After five years as his personal bodyguard, I can pretty much guarantee I'm not interested in him."

Miu stared at Victoria blankly, as if she didn't believe a word of it.

Reaching up with one hand, he pressed it to Miu's shoulder and eased her back into her seat. "I'll have a meal with Victoria, and I'll let Lily know about it personally. Now, let's get a move on, yeah?"

***

Felix glanced at the screen that was always open now, hovering just off to the side in his peripheral.

	Received	Spent	Remaining
Daily Allotment	250	0	250
Miu Miki	125	0	125
—Direct reports	2,500	0	2,500
Ioana Iliescu	110	0	110
—Direct reports	4,500	0	4,500
Kit Carrington	280	0	280
—Direct reports	6,200	0	6,200
Lilian Lux	300	0	300
—Direct reports	2,250	0	2,250
Andrea Elex	175	0	175
Felicia Fay	260	0	260

–Direct reports	8,000	0	8,000
Eva Adelpha	650	0	650
Mr. White.	40	0	40
–Direct reports	8,500	0	8,500
+ Loyalty Bonus	15,800	0	15,800
DAILY TOTAL	**49,840**	**0**	**49,840**

"No change," Felix said after he'd looked it over for a second. "I'm still being suppressed today. The point valuations are down."

Kit clicked her tongue and tapped a fingernail against the tabletop.

"It would seem they're dead set on keeping our losses from coming back right now," she said. "That's two days more than normal given the pattern you worked out. Isn't it?"

"Yeah, it is."

Felix lifted a spoonful of soup from his bowl and shrugged his shoulders.

"Definitely an outlier against the pattern. And yeah, I kinda felt the same. I had Victoria alert her people, and Ioana as well, to the situation," Felix said.

Miu was watching Felix eat his soup, her eyes fixed to him like a hunting hound.

"Lily, Ioana, and Victoria all confirmed they received my message," she said. "Preparations are being made already to take care of the situation and any possible contingencies."

Kit smiled, then chewed at her lower lip.

"Spit it out," Felix said, watching her.

After glancing up at him and then back down to her bowl, Kit sighed softly. Leaning back in her chair, she looked around.

She'd let her hair grow long over the years. Eventually long enough that she'd pulled it back into a ponytail.

In fact, now that he thought about it, he hadn't seen her in her Augur outfit since they'd fled. She'd packed it away and promptly settled into a life at Legion HQ in Wal.

"I begin to wonder if you need me anymore," Kit said, her eyes watching the Legionnaires moving around them.

Old Legion city was always a bustling place. It was the only thing they'd left behind in Skippercity, and it was so far deep underground that there was no risk of radiation.

If anything, it was one of the safest places they had because of what had happened far above them on the planet's surface. No one could even get close.

"I'm useful as a mind reader, but now you have much more talented people in place. I do little more than manage my team and sit around waiting," Kit said.

"Sounds like normal leadership to me," Felix said, setting his spoon down. "Realistically speaking, if you can be absent from your team and eighty percent of the time they function as if they didn't need you at all, you've succeeded as a leader.

"You don't need or want to save the day. You want them to run perfectly without you and only need you to guide, lead the way, or remove obstacles. That's the sign of a good leader."

Kit's mouth flattened into a line. She clearly didn't quite believe his words.

"Micro-managers are actually the worst kind of bosses. Their employees don't grow; they never get a chance to explore themselves as independent contributors."

Kit seemed to consider his statement more now than she had previously.

"And while you're thinking on that, I had a thought this morning. Back in Tilen, I met a Detective Torres," Felix said. "I was wondering if you or your team could dig up whatever happened to her. I was curious and—"

Felix's wrist device chimed, then let out a low buzzing noise while vibrating violently.

Tapping it quickly, Felix saw two screens overlaid. One was Legion Headquarters in Wal, and the other was a power-usage gauge.

There was a single column that had spiked to the top—a monitoring device left in the old Legion HQ building. He'd set it up to watch for a portal opening.

Pressing the button he'd put next to that column, he heard the chime of his line connecting to someone else.

He'd told Andrea to post a guard there and have her keep a personal device on her. Just in case something like this happened.

"Felix to portal drop, come in," Felix said. "There was a power fluctuation. Did the portal open again? Are there people?"

"Hi dear!" Andrea said excitedly, her voice coming over the speakers in his wrist device. "Yup! They opened the gate and they're staring at me."

"Wait, they can see you right now?"

"Yes. I wanted to say hi. I thought if I did, they wouldn't close it again."

"They look interesting. Though one of them looks a lot like you. A lot," Andrea said.

"Really? Huh. Uhm… what do they want?"

"I don't know! Let me ask," Andrea said. There was a pause. "What do you want?"

"Andrea, I swear to god… Did you put me on speaker phone?"

"Yes?" said the Beastkin. She sounded quite guilty.

"Ok… I'll just… why don't… ok. Hello, my name is Felix. Would you be interested in having a chat? I'd like to discuss an opportunity with you."

"I'll stay here," said a female voice. "Make sure it remains open."

"Red will go with you. Red wants to spar with the house cat, if possible," said a second, more gravelly voice.

"My name is Vince, and I'd be willing."

The sound of rapid hand claps cut through the air.

She's clapping. She's actually clapping that they said yes.

"I'll make pancakes!" Andrea shouted.

Yeah. She was clapping.

Kit and Miu were staring at Vince. Not quite sure of what was going on.

Suddenly, a bright flash lit up the main screen he'd been ignoring. He could see almost nothing through the glare of white light.

Then there was a rumbling crashing noise he could hear through the microphone pick up, and the video started to short and crackle wildly.

It had sounded like an explosion and looked like one, too.

"What the… shit," said Felix. "Andrea, Vince, I'm sorry, but I'm going to have to cut this one short. I have to deal with something."

"Andrea, give him the pack?"

"Vince, I truly look forward to meeting you in the future. Please don't be a stranger!"

Tapping the button, Felix closed the view and looked to Miu.

She was already talking into her communication device and relaying orders.

Turning to Kit, he found her doing the same while she opened a portal with her left hand.

It led straight into Legion HQ back at Wal.

No rest for the weary.

Here we go again.

- 507 -

Chapter 2 - Reaper -

Felix stepped through the portal Kit had created and straight into the newest iteration of the war room.

It was staffed by Andreas, Adrianas, and a number of specialists.

"Massive explosion at the entry to Wal HQ," an Andrea off to one side said. "The street was cleared immediately of hostiles by the defenses.

"Six reported enemy kills and a single vehicle disabled. Our defenses are clearing off the roofs, though. There were several alerts from the surrounding areas of Faith magic usage."

Of course there were.

Faith magic was almost always an indication of a strike from the heavens. One that couldn't be stopped with traditional magic as a defense.

"Fatalities?" Felix asked, dropping down into his "command chair" that sat in the middle of the room.

"Four. Hostess, two guards, one clerk," a different Andrea said. "Their remains have been secured and put with the fifty percent destroyed resurrection wave.

"The count for that wave is at seventy-six."

Seventy-six people who need a major number of points to be able to be returned to life.

Felix didn't say anything. He didn't need to.

Most everyone in Legion knew what was going on.

There weren't enough points to get people back up who had died in ways that destroyed their bodies beyond just losing a limb.

There were barely enough points to get someone back who had died a non-violent death during suppression.

Those who died and needed more points were being stored in a large morgue-like area. To be brought back in waves when whatever force that was keeping Felix's points down let up.

There were also a few people who had been almost completely destroyed. Truly destructive deaths, where the amount of points to get them back was beyond sizable in number.

Whenever possible, Felix stored points by converting garbage into gold. That same gold was then turned into points when he got the chance to fully utilize his power.

Usually it was about three weeks before he got a chance to bring anyone back. It was going on four weeks now, though. Longer than normal.

"The damage to the entry is extensive. It isn't something we can get repaired quickly," the Andrea directly in front of him said, turning in her chair to face him.

"Which means we have an open point of entry they can use," Felix said. "What about our defenses?"

"All clear. Everything was switched over to automation, but..." The Adriana who was talking paused and tapped her way through two screens.

"But there's interference from the explosion," Ioana said, stomping out of a back office. "They loaded the damn fucking van with religious relics and some type of blessed substance."

Felix sighed and pressed his fingertips to his brow.

"In other words, whoever it is this time is launching a full-scale attack. Probably in the next thirty minutes," Felix said.

"That'd be my assumption," Ioana said, shaking her head. "For all our planning, we're just not able to limit their faith magic."

Felix didn't know what to say. It was the simple truth. Faith magic had a way of slicing right through practical magic and technology alike.

Which left physical strength and super powers. Both of which were much harder for Felix to get his hands on since his own ability was so handicapped.

Kit folded her arms across her chest and sighed. "It isn't as if we're not holding our own."

"But we're losing," Felix said, cutting to the root of what wasn't being said. "This is a war of attrition, and we're getting chipped away at."

"Incoming," said the Adriana watching a bay of monitors. "A large number of vehicles heading our way."

"Panel vans."

And probably packed with combatants.

"Status on HQ defenses?" Felix asked.

Miu stepped closer to Felix, getting his attention.

"Victoria is assembling her people, and mine. She and I will move to the first bottleneck and work to hold them there," Miu said. "Lily and her team are moving to support, but they will take a few minutes. They were in a group practice, and there is no active portal from where they were."

Felix took the report with a nod and looked to Ioana.

"My people are more than ready, and we've brought up everything with simple mechanisms."

"Things we've found take a lot of effort for their priests to foul up," Ioana said. "The Wardens are being left in their bays."

"The Legion battalions on detached duty at the police stations are mobilizing, but they'll be at least an hour or two out. That's assuming there is nothing preventing them from getting here quickly."

That's pretty unlikely. I'd bet on them being delayed for hours and hours. If not attacked outright.

Like the engines in the vehicles failing outright. Just like the Wardens would fail if used.

It was an early lesson that Legion had learned in this war. Technology was vulnerable to faith magic.

Very vulnerable.

The more complicated, the more engineered, the more likely it would simply fail outright.

"I'm open to suggestions," Felix said. "I really don't see much we can do other than a standard hold out and wait for the enemy to take enough losses to leave, or for our reinforcements to arrive."

All around the room were pensive faces. One by one, they all shook their heads.

There really wasn't much to do.

"So… how about we talk about business instead?" Felix asked. "Tell me about our dumps."

"Last I heard, we were starting to fold over some of the deeper and narrower pits, and refining the methane."

Andrea Prime, denoted right now by her silver earrings, tapped open a light-computer pad and smiled.

"Everything is going exactly as you said. We're processing the metal and refining it as quickly as we can, now that we got the contract for trash-pickup as well as owning the dump and junkyards," Andrea said.

Then she started to flick through multiple screens, looking for something.

The lights in the war room went out, and then the emergency lights kicked in as apparently the HQ lost power.

"Intruders," said an Adriana further away. "Thirty or so just appeared in the dorm hallways. They're spread out, though."

"Some type of item with them is generating a field of faith magic that is interfering with the power generators in the base."

Oh.

Shit.

Felix looked to Miu, who would probably be the first able to respond right now since Victoria was already in the choke point.

Miu had been talking into her com device during the exchange.

"Lily is moving to engage. She picked up a squad or two of base soldiers to offset her team," Miu said, looking to Felix for a second. "They should be on the intruders before they can do anything more."

"Enemy vans are a minute out or less," an Adriana called out.

Felix thumbed the button on his wrist computer that was wired into the communication system.

"Enemies inbound," Felix said. "Everyone get into positions for main entry defense.

"We also have infiltrators in the dorm hallways. Use caution when traveling from area to area."

Closing the communication channel, Felix looked at the screens on the desk of the Andrea in front of him.

"I'm going to suit up and go to the line," Kit said.

"I will join you," Miu added.

Ioana stepped up into Miu's position next to Felix. "I'll remain."

"Stay safe; I can't afford to lose you. And if you do die, make sure it's in one piece," Felix said, not looking away from the screens.

The sound of the elevator opening and then closing was the only response he got.

Ioana slowly began walking away from Felix, looking over multiple displays.

Andrea Prime and Adriana Prime stepped in close to Felix.

"Felix—" whined Andrea, her ears flat to her head and her tail low behind her.

"I don't like this anymore," said Adriana, her posture not as submissive, but certainly leaning towards the same feeling.

"I want to leave. Can we leave and go live somewhere else?" they said in unison.

Felix immediately wanted to deny her request. This was home now. They'd fought to build it, and then to maintain it.

He'd already fled Skippercity. Tilen as well.

Fleeing again sounded awful.

The sound of scattered gunfire from the trio of Elex sisters at desks in front of him diverted his attention.

"Choke point one has been activated," said the Adriana of the three.

"They brought portable defensive barriers," said one of the two Andreas.

"Priests spotted amongst their number," said the last of the three.

"This is an all-out attack then," Felix said. "This isn't a probe or a feint; it's a real attack."

"Tell the battalions coming from the police stations to take a longer route. They're more likely to be attacked on a straight path home than they are delayed."

"On it!" chirped Andrea Prime, looking to her light-pad.

Felix was watching the screen. He saw the two forces deploy themselves behind bunkers and begin firing over the tops at the opposing side.

Kit was on the far edge, in her Augur outfit, deflecting bullets away from Legionnaires.

On the far-left side, a large melee was forming. The two sides had closed on one another before they had gotten the barriers up.

He could see Miu and Victoria on that end, already fighting.

"Felix," called the familiar voice of Lily through his com. "We just took down one of the infiltrators."

"They're from the government of Wal."

Frowning, he considered Lily's words.

"Wal itself," Felix muttered. "Which means they're either tired of us or they have someone trying to launch a coup.

"Has there been any word or warning from the government building assets?"

"Nothing," Adriana Prime said. "Wait—"

"Oh, heavens forbid," Felix said, pressing his hands to his head. He didn't need more bad news right now, and if the government buildings were really under attack, it meant Wal was about to disintegrate around itself.

"The man named Vince just walked back out of the portal," Adriana said.

"Vince?" Felix asked.

"Yes. Andrea sixty-seven took a photo of him and updated our files. Adriana ninety-three took her place. He just walked in through the paired portal and left the arrival room."

"He's in the hallways of the dorms."

"What do you mean he left?" Felix asked.

"Ninety-three gave him a vest and her sidearm, and sent him to find you," Adriana said with a frown.

"Remind me to trade ninety-three with you, sister," Adriana said, glancing to Andrea.

"She's nice," Andrea said with a grin. "I like her. I'll trade. Would you take twenty-two?"

"Wait, wait. Vince is walking around in the hallways with a gun. We don't even know what he'll do!" Felix growled.

"He just killed a Wal infiltrator with a sword," Adriana said.

"A sword?" Vince parroted.

"Vince has a sword. He just killed three more people and he's heading toward Lily," Adriana said.

Lily!?

"Vince just walked past her. He's heading to the choke point. Lily is following him."

Felix looked to the cameras; he should be able to see this man named Vince now.

Just on the edge of the camera, Felix saw a man dressed in what looked like medieval armor to his eyes. He was wielding a curved sword, and he had a handgun.

Lily was beside him, clearly trying to talk to him.

The man looked at Kit, then at the opposing soldiers on the other side. And charged at them at a full sprint.

"Oh my," Andrea Prime said.

Vince was moving fast. Extremely fast. Speeding across the gap between the two sides.

Then he was shot. It looked as if he was struck by six or seven rounds in the chest.

Except he kept going as if he didn't feel it.

Watching with something akin to awe, Felix saw the man hop the barrier in a smooth leap.

Like a flash of light, his sword struck out and skewered an enemy. Then he slashed his blade through the guts of a second.

"So fast," Adriana said.

Lifting the handgun, Vince began to march forward, the gun flashing as he began putting rounds into enemy heads.

Dropping the gun, he stabbed someone and stole their gun. Letting go of his blade, he stepped back, racked the gun, and began shooting everyone in front of him.

The slide slammed backward as the gun went dry, and Vince pulled the sword out of the dying foe and took their rifle.

"Who is he?" Ioana asked.

"I don't know," Felix said. The man on the screen held the rifle low and began moving forward again. Spewing out a quick burst of fire, he mowed down those who stood before him.

"He's like death," Ioana said.

Vince reached the melee brawl and promptly stabbed a battle priest, his saber breaking in the enemy's guts.

Snatching the empowered sword from the priest's grasp, Vince beat him against the head with the stolen weapon's pommel.

Felix lost sight of Vince as he turned and began wading into the enemy force.

"He's faster than Victoria," Adriana said.

Felix stared into the mob, hunting for a hint of Vince.

"There, in the rear," the Andrea manning the desk said. She was pointing to another monitor and a view of the back of the fight.

A superhero in a silver suit stood in front of Vince.

"Who is that? I don't recognize them and—" Felix's voice stuck in his throat as Vince appeared a foot away from the super.

The glowing empowered weapon flashed out, and suddenly the super's head was flying away from his body as if it had wings.

Vince threw out his arms and seemed to shout something.

Then a burst of green magic exploded out of him in a ring.

The cameras fuzzed over for a second as the magic passed through it.

When the view came back on, Vince was stabbing downed enemies. Foes who were surrendering.

Making short work of anyone in his way.

In every camera, the enemy was surrendering. Surrendering and dropping to the ground with their arms up.

"Miu, if you can get him to stop, please ask him to join me," Felix said into his wrist communicator after tapping the line open for her.

Miu nodded, then darted out from the Legion forces in front of Vince.

Something passed between them, ending with Vince outright murdering an enemy who had surrendered and was lying on the ground with their hands on the back of their head.

Another exchange and Vince lifted his stolen weapon, eying Miu.

Holy shit, is he going to attack her too?

Several tense seconds passed before Vince stood up and let his posture change.

Vince began walking back toward Legion, looking for all the world as if he hadn't almost single-handedly solved the situation.

"Felix, he asked if you had a machine that could heal people," Adriana Prime said, getting his attention. "That's what ninety-three said."

"A healing machine," Felix said. "He uses a sword, wears armor outdated here, and wants a healing machine."

Clicking his tongue, Felix began to think.

This might be a possible exchange. What would he want beyond that?

Looking to the man once more, Felix tried to pull up a window as if he owned him.

Name: Vince (Demi-God: Shared Portfolio)	Power: Absorption through Digestion	
Alias: King of Yosemite	Secondary Power: None	
Physical Status: Lightly Wounded	Mental Status: Slightly worried	
Positive Statuses: Sated	Negative Statuses: Slightly tired	
Strength:	97	Upgrade? (970)
Dexterity:	94	Upgrade? (940)
Agility:	98	Upgrade? (980)
Stamina:	175	Upgrade? (1,750)
Wisdom:	76	Upgrade? (760)
Intelligence:	74	Upgrade? (740)
Luck:	31	Upgrade? (310)
Primary Power:	8,789	Upgrade? (878,900)
Secondary Power:	--	Upgrade? (--)

Felix took in a slow breath.

"He's a Demi-God," he said. "And… very, very powerful."

"Felix," Miu said, her voice cutting through his thoughts. "I'm going to take Vince to your study. You should join us as quickly as possible.

"If he decides he wants to cause a scene, I don't think I could stop him."

Felix rubbed a hand against his jaw and chin, thinking.

Making a decision, he tapped his communicator and punched in the line for Mr. White.

Two seconds later he heard the devices connect.

"Mr. White here; my lab is secure," said the man. He was a direct peer to Felicia, and he ran a separate lab in addition to a second he shared with her.

"Great. I'm glad to hear it," Felix said. "I have a request, Mr. White. I need you to put together a healing bed. Preferably one that can work for a mobile type of need. I imagine it might travel a bit. Assume that wherever it is won't have a power source as well."

"Alright. I can pull one out of storage that'd work. Anything else?"

"I'll need someone who can operate it, and I'll probably have some other things I need to put together later. This might be an off-world mission," Felix said, trying to be honest with the man.

He wasn't sure where the portal was going to go.

"Off world? Hmm. Alright. I'll get it taken care of. White out."

Leaning back into his chair, Felix scratched at his head.

He felt tired. Tired and worn out, and he hadn't even done anything.

Adrenaline is wearing off. It went from three thousand miles an hour to nothing.

"You should get going, dear," Andrea said, leaning down in front of him. "It sounds like we shouldn't keep him waiting."

Then she gave him a kiss and patted his cheek. "Play nice!"

Chapter 3 - River of Trade -

Felix stood in front of the door to his study, rubbing a hand back and forth across the back of his neck.

He wasn't quite sure how to handle the situation.

What basically amounted to a Demi-God of battle was on the other side of the door. One who had single handedly taken out an enemy elite force.

Somewhat of a rapid change from long lunch meetings. Then again, this was fast and furious, but done.

I'm not sure which I prefer.

Taking a deep breath, Felix opened the door and stepped inside his study.

"Good afternoon," he said, closing the door behind him.

The Demi-God was sitting in one of the chairs in front of Felix's desk. He turned in his seat to face Felix.

Immediately, he was struck by how similar this man looked to himself.

Though the Demi-God was significantly broader in the shoulders, seeming to radiate power and barely restrained violence.

It's like standing next to a wolf. One with its teeth bared, but not growling.

"Hm. We really do look alike, just like they kept saying," Felix said, scratching at his jaw. "It's uncanny."

"I thought the same when I saw you," said the man.

Felix moved over and took the chair directly next to the man. Leaning forward, he reached out with his hand.

"I'm Felix."

"Vince," said the man, taking Felix's hand in his own. His handshake was firm and strong, but not crushing.

"First off, thank you for your assistance back there. I can't tell you how much it helped. I have no doubt your actions saved the lives of many of my people," Felix said.

"Mm. I wanted to blow off some steam. I haven't been able to fight my own foes as directly as I'd wish," Vince said, his face showing a bit of annoyance. "The Beastkin at the portal gave me the gun and told me anyone without a patch or the black vest was an enemy. Seemed straightforward enough."

"Adriana. Yeah, I could see her doing that." Felix nodded slightly with a strange grin. "She tends to view things fairly differently."

Even more so than Andrea sometimes.

"Forgive me for getting straight to the point, but honestly, I came here for help."

"From anyone I could find," Vince said, leaning forward in his chair. "I was hoping I could get my hands on some technology. Technology that could help me and my people."

Direct.

That's rather refreshing.

Felix folded his hands into one another and didn't immediately respond.

"What kind of tech did you need?" he asked after a second to collect his thoughts.

"First and foremost, medical. One of my wives is... dying. Others are attempting to heal her, but... they can't. It's too much for their magic. She's slowly dying.

"They said it's in her blood and they can't seem to stop it, no matter how much magic they use," Vince said.

He's really laying everything on the table. There's nothing in his body posture that would indicate he's lying or hiding anything.

Maybe it really is exactly what he's saying.

"That's not a problem at all. Consider it done," Felix said. Reaching over the desk, he pressed a button on the intercom. "Andrea?"

"Yes?" came back the ever-eager reply.

"I need Mr. White, a healing pod, and some people to carry it through the portal. Take a portable energy source as well. Tell Mr. White he's on detached duty as a special favor for me," Felix said.

"Okay! Oh, there's three more guests that just came through the portal."

"They're on their way over to you with Prime, Adriana Prime, Kit, and Lily."

"More guests?" Felix asked curiously, letting go of the button. "Were you expecting more people?"

"No. I left orders to not follow me, to be honest," Vince said, his nose wrinkling.

Both Vince and Felix looked to the door as it suddenly opened. Seven women trooped in and stood staring at the two of them.

Adriana Prime, Andrea Prime, Kit, and Lily had walked in with a group of women Felix didn't know.

One looked like some type of Beastkin, except her flesh was pale. Her brown hair made her look even whiter as it hung around her face and shoulders. The strangest part was her eyes, though. They glowed with an inner red light.

The second seemed like she had fallen out of someone's wet dream, with dark curls, green eyes, and green skin. She was all curves and slim at the same time. She was also one of the prettiest women Felix had ever seen. It was as if she oozed sexuality.

The third looked like an Elf, though her skin tone was significantly darker than any Felix had ever met. It was almost pearl gray. She also had dark eyes and pitch-black hair. Though she seemed the most normal of the three.

"They look like brothers," said the Elex sisters in unison.

"I don't have a brother," Vince and Felix said, also at the same time.

Swift and silent, the pale-skinned Beastkin leapt forward and leaned over Felix, audibly sniffing him.

Then she turned and cuddled in close to Vince, nuzzling him while smelling him loudly.

"Red thinks they smell like each other," she said, then scooted around behind Vince and laid her hands on his shoulders.

What in the shit?

"Ok, before this gets any weirder," Felix said. "My father died quite young, and as far as I know, I have no siblings. The end."

Vince nodded. "My father vanished when I was in my twenties, but I have no siblings that I know of."

"On top of that, we're from different planes of existence," Felix added, folding his arms in front of his chest.

"Well, that doesn't seem to matter," Vince said with a shake of his head. "Apparently my father wasn't from my... plane of existence... as you called it. The portals were an experiment, I think. They found my father with one."

Felix frowned at that, his mind racing ahead.

Is that why he didn't want me playing with portals? This isn't the first time something has happened, is it?

"You said... they found him?" Lily asked.

"Yes. They opened a portal and brought him through, I believe. And you are?" Vince asked.

"Oh, ah, Lily," Lily said, bobbing her head slightly to Vince.

"That makes you Kit," Vince said, looking to her.

"Yes, I am," Kit confirmed.

"This is Red," Vince said, pointing at the Beastkin who had moved around behind him.

"That's Mouth," he said, pointing at the green-skinned sex goddess. "And Felicity," he continued, pointing at the Elf.

"The portals were an experiment on your world?" asked Lily.

"Yes. They ruined my world in doing it. Much of what used to be the United States is a mess of other races all battling for supremacy."

"The United States? What's that?" Kit asked.

"A country. It was a country many years ago," Vince said.

Felix raised a hand and started to rub his chin, as if in thought. "Oh?"

"Felix?" asked Andrea.

"Hm?"

"Mr. White, the pod, and the guards will be ready in about ten minutes. They're getting it all packed up now."

"Great," Felix said, not looking at anyone or anything in particular.

His mind was elsewhere, churning with thoughts about how to make this sudden ability to access another world benefit Legion.

"Would you be willing to make a trade with me?" Felix asked, looking at Vince.

"Depends on what you want," Vince said. To Felix, it was clear he was used to dealing with predators.

"Gold. As much as I can get my hands on. It'll help me and my people immensely. What do you need?" Felix asked.

"Weapons," Vince immediately replied. "I'm fighting a war against those with weapons I cannot match. They have guns, artillery, and bombs. I have... very few of those for my country."

"Your country?" Andrea asked.

"Yes. Yosemite. It's my—our—country."

"Ooooh! I wanna visit!" Andrea said, looking at Adriana.

"I do, too!" said Adriana.

They both turned and looked at Red. "Feral friend, will you give us a tour?"

Red looked at the two Beastkin as she continued to hold Vince.

"If Bringer says it's ok, then Red will do so," Red said.

Weird way of talking. I wonder what she is.

"Hm? That's fine; go now if you like," Vince said, leaning forward towards Felix.

Eager to continue. Looks like I'll be an arms dealer again.

"Yay!" the Elex sisters said, looking quite pleased with themselves.

Red let go of Vince and started to walk away.

"Bringer, why is there a picture of your father?" Red asked suddenly.

Vince frowned, shaken from his deep desire to talk about a trade, and looked to Red. Felix looked as well, curious what she was talking about.

The pale Beastkin was pointing at a bookshelf with a framed picture of Felix's uncle.

"Huh?" Vince asked.

"Red remembers Bringer's father. This is him," Red said. She moved forward, grabbed the picture and brought it over to him.

"See?" she said.

Vince looked down at the picture and looked lost.

Very lost.

"I don't understand," Vince said, looking up from the picture to Felix.

Shocked at the possibilities, Felix reached out and gently took the picture from Red's hands.

"This is my uncle. Miles, Miles Campbell," Felix said, looking from the picture to Vince.

"This is your father?"

Vince nodded.

That doesn't make any sense. The time doesn't add up.

It's impossible. There's no actual way this is even remotely possible.

Unless... my dear nameless godlike benefactor has been playing with the flow of time.

"Mother only called him Campbell. On the deed in the house, though, it says Miles Campbell," Vince said.

Dad and Miles were twins. If it's true... doesn't that make him more of my half-brother of sorts?

Grinning, Felix set the picture down on his desk and looked at Vince.

"Well, I suppose I have another surprise for you, then. My dad and your dad were twins," Felix said. "Genetically, we're probably closer to half-brothers than cousins, I guess."

"I'd wonder if all this was only a coincidence. Especially considering there are some concerns with time, if one thinks about it.

"Doesn't quite match up, really," Felix said, looking up towards the ceiling. "Though I'm betting it isn't as much a coincidence as I would originally think." Shaking his head, he looked back to Vince with a smile. "Let's talk about what you need, and what I need, and let's figure out how we can help one another, little brother."

"Ah, I'm afraid my lord is apt in the ways of war, but he has me and my sisters for the needs of the kingdom. I'll be happy to work through Yosemite's needs with whoever your representative is," said the woman Vince had named Felicity.

"That's me," Lily said, her eyes still moving between Vince and Felix for a second before looking to Felicity.

***

"I think we should have a chat," Felix said, sitting alone in his study. Staring up at the ceiling. "Because the time involved doesn't add up. That and it sounds like there's a lot more going on than meets the eye.

"So... let's have a chat."

"As you like," said the man Felix had come to refer to in his head as his benefactor, since he hadn't named himself.

He'd simply appeared in the chair directly in front of Felix's desk. Where Vince had been sitting only an hour previous.

"I think I deserve some answers at this point. Especially if you want me to do my best with whatever favor you ask of me in the future," Felix said. "Because things are starting to go pretty bad for me here, and now this happens.

"It's all a bit... odd, to me."

Felix's benefactor sighed and slumped into the chair. He pressed his right hand to his temple, leaning to one side.

"Right, then. Where to begin?" he said. "As to your problems here in the world, can't help you there.

"I have an agreement with the deities to not get involved if they don't get involved."

"They're very much involved," Felix said, his emotions leaking out in his tone.

"From your point of view, it probably feels that way. But up to this point, they're really just acting through belief and some cryptic messages," said the benefactor. "They've summoned and used no avatars, they've granted no holy weapons, nor demanded any crusades.

"This is all mankind simply turning on itself as soon as it's gotten a taste for power. Power it can tap into and believe in."

Felix grit his teeth together rather than reply. He wasn't sure he could say anything that would be even remotely construed as polite.

"Be that as it may, I won't get involved. But I can at least give you some answers you could easily get yourself," said the man, sitting upright in his chair. "So let's start there. What questions do you have?"

"Why does practical magic fail against this religious magic?" Felix asked.

"Because the god of magic for this plane is dead. He perished a long time ago, and in such a way that no one could inherit the mantle," said the benefactor. "There is nothing backing the magic up. No amount of faith in practical magic will give it anything more than its base value."

"Faith magic, though, is empowered by that faith."

Ok. That makes sense. It's... a little strange, but ok. It's an answer. Let's keep going.

"How many gods are actively suppressing me and my power? It seems a bit unfair when I can't even use my abilities and a god is holding me down," Felix said bitterly.

"Twelve," the benefactor said. "They take turns in keeping you from your full power. They're required to give you breaks directly relative to how long they've kept you down.

"At this rate, they're going to have to give you an entire week."

"Required?" Felix asked.

"Required by me. I felt their plan was too much for a group of deities to put upon one such as yourself, so I limited their actions," the benefactor said.

Good to know he's working on my side to keep things "fair" at least. Never really considered why they stopped every now and then.

"Is Vince reall—"

"Yes. Yes, he is. Genetically he's your half-brother; relationally, he's your cousin," the benefactor said. "And no, I can't get too deep into the details, but I can tell you some of it."

Felix nodded and held his hands out in front of him.

"Please then, tell me all that you can. I would love to know what's going on, because honestly it's just... confusing," he admitted.

Felix's benefactor sighed and looked up at the ceiling.

"Part of this story has more to do with me, but... I don't think we'll get into that yet.

"We'll keep it to you and your family.

"First, on the plane Vince comes from, they were conducting experiments with portals.

"They built several labs, then opened portals at the same time—thinking they would go from one to the other.

"Portal jumpers, or sliders, as it were."

Felix's benefactor tapped his thumb against the arm of the chair, clearly thinking on his words.

"The simplest answer, though it isn't completely right, is they didn't lock the portals in place. Several of them went spinning off through the planet, then into space.

"While others opened up into other worlds and... did the same thing there, ripping out giant chunks and sending them to the other side.

"Then the experiment just... got worse. Random portals began opening all over, across multiple planes, universes, planets.

"Entire cities were ripped out and flung into other worlds. Whole populations of people. For a number of planes, it was the end of their existence.

"One planet ended up having its core pulled inside out and emptied into the vacuum of space."

Is that even possible? What he's describing sounds more like something out of a religious text describing the end times.

"Even deities were ripped from their home planes and flung around," the benefactor said. "Then I closed it. All of it. Every portal.

"I put back everything I could. Even whole planes I wasn't willing to give up on. Though there were some things I couldn't fix... but that's another story for another time.

"Your uncle was pulled across into another plane many years after the original experiment. Apparently, some of the scientists had survived and kept trying to finish their ancestors' work."

"Pulled across. But what about my aunt?" Felix asked.

"Yes, he was pulled across from your plane to that plane.

"Happened while he was visiting a site where a portal had opened. There's a particularly nasty little critter there that tore your aunt apart, though, which is how she died.

"Your uncle escaped that fight, and during his escape, he was grabbed by the team of scientists.

"Hence, eventually creating Vince on that plane with one of those very same scientists."

Felix shook his head, pressing his hands to the sides of his temples. "You realize this sounds crazy, right?"

"You asked. And as to your next question: yes, the time doesn't add up right. Each plane runs on its own time.

"Their world was running at a different pace than yours for quite a while."

Closing his eyes, Felix tried to process all that into something more comprehensible.

"Ok. Vince really is my half-brother, the gods are holding me down here, and you're playing referee," Felix summarized.

"More or less. Definitely a soup sandwich there, bud. Seems like you're getting a handle on it, though. I would probably—"

The benefactor paused, his head swiveling around toward the study door. A second later and he simply vanished.

The door opened, and in walked Felicity, Adriana, and a curvy diminutive woman with green skin. She seemed very similar to the one Vince had called Mouth.

"Hi dear," Adriana said cheerily.

"Mr. Campbell," Felicity said, a paper ledger held in one hand tucked up into her side. "I have with me a Dryad by the name of Betty."

Felicity was pointing to the woman next to her. Her hair was cut quite short, and her eyes were a bright green. She was painfully pretty, though she didn't seem to radiate sexual desire like the other one had.

"A Dryad," Felix said, standing up. "Before today, I didn't know of your kind at all."

Holding his hand out for a handshake, he smiled at the woman.

Betty stepped up close to the desk, grabbed Felix's hand with both of hers, and clasped it to her chest.

"I am Betty, grove mother and leader of my people. You reek of power," she said, her eyes gazing up at him in a strange, fanatical way.

Felix blinked owlishly and slowly looked to Felicity.

The Elf woman gave him a wide smile and flipped open her ledger, looking down at it.

"Betty comes with three hundred and twenty-four of her grove sisters. All are priestesses and worship nature. Their magic is empowered through it," Felicity said. "I believe they will be suitable as troops, combat medics, and soldiers with a modicum of training in whatever usage you see fit."

Adriana bounced lightly up and down, her SMG swaying back and forth at her side.

"Vince said he sends them with his regards!" Adriana said. Then she started giggling. "We have so many nieces and nephews, by the way. I want to have a litter."

Betty looked to Adriana without releasing Felix's hand, keeping it wedged in her chest.

"You are cursed. You cannot bear children," Betty said simply. "I can wipe it free of you with only a minor prayer once I have my grove planted. The power it has is limited."

Adriana froze mid-bounce, her eyes locked on Betty.

"You can fix me?" she whispered.

"Yes. But I need to plant my—"

Adriana grabbed Betty and bodily pulled her out of the study. Betty practically dragged Felix over the desk when she wouldn't immediately release him.

"I'll show you where to plant trees! We have a world that is very pretty and lots and lots of nature. It'll be perfect! We named it Legion Prime," Adriana said, hustling the small Dryad away.

Felix found himself alone in his study with Felicity.

"Mm. She is rather excitable," Felicity said, tapping a pencil against her ledger. "Ah, I've asked to be transferred temporarily into your service, Mr. Campbell. I feel I can be of use in managing the Dryads. I'm also an accomplished mage and assistant."

Righting himself and adjusting his clothes a bit, Felix looked to the Elf. "Uh huh. Why do I get the impression the Dryads are going to be a problem?"

"Ah, because they also have another name that is entirely accurate," Felicity said, tucking her pencil behind her elongated ear and pressing her ledger to her side.

"And what's that?" Felix asked, not quite able to shake the heat Betty had ignited in his body with the way she'd held his hand.

"Nymphs," Felicity said with a grin. "Don't worry. I'll have a word with Betty later and let them know you're off the table as far as a potential mate."

Great.

Chapter 4 - Openings -

Felicity was scratching away at her ledger with a modern-day pen. He wasn't sure where she'd gotten it, either.

She's adapting quickly. Very quickly.

Setting her ledger aside, she picked up the tablet Andrea had given her only thirty minutes before, then began to peck and poke at it with her finger.

Watching her, Felix never would have figured she came from a world where technology didn't really exist. She was actually figuring out the tablet with a driven intensity.

Hooking her thumb into the stylus set into the side, she drew it out and then held the tablet like her ledger. Hesitantly, she began to write on it.

With a smile on her face, she quickly fell into the same flow with which she used her paper ledger.

"You can sort things as well," Felix said, interrupting her discovery. "At the top, there's a small area that's blank. It has an add file and folder function. You can create a hierarchy with it."

"Oh?" said the Dark Elf.

It had been surprising to hear what race she was. Felix had worked up the courage to ask her directly only minutes earlier.

Felicity lifted the stylus up and began tapping away at the top. "Ah, it's the simple drag-and-drop connection system Andrea showed me earlier for the other program.

"Your technology is very intuitive to new users."

Ha. I don't think it's as intuitive as you are intelligent.

"I can feel your eyes on me," said the Dark Elf, not looking away from the tablet. "Is it my form of dress? I was speaking to Andrea and she promised to take me to get more fitting clothes after this meeting."

"Ah, no, sorry. Just... interested. You're very different. Elves aren't very common here," Felix admitted. "They exist, but they live in very small groups and keep to themselves."

Felicity smiled at that and looked up at him for a second. "Hm. Interested, you say. We'll see.

"You're certainly as handsome as your brother, but you do tend to favor your mind over your arms, it seems.

"I'll not say no at this time, but I think it would be prudent to get to know one another more, Mr. Campbell."

When she turned her gaze back to the tablet, Felix wasn't sure what to say.

I think she believes I just propositioned her.

Alright... not really the intent. I'll have to be wary. Her world seems exceedingly different.

And geared towards sex.

The door to the meeting room opened, and Adriana Prime, Andrea Prime, Lily, and Dimitry all walked in.

This was everyone he had asked to meet. He needed to get on this attack as soon as possible.

"Felix," Dimitry said, giving him a sardonic grin. "Good to see you."

He'd had Felix modify him a single time more so he could change his hair color, eye color, and some minor features at will.

Right now, he had his meeting-with-Felix Dimitry face on. Steel-gray eyes, dark-brown hair, and looking very corporate. In the dark-gray suit he was wearing.

He'd taken to his role in Legion very well. There were very few places the "Maintenance" department of Legion hadn't spread itself out into.

Having his own department of Minders and Fixers had only helped speed the process along.

Anything involving crime, organized or not, fell into Dimitry's sphere of influence.

"Likewise, Dimitry. How's the wife and kid?" Felix asked.

Chuckling, Dimitry raised a hand and moved it back and forth.

"So, so. I swear we just got him to sleep in his own bed, and now he wants to sleep in ours every night.

"Two steps backward, one step forward," Dimitry said, looking pleased all the same.

Corporate life in Legion agreed with Dimitry. Surprising everyone but Felix, Dimitry had a knack for it. He'd said several times it was a lot like organized crime, just without the beatings and shootings.

Lily took a seat next to him and Andrea took the one on his other side. Adriana Prime stayed near the door, weapon in hand.

This was everyone who would be here, as everyone else had too much going on in one way or another to attend or work this project.

Despite it being a full-blown attack he wanted to talk about, Felix's resources were a bit stretched.

"Well, let's get started then. I assume you read the meeting notes I attached?" Felix asked, looking at the attendees.

"Yeah," Dimitry said as he leaning to one side in his chair.

"Alright. Lily, could you restate what you learned during the attack?"

The dark-haired, dark-eyed beauty looked at Felix while clearly gathering her thoughts.

She pursed her lips and then sighed.

"Honestly, it was strange. The Fixer in my group identified the enemies almost immediately as government contractors. There was no effort to conceal the information," Lily said. "It was as if it was at the forefront of their minds.

"To the point that nothing else was readable. And I question it. It's too easy. Too clean."

Dimitry nodded, a finger scratching up along the side of his head.

"Feels like a setup," said the ex-crime-boss.

Felix couldn't help but agree, but he also wasn't about to underestimate his opponents.

"And maybe that's what they want us to think. That it's so obvious we discount it.

"Which leaves us with really only one option that fits. Investigate it as if it's real until we can prove it isn't," Felix said with a shrug of his shoulders.

Dimitry nodded once.

"Is a good way to do it," he said. "How do you want to start?"

"Money. The same as ever. Someone had to supply the hardware, the vehicles, the bodies," Felix said. "So, let's track the money. Use whatever resources we have on hand, and if you need to, get some contractors signed on to a Legion standard for temp work."

Lily tapped her chin with a finger.

"Or their magic," Felicity said, looking up from her tablet. "They appeared in your fortifications suddenly. Use the Dryads to trace their magic back.

"I would surmise that whatever you find will be empty and barren, but at least it's more than nothing."

All eyes were on Felicity, who returned each gaze evenly.

"What? Dryads are very sensitive to magic. It's how they choose mates," Felicity said. "Use them like hounds and have them run it down."

"Alright. I'll leave it to you then, Felicity," Felix said, gesturing at her with one hand.

"As you like," said the Dark Elf, jotting something down.

"You're nice," Andrea said, suddenly leaning in close to Felicity. "You smell good. Like flowers and grass. Shadows, too."

Felicity looked askance to Felix, then back to Andrea.

"You remind me of Red," Felicity said.

"Oh, that's my Feral Friend, right? The one with the red eyes?" Andrea said, scooting even closer.

"Yes. That would be her."

"I like her. We play sometimes."

"Did you think on my question?" Andrea said.

What?

"I have. Though I'm not really sure what you described would really entail. It sounds very similar to the function I served to... to Vince," Felicity said.

- 521 -

"Probably!" Andrea said, then she reached out and grabbed Felicity's wrists. "I think you'd make a great personal assistant secretary admin to Felix."

"I don't want to do it anymore. I want to do the Andrea-net and nothing else."

What what?

Felicity gave Andrea a strained smile and looked to Felix. "It would appear you have an opening."

"Apparently," Felix said, not sure how to take it. He hadn't even realized she'd been unhappy with her role.

"You don't even have to sleep with him," Andrea said. "I made sure of that point before I took the job myself. Though in the end, I decided I wanted to. He smells amazing."

"Actually, you should smell him. Maybe you'll want to sleep with him, too. It makes the job easier. Whenever I do something bad I just pull him into the bed or somewhere quiet."

"Here, smell him!"

Andrea's hand snapped out and grabbed Felicity by the neck, and she began dragging her toward Felix.

Adriana had taken several steps toward the pair, looking like she wanted to help her sister.

"Andrea, that's enough, I'm sure she can smell me fine from there," Felix said before she could wrestle the Dark Elf over. "Let's call this meeting for now and get to work. We have a lot to do."

Andrea whined unhappily but stopped pulling on Felicity.

"Oh, and if I've done a very bad thing, he likes it when I use my mouth," Andrea said in a loud whisper to Felicity.

"I'll keep that in mind," Felicity said, carefully pulling away from Andrea. "Far too much like Red."

Andrea and Adriana took Felicity by an arm each and practically dragged her from the room, not giving her a chance to respond. They were already chattering at her before the door even opened.

Dimitry gave Felix a wave of the hand and left as well.

"She's been talking about it for a while," Lily said as soon as the door closed. "She wants to be more your wife and less your employee."

"The Primes and Seconds will probably both stop working and go tend to the home after this. Apparently that little Dryad fixed up whatever problem the gods had thrown on them. Though I'm curious why they'd do such a thing. I was not cursed at all, apparently."

"I expect she'll be begging me to trade turns with her tonight. She's been dying to have her 'litter' you know."

Good thing I took care of that barren issue I put on her years ago. This had nothing to do with me.

Then Lily was behind him, her chin resting on his shoulder, her arms draped around him. Her fingers lightly began to play up and down his chest.

"To be honest, I've been thinking about it myself," Lily said softly. "I think I might be ready soon to start trying. I kept telling myself I wanted to wait till we were safe."

"Secure."

Reaching up, Felix placed his hand atop one of Lily's.

They'd had a number of late-night bedroom talks about children. He'd gotten the impression she wanted a kid far more than she let on, but that she didn't want to have it in this environment.

"I don't think we'll ever have that. And from what I got out of that little sex-monster your brother brought with him, he has... a lot of kids," Lily said.

"What do you think, dear?" she asked, her lips nuzzling his ear.

"I think you keep doing that and I'll throw you up onto this table and we'll find out where it goes, protection or not," Felix said in all seriousness. Lily had a way of making his skin light up. "As to having kids... I mean, my answer is the same as ever. I like the idea of having children, but... up to you. Your body."

Lily sighed dramatically. "Must you always be so... kind to me? You make me worry that I'm going to be punished for having something as good as you, with how badly I've lived my life," she said as she started to kiss and nibble his ear more intensely.

"I'm a bad girl after all. Now, go lock the door," she said.

***

"Felix?" came Kit's voice from his wrist.

"What's up, Kit?" Felix asked. He was going through the current casualty lists of everyone who needed to be brought back.

The number was growing ever higher.

Getting up, he walked over to a window and looked out upon old Legion City below.

His primary office was still here, and it had a portal he used to go back and forth from Wal HQ.

"I just got an email from the prime minister. She'd like to see you today about the attack that happened," Kit said.

"Of course she does," Felix said, drumming his fingers against his chest. "Alright. Prep our standard retinue for the meeting, but include Felicity."

"I'll take care of it," Kit said, and then the line cut off.

"Kit is not herself lately," Miu said, pressed in close to Felix's side. One of her hands slipped up the back of his shirt, her fingers playing along the muscles of his back. "She never completely identified with Legion. She was a hero too long."

Miu always got a bit handsy with him in private. Most especially when they sparred. She took special delight in causing him to sweat or bleed.

Then in devouring either.

Miu was well and truly insane. And despite his many offers — pleas even — she didn't want him to fix her.

"I can smell Lily on you," she said, pressing her nose into his side and inhaling deeply. "She doesn't deserve you. I deserve you. I'd do anything for you, and let you do anything you wanted to me."

"Anything. I'm yours. All yours. Tell me what you want."

Except let me fix you, you crazy lady.

"You made an agreement with Lily. Are you saying you want to break it?" Felix asked, not bothering to push Miu away. When he did, she just got more wound up and tense till she was useless.

Where Andrea was clingy, Miu was simply an appendage.

"No. I will abide. It's already been five years since I swore to her. Only five to go."

"I haven't killed anyone or hurt anyone around you. At all. Not even an Elex twin," Miu said, her voice a breathy whisper. "Only five years to go and I get my time with you."

Certainly not what I expected from Lily. Then again, I think she believed Miu wouldn't last a week before I'd have to put the restrictions back on her and she'd have to abide by her agreement.

"I want to taste you," Miu said.

"Uh huh. Ok, come on my little psycho. We need to get ready for the trip. You behave and I'll let you spar with me tonight," Felix said. It'd been a long day. He hadn't slept since the attack the previous night.

A quick and dirty brawl with Miu sounded like a pretty good tension release, though. He'd gotten pretty good in hand-to-hand combat.

So long as Miu didn't push her super ability, he could hold her off for a while.

"I'm going to make you bleed and lick your wounds," Miu said in a strange tone.

"Course you are," Felix said.

He was used to her eccentricities at this point. Though he couldn't tell if that was a good thing or a bad thing.

Patting Miu on the head, Felix left his office. Knowing the prime minister for the little petulant child she was, Felix needed to get moving as quickly as he could.

Which, in the end, wasn't fast enough.

Sitting in the lobby outside her office, he realized she was clearly making him wait for an audience she'd summoned him to.

"This seems... unprofessional," Felicity said, working away steadily at her tablet. Her expertise with it was increasing by the hour, it seemed.

"It's normal," Lily replied, uncrossing her legs and re-crossing them with the other leg on top now. "She doesn't much care for us, but she needs us.

"We're probably the only reason she's kept her job."

Felix glanced around the room to make sure they were alone.

Kit, Victoria, Miu, and an Adriana were here along with Felicity and Lily.

"Politics here seem to be the same as back home," Felicity said. She tapped at something on her screen, then closed a leather case over the front of it and tucked it into a bag at her side.

Andrea had apparently made good on her word, because Felicity looked as smartly dressed as Lily right now.

In fact, it looked like almost the exact same fashion sense, now that he paid it any mind. Even down to the tight-fitting pencil skirt.

"Though back home, Vince would probably simply kill her, dump her body to the Goblins and move on," Felicity said, giving Felix with a smile. "It's somewhat refreshing to see a more... expected exchange in politics."

Note to self: remain direct and open with Vince.

"I've sent a note back home saying I'd like to remain here permanently," Felicity said after a moment. "I'd like to take you up on that job offer.

"I don't think my sisters will miss me. And what I've heard back from the grove mother is very positive already."

"Grove mother?" Felix asked. "You mean Betty?"

"Ah, no. Vince has a grove in Yosemite. Her name is Meliae. She's more or less his primary wife. Though Fes is of course Fes," Felicity said with a shrug of her shoulders. "Fes means first wife. It's a title rather than a name.

"But anyway, Meliae seems to think it'd be good for me to remain here.

"And apparently Vince has already left on his mission."

"Mission?" Victoria asked, peering at a magazine in her lap.

"Vince needed weapons," Felix said. "I sent him all the original Warden models, some armory dispensers, and Mr. White.

"In return, he's apparently going to go... kill a Dragon and send me back half its hoard."

Victoria lifted her head up, her eyebrows attempting to crawl into her hairline.

"He's going to kill a Dragon?" she asked.

"Apparently. I'll be happy to have the gold, though. That always converts so easily into points," Felix said. "Anyways, you were saying, Felicity?"

"Ah, yes. He already left. It would be good if you could make time to visit Yosemite, if only to see it. The morale boost caused by your involvement is no small thing," Felicity said. Then she gave herself a small shake, as if she'd remembered something. "That reminds me. Will I be paid for my work as your personal assistant secretary admin?"

"Let's just go with... personal admin as far as a title goes, and yes. Paying you isn't really a problem," Felix said.

"I'll take care of it and get her enrolled appropriately in the records," Kit added as she turned the page in her book.

"Ah, as to sleeping with you and your interest in me," Felicity said, smiling at Felix. "I'll keep the option open for now, if you don't mind. The idea is intriguing, and it might be fun. You're rather handsome and that mind of yours is curious."

He could practically hear Miu's attention. Could feel it burning a hole in the back of his head.

"It was Andrea," Lily said, her voice directed off to the corner of the room. "Not Felix."

"Ah. That would make sense," Miu said, her voice uneven. "I will try to remember that later."

Later as in when she's beating me and trying to eat my blood.

The door to the office opened slowly.

"Mr. Campbell? Prime Minister Heather will see you now," said her assistant, a young man.

Sighing, Felix stood up and fastened the top button on his coat.

"You're only allowed two of your people; the rest can remain here," said the assistant. "The Prime Minister can assure you of your safety in her office, at least.

"Though the same can't be said of your own HQ, now can it?"

Felix stared flatly at the assistant, not responding.

After ten seconds passed, the assistant finally looked away, cowed.

"Kit and… Felicity, come with me. The rest of you, wait here. Do what you need to do should the situation change," Felix said.

He hadn't originally planned on taking Felicity with him, but suddenly it seemed like a good idea. Having someone new in there might give him a better read on the situation later.

"Let's go then, assistant," Felix said, still staring at the man. "And while you're at it, get me and my people some coffee. Two sugars, cream till it's brown."

Reaching up, Felix smoothed the knot in his tie and marched into the prime minister's office.

Chapter 5 - Relations -

The prime minister was surrounded by her bodyguards, assistants, advisers, and her personal inner circle.

Ranging from the general of her military, whom Felix had met several times, to the assistant prime minister, who was like her second-in-command.

By and large, they were a singular group of bootlickers who seemed intent to do anything she asked as quickly as possible.

"Hello, Felix," said the prime minister, leaning back in her chair.

She was an older woman, probably in her late forties or early fifties. Blond hair going gray, a pinched face, and as thin as she was petty.

"Madam Prime Minister," Felix said politely, stepping up behind the chair in front of her desk. It was uncomfortable, lower than the desk, and seemingly picked for the singular function of making people feel awkward.

"Please, take a seat," said the prime minister, gesturing to the very much hated chair.

Kit made an almost imperceptible move of a finger.

In an instant, the chair was gone, and a comfortable executive chair had appeared on top of it. Kit simply submerged the entire thing in her real-life illusion.

"Thank you, Kit," Felix said, unbuttoning his coat.

Taking a seat in the newly made chair, Felix smiled at the prime minister.

Leaning back, he tented his hands in front of him, elbows resting on the armrests.

The prime minster had always tried to position herself as Felix's boss. To get him to bend to her will and her desires.

So far, she'd been completely and utterly unsuccessful, but that didn't stop her from continuing to try.

Working every situation to her benefit to gain power and leverage.

Which means this is no different, and she's about to question Legion and its ability to protect itself.

"I'm sure you know why you're here," the prime minister said, her nose moving up slightly so she could continue to look down at him despite the chair having been changed.

Felix didn't respond.

Instead, he tilted his head to one side, his fingers tapping together lightly.

Blinking slowly, deliberately, Felix waited.

He was in no hurry, and there wasn't anything the prime minister could do to him. Legion wasn't just protected by the laws of Wal, it had taken an active hand in many of the recent changes in the last five years.

Laws that would help protect Legion and its interests, people, and way of life.

Wal had been slowly corrupted from the inside out to favor Legion.

Luckily for Wal and its people, Felix didn't abuse this power. He simply used it to protect his people from politicking.

The prime minister stared back at Felix, seemingly intent on making Felix respond.

A soft chime alerted Felix to a notification from his phone.

Turning his wrist over, Felix broke eye contact with the prime minister and looked at the bar at the top.

Adriana sent a message... I wonder if it's another sketch or another nude of herself. She's so different from her sister.

Opening the message, Felix raised an eyebrow.

Hi dear, I hope things are going well.

Vince's primary wife is visiting and she seems quite nice. I'm trying to keep her here long enough for you to meet her, but she may have to meet you next time.

Also, Andrea's second is pregnant! I'm very excited to be an aunt.

With all my love, hugs, kisses, and other things I'd like to do but won't write right now as you're in a meeting, Adriana's second.

Come home. It'll be worth it.

I'll make sure of it.

Felix took in a slow breath as he reread the message.

Andrea is pregnant. So the Dryad fixed her after all.

Which means I'm going to be a dad.

Suddenly I have a brother, nephews, nieces, and a kid on the way.

Quite a bit of change in a short time frame.

Looking up from his watch, Felix focused on the prime minister. Suddenly he had a thought strike him hard as the other half of the message scurried through his mind again.

I think I'd rather go home and play with Adriana.

"Right, have a good day," Felix said, then stood up.

"You can't leave," said Heather.

"Sure I can," Felix said, buttoning his coat's top button. "I'm not a government employee, and you're not my boss."

"Wait—sit," Heather said, pointing to the chair.

Felix ignored her completely, turning around and heading for the door.

Never be afraid to walk away from a negotiation or a deal.

Felicity's eyes followed him as he went by, a feral smile on her face. She seemed to approve of his tactic, and maybe she even understood it.

"Please, wait. Please," Heather said.

Felix only stopped when he had his hand on the doorknob.

"What?" Felix asked simply.

"We're going to be hosting a summit. On religions and for multiple government heads. I want you to run security for it. It's going to be held at Wal's national stadium," Heather said. "There will be twenty some-odd heads of state attending. We were selected since we have the least religious problems, despite not having outlawed all religion."

A summit? A multi-national summit?

Hm. That's not going to be easy.

"Send me the contract and I'll consider it," Felix said, opening the door. "Good day."

He stepped out of the prime minister's office and quickly left the building entirely.

After clambering into the back of the middle sedan outside, he sighed and leaned his head back onto the seat.

"That was well done," Felicity said, pressing in close to his side in the back.

Confused at her presence, as that seat was normally reserved for Miu, he looked to the Elf.

"I promised her I'd assist her in her goals and desires. She is very simple and easy to read," Felicity said with a wave of her hand.

The Andrea chauffeur in the driver's seat giggled to herself and turned her head to say something to the Adriana next to her.

Lily slid into the back seat on Felix's other side.

"I can't deny that," Lily said. "Though you're a bit harder to pin down. You're also starting to make me worry about what your intentions are."

The sorceress leaned her head to one side to look around Felix at Felicity.

"My intentions are simple. To find a place for myself. And Felix has offered me a job, which I've accepted, as you know," Felicity said. "Beyond that, I find myself wanting to know more of your man. He's intelligent, cynical, and quite deft at manipulating others."

"I'm not sure I want you to know more of, as you say, my man," Lily said, her lips pressed tightly together.

She'd said many times she didn't like the idea of sharing Felix with anyone, even Andrea. It'd taken a long time for her to get used to the fact that if she wanted Felix, she'd be sharing with Andrea and Adriana.

"I'd be willing to recognize you as Fes, Lily," Felicity said calmly. "I wouldn't even mind being last amongst his wives. Though I do think you're limiting him by not allowing him to take more women to bed."

Felix held up a hand and then coughed once.

"Look, I'm not exactly good at relationships and I have a hard enough time managing the three I have. Let's just call this conversation done for now and head home."

"Apparently Vince's primary wife is there," Felix said.

"She is? Good. She is his Fes; you would do well to speak with her, Miss Lily," Felicity said. "I think she can help you understand how you're limiting Felix."

Biting back a sigh, Felix rested his head on the seat.

***

Stepping through the portal, Felix looked around.

He was in an empty room, but it was clearly well used.

It was a corridor of sorts that seemed to cross from one side of a house to another.

Outside the doorways, he could hear the sounds of voices and people.

Upon getting home—or at least to his section of HQ—he'd found that everyone had apparently gone for a tour of Vince's world.

Felicity had elected to stay at HQ and work with the Dryads.

Apparently, they'd settled on a single man to serve as their center, but only after having an orgy. Many single men of Legion had been dragged to Legion Prime for a few hours.

The Dryads had called the massive settlement on that plane home and planted their trees.

Following the sound of laughter and talking, Felix started to wander.

He slowly made his way through several rooms before exiting through what was apparently the "back door" to a wide, open grassy field.

Innumerable children ran around, darting this way and that. Everywhere he looked there were beautiful young women with green skin. Many of them accompanied small children while others were grouped together chatting as children ran about in the grass nearby.

Andrea Prime, Adriana Prime, Lily, Victoria, and Miu were all talking with a group of women Felix didn't know.

"Ah! Dear!" came a high-pitched squeal.

Andrea turned from the group and rocketed into him, pressing her head into his chest.

"We have a litter on the way!" she said excitedly. "My second is pregnant, so she won't be able to merge for a while. We don't want to risk the little ones."

An Orc woman broke away from the group and hobbled his way. She was missing an arm and a leg, and used a cane to get around.

"Ah, you must be my husband's brother. You look amazingly similar to him," she said. She gave him a tusky grin as she got closer. "Forgive me, I'd offer you my arm but I'd likely fall over. I am Berenga, once Fes for Vince."

"Ah... sorry, second time I've heard that term lately. Could you give me a bit more context?" Felix asked, gently stroking and petting Andrea's ears.

Glancing over Berenga's shoulder, he looked to Lily, Miu, Victoria, and Adriana. They were talking with the remainder of the group.

Adriana caught his eye, giving him a slow wink and a wide smile.

Damn, she's not going to stop till she gets her own litter.

"...term roughly translates to first wife," Berenga said. "Vince has many wives, and I was the leader of them until I was wounded. Now I must step aside."

- 528 -

"Can't say I understand completely, but it's a pleasure to meet you," Felix said, giving her a wide smile.

"Likewise, though I'm surprised at how few wives you have. For one with as much power as you, you should have as many as Vince does at the least," Berenga said with a frown.

"Felicity said something similar. Can't claim I understand it. I think it's a cultural difference," Felix said.

Out of the corner of his eye, Felix saw a familiar face.

Ambling his way was Mr. White, looking rather happy and even with some color to his skin.

"Mr. Campbell, good afternoon," Mr. White said.

"Afternoon, Mr. White. How goes it here?"

"Well. The armories work perfectly here. No faith magic to impede anything. As force multipliers, much of the tech we've brought here is significant," Mr. White said, pushing his glasses up further on his nose. "I would hazard we could easily empty our retired armory here and it'd be the likes of dropping a tank in a war of sticks and clubs."

"Ah," Felix said.

As Mr. White had walked up, the group of women a bit further off had been heading his way as well.

Andrea gently pushed away from Felix, then went and stood next to Adriana.

Everyone was watching him now.

Apparently this wasn't just a casual statement. Mr. White planned on saying that first, then probably asking to take the retired armory. Clearly he'd shared his plans with everyone here first.

"Can't begrudge my little brother assistance if it's easy for us to give. Strip the retired armory of anything that would be useful here," Felix said. Then he gestured to Berenga with a finger. "And let's get my sister-in-law fitted up with some one-off tech. Put in a request to Felicia on my behalf, cc me on the form."

Mr. White blinked twice, then grinned at him. "Of course, Mr. Campbell. I'll do that."

A very full-figured, green-skinned woman who was pregnant to the point of bursting moved up to him.

She took his hand in both of hers and shook it gently, smiling at him.

"Hello, Felix. I'm Meliae," she said, holding his hand tightly. "I'm your brother's second wife."

"Let me introduce you to some of your nephews and nieces. They've been very excited to find out they have an uncle."

Taking hold of Felix's arm, Meliae began leading him deeper into the green glade, where children ran around freely.

Glancing back over his shoulder, Felix looked at the building he'd come out of.

It was a home.

One that was filled with family.

Frowning, Felix suddenly wondered about his own life.

His quarters were minimal at best, and indoors.

Looking back to the glade, he saw a green-skinned young girl shyly walking straight toward him.

Behind her were a number of other children, with grass stains and messy hair, watching. They stood behind the girl as if she was their leader.

Is Legion HQ even suitable to raise kids? Would it be better to shift everything to Legion Prime as HQ? We'll talk to Felicia when we get back.

Meliae waddled to a stop and gave Felix a smile. The small green-skinned girl was directly in front of him.

"Berest, this is Felix," Meliae said, patting Felix on the shoulder.

The small girl gave him a wide grin, small tusks slipping free of her lips.

Ah – Orc, not Dryad.

"Ah, you must be Berenga and Vince's daughter, then," Felix said with a smile, going down to one knee in front of her.

"And you're Uncle Felix," said the girl.

Before he could respond, Berest walked in close and gave him a hug around the middle.

Right. Ok. Yes.

Yes.

Hugging the girl in return, Felix let his thoughts wander to the idea of having kids.

***

"Felix."

Blinking and shaking himself out of his thoughts, Felix looked up from his desk.

Felicity stood in front of him, digital pad tucked under her arm. She had ditched her jacket, and her white blouse did little to draw the eyes away from her figure.

Forcing his eyes to Felicity's face, he made a mental note to have a conversation with whoever was supplying the Elf with her fashion sense.

"Betty is ready to lead a magical hound party. I took the liberty of assigning resources to this mission on your behalf. Since I was told you'd be part of the mission, I did requisition more than what Victoria recommended," Felicity said. "Andrea and the ANet did a wonderful job up to this point. It was quite easy to settle in to this role and they've been an enormous help."

"Oh. Glad to hear it, Felicity," Felix said, turning his display off with a flick of his thumb.

"And may I say, the way you handle your people, allies, and enemies is very impressive. Especially so since you've built this organization from the ground up and have actively led it," continued the Elf. "It's... most admirable."

"Thank you. Though I couldn't have done it without those I trust."

"That may be so, but it is one thing to rely on others; it's another to provide leadership, direction, and action, all while cultivating your followers to be leaders themselves," Felicity said. "Vince is a great leader, but a poor manager of people."

Felix shrugged.

"That's not exactly uncommon. He's a charismatic and admirable leader, from what I can tell. But it's all based on him and what he can do. Little of it is trained or learned.

"It just is who he is."

Felicity looked like she had fallen into deep thought. Her brow furrowed and her eyebrows came down.

"That's rather accurate," she said after several seconds had passed. "It's... magnetic. People want to follow him. To be with him and be part of his goals. But it isn't something he consciously does."

Smiling, Felix nodded and then pressed his hands to his face, scrubbing them up and down. He felt tired and worn out.

His nephews and nieces had run him around for a while. Apparently they'd realized very quickly that Felix couldn't say no to their requests.

He had suddenly become Uncle Horse, giving kids rides by the twos and threes.

"They were very excited to have another male older relative," Felicity said.

Pulling his hands down from his eyes, Felix looked over the tips of his fingers at the Elf.

"The children. They're all treated like the royalty they are. They have each other, their mothers and aunts, the Dryads, and Vince.

"You being Vince's brother makes you much closer to their father," Felicity said. "Though it was rather cute the way Berest and Mia had you wrapped around their fingers within minutes."

Felix snorted at that and dropped his hands with a grin.

"They were cute. Though I think Berest is going to lead the rest of them. They look to her for direction already," Felix said.

Felicity lifted a hand and curled her hair behind her pointed ear.

"Well? Shall we begin the hunt? Or would you rather wait for tomorrow morning? It's already deep in the night," Felicity said. "Your Beastkin seemed rather eager to try and take you off to bed earlier."

"I imagine she's desperate to get her own litter."

Ah... it is rather late, isn't it?

Adriana won't leave off. If I don't let her corner me tonight, she'll just come back until she gets what she wants.

"I think the morning would be ideal, actually," Felix said. Standing up, he picked up his coat and flipped it over his shoulder.

"I would certainly agree, which is why I already scheduled everything accordingly with that in mind.

"I assumed I'd be able to talk you out of going tonight if you had that as your intended direction."

"Oh?" Felix murmured with a grin for the Elf. "Thinking you can start pushing me around already? On day one?"

"Yes, I do. All I have to do is appeal to the pros, list the cons, and be sure to emphasize efficiency, cost, and dangers," Felicity said, grinning at him the entire time. "That or undo a few buttons on my blouse and get closer to you."

"Hm. I'm going to find out who's been giving you all this advice and skin them," Felix muttered.

"Well, Andrea introduced me to the internet, and that helped with my wardrobe," Felicity said, looking down at herself. "As to the rest, that's mostly just studying under my sisters. They are well versed in being House Elves and come from many generations of such. From different family branches."

Felix walked to the door of his office, wanting only to get to his personal bedroom.

"You never did say anything about my clothes, by the way. Isn't that rude?" Felicity asked.

Pausing at the door, Felix thought for a second.

"You look great—stunning, even.

"But if you're always this aggressive, Miu or Lily might not be happy," Felix said. He was hoping to side-step Felicity. He'd never had someone pursue him this determinedly so quickly.

Outside of Miu, at least, but she was insane.

"Miu isn't a problem; I've already secured her assistance in regard to you. I promised I'd help her earn your affections if she assisted me. Remember?

"As for Lily, that's another conversation for another time.

"Have a nice night... Felix."

Chapter 6 - Pencil Whip -

Felix flipped his rifle up to eye level and gave it a once-over.

It was one of Felicia's special jobs, maintained by the armory officers for him.

He still wouldn't take it out into the field without an inspection.

His helmet rapidly laid out his weapon and several windows popped up from the ANet's automated systems.

One window was a maintenance checklist performed the previous night because he had put in a requisition for his weapon.

A group of five Dryads in Legion combat armor were checking out similar rifles. Apparently, one and all of them were martial; they lived for combat and worshiping nature.

The cluster-fuck of an orgy had Felix annoyed, though. The amount of uncontrolled shrinkage it had caused blew out his efficiency for the entire month in almost every department.

Let's see if they're as good as Felicity seems to think they are.

Satisfied that his weapon was in working order, especially since it only had a limited number of working parts, Felix let it hang at his side.

Pulling out his sidearm, he eased the slide back several inches and made sure it was empty and clear.

Finding it in proper condition, Felix chambered the initial round, checked the safety, and holstered it.

"I admit I wasn't expecting this."

Felix looked up from his belt and webbing to see Felicity standing next to him.

"Which part?" Felix said.

"Your suit, the armaments, even this." Felicity indicated her own combat armor.

She was decked out in Legion body armor, the same as everyone else. Though it was the type usually given to magicians, loaded with the tools of the trade Lily had designated specifically for casters.

Her hair was tied up in a bun at the back of her head, and an earpiece was clearly fitted into her Elven ear. A combat helmet hung against her hip, attached to her belt.

"Some of these items are so loaded with magical energy I'm tempted to drain them," Felicity said, a fingertip dragging along an energy grenade.

"Drain them?" Felix asked.

"Empty them of power. Then again, that's just my impoverished childhood rearing its head," Felicity said, looking to Felix. "Once your brother established Yosemite, my family gained access to many artifacts he had the care of that simply transfer energy over to the user. I have enough energy to last at least sixty-thousand years right now, and I'm always gaining more."

Felix didn't know how to respond to that. Elves here on this world were rare and kept to themselves. It seemed they were much more populous on her plane.

"Sir," Betty said, coming to attention in front of him. "We are ready for service."

Looking from the armor-clad Dryad to the Fixer in charge of the mission and his Minder second, he waited.

"Ready to roll out, sir.

"The Wardens are suited, our Magicians are ready, Miu and Victoria are waiting in the support vehicle, and we've alerted all the appropriate contacts," said the Fixer.

"Make the call, then. I'm just here for the ride and to do some sleuthing," Felix said.

For a moment, the Fixer didn't say anything, and Felix assumed he was transmitting messages to his team. Then everyone turned and headed for the exit.

"They're very well trained," Felicity said, pulling her helmet off her hip.

"Ioana would be the reason for that. She became our impromptu security implementation and coordination officer.

"Victoria took on the role of my team leader for bodyguards, and Miu took on internal security. They often overlap in their duties, but they seem to have worked out any problems years ago," Felix said.

Moving forward, Felix felt a sense of giddiness. It'd been a very long time since he'd been on a possible combat mission.

Lily had only given her grudging approval of the whole thing after she'd looked over Felicity's arrangements.

Apparently, whatever misgiving she'd had was mostly ameliorated by whatever she found there.

"Fes had a very long conversation with Lily," Felicity said, fastening the chin strap to her helmet. "I think it was successful."

"Still going on about that, huh?" Felix asked.

"Yes. I'm not going to be denied without you coming out and telling me to stop," Felicity said. "I truly believe you and your brother are destined for greatness."

There's that cultural gap again. Greatness doesn't mean having more wives than there are days in the month.

Reaching the entrance of Wal Legion HQ, which had recently been repaired and painted, Betty got down on one knee.

She stripped the glove off her right hand and began to drag her fingers along the pavement.

The two mark Four-One-F Wardens moved to either side of the building, weapons lifted and ready.

"Those are much newer versions of the ones you sent to Yosemite?" Felicity asked, eying the Wardens as well.

"Yeah. These were developed specifically to work in the conditions we're facing right now."

"Faith magic," Felicity said.

"Yeah."

Felix looked back to Betty, wondering if this was even worth the time.

Betty was conferring with another green-skinned woman. Several exchanges later and Betty looked to Felix.

"We have the track grove-master. We'll be moving as quickly as we're able. What do you wish to be done if we find them?" Betty asked.

Oh? Huh.

"Rules of engagement are fire if fired on; otherwise, challenge and treat as possible hostile," Felix said.

Betty blinked twice and then nodded her head, as if someone had translated something for her that he couldn't hear.

The woman Betty had been talking to turned and jogged off down the sidewalk. The Wardens fell in beside Felix as he moved to follow.

An armored personnel carrier rolled out of the garage nearby and began stalking them from the road. Hazard lights on the rear of the vehicle warned people away.

"Your people are covering for the Dryads," Felicity said, jogging along lightly next to Felix.

"They are?"

"Yes. I think they understand you better than you realize. They're aware that you're not exactly fond of the Dryads yet, and they're working to cover their disadvantages.

"Your Minder was rapidly filling Betty in on the situation. I could hear it through her link," Felicity explained.

Hm. They don't normally take to others so quickly.

"Ah, apparently Betty and her entire grove signed the Legionnaire contract yesterday. Hence you being the grove-master.

"As did I," Felicity said.

Ah… Legion first.

It'd been five years, and the mentality had grown. If you were Legion, you were family.

You were little more than sausage if you weren't.

Conversation fell off as people scrambled to get out of the way of the armed combat mission being carried out on the streets of Wal itself.

There was no way of hiding this action, and Felix was sure it'd make the rounds on the local networks.

He couldn't care less about that, though.

Not going to be a paper boat bobbing along the water. I refuse to wait for whatever comes next.

Twenty minutes passed before the lead Dryad turned down an alleyway.

Slowing up, Felix let himself fall to the rear part of the squad. Nearly at the same time, the support vehicle bounced up on the sidewalk and an Adriana and Miu slithered out from a door hatch that had opened.

Clanging shut, the vehicle shot off along the sidewalk, mowing down a parking sign with no regard in the process.

"They're moving around to the other side," Miu said, moving into Felix's side.

Betty was waiting for him when he turned the corner down the alley.

"We passed by the first location we arrived at. They had already vacated it, and it was obvious there was no one there," said the Dryad. "This is not where they launched the attack from, but it's where they fell back to. It is likely they are still here.

"I felt it would be best to move quickly given the number of eyes that were on us."

"Good call," Felix said after a second. "Nice work, Grove-Mistress. That's solid executive decision making."

Betty's chin came up a fraction, and a smile threatened the corner of her mouth.

"Mission leader," Felix said into his headset. "Move your team up and secure the perimeter of the building. Prepare for a dynamic entry with whatever plan you see fit."

"Confirmed," came the response over the ANet.

The rest of the squad moved up through the alley slowly. At the end of it, they stumbled out into what looked like a dilapidated industrial area. Several warehouses and an office building that was not much more than a frame sat in the overly large lot.

"The warehouse there," Betty said, indicating the building on the far left.

One by one, his team moved through the shadows, working to surround the building.

"Felix, this is Overwatch," said an Adriana through the earpiece. "There's a lot of strange phone traffic going on right now. We're trying to capture as much as we can for analysis, but it's clear something is going on out there."

"Understood. Keep me informed. Anything else I need to know?"

"Second is pregnant. Way to go, dear," the Adriana said.

Not... the best timing right now, but alright.

"Congratulations," Felicity said from next to him. Clearly able to hear what was being said inside his helmet.

"Your ears are too damn sensitive," Felix said, muting his link with Adriana as he said it.

"That's great. Give my regards to her, your Prime, and your sister. I know you've all been waiting for this," Felix finished, opening the line back to Adriana.

"Of course, dear. I look forward to sharing the memories with Second after it's all said and done. Especially the moment you impregnated her."

The Adriana dropped the line with that statement.

She's so very different from Andrea now.

"Felix, look there," Felicity said, getting his attention. He followed the line of her finger toward the warehouse.

The two Wardens were in position on each side of the warehouse.

"Tee-El to Throne, permission to go?" The sudden request was surprising; he hadn't realized everyone was ready.

Felix shook his head, clearing his thoughts.

"Permission granted, go," he said.

Both Wardens shot forward, crashing through the very walls themselves.

Betty and her Dryads fanned out in a semi-circle in front of the warehouse at a sprint, all leveling their weapons at the shuttered doors.

Several booms rang out, along with the sounds of weapon-fire.

Exploding outward, the front door of the warehouse crashed to the pavement and skidded along for several feet.

A man dressed in robes and covered in glowing blue light strode out into the lot itself.

"Battle priest!" Felix called into the radio.

The man spotted Felix and punched out a fist toward him, calling out to the heavens above at the same time.

A massive blue bolt of power scorched across the distance toward Felix.

Felicity knocked it aside with a flick of her hand. The strike went straight into the air above and dissolved to nothing.

Right behind the bolt came a bright blue fireball, which Felicity simply made a cupping hand motion at.

Snuffing it out as if it had never existed.

She did all this without runes, casting, calling, or asking for power.

It had only taken a few seconds for the priest to cast those spells. Before he could cast a third, a green, almost-solid aura jumped out of each and every Dryad. Their spells cut straight through his defensive shield, the protective aura, and his worn charms.

And flattened the man to the ground. Smashing him into the pavement itself. His guts spewed out the sides of his crushed torso like it was a ketchup packet under a tire.

The sound of rapid gunfire drowned out everything else. The Legionnaires were engaged in a gun battle with whoever else was inside the warehouse now.

"Contact. Multiple hostiles. Normals," came a call over the radio.

"Apprentice priest exiting front," called a second individual.

A man sheathed in a blue aura, much smaller than the first, stumbled out from the dusty entrance.

Looking around, the apprentice couldn't seem to figure out what was going on.

Betty lifted a hand and snapped it with a flick of her wrist.

A green spear of magic flashed out and passed straight through the priest.

His guts tumbling out of the sudden hole in his stomach, the priest fell to his knees and then slumped to one side.

Unmoving.

Holy fucking shit.

"Apprentice and master down," Felix said in the open lines. "Repeat, apprentice and master down."

Felicity was standing next to Felix, one hand partially held out in front of her.

"His magic wasn't that weak, but the structure was lacking," said the Elf. "Easy to pick apart."

Felix didn't respond. He honestly wasn't quite sure what to say.

Faith magic had been something of a bane to his people.

"Can all the Dryads do that?" Felix asked instead.

"What, cast magic? Yes, of course. From what I've gathered from Betty, it's very normal for their particular Dryad clan. They don't do as well with the sexual aspects of their magic, though."

"Ah, I'm going to move up and start working with the Dryads," Felicity said. She patted his armored forearm and moved off to join her plane-mates.

Watching her go, Felix chewed at his lower lip.

Plans were rapidly spreading out. Things he couldn't even have considered up to this point. Options that simply hadn't been reasonable.

Things just changed.

Changed and changed.

Just like when I got the girls way back when.

Felix grinned, feeling his longstanding despair blow away in a second.

Remind me to thank you, little brother.

***

They'd backtracked to HQ to tend to the wounded, unload the loot, put the enemy corpses on ice, and change their clothes.

Betty had sent one of her Dryads on ahead to follow the trail further while a second squad, coordinated with Victoria, was sent backward along the trail.

Where Betty had led them wasn't what he'd expected.

Peering up at the building in front of them, Felix wasn't quite sure what to say.

Miu sniffed, adjusting the holster under her jacket. "I wish I could say I was surprised, but I'm not."

"To be fair, I expected it to be someone in the government, but not the business and trade commission," Lily said, her arms folded in front of her chest. "That seems over the top and misplaced at the same time."

"Is it, though?" Felix asked. Looking to Betty and her companion, he waited quietly.

They'd led him here on the trail of the magic scent, and it seemed to go straight into the front door.

"If you think about it, and this is only a guess, mind you, but... someone has to foot the bill, right?

"We know for a fact that—" Felix paused and looked around himself, wondering if anyone was close enough to hear him.

Felicity made a small hand motion and smiled at him. "No one outside of eight feet of you will hear you. Please, continue."

Lily was staring at Felicity outright. Felix had made sure to express to her that it seemed Felicity could work magic without any type of requirement.

"We know for a fact that the government is broke. The police weren't even being paid.

"It's one of the reasons we got the contract and argued tax breaks and other things as part of the payment," Felix said. "If there really is a government agency working to end us, it stands to reason they'd have to get funding from somewhere. Right?

"What better place than a gathering of business leaders with too much money and a desire to gain power."

Felicity nodded her head and tilted it to one side.

"That feels valid, though I think you're missing a piece," she said. "If they're backing a religion they support in secret, I can only see it being far more than simply a wish for power."

"And every single one of them has a ring to blank their thoughts," Lily said, her tone sounding more like a curse. "I would take the souls of thousands to find out who made those damn rings and kill them."

"Rings?" Felicity asked, looking from Lily to Felix.

"That Legion ring you're wearing blocks people from reading your thoughts.

"It's unique to us," Felix explained. "Someone figured out how to make something similar, then flooded the entire continent with them. It makes the Minders and Fixers' job a lot harder.

"They can sometimes get through, but it takes a lot of effort, and usually the ring breaks. It makes it obvious when it happens."

Felicity frowned. "That seems oddly specific to limit Legion's effectiveness."

"Yeah, we figured the same," Felix said. "It came out the first year we moved here, and it's remained. Someone has been playing this game against us for a while."

"Grove-Master," Betty said, walking up to him. "We're ready, but I have a suspicion of what will happen once we go in."

"Oh? Anything you care to share?"

"The scent will go everywhere. Even from out here, it seems the whole thing is muddled," Betty said, watching him intently. "Confusing and back and forth. Old and new magical scents alike."

"In other words... it's more likely that many people who are involved are in there. That this has been going on for a long time," Felix summarized.

"Yes, that is my thought. By going inside, we confirm beyond any doubt that we're aware of the building," Betty said. "If we do not go in, we leave them with doubt about whether we know."

Felix looked away from the Dryad and found himself staring at Felicity's high-heeled feet.

It was a tough choice.

He internally agreed with Betty. It was likely the scent would just run rampant throughout the entire building.

From one conference room and committee to another, back and forth, floor to floor.

Because these business members could be on multiple committees and boards — they weren't limited to just one.

On the other hand, he wanted to push. He wanted to make them fear that he knew. To force them to make mistakes and chase then chase those mistakes down.

I hate being a paper boat. Hate it.

But in this case… it might be best.

"Let's go home," Felix said, giving up the chase for the moment. "And Lily? I have some requests for you."

"Oh?" Lily said, smiling to show him her bright white teeth. "Anything fun?"

"Hah, no. I need to find out how much control we have over a few things," Felix said. "Energy, waste, city maintenance, water, internet, phone lines, anything and everything that's a utility or could be leveraged as one.

"Fire hydrant placement, building inspectors. Anything.

"Everything."

"You're going to pencil-whip them to death," Lily said, still grinning at him.

"Damn right I am. I'm a manager at best. Middle management. I'm best at my worst, when I'm making another person's life hell.

"So… let's do that. Get me everything we have control over. For now… let's just go home," Felix said.

Chapter 7 - Panning for Gold -

After opening the door to the warehouse on Legion Prime, Felix paused. Looking from one end of the large open area to the other, he saw no end to the items that were spread out.

Everything was laid out on tarps. Each item had a small piece of paper tagged to it, and each was grouped with similar items.

It wasn't the first time he'd done this type of exercise, but it was certainly the largest so far.

Taking several steps inside, he looked at the closest tarp and the items laid out on it.

A sundry of office equipment, it looked like a secondhand store from a supply store's cast-offs.

"The Dryads led the teams to various buildings and storage facilities," Kit said, stepping up next to him. "It's by far the largest haul of information, items, and just... data... we've been able to find."

"It's honestly just what we needed. We've been working in the dark for a bit."

Felix nodded in agreement.

They'd been doing well for themselves, all things considered, but it was no small statement to admit they were struggling.

"They're not exactly the type of people I'd spend time with," Kit said. "But they're unbelievably useful so far, and generally very kind and friendly to those in the Legion."

"I sense a 'but' coming on," Felix said, getting down on his knees in front of the first tarp.

Kit sighed from behind him. The slow crunching of her shoes on the pavement came closer.

Picking up what looked like a pencil, Felix focused on it.

He wanted to know a very simple piece of information. If he wanted to purchase this pencil from its owner, who would that be?

Focusing on the small window that popped up, Felix got his answer.

"The pencil is owned by one... Peter Miller," Felix said into his wrist device.

A soft chime indicated the name had been recorded.

"It's not so much a 'but' as it is an 'um' I suppose." Kit got down next to him, her skirt sliding up from her knees as she did.

Felix began to slowly sort through all the items on the tarp. Checking each for its owner and recording the names that came up.

He also wasn't about to interrupt Kit and her thoughts. She couldn't read his thoughts unless he allowed her to. Which meant she actually had to sit down and think about what she wanted to convey to him, without knowing how he'd react.

It'd taken her quite a while to get used to the idea, but she hadn't asked to scan his thoughts in two years.

"I'm not happy," Kit said finally.

"Mm. That's not exactly surprising," Felix said. Picking up a coaster, he gave it a once-over and then checked the name.

"Daniel Seville," Felix said into his wrist device. The soft chime came once again.

"It isn't?" Kit asked, her face turned toward him.

"Not really. Legion has, and always will be, a corporation for the benefit of itself. You're an actual hero. Probably one of the only ones in all of Legion," Felix said, setting the coaster down. "You look at what's going on in the world and see things you want to fix. To Legion, it's more a question of how do we get through it and come out on top."

Kit was nodding at his words.

"And if I had to guess, you're slowly running out of ways to validate your hero status.

"I mean, let's call it what it is — Wal is slowly falling apart. Non-profit organizations are vanishing. Neutral parties are gone. The arts have been stripped out of education. There's even been talk about a mandatory service period in the military."

Picking up part of a coffee mug, Felix checked the name, then set it into the pile of confirmed items.

"I... I don't..." Kit muttered.

"Well, it makes sense to me, at least," Felix said. "That being said, not sure what I can do to help you. We've talked about this before. If you really wanted, I could release you from Legion.

"With so much pull in Wal, it's never really been a question of the legality of freeing you. Then you can go off on your merry way."

"But… I don't want to leave," Kit said.

"Then you have a few problems to solve and some decisions to make.

"Stick it out and figure out a way to make it work for yourself, or ask to be released and rough it alone.

"Legion isn't going to change its direction. Too many people counting on us and what we represent to do otherwise.

"You already head up every single possible charitable outreach program we have. There isn't much left Legion can do as a company that wouldn't hurt us in one way or another."

"Has… anyone else asked to be released?" Kit asked.

"Hmm? Oh.

"Lily did. Then immediately signed herself back over to me personally. If I had to guess, the fact that she'd been forced into it bothered her," Felix said with a shrug. "Though the contract she wrote up was more like a marriage agreement than anything. Andrea and Adriana did the same thing afterward."

"Oh. I didn't realize."

"Well, anyways. You figure it out; I'll support you however I can. As I've always done and will do.

"But this conversation isn't exactly surprising to me. Was there something I could do for you immediately?"

"Not for me, at least," Kit said, then slowly stood up. "Though I did want to warn you.

"Felicity isn't going to stop chasing you. You'll have to firmly shut her down if you want her pursuit to end.

"And from what I picked out of her thoughts, she's already convinced Adriana and Andrea to open you up to other women."

Leave it to HR to abuse the fact that they can see into the minds of Legionnaires. Ring or not.

"Pretty sure I've already made it fairly clear my hands are full. I don't think I'd even have the stamina for more," Felix said. "Besides, Lily will never agree."

Standing up as he finished with all the smaller items, he brushed his hands off against each other. Then he moved over to an office chair to check it.

"Apparently Felicity has already changed your bodyguard assignments to include several Dryads. And… and they… uhm." Kit's voice trailed off.

Finding that the chair belonged to a name he'd already recorded, Felix moved to a desk. Looking up, he saw Kit was blushing darkly.

"Spit it out. We're both adults, after all," Felix said.

"Betty has assigned Dryads who are virgins to your bodyguard detail, with the hope that you'll eventually take them to bed. Apparently they'll rotate new girls in every year or so. Or that was the plan I got from her mind.

"Even if you don't pick one, they're there to feed your libido and keep you… keep you… uh, up.

"Felicity is trying to eliminate any excuses you might have, apparently."

Felix's eyebrows went up as he checked the desk.

Maybe I do have to shut her down hard.

"And before you ask, Miu agreed. As did Victoria. Felicity convinced them simply by saying she believes she can convince you to agree.

"And she's also working on Lily, and has even managed to talk her into considering it instead of just yelling no."

What the actual fuck?

Felix was starting to get annoyed.

Quickly, too.

"I wouldn't be too angry. From what I've been able to pick up, Felicity is genuinely infatuated with you.

"It's not as dark or frightening as Miu's version of love, but it's definitely not in line with Lily's or the Elex girls', either."

Distantly, Felix heard a door open.

"Ah, that's your next appointment, I believe. Thank you for the time; I'll consider your words," Kit said, scurrying away to the nearby door.

"Now just wait a min—"

The door slammed shut, cutting off his words.

"Damn it, does no one listen to me?" Felix asked. Growling, he moved away from the tarp.

He shook his head, working to control his anger. It wouldn't do him any good right now. But he didn't want to let go of it, either.

He just needed to wait for a chance to talk to Lily. She was due to speak to him soon. Either the next meeting or the one after that.

Reaching into his pocket, he pulled out a green sticky notepad and flicked one of the notes onto the edge of the tarp.

Done.

He turned around and moved to the next tarp. It was full of weapons and bits of what looked like blood-stained armor.

The click of heels behind him told him it was only one of a few people. The vast majority of people around him wore combat boots or flats.

Picking up a very blood-stained glock, Felix thumbed the magazine release.

He'd found previously that magazines and rounds could often have different owners than the weapons themselves.

Unfortunately, there were no modifications or accessories otherwise to check.

"Hello darling," said a soft voice. Fingers carded lightly through his hair.

"Hello yourself, love," Felix said, looking over his shoulder at Lily with a grin. "I was just thinking about you."

"Was it a fun thought? Or a boring one?" Lily said, her lips curling up at the corners of her mouth.

"Originally, they were fun. Very fun.

"But they turned boring, I'm afraid. Kit told me Felicity is playing games behind my back," Felix said, a trace of heat in his voice.

Lily snorted, crossing her arms in front of her and leaning to one side, drawing his eyes to her torso and waist.

He'd realized long ago that Lily had a propensity to make herself eye catching to him. Both in the way she dressed and posed around him.

"Of course she did. She's still mad at me for telling her Kit didn't belong in Legion," Lily muttered. "I won't deny that Felicity is playing her own game.

"Though so far, it's entirely to your benefit and hasn't caused any harm."

"Even with you?" Felix asked. He ignored the remark about Kit being in Legion. Lily wasn't wrong, and her relationship with Kit was her own.

Checking the rounds one by one, he found he'd been right. There were several different names in this one weapon. One for the gun, one for the magazine, and one for the rounds.

Dropping everything to one side and starting a pile, Felix glanced to Lily.

She had an odd look on her face. Clearly realizing she hadn't answered, she shifted her weight to the other foot and smiled at him.

"Truthfully? No. No harm. Though she has forced me to question my own thoughts. Her and Berenga seem keen on getting me to agree to you having more women in your life. Which I'm keenly against, obviously," Lily said. "Or at least, I was. Now I find myself questioning it."

"Care to share any of those thoughts?" Felix asked.

"No. Not particularly. Someday, maybe. Anyways, I came here to talk about all those orders you put out.

"I have the Laurens running it all down."

Felix couldn't argue that. The first Lauren, Lauren Aston, had once been a problem for him. Working against him, right up until she'd gotten fired. For which he'd hired her.

The second Lauren he'd picked up in a warzone. Tilen, to be exact.

She, Steve, and Julia had come out on the other side as more than common. Lily had scooped her up within a week and turned her into a lawyer.

Steve and Julia were part of his security forces, currently deployed to Vince's mission.

Along with Eva, whom Felix was doing his best not to think about.

"Anything interesting so far?" Felix asked.

"What, about your orders? Nothing out of the ordinary.

"Finding a lot of shell companies, listings, holdings, boards, people. Lots and lots to work with and push through.

"We're going over all their contracts with a fine-toothed comb, and we've already started canceling a number of them. Most of them are losing utilities faster than they can complain about them.

"There is a very unfortunate reality here, though," Lily said. "It would seem almost every bank in Wal is against us. I've already taken the liberty of removing all our assets, converting it all to gold in your name, and then dumping it in the vault."

Dropping the rifle he'd been working over into the "checked" pile, Felix sighed. "I figured it'd be something like that."

Felix looked up to the ceiling above him.

Suddenly it felt like those long-ago plans for having to deal with Wal he'd had everyone go through were coming back.

"Alright. Just make sure we have enough cash on hand to pay everyone outside of Legion for the next year.

"Move all Legionnaires to the Legion standard and start minting accordingly," Felix said, looking to Lily.

She gave him a tight smile, one that seemed more annoyed than anything.

"I must confess I'll need help for that," Lily said. "I've already asked them to be here. I showed up a few minutes early just to get a moment alone with you."

"You did? Was it—"

The nearby door opened, and Felicity stepped through, computer pad resting against her forearm and in place of her ledger. Her eyes immediately moved to him.

Smiling brightly, Felicity closed the door and walked straight to him. She paused only briefly to bob her head towards Lily.

She was dressed immaculately again today. Almost identical to Lily, though she was showing a bit more of her leg and cleavage than the lawyer.

"Felicity, thank you for coming," Lily said. "Felix was just asking us to go ahead with the Legion standard."

"Ah, wonderful. I already have everything ready to go. When Andrea transferred everything over to me, I spent some time going over all the projects and picked out the ones I felt would be most likely to happen," Felicity said, flipping the leather lid off her computer pad and tapping at the screen.

"I made several purchases for bronze and silver through Legion accounts.

"I also had several different dies cast for the coins. The bronze coin has a picture of the Legion iconography on it. The silver is Legion HQ back in Skippercity and is read as 'in memorium.' For the gold coin, it's of course a side profile of you."

Felicity tapped something else on her screen and gave Felix a wide grin. "Done. I've transferred all pay to be done in Legion standard, notified all employees, and activated the press.

"Everyone should receive their notifications shortly."

Felix stared at Felicity. Andrea had been good at her job. Very good. But now he was finding that the young Elf woman before him took it to a whole new level.

"What about all the currency Legionnaires had in the Legion bank?" Felix asked, curious.

"In the notification I sent out, I advised everyone to please transfer their currencies into Legion standard as soon as possible. They have the next ninety days to do so at a rate that is in their favor with no exchange fee.

"After that, it'll be normal rates with a small fee," Felicity said. "On top of that, I've made contact with a credit union willing to exchange currency for gold at a favorable exchange rate with us, and they aren't part of the problem we've been digging through."

Felix glanced at Lily, who had the same annoyed smile on her face.

Ok, even she can't naysay Felicity, apparently. Which means she's not just doing her job, but doing it phenomenally.

"Great," Felix said. "Since you're here, Felicity, direct me. What do I have on my calendar that I need to be aware of? I think I'll be stuck here for a while."

"Ah, would you like it in order of time, suggested priority, or impact?" Felicity asked.

Huh. Uh…

"Suggested priority then, and we'll go from there," Felicity said, looking down at her pad.

"I've set up interviews you'll need to complete for me. They're going to be new recruits for your personal bodyguards.

"I'd like you to give me confirmation on at least ten, and a maybe status on twenty. That'll form the core of that addition," Felicity said. "After that, Miu and I would like you to commit to a reorganization of the interior security detail and the bodyguard unit as a whole. Victoria and Miu would like to change things up."

Oh. That does make sense.

Felix turned to face Felicity directly, interested now.

"Andrea and Adriana have organized a permanent residence change for you, them, and Lily to Legion Prime," Felicity continued. "I've contacted Felicia and organized the manpower, budget, and timetables accordingly. She estimates it'll be done in about two weeks."

"You got Felicia to agree to a project?" Felix asked.

"Of course," Felicity said, looking at him as if he were an idiot. "All I had to do was manage what she wanted in return, which was a small home for her and her wife to be made in conjunction in the same area.

"I've set aside a large piece of land for you, your closest advisers, and lieutenants to live in on Legion Prime. Your inner circle and sanctum, as it were.

"Beyond that, Meliae and Fes have requested a formal audience with you when you have time.

"Everything else I've handled on your behalf. The only pending item is that the ANet is actively searching for any name you're recording, as you record it. They should have results for most of the names by the time you finish your task," Felicity said, then flipped the leather lid closed on her computer pad.

Felix glanced at Felicity's ear and saw an earpiece wedged into it.

She's actively tied into the ANet, and the girls are acting on her orders.

How in the world did she move in and take over everything so quickly?

"Oh, there is one more thing," Felicity said. "Erica and Jessica have asked to have dinner with you separately.

"I intimated that they'd be willing to go together to dinner with you, so I accepted on your behalf. I've already made the appropriate arrangements. You'll be dining with both of them in the near future. Unsure on when yet. Though it'll be in Old Legion City.

"I've prepared them with a list of topics you'll likely discuss with them, and what projects coincide with them that they may need to initiate on your behalf."

Lily began laughing suddenly, pressing a hand to her temple.

"Goodness. I think you've met your match, my love," she said. "I think she just out-corporated you and has you more organized than you've ever been."

Felix snorted and turned back to the weapons he'd been going through.

Lily wasn't wrong, though. Felicity had neatly emptied his task list, fixed his calendar, and organized everything for him.

"I would prefer to call it keeping him on track. My only job is to make sure he's best utilized; I could never do what he does," Felicity said.

"Uh huh. Come on, lover-girl, you can stare at him later," Lily said, walking over to Felicity. "I want to talk to you about your magic, if you don't mind."

"Of course, Lily."

The two women left Felix alone with his work, sorting through the junk and identifying things.

"Afternoon, Felix."

Closing his eyes tightly, Felix didn't want to open them.

"I won't go away just because you can't see me," said his benefactor, "or at least pretend I'm not here.

"I mean, come on. Are you three years old?"

Chapter 8 - Opening Moves -

Felix grunted and opened his eyes. It wasn't as if he'd actually thought closing them would make the man go away.

But he had secretly hoped for it.

Looking to the voice, Felix found exactly what he'd expected.

Or *whom*, that was.

It was his benefactor, standing off to one side, playing with what looked like a coin. A very dirty and worn coin.

"Hi. Are we done playing hide-and-seek now? If you want, you can go first," said the man.

Accepting that he was there, Felix bent down and picked up a combat knife. Pulling the sheath off it, Felix looked from the sheath to the knife.

Ignoring the man.

"I figured I'd drop by since our conversation was interrupted last time," said his benefactor.

"Uh huh. You didn't talk to me—wouldn't talk to me—for five years. Now you show up when I ask for you one day, as if you were always here. Then you just... poof... vanish. And now you're even coming back because we didn't finish our conversation, or so you say.

"Forgive me if I'm not that interested. Because I'm not. Yet I can't really tell you to go away.

"I find myself annoyed while unfortunately unable to decline whatever it is you're here to say or do," Felix said. "I'm not a yoyo."

Finding the same name for the combat knife and the sheath as he had for the pistol, Felix flicked them onto the pile.

"Yes, well... that's actually rather reasonable. Sorry. I was hoping I wouldn't need to do anything or intercede before this. Things get complicated when I'm involved," said the benefactor. "The longer I'm involved, the worse it gets. It's like an escalating scale of tsunami-level bullshit. Exponential."

"Yeah, well, seems like my world is rapidly falling apart. Maybe it's time you stepped in anyways," Felix grumbled. "Maybe fix it and put it back together rather than letting itself get torn apart."

"I already have, actually. Several times, but you'd never know that because I fixed it.

"Though, due to their bickering, I've bound all the gods, and I had to do so here on this plane.

"They're not allowed to leave. Either back to Legion Prime, as you've called it, or Vince's world. I've also limited their influence further, because I found a few who had violated my laws.

"That doesn't change the fact that the populace here are killing each other for their deities, but there it is.

"They'll turn around eventually, since they'll be the ones who have to deal with the mess."

"Are... Desh and Abera alright?" Felix asked, changing the subject. "We haven't heard from them since the battle. They vanished."

"They're actually quite fine. They were abiding by the laws I gave them to the fullest intent I expected, so they've been rewarded. They'll not be coming back here, though. They've been moved to another plane that could use their help as deities who wish to care for their people."

At least they're okay. They were and weren't Legion at the same time.

"Now, we were talking about the planes and, I suppose, me, to a degree," said his benefactor. "Would you care to hear more of my story, or are you dead set on not listening?"

Felix shrugged, sorting the items in front of him.

"Might as well listen, I suppose. I don't have much else to do," Felix admitted.

"Right, then. I'll not start at the beginning, since it doesn't matter, but more towards the end." His benefactor crossed his arms and leaned up against a desk. "I'm a traveler of sorts. In my travels, I found I had the ability to create countless planes and worlds. And so I did.

"This plane is one of the first. I made around a hundred in the early days."

Felix paused in his sorting and checking, actually growing interested.

It wasn't every day one heard the origin of the universe.

"Except that I made a mistake. I fashioned all the worlds from an original world. One that came before all else. Including all that was wrong with it."

Sighing, the Overgod ran his fingers through his hair. "The planes started right and true. Good.

"But I didn't expect... well, I didn't expect an entity to appear. It didn't act immediately. It moved.

"And it moved slowly. It crept through all that I'd built. Spreading out through these core worlds. Spreading out and starting to work in the background.

"This individual was behind the original portal experiments, in fact."

Felix found himself staring at the Overgod now.

"After that fiesta of a shit-flavored birthday cake... I found that a number of core worlds were corrupted. Turned against me. And I couldn't work through anyone in them. They were essentially fortified against me specifically.

"I could always just... wipe out the planes, dismiss these core worlds completely. But that'd kill how many billions of innocents?

"Untold numbers."

And is that why you need a favor from me? Do I play into this game between you and this 'entity' somehow?

Giving himself a visible shake, Felix's benefactor, now confirmed as the Overgod and creator of all, gave Felix a bemused smile.

"Enough of story time. My apologies, I didn't mean to ramble on like that. I think that's all the time I want to spend here right now as well."

"Before you go then, is there anything you can share about my current predicament?" Felix asked. "Like if it's worth my while to dig through any of this?"

Smiling, the Overgod, Felix's benefactor, flipped the dirty coin at him.

"Nothing I can formally tell you. Though I will say this: I definitely think all the steps you've taken are the right ones so far. Up to this point."

Felix caught the coin in one hand and looked down at it.

"Oh, and you should have your power back in about ten days. It'll be available for six, give or take a few hours," said the Overgod.

The coin he'd just caught was a key ring. It wasn't a coin at all.

It just had so much dirt in it that the interior of the circle was filled with filth.

Destroyed was the best way to describe it. Rusted and rotting, it looked like it had been dug out of a mud pit.

"Very helpful. Now if I only you could—" Felix stopped talking when he looked up and found the Overgod was gone. "Whatever."

Frowning, Felix focused on the key-ring and activated his purchase request.

"Richard Munro," Felix said as the window popped up.

Dropping the key-ring onto the pile, Felix turned back to the weapons tarp.

"Dear, please confirm that last name?" asked an Elex sister over the ANet.

"Richard Munro," Felix said.

"Got a hit on that. Almost immediately. It's not a shell company, ghost, or false name. It's an actual person," said the voice Felix was starting to think belonged to an Adriana. She always sounded much less flighty than her sister.

"So? Who is it?" Felix asked.

"Ah... he's the committee leader for the banking committee, and CEO of the Hero International Bank."

Sighing, Felix looked down to his feet.

He gave me a lead after all; he just didn't want to say anything.

"Tell Lily, Kit, and Felicity about it. Sounds like this rabbit hole just got a lot deeper than I expected," Felix said somberly.

He'd expected people to be involved. Maybe some branch managers, a few middle-to-low-end upper management.

Not an actual CEO of a massive business.

An international bank, no less.

Then Felix paused, his thought process turning in a different direction.

We were just talking about the fact that we were moving off government-backed currencies.

That we were transitioning to gold.

Even if the banks had the same thought, they wouldn't be able to do anything about it. They're more invested in currencies than we are, I bet.

They'd protect it.

Like attacking a corporation that was poised to corner gold through pawn shops, buy up material, and transfer a lot of money into precious metals.

Felix scratched at his chin, not quite sure what to do.

He could easily see how he'd set himself up as a target for this, possibly pushing them straight into his enemies' pocket.

If he were in their position, he'd probably be forced to do the same. Though now he had to wonder how far it'd gone. If the government of Wal knew about this, where would they fall?

If the currency of Wal weakened, it definitely wouldn't help. But considering Legion deferred so much of their debt and upheld large portions of security, he couldn't imagine which way the prime minister would go.

"Are we going to rob a bank?" came Andrea's voice through his communicator. "It's been a while since I've done it, but it was a lot of fun!"

"Myriad usually ran those, but I have all her memories for them and the planning!"

"Can I be the first person in?" asked what sounded like an Adriana. "Point is always fun because it gives the biggest rush."

"Yeah, but that one almost always get shot," said another.

Rob the bank?

Felix grinned at the idea.

Rob the bank.

"Get those contractors we've been working with for cyber security and make them a deal they can't refuse to join the Legion," Felix said. "Get as many as you can."

***

Looking at the display, Felix watched as the drone continued to fly over the expo center.

"It's big," he said, shaking his head. "There's a lot of ways in and out, too."

"Yes. It will not be a pleasant duty," Ioana said, watching the screen from over his shoulder. "Though I believe in our people."

"Uh huh." Felix sighed and handed the display over to Ioana. "Honestly, I'm not sure on this one. It's obvious something is going to happen, either externally or internally, but I'm terrified that if we're not here to stop it, it'll succeed."

"A common worry, you've often said," the big warrior woman reminded him.

Glancing up at her, Felix couldn't help but compare her now to how he remembered her.

She'd softened considerably. Her brown hair was pulled back behind her head in a long ponytail. The hard-set quality to her features was gone, replaced by a woman heading into her thirties and settling into a comfortable lifestyle.

Catching his look, Ioana gave him a smile.

"What?" she asked.

"Nothing really. Just realizing how good Felicia has been for you. You look good, Ioana. Happy," Felix said, grinning back at her. "That makes me happy."

Ioana blushed deeply, then shrugged with a smile. "My wife is indeed the best thing that has happened to me. Second only to joining Legion.

"Now stop with the frippery and give me a direction."

Sighing, Felix looked to the ceiling of the armored personnel carrier they were sitting in.

"You take care of the external security just as we originally discussed. I defer to you in all things. Assume we could be under attack in any way, shape, or form.

"I'll give you two hundred of the Dryads as well; the other hundred will go to Miu and Vicky for internal usage," Felix said.

"We need more of them," Ioana said.

"You tell me where to get more, and I'll hire them personally through whatever means necessary. Until then, that's what we can do.

"Need anything else?" Felix asked.

"No. I'll run it all through Felicity and have her check and approve it," Ioana said, setting the display to one side.

Felicity? Even you, Ioana?

"I'm going to walk the perimeter and start my plans. Unless there's something else you need from me?" Ioana asked.

"No. I'll head inside to catch up with the others and start planning that out with them."

"Good. Tell Felicity Felicia said hi for me. She wants to know if you two are willing to come over for dinner this weekend," Ioana said, moving to the rear hatch.

"Uh, I'll ask her," Felix said, feeling very confused.

"Great, see ya then."

Ioana popped open the door and stomped out, her lieutenants falling in around her as she went.

Miu's head slid into view at the rear hatch. Her eyes locked on him, unwavering in their intensity.

"Can I come in?" she asked.

"No, I'm coming out."

"I should come in," she said, starting to mount the rear step.

"No, Miu. The last time you were in a small space with me, it didn't end well, remember?"

"Nightly," came the breathy response.

Grumbling, Felix moved to the rear hatch and got out. "Keep it running. No idea how long we'll be."

"Affirmative," called the driver in response to his request.

Hitting the ground, Felix turned toward the expo and started heading toward the doors.

"Felicity is waiting inside. She's already gone over the building several times with me and Victoria," Miu said. "We need you to check the work, offer your opinions, and give us the go ahead."

An Adriana, Andrea, several Dryads, and a magician all fell in around him as his personal bodyguard.

"Got it. What do you think of her, by the way?"

"Felicity? I like her. She understands everything immediately and knows what I want. She was honest with me and didn't shy away from what I told her," Miu said. "I would still pull her head off if you asked me to, but I would regret it."

"How's she fitting in with everyone else?" Felix asked. They were only twenty seconds away from the door now. Miu's acceptance of her was strange, but he'd been warned she'd been turned.

"Very well. Everyone likes her. It's as if she's always been here," Miu said.

And that's what worries me. Is she just that charming, lovely, and personable, or is she something much worse?

The door opened as he approached it. Felicity was standing there, a Dryad, Andrea, and Adriana standing just behind her.

Victoria was only a few feet away on the other side of the doorway.

They're deferring to her, aren't they?

"Welcome, welcome," Felicity said, smiling at him. "Come, I had lunch arranged for everyone as we walk around. Simple, portable things we can carry in a single hand."

Walking deeper in, Felix looked around. They were standing in a large, open entryway.

"So, be honest with me, do you really need me to look around?" Felix asked.

"I can reasonably assure you I've taken care of everything you would have been concerned with. Though I would please ask you to review a presentation I've prepared for you," Felicity said. "I've also made sure your inner circle has seen it and approved of the plan."

Felix turned to look to Victoria and waited.

She wouldn't lie to him; she would tell him the truth.

"It's as clean a plan as we can make it," Victoria said, giving him a lopsided smile. "Everything was worked out with all departments included, as well as providing the exterior team with what we can do to help them. Ioana is probably getting the same information right now that we're giving you."

"It's exciting," Andrea said, bouncing up to him. She was eating what looked like a pancake folded over itself. "I made pancakes! Felicity said it was delicious. She said I was beautiful and a great cook."

Andrea grinned at Felix with a mouth full of pancake, her tail swishing back and forth wildly behind her.

Adriana was nodding in agreement with Andrea's words.

"Then we'll move on to something else. Did you all review my request?" Felix asked. He turned to the glass doors that led back outside and walked up to them.

"The bank heist?" Victoria asked.

"Yes. The bank. Unless Andrea has something to add about our dear friend Dick Munro."

"No," Andrea said around her pancake. "It's looking like the entire board is in it with him as well."

"Then yes, the bank," Felix said. Lifting a hand, he pointed at a large single-story building across the way. "That one, to be specific."

"Huh? That one?" Adriana said, stepping up next to him and looking out the glass.

"Yes. It's listed as only a branch, but Lily and Kit were able to dig some things up," Felix said. "Apparently, it has a much larger underground footprint than you would think. And many more people on payroll than a simple branch office should.

"The reports they put together are available in my personal share drive."

Looking over his shoulder, he saw Victoria, Miu, and Felicity all reading something on her pad.

Felix figured they were looking for the report. Looking back to the bank, he set his hands together behind his back and waited.

"I love you," Andrea said suddenly, pushing up close to him. She leaned up and kissed him, giving him a bright smile. "Andrea and Adriana Prime and the Seconds are moving to Legion Prime right now.

"The house plans look great. I especially like the nursery. Thank you. I'm very happy. I'm going to reward you so much."

Right. Need to thank Felicity for her work.

Adriana stepped up on the other side of Felix and pressed her forehead to Felix's shoulder. "Love you. Thank you. Reward you too."

The Elex twins then stepped away at the same time, as if they'd never been there.

Must mean they heard the others coming to a consensus, for them to break off like that.

"I think we're ready for you to continue," Felicity said, confirming his thought.

"It's very simple. I want to clean out their vault, as well as their electronic bank accounts."

"At the same time, I want to wipe out their records on debts and negative balances," Felix said. "So we'll have several moving parts to this.

"The first part has already happened. A number of cyber-security contractors were made full-time Legionnaires. They put together a program that was likely to tempt someone to open it. A fun little bit of malware.

"Malware that does nothing other than record data."

"If all it does is log it, how do we retrieve it?" Miu asked.

"One of the contractors Kit secured is responsible for that bit. They're apparently powered with a unique power. They can chip a piece of themselves off and put it into the code. Making the code part of them.

"There's some risk of course, and if that code is lost, it'd hurt them significantly, but... that's the way this one goes," Felix said.

"Oh! Exciting," Andrea enthused. "What's next, then? How do we get this code and data back?"

"Funny you ask. That'll be a job for our lovely Elf over there." Felix pointed at Felicity. "She didn't have an identity here in Wal up until yesterday.

"Now you have one. All the appropriate papers and certificates."

Felix looked back out the glass to the bank.

"We've already prepped everything for you detail wise. Kept it fairly simple," Felix said. "You were born in what was once Tilen. In the local Elven enclave. They were small and close knit, so records, including birth certificates, seem to be hard to find.

"We know that because Tilen is little more than a ruin and we personally secured all the records available ourselves."

"Did any Elves from the enclave survive? That'd be a loose thread," Felicity said.

"Not sure. If they did, I'd be happy to welcome them into Legion.

"Regardless of that, though, I figure it's about time for you to open a bank account. What better bank than that one?"

The soft click of heels proceeded — what he assumed was Felicity drawing near.

"While I appreciate your faith in me, I'm not sure I've been able to completely jump the culture divide. It's easier with those in Legion, but..." Felicity stopped talking, letting the statement hang there.

Rewards are always best. And rewards that better their own goals are ideal.

"Complete the task without a problem, and I'll take you to dinner. I have an open invitation with Ioana and Felicia for this weekend," Felix said. "I'll even let you pick the location, but you'll have to work it out with those two if you manage it."

"I accept the terms for the time being, but I reserve the right to renegotiate depending on how difficult the task becomes," Felicity said.

Felix shrugged. "Fine. Though I'll ask for arbitration and let Kit decide if we can't find a middle ground. She's fairly impartial since she can read minds.

"After we get the code back out and all the data that comes with it, we'll plan our cyber attack to clean out some of their ledgers."

"Why just the debts and negative balances?" Andrea asked.

"Because then they'll not know how much money is owed to them. It'll strangle out their balance sheets," Felicity said.

"Yep. And at the same time that's going on, we'll attack the vault itself and clean everything out. They'll be insured against such a thing, so it won't hurt anyone who has their money there," Felix said. "And when it's all said and done, we'll have brought them to their knees. Because in the end, from what we can tell, they're the ones running all the money that was supporting that little party we had."

"Good. That means we can end this and move on," Victoria said.

"I'm afraid that only solves one part of it. We'll have eliminated the funding, but that still leaves the people who are illustrating the attacks, and those that are simply supporting it in government," Felix said. "We're apparently fighting a triumvirate of sorts.

"Or that's my expectation, at least. I suppose it could be two, or four, but I think three is accurate."

Chapter 9 - Usual Suspects -

Miu pushed open the large door and strode inside.

Before Felix had crossed the threshold, lights began to turn on, several bulbs flickering ominously before stabilizing.

It was a massive, empty room. It looked as if it would span at least three stories in height, and it took up enough space from wall to wall to be a football field.

"What is this place?" Felicity asked.

"Empty training hall. It'll probably see use in six months when we hire enough new classes to fill it.

"Until then," Felix said, looking around and seeing more than enough space to work with, "it's a bank waiting to be built."

"I don't understand," Felicity said.

Andrea squealed and skipped ahead of the group at a dead sprint. Her feet pounded against the hardwood floor until she started doing cartwheels. Those rapidly turned into backflips as she went rapidly tumbling away from the group.

"He wants to build a mock-up of the bank here," Kit said, watching Andrea as she moved. "Where on earth does she get the energy?"

Adriana was subtly gyrating in place, watching her sister as if she wanted to go chasing off after her. "Open spaces and fields. They're hard to resist," she said.

"A mock-up," Felicity said, bringing the subject back in line. "In other words, you want to practice the bank robbery here."

"Yep. And it'll make it much easier to do because—" Felix paused and looked at a series of massive screens that were spread out along every wall. "We can just throw your recording up there."

Looking down at the portable computer in his hand, Felix tapped the icon to connect to the wireless network.

A few seconds later, he had pulled up the recording Felicity had made during her trip through the bank.

"And there we are," Felix said, pointing up at the screen. "I say we start with the exterior of the bank.

"Tell me when to stop."

"Alright," Kit said.

All eyes turned to the closest monitor as what had been a play button became the view of walking up the front steps to the bank.

"Oh, I see," Felicity said. "I must admit, I'm growing so used to having such wonderful technology at my fingertips, I'm not sure I could go back home for any period of time."

"Just to make sure everyone is on the same page," Kit said. "This is Felicity going to the bank yesterday to open her account."

A Fixer, Minder, Sorcerer, and several Dryads nodded their heads.

Miu sidled in closer to Felix's side, her hand coming up to grab his jacket pocket and hold on to it.

As long as she doesn't do more.

Felicity's head rotated one way and then the other, the camera hidden in her glasses taking a good panorama of the front.

Kit waved a hand at the area to their right without turning away from the monitor. A replica of the bank front came to life from thin air.

A young man held the door open for Felicity and she went inside. Immediately, she began scanning the room.

Felix paused the video at this point. "Alright, let's head up the stairs and start matching it."

The Dryads, Fixer, and Minder all remained where they were. They were there to protect Felix, not take part in the robbery.

Moving up the illusory steps, Felix opened the door. "After you, Miss Kit."

Shaking her head with a smile, Kit looked in the open doorway and pointed a finger.

"Done with the floor," she said, taking the display from Felix and then walking through the doorway.

She's been practicing her illusions, it seems.

Miu, Felicity, Adriana, and a panting Andrea stopped in front of him.

"Sorry, dear," Andrea said breathily, fanning a hand in front of her red face.

"Don't be; it's who you are. Who I love," Felix said, pressing a hand to her lower back. "Now get in there."

Andrea spun lightly off his hand and kissed him roughly, then darted through the door, laughing.

She's so lighthearted lately.

"It's the pregnancy," Miu said as Felix followed behind her. "She's been wanting children this entire time."

That… makes sense.

Further into the building, Kit was moving the video back and forth, scrubbing for information on the placement of things.

"Thanks, Miu," Felix said, then offered her his arm. "Come on then, Kit looks like she'll be done sooner than we think."

Miu raised her eyebrows but then latched on to his arm and pressed herself to his side.

Felix himself was feeling rather buoyed as of late. The Dryads Vince had sent over had done wonders for Legion already.

So much had changed instantly on that one day.

"I think that's everything," Kit said, looking to Felix. Her eyes flicked to Miu and then back to him. "Do you want me to overlay the perspective of the cameras?"

"That'd be amazing and wonderful, Kit," Felix said. "After that, we'll move on."

Kit slashed a finger at the cameras and translucent green cones projected from each one. Covering the entire area.

Not unsurprising, given that the branch is far more than it appears.

Kit didn't ask for permission; she simply started up the playback.

Felicity was already seated in front of a middle-aged man's desk. He was the employee they'd set up the appointment with.

The one whose computer had all the data they'd been hoping to collect.

Kit was moving through the conversation at two times the speed. Felicity turned her head around whenever it seemed like she had the chance to do so, but she didn't spot anything new Kit hadn't already laid out.

Felix chuckled to himself when the man behind the desk clearly looked at Felicity's cleavage.

"He does look often, doesn't he?" Miu said.

"Hmph." Andrea crossed her arms in front of her chest. "This is why we can't wear nice things outside of Legion."

"The Legionnaires know better."

"No, they just know who you're sleeping with," Miu said.

Adriana and Andrea shrugged their shoulders at the same time.

"Same thing," they said in unison.

"I wasn't wearing anything scandalous," Felicity said defensively. "It's almost the same thing as today, just a different color."

Felix glanced over to Felicity.

She was once again dressed in clothing nearly identical to what Lily wore on a regular basis. It certainly did show some cleavage, but nothing she'd be hauled off to HR over.

"Don't blame him too much," Felix said. "You're rather pretty, after all."

The video jumped ahead rapidly as Kit flicked her finger across the bar.

"I think that's everything," she said. "Let's start constructing the rest from our blueprints and the stolen camera data.

"Well, go to the end just to make sure," Felix said.

She's getting testy. And has been.

Hm.

Didn't she say she felt nothing about me? We had that painful and ugly talk. I should know, since I initiated it.

It was years ago now.

She said she was happy with how things were.

Frowning, Felix wasn't sure what to make of the way Kit was acting, but it felt linked to Felicity.

Looking back up to the screen, Felix watched as Felicity finished up her account creation and headed back to Legion at what felt like four times the normal speed.

Slowing down the speed when Felicity entered the bathroom on Felix's personal floor, Kit seemed concerned about proceeding.

Not that he could blame her. A camera in the restroom wasn't a great idea.

Looking into the mirror, Felicity quickly gave herself a once-over. She'd clearly forgotten about the glasses.

With a quick adjustment of her blouse, she hesitated. Then she pulled it down just a bit, showing more of herself off. And then she quickly ran her fingers through her hair and adjusted her skirt.

Felix wasn't quite sure what to make of the primping.

Neither could anyone else, it seemed.

Felicity left the bathroom and then marched straight for Felix's study. Opening the door, she entered, and then she closed the door behind her.

Felix saw himself messing with a filing cabinet. Putting papers into a hanging folder inside, it looked like.

"Welcome back. How'd it go?" he asked Felicity on the video.

"Well. Very well," Felicty replied. Then the glasses tilted down a bit, the view centering on Felix's ass. "Mission accomplished."

Oh. Well, that's interesting.

In the second it took to register what they all saw Felicity looking at, Kit killed the feed. "Alright, let's move on to the data you brought back."

Glancing to Felicity, he couldn't see her face. But he could see her neck and ears.

They were bright red.

"From the data brought back, we're looking at a team of about ten supers," Kit said. "Most of them are in the sub-level, though two are at the elevator that goes down."

"What powers do they have?" Miu asked.

"The two at the elevator are on the super strength and a stamina variety. Meant to hold people back and stand their ground," Kit said. "The eight down below are much more varied.

"One is a Magician, two are Hyper-Sensitives, two Telepaths, and a what sounds like a Flamer. The last one, we're not sure—there's nothing listed."

The entire time Kit spoke, she was adding more and more to her massive construct. They were just now at the point that the elevator was being put in, along with two stand-in dummies with what looked like security-badge photos for faces.

Kit lifted a hand with a grunt, and Felix felt everything underneath him shift.

Then the elevator dinged and opened up.

"I moved the ground floor up, so we can now descend," Kit said, moving into the elevator.

Andrea and Adriana flanked Felix.

Miu disentangled her arm and then gave Felix a shove into the elevator.

Before he could turn around and complain, Felicity stumbled into him, suffering the same abuse from Miu's hand.

Felicity grimaced and took a step back from Felix, then turned around to the door.

Miu's never been subtle. She wants Felicity close to me.

- 552 -

The small psycho stepped into the elevator and pushed Felicity up into Felix's chest, then hit the elevator shut button.

Awkwardly, with Andrea and Adriana to either side, he couldn't do much other than stand there practically breathing in Felicity's hair.

Which did smell nice, honestly, if he thought about it.

"I'm fairly certain there's enough room, Miu," Kit said, her tone sharp.

Miu turned her head and gazed beyond Felix to what he supposed was Kit.

Unblinkingly, without saying a word, she just stared.

"Fine, fine," Kit said, as if Miu had said something.

Ok, I'm starting to get annoyed. Everyone has left my love life alone up till now.

I need to have a talk with Lily and just end this end.

The illusion elevator moved, and then the doors opened rather quickly.

Everyone piled out and found themselves in a very blank cement-covered room.

"Sorry, the elevator actually goes much further down, but we don't have the time or space for it. Now... where were we?" Kit said, looking around.

Suddenly, things started to pop into focus. Defensive hard-points, cameras, and a choke point. Everyone began wandering over to look at it.

"Sorry," Felicity said, hovering near Felix rather than following the others. "She means well, but she's forcing it."

"I know. In her head it was probably justified," Felix said with a shrug. He wasn't mad at her, as she wasn't the one who had done it. "Just who she is."

Kit and the others started moving down a hallway.

"We'll have to cut all the access points previous to this," Kit said, pointing down the hall. "Nothing beyond that point shows up on cameras, so I only have blueprints to go off."

Felix looked away from Felicity and nodded his head Kit.

"Already in place. We're going to kick this off the first day of the summit. Their garbage won't have been picked up for two weeks at that point, I should have my powers back, and they're expecting to have someone come out to work on their power and internet," Felix said.

"Oh?" Kit asked, tilting her head to one side with a smile. "That's convenient."

"Yeah. I had some of our engineers give 'em spotty internet and power for a while. There's one particular accounts manager who is apparently losing his mind at his nonexistent download speed," Felix said with a grin. "I never thought I'd enjoy being part of a telecom, but when you own the contract, the services, the lines for the power... well. Accidents happen."

"What about the supers and the unpowered citizens? There's a number of folks we'll have to get through," Kit said.

Miu nodded slightly, turning to look away from the machine gun to Felix.

"And why does it matter if your powers are back?" Miu asked suspiciously. "You're not going."

"Actually, I am. I plan on going with you," Felix said.

Immediately, the room turned hostile towards him. Even Andrea and Adriana looked angry.

"Wait—hear me out. My powers will be back. I'm going to take several of the Warden shields with me.

"They haven't seen any use here since the Faith magic just cut right through them," Felix said. "And before you say what's the point in the shields then, I'm going to have the Dryads bless them."

Miu's dark glare eased several degrees, but she still didn't look pleased.

"I'm also going to go in full body armor. The only bit that won't be armored is the mask, though I'm going to make sure to modify it before we head out.

"I want to be there just in case we have a sudden need."

That and he was tired of playing backfield. Doing nothing. Watching things fall apart around him.

He wanted to get in there.

"Who's going with you?" Kit asked. She shifted her weight from one foot to the other, looking rather annoyed.

"Miu, Felicity, a Fixer, a Minder, several Dryads, and Neutralizer. I gave him that phasing power about a year ago, you remember. He can cut through anything and get anywhere if he needs to," Felix said. "It covers all my needs and keeps our count low."

Everyone around him seemed to slowly ease up on their distaste for the situation.

"I wanna go," Andrea said, stomping a foot. Her ears were flattened on the top of her head as she pouted. "I liked robbing banks."

"I wish you could, but your ears and tail make you very identifiable. You're not Myriad anymore. You can't just run around and do what you want," Felix said. "Which goes for you as well, Adriana."

Adriana's ears were flattened as well, but she didn't look as upset.

"Besides, you'll need to run the ANet and everything else. That's where I expect your Primes to be. Because at the same time all this is going down, the summit will be kicking off," Felix said.

"You mentioned that. I take it I'll be there in your place?" Kit asked.

"Yes, please—sorry. You're the only person I can trust to be my body double, since you know how I think."

Kit sighed and nodded. "I can't say I much like the idea, but it does seem like you've worked the plan out for the most part."

"I had a bit of help from a few people. Lily was actually a big contributor to this," Felix admitted. "Her and Ioana."

"Yet neither are going with you. Why?" Miu asked.

"Too visible if they're gone. Same with Vicky," Felix answered.

"But not me," Miu said.

"No. Not you. You're rarely seen anyways. In fact, if you look at a lot of those websites that try to pin us down with info, there's only one photo of you."

"Hundreds of Vicky, Lily, Kit, Ioana. Thousands of Andrea," Felix said with a shrug.

"Alright, that all makes sense. But you said there was more to this," Kit said. "What else is there?"

Felix chuckled. "I may have put a challenge to Felicia."

"You didn't," Kit said.

"A small one," Felix said, grinning.

"Ioana won't be happy. Felicia is overworked as it is," Miu said.

"It really is a small one. And one she seemed quite eager to do. It's an implosion-explosive device built around a small bit of magic to power it that will summon a portal for about two seconds."

"The other end of the portal lets out into space. I had her attach it to a probe we shot up a few months ago, just in case."

"How small is small?" Kit said.

"About the size of their vault as it was listed in the blueprints. Anything we can't steal or take with us is going to get put into space. Hell, even if we take everything, I still want to detonate it in there to remove all the evidence," Felix said. "I don't want to just hurt them—I want to break them."

"Speaking of what we can't take," Felicity said, looking as if she'd regained her composure. "How are we going to get all our ill-gained loot back?"

"We're going to take a portal with us. A small one. It's the same thing the Fist uses—"

"The Fist?" Felicity asked.

"—and can easily act as a taxi for stuff we toss through. We won't be able to use it ourselves, but it'll be perfect for things no bigger than a dinner plate.

"Straight into our own receiving facility in Old Legion City."

Felicity was looking to Miu, who seemed to be explaining the Fist.

"After that, our contractors are going to slip into their system while it's isolated, download everything, and wipe everything we talked about previously," Felix said. "On top of that, we still have that hack in the hero's organization. We're going to put some stuff into their own servers that will make sure they don't get the right information from the bank for a while."

"It would seem you've planned all this out," Felicity said, looking at him.

"Of course. What guy hasn't thought about robbing his workplace or a bank at some point?" Felix said. "I just get to actually do it."

Felicity shook her head as a smile creeped over her face.

"You're far more interesting than you ever let on. And I think I'd like to see this 'Fist' you mentioned.

"From what was described, it seems impressive," Felicity said.

"Sure. Can't use it since Faith magic just shorts it and — actually, that's not right. We can have the Dryads cook something up, can't we?" Felix said, looking off to the side and thinking on it.

I forgot about it. I just wrote it all off as a loss.

We need to see what they can do to the new Wardens and the Fist.

Vince, my Brother.

I owe you more than I thought I did.

Chapter 10 - Payday -

"Seems too coincidental," Felicity said, fidgeting in her seat. "Almost like it's a trap."

"What, my power coming back? I suppose. If it hadn't come from the source it did, I'd probably suspect a trap, too," Felix admitted.

Leaning back in the bench seat, he grimaced. His body armor was digging into his sides again, forcing him to shift around until it got comfortable.

Miu took the opportunity to push herself up to his side, practically wedging him into the wall.

A lack of space tended to happen when you crammed twenty some-odd people into an RV. It was a large RV, but it was still rather full with all these people in full gear.

These twenty people were everyone going on the bank heist.

Neutralizer was already wearing his mask of Prime Minister Heather.

In fact, in a stroke of pettiness, Felix had made sure they were all going to wear masks of the prime minister.

Massive, wart-like mole on her chin included and over-exaggerated.

Sitting calmly on the ground in the middle of everyone, he seemed perfectly at ease.

"Report, branch manager has called to complain for the seventh time today that their internet continues to go up and down.

"She's demanding we send a technician out immediately," said an Andrea over the ANet.

Felix turned his wrist over and looked to his watch. The first delegates for the summit should be arriving in an hour.

That meant all the streets would be shut down in about thirty minutes for a few miles in every direction.

There'd be no traffic flow at all. Effectively locking down all the businesses nearby as well.

Including the bank.

The manager had decided to lock the doors up and go on an extended lunch for his people since there shouldn't be customers anyways.

Which suited Felix's needs perfectly.

"Go ahead and tell them we'll send someone out and they should be there in about twenty minutes.

"Let me know when they get on site and start disabling everything to perform 'maintenance,'" Felix said.

"Received. Power cut is ready to go once everything kicks off.

"The signals going out for their silent alarms and security triggers should be disabled as well once the tech hooks in." Andrea sounded prim and proper over the ANet, as she always did. Far different than the exuberant young woman who had done cartwheels across an empty warehouse.

Now it was just a waiting game for the tech to arrive.

Closing his eyes, Felix felt pretty good today.

This morning he'd emptied their gold set aside for bringing people back.

A large number of Legionnaires were back on their feet and amongst the living once more.

Yet there were still more to get to. And they would need quite a bit more gold, due to the condition they were brought back in.

Or simply the fact that most of their bodies weren't brought back at all.

There were many people who had been carried back as fingers or toes through their comrades after finishing them off.

An insurance policy of everyone leaving fingers behind in a morgue-like vault was still in place, but it wasn't a quick process to retrieve them.

Legionnaires simply cut a finger off now and brought it back if they couldn't bring a body.

Bodies were often lost to circumstances that couldn't be dealt with. Usually battle priests caused those losses.

Felix closed his eyes and let his thoughts float away.

"Technician is on site," Andrea said, her voice jarring him awake.

Opening his eyes, Felix found his head propped up on Miu's shoulder.

She looked like she was experiencing pain and pleasure at the same time. Her eyes wide and staring at him.

"I was good," Miu said, her hands locked together in her lap. "Very good. I listened to Felicity."

"She was good," Felicity chimed in. "And did listen. She kept her hands to herself and merely enjoyed your presence.

"Now, I assume that's our cue to act?"

Sitting up straight, Felix cleared his throat and nodded.

Everyone in the RV looked his way, waiting for the order.

"Everyone get to your positions," Felix said, fighting down a yawn. "Flip your weapons to active and be ready.

"Remember, Electro-rifles first, ballistic second."

Getting to his feet, Felix picked up the small battle rifle that had been resting between his knees. It looked a lot like a ballistic rifle, but the real difference was in what it shot out.

He didn't understand the mechanics of it—didn't want to, either.

It was a custom job Felicia had put together several years ago. She'd made around fifty of them, but they'd found no purpose at the time.

Faith magic more or less negated their use entirely.

So they'd been shelved indefinitely. Right up till Felix had gotten the idea to have the Dryads bless them with their own faith.

Looking to the handle, he moved the selector to "coma," so helpfully named by Felicia, and slung the strap over his shoulder.

Neutralizer was standing near the front of the RV now, one hand held up in front of him.

A small portal was forming. Still no bigger than a coin.

Stopping it right there, Neutralizer leaned down and peered through it.

He held up a hand above his head, asking for silence and that the exit was clear.

As one, everyone pulled their oversized masks down over their bulletproof face masks and helmets.

Standing up, Neutralizer started in on the portal again.

When it was big enough to walk through, he stopped and made a small motion with his hand.

Stepping to one side, he pulled his weapon up in front of him. He'd be staying here to maintain and control the exit.

A group of six moved up to take his place in front of the portal. Two Dryads, two Fixers, and two Minders.

More than enough to sweep through a bank lobby and subdue everyone inside.

Behind them, everyone else stood in order of entry.

Stock still.

Waiting.

They couldn't move until they got the go-ahead from Andrea that the tech had severed the remaining lines linking the bank to the outside world.

"Lines are cut, point of no return reached," Andrea said.

"Go," Felix whispered.

The six at the front of the portal leapt forward. The sound of a door being flung open accompanied them vanishing through the portal.

Everyone in line rushed out after them. They were there to help sweep up the people in the lobby and bring everyone into the offices deeper inside the building.

An overly large man who seemed ill fit for this job was the last in line. He was a recent addition to Legion. Hired a week previously with the promise of bringing his family with him.

Given his power, Felix still felt it was a cheap deal.

Finally, even the heavy-set man known as Circuit-Breaker had passed through the portal.

Neutralizer was standing at the edge of the portal, peering through it. His rifle propped up against his shoulder.

"Good to go, boss," he said.

Miu stepped in front of Felix and led him and Felicity through the portal.

His people were posted up in the corners, guns drawn and watching.

Circuit-Breaker stood in the middle of the lobby, looking out of place. Turning to face Felix, he nodded his masked head at him.

"Everything's popped. It'll take them days to replace whatever I didn't want gone," he said. "All the data on the computers is safe and secure, though. I'll start rounding that up."

Felix nodded at the man, his eyes sliding around the interior of the bank.

The doors were locked by the bank staff, the windows shuttered, and from the outside, it would look exactly as one would expect.

A closed bank due to the ongoing circus of politics not too far away at the expo.

Two of the bank robbers filed in next to Miu without a word. Felix imagined they were part of his bodyguard detail and were now reporting in.

"This is Camper-Actual; Scrooge is secured and all information taken," said a voice over the localized ANet. "Waiting for next phase."

They found the bank manager quickly enough. And even got everything out of him. Fun.

"All teams check in," Felix said.

"Central-Actual," Andrea said. "Everything is green."

"Flash-bang, phase confirmed, ready," said the breach team of six who would remain in the lobby.

"Exit-Actual, ready and in standby," said Neutralizer.

"Camper-Actual, assets are secured, moving to secure ground-level vault, waiting for next phase for split," said the team who had rounded up the staff and would be playing babysitter in the offices.

"Prybar-Actual, ready and waiting at jump-off point one," said the squad of Dryads, Powereds, and Security personnel whose job it would be to take down the two supers in front of the elevator.

"EMP-Actual," said Circuit-Breaker, trundling over to a computer. "Everything is toast, collecting intel."

"Chair-Actual," Miu said, her head turning to Felix. "Ass is secure and ready."

No one laughed, but he could feel that everyone mentally had their own chuckle at his designation.

I wonder whose bright idea that was.

Whatever. Keeping them loose to have a chuckle.

If it's on me, so be it.

"Prybar, you're clear to activate," Felix said. Turning, he moved toward the elevator in the back of the branch that would lead him down into the underground.

"I'm so excited. I've never been on something like this," Felicity said. "And before you scold me, I'm using a private channel to you only. Andrea set it up for me. She's such a sweetie."

Marching along at his side, Felicity looked like any of his Legionnaires. Holding her weapon correctly, moving as if she'd spent hours training with Ioana, Victoria, and Miu.

"Prybar-Two," panted a voice into the ANet. "Phase complete with two non-lethal captures. No fatalities, one wounded."

Wonderful. That's an ideal situation.

"Vicky gave me a skill book she'd been holding onto," Felicity said, as if reading his mind. "She's very helpful."

No. No she's not. None of them are.

You're a poison that's seeped into the entire Legion and taken over.

Witch, you're a witch. Can you hear my thoughts, too?

"No, I can't read your thoughts, but Kit gave me a crash course on how you work and think," Felicity said as they entered a strange hallway.

It looked like little more than a looping path that led to the break room.

Except at the end of it, which had been a blank wall probably ten minutes ago, there was a steel frame with two doors wrenched off their hinges.

Moving past it, Felix found himself in the bay that led to the elevator.

Legionnaires were securing the area, tending to someone off to one side and locking down their captives.

"Phase three is a go, split Miner from Camper and merge with Prybar," Felix said, moving into the elevator directly.

"How are we looking, Central?" Felix asked.

"All reports are green. Board is clear. No problems," Andrea reported back.

"Phase three is a go," Felix said.

Members from both the Camper team, now Miner, and Prybar team began assembling in the elevator around Felix.

This group would be taking the plunge with Felix into the depths of the bank.

Down into the vaults of the branch to find out what was waiting for them here. What they had tried desperately to keep out of plans and off the radar.

In under twenty seconds, the elevator was absolutely packed. They'd measured out how many people they could fit inside during rehearsals, and this was it.

Everyone was extraordinarily friendly, ass to crotch. But it was exactly what they needed.

Much to Felix's displeasure, in a last-second move as the doors closed, Miu had wedged Felicity directly in front of him. And instead of it being a random Legionnaire, which would have eliminated any embarrassment, it was Felicity wedged up against his front.

The strange flutter in his stomach threatened to overwhelm him. Crawling up through his ribcage and wanting to tear itself loose.

Frowning at the odd feeling, one he hadn't felt with anyone else since he'd met Lily and Andrea, Felix tried to clear his head.

The elevator lurched and then started to move down.

"I'm sorry. This isn't really how I wanted it to be," Felicity murmured.

Felix grimaced, wishing he could actually reply to her.

"I mean, I'm flattered and happy that Miu tries so hard to put me into situations like this with you, but… it's not what I want.

"Not really, at least," continued the Elf. "I want you to care for me. I know I care for you, and I think it might be love but I'm not sure. I definitely want to explore my feelings with you. Figure out if this… strange heat I feel in my chest is more than just physical attraction.

"I don't want it to just be lust. Nor do I want you to feel like you're indebted, or like you've been forced into this. So, I'm sorry.

"I'll talk to Miu after this, see if she'll understand."

Felix chewed at his lip, thinking on her words.

He wasn't emotionally incompetent, but he didn't really understand why so many people wanted to share his bed. Outside of his abilities and powers, he wasn't exactly a great catch.

"And since you're probably thinking about it, it's your mind. It's your ability to see straight through to what matters and cut everything else out.

"To do the right thing, when it's the most evil thing to do," Felicity said. "That you balance it all out, top it off with what's best for Legion, and pull it back through. Everyone calls it being corporate; I call it being a very good leader.

"Your brother is a great warrior-king, but a terrible leader. If ever you two decided to join forces, I'd pity everyone who stood before you."

Join forces?

The elevator came to a stop, and the doors began to open.

The Dryads at the front of the elevator stormed out as soon as they could. Activating Warden shields held out in front of them.

Falling to their knees, the Dryads immediately enforced those shields with their Faith.

The rest of the elevator emptied out, everyone moving to get behind the shields.

Projectiles began to pound into the energy shields. They seemed like heavy rounds or even rockets, considering how bright the shields lit up.

Felix dropped down into the position designated for him. Flipping the selector to "vaporize," also named by Felicia, Felix brought the rifle up to his shoulder.

Nosing the tip of his weapon out beyond the shield, he aimed toward an intense muzzle flash and pulled the trigger on his weapon.

The kickback wasn't bad, but the bright blue stream of angry light that slammed out from the end of his weapon was explosive.

It snarled and whipped through the air, and the entire room turned blue as a number of other Legionnaires fired at the same time.

When the light from the shields dimmed like they were taking fewer hits, Felix released his trigger.

Pulling the weapon back through the energy wall of the shield, he glanced to the ammo box at the bottom of the gun.

The blue line was near the very bottom of the gauge. Pulling a new box from his utility belt, Felix pushed it into the loaded box, knocking it out, and slid the new one into place.

Picking up the nearly exhausted box, he put it into his belt while looking around him. Everyone else was seemingly going through the exact same motion, recharging their weapons and storing the spent cartridge.

Turning his attention to the areas ahead of him, he tried to see where the enemies were.

"Ass-actual. Eyes on?" he asked into his mic.

"Chair-three, I sense eight dead, two wounded," someone said.

"Odd-numbered teams, pull secondary shields and shift up. Even-numbered teams work at shifting up the primary shields," Felix said.

Working through sheer muscle memory from hours of practice, the Legionnaires began working to secure the area. The shields moved forward as others went ahead faster with portable shields.

"Seems like it was what we expected," Felix said, watching as his teams kept pushing up.

"Any fixed defense that is runs a risk," Felicity said. "It asks for someone to figure out how to break it, while it presents something to attack."

"One of the main reasons I keep pushing Felicia to finish up that portal-vator," Felix said. "I don't want the entryway leading into HQ at all."

"Portal-vator?" Felicity asked.

"Miner-one, room is clear. All foes are dark; ten is the count."

Felix turned his head toward the exit of the entry room. Now that everything was cleared and the room wasn't as hectic, Felix had to reconsider his previous words.

It wasn't quite what they'd expected. The emplacements were in the walls, behind shields that looked a lot like they were Faith enhanced.

Without the Dryads, they wouldn't have been able to move forward.

This would have been a dead end.

"Rush up and clear. Keep your shields up as you roll," Felix said. Reaching toward a pouch at his side, he pulled out two items.

One was a folded-up tripod with attached wheels. Unfolding it, he telescoped out the legs and the central pillar, then set it down in the middle of the room.

Putting the second device on top of the first, Felix fit the threaded insert into the bolt and spun it in.

Then he pulled up a bar that was attached to the middle and locked it into place.

Activating it, Felix stood back and gave it a look.

After opening up into a circle the size of a large dinner dish, a portal stabilized itself.

On the other side was a cleared-out room in the heart of Old Dungeon City.

"Miner-two, contact and resolution. Six more enemies, all dark."

That was surprising.

"Ass-Actual, coming up with the chute," Felix said.

Grabbing hold of the bar that was coming up and beyond the portal, Felix started off down toward the vault.

The reason they'd gone through with all this.

Legionnaires were dragging bodies of enemies to the sides, securing weapons, and checking pockets as he went by.

Anything could provide intel. Even something as simple as a wallet, or the receipts in their pockets.

People got lazy and tended to feel like they were safe and secure in places like this. Like nothing could ever happen.

Like someone would kill them and check their pockets.

Wheeling the portal past two large doors, Felix stopped in the center of a large room.

All along the wall were deposit boxes of various sizes. Some looked as if they could fit a body, and some looked more like shoeboxes.

Three things were clearly out of place, though. A desk, a chair, and a computer.

Frowning, Felix wasn't sure what to think. He'd been expecting boxes, a pile of gold — a single person in a cell, even.

Not deposit boxes and a computer.

"Central, we have a surprise. I need a repeat of operation Farmer, stat. Please send someone to the asset containment room. Notification on arrival, please," Felix said.

"Understood; operation Farmer to be repeated," Andrea said.

"Start opening the boxes," Felix said into the local channel. "Dump everything into the portal.

"Let's go, Legionnaires. We need to be out of here as soon as possible."

Flipping his wrist over, he glanced at his watch. It had only been five minutes since they'd entered. They had fifty-five minutes before the bank was due to reopen, but he wanted to be done within twenty-five.

It'd give him thirty minutes to schmooze at the summit.

And establish his alibi more firmly.

Chapter 11 - Parting Shot -

Felix stood watching as his people systematically continued to crack open deposit boxes. Each box got a cursory look, and then the contents were swept into a sack if they could be casually tossed around.

Anything that needed a second look got a blue tag around the handle for an inspector to come through.

If the inspectors couldn't figure something out, it got a red tag, which meant Felix needed to come by and give it a go.

There had only been a handful of those so far, and each one had looked like blackmail material owned by certain politicians. Felix had handed those over to Felicity to take care of with Lily and Kit.

It wasn't his area, but he knew the benefit in having that type of thing on hand whenever one needed.

"Contact," Andrea said over the ANet. "Three targets identified at the edge of the city heading inward. supers.

"Early trajectories show them heading toward your location. ETA is at fifteen minutes."

Felix took in a slow breath, considering the options.

Opening his channel to the entire team, he chose his course of action.

"Closing bell. Ten-minute fire sale. Done in nine, one to be out," Felix said.

He set a timer on the ANet for nine minutes and activated it.

Simply put, he ordered everyone to be out of the bank in ten minutes. That'd give them five minutes before the supers even showed up.

All around him and through the ANet, team leaders started calling orders as things were finishing up.

The ones in the vault seemed to focus and then pick out which deposit boxes they could smash open in the last rush.

Felix watched it all go down. When the timer got to three minutes, the Miner team smashed open a few last deposit boxes and started to hurry out of the room.

Felix pulled out his special present from Felicia and gave it a once-over to make sure he was holding it right.

At two minutes, the vault was empty of personnel.

Moving to the portal at the center, Felix turned the device off. Once the portal shut, he set down the black-hole bomb on top of it and pushed the button at the top.

A green circle appeared around the button. Felix held it down for several seconds.

The green circle turned red and began pulsing slowly.

And that's the five-minute timer.

Turning around, Felix started to jog back toward the elevator. Miu and Felicity were standing at the entry engaged in quiet conversation.

The rest of the team had already gone back up.

Both of them looked to him as he came closer.

"Time to go; I set up the bomb," Felix said, moving into the elevator. "Let's get in and go."

Miu and Felicity got in, Miu tapping the button to send them back to the top.

The silence between the two women was obvious, and Felix realized they'd been arguing about what had happened.

Switching his microphone off, Felix cleared his throat.

"For what it's worth, if the desired effect was to make me aware of Felicity as a woman, you succeeded, Miu," Felix said. "Just... don't throw her at me like I'm a starving dog and she's a bone, alright?

"You didn't do wrong, Miu. And you're being a good girl and behaving well."

In truth, Miu had been on her best behavior since Felicity had gotten involved.

"Listen to Felicity. She seems to be steering you in the right direction, and you two are working well together." The ding of the elevator stopped him from continuing.

Both women were looking at him now.

Miu looked as if she had been given a pat on the head and a treat, though. She was practically vibrating.

Activating his microphone again, Felix tapped into the ANet timer and looked at his watch. *One minute.*

"Time's up," Felix said. "Everyone out — go, go, go. Move to the last phase."

Moving at a quick trot, Felix headed toward the closet. The lobby was empty, and there were only a few Legionnaires left near the portal out.

Then Felix was through the portal, Felicity and Miu hot on his heels.

"Leaders, get a head count," Felix said, moving into the very full RV.

"Supers are two minutes out," Andrea said. "Technician has left the scene, and an assault and robbery report is currently being filed by someone else at the police station, according to plan."

"Everyone's on board," Neutralizer said. He held his hand up against the portal he'd been maintaining, and it suddenly closed shut. "Opening a portal to the clean zone; everyone out.

"Standard turn-and-burn protocol."

A new portal opened in the same place, but it was leading into Old Legion City.

Sighing, and feeling the collective drop in pressure from everyone, Felix marched through the portal.

Then he turned to one side and headed for an area Felicia had set aside for him personally.

As much as he tried to be "one of the Legionnaires," everyone did their best to separate him.

"This is Central; we made an error. The supers are heading for the summit, not the bank," Andrea said.

The summit? Shit.

***

Felix waited in the bathroom, adjusting his tie and feeling very anxious.

Kit would be here any minute to change places with him.

He needed her to work on the supers who had vanished off the face of the world after getting in range of the summit.

The bathroom door opened, and Felix watched himself walk through the door. He was dressed in a charcoal-colored suit with a simple gray tie.

Everything about the way he looked matched his own appearance right now in the mirror.

Closing the door, Kit-in-the-Felix-illusion looked at him and let out a breath.

"You have no idea how glad I am to see you. It's like being a shepherd for a bunch of angry dogs," Kit said in his own voice.

She gave herself a physical shake, the illusion was broken, and Kit stood there wearing a much more feminine-looking suit. Pulling at her in all the right ways.

Sighing, she pressed her hands to her jaws.

"It's a wonder you don't murder everyone around you at times. I mean, I've seen this happen to you before, but having it directed at me is very different," Kit said.

Snickering, Felix shrugged.

"It is what it is. You come to expect it after a while. Anything I need to know?" he asked.

"No, and I honestly can't remember their names, or even their designations."

"They all have telepathic blocks preventing their minds from being read. Thankfully, they'll have to reintroduce themselves once the summit formally opens in an hour," Kit said. "Though it seems like every one of them brought a pretty Beastkin woman along. And each seems poised to bounce you straight into a bed."

Snorting at that, Felix wondered if it had been wrong to not curb that rumor. They'd spent a great deal of time actually reinforcing it.

"Goodie. I'm sure Lily will be pleased," Felix muttered.

"Surprisingly, she didn't seem as annoyed about it," Kit said, a frown creasing her brow. "She's been with me the entire time, so I imagine she'll be able to guide you as needed."

"Now, if there's nothing else you need, it sounds like I have yet another job waiting for me."

"Yeah. Thanks, by the way, Kit. I couldn't have trusted that to anyone but you," Felix said. Walking over to her, he set his hand on her shoulder, forcing her to make eye contact with him. "I know you feel out of place sometimes, but honestly, I feel like you fit in perfectly as you are. Legion wouldn't be the same place without you."

Kit nodded, dropping her eyes to the ground.

"I know, and thank you. Alright, I'm going now."

Not waiting for a second, Kit turned, and with a casual wave of her hand, she walked through a portal.

And promptly shut it behind her.

Glancing into the mirror, Felix checked himself to make sure he looked the same as Kit had.

Then he smiled at himself and prepped mentally.

We're just security. We're not a national leader.

All I have to do is talk logistics, security, and what we're doing to protect them at the summit.

The only other possibility is them asking me to talk about security in Wal and how we're handling the problem with aggressive religions.

Expect them to throw their young Beastkin girls at you in an attempt to get some leverage.

And the girls probably won't even know why they were selected, other than it's part of a job.

Sighing, Felix felt tired and pressured. The supers were a concern for him, though. A big one.

A group of powered individuals lurking around the summit right after he'd robbed a bank didn't seem like a good thing.

Blinking once and clearing his mind, Felix walked to the door and left the bathroom.

Looking around, he realized he was in the large assembly hall they'd designated as an open meeting room.

It was meant to hold everyone while offering them refreshments and a chance to talk with others without cameras around.

All around the perimeter, posted at doors, even up in the rafters, Legion security was being run by Victoria.

On the outside, Ioana was running her own operation paired to Victoria's.

Men and women wandered around the open area, talking, sipping drinks, eating finger foods. They were all dressed in very professional attire. Looking every bit the heads of nations that they were.

Felix spotted Lily and three Dryads to one side.

Once more, the soul-stealing sorceress was dressed in a professional and very enticing skirt, jacket, and blouse.

She must have felt his eyes on her, because her head turned his way and she smiled.

Walking over to him, she reached out and ran her fingers along his lapel.

"Welcome back, dear," Lily said, moving up close to him.

"Is it that obvious?" Felix asked, grinning at the fact that she'd immediately known it was him and not Kit.

"Kit doesn't look at me the same way you do, silly. You tend to eye me the way a hungry man would look at a feast," Lily said, then gently pulled on his tie.

Felix couldn't help but notice the armed young Dryads watching the exchange with smiles.

"What do I need to know?" Felix asked, trying to change the subject.

"Nothing. Other than there's a horde of young Beastkin women looking for you and your bed."

"One or two per country, I believe," Lily said. "Otherwise, normal politics.

"The welcoming ceremony is going to be in about thirty minutes."

Felix smiled and then wandered over to a nearby table.

Picking up a glass of water, he looked toward the room again, wondering whom it would be best to talk to.

"Who's Kit already spoken with?" Felix murmured, Lily at his elbow.

"No one. She's made a point of checking security, walking the perimeter, and being aloof."

"Fitting for your personality to be honest," Lily said.

Makes it easy, then, to slip into this.

Picking out the prime minister of Wal, Felix grinned and set off for her. It wouldn't hurt at all to have her validate his whereabouts later on.

Heather was talking to a man in his late middle age. He was wiry. Thin.

To Felix, he looked like a problem and a half.

Walking straight up to Heather, Felix smiled at her when she turned to face whoever was on a crash course with her.

"Ah, Mr. Campbell. I must say I'm quite satisfied with everything you've put together so far for the summit," Heather said, her mouth pinching around the compliment as if it was sour.

Felix nodded to the woman and lifted his glass slightly.

"My pleasure, of course. We were hired to do a job, and we're happy to do it," Felix said. "Legion prides itself in its work and responsibilities."

"Hm. Have you met Daniel?" Heather said, lifting her free hand to indicate the man next to her. "He's here as an attaché to the nation of Meer."

Felix turned to the man and gave him a once-over. He had gray hair but looked younger than the color would imply. Otherwise, he was a fairly unassuming-looking man.

Holding out his hand, Felix gave him a normal corporate smile.

"I've heard quite a bit about you and your Legion, Mr. Campbell," Daniel said, shaking his hand.

"Oh? Good or bad? There seems to be little in the way of middle ground in the country of Wal right now," Felix said, giving his hand a few solid pumps before letting it go.

"Both, to be honest. From what I can tell after speaking with so many, though, it would seem as if you're predominantly working in favor of big government and their position on religion," the man said.

"I support whatever helps the most people and keeps the government running. I lived in Skippercity and Tilen when the Awakening happened," Felix said, with no false heat to his voice. "I think I can speak for the hundreds of thousands who died since then when I say there are a number of gods we could do without. They want only to dominate other religions and foster war.

"Religion is a good thing, and I support its growth and the good things it can do for its worshipers, but not the violent suppression of other religions."

Daniel didn't immediately respond; instead, he stared at Felix.

Deciding he didn't want to play the game he himself was so well trained at, Felix smiled at Daniel and turned to Heather.

"It was good to see you, Prime Minister. I'll leave you to it for the time being.

"I'm going to mingle some more, see if I can meet anyone interesting," Felix said. "Good day, Daniel."

Then Felix turned and moved away from the two. He wasn't about to be dragged into a religious debate right in the middle of a religious summit.

Especially when he was nothing more than the head of security for the event.

On the periphery of his vision, Felix saw a woman with red Fox-ears on the top of her head moving his way. A thick, bright red mane fell down her back. She wasn't dressed as professionally as so many others, but she certainly caught the eye in her slim black skirt and white blouse that had a few too many buttons undone.

Off to her side, several other Beastkin women with a myriad of attributes were also heading his way.

One and all, they were incredibly pretty.

Ah. There they are.

Unable to prevent the incoming event, Felix did his best to ready himself.

"Felix," came Ioana's voice over his earpiece. "I have several people at the entry who want to talk to you.

"Also, it appears Legion security is swarming all over the bank. We can see it from the steps."

Coming to a stop, Felix turned his head toward a hallway that would lead him out to the entryway.

"They have badges, and they seem as if they're here from the Heroes guild," Ioana said.

Oh? That's a bit of a surprise.

As the Fox walked up to him, Felix gave her a broad smile.

"Forgive me. You're a lovely looking Beastkin, and I'd be happy to entertain you another time, but I've just been called to the entry gate.

"Apparently we have some guests that would like to have a word with me.

"Could I have a rain check, Miss...?" Felix asked, staring into the Fox's eyes.

Blinking rapidly, the woman smiled at him, canines slipping past her lips in a ferocious smile.

"Sarah Riks. I'm a reporter. And yes, I'll take that rain check. I'll be sure to arrange an interview with your personal secretary immediately," said the Fox. She gave him a small finger wave, but she didn't walk away.

"On my way," Felix said into his microphone at his collar as he turned toward the entry.

"Any thoughts on what it could be?" Lily asked, matching him pace for pace.

"No idea. Seems quick for the other bit, but it could be. It'd mean we missed something, or they're just looking for an excuse," Felix said.

Stepping into the hallway, he looked toward the end to find a security checkpoint manned by Legion.

Off to one side was the office area—that would be where Ioana kept herself situated unless something was needed.

"It's something I'd do if I was in their position," Felix admitted. "Even if all it did was let me have a chance at interrogating someone I felt would be worthwhile."

Lily grunted and then started talking to someone on her own earpiece.

Passing through the security checkpoint without even a word from anyone, Felix turned toward the office area.

Several Adrianas were there, and they immediately stepped aside for him.

Moving into the room, Felix saw two people, a man and a woman, sitting with Ioana in her office. They were both wearing super suits that hid most of their features.

They really do need to get over the spandex.

"Hello," Felix said, moving over to stand beside Ioana. "I'm Felix Campbell. What can I do for you two?"

"We're investigators from the Heroes guild. We'd like for you to come with us back to the local precinct," said the male super. "We'd like to take a statement from you."

Both the man and the woman pulled a badge from somewhere—which was surprising, since it didn't seem like they had pockets—and set them on the desk in front of Felix and Ioana.

Glancing down at the shiny badges, Felix did a quick check with his powers.

They were both genuine, giving him their names. Both their real names and their super names.

"Well. That's awfully convenient," Felix said, looking back to the supers. "What would be the focus of the statement? The last time I had some of your kind show up, it ended in a lawsuit."

Smiling, Felix stared at the woman.

He knew she was the senior partner here, based on her rank that had been given back to him by his powers.

"I think that'd be best discussed at our local facility," said the male again.

"No," Felix said simply. "Unless Becky here can tell me what the actual reason is, this discussion is over.

"You have no legal recourse to take me anywhere without my permission unless you have some sort of charge to put against me."

The female super seemed to lock up in her seat. The eyes behind her mask were dull gray and unflinching as they stared back at Felix.

Her name was Rebecca, not Becky, but it demonstrated his point perfectly.

Blinking slowly, Felix turned his head to one side, not opting to fill the silence.

The male super stood up, looking like he was about to reach out to touch Felix.

"I wouldn't do that," Lily said from the doorway. "The last time one of your kind did such a thing, we got a nice payout from it.

"My client is well within his rights, and unless you have something relevant to discuss with him, it's best if you keep your hands to yourself."

"Unless you'd like to give us another payout," said a voice from behind Lily.

Lauren Aston, Lily's second in command, appeared, moving around the lawyer. Short brown hair and blue eyes gave her a very different look than Lily's, though every bit as attractive.

Glancing at the new arrival, Felix had to keep himself from smiling.

Lily had been keeping Lauren up to date on the comings and goings of the Heroes guild and law as far as he knew. If anyone knew all the ins and outs, it was Lauren Aston.

The male super looked at the female hero, and everyone waited.

"We'd like to talk to you about a bank robbery," Rebecca said finally.

"Oh? That's rather interesting. A bank robbery. I wasn't aware of one. Where'd it happen?" Felix said.

"Here. Right under your nose," hissed the male super.

"I haven't gotten a report on it yet. My apologies. I'll have to look into it. I've been tied up here all day with the summit, you see," Felix said. "Though I'm happy to give a statement. Just not where you want me to.

"If you want to take my statement here and now, I'll be happy to give it. Otherwise, I'll see what time I can book you in for tomorrow."

Felix patted Ioana on the shoulder and then left his hand there.

"Now, if that's all, you can leave. We're hosting a summit here to discuss global matters. We were asked to provide security for it since... well... the Heroes guild is little more than a clubhouse now.

"Isn't it?" Felix asked with a grin.

Chapter 12 - Worries -

The male super clenched his hands into fists and looked like he wanted to leap out of his seat.

"A clubhouse?" he growled from between his teeth. "It's because of people like you! People who sit on the sideline and take pot shots at us!"

Felix snorted at that.

"Hardly. You want to know why you've been reduced to under a hundred members?

"Why your resources are stretched so thin, you can't even afford to keep all your buildings open anymore?

"Why the Heroes guild, the mighty and invincible great hope that it was, has fallen and will be nothing more than a footnote?" Felix asked. "Because your leadership was full of fools."

Felix leaned over Ioana's desk toward the male super.

"Your leaders squandered your resources. If you want an example that's close to my heart, how about you go look up the incidents in Skippercity involving me.

"I'm sure you've heard about it."

"A rogue element, nothing more," said the male super, the heat in his voice rather subdued now.

"A rogue element. How quaint. Yes, that'd be what I'd claim, too. For a black-kite operation I launched but didn't want to own after the fact.

"Let's not forget what happened in Tilen afterward. The sheer scope of the surveillance that was put on myself and Legion. I wonder how much that cost? Both in manpower and resources," Felix said.

There was no response from the super this time.

"Now let's move on to the simple and easy-to-spot facts that are pretty available even to the layman on the internet.

"The guild waged a war it was never going to win against Skipper, the religious warlords, and every villain who tried to use the events in the world to their own gain.

"Your leaders frittered away lives like scraps from a plate. As if they were nothing more than replaceable pieces on a board game. And now, after spending years in this never-ending war, you've lost.

"Your resources are gone, your financial backing spent, and your members dead," Felix said, shaking his head. "For all the world to view, here lies the ruin and wreckage that was the guild. Died for an idea.

"That being right, or righteous, was all one needed to win. That doing everything honorably would lead to victory.

"And that's not the way of the world. The good guys can lose as easily as the bad guys, and who's who changes in a fraction of a second."

Standing upright, Felix let out a shuddering breath.

He hadn't meant to unleash such a tirade, but he was tired of them. Tired of what they represented.

Their goodie-goodie wholesome beliefs that would doom a world for the sake of an ideal.

It sickened him.

"I think it would be best if we got your statement another time," said Rebecca, standing up slowly.

Adjusting her suit, she continued, "For what it's worth, I believe you're right. The guild is under new leadership, and we're working to correct everything we can as rapidly as possible.

"Maybe it's too late, but it doesn't mean we'll stop either.

"Thank you for your time, Mr. Campbell."

Rebecca and her companion left the office without another word. The silence still and complete once they'd done so.

"It's odd that they're involving themselves," Lauren said, raising a hand to her throat. "Very odd. In fact—"

Lauren turned her head to one side, the hand at her neck going up towards her ear. It was obvious she was asking some questions to someone else entirely.

"You had the guy looking like he was doubting his profession," Ioana said, tilting her head to the side to look up at Felix.

"Chances are he went through sub-standard training and got pulled up into the active ranks too early. He probably has all the rah-rah stuff still in his head," Felix said. "He'll be dead before the year's out."

"Felix," Lauren said, getting his attention again. "I'd like to talk to you about this, but I don't like this location."

Ah, she's not wrong. This isn't the place to talk about anything that's Legion business.

There's no guarantee we're safe from people listening in.

"Right. Alright, let's go finish up this introductory event and get a leg back to base. We'll need to talk about this supposed bank robbery; I'm sure there's a report waiting for me with my name on it," Felix said.

***

Feeling strange, Felix rubbed his fingertips against his temples.

He felt like he should feel victorious. That simply having crushed the bank and the people who'd backed the attack on Legion was worth celebrating.

But he didn't feel it. Things felt wrong.

Off.

"Feeling like it was too easy?"

Of course, it's her.

Expecting Felicity, Felix looked up and found her in the doorway to his office.

"Feeling like something is wrong. We did exactly what we set out to do.

"We missed some loot in the end due to the supers arriving, which was odd, but that's how it goes," Felix said, then shook his head. "No, something doesn't feel right. I'm missing something. I know it."

Felicity frowned, her lips pursed. Taking a quick breath and letting it out, she walked over to him. When she stood directly in front of him, she looked down into his face.

"Felix Campbell, there will always be something you can't account for. Always.

"And for all we know, you're right," Felicity said. She reached up with both hands and began to gently drag her index fingers across his brows. "Maybe we've been outsmarted, and they did something we don't know of.

"Perhaps they know we did rob their bank."

Felix felt his skin immediately prickle at her touch. He felt the need to shiver and pull away involuntarily.

His eyes felt heavy and he closed them most of the way, not really sure what to do with himself.

Felicity pulled her fingernails down along his cheekbones, across his cheeks, and back up along his jawbone.

"And so what if they do? Let's assume they really do know it was us. That they even have some bit of proof or some idea of how we did it.

"Does it matter?" Felicity asked. "So long as we're always working as you've made Legion to do, we can change our direction and proceed. Jump tracks and fuck off, as Felicia would say."

Felix nodded his head a bit at that.

She was right. Even if they were caught out with their pants down, they could move and shift.

Felicity began to lightly use all her fingers to carefully scratch through Felix's sideburns and up into his hair.

"And when it's all said and done, we just move on to the next obstacle.

"From the files in your database, that seems to be the way of Legion in the past. Adapt and overcome," Felicity said. "This'll be no different."

Closing his eyes, Felix took in a slow breath. The anxiety he'd felt was draining away.

Felicity's fingernails methodically worked back and forth across his scalp. He could feel her fingers lightly sifting through his hair as they went.

"Now, I'd love to continue this, but I can hear the others coming. If you'd like, I'd be happy to pick it up another time," Felicity said, gently brushing what felt like her thumbs over his eyelids.

Then her cool hands were gone, and the chair next to him creaked.

Opening his eyes as a door opened, he watched as Lauren, Lily, and Kit trooped in.

"You look like you're feeling better," Lily said, smiling at him. "Needed a moment to yourself?"

"Ah, yeah. Something like that," Felix said, sitting upright in his chair.

Or just someone paying me a lot of attention I don't deserve.

"Alright, so what did you want to tell me?" Felix asked Lauren as she sat down.

"Several things. From what the IT department could pull out of that computer you found, it would seem the bank itself is going to go under," Lauren said, flipping through several documents she'd pulled out of a folio. "Their finances are skewed, and they were already going under. They also weren't completely up and up on their insurance."

Felix frowned and waved a few fingers at the paperwork.

"No need to show me. I trust you, Lauren," Felix said. "They weren't up on their insurance? How does that even happen?"

Lauren looked flustered, pushing the papers back where'd they'd come from.

"Uhm, I'm honestly not sure. I don't think it's ever happened before. It's always been backed up by the Deposit Insurance Corporation.

"But that's what it looks like through some loopholes they were exploiting. Everyone who had an account at that location probably won't get their money back from what we stole from them," Lauren said. "Some will; most won't. And the bank is probably going to go into closure."

Unable to comprehend her words, Felix shook his head. It didn't make sense. He'd never heard of a bank running all their accounts without the DIC backing them up.

Sometimes banks would offer special accounts without backing, but not everything.

Being DIC insured was a point of competition.

"Yes, it really is that bad," Lily said, clarifying the situation. "There's going to be an economic crash for all of Wal."

Felix pressed his hands to his face, thinking.

"I've prepared a few slides with some predictions," Lauren said. "I'd like to share them and get your thoughts."

Felix waved a hand at her to continue. He was still lost in his own thoughts, and this would buy him some time.

The lights dimmed, and the overhead projector came down out of the ceiling tiles.

A bright square of white light flared to life.

Lauren pivoted the projector around to the wall behind her and the others, then got up.

Everyone spun in their chairs to look at the slides.

Felix watched through his fingers.

Soft fingers trailed up along Felix's thigh, and then across his lower back.

He didn't have to look over to realize Felicity was petting him again.

And that was what she was doing. Petting him.

Soothing him.

Her fingers made small circles over his back and shoulders, unseen by all.

Adapt and overcome.

Our goal was to hurt those who hurt us.

Not those who weren't involved directly.

"...jected to turn into a large loss for everything invested in it," Lauren said, looking to the slide and indicating something on it.

Frowning, Felix interlaced his fingers and set his chin on them.

The simple answer was right there for him to take.

They'd lose nothing by returning the money they'd taken to those who were uninvolved. They could act the part of the DIC.

It'd even be viewed as assisting the citizens of Wal, and it might earn them some greater political currency.

Yes. This can be turned around to our advantage rather simply, can't it?

"Alright," Felix said when Lauren turned to open the next slide.

Felicity's hand on his back slid down and away from him, the Dark Elf leaning back into her seat as if nothing were different.

"I think that… sums it up for me. I also have an idea of what to do," Felix continued. "We have all their account information and what everyone had deposited, right?"

"Yes, I believe so," Lauren said, turning off the projector and taking her seat again.

"We'll act the part of the DIC. Buy a building we can rapidly turn over into a bank," Felix said. "Quickly as possible. I only want the Bank of the Legion to do one thing. Take deposits and hold them in trust. That's it.

"No loans, no investments — nothing."

Lauren and Lily looked at him blankly.

Kit was already hard at work taking notes, her pen scratching back and forth across the paper rapidly.

At his side, Felicity was also taking notes in her electronic ledger.

"Bribe or buy whatever officials you have to, but I want ATM cards that work at whatever ATM they go to so they can withdraw their cash as they need it.

"Hire whatever contractors and experts we need to as well," Felix said. "Use the proceeds from the belowground vault to fund all this. Put everything we took out of the main vault into a separate account as a slush fund to pay off those who were impacted by this."

Everyone was taking notes now.

"Any questions?" Felix asked.

"None," Kit said, looking at him with a wide and bright smile.

Lily looked less enthusiastic than Kit, but didn't seem put out about it.

Your inner hero is showing, Kit.

"Great. Get to work, everyone.

"I'm probably going to take the rest of the night off and work on converting as much as possible to points and getting our people back up on their feet. We still have some days of me with my powers, so I want to use it to the best of my ability," Felix said. "In other words, I'll be in my office."

Kit, Lily, and Lauren all filed out immediately, talking to one another about how to handle this most recent direction change.

Leaving him alone with Felicity again.

"Would you like me to follow you up and pick up where I left off?" Felicity asked as soon as the trio of women had left. "You seem starved for personal attention.

"I take it your wives treat you well, give you what they think you need… but they don't realize you need a bit more attention right now?

"Have you told them? Asked?"

Felix didn't respond. He didn't want to.

Lily, Andrea, and Adriana took wonderful care of him.

But by and large, they weren't as aware of when he was overworked. He was a bit too good at hiding it.

Kept it too deep down inside, it seemed.

"I'll take that as a yes. Go, away to your office. I'll join you shortly. I just want to pick up a few supplies," Felicity said. "Nothing that would even remotely be a problem. I promise it's innocent but will make this much better for both of us."

Apparently I'm just easy for you to read.

Getting out of his chair, Felix made his way to his office.

He'd made the mistake of looking at his inbox as he went. The number of unread emails was one thousand and sixty-three. And that was after they'd been sorted through, as it was still a function of the ANet right now.

"A never-ending parade of emails," Felix muttered. Settling into the seat behind his desk, he began to pick through them one by one.

"I leave you alone for a few minutes and you get right back to work," Felicity said.

Glancing up from his terminal, Felix was at a moment's loss. Then he glanced at the clock. It'd already been ten minutes and it had only felt like two.

The lock on the door turning got his attention, and he looked back to Felicity.

She was dressed in much more informal clothing now. A blue summer dress that came to her knees and a lighter blue sweater.

She had a small basket on her arm, her free hand on the door handle.

"I let Lily know I was here and asked Andrea and Adriana to do what they could for me," Felicity admitted. "Better to be obvious than underhanded."

Moving over to the couch he had in his office, Felicity sat down and patted the seat next to her.

"Come over here and put your head in my lap; we'll get back to where we were," Felicity said. "And you can talk to me about what's going on behind that mask of yours.

"Because honestly, it seems like you're keeping too much behind it lately, and you're not getting a chance to let it out."

Felix blinked, looking to the spot Felicity had indicated. He wanted to join her. He felt a strange need to sit there and be pampered.

To set down the weight of being the head of Legion for a few minutes and just be taken care of.

And he felt guilty for it. A strange, stomach-churning, self-loathing guilt.

It wasn't as if Lily, Andrea, and Adriana didn't take care of his needs. They did, and wonderfully so.

But he felt like so much couldn't be said. That they wouldn't understand.

That they needed him to be strong.

"I even made a small lunch for you as well," Felicity said. "Come on over and I'll feed you at the same time."

Felicity began to pull out what looked like small sandwiches. Cut into bite-sized squares from her basket. Next came small bits of fruit. It all went onto the small end table at the end of the couch.

"Well?" she asked, giving him a warm smile.

Surrendering to the strange need rather than the guilt, Felix gave in. He wanted desperately to put his head in her lap and give up for a time.

Felix got up and slowly went over to her.

"Take your coat and shoes off. Then lie down, put your feet up over there, and lay your head right here," Felicity said, patting her lap and setting her basket on the ground.

Doing as instructed, Felix found himself staring up into Felicity's face above him.

"There. Now… let's just—" Felicity's hands came down and lightly unbound his tie. Pulling the ends apart, she set them to each side of his collar.

Then she reached into his shirt and undid the top three buttons. She smoothed down his collar and turned her eyes back to him.

"Now, how about you start laying out all those fears in your head? I'll listen," Felicity said, her fingers sliding through his hair.

Not wanting to look into her eyes, Felix closed his own and let out a sigh.

"I'm tired," Felix said, surprising even himself when he started talking immediately. "For the last five years it's just been a constant battle. One that we were losing until Vince showed up.

"I'm blocked at every turn. My resources are being chipped away at, and I'm losing people."

Felicity began to trace along his hairline, her fingertips rubbing gently back and forth.

"Tell me all about it. All of it. I'll listen to anything you tell me without judgment," Felicity said, her voice pouring over him like a warm blanket.

Organizing his thoughts for a second, Felix decided to unload all his worries on her.

Small and big, petty and real.

Just like she'd asked.

Having children; worrying about parenthood; dealing with schools; wondering if Lily actually wanted to expand their relationship; Felicity herself; Legion; Legion's enemies.

Even something as simple as having dinner with Ioana and Felicia.

He let it out.

All of it.

Chapter 13 - Getting it Out -

Felix floated up from sleep. Within a second of his consciousness surfacing, he turned to the side and pressed his face closer into his pillow.

He really didn't want to wake up right now.

Snuggling into the soft warmth of it, Felix was determined to fall back asleep.

Barely, at the edge of his hearing, he heard a soft tap. Then two more.

A hand swept through his hair, followed by what felt like a finger brushing gently along his cheek.

Huh?

Opening his eyes, Felix forced himself to wakefulness.

As he stared into blue fabric, he didn't know what to think.

He turned his head slightly and found himself nuzzled up against Felicity's stomach.

She was quietly working on her pad, propped up on the arm of the couch. Her left hand was resting on his head, her fingers idly petting him.

As if feeling his eyes on her, she looked down at him and smiled.

"Good evening. Do you feel better? That was a fairly significant nap," Felicity said.

She slid the stylus into the pad and set it off to one side. Then she laid her right hand on the back of his head, her fingernails scratching his scalp lightly.

"What—" Felix started, feeling like his mouth was very dry. Moving his tongue around to work some moisture up, he tried again. "What time is it?"

"Mm, I think it's about five or six. You slept for around four hours." Felicity's fingers and hands hadn't stopped, smoothing his hair back and caressing his face.

"I'm sorry," Felix said, feeling embarrassed and unsure of himself.

"No reason to be. I'm flattered that you felt so secure after that deluge of concerns.

"Though if you want to apologize, I think you owe one to the Elex sisters and Lily," Felicity said, giving him a small smile.

"Huh?"

"Everything you told me is honestly everything you should have already been sharing with your wives," Felicity said, curling a finger around Felix's ear. "It isn't as if they wouldn't listen. I've had many conversations with them and think I have a fair idea about who they are as people. They'd listen.

"Which means you didn't include them for reasons that have nothing to do with them."

Blinking, Felix didn't know what to say.

"Your concerns are all valid. Even the ones about me. The guilt you feel for wanting to see where it goes with me, to fearing that I'm a spy," Felicity said, lips turning into a wide grin. "Which I'm not, by the way—but I definitely understand the thought.

"But as far as I know, you've told none of it to those you love.

"I feel like you trust me enough that I can scold you on this. If I'm overstepping, tell me."

He wanted to deny her words. To fight her, debate it and win.

But she was right. On all fronts.

Not sharing any of this with Andrea, Adriana, or Lily was an insult to them.

"No. You're... right. Kit used to play the role of my minder. Prodding me into action and the right things.

"She's... been in her own head lately," Felix said. "I can't rely on her to just pluck my thoughts out and force me. I need to be self-sufficient in stating my own needs."

"Indeed." Felicity tapped his temple with a thumb. "Now that lovely brain of yours is working in the right direction, I'm afraid you'll need to get ready for dinner. I let Jessica and Erica know you were in a good mood tonight and wanted me to ask them out for you.

"Considering how much political backing we're about to get with your bank move, it seemed like a good idea to 'butter them up' as it were.

"Get them prepped and ready."

Felix nodded, his eyes moving back to Felicity's dress in front of him.

She was right. With his most recent plan, he'd need to get both the news girls working. If he could shape the story on the first day, both good and bad, it'd be ideal.

"Tomorrow we'll have dinner with Ioana and Felicia. You'll need to say thank you for that bomb she made.

"I already bought you a present to give them," Felicity continued, as if knowing exactly when his thoughts had accepted the previous statement. "I also put together some subjects for you to prep on that they'd find interesting. They're all in the form of questions."

Uh...

Felix started to laugh softly, wondering if this is what it felt like for others when he did it for them.

"Thank you," Felix said, closing his eyes. "Let me know when we need to leave for dinner. I'm just going to... relax here."

"Of course," Felicity said. He felt her right hand leave his head, and he heard her pick up her pad again.

The fingers on her left hand started to lightly move through his hair again. Felix took in a slow breath and let it out, feeling much of the stress he'd internalized vanish.

Though one of his fears seemed to be growing.

Felicity had wormed her way into his life, and she was making herself too useful.

"Oh, I already went through your email box and physical correspondence.

"I responded to everything that needed an answer that I could handle, and I organized your inbox and email address by the things you'll need to decide on or sign," Felicity said absently as she worked at her pad, her thumb rubbing his jaw.

Far too useful, and apparently exactly what he needed.

***

Felicity was all eyes as Felix led her around Old Legion City. He'd decided to give her a formal tour once she'd admitted she hadn't really been out in the streets.

They'd started out an hour before dinner and wandered around. Felicity had taken some time out to give him a glamour before they'd left. She'd magicked his true face behind a mask so they wouldn't get swarmed or need protection.

Just as Lily had done the first time they'd gone out to Old Legion City.

"You had all this built," Felicity said. It wasn't a question.

"Yes. It only took us a year. We keep adding more to it, but we have two cities now. Old Legion City and New Legion City. They're connected at the portal plaza," Felix said.

"You need to work on your naming conventions," Felicity muttered.

They were slowly wandering down the main boulevard that led through the middle of the city.

All around them, Legionnaires moved about their business. Whether personal or Legion.

"You can build a city in under a year. Then... why are you still here? I've seen the reports. You've built a city and recruitment location on Legion Prime," Felicity said. "There is nothing on that world that can pose a threat to you."

"Because... this is home. I'd be giving up on everything here," Felix said. "Giving up on everything we've fought for already and built for here.

"And I've already run away once. I'll not do it again."

Felicity shrugged lightly, her eyes roaming over a building to their left.

A soft chime from her wrist stole her attention away.

She lifted a hand and flipped her wrist over, looking to the small watch there. "Oh, it's time to leave so we can meet Jessica and Erica on time."

"So, where are we going?" Felix asked.

"Legion's," Felicity said, looking at the street signs.

Felix chuckled and then tapped Felicity's forearm. "This way. I know the place well. Lily and I go there for our anniversary."

"Oh? That sounds like a story," Felicity said. Before Felix could get away, she slipped her arm into his and started walking with him at his side.

"It was where she took us for our first real date. When we started down the path to where we're at now," Felix said.

Then he started to worry. Started to worry about how much he hadn't been telling Lily.

And how he'd break it to her.

"I already let Lily and the Elex girls know about everything you told me about. Especially the part where you worried for them and their wants," Felicity said. "I imagine you'll get a fond greeting when you get home tonight. You're welcome in advance."

Unable to help himself, Felix found himself sighing. Again.

Felicity hadn't just maneuvered him, she'd solved it for him at the same time.

"Was she angry?" Felix asked.

"Who, Lily? No. She had suspected for a while, but I don't think she wanted to bring Kit in. She was quite grateful to me.

"I imagine she'll want to spend some time with me as well, if only to get to know me better," Felicity said. Then she shrugged. "Lily is very pretty. I wouldn't mind getting in her bed after I've secured you, if you'd agree to it."

Vince's world is so very strange.

Felix turned the corner and led Felicity on.

At the end of the street, on the corner of Felix and Legion, sat Legion's.

The restaurant had grown over the years. Apparently it had somehow gotten out that Felix frequented it for special occasions. Its popularity had already been high before then, and afterward it had exploded.

That hadn't changed its menu, service, or feel, though.

A larger layout, decorated with more expensive versions of its previous decor, and far more seating—but still Legion's.

"It looks inviting," Felicity said.

Grinning, Felix walked up to the podium on the inside of the eatery.

"Ah, welcome to Legion's. Do you have a reservation? If you do, we can seat you immediately.

"If not, we can get you a table within twenty minutes or so," said the hostess with a brilliant smile.

After a moment of déjà vu, Felix realized it was one of the high-schoolers from Tilen they'd brought with them.

He couldn't remember her name, but he remembered her.

He glanced down at her name tag when she turned to her display.

Camille.

Apparently she had graduated from Legion High and decided to work in the city, rather than the company.

"Yes, we do. It's under Felicity," Felicity said without preamble. Still holding Felix's arm.

Camille looked at Felicity and then froze. Her eyes locked on the Dark Elf, momentarily flicking to her ears.

Shit.

If he was lucky, people didn't know who Felicity was yet.

But he was betting he wasn't lucky. In fact, he was betting on everyone knowing exactly who Felicity was.

"Ah... of course. Welcome to Legion's, Felicity, Mr. Campbell," Camille said, clearly knowing exactly who he was now. "I believe you're the first of your party to arrive. Let me take you to your table."

Felicity looked at Felix with a sheepish grin. "Sorry."

"'S alright. Just drop the glamour," Felix said, then looked to the hostess. "It's good to see you again, Camille. Haven't seen you since Tilen."

"Decided you wanted to work residential rather than business?"

Felix reached out and offered her his hand as he spoke.

Smiling brightly, Camille nodded, clasping his hand in both of hers.

"Yes, sir. I did, sir. I'd heard you came here but I didn't actually think you'd show up while I was working."

"And here I am. Mind showing me to a table? We're also expecting two more people to join us, as you probably know. I'm sure they're under Felicity's name as well."

Camille scooped up four menus and then led them into the main ground floor dining room.

As they passed by numerous tables, Felix wondered where she was taking them. More often than not, he and Lily sat at tables like the ones they were passing.

Then again, we're usually in disguise.

Camille took them up to a larger and partially private corner booth, which had always been reserved one way or another.

He'd only seen people at it once, and amusingly enough it had been Adriana and Andrea eating with Lily.

Camille flipped the wooden, red-and-black reserved sign off the table and set the menus down.

Smiling, she gestured to the booth. "Your waitress will be right along shortly."

Felicity motioned for him to go first. "I want to be on the end."

Felix didn't bother to argue—he really didn't care—and clambered in. Scooting to the interior, he gently pushed away the menu in front of him.

"You already know what you want?" Felicity asked, sitting down next to him and putting her purse between them.

"Yep, same thing every time. It's delicious."

Felicity clicked her tongue and picked up the menu, starting to read it. "That's no fun. How would you ever know if you're missing out on something?"

Well.

It's not like it'd hurt me. And worst case, I can always send it back and order the normal if I don't like whatever I get.

The price of two meals here in old town is less than the price of a fourth of a meal in Wal.

Felix stared at the menu, then shrugged and picked it up.

"Why not?" he said.

Flipping it over, he began to read through it in earnest.

Felicity glanced at him and gave him a smile. She reached over with her right hand under the table and patted him on the thigh, then began to lightly rub it. "Good to see you being adventurous."

Rolling his eyes, Felix didn't bother to fight the grin.

Well, this sounds different. We'll try it.

Setting the menu down, Felix wondered briefly at the fact that he didn't feel strange about Felicity's overly familiar touching.

Then he thought about the fact that she'd had her hands all over him earlier.

None of it bothered him.

Whatever.

Looking out into the dining area, he saw a sea of faces turned his way.

Everyone could see him and was watching. He briefly waved, smiling at the patrons and acknowledging them.

"It's odd. Vince had a similar effect on the people of Yosemite, but it quickly turned into a more familiar response," Felicity said, closing the menu.

"For many, that's a more appropriate management style," Felix said, letting his hand fall.

Then he saw Erica and Jessica standing at the entry in front of the booth, hand in hand.

The dark-haired, brown-eyed Rabbit Beastkin Erica and the brown-haired, hazel-eyed Fox Beastkin were clearly in a relationship. Or so Felix believed from this point of view.

Both were pretty, though Erica was softer where Jessica had a sharp predator's look.

Ah, that explains a lot. Good for them.

When Camille started leading them over to the table, they both seemed to realize Felix was watching them.

And then that the entire restaurant was watching them being led over to Felix.

Erica turned a deep, dark scarlet, and a smiling Jessica had to pull her along.

Pushing Erica bodily into the booth until she was next to Felix, Jessica moved in behind her.

"Felix, I'm absolutely floored that you're having dinner with us publicly," Jessica said. "And flattered. You never eat with anyone like this.

"You even invited us."

Realizing the political opening was there, Felix decided to take it.

"What can I say? Erica is always so determined to get me to go to dinner. So why not take the two prettiest Beastkin TV personalities out at the same time?" Felix said.

Both Beastkin women stared at him, unsure of what to say.

"It's good to see you two," Felicity said, giving them a chance to respond.

"Ah, yes. It's good to see you, too," Erica said breathlessly, leaning toward Felicity as if she were a life boat.

Jessica nodded quickly in response.

"Good evening. My name is Amy, and I'll be serving you today," said a waitress as she sidled up to the table. "Could I possibly get you started on drinks?"

She was deliberately talking to Felix, who nodded at Felicity, who smiled at him in return.

"Could I have some of your house wine?" Felicity asked.

"Me too," Erica and Jessica said in unison.

The server turned to Felix.

He was about to decline when the words died on his lips.

"Bring several bottles, please. I think we'll end up putting them down quickly," Felix said, giving in.

The server made a note, smiled, and left quickly.

Sighing, Felix looked to the two Beastkin.

"If you ladies don't mind, I'd like to get business out of the way so I can enjoy your company tonight," Felix said.

All three women were watching him now.

"Nothing spoils an evening like work, right?" he asked, grinning at them.

Still no response, which meant he needed to keep going.

"I'll keep it simple, then. You both know we're responsible for the bank robbery," Felix said, moving on. "It seems the bank wasn't insured half as well as it claimed. It's going to go under."

Both Beastkin blinked at that. Their ears perking up.

Can't keep their inner reporters down.

"Under?" Erica asked.

"Under. As in, everyone is probably going to lose their money. So we're going to act the part of the DIC. Anyone with an account and a statement can come to the newly established Bank of the Legion and start an account.

"It'll match what they lost," Felix said.

Jessica nodded. "Giving them back what we basically stole from them. Right?"

"That's right. I wanted to get you on this now, so you could start developing your own spins on it."

"I've prepped a number of reports and data for you," Felicity said as both women seemingly went for notepads in their purses. "As well as summarized notes and points each of you can take that are unique to your positions and channels."

Of course she did.

Jessica and Erica put their bags back down.

"Oh. Alright. Thank you," Erica said.

"Yes, thank you," Jessica said.

"You two make a lovely couple," Felix said, forcing the topic away from work as quickly as he'd brought it up.

Erica and Jessica both smiled at him, the former blushing once again.

"Thanks, Felix," Jessica said. "We make time for each other here in Old Legion City whenever we can."

A small stockinged foot slipped up the inside of his calf and began to gently rub against his leg.

"But… we both agree we'd love to join your own relationship," Erica said, leaning over table towards him. Her long ears dipped towards him as well.

"Oh, that'd be fun. You're both so pretty, I'd love to explore that with you two and Felix if you're willing," Felicity said, patting Felix on the shoulder and then gently rubbing his back. "But only after I'd made sure everything was stable with Felix here and that he agreed. I wouldn't want him thinking I was cheating on him."

Not quite sure how to respond to that, Felix looked at Felicity, who continued to rub his back between his shoulder blades.

"Here we are," Amy said, setting down three bottles and four glasses. "Are we ready to order?"

Yes, please. I'd like to move this along.

I suddenly regret all of this.

It's almost as bad as when Lily was in her temptress phase.

Chapter 14 - Needs -

The soft, chirping noise of Felix's alarm clock roused him from his sleep.

Lifting his head up, Felix looked at the offending device on the night stand.

Or tried to.

He was buried under an unconscious mass of naked Elex twins. It seemed to be made of arms and legs, mostly.

Tilting his head to one side, he could see out of the tangle.

There were two Dryads dozing on the couch, and a third was on guard, apparently on duty.

She was quietly watching him sleep naked amongst the press of Beastkin bodies.

"Could you get the alarm?" Felix asked.

The Dryad nodded once and reached over to the night stand. She tapped the button on the clock before it got louder.

Sighing, Felix let his head slip back into his pillow.

He remembered escorting Jessica and Erica back to the portal plaza. Then taking Felicity to her room, where she kissed his cheek and bid him good night.

Then he'd gotten home and... was attacked by sad and upset Andreas and Adrianas. After a brief discussion and him giving them a quick rundown, they'd seemed pacified.

Right up until they'd mauled him in the bed, then coerced the Dryad bodyguards to help keep Felix "active" all night long.

"Your device is going off, not the alarm," murmured the same Dryad guard. "It has a picture of Kit on it."

Kit's calling me?

"Mind picking it up and bringing it over here?" Felix asked. "I'm somewhat pinned and she's a very heavy sleeper."

The Dryad raised her eyebrows at that, but picked up the phone and came over to him.

She held it out while letting her eyes roam over both Felix and the naked Beastkins.

They really don't have much in the way of sexual morality, do they?

Taking the phone from the Dryad, Felix checked the screen.

It was Kit.

Tapping the green receive button, he pressed it to his ear.

"Felix here."

"Ah, I see you woke up with your alarm after all," Kit said. "I wanted to talk to you as soon as possible. We might have a lead on two other people behind the attack on us."

"Oh? I'm all ears," Felix said, shoving a fluffy tail out of his face.

"The computer you found inside the lower vault had a wealth of information on it.

"It took a bit for our people to crack through the encryption without damaging anything, but... they managed it," Kit said. He could hear paper shuffling around in the background, like she was sorting things. "In the end, we were able to dig up a few names that seem like they're supporting efforts from a government, political, and public-facing side.

"Care to guess?"

Looking up, Felix found the Dryad looking at him with lidded eyes and her lower lip stuck between her teeth.

"Not really. Care to clue me in?" Felix asked.

The blonde Dryad reached up and started to fiddle with the zipper on her ballistic armor, as if contemplating unzipping it.

"It's the assistant prime minister. He recently detached himself from Heather and is running his own platform for future elections," Kit said.

"Wait, the assistant?" Felix asked, watching the Dryad as she seemed to debate stripping down.

"Yes. His name is Blake Gresham. It's thin, but... we were able to match some of the money backward to him.

"It's a lot more complicated than that, but... this feel right, but thin."

Making up her mind, the Dryad quickly unzipped her vest and began pulling it off, freeing herself from the material.

Pressing the phone to a tail nearby, Felix smiled at the Dryad.

"You're awfully pretty, but I really don't think that's a great idea. I've got too much to handle as it is," Felix said in a whisper to her. Then he pressed the phone back to his ear. "Alright. Got it. So we need to figure out a course of action to take regarding the assistant and his bid for the prime minister position."

"Are you thinking of running against him?" Kit asked.

"Hell no. Last time I ran in a race, I kicked off a war that got a city nuked. Pass," Felix said.

Watching the Dryad warily, he waited as she clearly warred with a desire to strip further. Then get into the bed.

Or actually listen to his order. The vest was unzipped, hanging off her elbows. Her hands were holding the bottom hem of her tank top.

"Though I think we can work in the background on this one. Dig up everything you can on Blake and let's meet up in a bit," Felix said.

"I've already booked a meeting with Felicity for you later today," Kit said. "Oh, and Eva came back last night. I'm sure she has a story for you."

Felix let out a sigh, then smiled. Eva was back, safe and sound.

Wait, doesn't that mean Vince is back, too?

I wonder if he killed that Dragon.

"He also sent over a massive shipment of gold. I've had it prepared for you to turn and burn down into points," Kit said. "Just waiting on you to play Necromancer."

"On my way. And tell Vince I would love to see him," Felix said turning the phone off. He started to push the Elex sisters out of his way.

He wanted to get his people back on their feet.

Immediately.

The Dryad gave him a sad look, then pulled the vest back on and zipped it up. Grabbing her SMG, she gave him a flirty smile.

"Next time?" she asked.

Felix ignored her question.

Great.

At least she's got her head on straight when it's time for business. Though she did kind of abandon her post.

***

Felix's morning was the very definition of busy.

The gold Vince had sent over was vastly more valuable than gold from this plane. So much that Felix had just burned it all immediately to points and resurrected his Legionnaires.

All of them.

It was the first time in a long time that the casualty list was empty.

That there was no one in the morgue.

That all his people were up and alive.

And now for the last hour, he'd been listening to Eva spin him what sounded like a fantasy story. Most of it seemed impossible and unlikely, but since Eva was telling it to him, he believed it.

"...then we came here. Sent the gold over, and we've been recovering," Eva said.

"It just seems so incredible. To fight a Dragon, win, marry it, and wage a war with limited forces while on the run," Felix said, shaking his head.

"Vince seemed absolutely determined to fulfill his end of the bargain for the tech you sent over," Eva said. "I get the impression he feels indebted to you in a way he can't repay."

"Mm. I can almost say the same," Felix said, shaking his head. "Everyone is up, Eva. Everyone. And the Dryad's magic cuts right through Faith magic. As if it weren't there.

"We're... winning. Or if we're not winning, we're not losing anymore."

"Wait, everyone is up?" Eva asked, peering at him.

"Yeah. Everyone."

"How?"

"Vince's gold. It's worth more than normal gold. It's a planar import. It isn't even from this world. Or universe. Or whatever it is. But it's completely foreign, so it was worth a lot more."

Eva opened her mouth, then closed it. Then she started to laugh softly.

"So... what the Campbell brothers needed was each other?" Eva asked. "That's oddly coincidental."

Hm. No. It isn't.

Or at least, I don't think it is.

Another question to ask you, Mr. Benefactor.

"Felix, Vince is here," said the Andrea manning his secretary desk.

"Send him in immediately—great," Felix said.

Seconds later, the door opened, and Vince walked through it.

Smiling warmly, Felix stood up.

"Brother," Felix said.

Behind Vince was a pretty and dangerous-looking woman. She had black horns coming out of her head and looked to have scales covering parts of her face.

This must be Taylor. The black Dragon Vince defeated and bedded.

He went to slay the Dragon and lay with it instead.

Covering the distance quickly, Felix wrapped his arms around Vince and gave him a tight, brotherly hug.

"It's so good to see you. I was just talking to Eva about your trip. I'd not been able to really sit down and hear the tale until now.

"Would you and your companion join us?"

Felix could practically feel Vince try to flinch away from the hug. Clearly he wasn't used to anyone being familiar with him who wasn't one of his wives.

"Yes, we will. This is Taylor, my black Dragon," Vince said, nodding his head to the woman beside him.

"Hello," said the black Dragon named Taylor.

"She's the black Dragon he fought and proposed to," Eva said, confirming Felix's earlier thought.

Taylor smiled wide at that and nodded quickly.

"He defeated me in martial combat as my Dragon. It was very... impressive," she said.

The sexual desire in her voice was like a taut violin string having a bow drawn across it.

Their home must really be sexually charged.

"Come, sit, sit," Felix said, gesturing to the chairs and releasing Vince.

"First, let me just say thank you. Those Dryads you sent to assist us—me—were exactly what we needed.

"Exactly what we needed when we didn't even know we needed it. Their spells and belief cut through the enemy as if they were nothing.

"And the fact that they're all able to fight, heal, and use magic makes them beyond useful. It only took them a day to adjust and adapt to firearms and body armor," Felix said, wanting to give Vince his thanks before anything else could be said.

"At least, it worked out after that day-long orgy. I had no idea Dryads were actual Nymphs," Felix said, remembering the reports he'd gotten the next day.

"Did they settle on one man? My understanding is a grove calms down considerably once they've settled on one man," Vince asked.

"They did and you're right. They calmed right down after that.

"Amusingly enough, Eva's brother. Evan," Felix said smirking. "He's, uh... been indisposed ever since.

"Though I'll gladly trade him for the Dryads and consider myself light years ahead."

"Evan won't complain. I managed to get him to pick up the phone. He sounded exhausted, but… happy," Eva said, her tone amused.

Standing up, Eva clapped her hands together. "Alright Taylor, you come with me and we'll leave them to chat without us."

Taylor frowned, looking at the younger woman. It was obvious she didn't want to leave.

"It's alright, we won't go far," Eva said. "I promise."

Putting a hand to Taylor's back, Eva led the other woman from the room.

When the door closed behind the two women, Felix looked to Vince.

"So… you came through for me with flying colors, Vince."

"Your Dryads are the perfect accompaniment to my own forces, and the amount of gold you sent over is… astounding. I'm also told it isn't completely done yet, and more is being sent.

"On top of that, since it's from a different… plane… it's worth a lot more to me than regular gold. Even if it's the same thing."

"Huh. Does that mean you want to exchange gold for gold then?" Vince asked, jumping to a thought Felix hadn't even considered yet. "As for me, I'd say the same. Your Wardens and artillery managed to change the battlefield for me.

"We pushed everyone back from the front and retook what we'd lost."

Chuckling, Felix wasn't quite sure what to say at first.

"It seems we both gave the other what he needed, then.

"And yeah, I'd be willing to pay extra gold to get more of your gold in exchange for it," Felix admitted.

"Alright, we could do that. I'll just need to get someone to work on it," Vince said dismissively.

"I'll talk to Felicity. She's… an amazing woman," Felix said, wondering again at how quickly she'd inserted herself into his daily thoughts.

He hadn't even considered going to anyone else.

"Yes, she is. Is she working out well as an envoy?" Vince asked.

"Very much so. Now, enough about business. I hear I have a massive number of nephews and nieces," Felix said, leaning forward. "When can I come meet them? I've gone to your world once or twice, but I haven't managed to stay long enough for them to all be brought together.

"I admit, I'm rather excited to have family."

"Whenever you want to drop by," Vince said with a grin. "And yeah… there's… a lot.

"But I'm sure they'd all be happy to meet their uncle."

I'm going to spoil them rotten, fill them up with sugar, and tell them you want to play hide and seek. Then sit back and watch.

***

Felix was sitting at his terminal, working through paperwork that needed his signature.

Things Felicity couldn't do without him.

He needed to get most of this done tonight, because after tomorrow it was unlikely he was going to have much time to himself.

So many planned interviews, it's not even funny.

Interviews, board takeovers, contract pull-outs, and lobbying. Going to be a busy, busy election period.

All while managing the summit.

Tapping the pen against the paper in front of him, Felix double-checked his signature. Finding it to be exactly what he'd expected, he picked the paper up and dropped it in his outbox.

Then he grabbed the next in the stack.

Reading it over, he slowed down as he started to digest its contents.

Felix frowned, not sure what to think of it.

Mr. White had put in a letter to request a formal transfer over to Vince.

As if Vince and Felix, Yosemite and Legion, were part of one larger company. And one could just put in a transfer request and be moved over, as simple as that.

Setting it to one side, Felix picked up the next paper in the stack.

When he got to the bottom of it, he was just as perplexed.

It was a carbon copy of a similar request Felicity had sent to Vince and his people. For her to be formally transferred into Felix's service.

Closing his eyes, Felix set his chin in his hands and thought.

Losing Mr. White would be a blow; he's very useful. His apprentices aren't bad, but he himself is quite a creative man.

Gaining Felicity would be a nearly equal worth in exchange though, wouldn't it?

Trade one for one, and it almost seems I might be getting the better deal.

But... am I being biased? Is it because I might have some burgeoning feelings for the girl?

Felix grimaced, feeling his eyebrows press together.

His thought felt like a lie.

I'm biased. Because she's interesting, pretty, smart, and has interest in me. She's not crushing me into the ground like Lily and Andrea did, but she's cornered me and is letting me make the moves.

If I tried to slip away, she'd come for me.

But if I told her no, she'd back off.

Do I want to tell her that anymore, though?

Wait, no — this is all garbage. We need to evaluate the trade on its merits. On what's offered and —

Felix growled and snatched up his pen. Rapidly, he signed both documents and flicked them into his outbox.

"That seems rather aggressive for you, love," purred a voice from in front of him.

Looking up, he found Lily at the door, leaning against the frame and watching him.

"Care to share?" she asked.

Immediately, Felix wanted to say it was nothing. That it didn't matter.

Except that'd be exactly what he'd been doing up to this point.

"I was having difficulty keeping my head clear in debating if Mr. White was worth Felicity in trade," Felix said, gesturing at the paperwork. "They both put in for a transfer and they happened to hit my desk at the same time."

"Well, no, that's not true. I'm sure she did it that way on purpose."

Lily smiled with one side of her mouth and nodded her head a bit. "It does sound like Felicity. She's every bit your equal in administration. Not so strong on the leadership side, or on figuring out how to really screw the other guy over, but definitely an administrator."

Pressing a hand to his face, Felix pulled it down as if to scrub away his thoughts.

"And the other bit doesn't concern you? That I'm biased and predisposed to want to keep Felicity nearby?" Felix asked.

"It did," Lily said, nodding slowly. "And it still does. A little. But not much.

"I've had a few Minders poke around in her head. Kit, too. She genuinely has feelings for you, though they're all tied up with a strange... carnal desire that no one can seem to explain."

Lily pushed off from the door frame and came his way.

"From everything I can tell, she just wants you for you. She's willing to do whatever she has to — to get you," Lily said, pausing to sit in the seat across from him. "Though I'm flattered that she's actually interested in me as well. She thinks I'm gorgeous and has even fantasized about me a few times."

Felix chuckled at that and set his elbow down on his desk, propping his chin up on it. "You are gorgeous though, idiot. I've told you that many times."

"You don't count as much anymore. My charms no longer matter to you, and you'll just say whatever you can to bed me," Lily said, grinning at him.

"Well, the last bit is true, but the first part is wrong. Your charms are ever charming," Felix said. Then he reached out with his free hand and tapped the paper. "I'm going to go through with the exchange unless you have a reason I shouldn't."

"I don't. Not really. Now, how about you come to bed?" Lily said. "I'm feeling needy for your attention, and there's this busty little blond Dryad that keeps making eyes at you.

"I'm feeling particularly awful and a bit territorial. Since she's your bodyguard, she'd have to watch... wouldn't she?"

What the...?

Lily gave him a wicked smile, her fingernails lightly tapping along his desk.

Things were changing around him more than he realized.

Even Lily seemed like she was changing.

Taking in a quick breath, Felix looked at his papers. "Alright. I might as well. We'll be making some moves tomorrow, so I might as well hit the sack."

"Oh? Moving ahead with your plan to get Blake out of the picture?" Lily asked.

"Yeah. I also want to contact the person running against him. One... Kevin Dane.

"This'll be a complicated nightmare of trying to get public opinion going for our candidate and against Blake. On top of that, I'll be doing everything in my power to pressure the governing bodies to be on our side, since they can cause problems," Felix said, getting up from behind his desk. "Now... you were saying something about a bed and the Dryad?"

Chapter 15 - Reset -

"Here you go, dear!" chirped Andrea happily, setting down a Styrofoam container in front of him on the counter.

"And equally as important, here's mine, dearest," Adriana said equally as happy, setting down another Styrofoam container next to the first.

Picking up both containers, Felix turned and moved away before they could start trying to convince him one was better than the other.

This breakfast civil war is... just too tiring to deal with anymore.

Though I'm glad to see their food truck venture is doing so well.

Glancing to the long line sprawling out from the truck, he chuckled to himself.

Miu, Felicity, and Victoria were moving around him in a triangle. His normal bodyguard group a was bit further out, but still encircled him.

"We're not going to eat?" Felicity asked. In one hand, she had two containers of her own, in the other a carrier with multiple coffees.

Glancing back at the food truck in front of the expo-center, Felix shook his head.

"Nope. Andrea believes world peace could be achieved through pancakes.

"Adriana defied the world order last year when she proclaimed waffles were better," Felix said. "I can't eat one or the other in front of them without having to eat both completely."

"Oh. I see," Felicity said, clearly not quite understanding.

"I prefer Adriana's waffles," Miu said.

"I still like the pancakes," Victoria countered. "Reminds me of when I first joined Legion."

Glancing at the two, he wondered at the change in them recently.

Victoria had taken to acting as his personal bodyguard again lately. Taking every opportunity to do so without wearing a helmet.

Miu had become less aggressive with others, but far more clingy, and had given up her own responsibilities to be his personal bodyguard as well.

Feels a lot like it used to back in the day. Not sure if that's a good thing or a bad thing.

"Then when are we eating?" Felicity asked.

"Soon as we turn the corner," Victoria said. "Just can't let them see us is all. Felix likes to eat some of both, but he can't finish either one."

Felix shrugged, not arguing.

"Give me the rundown on this. I read the report, but I'd love a direct explanation," he said.

"There's been an ongoing disturbance back here. The number of days between each occurrence varies and it's always at different times," Victoria started to explain. "The cameras don't pick anything up, and there's nothing actually visible. Except the tech team swears up and down that when they point some equipment in that area, they get readings. They just can't catch it right as it happens."

"Ok, so why don't we just drop a team on it and call it done? Don't we have people on staff for exactly this?" Felix asked.

"We do, but they're all busy. With our recent contract acquisitions, namely the summit, everyone who can be committed *is*. Those who aren't were in the morgue for a while. They're a bit out of date, and there's no one with enough experience amongst them to lead this."

"Suppose that answers my next question," Felix said. "I was curious why you scheduled an interview for the same time period. I thought you'd just double-booked me or made a scheduling error."

"Of course not. I make sure to be very careful with everything I put on your calendar," Felicity said.

"I trust Felicity. She's impeccable," Victoria said.

"Felicity wouldn't make a mistake," Miu said at the same time.

Felix raised a brow and looked to the other two women. Neither had even considered for a second that Felicity had done something wrong.

And they'd defended her instantly.

"Right. That wasn't strange at all," Felix said under his breath, turning around the corner. They were officially out behind the expo now.

Security was tight all the way around the building, but the back and side yards didn't have immediate or direct access to the entry points.

Which meant security was a bit less over here. If something were to happen, it would probably be here.

Though technically there wasn't much someone could do here. Hence the lower security level.

"Right there." Victoria pointed to a rather ugly modern-art sculpture. It looked almost like someone had just started smashing at a stone block with a hammer to Felix's eyes.

Random areas were flattened out like cubby holes.

There was a pedestal next to it that probably explained the art.

Damn well guarantee I'd need that, since these things never make sense to me.

"What, the broken column thing?" Felix asked.

"Yes, that. The origin point for the disturbance is right behind it," Miu said.

Wandering over, Felix gave the area a once-over.

He didn't see anything out of the ordinary.

"And the cameras don't see anything?" Felix asked, looking up to the corner of the building. There was a camera trained on this exact spot.

"Not a thing," Victoria said.

"Right... so... why am I here?" Felix looked from Victoria to Felicity.

Sighing, Felicity set one of the containers on the pedestal and set the carrier full of coffee on the edge of the stone platform the art was on.

She opened her container, reached in, and pulled out a pancake. Folding it over on itself, she began eating it dry.

"Because I need you to hire someone to take on this investigation and then assign resources to them," Felicity said after swallowing. "I don't have the ability to do that for you."

Felix thought on that.

It was true, of course. Ultimately, almost everything came down to him and his choices.

Kit, Lily, Miu, Ioana, Felicia, and Victoria could all make hirings without him for their respective departments. And they could requisition resources.

As his admin, Felicity dealt with larger things but needed permission.

"When we get back, draw up some type of authorization that lets you act in my stead for all things up to company-wide decisions. Equivalent to any other department head, really," Felix said. "No, you said I was interviewing someone. Where are they?"

Felicity, Miu, and Victoria had gathered around the coffee carrier and were pulling coffees out for themselves.

"I'll draw up the paperwork as soon as we get back. Thank you... for that.

"As far as your interview, it's Detective Torres."

"I found a request you had made to find her. So I did," Felicity said, taking a sip of her drink. "Then this came up, so I decided I'd answer your request, see if she was interested in a job, and possibly solve two for one."

"She needs a job?" Felix asked, puzzled.

"After Tilen fell, she moved around a bit. Landed a few police jobs but was only ever a recruit," Felicity said. "They didn't take her time into consideration with Tilen and almost seemed to fault her for it.

"Or so it read on her personnel files that we looked into."

Miu and Victoria wolfed down their food and drink like ravenous wolves, then immediately returned to their duties of guarding Felix. Both women scanned the area around Felix as if the loose circle of bodyguards thirty feet away wasn't there.

"Odd," Felix said.

"Not really. I looked into some of the official records. The number of refugees moving into Wal has been considerable. This has put a fairly large strain on the economic situation here." Felicity nibbled at her pancake while talking. "Honestly, half the stability Wal enjoys is simply due to the fact that Legion moved in. The company practically single-handedly propped everything up."

Felix couldn't argue that. He could remember loaning the government a substantial amount of capital in the early years.

They'd pay him back—and with interest since then, of course.

"So where did she end up?" Felix asked.

"Working as a coffeeshop barista," Felicity said. "She has no family, no attachments, and a small social circle.

"With her highest form of education being a master's in criminal justice, I felt she would be an excellent Legion candidate."

That's a lot of degree for very little wage.

Such is the way of the world. Take on a truckload of debt for the slim promise of a better job, then watch as everyone with experience take those jobs.

Legion is definitely in the wrong business. College degrees are a surefire, easy way to make money.

Get-rich-quick scheme to sell those educations.

"Ah, here she comes." Felicity's eyes moved behind Felix as she spoke.

Looking over his shoulder, Felix saw Detective Torres heading his way.

She was dark skinned, with brown eyes and short, straight black hair. He remembered her as pretty, and she still was, but she looked as if the world had beaten her down a few too many times lately. Aging her prematurely, putting years on her.

She was dressed in a white shirt and black slacks, with a coat. Dressed for an interview and looking well put together.

But Felix could see it in the way she was carrying herself. In the slight wear of the elbows on her coat. That her collar wasn't quite crisp.

She's on the edge of giving up, isn't she? Let's move this from temporary employment to permanent. Hate to see a talent wasted.

Putting both his containers down on the podium, Felix turned to face Detective Torres.

Well, she's not really a detective anymore, is she?

What's her first name, then? I can't call her detective.

"Her first name is Edith," Felicity said.

"Get out of my head. It's dangerous in there. Full of rusty bear traps and disturbing thoughts," Felix muttered.

"'Shower thoughts' is what Kit said they were. Apparently you have a very active imagination," Felicity said, to which Miu and Victoria chuckled.

Edith was picked up by the Dryad portion of his bodyguards and brought in to him.

"Miss Torres, a pleasure to see you," Felix said, holding out his hand to her.

"Mr. Campbell." Edith's eyes locked on him as she shook his hand. He figured she was trying to determine whether this was a real interview or not, given the location.

"It's a real interview, but not in the way you think," Felix said.

Edith let go of his hand and looked at the women around him, then finally back to him.

"Do tell," she said.

"I want to call in that favor you owe me," Felix said, getting straight to it. "I have a job I want you to do. An investigation.

"After that, we'll see where you end up. But you'll be in the Legion. A Legionnaire.

"I haven't needed a police force up to this point. Not really. But I imagine it wouldn't be a bad idea to start putting one together.

"So depending on where this goes, I might need a police chief."

Turning to Felicity, he gave her a smile and held out his hand to her.

He figured she already had an entire pay folder put together for Edith. If she didn't, he'd be damned surprised.

Shifting her coffee to her right hand and digging in her bag with her left, she dug out a single folder with three tabs and handed it over to him.

Flipping open the cover, Felix read the tabs.

Twenty-fifth percentile, fiftieth percentile, eightieth percentile—that was what they read.

Adjusted salary against the market value. You're a treasure, Felicity.

Flipping to the red one, which was the max, Felix found a standard Legion contract.

"Felicity, do you happen to have a modified contract in your bag? I would have probably called it a 'Buildup package' in the HR database," Felix said.

"I do; one second."

Felix smiled at Edith and gestured at the container. "Care for some waffles or pancakes? Or a coffee? We have plenty of all of that."

"No thanks. I've grown a distaste for coffee and I already ate," said the grim-looking Edith.

Felicity held a small pack of papers out to Edith.

"Great, so here's the deal, Edith. I want to hire you to figure something out. That's the contract."

"It comes with a number of perks and benefits. Feel free to read it over and—"

Edith pulled a pen out of her jacket pocket, flipped to the last page, signed it, and held it back out to Felicity.

"Now what?" asked the woman who was once again Detective Torres. She was clearly beyond her wits end. She didn't even ask what her salary would be.

Felix chuckled and gave his head a shake.

"Well, for starters, we wind your clock back a number of years, fix you, and give you some powers, Detective Torres. After that, I have a folder for you to read over with your job duties, salary, and current project," Felix said.

He had one more day before he would lose access to his powers. He'd spent all of yesterday doing maintenance and upkeep on various projects he'd had his eye on. Today his points were free until close to midnight, when he'd convert them to gold.

"What?" she asked.

"Probably should have read your paperwork. That's on you, though," Felix said, then stabbed the accept button on the build-up window he'd created for her.

Detective Torres locked up as if she'd been hit by a taser, then slumped to the ground.

"Right. Time to eat, then," Felix said, turning to the container. When he popped it open, he found it was the Adriana waffles.

He picked one up, taking a deep smell and then a big bite.

If only they could cook anything other than waffles and pancakes.

Although this is still better than just pancakes. Having alternatives is great.

Chewing happily, Felix watched as Edith Torres literally shed years off. The lines and hard edges on her face smoothed out and simply vanished.

Soon, she looked like she was only twenty years old. Practically fresh out of college, even.

"Wow, she was younger than I thought," Felix said aloud.

"Her file said she was thirty-eight, but there is the possibility she lied on it to command greater respect? Is ageism a thing here?" Felicity asked.

"Yes. It very much is. Especially if things are run by a bunch of old people who think the generation after them is full of a bunch of lazy, directionless kids.

"Funny—they broke the world and created the problem, and somehow we're supposed to fix it for them." Felix shook his head. "Joke's on her, then, I guess. I had dialed it back to put her in her mid-twenties. She'll be lucky if she's twenty at all."

A single deep chime came from his wrist. Lifting his hand up, Felix flipped his wrist over and looked at the display screen.

Urgent email from Kit.

The screen buzzed, then chirped again.

Urgent email from Lily?

It buzzed three times more, and he saw urgent alerts from the HR department and both Laurens in the Legal department.

Rather than opening the email, Felix tapped the icon next to Kit's name and then pressed a finger to the earpiece he had in.

The line clicked once.

"This is Kit," said the voice on the other end.

"Hey Kit, what just happened? I got several email alerts. Urgent ones," Felix said, watching Detective Torres struggle to get to her feet. Her change having been completed.

"Felix! Good, great. I'm glad I got you on the line. We have to immediately act on this," Kit said.

"Act on what? I didn't read your email yet; I just called you instead."

"What? Oh. Oh! Ah, the Wal Supreme Court is hearing a case on Legion."

"A case was put forward for an anti-trust hearing. They want to break up Legion into smaller pieces," Kit said.

Felix's breath caught in his throat. He didn't quite know how to respond. The very idea of them moving on Legion was laughable. His company was so diversified that no one could ever hope to call them a monopoly.

But this wasn't about right or wrong. This was about someone trying to hurt him.

To hurt his people.

"Blake Gresham is on the plaintiff list," Kit said.

"Right. Ok," Felix said, his brain spinning up furiously as he thought through the situation. "Can we reach out to any governments to have them accept us as a corporation?

"Even if they attempt to break up Legion, if we just move our HQ to another country that accepts us, then we're fine as far as the legalities of being 'Legion' and everyone still being together."

Felix paused and thought on the situation.

"No. I already reached out to a number of embassies as soon as the news broke and we were served papers," Kit said. "They're all sitting on the sidelines here. Though the PM seems rather miffed about all this.

"If we go down, she goes down, too."

Pressing a hand to his head, Felix closed his eyes and thought.

Yosemite. That'd be legal, and my powers would remain active, right?

"Send a formal delegation and a company officer to Vince. See if he's willing to sign for Yosemite. That'll take care of our legal side for my powers," Felix said.

"Yosemite? I... no, that'd work. Ok, yes. I'll do that immediately. Anything else?" Kit asked.

"No, but get Lily as much in the way of resources as she asks for. This is going to turn into a real circus in the courts," Felix said. "We'll need to really pull out all the stops. See if we can't figure out if it's an individual judge from the Supreme Court hearing the case, or all of them.

"Then see what we have on them and how we can influence this. Alright?"

"Got it; on it. I'll update Felicity as I go," Kit said. Then the line clicked, and she was gone.

Tapping up a simple message with a few finger swipes, he sent an email off to Lily. Indicating he was now aware and she should link in with Kit.

When he turned back around, he found an angry-looking Detective Torres. She looked as if she was about to burst out of her coat and blouse, along with being decidedly younger.

She really did look like a college student.

"What'd you do to me?" she asked, and her voice even sounded different. Higher. Lighter.

"I hit reset on you, basically. I had you put to your 'default' state, as it were. What you would be if you hit all your genetic markers without influence from anything in your past.

"In other words, if a lack of nutrition in your youth caused your body to develop differently, I just removed that," Felix said, giving her the short version. "That and built you up some. You're a bit of a powered now."

"I don't understand any of this," Edith said, looking down at her much-larger chest. "Did you do this?"

That's kinda weird, actually. I wonder what happened there.

"Ah, no. I didn't.

"The simple answer is I made you the best version of yourself. And the cost of that modification is very high, as stated in the contract you signed. You're mine now," Felix said with a grin. "Welcome to the Legion, Legionnaire Torres."

Felix flipped open the folder still in his hand and fished out the project with all the reports.

"Your orientation to Legion will probably be today. That'll include everything you need to know and how to find answers for anything else.

"Your apartment will probably be cleaned out tonight and moved over to your new residence.

"You'll probably be squared away by tomorrow night, if I don't miss my guess," Felix said. "That's mostly handled by HR and doesn't require much from you. Here's your duty assignment."

Edith grimaced at him, stepping out of her shoes.

"Even my damn shoes don't fit," she complained.

"Yeah, something was seriously wrong in your childhood. You kinda grew... all over," Felix said, gesturing at her with a hand. "Anyways, welcome to the Legion."

Felix grinned at her and happily started eating his waffle again.

He was doing his best to put on the mask of himself that everyone knew.

The calculating boss that took delight in surprising his employees.

Even if he was panicking internally at the idea that Legion was under attack in more ways than one.

Chapter 16 - Curiosity -

Felix had his portable light-terminal out in front of him. His fingers rapidly tapped along the keys as he modified his internet search again.

He knew Lily was working on the same thing from her office, but he didn't want to sit around and do nothing.

Taking a second, he looked over his shoulder.

Edith, Victoria, Miu, and Felicity weren't far away, probably still going over the details of the case.

That or other cases they're assigning her. Who knows.

Looking back to the screen, Felix sighed.

He didn't have another meeting on the books for another thirty minutes.

Reaching across the picnic table, he opened the container and peeked inside.

Yep, still no more food.

He flicked a finger against his coffee cup and found it empty as well.

Briefly, he contemplated going back to the truck and getting more.

No, I don't need it. I'm nervous, anxious, and a little bored. I'm eating to fill the void.

Just... keep searching. If I can at least be well versed on similar cases, I can probably follow along with Lily's explanation later.

Maybe.

"I'll go get you another coffee and some fruit," murmured a voice next to his ear.

Looking to his side, he found the blue-eyed, blond-haired Dryad bodyguard who constantly invaded his space and his bedroom.

"Thanks," Felix said, genuinely thankful, even if she did get too close at times.

Bouncing away, the Dryad shouldered her battle rifle and pulled her Kevlar face mask down into place.

Felix turned his attention back to his screen.

Except he just didn't have the care or desire to complete his search. To dig through numerous results in his quest to find information on anti-trust cases.

Closing the terminal, and feeling a bit angry at his inability to do anything right now, Felix pressed his face into his hands.

He wasn't sure how long he sat like that, but eventually the soft tap of something against the table got his attention.

The Dryad was already walking away, but sitting in front of him was a coffee cup and an apple.

Picking up the cup, Felix took a sip and sighed.

I'm being childish. Leave it to the people who are paid to worry about situations just like this.

For all I know, Lily already has a plan in place. Hell, she might have already prepared for something like this.

I could be worrying over nothing at all.

Nodding, Felix looked back to the group by the art installation.

Except there was a child and a man standing there. Talking to Miu and Victoria.

He sensed some definite tension in the situation as well. It looked like the kid and Victoria were having a disagreement.

Miu took a sudden step forward, and the man held his hands up in front of him.

Before anyone could react, a bolt of lightning jumped from one hand to the other. A boom of thunder pealed out and made Felix's teeth ache. The hair on the back of his neck stood on end, and his skin prickled from head to toe.

Power radiated out of that simple spell. Pure, unadulterated power and a threat to use it.

Except the man was holding his hand out to Miu in the universal stop gesture.

Tapping his wrist communicator with Felicity's contact card, he watched as she glanced down at her own wrist and then looked across to him.

Felix waved a hand at her, beckoning her over.

The man and the child hadn't missed the gesture and beckoning, either. Turning, they started toward Felix.

Making Miu, Victoria, and Felicity all seemingly panic.

Then his bodyguards noticed it and went on instant alert.

Guns were drawn and leveled at the approaching duo.

The child seemed unfazed, walking unerringly straight toward Felix. Though apparently, he was aware of the situation, because he stopped twenty feet out from Felix. Just a few feet in front of the ring of his bodyguards.

"Hello, my name's Al," said the boy loudly, attempting to speak with Felix from this distance. "I wanted to look at the area, but they said I couldn't."

Felix gave the kid a quick once-over. He looked like he might be somewhere between eight and twelve, but Felix was awful at guessing kids' ages.

He had bright blond hair and green eyes. Dressed in jeans, t-shirt, and jacket, he otherwise appeared every bit a normal kid.

The man with him was a bit different, though. He had brown eyes, so dark they were almost black.

His straight black hair lay flat on his head. Though it had a strange "about to go bad" look to it. As if his hair was naturally wild.

Must have some wicked-to-control hair.

"Let them over," Felix called as the rest of his bodyguards spread out around the duo.

The child and the man walked over casually.

"Hi, I'm Al," repeated the child, smiling at Felix. Then he gestured at the man next to him. "This is Uncle."

The man smirked at the title and held out his hand to Felix.

"I'm Felix." Taking the other man's hand in his own, he gave it a firm shake and then looked back to the kid.

"And why would you want to look at the area? This entire location is currently under heightened supervision and security," Felix said.

"Because that's where the trail goes," Al said simply. "Extra security?"

"There's a summit being held. Foreign nations are all coming here to discuss the problem with certain religions," Felix said. "What do you mean by trail?"

"The trail. I'm following a trail. It led me here. I don't think I can follow it further, though. This seems to be the origination point," Al said.

"Uh huh." Felix looked to the man for help. Wondering if he could get any more information there.

Except the man was watching the Dryads nearby. It was almost as if he was unconcerned with everyone around him, more interested in other things.

"Don't mind Uncle. He likes to look, but he's married," Al said, apparently catching the look on Felix's face. "Can I look at the location?"

"It depends. You said you're following a trail. A trail of what? To what end? Why?"

"That location is under an investigation for us. We're attempting to make sense of what keeps happening there, but we can't seem to figure it out," Felix said.

"Oh. That's easy enough. If I help your people determine the cause, may I inspect the area?" Al asked.

Felix thought about it.

This entire situation was too strange. It felt more like the divine were getting involved here. There was too much unanswered and too many open questions.

Al was clearly being evasive, and the casual disregard "Uncle" had for everyone around him was unnerving. Not to mention the power he'd put on display.

"While we're working on the investigation, Uncle will help protect everyone. He's a very accomplished wizard," Al said, smiling and nodding. It almost seemed like pride.

"I'm gonna what?" Uncle said, looking back to Al. "Hey. What the hell, brat? If your Dad gets wind of this he's going to turn your ass red, and I'll get a chewing out I really don't want."

Al waved a hand at Uncle as if his concerns didn't matter.

"No, he won't. Dad trusts you and that you're with me," Al said. Then he looked back to Felix. "Well?"

As subtly as he could, Felix tried to pull open a window to see Al's stats.

Except it failed.

There wasn't even a message about not being able to. Nothing happened.

Repeating the same exercise for Uncle, Felix got the exact same results.

Ok, yeah, this is divine. Who's his dad, though? Did the delegates bring their own pantheon and divine problems with them?

Is Wal about to get turned into a holy war?

Shit.

Shit, shit. Fuck, shit.

"You can look at the site first. Then after that, you can help us figure it out and end the interference. I doubt whatever is happening here is to my benefit," Felix said. "If that's agreeable to you?"

Al nodded and then clapped his hands together once.

"It's agreed. A deal is struck," said the child. "Now, I'm starving. Is there some food around here? What I want to do is going to cost me some power, and I'd like to eat first."

Felix pointed back the way to the food truck.

"Back that way. Waffles and pancakes," Felix said.

Al followed the line Felix's arm created and immediately set off in that direction.

Uncle followed behind him lazily, looking unimpressed and rather bored.

Felicity walked up beside him, her eyes tracking the duo. She laid a hand on his shoulder, her fingers moving back and forth lightly over the fabric.

"Felix, I don't think I could have beaten 'Uncle.' In fact, I don't think Vince could have either," she said. "Or even Lily."

"Great. Grand. Goodie." Felix propped up his chin in his hand. "I suddenly feel like we're going to have a number of deities and champions with axes to grind showing up here."

"Care to wager that a number of these national leaders are priests in disguise?"

"No. Not really. I'd lose," Felicity said. "Are you ready for dinner with Ioana and Felicia tonight?"

Felix nodded. "Yeah, that'll be a nice diversion. Tomorrow I need to start up the press machine."

"True. You have back-to-back interviews with Erica and Jessica, and then I set one up with Sarah Riks," Felicity said. "Apparently she's a journalist from abroad doing a piece on the summit. If we can get her to speak in our favor, and then get it before it goes to press, we can launch it here through friendly press agencies at the same time."

"Fun."

"Then we need to head over to the court house. I believe the first open hearing is scheduled for tomorrow for the anti-trust case," Felicity said. "To formally state the grounds for the case and start going through the motions."

Ah, she knows. Knows and has already started to work it into my schedule.

"It's rather soon, but I get the impression this will be quick, to a degree. One way or the other," Felicity said.

Out of nowhere, Felix had a sudden idea that he thought might be able to help.

At least with their public image, which might play into their hearing.

Anyone who ever believed public perception doesn't play a role in the judicial system is a fool.

"Actually, if you don't mind, could you schedule Jessica, Erica, and Sarah to all meet us at the newly minted Legion bank for its grand opening?" Felix asked. "I think I'd like to take the opportunity to spin up the public opinion on that one, and what we're doing there."

"I can do that," Felicity said, still watching Uncle before he turned the corner.

She looked wary.

Felix didn't disagree with that sentiment, either. He had a lot more concerns in this hour than he'd had the hour previous.

***

The Bank of the Legion was a large building. In fact, it had once been a prison constructed in an older district of the capital.

This was right on the edge of what people called "New Legion City," once a wasteland of nothing but run-down warehouses, failed businesses, and burnt-up buildings. Newly purchased as a whole, turned into a gated city, and re-purposed by Legion entirely. Though the bank and New Legion City were still technically in Wal City.

Felix was standing in the lobby watching the operation of the bank.

They'd been able to hire the entire staff of a bank that had been going under in a different city. Felix wasn't up to date on the details, but he got the impression from what little he read that banks were closing up smaller locations around the country.

Or locations they no longer deemed relevant.

Everyone who had been hired from that bank was given Legion contractor jobs, which meant they weren't actually Legion.

Of course, there was always the possibility of earning that privilege, but it wasn't just given freely.

Jessica and Erica were both standing next to Felix, watching over the same thing he was.

"They look very relieved," Erica murmured.

"I imagine we would be, too," Felix admitted. "Our life savings wiped out in a moment that had nothing to do with us. Everything we'd worked to save and build up with."

Jessica nodded her head a bit. "Well, that's why we're doing this. Make sure those who were uninvolved remain uninvolved."

"Ah, there she is," Felix said, trying to stop the conversation. He wasn't sure how good Sarah's hearing was, but he remembered Jessica's being substantial.

Felix pointed to the front of the bank.

They were only allowing small groups of people in at a time to avoid overcrowding the lobby.

Magically, everyone had seemed to get random bank statements all at the same time. Listing out their balances the very day the bank heist happened.

As if by some miraculous force, every single customer of the bank had gotten an off-cycle statement.

Courtesy of Legion having everything needed to print off statements and mail them out without anyone even noticing.

The young woman they had been waiting for was at the front of the bank, talking to a security guard.

She was in a very professional business suit. Looking the part of a reporter—if you discounted the part where she seemed closer to one of Vince's Dryad wives—Sarah seemed ready to interview him.

"Hmph. They sent you a beautiful Red, did they?" Jessica asked. Her tail swished behind her ominously and then settled back into position. "Well, you already have a Fox, a gray one. Me."

Ruffle some feathers, did we?

Or territory, as it were.

Felix grinned and as surreptitiously as he could manage, he reached over and lightly scratched Jessica at the base of her tail.

"You're right. But be calm, Jess. She's here to help push the story for us. Make international news, and we feed it to the local stations.

"Play your part like normal," Felix said softly. "She's not Legion."

"Legion First," Erica said, responding automatically.

Jessica hadn't responded; she seemed lost in the sudden attention Felix was giving her. Her hip had swung over and was pressing into his side.

Sarah's head turned their way as she entered the lobby, her nose moving up and down.

Always surprising to see them acting more animalistic. Then again, that was always the argument, wasn't it?

Demi-humans aren't human.

The Legionnaires who had directed Sarah in hadn't given her a second glance. The lobby staff did though. They seemed to be considering her, as if they weren't sure she belonged here.

And that's why most of you will never be worthy of Legion.

"Sarah, welcome," Felix said, smiling as the reporter's eyes locked on him.

She briefly looked at Jessica and Erica, clearly assessing them as she came closer.

That's right, you're not alone, and they clearly have a better relationship. How do you handle it?

Sarah's black-tipped ears flexed down and then up as she came to a stop in front of him. Then she smiled, revealing her rather long canines.

"Good afternoon, Mr. Campbell—or can I call you Felix?" Sarah asked. He hadn't been able to pinpoint her accent last time, and he still couldn't. It gave her pronunciation an almost liquid quality, though. It flowed.

"Of course you can, Sarah. I invited you along as I think I'm going to be here most of the day," Felix said. "And since I'd invited local reporters, I figured I'd give you some face time as well."

"It is greatly appreciated." Sarah pulled a pen from an inner pocket and slid a small pad of paper out from her coat. "Especially since you recognized me for what I am."

Felix shrugged and gestured to an office behind him.

"Would you all care to join me? My admin prepared some light fare and coffee."

Turning to the door, Felix opened it and gestured inside.

"Ah, that is very appreciated, but I don't—"

"I believe she prepared something specifically for you, Sarah," Felix said.

"Oh?" Sarah asked, moving into the office with Erica and Jessica.

"Felix is very methodical with his guests and their needs," Jessica said, a slight edge to her voice.

"So I have noticed," Sarah said.

Felix didn't have the time or the luxury to try and get them to work together, and it honestly wasn't his problem.

"To begin with, the official statement from Legion has already been prepared for all three of you," Felix said, indicating the three manila envelopes sitting around a circular table in the corner. There was a fourth seat, but it lacked anything in front of it. Felix sat in it. "The details for everything are in there, inclusive of the amount set aside to cover this horrible situation."

Sarah, Jessica, and Erica were all sorting through the drinks and food Felicity had prepared for them. When each of them had found whatever the Elf had put in there specifically for them, they came to the table with it.

"My compliments to your admin," Sarah said, setting her cup down. "As to Legion… one could almost say two things of this situation."

Felix leaned back in his chair, tenting his fingers in front of him.

Waiting.

"It is very fortuitous that Legion is able to step in for the government and take up the slack. It's actually a PR miracle," Sarah said.

The hidden statement here being that it would proclaim quite loudly Legion is doing far better than projections.

"Sounds like a fairly expensive miracle," Felix said calmly. "Especially given what the financial wizards are claiming about Legion."

"I believe the headline this morning was something akin to 'Legion Cashing out Now; Expected Losses in Quarterly Call,' or something to that effect."

Jessica snorted and tapped a finger against the packet in front of her. "Something to that effect? It was far more disparaging and rude. It's getting increasingly obvious which side of the greased-up coin they fall on."

Erica's mouth had been pinched tight up to this moment. He'd been waiting for her to say something to back up those headlines, though. She was meant to play the opposing opinion for Legion.

"And yet, didn't Legion just dump almost all of their invested holdings for far more hard assets. Like gold?" Erica asked, doing her job. "If they're not in financial trouble, then I'd say they believe Wal to be in financial trouble."

"Any comment on that, Felix?"

Shrugging his shoulders minutely, Felix smiled at her. "As is ever the case, Erica, I'm afraid I can't comment on speculation. Though I will tell you this: Legion believes in the current government of Wal, and we're here to stay."

"That is closer to the second comment one would have on this situation," Sarah said, taking a sip of her drink. As it came away from her lips, she gave him a feral smile over the rim. "Perhaps this is all an attempt for Legion to take another business in hand. Further expand their holdings."

"An interesting theory, but... there's a problem with that," Felix said, feeling a bit on guard. Sarah was a bit more cunning and intelligent than he'd expected.

"And what's that?" she asked, her smile faltering.

"We're not taking new customers in our bank. Only those who were going to fall through the cracks." Felix spread his hands out in front of him. "No one else."

Sarah blinked and then jotted something down in her notepad.

One set of questions down... time for another, I suppose.

And then there's the first hearing.

That'll be fun.

Chapter 17 - Comes in Threes -

Sitting down at the table in front of the Supreme Court justices, Felix felt odd.

This was only the first hearing, and yet he was already being asked to sit and be questioned.

Lily, Lauren, and Lauren were with him.

Behind them was the entire legal department of Legion. Some thirty deep and ranging from the youngest intern, Jeff, a Tilen high-school graduate they'd picked up, to an ex-judge who had picked lawyering back up after the fall of Skippercity.

Opposing them was Blake, the attorney general, and a slew of others. There was even a list of people who supported the move but weren't able to appear. Due to constraints on their time, or there simply not being enough room at the table.

So many people either want a piece of Legion or to make it fail.

"Thank you for being a willing witness, Mr. Campbell," said one of the justices.

She was seated in the middle of the seven of them, and she looked to be the oldest one there.

"Of course, happy to be here to discuss my private and multi-national recognized company and its holdings," Felix said, immediately putting that front and center.

The simple fact that Legion was a private business would help obfuscate the matter. Legion wasn't publicly traded, and there was no one else in charge, or owning it, other than Felix.

Heck, we could argue we're non-profit since we have no stock.

Having it recognized by other countries also limited the court's ability to punish him fully.

All seven justices stared at Felix now, as if realizing this was going to be a no-holds-barred grudge match. Then they looked to the attorney general.

"Mr. Attorney General, before we begin, we have a series of questions we'd like to ask," said the same justice.

The man nodded, saying nothing in response.

"Mr. Campbell, it goes without saying that we're all well aware of what Legion has done for Wal. We're also well aware that Legion is a privately held company that indeed has a number of international countries recognizing it as a business," said the woman. "Though this hearing is primarily designed to determine if the company has gone further than anti-trust laws would allow, and if anti-competitive practices have been orchestrated by Legion or yourself."

Felix said nothing, sitting quietly at the table with his hands folded one into the other.

"Hopefully through the course of this hearing we can determine if your company is innocent and find the next course of action," said the justice to the right of the one who had been talking.

The woman who appeared to be leading the court looked angry for a fraction of a second. Almost like a wince.

And it was gone as quickly as it had been there.

But Felix had noticed it. Everyone probably had.

Is this a show trial, or do they want me to believe it is? Do they want us to just roll over and take this without resisting?

Fat chance of that.

Now I'm going to go after all of you personally.

Feeling the anger rise up inside him at the people lining up to take a shot at Legion, Felix contemplated standing up and walking out.

"I believe the burden of proof falls to the AG," Lily said, leaning toward her microphone. "Not Legion. Though I feel silly saying it, I must remind the court that Legion is innocent until proven guilty, even at the level of the Supreme Court."

"Or is what you're saying that you have already determined Legion as having committed anti-competitive practices or broken anti-trust laws without having heard a single word of the case?" said the Lauren on Lily's left into her own microphone.

"If that's the case, Legion can withdraw from Wal right now and move to another country, while severing all our contracts," said the Lauren on Lily's right.

The atmosphere of the room had rapidly grown more tense by the second. To the point that it felt more like a standoff with guns drawn.

For all intents and purposes, it would seem this was indeed a show-court. Whether intentional or not—perhaps he'd just lost his temper—the justice who had spoken had possibly revealed the court's machinations behind this.

The threat Legion had just made wasn't a small one, either. If the company simply packed up and left, there would be little the government could do to actually keep itself afloat.

Felix deliberately cleared his throat and stood up. Taking a moment, he adjusted his tie and buttoned his coat.

"It would seem Legion isn't wanted in Wal," Felix said simply. He wasn't about to sit here to hear a case that was presumptively being put together just to railroad them.

Taking action would be costly. So costly it would take years for Legion to recover, if they ever could. They'd end up sacrificing much of their wealth, technology, and ability. There was simply too much invested in the running of businesses and assets that wouldn't be able to move.

Everything would have to be started over from scratch with those. As if they'd practically never been in business at all.

"Now, let's not be hasty," said the female justice, clearly realizing this was rapidly turning against her.

"I don't think I'm being hasty. I think I'm being prudent. If a trial lawyer has to remind a Supreme Court justice of the burden of proof, I'd say this is little more than a farce." Felix said held up his hands in front of him. "When people ask where Legion went, be sure to step forward and identify yourself and this kangaroo court, would you?"

"I think you're bluffing; you're too deeply invested in Wal to pull out now," said the male justice who had let slip the direction the court was going.

Admittedly, Felix was bluffing, to a degree. He didn't want to do this. At all.

But it felt like his back was up against the wall.

"Not at all. We have zero penalty clauses for pulling out. Not one," Felix said. "We don't even have a time limit stipulation for contract break. Nor a need to notify in advance.

"Starting tomorrow morning, there will be no trash pickup. The police force will rely on its own department instead of the Legion. The same for the fire department and the emergency responders," Felix said, stepping out from the table. "The electrical grid will drop out after that, since the government gave the production of power contract to Legion when all the other companies fell through.

"After that, the internet will probably go down—we host the servers, after all.

"I'm only giving you till tomorrow so the news can pick this up and run with it. Preferably with your photos on the front page and every website."

Lily and the Laurens were clearing up their places, sorting papers into various folders and packing up.

"Now, wait—" said the female lead justice.

"Then, when the sewage fails, and people's toilets start backflowing with the shit of thousands, it'll be done. The systems Legion maintained in trust at cost, and its own expense, will have failed.

"Except, of course, that doesn't include all the businesses we actually own. So there goes all the employees, taxes, and revenue they generated.

"That'll tank the economy."

Felix looked to the name placard in front of the female justice, and the one to her right who had spoken out of turn.

Bissel for the woman, Kiss for the man.

"You'll be the justice who ran out Legion. Justice Bissel, the founder of the ruin that was Wal.

"And you can wear that lovely little moniker around your neck as you wade through the sewage in your living room.

"That you and your court got rid of Legion—good for you," Felix said, pushing his chair in at the table.

"While I, and Legion, will happily make use of our talents elsewhere for another location. One that would probably want a company that hands out no-interest loans to a government. Because we'll be calling in those markers as well, since Wal still owes me personally."

Lily and the Laurens had packed up quickly and were standing with Felix. News reporters were furiously taking notes as politicians who had once shown up for a spectacle looked like they wanted to jump into the center of the court and start shouting.

"You can't just leave," said Justice Kiss.

"Of course I can," Felix said with a grin. "I'm a citizen. I'm not a government employee, and it's my company. I'm recognized in other countries, and I owe no debts or fines to Wal."

"I can hold you in contempt," Kiss said, getting his feet.

"Mr. Campbell is here by invitation; he is not here under a warrant in any way," Lily said. "Unless you're declaring that Wal is under martial law, which I don't think is in your purview."

Justice Bissel was glaring daggers at Justice Kiss, her hand pressed to the microphone in front of her.

"Would you remain a moment, Mr. Campbell, if we cleared the court?" asked a third justice, seated to the left of Bissel.

Felix considered it for a moment. Looking like a man who didn't care one way or the other but was on the verge of agreeing for the sake of simplicity.

"Fine. My calendar was booked for the entire period anyways. It'll take time for the contract terminations to be drawn up and sent to the PM," Felix said. "We have a little bit of time I could give you."

The courtroom erupted into a chorus of protests as bailiffs began guiding people out of the hearing.

"Felix, we can't really leave," Lily whispered as softly as she could manage. "We really are too deeply tied in. Hardware, payable debts to us, investments. We can't take any of that with us.

"If we left, we'd lose a considerable amount of hard assets. I'm not sure Legion could recover in a reasonable time frame. There aren't too many other places we could go. Most of the world is closed off to us.

"And the moment we pull out, Wal will more or less shut us out, and they won't bother to pay all those debts."

Hm. Maybe I overplayed my hand a bit.

Giving her a wide smile, he didn't respond. He promised himself he'd never admit if he was bluffing one way or the other if she asked.

Glancing over to the AG and his team, Felix was treated to a sight of absolute chaos. Everyone over there was madly scrambling through paperwork.

They must be checking the fact that we have no penalties for pulling out.

With a thud that reverberated throughout the court, the hearing was cleared of all non-essential bystanders.

The justices had been in a conference during this time and were now turning back to Felix.

Taking the opportunity to make a point of his stance, he lifted his wrist a bit and turned it over. Checking the time, Felix let his hand fall back to his side, and then he waited.

Still standing behind his chair.

"Mr. Campbell, I believe this has gone terribly awry," said Justice Bissel.

"You mean when you and your cronies admitted this was a farce? Yes, it has," Felix said. "Anything else? Or new? Otherwise I'll be leaving."

"Do remember to point back to this moment when people ask you why there is a giant lake of shit spread around the city."

"What if Justice Bissel and Justice Kiss were removed?" asked the third justice suddenly.

All around him, the others turned to him in surprise.

Felix looked at the placard to check the name.

Justice Moran.

"I'd take my seat and we could continue for a time, Justice Moran. I might even put my contract cancellations on pause. Depending on how I feel about this court case and how it's going," Felix said. "I mean, let's be honest. If you find against me, I leave and take Legion with me, and you end up right back here.

"If you rule with me, I'll stay. But I won't be trusting the government in Wal with my wellbeing.

"It may just be a business to you, but it's my family. When someone pulls a knife on my family, things change. And you pulled a knife when you agreed to hearing this trumped-up political case."

"And if we cleared it here and now?" pressed Justice Moran.

"Suppose we'd find out," Felix said with a shrug.

Personally, he was hoping they'd throw the whole thing out now. He knew they were in bed with Wal, and deeply so, but he'd be damned if he was held hostage here.

"Justice Kiss, Justice Bissel, you're removed from the hearing," said Justice Moran.

The other four justices immediately nodded, voicing their agreement.

Felix gave the two a wave and a smile.

"Bye, bye. I look forward to explaining to the press why you've been removed from the hearing," Felix said. "How Justice Moran saved the city of Wal, and you two were the first willing to see it burn."

The two justices who had been kicked off the hearing looked stunned.

Then they were escorted out bodily by the bailiffs.

***

"Things are getting worse," Lily said, pressing a hand to her neck as she leaned back in her chair.

Felix, Lauren Aston, and Lily had retreated to her office in Old Legion City. The other Lauren had gone to her office to start double-checking contracts.

"And here I thought an anti-trust case was easy," Felix said with a chuckle.

"No, not that, but what happened in there," Lily said, tilting her chin down and meeting his eyes. "Justices have recused themselves before, but I don't think I've ever heard of one justice leading a coup against the others."

"It's unheard of," Lauren said.

"How is it worse, exactly?" Felix asked.

"Because it means the system of law that existed here is deteriorating," Lily said patiently. "It's a corruption, and it'll spread to lower courts. It sets a precedent. Especially for wealthy business owners."

Felix frowned. He hadn't considered it from that angle. Legion had admittedly been skirting laws here and there, but nothing to the detriment of the public.

It was usually bureaucratic laws they sidestepped and avoided entirely.

"Ok. What does that mean for us right now?" Felix asked.

"Nothing. We continue with the court case and hope they muddle their way through it without forcing us to abandon ship," Lauren said. "Realistically, we could cut ties with Wal and leave. Quickly."

"But it'd hurt. We'd have to leave almost every single physical asset behind except personnel."

"And that's if Wal doesn't make a move first. You said they pulled a knife on us… Well, you pulled a gun and leveled it at them," Lily said. "You put teeth to the threat that they're actually investigating.

"The fact that we can do what you said is a completely valid reason to break Legion up. Amusingly as it sounds, the threat you put on them against breaking up Legion is the reason they *would* break up Legion.

"They got to the right idea, just too late to do anything about it."

"Which leads us back to the original thought — get out of Wal," Felix finished for her.

"Right." Lily rubbed at her neck. "I need a drink. Several drinks. Because starting tomorrow, I think I'm going to be hip deep in case law and documentation on this one until it's over."

Lauren only nodded glumly.

A soft chime came from Felix's wrist.

Turning the device over, Felix tapped the icon. It was an urgent email from Kit.

Then Lily's device chirped, followed by Lauren's.

Shit. Now what?

Felix opened the email and read it over quickly.

"Is this even possible?" he asked aloud after giving it a second read-through.

It was easy enough to read, after all, being only three sentences.

The summit attendees have posted an addendum to their committee list. Committee to be headed by Blake. Goal of committee is to determine legality of Legion preventing worship of certain religions.

"It's entirely possible," Lily said, slumping into her chair, apparently having read a similar email. "Entirely possible and exactly what I would do if I were Blake."

"Why? I mean, I assume it's a way to somehow bring ruin to our international recognition," Felix said.

"It is," Lauren agreed. "But it's more than that. This gives everyone living in Wal an outlet for their inability to practice certain religions openly."

"Despite the law coming from Wal, we're the ones who enforce it."

"It'll die in committee," Lily said, pressing her thumb and forefinger to the bridge of her nose. "Die and be forgotten afterward. During, though... they're going to dig up every mistake possible we've ever made regarding religious worship."

"It might even go further than you think," Lauren interrupted. "Technically, the Dryad religion would be outlawed. It hasn't been declared, confirmed, or vetted. And the moment it does get inspected, it'll fail."

"Then it'll fall to us to remove the Dryads from Wal or get them to convert to a stabilized religion."

Feeling as if someone was expertly putting the pinch on him and Legion, Felix wasn't sure which way to go anymore.

"Right, that's enough bad news in one night for me," Felix said, clapping his hands together. "I'll leave it to you, as I have no idea what to even think on that one. Legal problems have never been my forte, and I don't think they ever will be."

Lily was already turning on her terminal while Lauren pulled out her light-terminal.

It wasn't until he opened the door that Lily seemed to notice.

"That'd be why you have me and my team. I'll let you know as soon as we figure something out, dear. I love you," Lily said, then gave him a beautiful smile.

"Love you, too, dear." Felix closed the door and moved out into the hall.

An anti-trust case and a legal challenge on our ability to enforce the law.

These things typically run in threes, don't they?

Felix didn't think anything more of it and started to move down the hallway. He was planning on heading back to his office.

There was a lot of work to get done, and he didn't have a whole lot of time to do it in.

He had dinner plans he couldn't duck out of.

Then his wrist device chimed.

The sound was soft and deadly.

Felix had violated one of the cardinal rules in Legion. Don't tempt fate. Don't jinx it.

And he'd done that, hadn't he?

Lifting his wrist with a grimace, Felix looked at the alert.

This time it was from Felicity, and marked urgent.

Opening it up, he prepared for the worst. Which was good, because when he read it, it didn't seem that bad.

At least, compared to what he thought it would be—or the previous two.

An emergency runoff was going to be held in two months. The current prime minister had just been recalled, and there was a need to immediately fill her position. The minimum time set forth was two months.

Until then, the assistant prime minister, Blake Gresham, would be the acting PM.

- 602 -

The very same man pushing for the AG to file the case, and now apparently running the committee to see Legion tangled up in the religious case.

Oh... my... shit.

Felix closed his eyes and pressed his hands to his face.

Then yelled loudly into them.

Chapter 18 - Alone -

Felicity had managed to arrange a meeting between Felix and Blake.

They had consented to each of them having one aide with them, if only to make sure the meeting could be documented appropriately.

At this point, everyone, from the citizenship to the PM, saw everyone else with daggers and conspiracies.

Felix didn't want to meet with Blake. At all.

But Felix was also the one who had requested that Felicity see what she could do.

He really needed to know if Blake was the enemy, or if this was all circumstantial.

They had no hard proof; it really just came down to the fact that Blake kept showing up in the unlikeliest of places.

Cool fingertips lightly brushed against the back of his hand. The touch was like electricity, crackling down his arm and straight into his brain. Felicity's fingers had only barely touched him, but his skin had prickled from head to toe, and it'd broken him from his thoughts.

"I share the same fears and thoughts," Felicity said when his eyes turned to her. "But there is little we can do one way or the other. We need to go in there and ascertain his intentions."

"Then act accordingly."

Felix nodded. He'd come to the exact same conclusion, of course. Though it was nice to hear Felicity echoing his thoughts.

"You're awfully in tune with me," Felix said bluntly.

Felicity smiled at that, tilting her head to one side.

"Really? I'm truly glad to hear that. Realistically, I'm just doing my best imitation of my family's role back home.

"I learned under my sisters for a number of years. Most especially Elyssia. You and she would get along very well," Felicity said.

Looking around the small waiting room they'd been put in until Blake was available, Felix wondered about that.

"She's your sister-in-law, as she's married to Vince. She keeps him on track, though she's been run down."

"As you yourself said, he's a masterful leader through direction and power. Though much of his decisions are simply based on how he feels rather than the politics of the situations. Or at least, not to the same level as you," Felicity explained.

"Sounds lovely. Wish I could do that," Felix admitted.

"Yes, right up until his personal charisma can't outweigh what he wants to do. I'm sure that time will come. He isn't balancing his... hm, I don't know if I could explain it, actually," Felicity said.

"His keys to power, maybe? Giving away too much 'treasure,' so to speak, from his vault without considering if he's giving it away as frugally as possible?" Felix asked.

"Yes. That... sounds about right."

"If you'd like an example, I balance the time I allow myself to spend with each department during business hours. I also make sure to take each group to lunch at least once a month.

"That doesn't change what I give to each group."

Felix flexed his hands out in front of him.

"Let's say one wants permission to make a move on a business and take it over through financial pressure. Another wants to do a purchase outright and bring it in house," Felix said. He could hear someone coming this way. Glancing at the clock on the wall, he saw it was time for their meeting. "I weigh out which group I've favored previously, and how. Which group hasn't received an agreement in their favor recently. Then I take into account what would be best for Legion. Blending the two together, I figure out what makes the most sense."

Felicity nodded, her face pointed toward the door.

She must be listening to their conversation. Those ears of hers are quite sensitive.

The tread of feet stopped.

Several seconds later and the door opened, right on time for the meeting down to the second.

"Blake is ready to see you now. Thank you for being patient," said a young male secretary. He gestured into the hallway beyond.

Felix stood up, buttoned a single button on his jacket, and smiled.

Felicity brushed a hand across her skirt and then led the way, Felix following along behind her.

"It's the third office on the left," said the man.

Felicity didn't need any more direction. She opened the door and went right in.

Coming in behind her, Felix didn't bother with the door. He assumed the secretary would be following along.

Blake Gresham stood behind his desk. He was a man in his middle years. Brown hair, brown eyes, clean shaven, neither handsome nor ugly.

One amongst the many.

Beside him was a woman in her early twenties. She had an almost vapid feel about her, and Felix wasn't sure what her purpose would be. She had dark black ringlets cut short with bright blue eyes.

She also had a very well-built figure that curved in the right spots.

Felicity walked right up to the desk and held out her hand to the woman.

"I'm Felicity, Felix's personal admin," she said, shaking the other woman's hand.

"Shirley," the woman replied, giving no title or position.

Felix felt odd about this Shirley woman. But there wasn't much he could do about it.

Maybe she's Blake's Felicity.

"Blake Gresham," said the man, shaking Felicity's hand when she moved to him.

"And you are Felix Campbell. I think everyone in Wal knows who you are," Blake said as Felix shook Shirley's hand.

"That I am," Felix said, moving to Blake. Felix didn't mistake noticing that Blake was wearing a null ring. A standard ring everyone seemed to wear that prevented mind reading. "Thank you for agreeing to meet with us. We've been seeing your name a lot recently."

"Yes… well, I suppose that's part of the reason I felt it'd be ideal to meet with you," Blake said. Releasing Felix's hand, he gestured to the two seats in front of his desk.

"I had no doubt you were aware of me by this point, and I felt it'd be a good idea to sit and talk. Clear the air," Blake said.

"That'd be most appreciated," Felix agreed. "To be sure, I'm wondering where you fall in all this. With how your name keeps coming up, I'm starting to wonder if you're not in favor of Legion remaining in Wal."

Felix didn't want to beat around the bush, and he sure as hell didn't want to deal with politics right now. His preferred tried-and-true method of letting others bring it up wasn't going to fit here.

He needed answers, now, before he went about skewering Blake and everyone backing him. He didn't have time to give Blake the normal foreplay he was probably used to in politics.

"I see. Perhaps I misjudged the timing of this meeting. Having it a few weeks ago—or perhaps even a month—would have been ideal, I think now," Blake said, closing the folder he had open in front of him and pushing it to one side.

"I'm neither in favor of Legion nor against it. I only want what's best for Wal. If that means attempting to break Legion up as a company in its Wal holdings, then that would be the goal," Blake said. "If it's attempting to remove Legion from the religious problems we're having in the country, then so be it.

"I'll do what's best for Wal. And if that means selling the entire country to Legion for safekeeping in these harsh and wild times, then that's what I'll do."

Frowning, Felix wasn't quite sure what to make of it.

Blake had cleanly and expressly told Felix what he was about, but it didn't fit. At least, it didn't fit with Felix's worldview.

Nothing Blake had just said matched what politicians actually wanted.

This sounded more like the open and broken promises given during elections.

The next of which was going to be actively held rather soon.

Is he trying to get the Legion vote? Is that what this is?

We do have a significant voting power in our members alone. It's no secret that we vote as a block, too.

"Right. So everything that's happening is coincidental, and you being on the list of every action against Legion is… circumstantial?" Felix asked.

"In my current position, I'm required to be present in many motions that I would otherwise not wish to be on. But I must, as a representative of the government," Blake said.

That's too easy. Many politicians would claim the same but simply have their name removed, delegating the action to a lesser functionary.

Felix smiled despite all his internal thoughts. "Of course."

"As far as the anti-trust case goes, while I do agree that Legion holds too much of Wal in check, I can only wonder about those who are pushing the case," Blake said, splaying his hands out. "It is no surprise about these contracts, or how much Legion holds. Each contract made its way through the various branches of government. In every case, it was supported by a majority."

And you've conveniently forgotten that your name was on those rosters in the majority.

"And the summit?" Felix asked.

"Not my choice, either. The prime minister put it on the books the day before she was told there would be an emergency recall. Odd timing, but there it is," Blake said.

That really is odd timing. Nor did he mention why she was being recalled.

In fact, no one seems to even know. Just that it's going to happen.

"And before you ask, no, I don't know why she was pulled. The reasoning has been kept between the prime minister and the majority leader," Blake said.

Not replying immediately, Felix weighed out his options.

He really only had two directions available to him.

Trust Blake—and believe he was really working for best of Wal.

Or distrust him—turning him into a political pariah and putting the fix in so he wouldn't be elected in the emergency runoff.

There were too many things working against Legion coming from Blake, though. This had all the classic hallmarks of being a political fluff job.

Assurances of innocence and support without the hint of any evidence or backing to the contrary.

In fact, he didn't actually assure his support. Just that he'd do what he felt was best for Wal.

He's a terrible politician.

Everything in Felix screamed at him that this man was lying. Lying and working against Legion.

There was a knock at the door.

"Come in," Blake called, looking from Felix to the door.

"Mr. Gresham, there are quite a few people here who want to see you about an emergency issue. What would you like to do?" asked the same male secretary from earlier.

Felix stood up, forestalling a conversation.

"No, it's quite alright. I think we said everything that needs to be said," Felix said, moving to the door. "Thank you for your time, Blake."

They hadn't even made it into the hallway before Felicity slipped her arm into his.

"There, I've sealed the area around us. No one can hear us talk without smashing through my personal shield," she said. "I take it you don't trust him?"

"Not at all. Either he's the best politician ever, or he's the worst and being completely honest with us. In either case, we didn't hear anything new, and he offered us nothing to take back for assurance," Felix said.

"I would agree… though I feel like I've missed something." Felicity shook her head."

"I've felt that way for a month now," Felix muttered.

Felicity sighed and patted his arm. "Other than lunch, what's next?"

"Do we have anyone on the voting district table? Or some name like that? The basic premise is they define the zones people vote in and where they go to vote," Felix said.

"I think so, but I'd have to check my notes. Why?"

"I want to do some gerrymandering. I want to create districts that'll favor… what's his name, again? Blake's opponent on stage?" Felix asked.

"Honestly, the name has slipped my mind. But I do know they reached out to Lily through some back-channel means. This morning no less.

"She has a meeting with you later today to discuss it," Felicity said. "From what I got from her when she asked me to book time with you, they're looking for a couple kickbacks and some concessions. She seemed bored by it."

"It's normal political process here in Wal. Maybe he wants me to open some businesses in his home districts and hire from them.

"It'd help him knock down some of his unemployment," Felix said.

Felicity nodded slightly. "I'm learning much from being with you. I think you would have Yosemite ironed out in little more than a month and possibly working better than it is today."

"Probably not; it sounds like it has a serious military bent. I'm not that great at anything regarding that. I'm trained in some limited combat, but I have no talent for it," Felix said.

Felicity's mouth became a thoughtful frown at that, and the conversation dropped momentarily.

"So, what do you want for lunch?" Felicity asked as they stepped out of the government building.

A horde of Legion bodyguards dropped into place around him. The blond Dryad who was constantly invading his space came in very close, standing directly at his side and looking at him, then at Felicity.

"She's very pretty, Felix, but you can't eat the Dryad," Felicity said, patting his arm. "Admittedly, she's from Betty's grove. Which means she's probably open to being eaten."

Realizing he'd been staring at the Dryad, Felix turned his face forward, thinking about food.

Recently, his libido had skyrocketed. Andrea and Adriana had been getting a workout producing more and more clones.

And he didn't feel quite sated more often than not.

I bet the Dryads are to blame.

"Speaking of Dryads, before Lily's meeting but after lunch, we're supposed to meet with Fes, Meliae, and Yarris to see about formal Legion recognition," Felicity said.

That'll help. Government recognition will prevent them from having control over Legion and how it sits with me.

***

The overly endowed and unbelievably pregnant Dryad that was Vince's wife Meliae came straight at him.

"Felicity, Felix. Welcome, welcome," she murmured, immediately latching on to his arm and leaning on him. "I'm so glad to see you, brother-in-law. Though I'm sorry to say your brother is already back in the field. He's down south now, working to end this war."

Smiling at the bubbly woman, Felix nodded. "Of course, Meliae. Is it going well? I've had a few reports here and there, but nothing concrete."

"Very well, actually. All those pieces you keep sending over have drastically changed everything. We're well on our way to ending this," Meliae said, slowly waddling through the large mansion the portal was still set up in.

"Much of this turning point is thanks to you," said Fes as they turned the corner into a large study.

She looked much healthier than the last he'd seen her. Even if she did look more like something out of a science fiction novel now.

Her missing arm and leg had been replaced with what looked a lot like a custom Felicia job.

"Felicity, it's good to see you," Fes said, looking over Felix's shoulder. "You look happy."

Glancing over his shoulder, Felix caught Felicity looking the same as ever. Her bag tucked up under her arm, dressed in the normal clothes he'd seen her in every day.

"Very happy, Fes." Felicity bobbed her head at the Orc.

A distinctly different-looking Elf woman Felix hadn't met crossed over to Felicity and gave her a hug. She had all the appearances of a High Elf, though a bit shorter.

"Sister, it's good to see you," said the woman. Then she leaned back, taking Felicity's face in her hands. "You do look happy. Things are working out?"

Felicity smiled and nodded.

"They are, sister. And before he asks," Felicity said, looking to Felix. "This is Yaris, Vince's queen, and my older sister. She's a Royal Elf."

Felix hadn't heard of that sub-species before.

She really did look similar to a High Elf, with her dark-blond hair, though the coloring wasn't the same throughout. The bright blue eyes only added to that opinion of species relation.

"Felix, welcome to our home," Yaris said.

"Thank you for having me. Though as much as I'd love to keep this a family meeting," Felix said, "I'm afraid I've come with my hat in hand. I'd like to request Yosemite formally recognize Legion as a corporate entity."

"I don't understand," Fes said, looking to Felicity.

"Legion really is just a business. It's like a military, but it isn't. It's not even a country," Felicity said.

Fes nodded and then looked to Yaris.

"It has no impact on Vince, so I defer to you," said the Orc.

"Would there be any unexpected needs? Anything we'd need to do?" Yaris asked.

"Nothing other than politically. My enemies would be your enemies," Felix said honestly.

Now it was Yaris's turn to look confused.

Meliae snorted and then giggled to herself.

"Brother dear, your enemies are already our enemies. Yaris wanted to know if we should prepare anything else. Was that really it? Just a declaration?" Meliae asked.

"For this, yes. That's really all we need. Recognition from another government so we don't fall under someone else's authority." Felix was touched that helping Legion had been a forgone conclusion for them.

"Then it's done." Yaris shrugged. "Now, how about we go out back? The Dryads have been preparing a very lovely after-meal tea, with some fruit as well.

"And the children would love to see their uncle, I know it."

There wasn't a response he could give that would have been faster than Meliae starting to pull him out of the study and out back.

"Oh, yes, yes. Many of the children who didn't get to see you last time said they wanted to meet Uncle Felix the next time you visited," Meliae crooned.

"This is true. Falaein was very unhappy he didn't get to meet you," Fes said. "Berest couldn't stop bragging about the fact that you let her ride you around."

Moving back through the portal room, Meliae paused for a second as she looked through it.

A Dryad was sitting next to it in a chair, nervously clutching a pack in her lap.

"You haven't left yet?" Meliae asked the Dryad.

Sitting up straight in her seat, the young woman looked to Meliae with a bit of panic in her face.

She looked a lot like Meliae, even with the same coloring to her hair. Her figure and stature were nearly identical, just a bit smaller.

Which made her look almost normal, instead of a hopped-up wet dream.

Almost.

"I'm sorry, sister. I'm just nervous," said the younger woman. "It sounds like such a strange place."

Meliae turned to Felix and smiled up at him.

"This is my sister. She's moving into your Legion today so she can find a place for herself. We arranged an apprenticeship with your wife, Lily," Meliae said. "Our father was part Elven. I took much more after mother, and only inherited a very small amount. Patricia took on much more.

"She won't fit in with a grove, as she's a sorceress as well. Her magic makes her incompatible with other Dryads. Somewhat like oil and water. They won't violently oppose each other, but... they won't mesh."

"Oh?" Felix asked, looking to the younger woman. "You'll be welcome in Legion. I know Lily always likes having new students.

"Personally, we can never have enough sorceresses. We take in all we find who wish it."

The Dryad looked from Felix to Felicity, and then to Meliae.

"Everyone has been telling me the same about Legion. I suppose it's time to just... muster up the courage and go then, isn't it?" said Patricia. "Ok. Uhm... I'm going to go now, then."

Meliae smiled patiently, waiting.

Patricia turned to the open portal, her hands clenching around her bag.

"Have a good trip, and if you need anything, reach out to myself or Andrea," Felicity said.

Patricia didn't respond; instead, she started running at the portal. As if she had to do it at a sprint or she'd lose her courage. She tucked in her chin, ducking her head down.

Poor thing. She's as nervous as could be.

The moment before she crossed through the portal, a small arc of blue lightning flashed out from Patricia and struck the portal's rim.

With a cascade of light, the exit shifted from Legion to somewhere else. It looked like a street, with a single car parked to one side. It was also the middle of the night.

Patricia rushed through the portal to the other side.

Then the portal snapped back to normal, the Legionnaires on the other side looking confused.

Then the portal turned off entirely, and nothing was there.

The portal had shut down completely.

What?

Chapter 19 - Disappointed -

"Where's Patricia?" Meliae asked. "Where's the portal?"

"I don't know," Felix answered honestly. Gently disentangling himself from the Dryad, he moved over to the portal device.

Getting down on one knee, he pressed the activation button.

The machine powered up, circulated energy, and then activated.

Only for the portal to fizzle out before it was even constructed.

Trying again, Felix pressed the button. And got the exact same results. There was no change.

Reaching into a breast pocket, Felix fished out a metal card. Felicia had made it so he could get back to Legion from wherever he was. No matter the distance.

His brush with being teleported against his will had created some new security toys.

Rolling his thumb over the activation square, he waited.

And waited.

But nothing happened.

It simply didn't work. It was as dead as the major portal device was. Felix frowned and pushed it back into his breast pocket.

"It would seem," he said, thinking about the problem at hand, "that I'm trapped here, and your sister is... somewhere else."

"It looked like she cast a spell as she went," Meliae said, her voice sounding subdued and a bit guilty.

"Yes, it did seem as if she set off a spell on accident. It struck the portal, sent her elsewhere, and... broke it?" Felicity asked.

"I'm not sure it's broken," Felix said. "It powers on correctly, but shuts off when the portal starts to form. That's never happened before."

"But it doesn't feel like it's broken, per se."

"I'm so sorry, Felix. I don't know what she did," Meliae said.

Taking a moment to spare her a glance, he confirmed she didn't look like she was going to fall apart, then looked back to the device.

"Don't worry about it. I have Mr. White here on site. He can take a look and tell me if it's a mechanical failure.

"Though I genuinely believe it isn't. I think this is more about deities taking an opportunity," Felix said.

Sighing, he got up and then checked on his point count.

	Received	Spent	Remaining
Daily Allotment	300	0	300
Felicity	4,850	0	4,850
+ Loyalty Bonus	1,300	0	1,300
DAILY TOTAL	**6,450**	**0**	**6,450**

Hm. No repression. Seems like they have no influence over here, exactly as my benefactor promised.

Speaking of, I wonder if there's any chance of him assisting me.

Then again, if he wanted to, he already could have.

Focusing on the idea of fixing the portal so that it opened immediately, Felix pushed mentally for a window to appear.

```
Status Correction: Non-working - Correct Status?
> Working                        (4,245,893,132,940,000 points.)
```

Felix grimaced and got the answer he had been expecting. For all intents and purposes, he was stuck here until his people could open a portal from the other side, or until the dirties holding it shut ran out of time.

It shouldn't take Kit long to figure it out and pop open a portal. I just need to wait.

Let's just hope there's no time dilation like what the benefactor mentioned.

Barely stopping himself from shaking his head in mute defeat for the moment, Felix turned to Meliae and smiled.

"How about I visit those nephews and nieces of mine for the time being," Felix said. "I'm not overly concerned about this. I think it'll work itself out one way or the other. It'd be pointless to sit here and worry over it when I can just go see family instead.

"Maybe we could even have a family dinner later if you're willing to play host for a bit."

Meliae gave him a slow, fragile smile and nodded slightly.

"Ok. We can do that," she said. It seemed her mood rapidly picked up as she realized Felix really wasn't that concerned. "Yes, we'll do that. I think it'd be a great idea. We'll have lunch in the grove with everyone, then a family dinner later."

Felix grinned at her, glad to see her perking up. He'd never be able to escape his mindset of the middle-manager, but at least he could make it work for him.

He even managed to keep that positive outlook all day. Past lunch, through dinner, and into the evening.

It was still there, right up until he closed the door on the room Fes had set aside for him to sleep in.

When it was clear the portal wasn't reopening, plans started to rapidly shift.

Felix let out a slow sigh, not sure what to do anymore.

The point value to open the portal would be astronomical.

"Any chance you can help me out, Mr. benefactor?" Felix asked, peering up at the ceiling.

There was no response. Not that he'd actually expected one. Felix was betting on a time dilation now between the two worlds, and that this one was running faster.

At least, that was what he'd do if he was the opposing gods against him.

The question was: how much faster?

Moving into the room, Felix looked around.

It was well furnished, and it seemed to have been cleaned and decorated specifically for someone of importance.

A hearth, couch, table, desk, and a rather large bed rounded it out for what equated to a small apartment.

Minus a kitchen, of course—but there were no appliances in this world.

I wonder if they were expecting me to stay at some point, or if this room is just put together in general.

Moving to the desk, he idly fingered through everything on top of it.

"Inkpot, quills, paper, and a strange… pencil," he said aloud. "No terminal, no spreadsheets, no employee files, no HR."

Running his tongue along the inside of his teeth, Felix really didn't know what to think.

Pulling out the chair, he sat down lightly in it.

"At least I have Felicity," Felix said, propping up his elbow on the desk. There wasn't much he could do.

He didn't feel down, but he definitely felt a lack of direction. There were a number of things he'd been putting into place that should send Blake on a crash course into the ground and make him untouchable.

And those who did vote for him were getting shuffled around with some classic gerrymandering to create districts unfavorable to him.

And now I'm here… unable to act.

Someone knocked on his door twice.

"Enter," Felix called, getting to his feet.

The door swung open and Felicity walked in. Her cheeks had a hint of color to them as she closed the door behind her.

She'd changed into clothes more fitting for this world, and she looked to fit in perfectly.

"Hello, Felix," she said, her hands disappearing behind her back.

"Good evening to you," Felix said, sitting back down on the desk. "Feel free to have a seat."

Felicity slipped some of her hair behind her ear and moved over to his bed. Sitting down on the edge of it, she set her hands in her lap.

"How are you settling in?" she asked.

"As well as I can, I suppose," Felix said with a shrug of his shoulders.

"You're not... upset or mad?"

"What, about the portal? No. It'll open as soon as they can open it. Me being angry or upset about it won't speed it up. I admit I'm a little disheartened and nervous, but who wouldn't be?

"And I don't think Meliae's sister had anything to do with it, before you ask. I think it was accidental, and then our foes seized on it," Felix said.

Felicity smiled and bobbed her head quickly.

"Yes, good. Yes. I'm glad to hear that. While it isn't the way people expected to get to know you better, I know for a fact no one is looking at this as a negative thing. They're happy you're here," she said.

Putting his chin in his hand, Felix leaned on the desk.

"Well, I'm happy to be here for the time being. Hopefully not much longer, but it isn't a problem so far either."

Felicity was fiddling with her thumbs, clearly somewhat unsure of what to do with herself.

To be sure, Felix wasn't quite sure what to do either. He was alone in his room with her, on a planet that was quite possibly in a different universe.

"Yaris and Fes are going to hold court tomorrow. They'd like it if you could attend," Felicity said. "I've learned quite a bit from you as an admin, but I don't have your eye for people. I'd like to get your opinion on everyone."

"Yeah, I'll be there," Felix said. Looking at the Dark Elf, he was suddenly curious.

He focused on her and opened her character sheet.

Name:	Power:	
Felicity	None	
Alias: None		
Physical Status: Quickened Heart Rate; Slightly Upset Stomach; Randy; Lustful.	Mental Status: Hopeful; Willing	
Positive Statuses: In Heat(Pheromones II); In Love(Emotional Boost X)	Negative Statuses: None	
Strength:	47	Upgrade?(470)
Dexterity:	96	Upgrade?(960)
Agility:	87	Upgrade?(870)
Stamina:	38	Upgrade?(380)
Wisdom:	57	Upgrade?(570)
Intelligence:	92	Upgrade?(920)
Luck:	15	Upgrade?(150)

| Primary Power: | — | Upgrade? (—) |

Taking a sniff of the air, Felix couldn't deny the only thing he could smell was Felicity. She had a naturally cool and dry smell that reminded him of the walk-in receiving fridge at a grocery store he worked at when he was a teen. It'd always been empty and smelled like fresh snow.

It wasn't unpleasant. In fact, it made his heart thud oddly in his chest. In the same way that Andrea's, Adriana's, and Lily's scents did.

"What are you looking at?" Felicity asked suddenly, her voice breaking into his thoughts.

"You. Or your stats. You're mine, so I can see everything about you," Felix said. "For an example, you have an incredibly low luck score. Lowest I've ever seen, I think."

"I do?" she asked curiously.

"Indeed. Though your intelligence is... very, very high."

"What else does it say?"

Felix smiled and closed the screen with a flick of a finger. "Just your basic things."

Feeling strange at having such a visual confirmation of her feelings for him, Felix gave her a smile.

"Oh. Does that mean you can modify me in any way you want?" Felicity asked, her head tilting to one side.

"Yep."

"But you can't modify yourself."

"Nope."

"Is there... anything about me you'd want to change?" she asked, her eyes pinning him to his chair.

"Ah... no. You're... lovely the way you are," Felix said and coughed into his hand. He was having trouble remembering why he'd been so resistant to Felicity's attention.

Other than Lily, that was.

"Ah... I think I'll take that compliment, and leave you alone for the night," Felicity said, standing up. "I'll see you tomorrow morning before the court, okay?

"Or, with any luck, we'll be back home sometime tonight."

Felix nodded and watched Felicity leave, forcefully prying his eyes away from her hips as she opened the door, spun to wave at him, and left. Closing the door behind her.

Sighing, Felix pressed his face into his hands and groaned.

Get it together, Felix, get it together.

"Damn she has a nice ass," Felix muttered as he realized he'd been staring at it.

***

Felix had arrived early to the Yosemite court and found Felicity already waiting for him.

She'd even come with some bread and fruit for an early light breakfast. Now they were ensconced in a booth to the right side of the raised dais that sat two thrones.

One was clearly for Vince, the other Yaris.

"Is it a traditional monarchy?" Felix asked, watching as members of the Yosemite public began filtering in.

"For the most part. Yaris is also the spiritual leader of Fes through combat, but has recognized Berenga as Fes instead," Felicity said, sitting next to him in the booth.

Watching as groups of people filtered into seats that had no markings or designations, Felix had to wonder. It seemed as if most of the leadership was determined by virtue of who Vince was, and it had little to do with arrangements, agreements, groups, or representation.

As long as an overwhelming majority supported Vince in his desires and pushed forth his wishes, there would be no issue.

Except… Felix had a strange feeling as he watched the people of Yosemite. It felt cohesive, but it felt odd.

Tenuous.

I wonder if it's being held together by the sheer force of Vince's will and unity of his purpose.

If he was gone for an extended period… what would happen?

Is that why I can sense the tension?

"Do you sense anything out of the ordinary?" Felix asked, watching as a group of Dwarves stumped their way to a set of seats. They looked no different than any other.

They're moving themselves into their own groups.

"No? Should I?" Felicity asked. "Everything seems normal."

"Do they normally sort into groups?" Felix asked.

"Yes."

"Do they vote in groups, or are they broken up by job and department?"

"No. They don't vote. They put forward requests and Vince makes decisions. Each race has a voice they rely on to speak for themselves."

"What happens if they disagree with Vince?"

"Nothing. They just let it go," Felicity said simply.

"What about those in the military?"

"They put their concerns up through their generals."

There's a lot of power in those racial groups, then. They need to be broken up into job types, finances, or background. Bracketed accordingly and given voices that let them channel what they want accordingly.

More groups, easier to manage.

A corporate meritocracy does well for things like this, as you simply kick down the ones who aren't playing by the rules.

If he did break everything out, they could move about and create their own alliances and factions with one another.

They'd work to keep their opponents out of power as often as they did to keep themselves in.

The trick is keeping them in check with proper oversight while still giving them perks for being in that position.

"Why? What's the problem?" Felicity asked.

"How long has Vince been gone? When was the last time he really stuck around here?"

"Uhm, not long. There's too much going on."

"And do they listen to Yaris in his place?"

"Mostly."

"Mostly? That doesn't sound good."

"Many feel she favors the Elves, which honestly she does."

"Sounds very similar to the problems I have with my security personnel," Felix said. "I'm no warrior. No fighter. There's a disconnect between me and them. Seems like Vince has a disconnect with those who aren't soldiers of Yosemite."

"Do you listen to your people in their complaints?" Felicity asked, an edge to her voice.

"No. I have HR do it, as that's their job. They have focus groups, surveys, and meetings to discuss problems. Pressure points. Figure out what's going on," Felix said, watching as soldiers began filling court. The atmosphere instantly changed. "Then I make choices and decisions based on that, and we move forward. It's usually quarterly and annually. The annual ones contain performance and merit reviews."

"Oh. That makes sense. Uhm…" Felicity's mouth turned into a delicate frown.

When it seemed no one else could fit in the hall, Yaris entered with her personal guard.

Entirely made up of Elves.

Yes… I can see where the cracks are going to start forming.

There's tension outside of the military.

"Her majesty Queen Yaris of Yosemite," called someone near the door.

Yaris reached the dais, stepped up to her throne, then turned and bowed to the audience.

- 614 -

Then she sat herself down. The respect she had for her people, and what those people had for her, was definitely present.

At least she's fostered a good relationship.

She seems to have a good sense for how to act as royalty, even if it doesn't seem like they have the infrastructure to support a long-term plan.

"Today we'll hear from a number of representatives, several reports, and a commissary from the emperor in the west," Yaris said.

A subtle murmur was spreading throughout the audience, though. Felix couldn't quite identify it, but he got the impression it involved him.

"They want to know who you are and what you're doing here," Felicity said.

Felix looked at her, and then at her ears.

"Is your hearing really that good?" he asked.

"Yes. And I'm glad you like my ass," she said, her eyes flicking to him for a moment before going back to the crowd.

Before he could process that comment, Yaris held up a hand, getting everyone's attention.

"We've also been graced by the presence of our Lord Vince's elder brother, Felix," said Yaris. "He's here as a visitor and to assist in deploying the technology, soldiers, and weaponry he's sent to our aide."

There was an almost universal nod at that. Everyone knew who Felix and the Legion were. Vince's brother from through the portal who had sent technology that might as well be magic.

But there was still something there. A strange sort of tension from certain people.

"Let's hear from Lord Felix then!" someone called out.

"Maybe without a warrior for a king, we wouldn't always be at war!" called a second.

Ah. They're war weary.

The strain is too much for the civilian population.

"We've only been fighting the Tri-lliance for a short time, but we've been at a general state of alert for six or so years," Felicity said softly for his ears alone.

Some type of victory needs to be declared. Some type of information relay.

"How much do they know of the fight?" Felix asked.

"Very little. The military is on an information blackout to protect troop movements. There is a distinct possibility of spies," Felicity said.

And that explains more. There's no way to confirm allegiance, as it's on word and bond only.

Nothing to magically enforce.

Legion contracts would be very useful here.

I'm betting a good portion of this is a lack of information, clarified direction, and a security force built to root out naysayers.

The rumbling of voices slowly drowned out Felix's thoughts, and he came back to himself. Looking through the crowd, he could see many people watching him.

Yaris's head slowly turned to him. It was clear she was unsure how to proceed.

Felix made a small gesture, asking her for permission. To which he immediately got a nod back.

Standing up, Felix folded his hands behind his back and walked out from the booth he was in.

Almost immediately, the room fell silent.

Saying nothing, Felix let his eyes roam over those in the audience while he slowly walked to the dais.

Mounting a single step, he stood in front of Yaris.

Like a shield.

He continued to eye the crowd, a slow frown spreading over his face. Stopping here and there on people who seemed to have energy in them.

Tension and energy.

Once he'd made a slow circuit of the room with his gaze, Felix shook his head once. Then he let a full frown take over his face before he drew in a slow breath, which he let out in a heavy, disappointed sigh.

"You would ask my thoughts?" Felix's voice was loud enough to carry, but it wasn't a shout, either. "My thoughts are simple and clear. Yosemite and its people have clearly failed in their support of Vince."

There was an outcry of disagreement, to which Felix did not respond.

It wasn't until everyone quieted down that he opened his mouth again.

"You cry out in denial, yet you asked me for my opinion.

"As your queen, Vince's wife, sits on the throne for you. Attempting to guide you in the events of the day provide you with information," Felix said. His tone was chastising, but neutral. Without heat.

Only disappointment.

It was obvious they had expected a fiery retort. Retribution. Angry denials.

Without emotions for them to latch on from Felix, their own would fail.

"Your support of Vince has failed. It saddens and disappoints me. When he needs you most, you ask for someone to speak other than the person he appointed. A person he loves and shares his trust with.

"And that's the simple truth of what you've done. There is no excuse, and no room for explanation," Felix continued. "It'll be depressing to tell him of this when he returns."

Felix shook his head again, broke eye contact as if he couldn't stand to look at them, and then went back to his booth.

Sitting down lightly, Felix folded his hands and turned his attention squarely to Yaris, as if no one else mattered but her.

Well. That'll help for the moment. Needs some long-term work, though.

Chapter 20 - Perception -

No one said anything. There was a decidedly dejected air throughout the hall.

To Felix this was normal, familiar.

He'd learned to identify this feeling long ago, when he'd first started out as a manager. When he'd figured out what management style worked for him.

This was the "disciplined child" feeling people gave off. Where the employees were left to contemplate what he had put on them.

Because it had absolutely no emotional charge when he did it, there was little for people to react to.

Yaris blinked several times under Felix's stare, then looked to her people.

"Thank you, Felix, for your honest words.

"We'll be moving on to the day's events now," Yaris said, her voice carrying clear over the complete silence over the crowd. "First, we'll start with news from the front…"

"That was well done," Felicity whispered in his ear, leaning in close. "I'm impressed. Very impressed."

Her lips touched his earlobe and made his entire body light up with goosebumps and tingles.

Pulling his head slightly away from her, Felix gave her a flat look. "It's little more than management and understanding people. There will be those my little drama did nothing for, and they'll need to be spoken to separately at a later time.

"I bought Vince and Yaris time to solve it. Little more than that, though."

Felicity was gazing at him with an emotion Felix couldn't identify. "This is why everyone follows you in Legion. You've given them what they need on a personal level.

"Even if all you're doing is listening to their complaints and talking to them personally."

Felix didn't respond to her, instead turning his attention back to Yaris. It wouldn't do to ignore her after having so recently pushed all the attention to her.

Pretending Felicity didn't exist, he listened. Unfortunately, it was a rather boring meeting.

The requests presented to Yaris were mostly selfish and did little to help Yosemite. Most of them were declined, or they were altered enough to provide positive results for Yosemite and then given back to the requesting party.

Beyond that, there wasn't much discussed that he hadn't already heard from Yaris, Fes, or Felicity directly.

Vince was in the south, waging a war on the Tri-lliance. It was going well, but there were no details.

The east had fallen after its king was assassinated, and the resulting warlords and local barons had carved the entire area up amongst themselves. Refugees were flooding into Yosemite's lands and crime was on the rise.

This was especially true for the smaller cities and towns strung through the wastes who were under the Yosemite banner.

Patrols of soldiers were being dispatched to make sure local militia forces were strong enough to take the situation in hand. So the cities and towns weren't simply overrun.

Felix had the distinct impression the underlying statement was that this had already happened, and these were now considered preventative measures so it wouldn't be repeated.

"Last, but not least, we have an emissary from the emperor. As this is probably the most important bit of news, I set it for the last item of the day. That way we could break afterward," Yaris said.

A young woman walked up to the dais and bowed at the waist. She was beautiful, showing an impressive amount of cleavage and legs.

Unfortunately for her, Vince wasn't in attendance, and clearly she hadn't prepared or cared enough to dress for Yaris instead.

"The emperor sends his greetings. He would invite a representative from Yosemite to come and meet with him regarding the recent situation involving the Tri-lliance," said the woman.

Felix didn't miss the undertones in that comment. There was a lot unsaid there. In fact, it almost felt like a statement rather than a request.

"The emperor is a human in the western part of the continent. He took over an arsenal, hired a mercenary company, and now rules from a fort of guns and cannons," Felicity said. "He's betrayed us before and is clearly a foe. Just not one we're attempting to provoke quite yet. He also supports slavery as they pay him a hefty sum.

"He rules everything that isn't 'the Wastes' along the west coast."

Felix nodded, putting that information away for later.

"...with a warm welcome. Yosemite has received the emperor's invitation, and will respond accordingly by the end of today," Yaris said.

The emissary nodded and then walked off to the same spot she'd been before being addressed. There was a brief second when her eyes met Felix's, only to leap away again.

"If there is nothing else for the day, we'll close the court and retire," Yaris said, looking around the hall.

No one responded. It was deathly silent.

In fact, no one seemed to want to look at Yaris for too long.

And no one wanted to meet Felix's gaze at all. Everyone's eyes skated away almost as soon as their meeting his was possible.

Everyone began to file out, the room cleared by command alone. The soldiers were the last to go. Leaving Yaris alone with Felicity and Felix.

"Felix," Yaris said, moving over to stand in front of the box he was sitting at. "Thank you for that."

He shrugged in response. "Wasn't that big of a deal, honestly. Though I do have some concerns for Yosemite. It seems like there's a considerable amount of tension building.

"And a number of things that could change or be manipulated to help offset it."

Yaris opened her mouth, then closed it again.

"I only know how to rule," she said finally. "To rule, and to do what I feel is best for my people. I don't think I could have achieved what you did with as few words."

"Yes, well, ruling people and managing them are different things, though they overlap often," Felix said with a shrug. "Being a ruler can forsake the possibility of being a manager at times."

Yaris took a slow breath. Then she looked as if she'd come to a conclusion in her thoughts.

"I'd like you to go see the emperor in the west. I can send any number of people, but I don't think any of them would do as well as you could for Yosemite," Yaris said. She paused for a beat and then sighed, reaching up to rub her hands together. "I don't think Vince could do as well, either. He'd just get mad and threaten to blow the place up."

With a single throwaway thought, Felix could definitely see Vince losing his cool. Losing his cool and possibly going on a killing spree.

Especially after having been in a long, dragged-out war and traveled extensively.

He's probably a hair's breadth away from turning anyone perceived as an enemy to ash.

"To be honest, Yaris," Felix said, looking up from his seat in the booth. "I'd like to go home as soon as possible."

"If I'm not here, it'd be pretty hard to see the emperor."

Yaris nodded at that, looking away.

"I had assumed that would be the answer, but I still needed to ask. There is so much going on and so much to do that I don't think this meeting isn't a planned attack in some way," said the Elf.

Felix could feel Felicity's eyes on the side of his face. Boring into him.

Imploring him to help, if not practically demanding outright that he do so.

"Can you give me the ability to open a portal?" Felicity asked suddenly.

"Huh?" Felix turned to her. Then his mind skipped ahead to the logical conclusion. "I can indeed. It'll cost some gold to do it, but it shouldn't be too bad."

But... wait.

"Before you get excited, let's run a thought experiment," Felix said, looking to the wooden railing of the booth.

How many points would it cost if I wanted to give Felicity the ability to open portals?

First Power (Unlock): Portal Control	Required Primary Power: 90 (Unmet) Required Intelligence: 90 (Met)	Upgrade? (10,000)

That seems about right, but… it doesn't seem complete. Almost doable even if I borrow some gold.
How many points would it cost if I wanted to give Felicity the ability specifically to open a portal home?

First Power (Unlock): Portal Control-Direct	Required Primary Power: 994 (Unmet) Required Intelligence: 90 (Met)	Upgrade? (5.5x10^8th)

Ok, yeah. Having the power required to open a portal back home is astronomical.
Does that mean it's just as hard for Kit? Or would it be easier from her side since this side has the pressure on it keeping things from opening?

"I can definitely give you the ability to open portals, but the amount of power required to pop one open to get home would be exorbitant, to say the least," Felix said, smiling at Felicity.

"That's fine. Give me the power to open portals, and we can do a daily check-in back here to see if there is any change with the portal to home."

"All the while going on a trip to see the emperor," Felicity said, looking pleased with herself for having solved the problem.

It'd work, I suppose. It'd also give us a bit more room to work with in the future if Felicity could do the same as Kit.

Felix sighed and then looked to Yaris.

"It would seem my enthusiastic admin has volunteered us for the job. Give us a day or so and we should be ready," Felix said. Getting to his feet, he inclined his head to Yaris and made his way for the exit.

He heard Felicity catch up to him and walk quietly at his side, a single step behind.

"What are you doing back there? I can't see you," Felix muttered as he opened the assembly door and stepped out into the streets of Yosemite.

"I shouldn't have volunteered us the way I did," Felicity said as the door shut behind them. "I should have saved that conversation for private."

"Yes, you should have. But it's done, and in the end, you weren't wrong." Felix looked back and forth down the street. "I have no idea where I am. So get in front of me and show me where we're going. We need to get home and put you somewhere safe."

"When I give people powers, they tend to pass out."

"Oh? Oh! Of course, yes." Felicity scurried out in front of him and began walking determinedly away. Her clothing fit in naturally here in Yosemite.

Those pants fit her like a damned second skin.

She cast a single glance over her shoulder, catching him as his eyes jumped back up to her face. Smiling, she looked ahead again.

***

The sudden knock on his door caused Felix to stop writing. He wiped the quill nub against the inkwell to get rid of the excess, then slid it into its place in the writing set.

Turning to the door, he cleared his throat.

"Enter," he called.

When the door opened, though, Felix was absolutely surprised. Vince was standing in the doorway, looking tired and run down.

But alive, and with a lot less stress in his face than the last time Felix had seen his little brother.

Getting to his feet, Felix immediately went over to Vince.

Only to have Vince hug him before Felix could.

"It's good to see you, brother," Vince said, then released him. "Though it's strange that you're here. I heard some of it from Yaris before I came over. I got in last night."

"Yeah, I'm not exactly here by choice, but I'm enjoying my stay so far," Felix said simply.

"I hear Berest, Falaein, and Mia are quite fond of their uncle." Vince gave him a brilliant grin. "Uncle Horse, huh?"

Snickering despite himself, Felix walked back over to the desk and took a seat. Picking up the quill, he got back to work. He was trying to pen out everything Vince would need to keep an eye on going forward.

Wish I had my damn light-terminal.

"What're you doing?" Vince asked, peering over his shoulder.

"Writing down things for you to do to solve some of the problems I'm seeing in Yosemite," Felix said. "Well, suggestions, really. You can use or lose them."

"Huh. Anyways. I hear Yaris roped you in to going west for me. To see the emperor."

"Felicity did it for her, but yes. That's the plan."

Felix finished the paragraph he'd been working on and contemplated continuing.

"Any chance you could put that away for now? Come with me to the grove? I'd like to talk more about this and get your opinion on a few things as well," Vince said.

Felix shrugged and left everything where it was on his desk. There was no need to do anything to it. He'd just let it air dry.

Felix didn't say anything as Vince led him through the manse and out the back step.

Everyone who saw them walking together watched for a few seconds before leaving or continuing with their chores.

A Dragon maiden with dark blue-black hair and bright blue eyes moved in next to Vince without a word. She trailed him several steps behind, clearly not willing to let him leave her presence.

She was waiting for him.

Giving her a quick once-over, Felix realized she was acting the part of bodyguard and dismissed her.

Vince finally came to a stop near what were clearly three graves.

"First, how's Eva?" Vince asked.

"Well. She's been moved off-world to a place we call Legion Prime. Or by the code word planet Campbell.

"She's doing coursework there with Michael Haglund, my on-site force commander. They're trying to get her ready to take over a location," Felix said.

"I'm glad to hear that. I think she has an amazing amount of latent talent." Vince grinned. "Second, thank you for heading out west. It seems I'll be heading out east myself to see what I can do about this refugee problem," he said.

"I'm here. I might as well help as I can," Felix said.

Vince only nodded, his eyes looking toward the middle space between them.

Not feeling any type of discomfort, Felix inspected his surroundings. Going through his mental notes on what he needed to prep for his trip.

"He's a slimy bastard," Vince said after a minute. "He'll do everything he can to trip you up. Do what you feel is best for Yosemite, and I'll agree to it. There's not much more to say about it or him."

"That emperor is almost as strange and wriggly as the god who granted me a favor."

Felix immediately felt sick.

"A god granted you a favor? Did he look fairly human—black hair, blue eyes, somewhat of an ass, and mildly exasperating?" Felix asked.

"Yes, yes he was. I take it you've met him?" Vince seemed mildly annoyed and shocked at the same time.

"I owe him a favor," Felix admitted with a sigh.

Frowning, he suddenly felt like someone was watching him. At first, Felix mildly hoped their conversation about the god had summoned the annoying deity.

Turning in the direction the feeling was coming from, he saw a troop of women with horns heading his way.

At the front was the lithe and athletic black Dragon, Taylor. He'd never really had a true sit-down conversation with her at this point.

Nor had he really evaluated her.

Doing a quick assessment, even flipping through her character table, he found she was exactly what he'd expected. She'd be aggressive, dominant, and determined.

The simplest way of dealing with her was non-confrontation and keeping his distance.

She wasn't a concern for him.

Pulling his gaze from her, Felix looked back to Vince. Except Vince was watching the Dragon maidens' approach.

Suppose I'll wait, then.

"Taylor," Vince said, resting an arm around the shoulder of the black-horned woman as she snuggled in close to his side. "Good timing. Felix and I were just talking about a trip he's going to be taking.

"He's going west to talk to the emperor on behalf of Yosemite while I travel east to take care of this refugee and warlord problem. I'll have our borders safe one way or the other."

"I've tasked one of mine to form a wing for Felix," Taylor said, standing up straight and looking at Felix. "It'll be led by a black like me."

"Interesting," Felix said. He wasn't quite sure what that meant, or why he felt like it wasn't a good idea, but he wasn't about to say no to handouts when he had nothing.

With any luck, I can use them as point farms.

"Good, that'll help. I was about to warn him that the emperor seems to be able to read minds as well," Vince said.

"Not a concern." Felix held up his hand. "Ring of the Legion prevents anyone from seeing anything inside my head."

Vince frowned, his brows coming together. Felix could feel Vince's mind press in on his own.

And slide right off.

"I can't get in," Vince said after several seconds. Felix felt him give up his attempt to break in.

"Indeed. Anything else I should know?" Felix asked, trying to turn the conversation to something useful.

"No, nothing we haven't discussed." Vince said. Then he looked to the graves.

Which was very little, but enough to know what to expect, I suppose.

"I'll depart this afternoon then," Felix said.

"Our mutual friend told me she was awake, but... no one agrees. The other Dryads have told me repeatedly that they sense no life from in there, and that digging them up to check would disrupt the regrowth," Vince said.

Felix clicked his tongue and assessed the graves.

"Sell me the bodies, dig them up, bring me some gold, and I can get them up and moving today. Depending on damage and decay, the cost would vary, but nothing terrible since I don't have the enemy pantheon pressing on me," Felix said. "Afterward, I'll sell them back to you on the cheap."

"You can return them to life?" Taylor's voice was sharp and quick in Felix's ear. "Why would you ask for payment, though? And to sell you their bodies?"

"I have to own them to bring them back, and the gold is to be sacrificed. I turn it to dirt and bring them to life.

"If it's that much of an issue about the gold, I can turn iron to gold later on if we sacrifice other things," Felix said. "I'll need time for it, though."

"They're yours, brother; as the king of Yosemite, I so decree."

"Taylor, dig them up. One of you others, go get me several bars of gold," Vince commanded.

Taylor stepped aside, disrobed, and turned into a large black Dragon. At the same time, another maiden ran off to probably get the gold.

Felix waited quietly, watching as the giant Dragon's claws functioned as shovels.

In no time at all, three corpses were laid out next to their graves.

Two were in pretty rough shape, though the third looked complete. Just extremely dirty.

"This one will cost almost nothing. She's intact," Felix said, pointing at the very curvy but young-looking Dryad. He didn't even need to check his points to know that. "The other two should cost about a gold bar in total. I can convert gold later if we need it after I recover my points."

"Bring her back. Please. Now," Vince said, moving down to get in front of the one that would cost nothing.

Activating his power, Felix tapped on the screen message that popped up. He was apparently bringing one Karya back to life.

"Done," Felix said immediately after he'd activated the ability.

"Karya?" Vince asked, leaning over the Dryad.

She suddenly coughed twice, turned her head, and started to throw up wet dirt.

"Oh, sorry," Felix said. Opening his menus for her, Felix got her cleaned and put to rights as quickly as he could.

He couldn't imagine that having mud and dirt in one's lungs was conducive to remaining alive.

The Dryad suddenly stopped coughing. She was also clothed, cleaned, and looked as if she'd spent a day being groomed.

Felix looked away from the scene and turned his head.

Behind him, a group of Dragon maidens were all eying him speculatively.

Feeling like he'd rather be done with this situation, he pulled up the screens for the other two women and brought them back just as quickly. Making sure to have them cleaned in advance this time.

"There—all yours again, brother. Sold for the use of that gold, and in exchange for the wing of Dragons behind me," Felix said, officially transferring them back to Vince.

"Accepted," Vince said in a choked voice, having pulled all three Dryads over into a single embrace.

Felix didn't know what to feel or think. Situations like this always made him feel awkward.

I wonder what the emperor is like.

Chapter 21 - When it Goes Wrong -

Felix looked around as they rolled into Sacramento. They were several days ahead of the schedule that had been shared in Yosemite.

The goal was to throw off anyone who wanted to use the information against them.

Apparently Vince had previously had a problem with the emperor and having his plans revealed to those who wished him harm.

"Is there anything you'd like to do?" Felicity asked at his side in the carriage.

The black Dragon whom Taylor had assigned to him, Kris, was sitting across from him. She looked very similar to the other woman, in fact.

Black hair, dark eyes, and athletic but very well endowed in comparison to Taylor.

Sitting next to her was a taller woman with bright gold hair and yellow eyes. Where Kris made Taylor look a bit under-developed, Goldie made both of them look masculine. She had an hourglass figure and looked like she had to be poured into her clothes for them to fit right.

Apparently, she was a gold Dragon. Her name was Goldie, which felt very uncreative even to Felix.

"Is there anything to actually do?" Felix asked. "If not, I'd rather just sit and work on my notes for Vince.

"There wasn't much to do back home until the election runoff, but there was a host of menial things I could work on. Here... I don't even have people to manage."

He could practically feel Kris and Goldie fighting themselves from something they seemed to desperately want to suggest.

Apparently Dragons don't hide their emotions well.

"Kris? Goldie? You seem like you have something you want to say," Felix said, looking out the window of the carriage.

Older buildings that looked sixty years out of the current tech from home lined the street on both sides.

The rusted-out hulks of what looked like cars had been shoved into alleys or pushed up against walls.

All in all, Felix was unimpressed. Whoever ran this city had focused on survival for so long that they hadn't planned for the future.

It isn't enough just to live; people need to thrive.

"I could suggest several things to pass the time," Goldie said, a long finger trailing along one of her horns.

Felix ignored her.

The Dragons were not hiding the fact that they wanted to get into his bed.

All of them.

And Felix wanted nothing to do with it.

"We could go to the slave auction," Kris said. "We could purchase some people. You said the more people you have under you, the stronger your power is, no?"

That's a pretty solid idea. Though I don't really have any currency.

"I spoke with Yaris before we left," Kris said. "She had some chests with the slave guild's bond notes. I put them in the room next to where Felicity has been checking for the portal. We can retrieve them as you like."

"Oh? That's some solid foresight on your part. I think it'd probably be best to have them exchanged into local currency in a different city, though.

"We should hide the trail and spread out the questions," Felix said. "Felicity, go with one of the Dragons and start getting it turned over through a few different cities when you can.

"I think I'll just go sit in the inn and work on my notes until you're ready," Felix finished, feeling a bit morose.

He missed home. Missed his things. Missed his luxuries and conveniences.

He missed his Legionnaires. His department heads, his specialists. Reading through reports and figuring out what needed to be changed to raise efficiency and employee happiness a few points.

Most of all, he missed Lily, Andrea, and Adriana.

"I'll go now," Felicity said. "I'll check on the portal and exchange the bonds."

"Thanks." Felix leaned into his hand to peer up at a taller building that was actually somewhat well cared for.

Well, that's odd.

The sound of Felicity opening a portal and then closing it was loud enough that people around the carriage looked over in confusion.

"It's the slavers guild," Kris said, leaning her head out next to him.

"Interesting that they have the capability and technology to maintain that building," Felix said. "Isn't it?"

"I... suppose. Though from what I understand, this is normal for them in the cities they operate out of," Kris answered.

"Curiouser and curiouser. I wonder what they have to hide." Felix looked at the building's front entrance.

A banner was hanging over the entryway.

"Auction tomorrow," Felix muttered. "Special specimens guaranteed. Yosemite not welcome."

"Vince tends to buy out every slave whenever he can. Sends people on his behalf to every auction that'll take Yosemite's coin," Kris said. "He's single handedly cornered the buyers' market to a degree."

"Hm. Now I'm very interested. Good thing I'm not part of Yosemite, but Legion," Felix said.

Then his eyes focused on someone. Someone that looked so familiar to him. A man who was walking up the steps to the slave guild.

Felix couldn't place it, but he knew he recognized the man. He'd swear it.

Then the man glanced over his shoulder and saw Felix. The recognition was there in his eyes as well. Hurrying ahead, he opened the door and slipped inside before Felix could pull up a hypothetical owner window.

Now I'm very curious. So curious it hurts.

I think this auction will be more interesting than I thought.

Who would I know in this world?

And if I know him, that would mean he's a portal traveler too, right?

I should have asked Vince if he got the benefactor's name. I'd be shouting at him right about now.

Feeling some of his ennui burn off instantly, Felix noticed his inner problem solver sitting up. He wanted to figure out what this was, fix it, solve it, and put it back down.

It was why he enjoyed management. Everyone was a problem to be fixed.

***

"Just place your hand on this tablet and recite your affiliation," said a man in blood-red leather armor. He was holding out a black slate in front of him that clearly had an impression for a hand.

"Owner and proprietor of Legion, a business that specializes in re-purposing everything it can," Felix said easily and honestly.

Felicity, Kris, and Goldie were with him. He was allowed three bodyguards for the auction. They were also all sporting thin slave collars. Magical devices made to limit the ability of the wearer to act contrary to their owner's wishes.

It would even kill them if they ran far enough away.

The command Felix put on his people was to simply be themselves. He was curious about the collars, though. Since he owned them, he planned on taking them back to Felicia and letting her peel them apart. She often got ideas from other things that inspired her power.

Before his thoughts could stray into dangerous homesickness territory, he turned his mind back to the situation at hand.

The law in the emperor's lands was that all non-humanoids had to wear slave collars.

If non-humanoid treatment had been poor in his home plane, it was downright abysmal here.

"And them?" the guard asked, pointing to the women.

"My personal bodyguards. They can swear the same if it pleases you," Felix said with his hand still on the plate.

The guard glanced down at the plate. Whatever he was expecting or looking for, he didn't find it. Without an excuse to detain or turn them away, the guard waved Felix and his people inside with a lazy wave of his hand.

"Go on in. Seating is undetermined, so feel free to sit wherever," said the guard.

Appreciative of the dismissal, as it confirmed that he had passed muster as a "nobody," Felix wandered inside. He immediately spotted a sign that read a listing for two different directions.

One was for deposit security, the other the bid.

Turning off towards deposit security, Felix adjusted the coat he was wearing. It felt strange—not very modern—and looked awful.

At least to his own tastes. Supposedly it was high fashion here, and he put out a certain amount of "wealth" in wearing it.

Felicity was wearing a dress that revealed far too much, and Kris and Goldie were in soft leather armor that seemed designed more to fit an aesthetic sense than for actual use.

Kris was also carrying a massive iron-bound chest around on her shoulder. It held all the coin they were willing to spend at the auction.

"Why are we going this way, nest-mate?" Kris asked.

"So you don't have to lug that box around on that shoulder of yours," Felix said immediately.

"It's not that heavy," Kris said.

"Yeah, and I'd rather not see you carrying it around all the same," Felix said, queuing up at the end of the line.

It only took a minute before he was at the front.

A young man looked from him to Kris. "I take it you'll be depositing that with us?"

"That'd be the case. This is our count." Felix pulled out a slip of paper and handed it over. "Feel free to confirm it."

Kris dropped the chest with a crunch of wood onto the ground in front of the teller window.

"Ah… that is… I'm sure it'll be fine," said the teller, eying the chest.

Kris rolled her shoulder and gave her hand a flex. Felix quirked a brow, smiling at the Dragon.

"No, it wasn't heavy. But not very comfortable," Kris said, answering his question before he could ask.

Felix looked back toward the way they'd come.

Goldie turned and started heading toward the auction area, her head swiveling one way and then the other. She'd apparently decided it was time to move this forward.

"She has better senses than I," Kris said, moving in behind Felix.

Felicity slipped her arm into Felix's and pulled him along after Goldie.

"This is rather nice, having you here in my homeland. All to myself," Felicity said, her fingernails grazing along the back of Felix's wrist. "Even if it does sound incredibly selfish."

"Selfish, certainly. Normal? Very." Felix patted her hand with his own. "Besides, you're good company.

"Though I'm curious about this auction. They seem to be dead set on preventing Yosemite from being here. But admittedly their precautions were easy to sidestep.

"And I think I recognized someone."

"You… recognized someone?" Felicity asked, her voice strained.

"I believe I did. Which doesn't bode well, does it?"

"No. It doesn't," agreed the Dark Elf.

Goldie and Kris kept Felix moving and somehow divided from the other auction-goers. Either with a glare, a shove, or a word, they kept everyone away from him.

When they got to the seats, Goldie went four seats into the last row and sat down.

Felix was moved in next and sat down next to her, with Felicity put on his right. Kris took the aisle seat.

Looking around, he wondered if this would be a full house in the end, or if these seats would remain empty.

"It's because they're Dragons," Felicity said, watching Felix.

"Huh?"

"You're wondering why everyone is getting out of the way. Why you have a literal zone of empty seats around you," Felicity said. "You have Dragons with you. Other than Vince personally, there is very little that could compete with a Dragon one on one."

"Oh. Good to know," Felix said, looking at Goldie next to him.

She was busy glaring a woman into a puddle of goo who had gotten within ten feet of Felix.

Looking across the seats to Kris, he was treated to her giving a gentleman similar treatment who had remained in the aisle nearby.

"We have two purposes. Find out why they didn't want Yosemite here, and if we can't find that person I recognized," Felix said, putting his elbow on the armrest and leaning to one side.

Goldie immediately moved in closer to him since he'd leaned her way, and her hair tickled his ear.

Ignoring her completely, Felix waited.

The normal process started up. Pandering to the audience, hyping up certain "products" coming up today, and the next auction's date.

Felix had seen the same or similar back home.

Actually, it's identical in some ways. That's rather odd, isn't it?

The auction proceeded slowly. Felix purchased several people who had unique skills or abilities that he could harness or tweak accordingly.

He wouldn't even have to feed or clothe them. He could just have Felicity open a portal and send them home to Yosemite.

"For your pleasure today, our final auction is a set of Elves. The hunter has been collecting these specimens for the last several months," said the auctioneer from offstage. "We can guarantee their... freshness... and that they've been well cared for since we acquired them."

A group of young women that looked to be in their twenties were marched onto the stage. One and all, they were Elves. Their hair colors ranged from black as night to white as snow.

Tall, short, medium, and with every body type in between as well. There were even two with wings that looked as if their feathers had been clipped to prevent flight.

Felix wasn't sure, but to him it seemed they had two of every type of Elf on stage. Though he couldn't identify them all.

"For those who may not know all the sub-races, this includes: Dark, Wood, High, Snow, Desert, Winged, and Royal."

"Royal Elves?" Felicity asked disbelievingly.

"This is a special sale from the emperor himself. Acquired through personal hunting teams he put together. The majority of the proceeds will, of course, go to him.

"Starting price is one thousand standards."

"If they really do have Royals, we need them," Felicity said. "This is why Yosemite wasn't invited. Royals exert a magical pressure on other Elves. If Vince had more of them, he'd draw in Elves from everywhere.

"They'd need to remain separate from Yosemite as they're likely a different family, or branch family, and they would fight with Yaris and her children. But we could use them in Legion. We could use them to recruit more Elves."

Oh? Hm.

I wonder if that means Elves are more like insects. With each race having subsequent tasks and requirements they're best suited for.

Waiting, Felix watched as others bid against one another. Driving the price higher and higher.

- 626 -

Felix had started with about fifty thousand gold standards, and he'd already spent ten thousand so far.

That left him with a forty-thousand-standard bracket to work in.

Those bidding were moving the price up in one hundred and two hundred standard increments. They seemed intent to keep going higher and higher, but at a slow rate.

Let's jump it up and see if we can't run them off.

"Twenty thousand standards," Felix called out. He'd just bumped the price up by fifteen-thousand standards in one go.

"Ah… twenty thousand to the gentleman at the rear," called the auctioneer.

"Twenty thousand one hun—"

"Twenty-five thousand," Felix said, interrupting the man as he tried to bid up a smaller amount.

"Twenty-five thousand and—"

"Thirty thousand," Felix interrupted again.

"Thir—"

"Forty thousand," Felix said, scratching at his nose with his right hand.

Internally, he was already working through the calculations of his points to determine how much more gold he could create today.

And from that gold, how many standards he could then convert that to.

I could convert enough to make a smaller bid from here, but it'd be obvious it was my ceiling.

If I haven't intimidated the other bidders off by now, I doubt I'll do it with a dinky little thing.

"Current bid is forty thousand standards. Do I have anyone else?" the auctioneer asked when no one responded.

"I'll leave it at that and conclude the auction." The sharp rap of a gavel signified that Felix now owned a zoo exhibit's worth of Elves.

"We'll have a word from the emperor's personal slave handler, and then the auction can finish out," called the auctioneer.

"Go ahead and get them back to Yosemite as soon as this is over, Felicity," Felix said, facing her. "Buy a building if you have to, but get our people stashed away where they can't be seen.

"I don't want the emperor to think Vince somehow conned him on this one. I imagine he has spies in the city."

"But… we can check the thoughts of people. We should be able to find spies, shouldn't we?"

"With both Dryads and Dragons…" Felicity shook her head.

"Uh huh. And I can circumvent both of them with a Legionnaire's ring. You yourself wear one," Felix said.

"Ah… yes. Ok. I'll get it taken care of immediately after this," Felicity said.

"Great, thanks."

Turning his focus back to the stage, Felix froze.

Standing on the stage was the man he recognized. A man he now remembered.

Could put a name to.

Daniel. He was there at the summit.

Felix ducked his head down as subtly as he could. "Felicity, put a glamour on me, quick. Make me look like anyone but me."

"I think he already saw you," Goldie said before Felicity could respond.

"Why's that?" Felix asked, looking up to her.

"He's staring at you and isn't speaking," Goldie said.

Sighing, Felix sat upright.

Daniel was indeed staring at him. Smiling at the man, Felix waved a hand negligently. As if seeing Daniel was unsurprising.

"Mr. Seville, aren't you going to speak for the emperor?" called the auctioneer.

"Seville?" Felicity asked, her tone turning cold at the edge.

Daniel's eyes flicked to Felicity, then back to Felix.

Then Daniel brought his hand up and a ball of what looked like static formed there.

He flipped his hand forward, and the ball of crackling fuzz zipped toward Felix.

Felicity batted it to one side while Felix dove past Goldie and rolled down into the gap between the seats.

A boom sounded as the ball of static struck the ceiling instead of Felix. As if it were made of a child's interlocking brick toys, the ceiling simply disintegrated, leaving behind small jagged squares.

The mass of energy turned into motes of green and vanished as if it had never been there.

Then a giant peal of thunder cracked the air in almost the same position.

A beautiful white-winged woman with dark hair and dark eyes was simply there where she hadn't been moments ago.

Wielding a lance lazily in one hand, she brought up her other one. A wad of black lightning formed there. She tossed it ahead of herself and it scorched through the air toward Daniel.

Who winked out of existence with one hand in his pocket.

His clothes, some minor items, and a few coins clattered to the ground where he'd been.

The winged woman made a harrumphing noise and landed with a soft pat in the aisle behind Felix's seat.

Her eyes moved to him, skewering him to the ground.

"I know you," she said, her eyebrows drawing together. Then her eyes left him and began to scour the room.

"Runner, I'm going to need a hand sorting through this," said the woman. "And one of your pet projects is here where they shouldn't be. The designation doesn't match."

The world became still, turning dark gray in a single heartbeat. Felix couldn't even hear the sound of breathing.

Goldie looked like a corpse, her chest no longer rising or falling.

No one's was. Only Felix seemed to be able to breathe and move.

Looming over him was his benefactor.

"Right, then.

"You and your brother are becoming positively annoying," said the man. "I have half a mind to leave you here, but I think you'd end up causing more mischief here than on your own plane.

"In fact, now that I'm looking at it, you've been missing from your home for almost three months. What happened?"

Three months?

"Runner," said the angel, diverting the conversation. "It was the same one as last time that you almost caught.

"He came back."

"Did he now?" said the man, who was apparently named Runner. "Well, that's a shit show, ain't it?

"Especially if he recognized this one here."

"I... what?" Felix asked when Runner indicated him.

"He also did that," the angel said, pointing at the ceiling.

Runner looked up and sighed.

"Right, then. Shit show would have been easier. This is now a clown fiesta."

Chapter 22 - Display -

Felix got his feet and looked around. Everyone was frozen in place in the grayness. As if they'd had their souls stolen away.

Reaching out, he pressed a finger to Goldie's face. Her warm skin depressed under his fingertip. Her head didn't move much, but she was clearly still human. She hadn't been turned to stone or anything.

He let his hand drop and her head moved back to where it had been, her skin resuming its original shape.

"Hey, don't get any funny ideas," Runner said as he walked to the front of the room.

"What'd you do?" Felix asked, turning around and looking at Felicity. She was standing above where he'd fallen. Her arm was thrown out in front of herself, magic suspended in midair. A shield was rapidly forming around Felix and moving up toward Felicity.

"I put the world in time-out. It's having a nice nap time right now," Runner said, sorting through the items that had fallen to the ground. "Why — you wanna go nap-nap, too?"

"Ah... no. Just... curious. Sorry." Felix suddenly felt completely overwhelmed.

With a fingertip, he gently pressed Felicity's lip. It shifted under the weight of his finger. She felt normal to the touch, just like Goldie had.

Reaching out, he pushed a hand to her shoulder and gave her a very light shove.

Her upper body moved, then returned to its original location. It was a strange state she was in. *Funny ideas. Hah.*

I wouldn't have even had any if you hadn't put my mind on that path in the first place.

Felix shook his head and tore his eyes away from Felicity's face.

"I suppose that's true," Runner said, picking up something from the pile of clothes. "But you still took your thoughts there anyways. I only pointed in a direction."

"Yes, he can read your mind. Yes, he's an ass. Yes, he's very confusing. But he also owes you a few answers, so press him," said the angel. Then she sighed and leveled her spear at Runner. "I'm going to see if I can trace this back somewhere, Lord-Husband. Do not forget that it's d — that I have your time tonight, and have arranged it to be so."

Then she seemed to turn into herself and vanish with a soft pop. Nothing more was left of her.

"Her time tonight, nuh nuh nuh," Runner said in a mocking tone, bobbing his head back and forth. "As if I'd forgotten."

Grumping, Runner stood up and looked at Felix. Then he gave him a wide smile.

"I imagine you've spoken to your brother?" Runner asked.

Felix looked away from the god to all the frozen people around him.

"Yes. He mentioned you briefly. I assumed you were one and the same," Felix said. "It only makes sense, when I think about it."

"Hm. I suppose it does at that," Runner said and wandered over to stand next to Felix.

"You froze the world?" Felix asked, still not quite able to comprehend that.

"I froze all of existence, actually. Your home plane, this one — every plane is frozen in time right now," Runner said.

He walked up to Kris and leaned in close to the Dragon, looking her over.

"This one's a treat for the eyes, isn't she? I like the horns. Kinda like handlebars," Runner said. Then his eyes slid over to Goldie. "And that one looks like it fell out of a damn skin mag."

Standing up, Runner looked briefly to one side. Seemingly inspecting nothing.

"Of course she did that. Because she'd think it was hilarious. Eh... I could have checked earlier, I guess — that's on me," Runner said to what Felix thought was nobody.

Is he crazy?

"No. I'm not. I'm just realizing that a lot more slipped through my fingers than I thought, and I owe my wife a punishment. Hopefully one she won't enjoy this time," Runner said, then looked back to

Felix. "So. Looks like you've been trapped in here for about a week in plane time. Been gone for three months in your home plane's time. Someone was playing with the time involved.

"And before you ask, Patricia is kinda a question I don't want to answer right now, so don't bother. Maybe later."

"I had no idea. The portal closed and we've been unable to open it. Apparently from either side," Felix said. He hadn't realized it until it was said, but he had been wondering if he could ask about Patricia.

"Yes. Your people have tried a number of things to open it," Runner said.

"Any chance you can just... cut open a slit in the plane for me to slide through?" Felix asked. "It's starting to feel like me against an entire pantheon at this point."

"It is. You really are fighting a pantheon. It's mildly disconcerting to me that they're all working against a single mortal, but that's how it is," Runner said simply. "And no. I can't just let you back through.

"As long as I abide by the commandments I put down, they have to adhere to them as well. They cannot violate them."

Felix felt the blood rush to his head suddenly and he clenched his hands at his side. He wanted to shout at this god. To scream at him with his bloody frustration.

He'd lost three months now. The special runoff for the prime minister would be over. His people would have had to face the anti-trust case without him, and then the anti-religion case as well in the summit.

This god, this Runner, was grating on him.

And he wants to argue semantics!

"Though there was one instance when realistically, it probably should have opened. I have a feeling someone interfered there," Runner said. "Not exactly violating the laws I put down, but probably pushing the gray area a bit too far."

Felix had his tongue stuck between his teeth. It took everything he had to maintain his composure and not speak right now.

"Tell you what I'll do. I'll reverse the flow of time back to that point and let you cross over at that moment in time," Runner said. "That meets the regulations I put down and gives you what you want, and I don't have to look at that grumpy face of yours."

"And how much time would I lose at that juncture from the point when I came here?" Felix asked.

"About three weeks. More than enough time to get back to Legion and set things as you would wish them."

"And what about this world? You can't really push it back, can you? If you rewound time here, it would create a paradox.

"I mean, if you rewound time, the initiating event that would cause you to rewind time wouldn't happen.

"Right? Nothing would happen, and we'd just be right back here. I mean, that's logical, isn't it?" Felix asked.

"Right. This world will remain the same," Runner confirmed after staring at Felix for a full three seconds.

"Then I want you to keep the rest of all existence—every plane—frozen until I can meet with the emperor," Felix said.

Runner raised his eyebrows at that, watching Felix.

"If you can't police your own policies, and I have to keep suffering for them, I think I deserve some sort of renumeration," Felix said, unwilling to budge on this. "I promised Vince I'd see the emperor. He's my brother. I won't break that promise."

Looking to one side, Runner was lost in his own thoughts.

Or so Felix believed.

He didn't dare think anything about the situation otherwise, since it was clear Runner would simply pluck the thoughts right out of his head as if they were chat bubbles in a comic book.

"Fine." Runner turned back to Felix. "One day's worth of time to meet the emperor and portal back to Vince to give him the news. Then I open a portal for you to go home. What happens after that is on you."

Felix let out a slow breath as subtly as he could.

"It's a deal," he said.

Runner waved a hand at him and moved around to stand outside of the row.

"Go ahead and lie back down where you were. We'll get this show on the road," Runner said. "As far as Daniel goes – or Seville, as Felicity and Vince know him – don't speak of him. To anyone. At all. It never happened.

"I'm going to poke around in your wife's head a bit and remove some memories."

"She's not my wife.

"And I've seen him on my own plane," Felix said, getting down on the ground. "What do you want me to do if I see him again?"

"Ha. I tried that game, too. Didn't work out very well. Now I have more wives than days in the week.

"As to seeing him again, just call out to me. Say my name. Runner Norwood," said the god. He moved around behind the seats to look down at Felix.

Felix shifted around on the ground, getting as comfortable as he could.

"Great, that looks about right," Runner said. "With all that, I'll see you in a day. I'll also make sure this world and your home world have matching times going forward. And here's a parting gift. Give her a kiss and a squeeze. She'll like it."

Reaching over, he slapped Felicity on the side of her shoulder.

The world jumped to color again, and the shield Felicity was casting winked out as she toppled toward him unexpectedly.

Unbalanced and unable to recover, Felicity collapsed right atop him. At the same time, Kris and Goldie launched to their feet, moving to stand above Felix.

Not expecting Felicity to crash into him, Felix hadn't been able to brace himself, and the wind was knocked out of him.

"Oh, I'm sorry, Felix! I don't know what happened," Felicity said, lifting her head up to look around. Her hands were pressed to his shoulders and she was practically laid out flat on top of him.

"He's gone," Goldie said.

"We should leave after we get our purchases," Kris added.

Felix could only nod.

Fucking Runner.

***

Somehow, Felix had kept his mouth shut about everything. He hadn't told anyone about his encounter with the god known as Runner.

That everything had actually already gone wrong, and he'd been locked out of his home for three months.

This was more like having a "get out of jail free" card and using it. Felix had erred in not treating the portal as a trap. That he could literally be cut off from his people as he had been.

He hadn't been paranoid enough.

"Leave your weapons here," said a guard with a large rifle in his hands.

Felix looked it over and then back to the guard. His weapon looked like something from a bygone era that had been modified extensively.

Except the modifications looked more like they'd come from his own world. Or somewhere very similar.

Alright. So there're some portal games going on here. Someone else is playing portal emissary for the emperor, as I am for Vince.

Except they're keeping it limited while I sent over mechs, basically.

Felix unfastened his hunting knife and pistol holster, then placed them on the tray that was set to one side of the big double doors.

They were standing outside the entry to the keep for the emperor. Felix had been singularly unimpressed with the giant paranoid fort of cannons pointing out in every direction.

It looked like something a crazy person would put together and somehow think they were safe. *All it would take is a few Dragons with bombs and this whole building would be gone.*

"I have no weapons," Kris said simply, holding up her hands.

"Nor I," Goldie agreed.

"Or me," Felicity offered.

The two guards looked at the single pistol and the knife on the tray, then to the women.

They were all dressed in tight clothes. Leather armor for the dragons, and a dress for Felicity.

There wasn't really much room for them to hide anything, anywhere. For a brief moment, the guards seemed to contemplate frisking the women.

That quickly ended when a rather bright aura of anger began to ooze out of Goldie. She apparently had caught the attention they were giving her and was displeased.

"Fine, go in then. The Dragons will wait in the antechamber. You can take the Elf to see the emperor, though," said the guard who hadn't spoken yet.

"I will not leave my nest-mate," Kris said, her voice pitched low and deadly. There was a growling edge to it that Felix didn't want to consider.

"Nor I," Goldie agreed, her voice sounding much more normal.

"Then you'll not be seeing the emperor," the guard said simply.

"Is there any way you'd allow them in with me? I'd prefer not having to beg you for your kindness, but I'm not much of a warrior and depend on their company, much as the emperor does for you," Felix said. He imagined the guards wouldn't mind letting Felix debase himself to a degree in asking.

"Huh… well… if they swore to their Dragon's word that they wouldn't hurt the emperor, we could let them in, right?" asked the first guard to the second guard.

"You see? Perfect," Felix said. "Girls, please swear to the nice guards on your Dragon word that you'll not harm the emperor during this visit unless in self-defense."

Felix turned back to the guards. "That'd be agreeable and fair, would it not? For the emissaries of a friendly country?"

The two guards seemed to be mulling that over individually.

"Great," Felix said, not giving them a chance to respond. "Ladies, go ahead and swear to that, and let's head on in."

Kris and Goldie glanced at each other, then both spoke at the same time.

"I do so swear as you stated, on my Dragon's word."

Not waiting for the guards, Felix immediately moved into the room.

Unable to respond, or at least unwilling to stop him physically, the guards let him proceed. His bodyguards trailing along behind him as he went in.

Several weapon-sporting soldiers were positioned along the hall as it wound deeper into the cannon fort. They all wielded similar weapons to those Felix had seen at the front door.

They were all older weapons that had all been heavily modified into clumsy, would-be current tech. Each had a sword belted at their waist as well.

When Felix really looked at them, though, they all had the look of men living on their position. That their job had become rote. Expected.

Taken for granted.

No one challenged the fact that two Dragons were walking down the hall with Felix.

Everyone seemed intent to guard their post. Stuck in their own affairs.

Perhaps it was something the emperor himself encouraged. That he didn't want individual or executive thinkers amongst his people.

A failing on his part and a short-sighted loss.

Walking sedately along, Felix took turn after turn. One twisted corridor after another. Finally, he reached an arched doorway that led into a massive throne room.

It was decorated in a style Felix would only describe as "self-interest," as it mostly contained things one would associate with wealth.

Banners, weapons, armor, expensive knick-knacks. Platters of food that looked untouched.

Innumerable objects locked away but visible in glass cases.

Well aren't you a self-important little toad of a man?

The guards here were different than the ones outside. These were armed with rifles clearly not from this plane that looked as if they'd been imported directly rather than modified.

Several women stood at the emperor's sides. All naked as the day they were born.

At least he values my opinion. Otherwise he wouldn't have planned all this. He wants it to influence me.

Clasping his hands behind his back, Felix walked lazily up toward the throne.

He was here as an invited emissary, not a subject.

Reaching the foot of the dais, several steps beyond a rather thick rug, Felix bowed at the waist to the emperor.

"Emperor. I am Felix Campbell, brother to Vince. I'm here as his emissary," Felix said simply before standing up straight.

Sitting in his oversized throne was the emperor himself.

He was a small man. With small eyes and a frown. Black hair, dark eyes, and a thin face.

"You dare?" he said around a scowl.

"Dare what?" Felix asked.

"You dare not kneel before us?" asked the emperor.

Felix frowned for a moment, considering the man. Given all he'd seen and heard of the man, he was truly concerned with how he was viewed.

In Felix's world, this was a man who had reached the height of the Peter principle. Who practically lived in it.

He'd reached the level of incompetence that would prevent him from achieving anything further.

Surrounding himself with all the trappings of power that he himself respected and wanted. Putting people around him that would serve and lick his boots, but never challenge him.

Except his position had been attained through birthright. There was no one to cast him down from the top.

"I am not a subject to the empire," Felix said simply. "I wasn't even born on this continent. I'm not even a citizen of Yosemite."

The emperor shuddered in his seat. Rage and anger exuding from his posture.

"You will kneel now before us, or we will have you kneel," said the emperor.

Alright. I suppose this is done. It's nothing more than him wanting someone to come kiss his ring and make him feel important.

Possibly because Yosemite stomped out the enemy armies and came back safe.

Whereas the emperor never beats his foe, and he ends up having to rely on others. Other countries, and men stronger than him.

He looks incredibly weak.

Now that Felix thought about it, he realized Daniel Seville had likely been someone in this court. Someone the emperor had relied on. Or at least here in some capacity.

This is pointless. He just wants someone to bend the knee. Time to go.

"I see. I'll let Vince know that your desire to speak with him was only to have him kneel before you," Felix said. "I'll be taking my leave. Good day to you, Emperor."

Felix turned on his heel and started to walk away.

"You will stop! We have not dismissed you," shouted the emperor.

Felix didn't respond. He kept walking for the exit.

"Stop him! Bring him before us and make him kneel," squealed the emperor in his high-pitched voice. "We'll send his head back to his brother as a present."

"Drop a cloud or something to obscure what we're doing. Don't attack him; he's not worth the risk," Felix said to Felicity and the Dragons. "Then open a portal. We'll just open it up and be gone. There's nothing left to do here."

Felicity nodded, her eyes moving to the emperor. The Dragons looked like they wanted to jump over to the emperor and pull his head off.

Curling her fingers, Felicity made a gesture, and a dense fog exploded out from her. It literally swarmed over everything and everyone. Blanketing the entire throne room in dense, split-pea-soup-like fog.

Then a portal opened in front of Felix. It led straight back to Yosemite.

"Everyone in," he said, and he stepped through.

Moving to one side of the portal, Felix waited.

Kris and Goldie came through. Then Felicity did as well. She turned back toward her portal and made a small gesture, and it closed up as if it had never been there.

"Well done. Though I suppose that was a failure," Felix said with a sigh. "The emperor just wanted someone there to kiss his ring, and little else."

Around him, Dryads were moving in to check on him. Felix caught sight of one exiting the hall and vanishing around a corner.

Off to tell Vince we're back. Well, that was about as bad as it could have been.

Other than the thing with Runner, that is. Going home sounds great.

As if on cue to his thoughts, the dormant portal sprang to life with a small crack of thunder.

There, standing on the other side, seemed to be every single magical caster in Legion that could fit in the portal receival room.

Oh. I see. I can definitely agree on how that probably should have opened. That kind of magical power would have poked a hole right through if Felicia made some type of input or funneling contraption.

- 634 -

Chapter 23 - Villainy -

Felix immediately turned, walked to his home plane's side of the portal, and looked back through to Vince's.

"Kris, go get the other Dragons," Felix said to the black Dragon.

She nodded and fled out of the hallway immediately.

"Goldie, go get the Elves. Felicity, go get Vince," Felix ordered.

The Dragon woman lifted her chin, then nodded with a smile. "Time to see our home, nestmate," murmured the gold Dragon before she turned and left.

Felicity was gone without a word or gesture, practically sprinting out of the room.

Felix turned back to his people who had opened the gate.

Standing in front of him, glaring up at him as if he were the most hated person in the world, was Felicia.

Her dark curly hair was cut short, her brown eyes locked on him. Arms crossed in front of her impressive bust.

"Hey, Felicia," Felix said, smiling at her. "I'm betting I have you to thank for my rescue?"

Felicia's face screwed up from anger to a strange look of desperate relief.

"Where have you been?" she asked. Her voice had started to quaver as she spoke. "You've been gone for three weeks. No one knew what happened to you. We knew you were alive since the contract magic of Legion still existed, but we didn't know where you were."

By the end, her words had degenerated into a blubbering sob.

Getting down a bit, Felix wrapped the smaller Dwarven woman in a tight hug.

"I'm sorry. I was trapped on the other plane by the deities from this plane," Felix explained. "There wasn't anything I could do to get back."

"Don't you understand? Without you we'd lose everything. This is my home. My family. I met my wife here," Felicia said, her small, thick fingers digging into his back painfully. "If you ever do that again I'll make a machine to track you down just so I can kill you."

"Got it. I'm open to any ideas you come up with to make sure I don't get lost again," Felix said. "Implant, tracker, spell, or anything."

"Good. I'm going to make sure it happens through an anal probe, you insufferable wart on a frog's asshole," Felicia said. Then she backed up and wiped at her face with her hands.

"Come over for dinner this weekend. Bring Felicity. It was nice having you two over," said the Dwarven woman. Then she thumped him on the shoulder and pushed her way into the crowd.

I don't think that was something I'd ever expect to see.

Then Felix was bowled to the ground under a horde of mewling, whimpering Elex women.

Looking just beyond them, he saw a smiling Lily and Kit. They looked extremely relieved.

Ioana was standing beyond them, comforting a shuddering Felicia. She gave him a half smile and a shrug of her shoulders.

Miu was standing off to one side, her body shivering as she stared at him. It was clear she'd not slept in days, and it looked as if she hadn't even showered.

Victoria was right next to her, and she looked as if she'd withered as well. Though she didn't look like she'd gone without showering, she did seem pale and thin. As if she wasn't eating very well and sleeping even less.

Even Jessica and Erica were here. Their hands were clutched together tightly, but they were smiling, and dressed as if they were ready to conduct an interview.

"Alright. Come on, get off me, my loves," Felix said, kissing the closest Andrea and then the closest Adriana. Then he started petting them and scratching at the ears of any he could reach. "I need to make some plans with Vince and then we can catch up."

Felix said the last bit looking around at his inner-circle lieutenants.

"We'll all have a quiet meeting somewhere, some food, and talk. I'm sure a lot's happened," he continued. "I also have a lot to tell you all."

Slowly, the Elex sisters started getting up, their tails happily moving back and forth behind them despite tear-stained eyes.

Getting to his feet, Felix brushed himself off quickly.

Andrea Prime and Adriana Prime didn't move too far off, though. Andrea was still holding on to his hem, and Adriana looked like she wanted to as well.

Gotta remember I knew I was safe. They didn't. They didn't even know where I was.

From their point of view, it's been three weeks of not knowing.

Not pushing them away, Felix took a step closer to the two Beastkin and waited.

He could hear the Elex sisters sniffing lightly. Looking to one side, he caught Erica and Jessica doing the same.

Maybe it's a Beastkin thing. That they need to touch and smell?

Is that why Andrea and Adriana had to dogpile me?

When they realized Felix was watching them, Jessica and Erica became motionless.

He waved them over.

Jessica moved in an instant, practically dragging Erica behind her when she didn't let go of her hand.

Then the Fox and the Rabbit Beastkin latched on to him. Hugging him tightly in the same way Adriana and Andrea had.

Yeah, must be a Beastkin thing.

And since we're thinking about it this way... let's make it easy for Kit. She'll undoubtedly talk to Lily.

With a quick thought, Felix opened his mind up to Kit. He never needed to tell her when he did it. He imagined she was always passively scanning everyone now.

She'd be rifling through his thoughts and experiences any second, then relaying the more salient points to Lily and the others.

She'd even gotten to the point where she could do it without him noticing.

After a few seconds, Erica and Jessica let go and moved around behind him. He got the impression they were standing just behind the Elex sisters, but he didn't look to confirm it.

"Thank you," murmured Erica. "I didn't think we'd get a chance to see you."

There were small grunts of agreement from the Elex sisters, and a softer one that was likely Jessica.

"Yeah, well, I'm not good at this. But even I can realize Beastkin have different needs. Ah, here they come," Felix said.

Kris came around the corner. With her were several beautiful and lightly dressed women.

One and all, they looked somewhere between Kris and Goldie in body shape and size.

Their horn colors of course designated their sub-species of Dragon, but also seemed to dictate what their hair colors and eye colors could be.

They all passed through the portal and went to one side. Then they formed two rows, presumably by their rank in the wing.

"All are here, nest-mate, except for Goldie," Kris said.

Felix nodded, looking back into the portal. Half a minute later, Goldie came into the hall. Her eyes found him out immediately and she gave him a wide grin. Behind her came the Elven women.

When she passed through the portal, Goldie deliberately walked close to Felix and dragged a finger along his chest as she went.

The Elves formed two rows of their own next to the Dragons.

Goldie took her place next to Kris as the second-in-command.

"You will have to explain those. Lily isn't upset, but she isn't happy either," came the mental warning from Kit.

Felix couldn't push his thoughts back at her in the same way, so he just nodded instead. He was sure she could see the back of his head.

"Good. Thank you."

Felicity came back now with Vince. In tow with him were Yaris, Meliae, and Fes.

Vince stopped just on the other side of the portal while Felicity lightly hopped through and moved past Felix.

"I'm glad to see the portal is back open, brother," Vince said, smiling. "Felicity said you had news from the emperor?"

"Yes. He just wanted someone to take hostage, bend the knee to him, or kill outright," Felix said simply. "It would seem the emperor is not very happy with how your war turned out."

"Of course he isn't," Fes said with a snort. "He would have lost if not for us. Or at least, he would have had to actually strip the citadel of guards and weapons."

Vince sighed and nodded once. "I understand. Sounds like I need to fatten up my western border then, while holding back the wave of refugees from the east."

Shaking his head, Vince stepped through the portal and moved to stand in front of Felix.

"Thank you, brother. I appreciate you handling that for me," he said, reaching out and grabbing Felix by the shoulders.

"Of course. Now… as unbelievable as it may seem, three weeks have passed since the portal closed. I must tend to my own problems," Felix said.

Vince nodded and clapped Felix on the shoulder one more time, then turned and headed back to Yosemite.

He's become rather expressive with me. I feel like the awkward brother all of a sudden.

***

As he went to take a seat, Felix found himself looking down at the chair under him. It was incredibly inviting compared to what he'd been sitting in recently in Yosemite.

Making himself comfortable, he looked around the conference room.

Andrea, Adriana, Lily, Kit, Miu, Victoria, Ioana, Jessica, Erica, Kris, Goldie, Felicity, the blond Dryad who seems to stalk me… Where'd Felicia go?

"She was feeling really drained," said Ioana, who must have known what Felix was about to ask. "She went to go take a nap. She'd been working on that magical amplifier since the day you vanished."

Felix sighed at that. He was grateful for her effort and felt guilty at the same time.

He imagined they had all put in work on this.

Next to him, Miu sat down forcefully in the chair and stared at him. She reeked of body odor and sweat. Her breath also smelled, as if she hadn't brushed her teeth in a while. Her lips were cracked and her eyes bright red.

She was shivering from head to toe.

Before she could attack him, lose her grip on herself, or say anything, Felix leaned over and hugged her.

Then her gently kissed her cheek and pressed his mouth to her ear.

"Miu, my dear little psychopath. Would you do me a favor? I would feel infinitely better if you would take a nap. That way I could know you were watching over me later," Felix said. "Take some time to care for yourself and come back to me. I promise I won't go anywhere without you until you feel calm again.

"Alright?"

Miu's shivering had stopped as soon as he touched her. Her hands came up behind him and clenched into his back.

Then her head dipped down and she bit him on the neck. Hard and sharp. He felt her actually break the skin.

God damnit, really?

Here and now?

Grimacing in pain, Felix put a hand behind her head and looked to the others. The only way to keep her from freaking out at this point was to hold her, rather than try to push her off.

"She gets this thing where she needs to eat something of me," Felix explained to the shocked eyes of everyone around the room. They all knew she was five beers short of a six pack, but most of the others never saw it. "She'll break off in a little bit. We haven't had an episode like this in a while. A long while."

"First," Felix said, ignoring the crazy woman actually drinking his blood and gnawing at his flesh, "the Dragon maidens were given to me for protection. They're my Wing, as they call themselves, I suppose. They're more often in their human form than anything else. But they're Dragons."

"That will make protecting you easier," Victoria said. "Will they report to me like the Dryads, or…?"

Felix glanced at his stalker blond Dryad and quickly called up her character sheet. He just wanted to see her name.

Name: Faith	Power: None	
Alias: None		
Physical Status: Randy; Lustful.	Mental Status: Hopeful; Willing; Dazed.	
Positive Statuses: In Love (Emotional Boost XXX)	Negative Statuses: Nervous, Lonely	
Strength:	63	Upgrade? (630)
Dexterity:	89	Upgrade? (890)
Agility:	87	Upgrade? (870)
Stamina:	61	Upgrade? (610)
Wisdom:	78	Upgrade? (780)
Intelligence:	84	Upgrade? (840)
Luck:	69	Upgrade? (690)
Primary Power:	—	Upgrade? (—)

Her stats are impressive. No wonder she's the lead Dryad bodyguard.

"I'd like you and Miu to stop acting as bodyguards and focus on inner-security consultant work, plus whatever projects I assign you. I need you closer, more able to flex to my needs.

"Turn the bodyguard stuff over to Kris and Faith; they can handle it well between the two of them," Felix said, indicating the Dryad. "I get the impression their goals are the same, so they'll work well together."

Faith the Dryad looked stunned at his words.

"I'm… honored and flattered that you know my name, Felix," Faith said.

True, she never actually told me her name, did she?

This was also the first time he'd heard her speak. Her voice was warm and smooth. Lower toned but not masculine.

"I will make sure your Dryad bodyguard meshes with your Wing and your Elves. We will take care of all your needs," Faith promised.

Felix wasn't quite comfortable with how she hit "all" as hard as she did, but he understood where she was coming from.

She was a Nymph, after all.

"Speaking of the Elves, they're next. Felicity, could you give them a brief rundown?" Felix asked.

He needed a break to pry Miu off and get her situated. Felicity could handle explaining that the Elves were a point drop and a recruiting tool.

Turning his head inward, he pressed his lips up to Miu's ear.

"Can you let go now? I promise I'll not punish you in any way. I understand completely, and I know it was hard on you," Felix said soothingly. "Just… take a nap. Relax. Care for yourself. That's what I want.

"Ok? I'm telling you exactly what I want."

He was very careful about telling Miu what he wanted of her. Her reactions were almost always over the top. But this time she didn't seem like she was going to give up his neck anytime soon.

Her lips slowly peeled away from him, but she didn't move away yet.

"You want me to rest? And care for myself?" Miu asked, her voice a rasp.

"Yes. I want you to care for yourself. I want you to get some rest and then come back and take care of me. Ok? I need you, Miu," Felix said. "I need you, and I need you to be in tip-top condition for me."

Miu nodded her head minutely. "You need me."

"Yes. I do. Now… will you please take care of yourself?"

Miu nodded once more, then let go of him. Rather than moving away, though, she lay down on the ground right next to his chair, closed her eyes, and immediately fell asleep.

Underneath him, practically.

Sighing, Felix leaned back into his chair. Before he could do anything about the bite, Goldie had a cool hand pressed to his neck with some type of fabric.

Glancing down, he realized it was a bandage.

"Thanks, Goldie." Felix smiled up at the Dragon.

She gave him a bright smile and a wink.

"…bring in more Elves," Felicity said. She glanced at Felix as if to see if he was done with his situation.

"Great, thank you Felicity," Felix said, then looked to Kit and Lily.

"Now, what do I need to know immediately? I get the impression things are starting to spin out of control."

"The government canceled one of our contracts," Lily said. She looked like she was annoyed, but not upset. He imagined she wanted to pull him off somewhere alone and talk. She simply did better in one-on-one situations. "It was a police precinct contract.

"They brought in a whole bunch of rookies, retired cops, and military police to fill it out," she continued. "I get the impression this is a test for doing the same to the rest."

Felix thought on that. He didn't disagree with Lily's assessment, except he felt like it was actually much larger than a single contract.

This was a phased test and solution run. Figure out if they could handle canceling a contract, rapidly filling the gap, and taking over.

There were two options for Legion here. Let them take them over one by one and ease the band-aid off. Limiting the loss of resources from both sides.

Or cancel every contract he had with Wal. Cancel them all and let the country fall on its sword.

It'd eliminate the anti-trust case, remove Legion from the problem, and shoulder all the blame on the government.

He could get Jessica and Erica working on this tonight, even. They'd come dressed for an interview; he could give them one and let that work its way through the public.

Then do it.

Cut every contract, dump every hold, call in every debt, release every position Legion held.

Focus down to the businesses that were Legion owned and operated.

"We could pull out of every contract," Kit said. "It'd cost us, and public opinion, but I know you already have a thought on that.

"The financial cost would be worse than anything else. It might cripple the economy to a degree if public faith in the government drops too far, too fast."

Felix drummed his fingers along the armrest of his chair. The soft snore of Miu's deep sleep was the only other noise.

"Is the summit still ongoing?" Felix asked suddenly.

"Yes," Lily said. "And the chair on Legion's use of force to prohibit religion is still going as well."

"If we canceled all those contracts, they wouldn't have much of a leg to stand on for anything going forward," Felix said. "We'd be out of the government entirely."

Slowly, his thought crystallized into a single fact. He didn't want to work with Wal anymore. Felix wanted out. To hunker down and let whatever happened happen.

He had been playing this game with them for a while now, and it was time his business motto lived on.

"Legion First," Felix said aloud. "Drop all the contracts, cancel everything, and bring everyone back in.

"But before you do that…"

Felix paused to look at Jessica and Erica.

"I'd like to have some time with you two," Felix said. "An interview for each of you, here in Legion. We'll not cut the contracts until you two have the chance to drop your stories. Preferably at the same time."

Erica took in a slow breath and then nodded, her long ears bobbing.

"Sure thing, Felix." Jessica smiled at him. "We can do that."

Looking back to Kit and Lily, Felix coughed into his hand to clear his throat. He was starting to feel a bit parched.

"Let's pull everyone in who was working security. Military or civilian, get them armed, armored, and sent over the portal. Vince could use a hand, I think," Felix said. "I believe his general, Petra, would be the best person for them to roll up to for the time being.

"Though if I don't miss my guess, our people will probably just end up guarding a wall with rifles."

Ioana nodded, her hand moving slowly back and forth as she took written notes.

It was such a drastic change in her that he barely recognized her as War Maiden anymore.

In fact, that was the way of it for almost everyone in Legion. Who you were before didn't matter as soon as you become a Legionnaire.

"Anything else?" Felix asked.

Everyone shook their heads.

"Alright, then the last thing I want to do is sink Blake. I want the voting blocks gerrymandered in our favor. I want those blocks so twisted over, I don't even care if it looks like a garden hose.

"I want his constituents to think he's the devil incarnate," Felix said. "Pull out every trick in the book to get him off the winner's podium."

Kit and Lily nodded at that, though the former looked a touch unhappy about it.

"Great. Let's get this done with. I'd like to sit back and watch the flames burn comfortably from a distance," Felix said.

"Lunch?" Andrea asked, smiling at him from her place at the table. Her ears were perked up and her tail was moving gently behind her.

"Yeah… let's do that. I'd love to just… catch up with you all," Felix said, and he meant it.

He'd been pushing Legion upward to ever greater heights. Except there were too many people working against him now. He just wanted to sit back for a bit and let Legion catch a breath.

Then we'll move on.

Kris leaned down over him and pulled whatever Goldie had used as a bandage away from his neck.

Then she ducked her head in close and started to gently lick at the wound.

"It'll help it heal," Goldie said as Kris did it.

Felix didn't care anymore. It'd been a long month.

Instead, he reached up and gently stroked Kris's horns. The black Dragon didn't seem to react negatively to the touch, so he continued.

"What're we eating then?" he asked, feeling a bit like some sort of supervillain.

Except it's a black Dragon instead of a cat.

Hm.

Chapter 24 - Mending Fences -

Lily had caught Felix's eyes after they'd finished eating lunch. She'd clearly been waiting for him to look her way. It was then obvious she wanted him to meet up with her. She'd even tapped her wrist communicator once, giving him a smile.

Then Felix had been thrown into a whirlwind of activity and hadn't gotten a chance to check it.

First he had Miu delivered back to her room, with a five-second recording of him telling her what he wanted sent to her email box, her wrist communicator, and her television.

He'd sent a few Adrianas to do it. They wouldn't panic at Miu's living quarters. They were the more battle-hardened versions of Elex women from the original Myriad, after all.

Felix had seen it a few times, and it was exactly what you would expect from someone who probably needed to be locked in a cell for all time.

After that he'd changed quickly into some fresh clothes, then gone straight into an interview with Jessica and Erica, making sure to flirt shamelessly with them all the while.

The Beastkin vote was going to be important in the fight against Blake. With some well-placed gerrymandering, the Beastkin population in certain blocks should overwhelm the rest of the group they were lumped together with.

Now... some three hours after Lily had pantomimed her wrist, Felix was able to check it. Trying to do so at any other time would have just been too much, since he wasn't sure what he was looking for.

Flipping through his emails, he found nothing. Then he checked his appointments for the rest of the day.

Huh. She booked a meeting for me on my calendar.

One on one with Lillian Lux.

Topic: Repeated marital relations.

Location: In our bed.

Felix reread the invite once more just to make sure he got it right. Not that there was much to double check.

She's certainly being cute and playful, isn't she?

Closing the invite, Felix moved down the hall. His plan was to go straight toward his personal quarters he shared with Lily, Andrea Prime, and Adriana Prime. Which was two hallways, an elevator, a checkpoint, and another hallway away.

Glancing at his watch, he saw he had about twenty minutes to make what was a five-minute trip.

Ghosting along behind him as he walked were Goldie, Faith, and a High Elf. The rest of his bodyguards were on stand-down.

They were all bunked up in general quarters on the same level as his personal quarters that functioned as their base of operations.

Apparently all the old bodyguards had been detailed elsewhere, and the Dryads, Elves, and Dragons had moved in.

Amongst that group, they'd be able to handle anything thrown at Felix.

Stepping into the elevator, Felix dodged to one side and let everyone inside.

Faith tapped the appropriate button for his floor and pressed her personalized ring to the security scanner.

A soft beep recognized her permission, and the doors slid shut.

"Security looks good so far," Goldie said, her eyes moving to Felix. "You've developed a strong force of people. Even if they lack soldier experience."

Felix wanted to argue with that point, but after seeing Yosemite, he wasn't quite sure anymore. His people were great when using their tech to its advantage.

Brief skirmishes weren't a problem either.

But a full-out war? Felix wasn't so sure.

"Do you want me to heal the bite?" Faith asked.

"Hm? No. Miu will want to see it when she wakes up. She'll probably sniff it, too. Ask me if anyone saw it," Felix said with a sigh.

"I briefly touched her thoughts. She was playing with her ring and pulled it off for a second."

"Her love for you is… endless, and dangerous," Goldie said with a smirk. "I think she'd fight me in hand-to-hand combat if you promised her a kiss for it."

Dangerous. Well, that's one way to put it, I guess.

Also should probably get all the Dragons' HR rings so they can poke into the thoughts of those Legionnaires around me.

Just like HR.

The elevator dinged, and the doors slid open. There was a checkpoint right here.

The guards manning the entry made no exceptions for him, even if he was the reason for the checkpoint. Felix was forced to badge in and provide a retinal scan.

Goldie, Faith, and the Elf did likewise before they moved on into the next hallway around the bend.

At the end of the hall were two doors. One led to Felix's personal suite, and the other to the general quarters for his bodyguards.

Standing in front of those doors was Victoria.

"Ah. We'll stand down and do a shift change," Faith said. "Please let us know when you're ready to leave."

The three bodyguards had apparently gotten the hint that Victoria wanted to talk to him alone long before he did. They moved up ahead of him and marched into the bodyguard quarters without a word.

Victoria was standing perfectly still, dressed in casual wear. She had on a calf-length green dress with a black belt around the middle.

Her hair was done up as well, and for all the world, she looked more like a citizen than he'd ever seen her before.

She eyed the door to the bodyguard quarters as it closed, then looked back at Felix as he walked up to her.

"Welcome home, Felix." Victoria's fingers locked together in front of her. "We were all very worried about you."

Felix had an idea where this was going. He wasn't stupid or blind. Just reticent and slow to act.

Remember, they had no idea what was going on.

Be nice, give them attention.

"You look lovely, Vicky. That dress really pulls the eyes to the right spots and fits your frame.

"Would you mind if I asked you out to dinner tonight? Providing that you went as you are dressed right now, that is," Felix said, jumping straight to what he felt would be her question.

Her dark green eyes were glued to him now. She blinked twice and nodded slightly.

"Great. Would you mind if I took you to Legion's? Apparently they keep that booth open for me just in case I drop by. We wouldn't need reservations," Felix offered. "I'd just show up as me."

Victoria nodded a bit more forcefully now.

"Yes. That'd be—yes. Yes. Good." She smiled at him.

"Great. Would you like me to pick you up or meet you there?" Felix asked.

"Ah… meet me at the Fist monument?"

"Sure. How's seven o'clock sound?"

"Seven. At the Fist," Victoria said back to him, confirming the details.

"In that dress," Felix said, indicating her waistline.

"In this dress," she agreed, smiling at him.

"Until then." Felix gently moved past her. Opening the door to his personal quarters, he stepped in and closed it behind him.

Moving in past the entryway, Felix undid his tie and loosened the top several buttons on his shirt.

He'd dressed in a hurry for the interviews. With a shave and an impromptu sponge bath in a chair so they could hurry up.

It had left him feeling like he needed a real shower and to change his clothes.

Lily was sitting in what he'd affectionately come to refer to as her thinking chair. It was a comfy thing that sucked you into it. She seemed to prefer it when she wanted to think and not work.

"Pretty sure that's not the meeting location," Felix said, walking over to her.

"And you're early." Lily looked up at him with a small smile.

Coming to a stop next to her, he reached down and gently smoothed her hair back, his fingertips caressing her hairline and scalp.

"I missed you," Felix murmured.

Lily closed her eyes and leaned her head into his hand. "As I missed you. Though I'm not quite pleased at the company you brought back. Even if I do understand it."

"I didn't think you'd like it, but I didn't have many options at the time. I truly thought I'd be stuck there for a long while," Felix said, curling some of her hair around her ear.

"I know. I get it. I even agree with it. I just... I don't know." Lily sighed. She slumped deep into her chair, her skirt riding up to her hips and her jacket stretching at her chest.

She must really be frustrated. She usually takes great care not to muss her clothes.

"Talk to me," Felix said, gently rubbing his fingertips along her scalp.

"I had a really long talk with Fes, you'll remember," Lily said.

"I do."

"She talked to me about how I'm the Fes here and I need to bring more women into contact with you and bind them to our 'family.' That doing so would make you strong and keep you safe," Lily said. "That wasn't all of it, of course, and I'm paraphrasing, but that was the gist of it. I guess."

Lily was looking forward again now. Her pretty face wound up in a scowl.

"And the worst part is I understood it to a degree. Then I hated her. Then myself. Then you," Lily grumbled. She lifted her chin up and looked at him. "Was Vicky still outside the door? I got the impression she was waiting for you. Standing there in that pretty dress and all," Lily said.

"She was. I took the initiative and invited her to dinner, rather than put her through it. I've been making plans with all my inner-lieutenants to give them some face time," Felix admitted quickly.

"That's a good idea." Lily nodded. "Even if it isn't her intention."

"No, clearly it wasn't, but I'll not be taking that road," Felix said with a chuckle.

"Do I satisfy you? Do I give you everything you need? I try really hard to figure out what you like and want," Lily said, the subject veering to a different direction entirely. "I'm not as adventurous as Andrea or Adriana, but between the three of us, we hit your needs, right?"

Ah. I understand.

Leaning down, Felix kissed Lily tenderly and then tapped her nose with a fingertip.

"You give me everything I want and more. I was being dumb not long ago and didn't tell you about what was stressing me out.

"Felicity saw through it and cracked me open, despite my own wishes," Felix said. "That's on me, not you."

Lily chewed at her lower lip, her eyes looking into his face.

"Promise? I love you, Felix. I don't... want to think I'm failing you in some way. You've always done everything for me that I want, even when I don't know I want it. And that doesn't even take my brother into account.

"Did I tell you he's on Legion Prime with Eva? They're doing coursework under Michael together."

Lily shook her head with a bemused smile. "I think he has a thing for Eva.

"But that's... that takes me right back to my problem. I sometimes don't feel like I give back to you what you give to me."

"For one of the smartest people I've ever met, you're kinda dumb sometimes," Felix said with a grin.

Lifting her chin, Lily raised her eyebrows.

- 644 -

"I could always suck your soul out and give it back to you, you know, my love," she said. "I am, and will always be, Mab."

Snickering, Felix pressed his forehead to hers and kissed her again.

"Love you, Mab. You and your evil sultry ways.

"Now, how can I ease your burdens?"

Lily's eyes fluttered, her breath shortening.

"You're making me dizzy. Kiss me some more," she murmured, her hands coming up to grab at the sides of his coat.

***

Two Dryads in heavy sweatshirts and cargo pants moved into the civic center public library ahead of him. Their SMGs were snuggled up against their chests. The thick fabric distorting the small, boxy outline of the weapons entirely.

On his left, two Elves were engaged in a quiet conversation, moving in the same direction. They were both sorceresses, the magical support in his current bodyguard unit.

Behind him and to the right, two Dragons walked arm in arm. They both carried pistols inside their clothes, but they would primarily be relying on their enhanced physical abilities.

They were wearing a glamour like Felix was, though theirs was to make them look like Elves. Whereas Felix's was just to make him look like anyone other than Felix Campbell.

To everyone watching, it just looked like a small group of unrelated people all going to the library.

Moving inside, he saw the Dryads up ahead. They were moving toward a number of seats in front of a small café.

Detective Torres had picked this location and this time for some reason. She had been very explicit about the exactness of it.

In the corner of the café was Detective Torres, clearly trying to fend off a man's attention. She was sitting with a newspaper and a cup of what was likely not coffee.

Before Felix reached her, she said something that made the man leave quickly. Except not far away, a few other men sat watching her as well.

Felix walked over to the café and bought a cup of coffee with a small bag of donut holes. Without a word, he sat down at the same table as Detective Torres.

He clicked his tongue and took a sip of his coffee.

"So, do they always hover around you like flies?" Felix asked, enjoying the popularity his buildup had given her.

Growling, Torres pointed a finger at him.

"Don't you start with me, Felix. I admit I should have read the damn contract, but this is just ridiculous. I got told my ID was fake when I tried to buy some beer last night. I apparently don't even look twenty-one," she said.

"Well. Kinda? I mean, you're definitely eye-catching now, and you look really young, but I'd say you're probably twenty-one. Maybe. Could possibly be jailbait if you don't get your clothes and makeup right," Felix said with a shrug. "Now, what do you want me here at this exact time for, Detective?"

"I'm not a detective anymore. And are they following you on purpose?" Torres said, her eyes not leaving Felix.

"Yeah, bodyguards. No one will recognize me except you, but still. And yes, you are a Detective. Mine. My Detective Torres.

"Shall we continue now?"

Edith flipped open her newspaper and pulled out a single piece of paper. She then set it down in front of Felix.

"It isn't just one location this was happening at. There've been multiple ones. All over the city. Sometimes at the same time, others over different days," said Torres. She pointed to a column on the paper. "These are all the days something happened, and these are the locations they happened in; these are the times they happened at.

"That kid helped me track down a number of them."

Felix pulled a donut hole out and popped it into his mouth. Chewing slowly, he read over the data sheet.

"In other words, it's more than one person, or more than one group of people. Did you make any headway on that part?"

"Not yet. But that's why you're here. This is one of the locations. Right out there, in fact." Torres pointed out a window behind her with her thumb.

Glancing that way, Felix could only see a mass of Beastkin assembling.

"Yeah, I know. The times for this particular activity seem to always be when someone is using the venue. Easier to slip into the mob, I would imagine," Torres said. "That one is your fault, by the way."

"My fault?" Felix asked, pulling out another donut hole.

"That mob of Beastkin. Everyone is well aware of the shenanigans we're pulling with the voting blocks. It's made plenty of people angry at us. Let alone the contracts we dumped.

"Did you know some businesses haven't had their trash picked up in a week? You have no idea how much trash a coffee shop makes."

Felix chuckled at that and shrugged.

"Considering we've put the entire thing squarely on Blake, I'm sure he's up to his neck in this."

"Wouldn't know. I'm just doing my job and keeping my nose to the ground."

"And a great job you've done, Detective. After this, we'll have to see if we can't get you in charge of an internal police force."

"You really think anyone is going to listen to me as a police chief when I look like this?" Torres asked.

"To be honest, you're pretty enough that I imagine many men will do what you want based on that alone.

"Otherwise, with me as everyone's boss, yeah, I think so. I'll just make it clear I'm the one appointing you.

"Then I can have a private word with anyone who has a problem with it and offer them the Sausage Chute, the Walking Papers, or getting on the train," Felix said. "Not many options for them."

"Sausage Chute?"

"You haven't seen or heard of the power s—"

"Shut up," Torres said suddenly. "Armed gunmen. Five of them. They're moving through the library and heading straight for that organized chaos behind me."

"Seriously?" Felix asked.

Before he could go to tap his communication device, someone started yelling orders at him to put his hands up.

In about ten seconds, Felix, his bodyguards, and Edith were all being led out into the venue behind the library.

Men with rifles were there as well, rounding up all the Beastkin into groups.

The closest guard moved away from Felix and started to talk to another one.

Taking the opportunity for what it was, Felix tapped his communication device and covered it with a cough.

There was no response. He just got dead air. Not even a transmission signal.

"Jammers. They're placing them everywhere," murmured Torres. "This isn't just a robbery. This is a statement."

Felix could only watch as the gunmen went from rounding up the mob of people to sitting them down in orderly lines on the ground. Quickly separating out human from non-humanoid.

"Felix, they smell of anger. Righteous anger," said a beautiful green-horned Dragon maiden next to him.

"And faith magic," said the pretty red-horned Dragon next to the green. "A lot of faith magic."

Shit. Is this a straight-up hate crime? It feels like they're sorting them out to make sure it's only non-humanoids on one side.

The Dryads were slightly off to his left, the Elves right next to them.

"The Elves can hear us, and we can hear them," whispered the green Dragon. "The Dryads believe they can kill half, but after that it will turn into a blood bath."

Felix didn't say anything. Instead, he pressed his right shoe up against his left. It was an awkward pose. One no one should ever find themselves in. It looked and felt like he had a stick up his ass and was trying to get off it.

After giving the full ten seconds Felicia had told him to wait, Felix finally moved his feet apart. The extremely strong signal from the chip she'd put in every single pair of his shoes should now be transmitting his distress.

"I've signaled the rest," Felix said.

"You two, get over there with the rest of the humans," said one of the men with a gun. He grabbed Felix and Torres, then began leading them away from the rest.

Felix was separated from his guards, but he wasn't concerned.

It'd been a week or so since he'd returned from Vince's world. The Dryads, Dragons, and Elves had been working extensively for rescue situations.

Which this was clearly rapidly becoming.

Feeling like the helpless citizen he was pretending to be, Felix waited. He kept watching the men with the rifles. They seemed nervous, but trained.

Then a shot rang out.

Chapter 25 - Chasing Your Tail -

One of the gunmen dropped to his knees, then slumped to one side.

The shot had come from the crowd. Someone was attempting to play the hero.

Shit!

Knowing what would come next, Felix dropped down to the ground and lay perfectly flat. He wasn't about to take a random stray round when the inevitable happened.

By the time a third shot rang out from the crowd, the gunmen were running. But even as they went, they leveled their rifles at the crowd.

Six men with automatic rifles emptied their magazines in three seconds into a tightly packed crowd of non-humanoids.

They literally hosed the crowd down.

Everything became pandemonium then as people rushed away from the gunmen to try and get to safety.

Or hit the ground where they stood. Fainted, shot, or otherwise.

In the mad chaos of the situation, people went running in every direction. Nearby, Felix saw one of the jammers explode into a fiery mess for a few seconds.

Not sure which Elf did that, but I'll need to reward them.

When it was clear the gunmen weren't going to be coming back, Felix got to his feet. He pulled out the earpiece from his wrist device and crammed it into his ear.

Glancing down at the screen, he tapped it for a conference call, quickly flipped Kris, Lily, Victoria, and Kit onto the list, and then hit the call button.

"We should leave now," said one of his Dragons.

"We're following them. Get moving." Felix pointed the way the gunmen had gone. Then he looked to the Elves. "Stay here and help the wounded, and police the body of the dead gunman."

"The rest of you are going with me."

The green Dragon was already moving at a quick trot, chasing after the terrorists. She hadn't needed to be told her orders twice.

Felix started after her, and the two Dryads, Dragon, and Detective Torres ran with him.

Then the line started ringing and was instantly picked up.

"Felix?" Kit asked. "Is eve—"

"Felix?" Lily cut in.

"Are you ok?" Victoria got in somehow.

"What's wrong? I got the—" Kris started.

"Everyone, stop," Felix said. "I'm fine. There was an incident just now at the civic center. Gunmen fired into the event, and there's probably a lot of dead Beastkin and non-humanoids here. Send what resources we can spare to help out.

"My bodyguard detail and I are in pursuit. My tracker is active."

"Kit?"

"Yes. Alright. I'll see what we can do about getting resources there," Kit said.

"Great. I think this is going to be a public relations nightmare. Lack of security, lack of emergency responders, whatever may have you. Lily?" Felix asked. They were turning off from the green fields behind the venue and onto a side street. He could see his Dragon up ahead of him moving at an easier pace now.

Maybe they slowed down.

"I'll handle it. I'll have this spun up as a lack of planning on Wal's part. That their pressuring of Legion was behind the disappearance of resources that were once able to keep the city safe," said the villainous lawyer whom he loved.

"Great. Victoria, I need you to get on this. One of the gunmen got dropped. I need that body picked up, and we need to pick it apart," Felix said.

"On it," said the swordswoman. She sounded cheerful. Her mood had been incredibly positive ever since their dinner.

"Kris? I need you and Goldie, and whoever you need to bring with you," Felix said.

"We'll be arriving with the Dryads and some Elves," Kris said firmly into the line.

"Goldie!" Kris shouted. "Get your head out of his closet. He needs us!"

"What?" Goldie shouted back. "Let's go, then!"

"We need the Dryads and the Elves," Kris said.

"Uh, Kris, you need to close the line," Felix said.

"Fine! I'll get him," Goldie shouted back.

It was obvious neither Kris nor Goldie could hear him as they continued to shout back and forth about their plans.

"It's ok," Lily said. "I'll handle the rest."

Felix grunted and then just closed the line outright.

The green Dragon maiden was waiting on the side of the road up ahead. Her eyes seemed to be tracking something in the busy, traffic-filled street.

"Felix, I could briefly read one of their thoughts," said the red Dragon next to him.

"You could? How?" Felix asked.

"There was something around his mind that I couldn't get through, and then I suddenly could when I pushed hard against it," said the red.

She must have snapped the protection ring he was wearing. If they're not made well, they can break.

"Memorize it then, and be ready to talk about it later," Felix said, and then he got to the green. "Which way?"

"Brown... wagon thing," the green said, pointing at a dark brown van.

Alright, need to speed up that cultural training. Seems like we have some gaps.

"I've got it," said one of the Dryads, her head moving to follow the van the green Dragon had indicated. "I've put a small spell on it; we should be able to follow."

"Great," Felix said. "We're going to stay on it."

"Are you sure, nest-mate?" the red asked. "We should – "

"It's turning; let's go." Felix moved forward quickly.

All conversation fell off as everyone moved with him, walking along the sidewalk. It took a considerable amount of patience, as the van didn't move through traffic all that quickly.

Surprisingly, it eventually turned into a quiet neighborhood, moving off the main boulevard it'd been crawling along.

"Why aren't we turning?" asked the green as they crossed the street rather than chasing it in.

"Because the sign says 'no outlet' right there," Felix said. "Which means that van isn't coming back out."

"Oh," said the red. "That's... good to know."

Stopping at the other side of the entry street, Felix made a show of looking at his wrist device. "And if we followed them right in there, it's very possible they'd notice or realize."

"They've turned again," said the Dryad who had put the spell on the van. Her head was turning, as if she could still follow it deeper into the neighborhood.

"Yeah? Alright... seems like maybe we can go in then." Felix let his hand fall back to his side.

"What exactly are you planning to do?" asked the green.

"Capture them, then figure out who they are and who they're working for," Felix said.

"This has nothing to do with us," the red Dragon said.

"You're right. It doesn't; but in the same breath, it does. That was an attack on the voting base that is going to help spur us to victory.

"We need to treat this as a rallying cry, not a fearful wail," Felix explained, turning toward the street leading into the neighborhood.

"I don't understand," said the Dryad without the tracking spell. "We could do that without involving ourselves, couldn't we?"

- 649 -

"If this were an isolated event, certainly. But I'm not positive it is. That was too much planning, hardware, and training," Felix said. "I'd bet on this being the first of several, if not more."

"That seems like what Lily calls your paranoia surfacing," said the green Dragon.

"Heh, probably not wrong. But I'd rather waste some time making sure of that than pay the price later for negligence," Felix said.

"Hm. I can understand that. Like making sure you've checked every pocket on the bodies before you eat them, just to make sure there aren't any gold coins on their person," the red said.

"Oh, yes. That makes sense," the green agreed.

Right. Dragons. They've eaten… people. Yes.

Moving along the smaller streets of the neighborhood, Felix felt oddly exposed. They weren't a normal group of people to begin with. Moving around in such a large party in such a quiet set of streets seemed like an easy way to get flagged by the neighborhood watch.

"Right there," the Dryad said, indicating a squat, unassuming ranch house to the left. "The van is in that garage."

Felix made no pretense of hiding himself. He walked straight up to the side of the house, opened the gate, and moved around into the fenced-in backyard.

"Felix, I don't like this at all," said the green Dragon.

"I'm not exactly fond of it, either, but we need to know."

"Alright, any tactical plans?" he asked.

The two Dryads looked at one another and then unzipped their sweatshirts, pulling out their SMGs.

"We'll go in first," said the one who had used the tracking spell. "The Dragons behind us. You're last, Felix. If at all."

"Great. Let's get a move on, then." Felix pulled a small pistol out of the holster on the inside of his jacket.

He racked the slide and eased the safety off.

Then Detective Torres was there. Felix had somehow forgotten about her entirely.

"None of that now," she said, taking the pistol from him. She gave it a once-over and then held it in both hands. "I'll keep him safe and we'll come in last."

All four of his bodyguards looked gratified for the other woman's interference.

They stacked up on the door, the two Dryads in front.

Stepping forward, the red Dragon slammed a foot against the spot next to the doorknob.

With a sharp crack, the door tore loose from its hinges and collapsed inward.

Damn, they're strong.

Sweeping in with their weapons up, the Dryads entered the house. Immediately after them went the two Dragons.

When Felix tried to make his way in, Torres pressed him up against the side of the house. "Just wait.

"If they find anything, you'll just panic them if you're in harm's way. If they don't find anything, all the better. You can inspect it after."

A minute passed in near silence, except for the occasional door opening or closing.

The green came back up and waved him inside.

"Nothing here," she said. "Though it's clear they were using this place as a safe house for more than a little while."

Felix followed Torres inside and immediately agreed with the Dragon's assessment. The place was a wreck and looked as if squatters had lived there. That or hoarders.

It reeked of what smelled like a well-used port-o-potty.

Trash was piled up in neat stacks in the corners. Empty boxes of survival equipment, ammo, and what looked like gun-cleaning kits were packed in those towers of garbage.

"Right," Felix said with a sigh. "We missed them? How?"

"There's an open hole in the ground in the bathroom," said the green. "Big enough for someone to go down into. It looks like they entered the sewer system from there after tunneling into a large pipe."

That'd explain the smell.

"Fine. Flag the whole building for Kit and Lily to clean out for intel. I'll check everything like last time," Felix said, then turned to the red when she rejoined them. "Now tell me what you saw in their minds."

"They were part of an organization called Humanity Pure and had been ordered to take over the civic center." The red's eyes scrunched up as she clearly pulled on her memories about it. "Their goal was to kill as many of the non-humanoids as possible while making a statement about Legion and what we'd done to the voting blocks."

"It was supposed to take about thirty minutes."

"Alright... that all kinda makes sense. Anything about backing at all?" Felix asked.

"No. There was a name floating around, though—where they got the guns."

"A Peter Miller," the red said.

"Peter Miller..." Felix felt like he'd heard that name before. "Any mental image of his face attached to that?"

"Yes. I think I can do a decent job of presenting the image to someone with more creative talents who can draw it."

"Ah, we'll give it to Kit. She can make an actual illusion of the image, and we can go from there," Felix said. "I guess that's it for now."

"What an awful thing to do for almost no reason."

"Corporate terrorism is so much easier and less bloody." Felix shook his head. "Actual violence is pointless."

***

Felix sat down in the defendant's chair and unbuttoned his coat. Making himself comfortable, he reached out for the pitcher of water and poured some for himself into the paper cup next to it.

"Are you quite comfortable, Mr. Campbell?" asked a lawyer Felix couldn't identify. Nor did he care to.

"Getting there," Felix said amicably. Picking up the cup, he took a sip and set it back down. All around the edges of the court had gathered reporters, journalists, and anyone who wanted to be here to see this trial.

It was a bit of a circus, to be honest. One that seemed to have grown too large for the courtroom itself.

This was of course perfectly acceptable to Felix. It'd give him a chance to really hit Blake hard.

Felix settled into his chair and looked up to the justices on the bench in front of him, smiling at them.

Realizing Felix was ready to proceed, the judges slowly turned their heads to his side.

They were looking to Lily for direction, as she had already submitted a number of legal proceedings ahead of time for them to view her request.

"I believe you have a statement for the court?" asked a judge near the far-left side of the bench.

"Legion moves to dispose of the case against it, as the grounds that were being used to hold the case up are no longer valid," Lily said.

"And the attorney general says?" asked the same judge, looking at the other desk to Felix's right.

"Despite the fact that there are no longer grounds to hold them to an anti-trust case, we would like to proceed regardless," said the attorney general.

"Your honors, by his own admission he agrees that the case is now pointless. He's just fishing for something to use against Legion at this point."

"There's no point to proceed with this case at all," Lily argued.

The judges behind the bench seemed to be considering this, talking to one another in soft whispers.

Felix folded his hands in front of him, his fingers tapping against each other. There wasn't much he could do but wait. He was just the owner of the company, which meant his part was mostly to sit there and look non-threatening.

This was hopefully the end of the road for Blake, though. Other than the summit panel.

But that had no teeth to it. It was mostly a political move, more than likely to discredit Legion and Felix. In doing that, they'd be better able to put pressure on the company and force it to do what Wal wanted.

With Legion eliminating all the contracts early, they'd pushed Wal into a corner. The government didn't have a leg to stand on in court now.

It meant there truly was very little in the way of problems Wal could throw at them.

"As much as I'd like to see Legion be called to task for their actions," said a judge in the middle of the bench, "we find it hard to hold them accountable to contracts they held in trust and canceled in a legal fashion."

The attorney general muttered something under his breath and threw up a hand at the justices.

"Of course you won't hold them accountable. Maybe our dear friend Mr. Campbell has put you in his pocket as well," said the man.

"I'd like to caution you to not make such slanderous remarks," Felix said, looking fully at the attorney general. "Unless you'd like for me to take you to court over it."

"As far as what Legion has and hasn't done, I can tell you one thing."

Felix leaned back into his chair and tapped his thumb against the table.

"If Legion still held the contracts for security, emergency services, and first responders, the massacre at the green wouldn't have happened," Felix said. "Instead, Wal decided it wanted to start eliminating Legion contracts."

"Wal canceled one contract—one," said Blake, sitting just beyond the attorney general.

"Canceled one, with plans to cancel them all. I'm sure we've all read those lovely notes sent back and forth between offices about it all," Felix said with a smile. He'd had his people break into the servers and download everything, then feed it to the net for free. "Don't act blameless and innocent here, Mr. Gresham.

"Just because you got your hand caught in the cookie jar doesn't mean you can blame those who made the cookies."

Everyone in the room was hurriedly jotting down notes as cameras swung around and zoomed in on Blake.

The man said nothing, realizing any response he gave would only dig him deeper.

"Won't even defend yourself, huh?" Felix asked, standing up. "That's alright. It's not as if you could anyways.

"You got rid of the prime minister, who had been doing right by her people, only to try and replace her with yourself."

Buttoning his top coat button, Felix picked up the paper cup and downed what was in it.

Setting it back down, he smiled at Blake.

"Then you pushed Legion into a corner and got hit for it. Now all of Wal suffers for your hubris. Your greed. And all I can do is wish you luck as I consider pulling Legion out of Wal entirely."

"I wonder how the economy would do if I did that.

"Do you think it'd crash, maybe? Would the entire stock market implode? Or maybe not.

"Maybe I'm thinking Legion is bigger than it really is."

Felix sighed dramatically and shrugged.

"Or maybe I'm not, and Wal goes down hard, and the economy folds. And you'll be the one to blame, Blake. You and only you.

"Now, if you excuse me, I'm going to leave. I don't think I want to hear any more slanderous lies from the government of Wal."

Putting his hands in his pockets, Felix casually walked down the center aisle, past everyone watching, and out the door.

Well, that was fun.

Let's see you get out of that one, Blake.

Because personally, I don't think you can. In fact, I'd bet on this being the end of your political career.

Pushing the doors open, Felix left.

Chapter 26 - Hard Conversations -

Andrea Prime and Adriana Prime were waiting for him when the doors to the hearing closed behind him.

They were dressed up in comfortable-looking casual clothes, and they looked like any other Beastkin one might see on the street.

It was odd. Though now that he thought of it, he hadn't seen the Primes or their Seconds in a while. Not since the day he'd come back.

Then what are they doing here now, and what's wrong?

"Hi dear," Andrea chirped happily, wrapping him up in a hug.

"Hi dearest," Adriana said, hugging him in the same way from the other side.

"Hello, hello. What's up? Seems like you two were waiting for me," Felix said, hugging them back.

"Yes, we were." Andrea stepped back away from him. "Can we talk in the car? It'd be easier, and safer for you."

Felix nodded and gestured down the hallway toward the exit of the government building.

"Of course. Lead the way," he said.

Several Dragons, Dryads, and Elves were waiting in a circle. The Dryads and Elves were dressed in Legion security gear, with the Dragons wearing light versions of the same. Though it looked like it'd tear apart easily if they shifted into their Dragon forms.

Both Andrea and Adriana looked toward Kris, Goldie, and Faith, who were in today's lineup.

Goldie and Faith gave the Elex women a smile and turned to Kris, who nodded her head down the hall.

One of the Elves lifted a hand to her long ear, her masked face turning toward the long hallway ahead of them.

They've been training extensively on this. I wonder if the Dryads helped the Elves. Or if Victoria and Miu stepped in to help before they shipped out to the wild wastes of Vince's world.

"Have we heard from Miu or Victoria at all?" Felix asked. He'd left them alone since they'd left. Not wanting to distract them from their duties under Vince's general, Petra.

"Yes," Adriana said. "They're doing well. They've been sending up reports about the situation. There was a probing attack by what Petra believed to be the emperor's forces. They were turned around so strongly that they ended up leaving their wounded on the field.

"After that, another ambassador from the emperor came."

Andrea was nodding her head rapidly.

"Yes, yes," she said, taking over for her twin. Around them, the Dryads, Dragons, and Elves started leading Felix out of the building. "Petra told Victoria she thinks this'll be over before it really starts. The fact that Yosemite had so many troops with modern weaponry, in this case the Legionnaires, she thinks the emperor will reconsider before he even formally declares war."

"Huh. I can't imagine Vince as the type of person to let that sit," Felix said.

"Petra isn't, even if Vince was," Adriana said. "Apparently she sent a detachment of Orcs to secure a kingdom that was in a civil war with the emperor. She's going to bring them into Yosemite. She's also moved the garrison from Yosemite out, and down to the south west to secure the emperor's southern borders against him.

"Now that Legion holds Yosemite, that is."

Felix nodded at that.

This Petra seems formidable.

Stepping out into the sunshine of the day as the door was held open for him, Felix kept moving. He'd learned his lessons.

Stopping for any reason outside was always an invitation for a problem.

He wasn't going to hide away in his house to prevent people from trying to take his life. There would be no point in living at all, if one had to live in eternal fear of going outside.

Five black Legion sedans were waiting down at the curb. Moving into the middle one, Felix was surprised when everyone else left for other vehicles.

Faith and Goldie often took it as an opportunity to wedge themselves against him, with Kris in the front paying attention.

Chauffeur Andrea opened the door for him with a grin.

"Today's different!" she said enthusiastically. "And I got ice cream. It's in the cup holders in the console."

Ice cream...? Ok... sure.

Adriana got into the car first, moving to the far side of the bench seat. Felix took his customary position in the middle, and Andrea slid up on his other side.

Both the Elex women fussed over the ice cream in the cup holders.

They were testing each one to see what it was, then discussing who would get what.

With a pop, the door shut, and Felix looked to the front.

Felicity was sitting there with a smile. She gave him a small wave with her fingers.

"Before they steal away the conversation after they figure out the ice cream, I have a request from Petra of Yosemite.

"She asked that all books on modern-day and past military tactics be sent to her. Along with any other materials we could suggest," Felicity said. "I noticed there was no skill book for military tactics in our library.

"For now, I've approved the transition of a digital reader pad and a copy of every book I could get my hands on that fit her requirements.

"I'd like to create a skill book that would transfer all that over to her on its own, though."

Felix frowned at that. Petra was already a formidable general, as far as he knew.

Then again, giving her more isn't going to hurt me. Will probably help.

"Alright. Put it on the point calendar and allocate it accordingly. If the same time limits apply like they used to, I should have an open window to use my ability in a day or two," Felix said.

The driver's door opened and Andrea got in. Settling into her role, she tuned them out and acted as if they didn't exist.

Andrea set a small container of ice cream into his hands and pushed a spoon into his mouth.

"Here, dear! Chocolate," she said happily.

"You should probably move on to your conversation," Felicity said, sitting forward in her seat again. "We'll be moving shortly."

"Oh! Yes. You're right. Thank you, Fell," Adriana said.

Felix felt like he should be surprised at the nickname, but he realized he wasn't. Thinking about it, it made sense.

She vanished with me and came back with me. There was no change in the status quo while she had me cornered and alone.

If anything, they all probably trust her at this point. That was her opportunity to make a move, and she chose not to.

"We're not going to stay here," Andrea said, reaching over to pat him on the knee. "We're leaving."

What?

"It just isn't safe here for us as Primes, or for our Seconds," Andrea continued. "Adriana and I are going to move into our new home on Legion Prime."

"Our Seconds are already there," Adriana said. "So it won't be like we're alone. We'll still be connected to the ANet, but only our others will remain here."

Oh. That... makes sense, I guess. Especially if they're nervous about the current situation.

To be fair, the tension and air around Legion HQ and New and Old Legion City has been... a touch oppressive.

"Will you move with us? Lily said she would come if you did," Andrea said, making firm eye contact with him. "Felicity said she already set up everything. The houses for the inner circle, the bodyguard barracks, the Dragon vault, nursery, grove—everything."

Glancing to the front seat at Felicity, he paused before asking her about that. She had a map on her pad and was holding it to the side. She'd predicted his wishes once again. He was able to see the entire thing as it was laid out there.

It was exactly as Andrea had said.

Felix nodded slowly. Now that he really thought about it, he recognized the feeling of having been under siege for... a long time.

Then he thought about the manse and open life Vince enjoyed. Felix had felt envious of it.

And now he could live it.

It's not as if anyone will have a sniper rifle on Legion Prime.

Not to mention we can erect mage walls, shields, forcefields.

No one could tell us no or cite regulations.

"Alright," Felix said. "I can't quite move yet, as my office is in Legion HQ, but... let's start figuring out how we get everyone over.

"The ANet, Felicia's lab, and the vault are the three buildings we'd need immediately.

"As for personnel, all the department heads, their families, and everyone in the inner circle."

Andrea and Adriana were both watching him with eager eyes. Smiles plastered on their faces.

"Yeah?" they asked in unison.

"Yeah. We'll start moving out of Legion HQ today. Can I count on you, Felicity?" Felix asked.

"Of course," replied the Dark Elf as she pulled the pad back to her lap. "It'll be done."

Andrea snuggled in close to Felix's side and laid her head on his chest. Adriana snatched Felix's hand and held it in her own.

They're so different now.

"And by the way... the Royal Elves worked. We've been contacted from almost every Elven enclave on the continent. I give it a week before the news spreads overseas," Felicity added.

"Oh?" Felix asked.

"Indeed. I've sent them Legion contracts in response. If they want to join, they can sign and send them back.

"Then I'll ask Kris to use one of your girls to fly over a portal device so they can join us."

"Great. The Elves have been a great source of magical power. Lily and her people are strong, but they're so few."

"To be sure, Lily and Evan are terrifying. They have a lot of combat experience, and for human magicians, they are equally comparable to senior Elven mages," Felicity agreed.

"So... how many are we looking at so far?" Felix asked as Andrea rubbed her face against his chest, her head bumping his chin.

"Elves? Something to the order of two thousand or so. I don't think they'll all join, but... it's a possibility. The Elven enclave on Legion Prime is certainly going to be higher than I originally thought in priority," Felicity said. "Suppose that'll happen when there hasn't been a Royal Elf on a planet for hundreds of years."

That's a lot of Elves.

Turning into a real melting pot of people and cultures.

***

Felix was sitting on the couch in his office watching television. It wasn't something he did often. The TV on his wall was off more often than not, or someone was using it to show what was on their light-terminal.

Watching TV always felt like a waste of time to Felix. There were always other things to do, and television felt lazy to him.

Reading books took longer, but he always felt better for it.

Today was an exception. Today, the results would be announced of the runoff for the prime minister's position.

The volume was low right now, but Jessica was sitting behind the desk on the TV screen, apparently talking about what looked like an accident.

Or so Felix thought from the graphic next to her head.

The news had slowed a bit lately. The fact that it wasn't Blake was impressive.

Ever since the anti-trust hearing and how it ended, Blake's political currency had been spent hard and fast.

Though he'd hung on somehow.

Lily shifted her shoulders a bit, snuggling ever closer to Felix, her hand resting on his thigh.

"I talked to Vicky after your dinner date with her," Lily said.

"Wasn't a date," Felix said. Readjusting his arm around Lily, he slouched a bit further on the couch to adjust for her change in posture.

"She felt it was. She also said you were a perfect gentleman. Treated her like she was the only person in the world there, despite being interrupted repeatedly," Lily continued.

"Uh huh. Wasn't a date," Felix reaffirmed.

"She's probably going to ask you out again soon," Lily said, her fingers moving up and down his leg.

"If it's a date, I'll decline it," Felix said.

Jessica was apparently gaining more traction in her network. She'd gone from doing interviews and reporting pieces to also being a lead news anchor.

So far, they'd been keeping her front and center all day.

She was dressed smartly and attractively.

Picking up the remote, Felix flipped it to Erica's network to see what was going on there.

It was always a curious thing to flip between the two. They always had the same story presented from two political views. Except they were so radically different, they might as well have been different stories entirely.

Erica was in a similarly upward-trending position. Both women kept getting stories that catapulted them to the center of the news.

"Preliminary results seem to be coming in," Lily said as the picture next to Erica flipped to a map.

The colors chosen were a dull brown for Kevin Dane, Blake's major rival, and a soothing blue for Blake.

"Any thoughts on how it'll go?" Lily asked.

Glancing down at the woman next to him, he realized her eyes were closed. She looked like she was about ready to go to bed.

Small tears were forming at the corners of her eyes as she clearly fought a yawn back down.

"Mm, I think it'll be exactly like Kit's people running the polls found. Kevin will win by a ten-to-twenty-percent majority," Felix said, lightly combing his fingers through Lily's hair. "You should go to bed. It's going to be a long night after all. I kinda need to sit up and watch what happens."

"Even though you're so sure of the outcome, you're still going to watch it?" Lily asked, slowly sitting up next to him.

"Yeah. I kinda need to. I need to make sure we're ready to go despite whatever happens."

"Mmm. Alright, love. I'm going to go hit the hay, then. Don't stay up too late." Lily leaned in and gave him a kiss.

"Soon as I know we're in the clear, I'll join you."

"Good. Goodnight, love," Lily said. She quickly crossed to the door, opened it, and left.

Felix shifted around in the couch and got comfortable again.

The door opened and Felix looked over, wondering who it was.

Goldie stuck her head in and smiled at him.

"Hello, nest-mate. Everything okay?" she asked, her hair sliding over her shoulder and hanging there. Her eyes were moving around his office as if looking for something.

"Yes. Why?" Felix asked, looking back to the television. Felix picked up the remote and turned on the close captioning.

It bothered Lily to have it on, but Felix found it preferable.

Goldie walked into the office and closed the door. She was dressed in the light Legion security uniform the Dragon maidens had adopted.

She folded her hands behind her back and wandered over to him.

"It's strange for you to be alone," Goldie said. "Usually Felicity, Lily, the Elex girls, or one of the potential wives are here."

Felix shrugged his shoulders at that. She wasn't wrong.

He almost never had any time to himself, in any way.

"Yeah. Well, it's getting late. Most people finish up their shifts and go to bed. Legion is a company, after all," Felix said. "I don't really have that luxury. I'm practically Legion itself, so I have to be working all the time."

"Late at night, I'm usually by myself."

"Oh? Where are the on-duty bodyguards at this hour?" asked the Dragon. Her horns glinted golden as she came closer to him. "I'm only ever on the day shift."

"Usually in their barracks. Sleeping or resting. There's usually a few night guards outside the door," Felix said.

"Yes. There were two Elves and two Dryads out there, and a Dragon of course."

"They're playing cards," Goldie said. Turning aside, she continued to move but went behind the couch.

Felix could hear her stop just behind him. Looking over his shoulder, he saw the full-figured Dragon peering down at him with her bright eyes.

"I don't like cards. No one could tell me why I shouldn't come in here and spend time with you, though," Goldie said.

Felix didn't have an answer to that. Instead he looked back at the TV.

Erica was gone, a large map on the screen in her stead. Districts and areas around the country were starting to report in.

"You're welcome to join me," Felix said. "I'm just watching the results. Not exactly the most entertaining thing in the world."

Goldie's hands slipped over Felix's shoulders, and her fingers started to curl into him. Her thumbs pressed into his spine and moved upward.

"I've been speaking to Felicity," Goldie said as her fingers began to push and prod at his muscles. "She tells me you have intelligent women all around you. Strong women.

"Women who can lead without the need for someone to tell them what to do."

Felix couldn't deny that. Nor could he deny that Goldie's warm fingers were massaging his muscles in the right way.

"Kris is a strong leader, and Faith is an aggressive representative for her faction," Goldie continued. "Much like so many others around you.

"When I first realized this, I was concerned. I looked at all those women you had about and thought perhaps I'd made a mistake."

Felix sat up straight in the couch and rolled his shoulders forward as Goldie expertly tended to his back. He was only dimly watching the screen now as she spoke.

"Why's that?" Felix asked. Erica was pointing to several places on the map now as they were colored in. Brown was slowly filling in more and more, though the blue color had won some key areas as well.

"I'm a Dragon. I've eaten my fair share of humanoids and battled for gold more often than I would care to remember.

"But I never... craved it," Goldie said. "I always wished to settle down and just nest. Roost.

"I wish to care for another and be cared for. I'm much more similar to Felicity than I am to Kris.

"Kris and the others all want you to fight them and win. To see you crush your enemies as you've been doing. That would tame their Dragons and claim them to the point that they'd need to nest," Goldie said. "Or for you to outsmart them, outwit them. That'd be much the same."

Makes sense, given what they are and where they came from. That human form can be deceiving.

"My Dragon was interested in you when you brought back Green, Karya, and Daphne. For nothing.

"Just because he was your brother," Goldie said. "You could have demanded anything. Asked for anything. Desired anything. And received it."

Wasn't exactly complicated or hard. Cost me nothing.

"It was enough for me to join your Wing. From everything I saw of you in my homeland, and what I've seen here in your world, my Dragon has swooned," Goldie said, her fingers pressing into his skull.

Felix didn't say anything.

If anything, he felt worse for the situation. He hadn't expected the conversation, and he probably should have.

Lifting his head, he looked at the TV.

It wasn't done, but the map showed that the majority of the population had already voted, and Kevin was the victor.

The subtitles were underscoring that not all votes were in yet, and there was still a chance for Blake to pull through.

The likelihood of that was extremely slim, however.

Cutting from Erica, the screen moved to the face of an older man standing near Blake in his campaign center headquarters.

Felix felt like the man was familiar.

"Nest-mate, isn't that the face Jillian saw?" Goldie asked.

His mind locking up as he processed that, Felix stared at the face.

"It's not the same name, though," Goldie said, her thumbs digging into the base of Felix's skull.

"But it's him," Felix agreed with her.

Cameras switched, and the man Felix and Legion knew as Peter Miller stood there. In a general's uniform, next to Blake.

"Suppose that tells us who was handling the armed-forces side of our problem," Felix said. "Time for an all hands."

Chapter 27 - All Hands -

Felix was waiting in the conference room next to his office.

Felicia had put it together specifically for him, with a significant amount of electronic toys, bells, and whistles.

While it didn't see daily use, it did get used for anything more than an impromptu meeting that was larger than five attendees.

He was early. Very early. By about ten minutes.

It was always easier for him to be first, though. The extra time could be used to focus his thoughts on what he wanted to say.

This felt like a big meeting. They'd already broken two of the supposed three pillars, and they'd identified the third.

This was going to be the last bit of resistance in Wal, and then Legion could exert itself again.

If I did push us to the front again, I think I'd want to take Wal over completely.

Or turn it into a puppet state.

Playing nice-nice is what got Legion into this position to begin with.

No, Legion is done playing nice-nice. If this situation turns on us and the opportunity presents itself, we're taking Wal.

The door opened and Felicity walked in. She had her pad balanced in one hand, a messenger bag over her shoulder stuffed with paperwork, and a push cart trailing along behind her in her other hand.

She was dressed as she always was. Beautifully put together and eye catching.

Blinking, Felicity stared at him, looking rather confused.

Getting up immediately, Felix moved over to her and took the push cart from her. In it were several coffee travelers, donuts, bagels, cream cheese, and chocolate bars.

"Oh, thank you, Felix," Felicity said, letting him take it. "Cutlery and the like is below."

Nodding, Felix wheeled it to the side of the entry. He quickly unpacked the cups, plates, plastic forks, and plastic knives.

"Judging from the meeting agenda you sent over, I felt it'd be a good idea to get some snacks and things," Felicity said, pulling her bag from her shoulder.

"And that is one of the reasons I think you're amazing." Felix picked up a blueberry bagel.

"I appreciate the compliment." Felicity moved past him and set down her messenger bag in the seat to the right of his own. She pulled her light-terminal out and put it on the table top.

"Can I get you something?" Felix asked, pouring himself a cup of coffee.

"Ah… yes, please. I'll take the same thing you're having, from the looks of it," Felicity said, peering at what was in his hands. "Though a bit more cream cheese than that."

Felix shrugged and added more cream cheese to the one on his plate. Then he simply gave her everything he'd already prepared and went back for another.

With napkins this time, since he'd forgotten them in the first pass.

"You're awfully attentive to me today," Felicity said.

Felix didn't know what to say to that. He sat down next to her and placed a napkin by her plate, then one beside his own.

The door opened again and Faith, Kris, Lily, Kit, Andrea, and Adriana all walked in.

"Felicity brought treats," Felix said, gesturing toward the cart as he started breaking up his bagel into fourths.

"Goodie!" Andrea said happily, clapping her hands and darting to the cart. Adriana was a step behind her, bouncing excitedly.

Felix busied himself with his bagel as more people arrived, got their choices, and joined the table.

The soft chime of his wrist indicated the time for the meeting had been reached and brought Felix back to himself. He'd been lost in the methodical chewing of his bagel as he lingered over his topics.

Looking around the room, he found it was full of people.

Kit, Lily, Miu, Andrea, Adriana, Ioana, Felicia, Victoria, Dimitry, Erica, Jessica, Kris, Goldie, Faith, Michael Haglund from Legion Prime, a Elf he didn't know, and Felicity. Seems like everyone.

"Welcome. This isn't our normal timing for an all-hands meeting, obviously, but given what's been going on, it felt like the right time," Felix started. There were a few head nods around the room. "First, I'll cover a few topics I'd like to discuss, or at least reaffirm. Then we'll move from department to department, then person to person.

"Is there anything that needs to be stated before we begin?"

"Thank you, Fell, for getting snacks," Andrea said, pausing in her attempt to swallow more than half of a chocolate bar. "You're the best."

Felix grinned.

"Yes, thank you, Fell," Felix said, looking at Felicity, amused to no end by Andrea's nickname for her.

"Of course," she murmured without looking up from her terminal as she typed constantly.

"First then, moving from Legion HQ. It's been put forward to start moving critical facilities out of Wal and to Legion Prime.

"Obviously there're some problems with that, not least of all the fact that the infrastructure isn't ready for us yet. At least, not for all of us." Felix looked to Michael as the CO of the planet.

Sensing the unspoken request for an update, Michael cleared his throat.

"We've got wind turbines and solar panels up, as well as a small dam. We're able to meet basic electricity so far. Though it's nowhere near stable for all of Legion yet," Michael said. "It really comes down to how much of a footprint we want to make on the planet. We could easily throw together a coal or nuclear plant, but that's hard to move away from once we do it."

"Felicia," Felix said to the Dwarf. "Anything you can add?"

Rubbing at her jaw with a hand, she seemed to be considering the question.

"Well. We could always build a big-ass version of the Fist's power cell and its solar collectors. That wouldn't take me too long to put together," Felicia said.

"Think on it. With all that said, I want a few things moved to LP first."

Felicity tapped something and turned partly in her chair to look at the screen over Felix's shoulder.

Glancing that way, he saw the building plans for Legion Prime.

"Everything in blue has been deemed critical," Felicity said. "That includes Felix's home, the bodyguards' barracks, everyone in his inner circle's personal quarters, the R&D department, HR, Legal, Security, and Maintenance.

"Everything outside of that is a secondary priority or tertiary need."

Felix appreciated the quick summation. The problem, though, was that with so many priorities, they were limited by their own pool of available workers.

"Now, moving on to labor," Felicity continued. "I've put in a request with Yosemite. They have a large force of manpower that will happily work for pay. The citizenry isn't entirely made up of the military after all."

"That's a solid idea. Good work," Felix said. "Put it in motion and let's get them moving things. We might as well put up another portal between LP and Vince's world."

"What's the name of the world?" Andrea asked with chocolate-stained lips.

"It doesn't have one anymore," Felicity said. "The area Yosemite is in was once called the Wastes, though."

"Let's call it Yosemite," Andrea said, nodding quickly at her own words.

"Fine, let's get a portal between LP and Yosemite. No need to have them wander through HQ if they don't have to," Felix said. "Next. How's Richard and his bank?"

"Gone," Kit said with a shrug. "Richard vanished. The bank and all its assets are gone. It's simply no longer there."

"Great, and Blake?" Felix asked.

"He's done," Lily said. "After that debacle with the court and the terrorist attack, he was labeled pretty badly.

"Last I heard, he's moving out of Wal entirely."

"Two for two, then," Felix said. "And that brings us around to the newest problem. Peter Miller."

"Also known as Frank Kas," Kit said. "Three-star general for Wal. He's been in the armed forces his entire adult life. He was closely aligned with Blake.

"We've got some bits of things that point this back to him, but it's not very clean."

Felix thought on that. It was something to figure out, but he didn't want to rush it.

"Where we stand, then, is that we've crippled the economic backing our foes had, eliminated their political and public abilities, and have possibly identified where they're getting their offensive capabilities," Felix summarized.

"That's about right," Lily said. "By and large, we've carved out everything we identified with marginal impact to the citizens."

"Let's table Mr. Kas for the moment, then.

"Ioana, we'll start with your department. How's our security force looking?" Felix asked.

Ioana set down the donut she'd been chewing at.

"Not too bad. We had a major glut of manpower after we canceled all our contracts and there wasn't much to do.

"The summit is still ongoing, of course, but the amount of manpower needed there isn't going to change," Ioana said. "The rest of our people, as well as internal security who aren't on duty, are all in Yosemite."

Felix took that and turned to Miu and Victoria.

Miu looked healthy. She'd clearly been taking care of herself.

"We're following General Petra's orders and keeping to the wall. She won't let our people risk themselves. She moved off with the army and left her Lieutenant in place, a Dark Elf by the name of Eva, but she hasn't changed our orders," Victoria said. "It's all quiet on the Yosemite front otherwise."

"We're given a good amount of respect," Miu said suddenly. "It's clear they're appreciative of our presence."

Good.

"Kris? Faith? Which of you wants to speak for the bodyguard detail?" Felix said, deciding to keep with the armed parts of Legion.

"We are one hundred strong now," Kris said. "The Dryads have sent over thirty to be dedicated to you. We've also picked up a handful of Dragon maidens in the surrounding area that were attempting to escape notice. We now number seventeen."

Oh really? That's a surprise.

"They were in the area?" Andrea asked suddenly, her eyes curious.

It was easy to forget Andrea was a merc and had taken a number of contracts in her life.

Goldie shrugged. "We've cleared four hundred miles in every direction from this point. Some of the Dragons were males, or not maidens, or simply didn't want to join.

"We gave them all to Layla when they decided they'd rather fight than leave."

"She's a warlock," Felicity said before Felix could ask. "Trust me when I say it's both a good and bad thing."

"The rest are all Elven sorceresses," Kris continued. "I'm confident in our ability to keep you safe with our composition."

Felix looked at the Elex women.

"How's the ANet?" he asked.

Andrea blinked and then shifted her weight around in her chair.

"It's fine. We've been working on building a second command center on LP," Andrea said, her tone changing slightly. "Adriana has taken over all of our security and tactics side. I'm handling everything else. I've reached out to... to Myriad to see if she'll come home. I think we could use her.

"We know she read the letter, but she hasn't responded. Her signal locater is still moving further away as well."

Myriad... I can only wonder how you're doing since you don't write me back.

"Alright. Lily, how's our magic?" Felix asked.

- 662 -

"Significantly... stronger. The Elves are fantastic magicians. Combined with the Dryads, we have a very elite strike force. The losses we were taking from casual run-ins with master priests and their apprentices have sharply declined," Lily said. "No legal concerns at this time. Everything is working as it should."

Taking that with a single nod, Felix turned to Dimitry.

"And how's Maintenance?" he asked.

Dimitry let out an explosive sigh and spread his hands out in front of him.

"The underworld is taking over everywhere," he said. "From what I'm hearing, anywhere we're not entrenched, or the religion of choice isn't, is falling prey to organized crime."

Honestly, that was about what Felix was expecting. Until they could get a handle on this religious dilemma, the problem would continue.

Which is why we need that summit to actually get something done. They've been sitting there for so long already, I have no idea if they think they can even achieve anything now.

"Otherwise we're fine," Dimitry said.

"Kit?" Felix asked.

"We're seeing increased stress and tension across the board. People are deep into war weariness, and they're just exhausted," she said with a sigh. "We're doing what we can to keep everyone calm and on track, but we need a break."

"Legion needs to somehow take a breath for a bit."

"Working on it. I'm open to suggestions, of course," Felix said.

"Company picnic is coming up," Felicia said suddenly. "We'll just make it a big one. Lots of drinking. Lots of food. Lots of Felix getting dunked and taking pies in the face."

Felix chuckled. He wasn't going to argue. If that was what it took to cheer people up, he'd do it.

"Let's make it a big one then," he said. "A picnic to remember for years.

"Anything else, Kit?"

"Not really, but... I'm hearing some things from the Heroes guild. It's gotten even worse for them. It's unlikely there will be a legally sanctioned Heroes guild in a year."

That was sobering news. There had almost always been a guild in one fashion or another.

That it was simply going to vanish was more than a surprise.

"Any of the contacts I had have long since given up on me. From what I can gather, they're banding together in small groups and working in teams. Though it's not looking much better for them," Lily said with a strange smile. "In their eyes, I'm little better than a house wife. I went straight, gave up the villain life, and settled into a house with a white picket fence."

"Alright. How are our financials looking?" Felix asked.

"Painful, to be honest," Felicity said. "After we broke all our contracts, our revenue took a major hit. We're not taking a loss, but our margin for error is as thin as a razor.

"I don't think we'll be turning large profits for a while."

"We knew that'd happen though," Felix said. "Still sucks, but it's not outside expectation."

Felix turned to look at Felicia

"How's the lab?"

"Quiet," said the Dwarf, her mouth sporting a severe frown. "I miss Mr. White. He was a bit of a doof at times. Came across as a know-it-all and had odd moments, but he was a good and brilliant engineer.

"I didn't have to work half as hard when he could just swoop in with something he had already worked on or was working on."

That's quite a bit of praise.

"Find a replacement for him, then. Sounds like you need a mechanical engineer to keep you grounded."

"Just run it through Kit and Felicity; I don't need to be involved," Felix said.

"Jessica? Erica? Anything to know from the world of news?" Felix asked, looking at the two. Both shook their heads.

"No, Felix. Everything is pretty much the same. No news, as it were," Jessica said.

"Alright, let's do a quick round robin. Anyone have anything to add?"

Felix looked around the table as he spoke, meeting everyone's eyes.

"No? Alright then.

"That covers everyone for the basics and some of the larger and broader topics. Let's start digging through quarterly budget sheets and figure out where we can fix things. Sounds like we need to tighten the belt a wee bit."

***

"...itures in training are a necessary thing," Kit said calmly, pointing at the screen.

"It eats into their occupancy," Felicity said with a shake of her head.

"You yourself said we have time set aside specifically for training. That we had more than enough 'shrink' in the budget, as you called it," Kit continued.

"We do, and we did. Except you spent your entire budget on it. There's simply no more room to add *more* training to the calendar," Felicity said. "The only way you'd be able to manage that would be to change your expectations and how many people you need to get the job done."

"Alright, then let's talk about that. What are the projected—"

The door opened suddenly and Edith Torres stormed in.

She was dressed in professional clothes very similar to Lily and Felicity today.

At least she's settling into her age.

"Felix, I saw someone come out of the energy distortion," she said, her statement practically a shallow gasp.

"You saw someone walk out," Felix repeated back.

"Two people, actually," Edith corrected herself. "A man and a woman. I took a few pictures. I didn't get the woman very well, but I got a full front of the man's face."

She pulled a camera out of her jacket pocket as she moved over to him.

"Give it to Felicity; we'll put it up on the big screen," Felix said.

"What?" Edith said. Felicity took the camera from her outstretched hand and set it down next to her light-terminal.

With a flick of her fingers, she got her computer routed into the camera's wireless profile.

"Wait," Edith said.

The screen flickered and then changed.

On the display was a massive collection of photos. They were almost all of nature and had a definite artistic feel to them.

Some of them even looked quite good.

Never would have figured her for a photographer.

"I had no idea," Lily said.

"I like that one." Kit pointed toward what looked like a sunrise.

"Stop. Just... go to the most recent photos," Edith said, clearly flustered.

Felicity spared the woman and went straight to the indicated location.

The first photo that came up looked like a pair of legs in men's pants. They seemed to be appearing in the air. The bottom part of his body was materializing as the top half was still missing.

Progressing the selector, the next photo came up. It was the same pair of men's pants, though it now had most of a torso attached. It looked like he was significantly more filled in, just not quite there.

Felicity moved it forward again.

Standing in the middle of the frame, blocking the woman behind him, was Frank Kas.

"It was like he materialized from nowhere. Looking at it, it felt a lot like teleportation," Edith said. "I couldn't get a good picture of the woman. She stumbled to one side, threw up, and then vanished into the crowd."

Felix sighed and leaned back in his chair.

"I suppose that answers it for us. We start prepping for Frank," he said. "Let's start looking into everything he owns, his money, what he's in charge of, and who's visited him in the last six months.

- 664 -

"Get a Minder and a Fixer on him and let's see what's in his head, if we can, and what's he doing at home.

"Get to work, people. Meeting over."

Chapter 28 - Context -

Everyone was getting up from the conference table and starting to file out.

Felix smiled at those who made eye contact with him and nodded his head at them, remaining seated at the table.

He'd opened his mind as soon as he'd called the meeting to a close. Putting a giant, blaring thought in it that Kit should remain behind.

Even revealing the reason he wanted her to do so.

It took a few minutes for the room to clear out completely. Faith, Kris, and Goldie had caught his look and he'd guessed they'd taken position just outside the conference door.

They were the last out. The door clicked shut behind them.

"I'm not sure what to say, Felix," Kit said, giving him a smile.

"You can tell me what's going on in that pretty head of yours. I'm not the mind reader, remember?"

"It's nothing. Nothing you haven't heard or don't already know."

"Tell me again, then. Tell me in a different way. Tell me in a new way. Tell me in the same way."

"Just talk to me."

"Felix..." Kit sighed, pressing her head between her hands. "It's not that simple."

"Yes. It is. I deserve the honest truth. Just as I was direct and honest with you three years ago," Felix said. Breaching a subject neither of them had ever really wanted to talk about. "I told you how I felt, what I wanted, and what I was willing to do."

"You read all my thoughts on it in every way."

Kit's head dipped down; she was clearly hiding her eyes from him.

"We said we wouldn't talk about it," she muttered.

"I'm talking about it because you're not sharing your thoughts with me. You promised me you would when I asked. I've asked, and you're holding out."

"You said no to me at the time. That you needed time and space and you'd let me know if it changed. I agreed, so long as you shared your thoughts when asked."

Kit let out a sudden breath and started laughing darkly to herself.

"I'm literally reading your mind as you talk. It's interesting how often your thoughts are so much more violently put together than the words that come out of your mouth."

"Then you know I'm not letting this go. So... talk to me."

"It's the same as it always is," Kit said, shrugging. And still not looking at him. "I'm feeling a need to play hero, to go out and save the day. To be the good guy. To... get off... on that feeling. The power of it."

Felix didn't immediately respond. It sounded like she had more to say.

"And I know it's stupid. I know it's silly." Kit shook her head even as she spoke. "I know that mentality is the very reason the Heroes guild is pretty much done. They had to rush out and save everything, and now they can't save anything."

"Is that something you want to talk about? The guild?" Felix asked.

"No. Errr... maybe. Yes?" Kit sounded confused.

"Tell me about the guild. What's going on?"

"They're being hunted down. One by one. Every few missions, some heroes don't come back," Kit said. "It isn't every time. But it's adding up. Their losses keep mounting higher and higher.

"They really will no longer be a guild soon. They just don't have the backing, support, or finances for it."

Felix didn't give a damn if they were all turned into sock puppets. He had no use for them.

But he had a use for Kit.

"Would they be willing to sign on with Legion?" Felix asked. "I'd be willing to take them as a contract holder, so long as they followed Legion's rules and motto.

"I'm sure they could do some good operating as a Legion affiliate. I could easily bring them back from the dead if they fell."

Kit lifted her head up, her eyes piercing into him.

"You're only offering that because you love me. You'd rather see them all die and become worm food.

"Sock puppets," she said.

Felix took in a slow breath, then gave her a shrug and a smile. "Yeah. And?"

There was a small pressure in his head, and he realized Kit was rapidly scanning through his thoughts and memories again.

She tended to treat his brain like a search engine at times, trying to correlate one thing with others.

"Almost everything you do for me is because you love me. All the projects to give aid. The charities. The non-profits. You don't care about any of it," she said. "You do it for me."

"Come on, that's not exactly news. You've known that for years." Felix waved a hand in the air as he shifted his weight to one side. Propping his elbow on the arm of his chair, he put his chin in it. "Old news that's so out of date, it's pre-internet."

"I mean, I knew. But I'd never really sorted through it all." Kit was watching him. Her eyes unwavering.

"Anyways," Felix said, feeling awkward with the silence for once. "Do you think they'd take it? Protection, a budget, an armory to use, our intelligence network. They could do a lot of good in Wal."

Kit looked like she didn't want to change the subject. After several seconds, though, she sighed and broke eye contact.

"Maybe. I think they might. Most of the old guard is gone. Long gone. That woman you were actually polite to is probably the highest-ranking member now."

"Throw them an invitation, then. Though you should let them know I'm going to open an invitation to all unaffiliated Powereds. Villain or hero, I don't care. I'll take them and their families.

"If this is the end of an era, I want to sweep up as many people as I can into Legion," Felix said.

Kit grunted at that and tapped a finger against the table. "That might speed them along, to be honest. There's the distinct possibility a number of their people would take your offer if only for the sake of their families."

"And there you have it," Felix said simply.

"In other words, you're willing to save what's left of the guild for my sake. Because of how you feel for me," Kit said.

"I mean, if you have to put a point to it, yeah, that's pretty much what it is. Because I love you.

"I'm afraid I truly do believe in Legion first, otherwise. They're not Legion and they've worked pretty hard to end us."

"But you're Legion, Kit. And I'll do what I can for you."

Kit sighed and ran a hand through her short curls. "Why did I say no to you again?"

"I have no idea," Felix said with a grin. "I thought I was being rather charming at the time."

"You were. I'll put a message through to the guild and see what they say.

"Then I'll put together a public-facing broadcast from Legion about welcoming in all Powered individuals," Kit said. "I take it you'll want it to also go out from Dimitry and the reporters?"

"Yeah. If you don't mind putting together a packet for them all, I'd greatly appreciate it," Felix said.

Kit nodded and finally looked back to him.

"Sorry, Felix. I guess I've always been a problem. Constantly having to fix me."

"You're well worth fixing. Now, anything else you need to get off your chest? Anything you need to tell me?

"Or was the guild going under the vast majority of it?"

"It was. I'm sure my inner hero will be quite happy with the idea of saving the rest of the guild," Kit said, getting to her feet. She brushed at her blouse once, smoothing out the fabric.

Felix kept his thoughts neutral and bland as she moved for the door.

"You know… at this point… when you start thinking about that kind of blank stuff," Kit said, looking over her shoulder with a smile and stopping at the door. "I know you're staring at me and thinking shower thoughts—you're just not doing it directly anymore.

"By the way, Felicity is waiting for you outside the door. She has some plans for you that I think you should agree to.

"She's probably the best thing that's happened to you in years. And yes, I'm actually endorsing her."

Opening the door, she stepped out of the room and then closed the door before he could respond.

Suppose she's not wrong about the thoughts. It's a lot like how a word changes its form.

Can't use the word retarded because it's insensitive. Replace it with special.

Special is insensitive now. Use challenged.

Challenged is insensitive. New word.

When the word changes but the definition remains the same, it's only a matter of time before the new moniker gains the same stigma.

Frowning, Felix scratched at his cheek.

With that in mind, does that mean the Heroes guild will just become Legion? Or Legion will become the Heroes guild?

Should probably make them change the outfit name when they join, and make sure their procedure and protocol gets modified a bit.

The door opened and Felicity walked in. Through the doorway, he could see Faith and Goldie talking to each other on one side. And Kris's shoulder was just visible on the other side of the door frame.

Closing the door, the Dark Elf gave him a sad smile.

"Hello Felix," she said.

"Hey there," Felix said with a wave of his hand. He immediately started to think on what Kit had said before she left.

"When you didn't come out immediately, I figured you were trying to collect your thoughts," she said, walking over to him.

She put her bag down along with her terminal on the table next to him.

"Take your coat off, and face forward," she said, tapping the back of his head with a hand. "Make this easy for me and I'll make sure it's a good one."

"Yes, dear," Felix said with a mocking tone, doing as instructed. He shucked off his coat and set it down on the chair next to him, facing the empty chair in front of him.

"Time for your weekly therapy session. Care to share?" Felicity's hands settled on his shoulders. She started to lightly trail her fingernails up and down his neck.

Somewhere along the way, Felicity had slipped in closer to him than anyone ever had. She'd become his confidant and soothsayer, to a degree. He gave her all his problems, regardless of what they were. Even those involving other women.

Or her.

And she took it all with love and care.

"Kit probably isn't going to last much longer in Legion," Felix said, getting straight to the heart of his concern. "I don't think her heart was ever truly in it.

"She stayed around as long as she did out of loyalty to me. That and I kept giving her more opportunities to use Legion as a way to help others."

Felicity's cool fingers slid into his hair, her fingernails lightly trailing along his scalp.

"That makes sense. She's a very driven woman. I can appreciate her drive and her need to do good," she said after a moment of thought. "I would agree with your observation. I don't think she's going to be around for much longer.

"I've already been looking around in her department for those with a suitable aptitude to replace her. She's cultivated a… how did you phrase it last time… solid bench strength in her team. There are quite a few people who could step up and take her place," Felicity said.

"Good thing you're on my side. I don't think I'd survive a direct confrontation from you if you had your own company," Felix said, closing his eyes as Felicity's fingers slipped down from the crown of his head to his forehead. "That's lovely. You take care of me too much."

She was gently kneading the flesh there, slowly working down the bridge of his nose and to his cheeks.

"Somewhat counterintuitive. I wouldn't have been able to compete with you without having learned from you," Felicity said. "As far as taking care of you, well... if I don't, who would?"

"You'd just work yourself to death when you inevitably get stuck in your own head."

Felix didn't answer her. He just sat there and enjoyed the feeling of her fingertips pressing into him. Especially since she wasn't wrong.

He could identify several times over the last five years when he'd had a small breakdown, put himself back together, and marched back out into the forefront without anyone noticing.

"Now, everything seems to be moving as you wanted it. Is there anything in particular you want me to handle or watch out for?" Felicity asked.

"I think Faith and Goldie are going to try to sneak into my room," Felix said honestly.

"They already tried. Kris dealt with both of them. I spoke to her briefly," Felicity said. "Do not worry, she's being very professional about it. Though she did complain about the fact that she couldn't be as carefree as they are, even if she wished she could."

In other words, Kris wanted to sneak into my bedroom too, but is playing good soldier.

"I don't really understand it," Felix said finally as Felicity's fingers moved down to the hinge of his jaw.

"What, all the women throwing themselves at you? It's not so hard to understand given their point of view," Felicity said. "Everyone from my homeland is facing a slight gap in the male to female population, and death could be found around every corner for many years.

"It breeds a certain amount of honesty in desire and attraction. To propagate the species."

"I noticed. A certain Dark Elf has been chasing me to the ground daily," Felix said.

"Hardly. If I were truly giving you the full amount of pressure I could bring, I think I'd have more of your time than I do right now. I wouldn't have to settle for simply touching you in quiet moments.

"But I'm taking my time. Making sure you get your space as I slowly gather more and more of your attention." Felicity's tone was honest. "I don't want to scare you off with how I feel."

"It's... a little frightening. You seem almost as committed to me as Miu at times. I don't know what to do with it," Felix admitted.

"Miu is a different story. By the way, you owe her a kiss and a hug soon. As well as a pat on the head, and maybe take her out for a meal.

"She's doing incredibly well, and she took your words to heart. Have you looked at her lately? She's beautiful," Felicity said.

Felix had noticed.

Miu had translated "take care of yourself" to a whole new level. She'd been pretty before, but now she was almost unnervingly beautiful.

"Those amplification powers of hers are scary," Felix said. "Never thought they'd work on a level like that."

"As for my own feelings," Felicity said, bringing the conversation back around, "I'm just being honest. I desire you. I want to know you in many ways. And I think we'd be a very good match for one another. Especially in the long term.

"We balance each other quite well. I'm afraid I don't have any of your initiative to act, nor do I have much in the way of the ruthlessness or political intuition you have."

"And you know how to keep me moving and on track while balancing all the little things that typically build up on me and knock me over.

"Not to mention you've smoothed out every relationship in my organization that you encounter as well," Felix said.

"Like I said. We go very well with one another.

"And speaking of going with one another. You're having dinner with Jessica and Erica tonight with me. Then with the Elex girls for breakfast tomorrow morning.

"After that, we have lunch plans with Edith, Goldie, Faith, and Kris," Felicity said.

"Ugggh. Do I have to?" Felix asked.

"Yes. And flirt with all of them. Especially the new girls. I know you don't like doing it, but when you flirt with them, they get more interested, and then they work harder for you.

"Especially Goldie. I'm fairly positive her Dragon is utterly infatuated with you. If she submits and wants to nest, Kris won't be far behind her or the other Dragons. Goldie is stronger than all of them; she just doesn't have the same aggression."

"You want me to flirt with Detective Torres? She's more likely to pull a gun on me." Felix wasn't about to talk about Goldie to Felicity right now. His last encounter with the lovely Dragon had ended up making him a bit weak kneed in the end.

"No. I don't think so. Circuit-Breaker is my personal IT liaison when it comes to my needs. All I had to do was set him up with this sweet girl I knew back in Yosemite.

"After that, I had him set it up so anything I link to gets downloaded completely to a share drive of my own.

"That includes her camera I connected to," Felicity said. Her hands were trailing down his neck and out towards his shoulders.

Felix briefly wondered if Goldie had gotten her own idea to do this for him from Felicity.

"You didn't," Felix said.

"I did. And there were some photos taken of you from a distance. They were quite deep in the memory card, though, and under several folders. I kept a few I liked for myself."

"You're a terror, aren't you? Should I assume you've broken into Lily's computer? Andrea's? Adriana's?"

"Of course. How am I supposed to take care of you and alert you to problems if I don't know about them?" Felicity asked with a soft chuckle. "I'm sorry to say, Felix Campbell, I do not believe in Legion first."

Her breath tickled his face and Felix opened his eyes.

Felicity was right there, hovering over the top of him. Her face inches from his.

"I'm very much all about Felix first. Legion is second," Felicity said, and then she pressed a tender kiss to his lips.

"Now," she said, pulling away from him. "The only other thing you need to know is Andrea and Adriana are both sending letters to a 'Myriad' begging her to come home. Saying they want her back as a sister, and that she needs to get her Second pregnant.

"There's been no response yet, but I've been tracking where the signal ends up on Legion Prime each night."

Felix was still staring at Felicity, just a touch speechless.

"Her position hadn't changed for a while, it seems. Lately, though, it's begun to slowly come back towards the city. Then it stops and stays still for several days.

"I think she's considering returning, so you should prepare for that," Felicity said.

Then she stood up and gently ran her hands over his face.

"Come on, Felix my darling. Time to go." Felicity tapped him on the forehead with a finger. "We have meetings to attend and a great deal of work to do."

Chapter 29 - Buttering Up -

Standing in the hallway outside of Miu's quarters, Felix was nervous.

He'd taken Felicity's advice and sent Miu a note to please return to Legion, and meet up with him.

Truth be told, Felix had been avoiding Miu outright since her episode. In the past, giving her a few weeks to cool off after an "attack" had been the best thing for her. It gave her time to reassert her control and get herself back in order.

Meeting up with her earlier than that had caused problems in the past.

Which was why he was feeling a bit anxious. He wanted to take her out, give her more attention than he'd given her at any previous time, and give her a task.

Doing such a thing felt a lot like winding up a rubber band to the point where it looked like it would break.

Miu tended to overdo things.

His wrist communicator chirped once, causing Felix to flick his hand over and look at the screen. The message there was from Felicity.

Remember to be direct, give her attention, not too much, and give her the orders.

You look fine, be sure to compliment her on what she's wearing, take her out wherever she wants to go. Don't overthink this.

Quirking a brow, Felix looked around at the corners of the hall.

He saw what he was looking for at one end. A camera.

It was trained on the hallway and he was most likely completely in view.

After waving a hand at it, Felix gestured to his wrist with his other hand and bobbed his head.

Always keeping me on track. Are you watching?

Looking back to the door, Felix froze in mid action when his communicator chirped again.

Lifting his hand up, he looked at the screen.

There was another message from Felicity.

You're welcome. Stop fidgeting. I'm going to bed. Send me a message or come wake me when you're back.

Felix wondered about his life suddenly. Everything had rapidly changed so quickly. From his love life to his work life.

Lately he felt more like the leader of a country than a manager of a company.

He supposed they were very similar in the end, since the end goal was mostly the same.

The door opened in front of him, and Miu stepped out.

She was dressed in a very dark black dress that seemed to fit her athletic form very well. It showed off enough of her white skin and physique to flatter her, but it wasn't overly sexualized.

Her hair was pulled up behind her head and pinned in place. She'd gone light on makeup, though most of it was concentrated on or around her eyes. Making them seem large and dark.

"Felix," Miu said, her eyes staring into him. Pulling him in.

She looked more than healthy. She looked radiant. Her skin, her body, her hair—everything about her looked like it had been put together by a skilled artist rather than her own hand.

I swear to god, even her body dimensions changed.

"You look... really good, Miu," Felix said. "Really good."

Miu's face practically split in half with the smile she gave him, her cheeks coloring.

"Thank you. I'm trying very hard to take care of myself as you ordered. I'm doing everything I can to make myself appealing, healthy, fit, and more lethal." She lifted her arms and looked down at herself.

"You're definitely that." Felix remembered something Felicity had told him to do, and he moved in close to kiss her cheek.

Except somehow or other, Miu had turned to face him at the same time, and he ended up giving her a light kiss on the lips instead.

Pulling back quickly, he smiled at her, trying to hide the fact that he hadn't meant to do that.

Her eyes were wide now, pupils looking like they were going to start quivering. Her breathing had immediately become erratic and her entire face was bright red.

Holding out his arm to her, Felix cleared his throat. "Shall we go? I was hopping you'd tell me where you'd like me to take you."

Miu snatched at him, slipping her arm through his. She was pressed so tight to him he could feel her heart beating wildly in her chest against his arm.

"Legion's. It's where you take all your women," Miu said immediately, her lips parted as she waited for his response.

"Legion's it is. Did you want to go straight there or walk around for a bit?"

Miu blinked several times, as if processing his words.

"What do you want to do?" she asked.

"Honestly, I'm open to whatever suggestions you have. Other than that one episode, which was very understandable given the circumstances, you've been on extremely good behavior."

"Tell me what your heart wants. Because that's what I want."

Miu's delicate brows folded into one another and her eyes slowly moved away from his face. Then they jumped back to him.

"Pictures. I want pictures of us like this. I know where to go," she said.

"Lead on, then. I'm yours for the evening, Miu Mikki," Felix said.

Saying her full name had an impact. She started to walk forward only to stumble a bit, her eyes moving back to him.

"Say my name again," she hissed, moving in close. Her nose almost touching his.

"Ok, ok. Miu Mikki."

Shivering, she pulled him down with her freakish strength and pressed her forehead to his.

"Again," she said.

"Last time, then we need to go. Unless you don't want those pictures, Miu Mikki."

Her breath washed over his face in a wave. It smelled faintly of cinnamon.

"Pictures, yes," she murmured, slowly drawing back from him.

Patting her arm that was against his, he let her lead the way.

Hm. Either her crazy is getting easier to handle, or I'm getting used to it.

***

Miu had brought Felix to an actual photo studio. Apparently, she came here often.

Often enough that the man who owned the business didn't even bother asking her what she wanted after he'd spotted Felix. He just opened the door to the back room and flipped the sign on the front door to closed.

"There we go," said the cameraman, moving out from behind his setup. They'd been standing in various poses for the last hour or so, and Felix was starting to feel over it.

Pictures were hard enough for him, but an hour-long photoshoot seemed insane.

Miu just kept moving him around, making him sit, stand, lean with her and over her, hold her from behind.

Every single type of photo he imagined that could have ever been taken—they probably had done it.

"Good," Miu said. "Get it all to me as quickly as possible with an invoice."

The man waved a hand as if this was a common thing for her.

"Good to see you, sir," said the man to Felix. "Can I use one of the photos as advertisement?"

"Of course, no worries. Just make sure Miu signs off on it," Felix said. "Are we... done then?"

Miu moved to the door and exited to the front of the store without him.

Smiling, Felix nodded to the other man and left, following Miu.

She was already outside, and she looked like she was taking deep breaths. As if she'd been running miles.

"You alright?" Felix asked, walking up to her.

"Yes. Just… I think I'm losing myself. I've been allowed to touch you so much in such a short time.

"I feel like my skin is on fire and I can't breathe enough," Miu said, fanning at her face with one hand. "My entire lower body is tingling."

"Sure fooled me," Felix said with a chuckle. "You were cool as ice in there."

"I didn't want to ruin the pictures," Miu said. Then she groaned softly, pressing a hand to her neck. "And I have so many of them now. Did you see them?"

She spun in place, her eyes fastening on him.

"I did. Now come on, let's go get some food, alright?" Felix slipped his arm through hers.

Miu seemed to fall into a trance-like state as they made their way to Legion's.

It wasn't until they were seated in his reserved booth that she started to stir again. She'd been little more than a coat hanging off his arm until he sat her down.

Her head turned, and she looked out at all the tables in the center of the restaurant. After several seconds, she quickly looked back to him.

"They're all watching me," Miu whispered.

"I can't blame them," Felix said, reading over the menu. He made a point of trying something different every time he came now. "You're extremely pretty, Miu.

"Especially so in that dress."

"I'm not sure I like the attention," Miu murmured, picking up her own menu. "Most people ignore me."

Finding something he wanted to try, Felix set the menu to one side.

"If you like, I could distract you with some information. I know what mission I want to send you on next," Felix said, sensing this was a lead in he could use. "I wasn't planning on bringing it up tonight, but if it helps clear your head a bit, we could talk about work."

Miu stared at her menu for another second before she promptly closed it and laid it and her hands on the table.

"Yes, please. It would be good to give my mind something to focus on. I'm very overstimulated right now," Miu said, her eyes finding his own.

"We found out where Frank Kas is holed up, and what he's actually in control of," Felix said. It was all information Felicity had prepared for him earlier that day.

After reading it over, Felix had decided it was time to send in a strike team and eliminate Frank, along with everyone at the top of that military outfit.

It was going to be an assassination, more or less. And it would effectively eliminate the lead elements of those who were actively working against Legion.

A snake without a head was how Felix was hoping it would turn out.

He certainly wasn't going to mobilize an entire force to fight them head on. That was just stupid, and it would get his people hurt or killed. Not to mention drawing attention to Legion.

A surgical strike by Miu and a team of Minders, though? Much more likely to work, and not get anyone caught.

And once that's done, we should be able to make almost all of this blow away. There won't be anyone left to fight us.

Miu nodded.

"Do you want me to take care of it?" she asked.

"I do. I want you to take a team of Minders and eliminate him, along with the senior leadership that report directly to him," Felix said. "I think if we get rid of them, the rest won't be an issue."

Miu nodded slowly.

"Yes. If you were eliminated, and all your inner circle killed, much of Legion would fall apart," Miu said.

Certainly a… different way to look at it. But she's not wrong.

Amy walked up to their table, smiling at the two of them.

"You're back again," said the waitress. "Looks like you're ready to order. What can I get for you?"

- 673 -

Miu shook her head and turned to Felix when both he and Amy had looked at her.

"I'll take the chicken parmesan," Felix said, pushing the menu over to the waitress. "And I'll have a soda, please."

"I'll have the exact same," Miu said immediately, her eyes not moving from Felix.

"I'll get that put in," Amy said, leaving.

"So, yes," Felix said, redirecting the conversation again. "I want you to take a team of Minders in and take care of it for me."

"Of course. I'll not fail you," Miu said, quickly nodding . "But..."

Felix smiled at the tone. He was honestly expecting her to want a little extra motivation.

"If you do it without getting caught, without raising an alarm, without anyone even knowing you were there... I'll take you out again. Movie, dinner, lunch, whatever you like. We can do more photos again as well, or something else if you'd prefer variety," Felix said, moving straight to the carrot.

Miu looked like she was going to agree immediately. Her lips were already parted when she suddenly stopped. Then she closed her mouth and licked her lips, and leaned in closer to him.

"I want more," she said. "I've been very good. I deserve more. I listen to Felicity."

Felix couldn't deny that fact.

"Alright. And what do you want?"

Miu took in a quick breath, licking her lips again.

"I want to sleep in your bed once a week," she said suddenly. "Not sex, or anything, just... I just want to sleep next to you. It doesn't have to be alone. I don't mind Andrea, Adriana, Lily, or Felicity being in the bed."

Amusing that Felicity is apparently allowed in my bed before she's even in it.

He was already working out how to decline her request when he realized he might as well just accept it.

If she did what he asked of her, it'd bring an end to a headache. Not to mention her deal with Lily would lead down that road eventually.

Maybe getting her acclimated to it early would help things along.

"You're going to say no," Miu said, deflating in her seat. Literally wilting before his eyes.

"Actually, I'm going to say yes. But my bodyguards will remain with me in the room, if that's what they plan on doing. They don't always, but sometimes they do.

"So you'll have to play nice. Alright?" Felix asked, confirming it.

Miu had stopped breathing. Her fingers were clenched into the tablecloth.

She was clearly working to control herself.

Felix looked away, giving her time to get her control back. He knew if he looked at her for too long, she sometimes got worked up. And right now, she needed less stimulation.

My pet monster.

***

Shuffling into his room, Felix pulled off his coat and dropped it into the chair next to his desk.

Miu had worn him down and out. Her dedication, overwhelming devotion, and need for anything and everything of him was tiring.

Sighing, he rubbed his hand against the back of his neck.

Somewhat nostalgically, he wondered where the days had gone of him fretting more over if they were selling enough used cars to justify that arm of the business.

Instead of ordering straight-up assassinations of generals in the government's employ.

Looking around the entry room to his personal rooms, he found no one there. They hadn't been outside his room either.

It seemed his guards were further inside, or he'd managed to show up in the middle of a guard change.

Grumbling, he went over to his desk terminal and powered it on. Leaning over it, he unbuttoned his shirt with one hand and typed in his password with the other.

Quick as could be, he typed a brief note to Felicity about how it had all gone. Then sent it.

Standing up, he rubbed at his shoulder and moved into his bedroom. Thankfully, the day was over, and it seemed everyone was leaving him alone for once.

Maybe I can cancel my meetings in the morning and sleep in for once.

That'd be fun.

Yawning, Felix unbuckled his belt and kicked off his pants, getting rid of his socks at the same time. Picking them all up, he entered his bedroom.

He looked over to the spot where his Dryads tended to watch over him and doze in shifts, and he found… no one.

They weren't there.

"That's a relief and odd at the same time," Felix muttered and walked into his room. He dropped his pants with the belt still in them at the foot of his bed.

Sitting down there, he shucked his button-up shirt over his head and flipped it atop the pants.

Should put them away in the closet.

Mentally groaning at the amount of effort it'd take, Felix turned to the closet.

Goldie was sitting just in front of the closet in a chair. Watching him. She was dressed in what looked like a thin nightgown and little else.

She had one of his shirts in her lap. The sleeve had been pulled from the top of the shirt, and to Felix it looked like she was in the process of re-stitching it back on. The needle and thread were in her right hand, and her left was holding the fabric together.

"This one didn't fit you," Goldie said. "I thought I'd just… fix it up and put it back before you got home.

"I'm sorry, I really thought you'd be gone till later. I thought I'd have another thirty minutes."

Felix somehow wasn't surprised at the gold Dragon's presence. She seemed to be a very similar type of woman to Felicity. Just warmer and less work oriented.

"Miu was tired, and the more tired she gets, the worse her control. I think she was on the edge of invalidating the deal she made with Lily, so she asked me to take her home," Felix said honestly.

He got the impression Goldie wouldn't tell anyone.

"Oh. That makes sense. Her mind is a wild thing of violence, love, and desire for all of you," said the Dragon with a small nod. "The way you treat her is kind. Very kind. I know the minds of many men who would have done terrible things to her."

Goldie's eyes seemed to glow in the dim light. Her pale skin made the dark fabric of the gown she was wearing seem all the more devoid of color.

Shrugging his shoulders, Felix felt a little odd. He was sitting there in nothing but an undershirt and his boxers in front of a beautiful Dragon maiden.

"Miu is Miu. It's who she is. She's getting easier to deal with, the more I understand her," Felix said. "Uhm, I'm going to… go to bed now. Are you going to be alright?"

Goldie's horns faintly glittered as her head moved. "Yes, I'll be quite fine. I'll finish up with this and go to sleep myself. You don't mind, do you?"

He almost did. But in the same breath, it was endearing that she was doing such a thing for him without any expectation of a return.

Now that he thought about it, several of his shirts and pants had been fitting better lately.

"This isn't the first time you've modified my clothes, is it," Felix said. It wasn't really a question.

"Ah… no. I sneak in when you're out and go through your things," she said. "I try to fix, repair, or just maintain what I can. Well, for clothes, at least. I'm good with clothes.

"I promise that's all I do, though."

Felix felt like there was more there.

"Others do more?" he asked.

"Ah… Faith tends to get in your bed and… take care of her needs. Usually while holding one of your—"

"No, never mind. I don't want to know," Felix said, interrupting her.

Dryads are almost as bad as Miu.

"Thank you for the tailoring. I noticed the changes, but not the reason."

Felix pulled the sheets back from his bed and slid into them. He wasn't about to tell Goldie what to do. She seemed the most placid of his bodyguards.

Settling into his bed, he listened to the soft sounds of Goldie sewing. He could hear the needle passing through the fabric over and over.

He started to slowly drift off to the simple white noise. It was soothing. She also seemed to radiate a calm warmth into the room.

Felix lost himself in the comfort of the sound and her presence.

And then lost it when she slid into the bed with him. It woke him up immediately.

Opening his eyes, he watched her shift around in his bed.

She gave him a small smile and a tiny wave of her fingers, her eyes twinkling.

Except she didn't do anything further to him.

She rolled onto her side, put her back to him, snuggled into his sheets, and lay still.

He watched her, wary. Her side rose and fell slowly. Until he heard the distinctive change in her breathing that he associated with someone sleeping.

Fine. Whatever. At least she'll keep the others out.

Felix closed his eyes and had dropped back off to sleep in a minute.

Chapter 30 - Like a Violin -

Felix watched as the caterers were cleared through security and began wheeling in lunch for the summit.

The food served was high in quality and quantity.

Whoever is footing the bill for this is probably spending way too much. Especially with how long it's been going on.

I wonder how they're handling of it.

Faith, Goldie, Victoria, a Winged Elf, and a small Wood Elf were his guards today. They were standing around him in their gear, and even Goldie was wearing her light version of Legion body armor.

Victoria had been a surprise, showing up with her sword and specially made Warden armor.

Petra had apparently started sending Legionnaires home on furlough to take time off. Supposedly, the emperor was reevaluating his position.

Especially since the walls of Yosemite were so well armed.

The Winged Elf had been watching the tables closely as they passed. When one of the caterers turned their head, her hand shot forward and snatched something from the second level of the table.

Pulling it behind her back, her SMG dangling at her side, she looked as innocent as could be.

Felix gave her a questioning look.

She was as tall as a High Elf, with features to match. Blond hair, blue eyes, and a slim build. Though she had bright white wings on her back.

She grinned at him, her nose scrunching up.

When the last table went by, she pulled what looked like a t-bone steak from around her back. Then she started eating it right there.

Looking at the Wood Elf, Felix had to wonder if she would be equally problematic.

The smaller Elf seemed to be finishing chewing something as well, trying for all the world to look innocent. She had brown hair and brown eyes, with slightly tanned skin. The very appearance of a Wood Elf.

Not bothering with them any further, Felix turned to Victoria.

"They're always hungry. I noticed it while on their home world," said the swordswoman. "I think it's because for a long time, food was scarce in what they call the Wastes.

"Eat when you can eat."

"You ever notice that almost everyone from their world is beautiful or handsome?" Felix asked seriously. "It's a little strange."

Victoria looked thoughtful, then shrugged.

"I was a little intimidated by how pretty they all were at first. I thought for sure you'd just dump us to the side," Victoria admitted.

"Couldn't be further from the truth." Felix peeked inside the massive conference room to see how things were looking as the door swung shut.

He hadn't wanted to be here. His presence had been a last-minute request from several dignitaries who had felt the security for the summit would be better served with him there.

Except he truly wanted to be back in the ANet, watching Miu on her mission.

She was probably carrying it out right now. Risking her people and herself.

"I think you're rather pretty," Goldie said, standing behind Victoria with a wide smile.

"Where'd everyone go?" Felix said, moving to the door frame.

Holding open the door an inch, he peered inside, looking for his people.

All the Legion security members were gone. The places they had been along the edges and around the outer walls were now empty.

Touching his free hand to his wrist communicator, Felix tapped the transmit button.

"This is bureaucrat-actual," Felix said, hating the code names they'd given him. "Requesting a sit-rep for the main hall. Security forces are not present."

"Team leader one-actual here. We're posted outside the doors and preventing entry. They've stated they're going to hold a vote," said a voice on the ANet. "They got jumpy about us staying behind. Saw a whole lot of religious leaders in there that were part of that new group that arrived last night."

Something didn't feel right here. Not at all.

He looked to Victoria, who nodded and took off at a jog toward a door in the back. It'd lead her back out to the front of the expo.

Felix let the door slide shut and then motioned to Goldie, then the door.

"Kinda figure you're the strongest one here. Can you put your foot on this side and grasp the doorknob? Don't let anyone open it. Trying to pretend like it's locked in place," Felix said to the gold Dragon.

"Of course, my nest-mate," Goldie said, moving over to his side. She put her foot down in the place he'd asked. Grabbing the door knob, she leaned back a bit, holding it braced against her foot.

"That seems a bit odd," Faith said, moving closer to Felix and Goldie. "What're you thinking?"

"They're not supposed to kick security out. For any reason. The fact that they did it without involving me makes me nervous," Felix said. Giving his head a shake, he hoped he was overreacting. "Maybe it's paranoia, maybe it's not. I feel better with Goldie holding the knob."

"I'll hold your knob," said someone softly.

Glancing over his shoulder, Felix couldn't pinpoint who had said it. Though he suspected the Winged Elf. She seemed mischievous to him.

Frowning, Felix looked back to the door, wondering if anyone would check it.

"Don't fret, nest-mate. They're just nervous," Goldie murmured, watching him with that big smile of hers.

"Nervous?" Felix asked.

"Everyone other than your swordswoman is from my world. You make us nervous, and our skin tingles when you look at us.

"You have magic in you. We're all very sensitive to it," Goldie explained. "You're handsome to begin with, but the magic that is you calls to us."

Goldie suddenly stopped talking, her head turning down to the handle.

Felix looked down at the door frame and saw the hint of a shadow there, moving back and forth. Then he heard someone mutter something on the other side before moving on.

Wishing he could still see inside, Felix felt his paranoia slowly ramping up.

"Do you want to see in there?" asked a light voice.

Glancing over his shoulder, he found the Winged Elf there.

"Yeah, I do. Can you do something for that?" Felix asked.

Nodding her head, the Elf got down on her knees and pressed her hands to the bottom of the door. Then she lifted her left hand and held it up to him.

In her hand was what looked like a small magical window. It was showing a view that seemed to be on the other side of the door from her right hand.

"See? Very handy," said the Winged Elf with a grin. "We use similar spells for vision while flying."

Handy. Har, har.

Ok, you're the one who made the silly comment. Your humor is awful.

"Her name is Talia, and yes, she's always like that," Goldie said, watching him.

Felix wrapped a hand around Talia's wrist and stared closely into her hand.

"If you wanted to hold my hand, all you had to do was ask," Talia said, her folded wings quivering on her back.

"Hush, you silly thing." Goldie poked Talia in the back of the head with a finger. "Flirt with him later."

Ignoring her, Felix watched. So far, it all looked fairly mundane. Everyone was organizing themselves at their lunch tables. They seemed to be preparing to vote on something at the same time.

He didn't like it. Didn't like it at all.

It looked innocent enough, but it didn't feel right.

Two minutes passed like this, with him holding Talia's wrist and staring into her hand.

Finally, he felt like he could give up and leave this one alone.

"Alright, let it go, Talia," Felix said, releasing her hand. "We'll remain here just in case, but it seems like nothing's happening."

Talia nodded and canceled the spell.

"Of course, Felix," she said, slowly getting to her feet.

Felix grumbled under his breath, annoyed. He'd argued for a while with the prime minister about putting in cameras before everyone arrived.

He should have taken his argument up with Kevin the moment he was elected. Maybe he would have let him put them in after the fact anyways.

"I just wish—"

There was a loud crash from the room beyond the door. Loud enough that Felix could feel it in his feet and knees.

A flash of bright red light washed over everything and vanished as it passed through the walls behind them.

Reaching out, he grabbed Talia's wrist.

"No need for the rough stuff, I'll get down on my knees for you," Talia said, dropping down quickly. "Just don't pull my hair."

"Not now," Goldie said sternly, all trace of humor gone.

Talia pushed her right hand down to the ground and her left hand opened up.

Standing in the middle of the room was Skipper. She was holding a gun and waving it around lazily. Some Powered Felix had never seen before was standing next to her.

"Is that Skipper?" the Wood Elf asked, staring into Talia's hand next to him.

"Looks like it's her. The pictures from the database look like her," Faith said from Felix's other side.

She took the time to dig through the database? Good. I'm glad to hear it.

Talia shifted the view around, and it was apparent that the room was full of soldiers and Powereds.

"I don't think we can handle that much without the others," Talia said. Apparently she could see it without looking at it.

Felix tapped the transmit button on his wrist.

"This is bureaucrat-actual. We have contact with multiple hostiles," Felix said, letting go of the transmit button.

There was no response. Felix sat there waiting, listening to his earpiece for anything.

Pushing the transmit button, Felix tried again.

"I repeat, this is bureaucrat-actual. Multiple contacts; friendly targets are in danger," Felix said. "Require immediate evacuation and assistance."

Letting go of the button, Felix waited.

Nothing came back. There was only silence on the ANet.

Turning away from Talia's hand, Felix looked to his wrist display. Tapping it open with a finger, he moved straight to the wireless connection to the Legion satellite.

There was nothing there. It was as if he wasn't getting a signal at all.

Which was impossible.

Felicia had tinkered with their satellites before they'd sent them up. They were powerful enough to transmit through almost anything. The ANet depended on them and only rarely had any problems.

Those problems tended to be along the lines of a degraded connection for a short period of time. Usually around maintenance windows that were unavoidable.

A complete blackout of service was impossible.

Felix found a signal. But it wasn't his, or Legion's. It was a rogue signal he'd never seen before, and one he probably shouldn't be able to see.

Certainly not on Legion property.

Tapping it impulsively, he waited for it to connect.

When it did, his screen flickered and loaded up what looked like a webpage hosting a photo.

It was of a young woman. One that looked incredibly familiar to him. A play button was just below her chin, signifying that it was a video rather than a photo.

Suddenly Felix realized who he was looking at.

It was Blake's assistant. Shirley.

Or secretary. Or something. I never... looked into her that deeply. Her background was ordinary.
We picked her thoughts clean afterward, though. She wasn't even wearing a ring to protect herself.
There was nothing there.

He poked at the play symbol, and the button started to spin slowly as it loaded.

"Hello, Felix," Shirley said, waving a hand at him. The voice was coming over the connection to his earpiece. "If you're listening to this, you've already lost."

Uh huh. Isn't that what every villain monologues about?

"And in this case, I'm not monologuing. Before you start raging about Blake, or something else of that nature, it's best you realize that he had very little to do with this," Shirley said. She leaned back in her chair and gestured to herself. "The mastermind behind your downfall from the very start was myself and no other."

Felix looked at Talia's hand; the room beyond the door remained unchanged. Skipper was starting to move people around the room. Sorting them for something.

"Honestly, there was only one point in time where you made me nervous," Shirley said. "And you know what, I'll even explain it all to you. Because... it's already done.

"You've already lost. You're stuck in a zone of control, broken away from your protectors, and trapped with Skipper, who is looking for you.

"Aren't you?"

The smirk on the woman's face made Felix want to pull her head off.

"It was all rather simple. Beating you was just about understanding you.

"You have certain tendencies you fall into. Most especially when you feel like someone is attacking you," Shirley said. She got up and moved to one side of the frame, the camera tracking her.

"So... we attacked you. We left enough information and clues to get you to a healthy level of paranoia. To where you'd rather attack first and ask questions later," Shirley said. "This was where you surprised me. I thought for sure you'd buy the bank at a company level. Or go after it through political channels.

"Maybe discredit it and buy it through a leveraged stock purchase.

"Who would have thought you'd rob it? Rob it and steal all our blackmail data."

Shirley sighed as she walked over to a window, the camera still following her.

"So much work lost in that one hour. It was impressive on your part."

Not really. Runner helped me there. If it wasn't for him, I never would have known who was behind it the way I did.

It made it significantly easier.

"I almost scrapped my plan. Almost," Shirley said. She reached up and grabbed the drawstrings on the blinds. "You did do what we wanted, though. You eliminated the bank that was providing all the funding for the government of Wal.

"You effectively gutted their ability to do business, as their largest credit line was there. After that day, Wal had little capital to work with."

Shirley sighed and held up her arms. "What could we do at that point? We moved ahead and set Blake up."

Felix grimaced at that. All along, he'd actually felt like he was missing something. From the very beginning, in fact.

"Blake was an obstacle in our way. One we didn't want to move against, because that had the potential to reveal our presence," Shirley said. She was slowly drawing the pull-string down, raising the blinds up. "The original plan was to have you remove him, so we went back to it. A few tweaks later and we felt like we could pull you back in to do our dirty work."

When she'd finished drawing the blinds up, Shirley rubbed her hands together and looked back to the camera.

"And you did. Did it wonderfully. Blake was so crushed, so thoroughly beaten, that our candidate didn't just win, he became a political powerhouse," Shirley said. "Kevin was very appreciative of all the work you did for him. It's a shame he works for us."

Felix was feeling a bit sick to his stomach now. It seemed they really had been manipulating him from the very start.

"And that brings us to today. To now. To the fact that you sent your people to wipe out the last vestiges of what was keeping us back. Keeping us from simply… taking Wal," Shirley said.

The camera moved to the window. It was overlooking a short, squat building. There were clearly guards in front of the doors, and it looked more like a military base stuffed into an office building.

"Inside there, right now, is your team. Killing everyone who stood for Wal. Its defenders.

"Those we couldn't buy outright to our cause. And your people are in there, killing them," Shirley explained.

"Isn't it grand? I had you do all the work for me, without ever having to dirty my hands."

"You did it all. And now… we'll launch a coup, take the summit hostage, and kill Legion off."

"They're coming," said a voice off camera.

Shirley nodded and then pointed to the front of the building.

"Flip the little switch on the side," Shirley said.

The camera bumped to one side with a click. Then the frame was righted, except the view was strange now.

It looked more like a strange infrared view, showing heat but also details at the same time.

The door opened, and a group of nine slunk out of the building. Moving away from it quickly.

Felix knew it was Miu and her group. Without even seeing her face or anyone in her group directly. He could tell by their armaments and by the way Miu carried herself.

"Ah, looks like they're done. Which means it's time for us to take over Wal, and then… well… kill you all," Shirley said, pulling the camera back to herself.

"It's been fun, and interesting, but it's time for our game to end. Thank you for all the hard work you did, Felix. I couldn't have done it without you."

The video cut off abruptly, and Felix was left with nothing but his feelings about the situation.

He'd been played. Played expertly.

Predicted, used, and discarded.

"Hmph, we'll see about that," Felix muttered, looking back to Talia's hand.

There was no way he or Legion would bend over for Skipper or Shirley. There was no possibility of that on any level.

Felix licked his lips and started to think on what he and his small group of people could do. Preferably with the fewest amount of them dying.

Cutting off fingers sucks, and bringing people back from fingers is even worse.

Skipper raised a hand, leveled her pistol at a woman, and pulled the trigger.

The retort of the gun was loud.

The woman's head split open at the top of her forehead and deformed terrifyingly.

She dropped to the ground, dead long before she stopped moving.

Skipper shrugged her shoulders and looked at everyone else, waving the gun around a bit.

"She's asking where you are," Talia said. "You specifically, Felix."

"Great. Well, at least she doesn't know where I am. Which means Dragon telepathy works at least well enough to protect us in a similar way to Kit's," Felix said.

"Now we just have to kill her and get back home."

A large, loud explosion came from the opposite direction of Skipper.

To be perfectly honest, to Felix it felt like it was coming from outside the expo entirely.

Now what?

Another explosion went off, and Felix felt the very walls around him shake.

Damn me. It's all going to hell.

Chapter 31 - Tongue Tied -

"Oh shit," Talia muttered.

Felix's eyes shot back to the Elf's hand.

The many religious leaders who were there with national counterparts were now butchering them.

Some were using what looked like ritualistic weapons, while others were simply clawing at their faces with the bare hands. Others still were binding their victims up.

Skipper was gone.

"There is a lot of religious magic being thrown around in there," Faith said. "It's also rapidly building. Spiking. It's going to overwhelm everything in the area."

"Yeah. They're already all dead," Felix said, not wanting to get involved at this moment. "We need an exit."

Reaching into his body armor, Felix pulled out a slim metallic card and brushed a thumb over the activation square.

It was a new version of the portal generator Felicia had put together for him. After his forced trip to the wild wastes of Vince's home world, she had upgraded the device.

The card flickered and then turned a bright blue. As if literally ripping a hole through space and time, a portal popped open in front of him.

On the other side was the Legion portal receiving hall.

Vince stood in front of another portal, his glowing energy sword in one hand and his gifted sidearm in the other.

Felix couldn't see the other side of the portal, but he got the impression it led somewhere quite bad. The blood pooling out from the bottom of it was ominous, to say the least.

Vince stood there, firing into the portal. When the hammer locked back, he tossed the weapon underhand to a Legion security member nearby.

Whipping his sword around, Vince swung through the portal itself. There was a high-pitched squeal followed by a thump, and a black, chitinous-looking claw dropped through the portal.

The Legionnaire handed the reloaded sidearm back to Vince. Who began firing into the portal again.

Legion itself is under attack as well.

Then a red film slid over the portal Felix had made before he could even think of going through it. A bright red light spun out in every direction, then detonated.

Where the portal had been was now nothing. The metallic card had literally split in half and was smoldering.

"A god just intervened," Faith murmured. "Several of them. They do not want you to get back to Legion."

Talia got to her feet, brushing her hands off against one another. "They're all looking this way now; we need to go."

"Goldie, I need you to become a Dragon. Now," Felix said, then pointed at Faith and the Wood Elf. "You two, hold the door."

Releasing the doorknob, Goldie stepped away from it and moved over to Felix's side.

She pulled off the light body armor and handed it to Felix.

"I like these clothes. They fit and flatter me."

"If I change, I'll just destroy them," Goldie said as she quickly worked at her clothes. She unfastened her bra and undid her pants. "I'll need something to wear after anyways."

Then she shucked off her tank top and light pants, handing those to him too. Last came her undergarments.

Felix took everything and started putting them into his own clothes. The only thing he couldn't wedge in somewhere was her body armor.

For that, he buckled it together and slung it over his arm like a messenger bag. Looking back at her, he was momentarily at a loss for how lovely a naked gold Dragon could be.

Goldie gave him a bright smile before she went from completely naked to a Dragon.

She ducked her head and spread herself out as best as she could, but she wasn't going to fit in this small room.

Lowering her head as her face elongated, she slammed her horns into the wall.

A second later, she was stepping out of the expo and onto an open lawn, fully in her Dragon form.

She was massive, with golden scales from snout to tail tip.

Moving away from the hole in the wall, her head turned one way and then the other.

"Let's go." Felix put action to his command and jogged out of the room after the Dragon.

Faith, Talia, and the Wood Elf all came after him.

A bright red dome was high in the sky above them, spreading out as far as the eye could see.

"Is that why we can't get ahold of anyone?" Talia asked, pointing at the red shimmer.

"I would imagine so," Goldie growled as her head swung toward them.

"We need to get out of here and do some recon to figure out what is and isn't in the red thing," Felix said. Memories of something similar happening years ago popped into his head.

He was much more prepared this time around.

"Let's see if Legion HQ or New Legion City is in the dome first," Felix commanded, moving toward Goldie.

The Wood Elf next to him crumpled to the ground. Her chest turned inside out and a spray of blood and gore spewed out from behind her.

A distant boom followed, after she'd already hit the ground.

Sniper!

Goldie moved in front of Felix, Faith, and Talia, and squatted down.

Wasting no time, Felix bent over. Pulling out his belt knife, he flicked it open and cut the downed Wood Elf's thumb from her hand. After stuffing it in his pocket, he checked on the Elf.

There was no guarantee they'd be getting back to Legion anytime soon. Rather than risk it, he was determined to take a finger with him.

Besides, if he got lucky, he could resurrect her in the field.

She wasn't quite dead yet, her eyes moving around wildly.

Pressing a hand to her face, he got her attention.

"I'll bring you back," Felix said when her eyes turned to him. "I promise."

The Elf nodded slightly and then moved no more, her eyes unfocusing.

Standing up and turning to Goldie, Felix patted her mouth.

"Open that pretty mouth of yours. Faith, come over here. Talia, can you keep up with Goldie in the air?" Felix asked.

"Easily," said the Elf, her wings unfolding behind her.

Goldie opened her mouth a bit, her wickedly sharp teeth visible.

"Wider. Enough to fit Faith and me. You're playing taxi-cab for us rather than any of us trying to hold on to each other," Felix said, pressing a hand to her jaw.

"I bet you could fit in my mouth," Talia said.

Goldie opened her mouth wide, her tongue lying flat against the bottom.

"Are you ser—"

Felix grabbed Faith around the hips and tossed her into the Dragon's mouth before she could finish her sentence. Then he grabbed two teeth and levered himself up into Goldie's mouth.

Lying down flat against her tongue, he braced a boot against her molar. Pulling some thick paracord from his vest he looped it around one of her wide front teeth and tied it to his harness.

Faith was wedged up in the side of Goldie's mouth, watching him. When she figured out what he was doing, she immediately started doing the same.

"Alright Goldie, we're good in here. Try not to swallow. Would prefer it if you could keep your mouth cracked, but I understand," Felix called out.

"I'd have a hard time trying not to swallow you," Talia said, her tone nervous, her voice breaking at the end.

Goldie's mouth closed around them, and they were plunged into darkness.

"I'm sitting in a Dragon's mouth with a man I'm trying to talk into bedding me," Faith said aloud. "My life is very odd."

"Yeah, I hear ya there. I've had that thought more times than I can count. The odd part, that is. First time being in a Dragon's mouth," Felix replied.

There was a sudden lurching motion, and Felix felt his stomach rush up to meet his throat. Especially when he slid down toward Goldie's throat.

Her tongue came up and pushed him back up against the front of her mouth. His arms were pinned below his waist, her tongue wrapped up around his middle.

Faith was wedged up against the front of him. He couldn't see her in the dark, but he could feel her face against his own. Her nose was in his cheek.

Her body was pressed hard to his own, her hands trapped below as well, it seemed.

Goldie must be taking off. A lot of g-force there. She doesn't know we're tied in, or she thinks it'll be stronger than that.

Or she isn't taking chances on eating us.

Faith turned her face a bit, her lips brushing against his own. Then she kissed him.

Really? Right now? Not the time or place.

Damn Nymphs.

Unable to resist her, since he was literally trapped by a Dragon's tongue, Felix just accepted Faith and her determined kissing, which became heavier by the second.

Then she slipped her tongue in his mouth.

***

Eventually, Goldie let her tongue slide back into place, freeing Faith and Felix.

Breaking away from the Dryad, Felix moved to the side of Goldie's mouth. He couldn't see very well, but he could vaguely see Faith's outline. His eyes had adjusted as best they could.

She seemed to fall backward against the side of Goldie's mouth and sat down next to her molars.

"I'm so sorry. I couldn't resist myself. I'm so sorry. I'm sorry," Faith said, her voice high and fast. "You smelled so good, and then I could taste your attraction to me. I could feel your desire. I wanted it all so badly for myself."

"It's alright. No real harm done," Felix said. There was a very uncomfortable tightness to his pants that he didn't want to think of right now.

Sitting there in the gloomy dark of Goldie's mouth, Felix wasn't sure what to do next. He was effectively in time-out until she stopped.

Leaning his head back against a tooth, Felix let out a breath.

"Really? You're not upset with me?" Faith asked. Her tone had leveled out somewhat.

"No. I'm not upset with you. Annoyed, but not upset. It's partially in your nature, isn't it?" Felix asked.

"Uhm... I don't understand," Faith said.

"Never mind. Now we just—"

Goldie's jaw shifted and her teeth parted. There was an open airway, and it started to circulate around in her mouth. Which was honestly pretty welcome at this point.

The humidity had been getting unbearable.

That and there was also a bit of light coming in.

Moving to the front of her teeth, Felix peered out from between them.

They were high up in the air, looking down at the city. Goldie was flying lazily, her chin up so she wouldn't spill the contents of her mouth.

Talia's face appeared upside down between Goldie's teeth.

"Hey," she said. Her face was flushed. "We're as high as we can go and circling a bit. I've got an illusion around Goldie, so we're being left alone.

"As far as we can see, the area in the dome goes from where we were in the expo all the way to the bottom of the city. It covers almost the entire capital.

"It just doesn't cross over Legion HQ or New Legion City."

Felix sat back down on Goldie's tongue, contemplating Talia's words.

They'd built this little dome to lock Legion out as a whole, and everyone else in. That's... odd. Isn't it?

"In other words, we're effectively trapped in this zone until it vanishes or we break free."

Reaching up with a hand, Felix went to scratch at his head and thought better of it. It was covered in Goldie's saliva.

"That's about right," Talia said, agreeing with Felix's assessment.

"Great. Alright, I guess our first order of business is supplies and a place to lie low. Any libraries in the area?"

"A library?" Talia said, turning her head to one side, still looking at him from upside down. "I'm sure there is, but why?"

"After the last time something like this happened, I put some serious thought into it. Libraries were mostly left alone. People didn't think there was anything to take from them, and most of those buildings were so wide open they were hard to defend," Felix said. "So I quietly bought up a number of them and transformed them into bunkers below ground. They also connect to one another through subterranean tunnels."

"That... seems like a lot of work," Faith said. "And money."

"It was. Though it seems my paranoia was healthy and deserved. Alright, so... Goldie, can you spot a library and get us down somewhere we can get you back into human form?" Felix asked.

"Mmhmmm," Goldie mumbled, her mouth vibrating under Felix's ass.

"Oooh, that was interesting," Faith murmured, running her hands back and forth over Goldie's tongue.

Talia's head vanished from view, and Goldie closed her mouth again. All was darkness again.

Thankfully, Faith didn't do anything. She kept to her side.

They sat there in silence. In the quiet dark of a Dragon's mouth.

As the minutes inched by, Felix would swear he could feel his ears adjusting to what felt like an altitude change. Which meant they were probably on an approach to a library.

There was a thump, and then Goldie's head dipped forward and opened. Felix and Faith spilled out onto solid ground.

They were in a small, fenced-in area attached to a large building. A large trash bin sat to one side.

Getting to his knees, Felix watched as Goldie suddenly started to shrink, returning to her humanoid size.

Grunting, Felix stood up and started to pull her clothes out of the various crevices he'd crammed them into on his person.

They seemed drier than his own clothes.

"Blegh," Goldie said, followed by spitting noises.

"I know he said not to swallow, but I also know for a fact he'd like it if you did. No need to spit," Talia said from not far off.

"Talia," Faith muttered, pressing her hands to the lower part of her back. "I think even I'm tired of that right now."

"Sorry... she... she died. Ya know? We're stuck and... and I don't know..." Talia's voice had taken on a slightly frantic quality.

"Pish posh, Faith," Goldie murmured. "It's alright. Your joke was funny, Talia, just not the right time."

The nude and beautiful gold Dragon walked over to Felix and started to take her clothes back from him.

Turning away from Goldie as she got dressed, Felix moved over to the door set into the building. "I take it this is a library?"

"Yes. This is the rear of the building. Was that ok?" Talia asked. She was squatting down nearby, and shuddering a bit from head to toe.

Must be her first time in a bad situation. Or she was closer to the Wood Elf than I thought.

"You're doing fine, Talia," Felix said, reaching over to pat her on the head. "Just keep your chin up, alright?"

Talia slowly lifted her face up and looked at him.

She likes crude, immature jokes, right?

I can do that.

"See? It really gets me going if you look up at me when you're on your knees for me," Felix said.

Talia opened her mouth, then closed it. Then she started chuckling darkly. "Right? Need to see my eyes, yeah? Watch my lips stretch?"

Felix flicked her on the forehead and then pressed his Legion ring to the metal pad next to the key-lock.

"As if you would know. You're as much a virgin as I am," Faith muttered as she got close to Talia.

"I've seen movies. You can rent them from the ANet," Talia said.

There was a soft click in front of Felix, and the door unlocked. Stepping through the doorway, Felix started looking around for the basement.

The conversation between Talia and Faith continued. Felix ignored it, figuring that he really didn't want to know where it was going.

Finding a sign that indicated which direction the basement was, Felix set off toward it. He needed to get down there and find the lock-plate that'd open the bunker.

Goldie caught up to him as he was moving down the stairs.

"I take it what we're looking for is down here?" she asked.

"Yeah. It's a fairly secure little hidey hole."

After opening the door, he stood there for a moment, scanning the basement.

There.

On one side, there was a metal sign. It was bolted to the wall and had instructions for what to do in the event of an emergency.

Felix pressed his Legion signet into its corner. Right atop what looked like a bolt head.

"Seems a bit convoluted," Talia said.

Felix glanced over his shoulder to find Talia and Faith had caught up to him.

"It is," Felix said to Talia. "But it's also part of the mandatory emergency training. Everyone has ninety days to do it. I assume you haven't gotten around to it?"

"No. Been learning from the bodyguards and the Elex girls," Talia said. "No time."

The entire wall popped, then swung open as if it were on a hinge.

"There we are. Time to go down," Felix said. Stepping into the opening, he flicked the light switch on and moved down the stairs.

He'd half expected a comment from Talia about going down, so he was mildly surprised when she didn't make one.

When he hit the bottom of the staircase, Felix immediately went over to a terminal that was powering on.

The rest of the entry room was a very simple-looking staging area with more than a handful of doors leading elsewhere.

Talia and Faith kept moving past him. They looked like they wanted to explore the rest of the bunker.

Goldie eased up beside him, a hand coming up to rest on his lower back.

"Faith had a word with her," Goldie said softly. "She's very young. Eighteen. Apparently her species is incredibly isolated. She'll be alright, just… nervous."

"Thank you for giving her some leeway."

Felix shrugged, closing the door above them with the terminal.

Opening up the details for the bunker, he found it was exactly what he'd wanted. Just as he'd ordered these bunkers and safe houses built and installed.

Each one was independent, but also tied to every safe house and bunker nearby. They all had their own communication channels, portals, and controls. There were cables laid in the ground itself from location to location, creating a massive network that functioned independently.

Nothing depended on anything anymore.

He'd learned his lessons from the last go-round.

"Train is powering up. We'll get on it, ride it to the end of the line, and see if we can't get back home," Felix said.

"A train? This bunker seems rather complex and well stocked. How'd you get it all done? Or approved?" Goldie asked.

"A lot of money, years of unending work, and not asking Wal for permission or a dime. This was all done because I'm a paranoid man and experienced a similar situation before.

"I'm very glad to see that all that money I spent has been worth it so far."

Felix wanted to sit down and go through the bunker system to figure out who else was in the area. See if he couldn't get a survivor train going to Legion HQ.

Especially since Victoria had vanished in the expo.

Except he couldn't.

He needed to get back to Legion as soon as possible. It was under direct attack.

Every second that he wasn't there felt like a true disaster. He needed to be gone from here.

He needed to be back at Legion.

Now.

Chapter 32 - Distractions -

Felix had them moving along at a reasonable speed in the underground Legion tunnels.

The "train" as he had called it had four cars. Two for storage, two with seats, and the engine. It had hip high walls and the engine was a sturdy little thing, but there was no speed to it.

"This isn't very quick," Talia said. "And it looks like this is the maximum speed."

"It isn't meant to be quick," Felix replied. She was leaning over his shoulder, staring at the controls. "This is the fastest it'll go, but it'll go this speed no matter what load you put on it."

"One of Felicia's oddities. She doesn't quite understand it herself."

Talia didn't respond, just moved back into the passenger car.

Felix glanced down at the readout screen in front of him. They were coming up on another junction point. After this, he'd be able to get on the Legion railway. Which would require no further track changes.

There were no other trains on the rails. Either he was the fastest one to get down from the bunker into the system, or he was the only one to reach a bunker.

Felix couldn't help but feel like a coward. Running away from what was possibly his Legionnaires in trouble.

He knew logically that everyone would argue he was more important, as he could bring the others back. Therefore, his own safety was paramount.

But that didn't make it any easier for him.

Passing over the junction, Felix saw a red glow up ahead.

Realizing what it was, he smashed the brakes as hard as he could. Reaching over, he flipped the emergency brake as well.

There was the screech of iron wheels locking up and sliding along the rails. Behind him his bodyguards screamed as they were bodily thrown forward by the sudden change in speed.

The train slowed dramatically, but it still kept moving.

Up ahead, Felix could now actually see the dome. The red glow of it was distinct and obvious.

The speed of the train bled off quickly, and Felix felt his heart unclench when he realized they would stop short of the dome.

"Damnit," Felix muttered. Flipping the train into reverse when it came to a halt, he looked over his shoulder. "Sorry everyone, looks like we're not getting out by the rail either.

"Apparently it extends much further down than I thought. This thing is more of a sphere than a dome."

Faith, Talia, and Goldie were righting themselves and looking each other over.

Goldie looked the least perturbed about the whole situation. She flicked her hands over her clothes and sat herself back down.

"So, what's our plan now, then?" she asked.

"Back to the bunker. Last time I was in a situation like this, I played Mr. Run-and-Gun. Didn't go so well. Going to take up a firm defensive position this time and figure out our next moves," Felix said.

When they reached the junction, he maneuvered the train through the roundabout and got them turned around in the right direction.

It didn't matter that much since it was a train, but he didn't feel right going in reverse.

***

"How much does the bunker have stored away as far as food and water supplies?" Faith asked, stepping off the train and back into the bunker's loading dock.

"Enough for thirty people to survive a year without ever leaving," Felix replied, following her. "I figured anything beyond a year would mean there were much greater problems for Legion."

"That makes sense," Talia said, walking along behind them. She seemed much calmer now.

"What do you wish to do, nest-mate?" Goldie asked as they passed from the loading dock into the bunker's entry room.

"Not sure. Probably take a look at the cameras to see what's going on around the library and the surrounding streets. Maybe check in on the news to see what's what," Felix said. "Dial in to the Legion underground network to see if anyone else is on a terminal."

"All wise plans. I will handle the cameras. Faith, you go check the radio. Talia, the television," Goldie said, handing out orders.

The other two women immediately obeyed, moving off to do as instructed.

"Ah... you won't be able to look at the cameras while I'm on the network," Felix said, moving over to the computer terminal.

"I know. But I thought it'd be nice to get you alone to myself and give those two some time to process their thoughts," Goldie said, moving to stand next to him. She pressed a hand into his lower back and looked to the screen as he began going through the system.

Unable to help himself, Felix could feel his brows pressing together as he worked. Goldie's fingers were trailing up and down a short distance along his spine. It was making it a bit harder than normal to concentrate.

"You like to touch me," Felix said finally, pulling up the system screen to see all the other bunkers and safe houses.

"I do. It helps me connect with you.

"Though to be honest, I also took the time to sort through your wives' thoughts when I had the chance. As well as Felicity's.

"You enjoy being touched, but you don't ever ask for it," Goldie said.

Feeling a bit like a lab rat, Felix wasn't sure how to respond at first. Felicity and Goldie seemed to have both made concerted efforts to understand what he wanted and needed, without ever a word from him on the matter.

Maybe it's just their background. Their world.

"Ah, there we are," Felix said as he got the log to pull up. "And we have... several people in various safe houses. No one in other bunkers, though."

"How can you tell who's there?" Goldie asked, her fingers moving along his back to his neck.

"The rings everyone wears are security keys, through a form of RFID, as well as transmitters. They'll pick up anywhere in Legion networks," Felix explained.

Felix began to sort through each safe house roster and check their locations on the map.

He stopped at a safe house that was practically on the other side of the city.

It had three people listed as being inside.

"Oh, we should probably go collect them," Goldie said, tapping the screen with a fingernail. "Though I'd be curious how those three ended up together."

Edith Torres, Jessica Perreira, Erica Newberg.

Felix mentally flagged that safe house. They were part of his inner circle. He'd make the attempt to go get them.

Moving on, he kept reading through the lists.

He was looking for one name in particular, but he hadn't seen it yet.

Miu should be here, right? She was out on a mission. She's trapped in this dome, too. She'd move to a safe house or a bunker.

"Felix," Faith said, coming out from the media room. "It's a military coup. Kevin Dane just announced himself as King.

"Apparently the general in charge of the local forces here in Wal was murdered, along with his entire senior staff.

"Kevin just... stepped into the void and took over."

Closing his eyes, Felix did his best not to grimace.

He understood Shirley a bit better now. She'd put every obstacle in her way—in Felix's way. He and Legion really had been used as a tool to batter down all of Wal's defenses.

"There's a military curfew in effect right now. Anyone on the streets is considered an enemy of the state," Faith said.

"And Legion has been declared a terrorist organization," Talia added from the media room in a raised voice. "They broke into the HQ building, but they only seem to be in the lobby. Looks like they can't figure out the security elevator, so that's good."

"New Legion City was also a target, but apparently it was evacuated before they showed up."

Felix nodded, not sure what he was feeling. Everything he'd worked for had just been thrown out the window by his own actions.

All of his actions had been based on circumstantial proof and little more than paranoid feelings. Everything had been reasonable but never quite proven. There had never been a clear answer in any of it.

"Alright. We have to assume everyone is doing what they can to keep down and stay out of sight. First order of business is to start collecting all the Legionnaires we can. Or their bodies, or parts of them," Felix said. He could lament and regret his actions later. He needed to act now.

Opening his eyes, he found Talia, Faith, and Goldie all looking at him.

"Talia, you seem particularly well versed in illusions. Can you maintain one in front of people? When they're staring right at you?"

"Yes. That's actually how my people stay... out of sight for the most part. We don't do extraordinarily well around other races," Talia admitted. "And no, I wasn't caught because my illusion failed. I don't want to talk about it."

Felix stared at her for several seconds.

Slowly, Talia dropped her arms to her sides, her chin falling. "I was sleeping in a tree. They tracked me down with a Beastkin and stunned me."

"I need you to break into a military outpost and find out what their plans are," Felix said, not addressing her capture story. "Take one of the radios and earpieces from the supply crates. We'll all go to frequency Lima-Four-Two."

Talia nodded quickly, then moved back into the media room.

"Faith, I need you to take the train and go to this bunker here," Felix said, pointing to the screen. Moving around the side of the desk, she leaned over to look at what he was pointing to.

"Get it prepped and ready. I want it up and running as a fallback position. Make the weapons accessible, lay out the armor, and put together as many quick exit bags as you can," Felix ordered.

"I can do that," Faith said.

"Great. Goldie and I will go with you for the first part of the trip to get the second train. Then we'll be heading out to start picking people up." Felix shook his head. "Right now, I can't think of a way out of the dome.

"If it's anything like what they've been doing to my power set, it'll fail all on its own with enough time."

"That kinda feels like 'let's wait and see what happens,'" Talia grumbled.

Not hiding his sigh, Felix nodded. "Because that's kinda what it is."

***

Felix had parked the train in a pickup zone nearby the safe house Jessica, Erica, and Edith were at.

All the safe houses had been placed in locations that were relatively accessible by the Legion rail system.

The problem was there were a number of soldiers between the exit point and where they needed to go.

Sitting between a wall and a dumpster, Felix wasn't quite happy with the situation they were in. Everything smelled like rotting milk.

Goldie was wedged up next to him, with little space between the two of them. She was practically in his lap.

The way into the Legion rail system looked like a big vent on the side of a building. It led into a short drop and the actual vent system. The entrance to the rail was behind a giant steel plate in the wall inside the drop.

Felix slid the control stick to the left, and the aerial drone skimmed along the roof top. The view it provided on the screen attached to the remote showed him a scene he didn't want to see.

It was a near-perfect shot of the intersection below. A clear and solid viewing window of the entry to the safe house. A used book store on a corner lot.

Except parked practically in front of it was a tank. The rear of the metal monster was in the entryway to the shop itself.

In addition to the tank, there were several squads of Wal soldiers, and a machine-gun placement. There were a number of weapons facing each approach. It was clearly meant to be a checkpoint for anyone going in any direction.

Except almost every single intersection had a similar checkpoint.

Considering all of Wal was under martial law, that seemed a little odd to Felix.

"They're hunting us — Legion — aren't they?" Goldie said softly. It really wasn't a question.

"That they are. There's no other reason for all the checkpoints. Martial law more or less will keep the vast majority of the population indoors for now," Felix said.

"How do you want to handle this?"

"Really don't know. Though... how strong are you as a human? Can you knock down walls and the like?" Felix asked.

"I'm fairly strong in this form. Not as strong as Taylor or Kris, but blacks always keep more of themselves in human form than others.

"I don't think I could disable that... metal... thing, though. Human steel on this world seems much stronger than on my home world," Goldie said.

Setting the drone down on the edge of a building, Felix looked up from the display.

Turning his head to the side and up, Felix looked into the corner of the overhang on the building they were up against.

He knew there was a camera up in there that fed as a primary into the safe house his people were in.

With any luck, they were watching him right now, and they were hopefully aware he was trying to figure out a plan to get them out.

Because honestly, anything he did would rely on those three getting over to him as quickly as possible.

"I will cause a distraction," Goldie said. Crawling off of Felix and over him, she slithered out from behind the dumpster and to its side.

She pulled her body armor off and tossed it lightly to him. Her clothes quickly followed, until she was naked.

"Goodness, with your eyes on me like that I actually feel a touch of embarrassment," Goldie said with a soft laugh. Before he could respond, she gave her head a shake. "I'll rejoin you later, once I break contact. My magic isn't that far behind an Elf's."

"I'll keep an eye out for you," Felix said even as she transformed into her Dragon-self.

With a beat of her wings, she hopped the wall and launched herself toward the intersection.

There was a cry, the boom of the tank firing, and then a mass of rifle fire.

Felix squeezed out from behind the dumpster and peeked around the corner just as Goldie leapt away from the scene. Vanishing down a street.

Left in her wake was what looked like several dead or dying humans, a smashed machine gun, a tank with a bent cannon, and two dozen men with rifles who started chasing her.

The tank shuddered, and then the hatch opened. Men began pouring out of it as flames licked up from the inside the hull.

What the actual fuck did she do to it?

Felix watched from where he was. It wouldn't do him any good to expose himself. Goldie had acted just to give him a chance to do this without being seen.

Jessica, Erica, and Edith popped out of a broken window and crept around the far side of the tank. The three women looked disheveled, but intact.

Their clothes were clearly ripped and stained, and Edith's shirt looked like it had blood on it.

Moving low to the ground, they made a beeline for Felix and his position.

"It's so good to see you, Felix," Erica murmured, crushing him in a hug when she got close.

"Yeah, good to see you too — go, go," Felix said, peeling the Rabbit off him and pushing her toward the vent cover.

Jessica thankfully didn't stop to hug him, but she did kiss him quickly, chasing Erica down toward the vent.

Edith eyed him as she passed, but said nothing.

Then the tank detonated, and fire and flames erupted out of its top like an inferno.

Squeezing in behind Edith, Felix waited. When it became obvious she was having a bit of difficulty wiggling through the tight space, he put his hands on her rear end. Giving her only a second, he started pushing her roughly.

Goldie had encountered a similar problem and had been forced to go sideways instead of head on. They didn't have the time or luxury for that now.

"Felix, what're you doing?" Edith hissed.

"Getting us out of here — go already," Felix said, shoving at her bottom.

"I hate this. I hate what you did to me. My hips were never this big," Edith said between grunts as she forced herself forward. "Why did you have to put a dumpster here?"

"It wasn't here originally. It's not on the plans," Jessica said from ahead. "Hurry up Edie, we need to go."

After a minute of shoving and wriggling, Edith got through and into the vent.

Closing the cover behind him, Felix followed them through the security door and closed that as well.

After waiting till it locked, Felix started down the twisting stairway after the three women.

"I hope Goldie is ok," Erica said.

"She'll be fine. You saw her," Jessica replied. "I'm sure she'll be back before we know it."

"Out of curiosity," Felix said as they kept walking down the steps. "How'd you three end up together here? I didn't even know you knew each other."

"We were having lunch outside the office," Jessica said.

"We wanted to go over some photos Edith took. She has a really steady hand and seems to capture some great shots," Erica added quickly.

Edith only nodded.

The sound of their steps moving ever downward felt loud in Felix's ears. He could feel the tension in the three women in front of him. He doubted they'd had an easy go of it, judging from their torn and stained clothes.

Supposedly, she takes pictures of me.

"Got any good ones of me? If so, you could probably sell them to Miu and make a killing," Felix said.

"Ahhh…" the three women said in unison. The tightly constrained tension bled away immediately to pure embarrassment.

Felix started laughing and patted Edith on the shoulder.

She really does take pictures of me, doesn't she? Ha.

As they walked down the stairs, Felix chuckled to himself the whole way down.

Edith, for her part, remained absolutely silent.

The ride back on the train did manage to get them talking, but mostly about small things. It was clear to Felix the three of them were shaken up to a degree.

Edith was handling it better, but even she looked as if she'd seem something she hadn't wanted to.

The three of them crashed out pretty quick by the time they'd gotten back to the bunker. It didn't hurt that evening had settled over the city.

Talia and Faith both checked in to report things were progressing, but neither were quite done yet.

For Talia, she reported that she'd secured a station she could use the next day, but she couldn't access it today. She was sacking out in what she described only as a roost.

Faith slept in the bunker she'd been prepping for a fast evacuation. She felt she'd be done by the next day and would be back that night.

For this part, Felix sat and waited at the terminal. He took the time to put out an alert to all safe houses and bunkers, for everyone to make their way into the tunnels and head towards the bunker where Faith was.

If someone entered the tunnels, small alerts on the network would signal a need for a pickup.

All throughout this, though, his eyes were glued to the monitors.

He was waiting for Goldie to come back.

Chapter 33 - Photo -

Sometime in the small hours of the night, Felix got an alarm that jerked him awake.

He'd set up a number of alerts to trigger sounds if any movement was picked up on the external entry cameras. Sitting upright from behind the desk the terminal was on, Felix blinked several times.

Getting to his feet, he knocked over the speakers he'd attached to the terminal and set to each side of his head.

Looking at the screen, he saw Goldie. She was in her human form, hunched over at the rear entrance to the library.

Felix punched in the commands to open the rear door and the security door into the bunker.

Leaving the terminal, he took the steps two at a time and sped through the door as it was still opening.

He was practically on top of Goldie before she'd even managed to get inside.

"Felix?" she asked, her head coming up as he came toward her.

"Yeah, it's me. Come 'ere, you alright?" Felix queried, moving in close to her. Slipping under her left arm, he wrapped his right around her middle and started to bodily drag her forward toward the bunker.

"I'm wounded, but I'm alive and will live. I've returned to you as I promised.

"Though I must confess, the rifles of this world are much stronger than I expected," said the Dragon.

"Yeah, guns are rather dangerous even for most superheroes and villains." Felix shifted his hand around, trying to not to get a handful of her chest. It was hard to hold her without doing that, the way she was leaning.

"Stop moving your hand and just hold me," Goldie said, her tone pained.

"Sorry, just a bit awkward is all."

"I don't mind."

Felix took a firm grasp on Goldie and kept her moving. When they got to the stairs, he wasn't quite sure how to proceed.

"I can do it. Just... walk in front of me. Just in case," Goldie said.

Felix didn't argue with her. Letting her go, he went down two steps, took hold of the railing, and looked back at her.

Goldie's right eye had destroyed completely; a squashed-looking meatball was there instead. Blood covered her face and dripped down her shoulder and neck.

There were small holes all over her body as well, each one dribbling blood.

"What the hell—are you alright?" Felix asked, about ready to turn around.

"I will be. Dragons are hearty. I will heal. Even my eye. I just need time," Goldie said, swaying a bit on the top step. Then she slumped forward toward Felix.

Facing forward, Felix backed up a step into her while grabbing the hand rails on each side of the stairwell.

Goldie's face was resting on his shoulder now, her single golden eye looking at him.

"Just, uh... hang on. I'll carry you down like this, I guess." Felix reached back with both hands. Grabbing her rear end, he pulled her up onto his back and then started to shuffle down the steps as carefully as he could.

Remind me to thank Miu for always making me work out with her. I don't think I could handle this without all that training.

Felix's mind shied away from the thought that came next.

I wonder how she is?

Reaching the bottom, Felix glimpsed the medical room and carried her there.

After pushing the door open with a foot, he got her to the bed and slid her naked body into it.

Felix started grabbing bandages and medical tape from the nearby cabinet. Loading up a small bedside rolling table and tray.

"The entire army is out there in force. They're going from building to building, looking for anyone who might be in Legion, a sympathizer, or just against the new king," Goldie said. "I was forced to fight what seemed like two flying versions of that tank contraption. They had spinning blades on top of them."

"Helicopters," Felix said, pulling over a bottle of disinfectant.

"Can Dragons get infections? If you have an open wound, can it fester?" Felix asked.

"Of course," Goldie murmured softly. "We're still mortals. It's just unlikely."

"Are there any bullets or fragments inside you?" Felix asked, popping the top off the disinfectant.

"No. They were all pushed out with the change."

"And your eye, you said it'll grow back? Do I need to clear the wound or just leave it as is?"

When Goldie didn't immediately reply, Felix looked at her. Her one good eye was watching him.

"I don't know," she said softly after a few more seconds. "I've lost fingers, and they grew back. I think my eye is the same way."

"We'll leave it alone and have Faith look at it tomorrow when she gets back. I'll see if I can't modify it myself as well," Felix said. Taking the disinfectant in one hand and several gauze strips in the other, he gave her a grim smile.

"For now, though, it's time to clean and dress those wounds. Dragon or not, you need care.

"I'm sorry," Felix said sincerely. "This'll probably hurt."

***

"There's a military camp where they're sending anyone suspected of being in Legion," Talia whispered into the line. "They're also sending the remains of anyone suspected to be in Legion there as well.

"There is an unhealthy amount of fear that the bodies will come back to life."

Given that Legionnaires don't stay dead, and the enemy has no idea why, I could definitely see that concern.

"The side with the dead isn't that heavily guarded; it's just secured. The other building with the prisoners is much more heavily guarded," Talia continued. "There's also a list of incidents where they believe they had contact with Legion."

Felix sighed and rubbed his hands across his face.

Things definitely didn't seem as bad as he'd feared, but they weren't good either.

"Alright. Good work, Talia. If you end up coming across more information, get back in touch. Otherwise, stay there and keep an eye on them for me, and check back in at night," Felix said.

"Sure, sure, keep a girl on the hook for the late-night booty call, why don't you? Next you'll be telling me you'll respect me in the morning," Talia said.

"Of course I will. So long as you brush your teeth before you try to kiss me," Felix said.

Talia snickered and then closed the line.

"She likes that you don't get mad at her jokes, and that you give her some back," Goldie said, easing up beside him.

"Clearly. Though that's the mark of a good boss, isn't it? You can identify with them. Even when they're giving you orders, you still respect them.

"Anyways. How are you doing?" Felix asked, turning to address the Dragon. "You feeling better today?"

She'd endured him cleaning her up and bandaging everything he could find, only to pass out as soon as he was done.

She'd slept through the morning and into the early afternoon. It was just after one o'clock right now.

"Yes... I'm feeling better." One of her hands drifted up to the gauze eyepatch. "I'm a bit nervous about this, though. I'm not sure how good a bodyguard I'd be with only one eye."

"Guess we'd just have to find you a position with me that isn't a bodyguard. There's always seamstress," Felix said, turning back to the terminal. "That or I'll just regrow your eye myself. I can't do it right now because of the suppression, but I could do it once it goes away."

"There is that," Goldie said softly. She looked around the room with her one eye. "Where are the girls?"

"Faith picked 'em up and took them to the third bunker. Two are staying there to prep it like the one she was at. The third is going to help with hers.

"They'll be rejoining us when they're done," Felix said, slipping through multiple windows on the system.

"And what are you going to do?" Goldie asked.

"I'm going to go look for Miu," Felix said, then pointed to a spot on the map he'd pulled up. "There was an action here against Legion forces. The army threw in grenades and the whole damn thing came down.

"Chances are Miu and her people are inside there. I want to see if I can help them. You're going to stay here and play radio operator for us."

"No." Goldie's voice was firm, and she rested a hand on his shoulder. "You will not go without a bodyguard. Even if I must go myself, I will.

"Either call Faith or Talia back, don't go, or take me with you."

Felix wanted to snap at her. To shake her hand free. Push her away. Except she was right. Rationally, he knew she was absolutely right.

"Call Faith," Goldie said, her hand coming up to pet his cheek and jaw. "She'll do everything you need her to."

Felix grunted at that, then did exactly as she told him to and called Faith back to base.

She'd come immediately, of course, Edith taking the train back to the bunker they'd come from. On top of that, she'd insisted that she drive the train and have loaded it up with everything they might need for a search-and-rescue mission.

He wasn't quite sure how he felt about being treated like this, but he couldn't really argue with it, either.

The previous issue and Goldie's missing eye loomed in his mind.

"Faith, what'd you think of Goldie's eye?" Felix asked suddenly, breaking the silence as they walked up the spiral staircase to the exit.

Faith had taken the time to check Goldie for him on his request. She'd spent several minutes just standing there with her hand on the other woman's head.

"It's growing back, if that's what you're asking. It'll take some time is my impression, but she'll get her eye back eventually," Faith said. "Though I have no idea how long it will take. Guessing from the way her other wounds were healing, a few months."

Felix felt better with that information. Not great, but better. It meant he didn't have to feel guilty for possibly maiming her, even if he could make her eye just reappear.

"Besides, it's not like you couldn't solve it yourself if you really wanted," Faith said with a shrug. "You're practically a Demi-God."

"Your brother is all physical aspects. Physical dominance, charisma, and personal leadership," Faith said. "You're the opposite. You lead through emotion, intelligence, and exerting your control on others through changing them."

Hm. Vince's screen did list him as a Demi-God. If he's the same blood as I am, except for his mother, doesn't that mean I'm possibly a Demi-God, as well?

It wasn't the first time Felix had wondered about that.

"Be silent, darling," Faith whispered. She had stopped up ahead and seemed to be looking into a dimly lit display in the wall.

Staring up at her bottom mindlessly, he tried to control his breathing. These steps were killer, and he'd already done the massive climb twice in two days.

"We're clear," whispered the Dryad, pressing her Legion ring to the security plate.

The large and thick steel plate slid to the side, and the doorway showed a view of utter blackness.

- 696 -

Wherever it led had no direct outside access.

"Whoever chose these locations left something to be desired," Faith said, stepping through to the other side. "Though the two camera views make more sense now."

Felix followed her in, and he had to stop and agree with her. They were standing in a large access pipe, clearly in the sewer. Off to one side was a ladder that led up and out.

They kept silent and quiet as they made their way up to street level. There wasn't anything or anyone nearby.

"This way," Faith said, her battle rifle held low and ready. She'd traded out her SMG for the new weapon.

Her concern had been that to her, it looked like the armor the soldiers were wearing could probably stop smaller rounds.

Up ahead, Felix could already see the building that had been dropped down on Miu and her team. It looked like an apartment building.

"It's not what I'm particularly good at, but with so few people around, I can feel life in the building. Just not who," Faith whispered as they moved quickly down the sidewalk. They vanished down an alley that ran parallel to the destroyed building.

"How many?" Felix asked, keeping pace with the Dryad.

"Twenty, thirty. Something around that. They're spread through the building, though there's some out behind it as well."

Sounds like they're guarding it, or trying to find Miu and her team.

That or I'm much luckier than I thought, and it's just the Legionnaires with Miu waiting for orders or regrouping.

Faith slowed down when they got to the corner of the wall that separated the collapsed building from the one next to it. Slowly, she peeked out from around it.

Then she pulled her head back behind cover.

"Squad of six or seven. Fanned out and looking very bored. Not our people," Faith said, turning to face Felix. "We can try to enter another way and see what we can do. There's no guarantee we can even reach those alive inside."

Felix nodded, not quite sure what to do. He really wasn't cut out for active things like this. He did substantially better with corporate.

"That's our plan, then," Faith said, patting him on the shoulder with one hand. "Follow me; we'll go through a window. I saw it when we came. We'll try that and see if we can't work our way in."

Not arguing, Felix followed the Dryad back the way they'd come.

Picking their way around the side and up into the collapsed building, Faith got them into what was probably the remains of the third floor without issue.

"They're below us," she said, peering down and to the side. "Feels like it's probably the basement. Unsure."

Slowly, they started to make their way down. Slithering as quietly as they could through debris and shattered, broken rooms.

Suddenly, Faith held up a closed fist.

Felix froze in place, getting down into a low crouch and not making a noise.

He tilted his head around, listening. He could just barely hear people talking. Barely.

But he couldn't make out the words or what was being said.

He sincerely doubted it was his Legionnaires, though. There was a certain amount of lazy calm in the voices. It felt more like people comfortable in their position, rather than those in hiding. Especially in a building that had been knocked down.

It also sounded like they were getting closer to Felix and Faith's.

Faith turned her head and looked at him, then slowly shook her head.

Ok, got it. Not Miu. Time to go then.

Faith gestured toward a room they hadn't been in.

Moving quietly, the two of them eased into the small room. Felix immediately noticed there was a small crawl space between two collapsed walls that looked like it could hide them from view. He also noticed a piece of paper rustling slightly.

As if there was an airway back there.

Making a choice, Felix got down and started to shimmy through the space.

He heard Faith make a small hissing noise behind him as he got half his body in. Then he felt the floorboard shift under him as she apparently got down behind him.

Coming up on the other side, Felix saw what he'd been looking for. Getting to his feet, he brushed himself off as his eyes went straight to the light source.

It was a hole in the wall itself. It looked as if it'd been dug out by hand, the material shifted to one side of the room.

"Damn," Faith said as she got up next to him.

Glancing at the Dryad, Felix noticed she was looking down and to the side.

Following her gaze, he saw Miu there.

She was lying on her stomach in the corner of the room. He could see she was pinned beneath what looked like an I-beam twisted over her. It had her pinched from the hips down.

Except she was very clearly dead.

A pool of blood had spread out around her. It looked like it was seeping out from where she'd been crushed.

There were boot prints in the dust all around her. There were also clear smudges of hand prints all over the beam that had her pinned.

They must have tried for quite a while to get you out, didn't they?

And in the end, you made them leave.

Moving closer, Felix squatted down next to her. She was facing away from him, her left hand curled next to her shoulder.

Gently, he took her hand in his own and pried her fingers apart.

Except her pinky finger was missing. Cut from her hand.

You stayed here and died by yourself. And they left with one of your fingers just in case. Because that's standard protocol now.

Feeling morbid but determined, he pushed the blade into the webbing of her ring finger. He wasn't about to risk losing her like this either.

Pushing the blade in deep, he began to saw her finger off at the base. It only took a bit of effort, and it came free with relative ease.

He put the finger away in his pocket intending to add it to the Wood Elf's later. Then he leaned over her now that his grisly task was done.

He looked into her face and found it was still and calm. Her eyes were open and glassy, staring at the wall next to her. There was a strange, small smile on her face.

Following her gaze, he found she had wedged a picture of herself and Felix into a crack in the wall.

The photographer had taken it when she'd been fiddling with something on her dress. Felix had ended up laughing at her when she'd gotten frustrated and started cursing at the fabric.

In the end, the photo had looked very natural, with Felix smiling as Miu suddenly looked up into the camera.

"She is very… loyal… to you. I don't think anyone in either your wing or my detachment could ever match her," said Faith, who had apparently noticed the picture as well.

"She is absolutely insane. The things she does are on an order of magnitude that just isn't even… human. But she's mine. My little psycho," Felix murmured, running a few of his fingers through her silky hair. Reaching over, he gently pulled the photo from the wall and slipped it into a vest pocket. "And I'll be bringing her back as soon as possible."

There was a sudden crack of thunder from nearby, and Felix felt the hair on the back of his neck stand on end.

Faith snapped into action, her rifle coming up to her shoulder. She immediately went to the hole in the wall and pointed her weapon at it.

The sound of screaming reached Felix's ears.

"Someone is attacking the soldiers," Faith said.

"Let's go see who it is. The enemy of an enemy, after all."

Faith ducked low and crawled out of the hole, her weapon held firmly.

Felix looked down and checked his SMG slung low at his side. He wasn't sure how much it'd do against a soldier in body armor, but Faith had insisted he not carry a rifle.

If it came down to it, she wanted him to run, not fight.

Faith turned the corner and vanished toward the sounds of the fighting. Getting his legs under him as he got out of the hole, Felix followed suit.

When they got back to the back of the building where they'd seen the squad, they saw a man, a young boy, and a bunch of men in soldier uniforms all pressed together in a screaming, burning heap.

"Oh, hello, Mr. Campbell. It's good to see you," said Al. He was standing off to one side, his head turned toward Faith and Felix. "Uncle overhead them saying some things and decided they needed to die.

"Whether it was boasting, bravado, or simple trash talking, it doesn't matter to him."

Looking to Uncle, Felix watched as the man literally held eight men still in a bunch and roasted them alive.

The amount of magical energy pouring out of him was so high Felix could actually taste it.

"Are you here because of the energy disturbance as well?" Al asked.

"No... I was following one of my people. Energy disturbance?" Felix asked.

"Yes. There was a significant—" Al paused and looked up at the sky above him. "Uncle, look."

The screams abruptly died off when Uncle made a hand gesture. All eight men crumpled into one another, seeming to have been cut in half. Then he looked up as Al had.

Felix finally turned his eyes skyward, and he froze.

Snow was falling.

A lot of snow.

"I don't understand," Felix said simply.

"Your father wouldn't like this, Al. It's time for us to let this go and wait for him," Uncle said severely.

"Yes, Uncle. I think you're right," Al said, shaking his head.

"Wait, do you know what's happening?" Felix asked. "You said you'd share info with me. Our deal is still ongoing, is it not?"

Uncle snorted at that, reaching into his coat pockets.

"I suppose it is. It's the end of the world," Al said, catching several snowflakes in his hand. "It would appear the religious heads have been coerced into starting the end times."

"The end times for multiple religions."

"How does that have anything to do with snow falling?" Faith asked.

"Because that snow is passing through the dome," Al said simply. "Which means it's beyond the realm of the divine. I would seek shelter out if I were you."

Uncle flicked something out toward the wall of the building, and a spiraling blue portal opened.

Glaring at Faith and Felix, Uncle said nothing, but he was clearly waiting for Al.

"Good luck," Al said simply, nodding his head. "I hope to see you when it's all over, but the rules are the rules."

Walking through the portal, Al vanished.

Uncle took several steps to the portal and stopped just outside its edge.

Clearing his throat, the man shrugged a shoulder.

"This world is fucking toast. Hunker down and wait for the dome to fail if you can," Uncle said. "Won't last forever. Try not to die; you're mildly interesting."

Then he stepped through the portal and vanished.

Chapter 34 - The End Begins -

"Right. If they're getting the hell out of here, we need to as well," Felix said.

Shouldering his SMG, Felix set off at a quick trot back to the entry point for the Legion rail. Faith passed him by quickly, her movement swift and compact. It was a wonder to watch her.

She's actually really athletic despite her build.

Felix shifted his gaze from Faith to the alley they'd have to dive in to get to the sewer.

Ducking around the corner, the Dryad warrior took it at the same speed, her rifle coming up to her shoulder as she went.

Feeling like a slow-ass turtle given how far she'd gotten up ahead of him, it took Felix several seconds to catch up with her.

Turning the corner but having to drop speed, Felix saw Faith levering the manhole cover out with one glowing, green hand.

And incredibly strong. These Dryads are just too much.

Dropping the manhole cover to one side with a clang, Faith peered down into the sewer.

A dark hand lashed out from inside the shadowed interior.

Dodging backward with inhuman reflexes, Faith almost got out of range in time.

Black claws raked across her chest and stomach. The impossibly long arm whipped back into the sewers, dark smoke rising from it.

Stumbling to her rear, Faith lifted a hand and checked herself.

There were long gouges in the Legion body armor. The trauma plates underneath looked cracked, as if hit by an incredibly strong force.

Wheezing, Faith rolled to one side and crawled over to Felix.

Reaching down, he got his arms underneath her and hauled her to her feet. "Are you alright?"

"What the fuck," Faith got out between pants. "It felt... like a Dragon... punched me."

"Ok, got that part, but are you alright?" Felix asked, starting to undo the body armor to get a look at her.

"I'm fine... stop it. Didn't break... through the armor. Just winded," Faith said, hunching over.

Nodding at that, Felix spun Faith to one side and started working at the webbing on her hips that held her grenades.

"Felix, what... are you doing?" Faith asked, now bent over in front of him.

"Getting your HEs. Going to pop the pins and drop them down the chute. Whatever that was can enjoy a pineapple salad."

Before he could get the first one pulled free, Felix turned around to what sounded like someone walking behind him.

Then he was bowled over as if he were nothing more than a doll. Looming over him was Miu.

Her lower torso crushed and her intestines hanging out of her like a sweater unraveling.

Faith lifted her rifle, but before she could do anything, Miu had backhanded her, sending her flying and tumbling away.

The Dryad slid to a stop up against a wall and remained unmoving.

Then Miu dropped on top of him, her eyes glazed over with death and her mouth wide open.

"The fuck, Miu!?" Felix got out as her head bent down toward his face.

Her hands clawed at his body armor as she forced her head closer and closer, Felix's hands pressed to her throat and forehead to keep her back.

Damn me, it's like she's a zombie!

Miu's teeth clicked together once as she got within an inch or two of Felix's face.

Holy crap, she really is a zombie.

Al said it's the end of the world.

Her right hand grabbed hold of his shoulder and pinned him firmly to the ground. Her left hand came up and grabbed at his forearm.

"Miu, stop! Miu. Listen, it's Felix. Felix! Miu!" Felix shouted in her face. "Miu Mikki, stop!"

The zombie who had once been Miu stopped pushing closer. Her head slowly tilted to one side, her eyes focusing on him ever so slightly.

"Miu. It's me, Felix. You're Miu Mikki. You're mine. Remember? You gave everything to me. That includes when you're dead. You gave me your soul, remember?" Felix asked, unable to move her at all, still struggling with her casual strength.

Miu's mouth slowly closed, her head slowly tilting back the other way.

"Come on, Miu. Wake up. You're mine. I need you. Ok? I need you. Wake up already!" Felix shouted.

Her left hand closed around his forearm, her fingers feeling like clamps.

Miu's head shot forward the last two inches, her forehead pressing to his.

She wasn't breathing, and her skin felt hard and cold. Risking a glance at Faith, Felix realized she was still unmoving.

She was dead or unconscious.

Felix gave up and slumped to the ground. Everyone had warned him he'd come to a bad end with the Yandere known as Miu.

"Left me," came a hissing voice from between her teeth.

Blinking, Felix realized there was something of her left in there.

"No, I came back for you. Look at your left hand. You're missing two fingers, not one. The second one is in my pocket. I came for you. Just you," Felix said. "I have your photo as well."

Zombie Miu didn't move for several seconds. Then she moved back from him. Her eyes slowly focused in on her hand on his forearm. Her fingers flexed, the missing two becoming obvious.

"Look," Felix said, letting go of her shoulder and reaching into his vest pocket. He fished out her picture with two fingers and held it up to face her. "I took it because it seemed like it was important to you. I came for you, Miu."

Looking at the back of the photo, he saw the words "my love" written there in pen.

Miu's eyes were locked on the photo.

"Came for me," Miu wheezed. Then there was a slow, hissing noise as it seemed like she was forcing air into her deflated lungs.

Huh. Can't talk without air, right? I guess that makes sense.

Felix was mildly perturbed by the detached thought.

"Yes, Miu. I came for you. Because I need you. And I need you now," Felix said. Slowly, he put the photo back into his vest pocket.

She didn't seem as insane right now. Her eyes were focusing correctly, though belatedly.

"Need me," Miu repeated.

"I need you. Now, will you help me up? We need to get back to Legion," Felix said.

"Love you," Miu said suddenly.

Sighing, Felix reached up and put his hand behind her head. Pulling her down a bit, he pressed his forehead back to hers.

"Love you, too. Now get off me already," he said, patting the side of her head gently.

Miu's lips turned upward into a small smile, and she shambled up to her feet. Her hands came down and lifted him up off the ground.

He was covered in her blood and bodily fluids from the waist down.

Looking over to Faith, he realized she was just now getting to a seated position. Blood was trickling down from her temple.

"Miu?" asked the Dryad, looking very confused.

The zombie turned its head toward Faith. Her body posture slowly changed the longer she looked at the Dryad. Then she took a step toward her.

Felix moved in front of Miu and put both hands on her face. Her eyes had just started to lose some of the little comprehension they'd held.

"Miu, you must keep your eyes on me at all times," Felix commanded. "If I give you an order, I need you to follow it and then immediately look back at me. Ok?"

Miu's eyes unendingly gazed into his.

- 701 -

"Nod if you understand me, Miu."

She nodded her head incrementally.

"Good. Miu, something is trying to kill me. It's in the sewer. I'm going to drop grenades down there, and then I need you to go in and kill it for me," Felix said. "Do you understand?"

"Kill it. Save love," Miu hissed. "Look at love."

"Yes. Exactly right," Felix said. Releasing her face, he moved to Faith, keeping eye contact with Miu. "Give me your grenades."

He heard the pop of items coming free, and then he had several grenades in his hands.

Moving closer to the sewer entry, Felix looked down.

He pulled the pin on a grenade, flipped the lever off, and rolled it into the sewer. Then he proceeded to do it twice more.

He heard something snort in the sewer. Immediately followed by explosives detonating. One after the other.

Then all was silent.

In a strange, shambling gait, zombie Miu moved past and dove into the sewer.

The muffled sounds of fighting came up from the bottom.

Felix wasn't sure he wanted to go down there. Even if Miu seemed to be on their side, it seemed like she'd been moments away from killing him.

Or eating him.

"That was Miu," Faith said.

"Yeah. She's a zombie now," Felix said, staring at the sky above. Snow had continued to fall in ever-increasing amounts.

"Doesn't that mean the soldiers Uncle killed are zombies, too? And they might be coming this way?" Faith asked.

"Oh. That's a good point," Felix said.

Then a bright and fiery orange ring of flame opened in the sky over the center of the city. It was pitch black within the center, and out of it came a giant bulbous leg.

It was followed by another, and finally a waist.

When the truly massive creature dropped out, the portal slowly shut above it. What it left behind was what Felix thought of as a giant, froglike monster with thousands of teeth he could see from here.

It stood up, and Felix realized he'd underestimated its size.

"Oh... shit," Faith said, looking at the same thing.

Not far away, a black portal started to open in the wall of a building.

Right, ok. Yeah, time to go.

Moving to the sewer, Felix got his legs in, grabbed the side rails of the ladder, and slid down. He'd seen Andrea do it over and over, and he'd never tried it.

But the idea of standing above on the street seemed worse.

Hitting the bottom, his boot heels cracked against the slimy concrete. He moved to the side quickly so Faith could join them, then scanned the area.

A massive black-skinned monster lay not far away, with gaping wounds in its flesh from the grenades.

Its head had also been torn from its shoulders. Apparently Miu had practically landed on it and set to work making sure it was dead.

Miu wasn't far away, though her spine had been severed. The lower half of her body was wedged under the creature, one of her legs clutched in its clawed hand.

She was little more than a torso now, having lost everything below her navel.

And she was crawling towards him, her eyes only on him.

Damnit, Miu.

Moving over to her, he scooped her up and flung her around his shoulders like a backpack.

"Hold on, Miu," Felix said, patting one of her cold hands.

Faith clacked to the concrete in the same way he had, her eyes wide.

"There's a fireball heading for the city," she said, then turned and sprinted for the staircase that led into the rail system.

"What?!" Felix called after her.

He could feel Miu's cold face against his neck, bobbing against his skin as he chased after Faith.

"It was a giant ball of flame. Huge. Heading for the center of the city." Faith jammed her ringed hand to the railway security door.

The door slid open, and they hurried inside.

"We need to get to the train and contact everyone," Felix said.

The security door slid shut behind them, and then the entire world shook and rumbled.

Felix wedged himself up into the corner of the stairwell, reaching out and grabbing Faith by the hair.

He dragged her up the stairwell and pressed her against the wall next to him.

The world continued to tremble, and the lighting from the rail system flickered several times. Then it went out.

***

Making it down the staircase in the dark had been a trying time. There was no way to validate that the step below was still there without stepping on it.

Still, they'd managed to reach the bottom without incident.

Miu remained a mostly inert backpack. She didn't move, breathe, or say anything.

"Will it work?" Faith asked as she got into the train's first passenger seat.

"Yeah. It's powered by the engine, remember? It runs off a power source she made specific for this. It'll last for a very long while," Felix said, getting on the train. As gently as he could, he pulled Miu from his shoulders and set her torso down in the corner of the engine cabin.

He braced her up against the wall by pushing a heavy ammo can in front of her.

"Sorry, Miu. Best I can do for now. You alright?" he asked, looking down at the zombified woman.

She nodded her head a fraction, her eyes glued to him.

As soon as it felt like everything was secured, Felix sat down in the engineer's seat and sighed. Then he lifted his head to the ceiling of the rail tunnel.

"Runner! Runner Norwood! This is a... a clusterfuck!" Felix shouted at nothing. "I could use a hand right now, because this feels a lot like people interfering in ways you wouldn't approve of!"

Felix waited, growling.

Except nothing happened.

"RUNNER!" Felix screamed at the top of his lungs.

There was no response.

Nothing.

"Are you alright?" Faith asked.

"Runner is the name of the god of this entire world. The god of gods. I've met him a few times," Felix said, sinking into his seat. "I was hoping that... well... he could intervene."

"It would seem he cannot hear you."

Shaking his head, Felix pressed the starter for the train and waited as it powered to life.

The screen flickered twice, and then alerts began flooding into his system notification window.

"What the..." Felix watched as hundreds of red exclamation points showed up in the middle of the railway system. "There's been a breach. A big one."

"A breach...? The fireball, maybe?" Faith asked.

"That'd be my guess. I didn't think it would penetrate that deeply, but apparently it did. Let's see where... oh." Felix frowned at the screen and continued to flip through the windows available to him.

The information wasn't changing, however. It seemed to be exactly what was presented.

"Oh, what?" Faith pressed.

"Everyone evacuated into the tunnels. Everyone. They're all heading to the closest train tunnel to Legion.

"The safe houses that could reach the rails, Jessica, Erica, Goldie, Edith—everyone. Literally everyone is in the tunnels," Felix said.

"If they did that without an order from you, that means they're seeing something we're not.

"What would that be?"

Felix didn't know. The only thing they could access that he couldn't was the cameras.

Tapping into the communication system, he pulled up one of the trains. It was marked as the one Edith would have had access to, and the one Goldie was apparently on.

He could see it slowly moving forward down the track toward Legion HQ.

"This is Felix to train two. Come in train two," Felix said as he held down the transmit button.

"Felix? Where are you!" Edith just about shouted over the line.

"I'm on the train. I found Miu, or... what's left of her, at least," Felix said, looking down at the undead Miu. He gave her a small, sad smile.

She didn't return it, of course, but she watched him as he'd ordered her to. "Now I'm wonder—"

"Get the fuck out of there. Get to the Legion HQ tunnel as quickly as you can," Edith said.

"Why? What's going on? I don't understand."

"The city is filled with undead and monsters and... and lots of things. Lots and lots," Edith said. "There's so much wrong up there that I don't know what to do. There's also things in the dark. If you have lights, turn them on. Now. Turn them on as bright as they'll go.

"As many as you can."

Felix frowned and then flicked the switch for the lights on the train, moving it over to maximum illumination.

Out ahead of him, creatures and things fled and howled as the headlights kicked on.

Feeling an entire freak-out building up inside him, Felix crushed it down as hard as he could. He didn't have time to lose his mind.

His sanity was all he really had going for him.

Looking over his shoulder, he made eye contact with Faith. She was looking back at him as wide eyed as he felt.

"If you have a light spell, I'd really appreciate you using it right now," Felix said.

Faith only nodded. Her hands held close to one another. She must have already been doing exactly that.

"What else can you tell me?" Felix asked, pressing the transmit button.

"Jessica and Talia are dead. I cut their thumbs off and got the finger from your bunker. Goldie told me about it," Edith said.

"What? How'd that happen?"

A brilliant light burst out from Faith, lighting the tunnel in both directions.

"A creature came out of the shadows and ate Talia. Jessica got split in half when she grabbed Talia's arm and got slapped away for it.

"Thankfully she came away with the Elf's arm and her own. I got the thumbs, got on the train, and left with Goldie.

"Seemed like it was time to go. I told everyone to hit the rails, with lights, and get to the Legion tunnel ASAP."

Felix pulled the lever to get the train going and started pulling it around to head in the same direction Edith had stated.

It was as good a plan as any. They'd be trapped, but they'd also limit the approach vector.

"We're heading into a dead end," Faith said.

"Yep."

"With only one way in and one way out."

"Yeah."

"Unless the dome falls, it's very likely we'll die."

"Definite possibility."

- 704 -

"If the time comes, will you make love to me? I'd really like to not die a virgin," Faith asked. "I'd like to feel a child growing in me, too. At least once for both."

Felix didn't respond. He really didn't want to consider the end.

Nor the idea of trying to have sex as hordes of zombies were rushing down the tunnels.

You need to get your priorities straight, my lovely Nymph.

Chapter 35 - A Brief Glimpse -

They'd been hunkered down at the end of the tunnel for six days now.

A number of Legionnaires had joined them, along with Edith, Erica, and Goldie.

In her infinite wisdom, the Dragon had hauled some crates onto the train while recovering. She'd figured if Felix was having them get a bunker ready, why not a train?

To that end, she'd loaded a five-five six round dispenser, a crate of battle rifles, a field-grade med lab, several machine guns, and a generator.

Without her forethought, the defense of the tunnel wouldn't have lasted long.

Felix was on a watch shift, staring down the tunnel with one of the mounted machine guns she'd brought. Down the train line, ten or so zombies were shuffling around amongst the corpses there.

"Might be time to clear them out," Goldie said, stepping up next to him.

"Probably. I was waiting for one of them to start walking this way," Felix admitted, looking up from the weapon to the Dragon.

She was still wearing a gauze eyepatch, though the eye was clearly healing. The rest of the wounds she'd picked up had long since closed.

Turning his gaze back on his zone of control, Felix sighed.

"We can't stay here forever. The dark ones keep pushing closer every chance they get," Felix said.

The dark ones were the creatures that lived in the shadows. They came whenever there was a break in the light. If the generator had even the slightest hiccup, they were there.

Thankfully, one of the Legionnaires had enough know-how to strip one of the train engines and attach it to the grid they'd jerry-rigged together. When the generator dipped for even a second, the train engine source picked up the slack.

"True. Though we do have the other train engine. So that'll buy us some time."

Felix couldn't argue her point. They'd cannibalized two trains and their cars, turning them into barricades. Which meant they had an extra engine power source they weren't using right now. The same Legionnaire who had linked the other into the grid had put it in a secondary position with an on/off switch.

A tremendous boom came from somewhere above them. Whatever had been going on in the city, it was still happening. The strength of the explosions must be considerable if they rattled even the Legion rails this far down.

"They're getting louder, and more frequent," Goldie said, her eyes on the ceiling above them. "I worry and wonder. Were the tunnels designed to take such abuse?"

As do I. But that's neither here nor there since we don't have a choice. That and I have to be the rock to support everyone else.

Felix cleared his throat.

"Center position, opening fire to clear hostiles loitering nearby," Felix declared loudly.

The other machine-gun positions acknowledged his statement.

Felix lined his weapon on the zombies and pulled the trigger. Rounds began spewing out the end of the big weapon, and he began to sweep it from one side to the other.

He could see the zombies drop as they were practically cut in half. They toppled where they fell.

What was unnerving for Felix wasn't the zombies, though.

It was the things just beyond the edge of the shadows that he could see with the flashes of the muzzle.

They didn't to go down easily, either. The machine guns could drop them, but it wasn't a sure thing that it'd happen before the creatures turned and ran away.

Letting go of the trigger when his ammo went empty, Felix stood and looked down the rail line. There were no zombies standing.

Picking up a full ammo box from the pile nearby, he pulled the old one out and set it to one side.

Goldie picked up the box, secured it under an arm, and walked toward the rear of the fortification, where it would be recycled through the arsenal and refilled.

Giving his head a shake, Felix went through the process of getting his weapon back into action.

Pulling the bolt back and letting the first round cycle, Felix got back into position.

There was no change in the tunnel. Everything was the same.

Minus the zombies and some of his hearing. All he could hear now was ringing. It would fade in time, but he also knew it was a precursor to permanent hearing loss.

So everyone was spending a few minutes a day with the field lab getting their hearing fixed.

"Felix!" someone shouted from behind him.

Peering over his shoulder, he didn't see who was talking to him at first.

Because he was watching the bright red wall of light that was the back of their encampment flicker wildly.

Is it… failing?

Then he looked at the speaker. It was Faith.

"Faith, I need you to become a human beacon on the dome wall," Felix said, standing up. "We haven't put any big lights or defenses facing that way."

Faith froze in her tracks for a second, then turned ducked her head and sprinted in the other direction when his words sank in.

If there were creatures waiting on the other side of the dome wall, the camp could be destroyed outright. There was some light, sure, but not much.

They'd figured out early that the creatures could cross the dome, but not without catching fire. *That's an oversight on my part. I don't think anyone actually expected the dome to fall.*

A Legionnaire on backup hurried over to Felix and took over his position without a word.

Felix patted the man on the shoulder and hurried toward the back of the camp.

Stopping for a second to pick up his Miu backpack, he hoisted her over his shoulder.

She'd become almost unresponsive by this point. Her eyes followed him wherever he went, but little else. She didn't even hold on to him anymore as she had originally. Forcing him to stuff her into a rucksack after putting her lower body into a trash bag

He'd be damned if he left her behind, though. She'd given him her all and then some. Zombie or not.

Though thankfully, he'd long since become deadened to the smell of her.

He caught up to Edith, who was talking with several other people.

"Edith," Felix said, stepping in close to her. "The dome is failing. I need everyone armed, armored, and ready to move. We're loading up on the train."

"Right now."

Edith blinked and then nodded. "Got it."

Swinging wide toward where the arsenal was, he saw Goldie.

He moved at a jog to catch up to her and wrapped an arm around her waist, pulling her away.

"I need you to start getting everyone on the train," Felix said to her. "Make sure we don't leave anyone—or anything we need—behind. Ok?"

"I understand, nest-mate. I'll collect the fallen and make sure Erica is on board." Goldie smiled at him.

Thank goodness she knows how I think.

Felix internally fretted at the fact that he was prioritizing certain people, but even he wasn't above a certain amount of favoritism.

Letting go of the gold Dragon, he moved to the train engine.

He sat down in the driver's seat and booted the system up. While he waited for it to load, he pulled Miu's pack off his back and set her down in her corner.

"You ok, Miu?" he asked, glancing at her.

There was no response, but her eyes continued to track him.

"We'll get you fixed up soon. Then we'll go get something to eat or something," Felix said, looking back to the display.

The entire rail system was flooded with undead now. Undead, dark creatures, and monsters. The interface had been pointless after that, since it was all warning messages.

The fireball had ended up being a meteor. One that had impacted the city and torn a hole into the earth. Which went straight into a rail exchange point. People had begun entering after word spread that it might be an escape.

Which led to thousands of people dying in the tunnels to the dark beasts.

Switching to the radio interface, Felix immediately called up the Legion HQ frequency and dialed into it.

There was nothing but static.

Looking up to the dome wall, Felix caught it just as it flickered again. Fading to almost nothing and growing bright again.

Behind him, he could hear people clambering into their seats. Everyone getting in their assigned positions. Some would be wedged between the seats, and others between the low walls and the seats. There would be little to no room for anyone.

This was the last train out of hell, so to speak. There wouldn't be a second trip.

Felix stared at the shining red wall. The intensity of his gaze would have blown a hole through concrete.

Then the evil red light began to fade again.

Faith stepped up to his left side and put a hand out in front of herself. A bright beam of light shot out from her palm in a cone. Illuminating the dark beyond the red light.

Squeals and shrieks could be heard.

They were there after all.

Goldie stepped up on his right side, Miu now shouldered on her back. The zombie's gaze still locked on Felix.

Diminishing by the second, the glow of the dome faded away.

Finally, it vanished into nothing.

Felix sat there, waiting. After four breaths, he pushed the train into gear and they got rolling. They passed from their camp into the Legion tunnels, heading straight to HQ.

Glancing back over his shoulder, Felix watched as their well-lit home grew more and more distant.

Looking forward to the path ahead, they rode on.

***

As they got closer to Legion HQ, the radio frequency it was broadcasting out of slowly came to life.

First it was little more than clicks and whistles. But it was more than just static.

Now, though, it was a looped message.

"Full evacuation protocol. A-Zero-One," said Kit on the recording, followed by ten seconds of silence, only to then repeat.

Pulling into the lower receiving yard of Legion HQ, Felix was at bit of a loss.

The bay was in shambles. Signs of violence were everywhere. Shell casings, scorch marks, and corpses strewn about.

"Everyone out," Felix called as the train came to a full stop. "Evacuation protocol is engaged. A-Zero-One. That means everyone is heading for the emergency portal to Legion Prime.

"If it's not in Legion colors, shoot it. If it is in Legion colors, do a verbal challenge and then shoot."

Felix stood up and took Miu from Goldie, swinging her pack into place on his back.

Edith was marshaling their forces, getting them off the train and into formation.

As he got down from the engine, Felix wasn't sure what was waiting for them.

Erica joined him, holding a rifle out to him.

"You doing alright?" Felix asked, taking the weapon from her. He turned it over, pulled the bolt back and flipped the safety off.

"Yeah... I miss Jess, but... yeah. You have her..." Erica's voice trailed off.

"Yes. I have her. We'll see her back soon enough. Just have to get to Legion Prime," Felix said.

Edith came over and sighed.

"Well, at least it isn't far. We just have to get through the lab and the choke point," Edith said.

"True enough. For now I'm going to see if there's anyone here," Felix said, walking toward the bay exit doors.

Legionnaires were going about their business, clearing and marking the area.

Stopping in front of the panel next to the door, Felix pressed his ring into the security plate.

With a chime, the computer display turned on.

As quickly as he could, he moved to the communications part of the system and then tapped into it.

There were four signals he could see. They were all in the portal evacuation room.

Felix tried to call any of the signals up, but failed. Either they had their radios off, or the portal was causing interference.

It's done that before, but... not normally.

"Looks like the portal room is being held. Possibly by Legion forces," Felix said, looking to the women around him.

"Right. Then we push on in and get out of this hell hole," Edith said. "I'll go get the troops and tell them to stack up and get ready to move."

Nodding at that, Felix waited beside the door. He wasn't about to go charging in.

"You think it's our people?" Faith asked.

"They didn't respond," Felix said honestly. "So either they're there but can't be hailed, or it's a bunch of Wardens that weren't deactivated."

Goldie nodded and then made eye contact with him.

"You should remain behind me at all times, then," she said.

"Yeah, got it."

Edith tapped the door button to open, and the Legionnaires moved into the hall beyond the bay. Immediately, there was gunfire. It didn't sound like there was any return fire, though.

Zombies, I guess. Or... dark beasts.

Taking in a slow breath, Felix moved into the middle of the column as it went by. Faith, Erica, Edith, and Goldie moved with him.

Stepping over corpses of soldiers that confirmed his thoughts about zombies, Felix kept moving.

As they walked, sounds came from inside the rooms around them, but nothing that seemed living.

Slowly, they crept past the darkened lab. It looked like a fire had swept through it, followed by enough explosives to knock out a building.

"Do you think Felicia did it?" Erica asked.

"Probably. She was always very protective of our tech," Felix said.

Coming to a stop at the entryway to the evacuation point, the column didn't move any further.

The Legionnaire in front of him turned to face him.

"Door's locked. Should we proceed?" asked the man.

"Yeah, pop it open. But don't enter. Tell whoever's up there to see if anyone responds instead. They're probably just as jumpy as we are," Felix commanded.

Turning back to the front, the Legionnaire passed the message up.

"I suppose this is it," Goldie said.

"Don't jinx it," Felix and Faith said at the same time.

Looking ahead as best as he could, Felix was able to see the moment the door slid open. But he couldn't see what was going on beyond that.

A minute passed, and then suddenly the column moved forward.

Felix felt like his heart was about to race out of his throat.

Turning the corner, Felix saw four of the newest Wardens standing guard over a swirling portal. On the other side of the portal, he could see numerous Legionnaires waiting from behind defensive positions.

Before he could get through it, Kit, Felicity, Andrea Prime, Adriana Prime, Lily, and Vince all stepped through. They moved to one side and immediately spotted him.

Breaking away from the column, Felix moved to join the others.

Smiling as he went to them, Felix felt relieved.

A loud, hissing crack boomed through the air.

Across from the bay, a massive orange portal sprang into life. At the same time, the portal to Legion Prime winked out.

On the other side of the orange portal was an empty backlot. In the distance, Felix could see a billboard with a man drinking what looked like a sports drink.

Beyond the backlot, he saw a number of people quickly moving their way.

"I can't close it," Kit said, her hand flicking out at the portal repeatedly.

"I can't either," Felicity said.

"Damnit," Lily swore.

"I can solve it," Kit said suddenly, her head turning to Lily.

The magician winced and looked at the portal.

"Yeah. I can," Lily said aloud.

"Can what?" Felix asked, getting closer to them. "How can you solve it?"

Lily turned to him and gave him a deep kiss.

"I love you, Felix," she said. "Don't give up."

Kit typed something into her wrist communicator quickly, then looked to the portal.

"Ready when you are," Kit said.

"Wait, ready for what?" Felix asked.

Lily took a step away from Felix and sprinted for the portal.

"Lily!" Felix called after her. Then he started to chase.

Only to feel something wrap up around his ankles. Glancing down, he saw an illusionary metal band encasing his feet.

Kit was a few steps behind Lily as they both ran through the portal. Felix saw them standing there, completely at a loss.

Lily clapped her hands together, and a purple shield of magical force expanded around them.

Almost at the same time, weapon fire started to impact the shield.

Kit wasn't idle during all this. She gestured at the portal and then looked to Lily, who nodded.

A portal appeared beneath their feet, and the two women vanished through it.

The portal closed up behind them, and they were gone.

Soldiers in uniforms swarmed up to the portal from around the other sides. Then they stopped, staring at Felix and his people.

One man lifted a hand and slowly stepped through the portal.

Except he didn't. He winked out of existence as he walked through.

"She made a portal in front of the other one," Felicity said. "It's almost on top of it. They can't go through the portal to get here, because she put one in front of it and locked them together."

"Where are they, then? Did they portal back here?" Felix asked.

"No... she tried. I felt it. But it seemed to rebound off the dual portal and... fizzled out. She opened a portal to the billboard, then again somewhere else from there," Felicity explained.

"What do you mean?" Felix asked. His mouth was dry, and he felt lightheaded.

"They... they went deeper into wherever that is," Felicity said.

Numerous soldiers were milling around the portal. But they couldn't get through.

Opening his mouth and then closing it, Felix didn't know what to do. His brain refused to work.

A giant silhouette made of crackling static simply appeared beside the portal.

The strange creature's hand flashed out, and an orb the size of a beach ball made of black and white flashing light zipped out toward Felix.

With a boom, a woman came into existence ten feet in front of him.

She was tall. Very tall. Towering in front of Felix. She had an hourglass figure that would have come close to some of the Dryads' figures he'd seen. Long blond hair fell down her back and hung nearly to her hips.

She backhanded the ball of energy to one side, and it flew off and down the hall. Her other hand flicked out, and a bright blue lightning bolt shot from it and blasted into the strange silhouette.

Crumpling to the ground, the giant flickered and simply ceased to be.

"Sunshine," whispered a voice from Felix's right.

Felix's head whipped around, and there was Runner. Beside him were Al and Uncle.

Looking back at the woman, Felix watched as she turned her head to face Runner.

"Darling," she said with a smile.

"I'm almost done, mother," Al said, taking a step forward.

The woman smiled at the child, then simply vanished. The spot where she had been was gone. When he looked back to his side, Runner, Al, and Uncle were gone as well.

"What… the fuck?" Felix asked, and then his world turned white.

***

"It would seem I've once again failed your world."

Felix looked up and found Runner standing in front of him.

"Bring Kit and Lily back. Now!" Felix shouted, quickly moving toward Runner.

Getting a hold of the Overgod, Felix leaned in close, feeling rage and unending fury in his veins.

"I can't. That portal will never close, and that means I can't roll time backward. This world is… what it is now. I can't fix it," said Runner. "Though it is of little worth to you, I can promise you no other world will ever fail like this again. I know how he did it. I can stop it from ever happening again."

Felix lifted his hand and punched the god. Then he did it again, and again, and again.

He wailed on Runner as if the Overgod were a punching bag.

After what felt like an eternity of beating, Felix slumped to his knees, panting.

"Believe me… I truly understand what you're going through. I'm not much different than you are," Runner said, kneeling down in front of Felix.

He was completely unharmed.

"I can make you a promise, though. The favor I asked of you? It's to help me kill that… man… you saw. He's the god of the world on the other side of that portal. An Overgod in his own right, I'm afraid.

"My goal is very simple. Kill him, take his world, and take back what's mine. The moment we do that, I can find Kit and Lily. Return them to you completely unharmed."

"What good are you as a god if you can't even fight that devil?" Felix asked, his chin sinking down to his chest.

"Never were truer words spoken. I give you my promise, though, Felix, that once I take back that world, I'll return them to you. Just as you saw them today.

"I can't bring them back. But I did modify their souls before my enemy exerted full control over his world again," Runner said. "I made them immortal. They can't die. We need only take back that world, and they'll return to you. Even he can't change what I did, or even find them."

Felix closed his eyes and shook his head.

"By the way, that zombie you're carrying around is terrifying. The soul is still inside. It refused to leave.

"My collectors actually had to leave it alone given how violently she responded. The magic holding the whole thing together should have failed, but it held on by force of will," Runner said. "Absolutely terrifying."

Felix ignored the god. He didn't care.

All he wanted in the end was to have a family and get out of all the business he kept putting Legion in.

Except, when he'd thought of a family, his thoughts had included Lily and Kit.

Now they were gone.

Epilogue

Felix was sitting in his office. In front of him on his desk was a stack of very mundane-looking papers.

Without warning, the door opened and Vince walked in.

"Brother," Vince said, coming to stand next to the desk.

"Brother," Felix said, his voice feeling rusty and unused.

"I brought the contract. I've already signed my part. Time for you to do yours." Vince set down a packet of papers in front of Felix.

The very top page read: "The Legions of Yosemite Act."

It was an agreement between Yosemite and Legion to become one unified body. Felix would oversee all government functions at the top.

Yaris and Vince's progeny would act as the leaders to Yosemite.

Felicity and Andrea were in charge of Legion on Legion Prime. The city leaders and feudal lords would roll up as they had previously.

In essence, Felix had been made master over it all.

Ruling at his side was Vince, the general. He was in control of all security and military. From the door guards to the general of the armies. It all rolled to Vince.

There had been some personnel shuffling as well in the exchange. Two of the most notable in his mind were Ioana and Elysia.

Ioana and her entire organization now reported to Petra.

Elysia, a High Elf who had served as chamberlain to Vince, was now Felix's.

Only bodyguard departments remained as they had.

Vince set his rough hand on Felix's shoulder.

"I know, Brother. If I could fix it myself, I would. But you heard the Overgod. It isn't a question of if, just when," Vince said. "We'll storm across that portal and take them back."

Felix nodded. No matter how much he wanted to believe that, he knew it was still an if.

They would always be waiting for him, but there was no guarantee he'd find them.

Save them.

Shaking his head slightly, Felix tried to change his thought process.

It'd only been a week since he'd lost Lily and Kit. Everything still felt too raw. He'd more or less been secluded since then.

Other than Vince, only Miu had been able to see him, and that was because the moment after he'd resurrected her, she'd refused to leave his side.

He talked to Felicity on occasion through the door, but by and large, Felix was in voluntary seclusion.

Picking up the quill nearby, Felix dipped it into his ink pot and then signed his name to the contract.

The Laurens had drawn it up and made it into a Legion contract. So when Felix lifted the quill, suddenly, all of Yosemite was part of what was his.

Including Vince, even.

"Thank you, Brother. I appreciate this deeply. I've been wanting to step out of the limelight for a while. This'll make it significantly easier to do so. For you as well, since you can focus on your piece of it," Vince said. "Will you come to dinner tonight? Meliae would very much appreciate it."

Felix looked up at the younger man and gave him a tired smile.

"I'll see what I can do. No promises," Felix said.

Vince picked up the packet and nodded. "See you at the coronation, then. Yosemite does love its pomp at times."

Turning, the man left and closed the door behind him.

Miu oozed out of the shadows from nearby. Ever since the zombification, she'd seemed less insane than she had previously.

Or at least, Felix thought so.

"Love," she said, moving in close to him. She nuzzled him affectionately, pressing her face to his neck. "He means well. You should go to dinner. Take Andrea, Adriana, or Felicity. They want to see you."

Reaching up, he gently patted her on the back of her head.

"Not like you to tell me to see other women," Felix murmured.

"You're hurting. A lot. You won't even see Andrea or Adriana at all. That's not normal," Miu said. "You always sought comfort in those two. Or Felicity.

"You won't see anyone."

"I'm seeing you, aren't I?"

"Only because I threatened to kill everyone if you wouldn't."

Felix snorted at that. She had threatened him with that. He didn't quite believe her when she said it, but he wasn't going to risk it, either. Spending points on avoidable deaths seemed a bad idea.

"Will you please at least see Andrea? I grow tired of hearing her cry at night," Miu said.

Felix winced at that, his heart shuddering inside of him.

She was the last person he wanted to hurt or harm.

Miu is right.

"I'll go see her and Adriana immediately," Felix said, and then stood up.

Miu smiled at him and nodded her head sharply.

Following that line of thought, Felix immediately started to flesh out plans. He'd need a crash course on Yosemite. As well as starting the transfer work for everyone leaving and coming at the same time.

On top of that, he needed to get with Felicity and start arranging everything accordingly. Legion was going to grow and shrink.

"Right after I see Felicity, Faith, and Goldie, that is. I need to arrange a meeting and start getting everyone moving in the right direction. Rewards and awards to all those who performed above and beyond the call in the battle.

"Then I need to set up some one-on-one time with those we picked up in the transfer. I imagine there'll be a lot of tribal knowledge we'll need to learn."

"Goldie is outside the door. She never left," Miu said.

Felix sighed and ran a hand through his hair. It felt oily.

Then he brushed his hand over his jaw.

Need a shave, too.

"Let her in. I'm going to go take a shower and shave real quick," Felix said, and he went to his private bathroom.

By the time he'd gotten out of the shower and shaved, someone had hung some casual clothes for him on the inside of the bathroom door.

Probably Goldie.

Getting dressed in the suggested clothes, Felix felt... better.

He still hurt. A lot.

But he didn't feel like he was sitting in a pool of filth.

Walking out into the main part of his bedroom, he found Faith, Goldie, and Kris waiting for him.

"Ladies," Felix said, then smiled at them. "My apologies. I've grieved for them, and I'm ready to rejoin the living."

Walking over to Kris, he wrapped his arms around her and gave her a tight hug. "I understand I have you to thank for getting my inner circle out unharmed."

"Thank you, Kris."

The black Dragon seemed uncomfortable, but she slowly put her arms around Felix in return. Then she turned her head slightly and kissed his cheek.

"Anything for you nest-mate," grumbled the black. Clearly unused to being given direct affection.

Felix released her, then stood between Faith and Goldie.

"My loyal little Dryad," Felix said, then turned to Goldie. "And my lovely Dragon."

"Between the two of you, I had little to worry for or care about."

"I cannot express how much I appreciate you. And I need you further."

Goldie turned a deep red and smiled at him, twisting imperceptibly from side to side. "Will you hug me as well?"

"Yes, right after I hug Faith," Felix said, and then he wrapped Faith up in a tight hug.

The Dryad hugged him back just as forcefully, her hands pressed to the bottom of his lower back. *Any further south with those hands and she'd be getting a handful of... oh... there she goes.*

Smiling at the Dryad's antics, Felix let go of her and then opened his arms to Goldie.

Who promptly kissed him deeply, smothering him in a bone-crushing hug.

Ten seconds must have passed before she released him.

"Ooh. That was nice," Goldie said, wiping a finger across her lips.

Unable to even muster up the desire to reprimand her, because it *had* been nice, Felix only shook his head.

"Alright, come on. I decided on seeing Andrea and Adriana first. I think they're probably hurting as much as I am. After that, we need to see Felicity."

"Good. They need you, nest-mate," Goldie said with a nod of her head.

Leaving his own living quarters, he walked the short distance to Andrea and Adriana's shared rooms.

They were right next to his own.

Entering quietly, he closed the door with a soft click.

Andrea Prime and Adriana Prime were sitting next to their pregnant Seconds on a couch.

All four of them looked up when he entered the room. Their eyes were red, their ears and tails limp.

"Hello, my loves. First," Felix said, before they could say anything. "Let me apologize for keeping you out during my grief. I... didn't handle it very well. I should have realized you were equally hurting."

Felix went over to the four Beastkin and got down on his knees in front of them.

Before he could continue talking, all four of them moved in and pressed in close to him.

The bawling and wailing started almost immediately.

Listening to them, and doing his best to give them each attention, Felix settled in.

He figured it might be a while.

***

"Are they settled?" Felicity asked as Felix entered his office. She was sitting at a desk set to one side of what was apparently his own.

Must be hers.

"Yeah. Took some time. They, uh... cried themselves to exhaustion, then passed out. All four of them," Felix said, feeling sheepish.

"I've already taken care of a large number of personal tasks for you. A lot of the rest is... personnel and management things. I thought it'd be best to leave those to you," Felicity said.

Felix nodded and went to his desk. Grabbing the chair there, he dragged it over to Felicity's side and let go.

Then he took the seat and edged even closer to her.

Andrea had told him just how much Felicity had been doing in his absence and on his behalf. That she seemed to be running herself ragged for him.

And yet she'd still made time every day to check in on him frequently. He knew her feelings, and he was tired of running away from them.

She eyed him warily, setting the quill in her hand down in its holder.

"Thank you," Felix said simply, smiling at her. "You've done everything I could have ever asked of you. You kept everything running when I fell apart."

"Without you, I don't think I could do this. This is going to be a lot bigger than just managing Legion."

Felicity gave him a beautiful smile and shifted around in her chair, facing him directly.

"It won't be so bad. Between Elysia and myself, this'll be rather easy. We just don't have your knack for knowing what to do with people," Felicity said. "As for your thanks, you could always reward me."

"Oh? And what would you want?"

"Dinner. Several times this week. You and me," Felicity said immediately.

"Alright. Though I think I'm going to take a number of people out for meals this week. Any chance I could get you to limit it to once per week for four weeks instead?" Felix asked.

"What... just like that? You'll agree?"

"No reason not to," Felix said, and smiled sadly.

"Ah... yes... I see." Felicity's smile faltered. "Uhm, also, something came in your inbox. I needed something from the old Legion servers, so I had Talia sneak in — she's rather useful for stealthy needs, actually — and download all our data. Then wipe the servers clean."

"I... didn't read it past the first line once I realized what it was. I put it on your portable terminal. It's in your desk drawer."

"I'm going to go get some coffee. Can I get you something?" Felicity asked, standing up.

Felix lifted his chin and met her eyes. He gave her a smile.

"Yeah, but we'll talk about that later, over dinner tonight," Felix said, resting his hands on her hips.

Her eyes widened slightly, and then she gently ran her fingers through his hair. "You sure about that? One might worry they're just a replacement."

"I'm sure about it, and no. Not a replacement. Just me realizing something I already knew," Felix said, then shook his head with a chuckle. "Now, are you going to go get the coffee, or should I keep flirting with you?"

"I don't know. I kind of like this right now, but I think you should read that letter," Felicity said. She curled a finger around his ear and then tapped the tip of his nose. "You're a turd, dear. But I do love you."

Felicity pulled away from him and left the room.

Moving his chair back to his desk, he opened the drawer and fished out the terminal.

These were rather rare now. Most of their tech had been left behind in Legion HQ.

Going there at all was a risk. Dark beasts, undead, ghosts, and all sorts of nasties were crawling around everywhere now.

The portal area was the only permanently secured station.

Flipping it over, Felix powered it up. There were two files.

He focused on one that read "read me" and tapped it open.

Felicity tended to be as direct as possible. He ignored the second file for now.

Dear Felix,

If you're reading this, it means I did something stupid and probably heroic.
I'll start by saying I'm not sorry.
I was always a hero, first and foremost. It's who I am. Or was, possibly.
What I will apologize for, though, is lying to you. I was afraid of pursuing a relationship, even though Lily had agreed to me joining your little open marriage a long time ago.
I was afraid that if I agreed and admitted my love for you, I'd be trapped by it. I'd never be a hero again.
Maybe it isn't fair that I'm waiting to do this in a letter to be sent after I've possibly died in a way I can't be retrieved from, but that's what it is.
I'm a selfish coward. Sorry.
All I can ask and say is to please live on, and move forward.
If you can bring me back, do so. We'll talk about this letter then.

Maybe it's time I put up the hero title and become something new.
You were the most interesting thing that ever happened to me, and it's been a ridiculous and wild ride.

Yours Alone,
Kit

P.S.

Lily loves you, and she said you should love freely.
We'll find somewhere to hunker down. Bring a Dryad who can sense magic. I'll leave a trail.
Come get us!

"Just had to have the last word, huh, Kit?" Felix said, shaking his head with a smile.

Though the last bit was interesting. He got the impression that Kit had added that just before they'd jumped through the portal.

Leaning back in his chair, Felix thought on the situation.

"Well. Should probably start planning on how to storm through that portal, turn it into dust, and get them back," Felix said. "First, though... drones... satellite maybe... need to start recon.

"Can't save the princesses without knowing the lay of the land. Even if it's years away."

Felix went to set the terminal down and then looked at the second file.

When he opened it, a small window popped up first.

Who are the other two? Where did they go? the note read.

When Felix closed the note, there was a picture of Kevin Dane standing at what looked like a press conference.

There was no sound, but Kevin was talking.

Off to one side were three people.

"Seville, Shirley, and Skipper," Felix muttered, looking at the three of them.

Then there was an explosion off camera.

The three people Felix would love to see hurt looked surprised at something. Then they all pulled something out of their pockets. Felix leaned in close and squinted at the screen.

"Are those the cards?" Felix asked. He'd seen Seville use one just like that.

At the same time, Shirley, Skipper, and Seville simply vanished.

Frowning, Felix set the terminal down.

Skipper was in league with them all along.

Hm.

I should tell Runner.

Bonus Content: 2nd Epilogue

Peering down the lane, she wasn't quite sure what to think of everything.

Her first visit here had been a long time ago. It had been little more than a military enclave back then.

It'd even been called Fort One. Now she saw banners everywhere. The city had adopted the patently obvious lack of creativity Felix was known for.

"Legion Prime City, postal office," she said aloud, staring at the front of a stone building's display.

Adjusting the mask resting on her face, she looked around.

Members of Legion walked everywhere. They were dressed in clothes from their world as well as clothes made here on Legion Prime.

It would seem it really did happen, and the old world is simply no more.

Gritting her teeth, she began moving with the crowd. There was a definite flow of people going in one direction. From the conversations people were having, she could sense a significant amount of excitement going on.

And Felix would be publicly visible at this event. Listening to the people talk, they seemed to think it was because of what had happened back on their home world.

That he'd locked himself away for a week before he even started talking again. That now, a month after arriving, he was finally willing to start his duties again.

He must still be grieving deeply for Kit and Lily.

No one bothered her as she moved amongst them. A few gave her looks for the mask, but one and all, they immediately looked to her hand afterward.

A Legionnaire's ring sat there, obvious for all to see. The fact that she was able to move freely about the city and wore a ring was all most citizens needed.

She'd tried to move without a ring and had immediately felt sick to her stomach. She'd figured Felicia must have done something to the city walls and boundaries. Anyone without a ring would be fairly obvious to pick out.

I always felt like Felicia was the most dedicated. She just had the worst time showing it.

Easing around a group of people, she slid amongst them as if she wasn't even there. Moving up to the edge of what seemed like a giant amphitheater, she could see down into the center area.

Felix was standing there, next to a man who could only be Vince.

Even from this distance, she could tell they were a study of differences, even though they looked eerily similar.

Hopping down the steps, she kept herself out of Felix's line of sight. There was no doubt in her mind that he'd recognize her, mask or not, if he got a good look at her.

Getting halfway down the seats, she found a row with an open spot and immediately ducked into it. As she sat down amongst the Legionnaires, she felt a strange feeling bubbling up from inside her.

It reminded her of years ago. Before she'd escaped her own fear.

Now, though, it wasn't smothering like it had been.

It was like a pleasant heavy blanket sitting over her.

"Thank you for showing up. We'll give it another minute or two before we start," Felix said loudly, the sound of his voice immediately bursting through her thoughts.

It traveled straight down from her ears and practically out through her tail.

Shivering, Myriad leaned forward. It felt like he'd pulled on everything inside of her and laid it bare.

And she wanted it.

She'd missed him.

Desperately so.

His weekly letters to her had warmed her. She'd never been able to muster up the strength to write him back, though.

The words had simply failed her when she'd tried. What was in her heart for him, leaving Legion, abandoning Andrea—they were all tied up in shame and anger for her.

Leaving her no room or ability to say anything.

Except the letters had stopped one day. At the same time, she'd lost her connection to the main Legion databases.

It was as if a cord had been cut and she'd been on her own in truth.

In that dark minute, when she'd feared Felix had finally tired of reaching out to her, she'd realized the truth of her exile.

She'd never been alone. Ever.

Andrea, Adriana, Felix, and sometimes Kit and Lily all wrote to her. They'd never pressured her to respond, but they'd always said they'd love to hear from her.

Andrea and Adriana had become a bit frantic in the last few weeks before it had all gone dark.

It'd left Myriad feeling chilled once she was truly cut off, without any way of knowing what was going on.

Thinking they'd given up on her.

The database had kicked back in two weeks later, when she was only a week away from home, and she'd gotten her answer.

Kit and Lily were lost. Legion had suffered casualties. The home world was gone.

Felix was in pain.

Myriad had practically sprinted here from that point on, her Others collected inside of herself. She loved Felix. Deeply. Painfully. In her own way, separate from Andrea.

"First, welcome one and all. This is Legionnaire's meeting, so this is company wide, as it were."

"Second, I'm sure you all know the man standing next to me. My brother, Vince," Felix said.

Apparently, Vince had been crucial in the defense of the Headquarters during the apocalypse. He'd held an enemy entry portal by himself, battling it nearly single handed.

The response he got from the crowd was a sign of that respect. They roared, clapped, and stamped their feet for him.

He smiled and waved to the audience, but said nothing.

"He and I have talked for quite a while, made plans, scrapped them, made new ones, and scrapped those too," Felix said with a grin.

A vast majority of the Legionnaires chuckled at that. Most of them knew how corporate tended to work.

"In the end, I must confess I have a failing. I don't understand military or security as well as I probably should," Felix said, clasping his hands behind his back. "I rely on others to handle that for me, but I personally can't act fast enough, or early enough. I'm afraid that lack of experience and skill on my part has cost some of you dearly.

"And Vince has an equally problematic issue."

"I'm not Felix, and I hate politics and managing people," Vince said loudly. Except that was it. He had said his piece, in particular Vince fashion.

Everyone laughed. Even Myriad chuckled.

Vince and Felix were miles apart on personality.

"To that end, we're 'merging,'" Felix said, with air quotes, "Legion and Yosemite.

"I'll be responsible for everything non-military or security related, which Vince will take over."

The other man only nodded at this. Myriad got the impression Vince was happier with this situation than Felix was.

She could definitely empathize with that.

"I've already spoken with your leaders and department heads. Everything has been more or less worked out. All you need is to keep doing what you've been doing. The only difference is you may roll up to Vince instead of me," Felix said. "If you have any questions or concerns, I'll remind everyone that our open-door policy is always in effect, and please reach out to whomever you trust.

"That's all, everyone. I appreciate your time."

As one, the crowd got up and went back to their business. It was obvious to Myriad this had only been a formal statement of something everyone already knew.

Knowing him, he probably let it leak on purpose so people could acclimate to the idea long before it happened.

Smirking to herself, Myriad got up and moved into the city proper.

Though an interesting change had already happened.

At every government building where previously the red helmet of Legion had flown, there was now a blue shield with a sword plunged into the top of the red helmet of Legion.

Must be the combined banner. He really did plan it out in advance.

Ghosting into the crowd, Myriad filtered in amongst them and vanished.

***

Myriad wasn't sure what to think as she looked at herself in the mirror.

She looked exactly like Andrea. There was no difference whatsoever between her and her sister.

Adriana had her hair changed permanently by Felix. Maybe I could do the same?

I wonder what I'd look like with black hair.

Myriad sighed and pulled a strand of her hair. She'd cut it herself to roughly match Andrea's after the Legion meeting.

She'd done it to fit in and match with her sister, just in case someone recognized her.

It'd be easier to pretend to be Andrea — after all, she was her — than to try and explain how she looked different.

But I'm not Andrea... am I? That was the name my parents gave me. But I just... think of myself as Myriad now.

I wonder if Adriana thinks of herself as Adriana now.

They definitely seem very different from each other. Their letters are clearly from different people.

Letting her hair fall, Myriad looked into her own face in the mirror.

She'd broken into Andrea's room and stolen some of her clothes.

The Others in her head, she only had a contingent of ten, mostly comprised of Death-Others who came with her and kept complimenting her. Encouraging her.

Telling her to go to Felix as Myriad, not Andrea.

Except she couldn't. She was afraid. Afraid of what Felix would do.

He hadn't sent her a letter since the databases had turned back on. Even though Andrea and Adriana had started again. They'd even explained the situation.

Frowning, Myriad left Andrea's room and entered the hallway.

The manse had clearly been a recent addition. Though it was extremely well put together and seemed to be built with absolute love.

Which means Andrea did it.

Myriad grinned and ran her fingers over the wood. Her sister had devoted herself completely to being everything for Felix.

She could feel that unwavering dedication in her own heart for the man. It made her ashamed to think of what her sisters had done for him while she'd run away.

Putting on an Andrea face, Myriad left the hallway.

It only took a single turn to run into someone. And it was someone she didn't actually know.

An extremely well-put-together woman with gold eyes and golden horns coming out from her head. She was beautiful and womanly in ways that even Myriad had to admire.

"Oh! Andrea, there you are," said the golden-eyed woman. She immediately came in close and hugged Myriad tightly, pressing her head into a well-endowed chest. "Thank you so much for helping me out the other day. Everything went exactly like you said it would. Being direct and honest with him was exactly what needed to happen.

"He was extremely caring and took extreme efforts to not hurt me."

On a hunch, Myriad took a sniff of her.

Felix's scent was all over her.

He's sleeping with other women now. He was against it in the last letter he sent. He'd even mentioned it. The grief must be worse than I thought, or he's getting through it.

"Of course, happy to help," Myriad said in Andrea's chipper tone.

The Dragon—because clearly that was what she was now that Myriad has smelled her—made a cooing noise, hugging her even more tightly.

Then she let her go.

"I told Kris and Faith to do the same thing you told me. They'll probably come by to express their thanks to you. I know their own nights happened recently," said the woman. Then she leaned in and kissed Myriad on the cheek. "You're such a good woman for him. Thank you."

Then the Dragon left, moving past her with a gentle pat on the shoulder.

Apparently Andrea has really made herself the center of this little marriage.

Going out the front door, Myriad did her best to avoid everyone. She really couldn't afford any more strange encounters like the last.

She just wanted to see Felix, ask him how he was doing, and leave. To get back out into the wilderness.

Her plan was simple. Infiltration, information retrieval, and egress.

Keeping a smile on her face as she went, Myriad saw several horned women wandering around the mansion compound. In addition to that, she saw quite a few busty, green-skinned women in Legion security uniforms watching over the grounds. They were sporting SMGs and rifles at the same time.

Myriad only gave them a cursory glance because anything more than that and she was sure she'd alert them to the fact she wasn't Andrea.

They had the look of professional, hard-eyed soldiers.

Even if they look like sex dolls.

Felix has had some changes.

They gave her small, polite nods and waves of their hands. Seeing only Andrea and waving her on.

Turning the corner around the front of the house, she started to walk down the side wall. Up ahead, she saw a large number of Elven women. Elven women of every shape, size, and species. They were collectively working on a spell of some sort. The amount of power they were putting out made the air crackle.

Feeling like her smile was a bit brittle, Myriad kept moving.

Felix doesn't need me. I'm just a mercenary. He has powerful people all around him.

This is a mistake.

I'm just going to look foolish. Stupid and foolish and like a lovesick girl and—

Myriad turned the corner and found Felix. Her heart shuddered heavily in her chest. It felt like her blood had gone cold at the sight of him.

He was sitting in an outdoor lounge chair. He was clearly resting, slouched low in his seat.

Luckily, he was alone and seemed to be almost dozing.

This'll be easy. Just walk up, ask how he's doing, act like Andrea, and leave.

Myriad put one foot in front of the other and kept walking straight towards Felix.

Wait. What if he isn't just dozing?

What if he asks me questions and I can't answer?

What if he tries to kiss me?

What if he wants me to go to the bedroom with him! Andrea's pregnant. Adriana is pregnant.

I could easily get—

Felix slowly turned his head in her direction. His eyes locked on her, recognized her, and he looked straight ahead again, having seen only Andrea.

Then his head slowly turned back to her. His brows slowly came down. Suddenly his face split into a wide smile.

"Hi, dear!" Myriad said, exactly as Andrea would, when she was ten feet away.

"Hello. Have a seat. Let's talk," Felix said.

Reaching over, he patted the chair next to him.

This feels odd.

Myriad sat down in the chair and looked out at what Felix had been watching.

It was a simple open field. There was nothing there; it was empty of anything.

"That's where the vault, the nursery, the hatchery, and the grove is going. Nursery for the babies, hatchery for Dragon children, grove for Dryad children," Felix said. "The Dragons and Dryads are trying to get into my bed as fast as possible and get pregnant. I'd rather not, honestly, but if it turns out that way I'd rather have the childcare set up in advance.

"Though the weird part is the Dryads want to turn me into a grove for themselves, apparently. The Dragons want to live in the vault."

"No surprise there. Gold is their thing."

Myriad internally checked that information against everything she knew from the letters.

None of this had been mentioned at all.

Felix's hand moved over to hers, and his fingers slipped in between her own.

"I'm telling you all this because I doubt Andrea or Adriana would have included it in their letters to you.

"It's really good to see you, Myriad," Felix said, his head turning toward her.

Myriad slowly turned her head toward him, her Andrea smile faltering and then falling off.

"You knew?" she asked.

"Of course. How could I not tell my Elex women apart?" Felix said. "You're you, not Andrea."

Myriad wanted to hit him.

Hard.

He'd ruined everything by noticing her. By realizing who she was. She'd have to slip away again and it'd be even harder this time.

"You don't have to leave," Felix said, as if seeing her dilemma broadcast over her head. "I'd really prefer it if you stayed. Andrea and Adriana miss you, as I do."

Myriad sniffed once, detecting all the different scents on him.

"You have the scents of many women on you," Myriad said, her chin tilting up a fraction. "You don't need another Elex woman."

"Of course I do. Though you probably smell Miu, Goldie, Felicity, Faith, Kris, Jessica, Erica, and a strange little Elf named Talia. Though that one came out of nowhere, and I'm not sure if it was anything more than fun for her. Her humor is interesting," Felix said, with a strange look on his face. "Regardless of all that, though, I still would ask you to stay. You're not Andrea, but you are at the same time. I need all my Elex women. You and your Others. By the way, how are they? Are they doing all right?"

There was sudden cacophony in her mind as all the Others in her head talked happily at him asking about them. All of them trying to split from Myriad and smother him in their love and devotion.

"They're fine. Though I think you're asking for a mob of Elex women to come for you, if you really want to know," Myriad said, a smile slowly spreading across her face. Then she gently squeezed his hand. "You really want me to stay? I'm no use to you. You have Elves, Dragons, and Dryads watching over you."

"You don't need a use for me to want you to stay, you silly thing," Felix said. Then he leaned over the arm of his chair and kissed her tenderly.

Myriad felt like her head was heavy, and all the Others inside her suddenly locked up tight and went silent. Then Felix pulled away, the lingering warmth of his lips on hers making her feel dizzy.

"I want you to stay because I love you. You, your Others, your sisters, and their Others. All.

"Though we may want to see them sooner rather than later. They're going to be rather sore you didn't let them know you were coming.

"They desperately want to show you their pregnant Seconds," Felix said.

Wait, why did he stop sending me letters?

"I'll stay… if you can give me a good reason why you stopped sending me letters," Myriad said, her hand tightening into his.

"I didn't," Felix said, frowning at her. "I've been sending them every week. Even after the databases failed. I sent one the day they came back up."

Felix gently let go of her hand and pulled out a pad he had at his side.

He slowly started to tap through it, reading it.

"Oh. Huh. Looks like the settings had you listed as an external recipient, so it wasn't sending," Felix said. Tapping something, he looked at her.

Myriad's wrist communicator chimed, followed by a kissing noise.

"You put a special noise for my emails?" Felix asked with a grin.

Feeling absolute embarrassment, Myriad covered her wrist device as it continued to chime and then make kissing noises as each new email came in.

"You got about two more," Felix said, seemingly counting the number of times it had gone off.

"This is mortifying," Myriad said, closing her eyes.

Chuckling, Felix leaned over and kissed her again, wrapping an arm around her shoulders.

"Not really. It's endearing. For all that you try to be Myriad, you were still the original Andrea.

"And for that, I love you for who you are, as well as who you aren't. Now come on. Let's go see your sisters, or they'll tan my hide for not bringing you over," Felix said.

Myriad felt a strange panic and excitement rising inside her. It took a moment for her to realize it was her Second.

LITTER!

The force of the demand from her Second gave Myriad a moment of pause and reflection. Then she smiled and let Felix pull her up to her feet.

A litter.

***

Runner flopped into a chair and stared up at the ceiling.

"Motherfucking shit cock of a dumpster fire. What the actual shit just happened? Felix sent over a message, and it looks like there's three of those damn agents of Zeus running around," he complained. "And then you, 'Uncle,' are running around in the backfield with Al."

"Yeah. Well. Whatever," said Uncle, leaning up against a wooden pillar. "I'm supposed to watch him, so I am. Besides, he wasn't wrong.

"You do realize he's incredibly close to freeing his mom, right?"

Runner sighed and pressed his hands to his face.

Part of him was incredibly excited at the idea of Sunshine coming home.

It'd pained him dearly to see her. Standing there.

And he hadn't been able to help her at all.

But he'd seen her. And she'd seen him.

He'd heard her voice.

"I'm glad to hear it, but it still doesn't solve the problem, now does it?" Runner griped.

Uncle snorted at that.

"Don't be an ass-hat, Runner. Al's going to pull her out long before you mount your little assault team.

"Though I have to admit, the experiment worked pretty well. Those two are rather terrifying," Uncle said.

"Yeah... they really are. Though there's a couple others I'm looking at," Runner admitted, scratching at his stomach. "One's on a sub-world. He... was amusing, and changed himself.

"Then there's that thing my crazy one is doing."

Uncle grunted and then stood upright.

"I need to get home. Wife will pull my head off if I don't get home tonight," Uncle said.

"Which one?"

"All of them? You know how it is."

"Be sure to stop by and say hi; the kids wanna see you. You figure out how you wanna handle the mainland, by the way?"

"Yeah… more or less what we talked about. Not going to have a choice." Runner sighed and closed his eyes.

"See ya later, dickhead," Uncle said, poking him in the forehead as he walked by.

"Later, dipshit," Runner said, waving a hand in the air.

Lying there, he just let his mind drift.

I can't ever let him see Shirley. Ever. It'd break him.

A soft beep sounded in Runner's head. Cracking an eye open, he felt his AI-supported mind dive through the systems of the ship, rapidly peeling out what the alert noise was for.

The ship had just passed a boundary marker. It was on the edge of a solar system. It'd been dark, silent.

Cloaked.

Right up until the ship passed it by, at which point a small snippet of data was sent deep into the solar system.

"Guess we won't be surprising them," Runner muttered, charting the course of the signal.

It was following the same line the SOS Sunshine had sent them toward so many years ago.

"Right, then," Runner said.

Thank you, dear reader!

I'm hopeful you enjoyed reading Super Sales on Super Heroes. Please consider leaving a review, commentary, or messages. Feedback is imperative to an author's growth.

That and positive reviews never hurt.

Feel free to drop me a line at: WilliamDArand@gmail.com

Join my mailing list for book updates: William D. Arand Newsletter

Keep up to date—Facebook: https://www.facebook.com/WilliamDArand
Patreon: https://www.patreon.com/WilliamDArand
Blog: http://williamdarand.blogspot.com/
Harem Lit Group: https://www.facebook.com/groups/haremlit/
LitRPG Group: https://www.facebook.com/groups/LitRPGsociety/

If you enjoyed this book, try out the books of some of my close friends. I can heartily recommend them.

Blaise Corvin- A close and dear friend of mine. He's been there for me since I was nothing but a rookie with a single book to my name. He told me from the start that it was clear I had talent and had to keep writing. His background in European martial arts creates an accurate and detail driven action segments as well as his world building.

https://www.amazon.com/Blaise-Corvin/e/B01LYK8VG5

John Van Stry- John was an author I read, and re-read, and re-read again, before I was an author. In a world of books written for everything except harems, I found that not only did I truly enjoy his writing, but his concepts as well.
In discovering he was an indie author, I realized that there was nothing separating me from being just like him. I attribute him as an influence in my own work.
He now has two pen names, and both are great.

https://www.amazon.com/John-Van-Stry/e/B004U7JY8I
Jan Stryvant-
https://www.amazon.com/Jan-Stryvant/e/B06ZY7L62L

Daniel Schinhofen- Daniel was another one of those early adopters of my work who encouraged and pushed me along. He's almost as introverted as I am, so we get along famously. He recently released a new book, and by all accounts including mine, is a well written author with interesting storylines.

https://www.amazon.com/Daniel-Schinhofen/e/B01LXQWPZA

Made in the USA
Coppell, TX
07 January 2024